兎用心棒

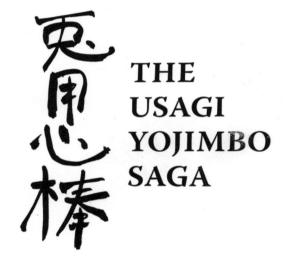

THE USAGI YOJIMBO SAGA

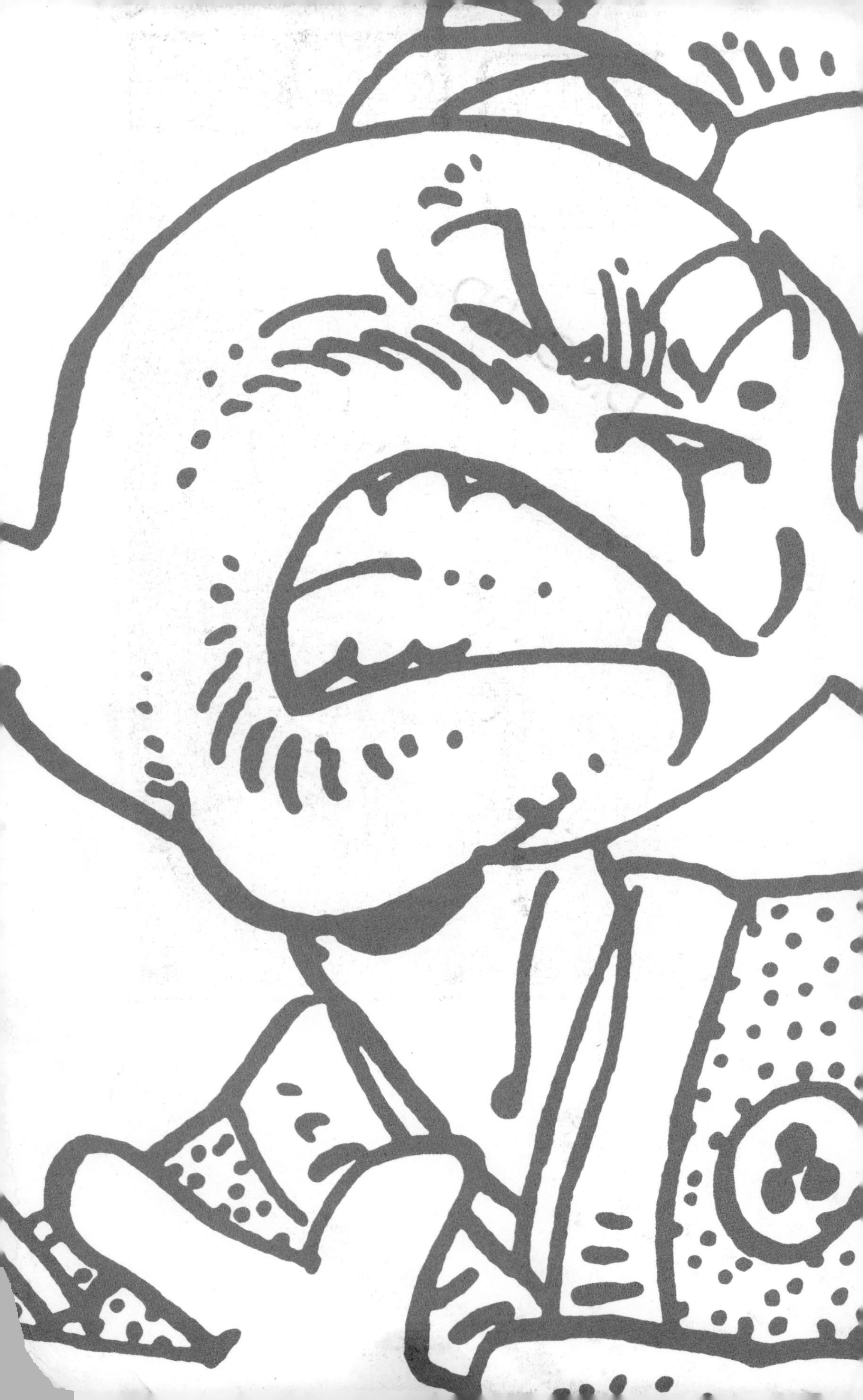

THE USAGI YOJIMBO™ SAGA

BOOK 9

*Created, written,
and illustrated by*

STAN SAKAI

Teenage Mutant Ninja Turtles *created by*
PETER LAIRD *and*
KEVIN EASTMAN

"The Crossing" written and illustrated by
PETER LAIRD

"Chibi Usagi" and "Chibi Tomoe" stories by
STAN SAKAI *and* JULIE FUJII SAKAI

DARK HORSE BOOKS

Publisher
MIKE RICHARDSON

Collection Editor
MEGAN WALKER

Collection Assistant Editor
JUDY KHUU

Original Series Editors
MICHAEL DOONEY, PHILIP R. SIMON, KIM THOMPSON, *and* **MEGAN WALKER**

Designer
CARY GRAZZINI

Digital Art Technicians
CARY GRAZZINI *and* **ADAM PRUETT**

THE USAGI YOJIMBO™ SAGA Volume 9

This volume collects issues #159–#172 of the Dark Horse comic book series *Usagi Yojimbo Volume Three* and the following stories: "Turtle Soup and Rabbit Stew," which originally appeared in *Turtle Soup* #1 (published by Mirage Studios in 1987); "The Crossing," which originally appeared in *Usagi Yojimbo Volume One* #10 (published by Fantagraphics Books in 1988); "The Treaty," which originally appeared in *Shell Shock* (published by Mirage Studios in 1989); "Shades of Green," which originally appeared in *Usagi Yojimbo Volume Two* #1–#3 (published by Mirage Studios in 1993); and "Namazu," which originally appeared in *Teenage Mutant Ninja Turtles/Usagi Yojimbo* (published by IDW Publishing in 2017).

StanSakai.com
UsagiYojimbo.com
DarkHorse.com

Published by Dark Horse Books
A division of Dark Horse Comics LLC
10956 SE Main Street
Milwaukie, OR 97222

To find a comics shop in your area, visit comicshoplocator.com

Library of Congress Cataloging-in-Publication Data

Names: Sakai, Stan, writer, illustrator.
Title: Usagi Yojimbo saga / written and illustrated by Stan Sakai.
Description: Second edition. | Limited edition. | Milwaukie, OR : Dark Horse Books, 2021- | v. 1:
  "This volume collects Usagi Yojimbo Volume One #1-#6" | v. 9: "This volume collects
  Usagi Yojimbo Volume 32: Mysteries, Usagi Yojimbo Volume 33: The Hidden, Usagi Yojimbo/Teenage Mutant
  Ninja Turtles." | Audience: Ages 10+ (provided by Dark Horse Books) | Audience: Grades 7-9 (provided by
  Dark Horse Books) | Summary: "Celebrate Stan Sakai's beloved rabbit ronin with the Second Edition
  collections of the comic saga featuring brand new original cover art by Stan Sakai"-- Provided by publisher.
Identifiers: LCCN 2020036007| ISBN 9781506724904 (v. 1 ; paperback) | ISBN
  9781506724911 (v. 1 ; hardcover) | ISBN 9781506725062 (v. 9 ; paperback) |
  ISBN 9781506725079 (v. 9 ; hardcover)
Subjects: LCSH: Graphic novels. | CYAC: Graphic novels. | Samurai--Fiction.
Classification: LCC PZ7.7.S138 Ur 2021 | DDC 741.5/973--dc23
LC record available at https://lccn.loc.gov/2020036007

First edition: April 2021
Ebook ISBN 978-1-50672-508-6
Trade Paperback ISBN 978-1-50672-506-2
Limited Edition Hardcover ISBN 978-1-50672-507-9

10 9 8 7 6 5 4 3 2 1

PRINTED IN CHINA

THIS ONE IS FOR MY FAVORITE
COLORIST, TOM LUTH. THANK YOU FOR
OVER THRITY-FIVE YEARS OF FRIENDSHIP.
HAPPY RETIREMENT.

MYSTERIES

THE HIDDEN

⋙⋘

TEENAGE MUTANT NINJA TURTLES

After the death of Lord Mifune in the battle of Adachi Plain, retainer **MIYAMOTO USAGI** chose the warrior's pilgrimage, becoming a wandering *ronin* in search of peace. Practicing the warrior code of *bushido*, Usagi avoids conflict whenever possible, but when called upon, his bravery and fighting prowess are unsurpassed.

A street performer who believes "a girl has to do what she can to get by," **KITSUNE** makes extra money as a pickpocket, but steals only from those who deserve it. She and Usagi have been friends for many years, since the day she stole his purse and he stole it back.

Apprentice and sidekick to the wily Kitsune, young **KIYOKO** is every bit as enterprising, mischievous, and cunning as her mentor. Kiyoko is one of a very few whom Kitsune calls friend, and their bond is as strong as that of a big and a little sister.

Using his keen mind to solve mysteries beyond the skills of his fellow detectives, **INSPECTOR ISHIDA** remains committed to justice, even when corrupt officials and other police find it inconvenient, a quality that has earned him enemies in the city government but also a true friend in Usagi.

Upon the death of her brother Shingen, **KASHIRA CHIZU** became leader of the Neko ninja, a clan serving the dark lord Hikiji but often pursuing its own agendas. Though Chizu is a skilled leader, several clan members resent being commanded by a woman and seek to remove her.

Trained in the art of *ninjutsu*, the four brothers **LEONARDO, DONATELLO, MICHELANGELO,** and **RAPHAEL** continually find themselves defending the world from the forces of evil—which sometimes leads to dimension hopping and teaming up with a familiar wandering rabbit *ronin*.

MYSTERIES

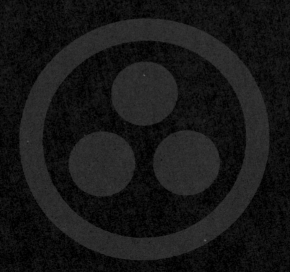

WHEN I WAS FIRST ASKED to provide the voice of Miyamoto Usagi for the 2012 *Teenage Mutant Ninja Turtles* animated series, I got cold feet. For many people around the globe, the character represented samurai. They started reading *Usagi* when they were young, and they grew up with him throughout the years, so Usagi's life was their alternate samurai life. Surely, voicing him would be a pretty daunting task for anybody. But, to my own surprise, my biggest fear was concerning a completely different reason: disappointing the creator, Stan Sakai-*san*, a Japanese American cartoonist icon. If I failed to represent Usagi properly, I failed him, thus wasting the biggest opportunity to contribute to showing the world an authentic samurai figure. This was my biggest anxiety and fear.

Ever since I came to the United States many years ago to pursue acting, I've constantly held myself responsible for overseeing everything that has to do with Japanese culture while on set. Sometimes it was the way the Japanese military saluted throughout history. Sometimes it was the way Japanese newspapers or signs were displayed. In a very limited amount of time, I had to research everything possible on set in order to correct mistakes out of the fear of letting the world see Japanese culture misrepresented. Eighteen years of this tiring work wore me out very much. But then, if you look at Stan-*sensei*, he's been doing it for over thirty years . . . and moreover, quite successfully! HOW?! THAT'S NOT POSSIBLE! To me, he's not just a master storyteller, but a master Japanese culture researcher.

When I first opened an issue of *Usagi Yojimbo*, the first thing I noticed was the level of research in the details: the shapes of *kasa* (hats), what people were wearing, what they carried, what toys kids were playing with, etc. Many people probably saw them just as background details, but to me they showed the determination of the creator to portray Japanese culture as truthfully as possible. And it was done in a subtle way so readers could immerse themselves in a realistic world instead of being distracted by those details. When you look at the pictures, you don't see everything drawn in the details, but you can definitely *hear* people shouting in the crowded streets; you can *smell* the food that vendors are selling; and when Kitsune performs and the townsfolk gasp, you can *imagine* how they spend their daily lives just by looking at their kimono. I was completely mystified by the fact that someone was able to accomplish such a feat.

But soon, my wonder faded—*not* because the book became less impressive, but because I stopped thinking about it being a manmade world. I found myself walking on the unpaved road with Usagi, listening to the sound of the breeze. Once Usagi settled into a seedy inn and started to eat his soggy rice, I cautiously looked around every corner of the panel to make sure there was no danger around him. I trembled whenever I heard Jei's haunting voice, and felt sorry for the plight of whoever was unlucky enough to share a roof with *him*. I laughed and laughed listening to Usagi and Gen talking. I was simply there. Like a skilled Neko ninja, the creator had vanished!

Voicing Miyamoto Usagi has taught me many things, but the biggest takeaway was being assured that good storytelling has no boundaries. It doesn't matter where the readers or the audience are from. As long as you succeed in creating a realistic world, people of any culture can submerge themselves into that world, and laugh, cry, and live.

YUKI MATSUZAKI
LOS ANGELES, CA
FEBRUARY 2018

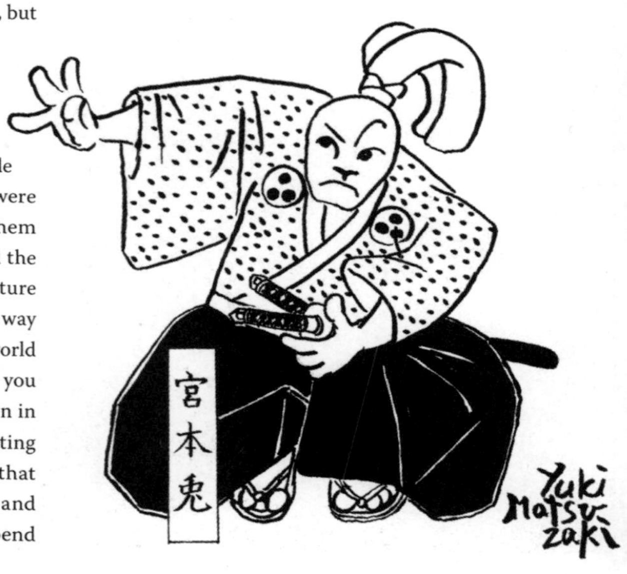
宮本兎
Yuki Matsuzaki

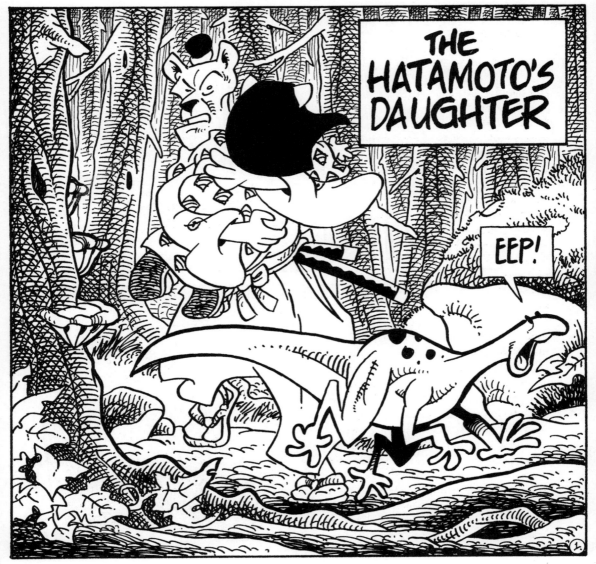

THE HATAMOTO'S DAUGHTER

EEP!

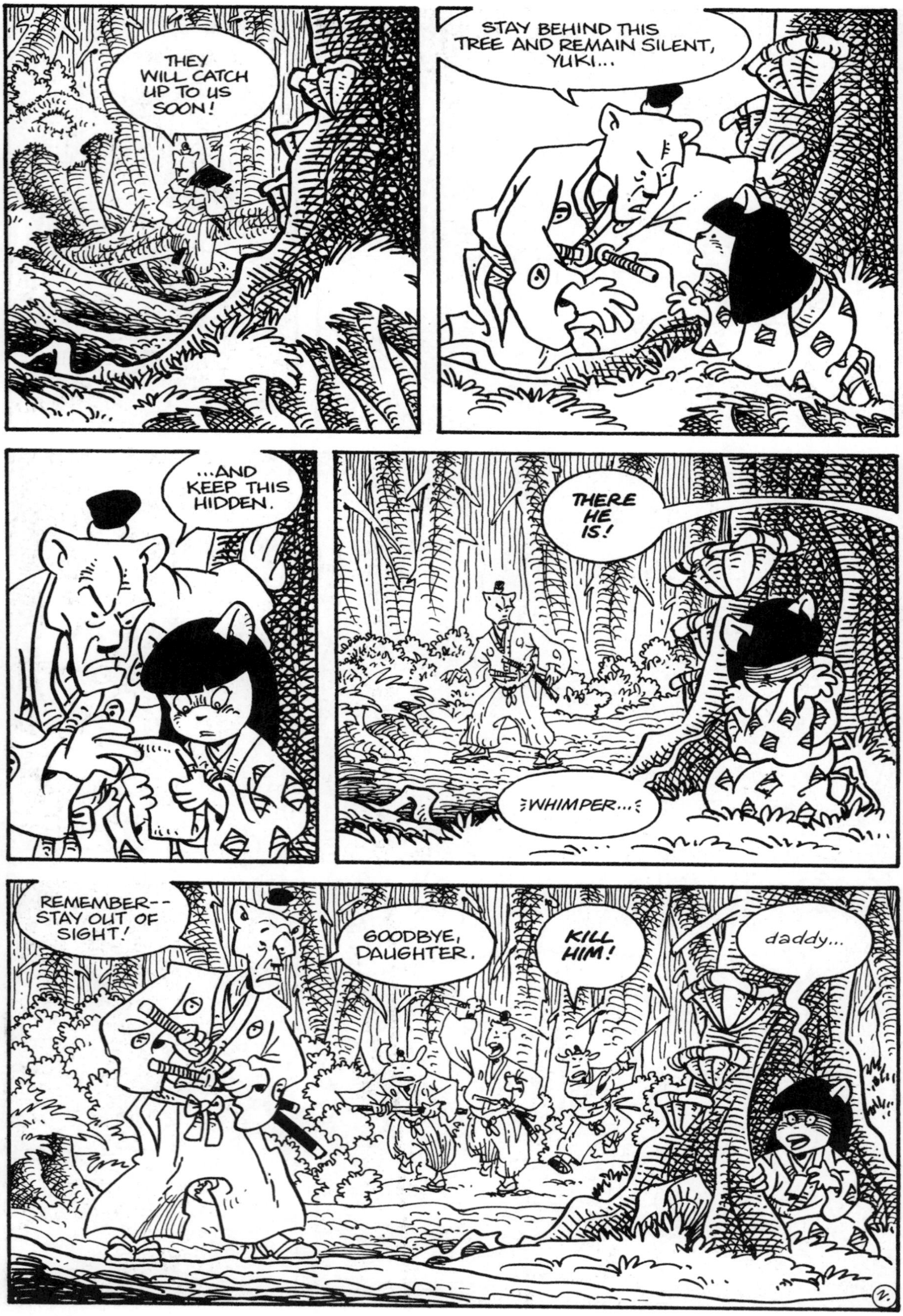
THEY WILL CATCH UP TO US SOON!
STAY BEHIND THIS TREE AND REMAIN SILENT, YUKI...
...AND KEEP THIS HIDDEN.
THERE HE IS!
WHIMPER...
REMEMBER-- STAY OUT OF SIGHT!
GOODBYE, DAUGHTER.
KILL HIM!
daddy...

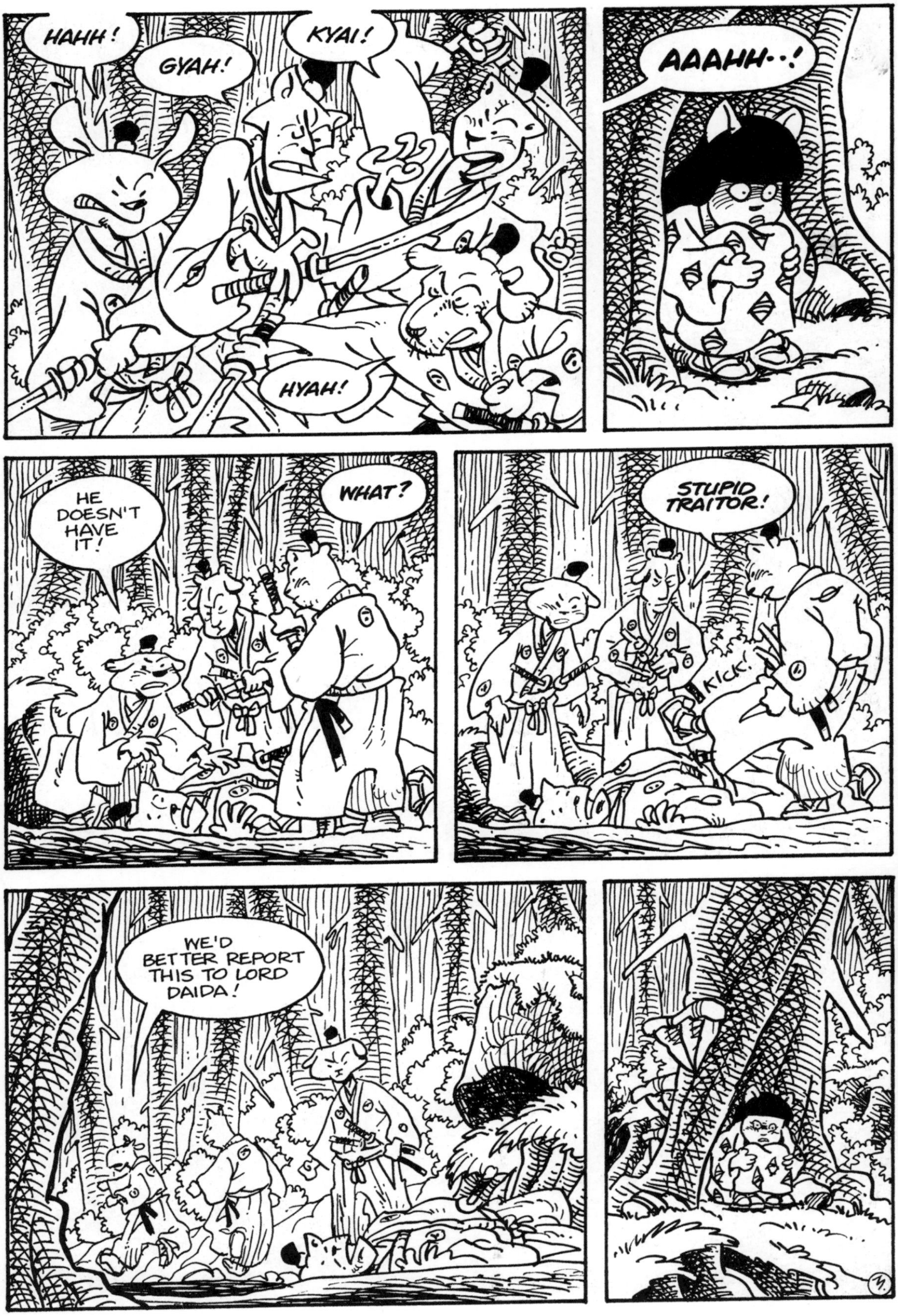
HAHH!
GYAH!
KYAI!
HYAH!
AAAHH..!
HE DOESN'T HAVE IT!
WHAT?
STUPID TRAITOR!
KICK!
WE'D BETTER REPORT THIS TO LORD DAIDA!

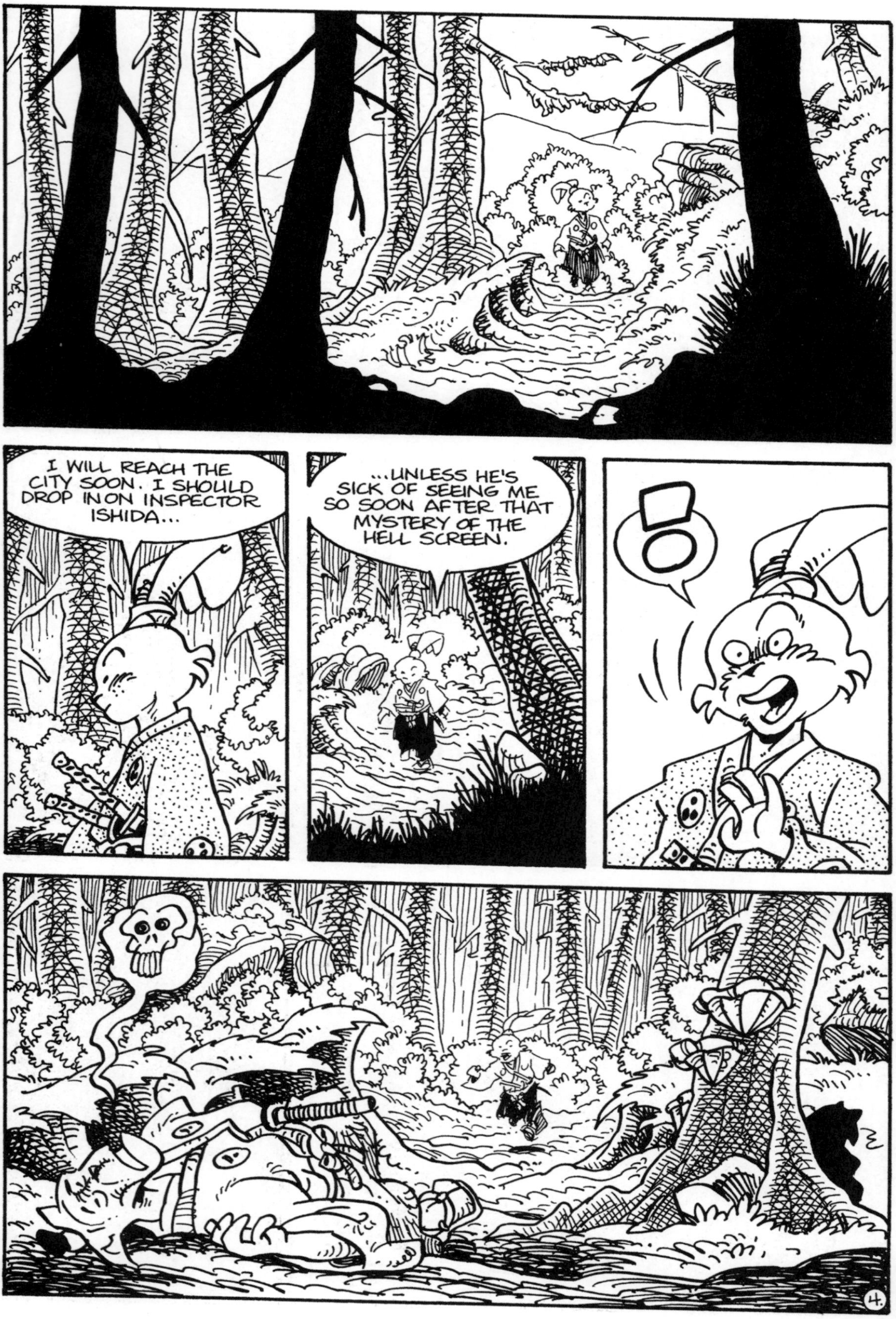
I WILL REACH THE CITY SOON. I SHOULD DROP IN ON INSPECTOR ISHIDA...
...UNLESS HE'S SICK OF SEEING ME SO SOON AFTER THAT MYSTERY OF THE HELL SCREEN.
4.

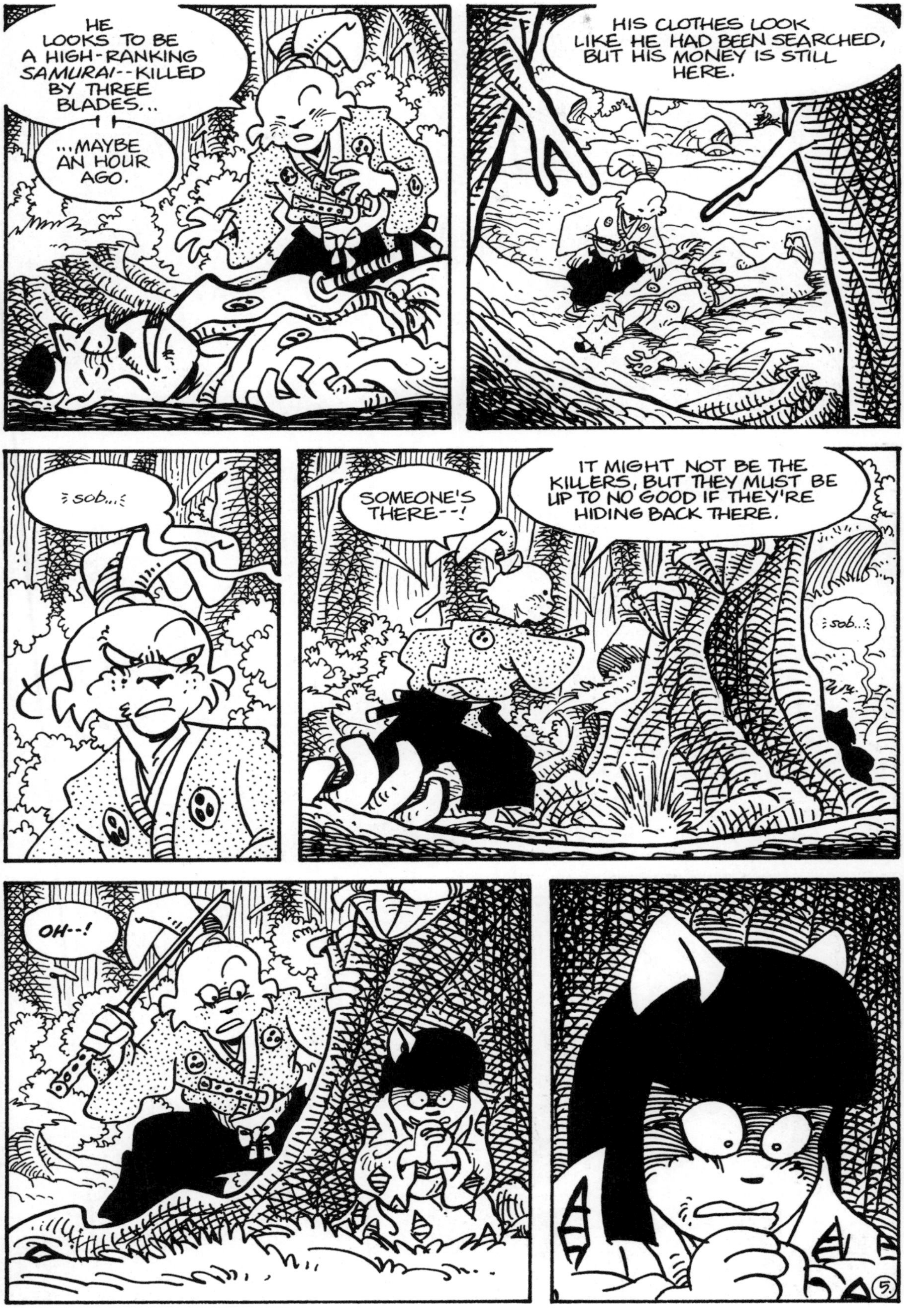
HE LOOKS TO BE A HIGH-RANKING SAMURAI--KILLED BY THREE BLADES...
...MAYBE AN HOUR AGO.
HIS CLOTHES LOOK LIKE HE HAD BEEN SEARCHED, BUT HIS MONEY IS STILL HERE.
sob...
SOMEONE'S THERE--!
IT MIGHT NOT BE THE KILLERS, BUT THEY MUST BE UP TO NO GOOD IF THEY'RE HIDING BACK THERE.
sob...
OH--!
5.

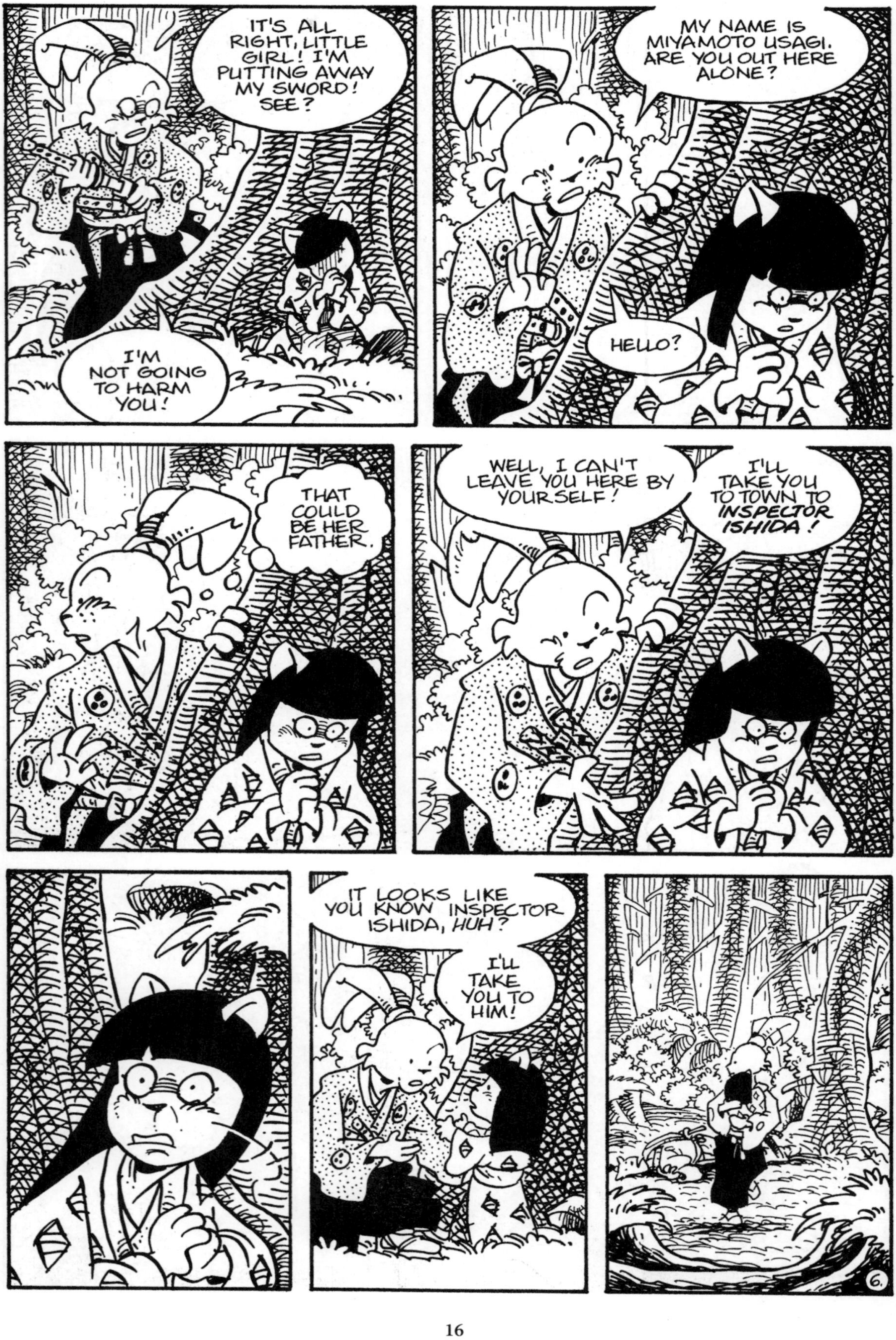
IT'S ALL RIGHT, LITTLE GIRL! I'M PUTTING AWAY MY SWORD! SEE?
I'M NOT GOING TO HARM YOU!
MY NAME IS MIYAMOTO USAGI. ARE YOU OUT HERE ALONE?
HELLO?
THAT COULD BE HER FATHER.
WELL, I CAN'T LEAVE YOU HERE BY YOURSELF!
I'LL TAKE YOU TO TOWN TO INSPECTOR ISHIDA!
IT LOOKS LIKE YOU KNOW INSPECTOR ISHIDA, HUH?
I'LL TAKE YOU TO HIM!
6.

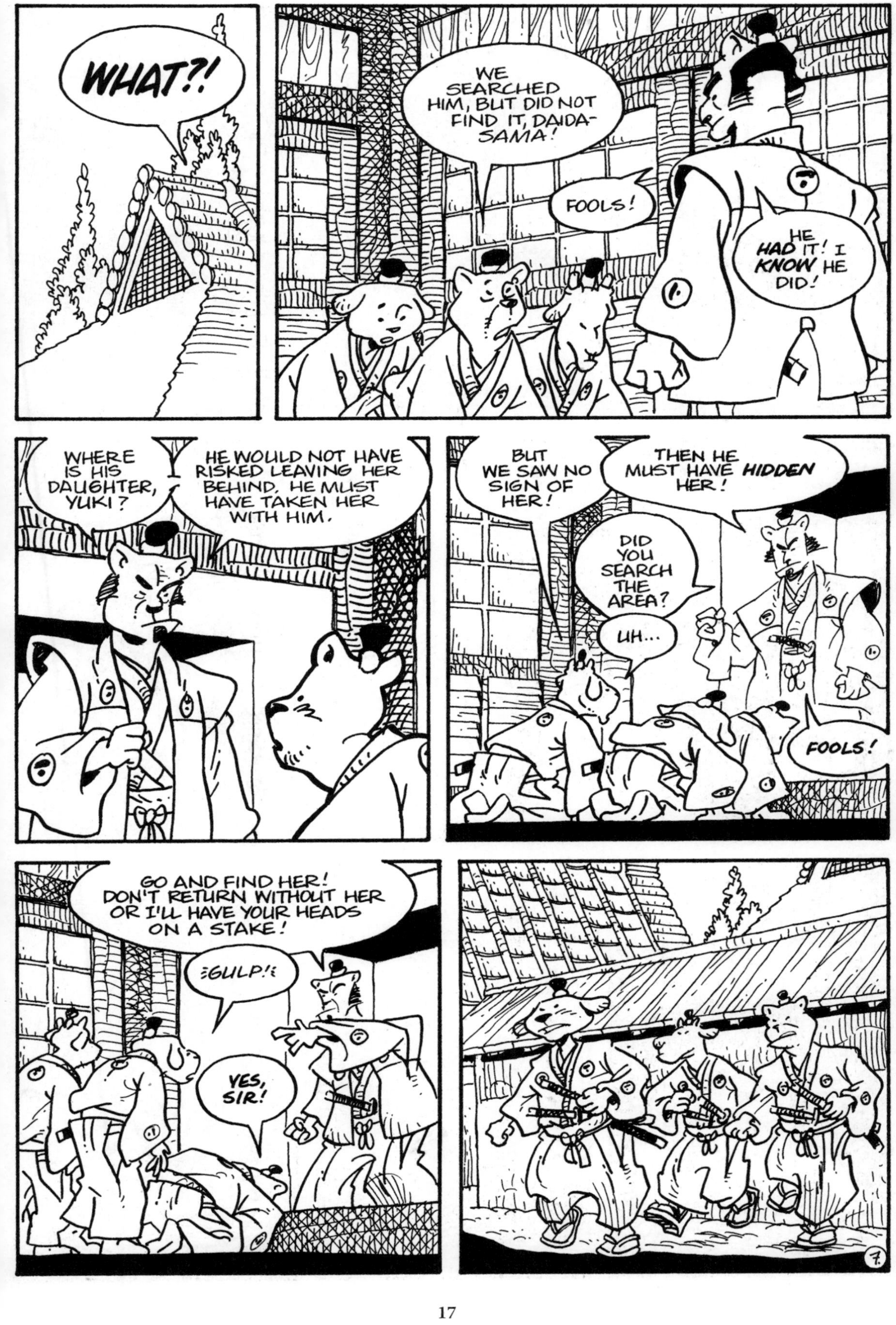
WHAT?!
WE SEARCHED HIM, BUT DID NOT FIND IT, DAIDA-SAMA!
FOOLS!
HE **HAD** IT! I **KNOW** HE DID!
WHERE IS HIS DAUGHTER, YUKI?
HE WOULD NOT HAVE RISKED LEAVING HER BEHIND. HE MUST HAVE TAKEN HER WITH HIM.
BUT WE SAW NO SIGN OF HER!
THEN HE MUST HAVE **HIDDEN** HER!
DID YOU SEARCH THE AREA?
UH...
FOOLS!
GO AND FIND HER! DON'T RETURN WITHOUT HER OR I'LL HAVE YOUR HEADS ON A STAKE!
GULP!
YES, SIR!
7.

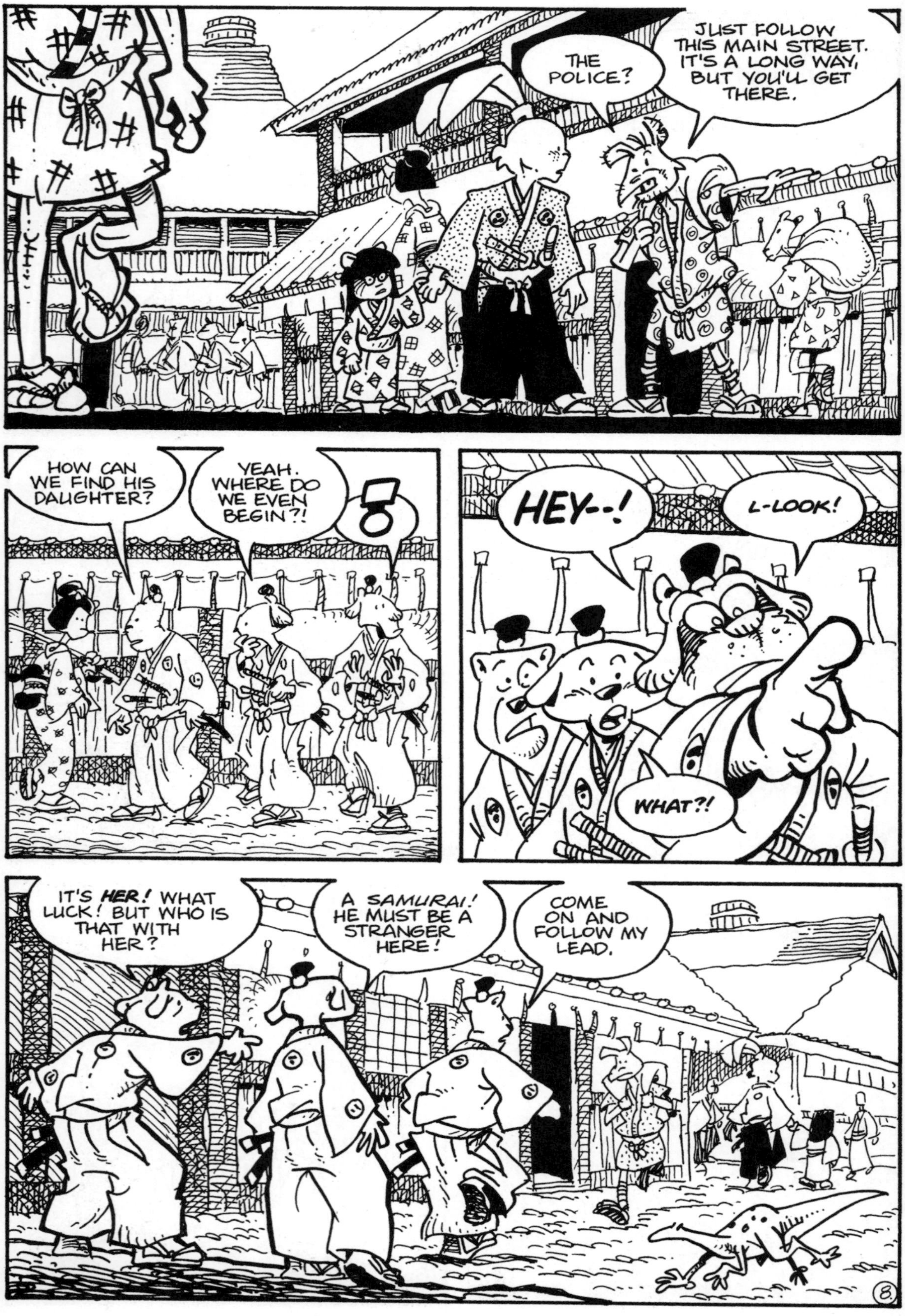
THE POLICE?
JUST FOLLOW THIS MAIN STREET. IT'S A LONG WAY, BUT YOU'LL GET THERE.
HOW CAN WE FIND HIS DAUGHTER?
YEAH. WHERE DO WE EVEN BEGIN?!
HEY--!
L-LOOK!
WHAT?!
IT'S **HER!** WHAT LUCK! BUT WHO IS THAT WITH HER?
A *SAMURAI!* HE MUST BE A STRANGER HERE!
COME ON AND FOLLOW MY LEAD.
8

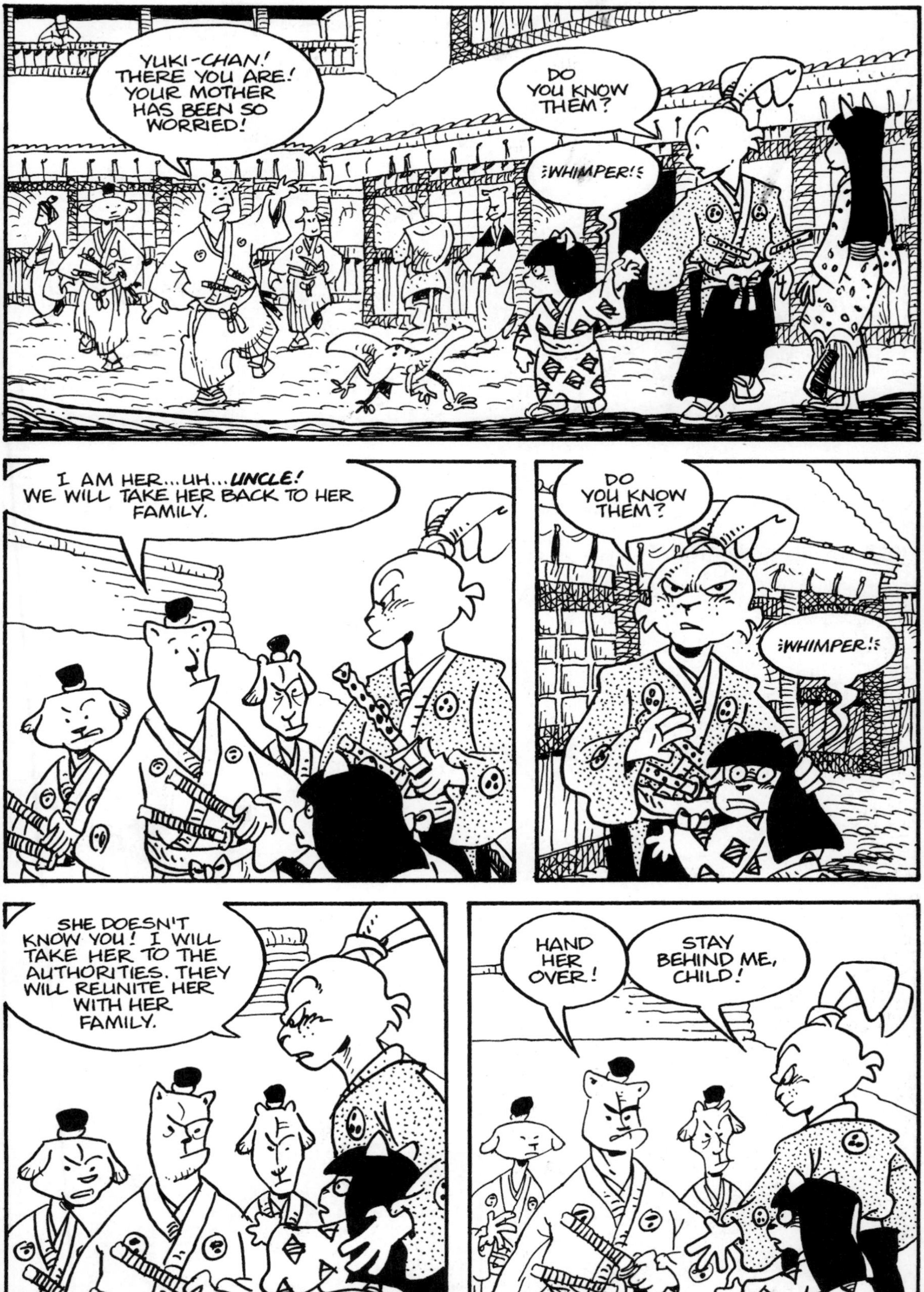
YUKI-CHAN! THERE YOU ARE! YOUR MOTHER HAS BEEN SO WORRIED!
DO YOU KNOW THEM?
WHIMPER!
I AM HER...UH...UNCLE! WE WILL TAKE HER BACK TO HER FAMILY.
DO YOU KNOW THEM?
WHIMPER!
SHE DOESN'T KNOW YOU! I WILL TAKE HER TO THE AUTHORITIES. THEY WILL REUNITE HER WITH HER FAMILY.
HAND HER OVER!
STAY BEHIND ME, CHILD!
9.

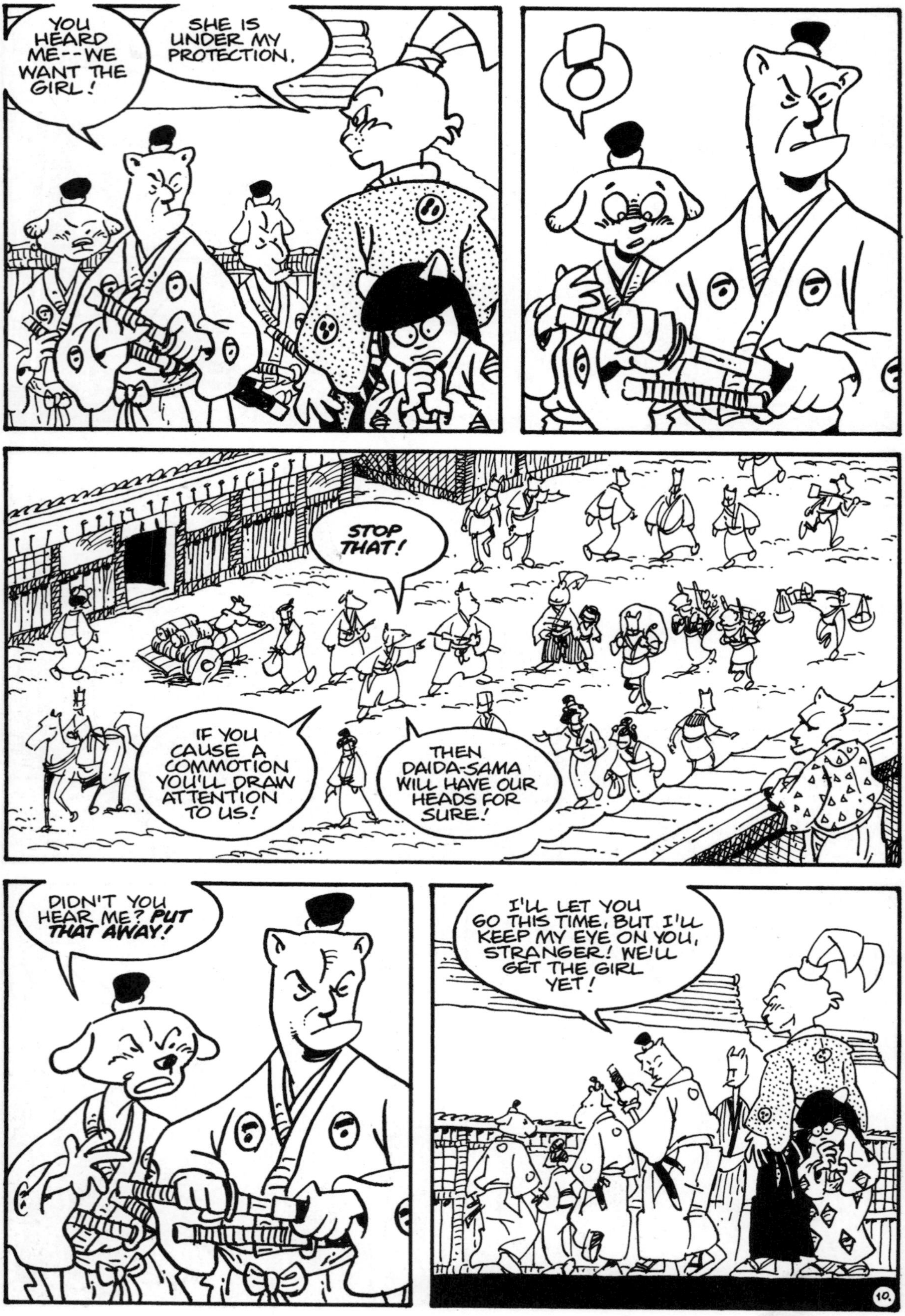
YOU HEARD ME--WE WANT THE GIRL!
SHE IS UNDER MY PROTECTION.
STOP THAT!
IF YOU CAUSE A COMMOTION YOU'LL DRAW ATTENTION TO US!
THEN DAIDA-SAMA WILL HAVE OUR HEADS FOR SURE!
DIDN'T YOU HEAR ME? PUT THAT AWAY!
I'LL LET YOU GO THIS TIME, BUT I'LL KEEP MY EYE ON YOU, STRANGER! WE'LL GET THE GIRL YET!
10.

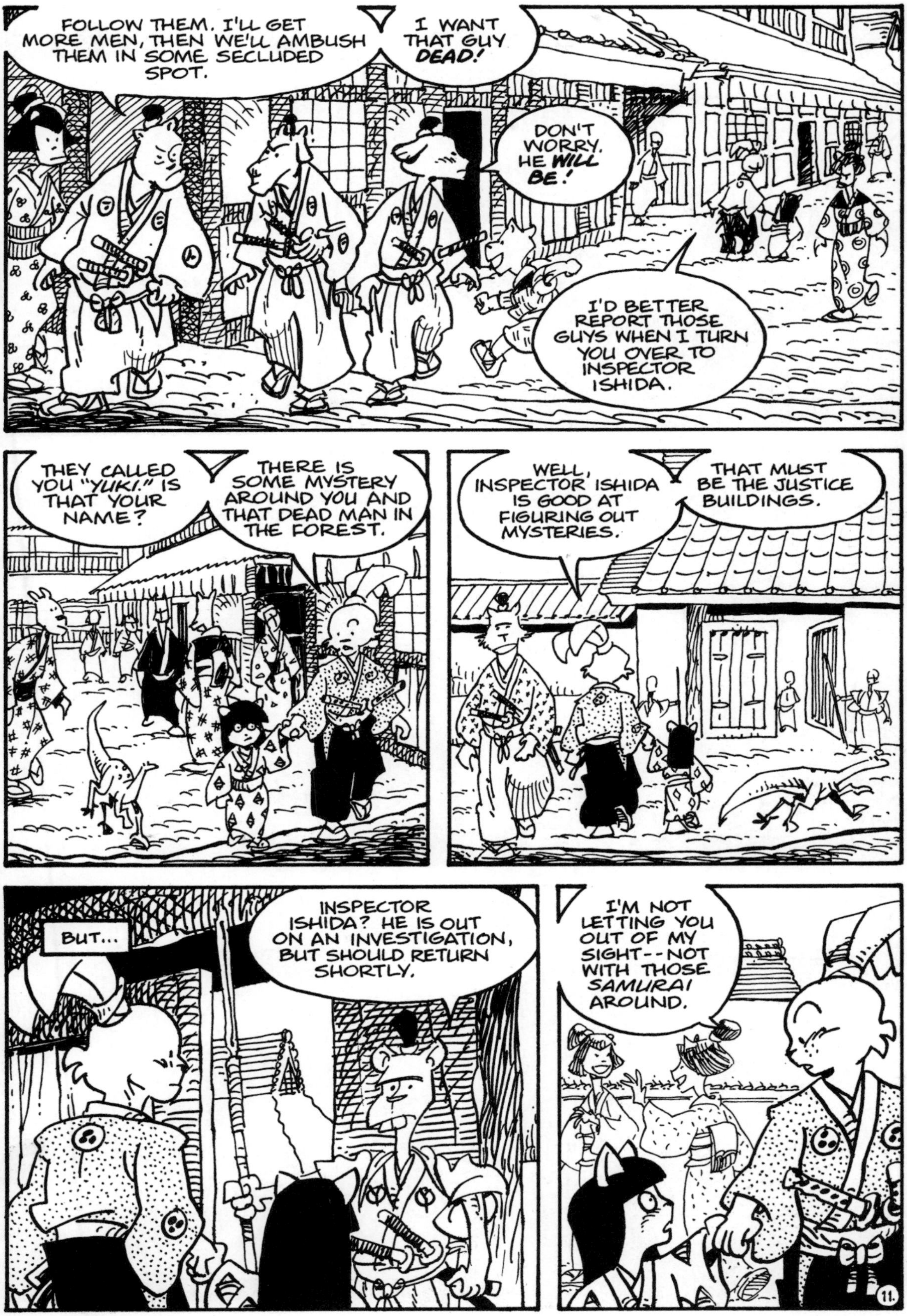

FOLLOW THEM. I'LL GET MORE MEN, THEN WE'LL AMBUSH THEM IN SOME SECLUDED SPOT.
I WANT THAT GUY *DEAD!*
DON'T WORRY. HE *WILL* BE!
I'D BETTER REPORT THOSE GUYS WHEN I TURN YOU OVER TO INSPECTOR ISHIDA.
THEY CALLED YOU "*YUKI.*" IS THAT YOUR NAME?
THERE IS SOME MYSTERY AROUND YOU AND THAT DEAD MAN IN THE FOREST.
WELL, INSPECTOR ISHIDA IS GOOD AT FIGURING OUT MYSTERIES.
THAT MUST BE THE JUSTICE BUILDINGS.
BUT...
INSPECTOR ISHIDA? HE IS OUT ON AN INVESTIGATION, BUT SHOULD RETURN SHORTLY.
I'M NOT LETTING YOU OUT OF MY SIGHT--NOT WITH THOSE *SAMURAI* AROUND.
11.

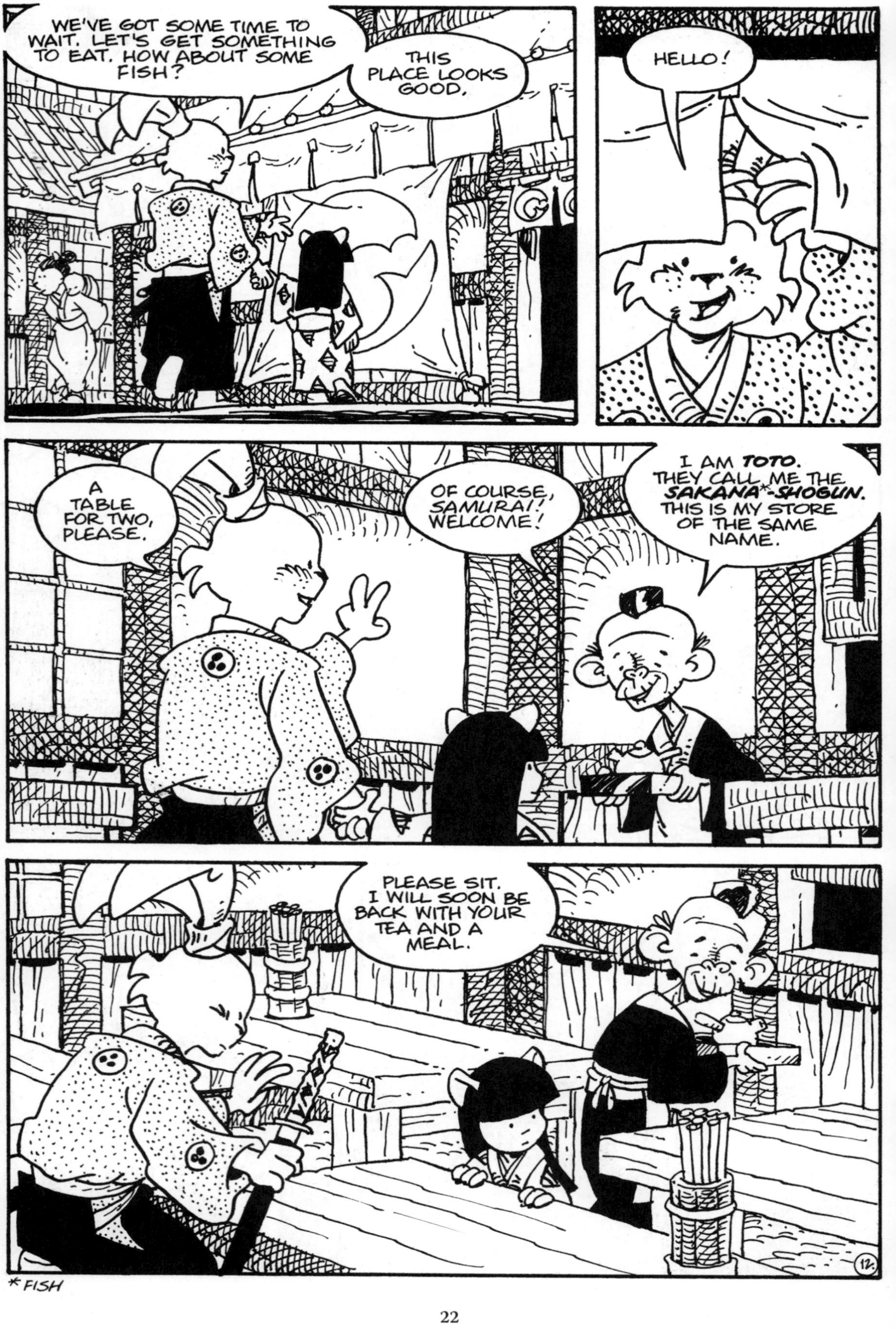
WE'VE GOT SOME TIME TO WAIT. LET'S GET SOMETHING TO EAT. HOW ABOUT SOME FISH?
THIS PLACE LOOKS GOOD.
HELLO!
A TABLE FOR TWO, PLEASE.
OF COURSE, SAMURAI! WELCOME!
I AM TOTO. THEY CALL ME THE SAKANA*-SHOGUN. THIS IS MY STORE OF THE SAME NAME.
PLEASE SIT. I WILL SOON BE BACK WITH YOUR TEA AND A MEAL.
12.

*FISH

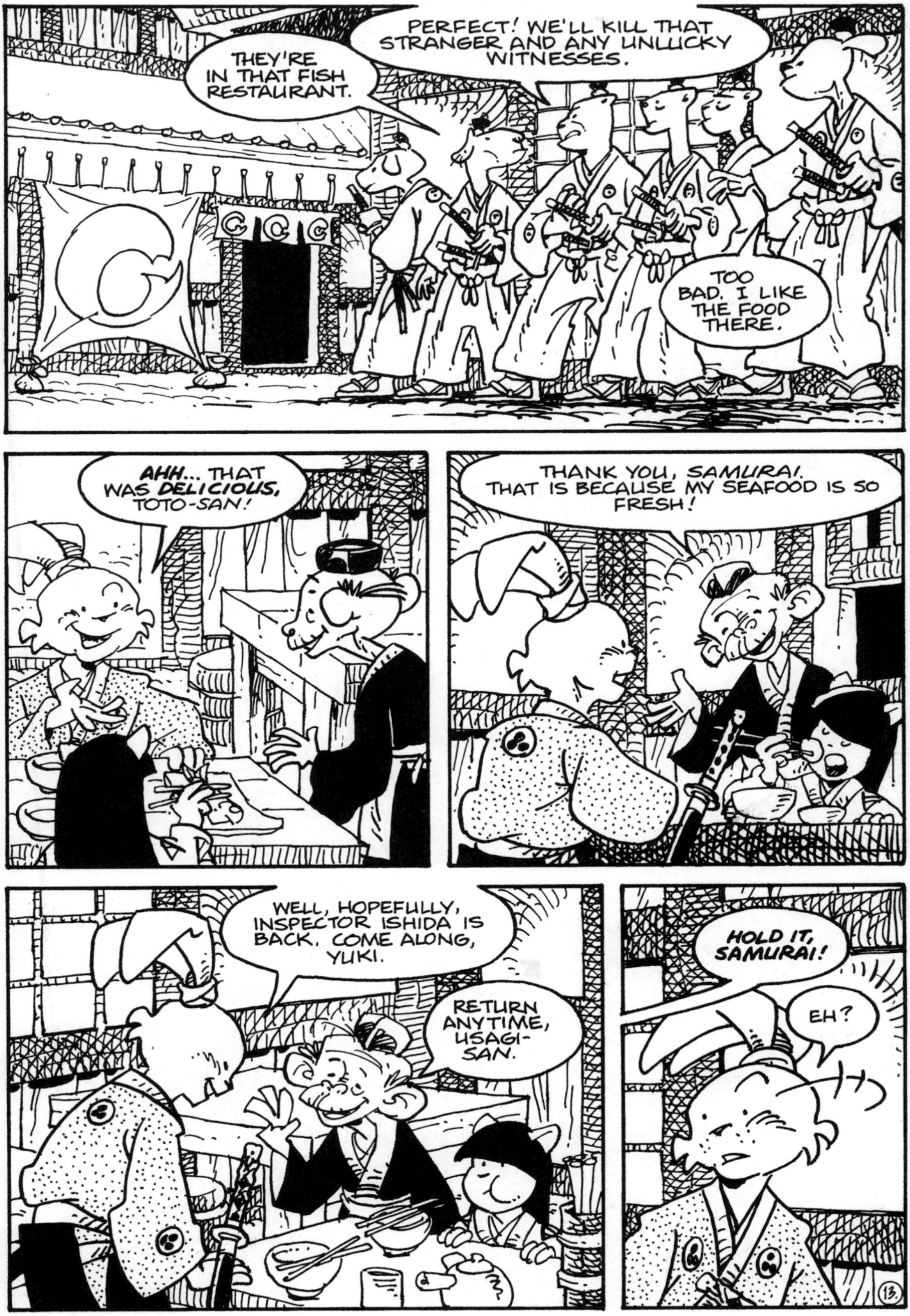
THEY'RE IN THAT FISH RESTAURANT.
PERFECT! WE'LL KILL THAT STRANGER AND ANY UNLUCKY WITNESSES.
TOO BAD. I LIKE THE FOOD THERE.
AHH... THAT WAS DELICIOUS, TOTO-SAN!
THANK YOU, SAMURAI. THAT IS BECAUSE MY SEAFOOD IS SO FRESH!
WELL, HOPEFULLY, INSPECTOR ISHIDA IS BACK. COME ALONG, YUKI.
RETURN ANYTIME, USAGI-SAN.
HOLD IT, SAMURAI!
EH?
13.

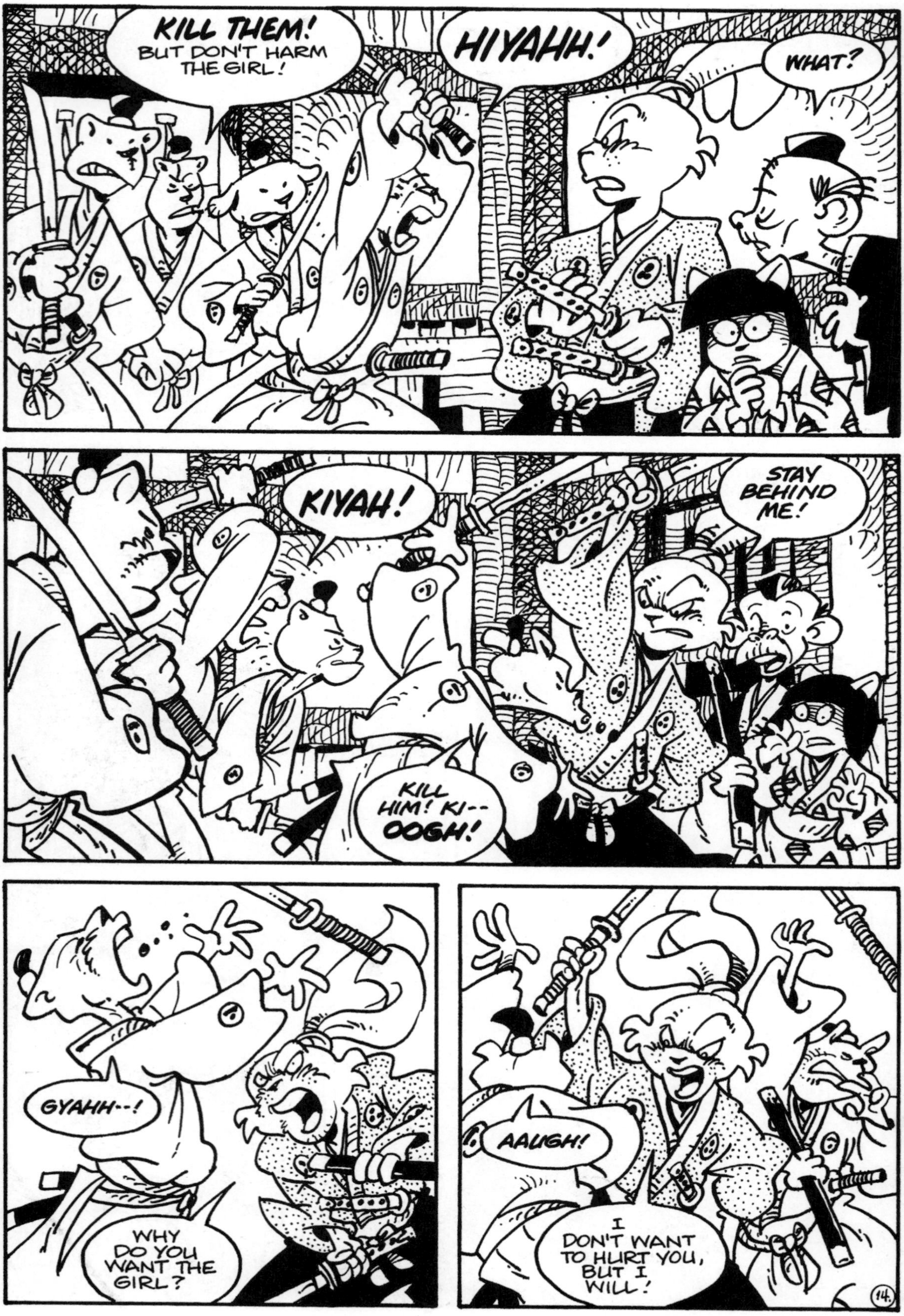
KILL THEM! BUT DON'T HARM THE GIRL!
HIYAHH!
WHAT?
KIYAH!
STAY BEHIND ME!
KILL HIM! KI-- OOGH!
...
GYAHH--!
WHY DO YOU WANT THE GIRL?
AAUGH!
I DON'T WANT TO HURT YOU, BUT I WILL!
14.

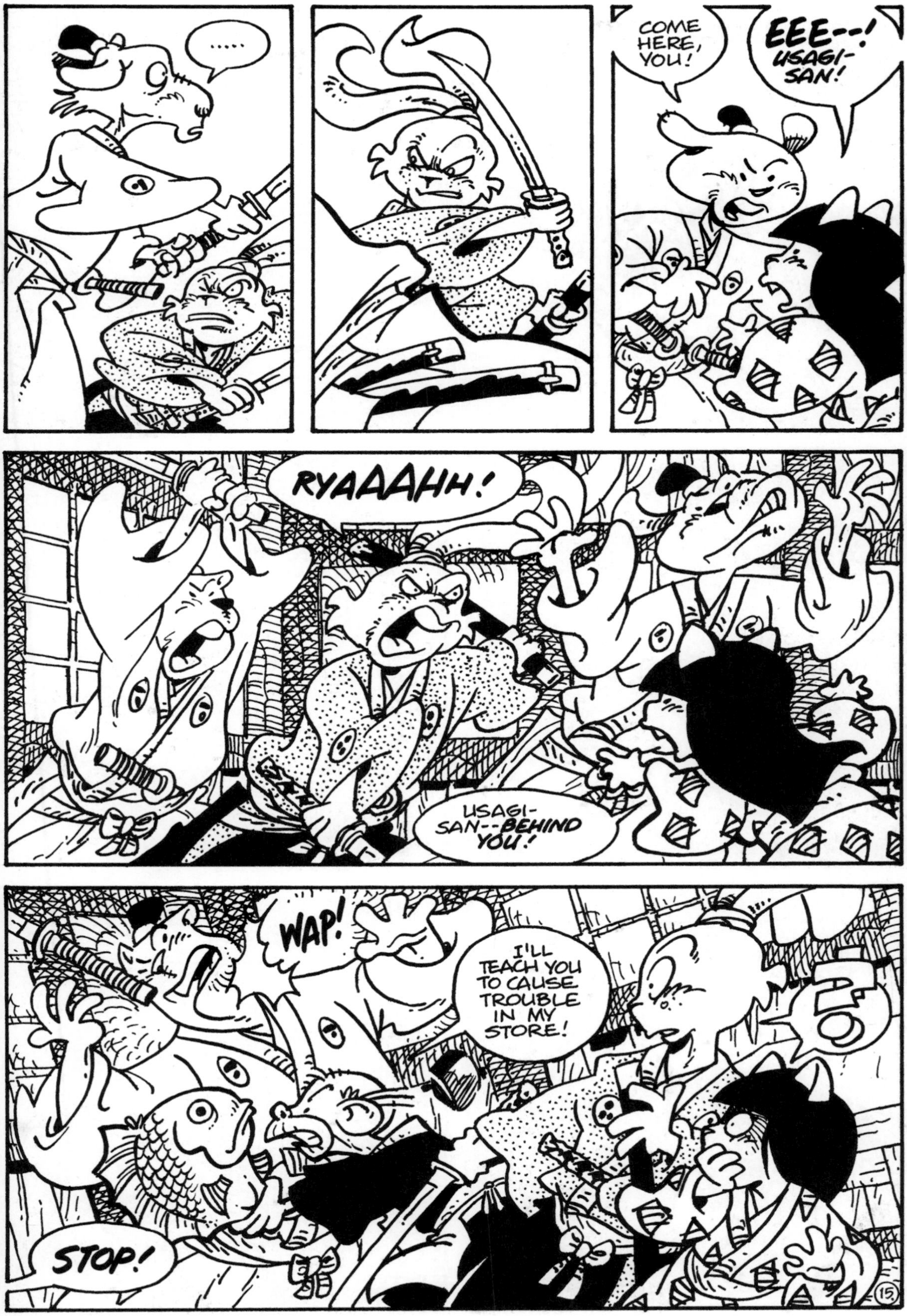
......
COME HERE, YOU!
EEE--! USAGI-SAN!
RYAAAHH!
USAGI-SAN--BEHIND YOU!
WAP!
I'LL TEACH YOU TO CAUSE TROUBLE IN MY STORE!
STOP!
15

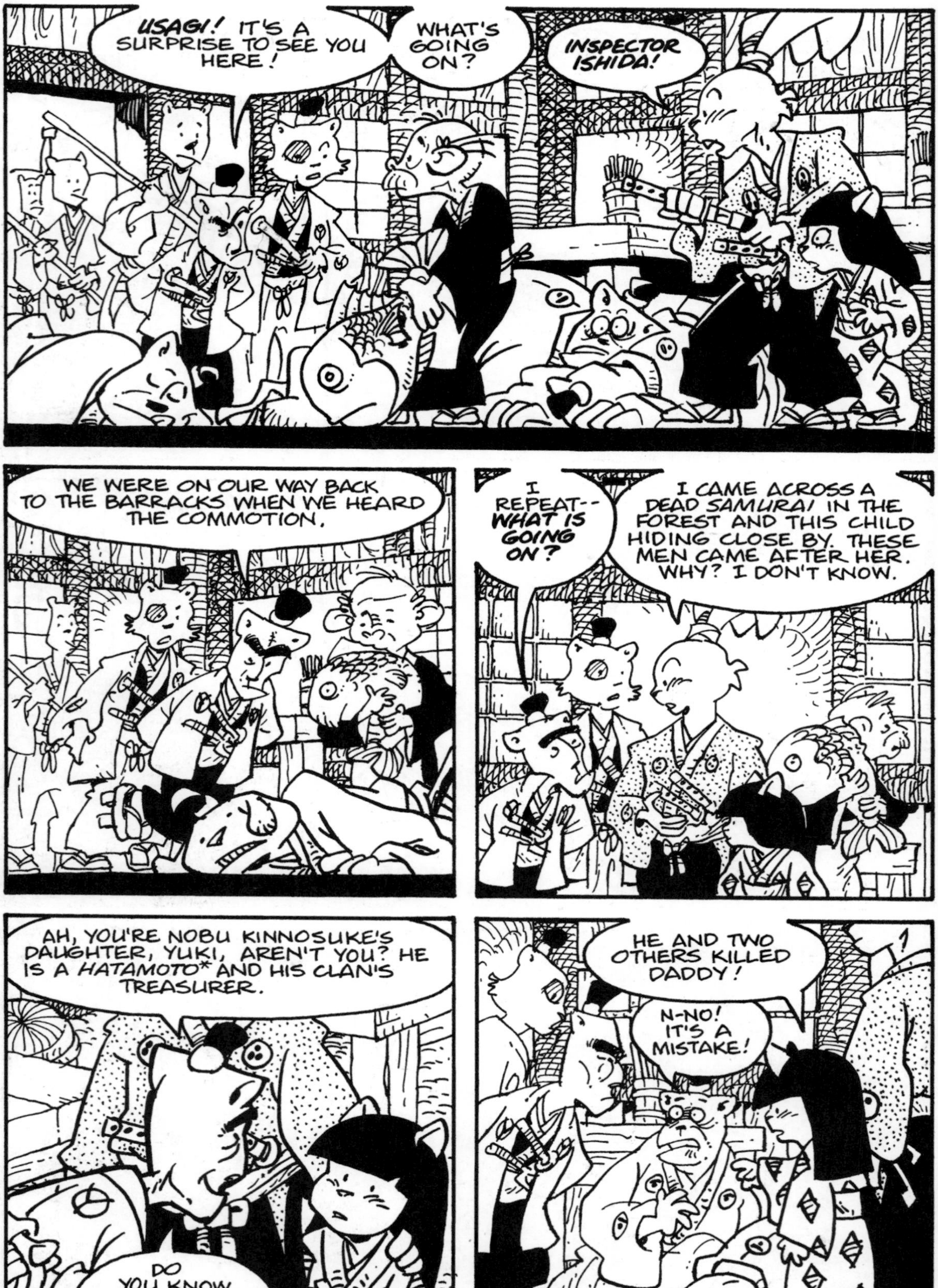
USAGI! IT'S A SURPRISE TO SEE YOU HERE!
WHAT'S GOING ON?
INSPECTOR ISHIDA!
WE WERE ON OUR WAY BACK TO THE BARRACKS WHEN WE HEARD THE COMMOTION.
I REPEAT-- WHAT IS GOING ON?
I CAME ACROSS A DEAD SAMURAI IN THE FOREST AND THIS CHILD HIDING CLOSE BY. THESE MEN CAME AFTER HER. WHY? I DON'T KNOW.
AH, YOU'RE NOBU KINNOSUKE'S DAUGHTER, YUKI, AREN'T YOU? HE IS A HATAMOTO* AND HIS CLAN'S TREASURER.
DO YOU KNOW WHO THAT DEAD SAMURAI IS?
HE AND TWO OTHERS KILLED DADDY!
N-NO! IT'S A MISTAKE!
16

* HIGH-RANKING SAMURAI

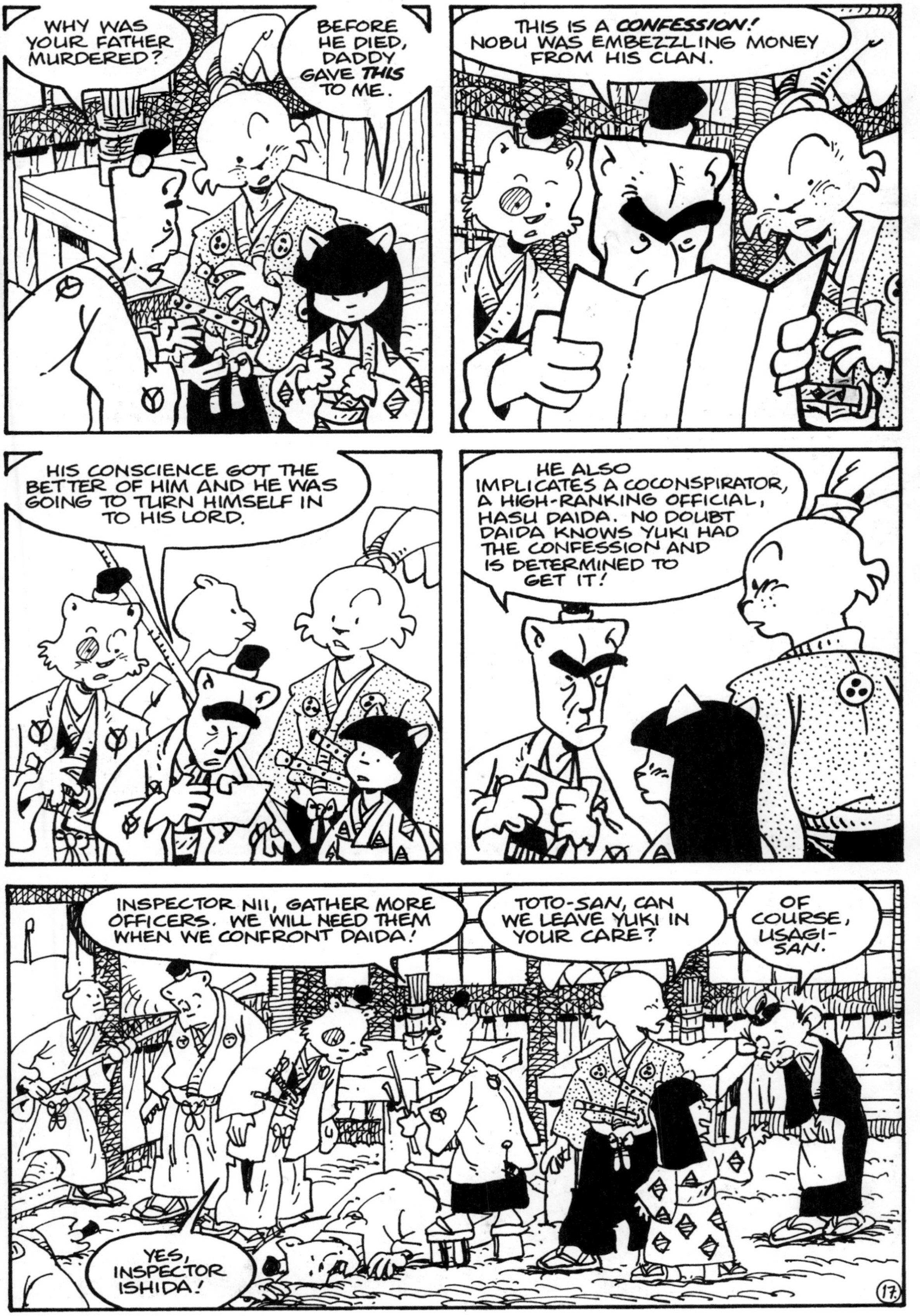
WHY WAS YOUR FATHER MURDERED?
BEFORE HE DIED, DADDY GAVE THIS TO ME.
THIS IS A CONFESSION! NOBU WAS EMBEZZLING MONEY FROM HIS CLAN.
HIS CONSCIENCE GOT THE BETTER OF HIM AND HE WAS GOING TO TURN HIMSELF IN TO HIS LORD.
HE ALSO IMPLICATES A COCONSPIRATOR, A HIGH-RANKING OFFICIAL, HASU DAIDA. NO DOUBT DAIDA KNOWS YUKI HAD THE CONFESSION AND IS DETERMINED TO GET IT!
INSPECTOR NII, GATHER MORE OFFICERS. WE WILL NEED THEM WHEN WE CONFRONT DAIDA!
YES, INSPECTOR ISHIDA!
TOTO-SAN, CAN WE LEAVE YUKI IN YOUR CARE?
OF COURSE, USAGI-SAN.
17

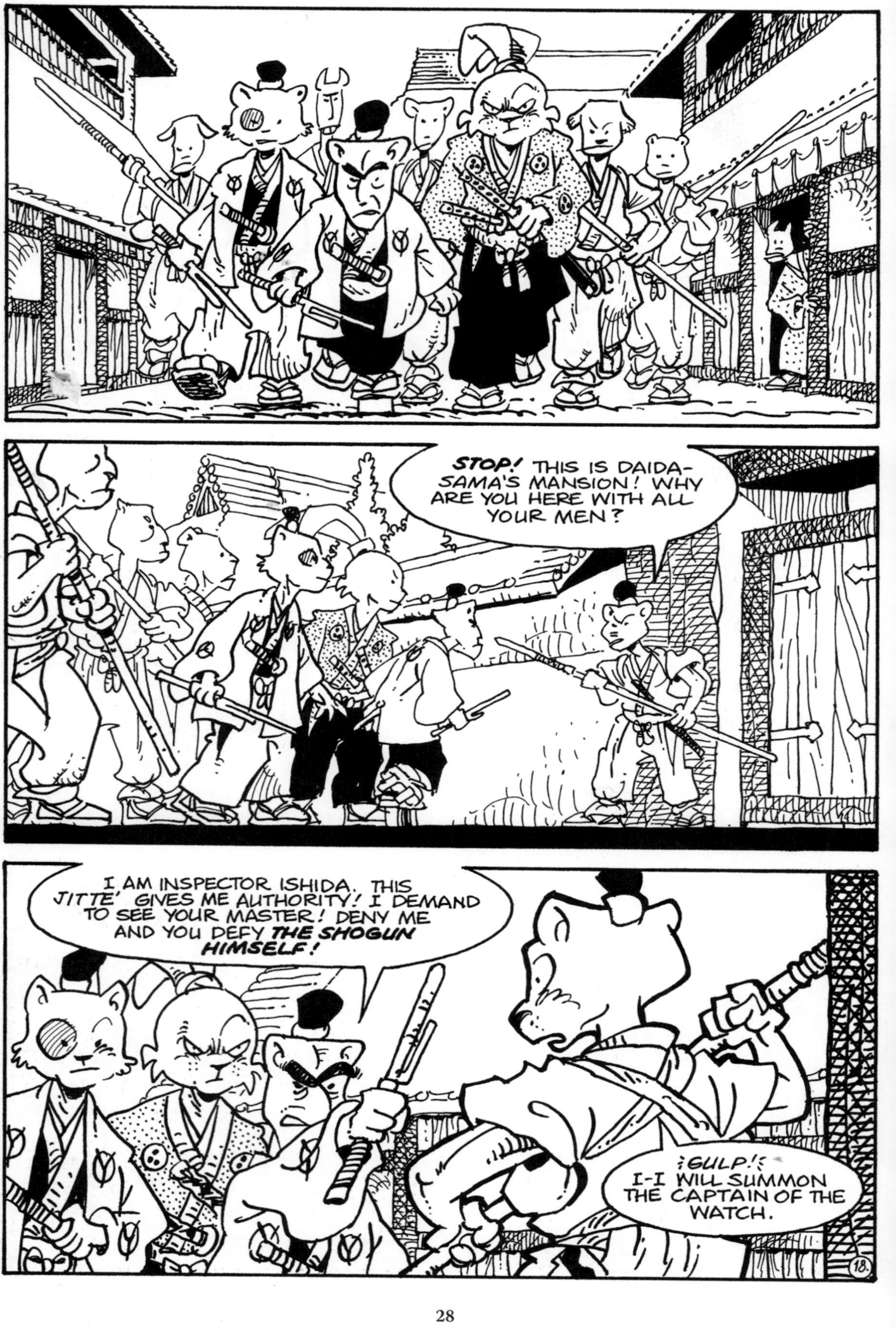
STOP! THIS IS DAIDA-SAMA'S MANSION! WHY ARE YOU HERE WITH ALL YOUR MEN?
I AM INSPECTOR ISHIDA. THIS JITTE' GIVES ME AUTHORITY! I DEMAND TO SEE YOUR MASTER! DENY ME AND YOU DEFY **THE SHOGUN HIMSELF!**
GULP!
I-I WILL SUMMON THE CAPTAIN OF THE WATCH.
18.

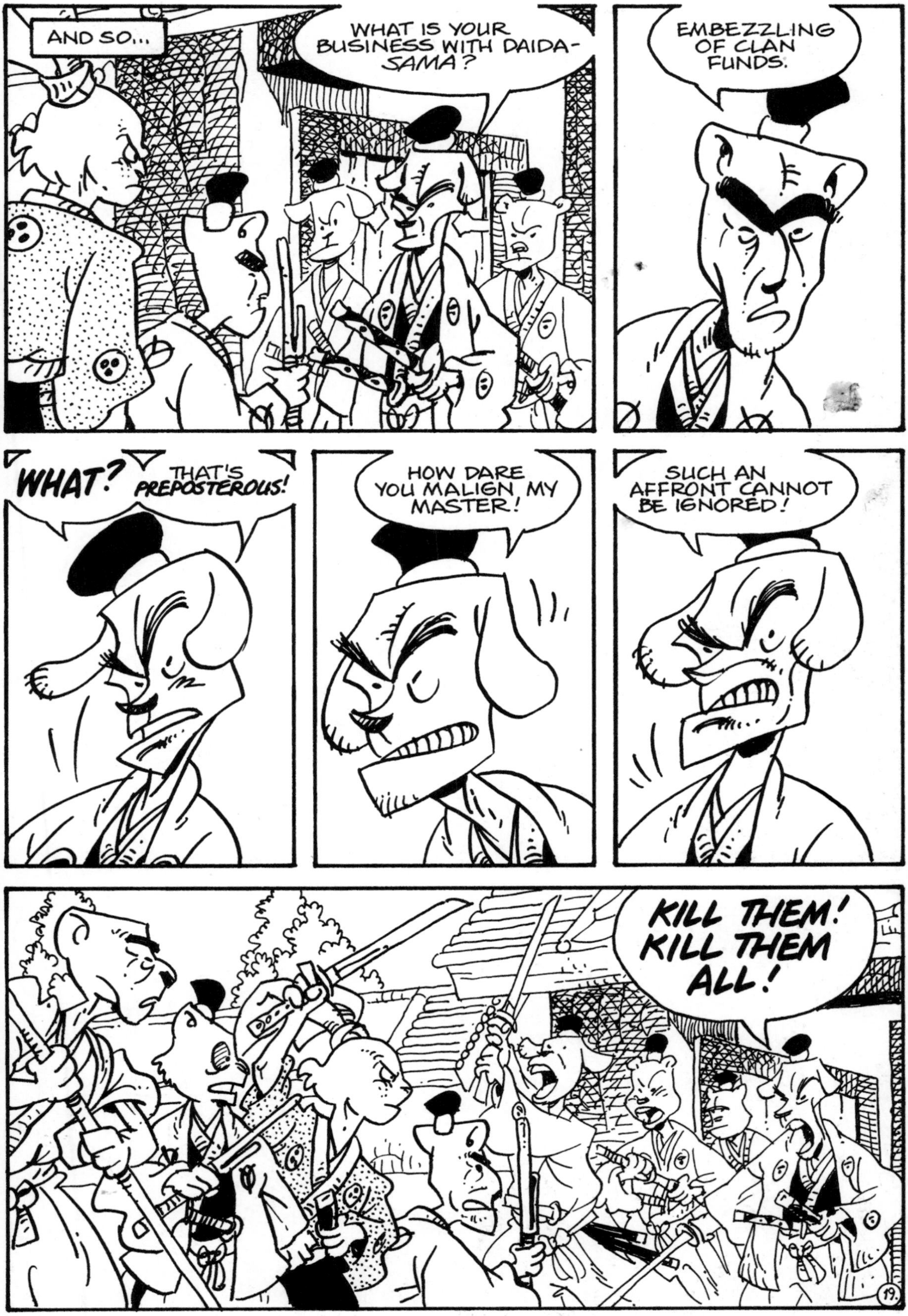
AND SO...
WHAT IS YOUR BUSINESS WITH DAIDA-SAMA?
EMBEZZLING OF CLAN FUNDS.
WHAT?
THAT'S PREPOSTEROUS!
HOW DARE YOU MALIGN MY MASTER!
SUCH AN AFFRONT CANNOT BE IGNORED!
KILL THEM! KILL THEM ALL!
19.

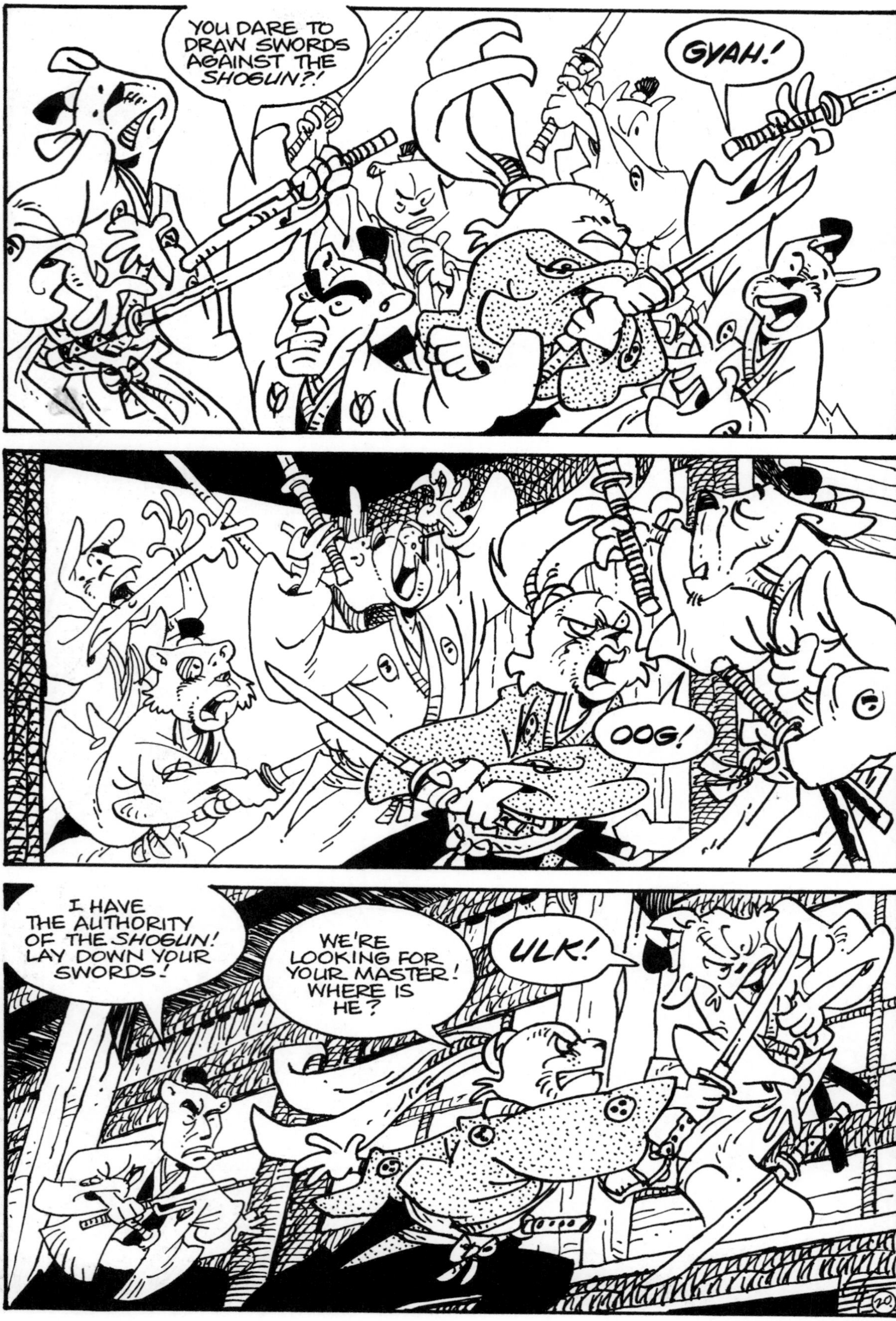
YOU DARE TO DRAW SWORDS AGAINST THE SHOGUN?!
GYAH!
OOG!
I HAVE THE AUTHORITY OF THE SHOGUN! LAY DOWN YOUR SWORDS!
WE'RE LOOKING FOR YOUR MASTER! WHERE IS HE?
ULK!
20.

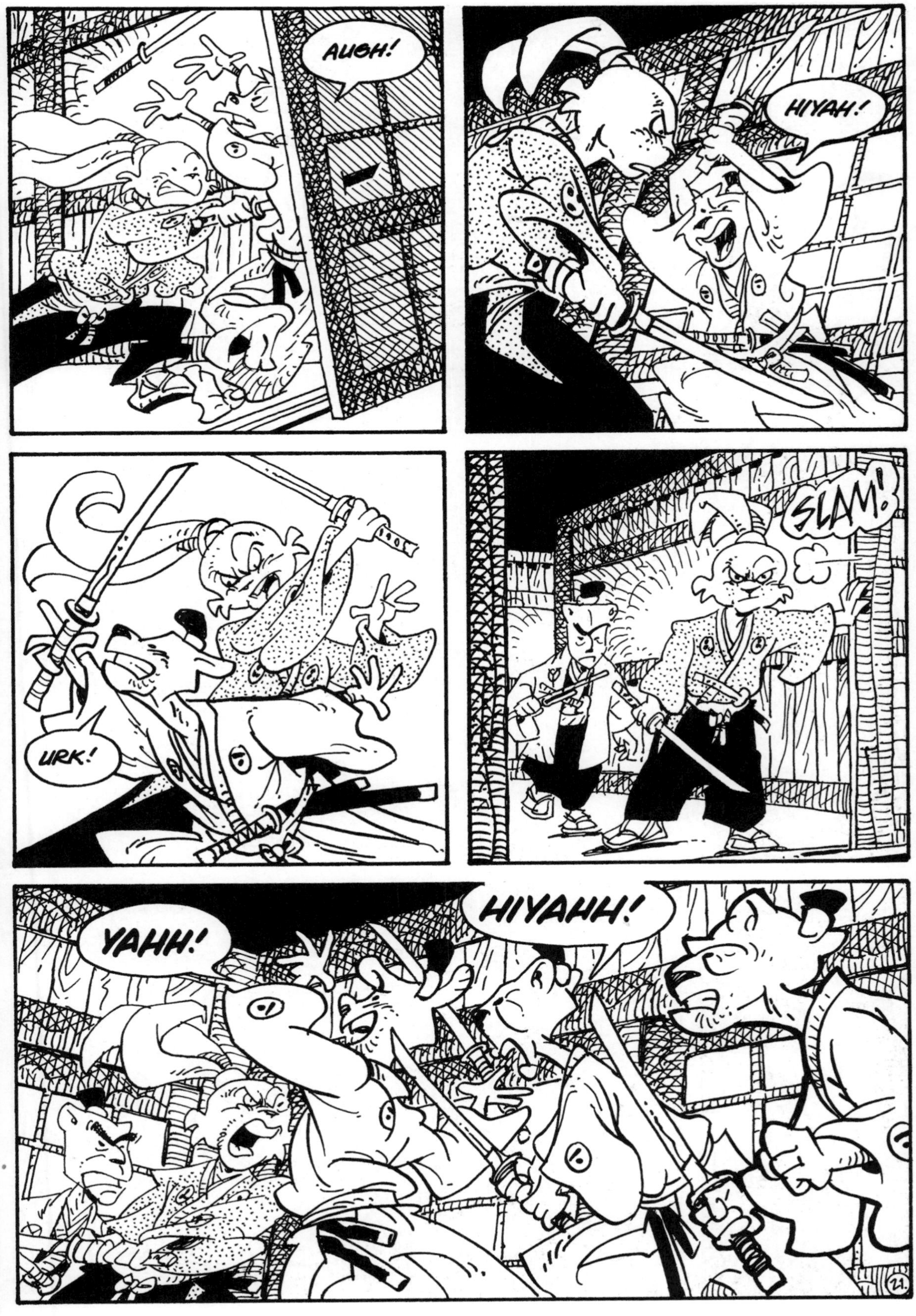
AUGH!
HIYAH!
URK!
SLAM!
YAHH!
HIYAHH!
21.

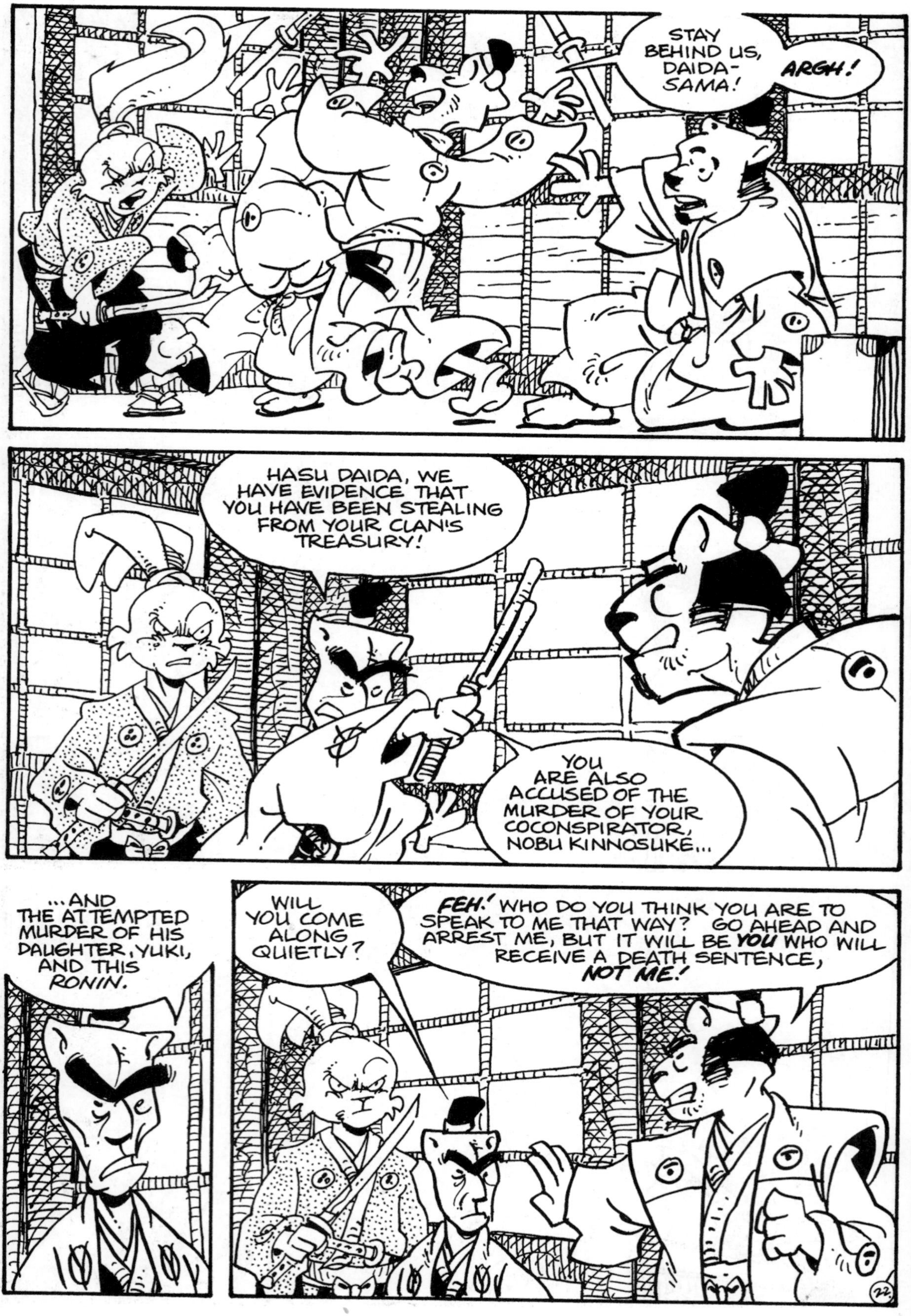
STAY BEHIND US, DAIDA-SAMA!
ARGH!
HASU DAIDA, WE HAVE EVIDENCE THAT YOU HAVE BEEN STEALING FROM YOUR CLAN'S TREASURY!
YOU ARE ALSO ACCUSED OF THE MURDER OF YOUR COCONSPIRATOR, NOBU KINNOSUKE...
...AND THE ATTEMPTED MURDER OF HIS DAUGHTER, YUKI, AND THIS *RONIN*.
WILL YOU COME ALONG QUIETLY?
FEH! WHO DO YOU THINK YOU ARE TO SPEAK TO ME THAT WAY? GO AHEAD AND ARREST ME, BUT IT WILL BE ***YOU*** WHO WILL RECEIVE A DEATH SENTENCE, ***NOT ME!***
22.

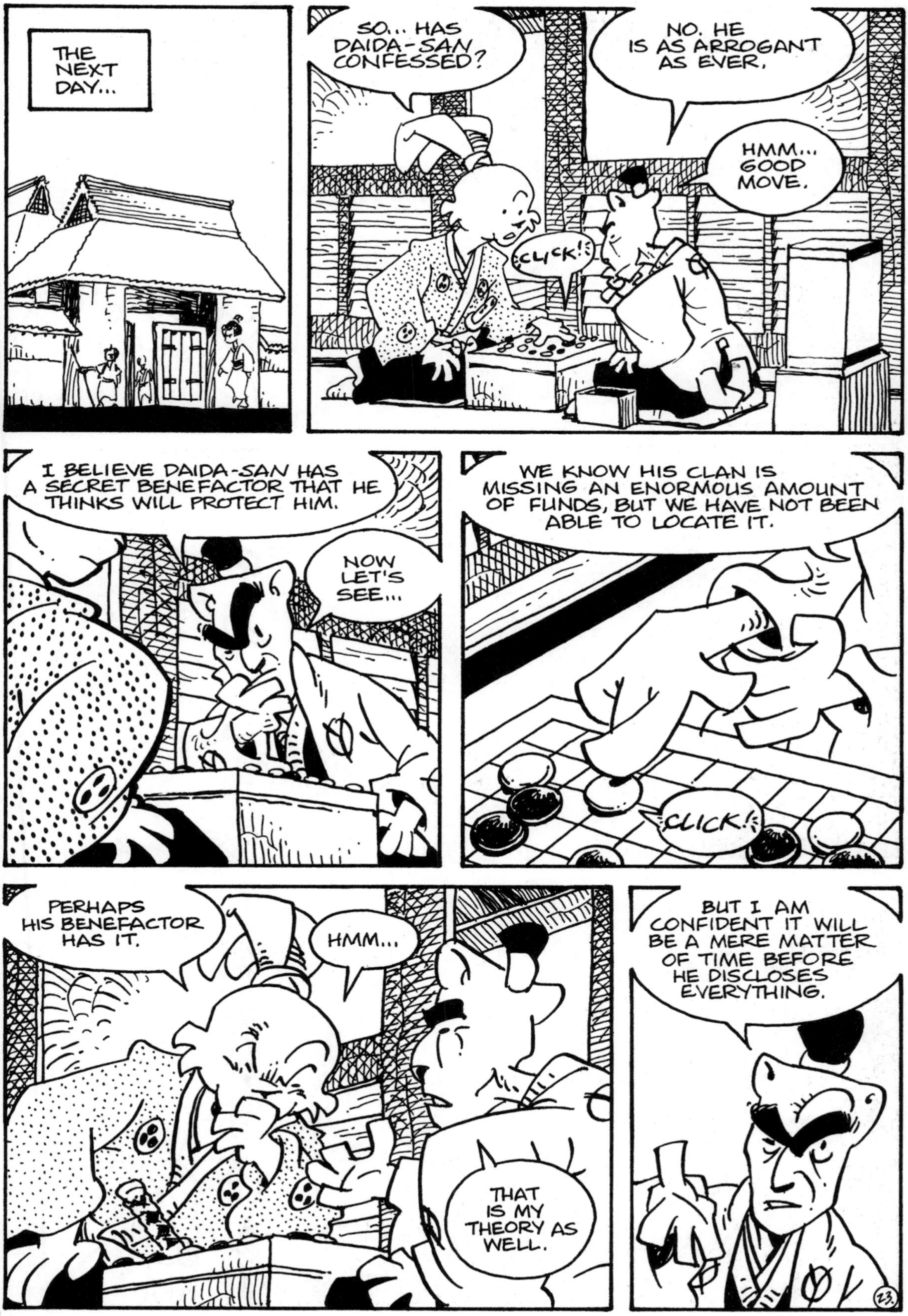
THE NEXT DAY...
SO... HAS DAIDA-SAN CONFESSED?
NO. HE IS AS ARROGANT AS EVER.
CLICK!
HMM... GOOD MOVE.
I BELIEVE DAIDA-SAN HAS A SECRET BENEFACTOR THAT HE THINKS WILL PROTECT HIM.
NOW LET'S SEE...
WE KNOW HIS CLAN IS MISSING AN ENORMOUS AMOUNT OF FUNDS, BUT WE HAVE NOT BEEN ABLE TO LOCATE IT.
CLICK!
PERHAPS HIS BENEFACTOR HAS IT.
HMM...
THAT IS MY THEORY AS WELL.
BUT I AM CONFIDENT IT WILL BE A MERE MATTER OF TIME BEFORE HE DISCLOSES EVERYTHING.
23

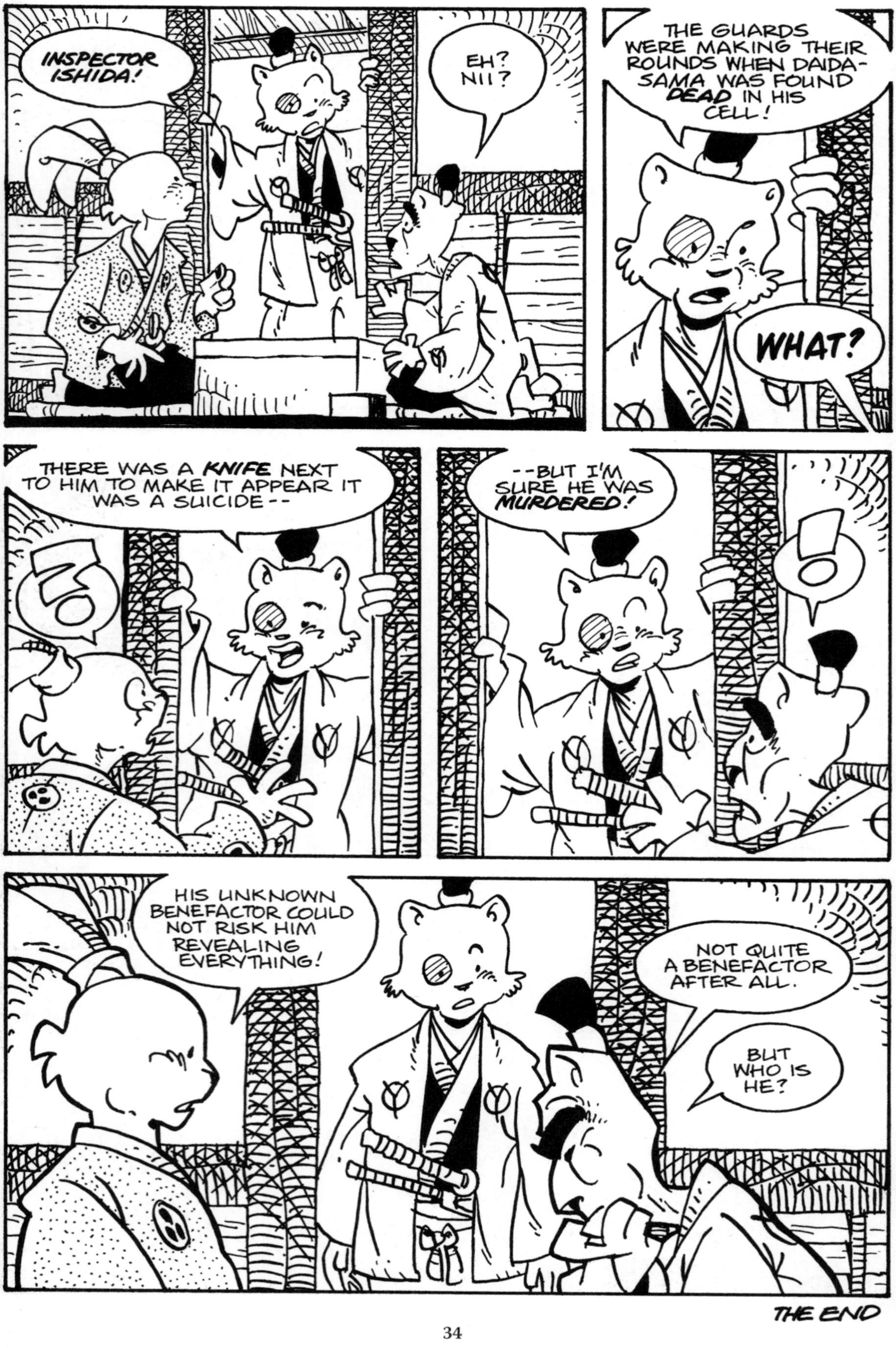
INSPECTOR ISHIDA!
EH? NII?
THE GUARDS WERE MAKING THEIR ROUNDS WHEN DAIDA-SAMA WAS FOUND DEAD IN HIS CELL!
WHAT?
THERE WAS A KNIFE NEXT TO HIM TO MAKE IT APPEAR IT WAS A SUICIDE--
--BUT I'M SURE HE WAS MURDERED!
HIS UNKNOWN BENEFACTOR COULD NOT RISK HIM REVEALING EVERYTHING!
NOT QUITE A BENEFACTOR AFTER ALL.
BUT WHO IS HE?
THE END

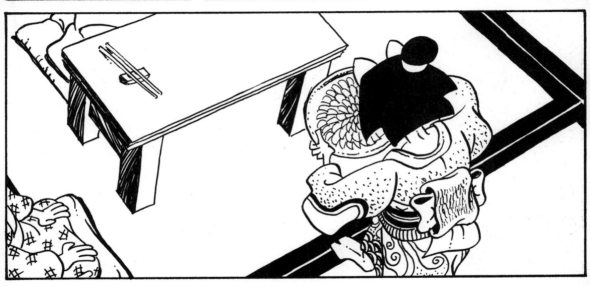

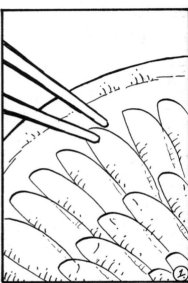

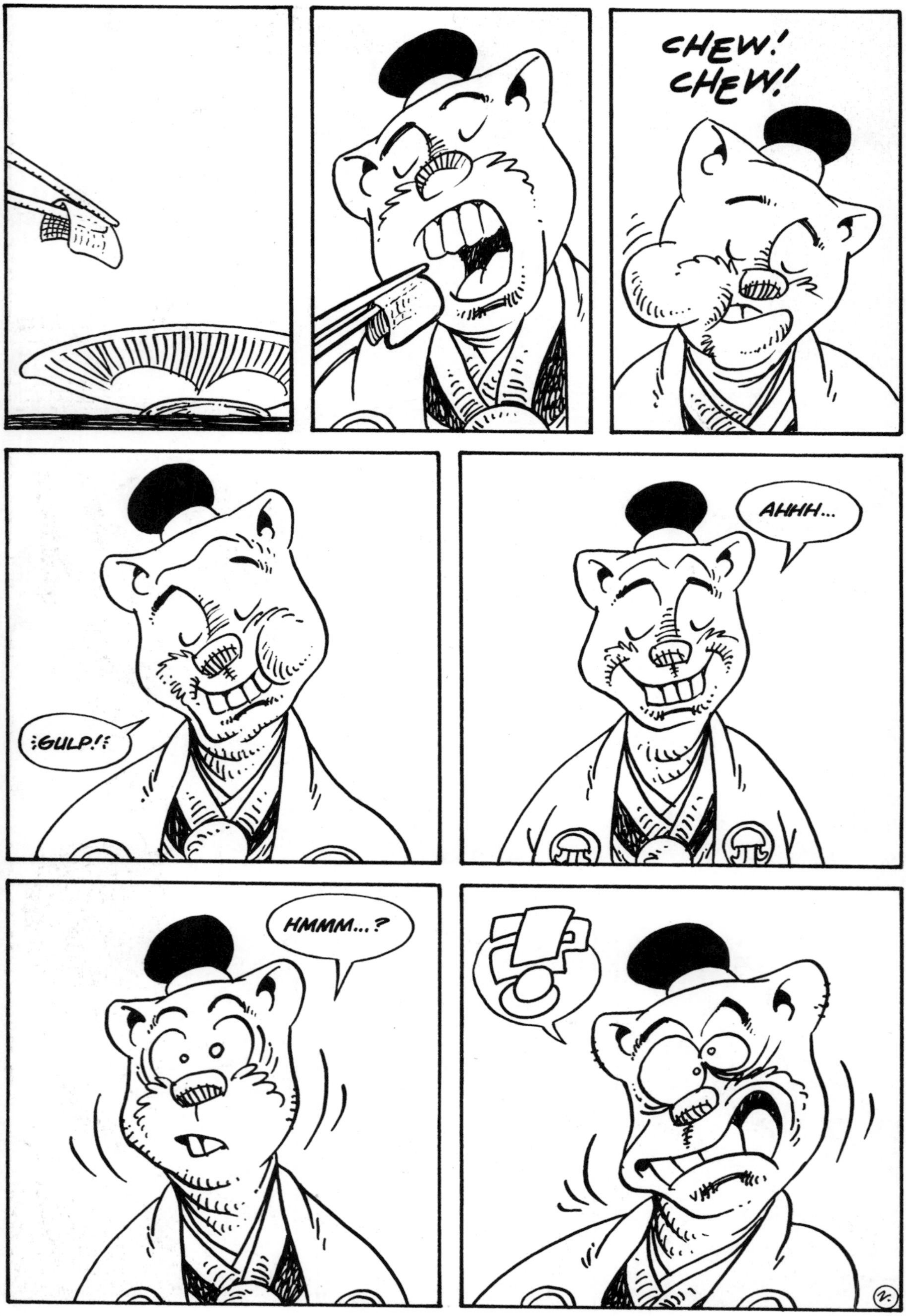
CHEW! CHEW!
:GULP!:
AHHH...
HMMM...?

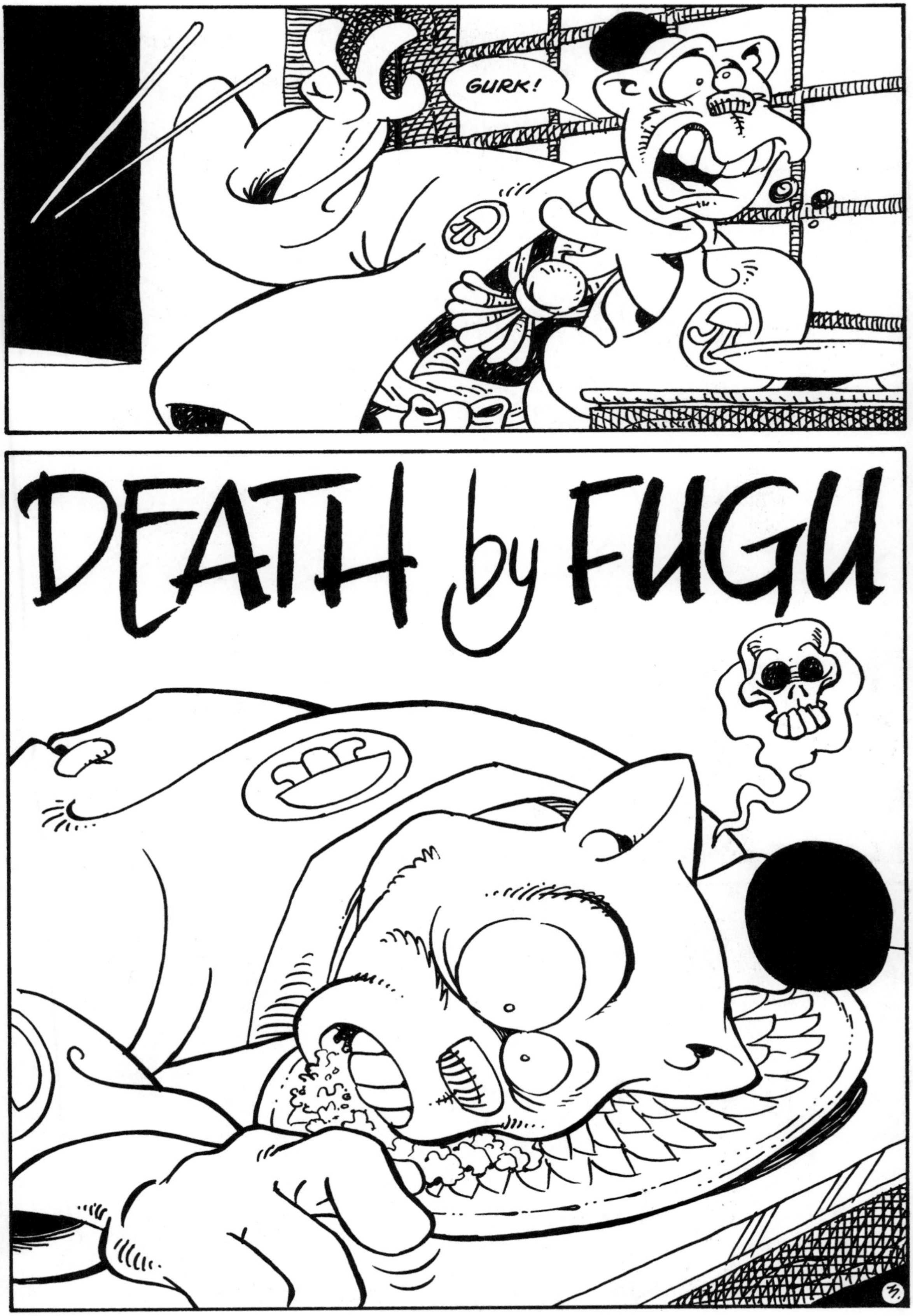
GURK!
DEATH by FUGU

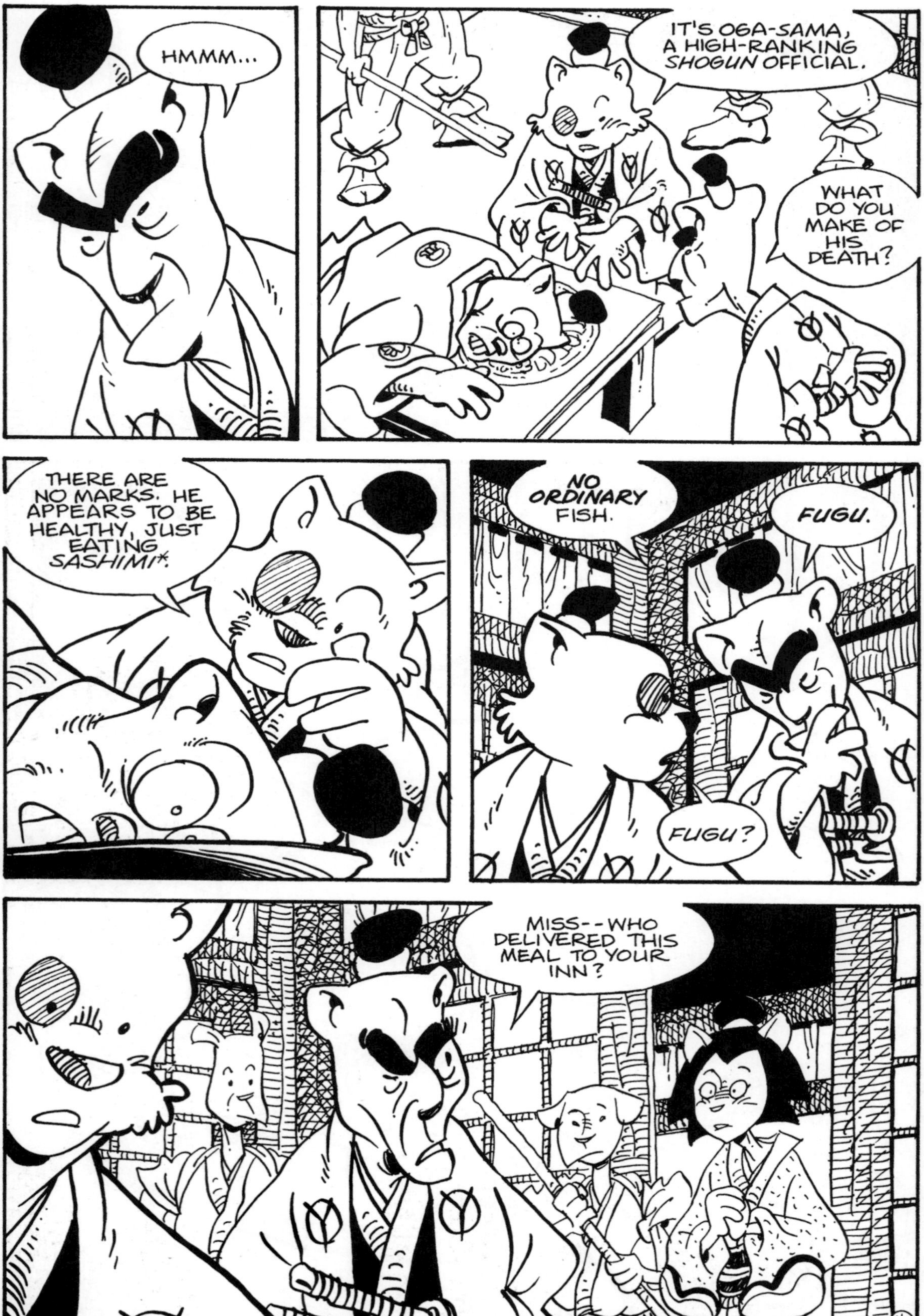
HMMM...
IT'S OGA-SAMA, A HIGH-RANKING SHOGUN OFFICIAL.
WHAT DO YOU MAKE OF HIS DEATH?
THERE ARE NO MARKS. HE APPEARS TO BE HEALTHY, JUST EATING SASHIMI*.
NO ORDINARY FISH.
FUGU.
FUGU?
MISS--WHO DELIVERED THIS MEAL TO YOUR INN?
4.

*RAW FISH

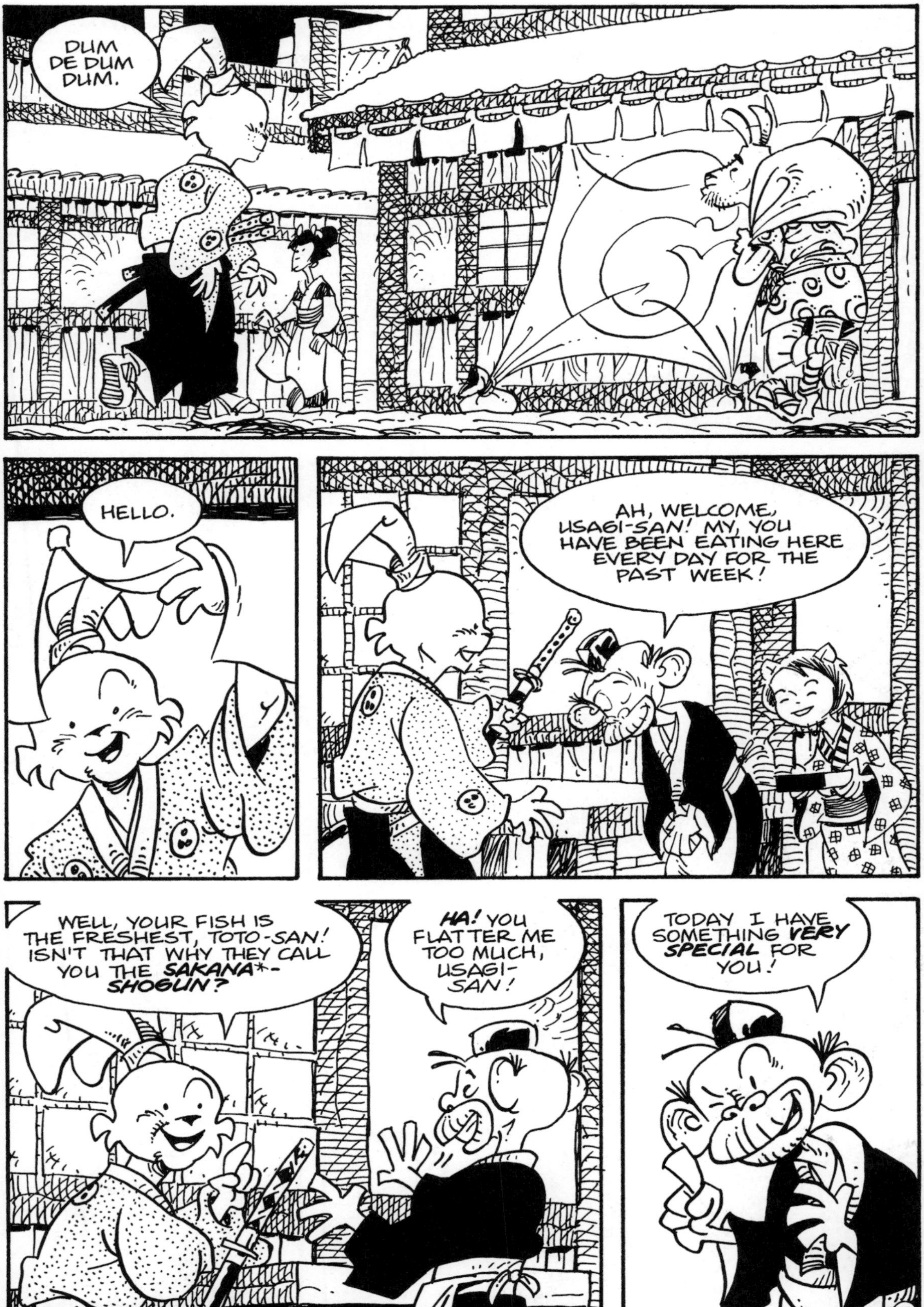
DUM DE DUM DUM.
HELLO.
AH, WELCOME, USAGI-SAN! MY, YOU HAVE BEEN EATING HERE EVERY DAY FOR THE PAST WEEK!
WELL, YOUR FISH IS THE FRESHEST, TOTO-SAN! ISN'T THAT WHY THEY CALL YOU THE SAKANA*-SHOGUN?
HA! YOU FLATTER ME TOO MUCH, USAGI-SAN!
TODAY I HAVE SOMETHING VERY SPECIAL FOR YOU!
5

*FISH

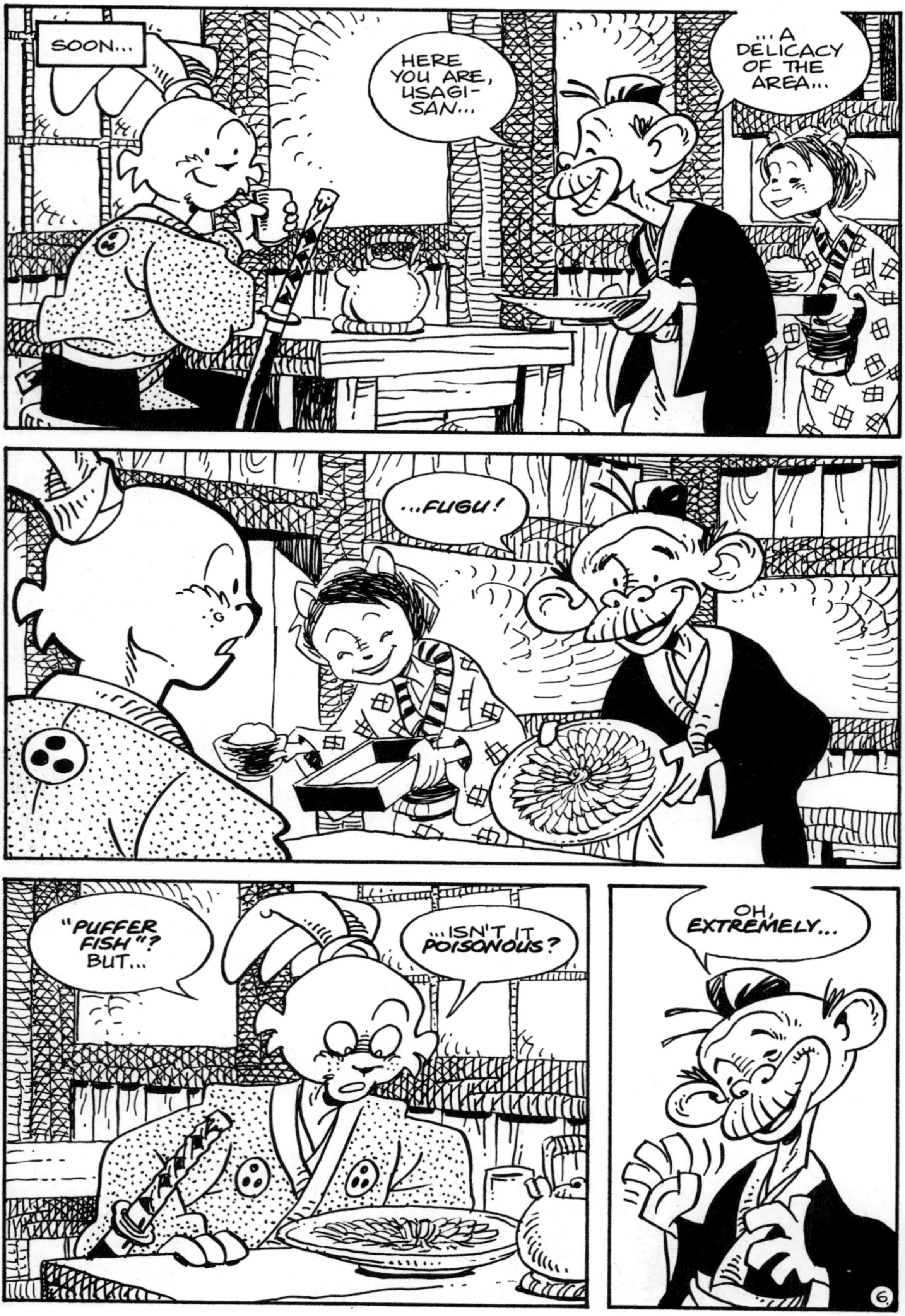
SOON...
HERE YOU ARE, USAGI-SAN...
...A DELICACY OF THE AREA...
...FUGU!
"PUFFER FISH"? BUT...
...ISN'T IT POISONOUS?
OH, EXTREMELY...
6.

...BUT ONLY IF IT IS PREPARED IMPROPERLY. THE *LIVER* IS ESPECIALLY DEADLY!

WE MUST BE CAREFUL NOT TO EVEN *NICK* THE LIVER. OF COURSE, I AM AN EXPERT WITH A KNIFE.

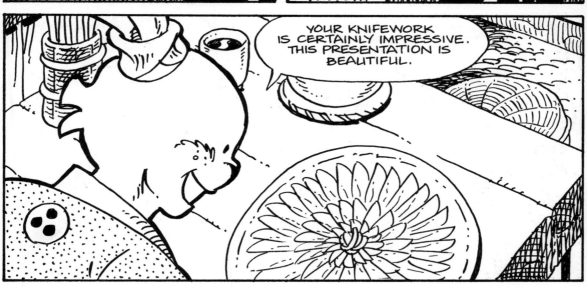

YOUR KNIFEWORK IS CERTAINLY IMPRESSIVE. THIS PRESENTATION IS BEAUTIFUL.

TRY A SLICE, USAGI-SAN! YOU'LL FIND THAT IT'S ALSO *DELICIOUS!*

STOP, USAGI!

HUH?

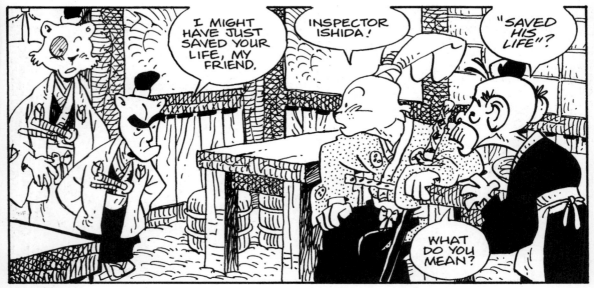

I MIGHT HAVE JUST SAVED YOUR LIFE, MY FRIEND.

INSPECTOR ISHIDA!

"SAVED HIS LIFE"?

WHAT DO YOU MEAN?

A *SHOGUNATE* OFFICIAL DIED THIS EVENING. *FUGU* POISONING MAY HAVE BEEN THE CAUSE.

MY *FUGU*?! IMPOSSIBLE!

DID YOU PREPARE A MEAL OF *FUGU* FOR OGA-SAMA OF THE *SHOGUN'S* STAFF?

OGA-SAMA? *DEAD?* OH, NO! HE ALWAYS ORDERS A *FUGU* PLATE FROM ME WHENEVER HE TRAVELS THROUGH TOWN!

MY ASSISTANT DELIVERED IT AN HOUR AGO.

8

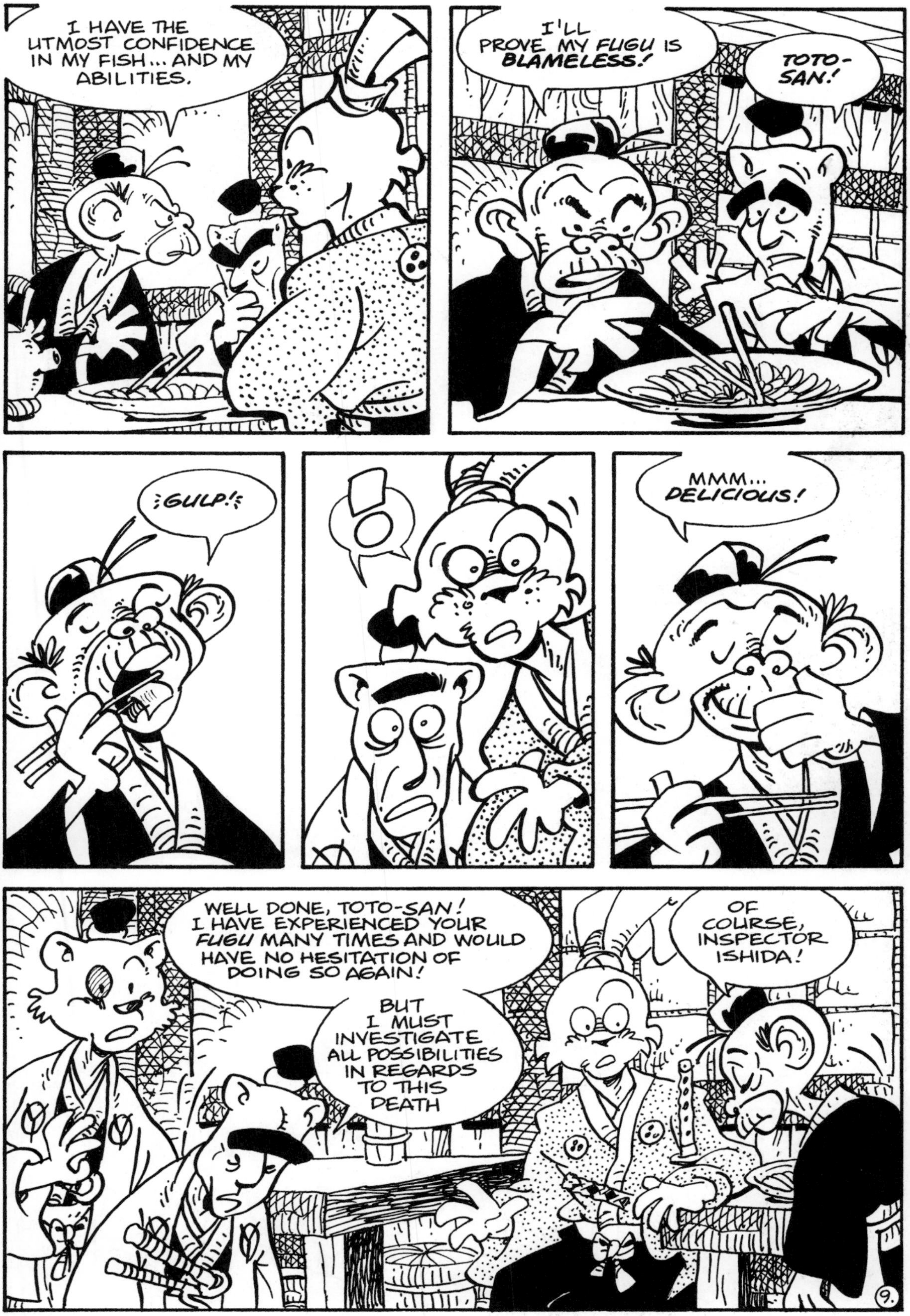

I HAVE THE UTMOST CONFIDENCE IN MY FISH... AND MY ABILITIES.
I'LL PROVE MY FUGU IS BLAMELESS!
TOTO-SAN!
GULP!
!
MMM... DELICIOUS!
WELL DONE, TOTO-SAN! I HAVE EXPERIENCED YOUR FUGU MANY TIMES AND WOULD HAVE NO HESITATION OF DOING SO AGAIN!
BUT I MUST INVESTIGATE ALL POSSIBILITIES IN REGARDS TO THIS DEATH
OF COURSE, INSPECTOR ISHIDA!
9.

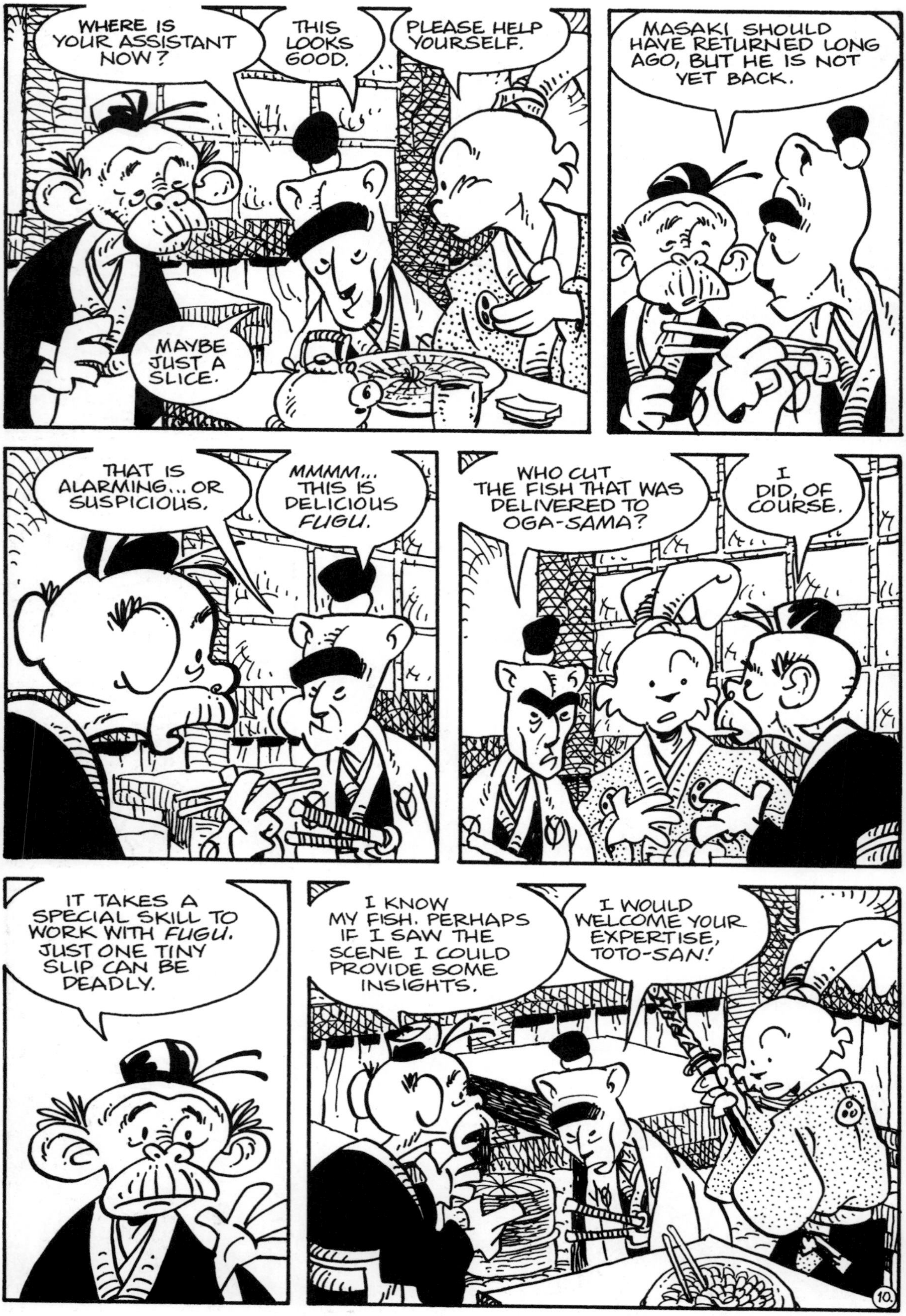
WHERE IS YOUR ASSISTANT NOW?
THIS LOOKS GOOD.
PLEASE HELP YOURSELF.
MAYBE JUST A SLICE.
MASAKI SHOULD HAVE RETURNED LONG AGO, BUT HE IS NOT YET BACK.
THAT IS ALARMING...OR SUSPICIOUS.
MMMM... THIS IS DELICIOUS *FUGU*.
WHO CUT THE FISH THAT WAS DELIVERED TO OGA-SAMA?
I DID, OF COURSE.
IT TAKES A SPECIAL SKILL TO WORK WITH *FUGU*. JUST ONE TINY SLIP CAN BE DEADLY.
I KNOW MY FISH. PERHAPS IF I SAW THE SCENE I COULD PROVIDE SOME INSIGHTS.
I WOULD WELCOME YOUR EXPERTISE, TOTO-SAN!
10.

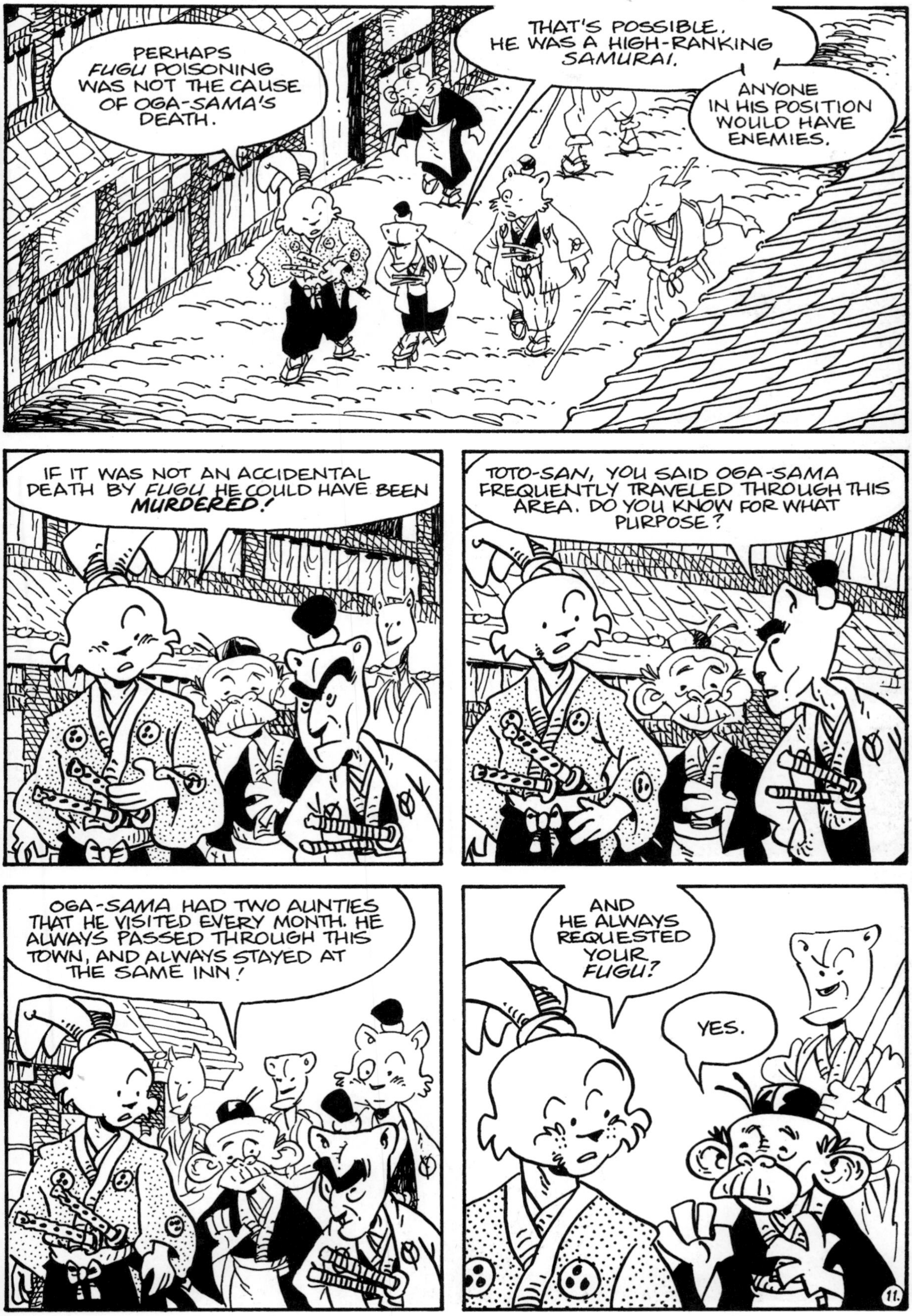
PERHAPS FUGU POISONING WAS NOT THE CAUSE OF OGA-SAMA'S DEATH.
THAT'S POSSIBLE. HE WAS A HIGH-RANKING SAMURAI.
ANYONE IN HIS POSITION WOULD HAVE ENEMIES.
IF IT WAS NOT AN ACCIDENTAL DEATH BY FUGU HE COULD HAVE BEEN MURDERED!
TOTO-SAN, YOU SAID OGA-SAMA FREQUENTLY TRAVELED THROUGH THIS AREA. DO YOU KNOW FOR WHAT PURPOSE?
OGA-SAMA HAD TWO AUNTIES THAT HE VISITED EVERY MONTH. HE ALWAYS PASSED THROUGH THIS TOWN, AND ALWAYS STAYED AT THE SAME INN!
AND HE ALWAYS REQUESTED YOUR FUGU?
YES.
11.

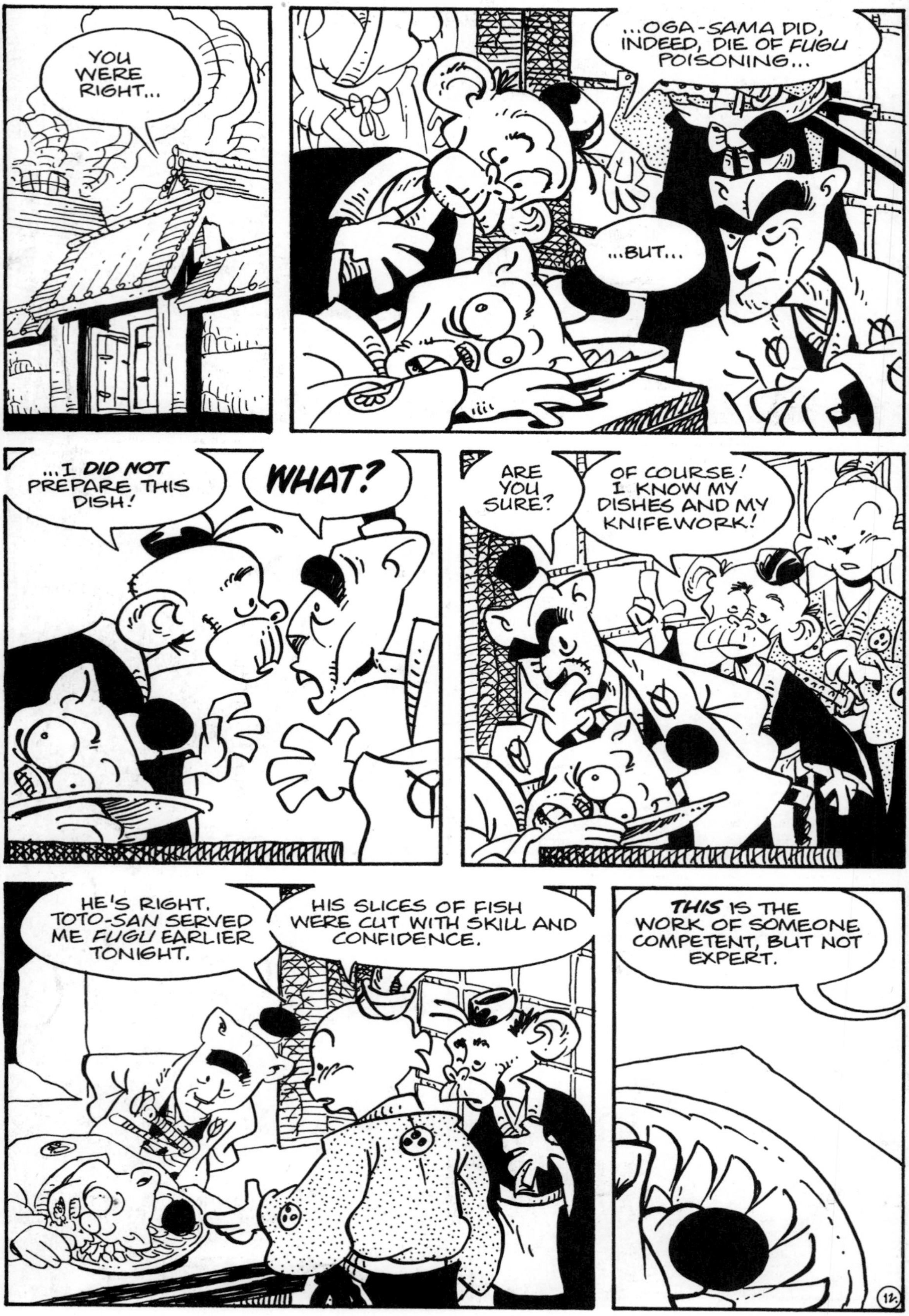
YOU WERE RIGHT...
...OGA-SAMA DID, INDEED, DIE OF FUGU POISONING...
...BUT...
...I DID NOT PREPARE THIS DISH!
WHAT?
ARE YOU SURE?
OF COURSE! I KNOW MY DISHES AND MY KNIFEWORK!
HE'S RIGHT. TOTO-SAN SERVED ME FUGU EARLIER TONIGHT.
HIS SLICES OF FISH WERE CUT WITH SKILL AND CONFIDENCE.
THIS IS THE WORK OF SOMEONE COMPETENT, BUT NOT EXPERT.
12.

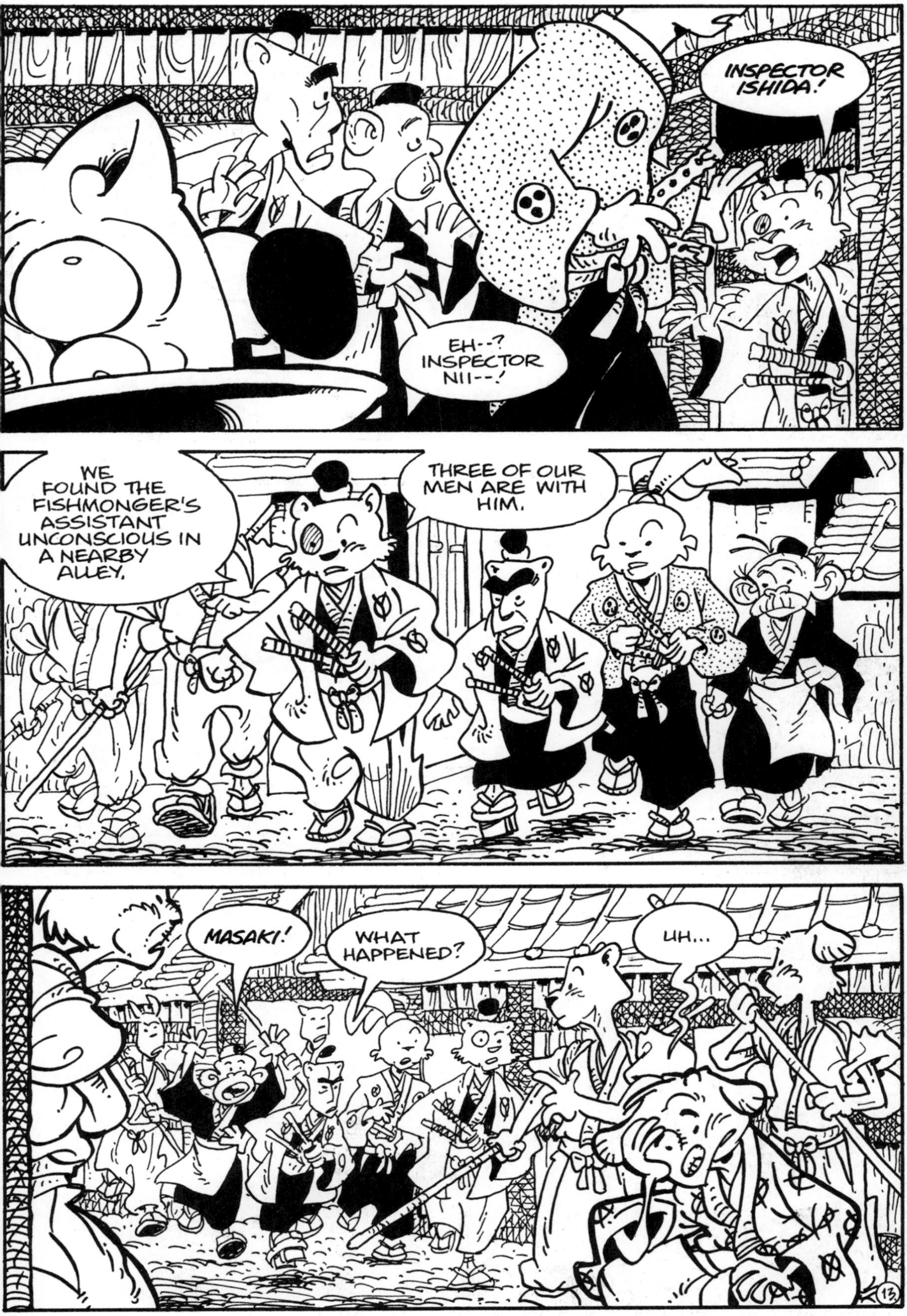

INSPECTOR ISHIDA!
EH--? INSPECTOR NII--!
WE FOUND THE FISHMONGER'S ASSISTANT UNCONSCIOUS IN A NEARBY ALLEY.
THREE OF OUR MEN ARE WITH HIM.
MASAKI!
WHAT HAPPENED?
UH...
13

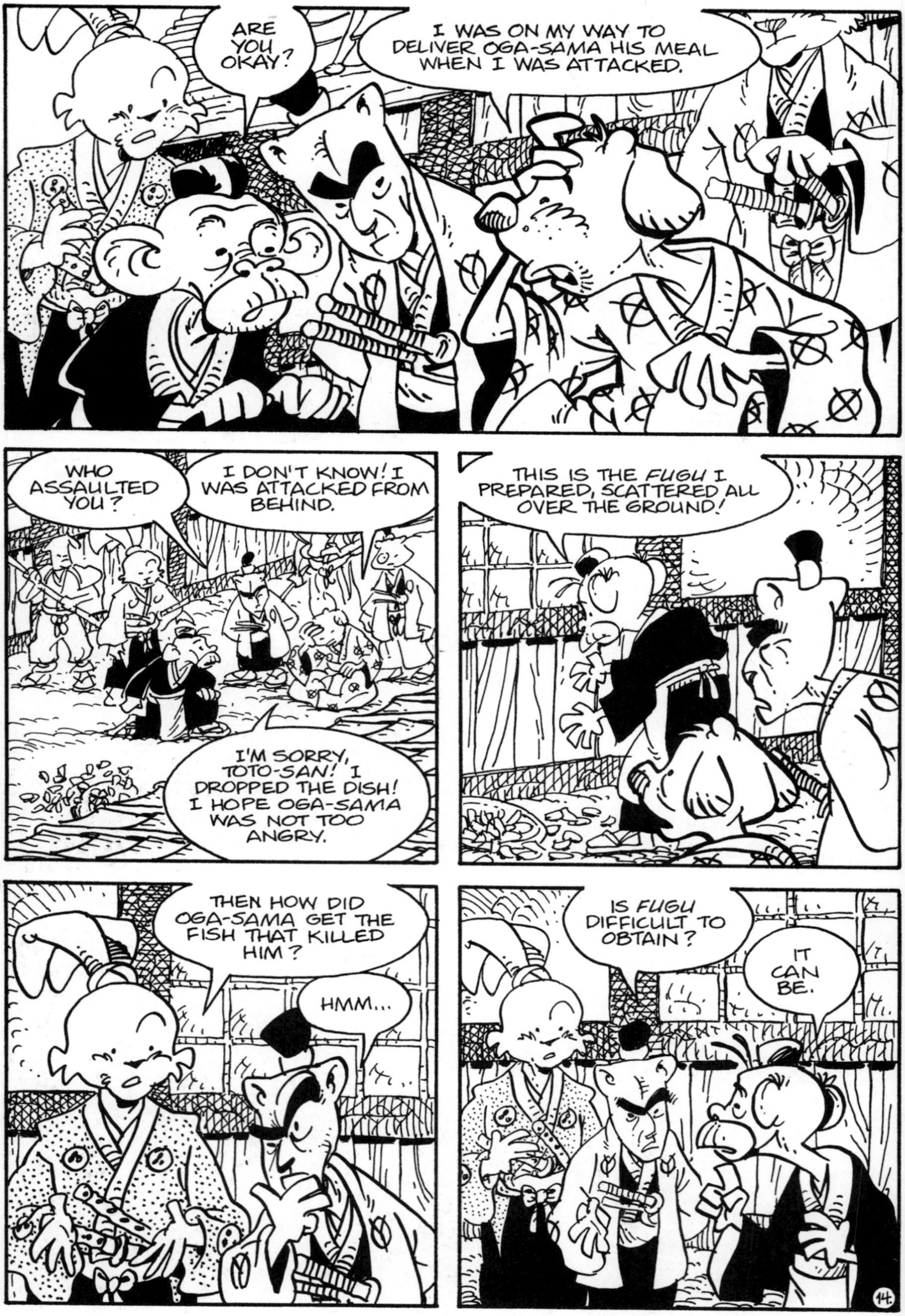
ARE YOU OKAY?
I WAS ON MY WAY TO DELIVER OGA-SAMA HIS MEAL WHEN I WAS ATTACKED.
WHO ASSAULTED YOU?
I DON'T KNOW! I WAS ATTACKED FROM BEHIND.
I'M SORRY, TOTO-SAN! I DROPPED THE DISH! I HOPE OGA-SAMA WAS NOT TOO ANGRY.
THIS IS THE *FUGU* I PREPARED, SCATTERED ALL OVER THE GROUND!
THEN HOW DID OGA-SAMA GET THE FISH THAT KILLED HIM?
HMM...
IS *FUGU* DIFFICULT TO OBTAIN?
IT CAN BE.
14.

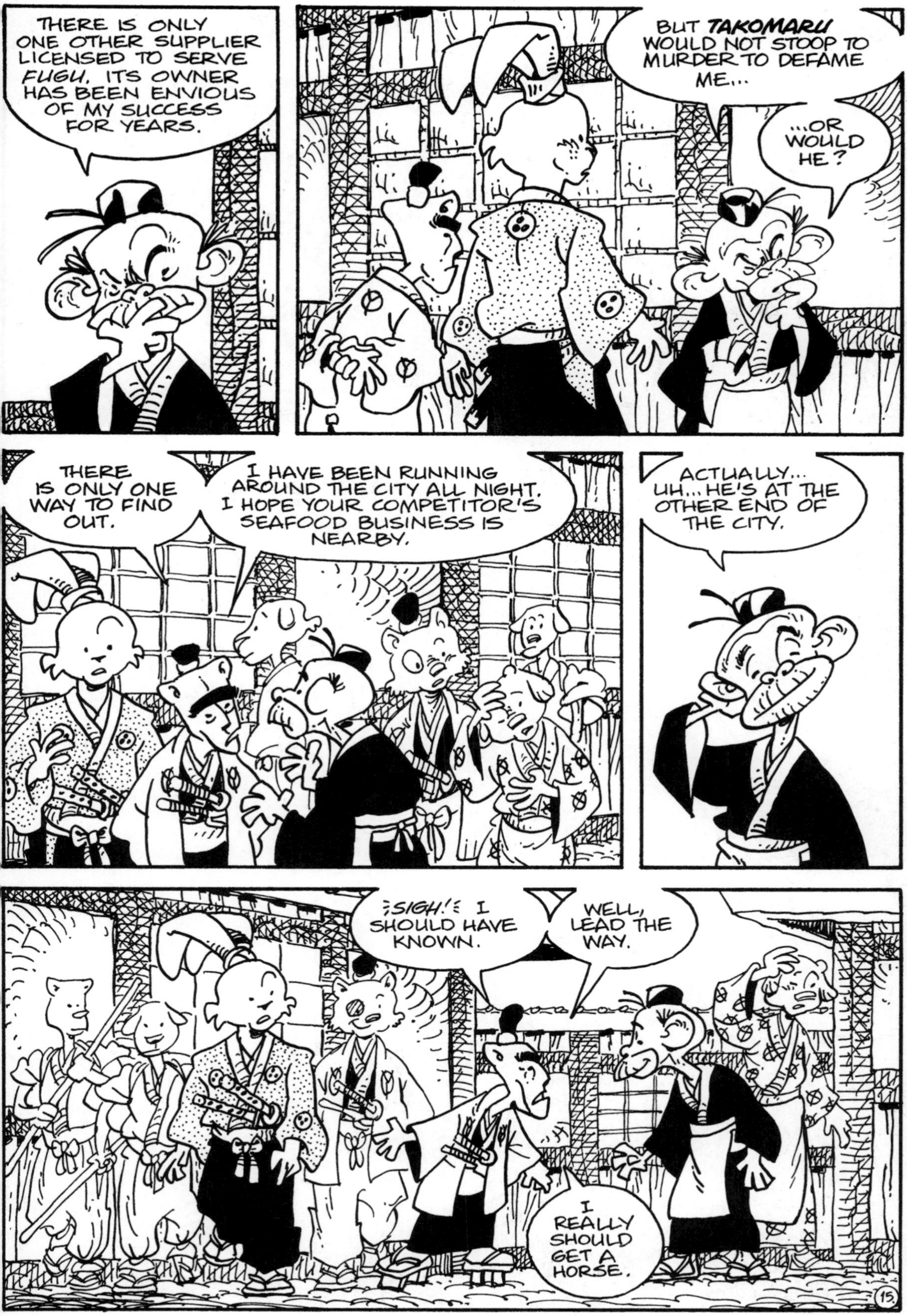
THERE IS ONLY ONE OTHER SUPPLIER LICENSED TO SERVE *FUGU*. ITS OWNER HAS BEEN ENVIOUS OF MY SUCCESS FOR YEARS.
BUT ***TAKOMARU*** WOULD NOT STOOP TO MURDER TO DEFAME ME...
...OR WOULD HE?
THERE IS ONLY ONE WAY TO FIND OUT.
I HAVE BEEN RUNNING AROUND THE CITY ALL NIGHT. I HOPE YOUR COMPETITOR'S SEAFOOD BUSINESS IS NEARBY.
ACTUALLY... UH... HE'S AT THE OTHER END OF THE CITY.
SIGH! I SHOULD HAVE KNOWN.
WELL, LEAD THE WAY.
I REALLY SHOULD GET A HORSE.
15

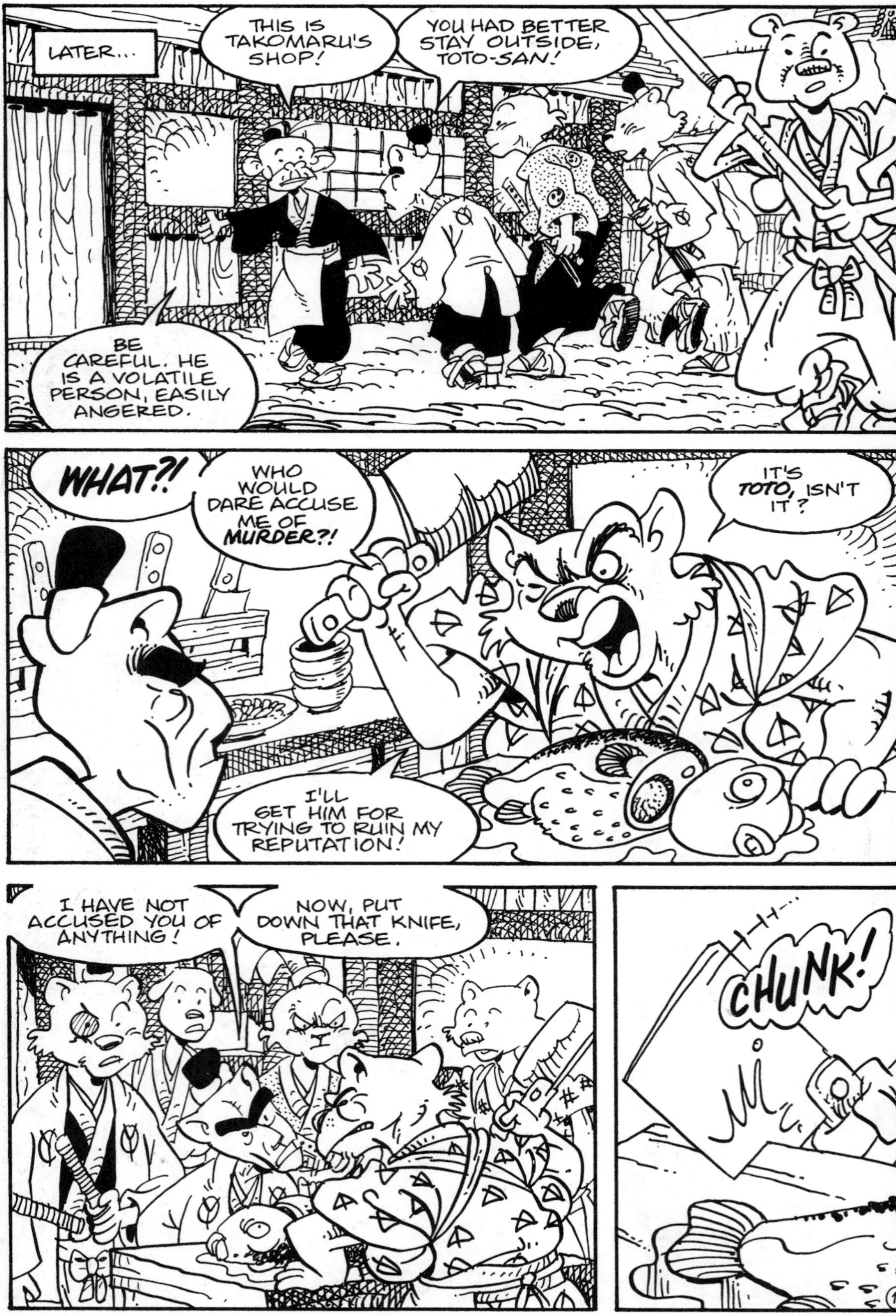
LATER...
THIS IS TAKOMARU'S SHOP!
YOU HAD BETTER STAY OUTSIDE, TOTO-SAN!
BE CAREFUL. HE IS A VOLATILE PERSON, EASILY ANGERED.
WHAT?!
WHO WOULD DARE ACCUSE ME OF MURDER?!
IT'S TOTO, ISN'T IT?
I'LL GET HIM FOR TRYING TO RUIN MY REPUTATION!
I HAVE NOT ACCUSED YOU OF ANYTHING!
NOW, PUT DOWN THAT KNIFE, PLEASE.
CHUNK!
16.

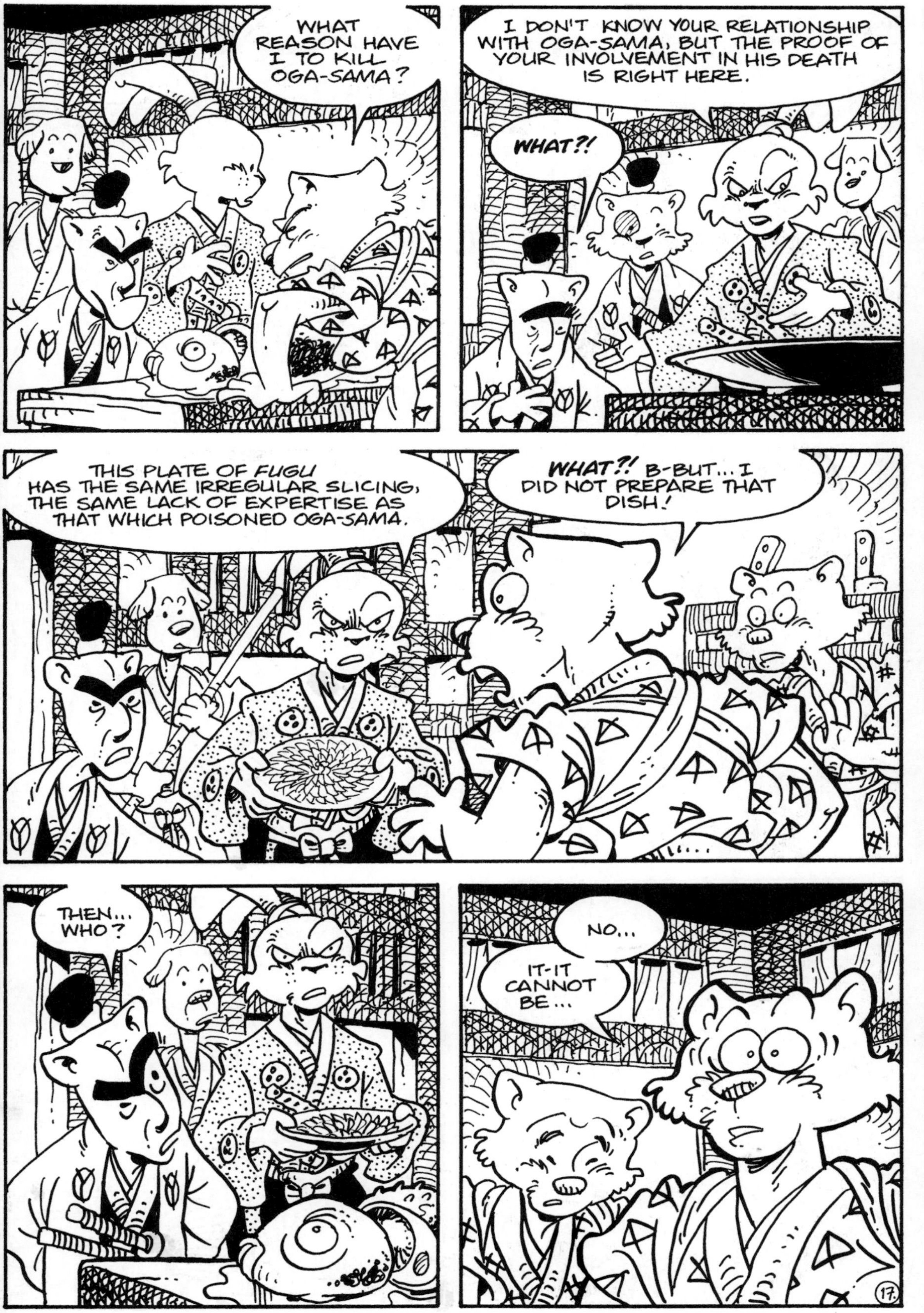
WHAT REASON HAVE I TO KILL OGA-SAMA?
I DON'T KNOW YOUR RELATIONSHIP WITH OGA-SAMA, BUT THE PROOF OF YOUR INVOLVEMENT IN HIS DEATH IS RIGHT HERE.
WHAT?!
THIS PLATE OF *FUGU* HAS THE SAME IRREGULAR SLICING, THE SAME LACK OF EXPERTISE AS THAT WHICH POISONED OGA-SAMA.
WHAT?! B-BUT... I DID NOT PREPARE THAT DISH!
THEN... WHO?
NO...
IT-IT CANNOT BE...
17.

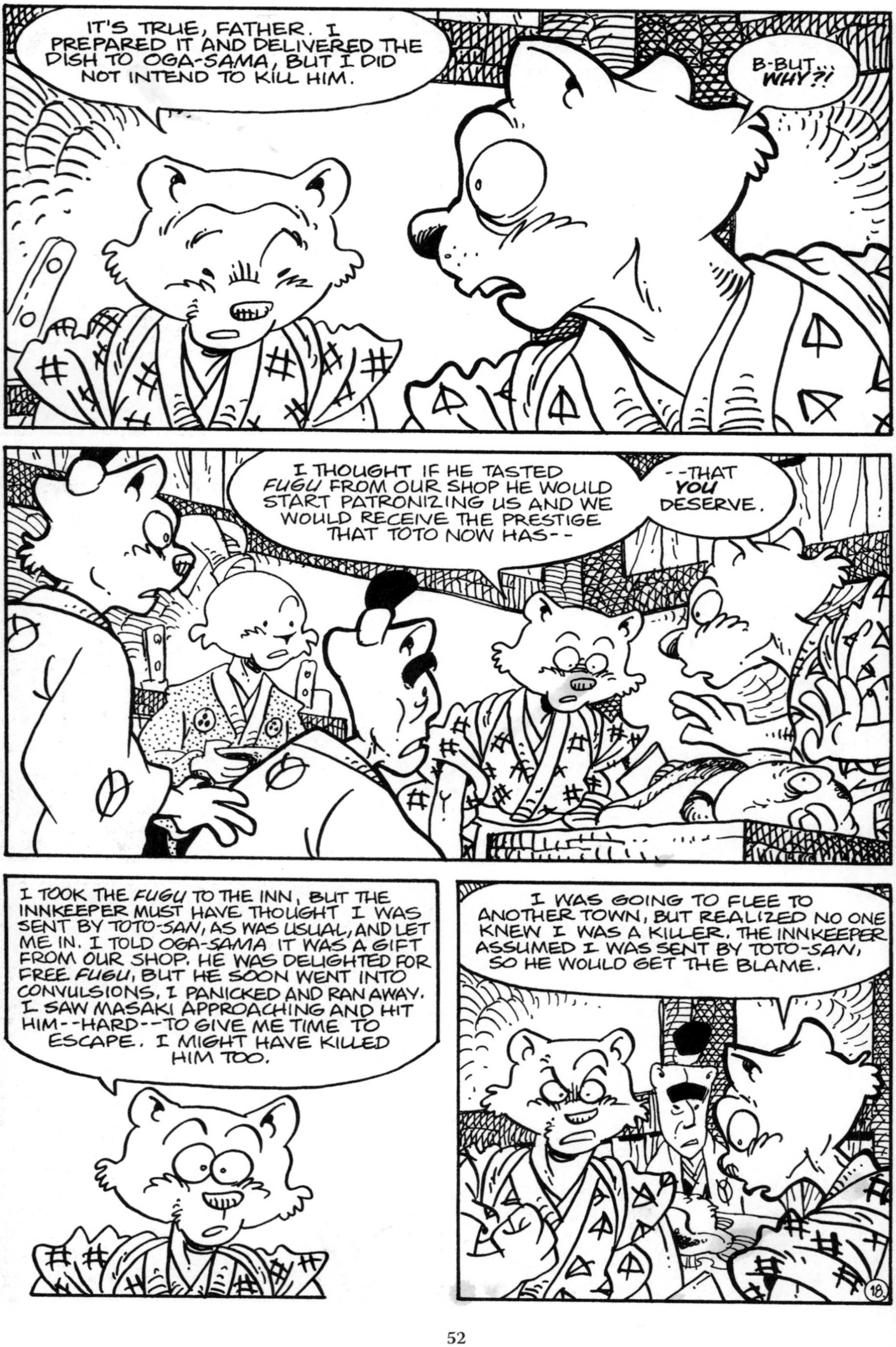
IT'S TRUE, FATHER. I PREPARED IT AND DELIVERED THE DISH TO OGA-SAMA, BUT I DID NOT INTEND TO KILL HIM.
B-BUT... WHY?!
I THOUGHT IF HE TASTED FUGU FROM OUR SHOP HE WOULD START PATRONIZING US AND WE WOULD RECEIVE THE PRESTIGE THAT TOTO NOW HAS--
--THAT YOU DESERVE.
I TOOK THE FUGU TO THE INN, BUT THE INNKEEPER MUST HAVE THOUGHT I WAS SENT BY TOTO-SAN, AS WAS USUAL, AND LET ME IN. I TOLD OGA-SAMA IT WAS A GIFT FROM OUR SHOP. HE WAS DELIGHTED FOR FREE FUGU, BUT HE SOON WENT INTO CONVULSIONS. I PANICKED AND RAN AWAY. I SAW MASAKI APPROACHING AND HIT HIM--HARD--TO GIVE ME TIME TO ESCAPE. I MIGHT HAVE KILLED HIM TOO.
I WAS GOING TO FLEE TO ANOTHER TOWN, BUT REALIZED NO ONE KNEW I WAS A KILLER. THE INNKEEPER ASSUMED I WAS SENT BY TOTO-SAN, SO HE WOULD GET THE BLAME.
18

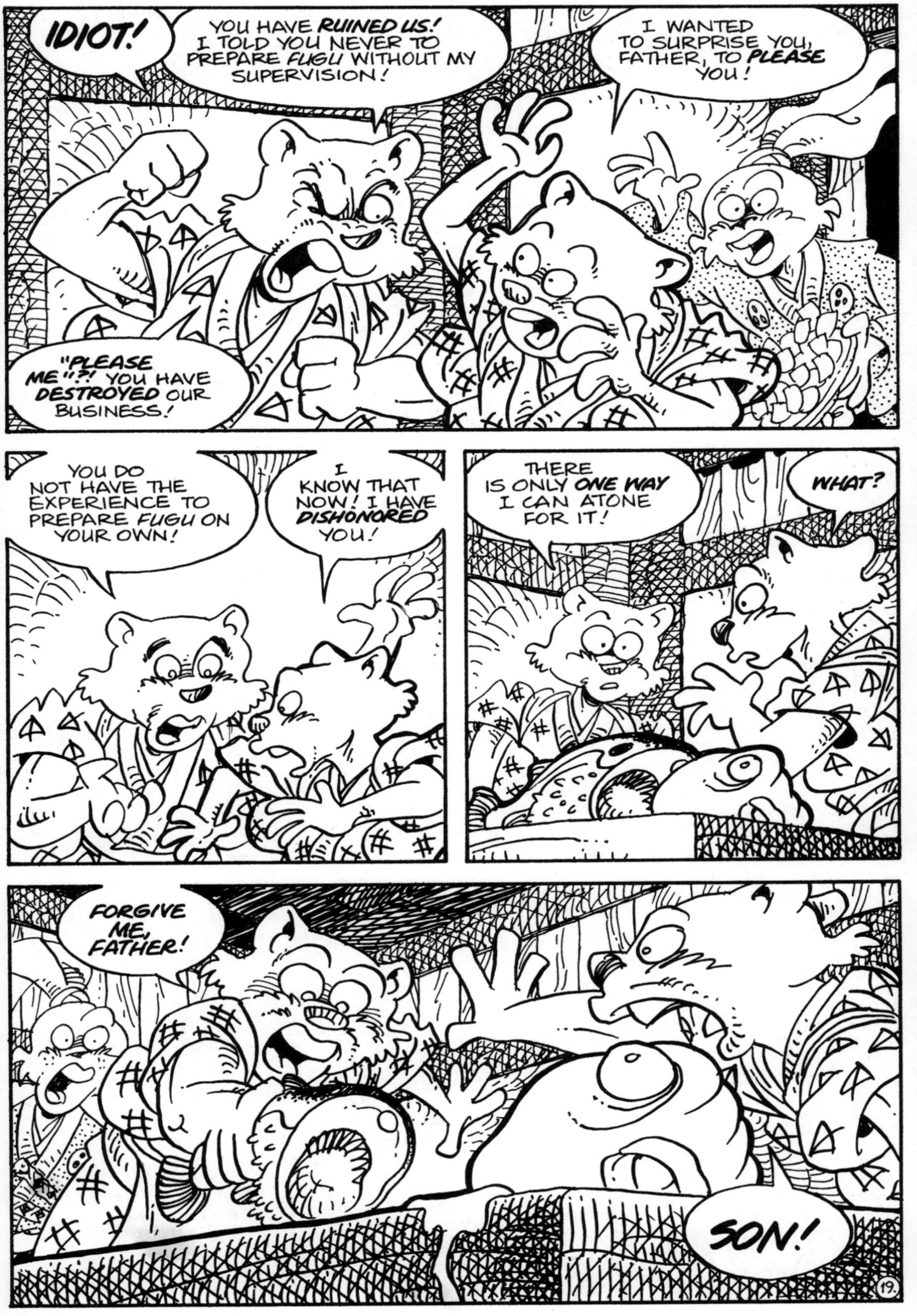
IDIOT!
YOU HAVE RUINED US! I TOLD YOU NEVER TO PREPARE FUGU WITHOUT MY SUPERVISION!
I WANTED TO SURPRISE YOU, FATHER, TO PLEASE YOU!
"PLEASE ME"?! YOU HAVE DESTROYED OUR BUSINESS!
YOU DO NOT HAVE THE EXPERIENCE TO PREPARE FUGU ON YOUR OWN!
I KNOW THAT NOW! I HAVE DISHONORED YOU!
THERE IS ONLY ONE WAY I CAN ATONE FOR IT!
WHAT?
FORGIVE ME, FATHER!
SON!
19.

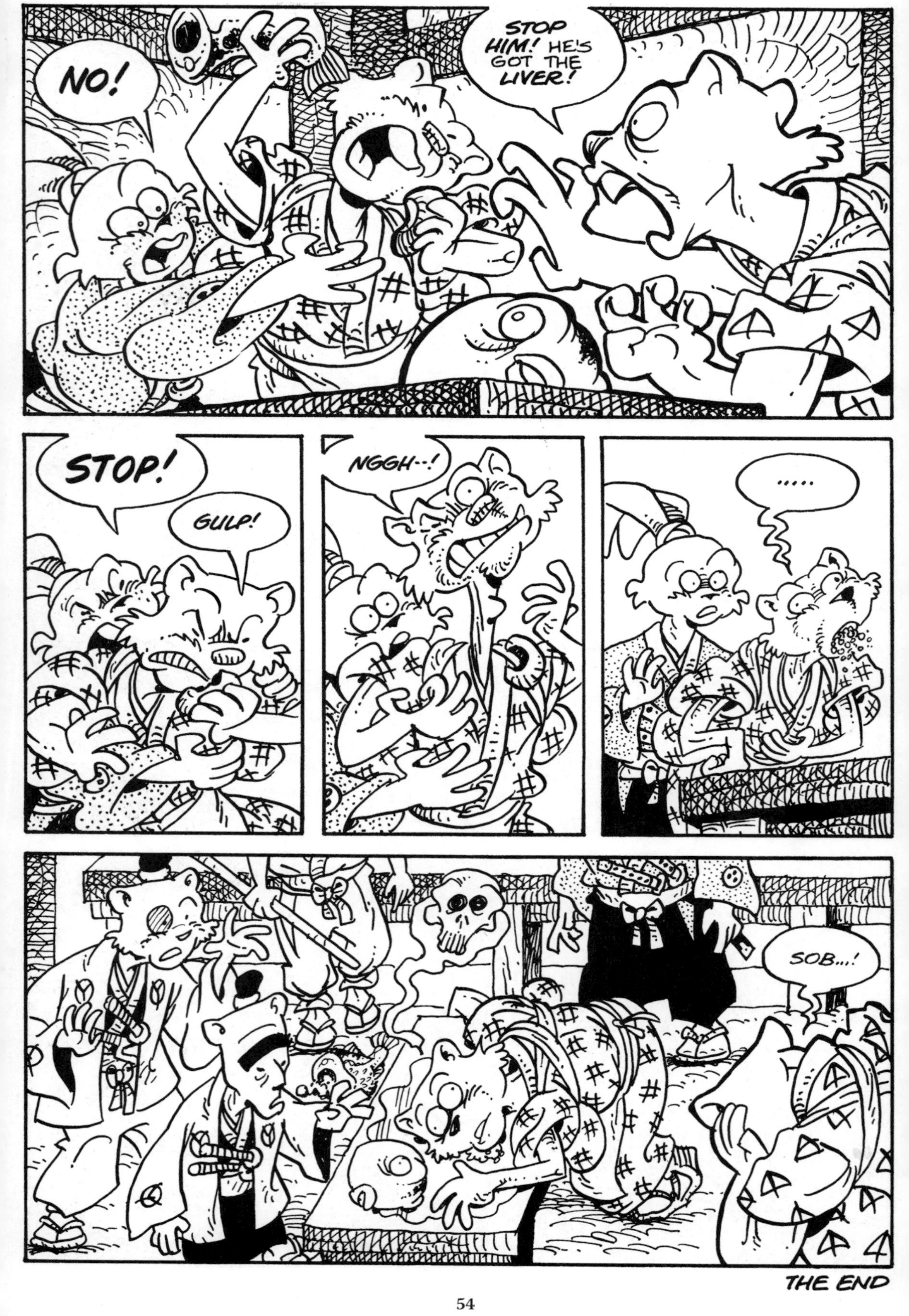
NO!
STOP HIM! HE'S GOT THE LIVER!
STOP!
GULP!
NGGH--!
.....
SOB...!
THE END

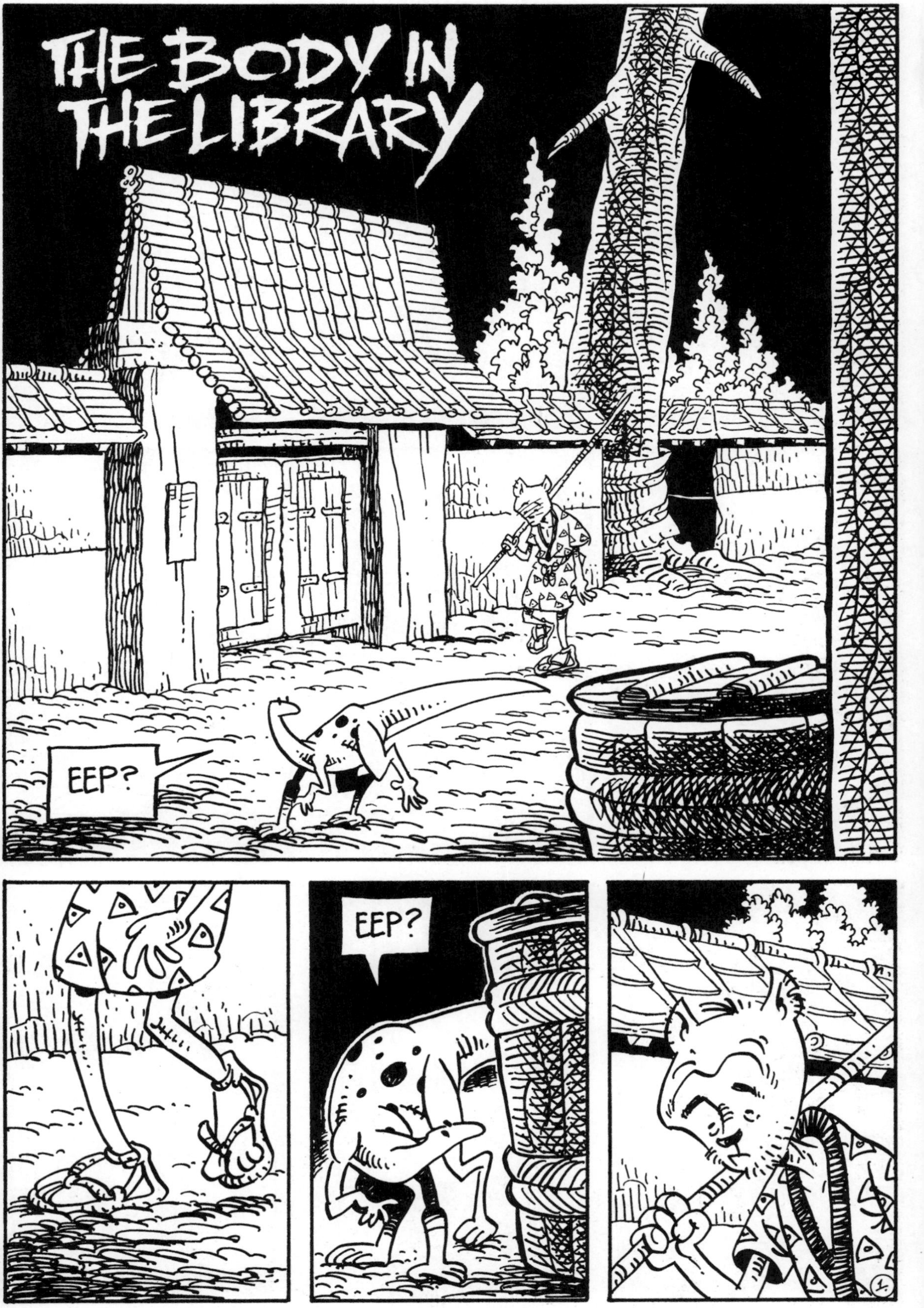
THE BODY IN THE LIBRARY
EEP?
EEP?
1.

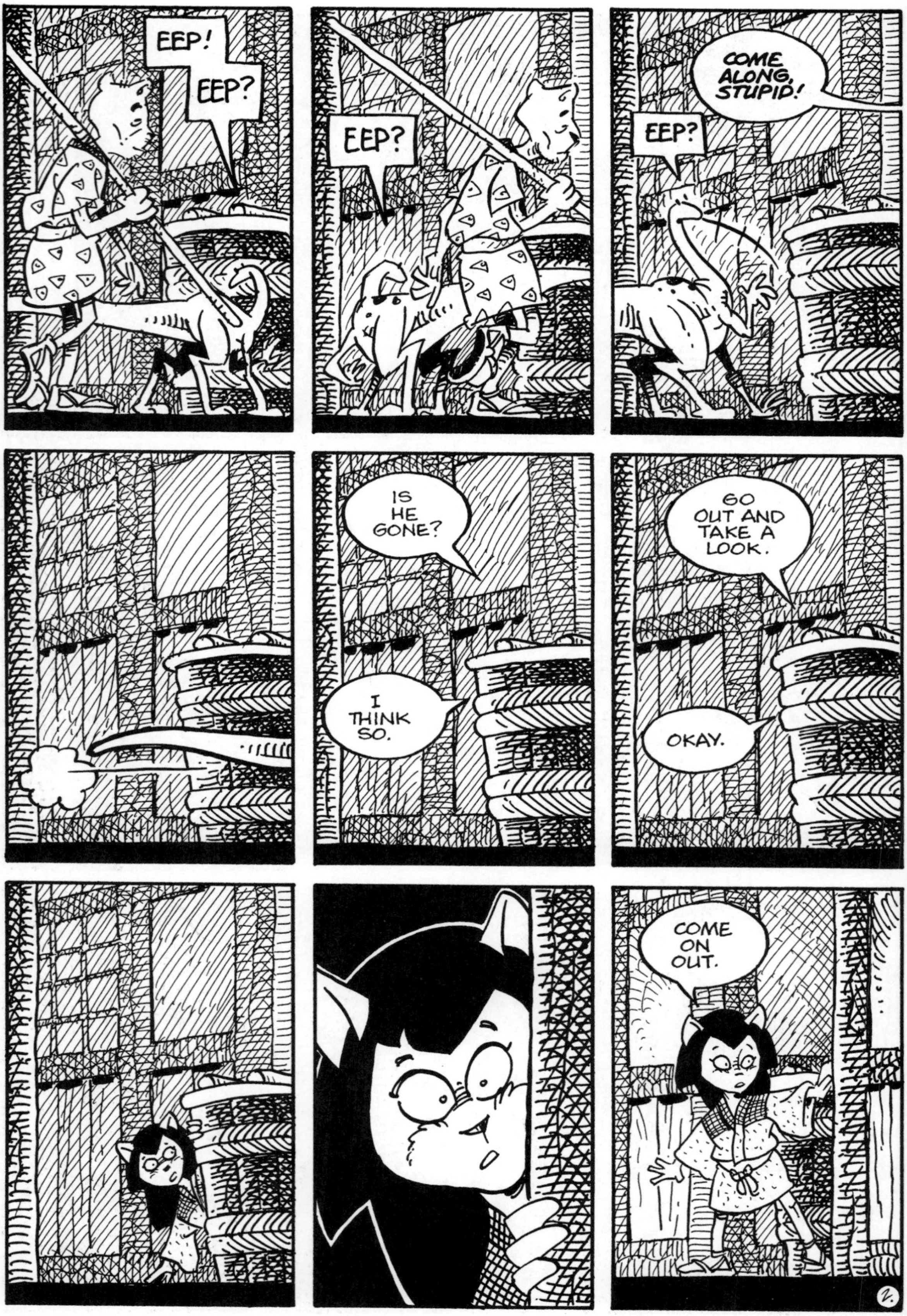
EEP!
EEP?
EEP?
COME ALONG, STUPID!
EEP?
IS HE GONE?
I THINK SO.
GO OUT AND TAKE A LOOK.
OKAY.
COME ON OUT.
2.

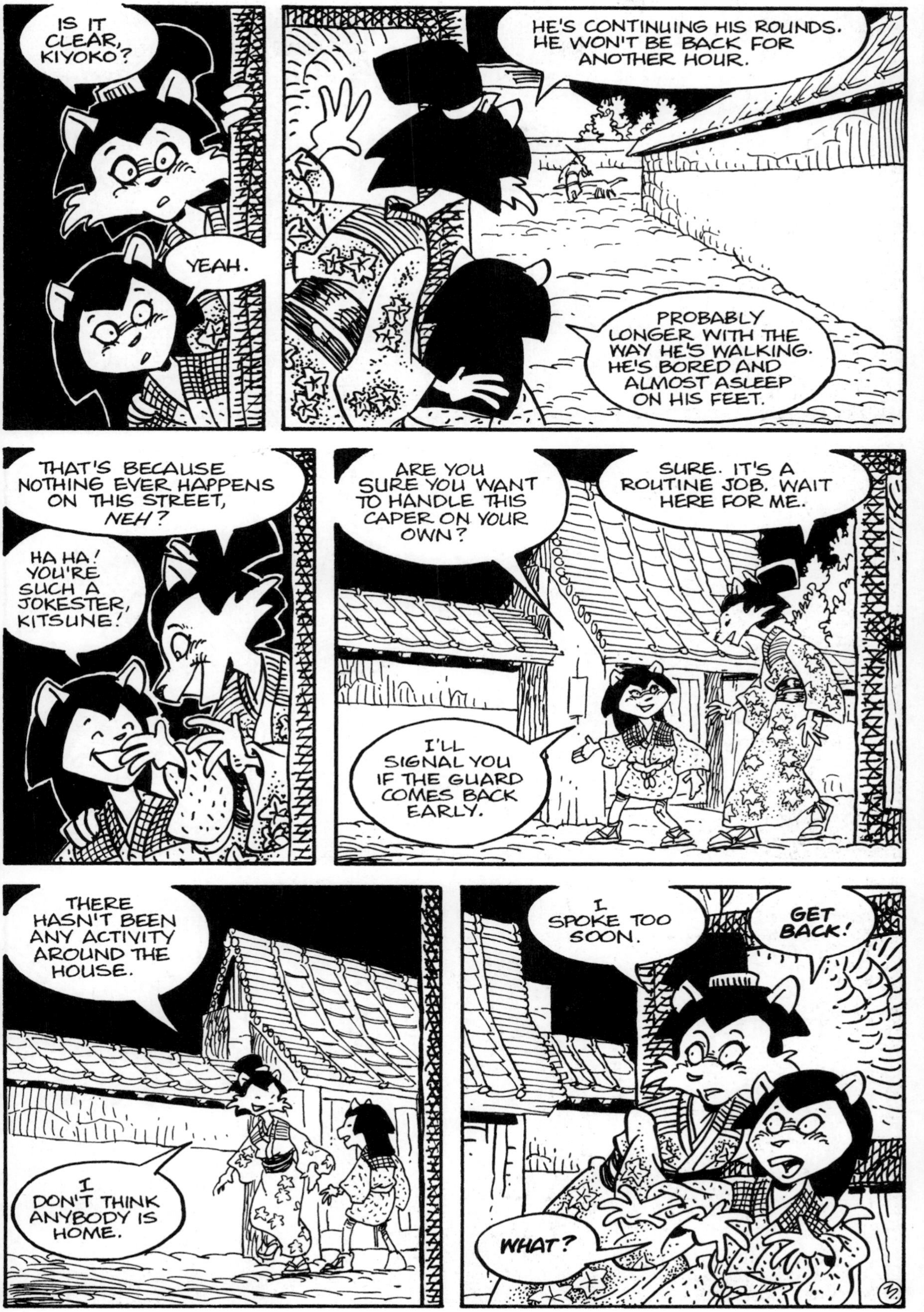
IS IT CLEAR, KIYOKO?
YEAH.
HE'S CONTINUING HIS ROUNDS. HE WON'T BE BACK FOR ANOTHER HOUR.
PROBABLY LONGER WITH THE WAY HE'S WALKING. HE'S BORED AND ALMOST ASLEEP ON HIS FEET.
THAT'S BECAUSE NOTHING EVER HAPPENS ON THIS STREET, *NEH*?
HA HA! YOU'RE SUCH A JOKESTER, KITSUNE!
ARE YOU SURE YOU WANT TO HANDLE THIS CAPER ON YOUR OWN?
SURE. IT'S A ROUTINE JOB. WAIT HERE FOR ME.
I'LL SIGNAL YOU IF THE GUARD COMES BACK EARLY.
THERE HASN'T BEEN ANY ACTIVITY AROUND THE HOUSE.
I DON'T THINK ANYBODY IS HOME.
I SPOKE TOO SOON.
GET BACK!
WHAT?

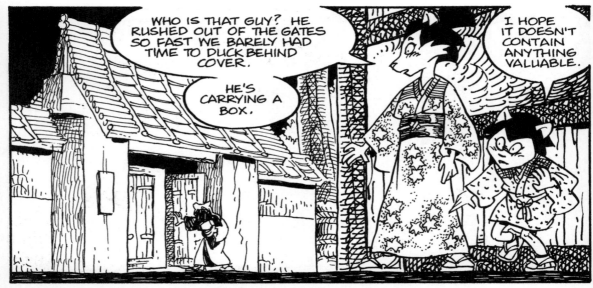

WHO IS THAT GUY? HE RUSHED OUT OF THE GATES SO FAST WE BARELY HAD TIME TO DUCK BEHIND COVER.

HE'S CARRYING A BOX.

I HOPE IT DOESN'T CONTAIN ANYTHING VALUABLE.

EVEN IF IT DOES, THIS IS A *DOCTOR'S HOME*. THERE MUST BE *LOTS* OF VALUABLES IN THERE!

OKAY. THAT GUY'S OUT OF SIGHT. WISH ME LUCK, KIYOKO.

YOU *DON'T NEED* MY LUCK, YOU'RE *KITSUNE*, THE BEST THIEF THERE IS!

OH, YOU FLATTERER, YOU!

THIS SHOULD NOT TAKE LONG.

I'LL BE BACK SOON.

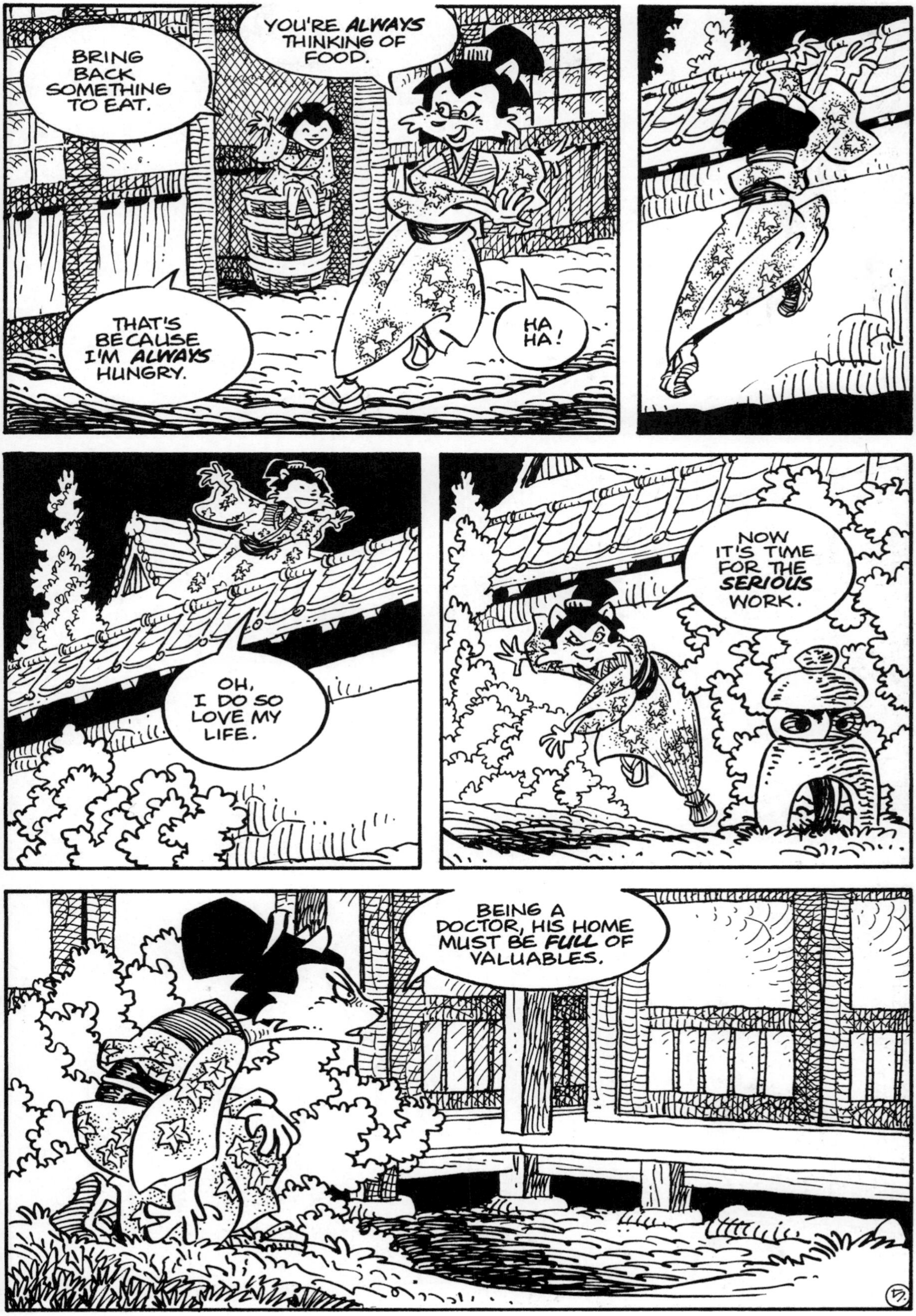
BRING BACK SOMETHING TO EAT.
YOU'RE ALWAYS THINKING OF FOOD.
THAT'S BECAUSE I'M ALWAYS HUNGRY.
HA HA!
OH, I DO SO LOVE MY LIFE.
NOW IT'S TIME FOR THE SERIOUS WORK.
BEING A DOCTOR, HIS HOME MUST BE FULL OF VALUABLES.

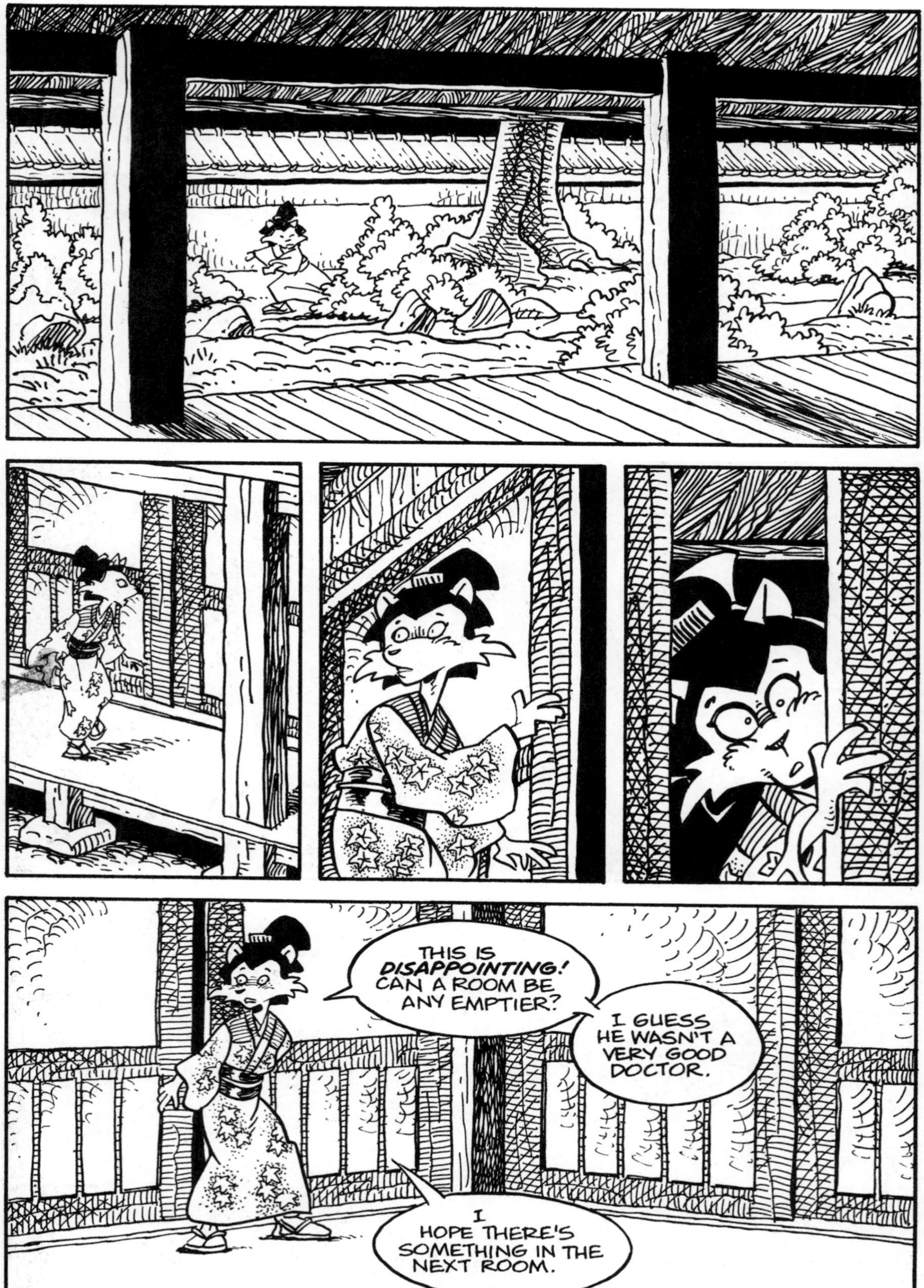
THIS IS DISAPPOINTING! CAN A ROOM BE ANY EMPTIER?
I GUESS HE WASN'T A VERY GOOD DOCTOR.
I HOPE THERE'S SOMETHING IN THE NEXT ROOM.
6.

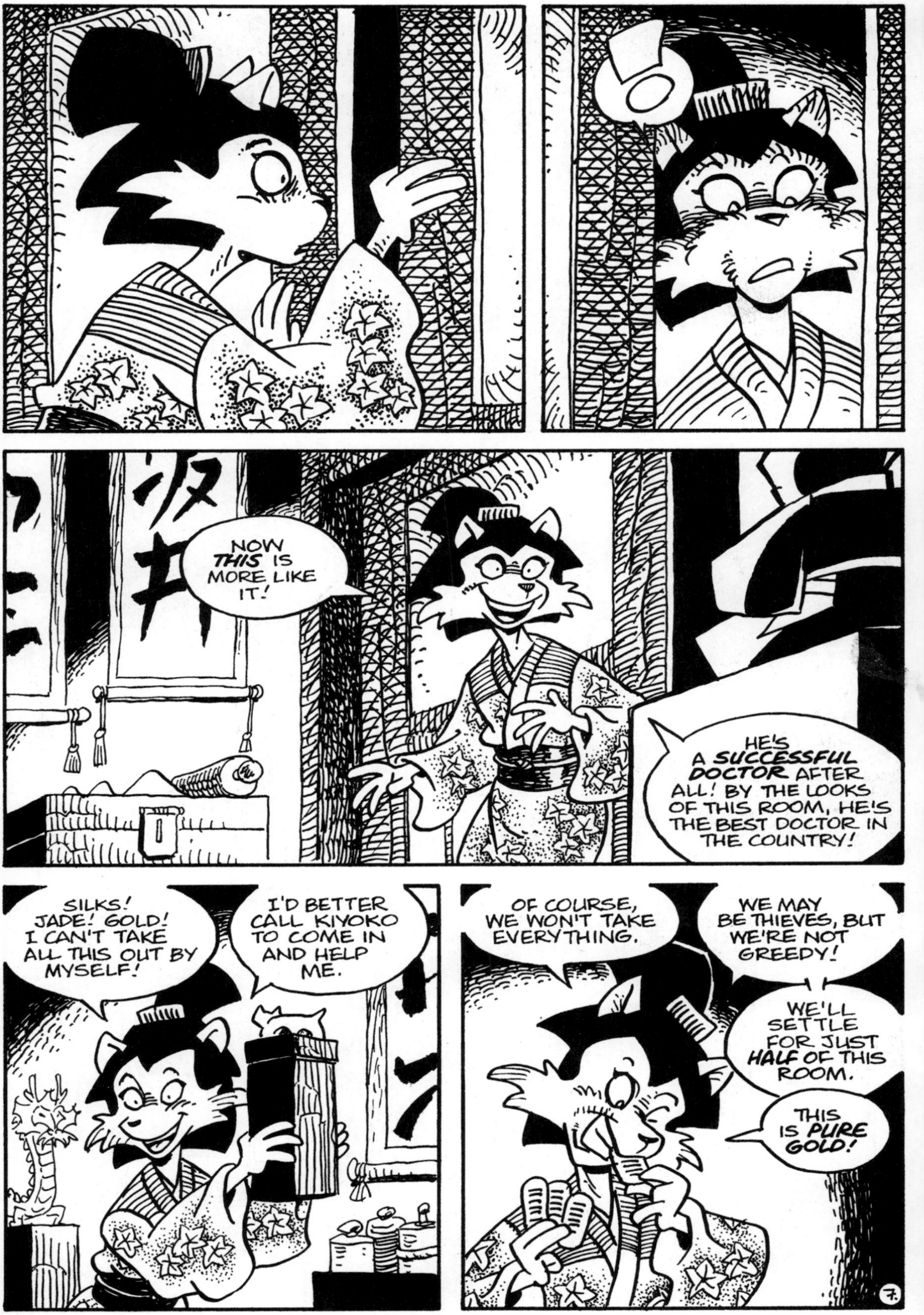
NOW THIS IS MORE LIKE IT!
HE'S A SUCCESSFUL DOCTOR AFTER ALL! BY THE LOOKS OF THIS ROOM, HE'S THE BEST DOCTOR IN THE COUNTRY!
SILKS! JADE! GOLD! I CAN'T TAKE ALL THIS OUT BY MYSELF!
I'D BETTER CALL KIYOKO TO COME IN AND HELP ME.
OF COURSE, WE WON'T TAKE EVERYTHING.
WE MAY BE THIEVES, BUT WE'RE NOT GREEDY!
WE'LL SETTLE FOR JUST HALF OF THIS ROOM.
THIS IS PURE GOLD!
7.

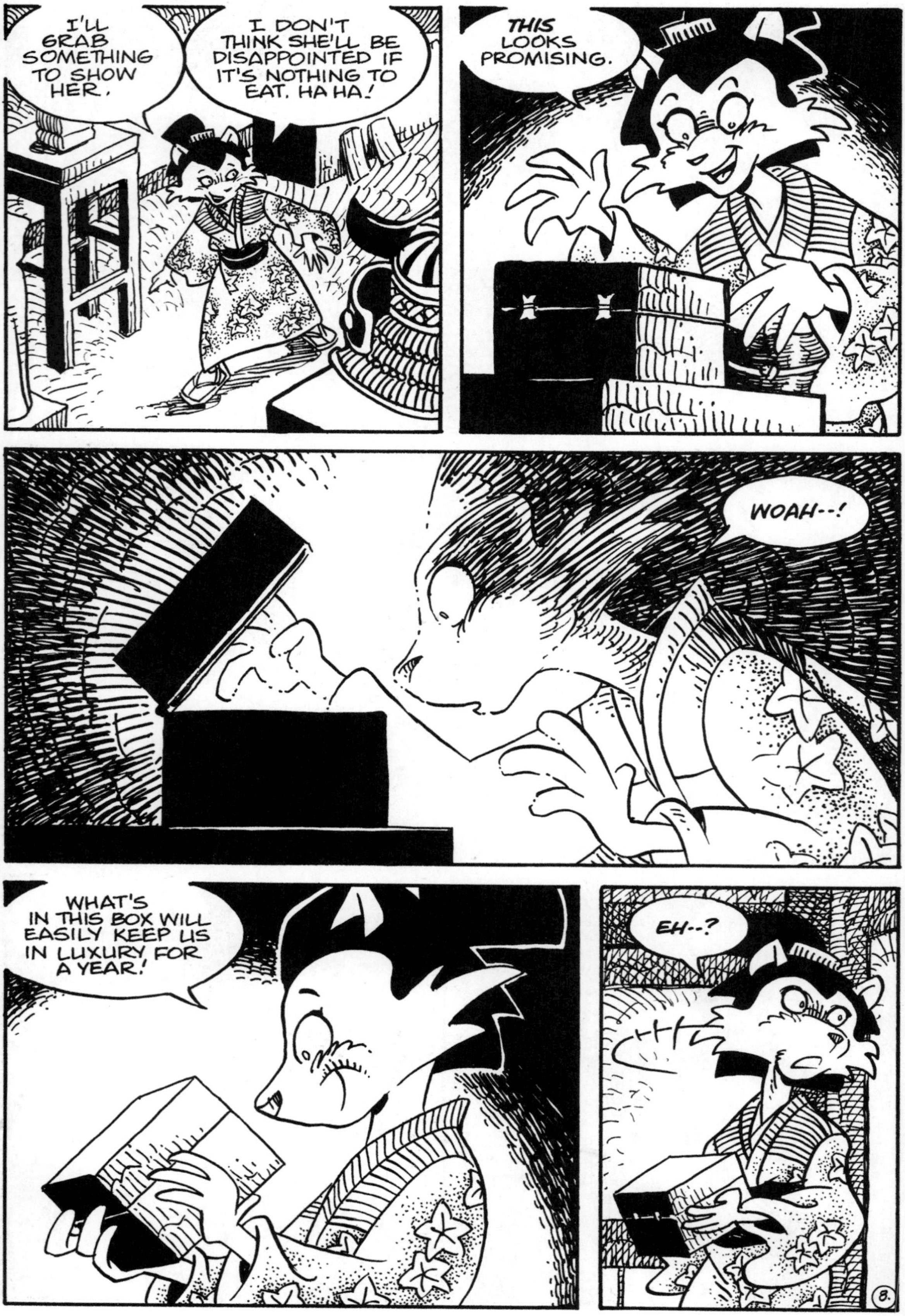
I'LL GRAB SOMETHING TO SHOW HER.
I DON'T THINK SHE'LL BE DISAPPOINTED IF IT'S NOTHING TO EAT. HA HA!
THIS LOOKS PROMISING.
WOAH--!
WHAT'S IN THIS BOX WILL EASILY KEEP US IN LUXURY FOR A YEAR!
EH--?
8.

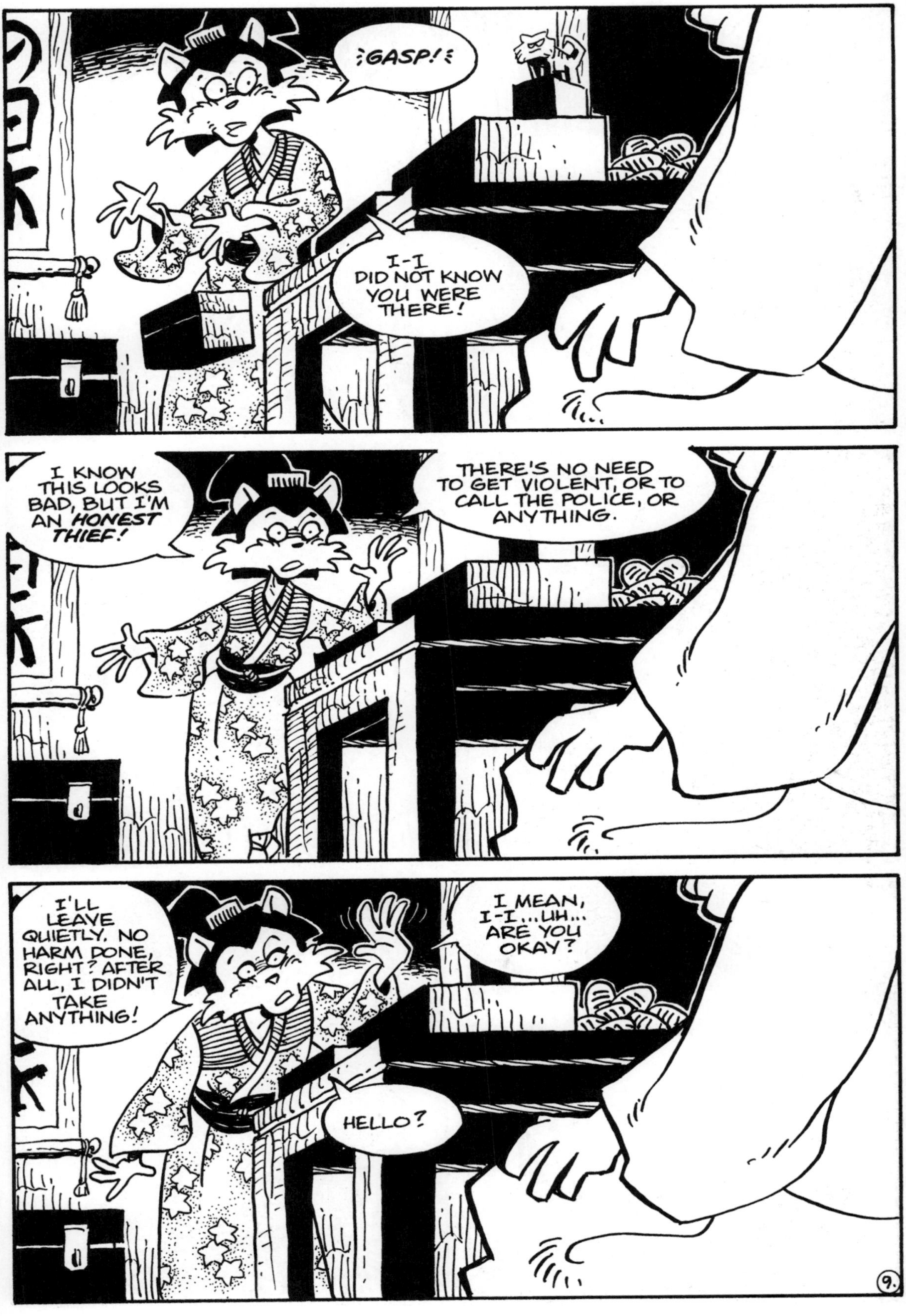
GASP!
I-I DID NOT KNOW YOU WERE THERE!
I KNOW THIS LOOKS BAD, BUT I'M AN *HONEST THIEF!*
THERE'S NO NEED TO GET VIOLENT, OR TO CALL THE POLICE, OR ANYTHING.
I'LL LEAVE QUIETLY. NO HARM DONE, RIGHT? AFTER ALL, I DIDN'T TAKE ANYTHING!
I MEAN, I-I...UH... ARE YOU OKAY?
HELLO?
9.

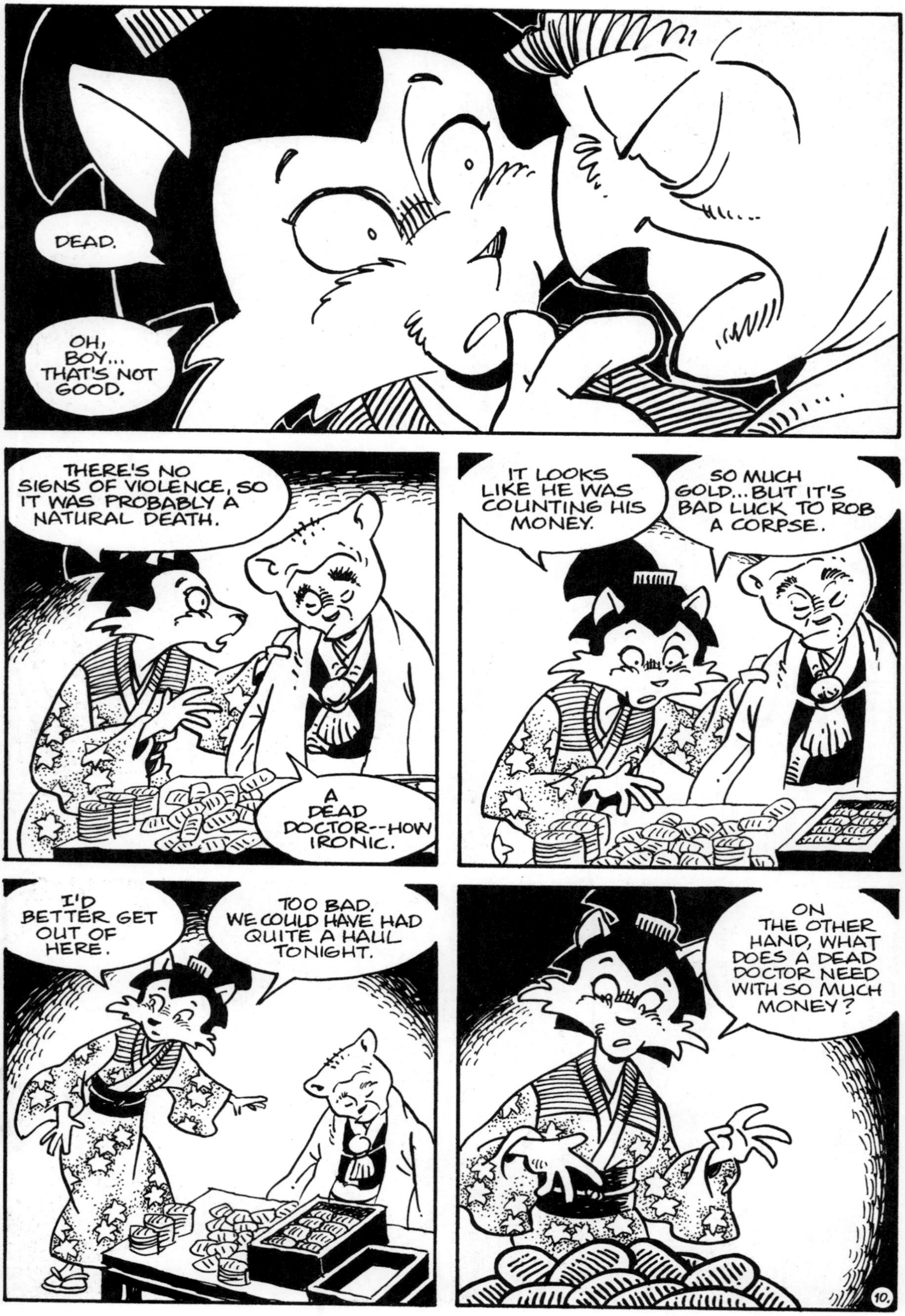
DEAD.
OH, BOY... THAT'S NOT GOOD.
THERE'S NO SIGNS OF VIOLENCE, SO IT WAS PROBABLY A NATURAL DEATH.
A DEAD DOCTOR--HOW IRONIC.
IT LOOKS LIKE HE WAS COUNTING HIS MONEY.
SO MUCH GOLD...BUT IT'S BAD LUCK TO ROB A CORPSE.
I'D BETTER GET OUT OF HERE.
TOO BAD. WE COULD HAVE HAD QUITE A HAUL TONIGHT.
ON THE OTHER HAND, WHAT DOES A DEAD DOCTOR NEED WITH SO MUCH MONEY?
10.

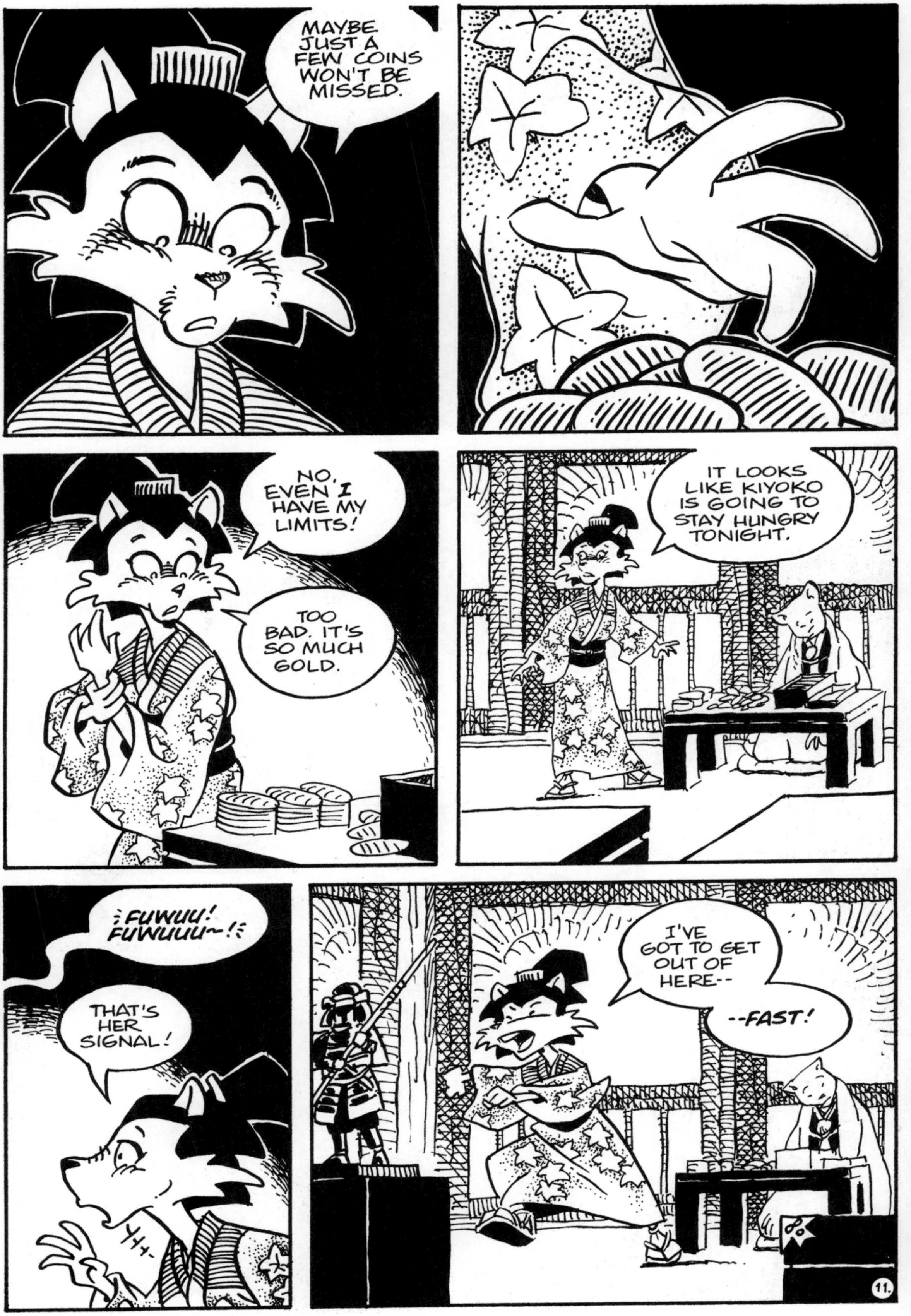
MAYBE JUST A FEW COINS WON'T BE MISSED.
NO, EVEN I HAVE MY LIMITS!
TOO BAD. IT'S SO MUCH GOLD.
IT LOOKS LIKE KIYOKO IS GOING TO STAY HUNGRY TONIGHT.
FUWUU! FUWUUU~!
THAT'S HER SIGNAL!
I'VE GOT TO GET OUT OF HERE--
--FAST!
11.

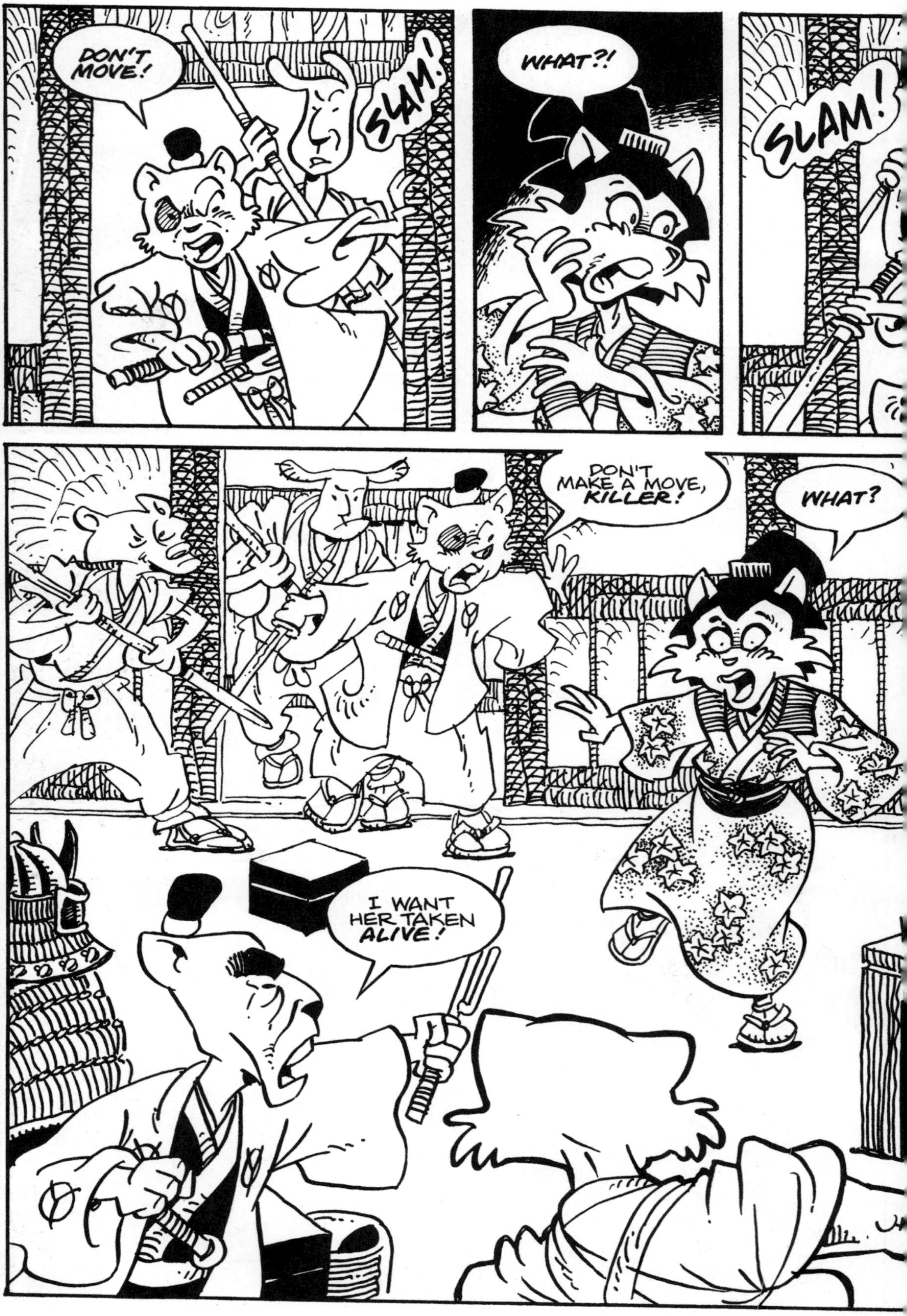
DON'T MOVE!
SLAM!
WHAT?!
SLAM!
DON'T MAKE A MOVE, KILLER!
WHAT?
I WANT HER TAKEN ALIVE!

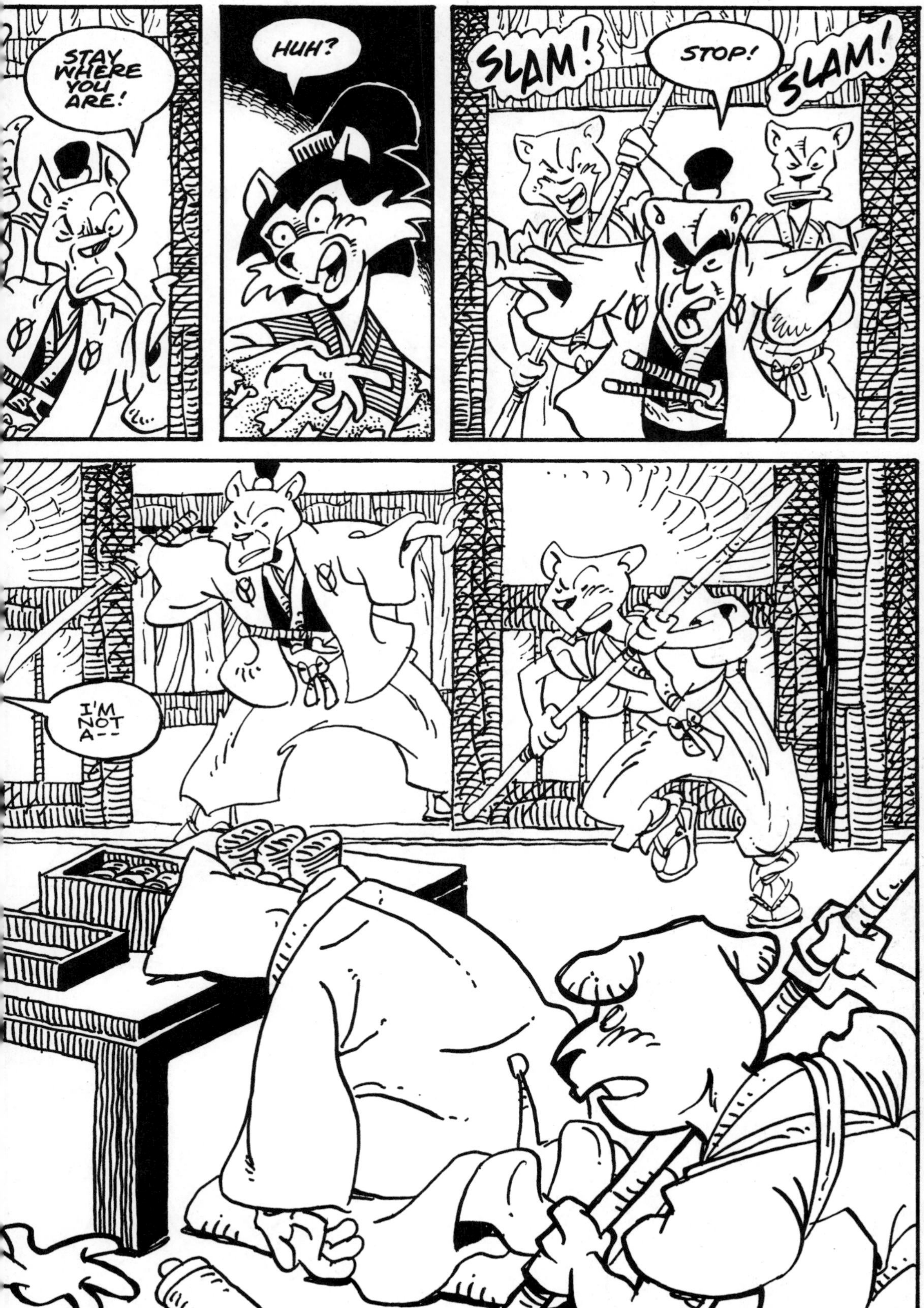
STAY WHERE YOU ARE!
HUH?
SLAM!
STOP!
SLAM!
I'M NOT A--
13.

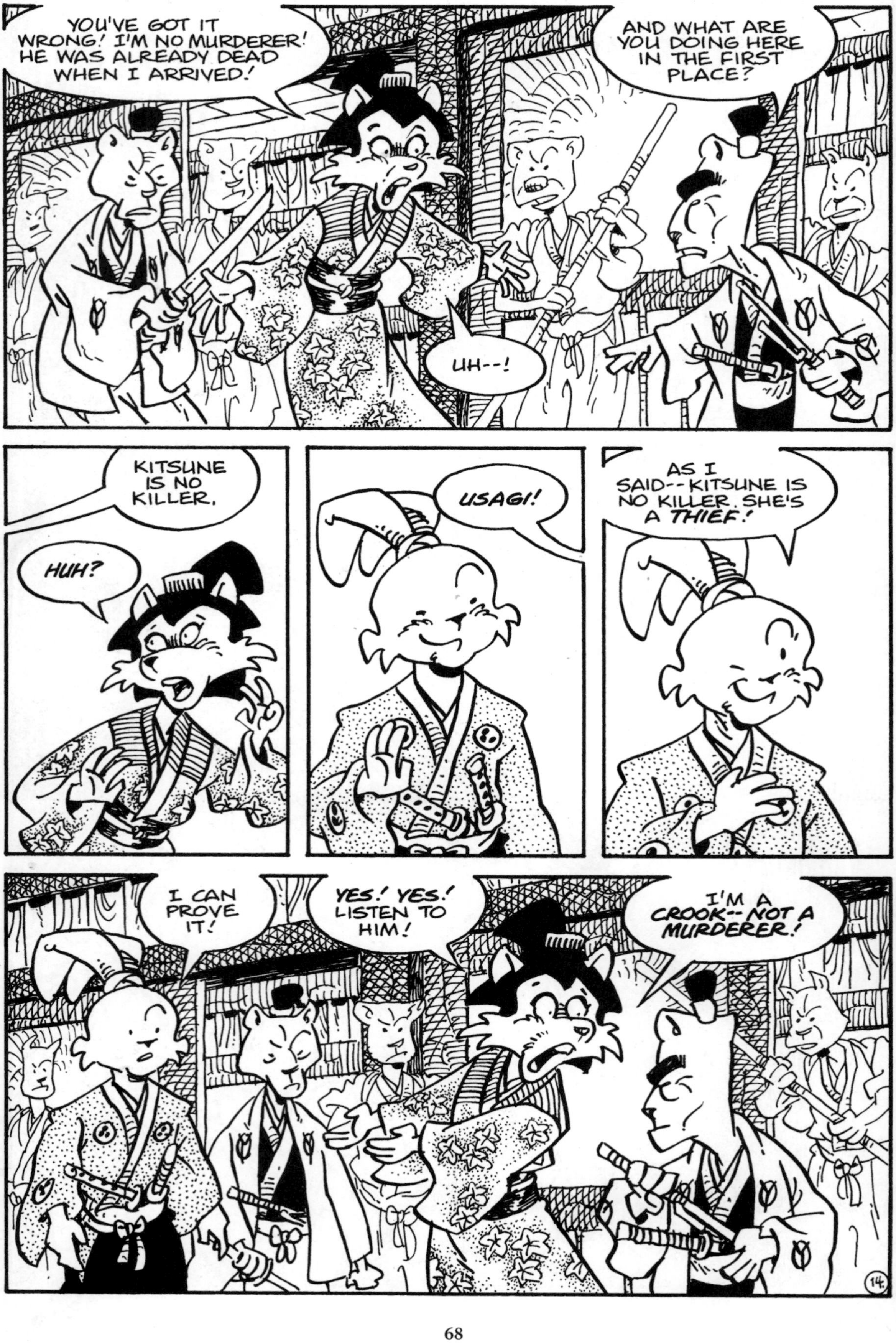
YOU'VE GOT IT WRONG! I'M NO MURDERER! HE WAS ALREADY DEAD WHEN I ARRIVED!
AND WHAT ARE YOU DOING HERE IN THE FIRST PLACE?
UH--!
KITSUNE IS NO KILLER.
HUH?
USAGI!
AS I SAID--KITSUNE IS NO KILLER. SHE'S A THIEF!
I CAN PROVE IT!
YES! YES! LISTEN TO HIM!
I'M A CROOK--NOT A MURDERER!
14.

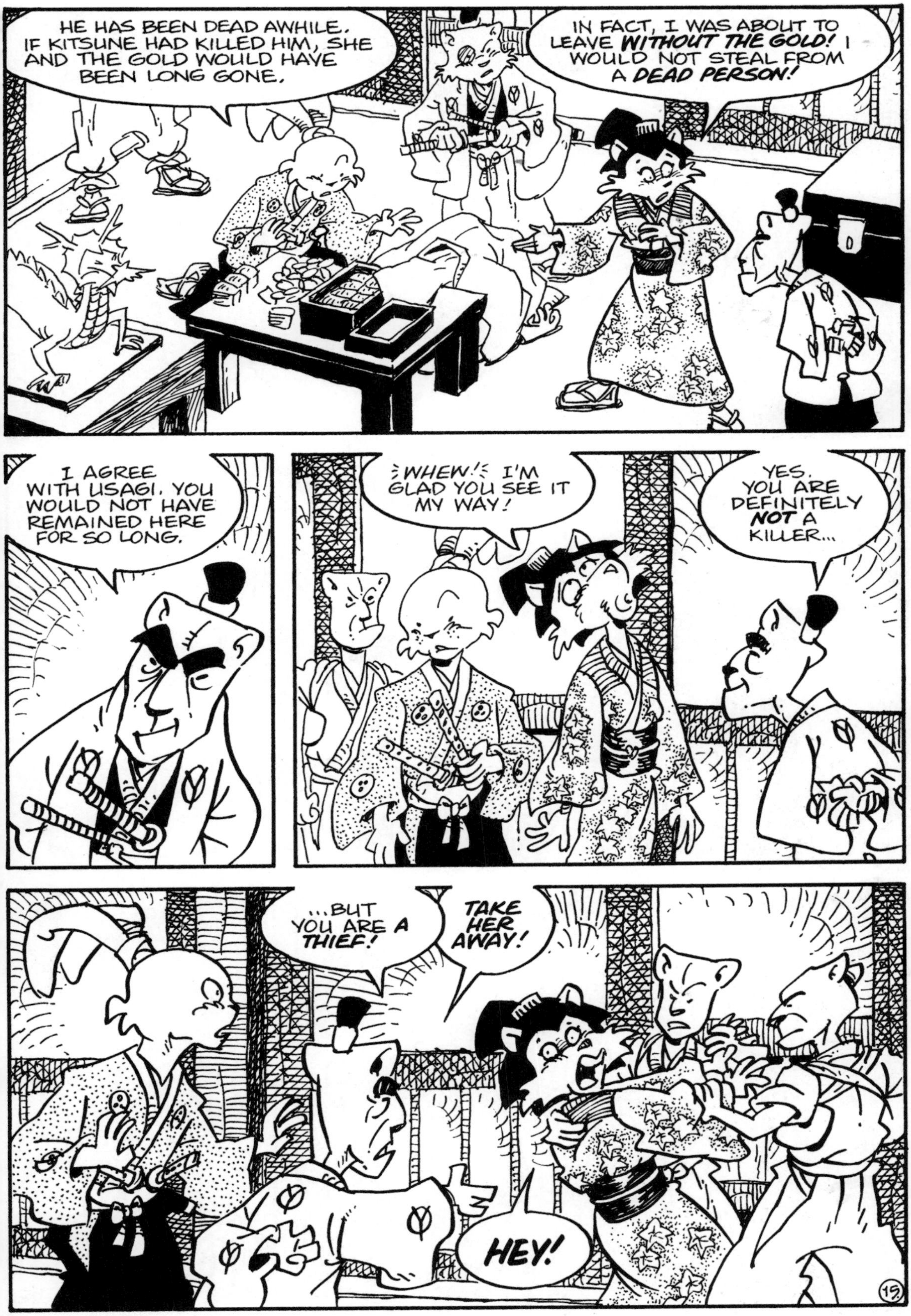
HE HAS BEEN DEAD AWHILE. IF KITSUNE HAD KILLED HIM, SHE AND THE GOLD WOULD HAVE BEEN LONG GONE.
IN FACT, I WAS ABOUT TO LEAVE **WITHOUT THE GOLD!** I WOULD NOT STEAL FROM A **DEAD PERSON!**
I AGREE WITH USAGI. YOU WOULD NOT HAVE REMAINED HERE FOR SO LONG.
WHEW! I'M GLAD YOU SEE IT MY WAY!
YES. YOU ARE DEFINITELY **NOT** A KILLER...
...BUT YOU ARE **A THIEF!**
TAKE HER AWAY!
HEY!
15

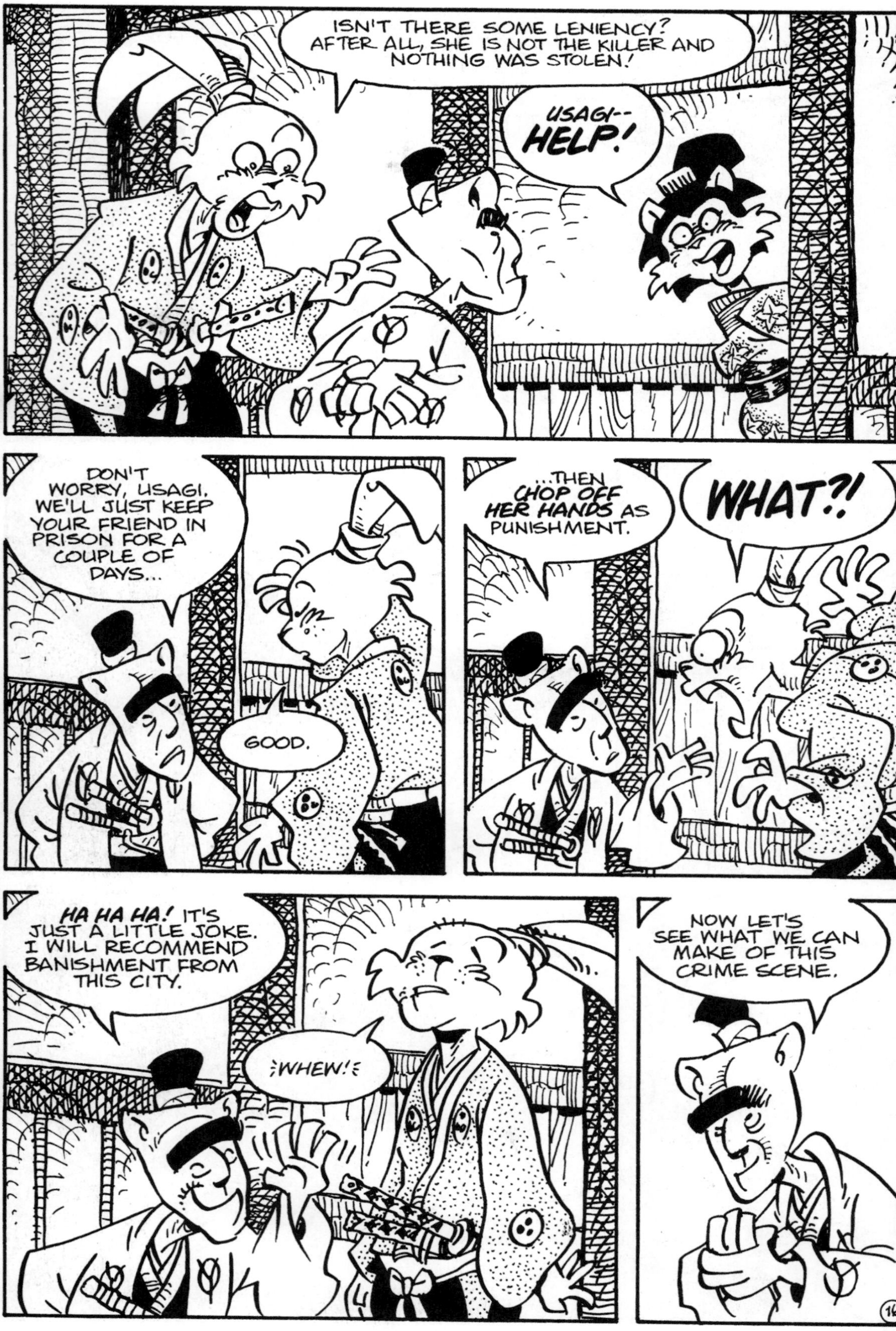

ISN'T THERE SOME LENIENCY? AFTER ALL, SHE IS NOT THE KILLER AND NOTHING WAS STOLEN!
USAGI-- HELP!
DON'T WORRY, USAGI. WE'LL JUST KEEP YOUR FRIEND IN PRISON FOR A COUPLE OF DAYS...
GOOD.
...THEN CHOP OFF HER HANDS AS PUNISHMENT.
WHAT?!
HA HA HA! IT'S JUST A LITTLE JOKE. I WILL RECOMMEND BANISHMENT FROM THIS CITY.
WHEW!
NOW LET'S SEE WHAT WE CAN MAKE OF THIS CRIME SCENE.
16

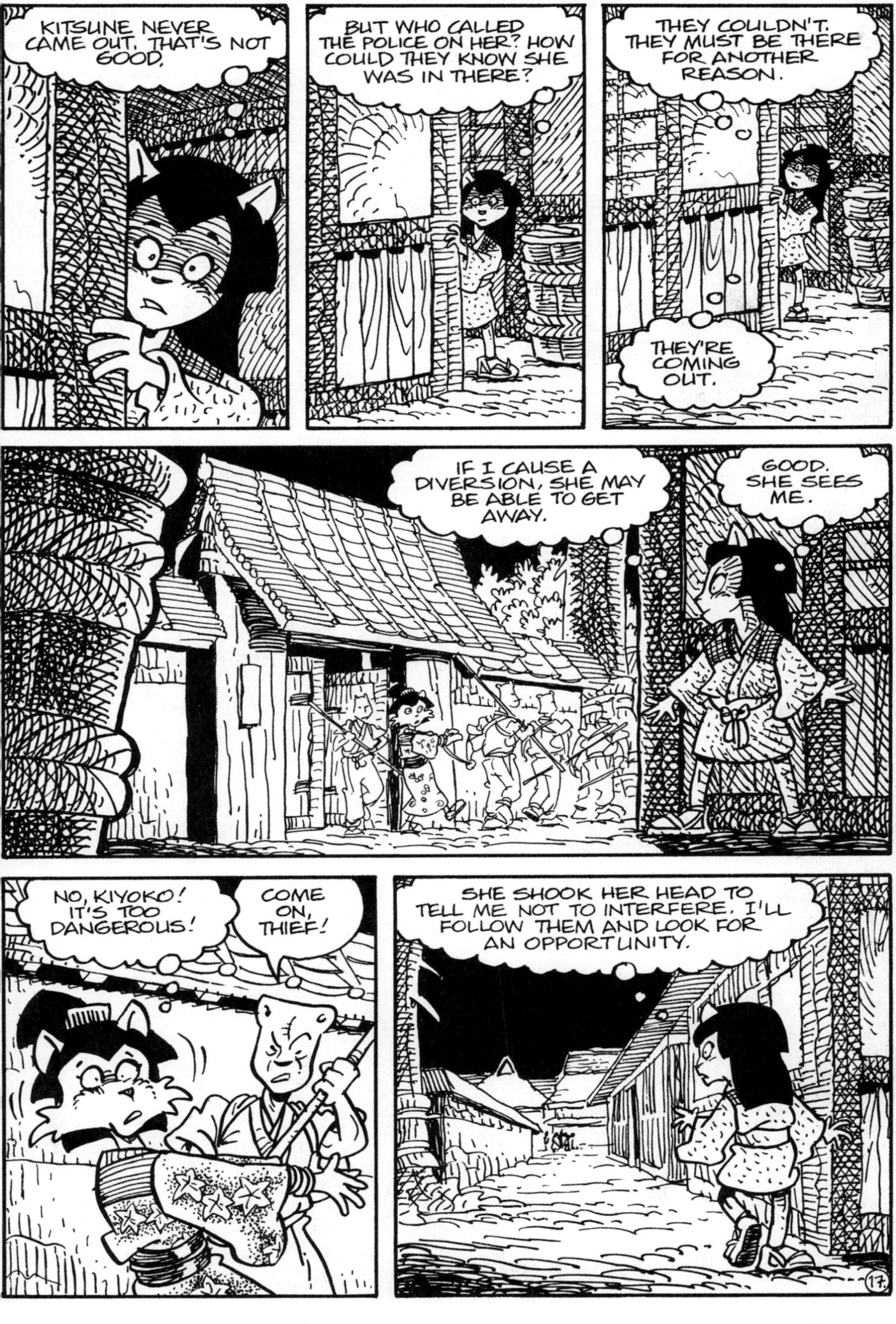

KITSUNE NEVER CAME OUT. THAT'S NOT GOOD.
BUT WHO CALLED THE POLICE ON HER? HOW COULD THEY KNOW SHE WAS IN THERE?
THEY COULDN'T. THEY MUST BE THERE FOR ANOTHER REASON.
THEY'RE COMING OUT.
IF I CAUSE A DIVERSION, SHE MAY BE ABLE TO GET AWAY.
GOOD. SHE SEES ME.
NO, KIYOKO! IT'S TOO DANGEROUS!
COME ON, THIEF!
SHE SHOOK HER HEAD TO TELL ME NOT TO INTERFERE. I'LL FOLLOW THEM AND LOOK FOR AN OPPORTUNITY.
17.

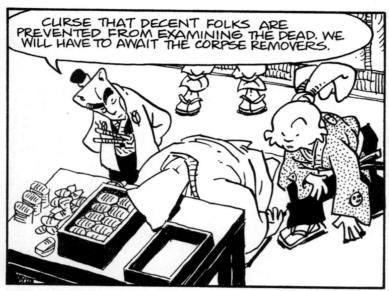

CURSE THAT DECENT FOLKS ARE PREVENTED FROM EXAMINING THE DEAD. WE WILL HAVE TO AWAIT THE CORPSE REMOVERS.

HE SHOWS NO OBVIOUS SIGNS OF VIOLENCE.

PERHAPS THIS IS JUST A NATURAL DEATH.

WHAT'S THIS?

LOOK AT THIS, INSPECTOR ISHIDA!

A SMALL PIN PRICK... WITH THE NEEDLE STILL INSIDE.

EH?

POISONED?

BRING IN THE DOCTOR'S ASSISTANT.

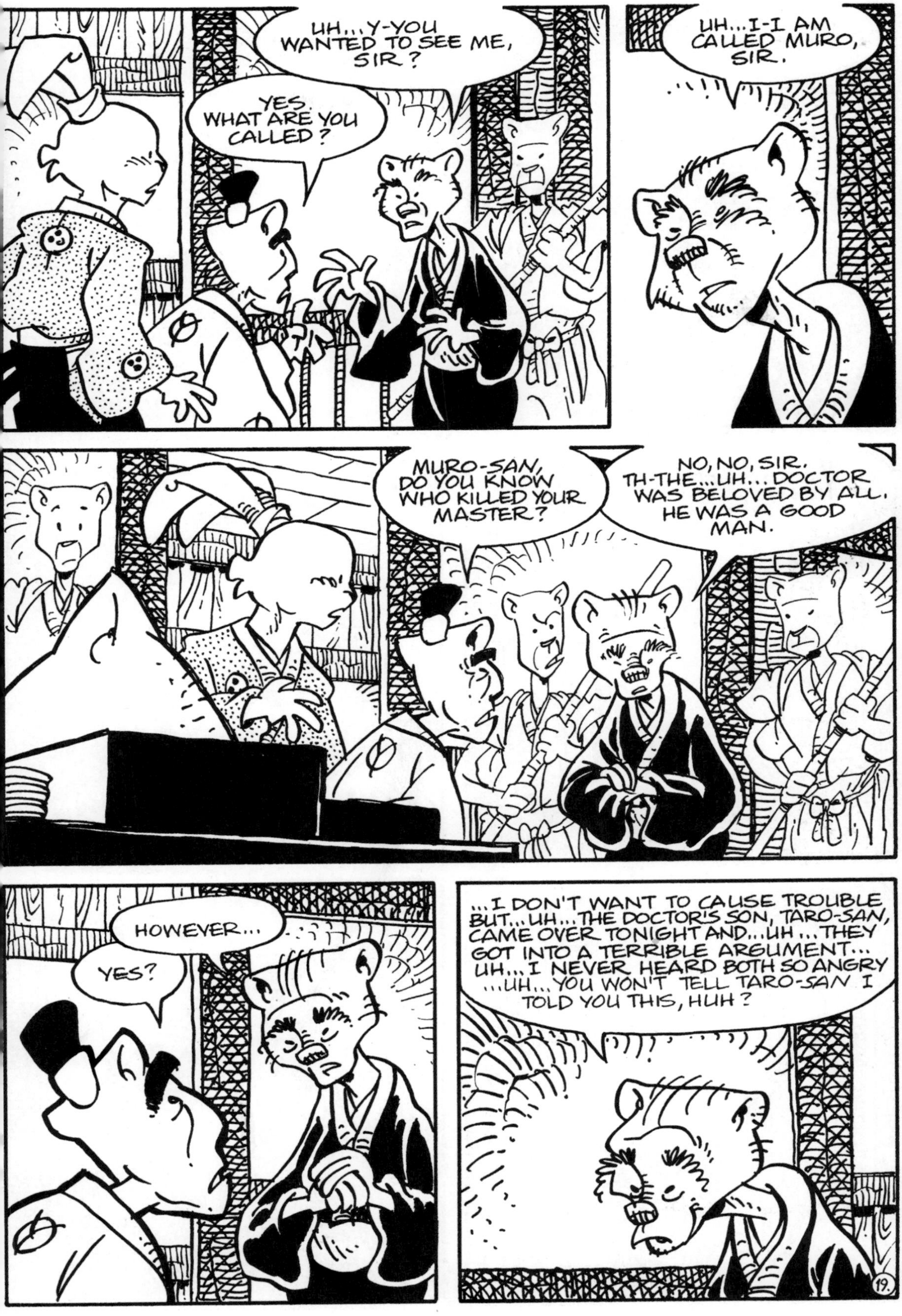
UH...Y-YOU WANTED TO SEE ME, SIR?
YES. WHAT ARE YOU CALLED?
UH...I-I AM CALLED MURO, SIR.
MURO-SAN, DO YOU KNOW WHO KILLED YOUR MASTER?
NO, NO, SIR. TH-THE...UH... DOCTOR WAS BELOVED BY ALL. HE WAS A GOOD MAN.
HOWEVER...
YES?
...I DON'T WANT TO CAUSE TROUBLE BUT...UH...THE DOCTOR'S SON, TARO-SAN, CAME OVER TONIGHT AND...UH...THEY GOT INTO A TERRIBLE ARGUMENT... UH...I NEVER HEARD BOTH SO ANGRY ...UH...YOU WON'T TELL TARO-SAN I TOLD YOU THIS, HUH?
19.

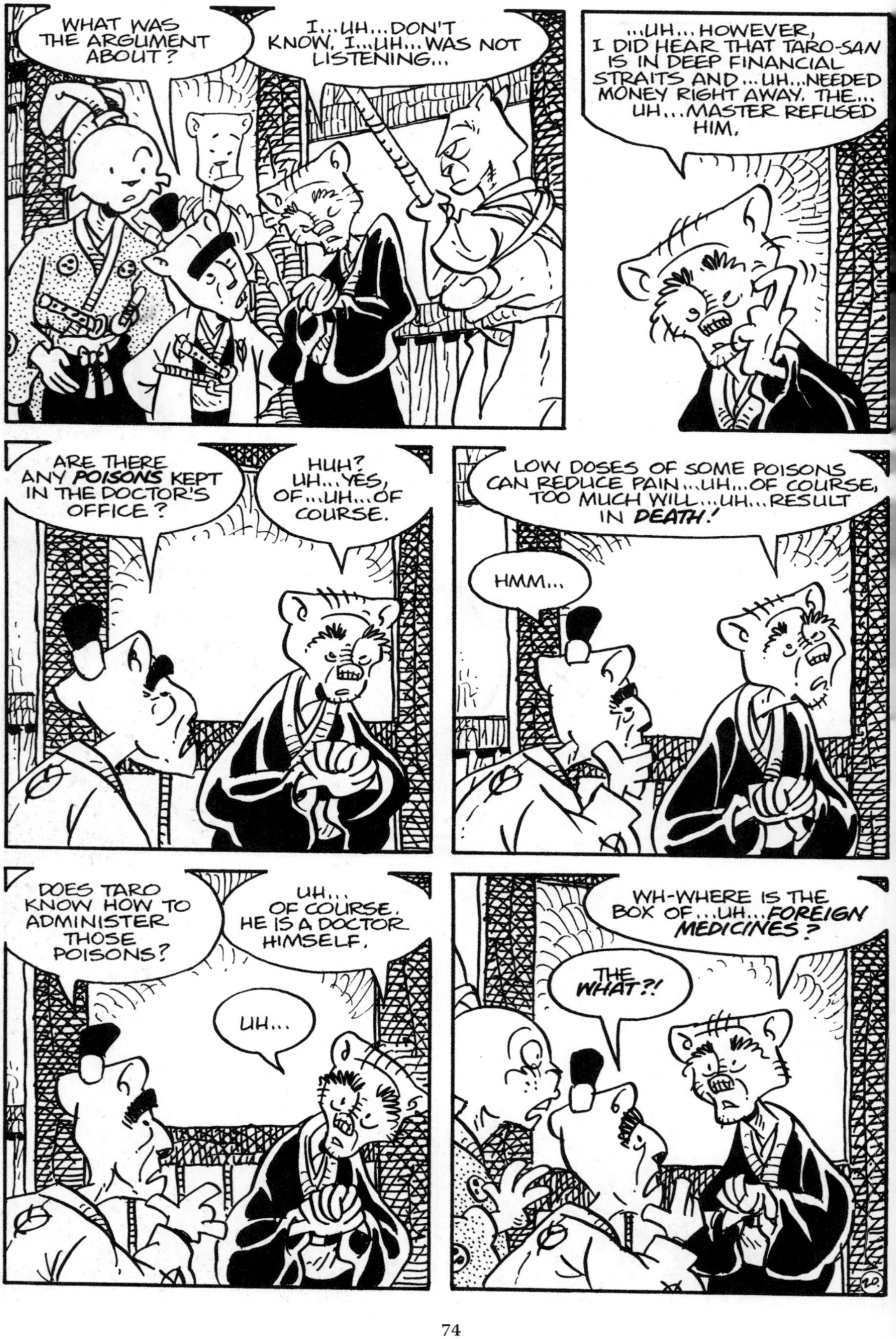

WHAT WAS THE ARGUMENT ABOUT?
I...UH...DON'T KNOW. I...UH...WAS NOT LISTENING...
...UH... HOWEVER, I DID HEAR THAT TARO-SAN IS IN DEEP FINANCIAL STRAITS AND...UH...NEEDED MONEY RIGHT AWAY. THE... UH...MASTER REFUSED HIM.
ARE THERE ANY POISONS KEPT IN THE DOCTOR'S OFFICE?
HUH? UH...YES, OF...UH...OF COURSE.
LOW DOSES OF SOME POISONS CAN REDUCE PAIN...UH...OF COURSE, TOO MUCH WILL...UH...RESULT IN DEATH!
HMM...
DOES TARO KNOW HOW TO ADMINISTER THOSE POISONS?
UH... OF COURSE. HE IS A DOCTOR HIMSELF.
UH...
WH-WHERE IS THE BOX OF...UH...FOREIGN MEDICINES?
THE WHAT?!
20.

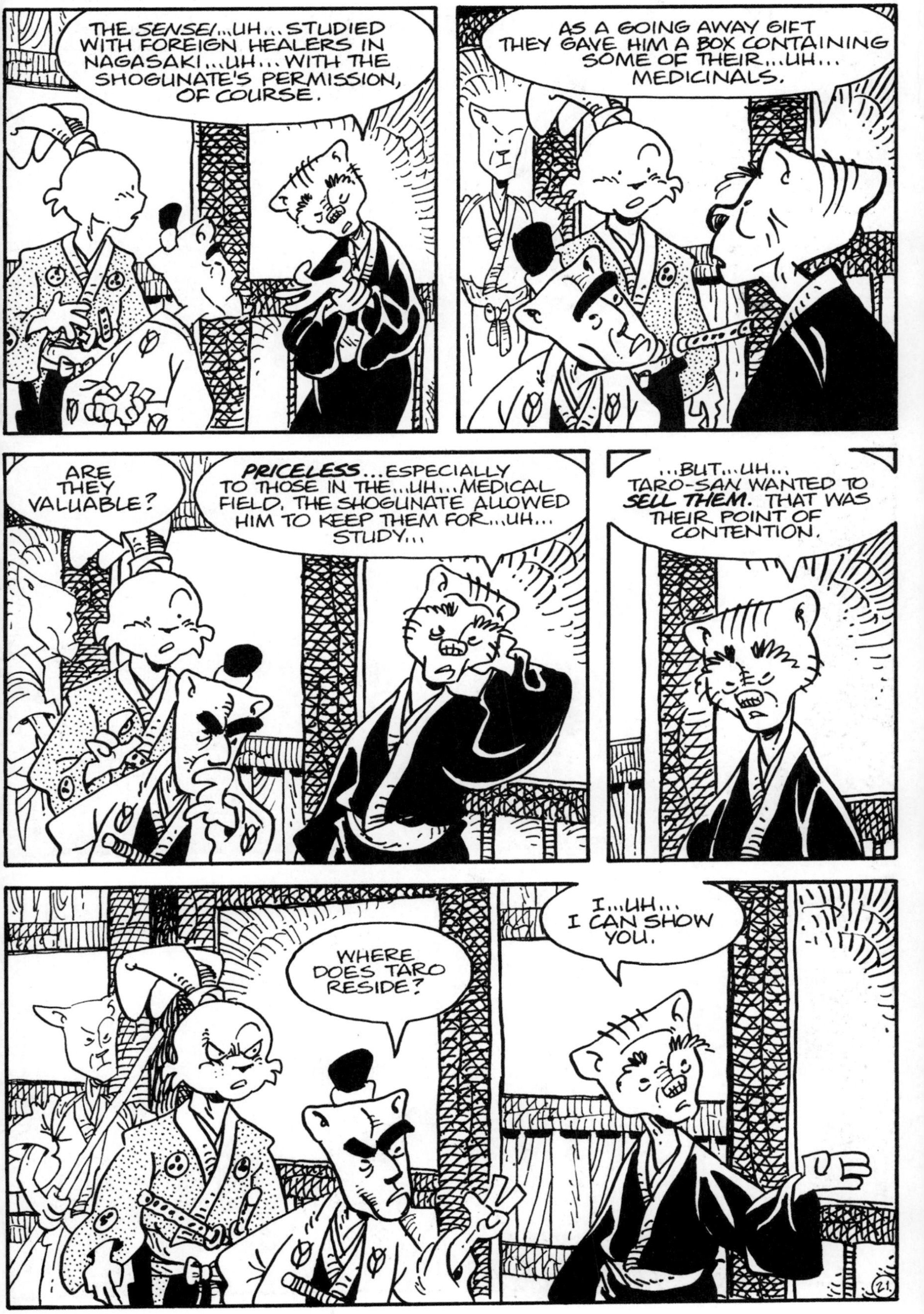
THE SENSEI...UH...STUDIED WITH FOREIGN HEALERS IN NAGASAKI...UH...WITH THE SHOGUNATE'S PERMISSION, OF COURSE.
AS A GOING AWAY GIFT THEY GAVE HIM A BOX CONTAINING SOME OF THEIR...UH... MEDICINALS.
ARE THEY VALUABLE?
PRICELESS...ESPECIALLY TO THOSE IN THE...UH...MEDICAL FIELD. THE SHOGUNATE ALLOWED HIM TO KEEP THEM FOR...UH... STUDY...
...BUT...UH... TARO-SAN WANTED TO SELL THEM. THAT WAS THEIR POINT OF CONTENTION.
WHERE DOES TARO RESIDE?
I...UH... I CAN SHOW YOU.
21.

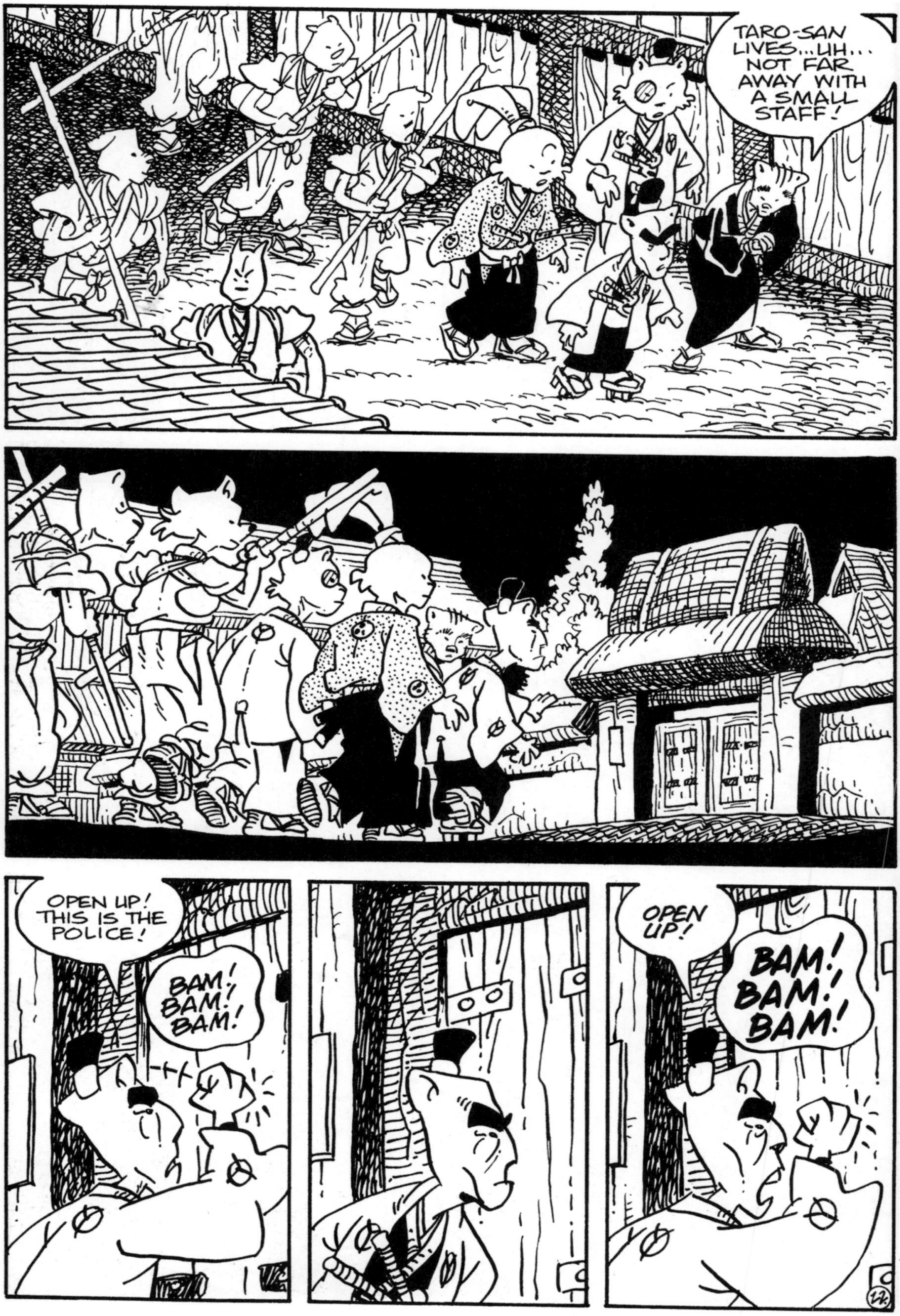
TARO-SAN LIVES...UH... NOT FAR AWAY WITH A SMALL STAFF!
OPEN UP! THIS IS THE POLICE!
BAM! BAM! BAM!
OPEN UP!
BAM! BAM! BAM!

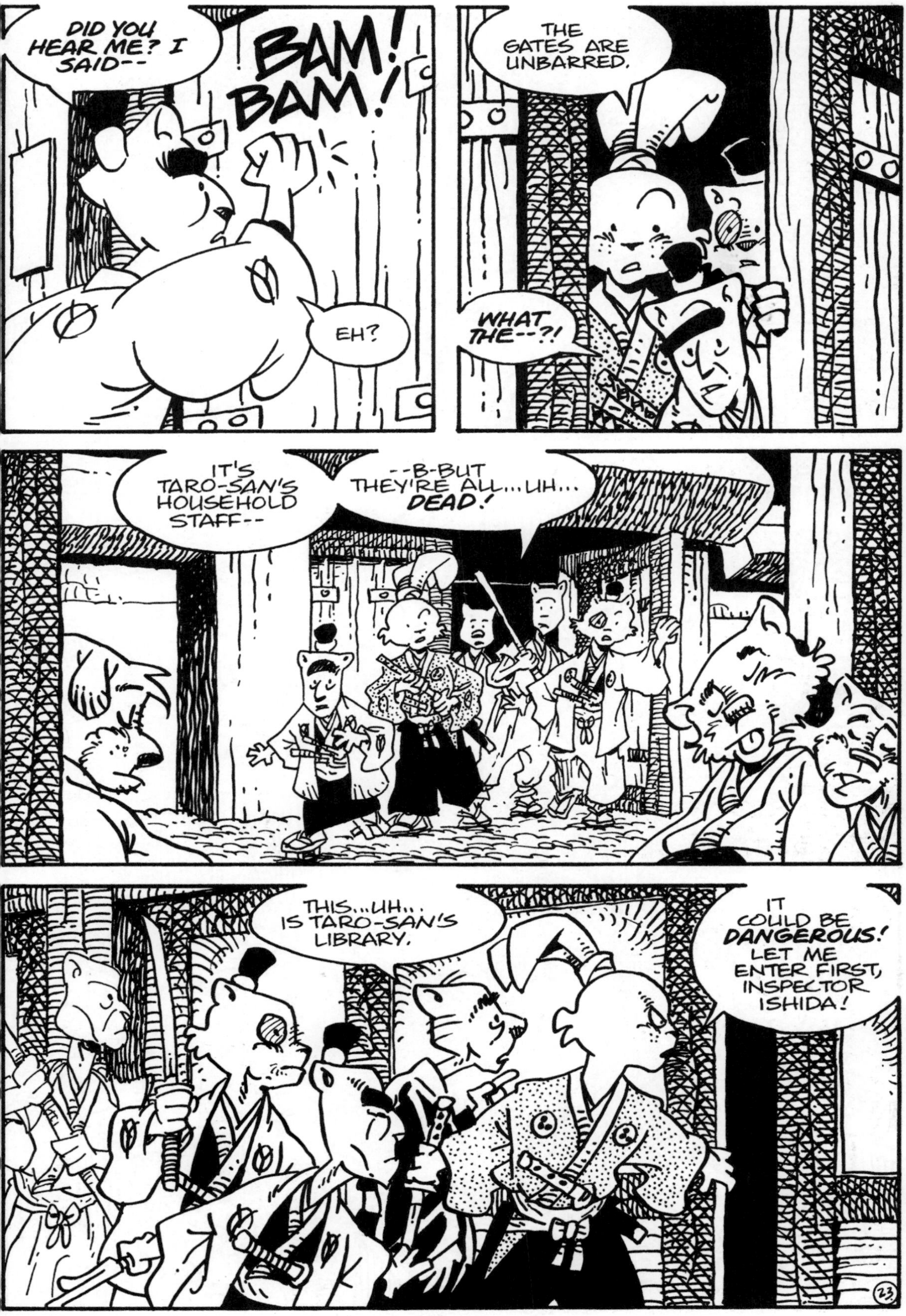
DID YOU HEAR ME? I SAID--
BAM! BAM!
EH?
THE GATES ARE UNBARRED.
WHAT THE--?!
IT'S TARO-SAN'S HOUSEHOLD STAFF--
--B-BUT THEY'RE ALL...UH... DEAD!
THIS...UH... IS TARO-SAN'S LIBRARY.
IT COULD BE DANGEROUS! LET ME ENTER FIRST, INSPECTOR ISHIDA!
23

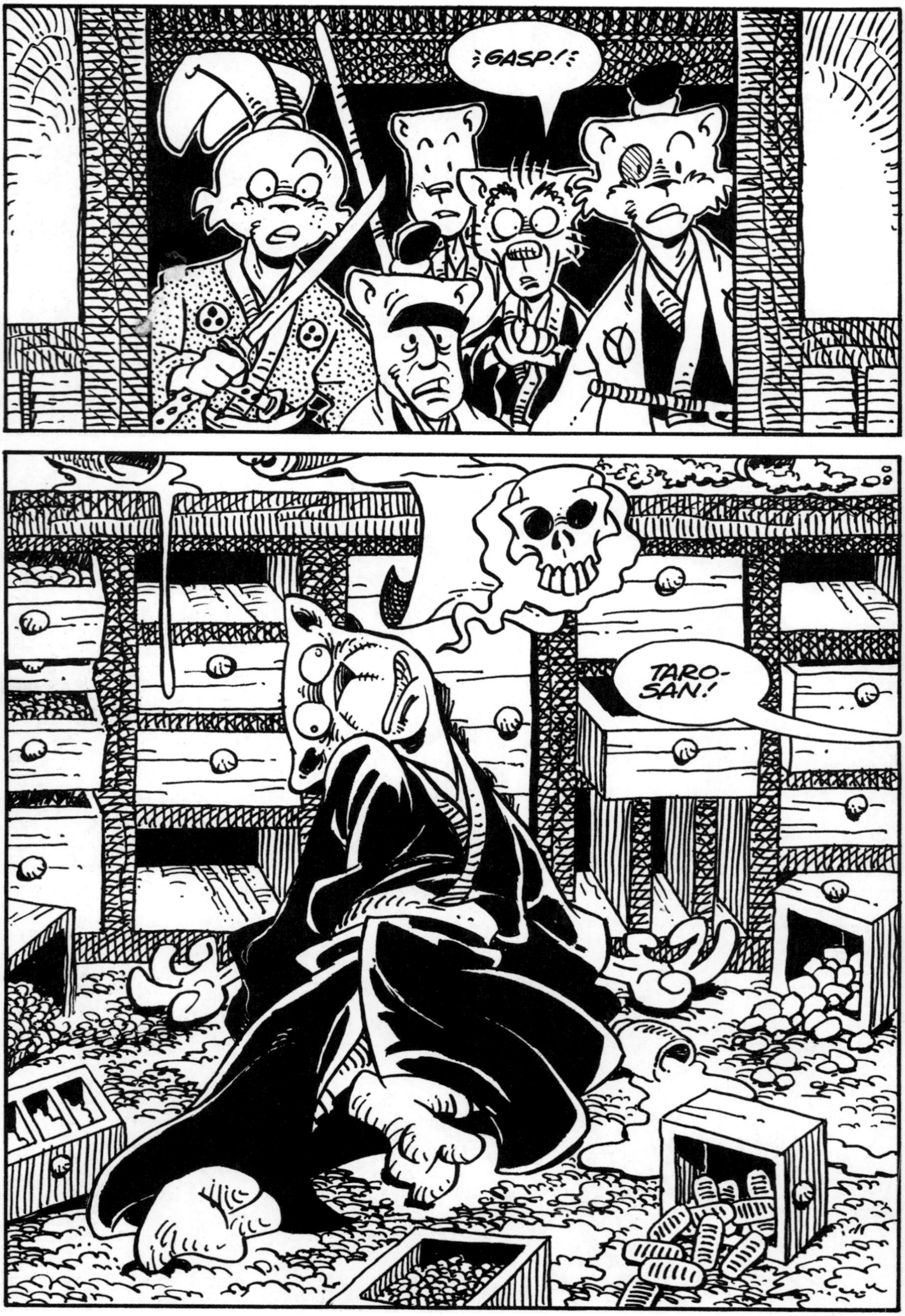
GASP!
TARO-SAN!

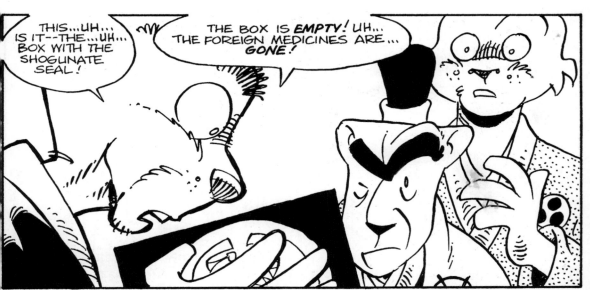

THIS...UH... IS IT--THE...UH... BOX WITH THE SHOGUNATE SEAL!

THE BOX IS *EMPTY!* UH... THE FOREIGN MEDICINES ARE... *GONE!*

THE BODY IN THE LIBRARY
PART 2

AND HIS FATHER WAS KILLED EARLIER TONIGHT.

TARO-SENSEI WAS MURDERED, AS WAS HIS ENTIRE STAFF!

YOU WERE THE ELDER DOCTOR'S ASSISTANT AND YOU DISCOVERED HIS BODY, MURO.

YOU KNEW BOTH VICTIMS.

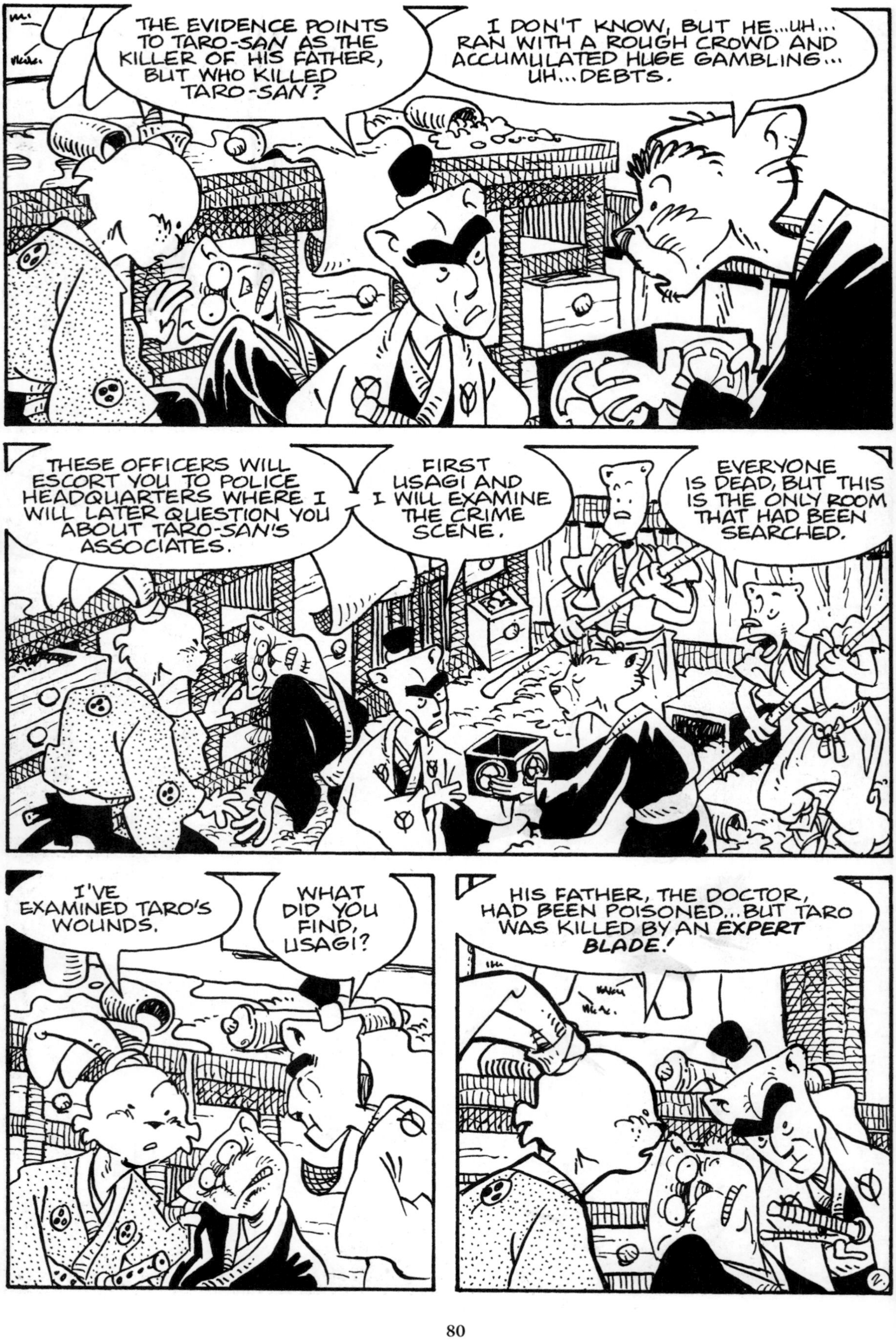
THE EVIDENCE POINTS TO TARO-SAN AS THE KILLER OF HIS FATHER, BUT WHO KILLED TARO-SAN?
I DON'T KNOW, BUT HE...UH... RAN WITH A ROUGH CROWD AND ACCUMULATED HUGE GAMBLING... UH...DEBTS.
THESE OFFICERS WILL ESCORT YOU TO POLICE HEADQUARTERS WHERE I WILL LATER QUESTION YOU ABOUT TARO-SAN'S ASSOCIATES.
FIRST USAGI AND I WILL EXAMINE THE CRIME SCENE.
EVERYONE IS DEAD, BUT THIS IS THE ONLY ROOM THAT HAD BEEN SEARCHED.
I'VE EXAMINED TARO'S WOUNDS.
WHAT DID YOU FIND, USAGI?
HIS FATHER, THE DOCTOR, HAD BEEN POISONED...BUT TARO WAS KILLED BY AN *EXPERT BLADE*!

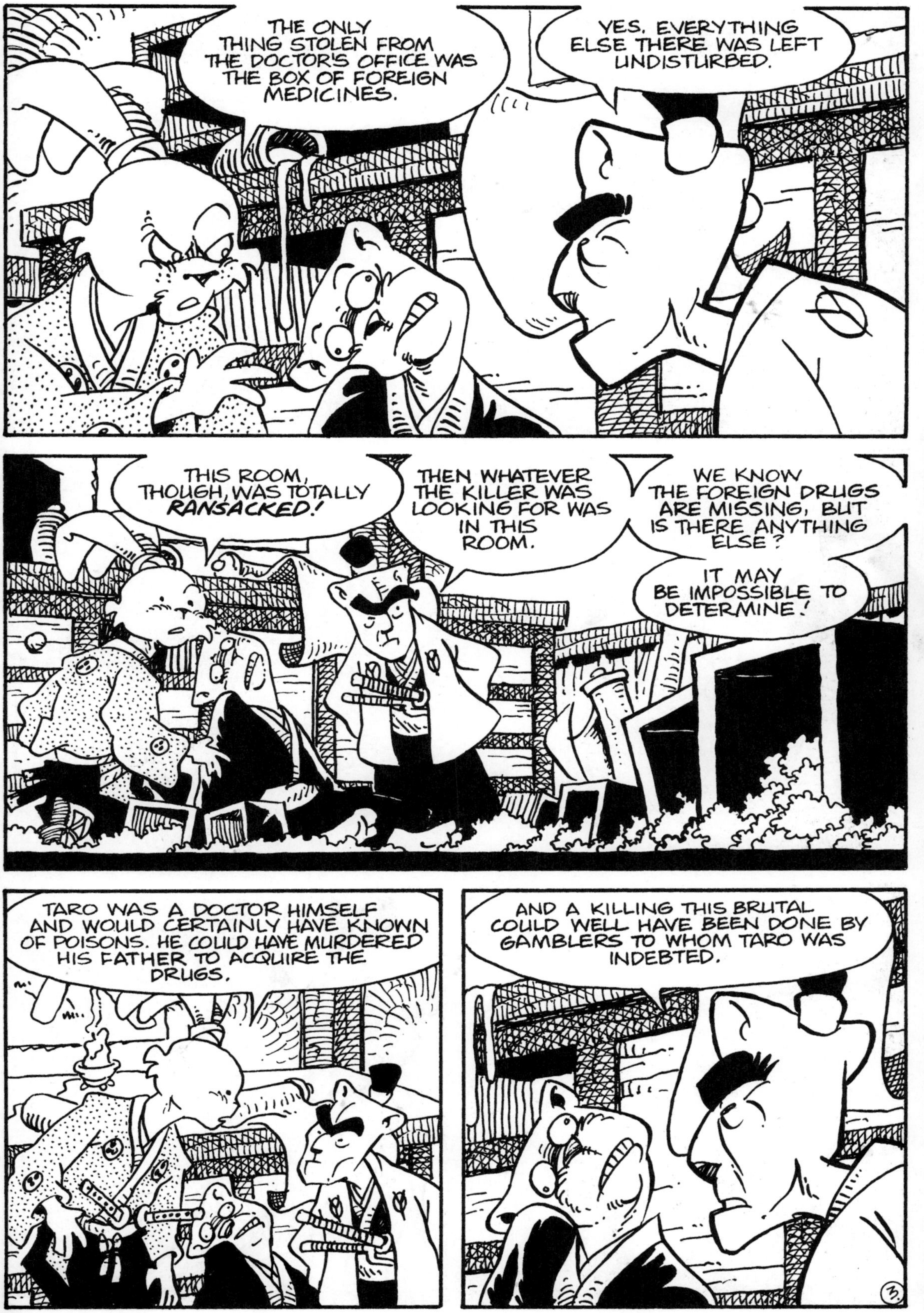
THE ONLY THING STOLEN FROM THE DOCTOR'S OFFICE WAS THE BOX OF FOREIGN MEDICINES.
YES. EVERYTHING ELSE THERE WAS LEFT UNDISTURBED.
THIS ROOM, THOUGH, WAS TOTALLY *RANSACKED!*
THEN WHATEVER THE KILLER WAS LOOKING FOR WAS IN THIS ROOM.
WE KNOW THE FOREIGN DRUGS ARE MISSING, BUT IS THERE ANYTHING ELSE?
IT MAY BE IMPOSSIBLE TO DETERMINE!
TARO WAS A DOCTOR HIMSELF AND WOULD CERTAINLY HAVE KNOWN OF POISONS. HE COULD HAVE MURDERED HIS FATHER TO ACQUIRE THE DRUGS.
AND A KILLING THIS BRUTAL COULD WELL HAVE BEEN DONE BY GAMBLERS TO WHOM TARO WAS INDEBTED.
3.

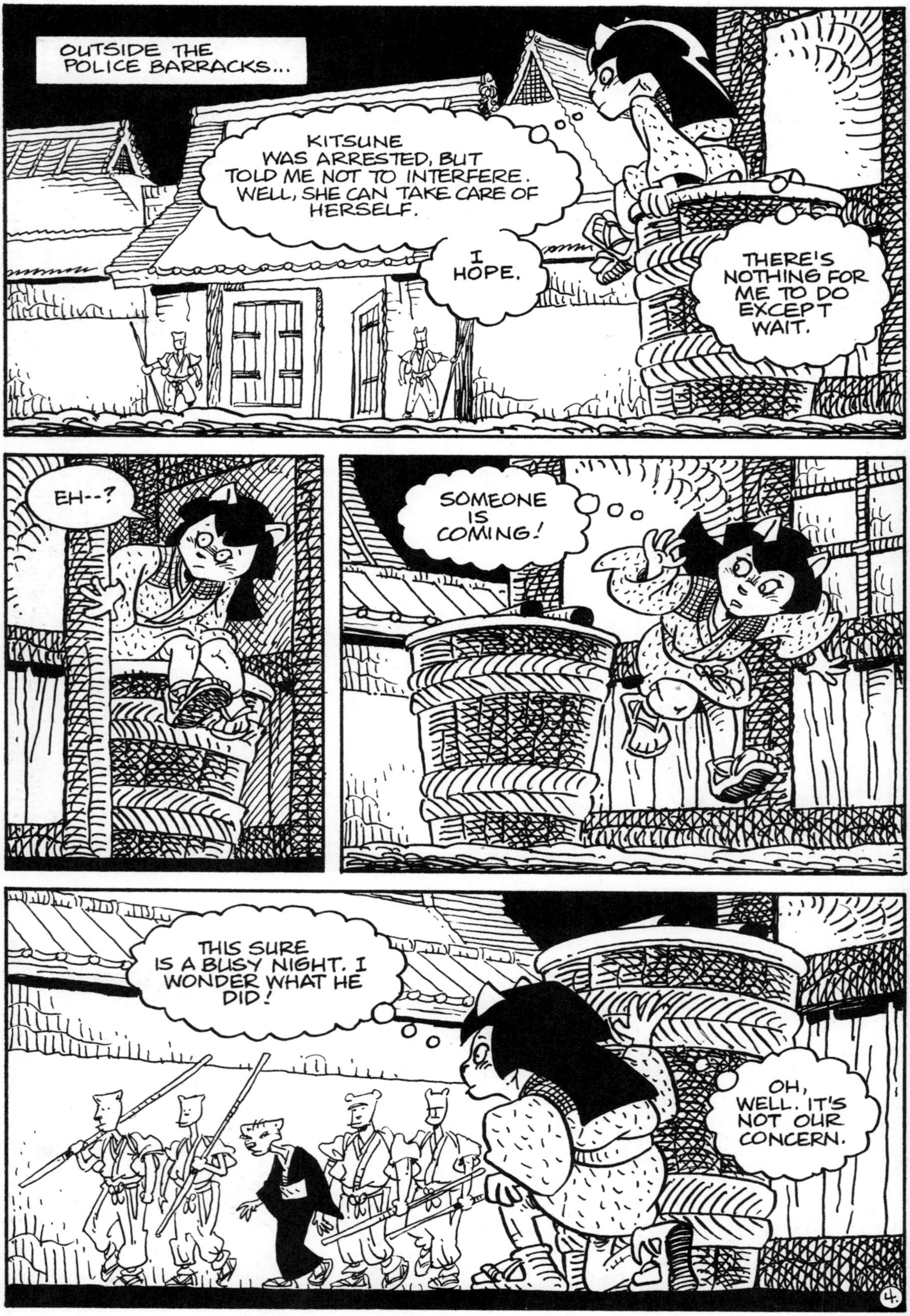
OUTSIDE THE POLICE BARRACKS...
KITSUNE WAS ARRESTED, BUT TOLD ME NOT TO INTERFERE. WELL, SHE CAN TAKE CARE OF HERSELF.
I HOPE.
THERE'S NOTHING FOR ME TO DO EXCEPT WAIT.
EH--?
SOMEONE IS COMING!
THIS SURE IS A BUSY NIGHT. I WONDER WHAT HE DID!
OH, WELL. IT'S NOT OUR CONCERN.
4.

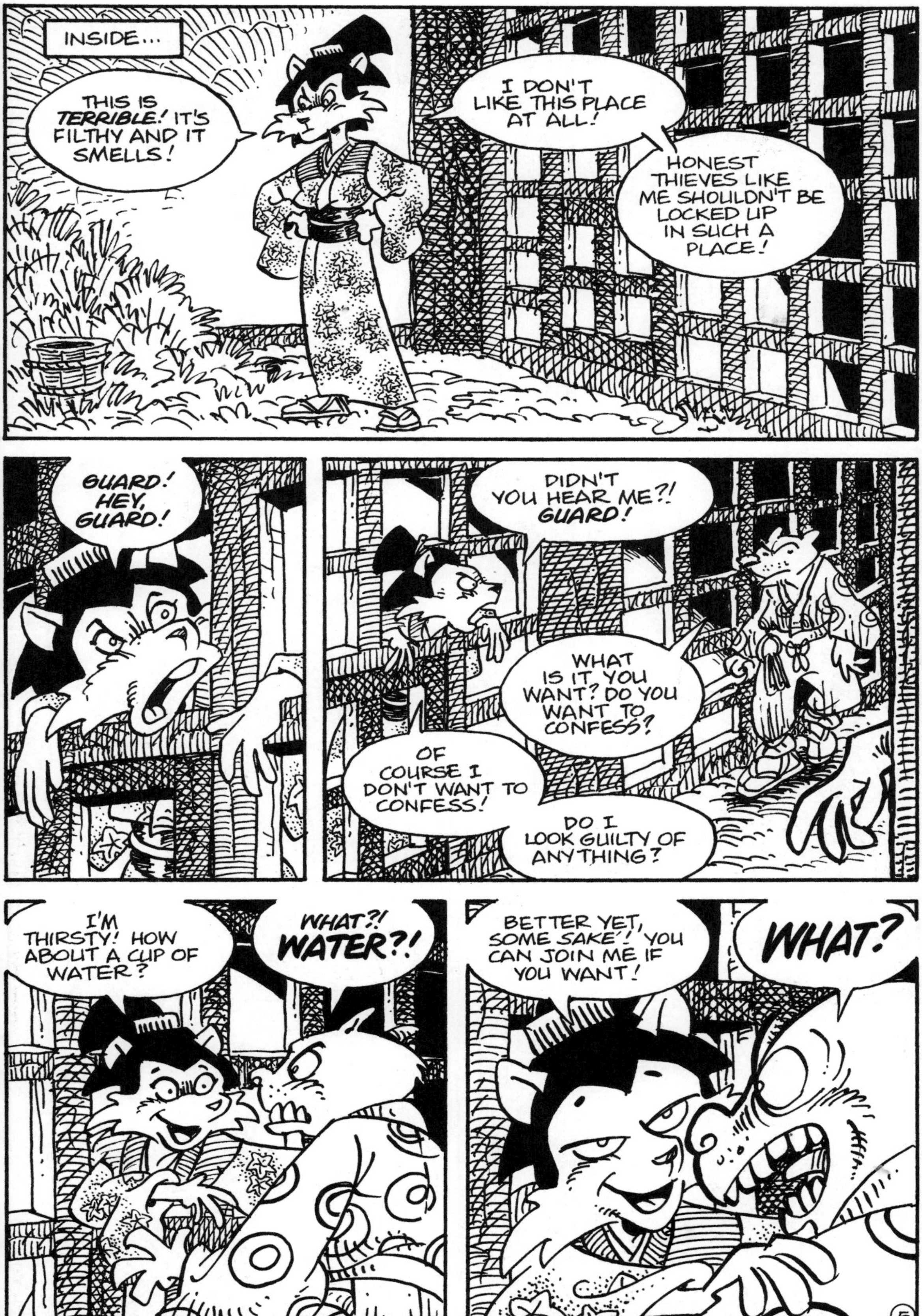
INSIDE...
THIS IS TERRIBLE! IT'S FILTHY AND IT SMELLS!
I DON'T LIKE THIS PLACE AT ALL!
HONEST THIEVES LIKE ME SHOULDN'T BE LOCKED UP IN SUCH A PLACE!
GUARD! HEY, GUARD!
DIDN'T YOU HEAR ME?! GUARD!
WHAT IS IT YOU WANT? DO YOU WANT TO CONFESS?
OF COURSE I DON'T WANT TO CONFESS!
DO I LOOK GUILTY OF ANYTHING?
I'M THIRSTY! HOW ABOUT A CUP OF WATER?
WHAT?! WATER?!
BETTER YET, SOME SAKE! YOU CAN JOIN ME IF YOU WANT!
WHAT?
5

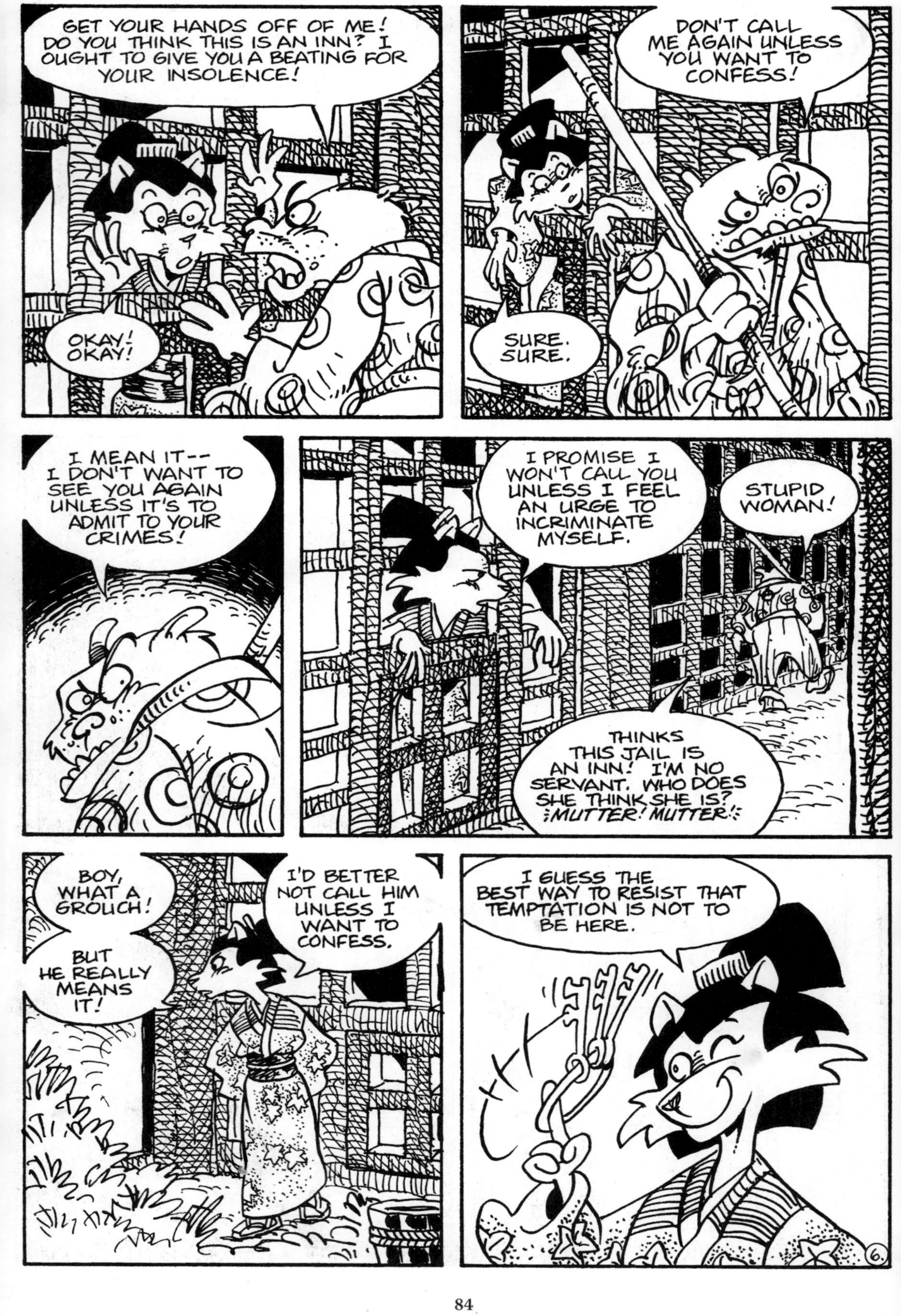
GET YOUR HANDS OFF OF ME! DO YOU THINK THIS IS AN INN? I OUGHT TO GIVE YOU A BEATING FOR YOUR INSOLENCE!
OKAY! OKAY!
DON'T CALL ME AGAIN UNLESS YOU WANT TO CONFESS!
SURE. SURE.
I MEAN IT-- I DON'T WANT TO SEE YOU AGAIN UNLESS IT'S TO ADMIT TO YOUR CRIMES!
I PROMISE I WON'T CALL YOU UNLESS I FEEL AN URGE TO INCRIMINATE MYSELF.
STUPID WOMAN!
THINKS THIS JAIL IS AN INN! I'M NO SERVANT. WHO DOES SHE THINK SHE IS? ;MUTTER! MUTTER!;
BOY, WHAT A GROUCH!
BUT HE REALLY MEANS IT!
I'D BETTER NOT CALL HIM UNLESS I WANT TO CONFESS.
I GUESS THE BEST WAY TO RESIST THAT TEMPTATION IS NOT TO BE HERE.
6.

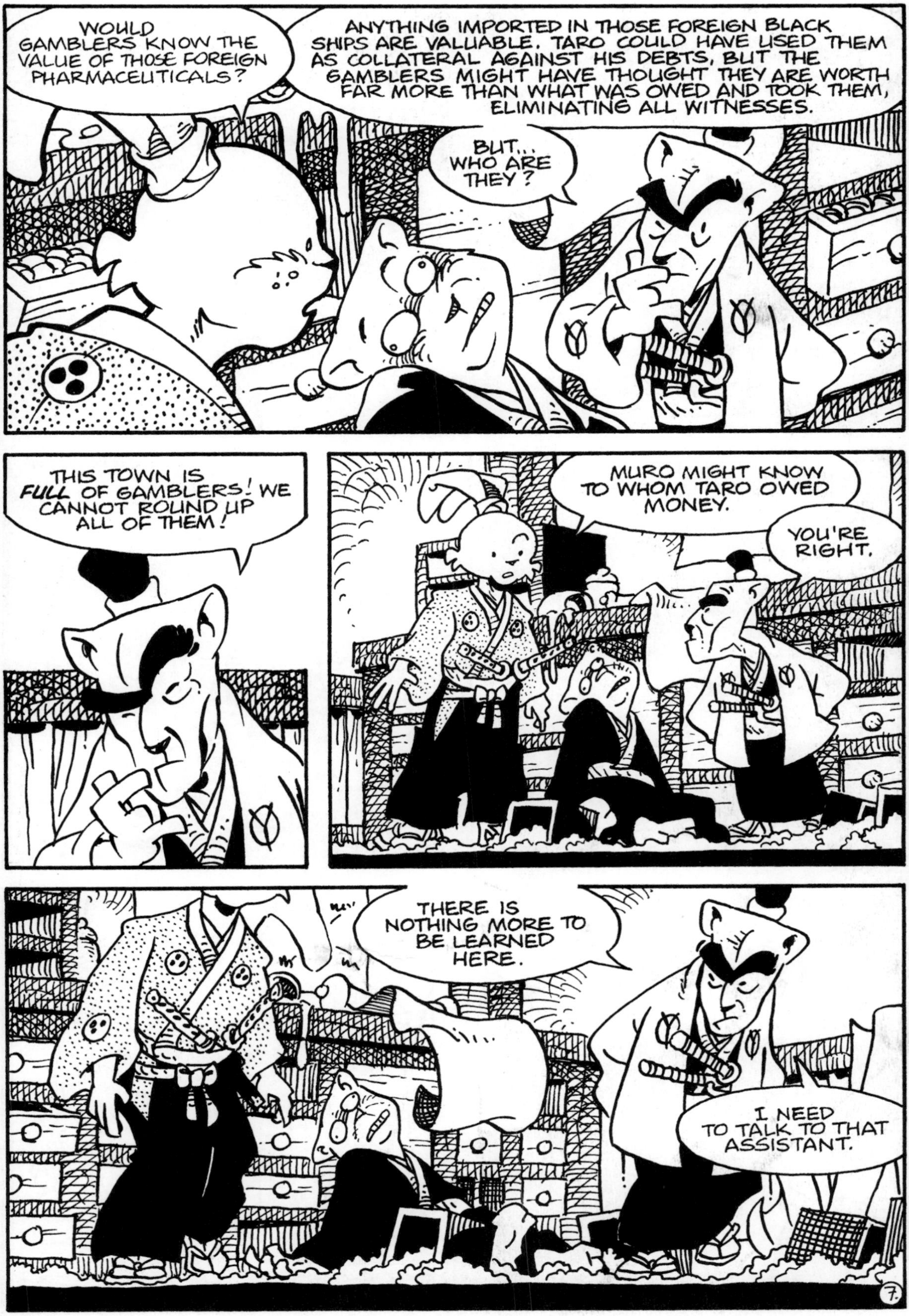
WOULD GAMBLERS KNOW THE VALUE OF THOSE FOREIGN PHARMACEUTICALS?
ANYTHING IMPORTED IN THOSE FOREIGN BLACK SHIPS ARE VALUABLE. TARO COULD HAVE USED THEM AS COLLATERAL AGAINST HIS DEBTS, BUT THE GAMBLERS MIGHT HAVE THOUGHT THEY ARE WORTH FAR MORE THAN WHAT WAS OWED AND TOOK THEM, ELIMINATING ALL WITNESSES.
BUT... WHO ARE THEY?
THIS TOWN IS FULL OF GAMBLERS! WE CANNOT ROUND UP ALL OF THEM!
MURO MIGHT KNOW TO WHOM TARO OWED MONEY.
YOU'RE RIGHT.
THERE IS NOTHING MORE TO BE LEARNED HERE.
I NEED TO TALK TO THAT ASSISTANT.
7.

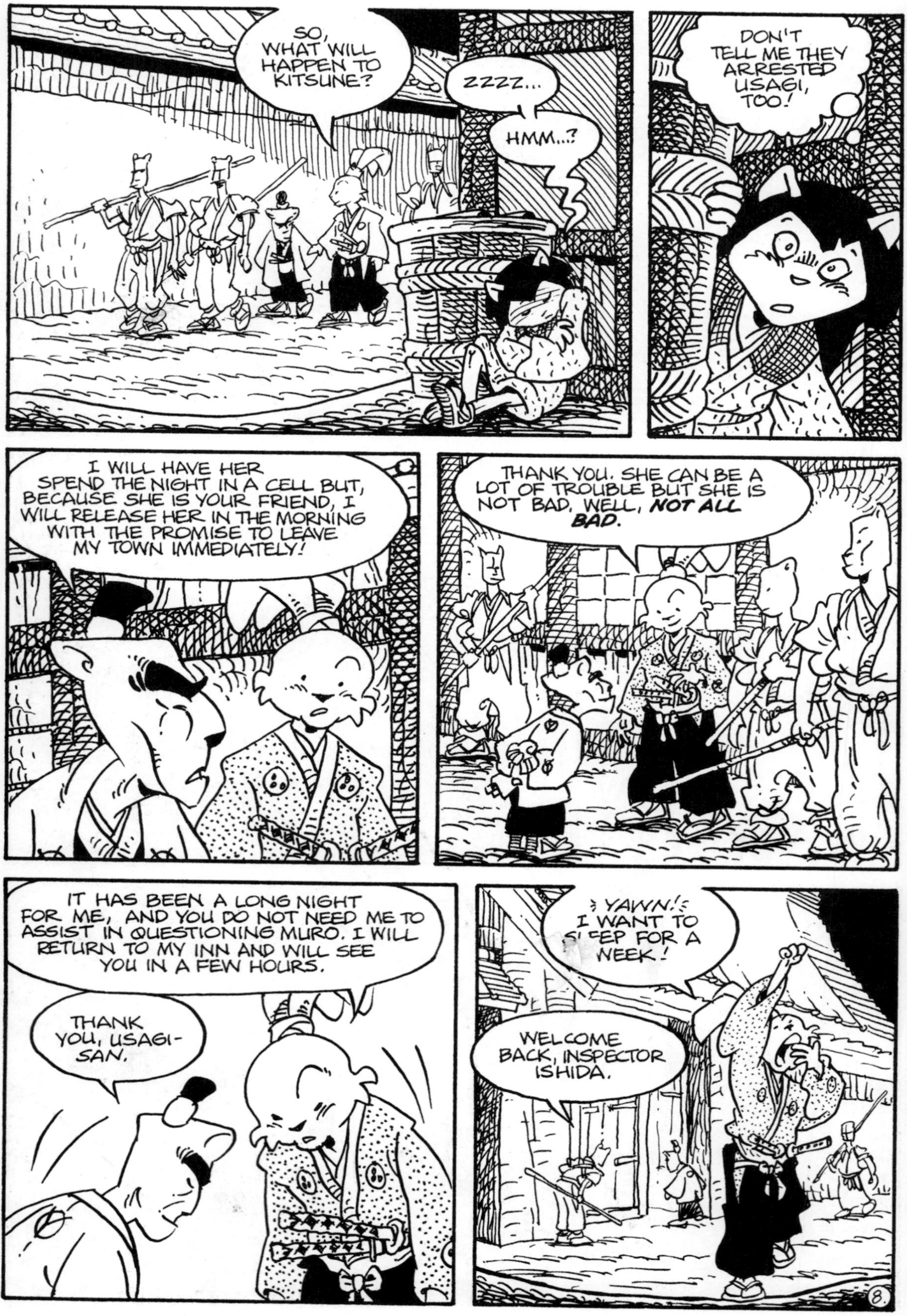
SO, WHAT WILL HAPPEN TO KITSUNE?
ZZZZ...
HMM...?
DON'T TELL ME THEY ARRESTED USAGI, TOO!
I WILL HAVE HER SPEND THE NIGHT IN A CELL BUT, BECAUSE SHE IS YOUR FRIEND, I WILL RELEASE HER IN THE MORNING WITH THE PROMISE TO LEAVE MY TOWN IMMEDIATELY!
THANK YOU. SHE CAN BE A LOT OF TROUBLE BUT SHE IS NOT BAD, WELL, ***NOT ALL BAD.***
IT HAS BEEN A LONG NIGHT FOR ME, AND YOU DO NOT NEED ME TO ASSIST IN QUESTIONING MURO. I WILL RETURN TO MY INN AND WILL SEE YOU IN A FEW HOURS.
THANK YOU, USAGI-SAN.
YAWN! I WANT TO SLEEP FOR A WEEK!
WELCOME BACK, INSPECTOR ISHIDA.
8.

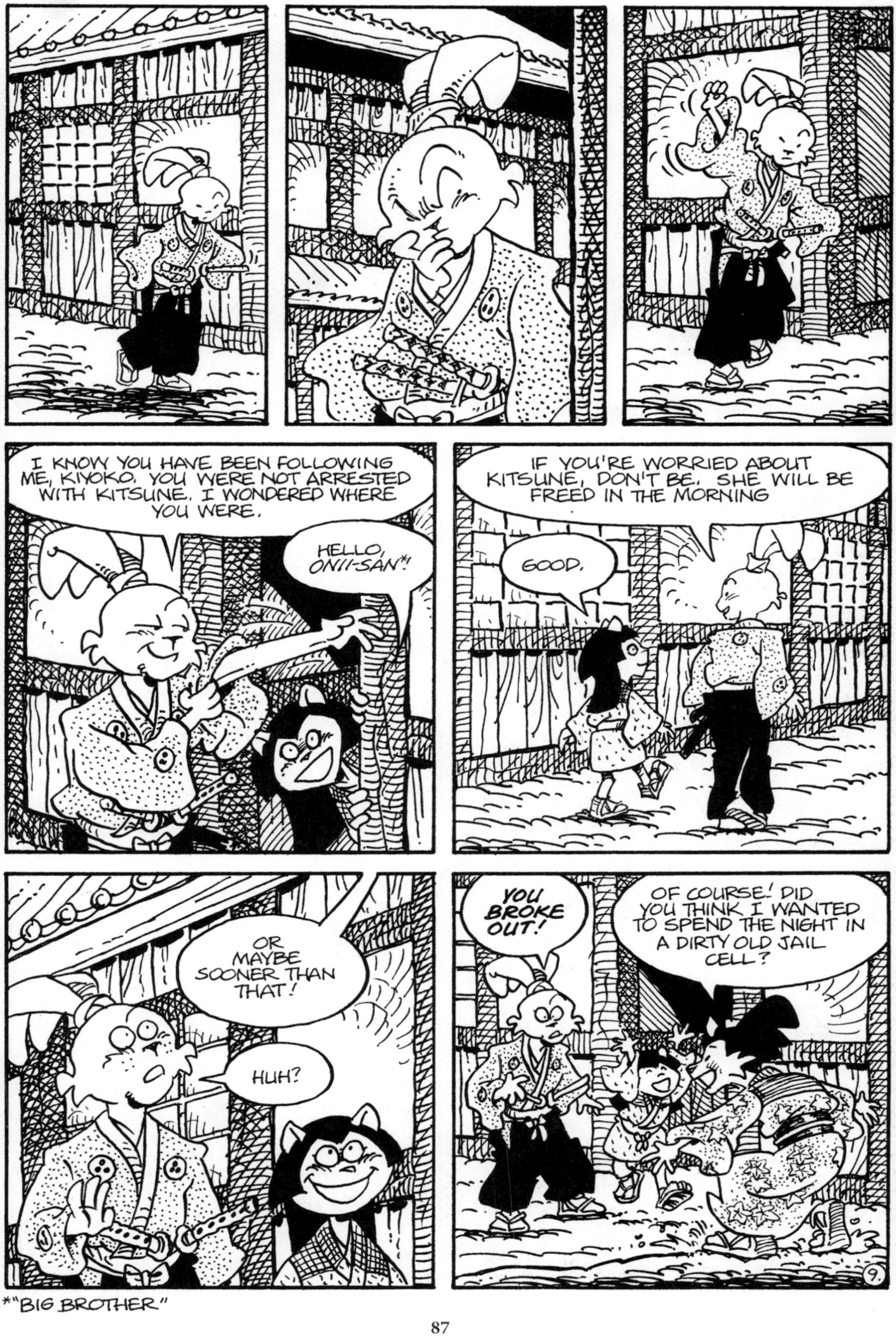
I KNOW YOU HAVE BEEN FOLLOWING ME, KIYOKO. YOU WERE NOT ARRESTED WITH KITSUNE. I WONDERED WHERE YOU WERE.
HELLO, ONII-SAN*!
IF YOU'RE WORRIED ABOUT KITSUNE, DON'T BE. SHE WILL BE FREED IN THE MORNING
GOOD.
OR MAYBE SOONER THAN THAT!
HUH?
YOU BROKE OUT!
OF COURSE! DID YOU THINK I WANTED TO SPEND THE NIGHT IN A DIRTY OLD JAIL CELL?
9.

*"BIG BROTHER"

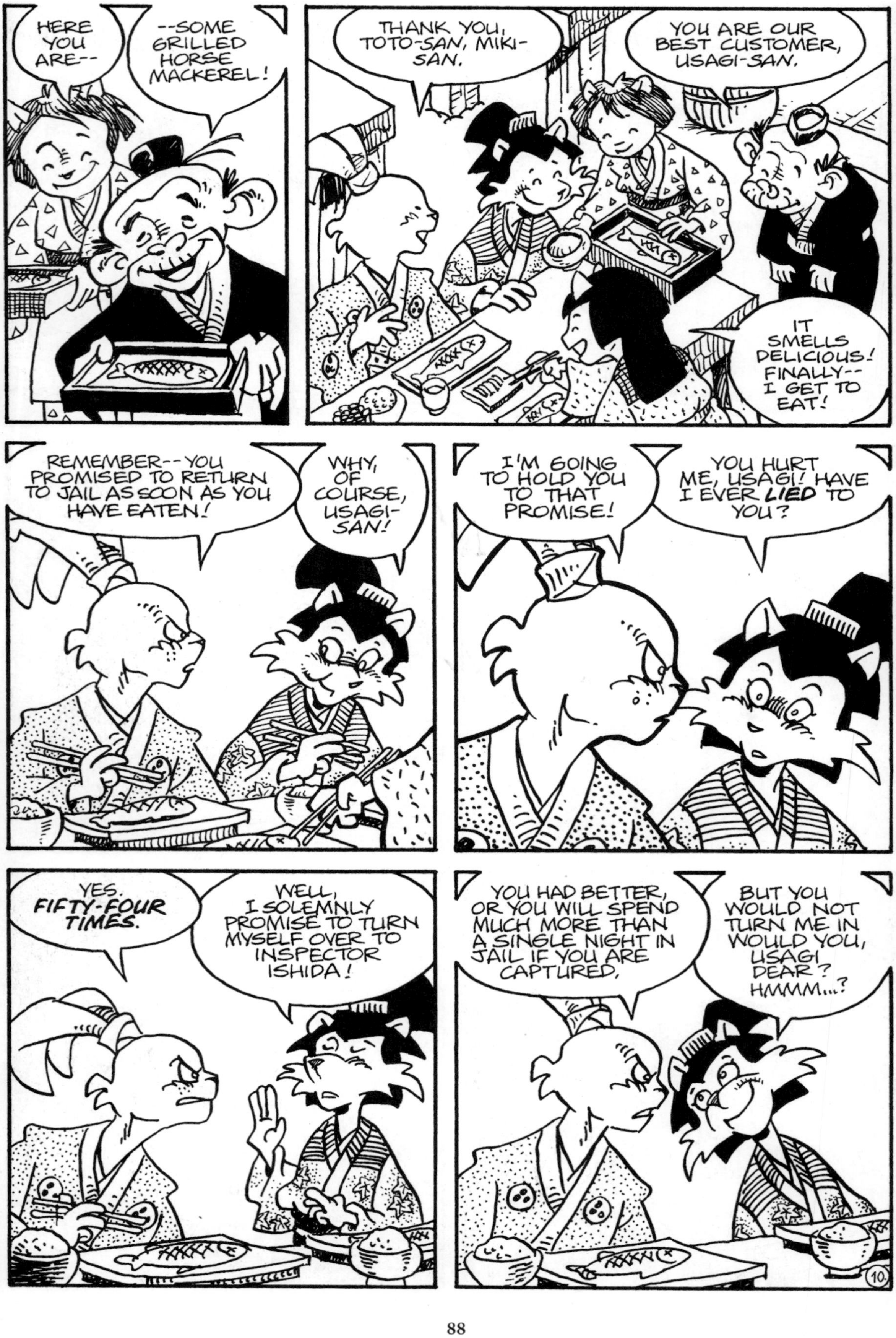
HERE YOU ARE--
--SOME GRILLED HORSE MACKEREL!
THANK YOU, TOTO-SAN, MIKI-SAN.
YOU ARE OUR BEST CUSTOMER, USAGI-SAN.
IT SMELLS DELICIOUS! FINALLY-- I GET TO EAT!
REMEMBER--YOU PROMISED TO RETURN TO JAIL AS SOON AS YOU HAVE EATEN!
WHY, OF COURSE, USAGI-SAN!
I'M GOING TO HOLD YOU TO THAT PROMISE!
YOU HURT ME, USAGI! HAVE I EVER LIED TO YOU?
YES. FIFTY-FOUR TIMES.
WELL, I SOLEMNLY PROMISE TO TURN MYSELF OVER TO INSPECTOR ISHIDA!
YOU HAD BETTER, OR YOU WILL SPEND MUCH MORE THAN A SINGLE NIGHT IN JAIL IF YOU ARE CAPTURED.
BUT YOU WOULD NOT TURN ME IN WOULD YOU, USAGI DEAR? HMMM...?
10.

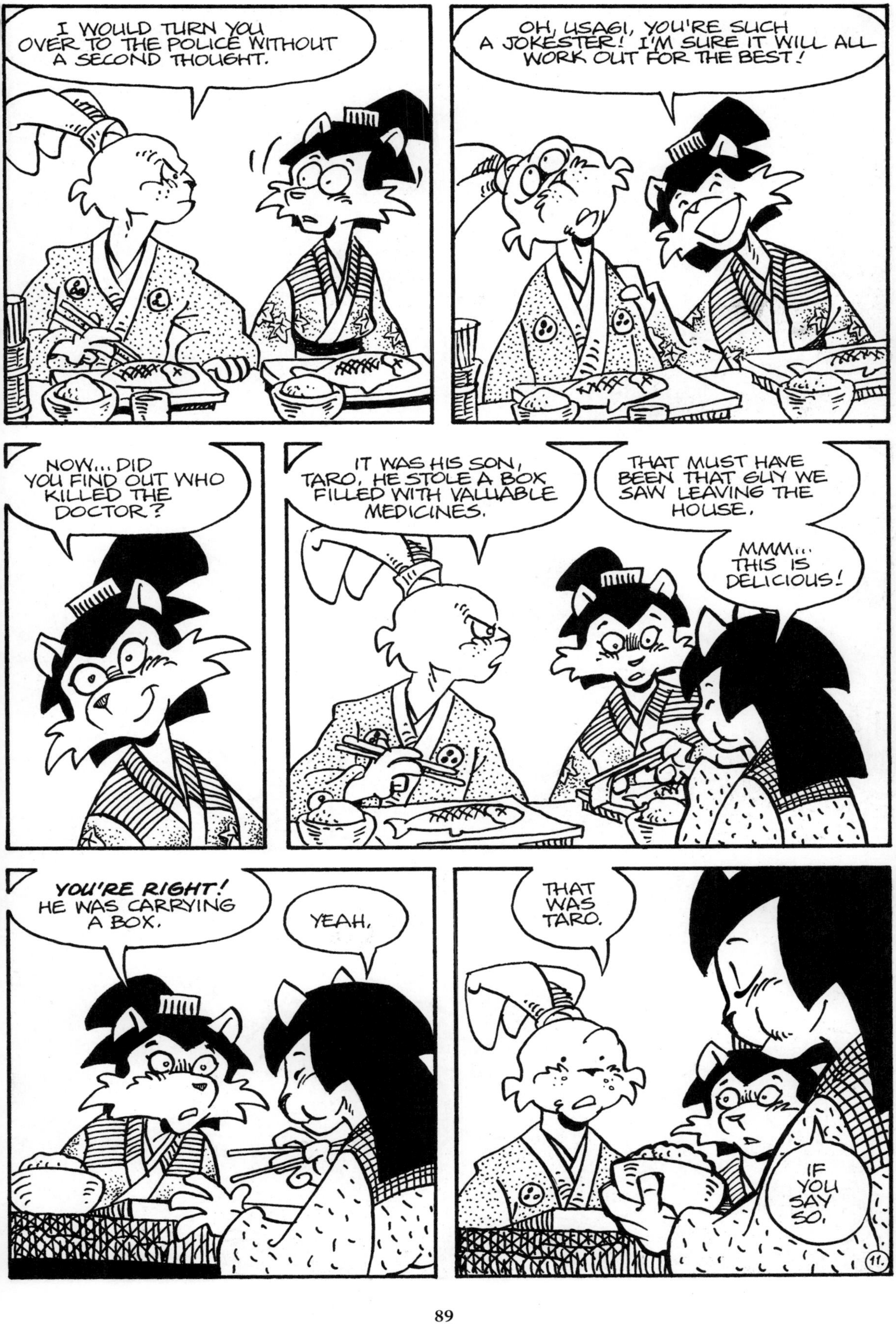
I WOULD TURN YOU OVER TO THE POLICE WITHOUT A SECOND THOUGHT.
OH, USAGI, YOU'RE SUCH A JOKESTER! I'M SURE IT WILL ALL WORK OUT FOR THE BEST!
NOW... DID YOU FIND OUT WHO KILLED THE DOCTOR?
IT WAS HIS SON, TARO. HE STOLE A BOX FILLED WITH VALUABLE MEDICINES.
THAT MUST HAVE BEEN THAT GUY WE SAW LEAVING THE HOUSE.
MMM... THIS IS DELICIOUS!
YOU'RE RIGHT! HE WAS CARRYING A BOX.
YEAH.
THAT WAS TARO.
IF YOU SAY SO.
11.

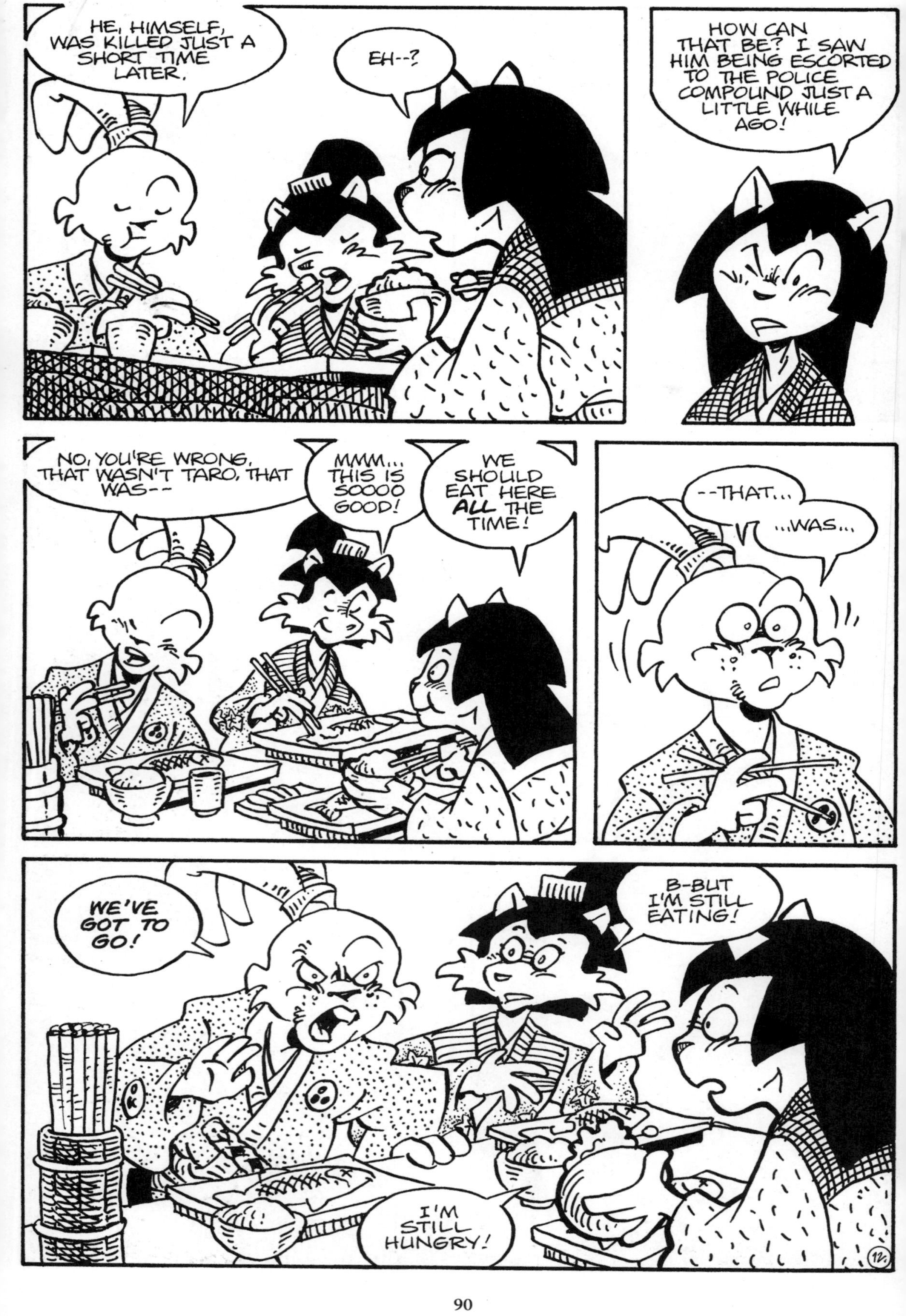
HE, HIMSELF, WAS KILLED JUST A SHORT TIME LATER.
EH--?
HOW CAN THAT BE? I SAW HIM BEING ESCORTED TO THE POLICE COMPOUND JUST A LITTLE WHILE AGO!
NO, YOU'RE WRONG, THAT WASN'T TARO, THAT WAS--
MMM... THIS IS SOOOO GOOD!
WE SHOULD EAT HERE ALL THE TIME!
--THAT...
...WAS...
WE'VE GOT TO GO!
B-BUT I'M STILL EATING!
I'M STILL HUNGRY!
12.

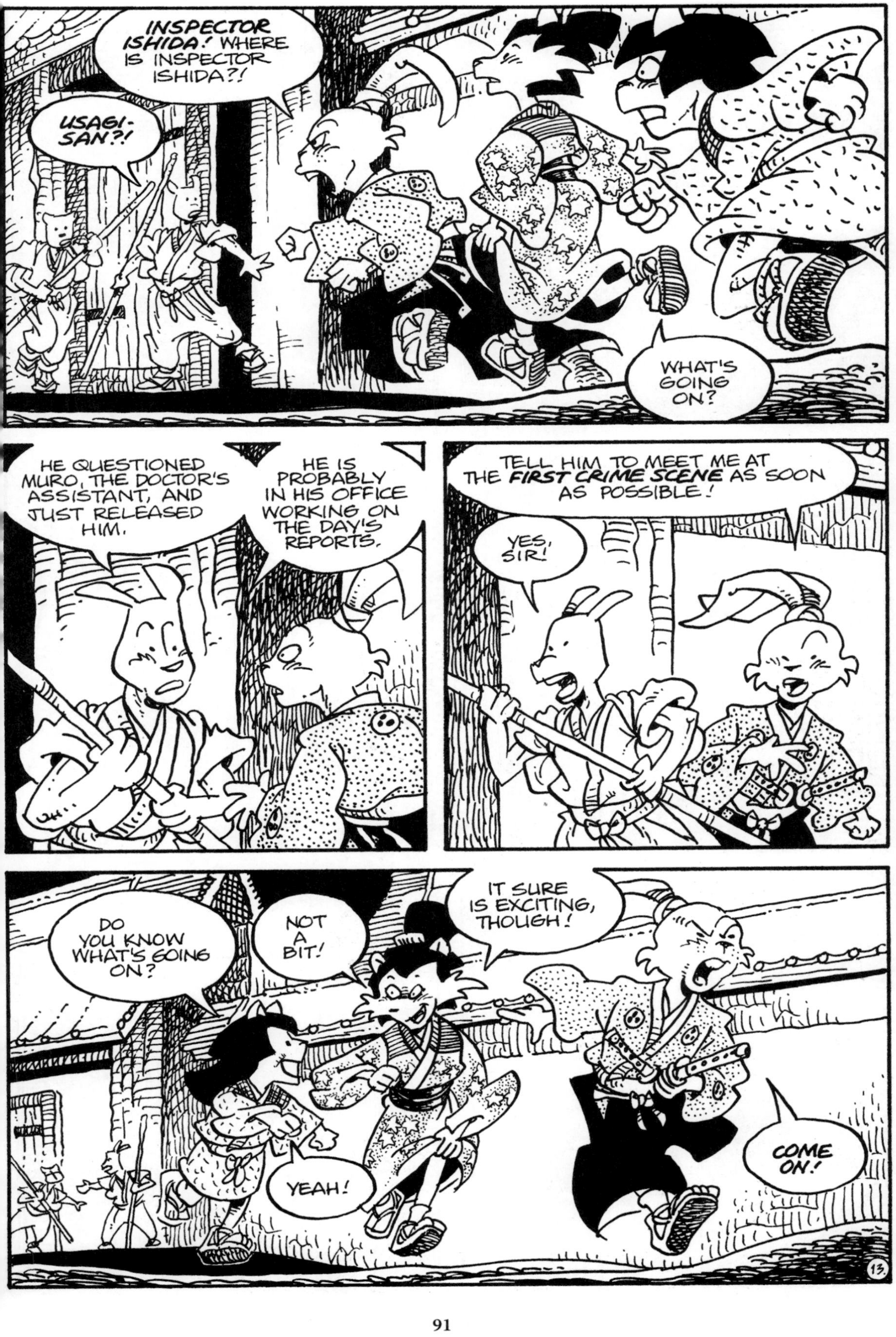
INSPECTOR ISHIDA! WHERE IS INSPECTOR ISHIDA?!
USAGI-SAN?!
WHAT'S GOING ON?
HE QUESTIONED MURO, THE DOCTOR'S ASSISTANT, AND JUST RELEASED HIM.
HE IS PROBABLY IN HIS OFFICE WORKING ON THE DAY'S REPORTS.
TELL HIM TO MEET ME AT THE FIRST CRIME SCENE AS SOON AS POSSIBLE!
YES, SIR!
DO YOU KNOW WHAT'S GOING ON?
NOT A BIT!
IT SURE IS EXCITING, THOUGH!
YEAH!
COME ON!
13.

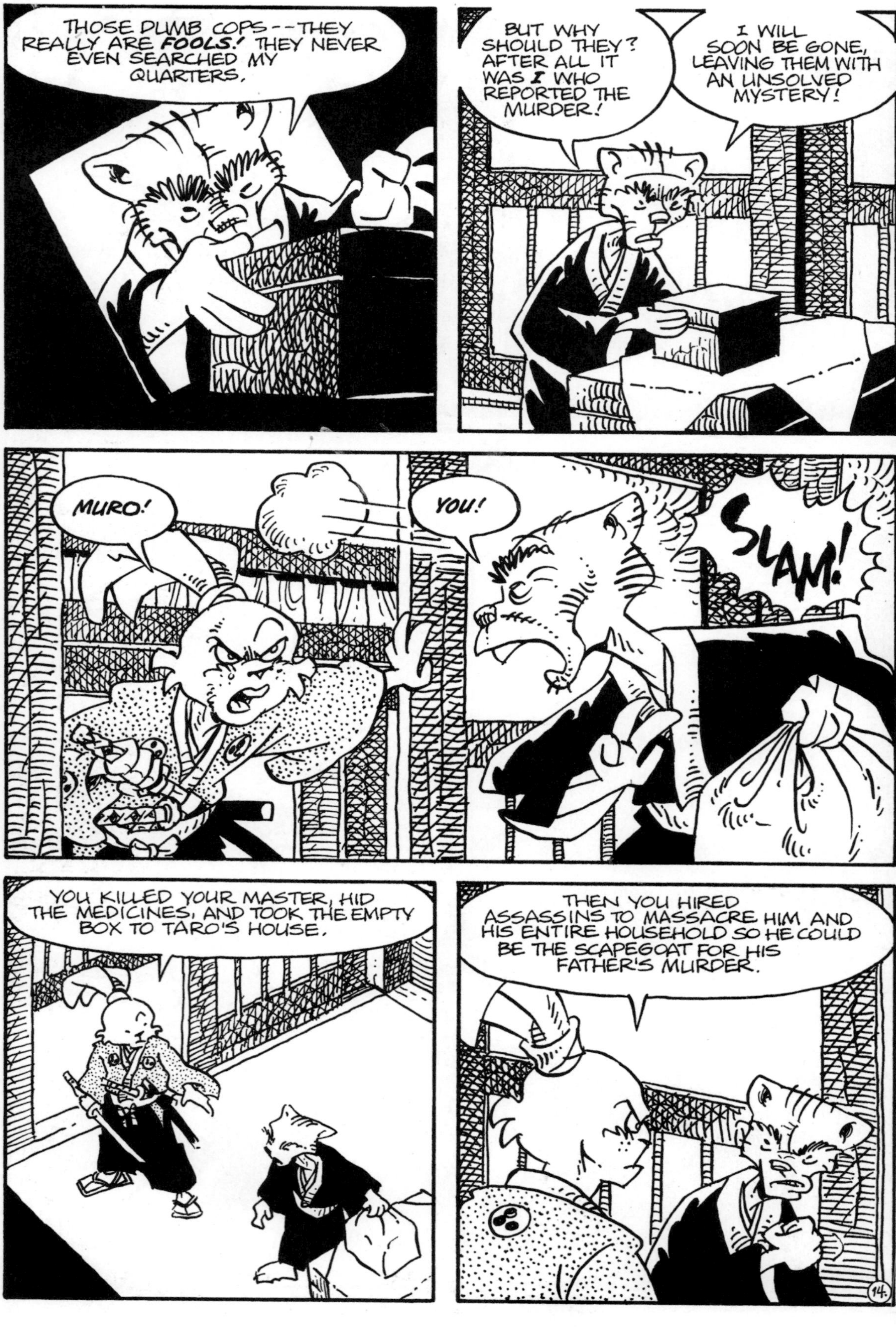
THOSE DUMB COPS--THEY REALLY ARE FOOLS! THEY NEVER EVEN SEARCHED MY QUARTERS.
BUT WHY SHOULD THEY? AFTER ALL IT WAS I WHO REPORTED THE MURDER!
I WILL SOON BE GONE, LEAVING THEM WITH AN UNSOLVED MYSTERY!
MURO!
YOU!
SLAM!
YOU KILLED YOUR MASTER, HID THE MEDICINES, AND TOOK THE EMPTY BOX TO TARO'S HOUSE.
THEN YOU HIRED ASSASSINS TO MASSACRE HIM AND HIS ENTIRE HOUSEHOLD SO HE COULD BE THE SCAPEGOAT FOR HIS FATHER'S MURDER.
14

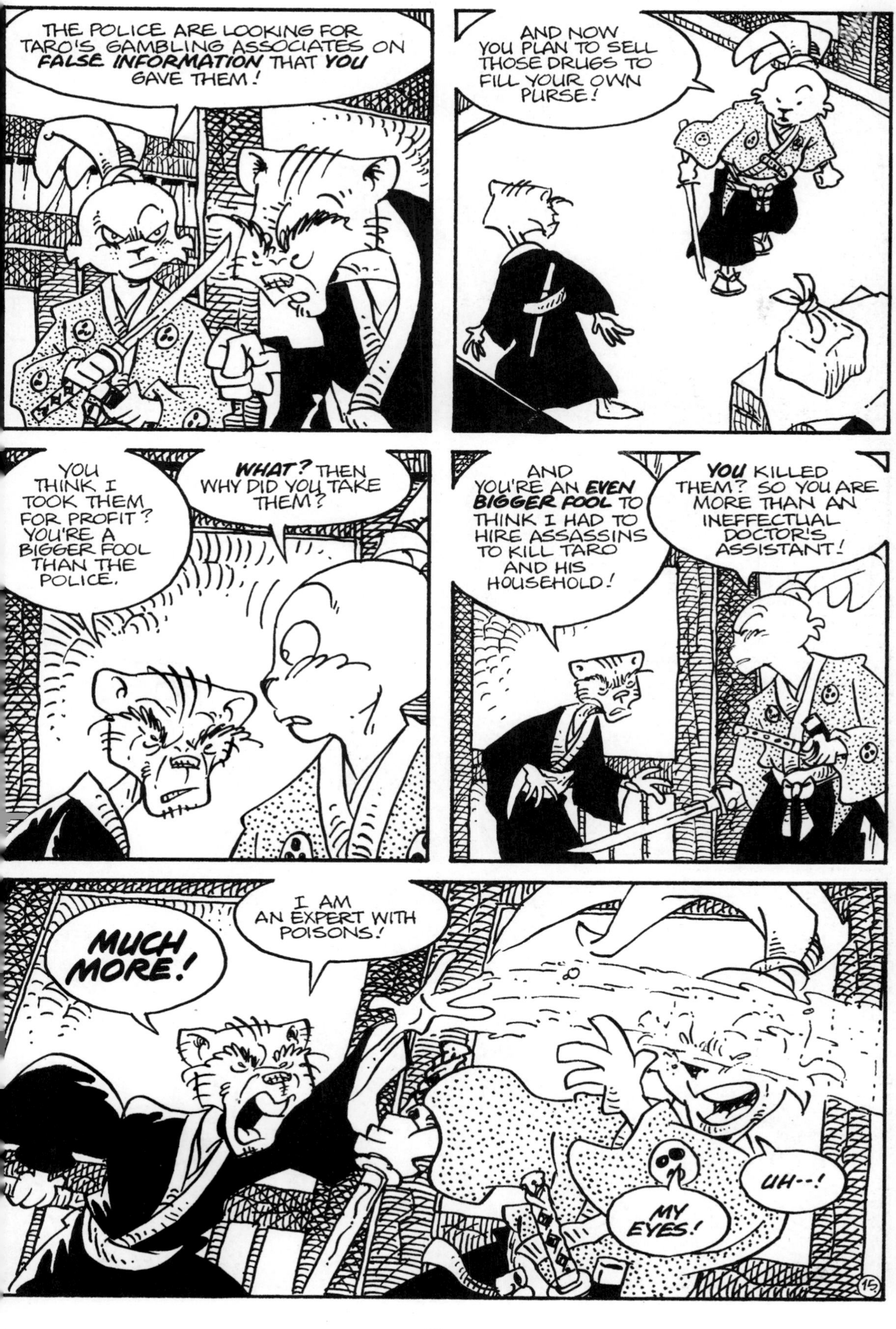
THE POLICE ARE LOOKING FOR TARO'S GAMBLING ASSOCIATES ON FALSE INFORMATION THAT YOU GAVE THEM!
AND NOW YOU PLAN TO SELL THOSE DRUGS TO FILL YOUR OWN PURSE!
YOU THINK I TOOK THEM FOR PROFIT? YOU'RE A BIGGER FOOL THAN THE POLICE.
WHAT? THEN WHY DID YOU TAKE THEM?
AND YOU'RE AN EVEN BIGGER FOOL TO THINK I HAD TO HIRE ASSASSINS TO KILL TARO AND HIS HOUSEHOLD!
YOU KILLED THEM? SO YOU ARE MORE THAN AN INEFFECTUAL DOCTOR'S ASSISTANT!
MUCH MORE!
I AM AN EXPERT WITH POISONS!
UH--!
MY EYES!
15

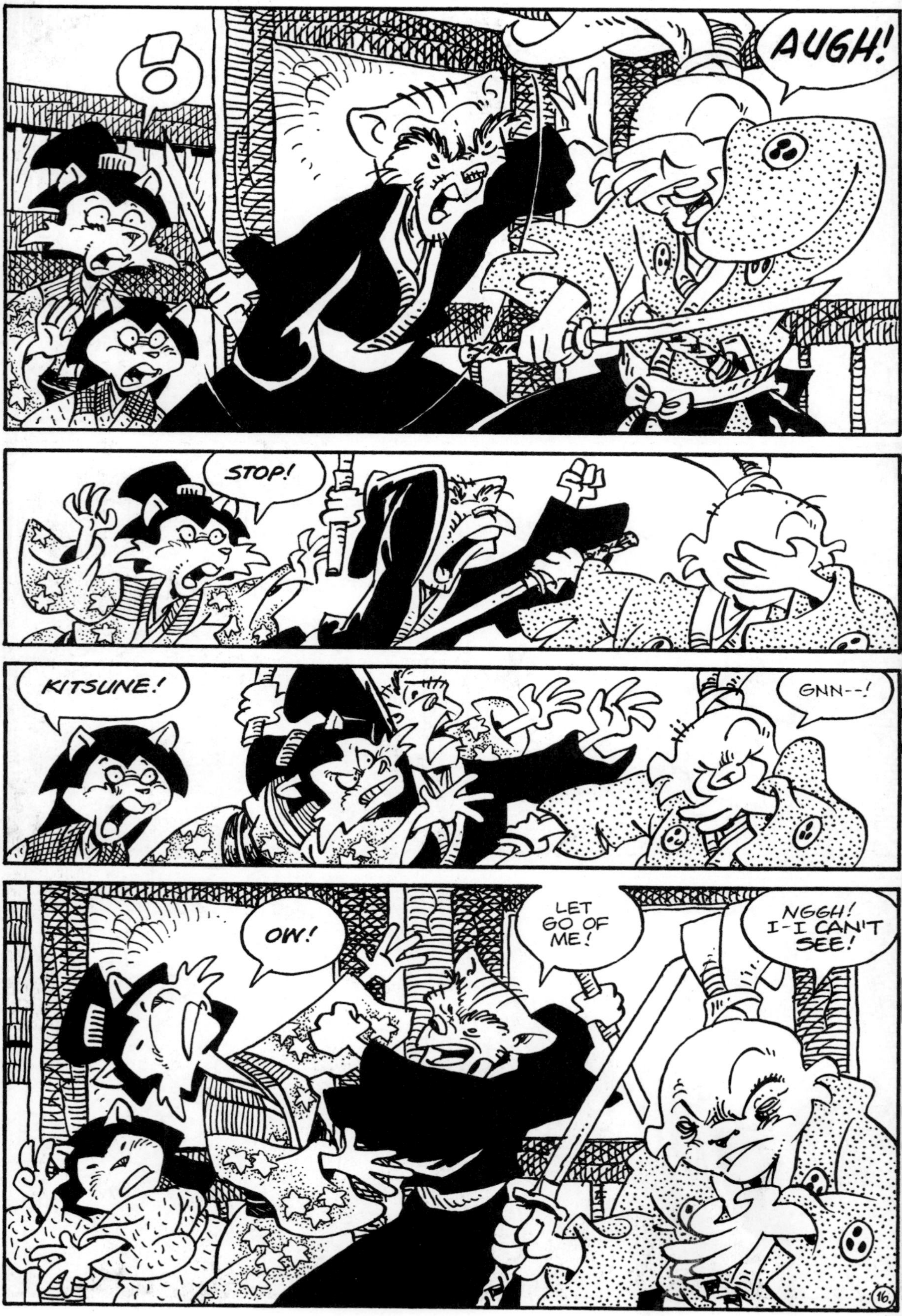
!
AUGH!
STOP!
KITSUNE!
GNN--!
OW!
LET GO OF ME!
NGGH! I-I CAN'T SEE!
16.

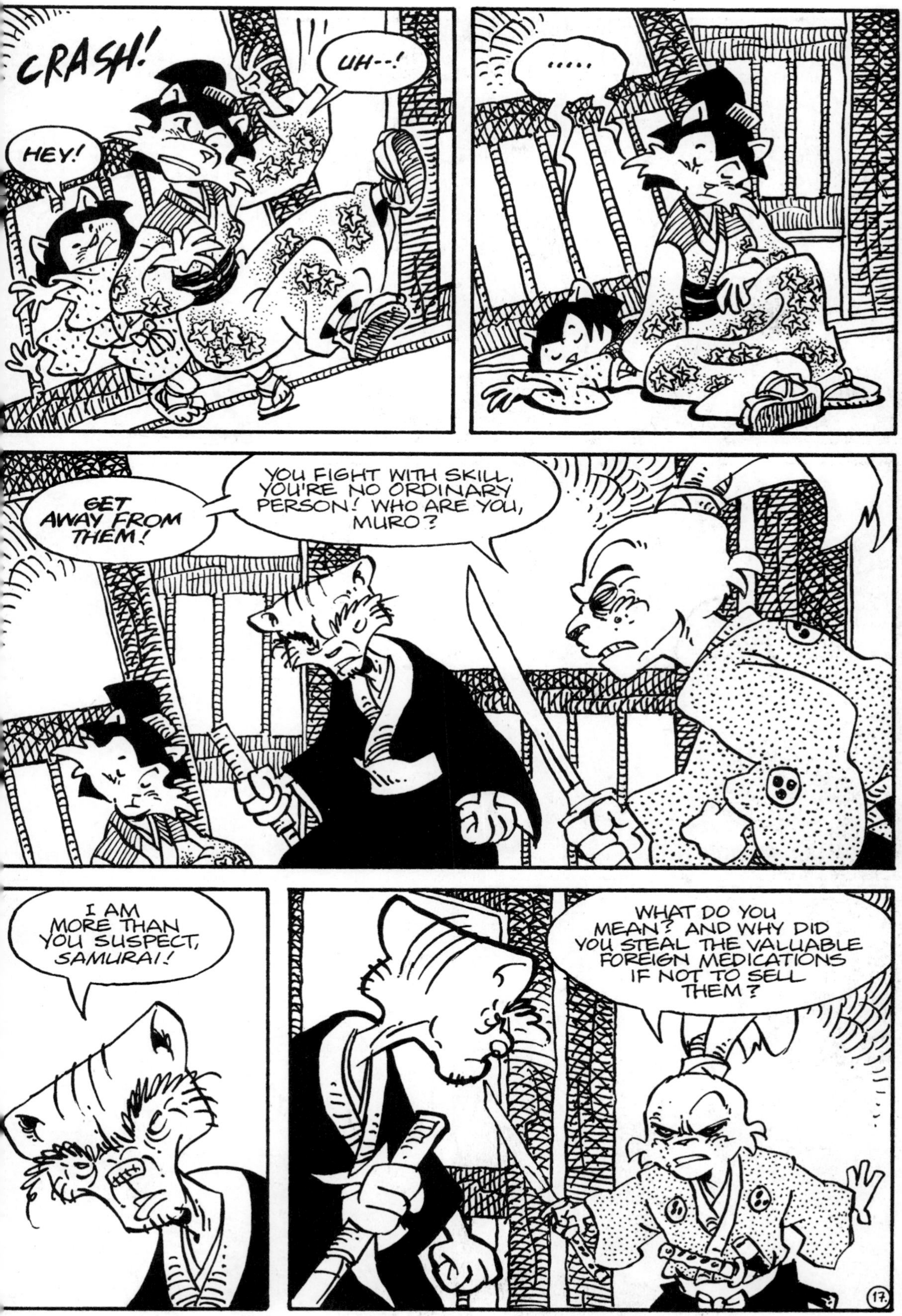
CRASH!
UH--!
HEY!
.....
GET AWAY FROM THEM!
YOU FIGHT WITH SKILL. YOU'RE NO ORDINARY PERSON! WHO ARE YOU, MURO?
I AM MORE THAN YOU SUSPECT, SAMURAI!
WHAT DO YOU MEAN? AND WHY DID YOU STEAL THE VALUABLE FOREIGN MEDICATIONS IF NOT TO SELL THEM?
17

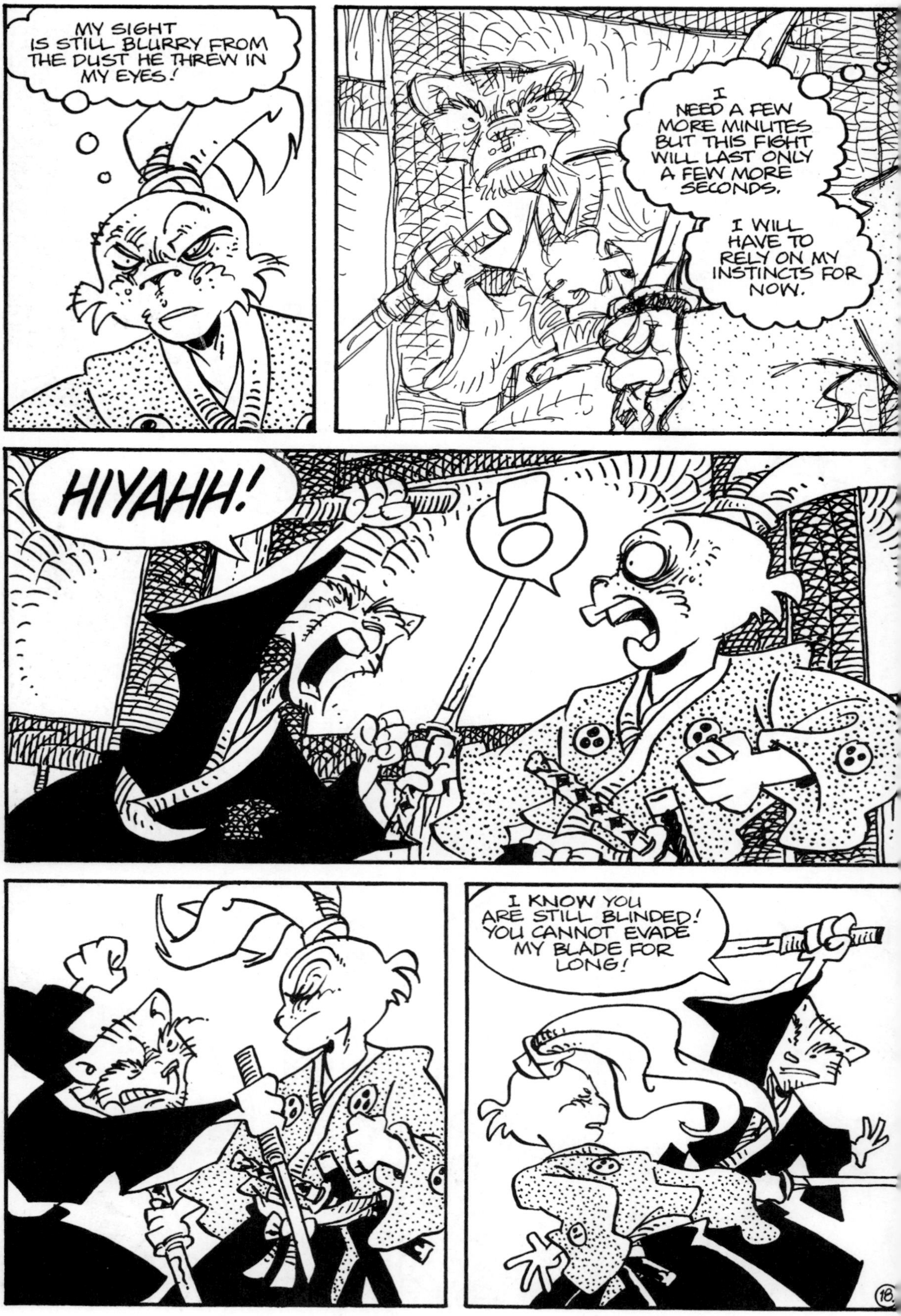
MY SIGHT IS STILL BLURRY FROM THE DUST HE THREW IN MY EYES!
I NEED A FEW MORE MINUTES BUT THIS FIGHT WILL LAST ONLY A FEW MORE SECONDS.
I WILL HAVE TO RELY ON MY INSTINCTS FOR NOW.
HIYAHH!
!
I KNOW YOU ARE STILL BLINDED! YOU CANNOT EVADE MY BLADE FOR LONG!
18

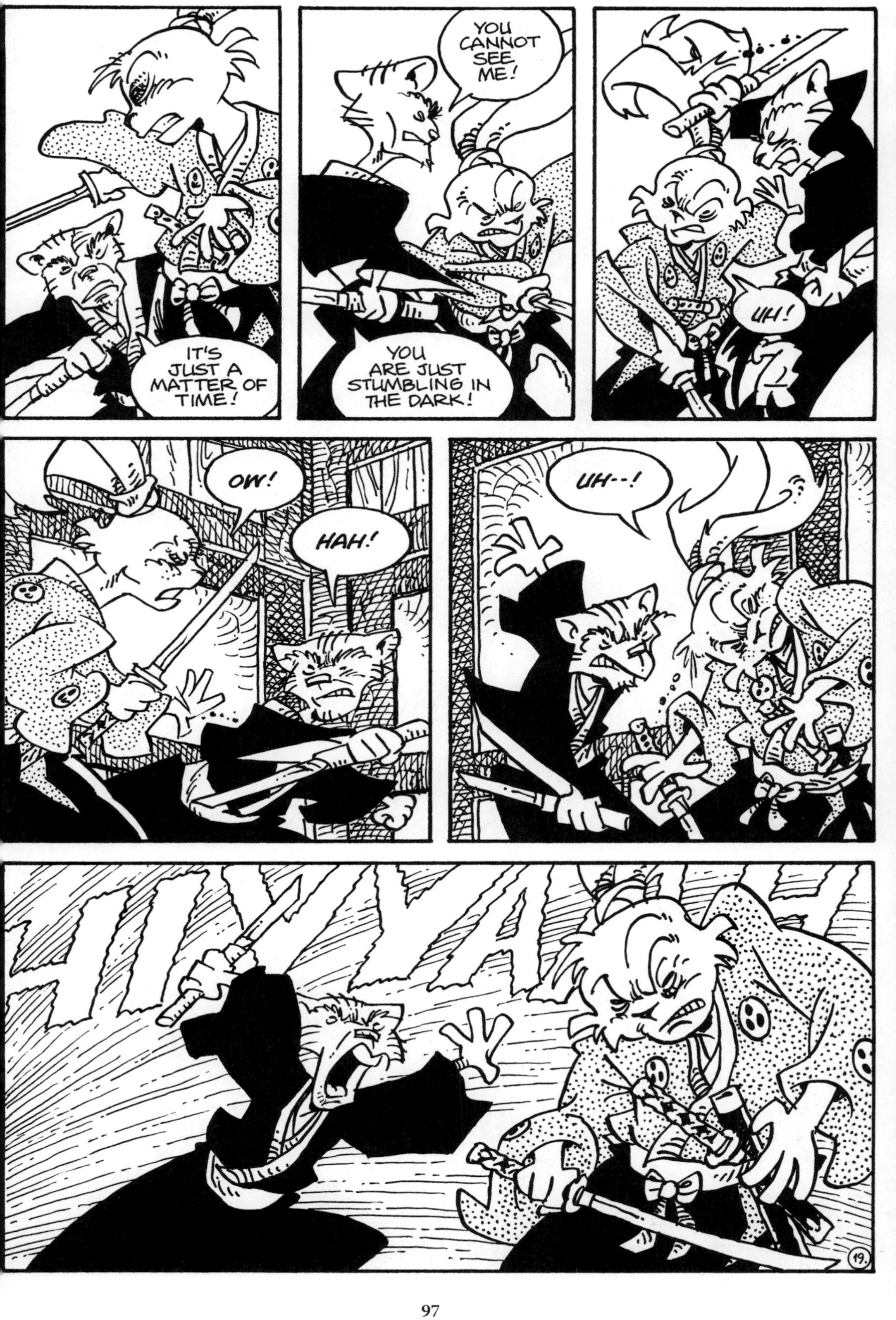

IT'S JUST A MATTER OF TIME!
YOU CANNOT SEE ME!
YOU ARE JUST STUMBLING IN THE DARK!
UH!
OW!
HAH!
UH--!
HIYA!
19.

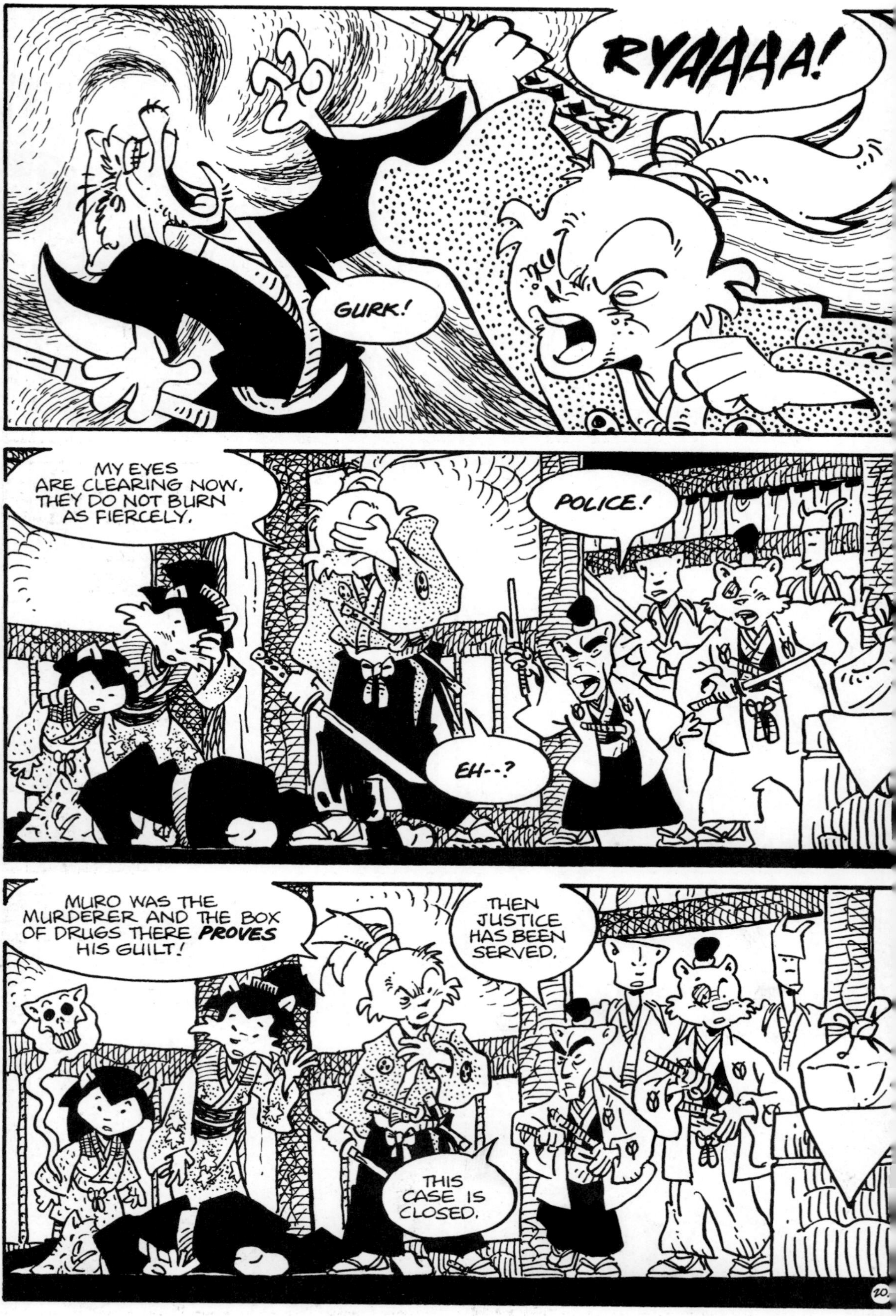
RYAAAA!
GURK!
MY EYES ARE CLEARING NOW. THEY DO NOT BURN AS FIERCELY.
POLICE!
EH--?
MURO WAS THE MURDERER AND THE BOX OF DRUGS THERE PROVES HIS GUILT!
THEN JUSTICE HAS BEEN SERVED.
THIS CASE IS CLOSED.
20

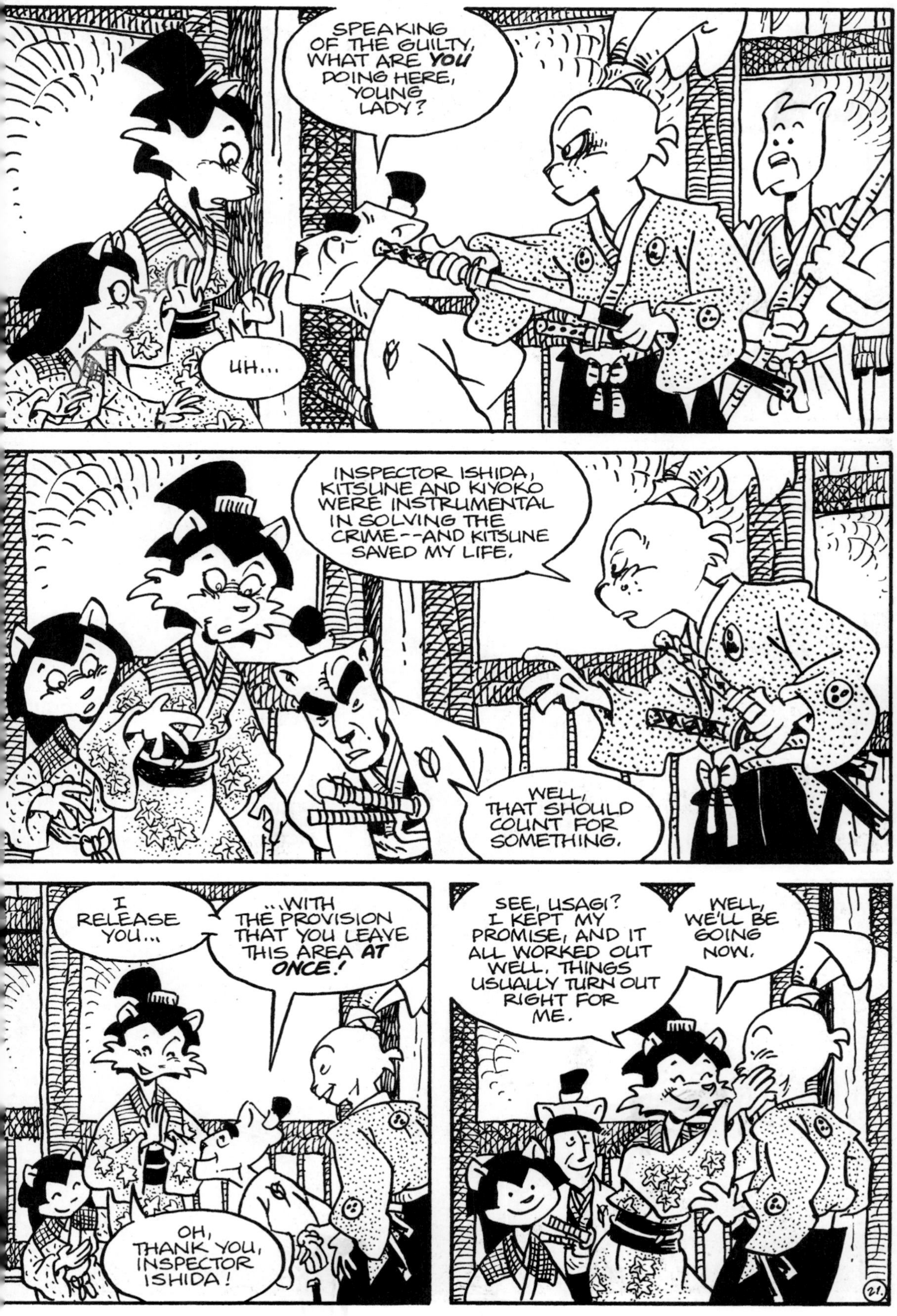
SPEAKING OF THE GUILTY, WHAT ARE *YOU* DOING HERE, YOUNG LADY?
UH...
INSPECTOR ISHIDA, KITSUNE AND KIYOKO WERE INSTRUMENTAL IN SOLVING THE CRIME--AND KITSUNE SAVED MY LIFE.
WELL, THAT SHOULD COUNT FOR SOMETHING.
I RELEASE YOU...
...WITH THE PROVISION THAT YOU LEAVE THIS AREA ***AT ONCE!***
OH, THANK YOU, INSPECTOR ISHIDA!
SEE, USAGI? I KEPT MY PROMISE, AND IT ALL WORKED OUT WELL. THINGS USUALLY TURN OUT RIGHT FOR ME.
WELL, WE'LL BE GOING NOW.
21.

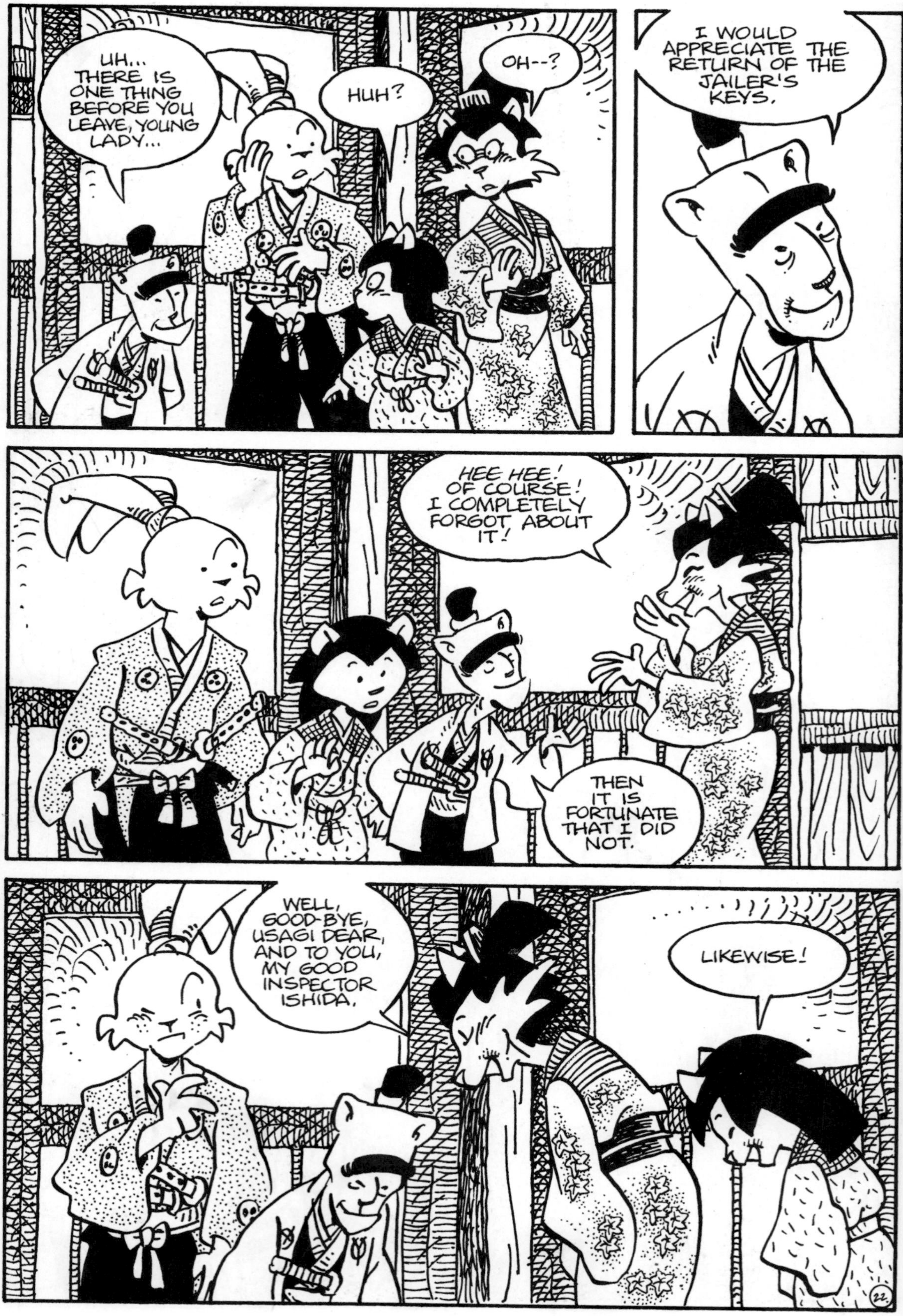
UH... THERE IS ONE THING BEFORE YOU LEAVE, YOUNG LADY...
HUH?
OH--?
I WOULD APPRECIATE THE RETURN OF THE JAILER'S KEYS.
HEE HEE! OF COURSE! I COMPLETELY FORGOT ABOUT IT!
THEN IT IS FORTUNATE THAT I DID NOT.
WELL, GOOD-BYE, USAGI DEAR, AND TO YOU, MY GOOD INSPECTOR ISHIDA.
LIKEWISE!
22.

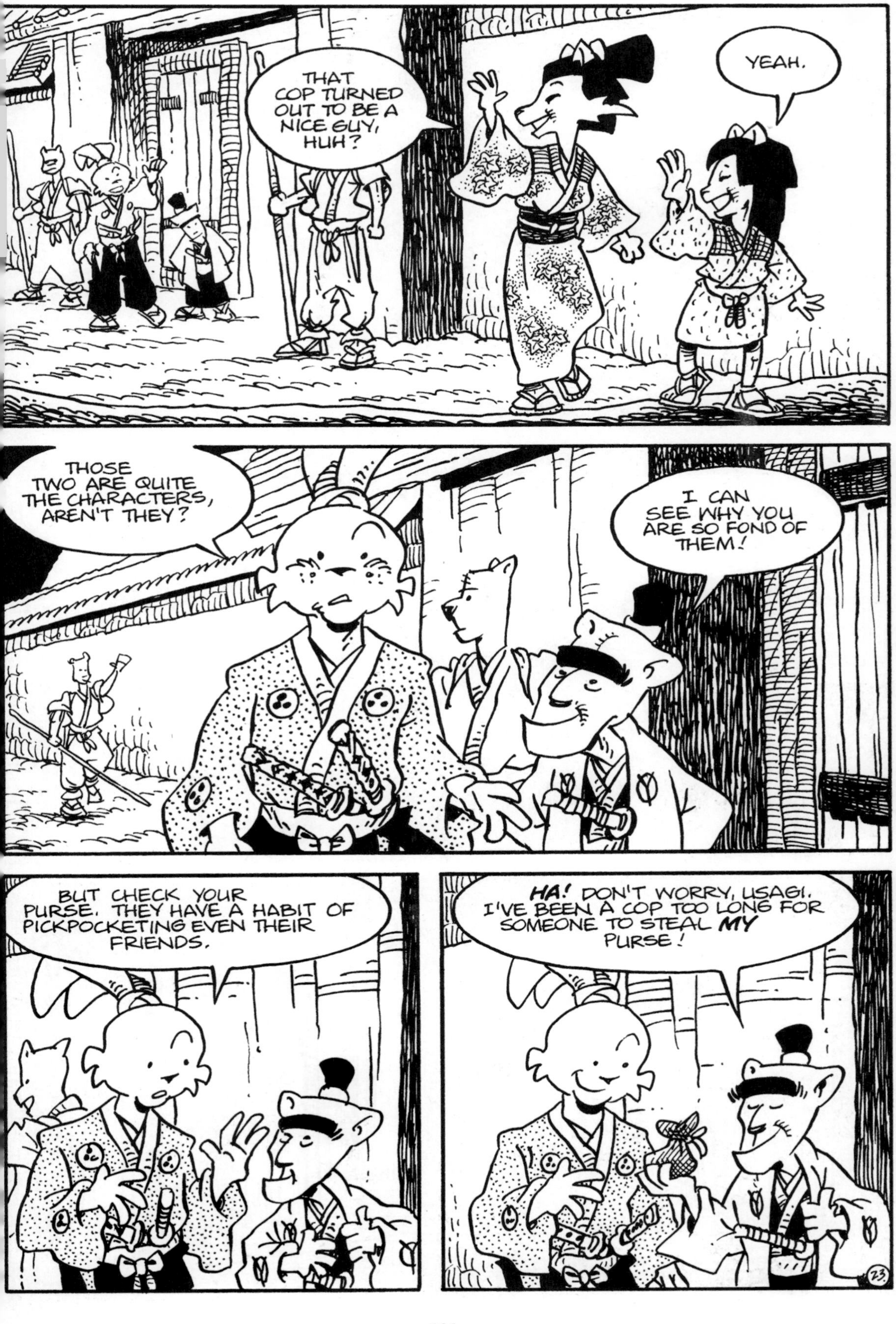
THAT COP TURNED OUT TO BE A NICE GUY, HUH?
YEAH.
THOSE TWO ARE QUITE THE CHARACTERS, AREN'T THEY?
I CAN SEE WHY YOU ARE SO FOND OF THEM!
BUT CHECK YOUR PURSE. THEY HAVE A HABIT OF PICKPOCKETING EVEN THEIR FRIENDS.
HA! DON'T WORRY, USAGI. I'VE BEEN A COP TOO LONG FOR SOMEONE TO STEAL MY PURSE!
23

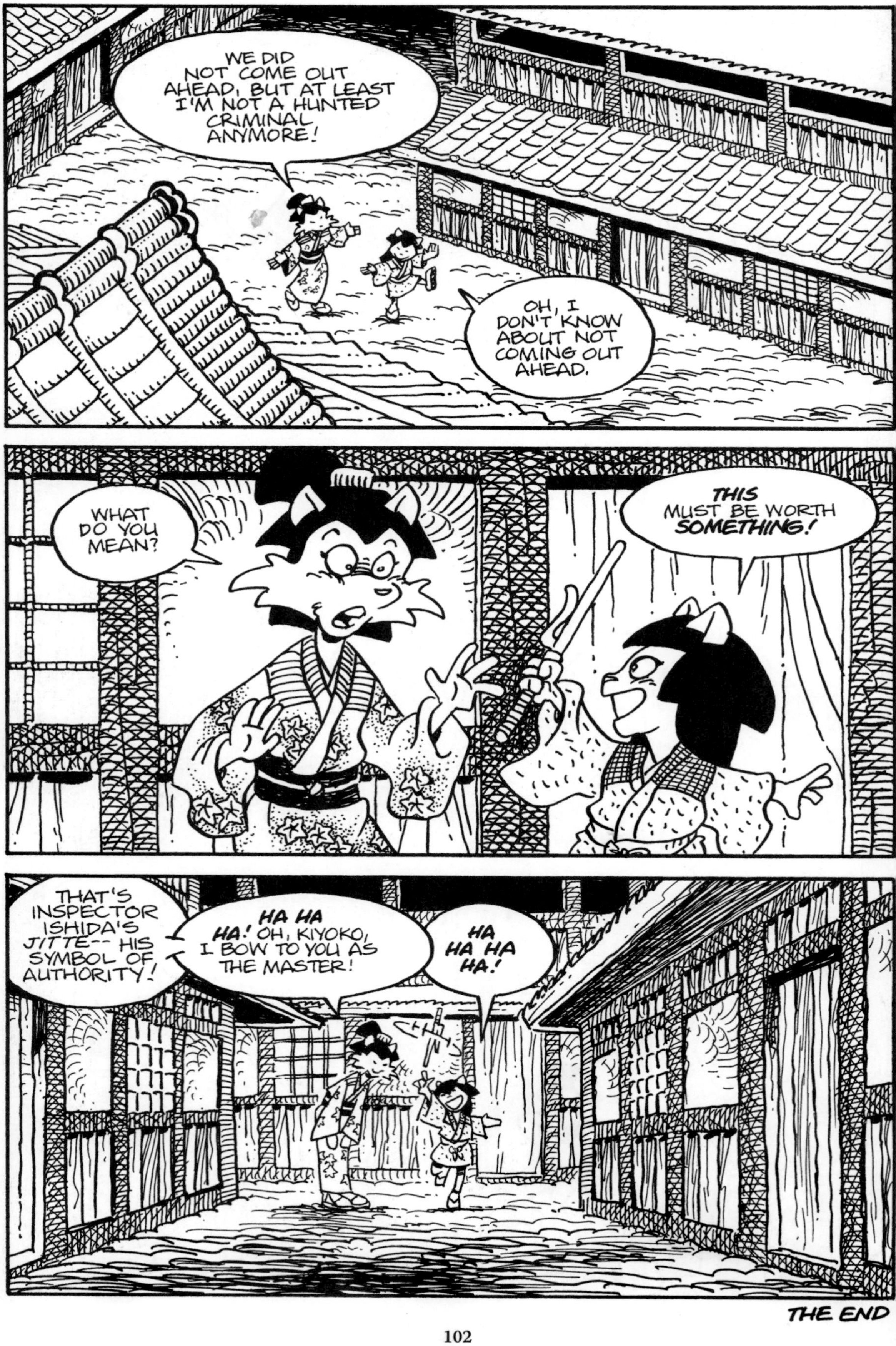
WE DID NOT COME OUT AHEAD, BUT AT LEAST I'M NOT A HUNTED CRIMINAL ANYMORE!
OH, I DON'T KNOW ABOUT NOT COMING OUT AHEAD.
WHAT DO YOU MEAN?
THIS MUST BE WORTH SOMETHING!
THAT'S INSPECTOR ISHIDA'S JITTE-- HIS SYMBOL OF AUTHORITY!
HA HA HA! OH, KIYOKO, I BOW TO YOU AS THE MASTER!
HA HA HA HA!
THE END

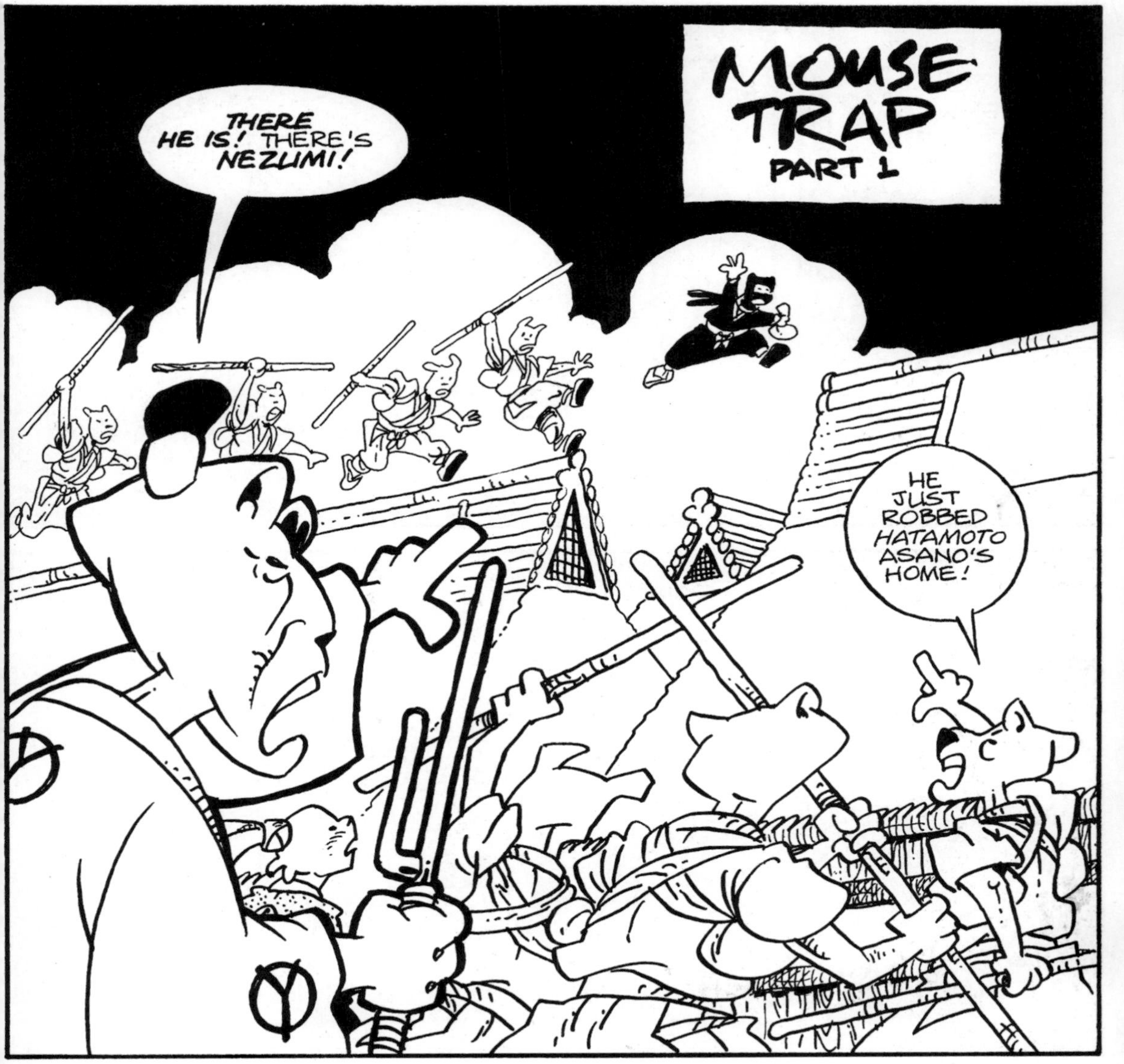
MOUSE TRAP
PART 1
THERE HE IS! THERE'S NEZUMI!
HE JUST ROBBED HATAMOTO ASANO'S HOME!

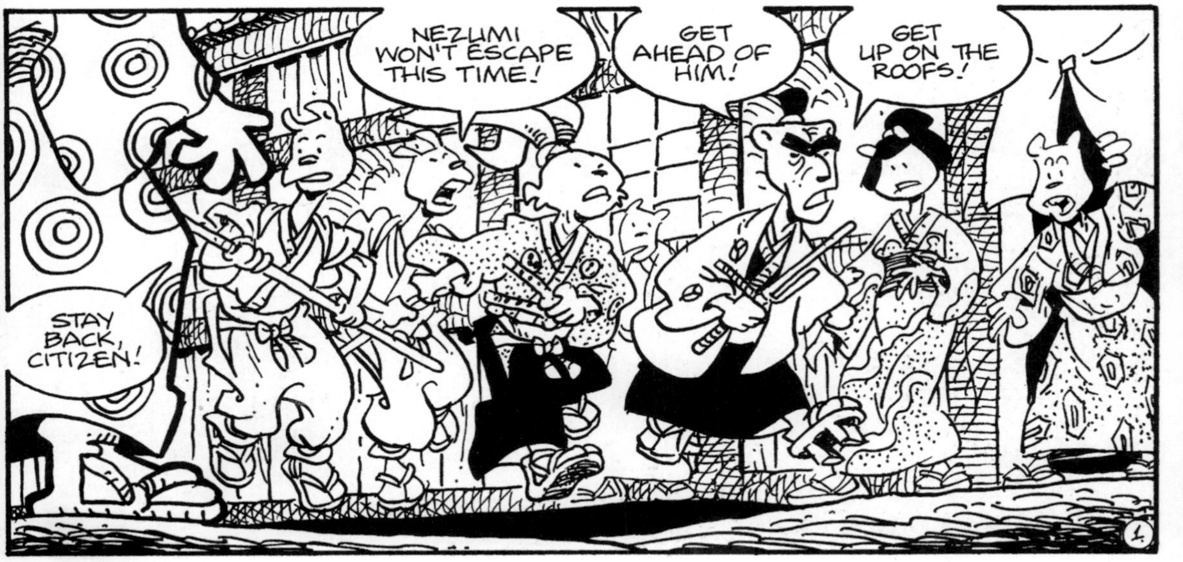
NEZUMI WON'T ESCAPE THIS TIME!
GET AHEAD OF HIM!
GET UP ON THE ROOFS!
STAY BACK, CITIZEN!
1

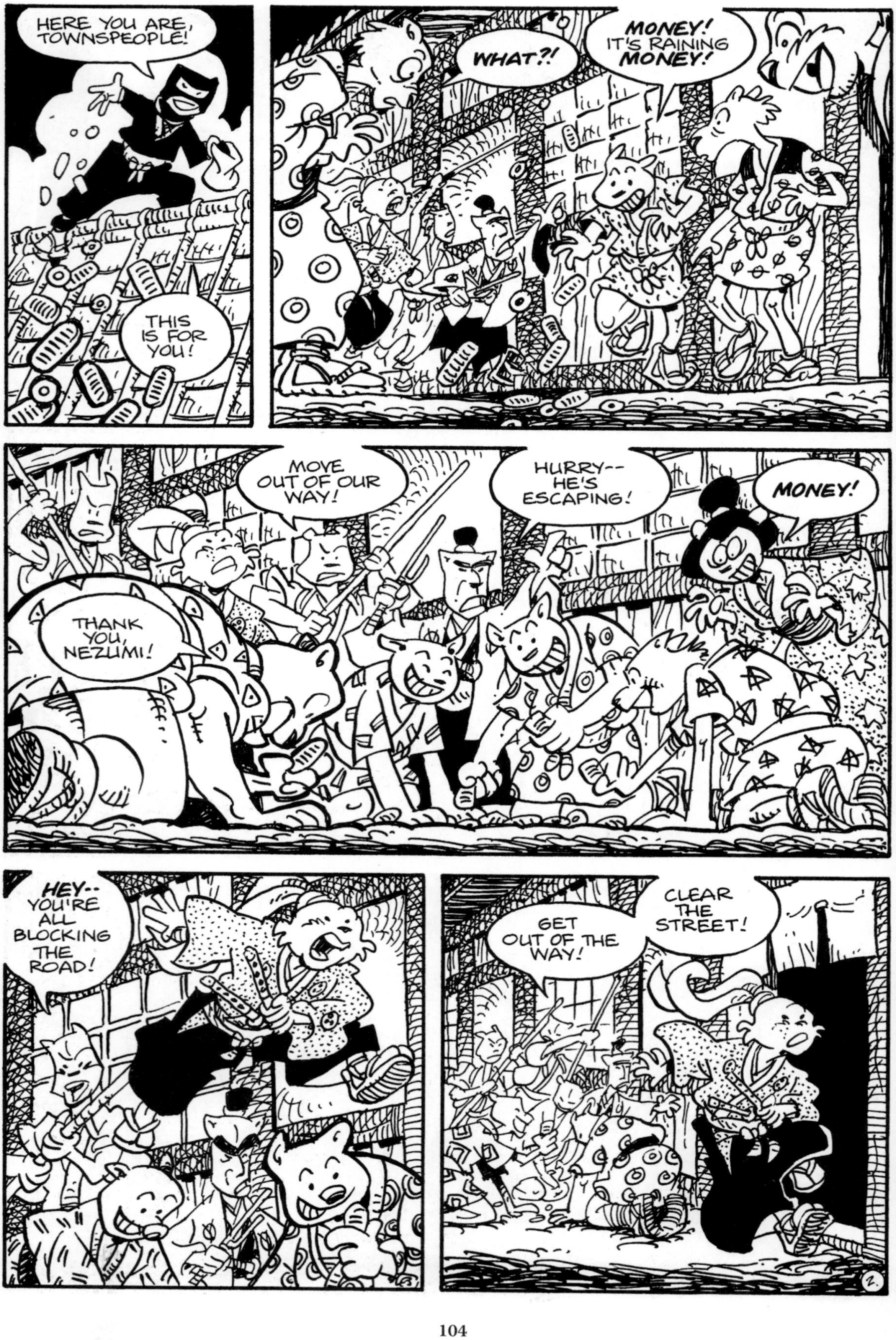
HERE YOU ARE, TOWNSPEOPLE!
THIS IS FOR YOU!
WHAT?!
MONEY! IT'S RAINING MONEY!
MOVE OUT OF OUR WAY!
HURRY-- HE'S ESCAPING!
MONEY!
THANK YOU, NEZUMI!
HEY-- YOU'RE ALL BLOCKING THE ROAD!
GET OUT OF THE WAY!
CLEAR THE STREET!
2.

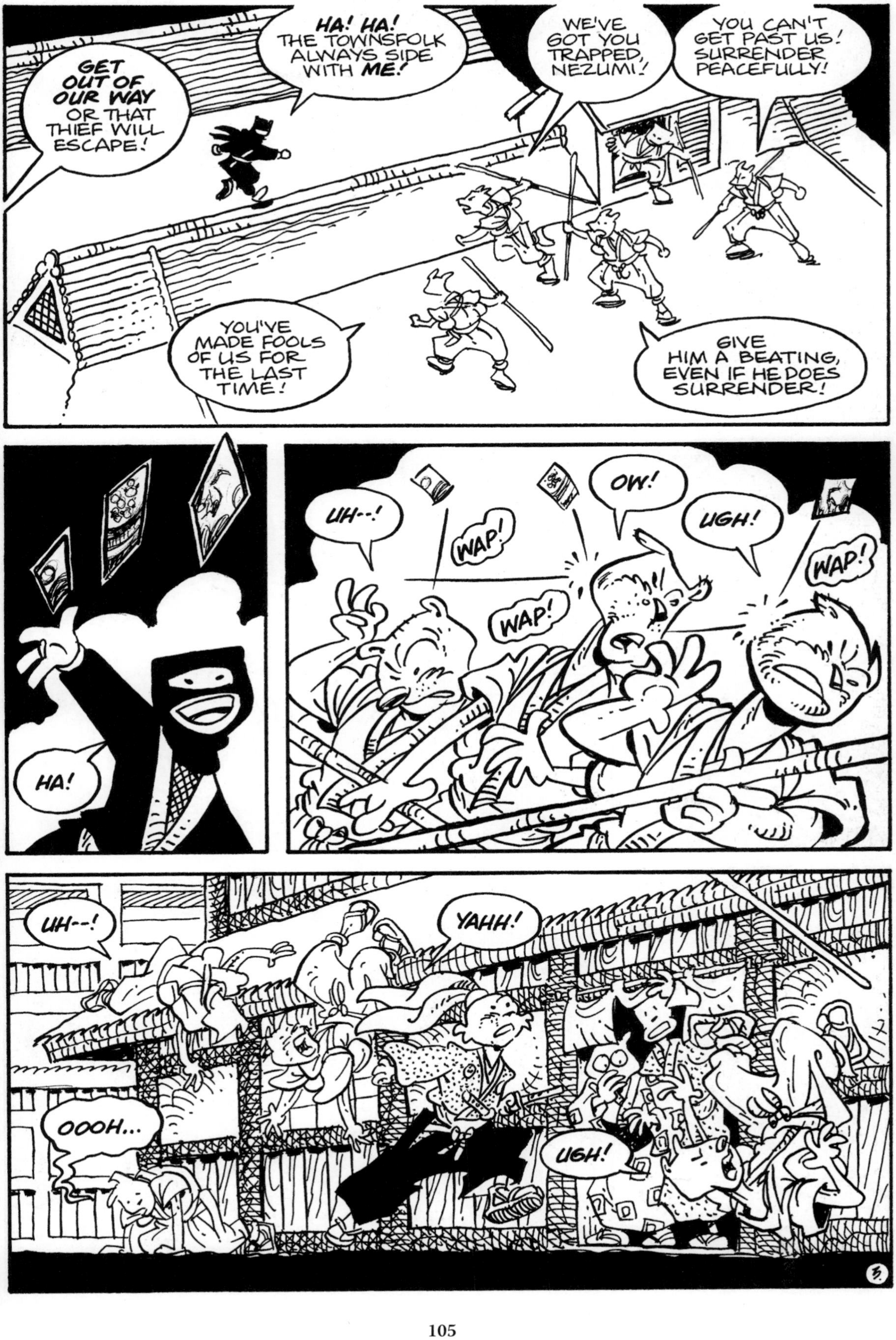

GET OUT OF OUR WAY OR THAT THIEF WILL ESCAPE!
HA! HA! THE TOWNSFOLK ALWAYS SIDE WITH ME!
WE'VE GOT YOU TRAPPED, NEZUMI!
YOU CAN'T GET PAST US! SURRENDER PEACEFULLY!
YOU'VE MADE FOOLS OF US FOR THE LAST TIME!
GIVE HIM A BEATING, EVEN IF HE DOES SURRENDER!
HA!
UH--!
WAP!
OW!
UGH!
WAP!
WAP!
UH--!
YAHH!
OOOH...
UGH!

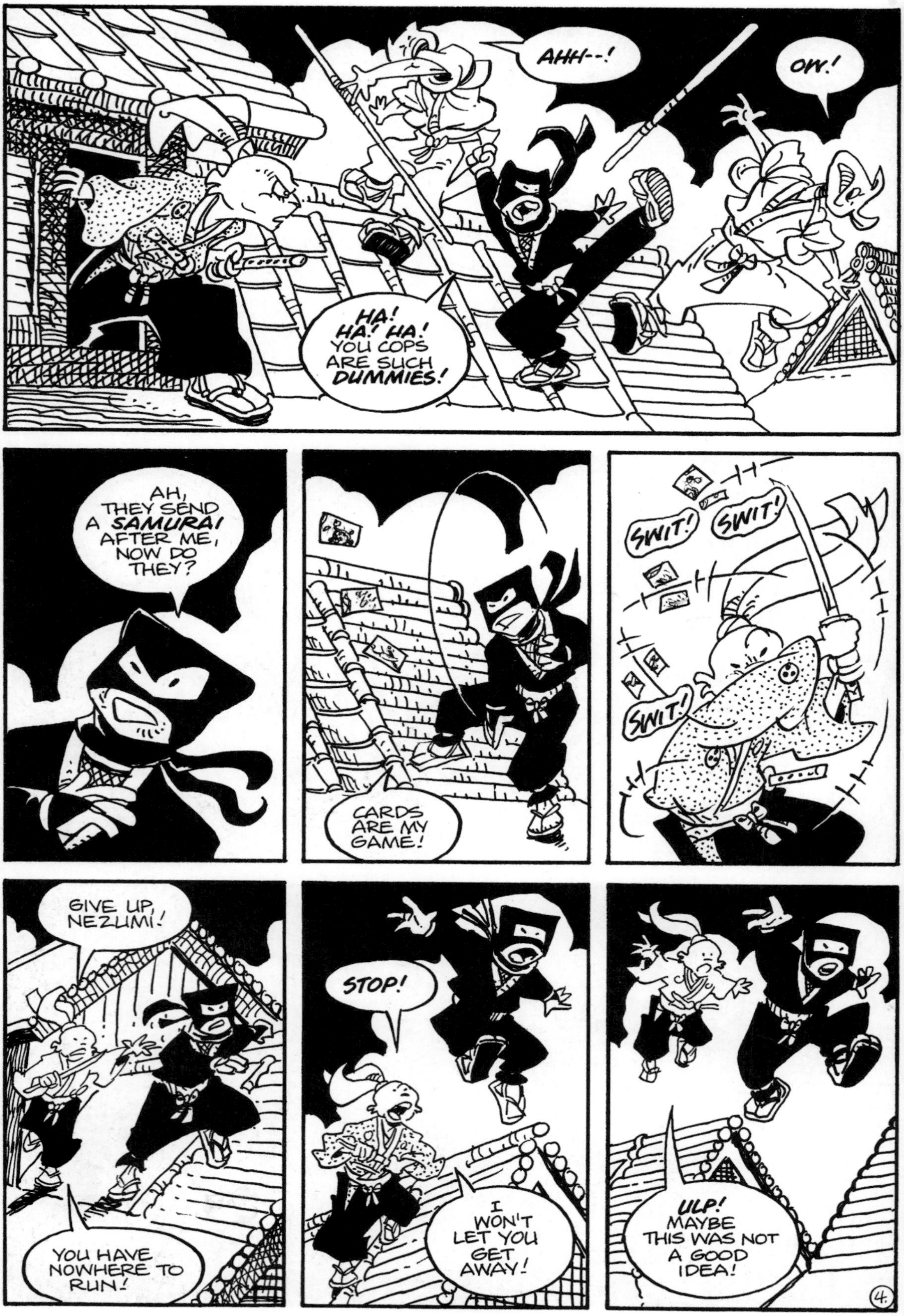
AHH--!
OW!
HA! HA! HA! YOU COPS ARE SUCH DUMMIES!
AH, THEY SEND A SAMURAI AFTER ME, NOW DO THEY?
CARDS ARE MY GAME!
SWIT! SWIT!
SWIT!
GIVE UP, NEZUMI!
YOU HAVE NOWHERE TO RUN!
STOP!
I WON'T LET YOU GET AWAY!
ULP! MAYBE THIS WAS NOT A GOOD IDEA!
4.

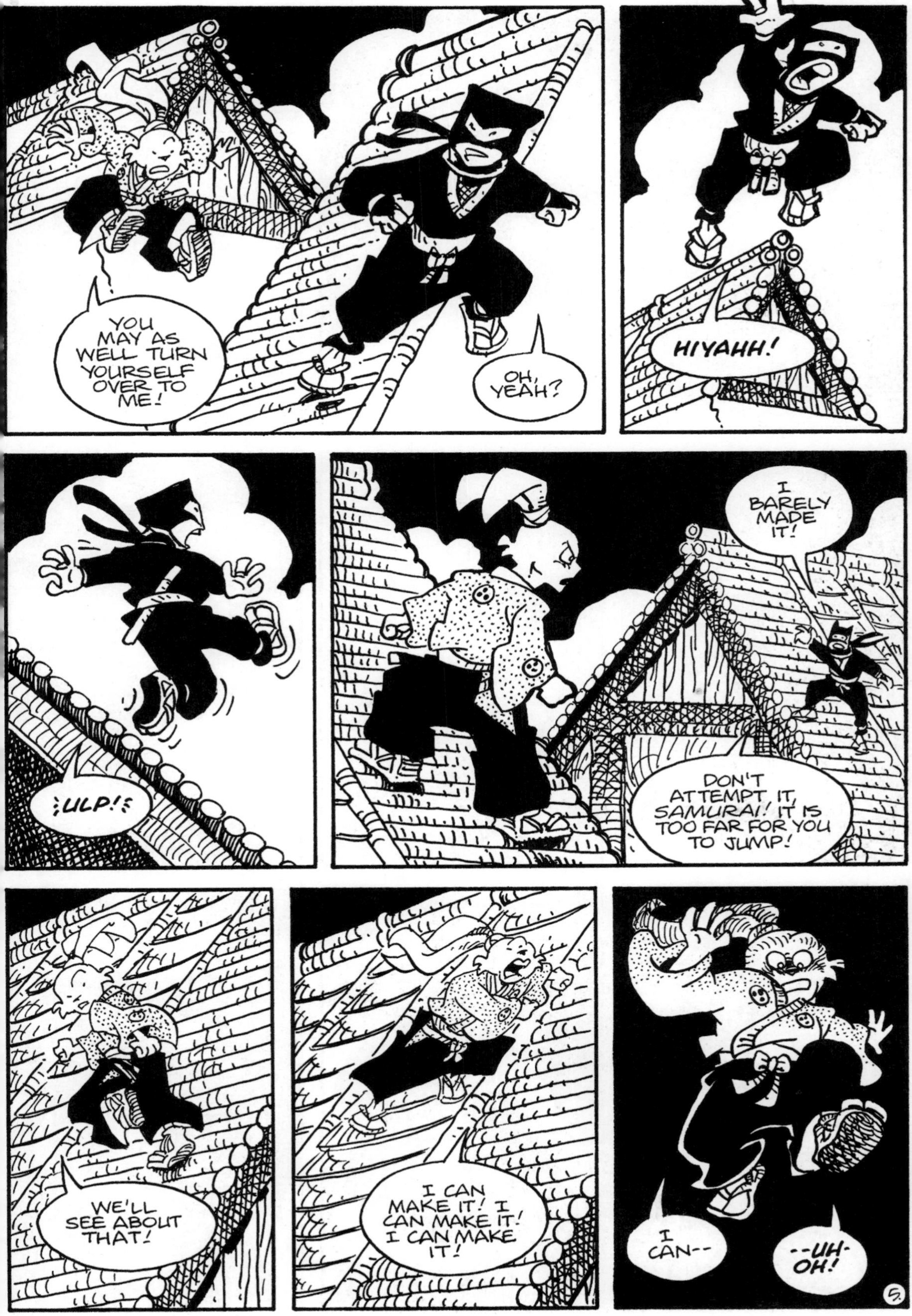

YOU MAY AS WELL TURN YOURSELF OVER TO ME!
OH, YEAH?
HIYAHH!
¡ULP!¡
I BARELY MADE IT!
DON'T ATTEMPT IT, SAMURAI! IT IS TOO FAR FOR YOU TO JUMP!
WE'LL SEE ABOUT THAT!
I CAN MAKE IT! I CAN MAKE IT! I CAN MAKE IT!
I CAN--
--UH-OH!
5.

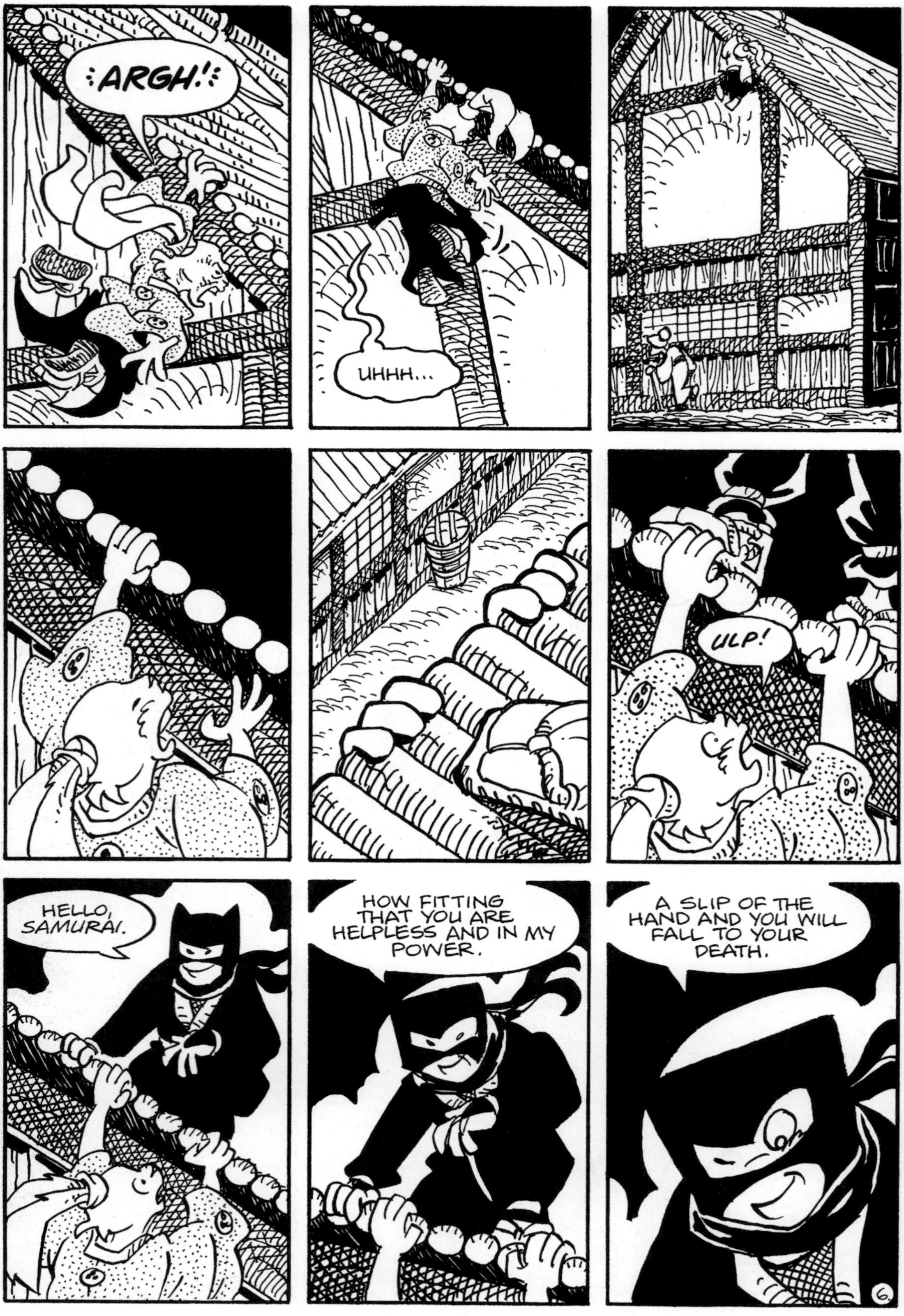
ARGH!
UHHH...
ULP!
HELLO, SAMURAI.
HOW FITTING THAT YOU ARE HELPLESS AND IN MY POWER.
A SLIP OF THE HAND AND YOU WILL FALL TO YOUR DEATH.
6.

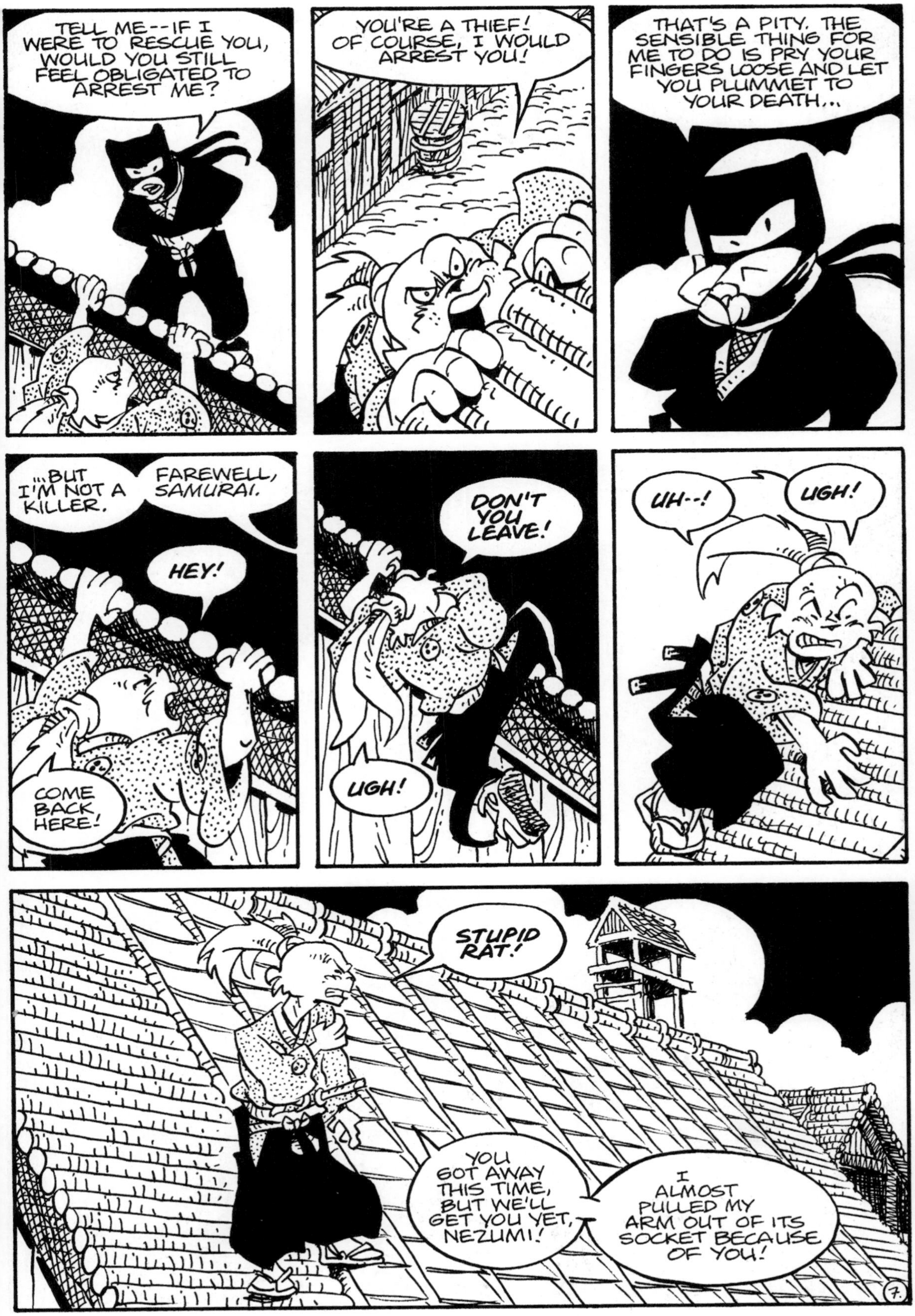

TELL ME--IF I WERE TO RESCUE YOU, WOULD YOU STILL FEEL OBLIGATED TO ARREST ME?
YOU'RE A THIEF! OF COURSE, I WOULD ARREST YOU!
THAT'S A PITY. THE SENSIBLE THING FOR ME TO DO IS PRY YOUR FINGERS LOOSE AND LET YOU PLUMMET TO YOUR DEATH...
...BUT I'M NOT A KILLER.
FAREWELL, SAMURAI.
HEY!
COME BACK HERE!
DON'T YOU LEAVE!
UGH!
UH--!
UGH!
STUPID RAT!
YOU GOT AWAY THIS TIME, BUT WE'LL GET YOU YET, NEZUMI!
I ALMOST PULLED MY ARM OUT OF ITS SOCKET BECAUSE OF YOU!
7.

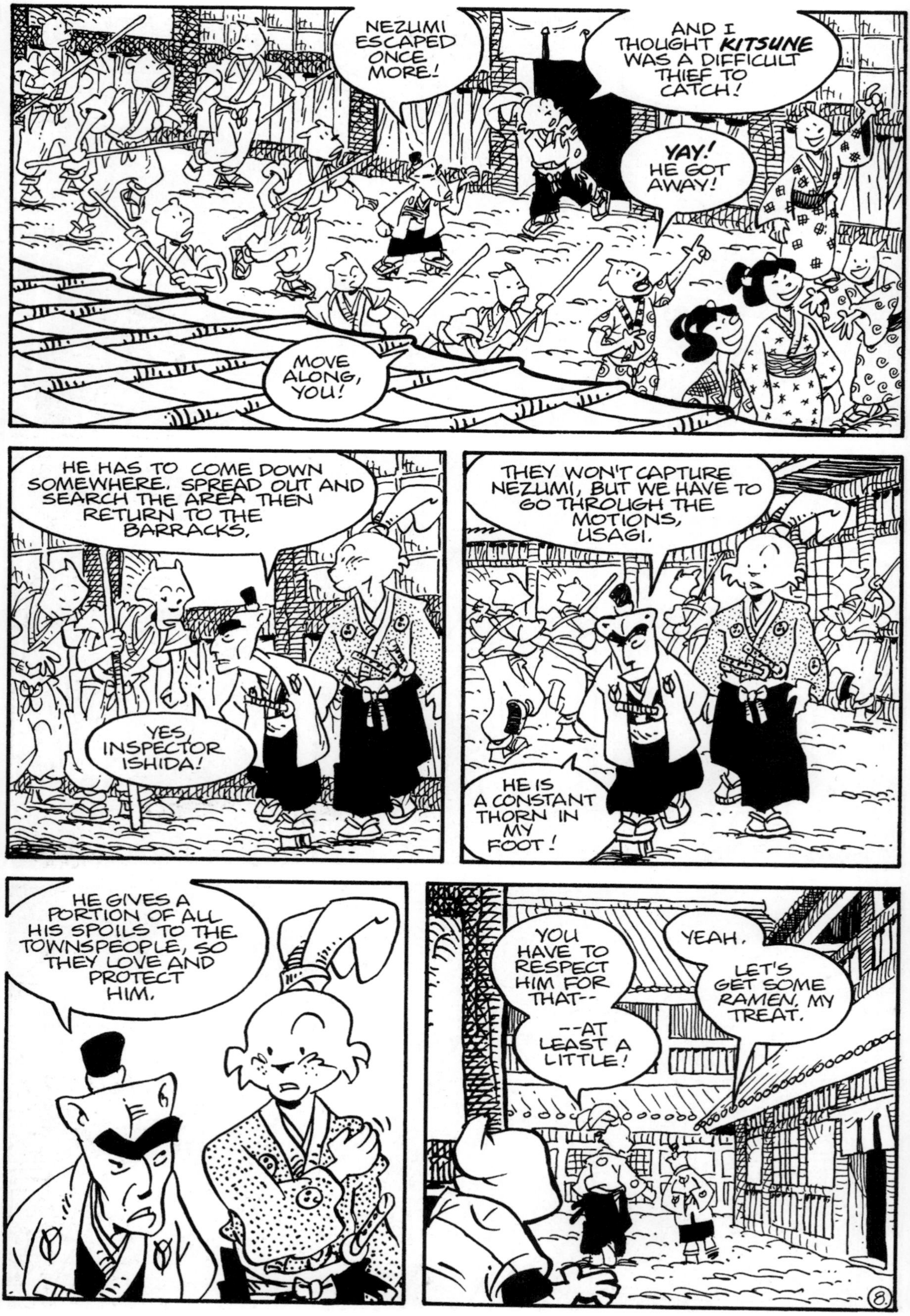
NEZUMI ESCAPED ONCE MORE!
AND I THOUGHT KITSUNE WAS A DIFFICULT THIEF TO CATCH!
YAY! HE GOT AWAY!
MOVE ALONG, YOU!
HE HAS TO COME DOWN SOMEWHERE. SPREAD OUT AND SEARCH THE AREA THEN RETURN TO THE BARRACKS.
YES, INSPECTOR ISHIDA!
THEY WON'T CAPTURE NEZUMI, BUT WE HAVE TO GO THROUGH THE MOTIONS, USAGI.
HE IS A CONSTANT THORN IN MY FOOT!
HE GIVES A PORTION OF ALL HIS SPOILS TO THE TOWNSPEOPLE, SO THEY LOVE AND PROTECT HIM.
YOU HAVE TO RESPECT HIM FOR THAT--
--AT LEAST A LITTLE!
YEAH.
LET'S GET SOME RAMEN. MY TREAT.
8.

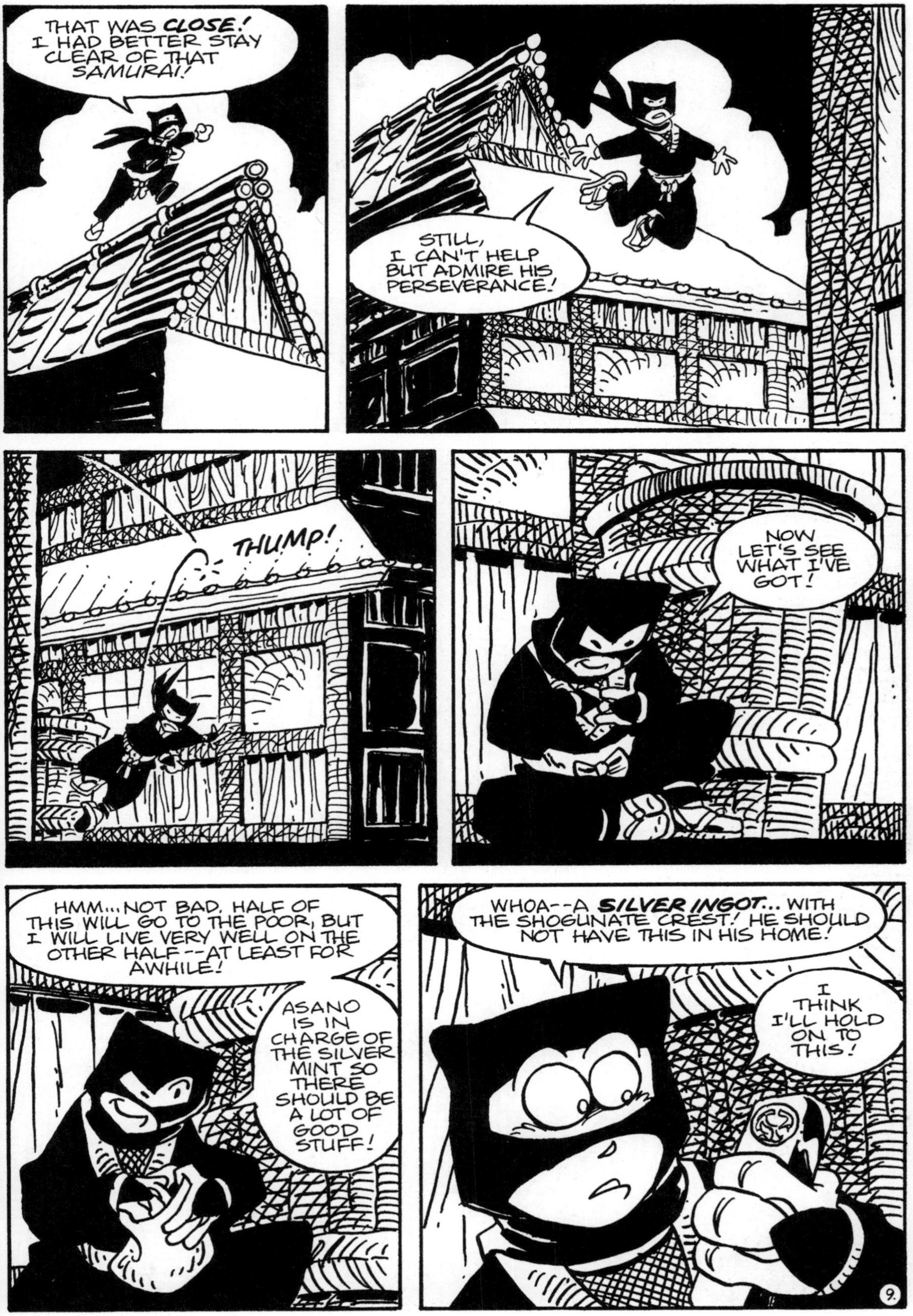
THAT WAS CLOSE! I HAD BETTER STAY CLEAR OF THAT SAMURAI!
STILL, I CAN'T HELP BUT ADMIRE HIS PERSEVERANCE!
THUMP!
NOW LET'S SEE WHAT I'VE GOT!
HMM... NOT BAD. HALF OF THIS WILL GO TO THE POOR, BUT I WILL LIVE VERY WELL ON THE OTHER HALF--AT LEAST FOR AWHILE!
ASANO IS IN CHARGE OF THE SILVER MINT SO THERE SHOULD BE A LOT OF GOOD STUFF!
WHOA--A SILVER INGOT... WITH THE SHOGUNATE CREST! HE SHOULD NOT HAVE THIS IN HIS HOME!
I THINK I'LL HOLD ON TO THIS!
9.

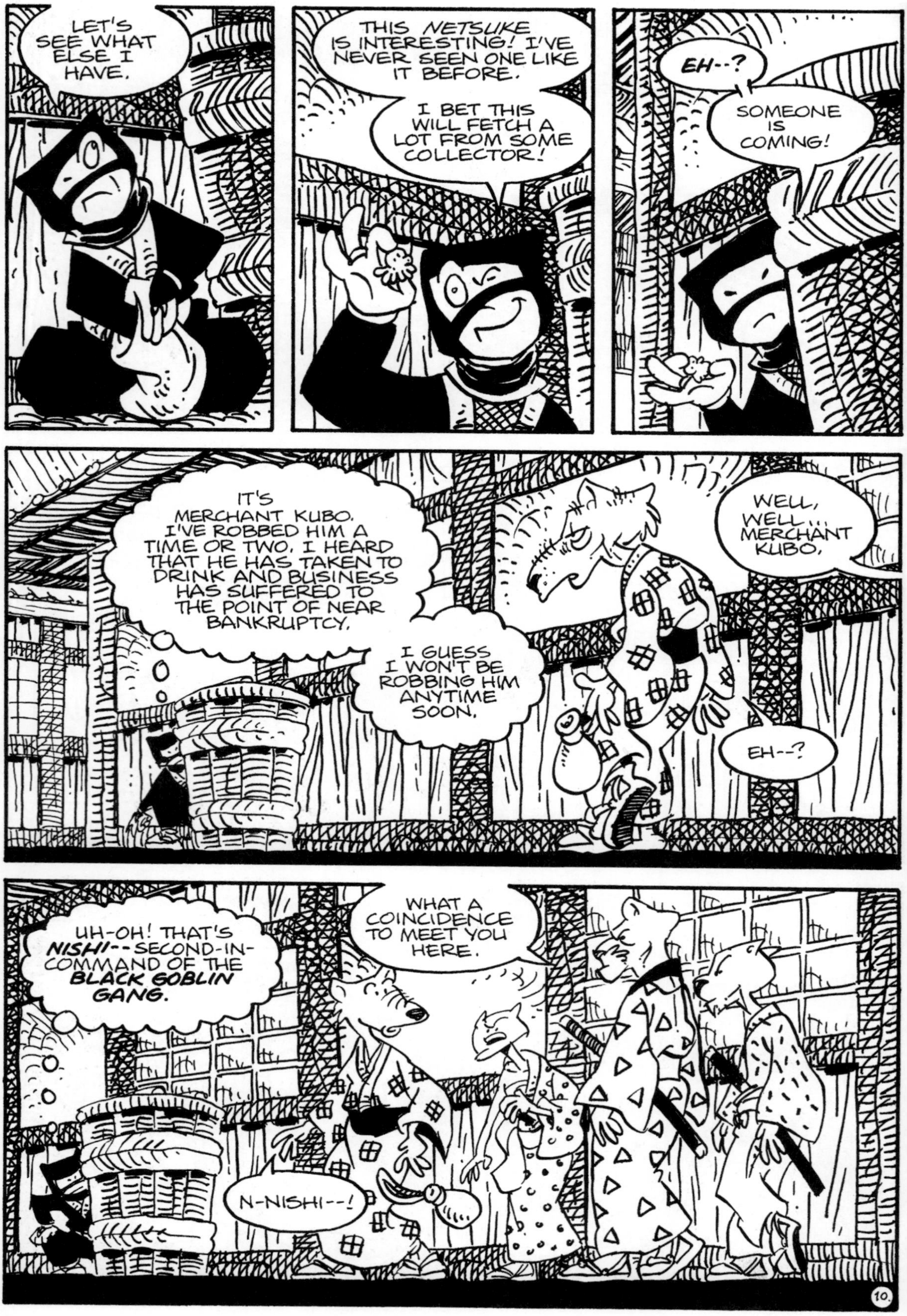
LET'S SEE WHAT ELSE I HAVE.
THIS *NETSUKE* IS INTERESTING! I'VE NEVER SEEN ONE LIKE IT BEFORE.
I BET THIS WILL FETCH A LOT FROM SOME COLLECTOR!
EH--?
SOMEONE IS COMING!
IT'S MERCHANT KUBO. I'VE ROBBED HIM A TIME OR TWO. I HEARD THAT HE HAS TAKEN TO DRINK AND BUSINESS HAS SUFFERED TO THE POINT OF NEAR BANKRUPTCY.
I GUESS I WON'T BE ROBBING HIM ANYTIME SOON.
WELL, WELL... MERCHANT KUBO,
EH--?
UH-OH! THAT'S **NISHI**--SECOND-IN-COMMAND OF THE **BLACK GOBLIN GANG**.
WHAT A COINCIDENCE TO MEET YOU HERE.
N-NISHI--!
10.

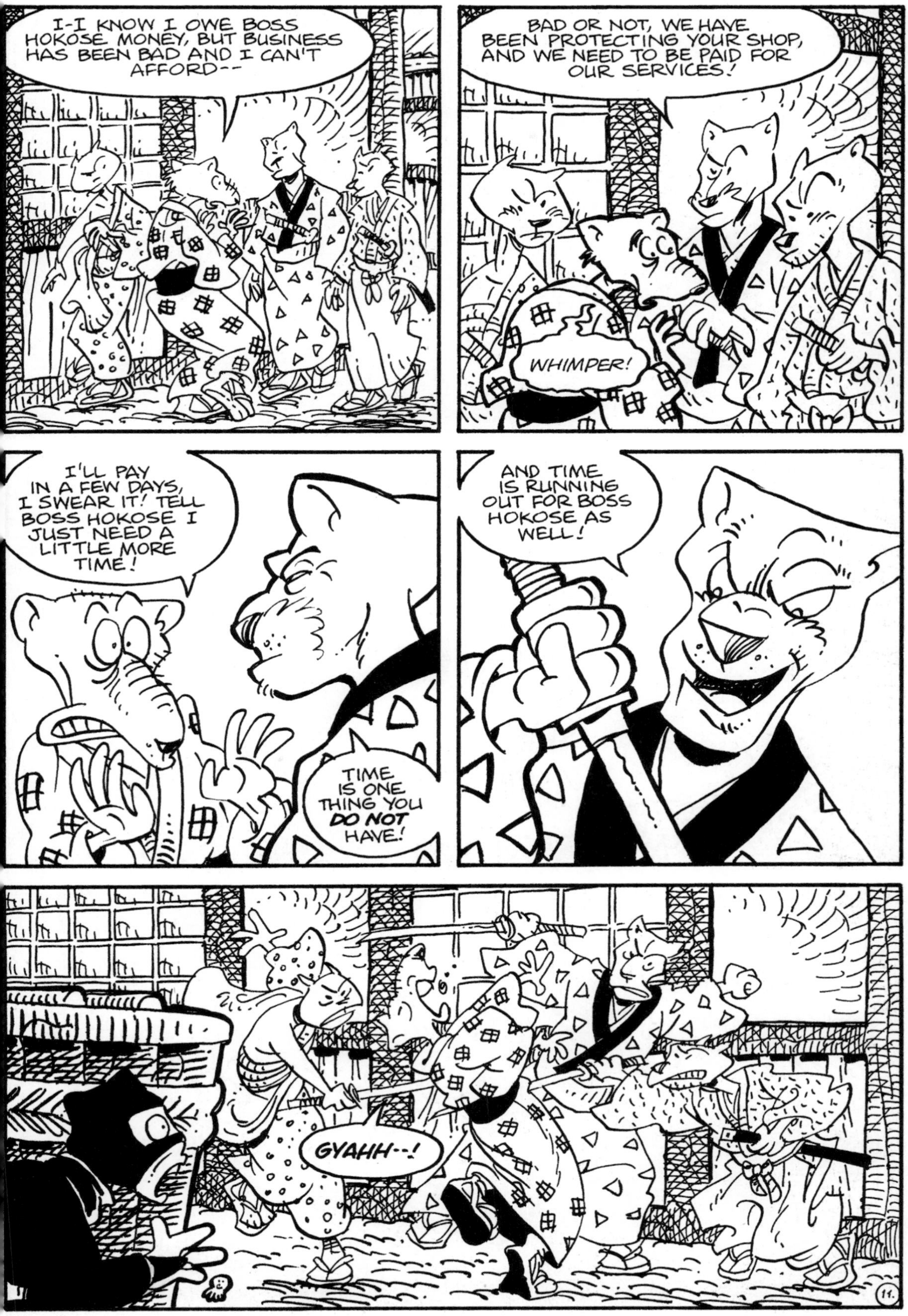
I-I KNOW I OWE BOSS HOKOSE MONEY, BUT BUSINESS HAS BEEN BAD AND I CAN'T AFFORD--
BAD OR NOT, WE HAVE BEEN PROTECTING YOUR SHOP, AND WE NEED TO BE PAID FOR OUR SERVICES!
WHIMPER!
I'LL PAY IN A FEW DAYS, I SWEAR IT! TELL BOSS HOKOSE I JUST NEED A LITTLE MORE TIME!
TIME IS ONE THING YOU **DO NOT** HAVE!
AND TIME IS RUNNING OUT FOR BOSS HOKOSE AS WELL!
GYAHH--!
11.

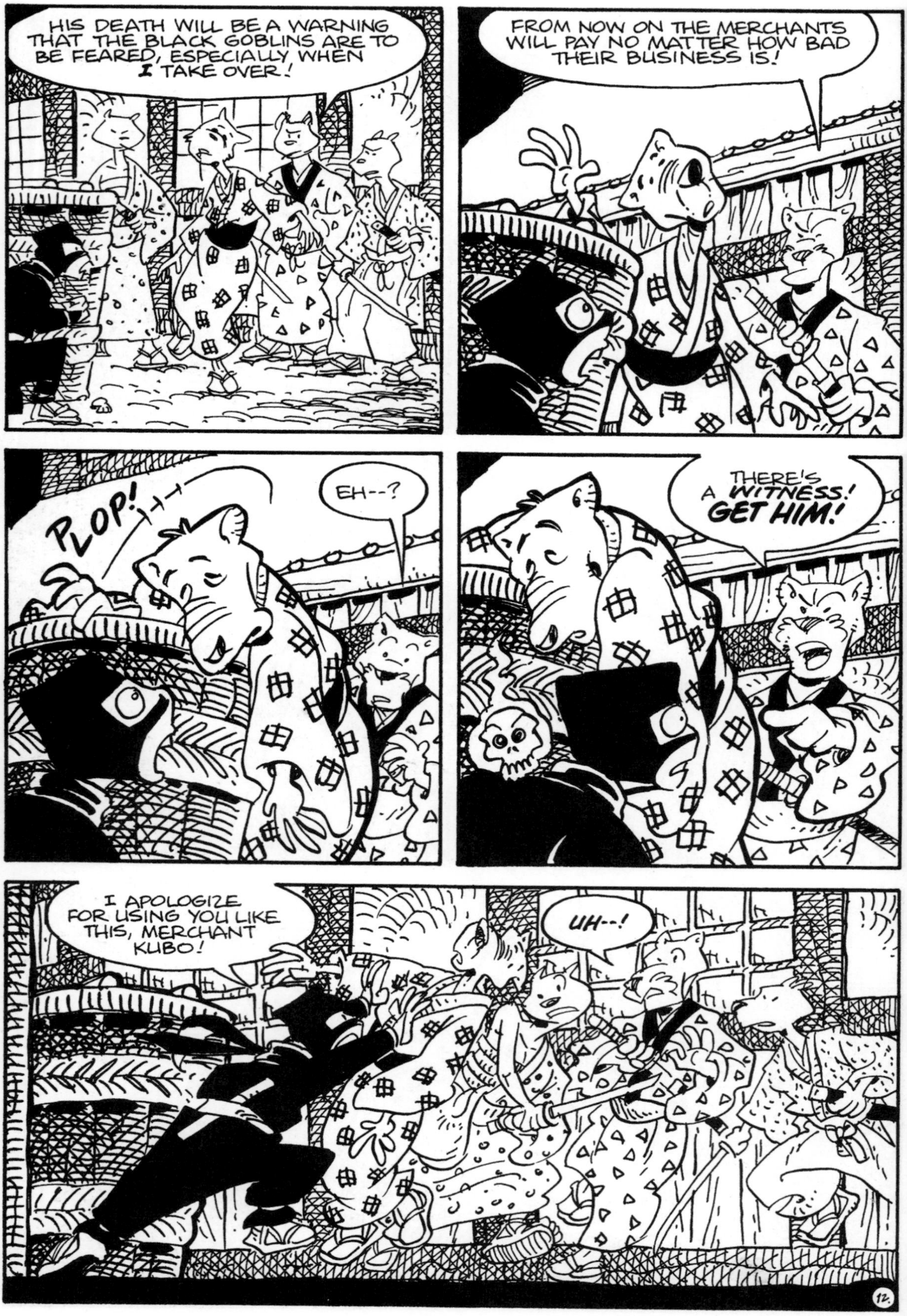

HIS DEATH WILL BE A WARNING THAT THE BLACK GOBLINS ARE TO BE FEARED, ESPECIALLY WHEN I TAKE OVER!
FROM NOW ON THE MERCHANTS WILL PAY NO MATTER HOW BAD THEIR BUSINESS IS!
PLOP!
EH--?
THERE'S A WITNESS! GET HIM!
I APOLOGIZE FOR USING YOU LIKE THIS, MERCHANT KUBO!
UH--!
12.

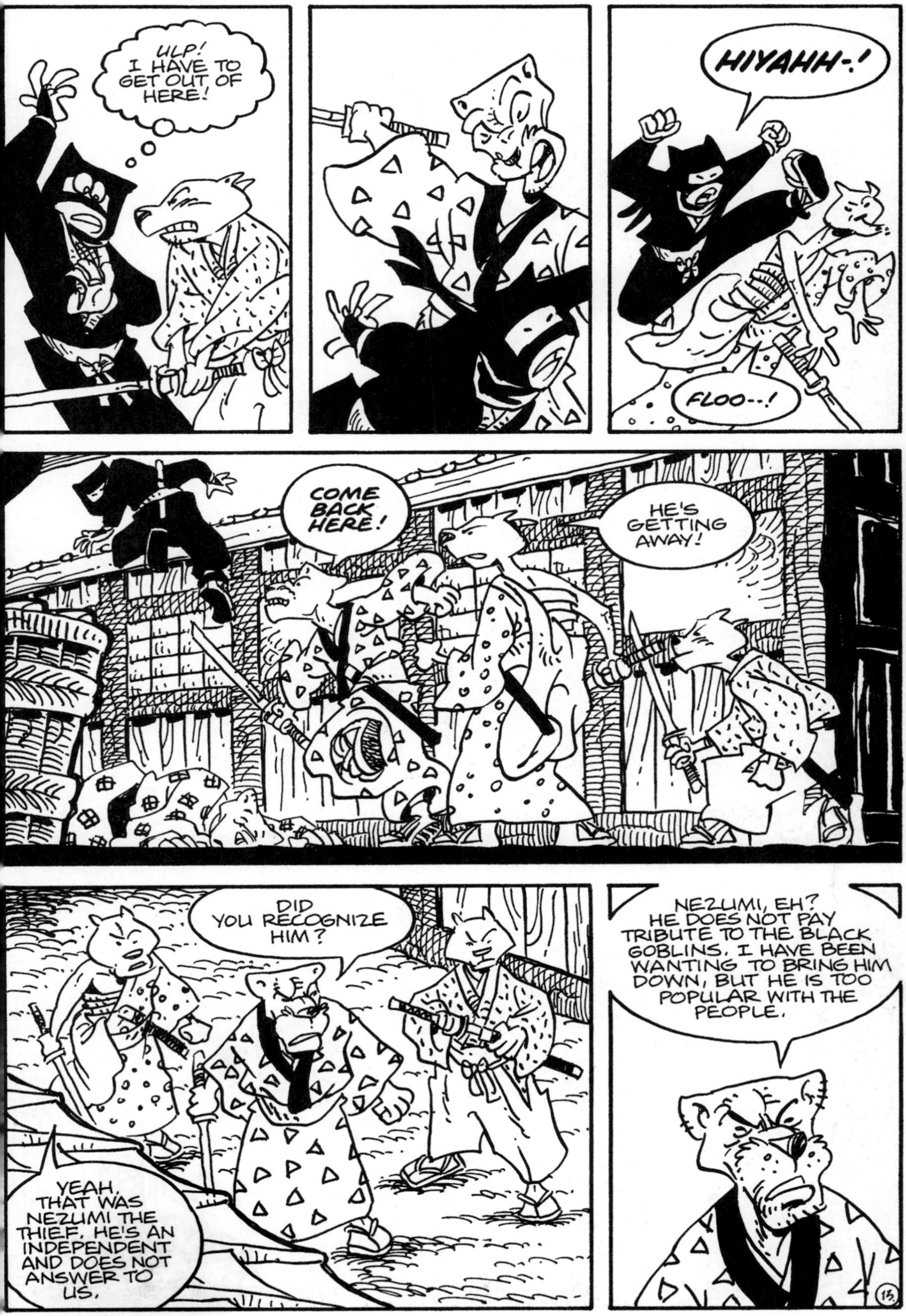
ULP! I HAVE TO GET OUT OF HERE!
HIYAHH-!
FLOO--!
COME BACK HERE!
HE'S GETTING AWAY!
DID YOU RECOGNIZE HIM?
YEAH. THAT WAS NEZUMI THE THIEF. HE'S AN INDEPENDENT AND DOES NOT ANSWER TO US.
NEZUMI, EH? HE DOES NOT PAY TRIBUTE TO THE BLACK GOBLINS. I HAVE BEEN WANTING TO BRING HIM DOWN, BUT HE IS TOO POPULAR WITH THE PEOPLE.
13.

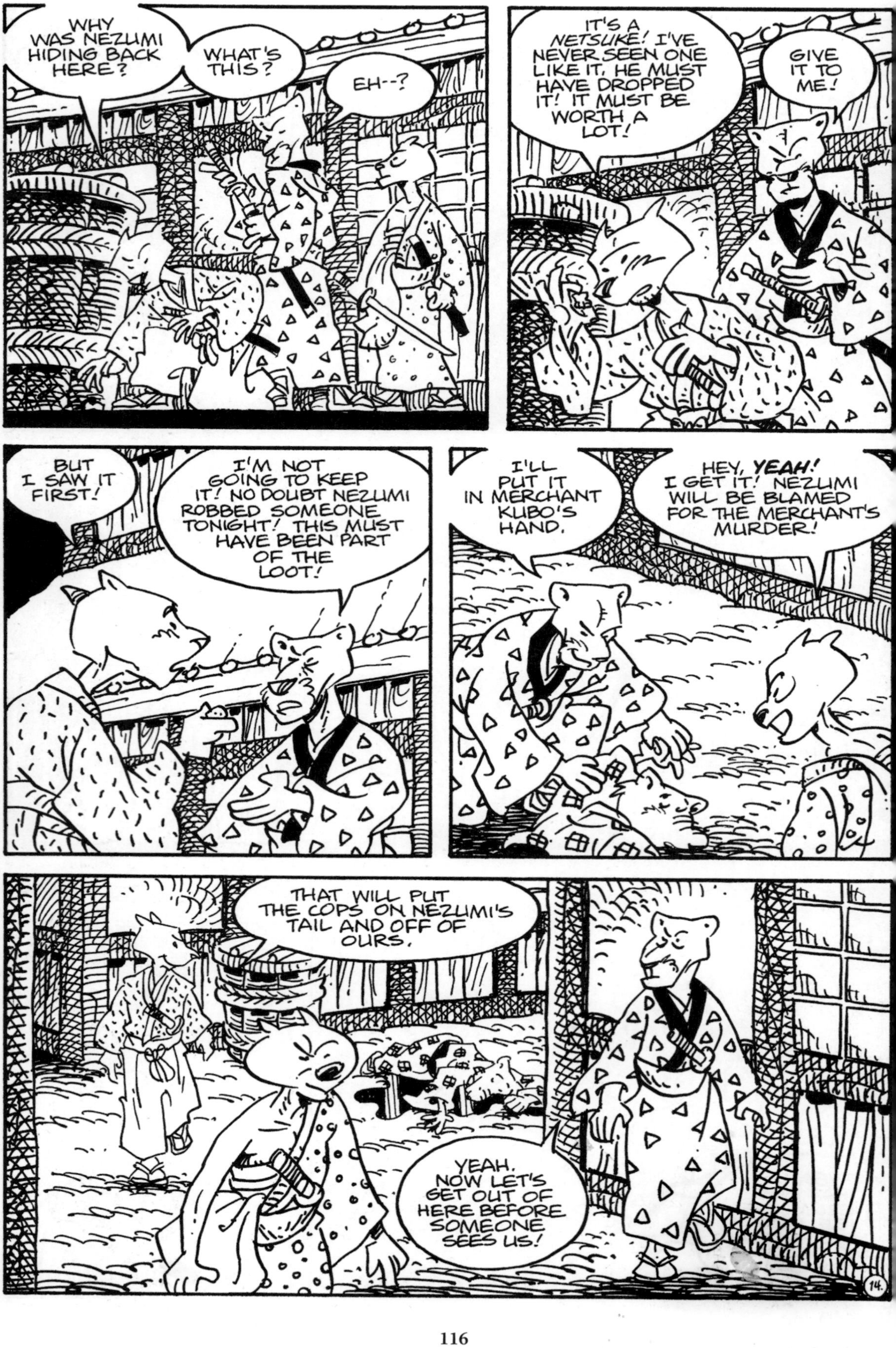
WHY WAS NEZUMI HIDING BACK HERE?
WHAT'S THIS?
EH--?
IT'S A *NETSUKE!* I'VE NEVER SEEN ONE LIKE IT. HE MUST HAVE DROPPED IT! IT MUST BE WORTH A LOT!
GIVE IT TO ME!
BUT I SAW IT FIRST!
I'M NOT GOING TO KEEP IT! NO DOUBT NEZUMI ROBBED SOMEONE TONIGHT! THIS MUST HAVE BEEN PART OF THE LOOT!
I'LL PUT IT IN MERCHANT KUBO'S HAND.
HEY, ***YEAH!*** I GET IT! NEZUMI WILL BE BLAMED FOR THE MERCHANT'S MURDER!
THAT WILL PUT THE COPS ON NEZUMI'S TAIL AND OFF OF OURS.
YEAH. NOW LET'S GET OUT OF HERE BEFORE SOMEONE SEES US!
14.

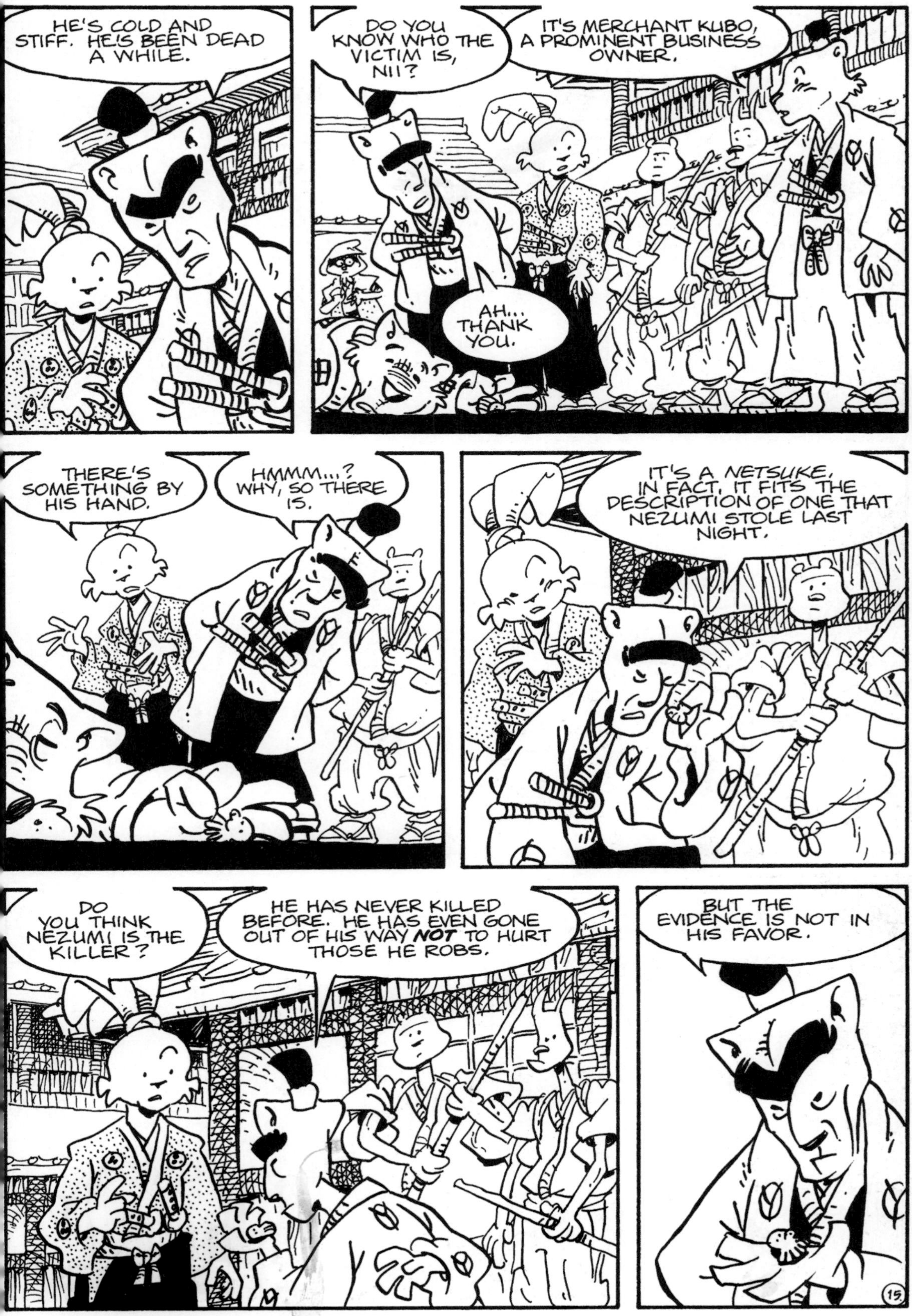
HE'S COLD AND STIFF. HE'S BEEN DEAD A WHILE.
DO YOU KNOW WHO THE VICTIM IS, NII?
IT'S MERCHANT KUBO, A PROMINENT BUSINESS OWNER.
AH... THANK YOU.
THERE'S SOMETHING BY HIS HAND.
HMMM...? WHY, SO THERE IS.
IT'S A NETSUKE. IN FACT, IT FITS THE DESCRIPTION OF ONE THAT NEZUMI STOLE LAST NIGHT.
DO YOU THINK NEZUMI IS THE KILLER?
HE HAS NEVER KILLED BEFORE. HE HAS EVEN GONE OUT OF HIS WAY **NOT** TO HURT THOSE HE ROBS.
BUT THE EVIDENCE IS NOT IN HIS FAVOR.
15

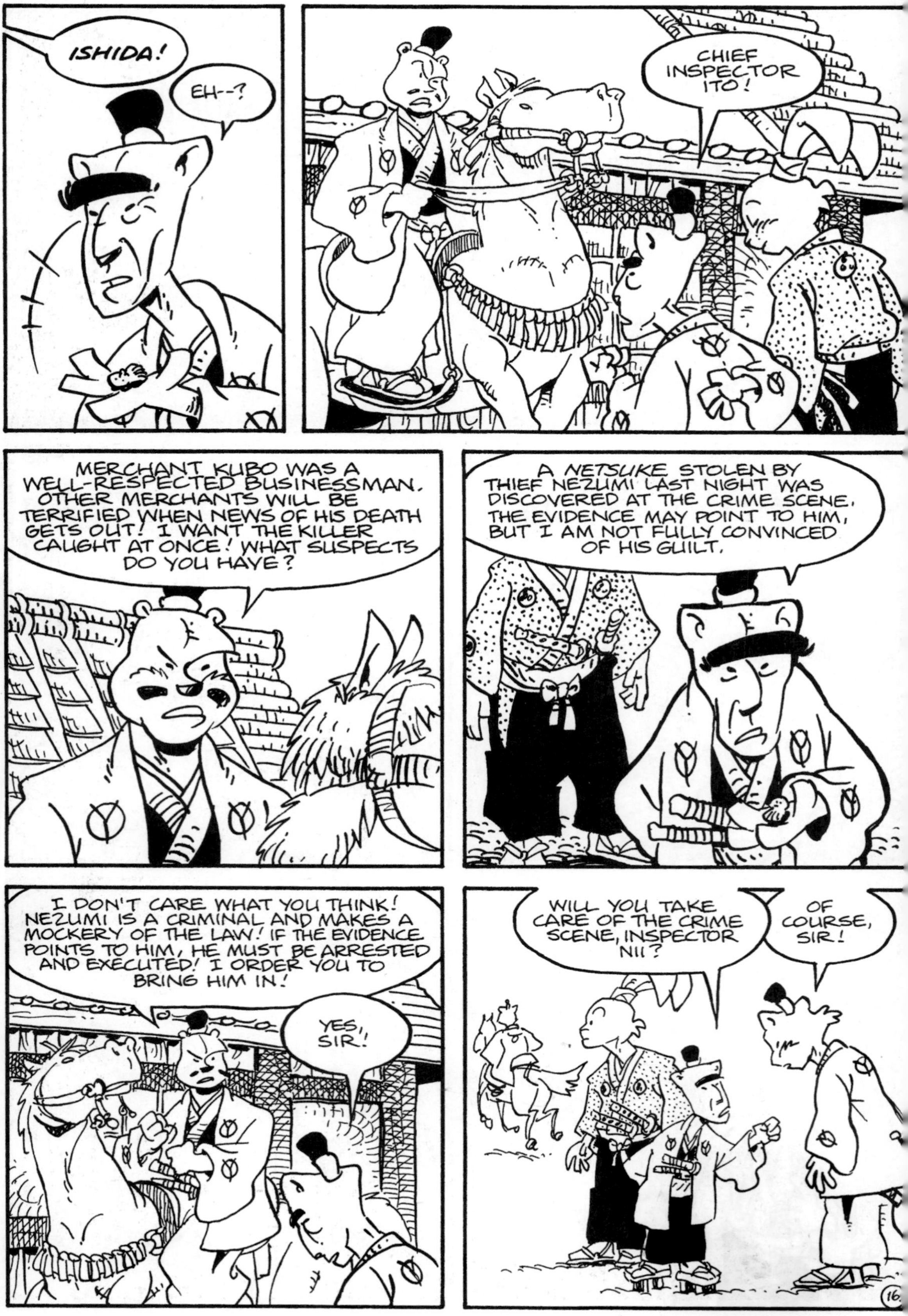
ISHIDA!
EH--?
CHIEF INSPECTOR ITO!
MERCHANT KUBO WAS A WELL-RESPECTED BUSINESSMAN. OTHER MERCHANTS WILL BE TERRIFIED WHEN NEWS OF HIS DEATH GETS OUT! I WANT THE KILLER CAUGHT AT ONCE! WHAT SUSPECTS DO YOU HAVE?
A *NETSUKE* STOLEN BY THIEF NEZUMI LAST NIGHT WAS DISCOVERED AT THE CRIME SCENE. THE EVIDENCE MAY POINT TO HIM, BUT I AM NOT FULLY CONVINCED OF HIS GUILT.
I DON'T CARE WHAT YOU THINK! NEZUMI IS A CRIMINAL AND MAKES A MOCKERY OF THE LAW! IF THE EVIDENCE POINTS TO HIM, HE MUST BE ARRESTED AND EXECUTED! I ORDER YOU TO BRING HIM IN!
YES, SIR!
WILL YOU TAKE CARE OF THE CRIME SCENE, INSPECTOR NII?
OF COURSE, SIR!
16

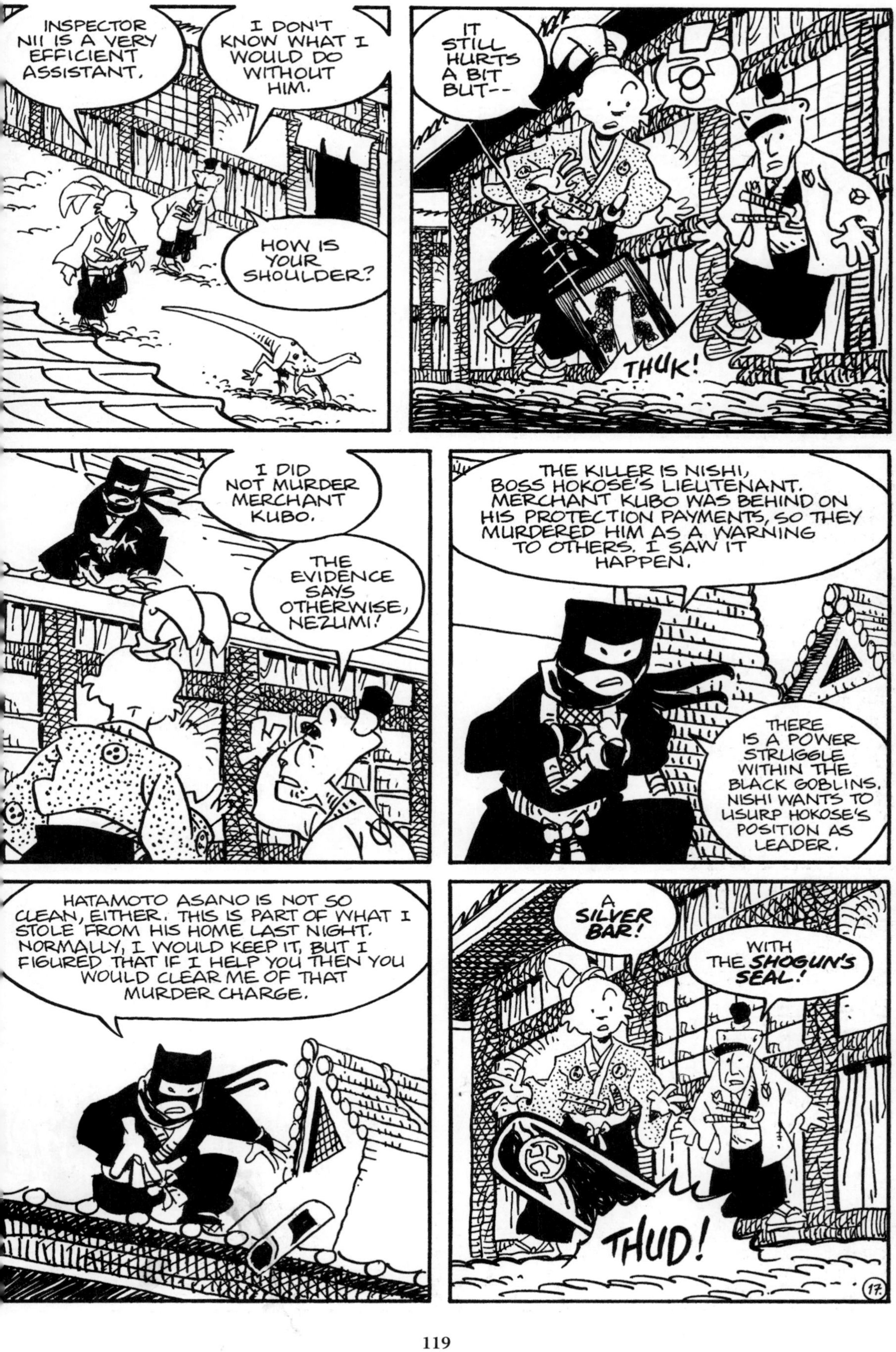
INSPECTOR NII IS A VERY EFFICIENT ASSISTANT.
I DON'T KNOW WHAT I WOULD DO WITHOUT HIM.
HOW IS YOUR SHOULDER?
IT STILL HURTS A BIT BUT--
THUK!
I DID NOT MURDER MERCHANT KUBO.
THE EVIDENCE SAYS OTHERWISE, NEZUMI!
THE KILLER IS NISHI, BOSS HOKOSE'S LIEUTENANT. MERCHANT KUBO WAS BEHIND ON HIS PROTECTION PAYMENTS, SO THEY MURDERED HIM AS A WARNING TO OTHERS. I SAW IT HAPPEN.
THERE IS A POWER STRUGGLE WITHIN THE BLACK GOBLINS. NISHI WANTS TO USURP HOKOSE'S POSITION AS LEADER.
HATAMOTO ASANO IS NOT SO CLEAN, EITHER. THIS IS PART OF WHAT I STOLE FROM HIS HOME LAST NIGHT. NORMALLY, I WOULD KEEP IT, BUT I FIGURED THAT IF I HELP YOU THEN YOU WOULD CLEAR ME OF THAT MURDER CHARGE.
A SILVER BAR!
WITH THE SHOGUN'S SEAL!
THUD!
17.

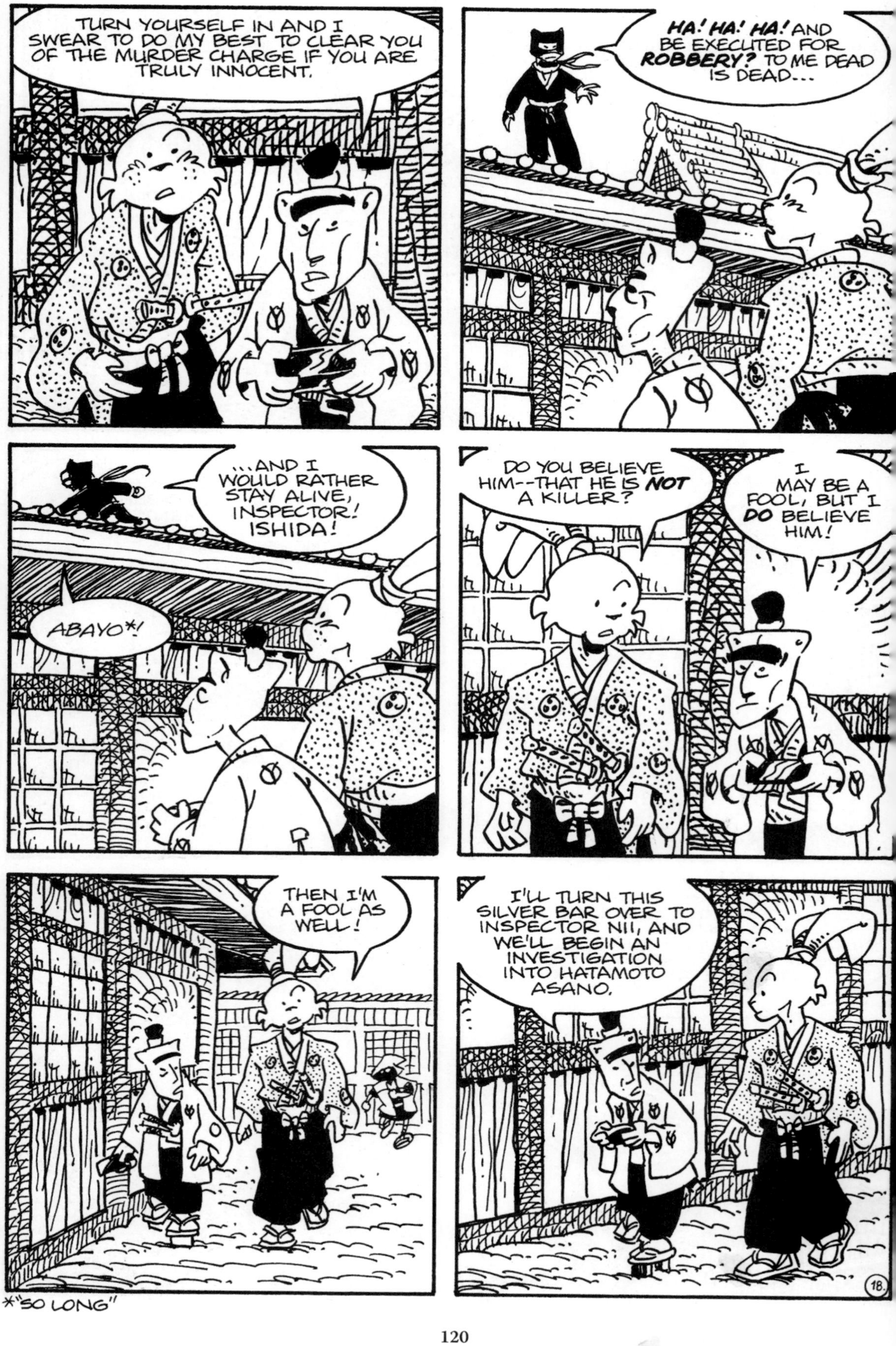
TURN YOURSELF IN AND I SWEAR TO DO MY BEST TO CLEAR YOU OF THE MURDER CHARGE IF YOU ARE TRULY INNOCENT.
HA! HA! HA! AND BE EXECUTED FOR ROBBERY? TO ME DEAD IS DEAD...
...AND I WOULD RATHER STAY ALIVE, INSPECTOR! ISHIDA!
ABAYO*!
DO YOU BELIEVE HIM--THAT HE IS NOT A KILLER?
I MAY BE A FOOL, BUT I DO BELIEVE HIM!
THEN I'M A FOOL AS WELL!
I'LL TURN THIS SILVER BAR OVER TO INSPECTOR NII, AND WE'LL BEGIN AN INVESTIGATION INTO HATAMOTO ASANO.
18.

*"SO LONG"

KILLING MERCHANT KUBO WAS *FOOLISH!* YOU CAN'T EXTORT MONEY FROM A DEAD MAN! ON TOP OF THAT, THE COPS WILL BE SNOOPING AROUND OUR AFFAIRS!

THE COPS ARE AFTER NEZUMI, BUT WE HAVE SPREAD IT THROUGHOUT OUR CIRCLES THAT KUBO WAS KILLED BECAUSE OF NON-PAYMENT!

STILL, YOU DARED TO TAKE SUCH A DRASTIC ACTION WITHOUT MY APPROVAL? DO IT AGAIN AND YOU WILL REGRET IT, NISHI!

YOU ARE TOO SOFT-HEARTED, BOSS HOKOSE. THE BLACK GOBLIN GANG WOULD DO BETTER UNDER A STRONGER LEADERSHIP!

WHO ARE YOU TO SAY SUCH THINGS TO ME?

DON'T FORGET--I HAVE THE BACKING OF *THE MASTER!* WITHOUT HIM WE WOULD NOT BE AS FEARED AS WE ARE!

NOW GET OUT OF HERE! I HAVE A MEETING WITH HIM THIS AFTERNOON.

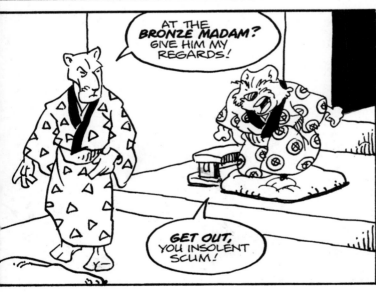

AT THE *BRONZE MADAM?* GIVE HIM MY REGARDS!

GET OUT, YOU INSOLENT SCUM!

GRR... IT'S ABOUT TIME I TOOK CARE OF NISHI!

19.

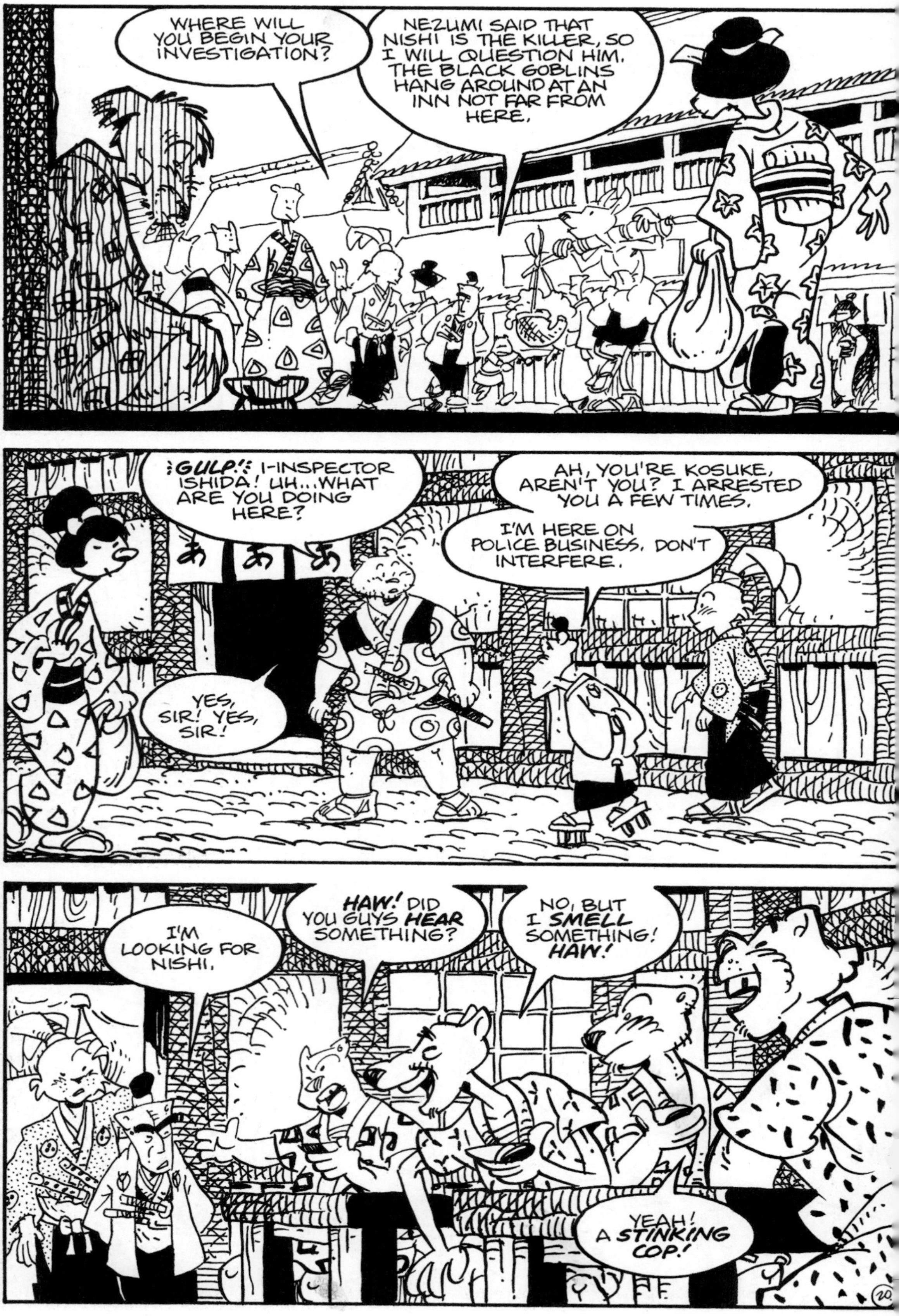
WHERE WILL YOU BEGIN YOUR INVESTIGATION?
NEZUMI SAID THAT NISHI IS THE KILLER, SO I WILL QUESTION HIM. THE BLACK GOBLINS HANG AROUND AT AN INN NOT FAR FROM HERE.
GULP! I-INSPECTOR ISHIDA! UH...WHAT ARE YOU DOING HERE?
AH, YOU'RE KOSUKE, AREN'T YOU? I ARRESTED YOU A FEW TIMES.
I'M HERE ON POLICE BUSINESS. DON'T INTERFERE.
YES, SIR! YES, SIR!
I'M LOOKING FOR NISHI.
HAW! DID YOU GUYS HEAR SOMETHING?
NO, BUT I SMELL SOMETHING! HAW!
YEAH! A STINKING COP!
20

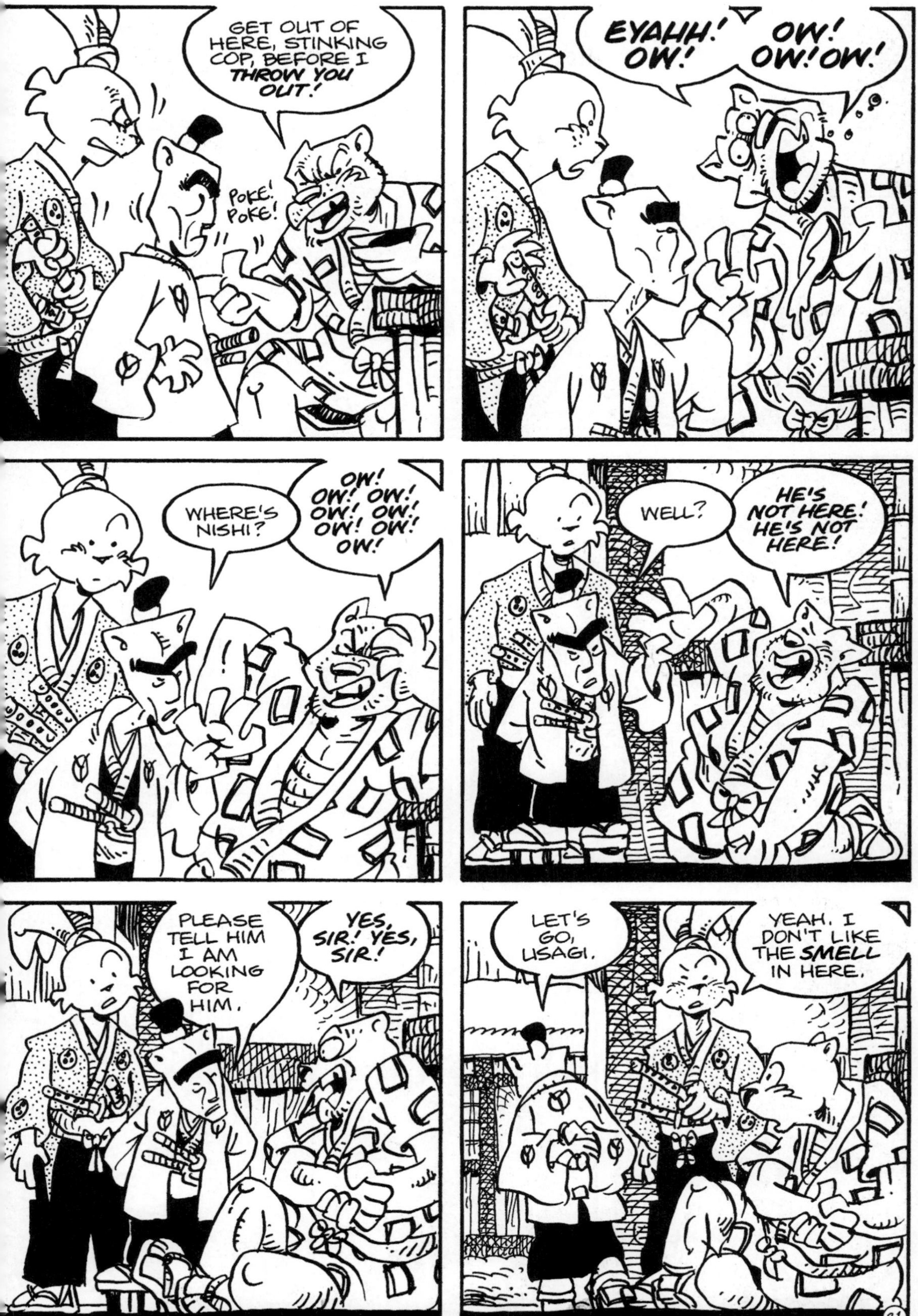
GET OUT OF HERE, STINKING COP, BEFORE I THROW YOU OUT!
POKE! POKE!
EYAHH! OW!
OW! OW! OW!
WHERE'S NISHI?
OW! OW! OW! OW! OW! OW! OW! OW!
WELL?
HE'S NOT HERE! HE'S NOT HERE!
PLEASE TELL HIM I AM LOOKING FOR HIM.
YES, SIR! YES, SIR!
LET'S GO, USAGI.
YEAH. I DON'T LIKE THE SMELL IN HERE.
21.

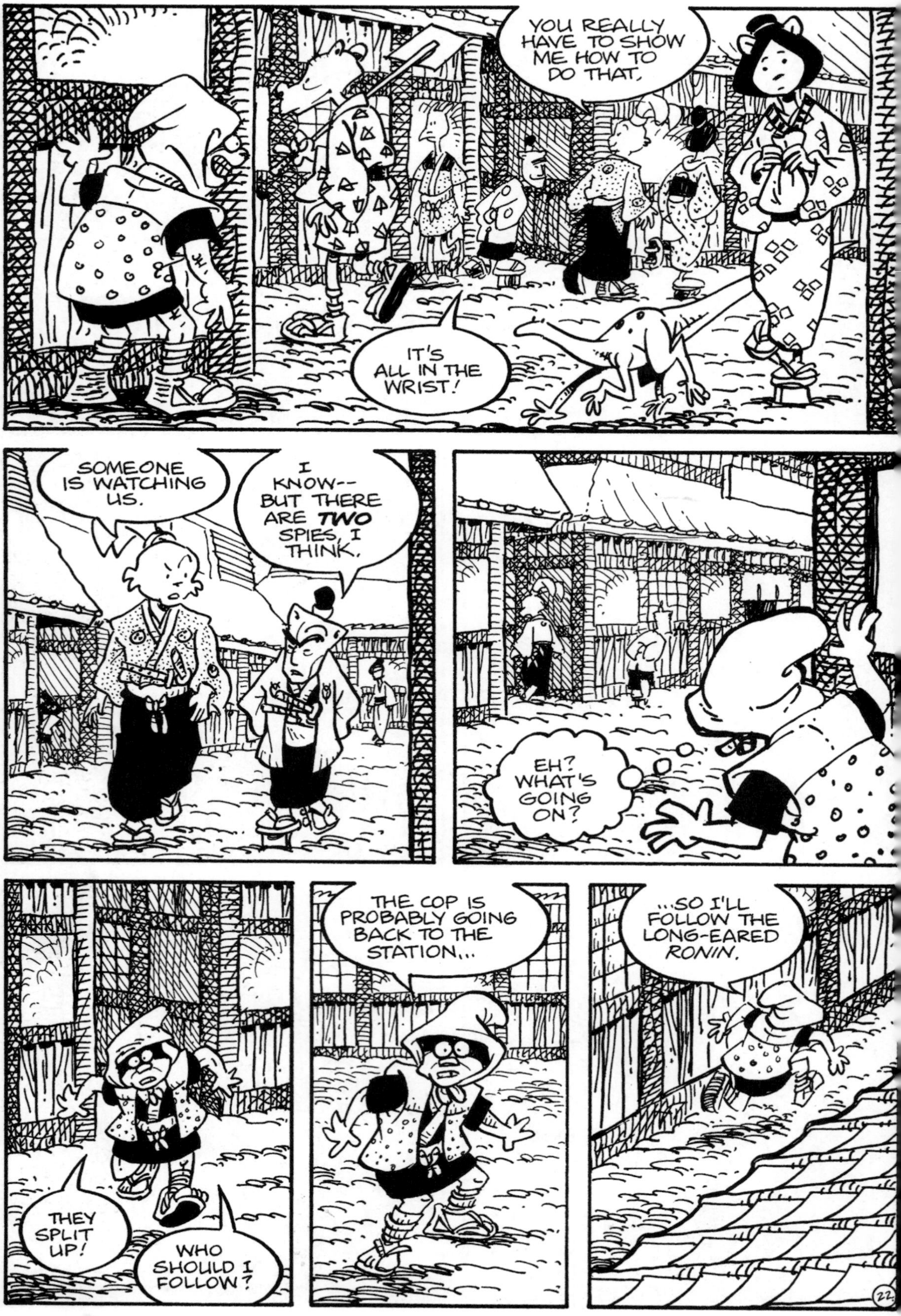

YOU REALLY HAVE TO SHOW ME HOW TO DO THAT.
IT'S ALL IN THE WRIST!
SOMEONE IS WATCHING US.
I KNOW-- BUT THERE ARE **TWO** SPIES, I THINK.
EH? WHAT'S GOING ON?
THEY SPLIT UP!
WHO SHOULD I FOLLOW?
THE COP IS PROBABLY GOING BACK TO THE STATION...
...SO I'LL FOLLOW THE LONG-EARED *RONIN*.
22

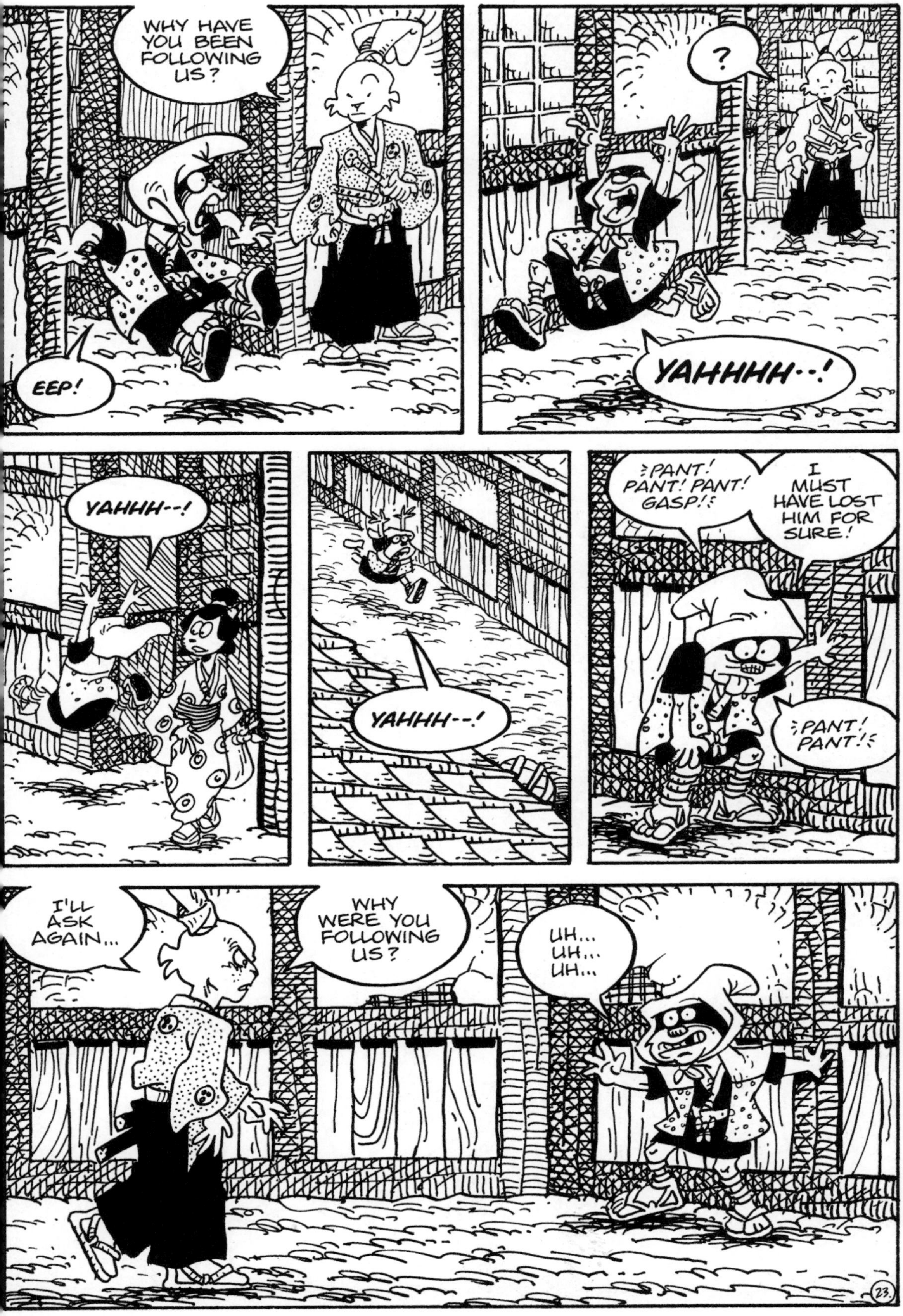
WHY HAVE YOU BEEN FOLLOWING US?
EEP!
?
YAHHHH--!
YAHHH--!
YAHHH--!
PANT! PANT! PANT! GASP!
I MUST HAVE LOST HIM FOR SURE!
PANT! PANT!
I'LL ASK AGAIN...
WHY WERE YOU FOLLOWING US?
UH... UH... UH...
23.

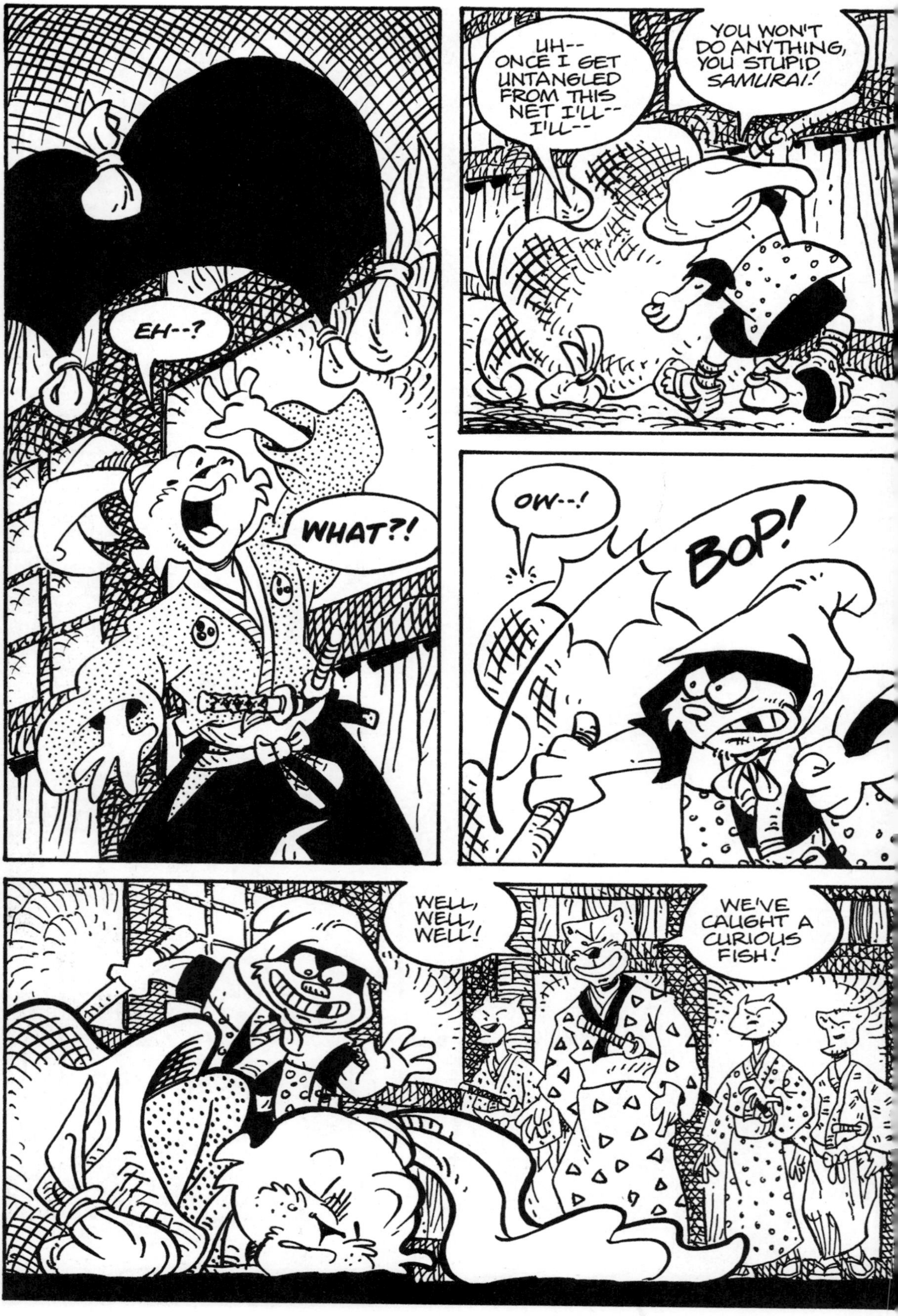
EH--?
WHAT?!
UH-- ONCE I GET UNTANGLED FROM THIS NET I'LL-- I'LL--
YOU WON'T DO ANYTHING, YOU STUPID SAMURAI!
OW--!
BOP!
WELL, WELL, WELL!
WE'VE CAUGHT A CURIOUS FISH!

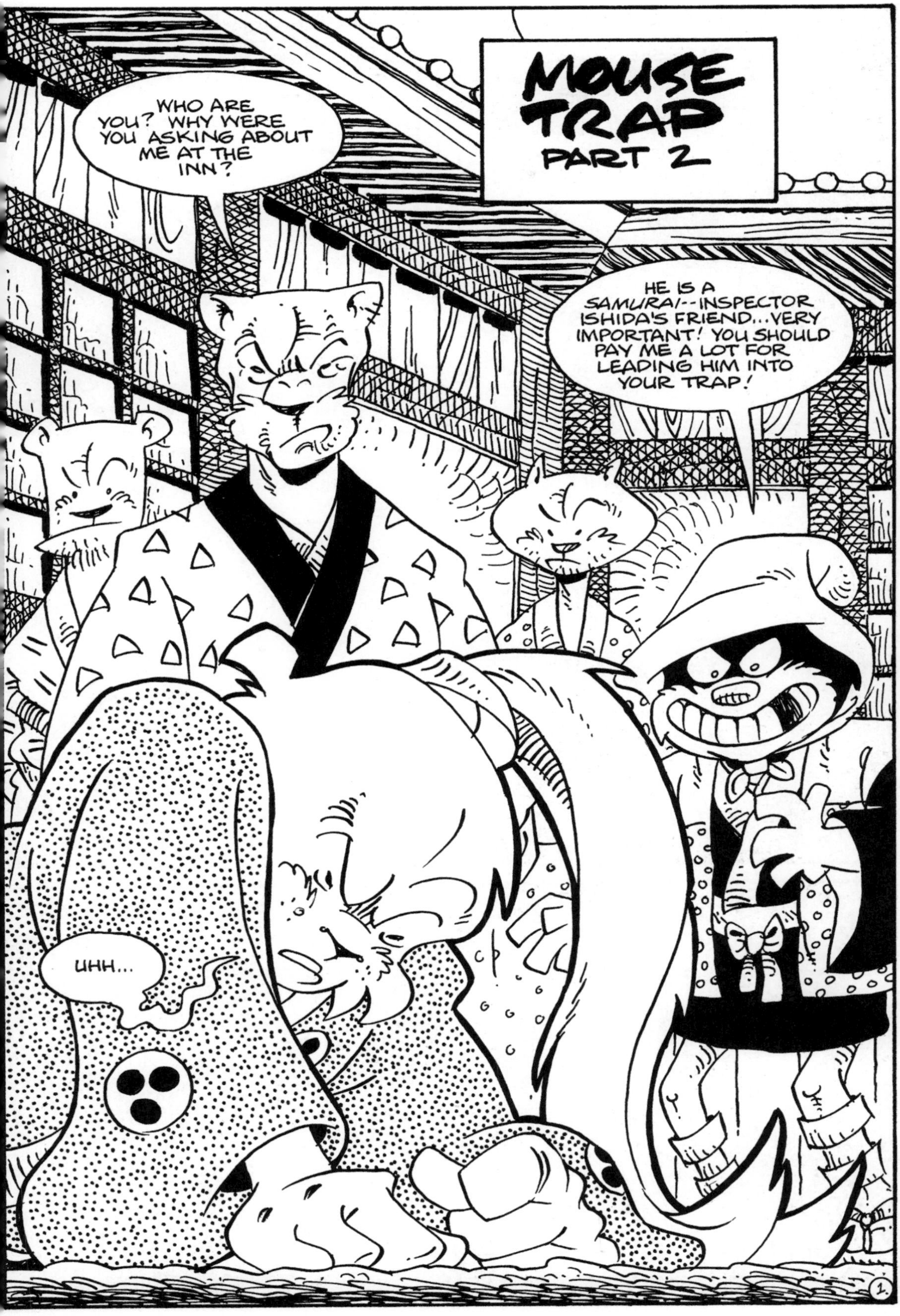
MOUSE TRAP
PART 2
WHO ARE YOU? WHY WERE YOU ASKING ABOUT ME AT THE INN?
HE IS A SAMURAI--INSPECTOR ISHIDA'S FRIEND...VERY IMPORTANT! YOU SHOULD PAY ME A LOT FOR LEADING HIM INTO YOUR TRAP!
UHH...
1.

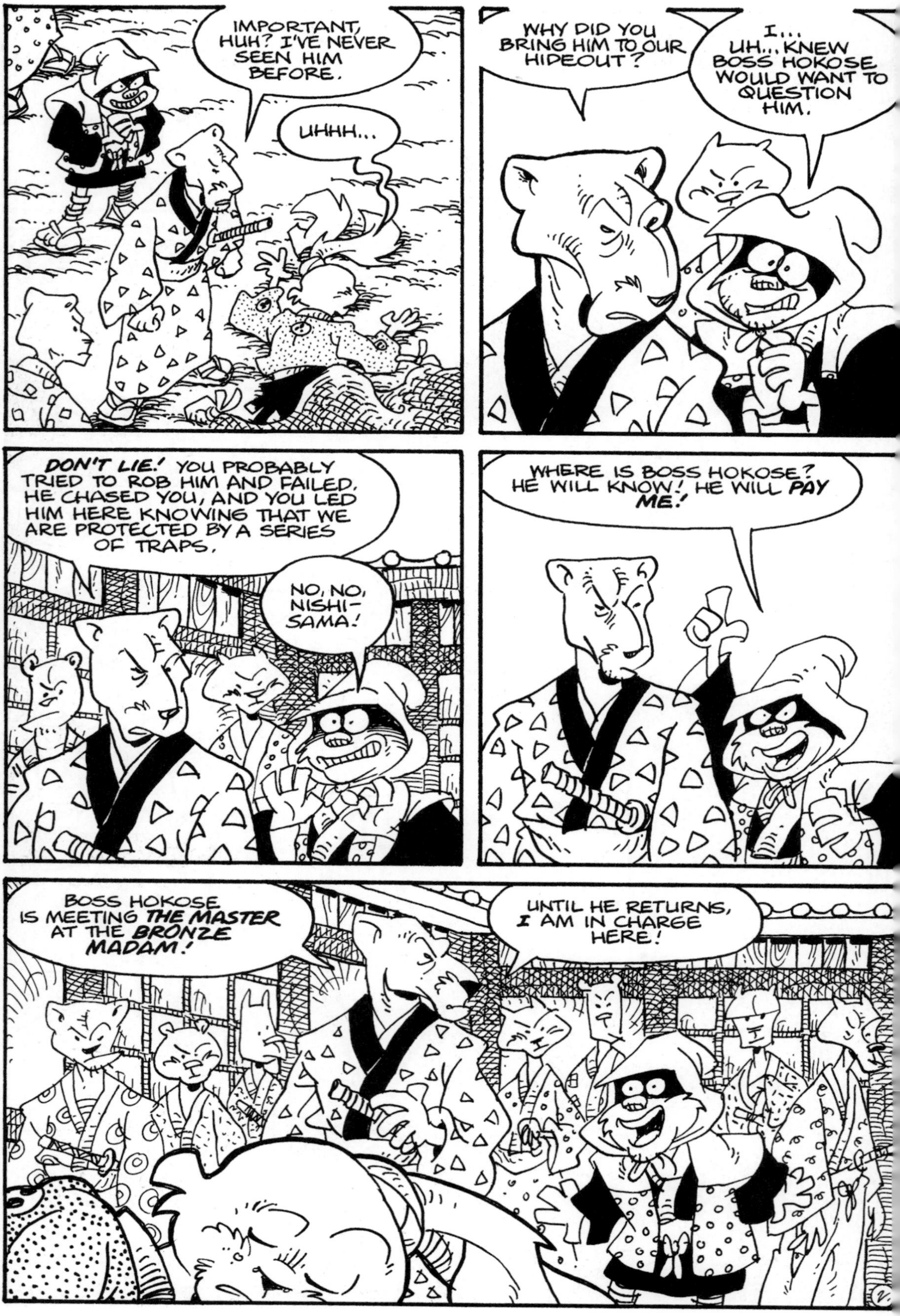
IMPORTANT, HUH? I'VE NEVER SEEN HIM BEFORE.
UHHH...
WHY DID YOU BRING HIM TO OUR HIDEOUT?
I... UH... KNEW BOSS HOKOSE WOULD WANT TO QUESTION HIM.
DON'T LIE! YOU PROBABLY TRIED TO ROB HIM AND FAILED. HE CHASED YOU, AND YOU LED HIM HERE KNOWING THAT WE ARE PROTECTED BY A SERIES OF TRAPS.
NO, NO, NISHI-SAMA!
WHERE IS BOSS HOKOSE? HE WILL KNOW! HE WILL PAY ME!
BOSS HOKOSE IS MEETING THE MASTER AT THE BRONZE MADAM!
UNTIL HE RETURNS, I AM IN CHARGE HERE!

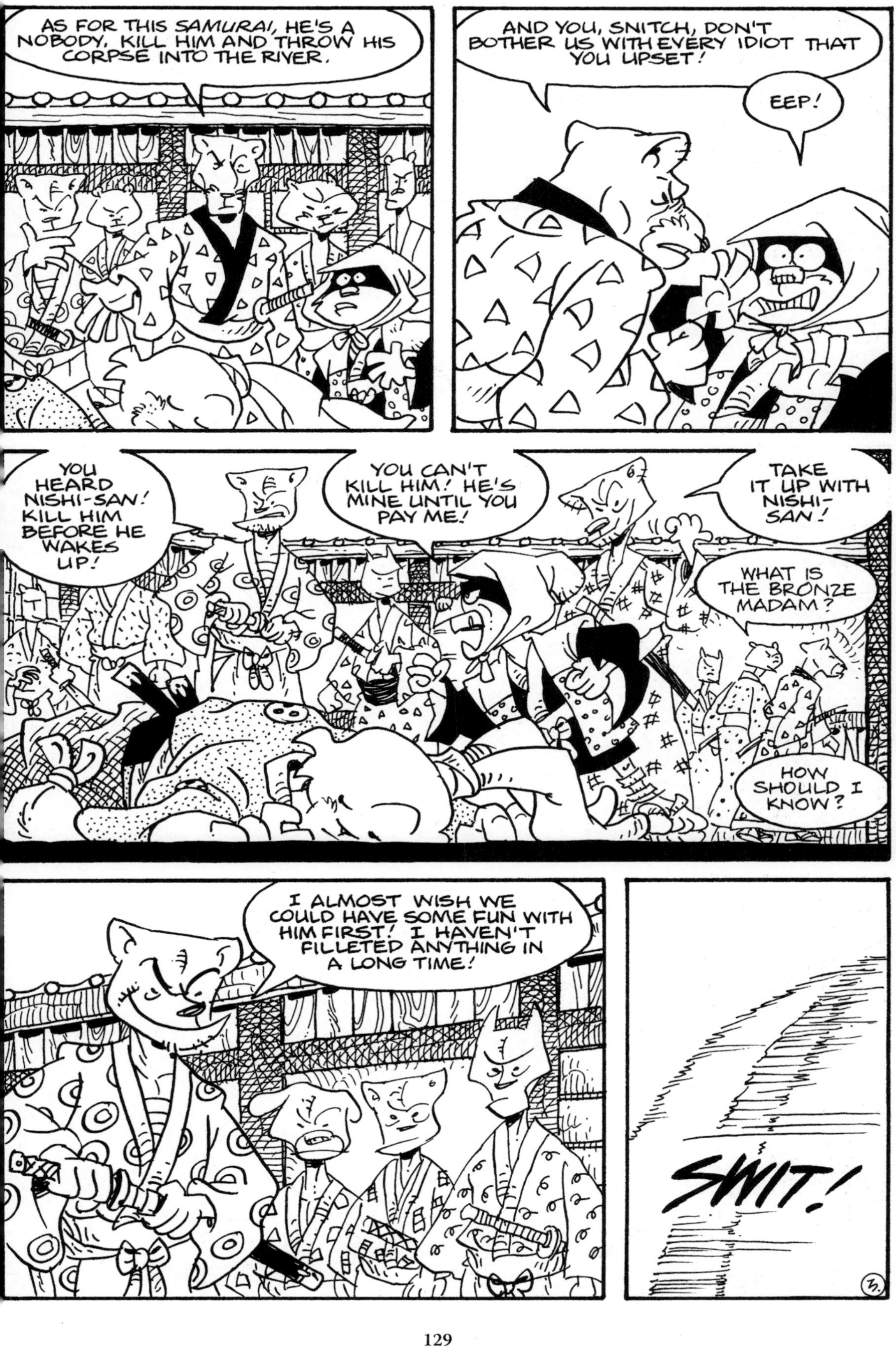
AS FOR THIS SAMURAI, HE'S A NOBODY. KILL HIM AND THROW HIS CORPSE INTO THE RIVER.
AND YOU, SNITCH, DON'T BOTHER US WITH EVERY IDIOT THAT YOU UPSET!
EEP!
YOU HEARD NISHI-SAN! KILL HIM BEFORE HE WAKES UP!
YOU CAN'T KILL HIM! HE'S MINE UNTIL YOU PAY ME!
TAKE IT UP WITH NISHI-SAN!
WHAT IS THE BRONZE MADAM?
HOW SHOULD I KNOW?
I ALMOST WISH WE COULD HAVE SOME FUN WITH HIM FIRST! I HAVEN'T FILLETED ANYTHING IN A LONG TIME!
SWIT!
3.

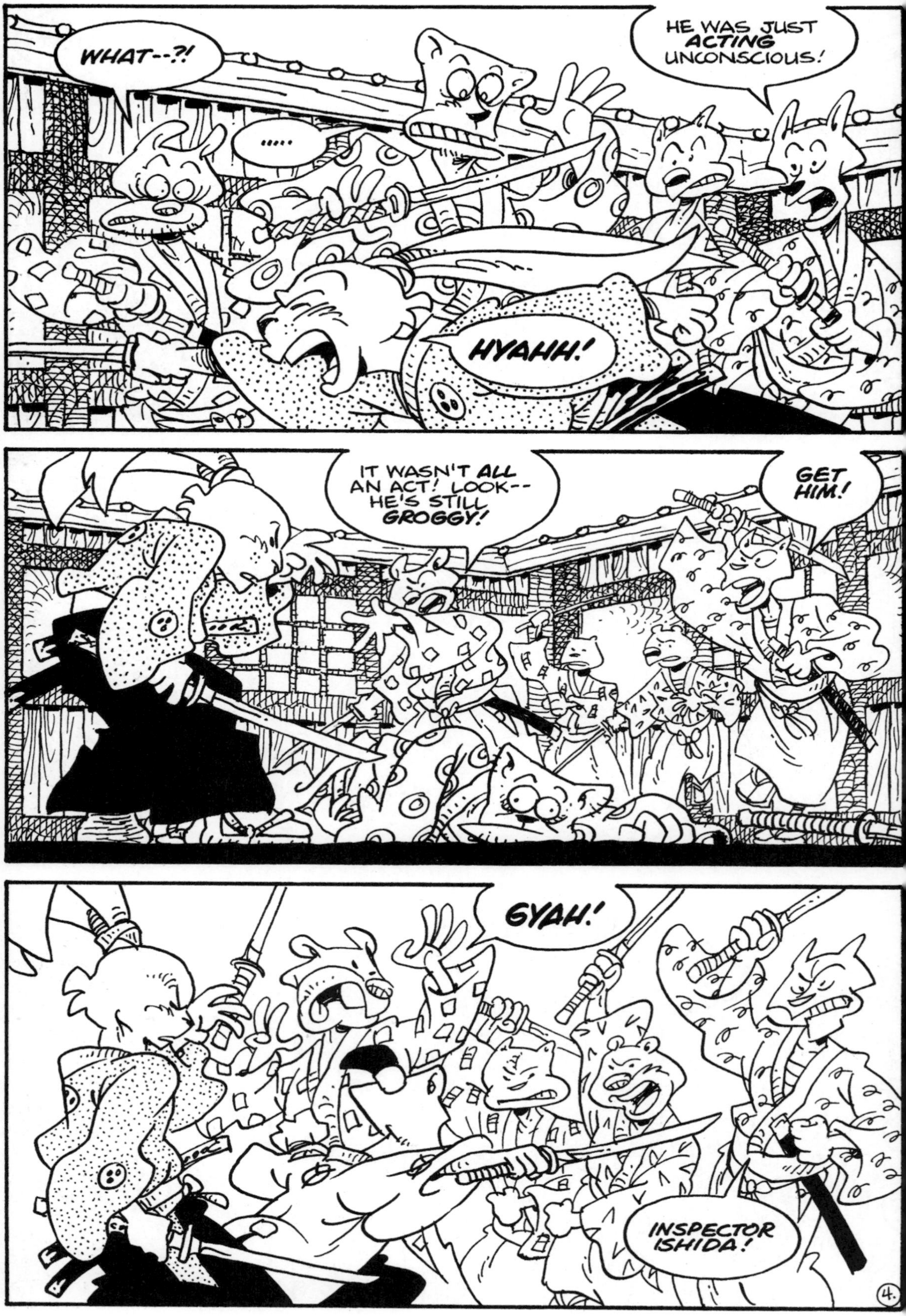
WHAT--?!
.....
HE WAS JUST ACTING UNCONSCIOUS!
HYAHH!
IT WASN'T ALL AN ACT! LOOK-- HE'S STILL GROGGY!
GET HIM!
GYAH!
INSPECTOR ISHIDA!
4.

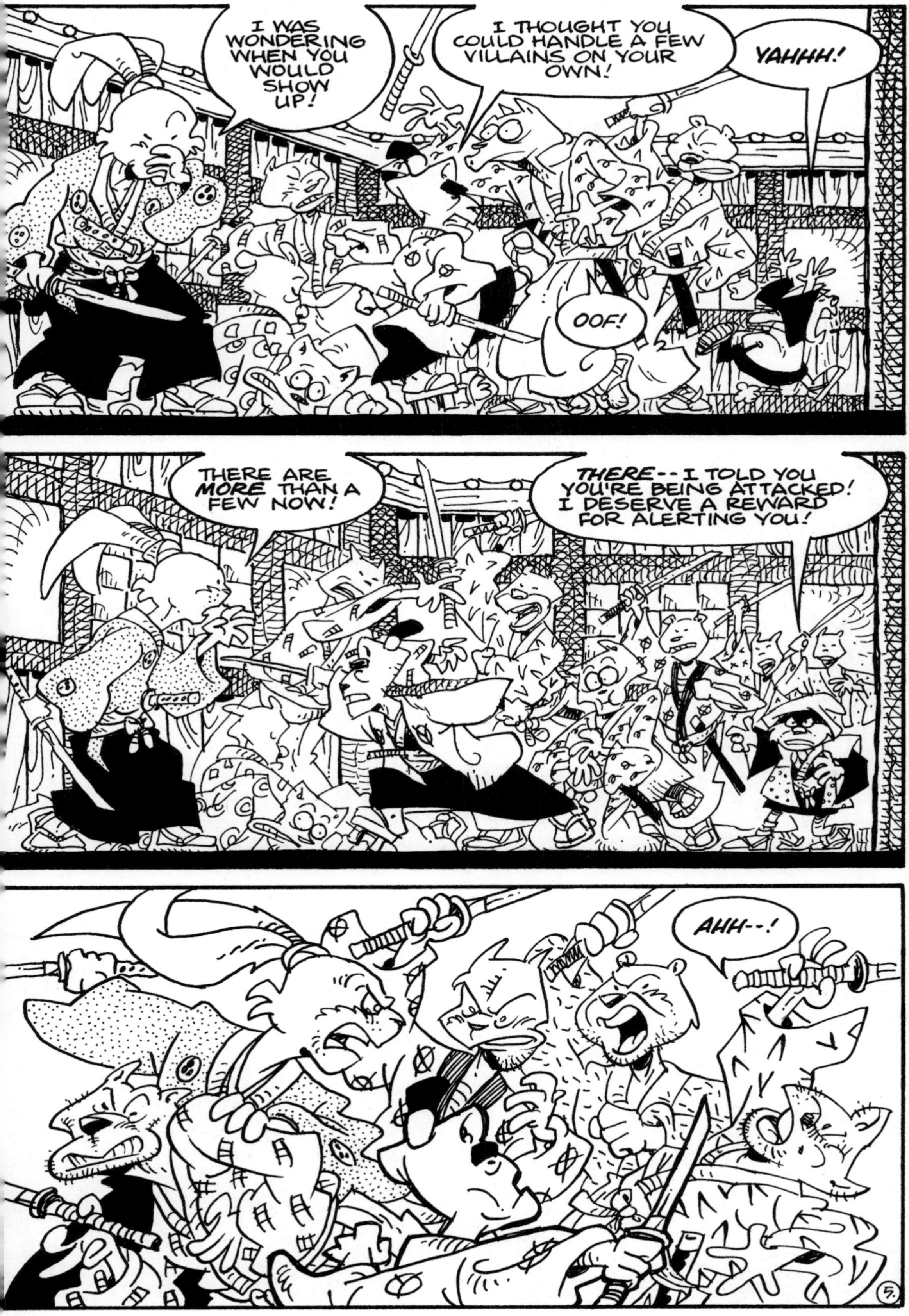
I WAS WONDERING WHEN YOU WOULD SHOW UP!
I THOUGHT YOU COULD HANDLE A FEW VILLAINS ON YOUR OWN!
YAHHH!
OOF!
THERE ARE MORE THAN A FEW NOW!
THERE-- I TOLD YOU YOU'RE BEING ATTACKED! I DESERVE A REWARD FOR ALERTING YOU!
AHH--!
5.

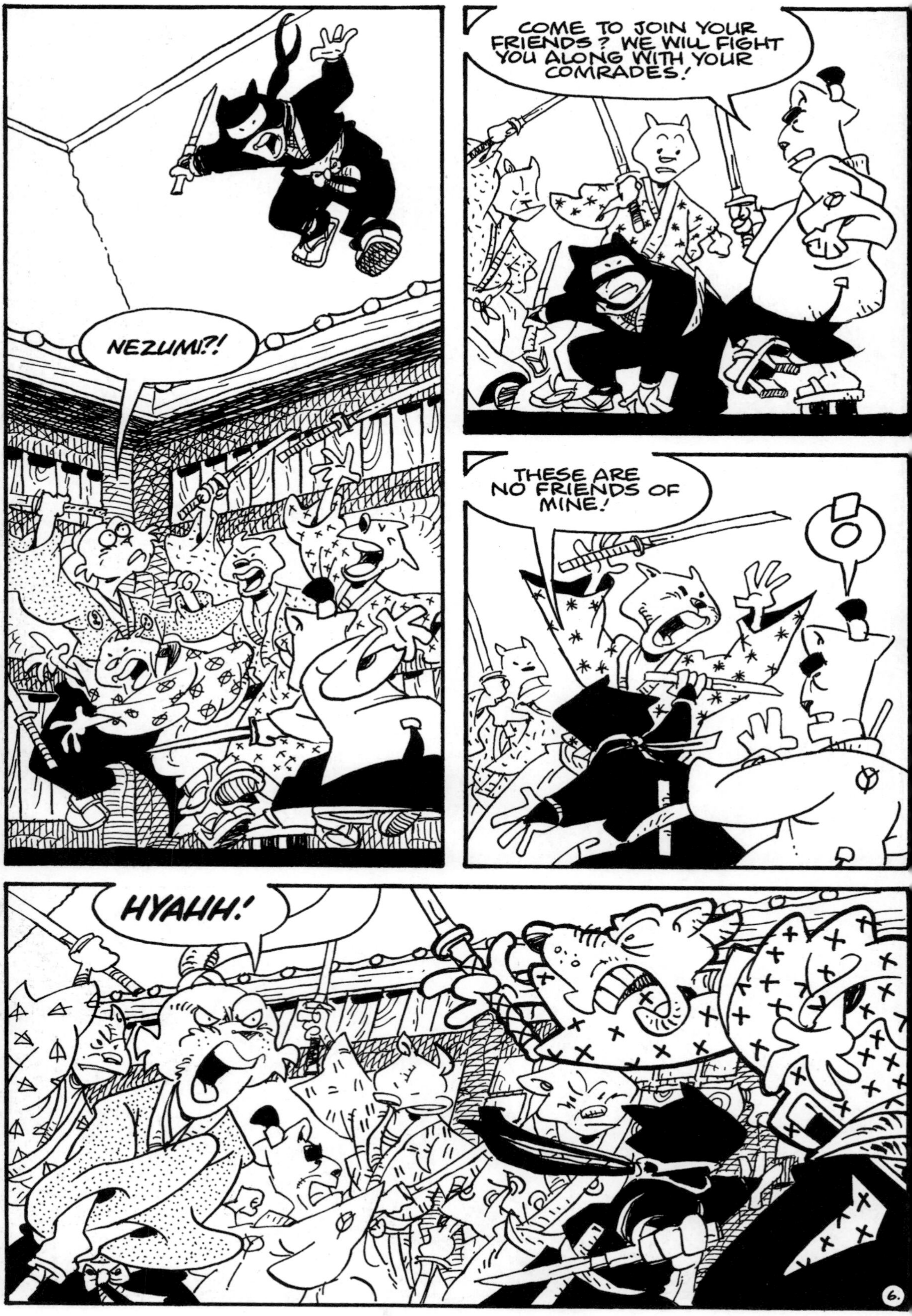
NEZUMI?!
COME TO JOIN YOUR FRIENDS? WE WILL FIGHT YOU ALONG WITH YOUR COMRADES!
THESE ARE NO FRIENDS OF MINE!
HYAHH!
6.

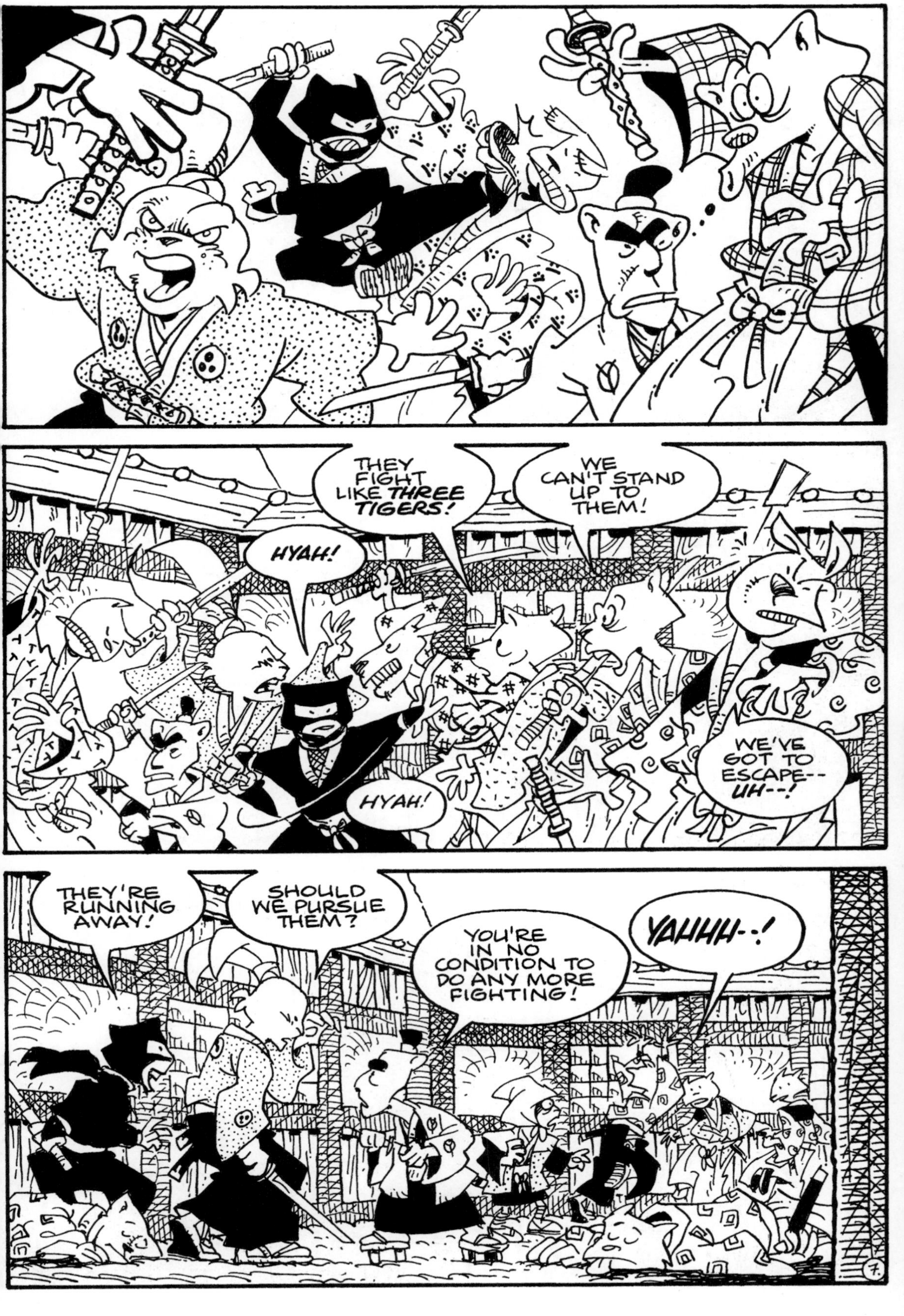
HYAH!
THEY FIGHT LIKE THREE TIGERS!
WE CAN'T STAND UP TO THEM!
HYAH!
WE'VE GOT TO ESCAPE-- UH--!
THEY'RE RUNNING AWAY!
SHOULD WE PURSUE THEM?
YOU'RE IN NO CONDITION TO DO ANY MORE FIGHTING!
YAHHH--!
7.

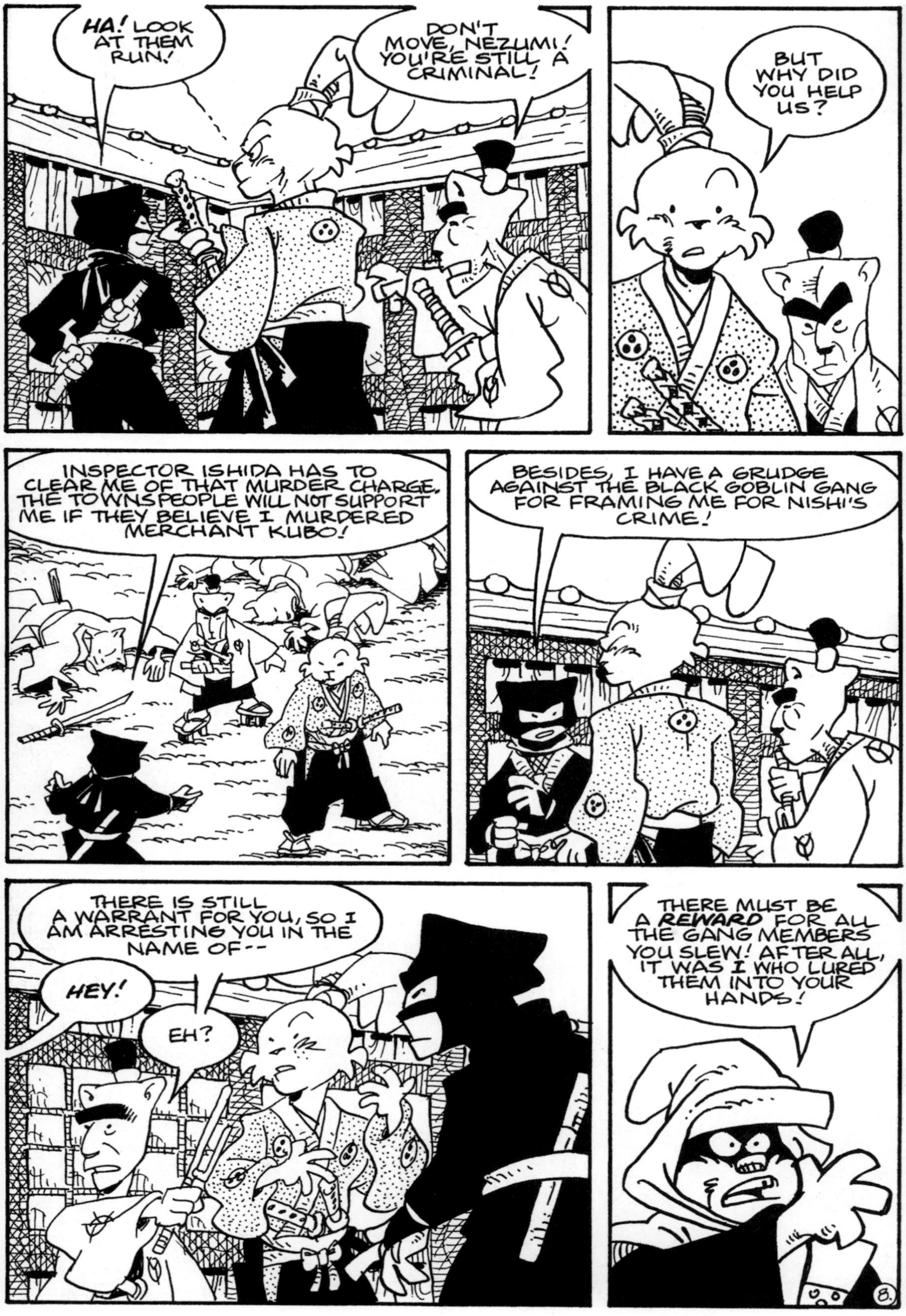
HA! LOOK AT THEM RUN!
DON'T MOVE, NEZUMI! YOU'RE STILL A CRIMINAL!
BUT WHY DID YOU HELP US?
INSPECTOR ISHIDA HAS TO CLEAR ME OF THAT MURDER CHARGE. THE TOWNSPEOPLE WILL NOT SUPPORT ME IF THEY BELIEVE I MURDERED MERCHANT KUBO!
BESIDES, I HAVE A GRUDGE AGAINST THE BLACK GOBLIN GANG FOR FRAMING ME FOR NISHI'S CRIME!
THERE IS STILL A WARRANT FOR YOU, SO I AM ARRESTING YOU IN THE NAME OF--
HEY!
EH?
THERE MUST BE A REWARD FOR ALL THE GANG MEMBERS YOU SLEW! AFTER ALL, IT WAS I WHO LURED THEM INTO YOUR HANDS!
8.

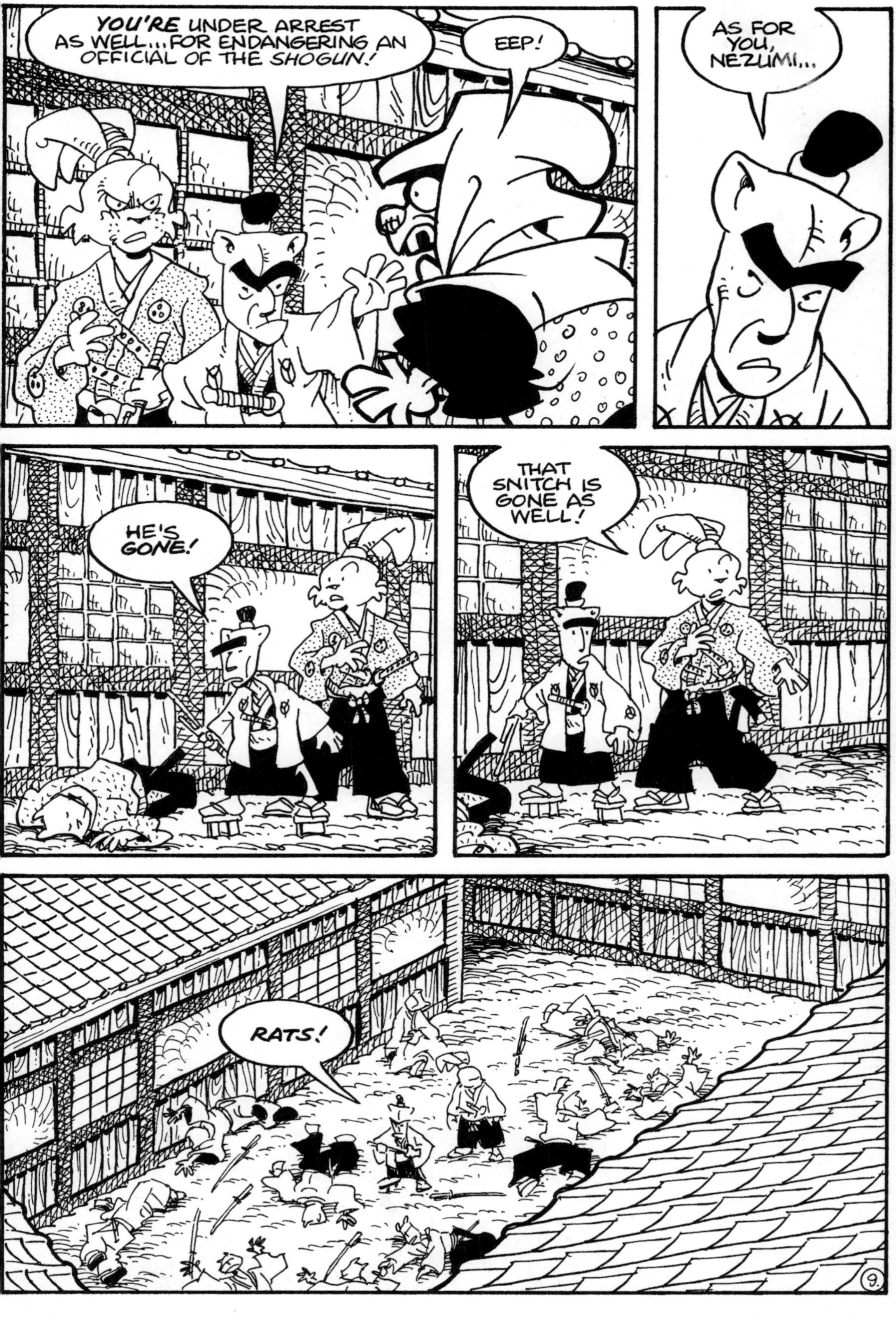
YOU'RE UNDER ARREST AS WELL...FOR ENDANGERING AN OFFICIAL OF THE SHOGUN!
EEP!
AS FOR YOU, NEZUMI...
HE'S GONE!
THAT SNITCH IS GONE AS WELL!
RATS!
9.

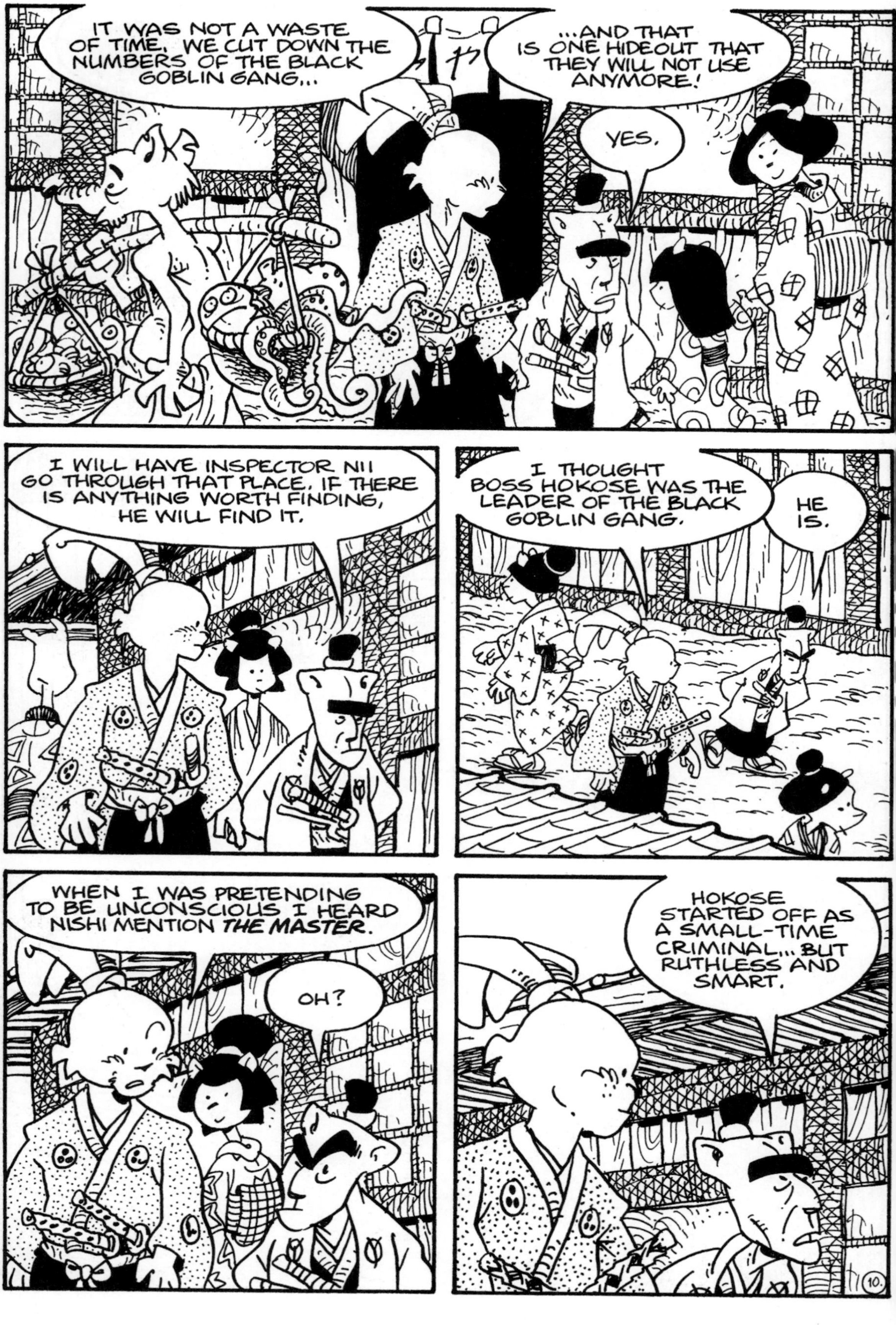
IT WAS NOT A WASTE OF TIME. WE CUT DOWN THE NUMBERS OF THE BLACK GOBLIN GANG...
...AND THAT IS ONE HIDEOUT THAT THEY WILL NOT USE ANYMORE!
YES.
I WILL HAVE INSPECTOR NII GO THROUGH THAT PLACE. IF THERE IS ANYTHING WORTH FINDING, HE WILL FIND IT.
I THOUGHT BOSS HOKOSE WAS THE LEADER OF THE BLACK GOBLIN GANG.
HE IS.
WHEN I WAS PRETENDING TO BE UNCONSCIOUS I HEARD NISHI MENTION *THE MASTER*.
OH?
HOKOSE STARTED OFF AS A SMALL-TIME CRIMINAL... BUT RUTHLESS AND SMART.
10.

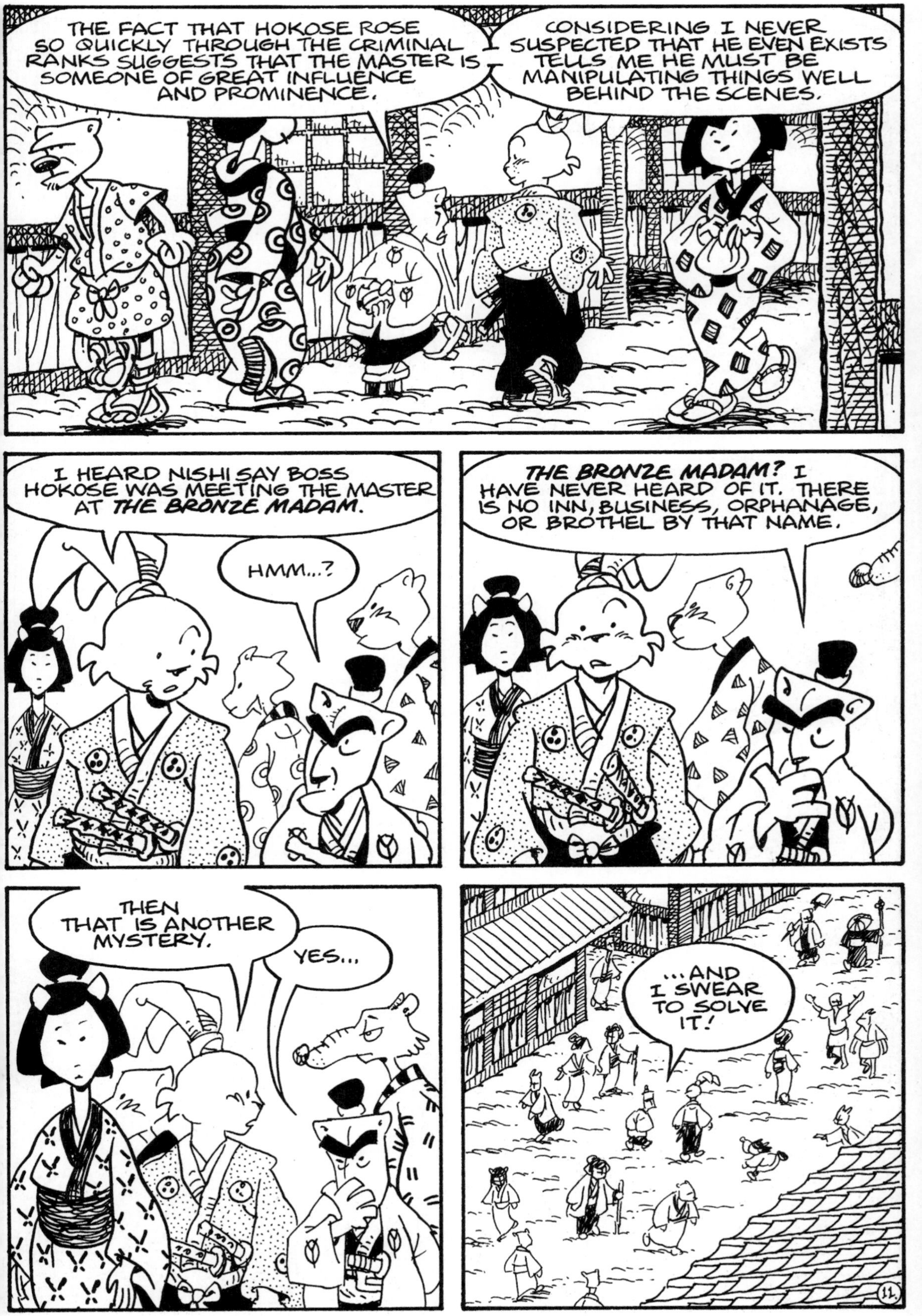
THE FACT THAT HOKOSE ROSE SO QUICKLY THROUGH THE CRIMINAL RANKS SUGGESTS THAT THE MASTER IS SOMEONE OF GREAT INFLUENCE AND PROMINENCE.
CONSIDERING I NEVER SUSPECTED THAT HE EVEN EXISTS TELLS ME HE MUST BE MANIPULATING THINGS WELL BEHIND THE SCENES.
I HEARD NISHI SAY BOSS HOKOSE WAS MEETING THE MASTER AT *THE BRONZE MADAM*.
HMM...?
THE BRONZE MADAM? I HAVE NEVER HEARD OF IT. THERE IS NO INN, BUSINESS, ORPHANAGE, OR BROTHEL BY THAT NAME.
THEN THAT IS ANOTHER MYSTERY.
YES...
...AND I SWEAR TO SOLVE IT!
11.

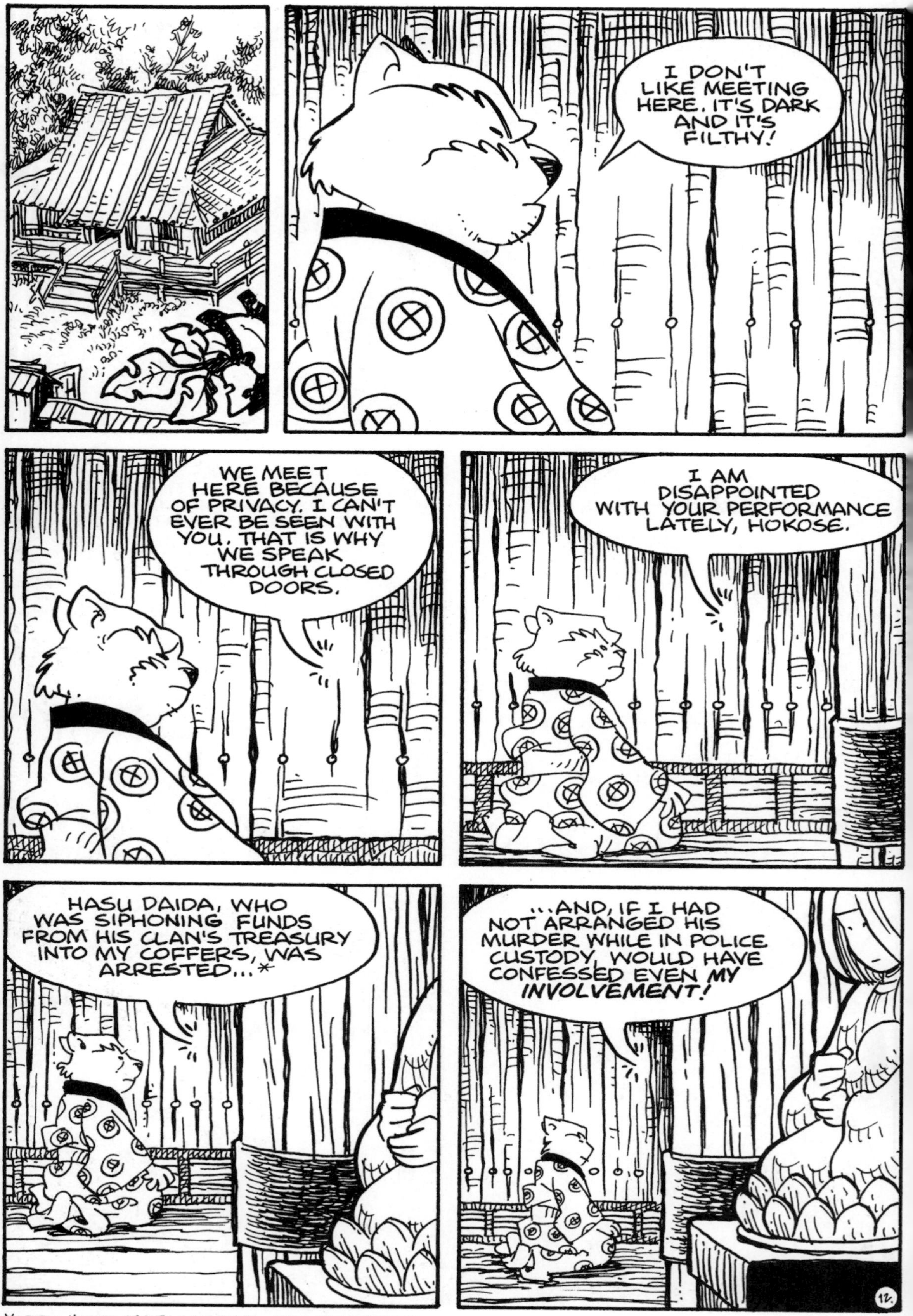
I DON'T LIKE MEETING HERE. IT'S DARK AND IT'S FILTHY!
WE MEET HERE BECAUSE OF PRIVACY. I CAN'T EVER BE SEEN WITH YOU. THAT IS WHY WE SPEAK THROUGH CLOSED DOORS.
I AM DISAPPOINTED WITH YOUR PERFORMANCE LATELY, HOKOSE.
HASU DAIDA, WHO WAS SIPHONING FUNDS FROM HIS CLAN'S TREASURY INTO MY COFFERS, WAS ARRESTED...*
...AND, IF I HAD NOT ARRANGED HIS MURDER WHILE IN POLICE CUSTODY, WOULD HAVE CONFESSED EVEN MY INVOLVEMENT!
12.

*SEE "*THE HATAMOTO'S DAUGHTER*"

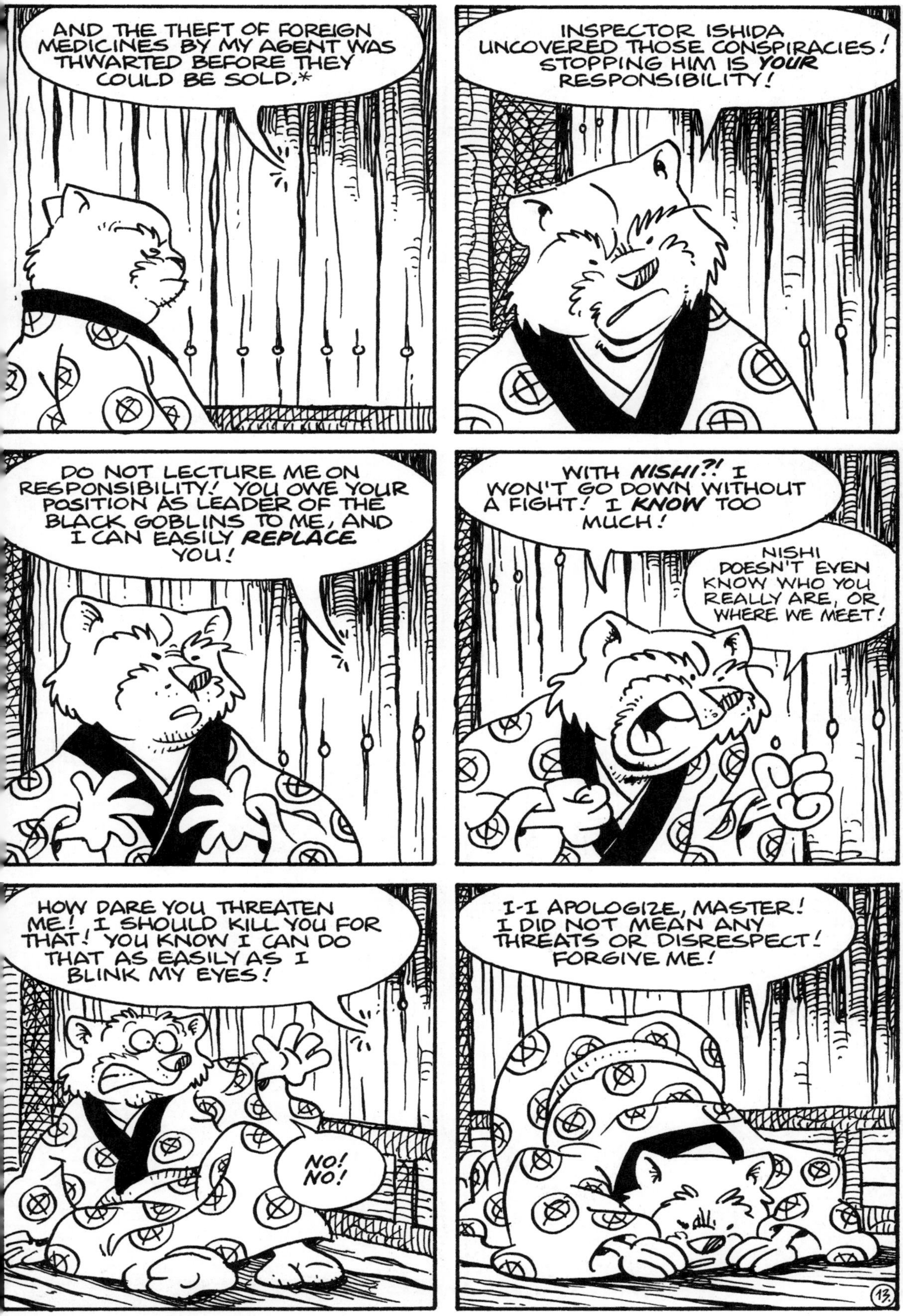
AND THE THEFT OF FOREIGN MEDICINES BY MY AGENT WAS THWARTED BEFORE THEY COULD BE SOLD.*
INSPECTOR ISHIDA UNCOVERED THOSE CONSPIRACIES! STOPPING HIM IS YOUR RESPONSIBILITY!
DO NOT LECTURE ME ON RESPONSIBILITY! YOU OWE YOUR POSITION AS LEADER OF THE BLACK GOBLINS TO ME, AND I CAN EASILY REPLACE YOU!
WITH NISHI?! I WON'T GO DOWN WITHOUT A FIGHT! I KNOW TOO MUCH!
NISHI DOESN'T EVEN KNOW WHO YOU REALLY ARE, OR WHERE WE MEET!
HOW DARE YOU THREATEN ME! I SHOULD KILL YOU FOR THAT! YOU KNOW I CAN DO THAT AS EASILY AS I BLINK MY EYES!
NO! NO!
I-I APOLOGIZE, MASTER! I DID NOT MEAN ANY THREATS OR DISRESPECT! FORGIVE ME!
13.

*SEE "THE BODY IN THE LIBRARY"

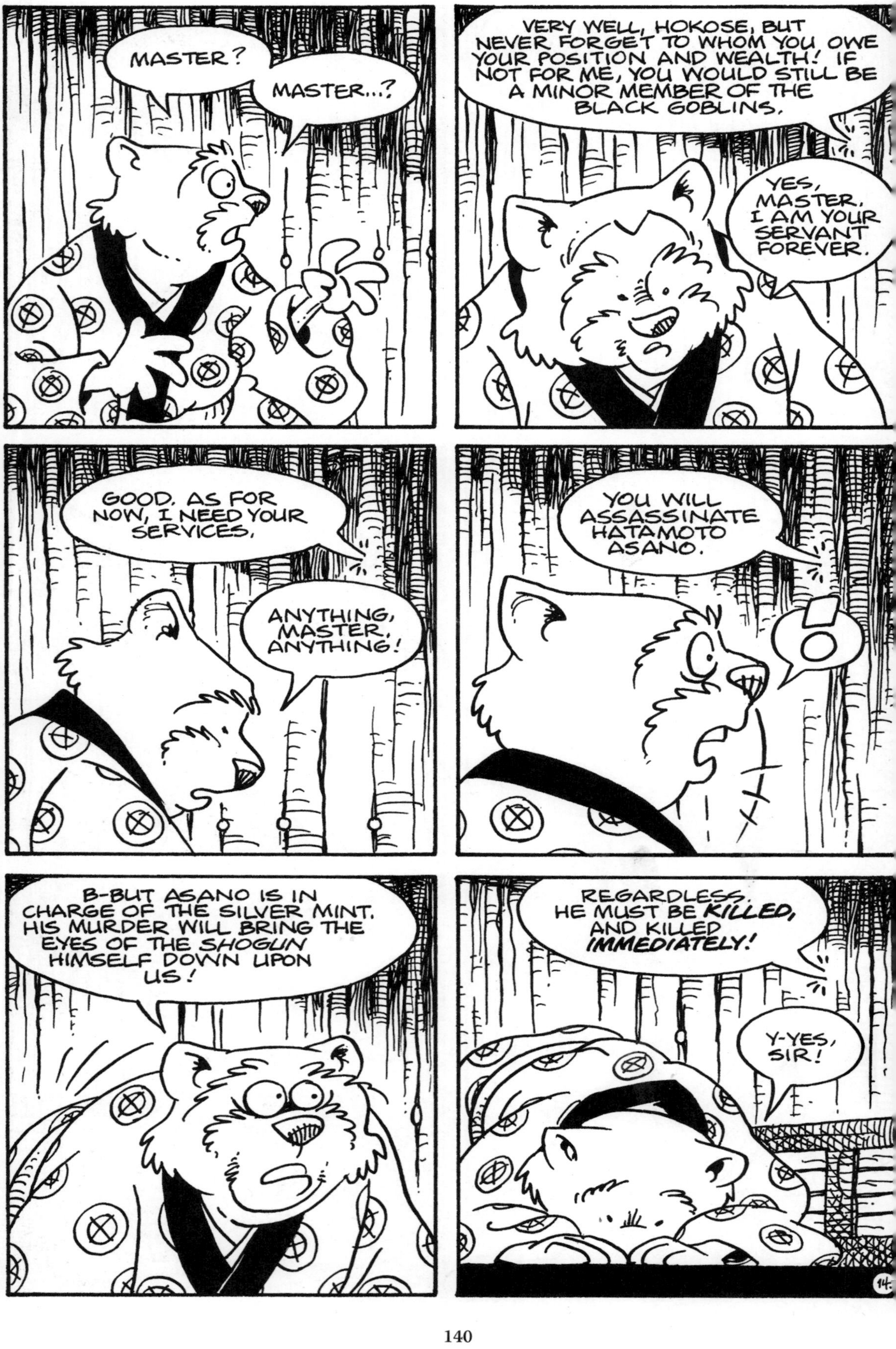
MASTER?
MASTER...?
VERY WELL, HOKOSE, BUT NEVER FORGET TO WHOM YOU OWE YOUR POSITION AND WEALTH! IF NOT FOR ME, YOU WOULD STILL BE A MINOR MEMBER OF THE BLACK GOBLINS.
YES, MASTER. I AM YOUR SERVANT FOREVER.
GOOD. AS FOR NOW, I NEED YOUR SERVICES.
ANYTHING, MASTER, ANYTHING!
YOU WILL ASSASSINATE HATAMOTO ASANO.
!
B-BUT ASANO IS IN CHARGE OF THE SILVER MINT. HIS MURDER WILL BRING THE EYES OF THE SHOGUN HIMSELF DOWN UPON US!
REGARDLESS. HE MUST BE KILLED, AND KILLED IMMEDIATELY!
Y-YES, SIR!
14.

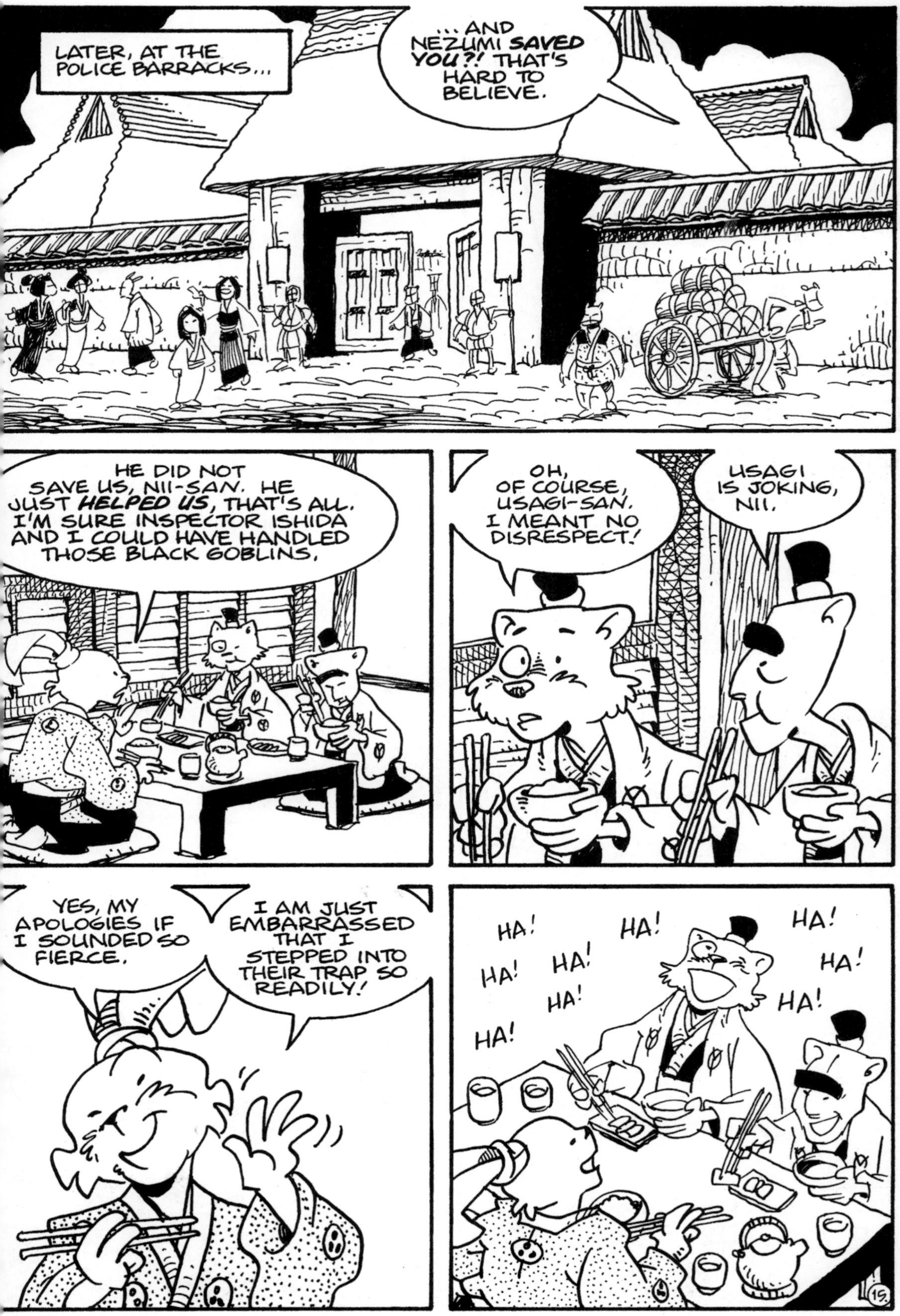
LATER, AT THE POLICE BARRACKS...
...AND NEZUMI SAVED YOU?! THAT'S HARD TO BELIEVE.
HE DID NOT SAVE US, NII-SAN. HE JUST HELPED US, THAT'S ALL. I'M SURE INSPECTOR ISHIDA AND I COULD HAVE HANDLED THOSE BLACK GOBLINS.
OH, OF COURSE, USAGI-SAN. I MEANT NO DISRESPECT!
USAGI IS JOKING, NII.
YES, MY APOLOGIES IF I SOUNDED SO FIERCE.
I AM JUST EMBARRASSED THAT I STEPPED INTO THEIR TRAP SO READILY!
HA! HA! HA! HA! HA! HA! HA! HA! HA! HA!
15.

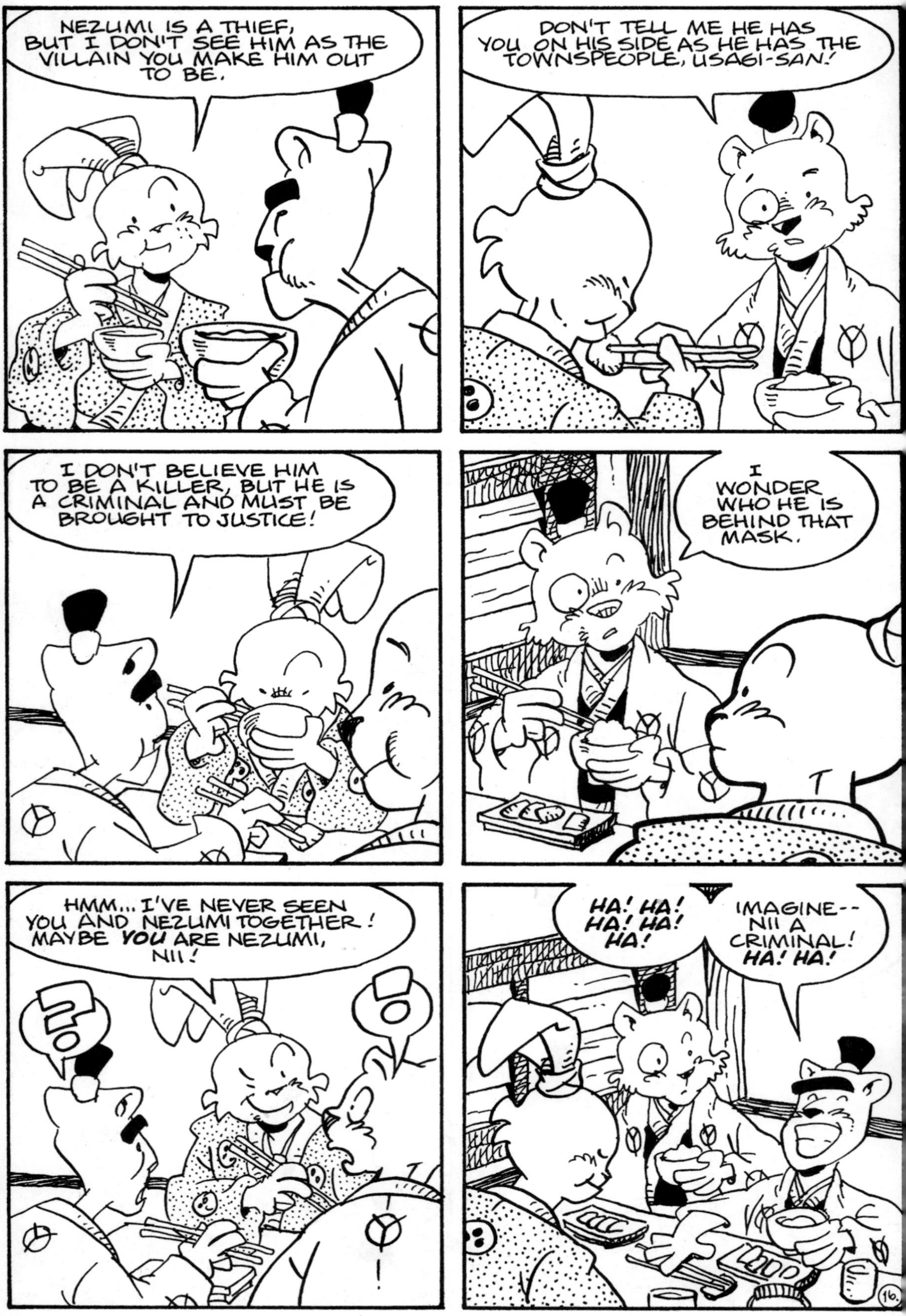
NEZUMI IS A THIEF, BUT I DON'T SEE HIM AS THE VILLAIN YOU MAKE HIM OUT TO BE.
DON'T TELL ME HE HAS YOU ON HIS SIDE AS HE HAS THE TOWNSPEOPLE, USAGI-SAN!
I DON'T BELIEVE HIM TO BE A KILLER, BUT HE IS A CRIMINAL AND MUST BE BROUGHT TO JUSTICE!
I WONDER WHO HE IS BEHIND THAT MASK.
HMM... I'VE NEVER SEEN YOU AND NEZUMI TOGETHER! MAYBE **YOU** ARE NEZUMI, NII!
?!
!
HA! HA! HA! HA! HA!
IMAGINE-- NII A CRIMINAL! **HA! HA!**
16.

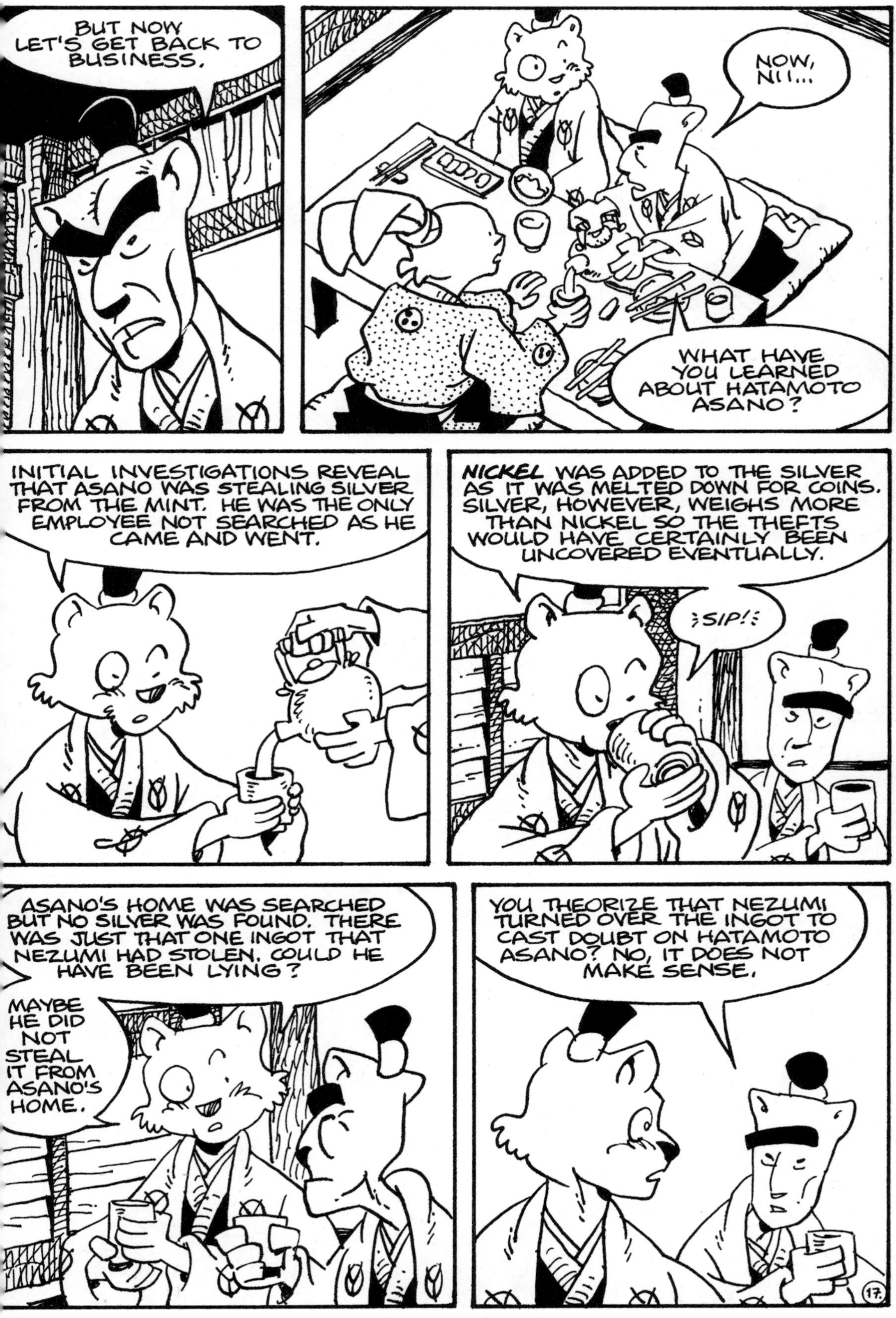
BUT NOW LET'S GET BACK TO BUSINESS.
NOW, NII...
WHAT HAVE YOU LEARNED ABOUT HATAMOTO ASANO?
INITIAL INVESTIGATIONS REVEAL THAT ASANO WAS STEALING SILVER FROM THE MINT. HE WAS THE ONLY EMPLOYEE NOT SEARCHED AS HE CAME AND WENT.
NICKEL WAS ADDED TO THE SILVER AS IT WAS MELTED DOWN FOR COINS. SILVER, HOWEVER, WEIGHS MORE THAN NICKEL SO THE THEFTS WOULD HAVE CERTAINLY BEEN UNCOVERED EVENTUALLY.
SIP!
ASANO'S HOME WAS SEARCHED BUT NO SILVER WAS FOUND. THERE WAS JUST THAT ONE INGOT THAT NEZUMI HAD STOLEN. COULD HE HAVE BEEN LYING?
MAYBE HE DID NOT STEAL IT FROM ASANO'S HOME.
YOU THEORIZE THAT NEZUMI TURNED OVER THE INGOT TO CAST DOUBT ON HATAMOTO ASANO? NO, IT DOES NOT MAKE SENSE.
17.

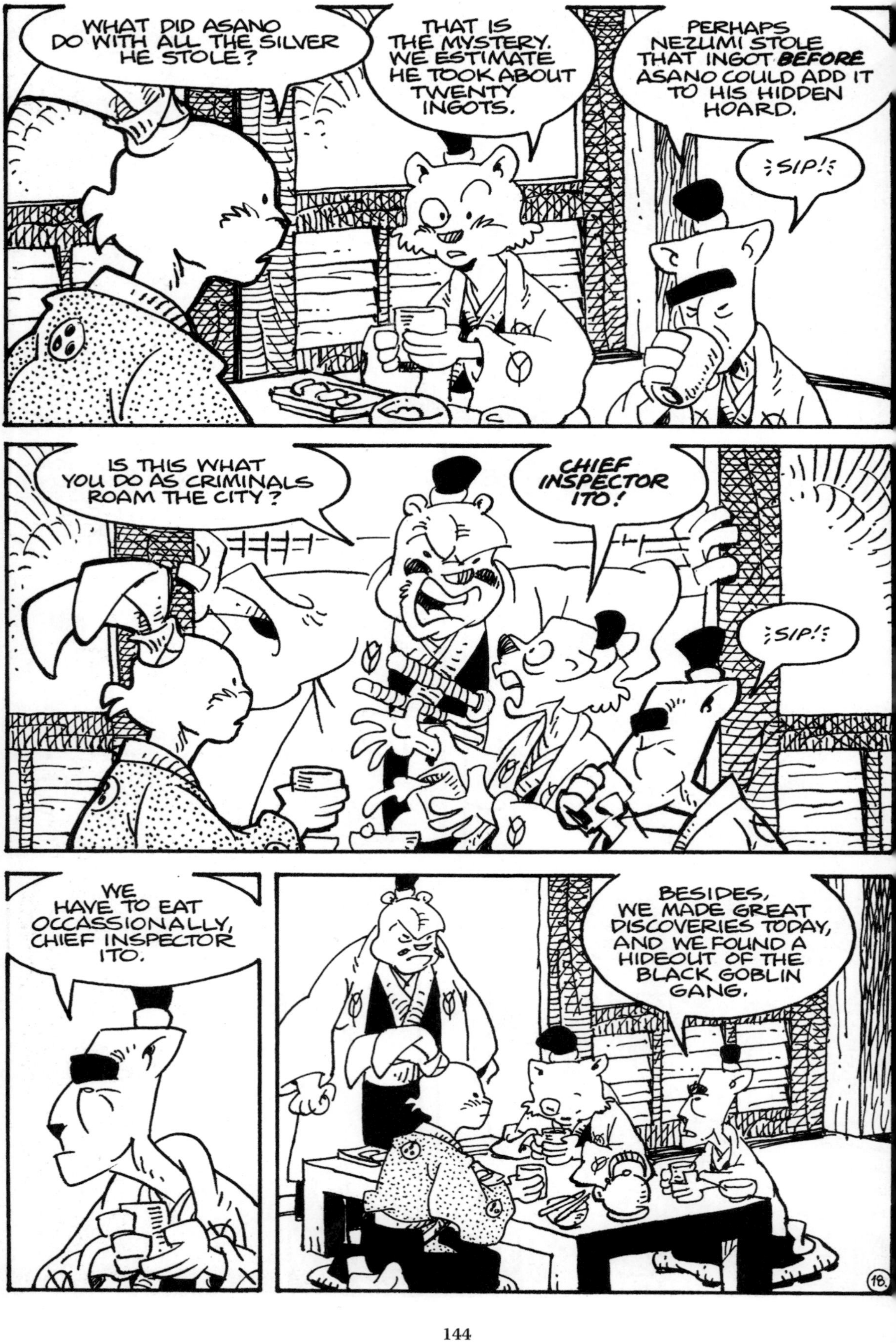
WHAT DID ASANO DO WITH ALL THE SILVER HE STOLE?
THAT IS THE MYSTERY. WE ESTIMATE HE TOOK ABOUT TWENTY INGOTS.
PERHAPS NEZUMI STOLE THAT INGOT BEFORE ASANO COULD ADD IT TO HIS HIDDEN HOARD.
SIP!
IS THIS WHAT YOU DO AS CRIMINALS ROAM THE CITY?
CHIEF INSPECTOR ITO!
SIP!
WE HAVE TO EAT OCCASSIONALLY, CHIEF INSPECTOR ITO.
BESIDES, WE MADE GREAT DISCOVERIES TODAY, AND WE FOUND A HIDEOUT OF THE BLACK GOBLIN GANG.
18.

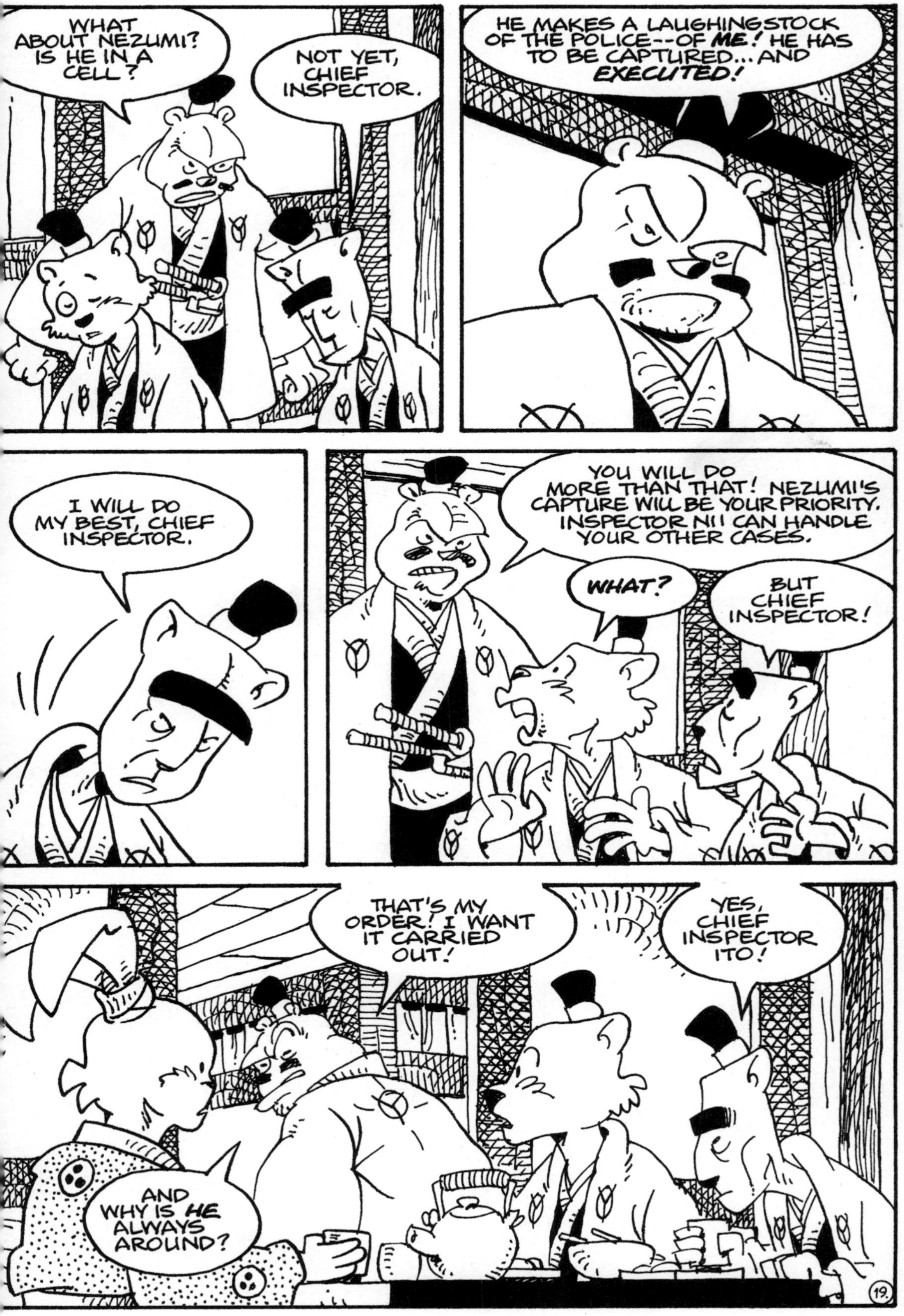
WHAT ABOUT NEZUMI? IS HE IN A CELL?
NOT YET, CHIEF INSPECTOR.
HE MAKES A LAUGHINGSTOCK OF THE POLICE--OF ME! HE HAS TO BE CAPTURED... AND EXECUTED!
I WILL DO MY BEST, CHIEF INSPECTOR.
YOU WILL DO MORE THAN THAT! NEZUMI'S CAPTURE WILL BE YOUR PRIORITY. INSPECTOR NII CAN HANDLE YOUR OTHER CASES.
WHAT?
BUT CHIEF INSPECTOR!
THAT'S MY ORDER! I WANT IT CARRIED OUT!
YES, CHIEF INSPECTOR ITO!
AND WHY IS HE ALWAYS AROUND?
19.

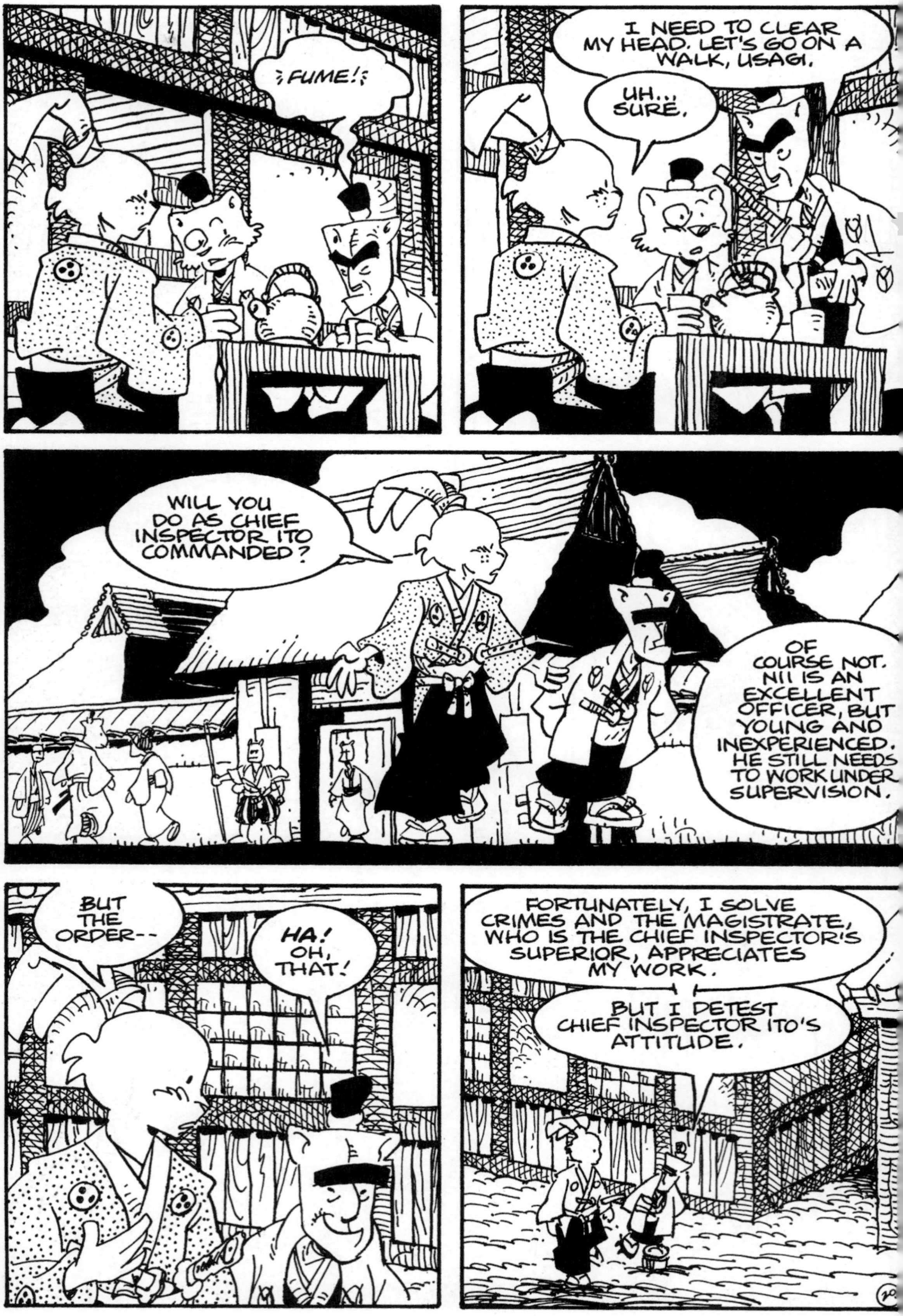
FUME!
I NEED TO CLEAR MY HEAD. LET'S GO ON A WALK, USAGI.
UH... SURE.
WILL YOU DO AS CHIEF INSPECTOR ITO COMMANDED?
OF COURSE NOT. NII IS AN EXCELLENT OFFICER, BUT YOUNG AND INEXPERIENCED. HE STILL NEEDS TO WORK UNDER SUPERVISION.
BUT THE ORDER--
HA! OH, THAT!
FORTUNATELY, I SOLVE CRIMES AND THE MAGISTRATE, WHO IS THE CHIEF INSPECTOR'S SUPERIOR, APPRECIATES MY WORK.
BUT I DETEST CHIEF INSPECTOR ITO'S ATTITUDE.

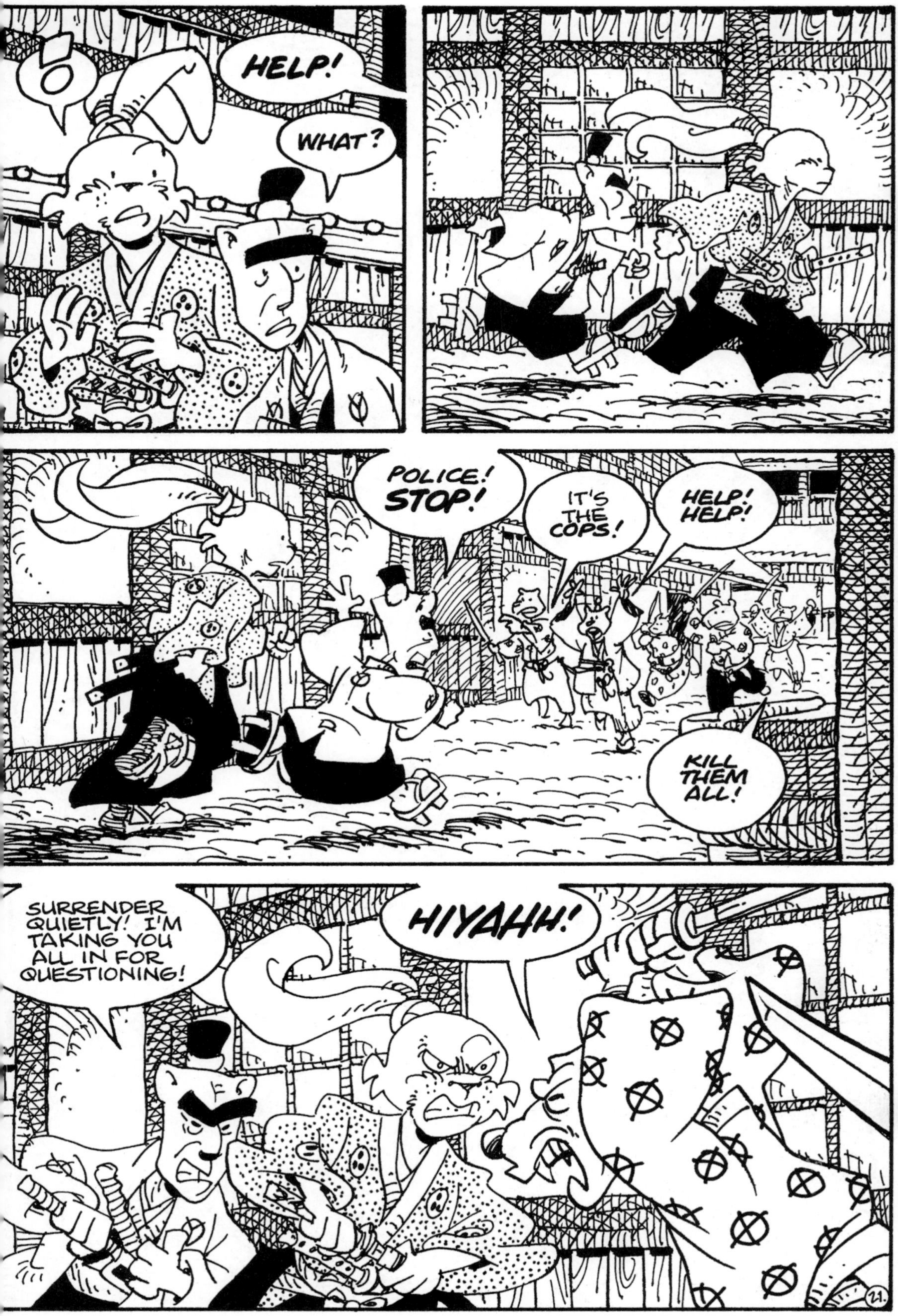

HELP!
WHAT?
POLICE! STOP!
IT'S THE COPS!
HELP! HELP!
KILL THEM ALL!
SURRENDER QUIETLY! I'M TAKING YOU ALL IN FOR QUESTIONING!
HIYAHH!
21.

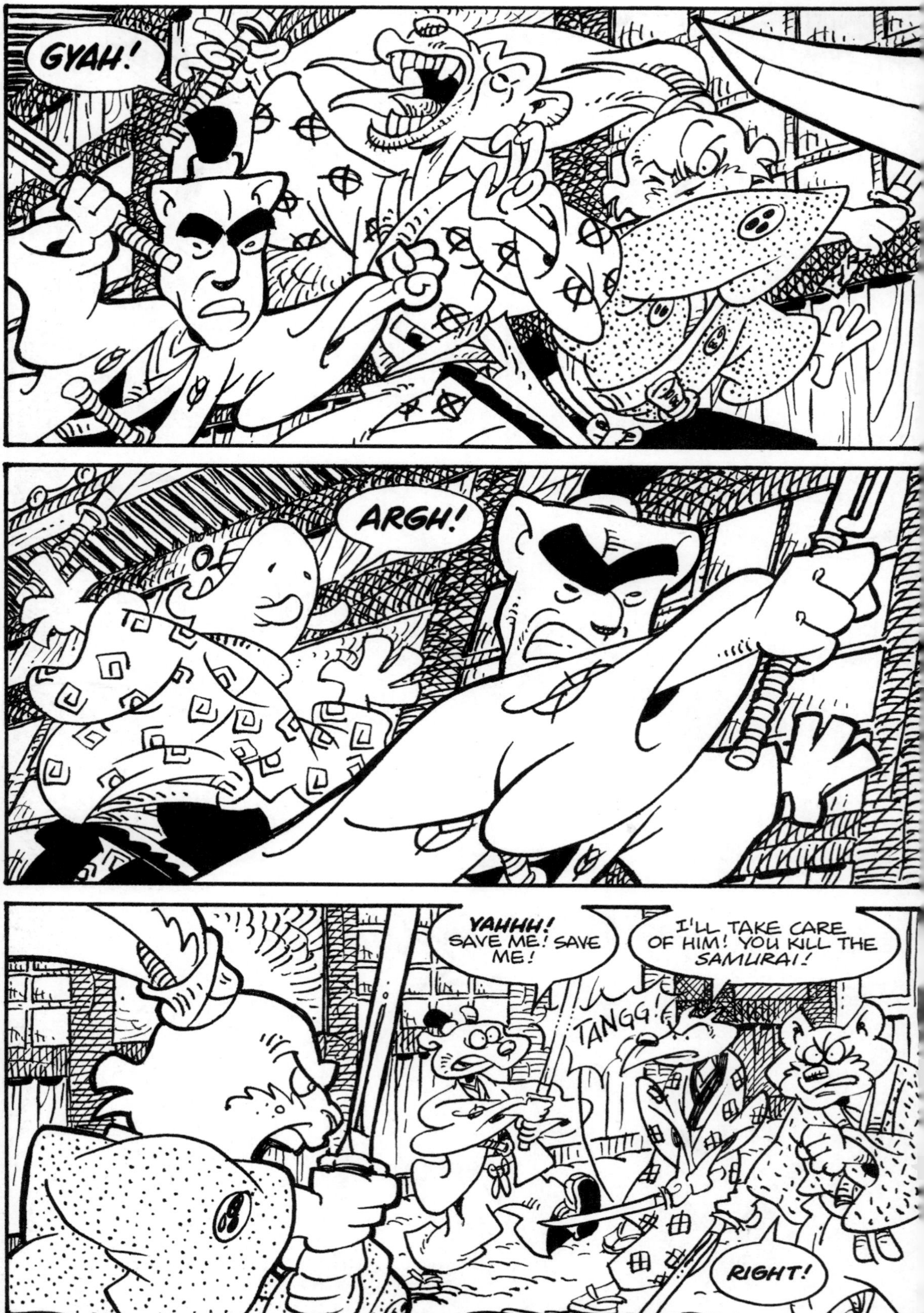
GYAH!
ARGH!
YAHHH! SAVE ME! SAVE ME!
I'LL TAKE CARE OF HIM! YOU KILL THE SAMURAI!
TANGG!
RIGHT!
22

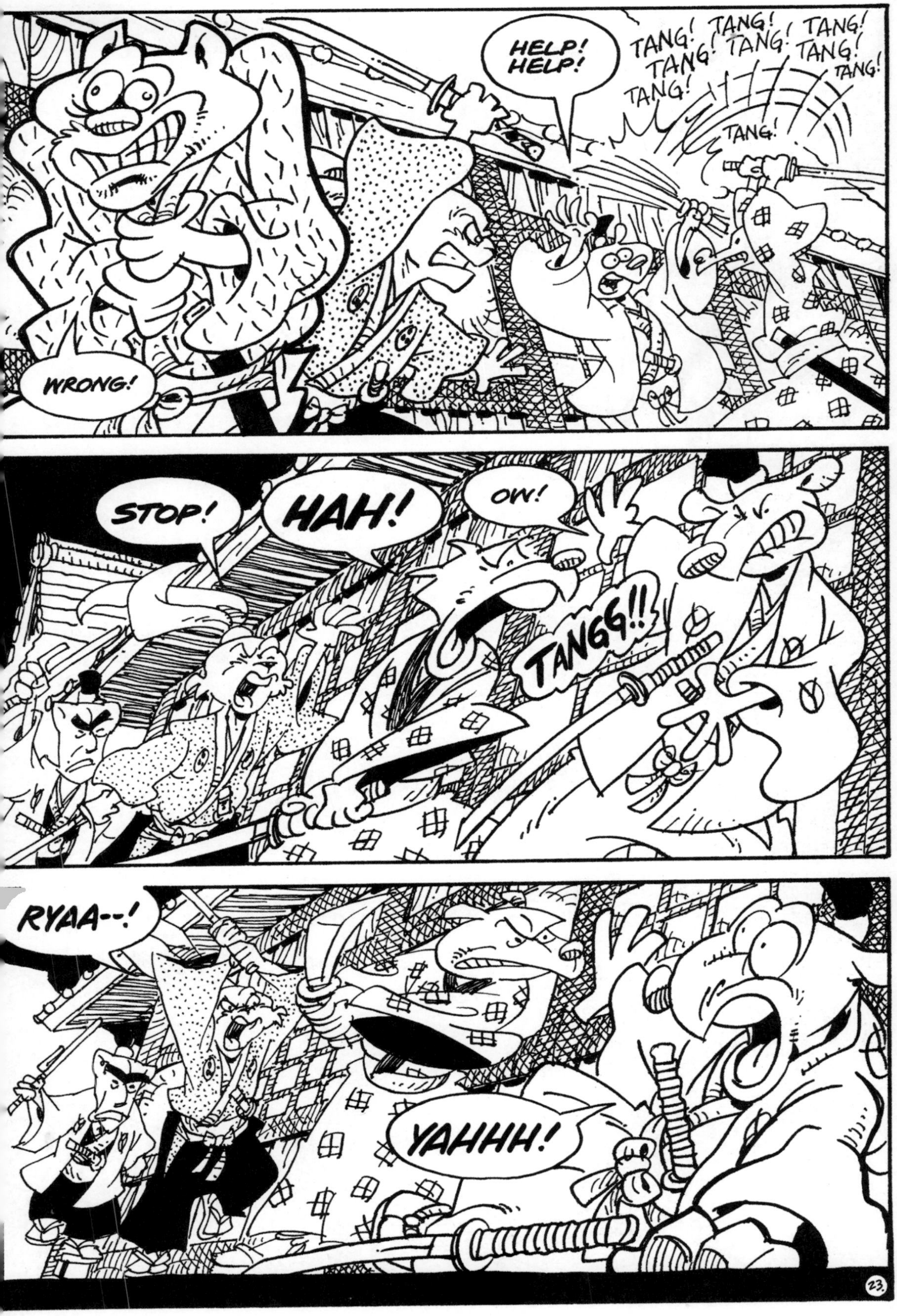
HELP! HELP!
TANG! TANG! TANG! TANG! TANG! TANG! TANG! TANG! TANG!
WRONG!
STOP!
HAH!
OW!
TANGG!!
RYAA--!
YAHHH!
23.

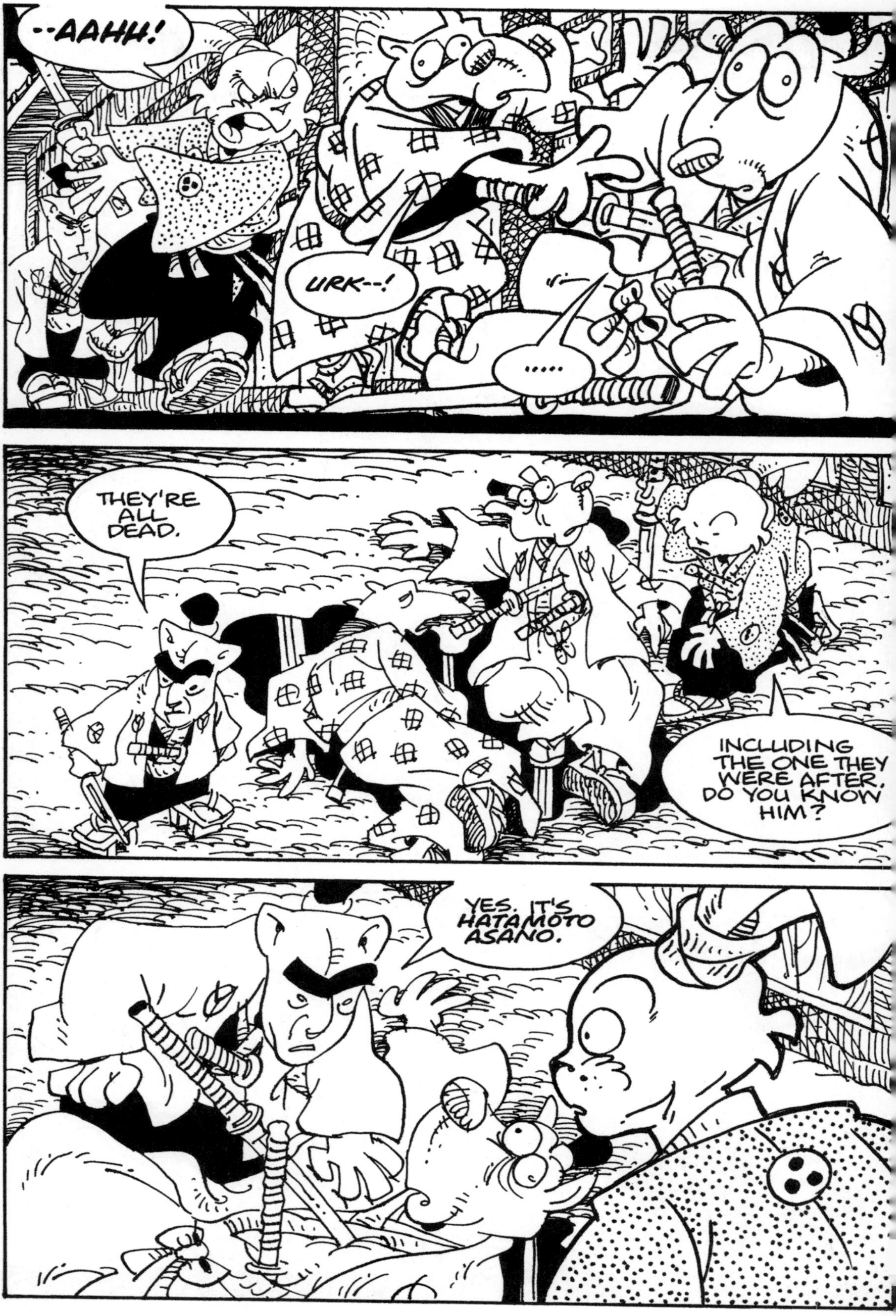
--AAHH!
URK--!
.....
THEY'RE ALL DEAD.
INCLUDING THE ONE THEY WERE AFTER. DO YOU KNOW HIM?
YES. IT'S HATAMOTO ASANO.

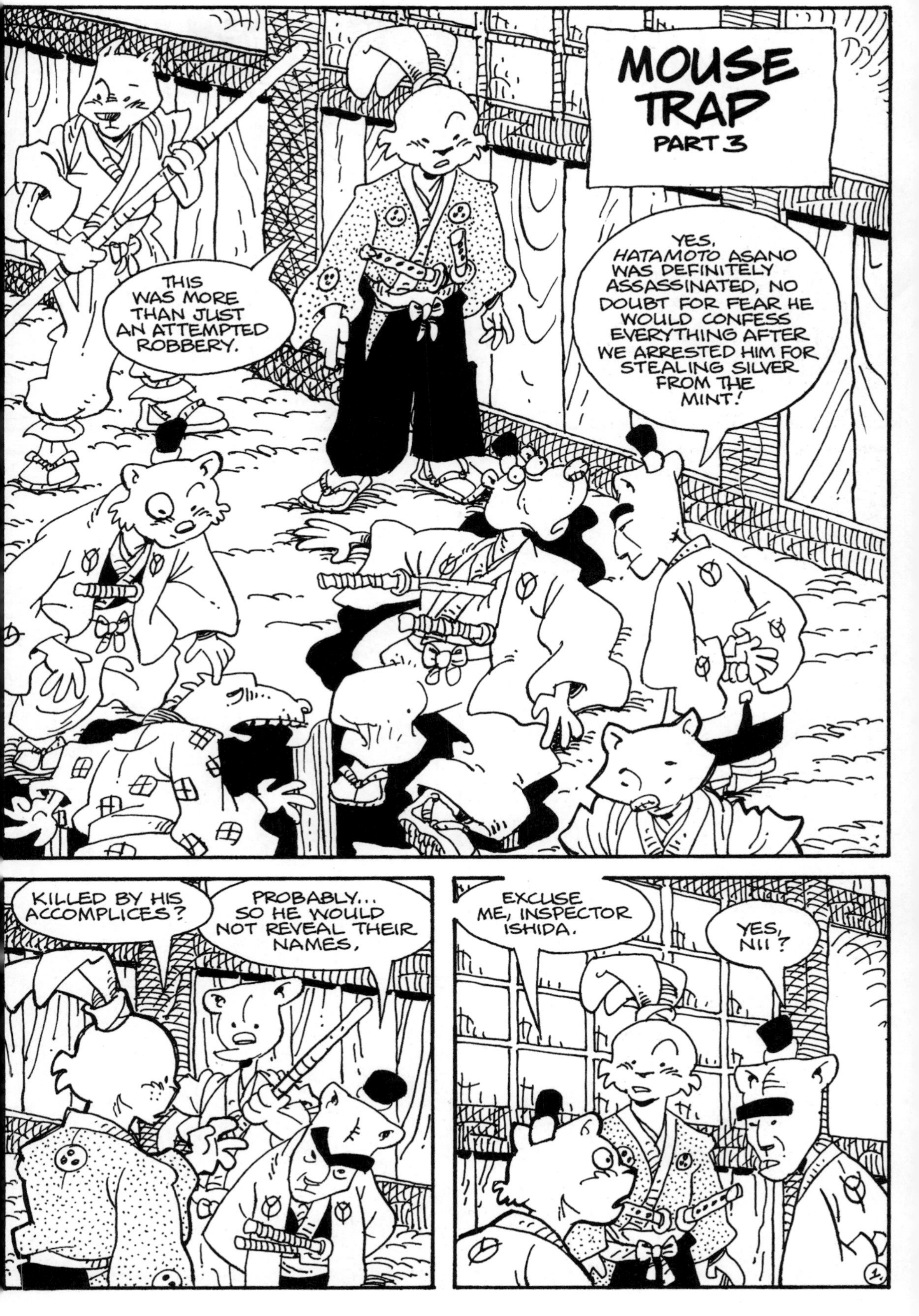

MOUSE TRAP
PART 3
THIS WAS MORE THAN JUST AN ATTEMPTED ROBBERY.
YES, HATAMOTO ASANO WAS DEFINITELY ASSASSINATED, NO DOUBT FOR FEAR HE WOULD CONFESS EVERYTHING AFTER WE ARRESTED HIM FOR STEALING SILVER FROM THE MINT!
KILLED BY HIS ACCOMPLICES?
PROBABLY... SO HE WOULD NOT REVEAL THEIR NAMES.
EXCUSE ME, INSPECTOR ISHIDA.
YES, NII?
1

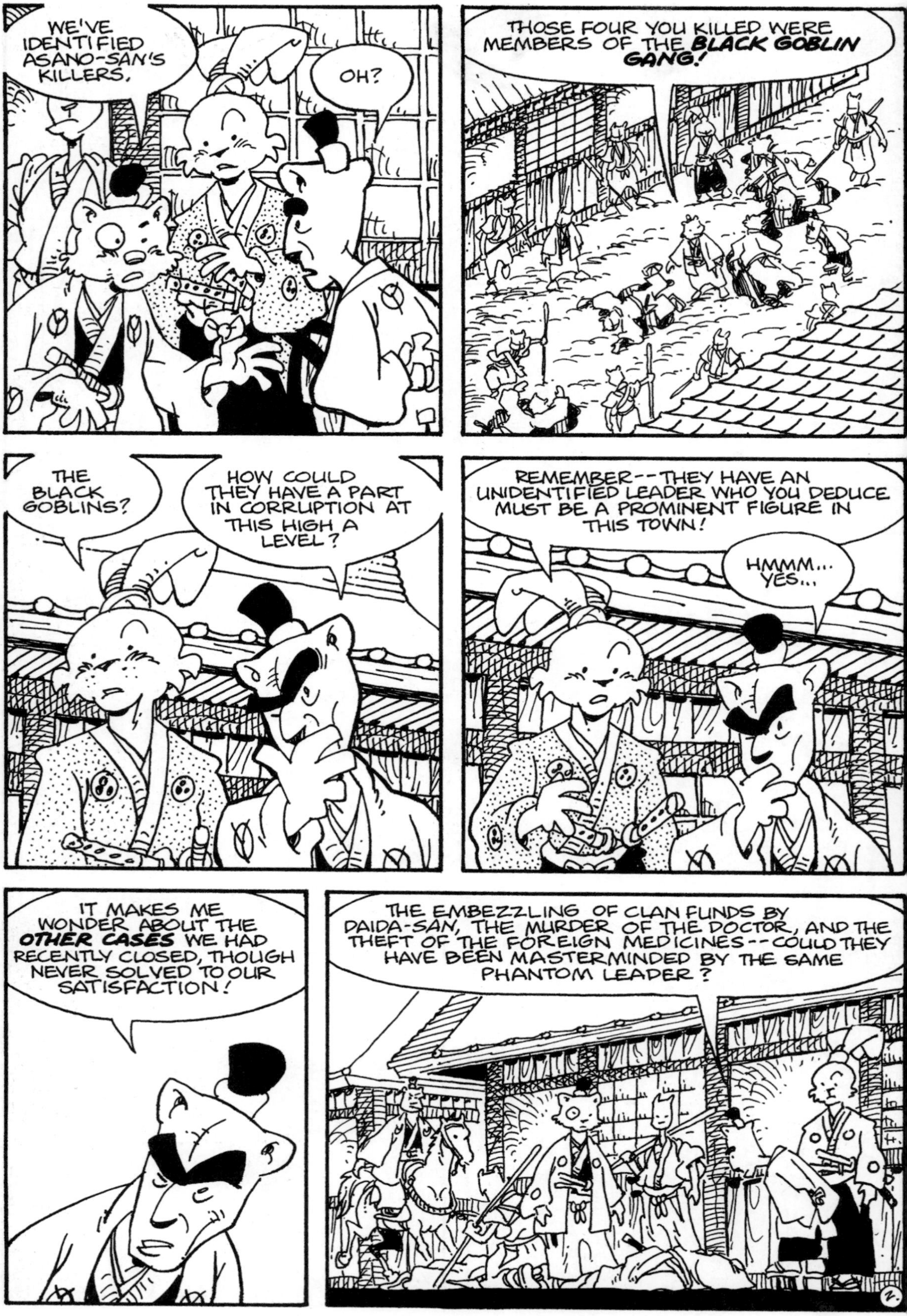
WE'VE IDENTIFIED ASANO-SAN'S KILLERS.
OH?
THOSE FOUR YOU KILLED WERE MEMBERS OF THE BLACK GOBLIN GANG!
THE BLACK GOBLINS?
HOW COULD THEY HAVE A PART IN CORRUPTION AT THIS HIGH A LEVEL?
REMEMBER--THEY HAVE AN UNIDENTIFIED LEADER WHO YOU DEDUCE MUST BE A PROMINENT FIGURE IN THIS TOWN!
HMMM... YES...
IT MAKES ME WONDER ABOUT THE OTHER CASES WE HAD RECENTLY CLOSED, THOUGH NEVER SOLVED TO OUR SATISFACTION!
THE EMBEZZLING OF CLAN FUNDS BY DAIDA-SAN, THE MURDER OF THE DOCTOR, AND THE THEFT OF THE FOREIGN MEDICINES--COULD THEY HAVE BEEN MASTERMINDED BY THE SAME PHANTOM LEADER?

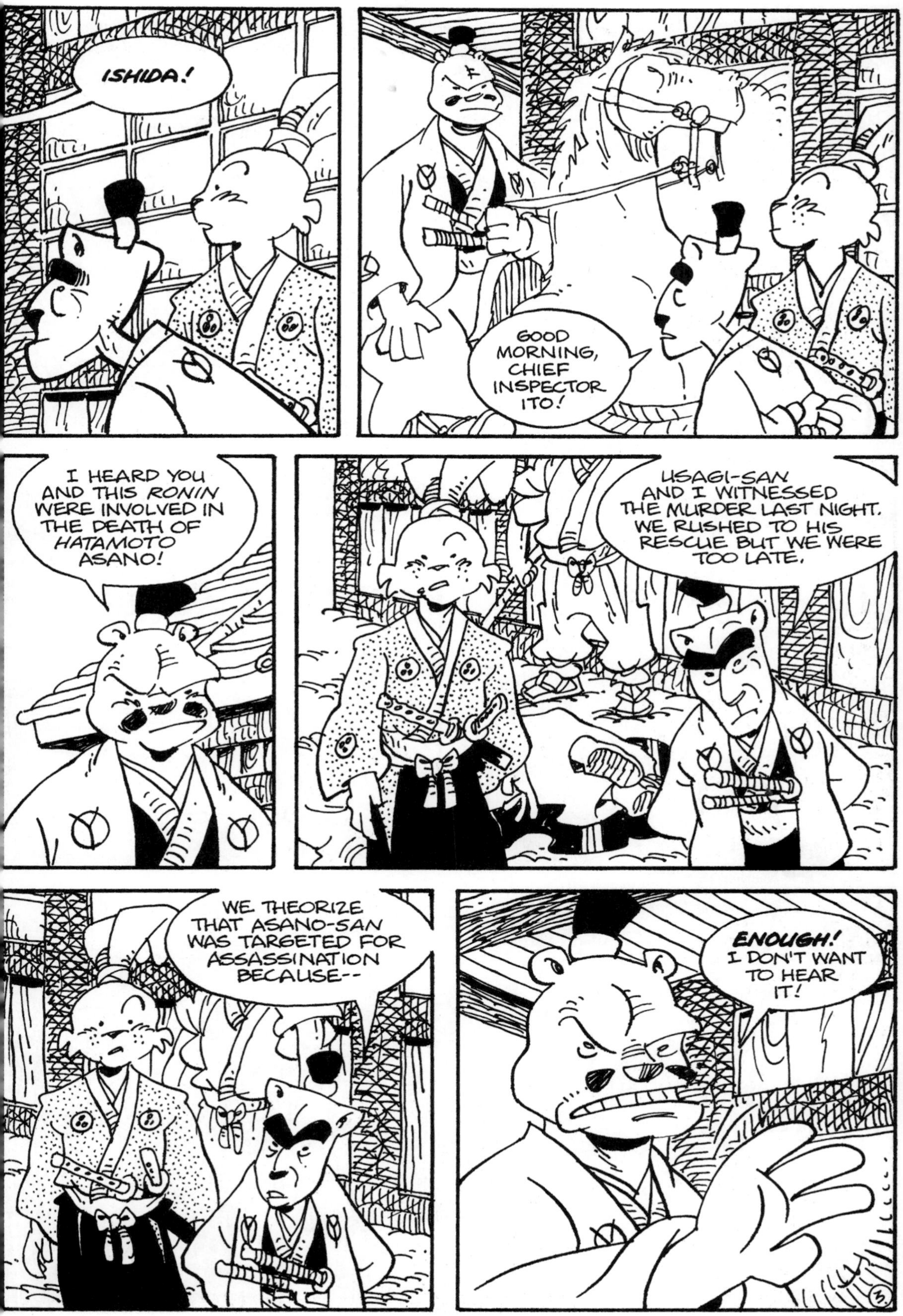
ISHIDA!
GOOD MORNING, CHIEF INSPECTOR ITO!
I HEARD YOU AND THIS *RONIN* WERE INVOLVED IN THE DEATH OF *HATAMOTO* ASANO!
USAGI-SAN AND I WITNESSED THE MURDER LAST NIGHT. WE RUSHED TO HIS RESCUE BUT WE WERE TOO LATE.
WE THEORIZE THAT ASANO-SAN WAS TARGETED FOR ASSASSINATION BECAUSE--
ENOUGH! I DON'T WANT TO HEAR IT!
3.

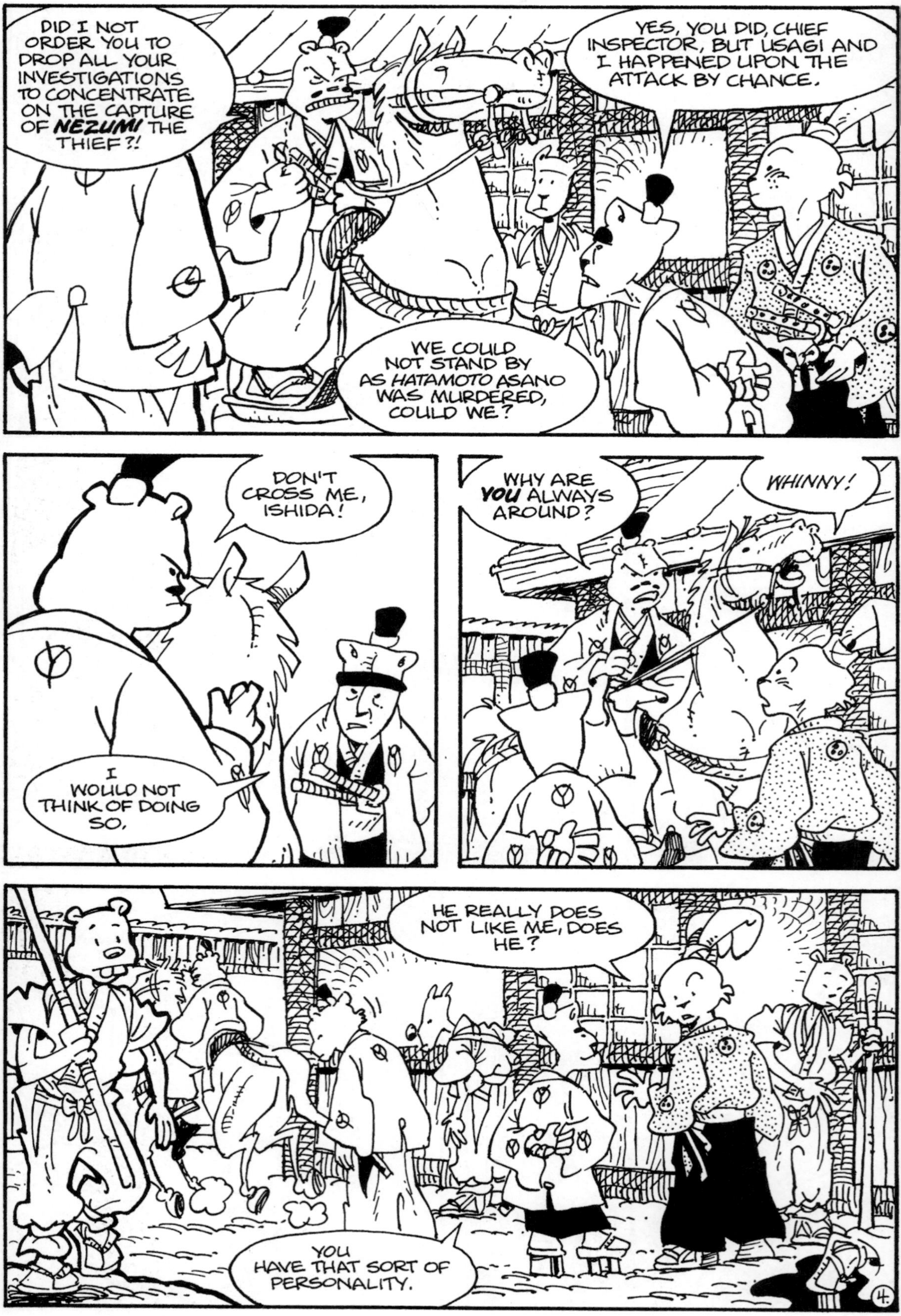
DID I NOT ORDER YOU TO DROP ALL YOUR INVESTIGATIONS TO CONCENTRATE ON THE CAPTURE OF NEZUMI THE THIEF?!
YES, YOU DID, CHIEF INSPECTOR, BUT USAGI AND I HAPPENED UPON THE ATTACK BY CHANCE.
WE COULD NOT STAND BY AS HATAMOTO ASANO WAS MURDERED, COULD WE?
DON'T CROSS ME, ISHIDA!
I WOULD NOT THINK OF DOING SO.
WHY ARE YOU ALWAYS AROUND?
WHINNY!
HE REALLY DOES NOT LIKE ME, DOES HE?
YOU HAVE THAT SORT OF PERSONALITY.
4.

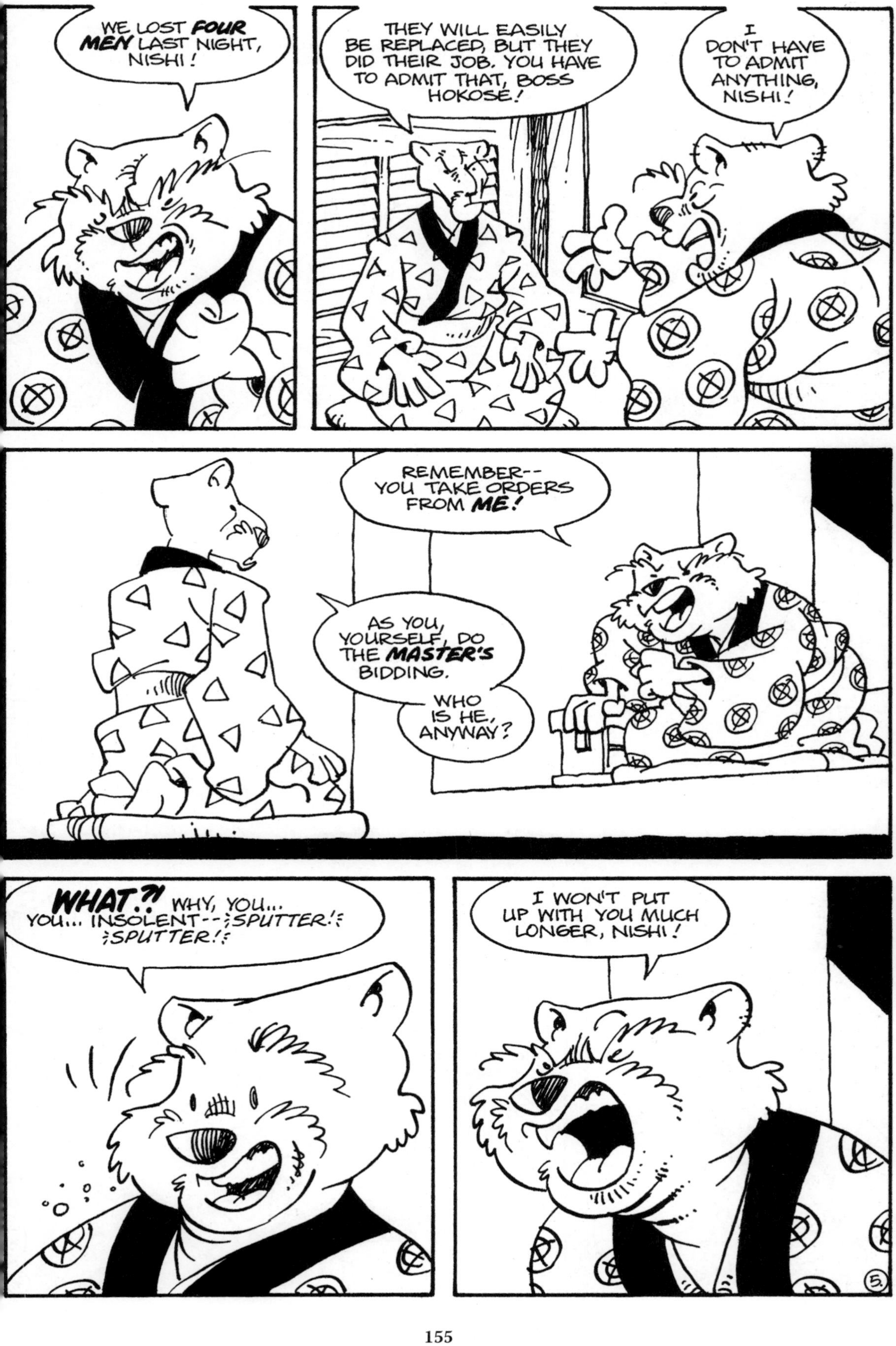
WE LOST FOUR MEN LAST NIGHT, NISHI!
THEY WILL EASILY BE REPLACED, BUT THEY DID THEIR JOB. YOU HAVE TO ADMIT THAT, BOSS HOKOSE!
I DON'T HAVE TO ADMIT ANYTHING, NISHI!
REMEMBER-- YOU TAKE ORDERS FROM ME!
AS YOU, YOURSELF, DO THE MASTER'S BIDDING.
WHO IS HE, ANYWAY?
WHAT?! WHY, YOU... YOU... INSOLENT-- SPUTTER! SPUTTER!
I WON'T PUT UP WITH YOU MUCH LONGER, NISHI!
5.

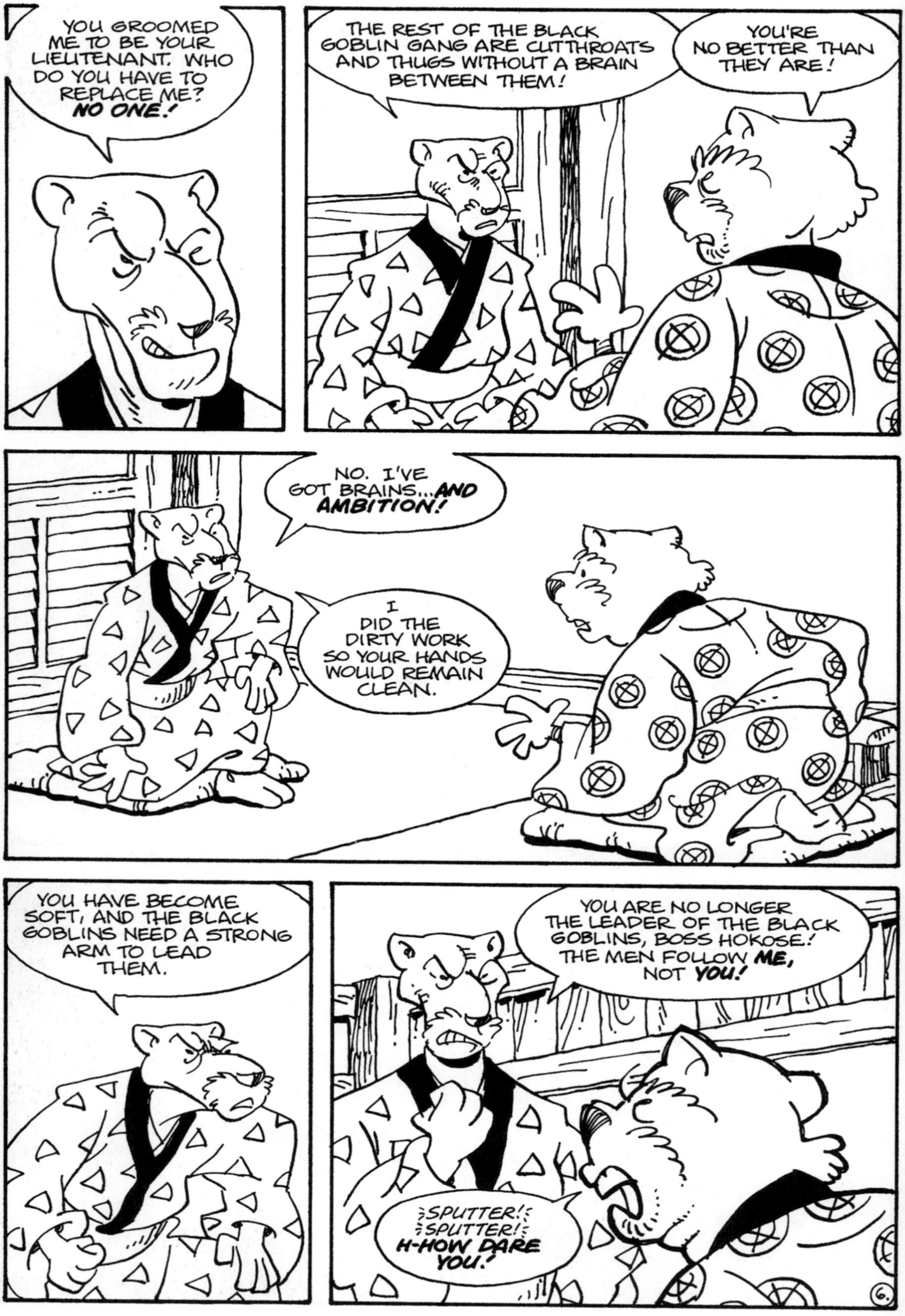
YOU GROOMED ME TO BE YOUR LIEUTENANT. WHO DO YOU HAVE TO REPLACE ME? **NO ONE!**
THE REST OF THE BLACK GOBLIN GANG ARE CUTTHROATS AND THUGS WITHOUT A BRAIN BETWEEN THEM!
YOU'RE NO BETTER THAN THEY ARE!
NO. I'VE GOT BRAINS... **AND AMBITION!**
I DID THE DIRTY WORK SO YOUR HANDS WOULD REMAIN CLEAN.
YOU HAVE BECOME SOFT, AND THE BLACK GOBLINS NEED A STRONG ARM TO LEAD THEM.
YOU ARE NO LONGER THE LEADER OF THE BLACK GOBLINS, BOSS HOKOSE! THE MEN FOLLOW **ME,** NOT **YOU!**
SPUTTER! SPUTTER! **H-HOW DARE YOU!**
6.

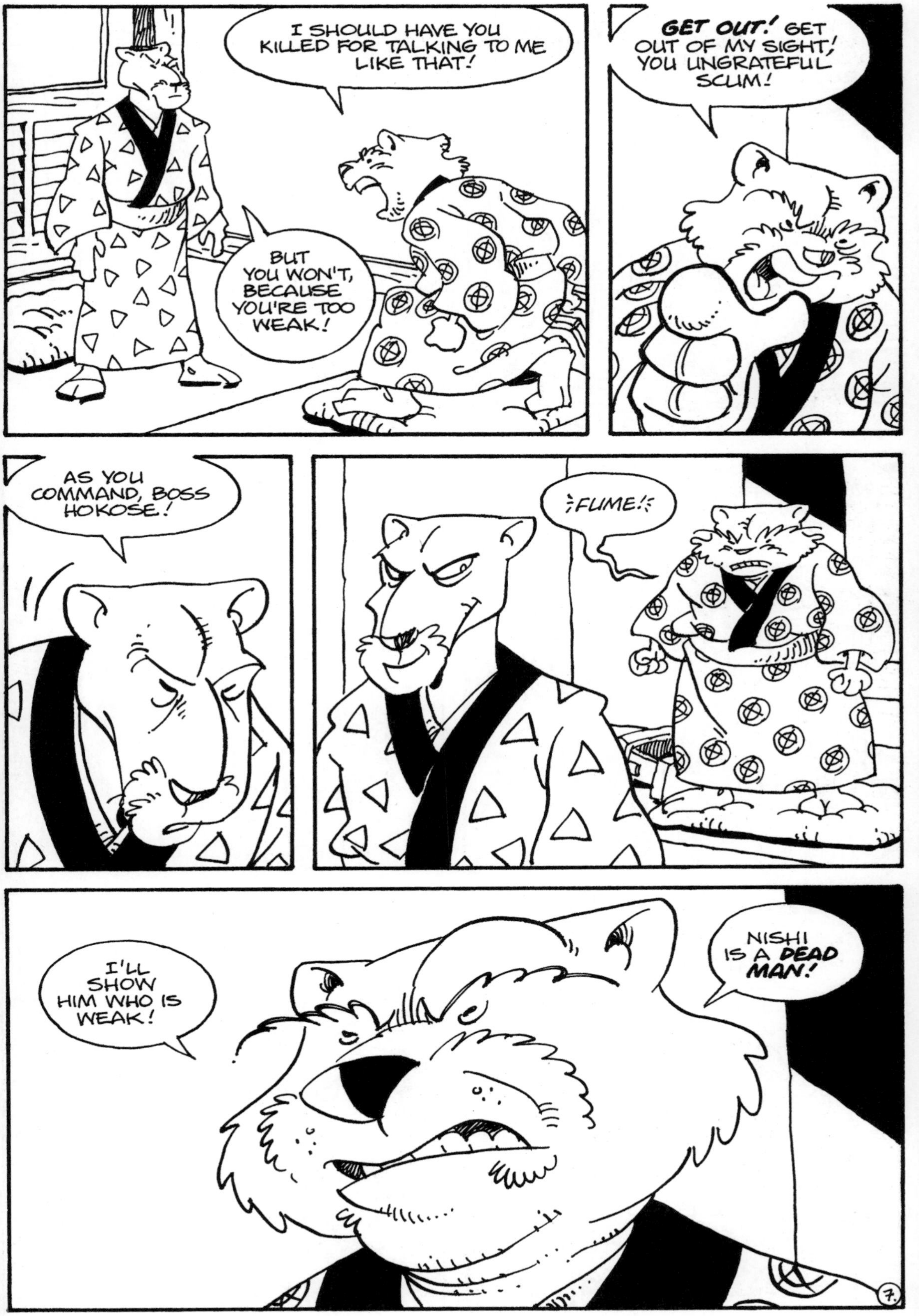
I SHOULD HAVE YOU KILLED FOR TALKING TO ME LIKE THAT!
BUT YOU WON'T, BECAUSE YOU'RE TOO WEAK!
GET OUT! GET OUT OF MY SIGHT! YOU UNGRATEFUL SCUM!
AS YOU COMMAND, BOSS HOKOSE!
FUME!
I'LL SHOW HIM WHO IS WEAK!
NISHI IS A DEAD MAN!
7.

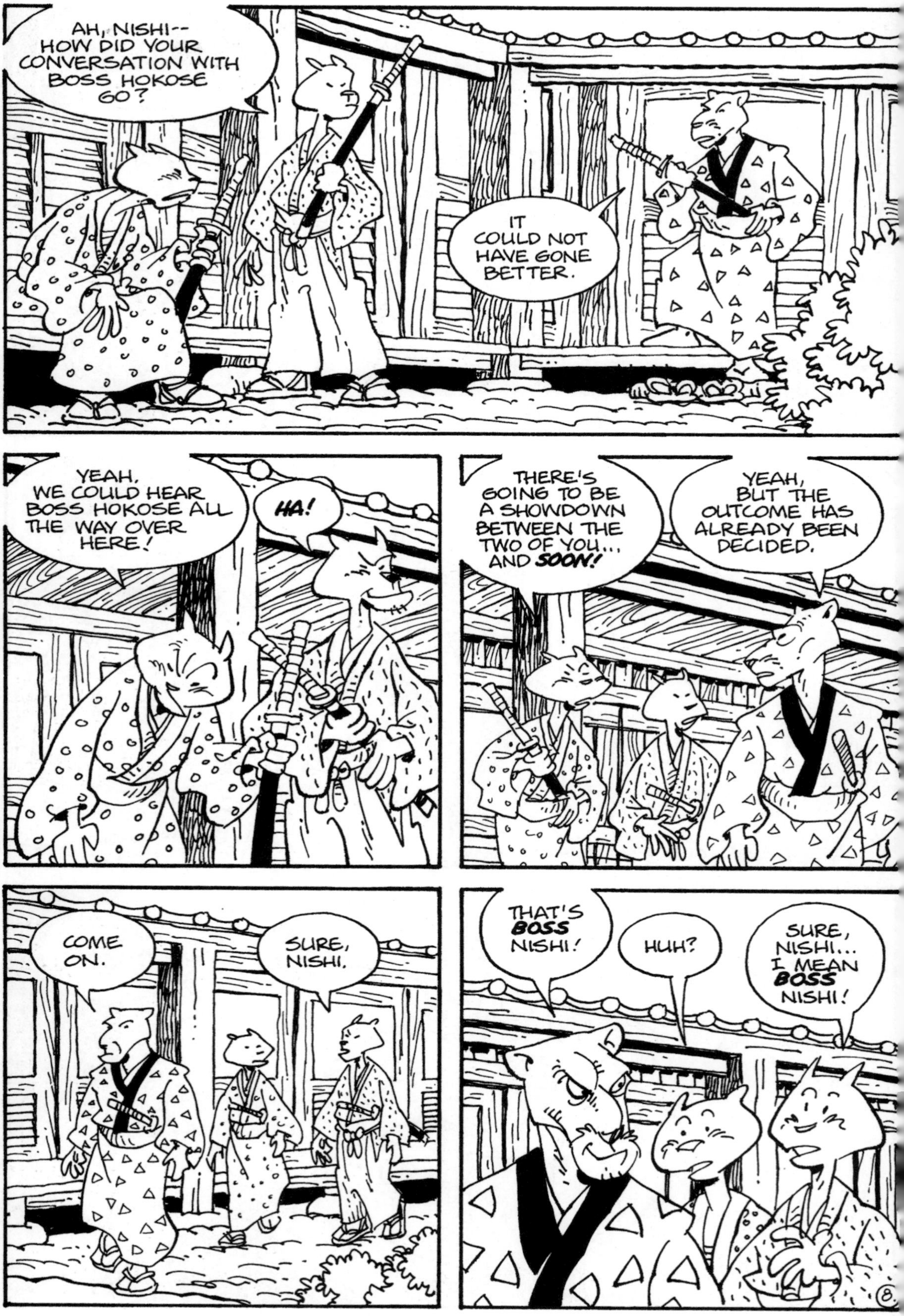
AH, NISHI--
HOW DID YOUR CONVERSATION WITH BOSS HOKOSE GO?
IT COULD NOT HAVE GONE BETTER.
YEAH, WE COULD HEAR BOSS HOKOSE ALL THE WAY OVER HERE!
HA!
THERE'S GOING TO BE A SHOWDOWN BETWEEN THE TWO OF YOU... AND SOON!
YEAH, BUT THE OUTCOME HAS ALREADY BEEN DECIDED.
COME ON.
SURE, NISHI.
THAT'S BOSS NISHI!
HUH?
SURE, NISHI... I MEAN BOSS NISHI!
8.

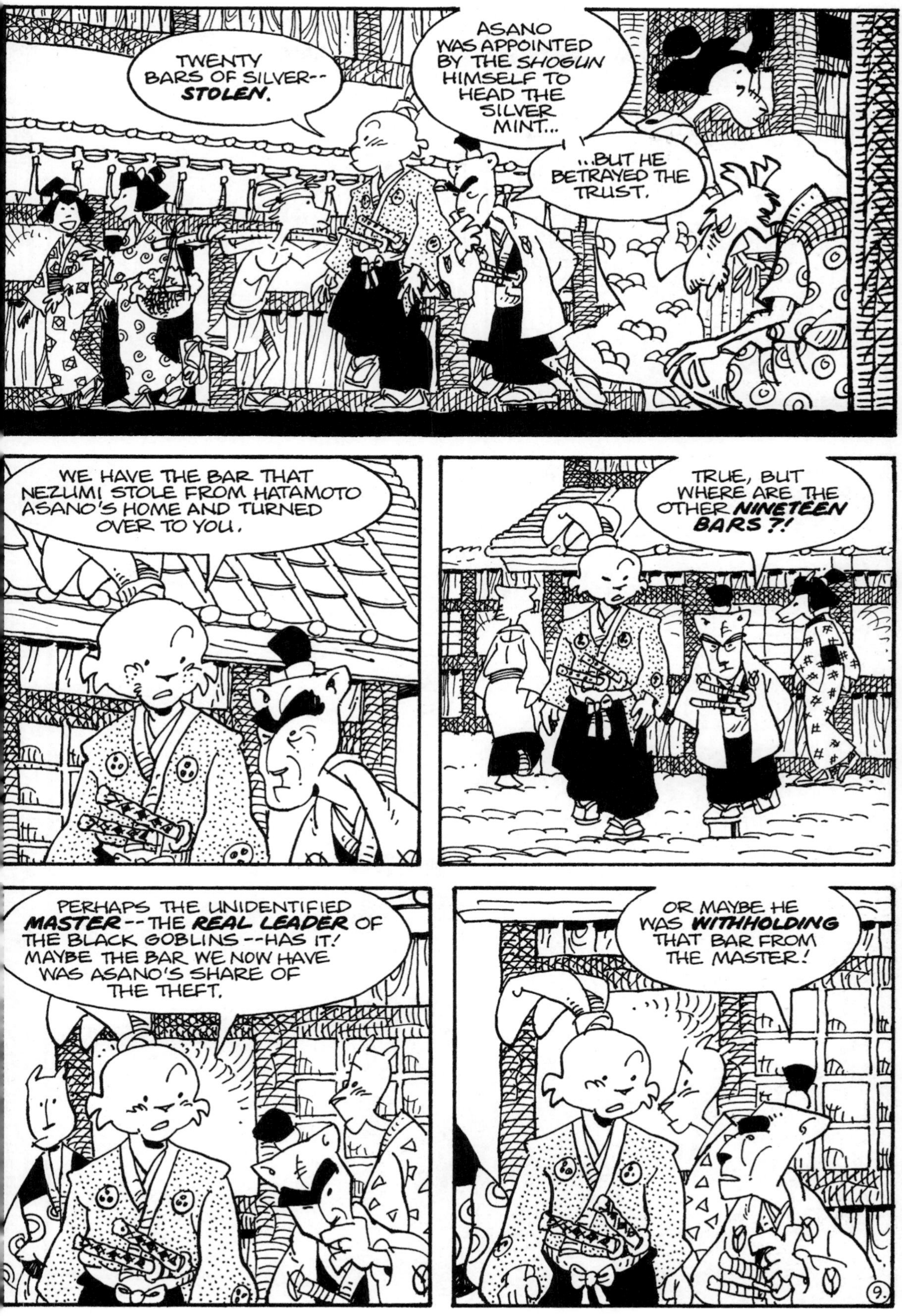
TWENTY BARS OF SILVER-- STOLEN.
ASANO WAS APPOINTED BY THE SHOGUN HIMSELF TO HEAD THE SILVER MINT...
...BUT HE BETRAYED THE TRUST.
WE HAVE THE BAR THAT NEZUMI STOLE FROM HATAMOTO ASANO'S HOME AND TURNED OVER TO YOU.
TRUE, BUT WHERE ARE THE OTHER NINETEEN BARS?!
PERHAPS THE UNIDENTIFIED MASTER -- THE REAL LEADER OF THE BLACK GOBLINS --HAS IT! MAYBE THE BAR WE NOW HAVE WAS ASANO'S SHARE OF THE THEFT.
OR MAYBE HE WAS WITHHOLDING THAT BAR FROM THE MASTER!
9.

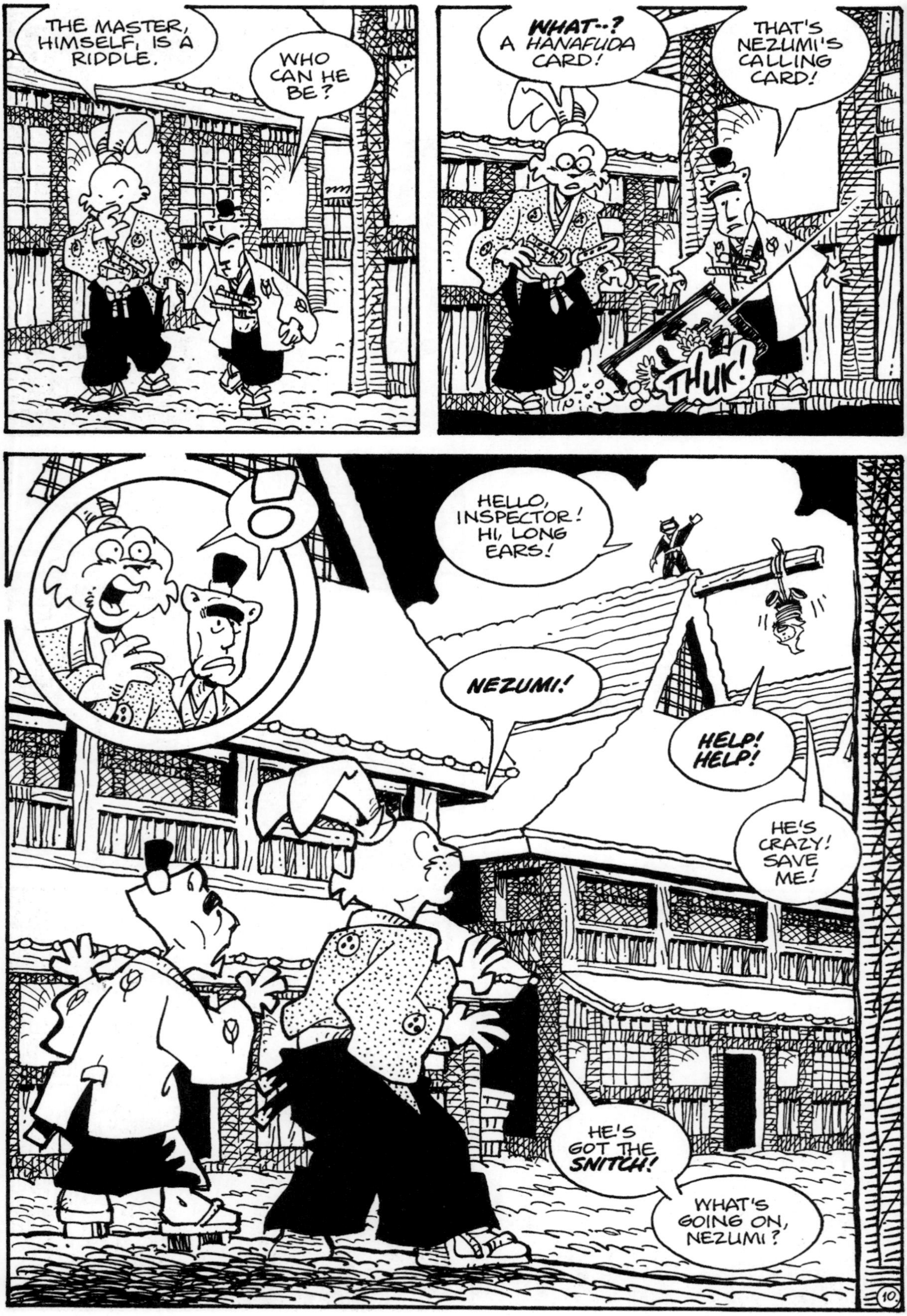
THE MASTER, HIMSELF, IS A RIDDLE.
WHO CAN HE BE?
WHAT--? A HANAFUDA CARD!
THAT'S NEZUMI'S CALLING CARD!
THUK!
!
HELLO, INSPECTOR! HI, LONG EARS!
NEZUMI!
HELP! HELP!
HE'S CRAZY! SAVE ME!
HE'S GOT THE SNITCH!
WHAT'S GOING ON, NEZUMI?
10

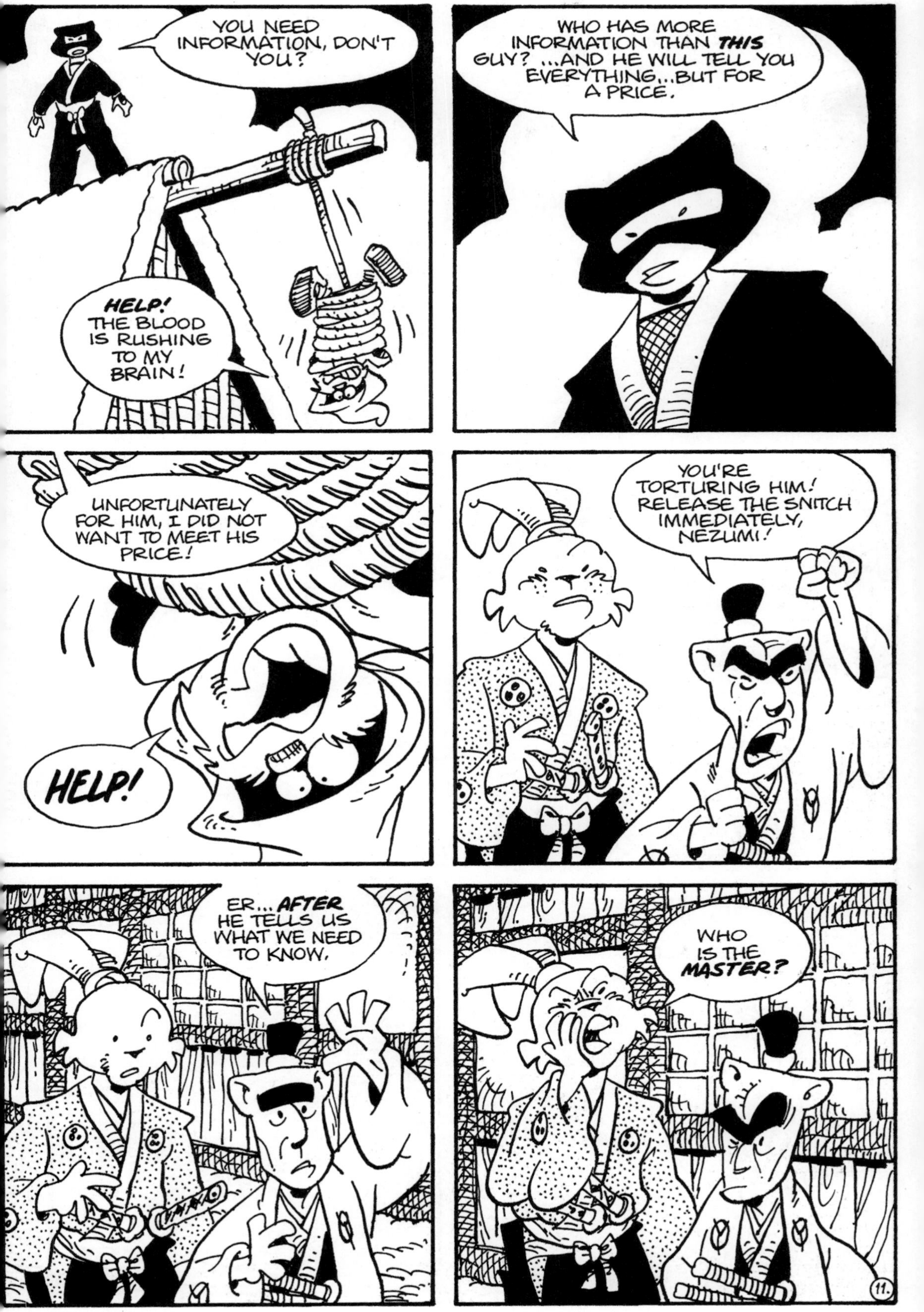
YOU NEED INFORMATION, DON'T YOU?
HELP! THE BLOOD IS RUSHING TO MY BRAIN!
WHO HAS MORE INFORMATION THAN THIS GUY? ...AND HE WILL TELL YOU EVERYTHING...BUT FOR A PRICE.
UNFORTUNATELY FOR HIM, I DID NOT WANT TO MEET HIS PRICE!
HELP!
YOU'RE TORTURING HIM! RELEASE THE SNITCH IMMEDIATELY, NEZUMI!
ER... AFTER HE TELLS US WHAT WE NEED TO KNOW.
WHO IS THE MASTER?
11.

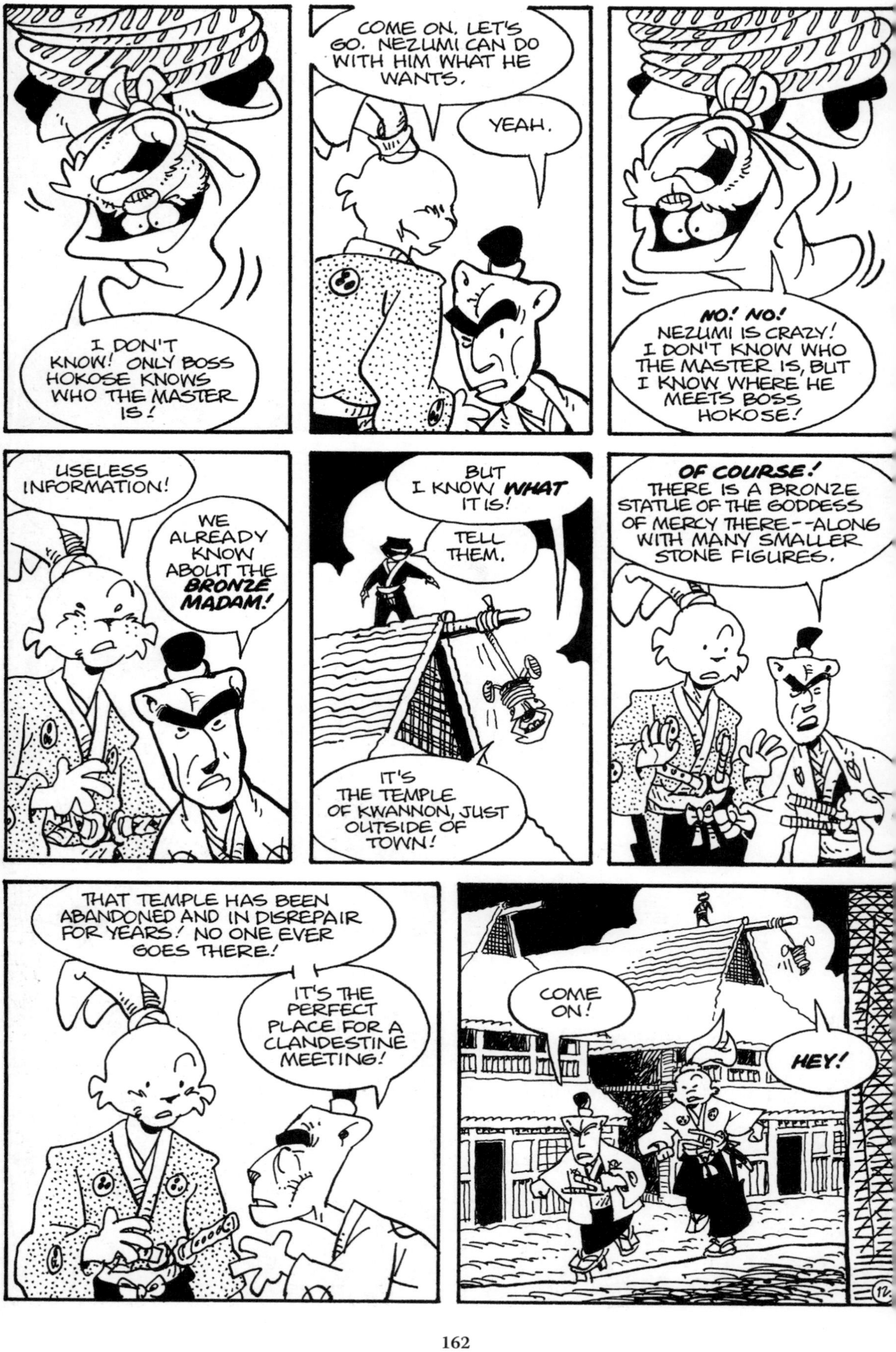
I DON'T KNOW! ONLY BOSS HOKOSE KNOWS WHO THE MASTER IS!
COME ON. LET'S GO. NEZUMI CAN DO WITH HIM WHAT HE WANTS.
YEAH.
NO! NO! NEZUMI IS CRAZY! I DON'T KNOW WHO THE MASTER IS, BUT I KNOW WHERE HE MEETS BOSS HOKOSE!
USELESS INFORMATION!
WE ALREADY KNOW ABOUT THE BRONZE MADAM!
BUT I KNOW WHAT IT IS!
TELL THEM.
IT'S THE TEMPLE OF KWANNON, JUST OUTSIDE OF TOWN!
OF COURSE! THERE IS A BRONZE STATUE OF THE GODDESS OF MERCY THERE--ALONG WITH MANY SMALLER STONE FIGURES.
THAT TEMPLE HAS BEEN ABANDONED AND IN DISREPAIR FOR YEARS! NO ONE EVER GOES THERE!
IT'S THE PERFECT PLACE FOR A CLANDESTINE MEETING!
COME ON!
HEY!
12

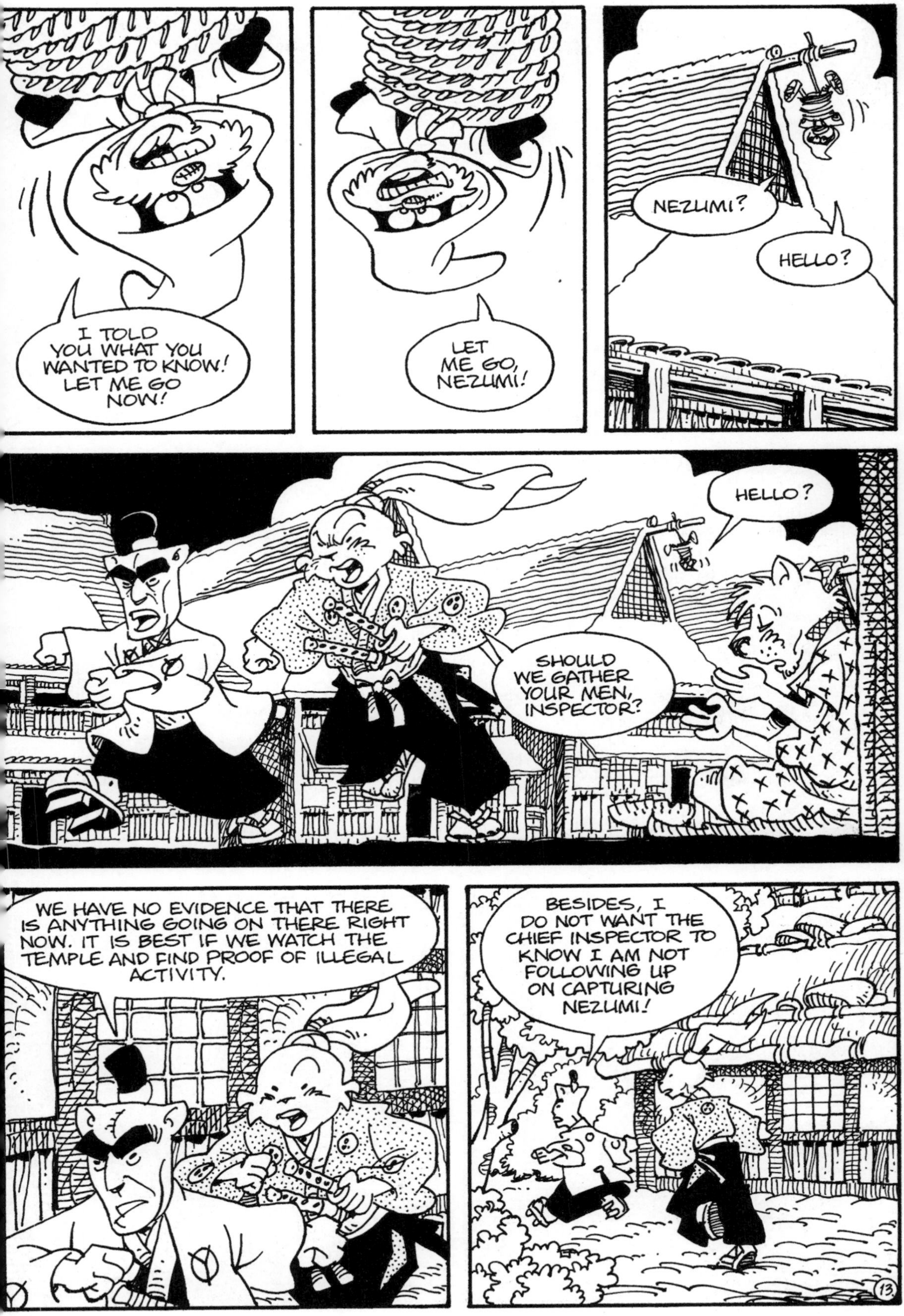
I TOLD YOU WHAT YOU WANTED TO KNOW! LET ME GO NOW!
LET ME GO, NEZUMI!
NEZUMI?
HELLO?
HELLO?
SHOULD WE GATHER YOUR MEN, INSPECTOR?
WE HAVE NO EVIDENCE THAT THERE IS ANYTHING GOING ON THERE RIGHT NOW. IT IS BEST IF WE WATCH THE TEMPLE AND FIND PROOF OF ILLEGAL ACTIVITY.
BESIDES, I DO NOT WANT THE CHIEF INSPECTOR TO KNOW I AM NOT FOLLOWING UP ON CAPTURING NEZUMI!
13

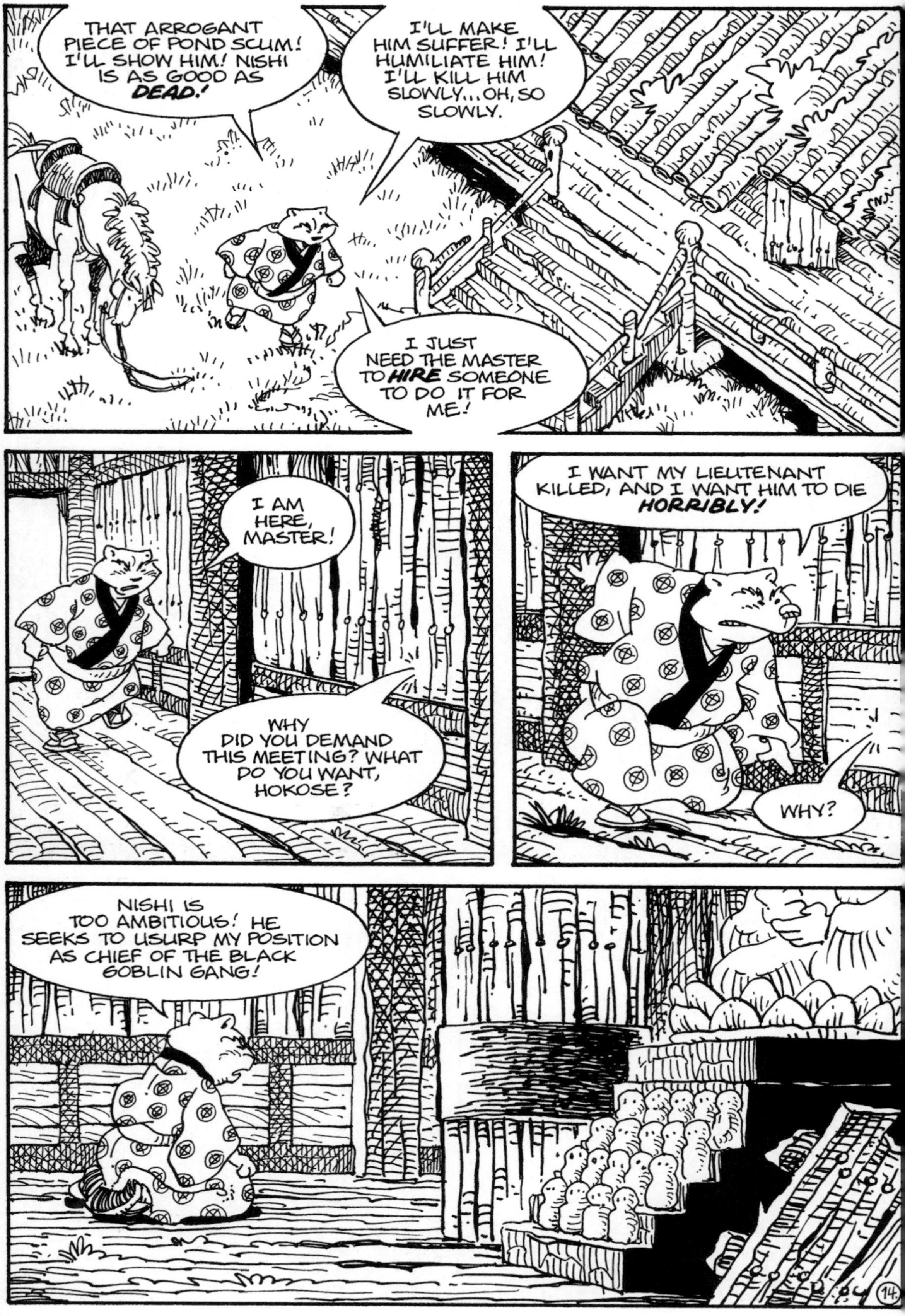
THAT ARROGANT PIECE OF POND SCUM! I'LL SHOW HIM! NISHI IS AS GOOD AS DEAD!
I'LL MAKE HIM SUFFER! I'LL HUMILIATE HIM! I'LL KILL HIM SLOWLY... OH, SO SLOWLY.
I JUST NEED THE MASTER TO HIRE SOMEONE TO DO IT FOR ME!
I AM HERE, MASTER!
WHY DID YOU DEMAND THIS MEETING? WHAT DO YOU WANT, HOKOSE?
I WANT MY LIEUTENANT KILLED, AND I WANT HIM TO DIE HORRIBLY!
WHY?
NISHI IS TOO AMBITIOUS! HE SEEKS TO USURP MY POSITION AS CHIEF OF THE BLACK GOBLIN GANG!
14.

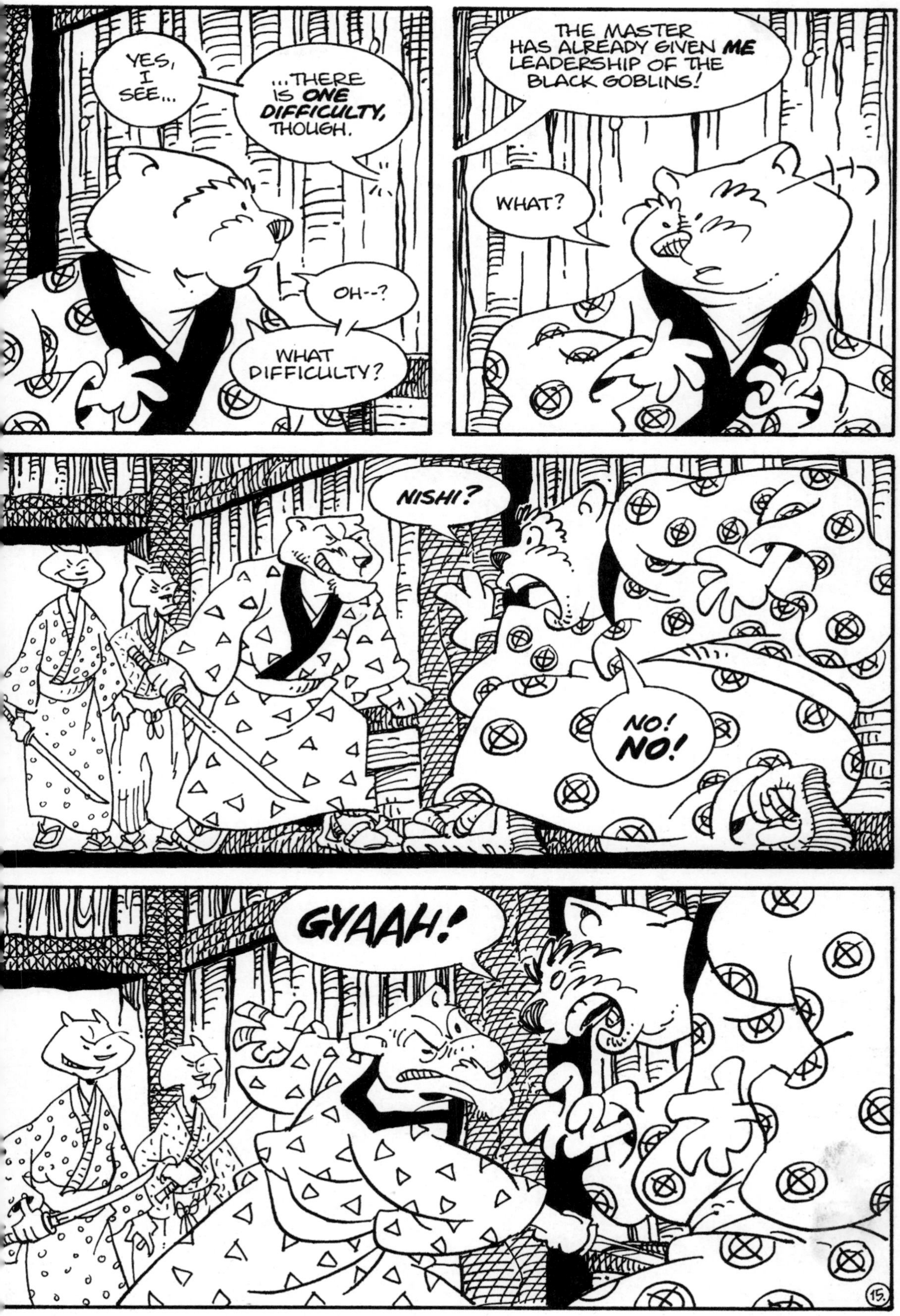
YES, I SEE...
...THERE IS ONE DIFFICULTY, THOUGH.
OH--?
WHAT DIFFICULTY?
THE MASTER HAS ALREADY GIVEN ME LEADERSHIP OF THE BLACK GOBLINS!
WHAT?
NISHI?
NO! NO!
GYAAH!
15.

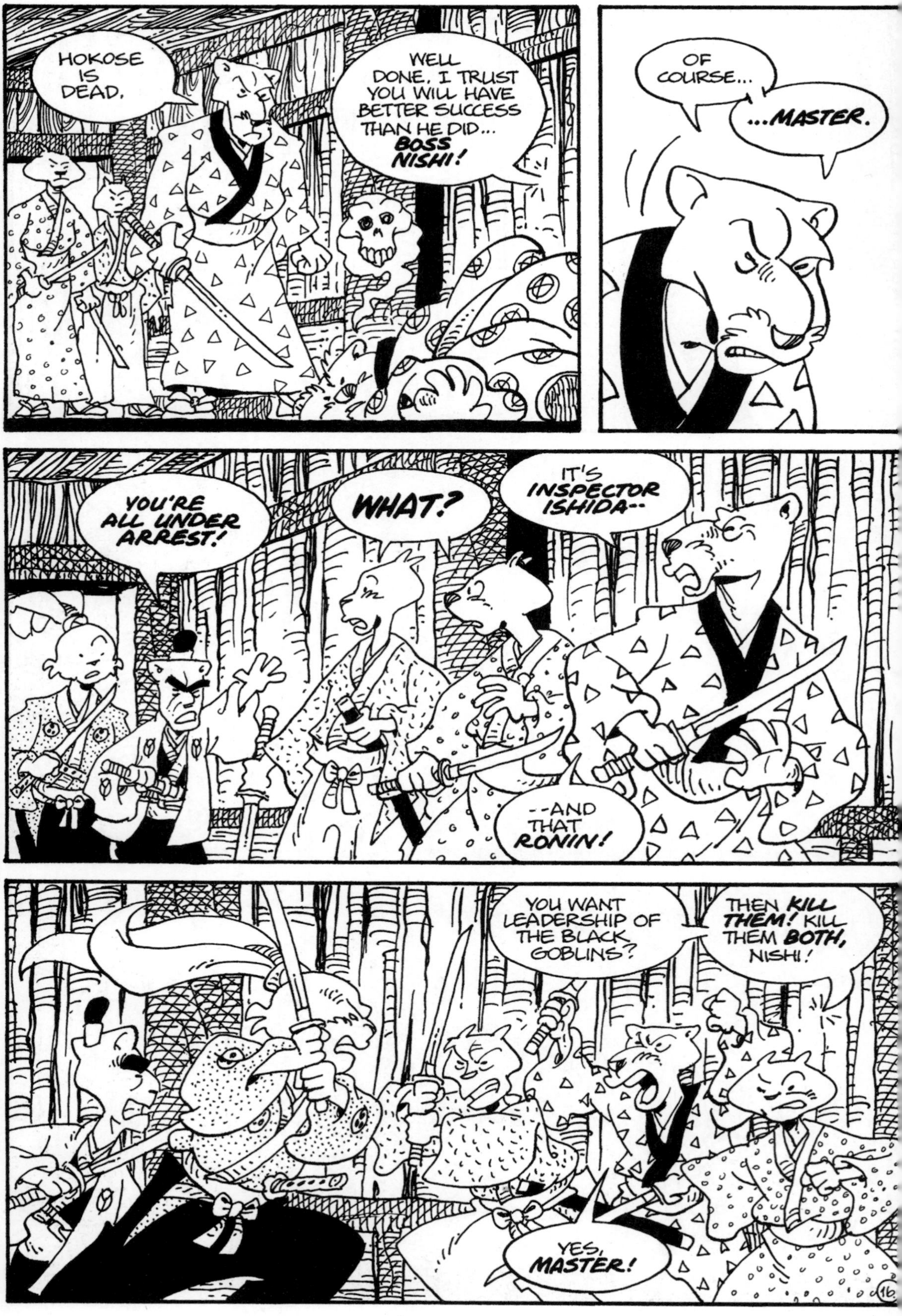
HOKOSE IS DEAD.
WELL DONE. I TRUST YOU WILL HAVE BETTER SUCCESS THAN HE DID... BOSS NISHI!
OF COURSE...
...MASTER.
YOU'RE ALL UNDER ARREST!
WHAT?
IT'S INSPECTOR ISHIDA--
--AND THAT RONIN!
YOU WANT LEADERSHIP OF THE BLACK GOBLINS?
THEN KILL THEM! KILL THEM BOTH, NISHI!
YES, MASTER!
16

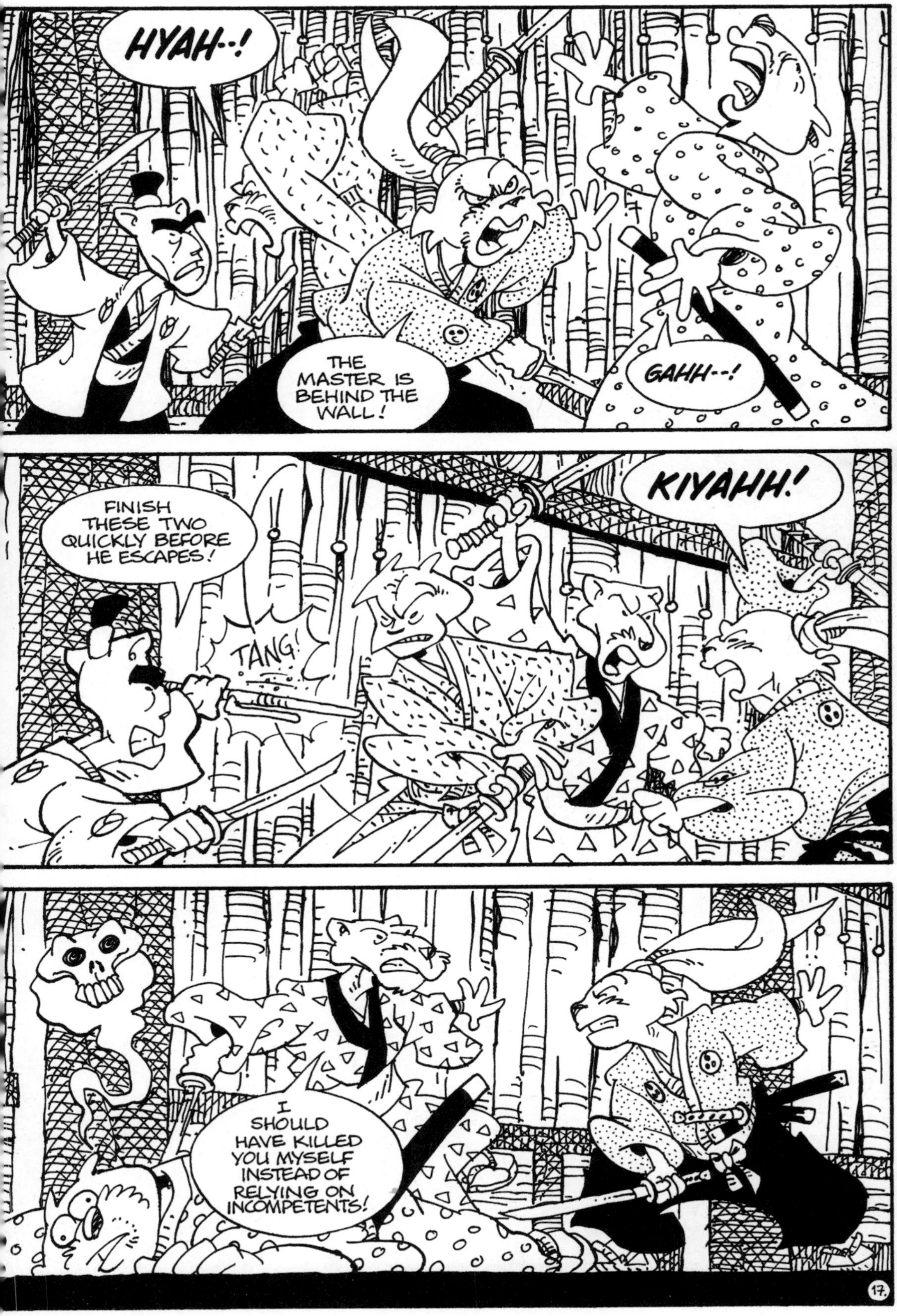
HYAH--!
THE MASTER IS BEHIND THE WALL!
GAHH--!
FINISH THESE TWO QUICKLY BEFORE HE ESCAPES!
KIYAHH!
TANG!
I SHOULD HAVE KILLED YOU MYSELF INSTEAD OF RELYING ON INCOMPETENTS!
17.

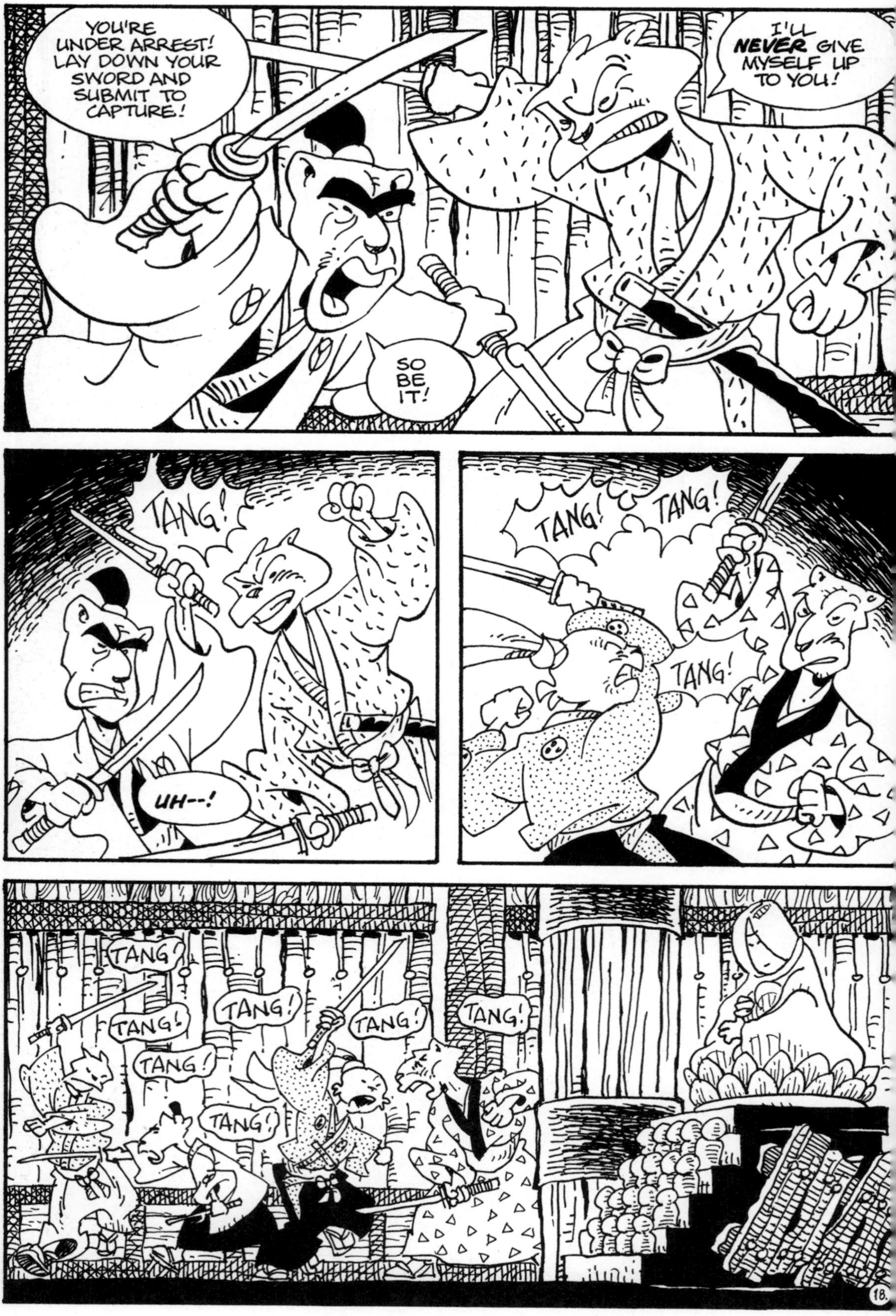
YOU'RE UNDER ARREST! LAY DOWN YOUR SWORD AND SUBMIT TO CAPTURE!
I'LL NEVER GIVE MYSELF UP TO YOU!
SO BE IT!
TANG!
UH--!
TANG!
TANG!
TANG!
TANG
TANG!
TANG!
TANG!
TANG!
TANG!
TANG!
18.

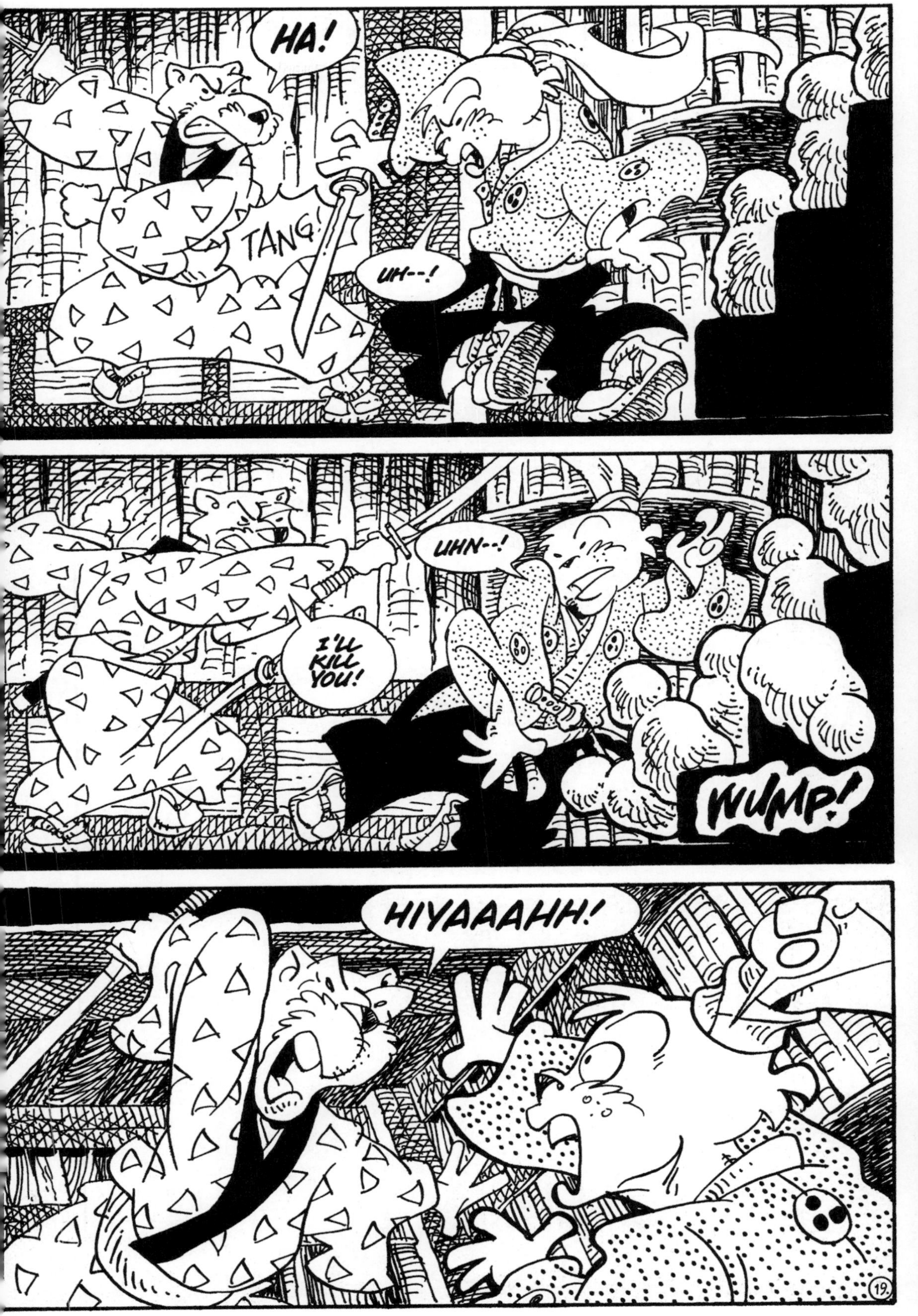
HA!
TANG!
UH--!
UHN--!
I'LL KILL YOU!
WUMP!
HIYAAAHH!
19.

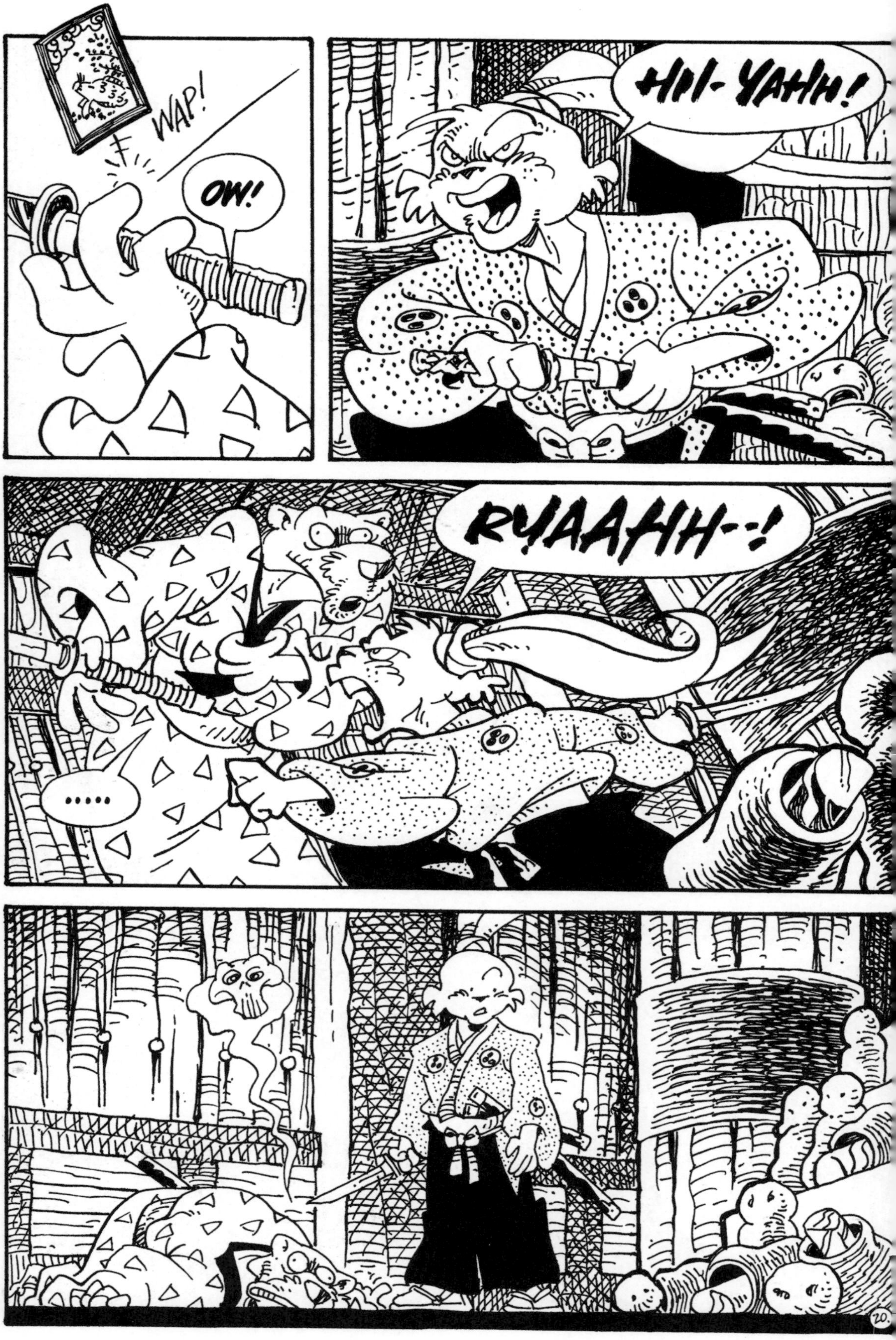
WAP!
OW!
HII-YAHH!
RYAAHH--!
.....
20.

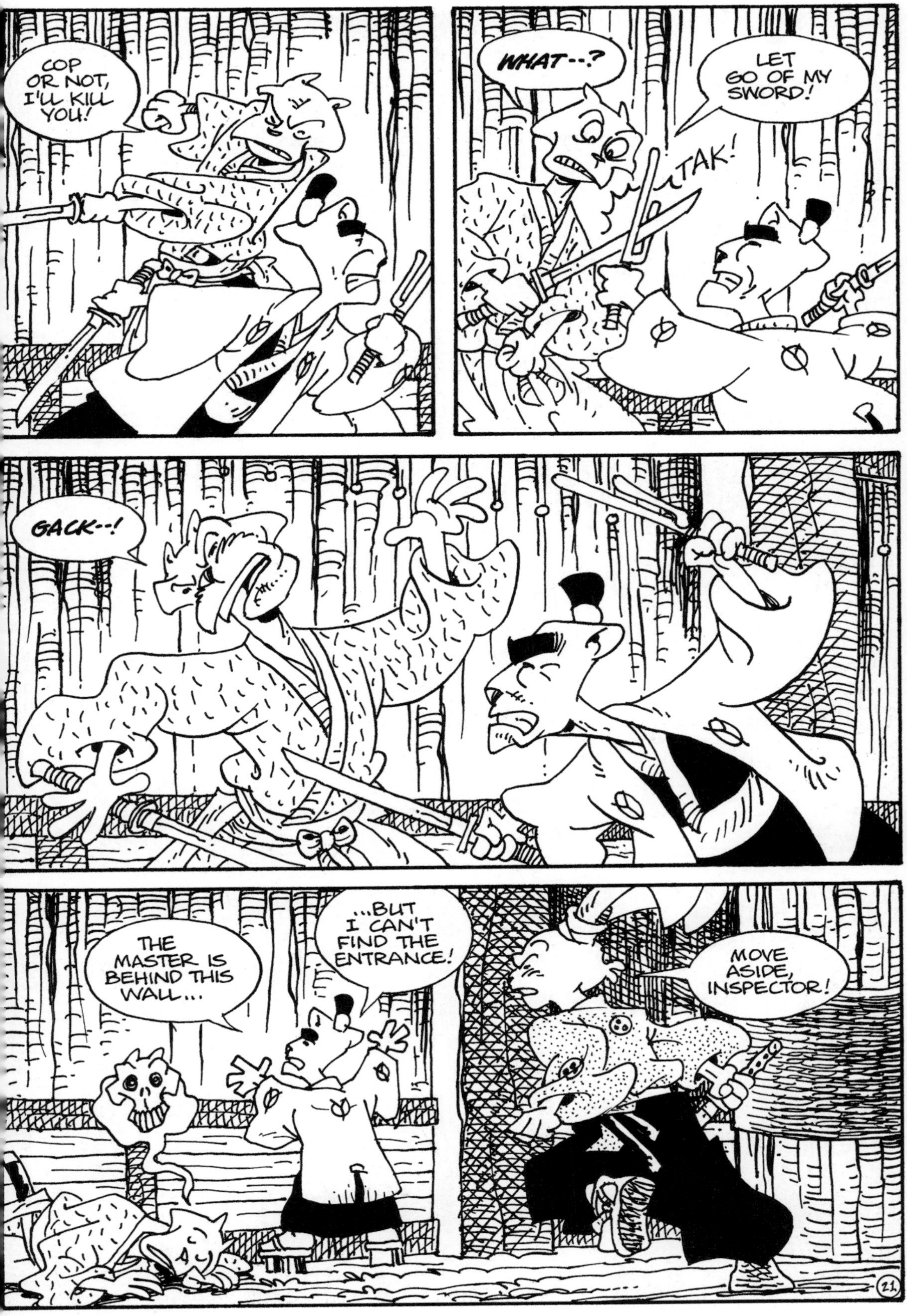
COP OR NOT, I'LL KILL YOU!
WHAT--?
LET GO OF MY SWORD!
TAK!
GACK--!
THE MASTER IS BEHIND THIS WALL...
...BUT I CAN'T FIND THE ENTRANCE!
MOVE ASIDE, INSPECTOR!
21

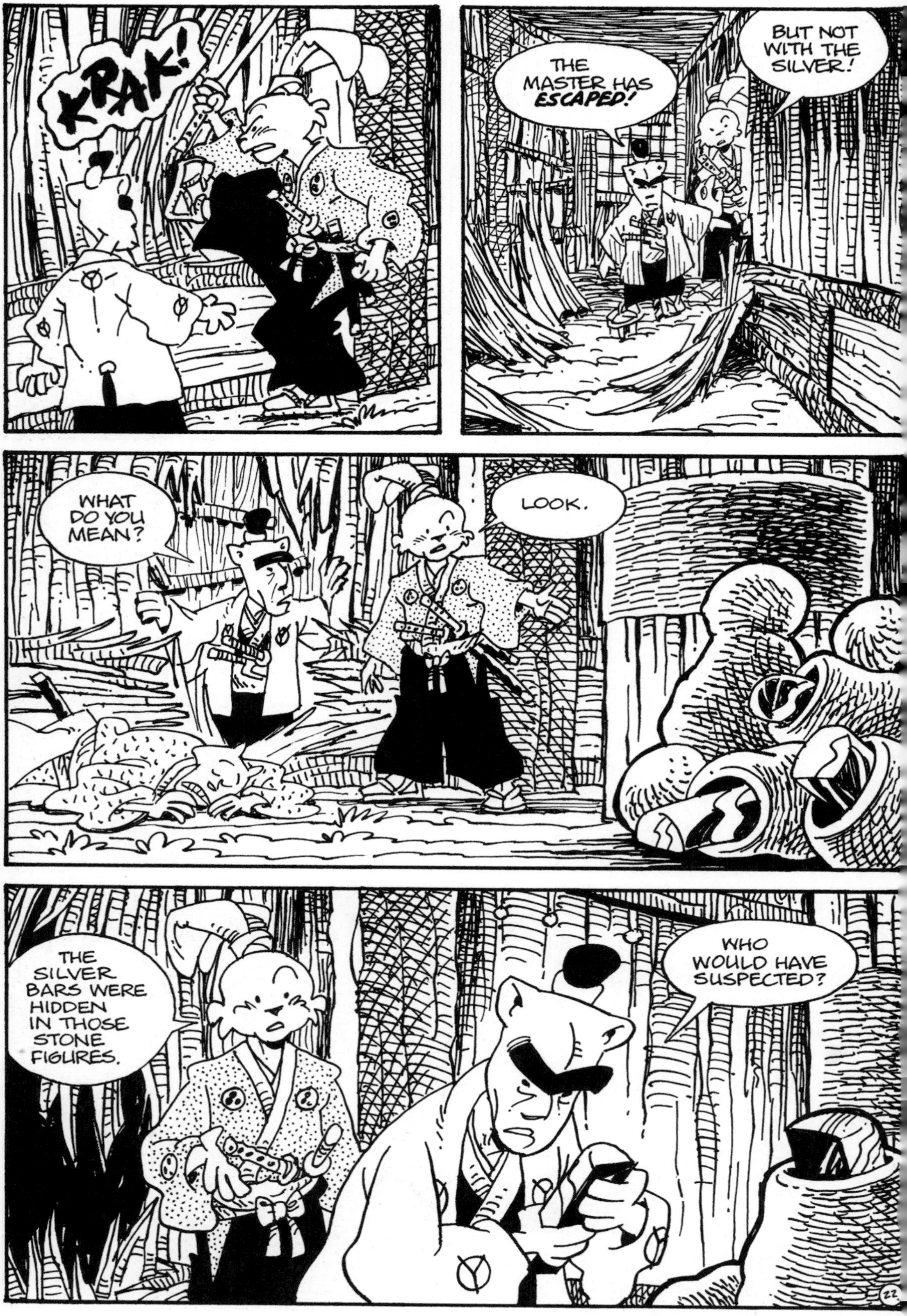
KRAK!
THE MASTER HAS ESCAPED!
BUT NOT WITH THE SILVER!
WHAT DO YOU MEAN?
LOOK.
THE SILVER BARS WERE HIDDEN IN THOSE STONE FIGURES.
WHO WOULD HAVE SUSPECTED?
22

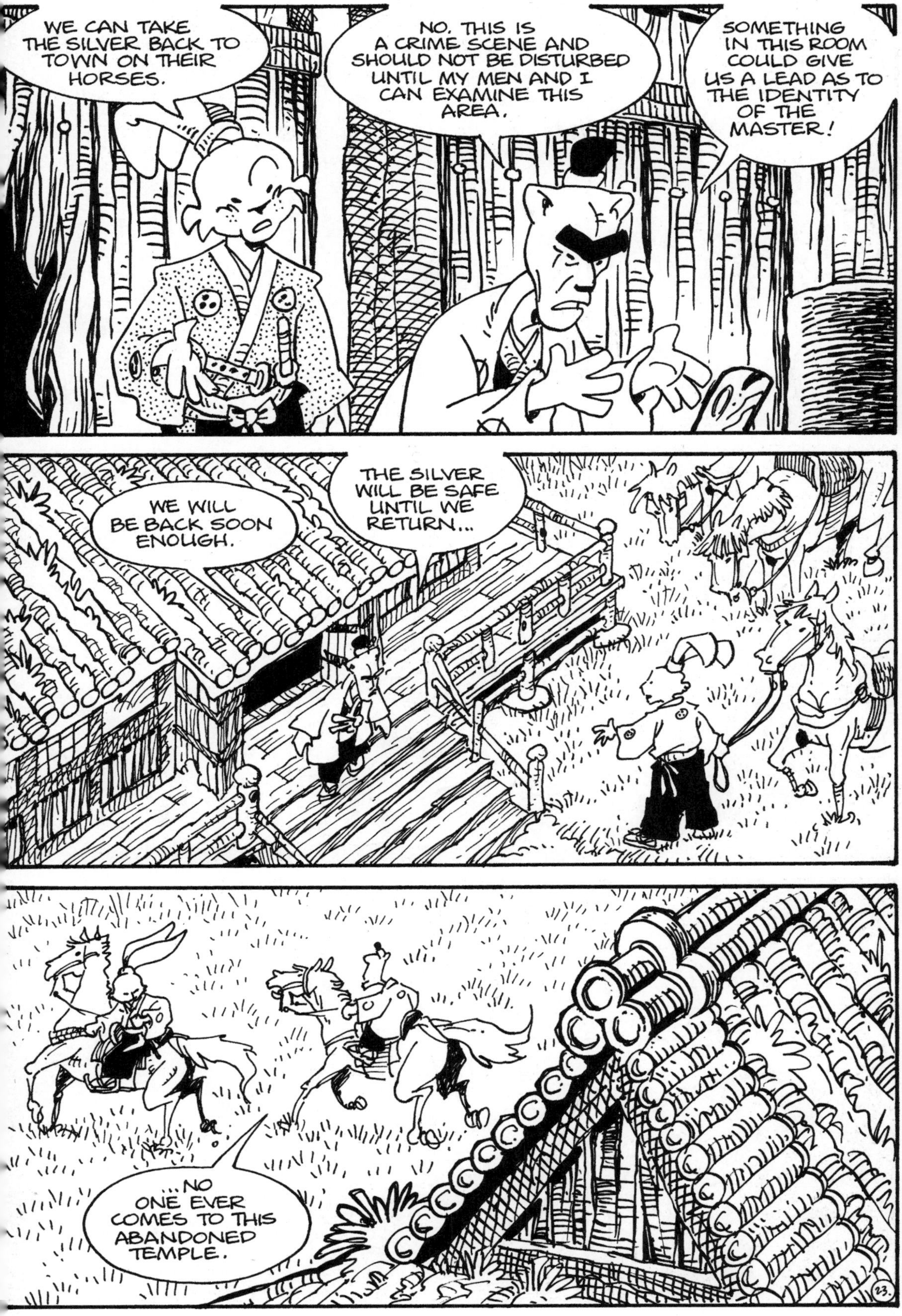
WE CAN TAKE THE SILVER BACK TO TOWN ON THEIR HORSES.
NO. THIS IS A CRIME SCENE AND SHOULD NOT BE DISTURBED UNTIL MY MEN AND I CAN EXAMINE THIS AREA.
SOMETHING IN THIS ROOM COULD GIVE US A LEAD AS TO THE IDENTITY OF THE MASTER!
WE WILL BE BACK SOON ENOUGH.
THE SILVER WILL BE SAFE UNTIL WE RETURN...
...NO ONE EVER COMES TO THIS ABANDONED TEMPLE.
23.

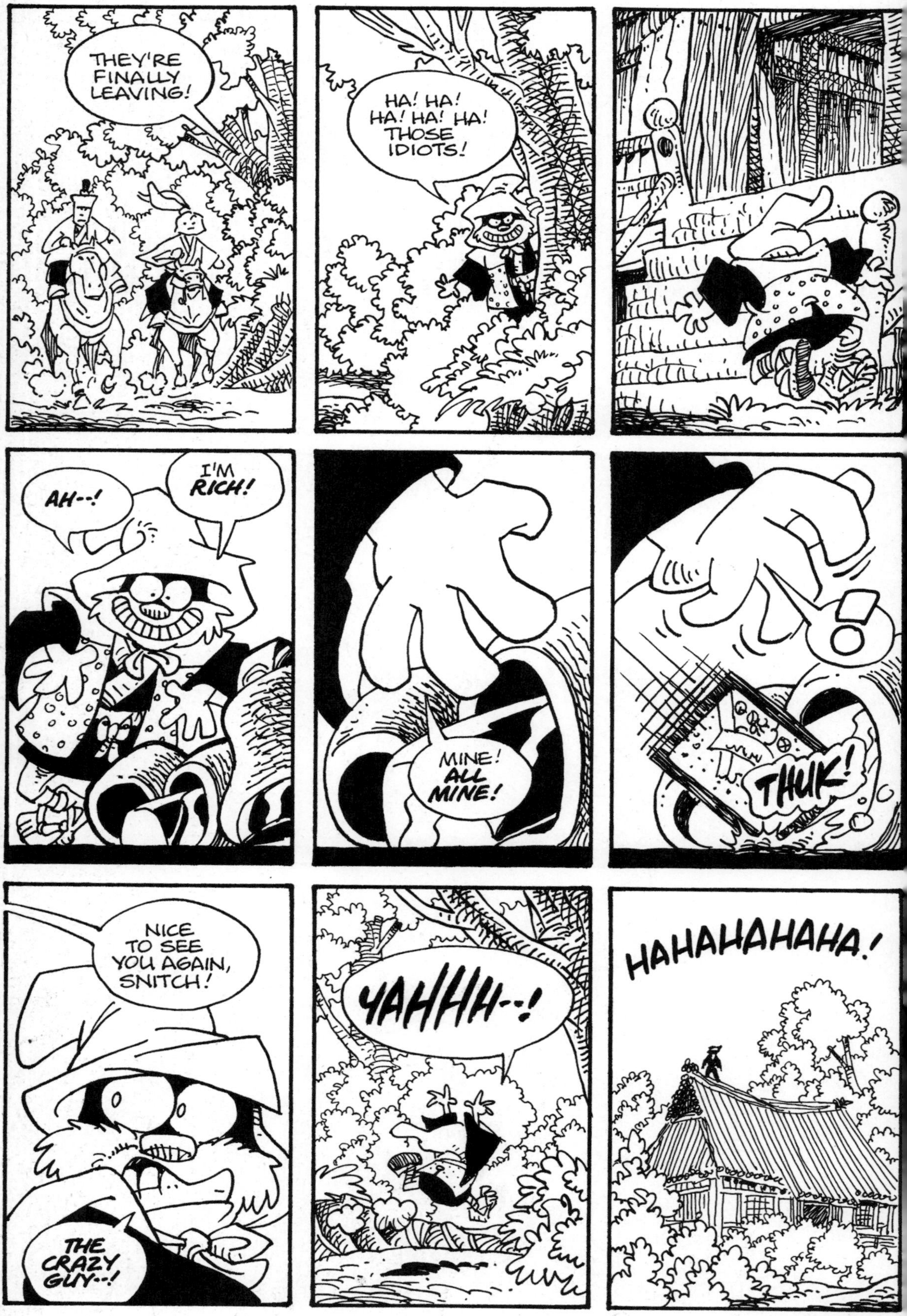

THEY'RE FINALLY LEAVING!
HA! HA! HA! HA! HA! THOSE IDIOTS!
AH--!
I'M RICH!
MINE! ALL MINE!
THUK!
NICE TO SEE YOU AGAIN, SNITCH!
THE CRAZY GUY--!
YAHHH--!
HAHAHAHAHA!

THE END

THE HIDDEN

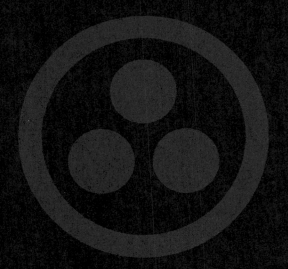

OF THE MANY THINGS I ADMIRE about Stan Sakai, ranking up there at the very top is his ability to so nimbly navigate so many different fictional genres.

That skill is a major reason why *Usagi Yojimbo* has remained so enjoyable—so relevant—for so long. Stan has never allowed his defining series to grow stale. My admiration for how carefully he has constructed Usagi's world is boundless. He has fashioned characters and a time and place which have allowed him to take his stories and ambitions in different directions—historical adventure, political intrigue, war, science fiction, fantasy—*Usagi Yojimbo* has been a very elastic premise that Stan has artfully deployed to many ends.

The Hidden is a detective story, and what with the high body count and degree of corruption, I'd say it qualifies as hard boiled. I mean that in the classic sense—there's a brutal precision and lack of sentimentality that goes straight back to Dashiell Hammett. Most importantly, though, it's about character. That makes it a genre story with a purpose, and from beginning to end the story belongs to Inspector Ishida. Stan makes the bold choice to relegate Usagi to a secondary role, having his usual alpha serve as the reader's surrogate, an outsider like us, to whom must be explained police procedure (including Ishida's sometimes unorthodox investigative techniques), as well as the complicated relationships of various cultures living under the shogunate. Usagi does get to go all *yojimbo* when needed, serving as Ishida's strong-arm man, but it is the inspector who is the story's driving force and its emotional center. He has become a fascinating personality (and I would love to see more stories centered on him!).

That Stan can present all this story's historical and plot-specific information in a compelling manner is a testament to his mastery of the comics medium. The very nature of a detective drama told within the static panels of a comic poses a problem: how do you make the repetitiveness of all the necessary verbal interactions visually interesting? It would be easy to succumb to a staccato gallery of talking heads. But Stan understands rhythm and flow, he is a maestro at manipulating the time and space implied in our two-dimensional, image-progressive medium. Stan has absorbed and transformed any number of influences, but I particularly see those of Harvey Kurtzman and Roy Crane here. The storytelling is always inventive and propulsive—every panel, every scene gives detailed information, throwing the story forward. That's real artistry.

Ultimately, Stan has taken his tale, set in a very specific time in the history of feudal Japan, and quietly reminded us that its underpinnings of cultural and class divide, state-sanctified corruption, and persecution fueled by fear of the "other" are not bound to that time and place. The persecuted, under another set of conditions, can easily become the persecutors. Power and the status quo shift, and only the individual who sees past prejudices and futile resistance to change gives us hope of finding a better way.

The Hidden is certainly entertaining, but it's more than that. It's genre storytelling at its best.

MARK SCHULTZ

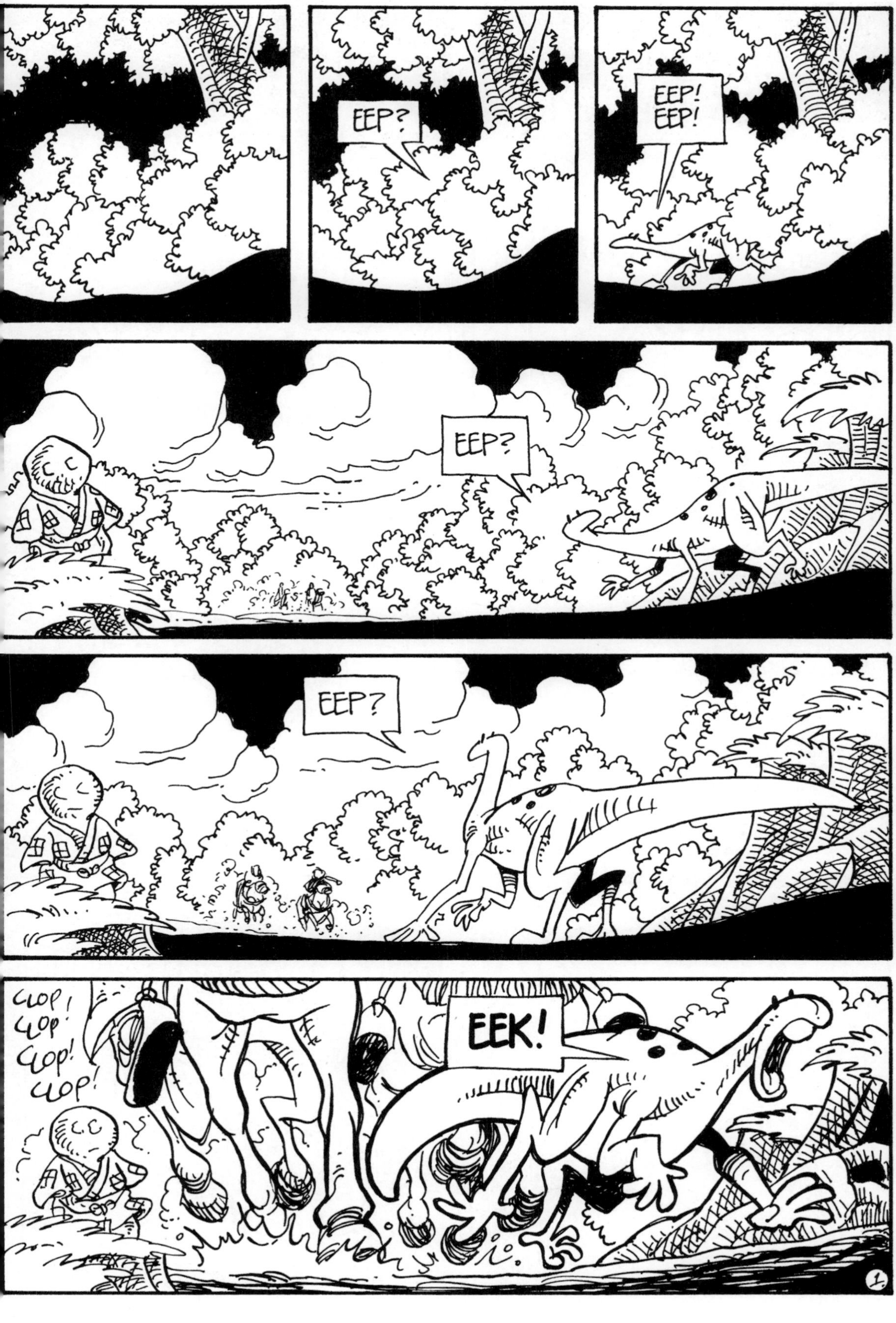
EEP?
EEP! EEP!
EEP?
EEP?
CLOP! CLOP! CLOP! CLOP!
EEK!
1.

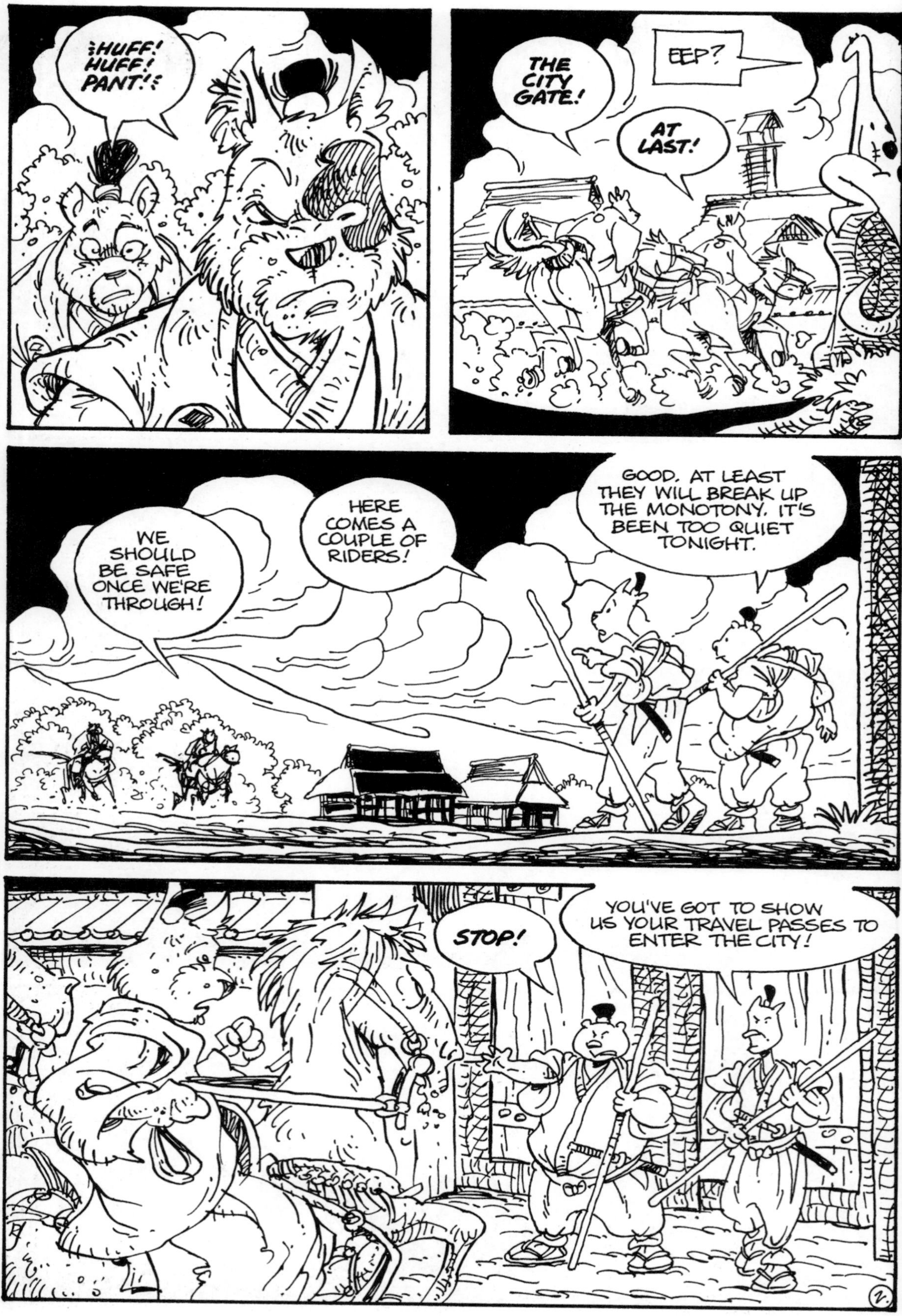

HUFF! HUFF! PANT!
THE CITY GATE!
EEP?
AT LAST!
WE SHOULD BE SAFE ONCE WE'RE THROUGH!
HERE COMES A COUPLE OF RIDERS!
GOOD. AT LEAST THEY WILL BREAK UP THE MONOTONY. IT'S BEEN TOO QUIET TONIGHT.
STOP!
YOU'VE GOT TO SHOW US YOUR TRAVEL PASSES TO ENTER THE CITY!
2.

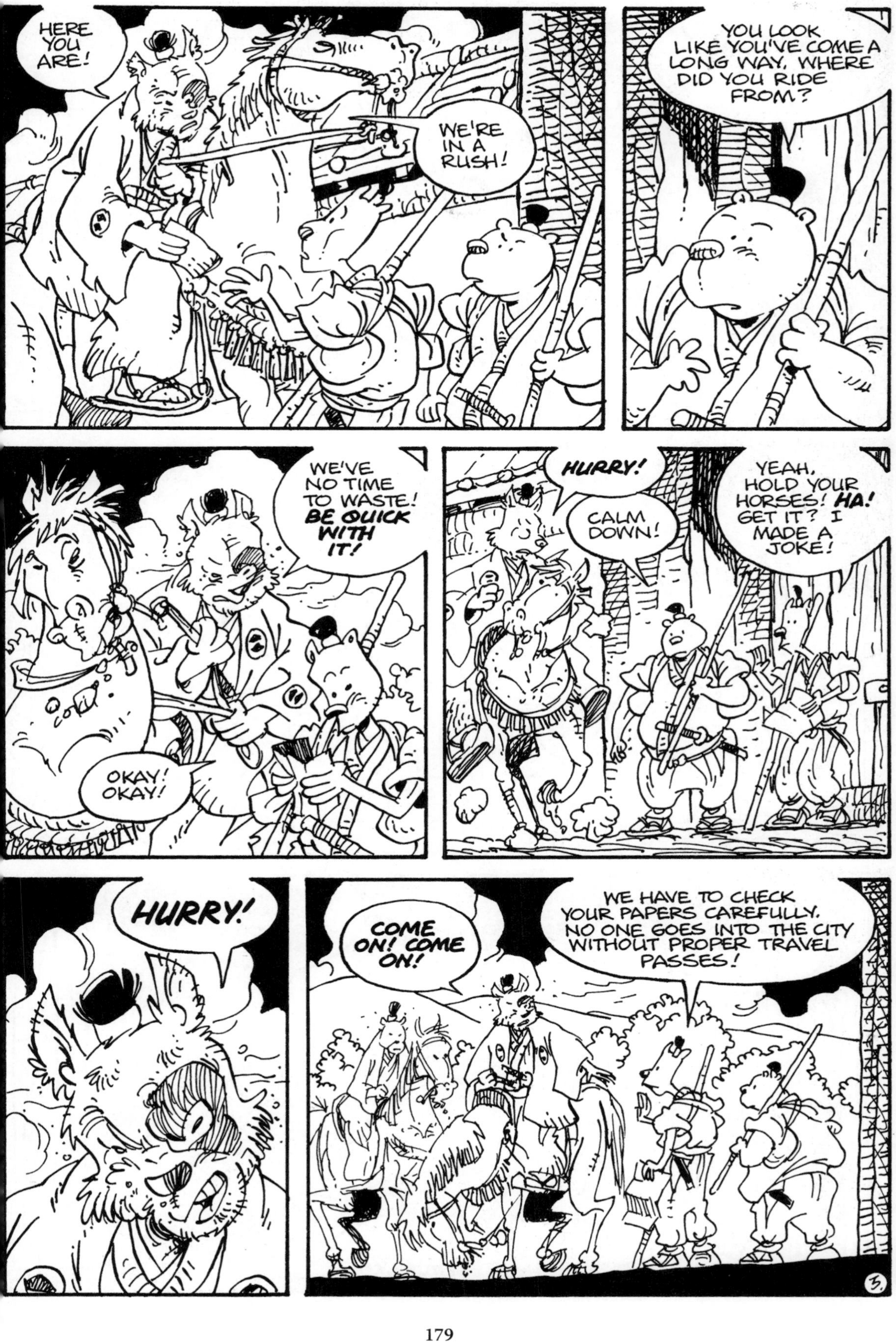
HERE YOU ARE!
WE'RE IN A RUSH!
YOU LOOK LIKE YOU'VE COME A LONG WAY. WHERE DID YOU RIDE FROM?
WE'VE NO TIME TO WASTE! BE QUICK WITH IT!
OKAY! OKAY!
HURRY!
CALM DOWN!
YEAH, HOLD YOUR HORSES! HA! GET IT? I MADE A JOKE!
HURRY!
COME ON! COME ON!
WE HAVE TO CHECK YOUR PAPERS CAREFULLY. NO ONE GOES INTO THE CITY WITHOUT PROPER TRAVEL PASSES!
3.

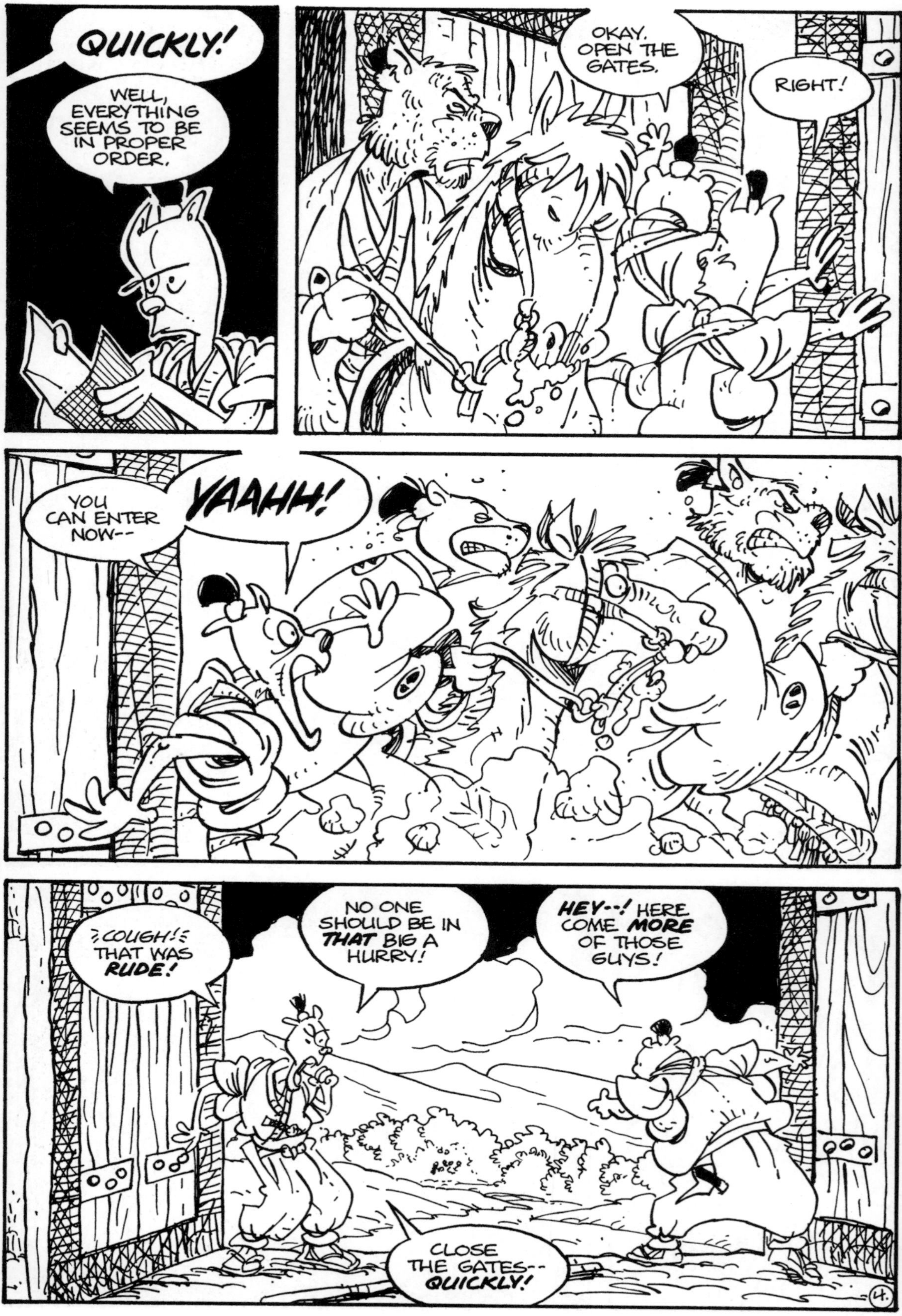
QUICKLY!
WELL, EVERYTHING SEEMS TO BE IN PROPER ORDER.
OKAY. OPEN THE GATES.
RIGHT!
YOU CAN ENTER NOW--
YAAHH!
COUGH! THAT WAS RUDE!
NO ONE SHOULD BE IN THAT BIG A HURRY!
HEY--! HERE COME MORE OF THOSE GUYS!
CLOSE THE GATES-- QUICKLY!
4.

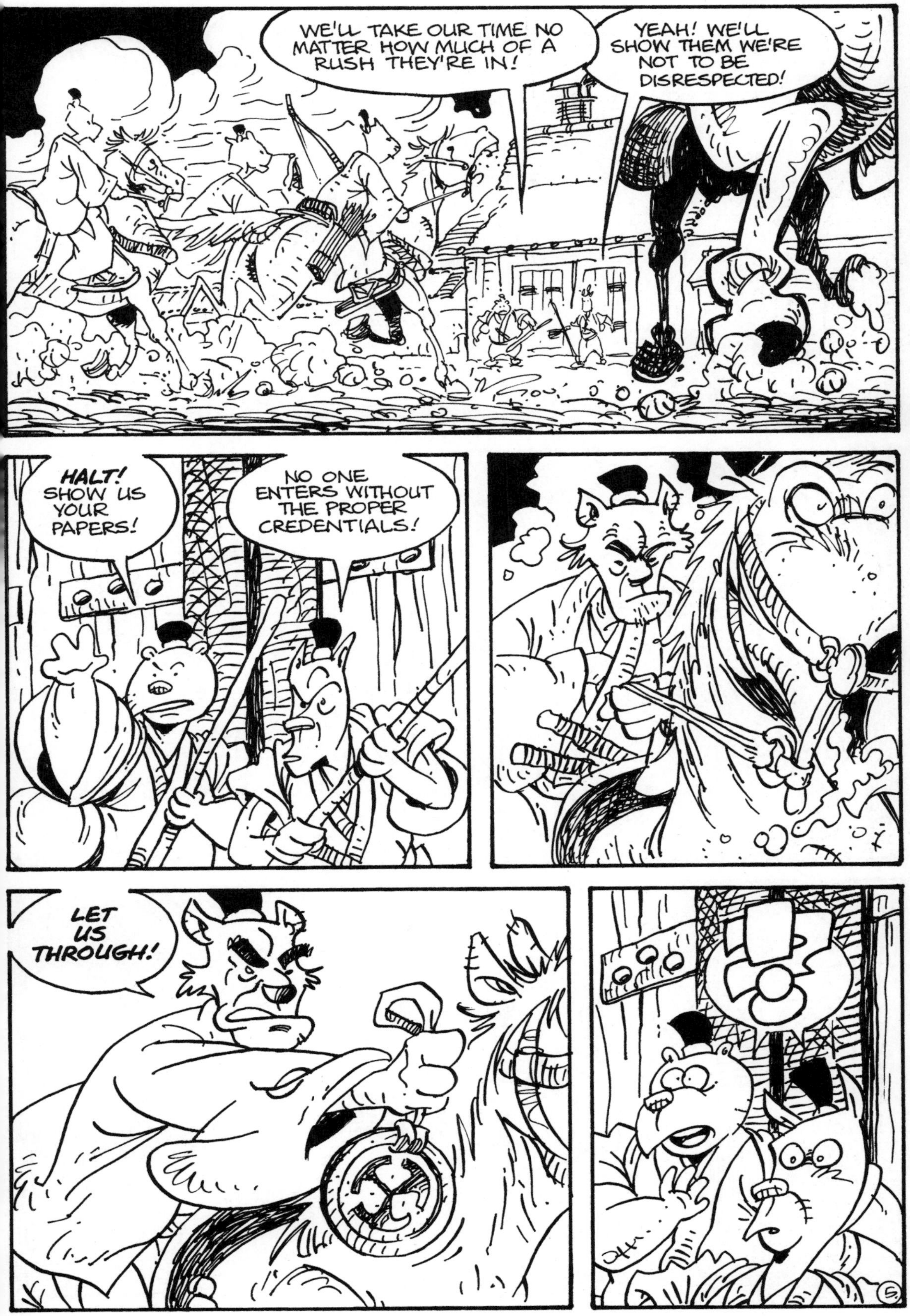
WE'LL TAKE OUR TIME NO MATTER HOW MUCH OF A RUSH THEY'RE IN!
YEAH! WE'LL SHOW THEM WE'RE NOT TO BE DISRESPECTED!
HALT! SHOW US YOUR PAPERS!
NO ONE ENTERS WITHOUT THE PROPER CREDENTIALS!
LET US THROUGH!

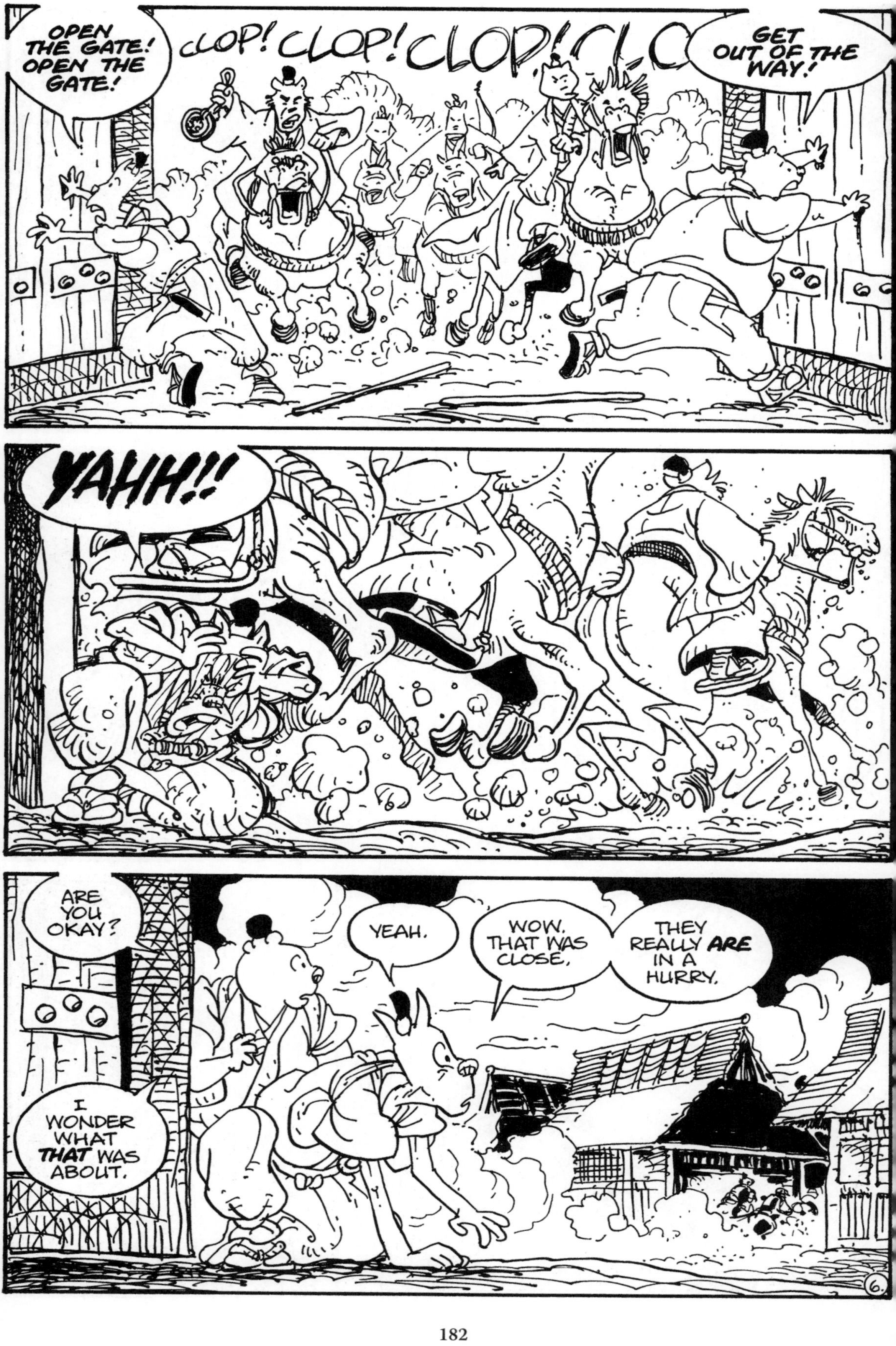
OPEN THE GATE! OPEN THE GATE!
CLOP! CLOP! CLOP! CLO
GET OUT OF THE WAY!
YAHH!!
ARE YOU OKAY?
YEAH.
WOW. THAT WAS CLOSE.
THEY REALLY ARE IN A HURRY.
I WONDER WHAT THAT WAS ABOUT.
6.

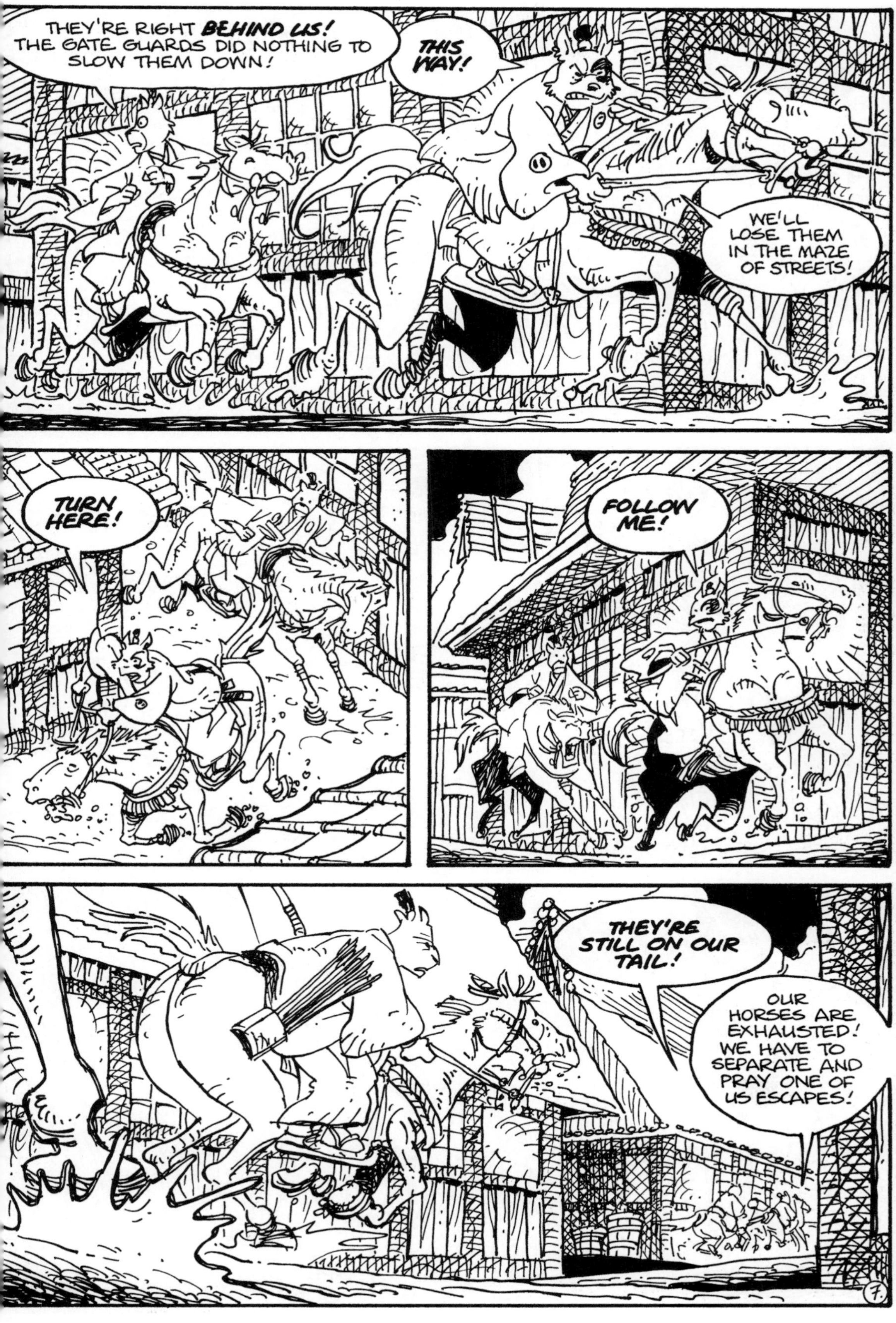

THEY'RE RIGHT BEHIND US! THE GATE GUARDS DID NOTHING TO SLOW THEM DOWN!
THIS WAY!
WE'LL LOSE THEM IN THE MAZE OF STREETS!
TURN HERE!
FOLLOW ME!
THEY'RE STILL ON OUR TAIL!
OUR HORSES ARE EXHAUSTED! WE HAVE TO SEPARATE AND PRAY ONE OF US ESCAPES!
7.

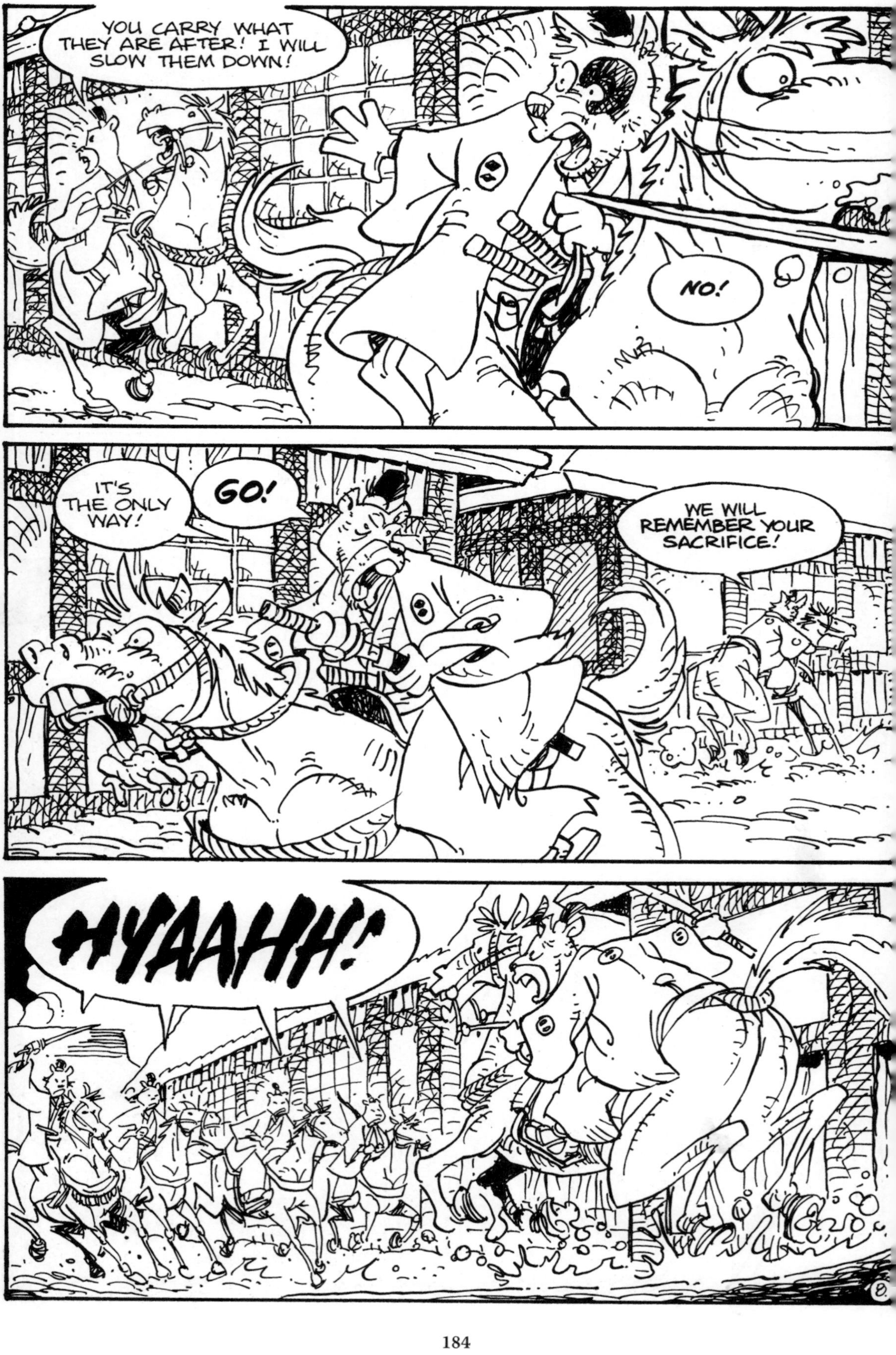
YOU CARRY WHAT THEY ARE AFTER! I WILL SLOW THEM DOWN!
NO!
IT'S THE ONLY WAY!
GO!
WE WILL REMEMBER YOUR SACRIFICE!
HYAAHH!

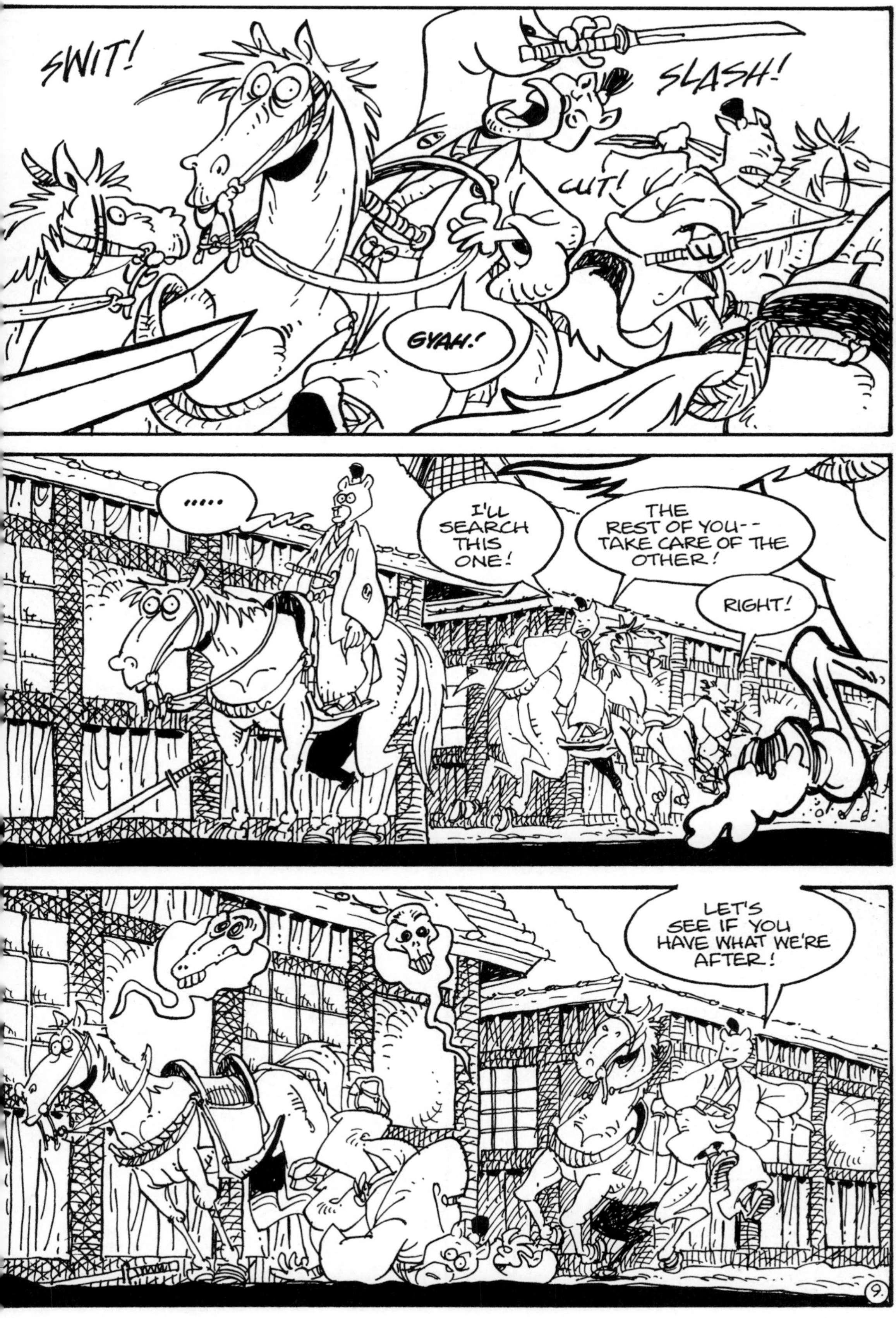
SWIT!
SLASH!
CUT!
GYAH!
.....
I'LL SEARCH THIS ONE!
THE REST OF YOU-- TAKE CARE OF THE OTHER!
RIGHT!
LET'S SEE IF YOU HAVE WHAT WE'RE AFTER!
9.

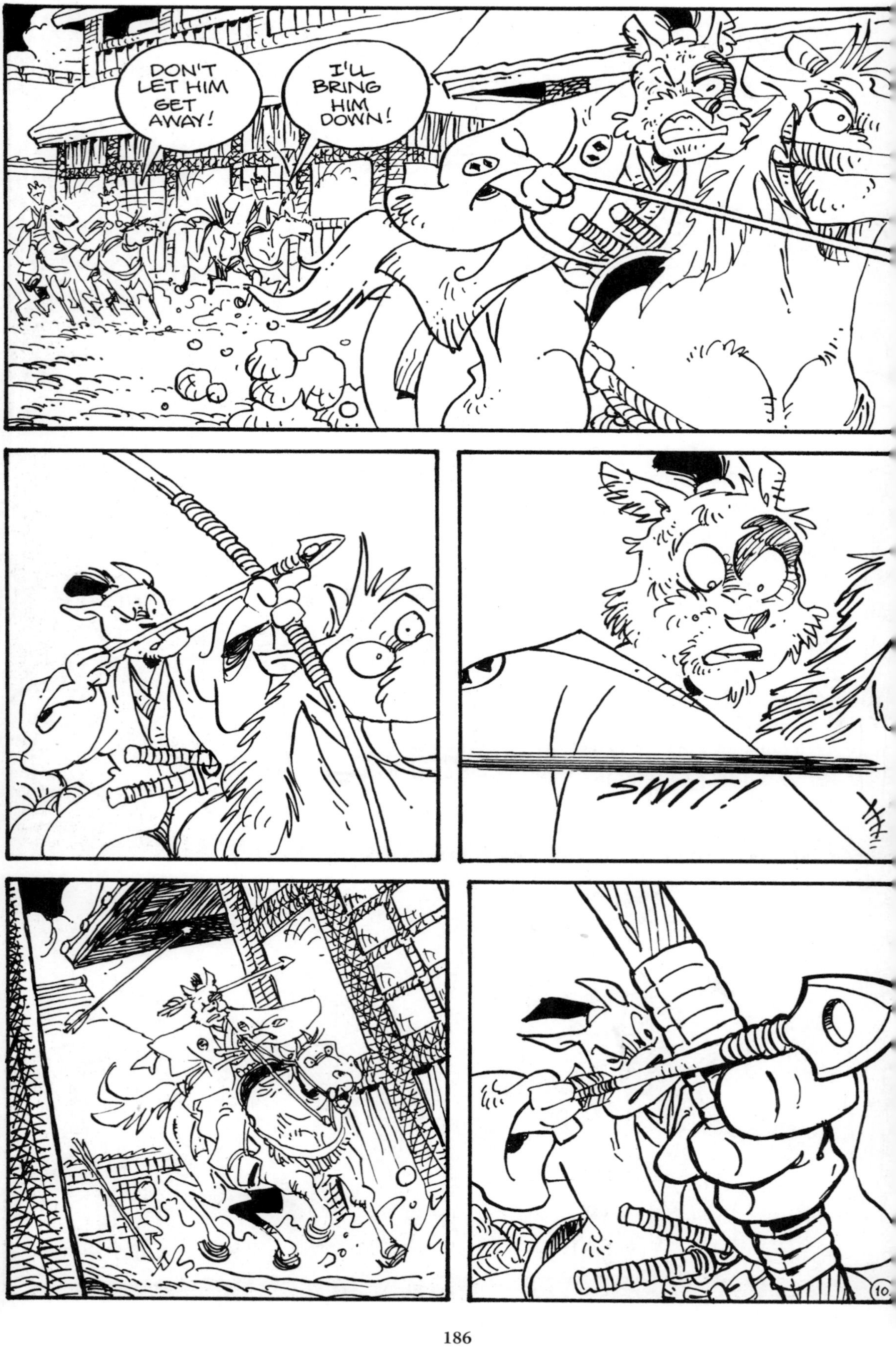
DON'T LET HIM GET AWAY!
I'LL BRING HIM DOWN!
SWIT!
10.

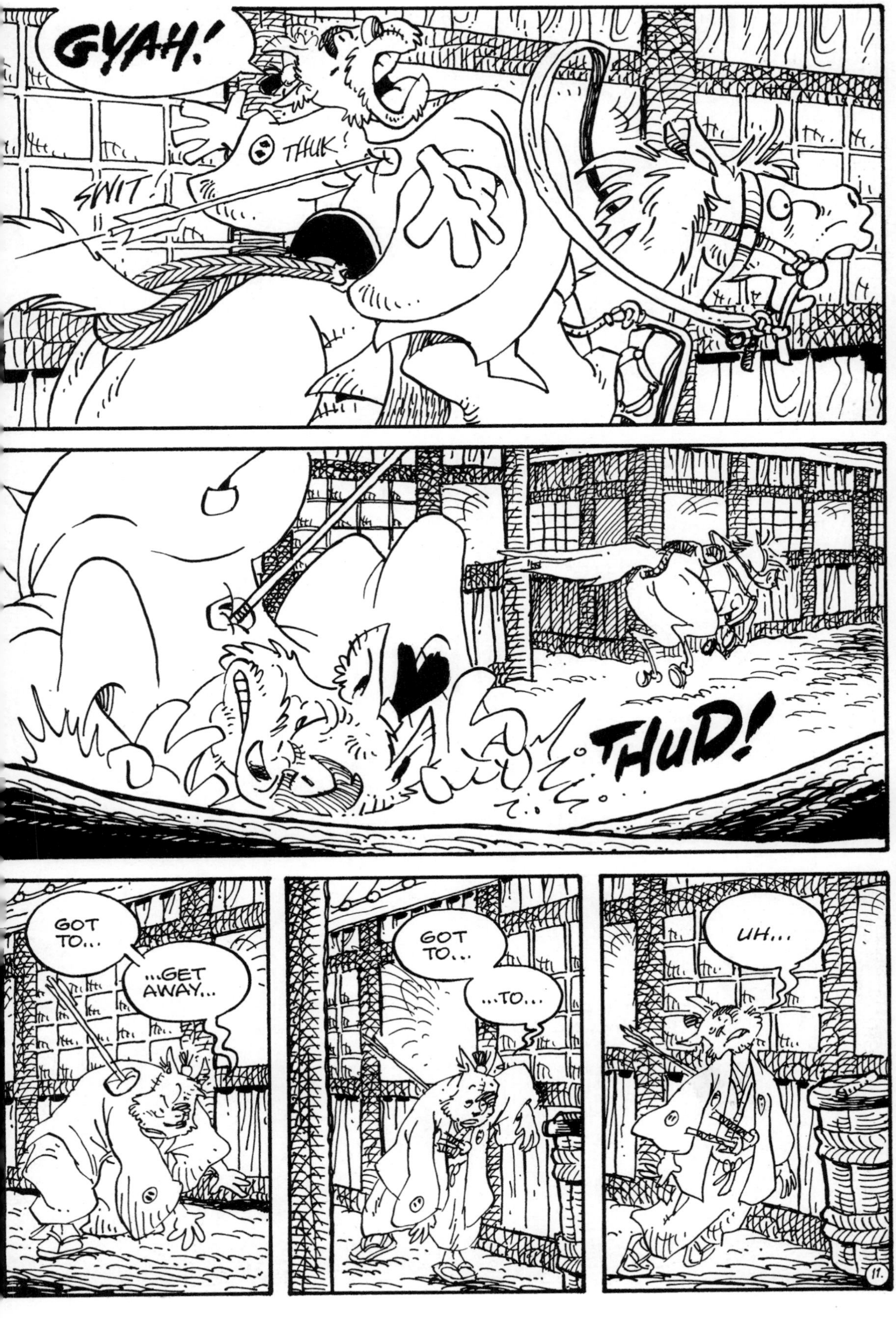
GYAH!
THUK!
SWIT
THUD!
GOT TO...
...GET AWAY...
GOT TO...
...TO...
UH...
11.

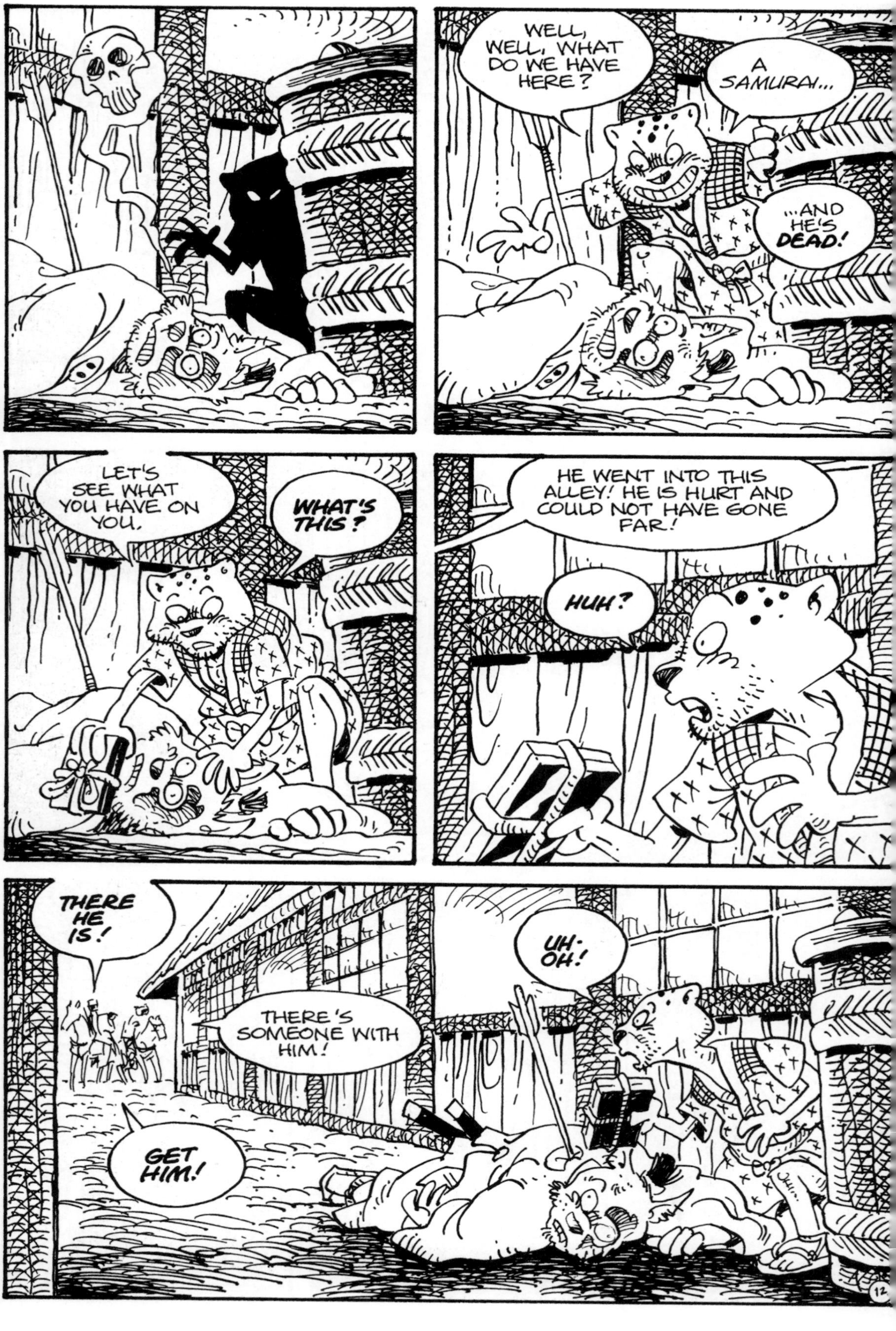
WELL, WELL, WHAT DO WE HAVE HERE?
A SAMURAI...
...AND HE'S DEAD!
LET'S SEE WHAT YOU HAVE ON YOU.
WHAT'S THIS?
HE WENT INTO THIS ALLEY! HE IS HURT AND COULD NOT HAVE GONE FAR!
HUH?
THERE HE IS!
THERE'S SOMEONE WITH HIM!
GET HIM!
UH-OH!
12

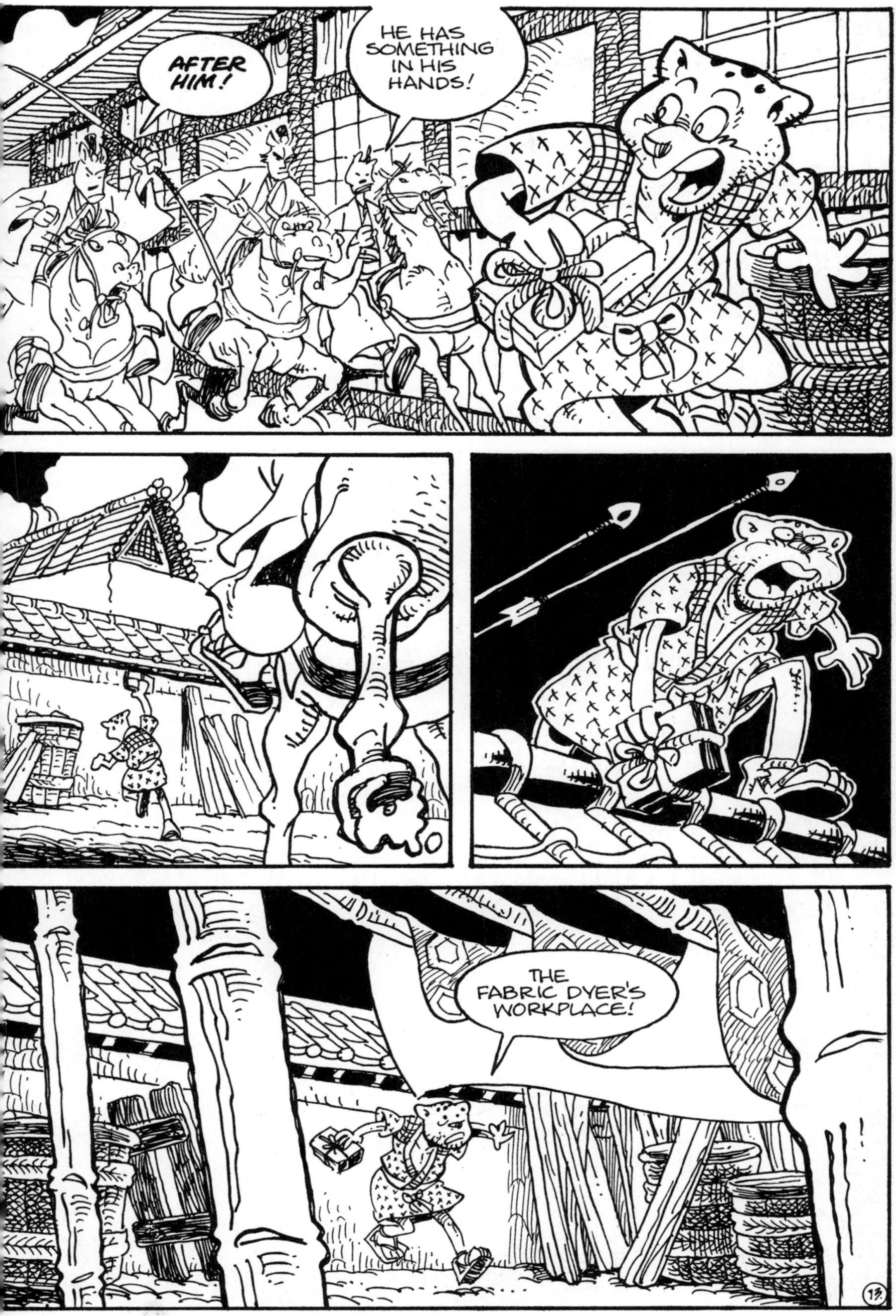

AFTER HIM!
HE HAS SOMETHING IN HIS HANDS!
THE FABRIC DYER'S WORKPLACE!
13

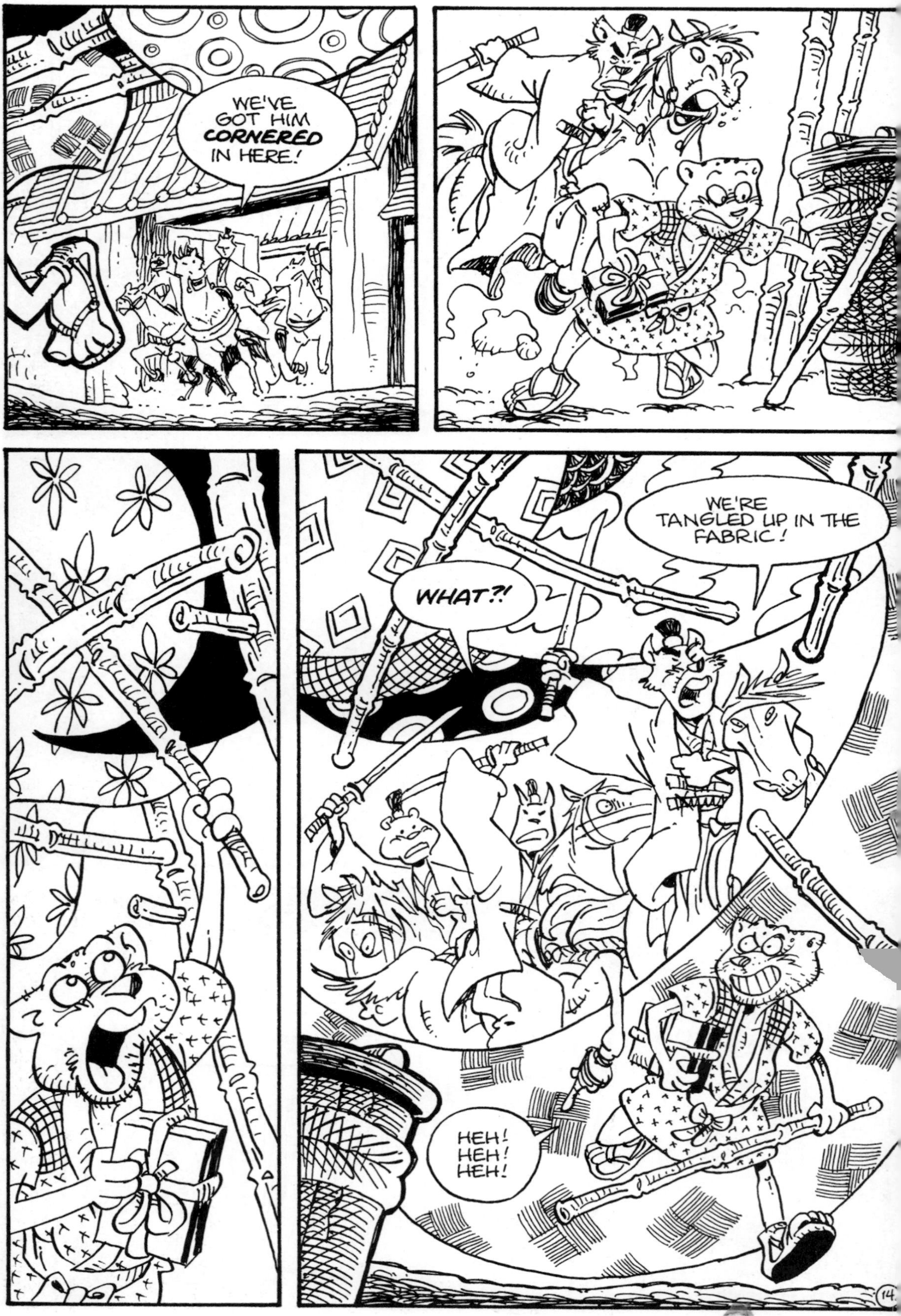
WE'VE GOT HIM CORNERED IN HERE!
WE'RE TANGLED UP IN THE FABRIC!
WHAT?!
HEH! HEH! HEH!
14.

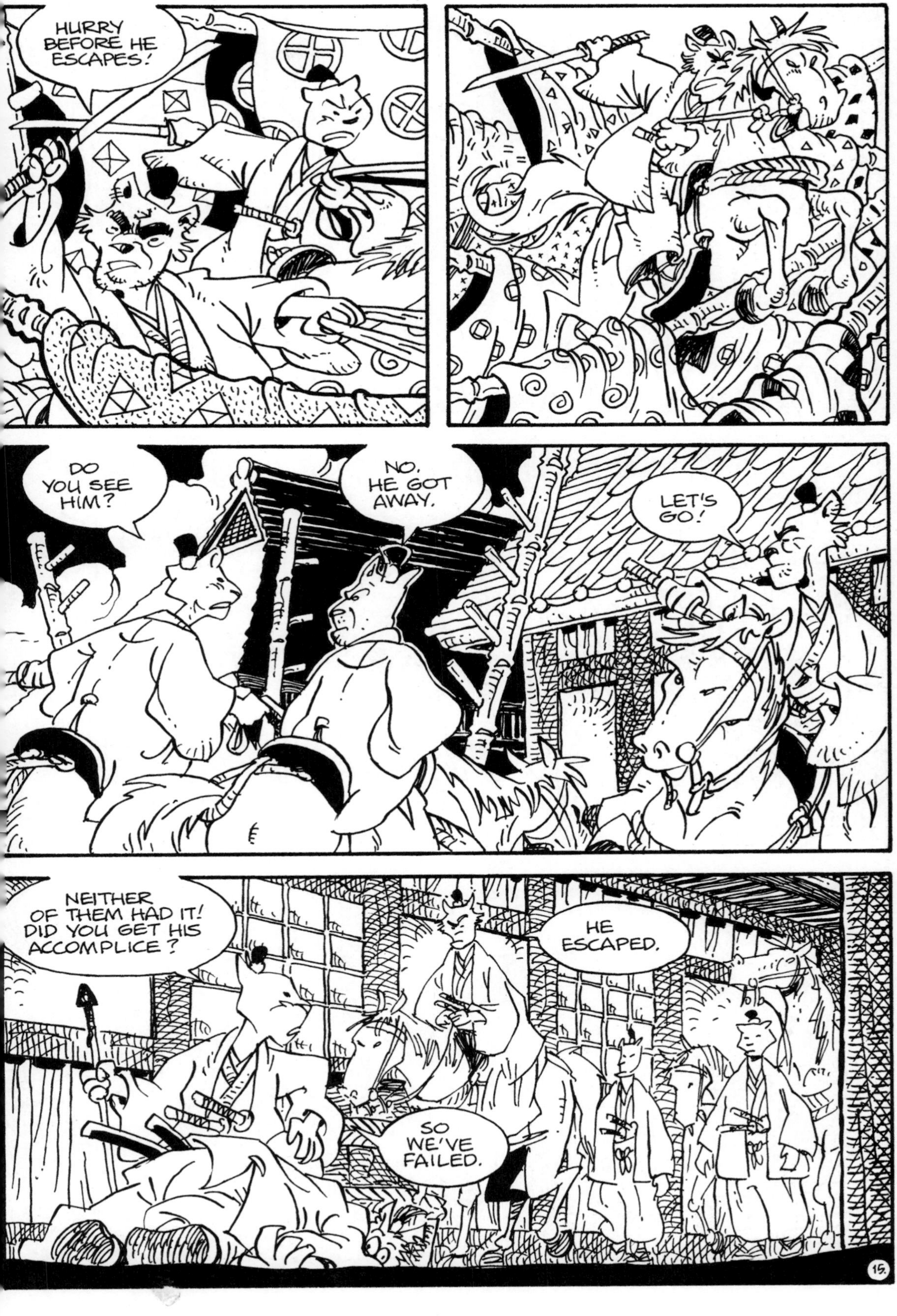
HURRY BEFORE HE ESCAPES!
DO YOU SEE HIM?
NO, HE GOT AWAY.
LET'S GO!
NEITHER OF THEM HAD IT! DID YOU GET HIS ACCOMPLICE?
HE ESCAPED.
SO WE'VE FAILED.
15.

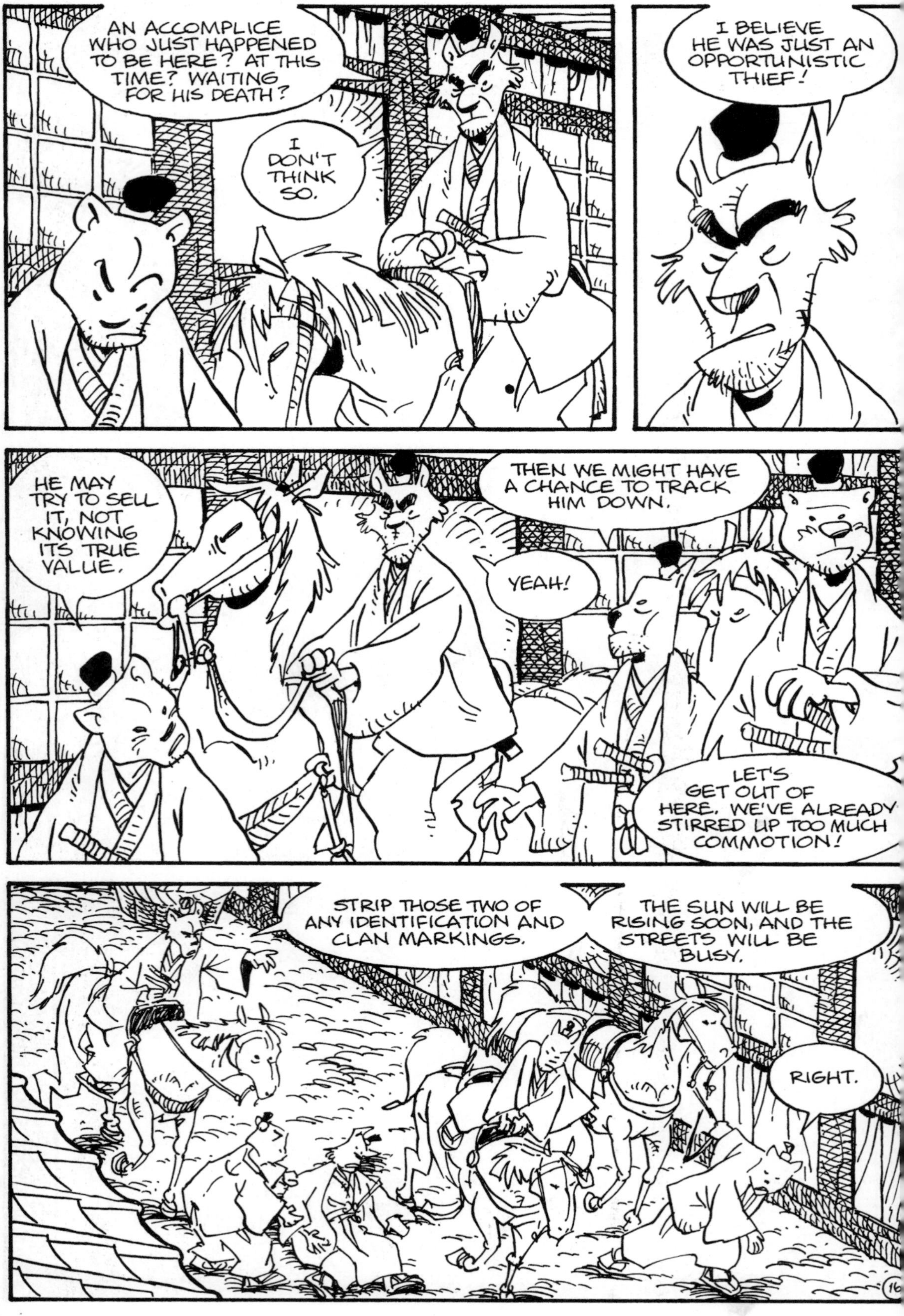
AN ACCOMPLICE WHO JUST HAPPENED TO BE HERE? AT THIS TIME? WAITING FOR HIS DEATH?
I DON'T THINK SO.
I BELIEVE HE WAS JUST AN OPPORTUNISTIC THIEF!
HE MAY TRY TO SELL IT, NOT KNOWING ITS TRUE VALUE.
THEN WE MIGHT HAVE A CHANCE TO TRACK HIM DOWN.
YEAH!
LET'S GET OUT OF HERE. WE'VE ALREADY STIRRED UP TOO MUCH COMMOTION!
STRIP THOSE TWO OF ANY IDENTIFICATION AND CLAN MARKINGS.
THE SUN WILL BE RISING SOON, AND THE STREETS WILL BE BUSY.
RIGHT.
16

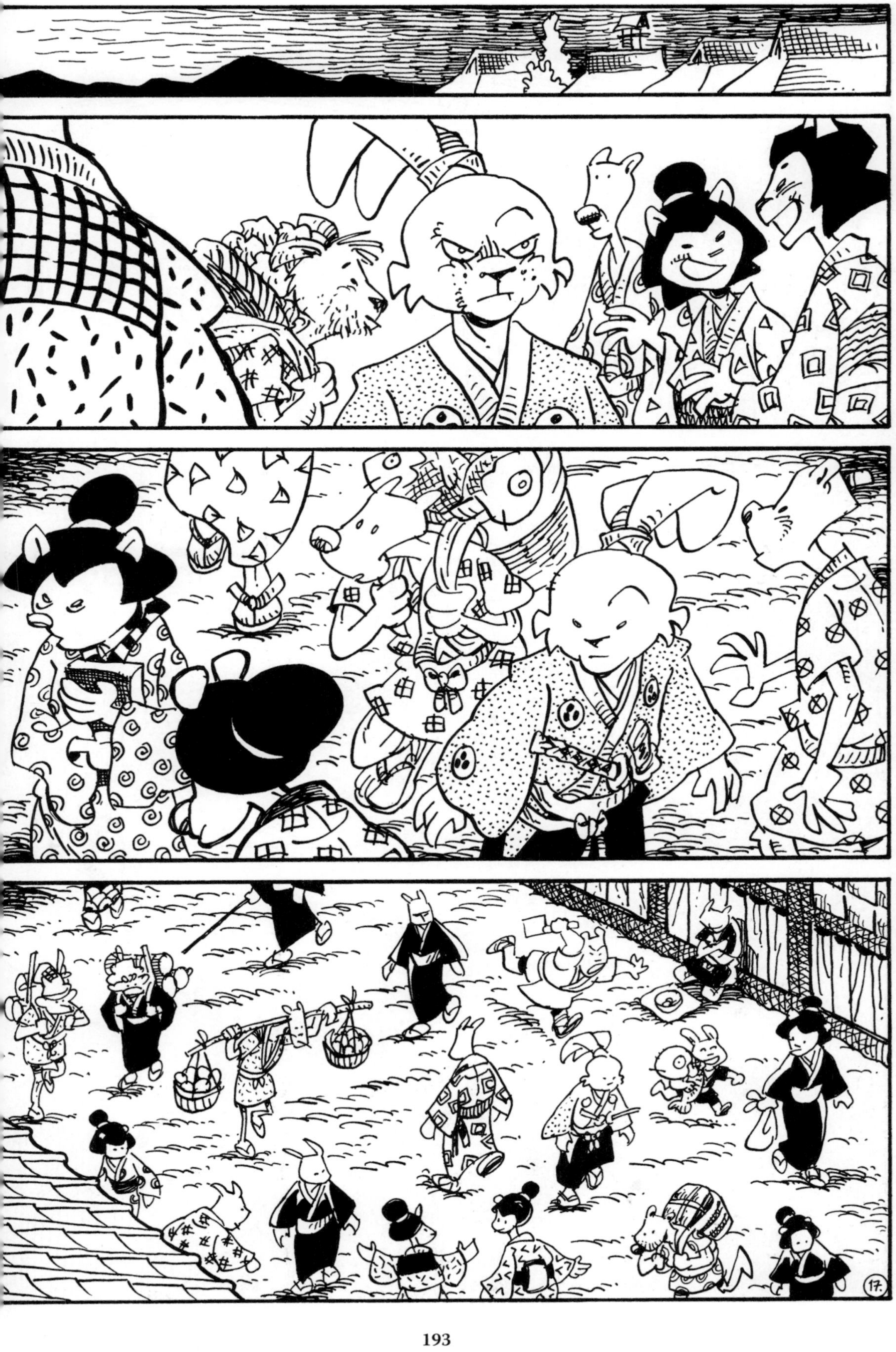
17.

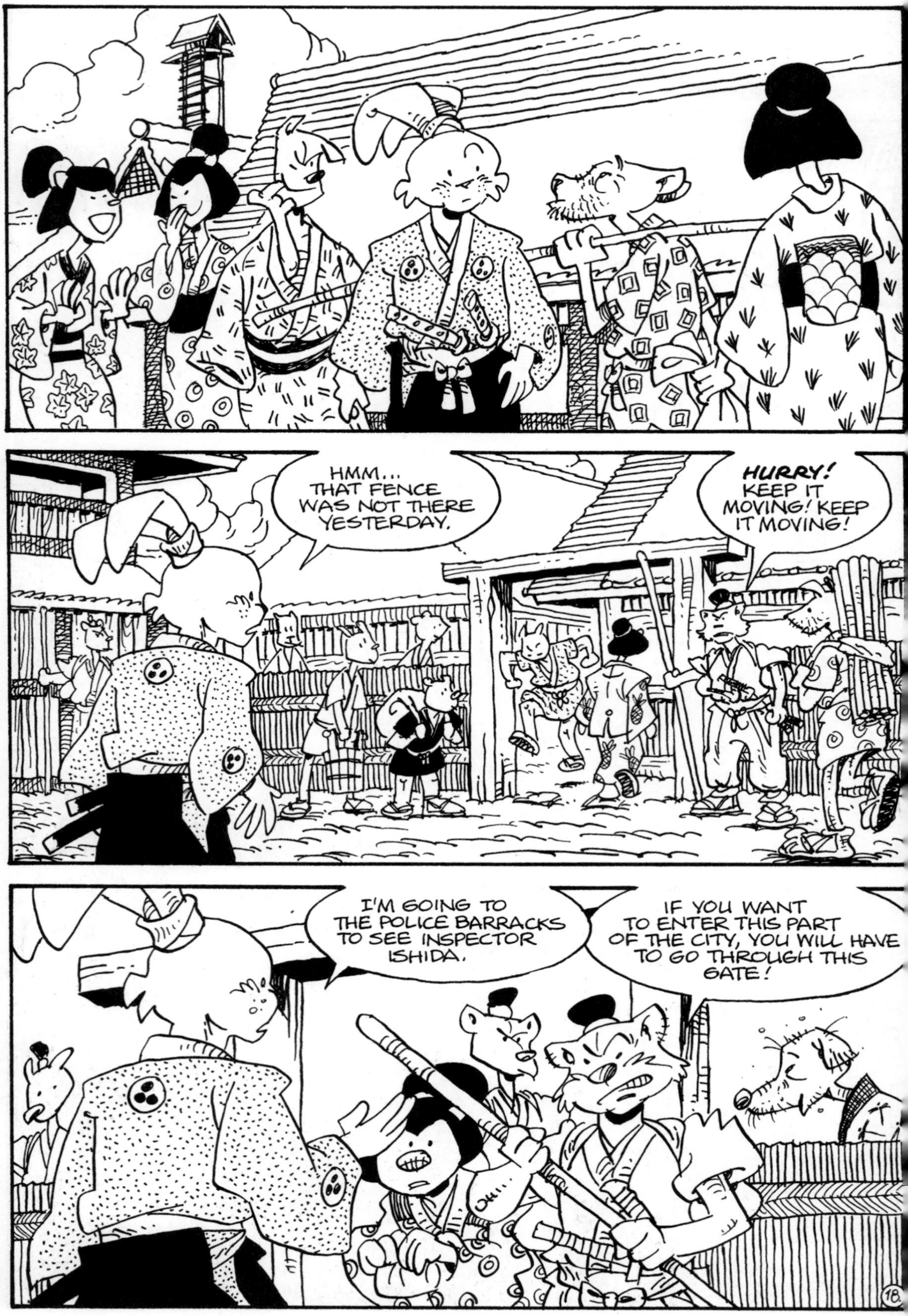
HMM... THAT FENCE WAS NOT THERE YESTERDAY.
HURRY! KEEP IT MOVING! KEEP IT MOVING!
I'M GOING TO THE POLICE BARRACKS TO SEE INSPECTOR ISHIDA.
IF YOU WANT TO ENTER THIS PART OF THE CITY, YOU WILL HAVE TO GO THROUGH THIS GATE!
18

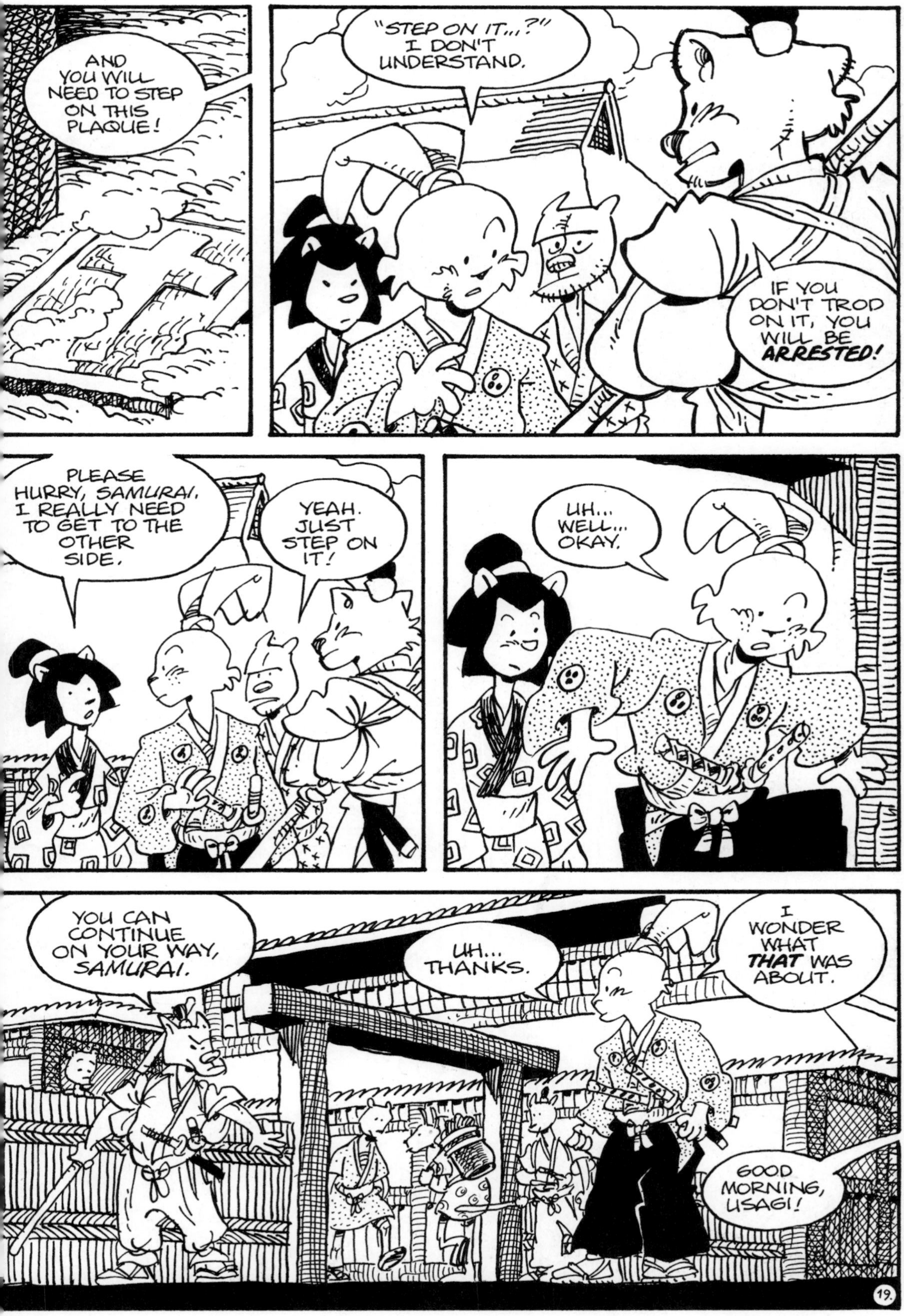
AND YOU WILL NEED TO STEP ON THIS PLAQUE!
"STEP ON IT...?" I DON'T UNDERSTAND.
IF YOU DON'T TROD ON IT, YOU WILL BE ARRESTED!
PLEASE HURRY, SAMURAI. I REALLY NEED TO GET TO THE OTHER SIDE.
YEAH. JUST STEP ON IT!
UH... WELL... OKAY.
YOU CAN CONTINUE ON YOUR WAY, SAMURAI.
UH... THANKS.
I WONDER WHAT THAT WAS ABOUT.
GOOD MORNING, USAGI!
19.

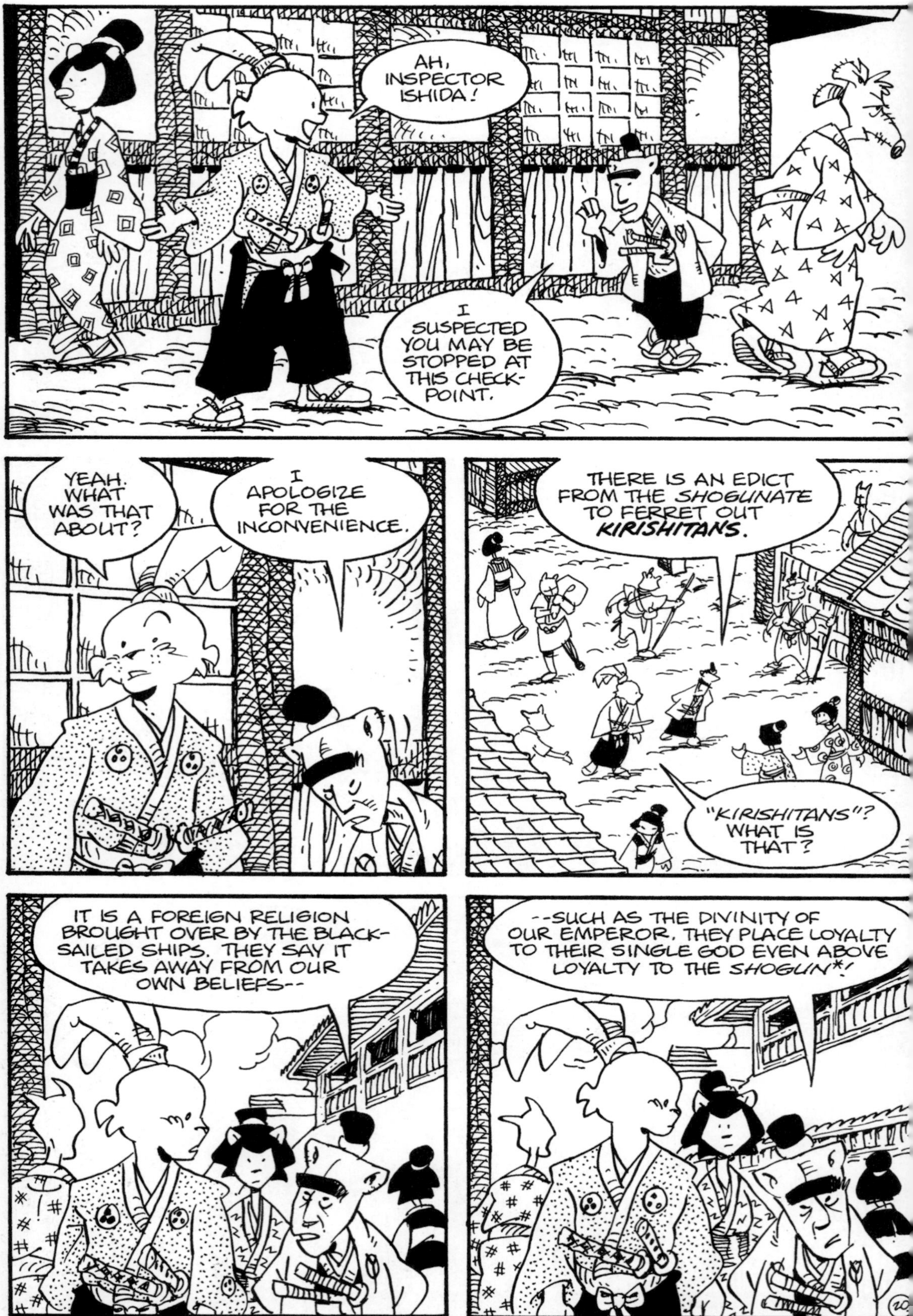
AH, INSPECTOR ISHIDA!
I SUSPECTED YOU MAY BE STOPPED AT THIS CHECK-POINT.
YEAH. WHAT WAS THAT ABOUT?
I APOLOGIZE FOR THE INCONVENIENCE.
THERE IS AN EDICT FROM THE *SHOGUNATE* TO FERRET OUT **KIRISHITANS**.
"*KIRISHITANS*"? WHAT IS THAT?
IT IS A FOREIGN RELIGION BROUGHT OVER BY THE BLACK-SAILED SHIPS. THEY SAY IT TAKES AWAY FROM OUR OWN BELIEFS--
--SUCH AS THE DIVINITY OF OUR EMPEROR. THEY PLACE LOYALTY TO THEIR SINGLE GOD EVEN ABOVE LOYALTY TO THE *SHOGUN**!

*MILITARY DICTATOR

TEMPORARY FENCES ARE ERECTED BY SHOGUNATE OFFICIALS AND MANNED BY THEIR *SAMURAI*.

THEY ARE LITTLE BETTER THAN THUGS, IF YOU ASK ME!

YOU MUST STEP ON A *FUMI-E** TO SHOW YOUR CONTEMPT FOR THAT RELIGION BEFORE BEING ALLOWED TO PASS THROUGH THE GATE.

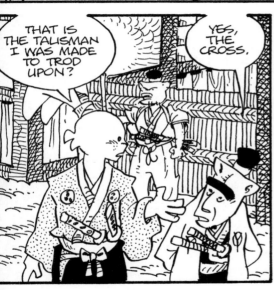

THAT IS THE TALISMAN I WAS MADE TO TROD UPON?

YES, THE CROSS.

IT REPRESENTS THEIR GOD, WHO CAME TO OUR WORLD AND WAS CRUCIFIED.

OH?

CRUCIFIXION IS A PUNISHMENT RESERVED FOR CRIMINALS.

AND SO THEIR GOD WAS JUDGED.

THEY WORSHIP A *CRIMINAL*?

HA! HA! THEIR BELIEFS CAN BE VERY COMPLICATED.

*TRAMPLING IMAGE

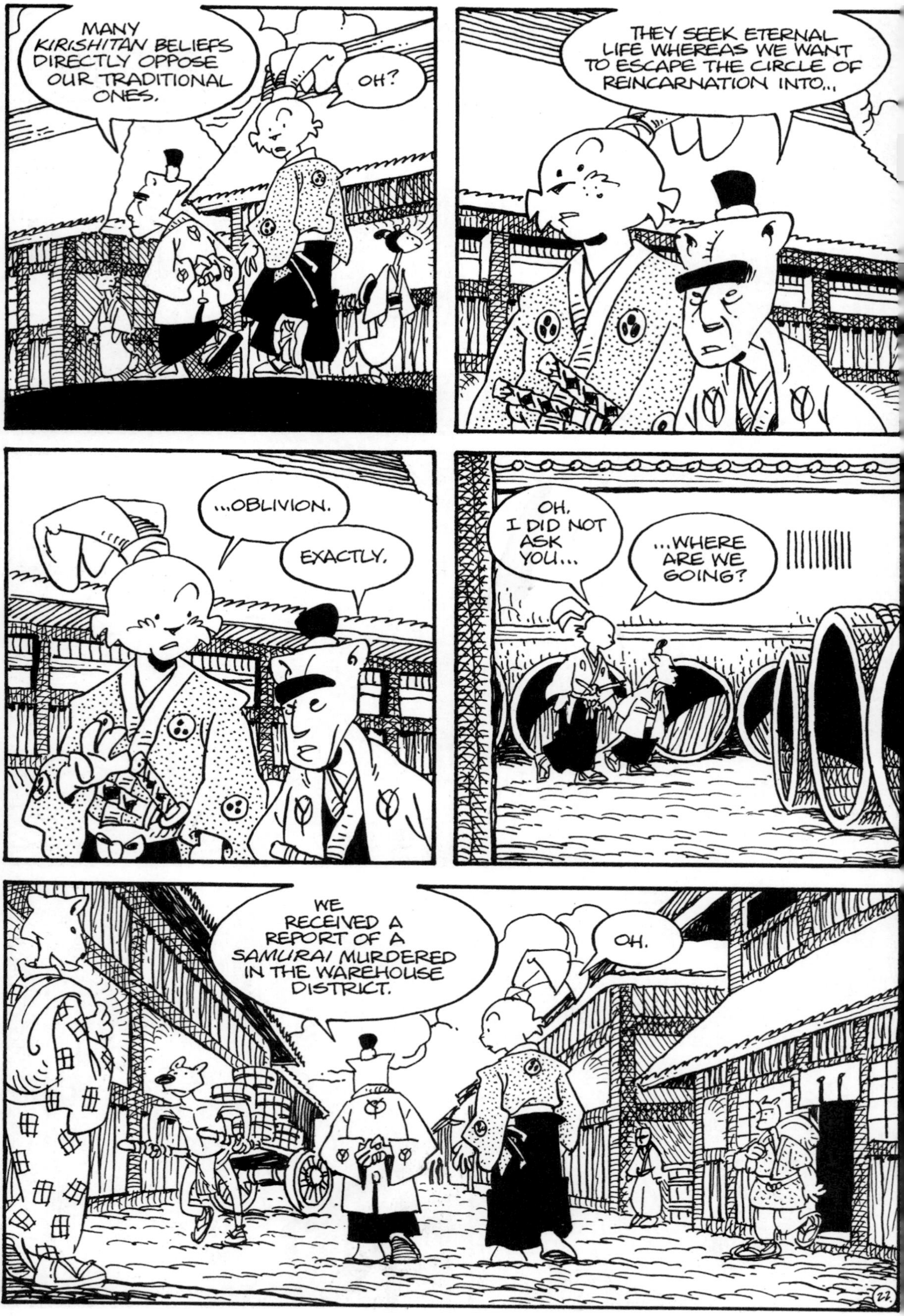
MANY KIRISHITAN BELIEFS DIRECTLY OPPOSE OUR TRADITIONAL ONES.
OH?
THEY SEEK ETERNAL LIFE WHEREAS WE WANT TO ESCAPE THE CIRCLE OF REINCARNATION INTO...
...OBLIVION.
EXACTLY.
OH. I DID NOT ASK YOU...
...WHERE ARE WE GOING?
WE RECEIVED A REPORT OF A SAMURAI MURDERED IN THE WAREHOUSE DISTRICT.
OH.
22

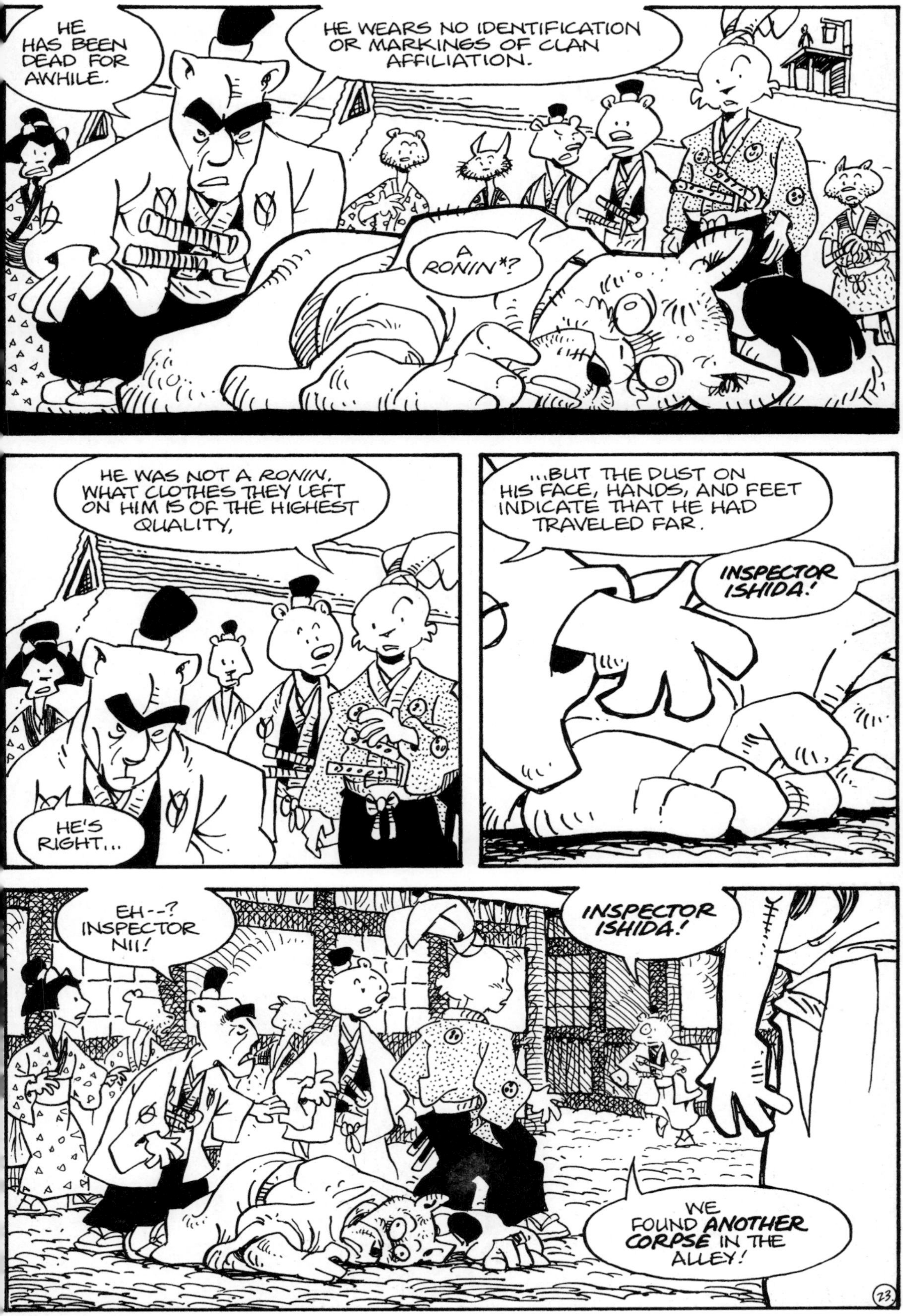
HE HAS BEEN DEAD FOR AWHILE.
HE WEARS NO IDENTIFICATION OR MARKINGS OF CLAN AFFILIATION.
A RONIN*?
HE WAS NOT A RONIN. WHAT CLOTHES THEY LEFT ON HIM IS OF THE HIGHEST QUALITY,
HE'S RIGHT...
...BUT THE DUST ON HIS FACE, HANDS, AND FEET INDICATE THAT HE HAD TRAVELED FAR.
INSPECTOR ISHIDA!
EH--? INSPECTOR NII!
INSPECTOR ISHIDA!
WE FOUND ANOTHER CORPSE IN THE ALLEY!
23

*MASTERLESS SAMURAI

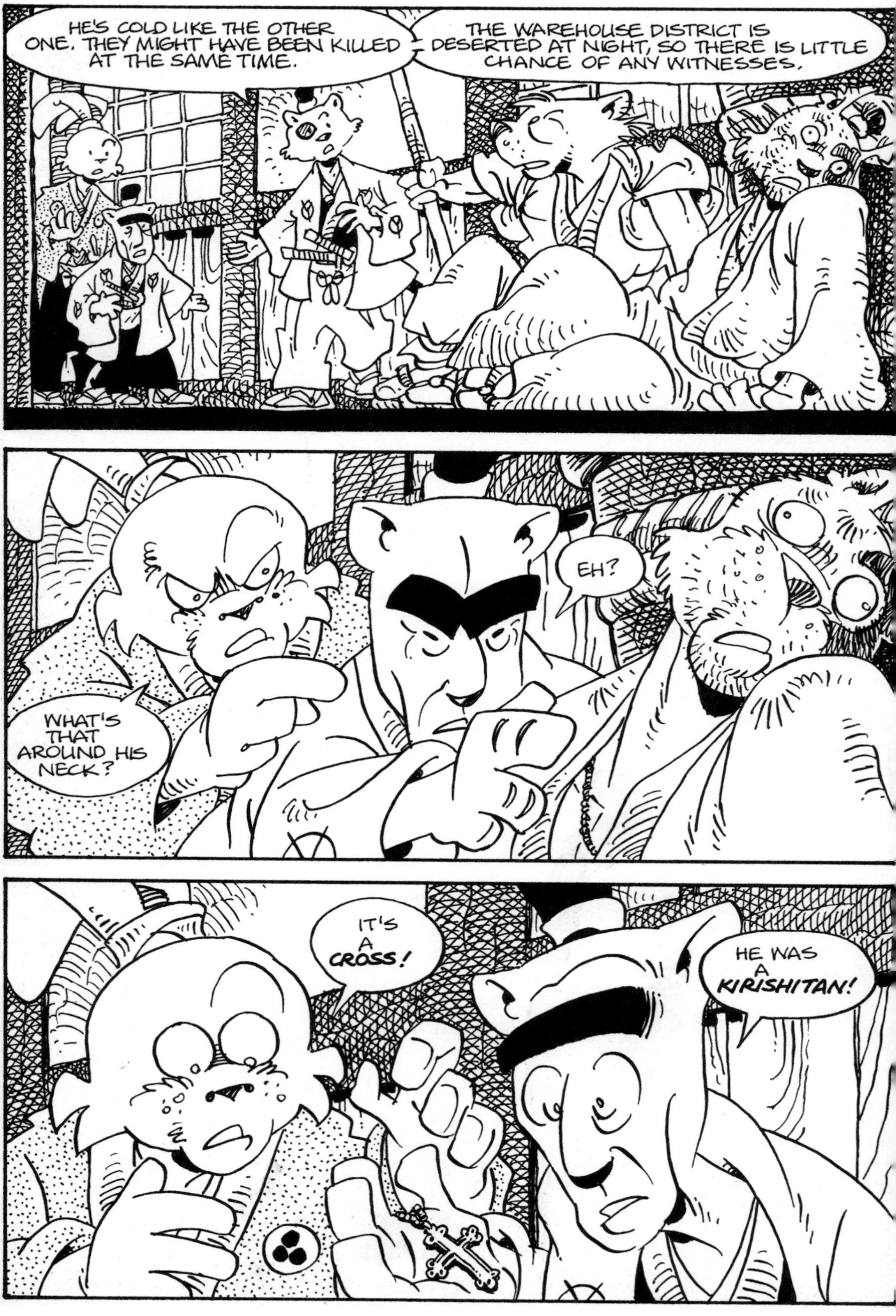
HE'S COLD LIKE THE OTHER ONE. THEY MIGHT HAVE BEEN KILLED AT THE SAME TIME.
THE WAREHOUSE DISTRICT IS DESERTED AT NIGHT, SO THERE IS LITTLE CHANCE OF ANY WITNESSES.
EH?
WHAT'S THAT AROUND HIS NECK?
IT'S A CROSS!
HE WAS A KIRISHITAN!

THE HIDDEN PART TWO

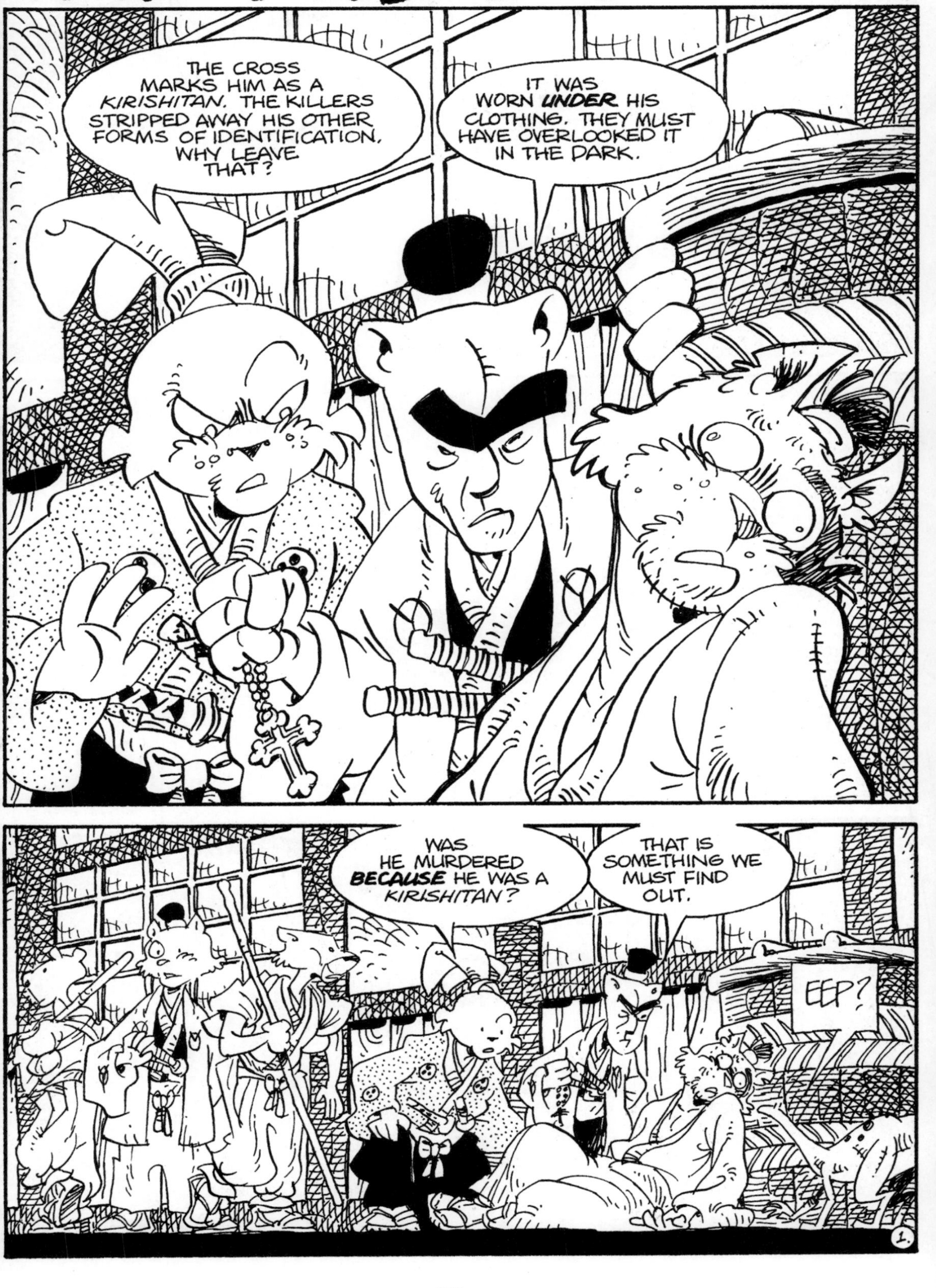
THE CROSS MARKS HIM AS A *KIRISHITAN*. THE KILLERS STRIPPED AWAY HIS OTHER FORMS OF IDENTIFICATION. WHY LEAVE THAT?
IT WAS WORN ***UNDER*** HIS CLOTHING. THEY MUST HAVE OVERLOOKED IT IN THE DARK.
WAS HE MURDERED ***BECAUSE*** HE WAS A *KIRISHITAN?*
THAT IS SOMETHING WE MUST FIND OUT.
EEP?
1.

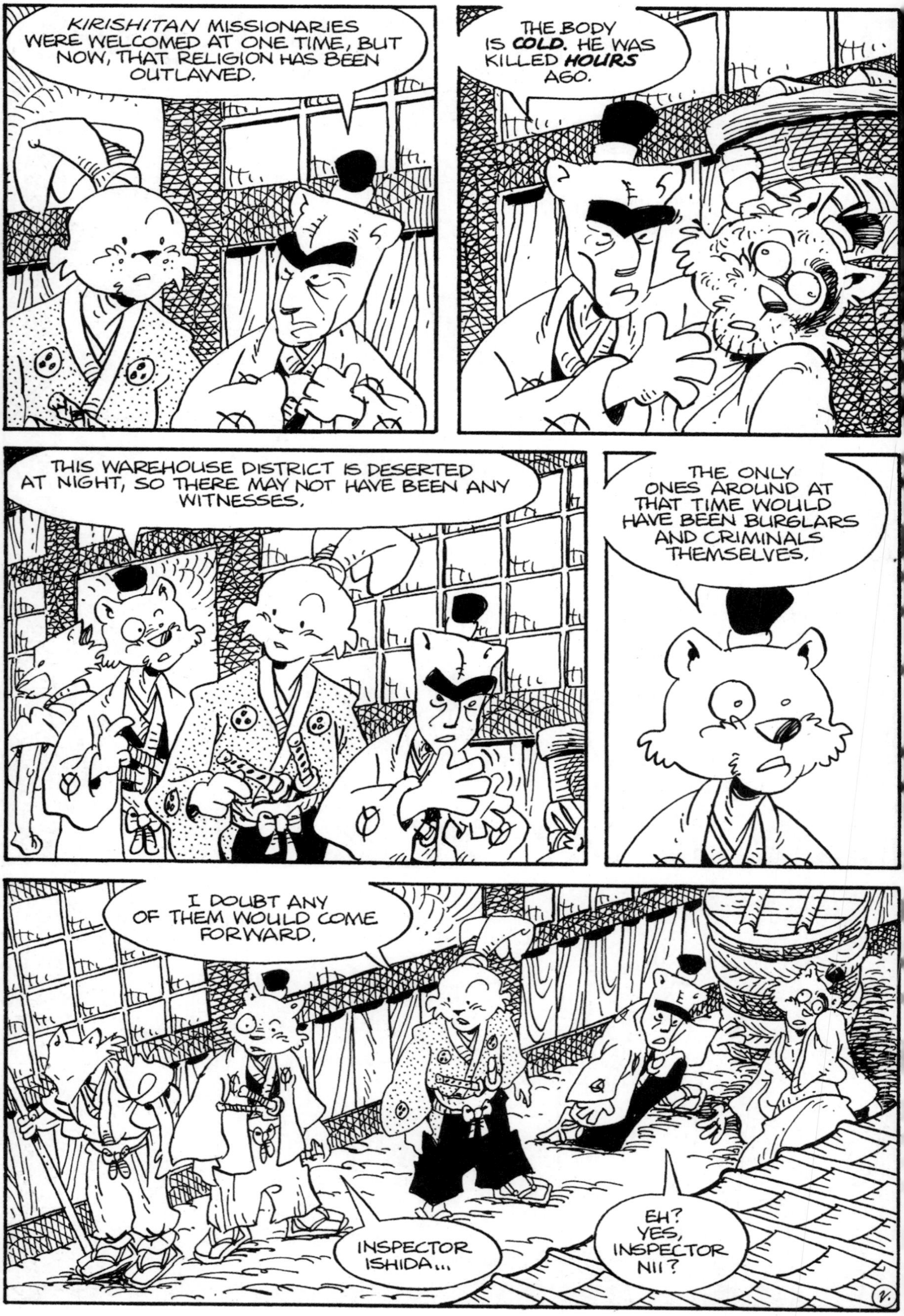
KIRISHITAN MISSIONARIES WERE WELCOMED AT ONE TIME, BUT NOW, THAT RELIGION HAS BEEN OUTLAWED.
THE BODY IS COLD. HE WAS KILLED HOURS AGO.
THIS WAREHOUSE DISTRICT IS DESERTED AT NIGHT, SO THERE MAY NOT HAVE BEEN ANY WITNESSES.
THE ONLY ONES AROUND AT THAT TIME WOULD HAVE BEEN BURGLARS AND CRIMINALS THEMSELVES.
I DOUBT ANY OF THEM WOULD COME FORWARD.
INSPECTOR ISHIDA...
EH? YES, INSPECTOR NII?

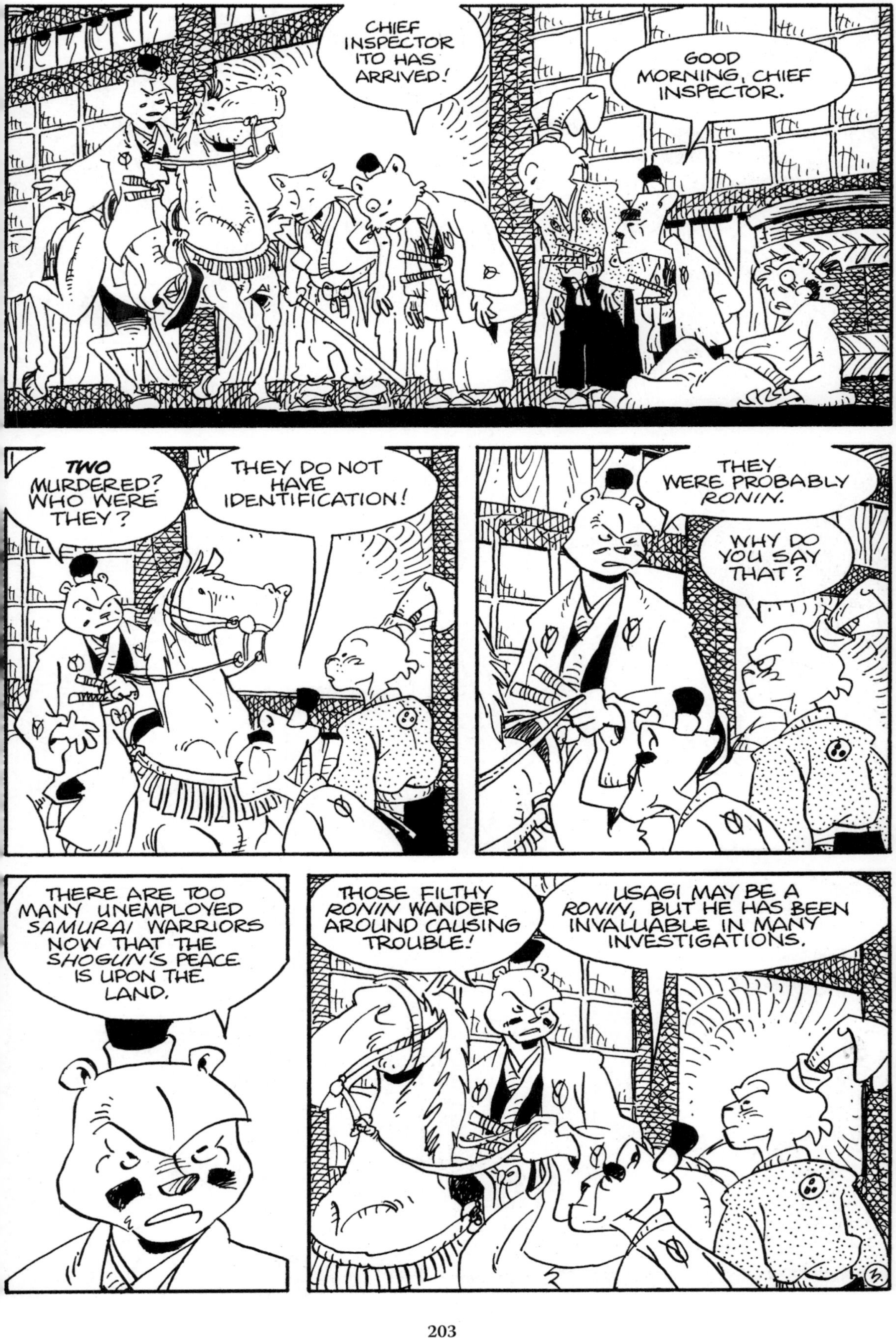

CHIEF INSPECTOR ITO HAS ARRIVED!
GOOD MORNING, CHIEF INSPECTOR.
TWO MURDERED? WHO WERE THEY?
THEY DO NOT HAVE IDENTIFICATION!
THEY WERE PROBABLY RONIN.
WHY DO YOU SAY THAT?
THERE ARE TOO MANY UNEMPLOYED SAMURAI WARRIORS NOW THAT THE SHOGUN'S PEACE IS UPON THE LAND.
THOSE FILTHY RONIN WANDER AROUND CAUSING TROUBLE!
USAGI MAY BE A RONIN, BUT HE HAS BEEN INVALUABLE IN MANY INVESTIGATIONS.

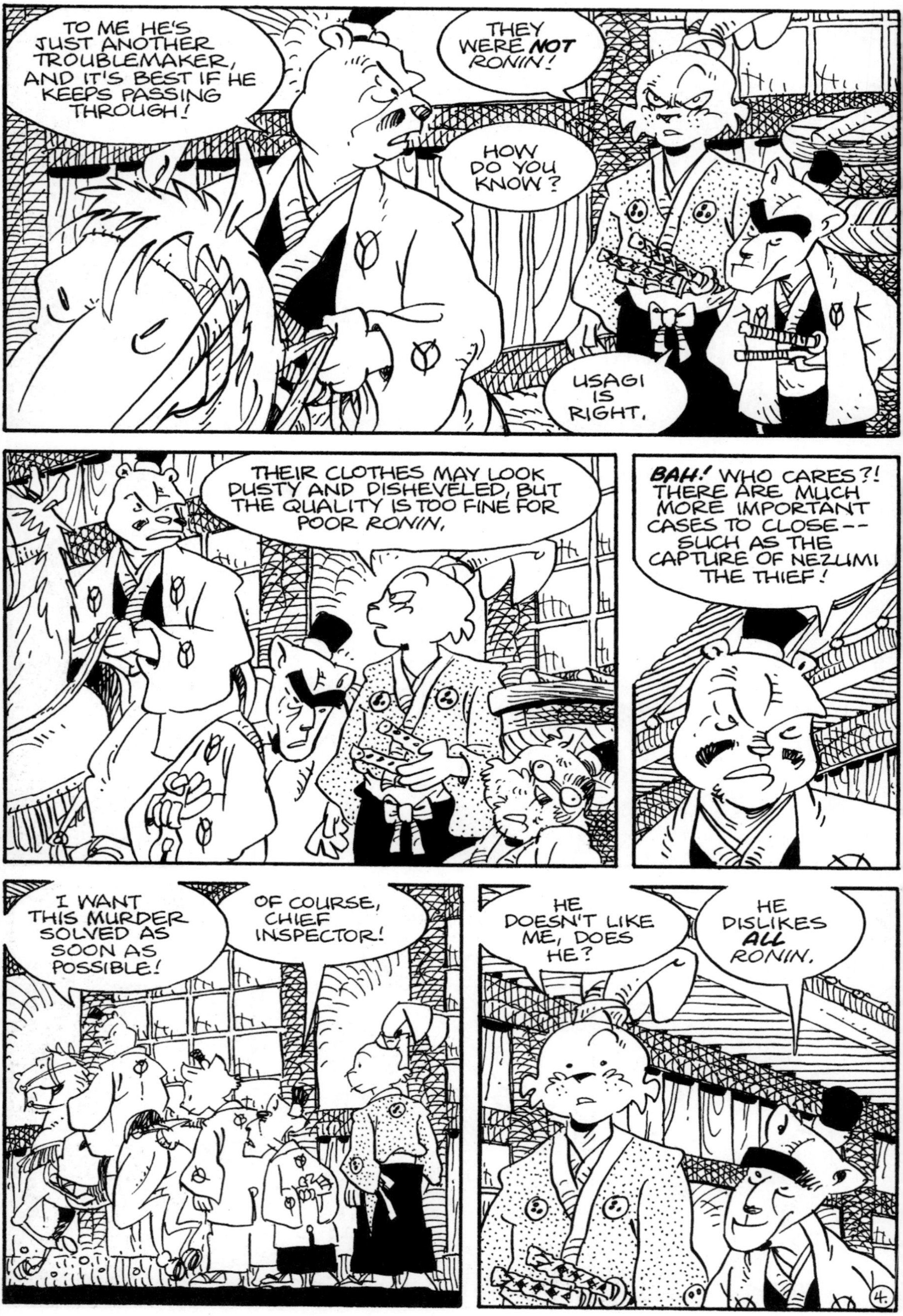
TO ME HE'S JUST ANOTHER TROUBLEMAKER, AND IT'S BEST IF HE KEEPS PASSING THROUGH!
THEY WERE NOT RONIN!
HOW DO YOU KNOW?
USAGI IS RIGHT.
THEIR CLOTHES MAY LOOK DUSTY AND DISHEVELED, BUT THE QUALITY IS TOO FINE FOR POOR RONIN.
BAH! WHO CARES?! THERE ARE MUCH MORE IMPORTANT CASES TO CLOSE-- SUCH AS THE CAPTURE OF NEZUMI THE THIEF!
I WANT THIS MURDER SOLVED AS SOON AS POSSIBLE!
OF COURSE, CHIEF INSPECTOR!
HE DOESN'T LIKE ME, DOES HE?
HE DISLIKES ALL RONIN.
4.

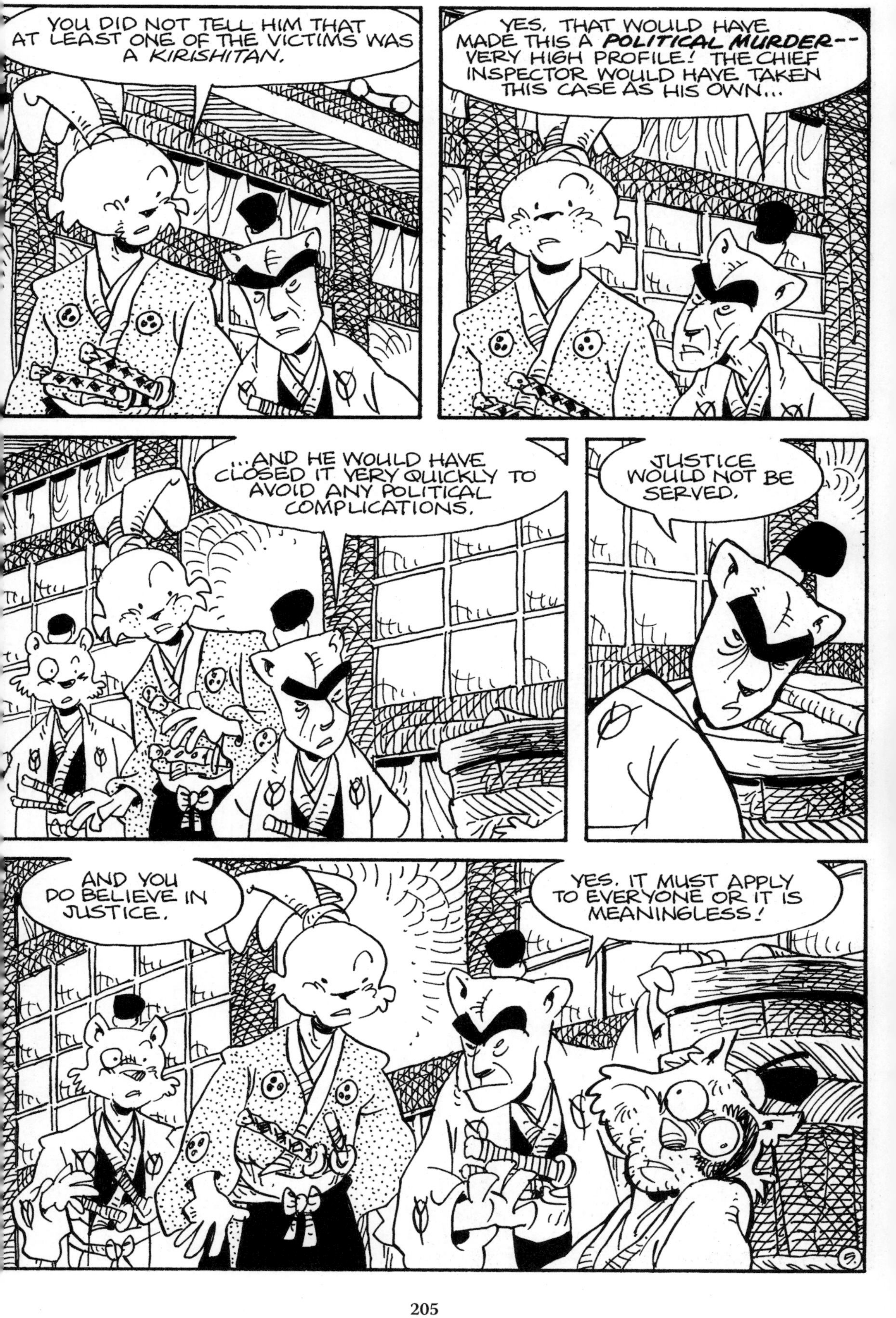
YOU DID NOT TELL HIM THAT AT LEAST ONE OF THE VICTIMS WAS A KIRISHITAN.
YES. THAT WOULD HAVE MADE THIS A POLITICAL MURDER-- VERY HIGH PROFILE! THE CHIEF INSPECTOR WOULD HAVE TAKEN THIS CASE AS HIS OWN...
...AND HE WOULD HAVE CLOSED IT VERY QUICKLY TO AVOID ANY POLITICAL COMPLICATIONS.
JUSTICE WOULD NOT BE SERVED.
AND YOU DO BELIEVE IN JUSTICE.
YES. IT MUST APPLY TO EVERYONE OR IT IS MEANINGLESS!
5

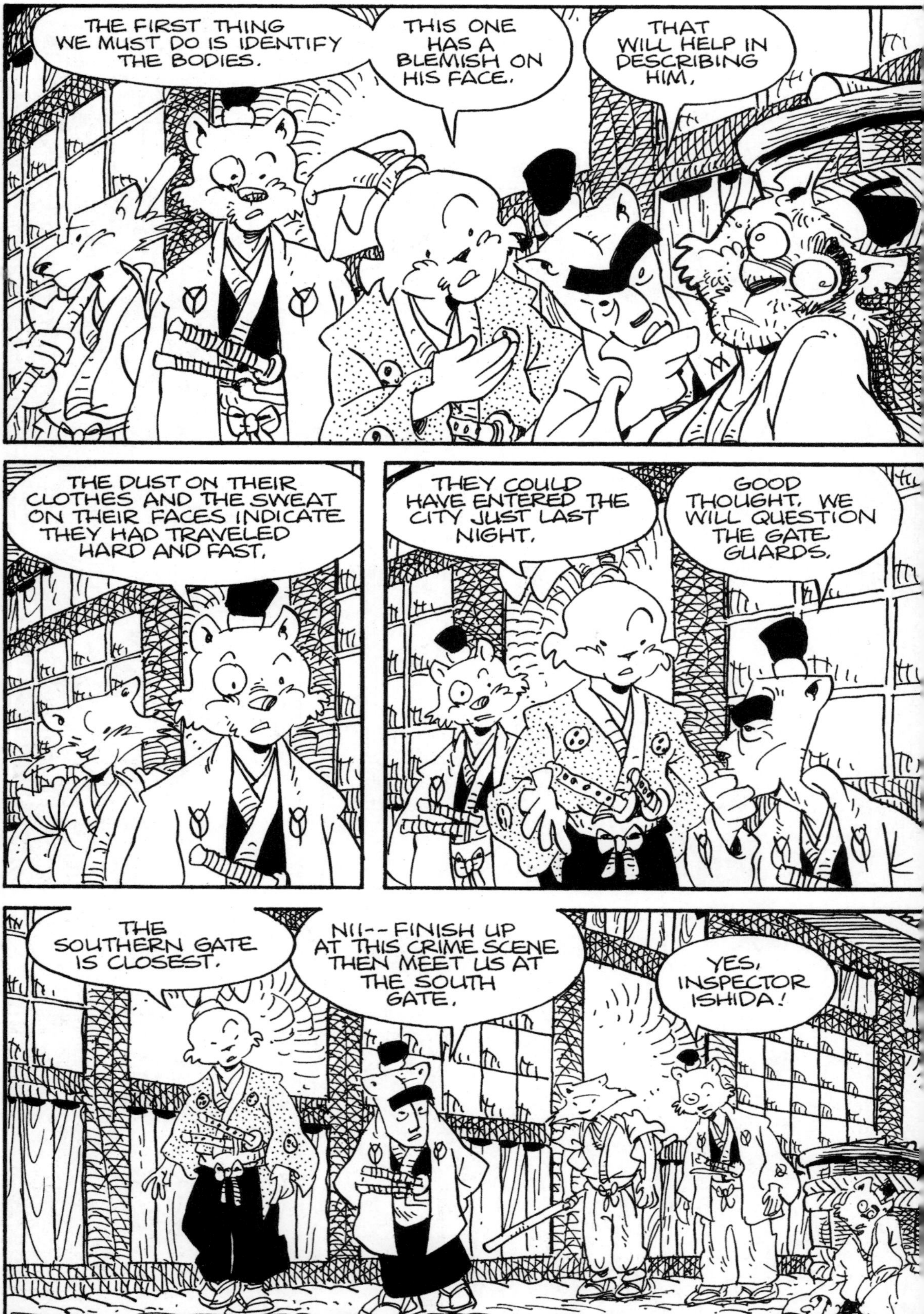
THE FIRST THING WE MUST DO IS IDENTIFY THE BODIES.
THIS ONE HAS A BLEMISH ON HIS FACE.
THAT WILL HELP IN DESCRIBING HIM.
THE DUST ON THEIR CLOTHES AND THE SWEAT ON THEIR FACES INDICATE THEY HAD TRAVELED HARD AND FAST.
THEY COULD HAVE ENTERED THE CITY JUST LAST NIGHT.
GOOD THOUGHT. WE WILL QUESTION THE GATE GUARDS.
THE SOUTHERN GATE IS CLOSEST.
NII--FINISH UP AT THIS CRIME SCENE THEN MEET US AT THE SOUTH GATE.
YES, INSPECTOR ISHIDA!
6.

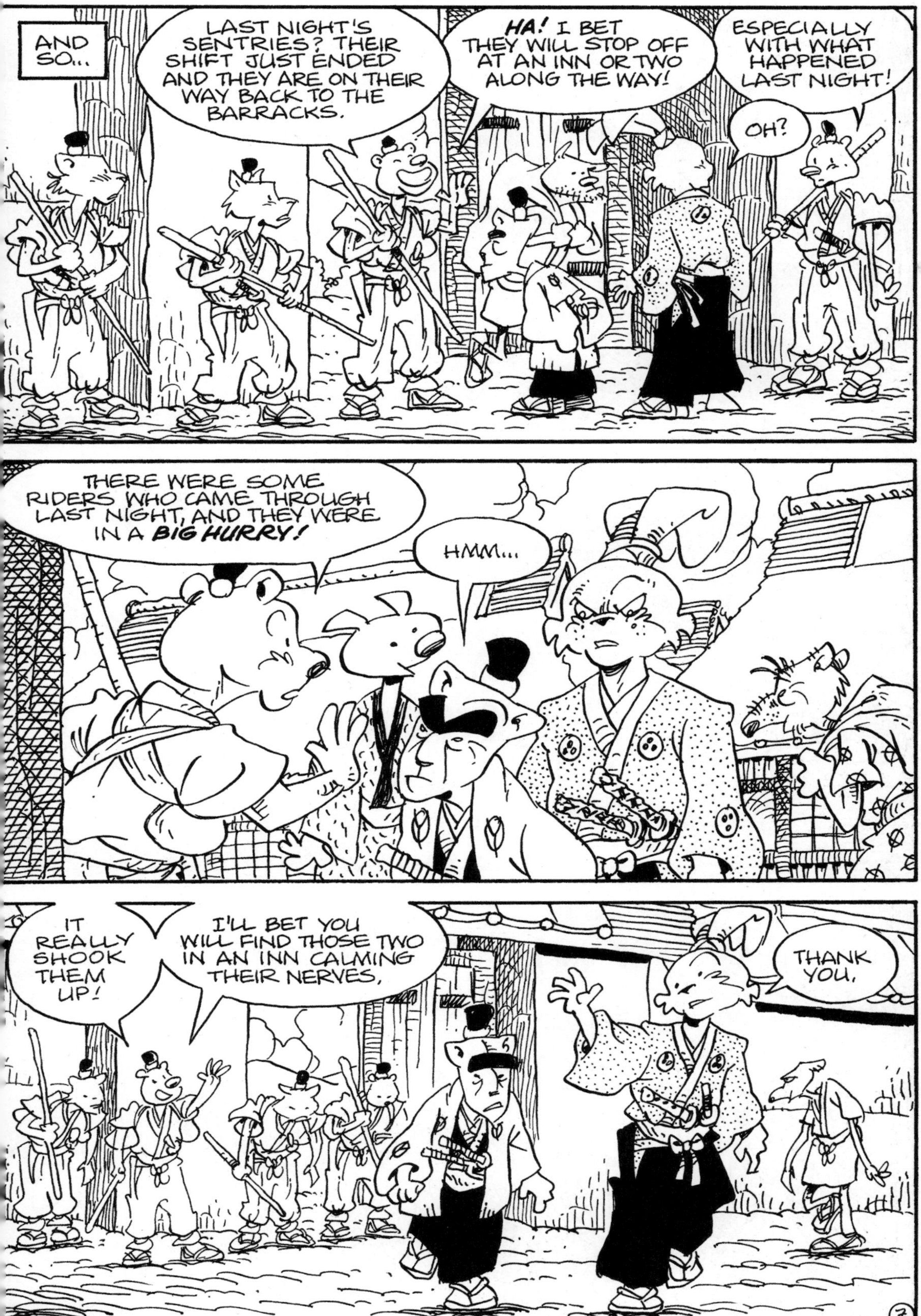
AND SO...
LAST NIGHT'S SENTRIES? THEIR SHIFT JUST ENDED AND THEY ARE ON THEIR WAY BACK TO THE BARRACKS.
HA! I BET THEY WILL STOP OFF AT AN INN OR TWO ALONG THE WAY!
ESPECIALLY WITH WHAT HAPPENED LAST NIGHT!
OH?
THERE WERE SOME RIDERS WHO CAME THROUGH LAST NIGHT, AND THEY WERE IN A BIG HURRY!
HMM...
IT REALLY SHOOK THEM UP!
I'LL BET YOU WILL FIND THOSE TWO IN AN INN CALMING THEIR NERVES.
THANK YOU.
7.

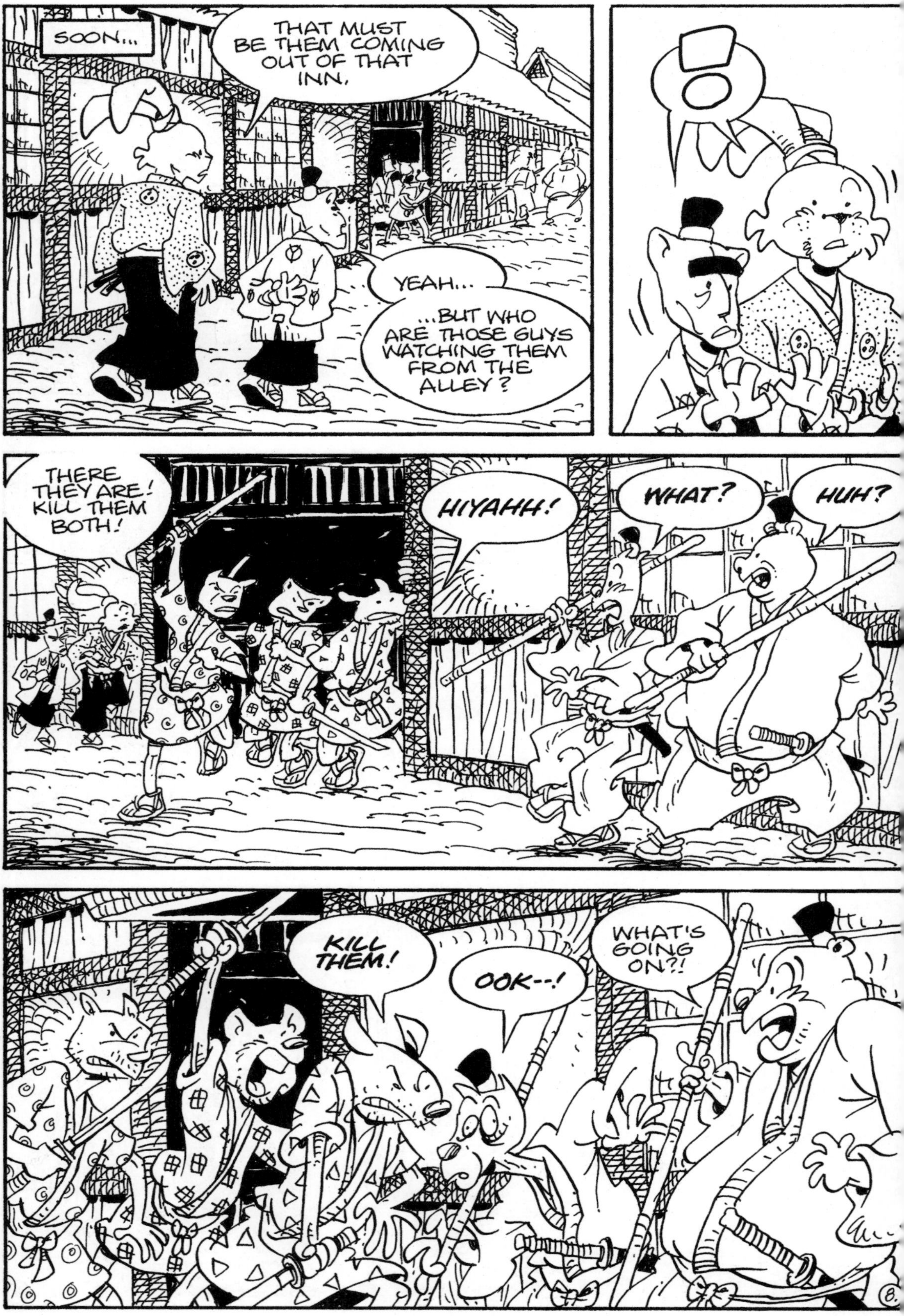
SOON...
THAT MUST BE THEM COMING OUT OF THAT INN.
YEAH...
...BUT WHO ARE THOSE GUYS WATCHING THEM FROM THE ALLEY?
!
THERE THEY ARE! KILL THEM BOTH!
HIYAHH!
WHAT?
HUH?
KILL THEM!
OOK--!
WHAT'S GOING ON?!

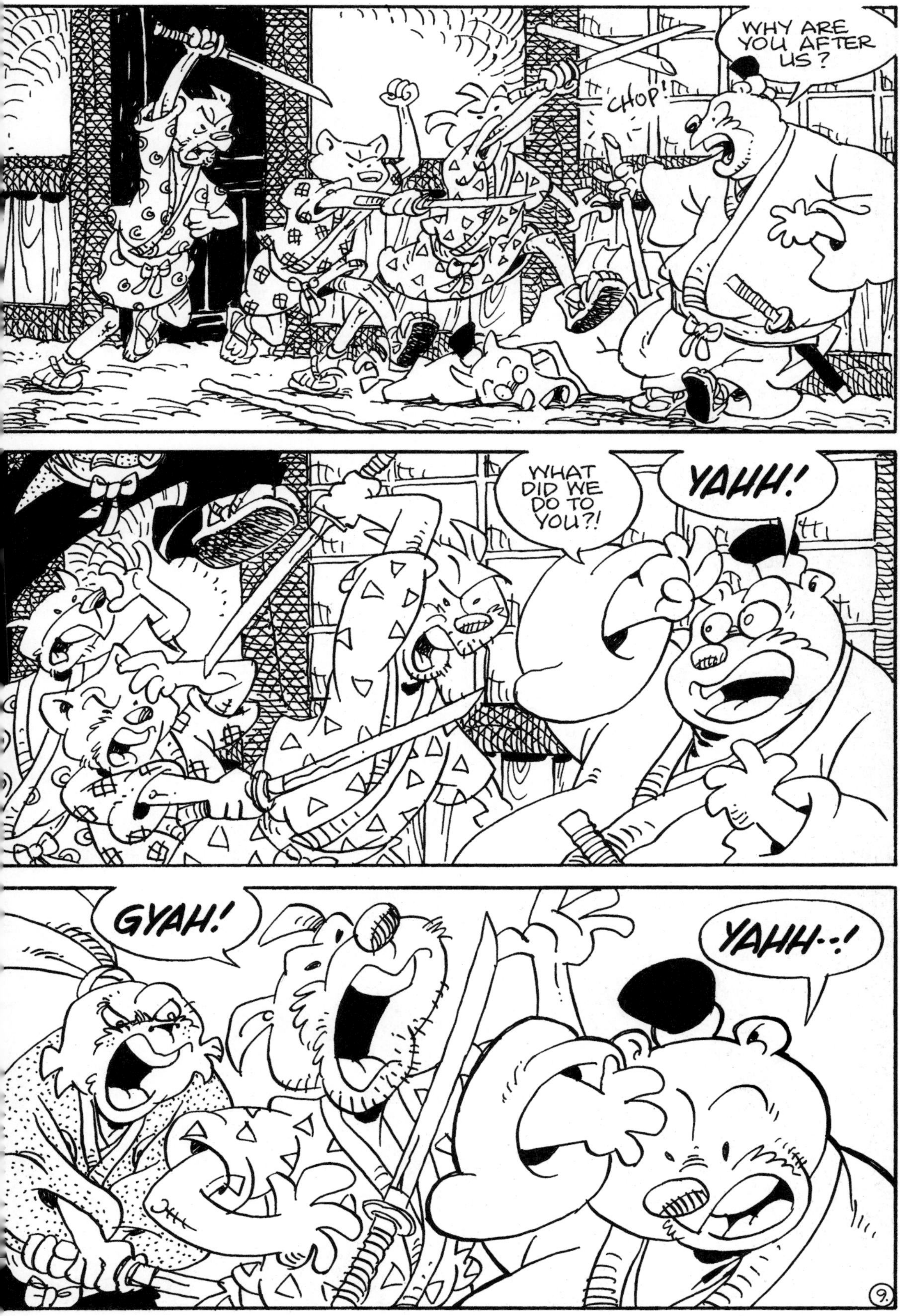
CHOP!
WHY ARE YOU AFTER US?
WHAT DID WE DO TO YOU?!
YAHH!
GYAH!
YAHH--!
9.

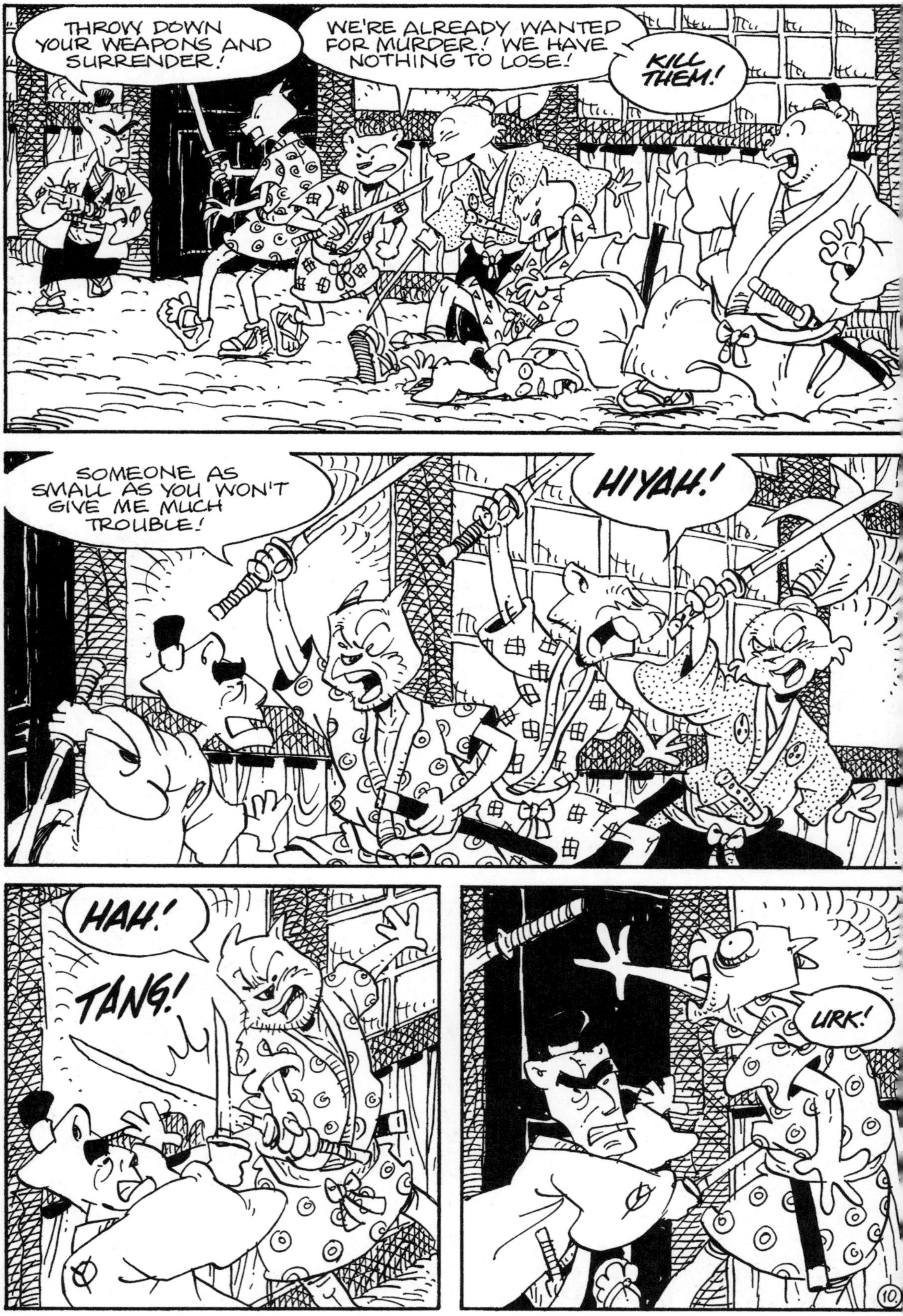

THROW DOWN YOUR WEAPONS AND SURRENDER!
WE'RE ALREADY WANTED FOR MURDER! WE HAVE NOTHING TO LOSE!
KILL THEM!
SOMEONE AS SMALL AS YOU WON'T GIVE ME MUCH TROUBLE!
HIYAH!
HAH!
TANG!
URK!
10.

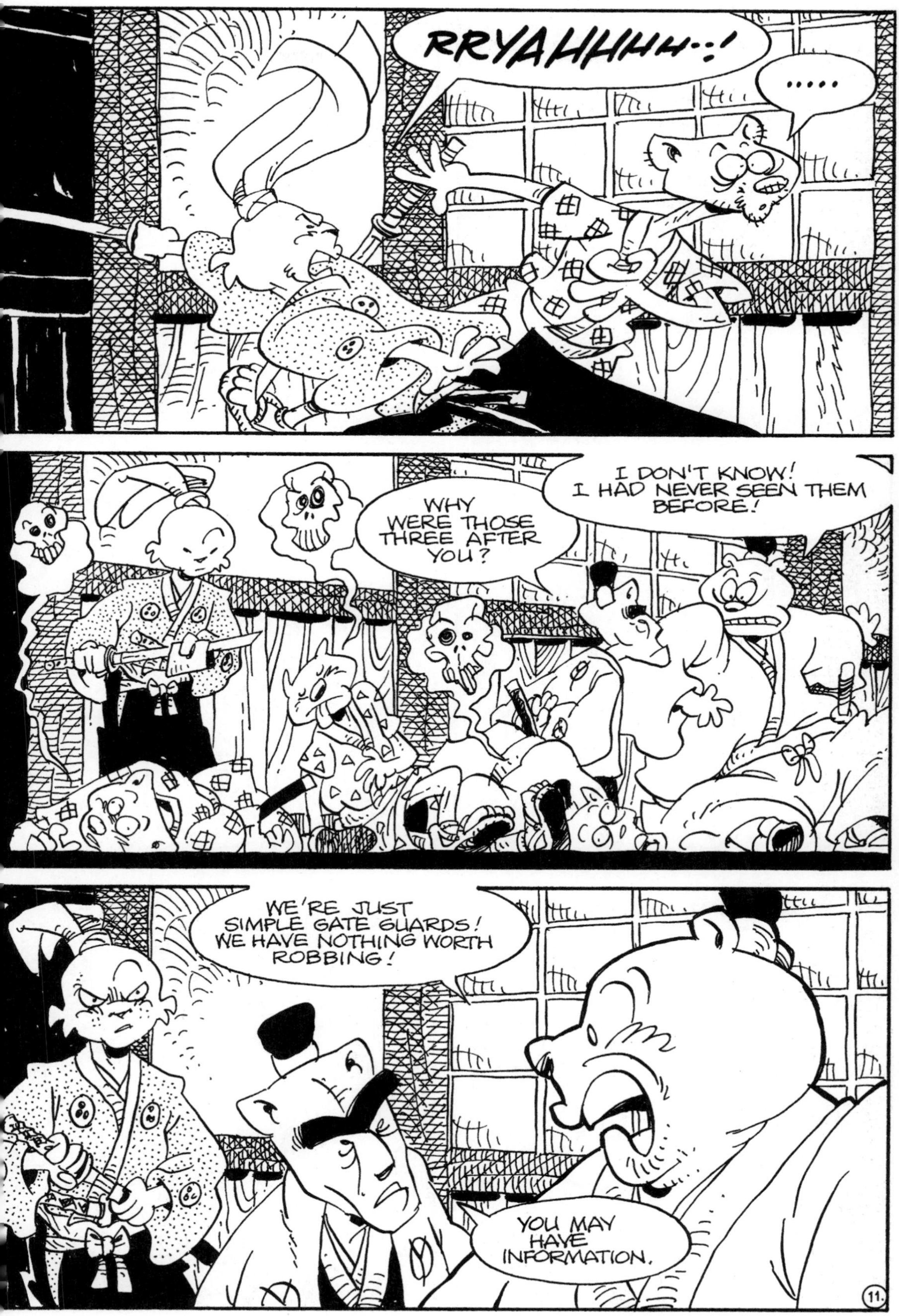
RRYAHHHH...!
.....
WHY WERE THOSE THREE AFTER YOU?
I DON'T KNOW! I HAD NEVER SEEN THEM BEFORE!
WE'RE JUST SIMPLE GATE GUARDS! WE HAVE NOTHING WORTH ROBBING!
YOU MAY HAVE INFORMATION.
11.

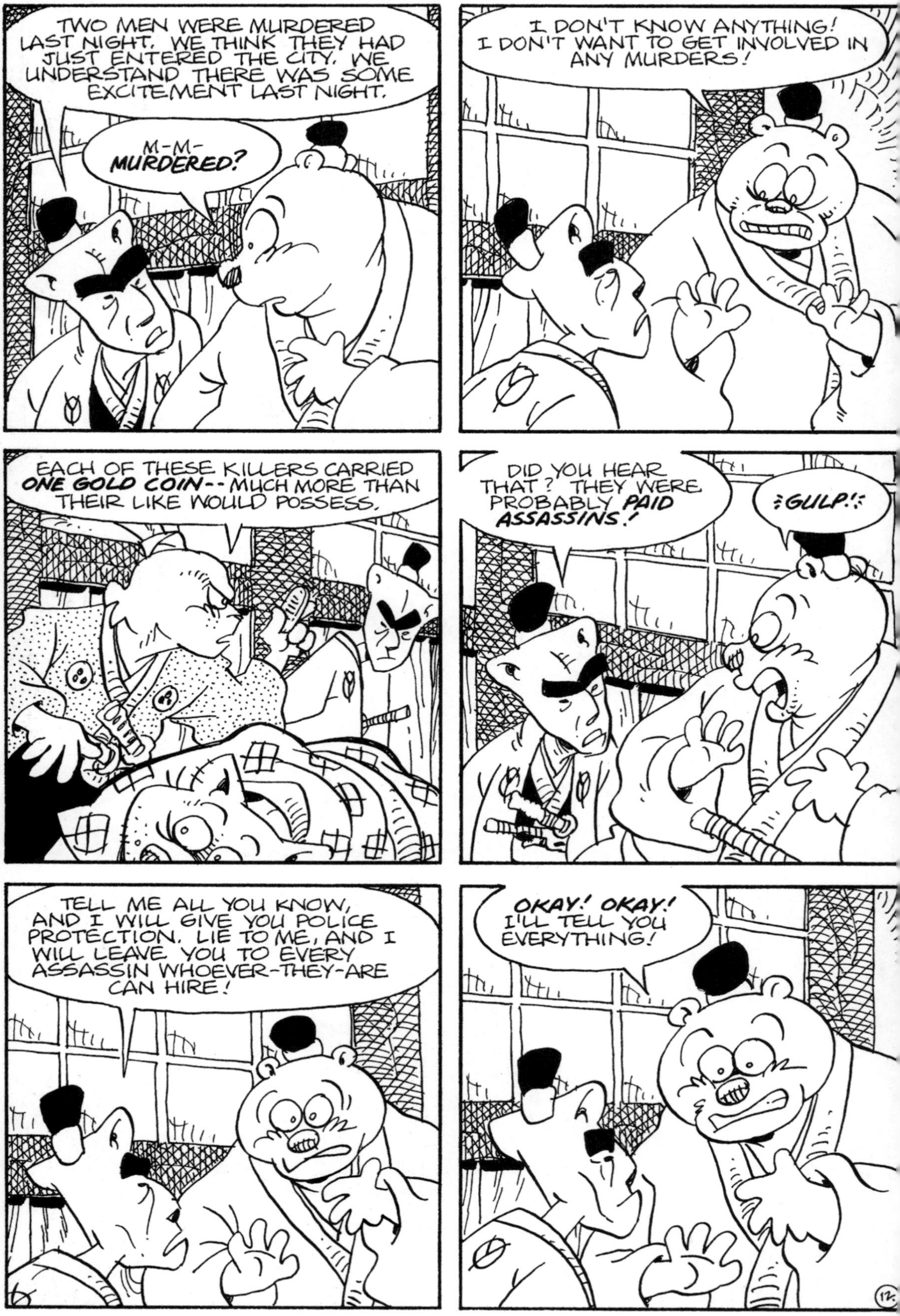
TWO MEN WERE MURDERED LAST NIGHT. WE THINK THEY HAD JUST ENTERED THE CITY. WE UNDERSTAND THERE WAS SOME EXCITEMENT LAST NIGHT.
M-M-MURDERED?
I DON'T KNOW ANYTHING! I DON'T WANT TO GET INVOLVED IN ANY MURDERS!
EACH OF THESE KILLERS CARRIED ONE GOLD COIN--MUCH MORE THAN THEIR LIKE WOULD POSSESS.
DID YOU HEAR THAT? THEY WERE PROBABLY PAID ASSASSINS!
GULP!
TELL ME ALL YOU KNOW, AND I WILL GIVE YOU POLICE PROTECTION. LIE TO ME, AND I WILL LEAVE YOU TO EVERY ASSASSIN WHOEVER-THEY-ARE CAN HIRE!
OKAY! OKAY! I'LL TELL YOU EVERYTHING!
12.

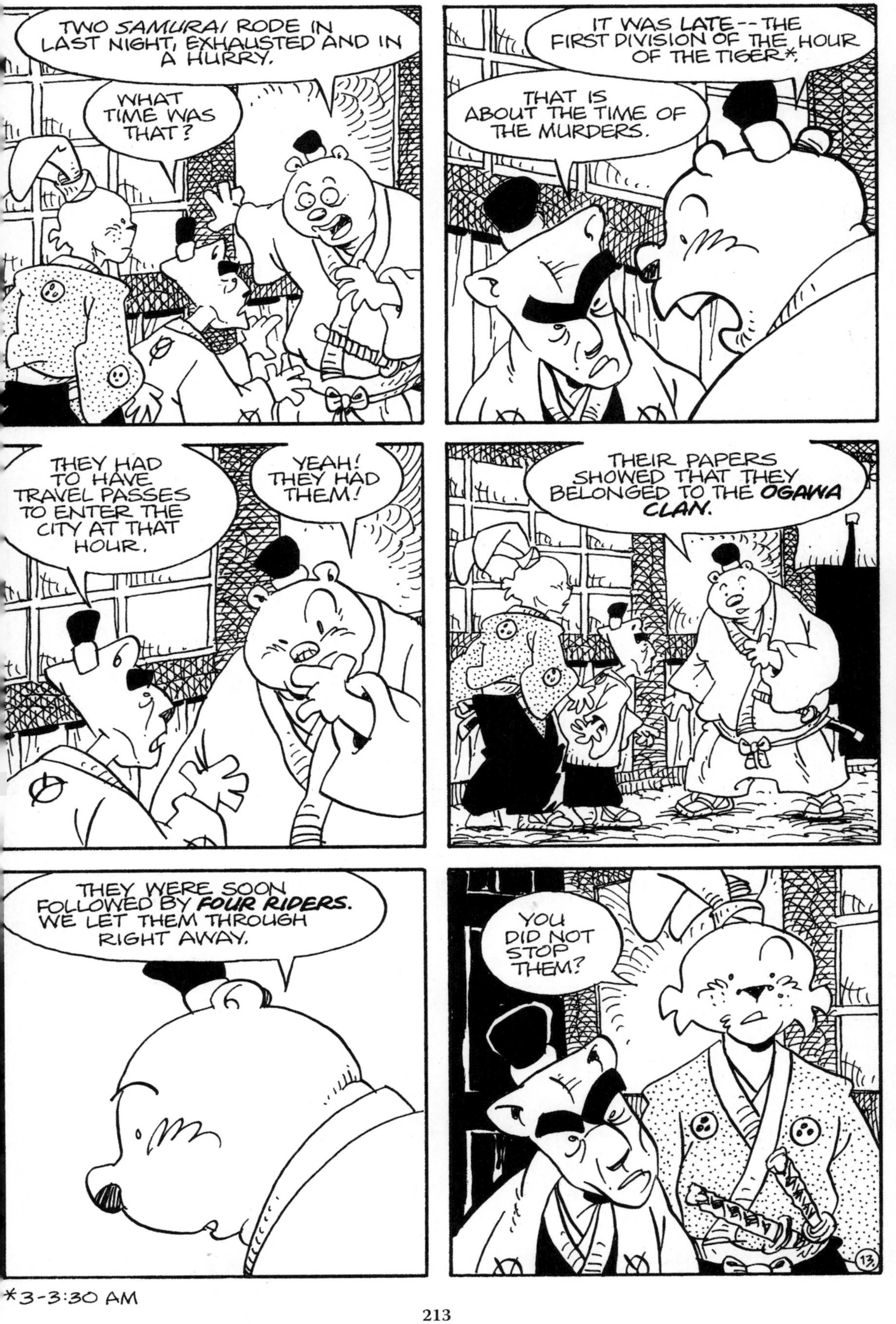
TWO SAMURAI RODE IN LAST NIGHT, EXHAUSTED AND IN A HURRY.
WHAT TIME WAS THAT?
IT WAS LATE--THE FIRST DIVISION OF THE HOUR OF THE TIGER*.
THAT IS ABOUT THE TIME OF THE MURDERS.
THEY HAD TO HAVE TRAVEL PASSES TO ENTER THE CITY AT THAT HOUR.
YEAH! THEY HAD THEM!
THEIR PAPERS SHOWED THAT THEY BELONGED TO THE OGAWA CLAN.
THEY WERE SOON FOLLOWED BY FOUR RIDERS. WE LET THEM THROUGH RIGHT AWAY.
YOU DID NOT STOP THEM?
13

*3-3:30 AM

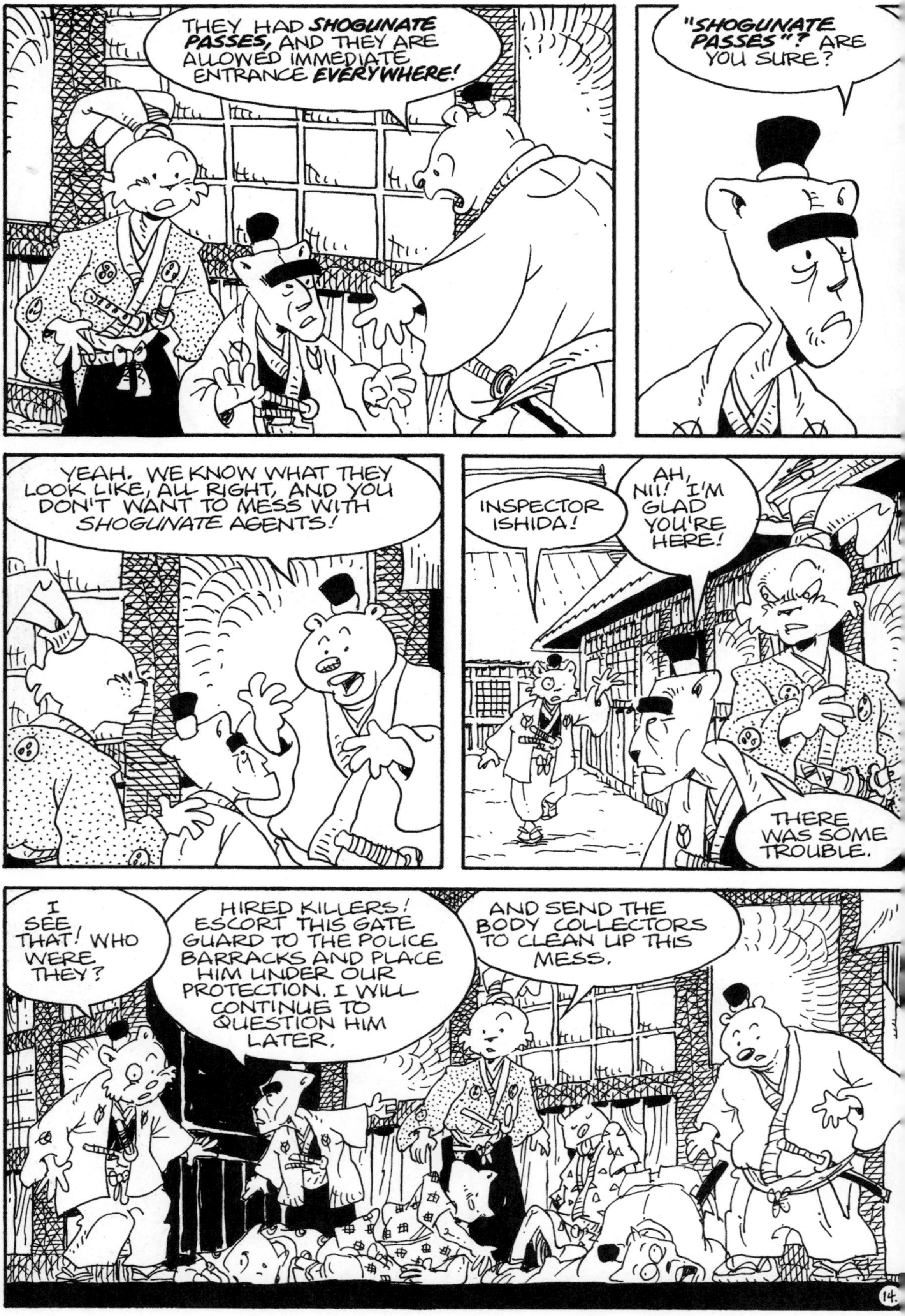
THEY HAD SHOGUNATE PASSES, AND THEY ARE ALLOWED IMMEDIATE ENTRANCE EVERYWHERE!
"SHOGUNATE PASSES"? ARE YOU SURE?
YEAH. WE KNOW WHAT THEY LOOK LIKE, ALL RIGHT, AND YOU DON'T WANT TO MESS WITH SHOGUNATE AGENTS!
INSPECTOR ISHIDA!
AH, NII! I'M GLAD YOU'RE HERE!
THERE WAS SOME TROUBLE.
I SEE THAT! WHO WERE THEY?
HIRED KILLERS! ESCORT THIS GATE GUARD TO THE POLICE BARRACKS AND PLACE HIM UNDER OUR PROTECTION. I WILL CONTINUE TO QUESTION HIM LATER.
AND SEND THE BODY COLLECTORS TO CLEAN UP THIS MESS.
14.

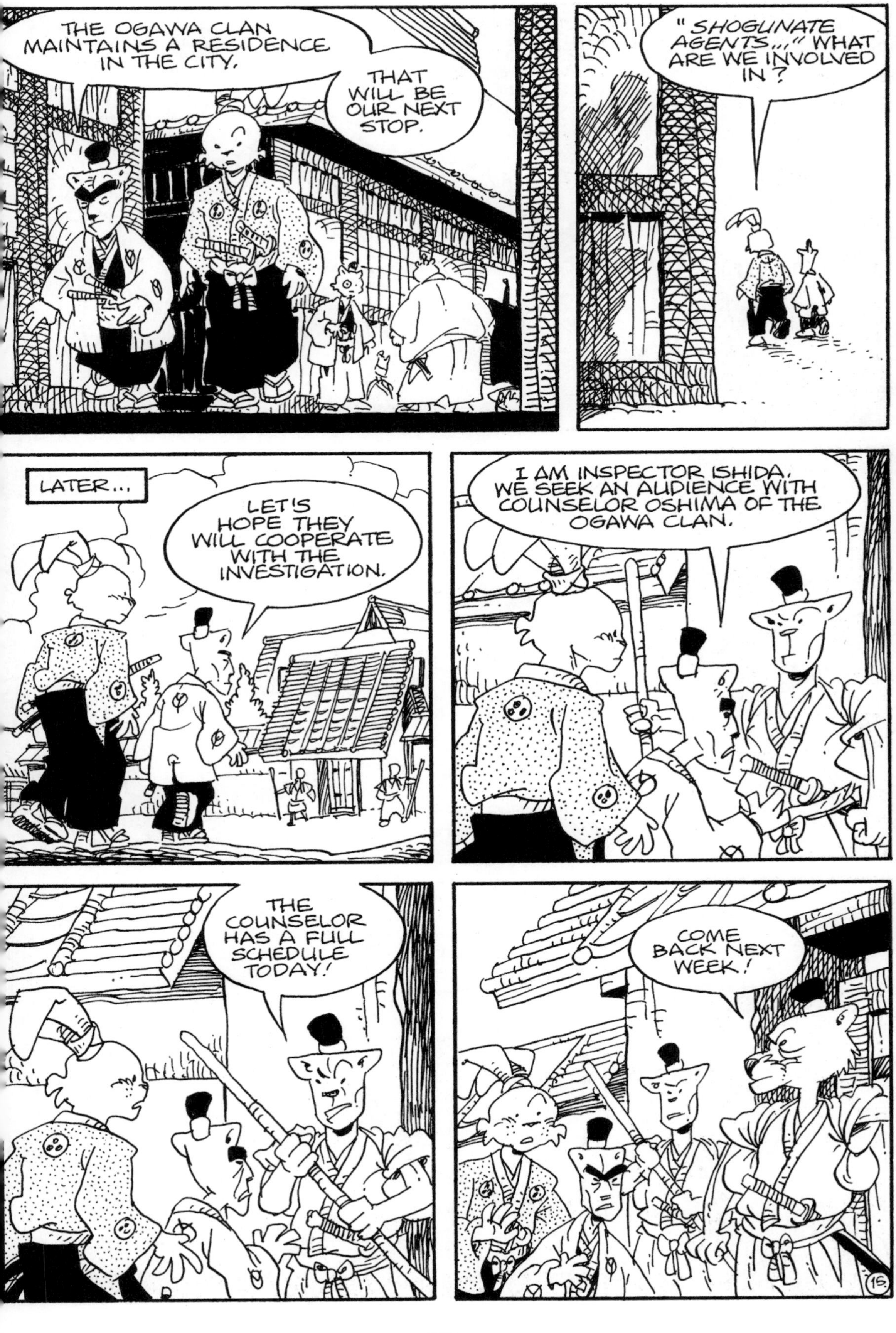
THE OGAWA CLAN MAINTAINS A RESIDENCE IN THE CITY.
THAT WILL BE OUR NEXT STOP.
"SHOGUNATE AGENTS..." WHAT ARE WE INVOLVED IN?
LATER...
LET'S HOPE THEY WILL COOPERATE WITH THE INVESTIGATION.
I AM INSPECTOR ISHIDA. WE SEEK AN AUDIENCE WITH COUNSELOR OSHIMA OF THE OGAWA CLAN.
THE COUNSELOR HAS A FULL SCHEDULE TODAY!
COME BACK NEXT WEEK!
15.

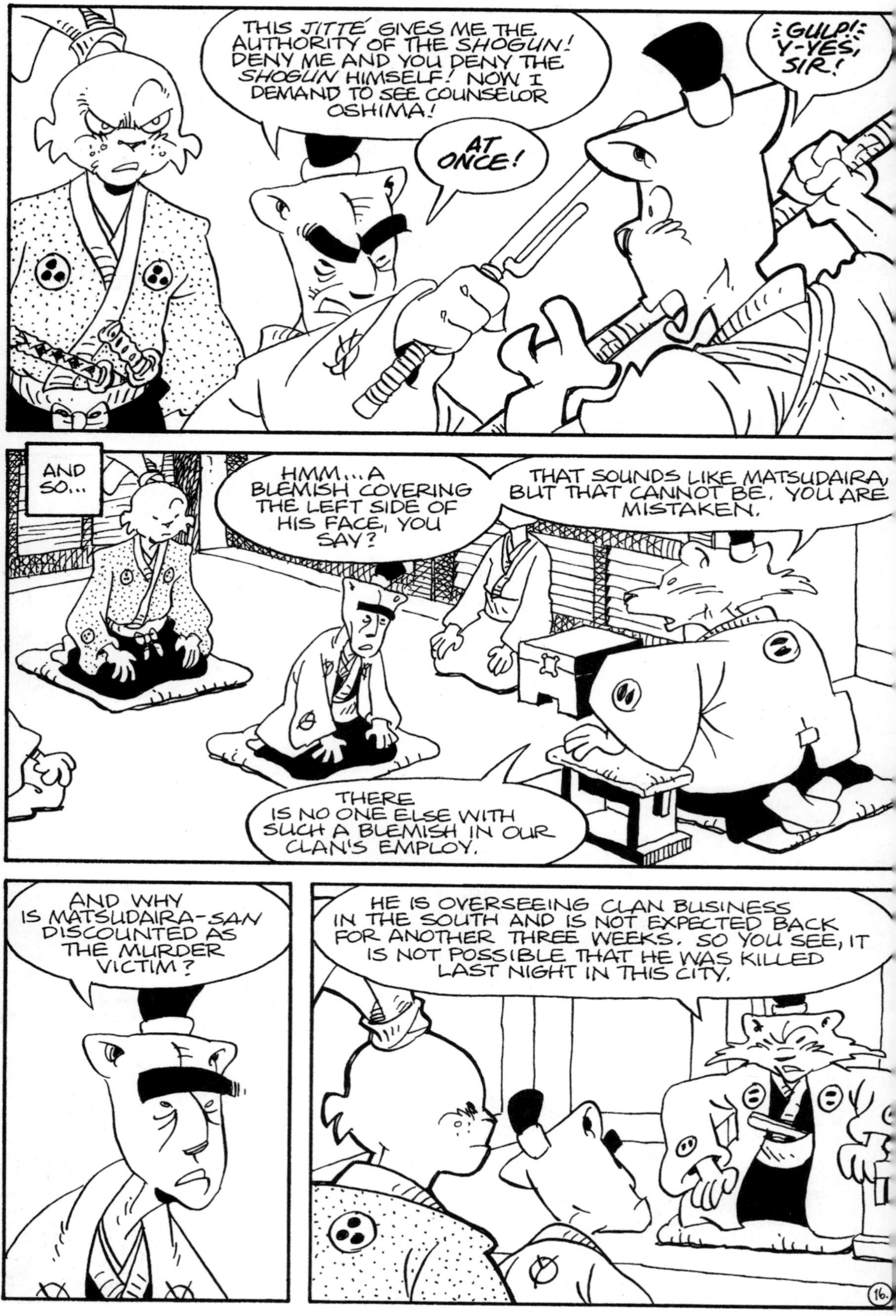
THIS JITTE GIVES ME THE AUTHORITY OF THE SHOGUN! DENY ME AND YOU DENY THE SHOGUN HIMSELF! NOW I DEMAND TO SEE COUNSELOR OSHIMA!
AT ONCE!
GULP! Y-YES, SIR!
AND SO...
HMM... A BLEMISH COVERING THE LEFT SIDE OF HIS FACE, YOU SAY?
THAT SOUNDS LIKE MATSUDAIRA, BUT THAT CANNOT BE. YOU ARE MISTAKEN.
THERE IS NO ONE ELSE WITH SUCH A BLEMISH IN OUR CLAN'S EMPLOY.
AND WHY IS MATSUDAIRA-SAN DISCOUNTED AS THE MURDER VICTIM?
HE IS OVERSEEING CLAN BUSINESS IN THE SOUTH AND IS NOT EXPECTED BACK FOR ANOTHER THREE WEEKS. SO YOU SEE, IT IS NOT POSSIBLE THAT HE WAS KILLED LAST NIGHT IN THIS CITY.
16.

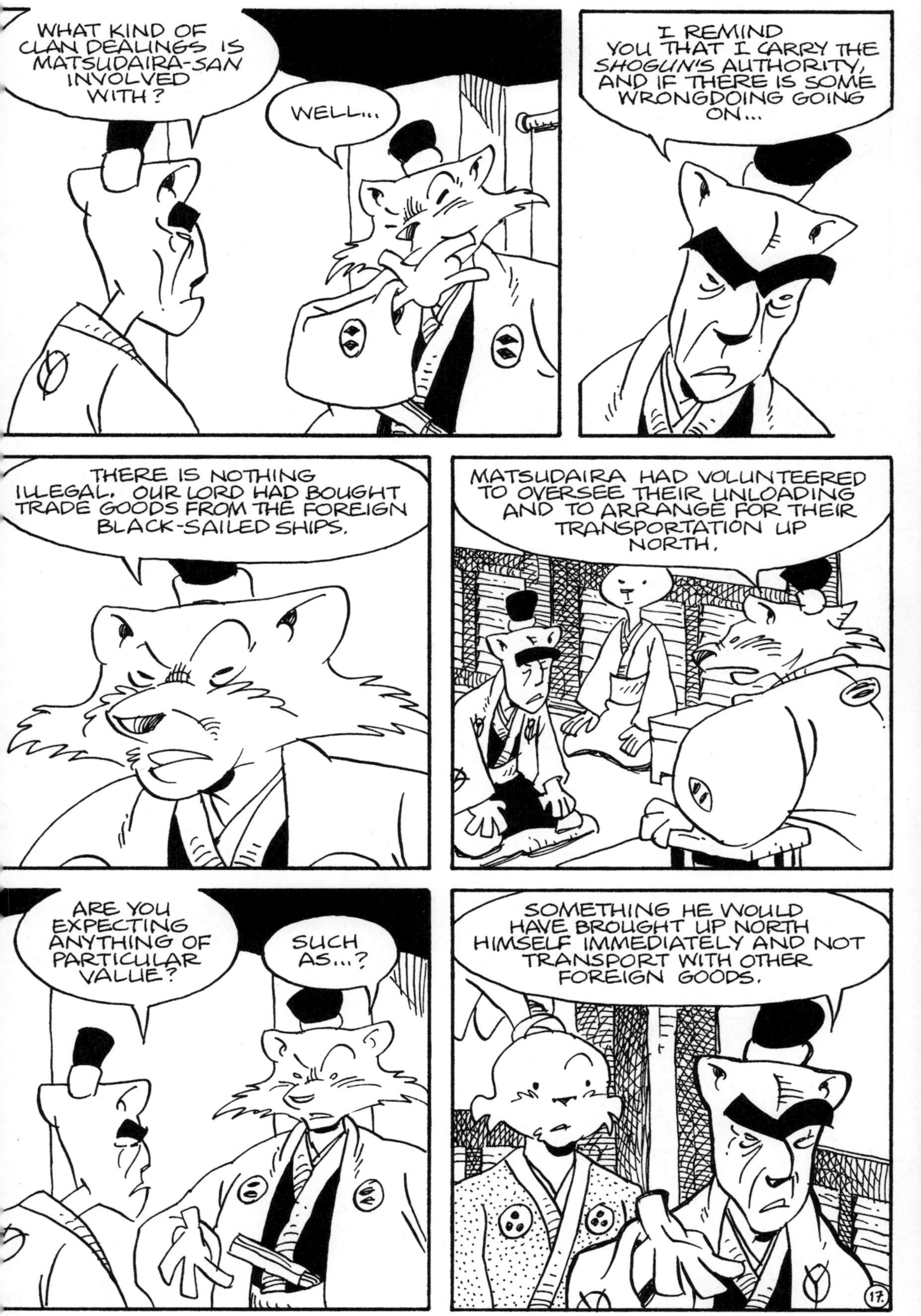
WHAT KIND OF CLAN DEALINGS IS MATSUDAIRA-SAN INVOLVED WITH?
WELL...
I REMIND YOU THAT I CARRY THE SHOGUN'S AUTHORITY, AND IF THERE IS SOME WRONGDOING GOING ON...
THERE IS NOTHING ILLEGAL. OUR LORD HAD BOUGHT TRADE GOODS FROM THE FOREIGN BLACK-SAILED SHIPS.
MATSUDAIRA HAD VOLUNTEERED TO OVERSEE THEIR UNLOADING AND TO ARRANGE FOR THEIR TRANSPORTATION UP NORTH.
ARE YOU EXPECTING ANYTHING OF PARTICULAR VALUE?
SUCH AS...?
SOMETHING HE WOULD HAVE BROUGHT UP NORTH HIMSELF IMMEDIATELY AND NOT TRANSPORT WITH OTHER FOREIGN GOODS.
17.

ALL FOREIGN GOODS ARE VALUABLE, BUT THERE IS NOTHING OF UNIQUE VALUE.

I WILL GET YOU A LIST OF THE GOODS WE PURCHASED.

I HAVE IT HERE, SIR!

CLOTHING... FURNITURE... ORNAMENTATION... HMM... NOTHING HE WOULD BE KILLED FOR.

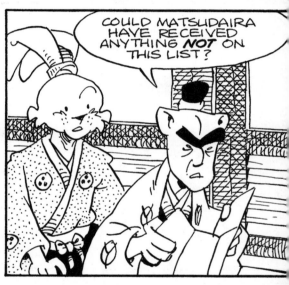

COULD MATSUDAIRA HAVE RECEIVED ANYTHING NOT ON THIS LIST?

YOU DARE INSINUATE THAT THE OGAWA CLAN COULD BE GUILTY OF SMUGGLING? THAT WOULD BE AN ACT OF DISLOYALTY AGAINST THE SHOGUN!

SUCH AN ACT COULD BE PUNISHABLE BY DEATH, AND THE CLAN COULD BE ABOLISHED! BE AWARE OF YOUR ACCUSATIONS, INSPECTOR ISHIDA, OR I WILL REPORT YOU TO YOUR SUPERIORS!

18.

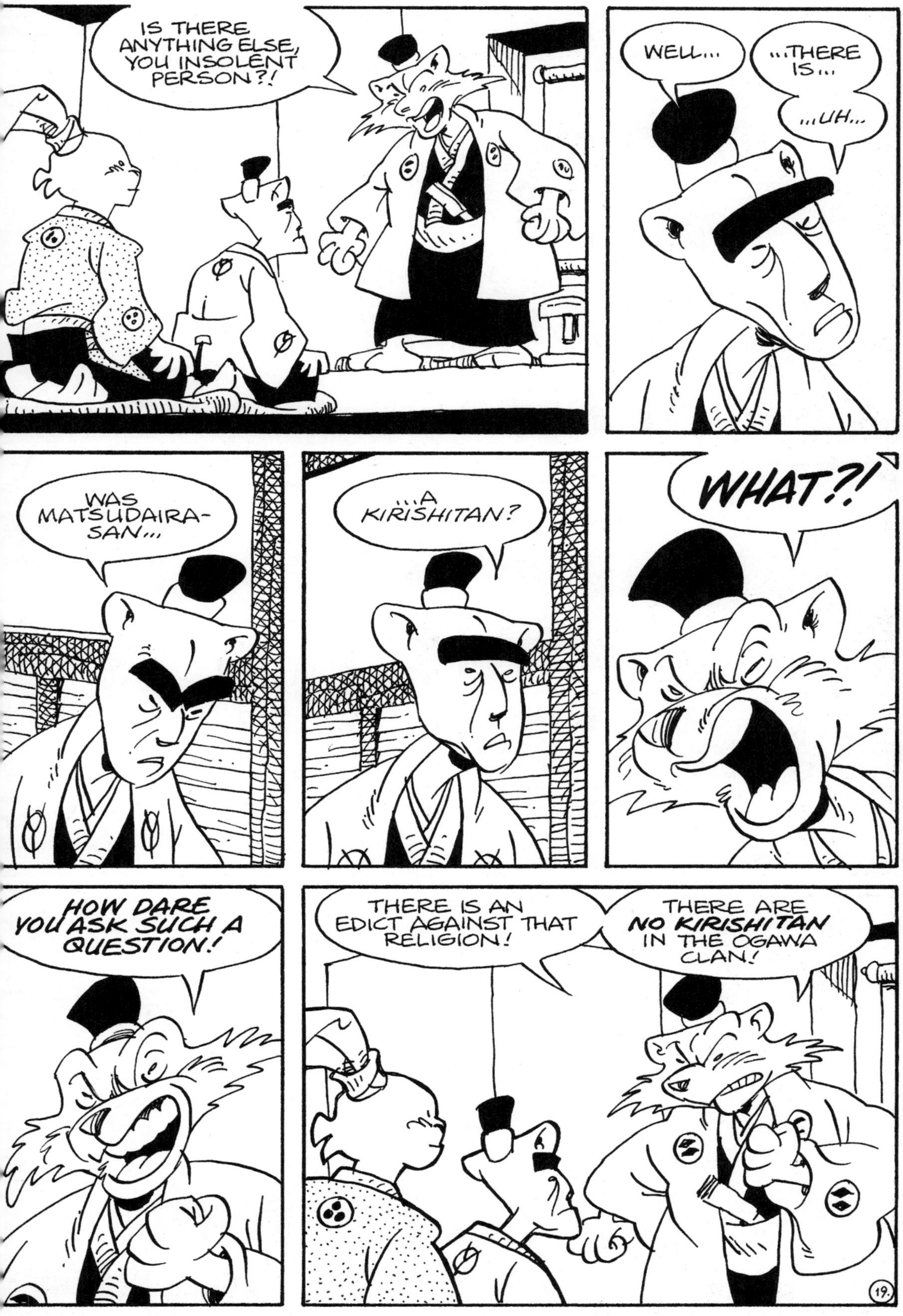
IS THERE ANYTHING ELSE, YOU INSOLENT PERSON?!
WELL...
...THERE IS...
...UH...
WAS MATSUDAIRA-SAN...
...A KIRISHITAN?
WHAT?!
HOW DARE YOU ASK SUCH A QUESTION!
THERE IS AN EDICT AGAINST THAT RELIGION!
THERE ARE NO KIRISHITAN IN THE OGAWA CLAN!
19.

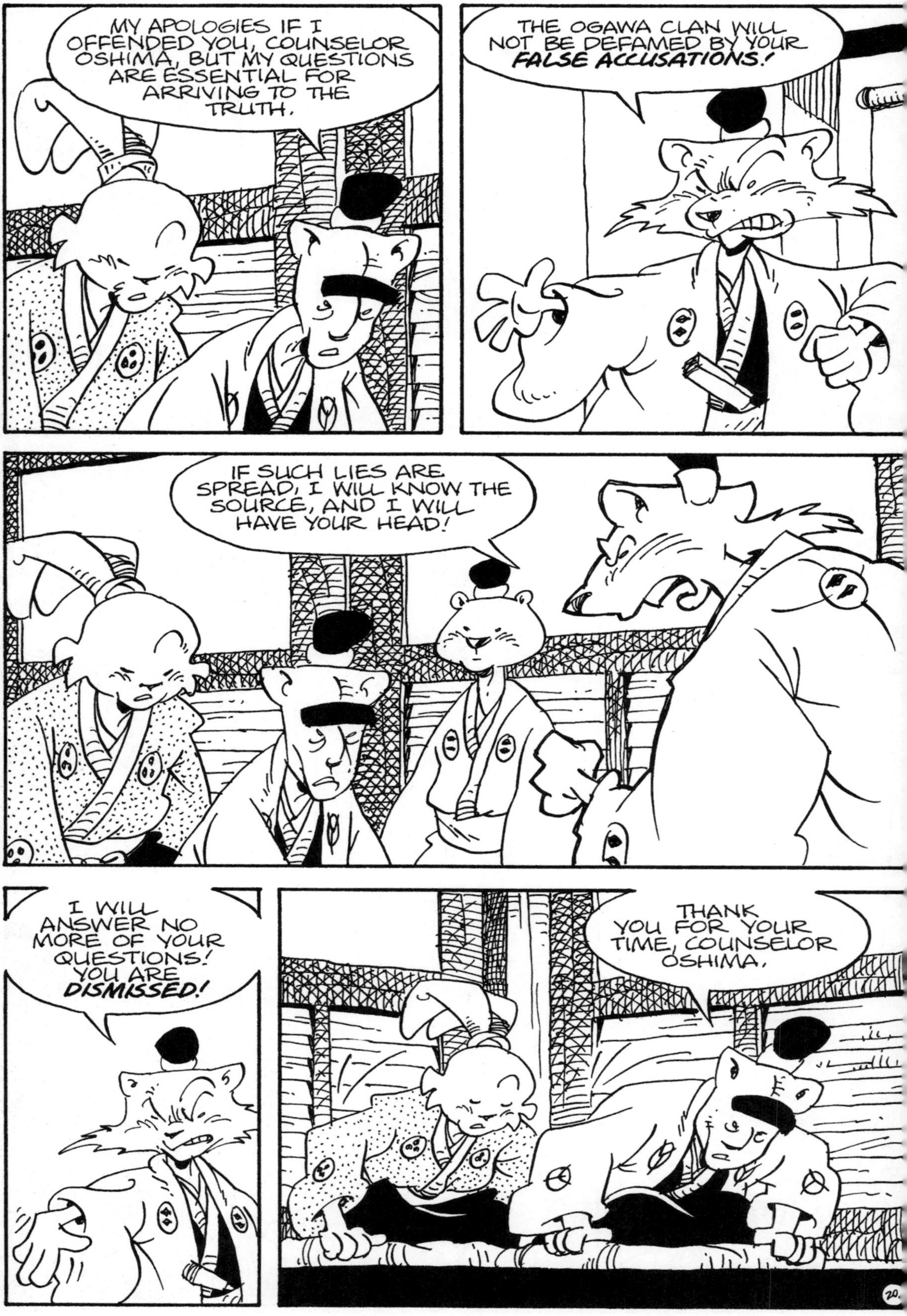
MY APOLOGIES IF I OFFENDED YOU, COUNSELOR OSHIMA, BUT MY QUESTIONS ARE ESSENTIAL FOR ARRIVING TO THE TRUTH.
THE OGAWA CLAN WILL NOT BE DEFAMED BY YOUR FALSE ACCUSATIONS!
IF SUCH LIES ARE SPREAD, I WILL KNOW THE SOURCE, AND I WILL HAVE YOUR HEAD!
I WILL ANSWER NO MORE OF YOUR QUESTIONS! YOU ARE DISMISSED!
THANK YOU FOR YOUR TIME, COUNSELOR OSHIMA.
20.

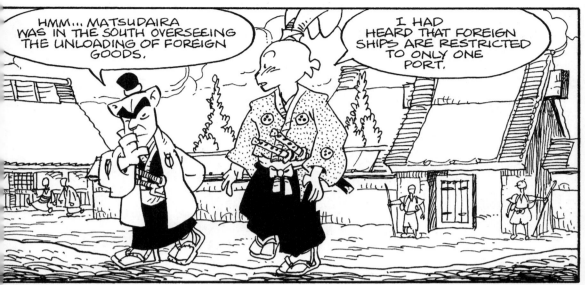

HMM.... MATSUDAIRA WAS IN THE SOUTH OVERSEEING THE UNLOADING OF FOREIGN GOODS.

I HAD HEARD THAT FOREIGN SHIPS ARE RESTRICTED TO ONLY ONE PORT.

YES, THEY ARRIVE IN THEIR BLACK SHIPS TO THE PORT OF NAGASAKI FROM MACAU TO THE SOUTH.

WITH FEW EXCEPTIONS, FOREIGNERS ARE CONFINED ON THE MAN-MADE ISLAND OF *DEJIMA*.

FOR THE MOST PART, OUR COUNTRYMEN ARE FORBIDDEN TO INTERACT WITH THEM.

I HAVE HAD AN ENCOUNTER WITH *ONE* FOREIGNER *.

...MUCH TO MY REGRET.

* UY BOOK 30: THIEVES and SPIES

221

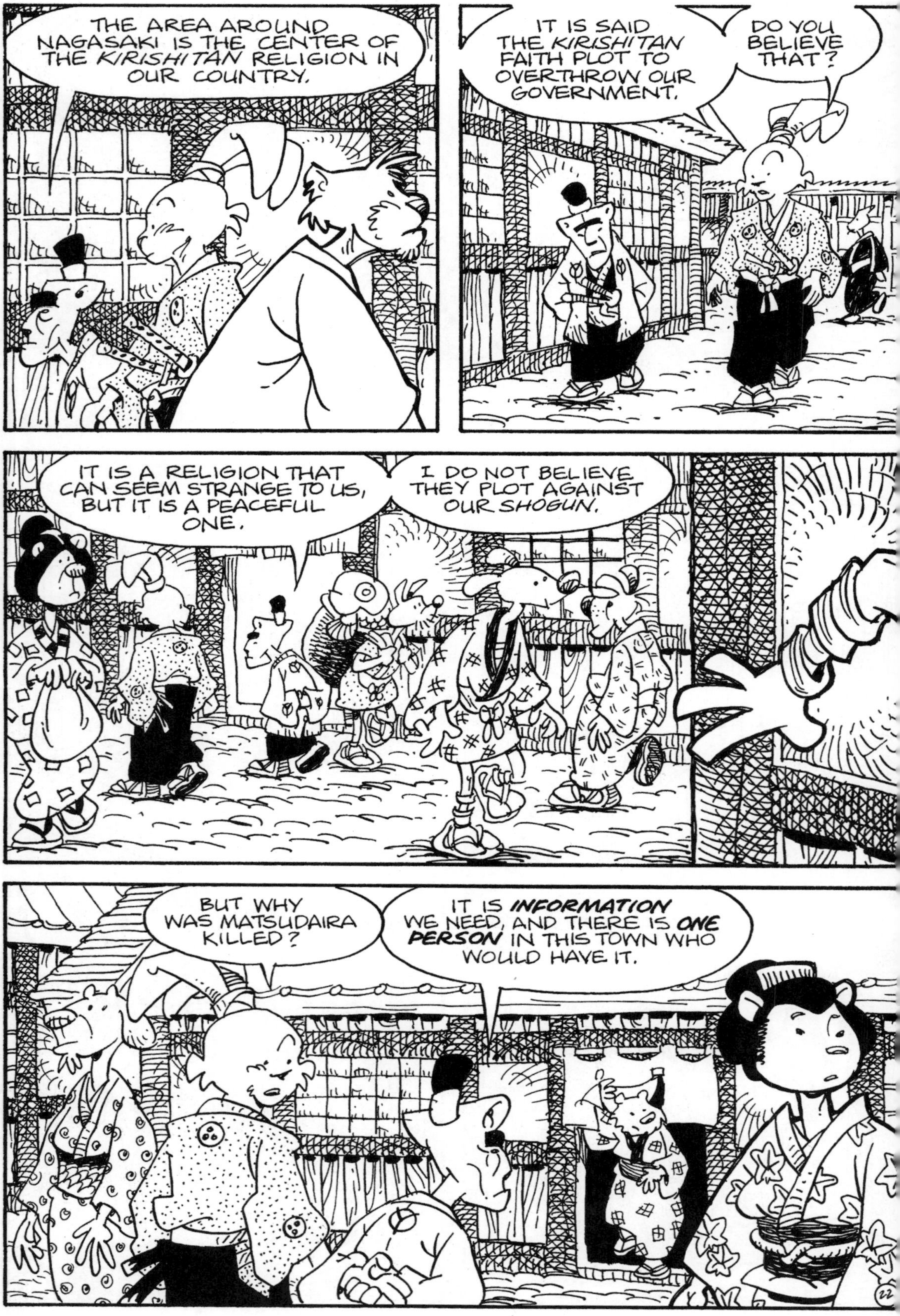
THE AREA AROUND NAGASAKI IS THE CENTER OF THE *KIRISHITAN* RELIGION IN OUR COUNTRY.
IT IS SAID THE *KIRISHITAN* FAITH PLOT TO OVERTHROW OUR GOVERNMENT.
DO YOU BELIEVE THAT?
IT IS A RELIGION THAT CAN SEEM STRANGE TO US, BUT IT IS A PEACEFUL ONE.
I DO NOT BELIEVE THEY PLOT AGAINST OUR *SHOGUN*.
BUT WHY WAS MATSUDAIRA KILLED?
IT IS ***INFORMATION*** WE NEED, AND THERE IS ***ONE PERSON*** IN THIS TOWN WHO WOULD HAVE IT.
22

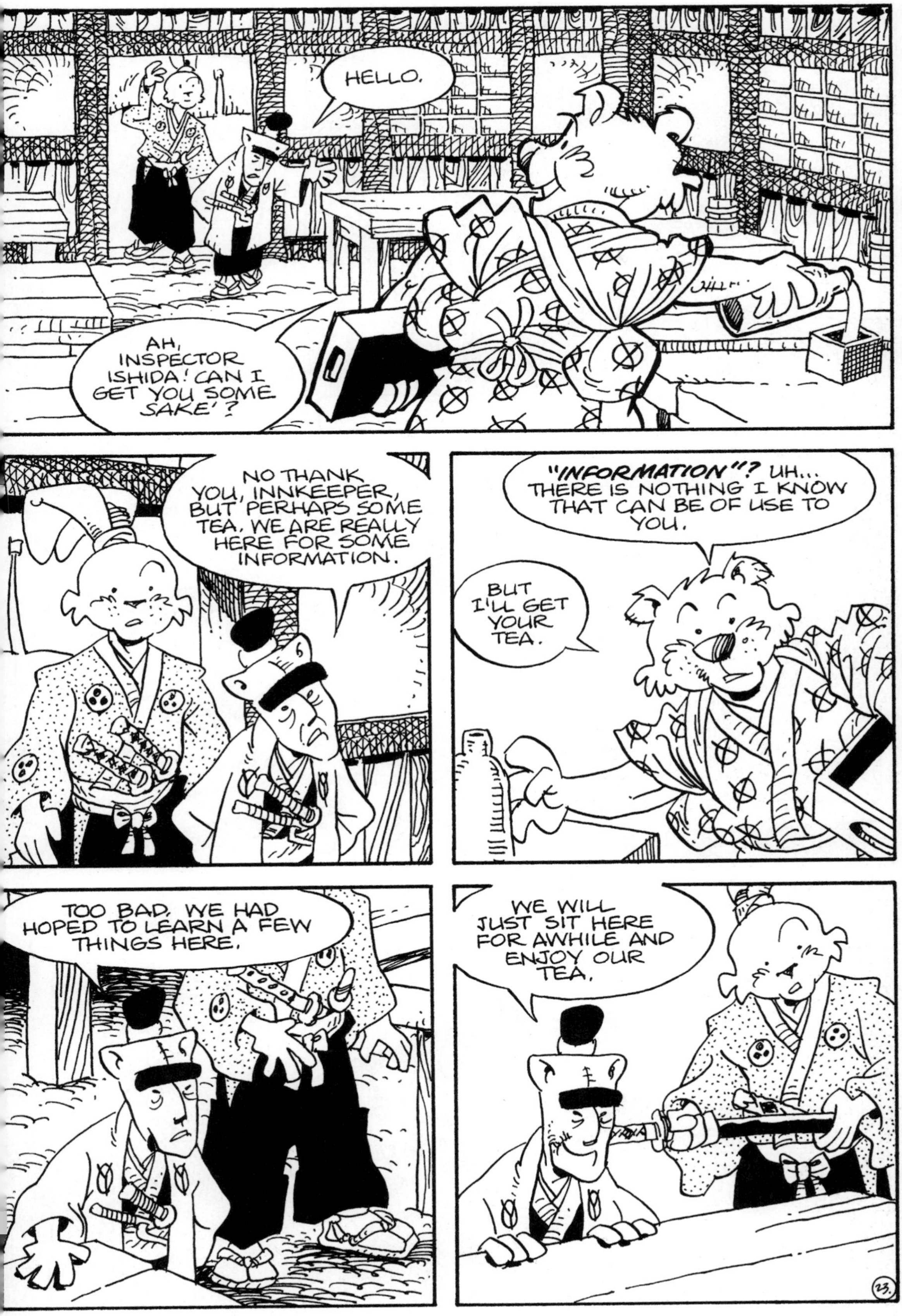
HELLO.
AH, INSPECTOR ISHIDA! CAN I GET YOU SOME SAKE'?
NO THANK YOU, INNKEEPER, BUT PERHAPS SOME TEA. WE ARE REALLY HERE FOR SOME INFORMATION.
"INFORMATION"? UH... THERE IS NOTHING I KNOW THAT CAN BE OF USE TO YOU.
BUT I'LL GET YOUR TEA.
TOO BAD. WE HAD HOPED TO LEARN A FEW THINGS HERE.
WE WILL JUST SIT HERE FOR AWHILE AND ENJOY OUR TEA.
23.

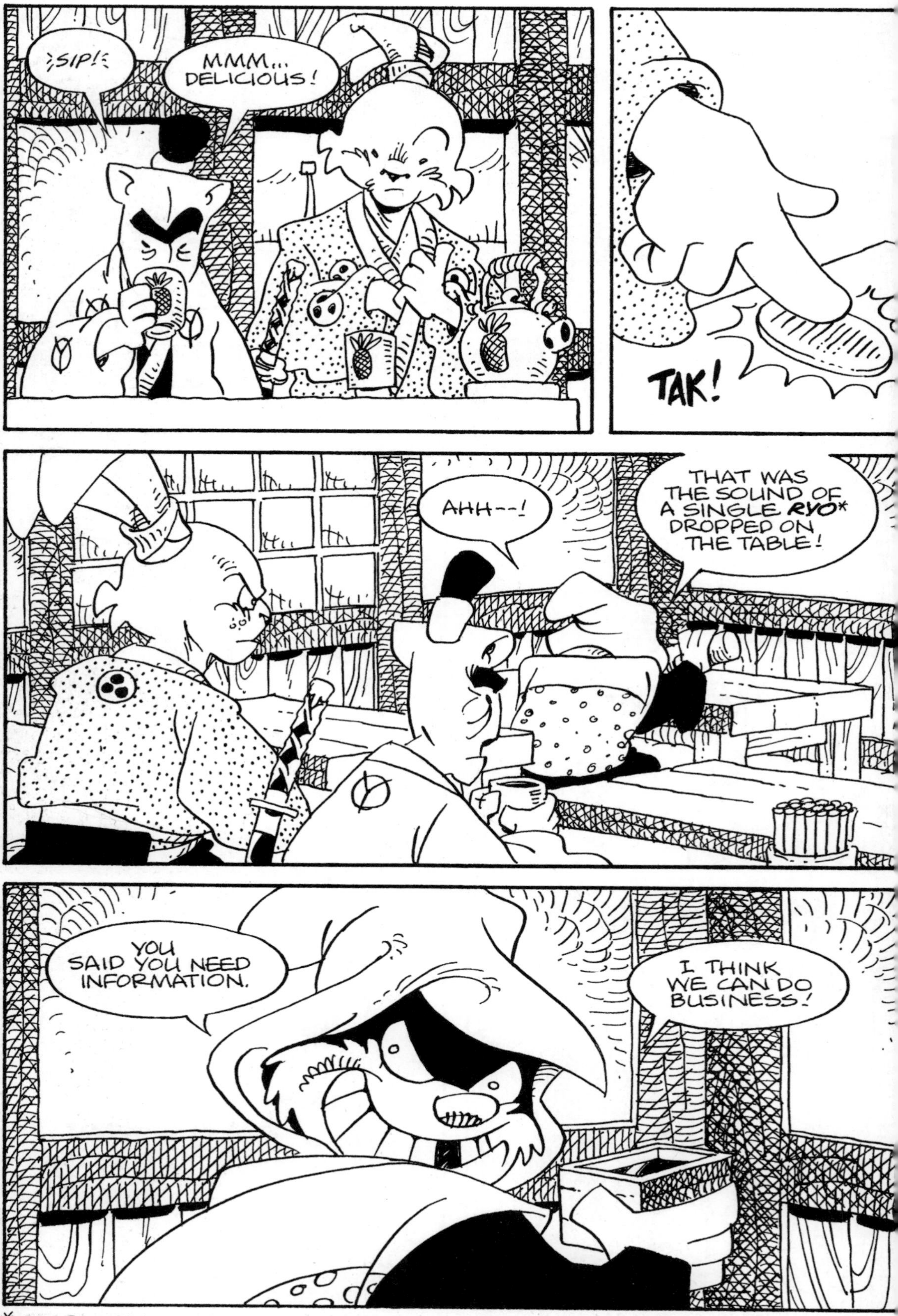

SIP!
MMM... DELICIOUS!
TAK!
AHH--!
THAT WAS THE SOUND OF A SINGLE RYO* DROPPED ON THE TABLE!
YOU SAID YOU NEED INFORMATION.
I THINK WE CAN DO BUSINESS!

* GOLD COIN

THE HIDDEN PART THREE

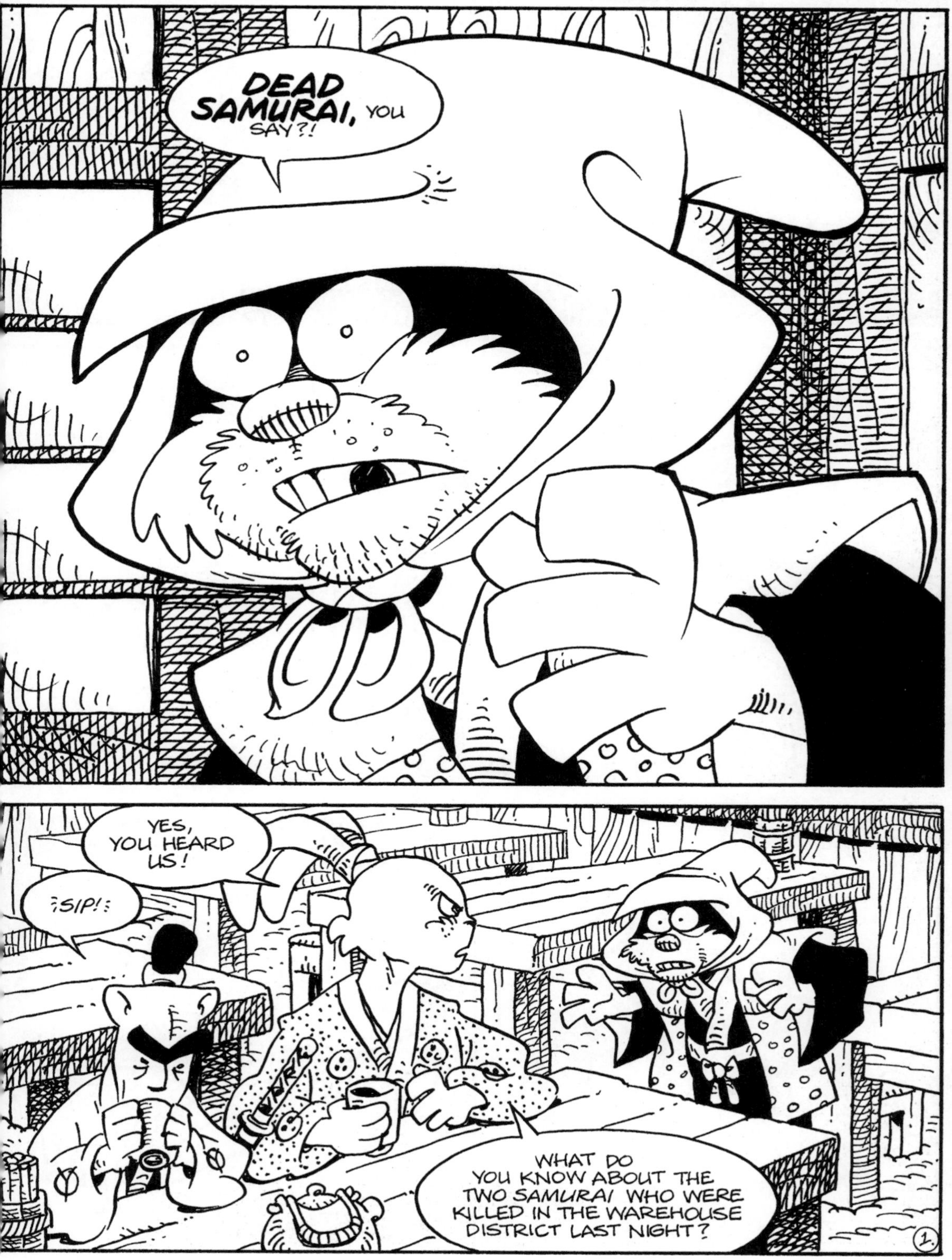
DEAD SAMURAI, YOU SAY?!
YES, YOU HEARD US!
SIP!
WHAT DO YOU KNOW ABOUT THE TWO SAMURAI WHO WERE KILLED IN THE WAREHOUSE DISTRICT LAST NIGHT?
1.

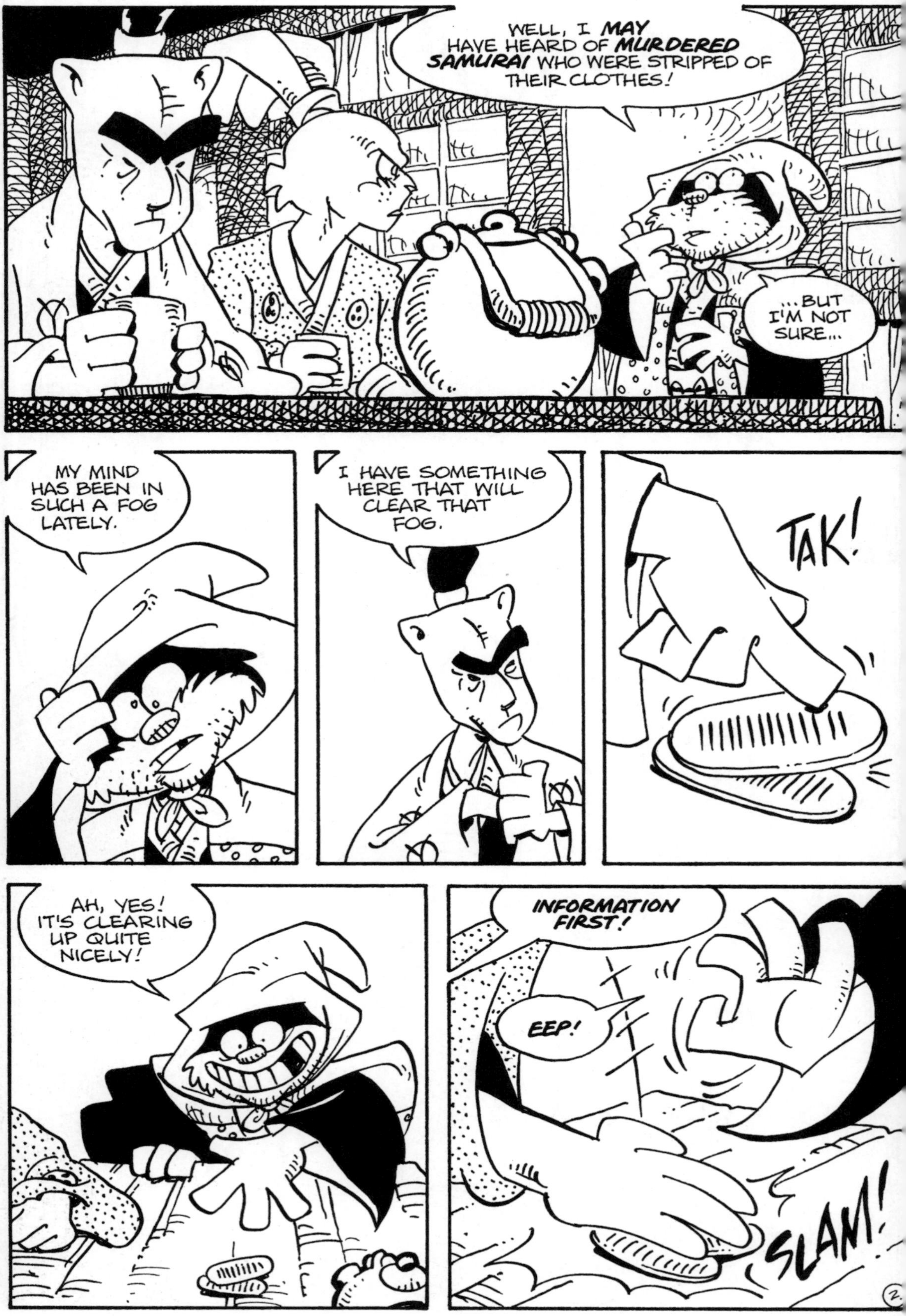
WELL, I MAY HAVE HEARD OF MURDERED SAMURAI WHO WERE STRIPPED OF THEIR CLOTHES!
...BUT I'M NOT SURE...
MY MIND HAS BEEN IN SUCH A FOG LATELY.
I HAVE SOMETHING HERE THAT WILL CLEAR THAT FOG.
TAK!
AH, YES! IT'S CLEARING UP QUITE NICELY!
INFORMATION FIRST!
EEP!
SLAM!
2

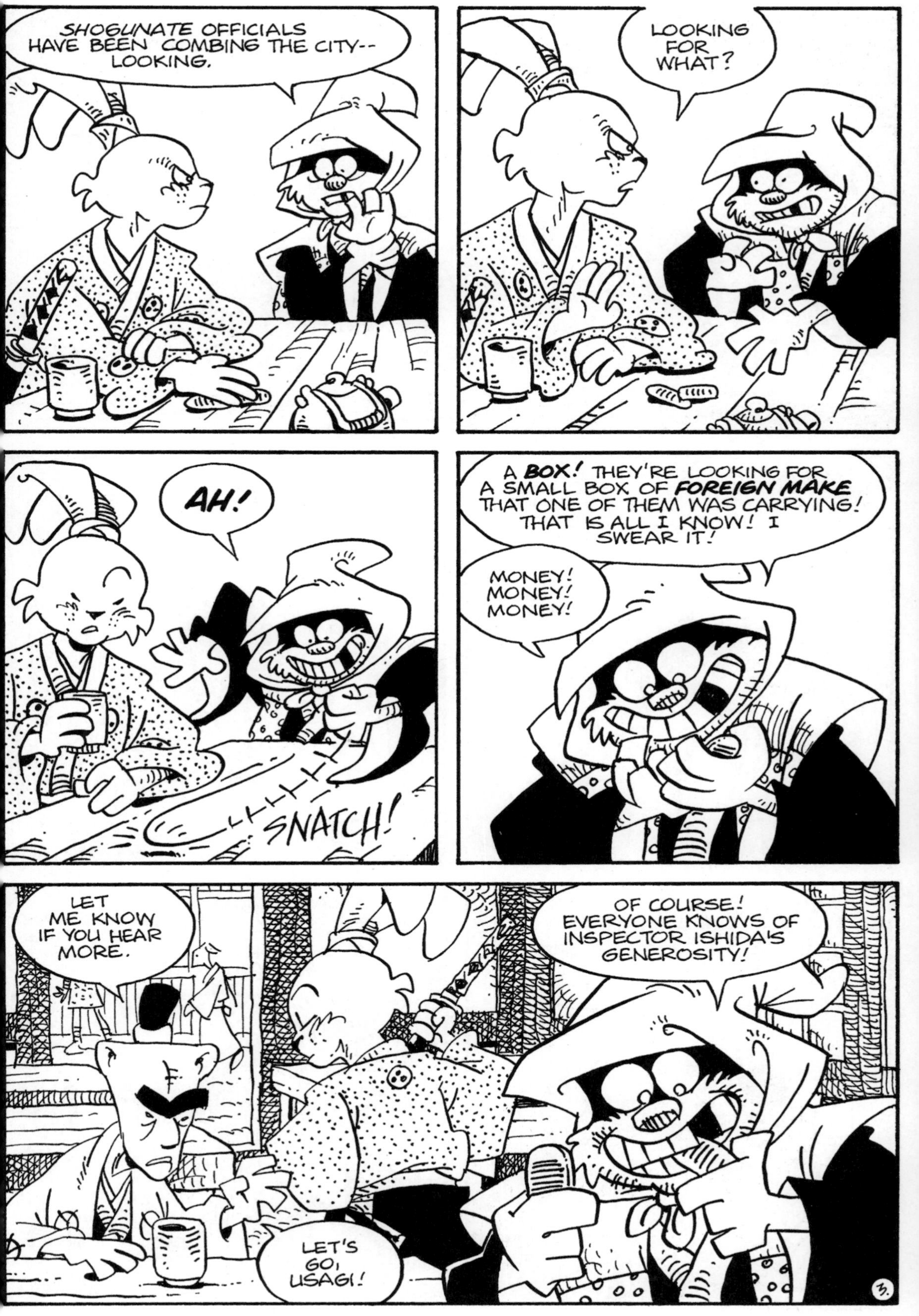
SHOGUNATE OFFICIALS HAVE BEEN COMBING THE CITY-- LOOKING.
LOOKING FOR WHAT?
AH!
SNATCH!
A BOX! THEY'RE LOOKING FOR A SMALL BOX OF FOREIGN MAKE THAT ONE OF THEM WAS CARRYING! THAT IS ALL I KNOW! I SWEAR IT!
MONEY! MONEY! MONEY!
LET ME KNOW IF YOU HEAR MORE.
OF COURSE! EVERYONE KNOWS OF INSPECTOR ISHIDA'S GENEROSITY!
LET'S GO, USAGI!
3.

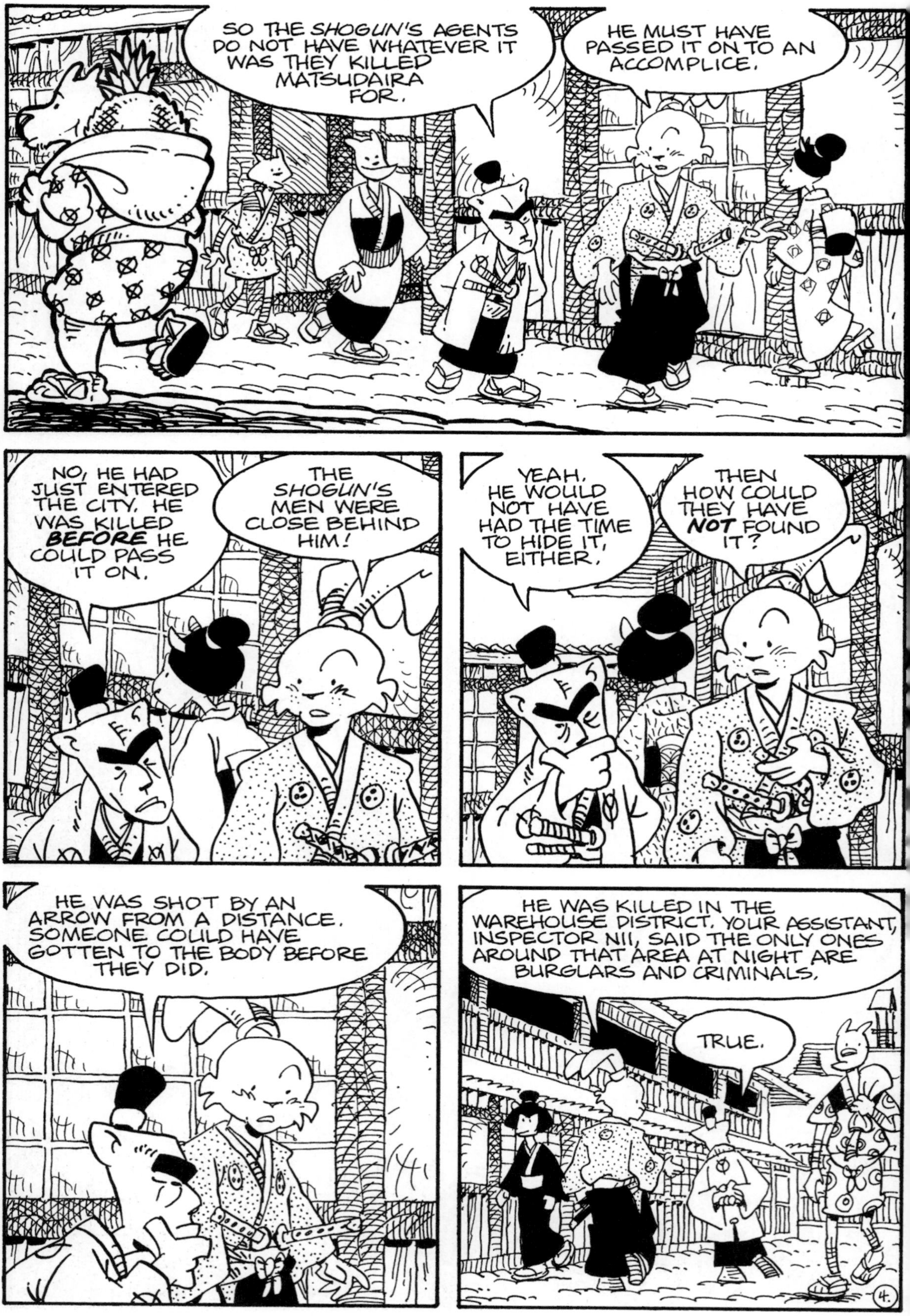
SO THE *SHOGUN*'S AGENTS DO NOT HAVE WHATEVER IT WAS THEY KILLED MATSUDAIRA FOR.
HE MUST HAVE PASSED IT ON TO AN ACCOMPLICE.
NO, HE HAD JUST ENTERED THE CITY. HE WAS KILLED ***BEFORE*** HE COULD PASS IT ON.
THE *SHOGUN*'S MEN WERE CLOSE BEHIND HIM!
YEAH. HE WOULD NOT HAVE HAD THE TIME TO HIDE IT, EITHER.
THEN HOW COULD THEY HAVE ***NOT*** FOUND IT?
HE WAS SHOT BY AN ARROW FROM A DISTANCE. SOMEONE COULD HAVE GOTTEN TO THE BODY BEFORE THEY DID.
HE WAS KILLED IN THE WAREHOUSE DISTRICT. YOUR ASSISTANT, INSPECTOR NII, SAID THE ONLY ONES AROUND THAT AREA AT NIGHT ARE BURGLARS AND CRIMINALS.
TRUE.
4.

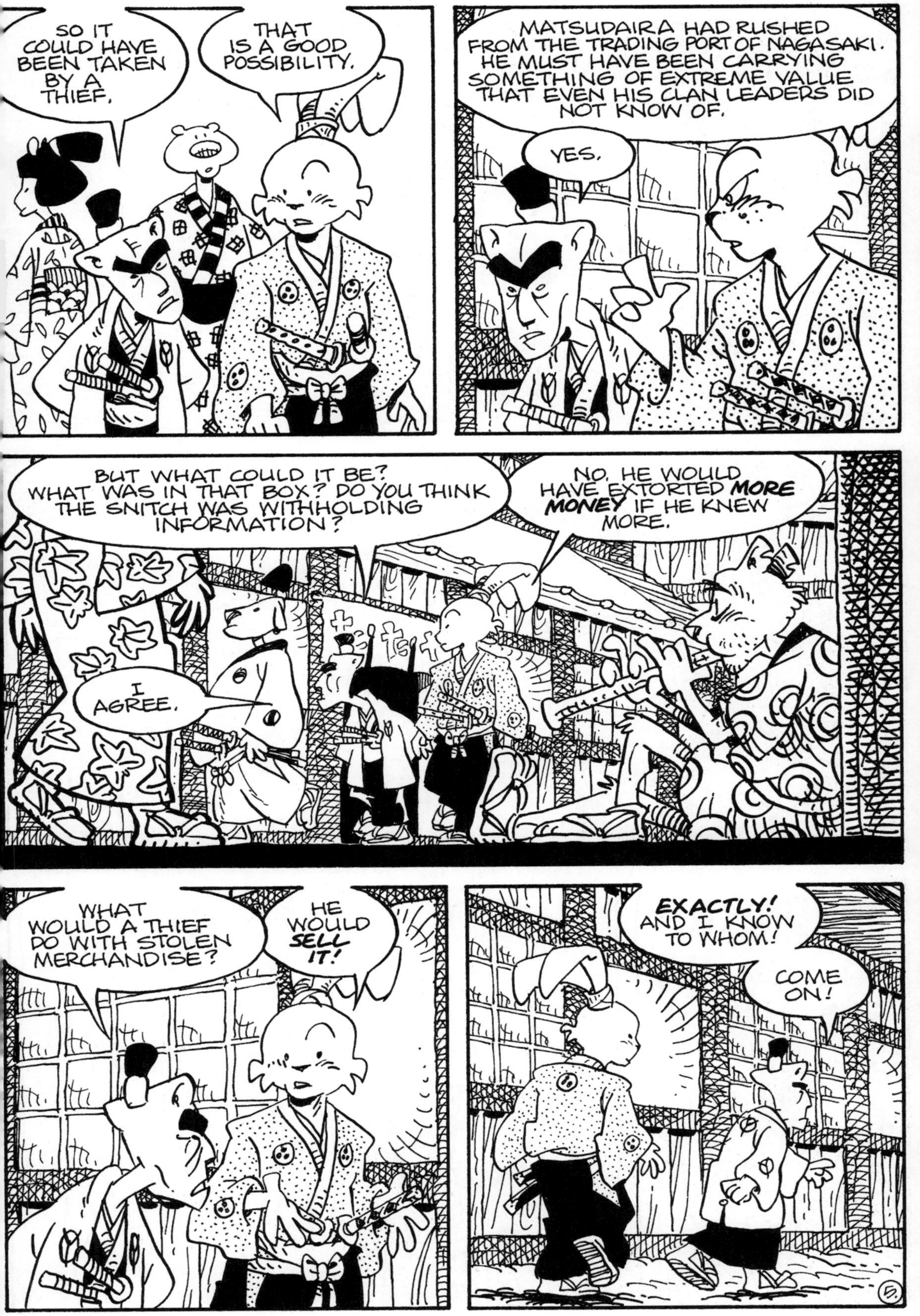
SO IT COULD HAVE BEEN TAKEN BY A THIEF.
THAT IS A GOOD POSSIBILITY.
MATSUDAIRA HAD RUSHED FROM THE TRADING PORT OF NAGASAKI. HE MUST HAVE BEEN CARRYING SOMETHING OF EXTREME VALUE THAT EVEN HIS CLAN LEADERS DID NOT KNOW OF.
YES.
BUT WHAT COULD IT BE? WHAT WAS IN THAT BOX? DO YOU THINK THE SNITCH WAS WITHHOLDING INFORMATION?
NO. HE WOULD HAVE EXTORTED **MORE MONEY** IF HE KNEW MORE.
I AGREE.
WHAT WOULD A THIEF DO WITH STOLEN MERCHANDISE?
HE WOULD ***SELL IT!***
EXACTLY! AND I KNOW TO WHOM!
COME ON!
5

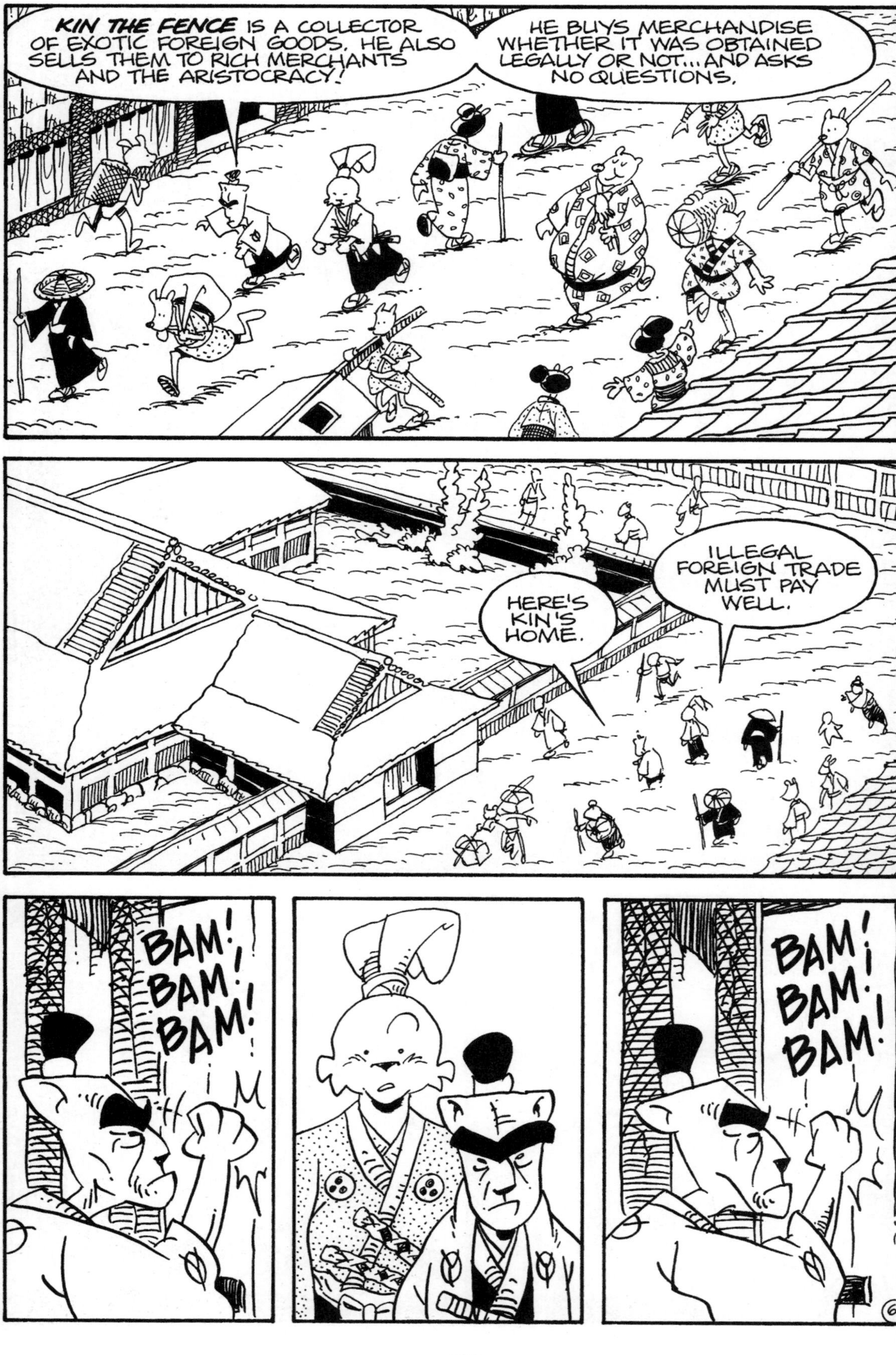
KIN THE FENCE IS A COLLECTOR OF EXOTIC FOREIGN GOODS. HE ALSO SELLS THEM TO RICH MERCHANTS AND THE ARISTOCRACY!
HE BUYS MERCHANDISE WHETHER IT WAS OBTAINED LEGALLY OR NOT... AND ASKS NO QUESTIONS.
HERE'S KIN'S HOME.
ILLEGAL FOREIGN TRADE MUST PAY WELL.
BAM! BAM! BAM!
BAM! BAM! BAM!
6.

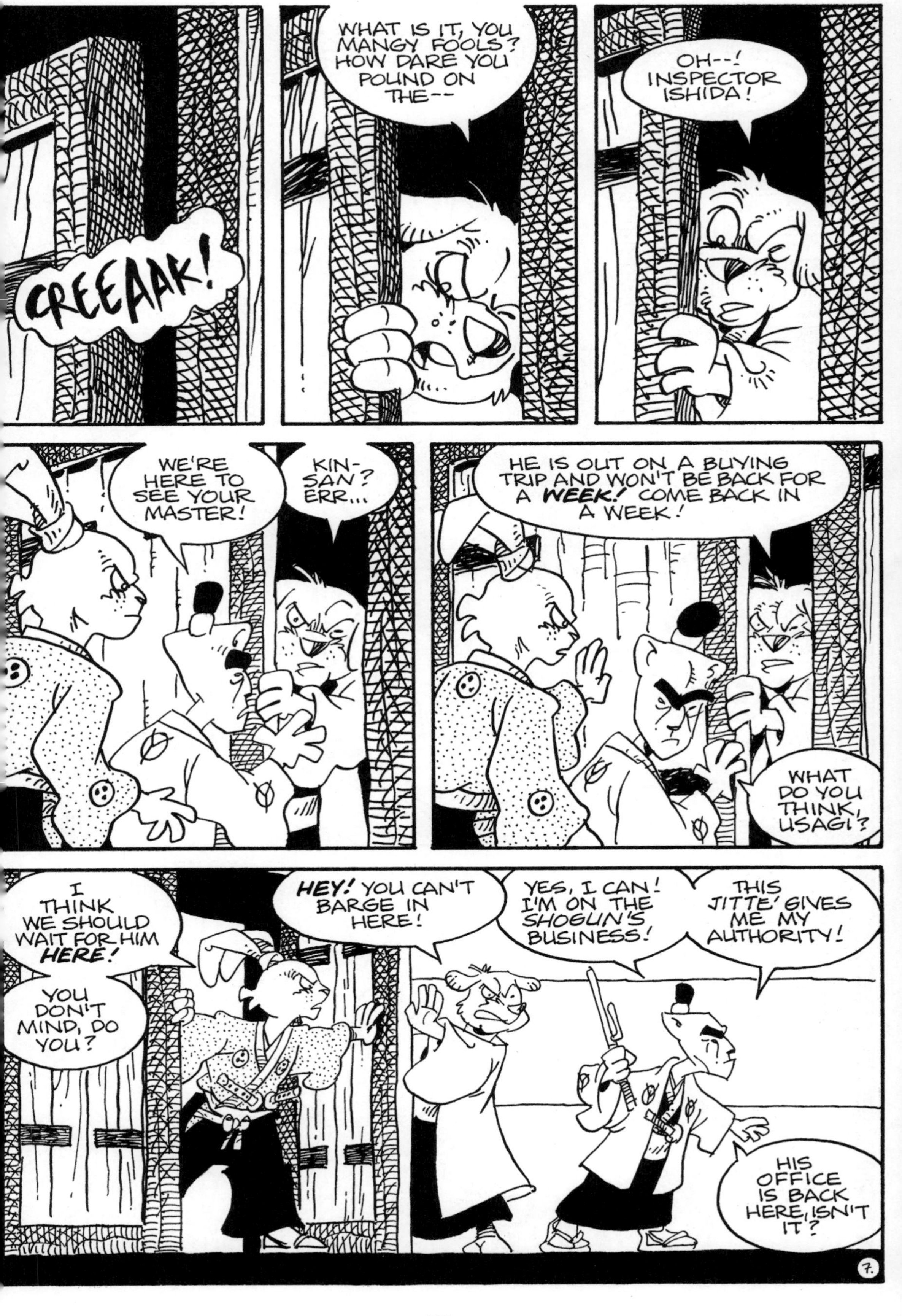
CREEAAK!
WHAT IS IT, YOU MANGY FOOLS? HOW DARE YOU POUND ON THE--
OH--! INSPECTOR ISHIDA!
WE'RE HERE TO SEE YOUR MASTER!
KIN-SAN? ERR...
HE IS OUT ON A BUYING TRIP AND WON'T BE BACK FOR A WEEK! COME BACK IN A WEEK!
WHAT DO YOU THINK, USAGI?
I THINK WE SHOULD WAIT FOR HIM HERE!
YOU DON'T MIND, DO YOU?
HEY! YOU CAN'T BARGE IN HERE!
YES, I CAN! I'M ON THE SHOGUN'S BUSINESS!
THIS JITTE GIVES ME MY AUTHORITY!
HIS OFFICE IS BACK HERE, ISN'T IT?
7.

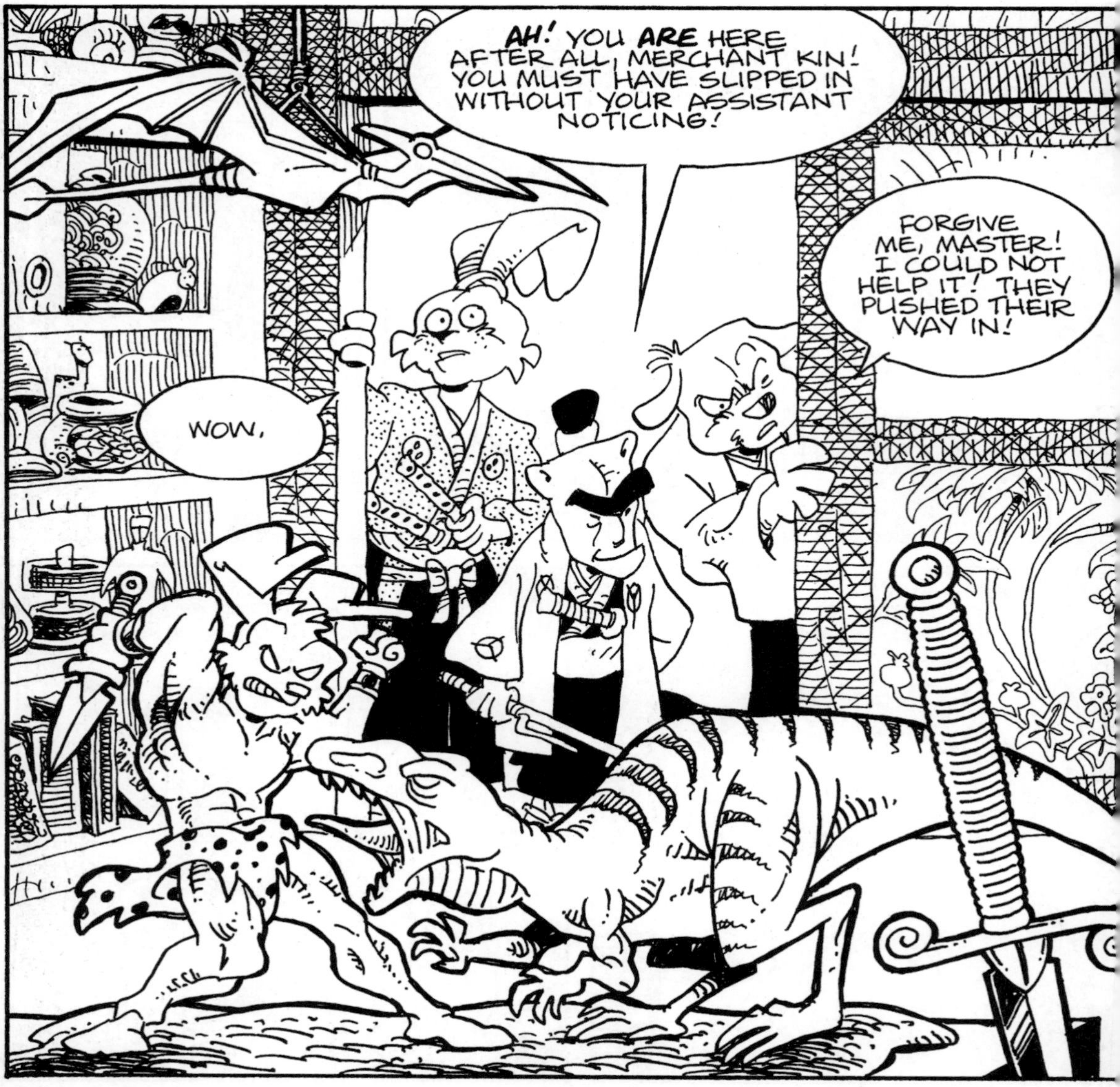
AH! YOU ARE HERE AFTER ALL, MERCHANT KIN! YOU MUST HAVE SLIPPED IN WITHOUT YOUR ASSISTANT NOTICING!
FORGIVE ME, MASTER! I COULD NOT HELP IT! THEY PUSHED THEIR WAY IN!
WOW.

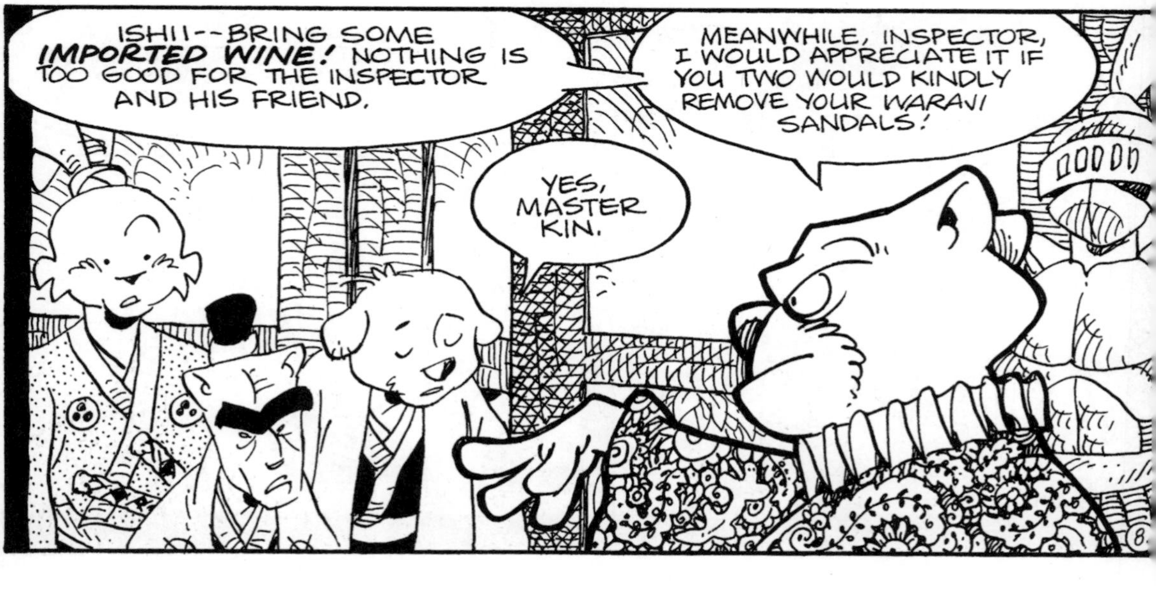
ISHII--BRING SOME IMPORTED WINE! NOTHING IS TOO GOOD FOR THE INSPECTOR AND HIS FRIEND.
MEANWHILE, INSPECTOR, I WOULD APPRECIATE IT IF YOU TWO WOULD KINDLY REMOVE YOUR WARAJI SANDALS!
YES, MASTER KIN.
8

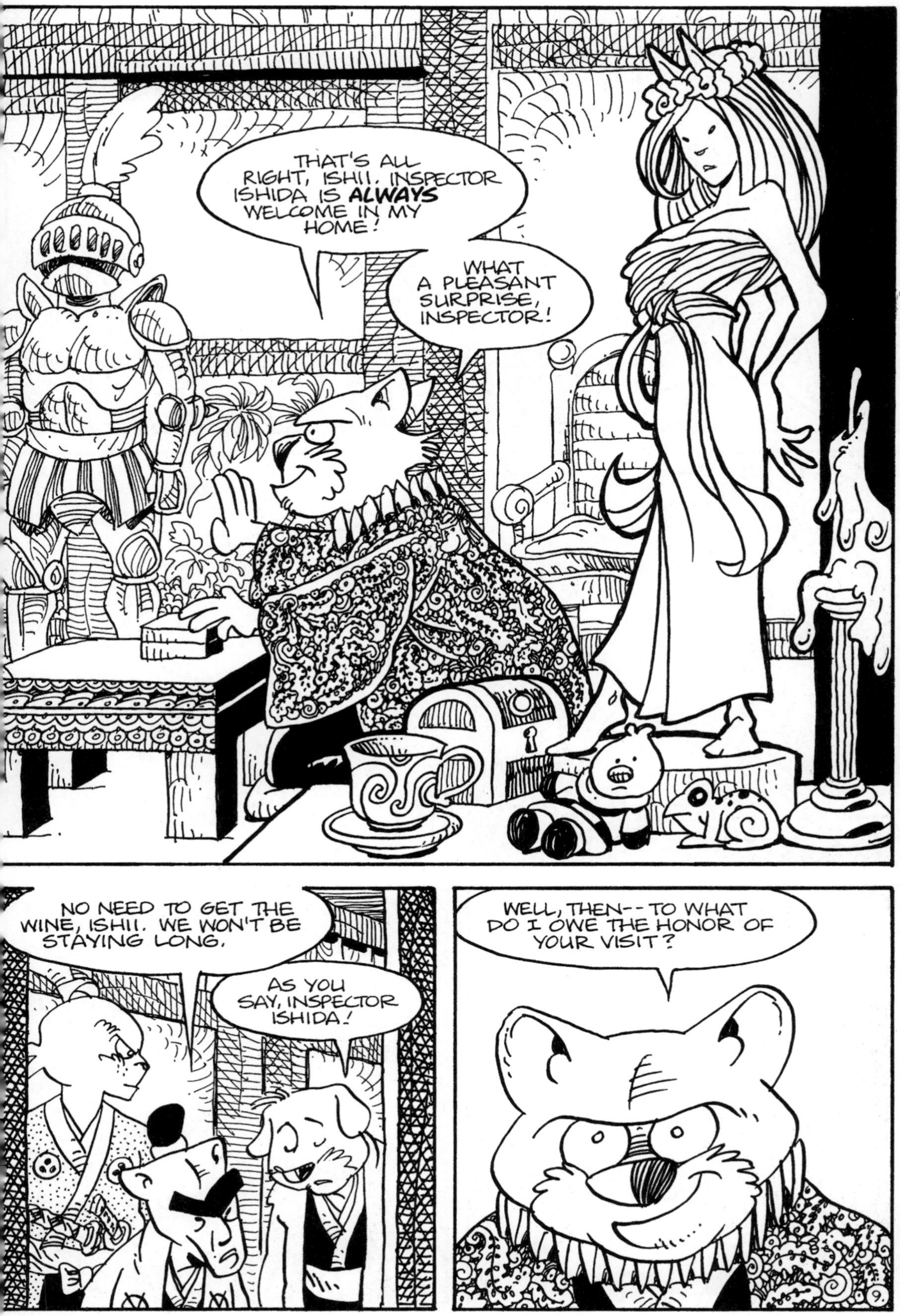
THAT'S ALL RIGHT, ISHII. INSPECTOR ISHIDA IS **ALWAYS** WELCOME IN MY HOME!
WHAT A PLEASANT SURPRISE, INSPECTOR!
NO NEED TO GET THE WINE, ISHII. WE WON'T BE STAYING LONG.
AS YOU SAY, INSPECTOR ISHIDA!
WELL, THEN-- TO WHAT DO I OWE THE HONOR OF YOUR VISIT?
9.

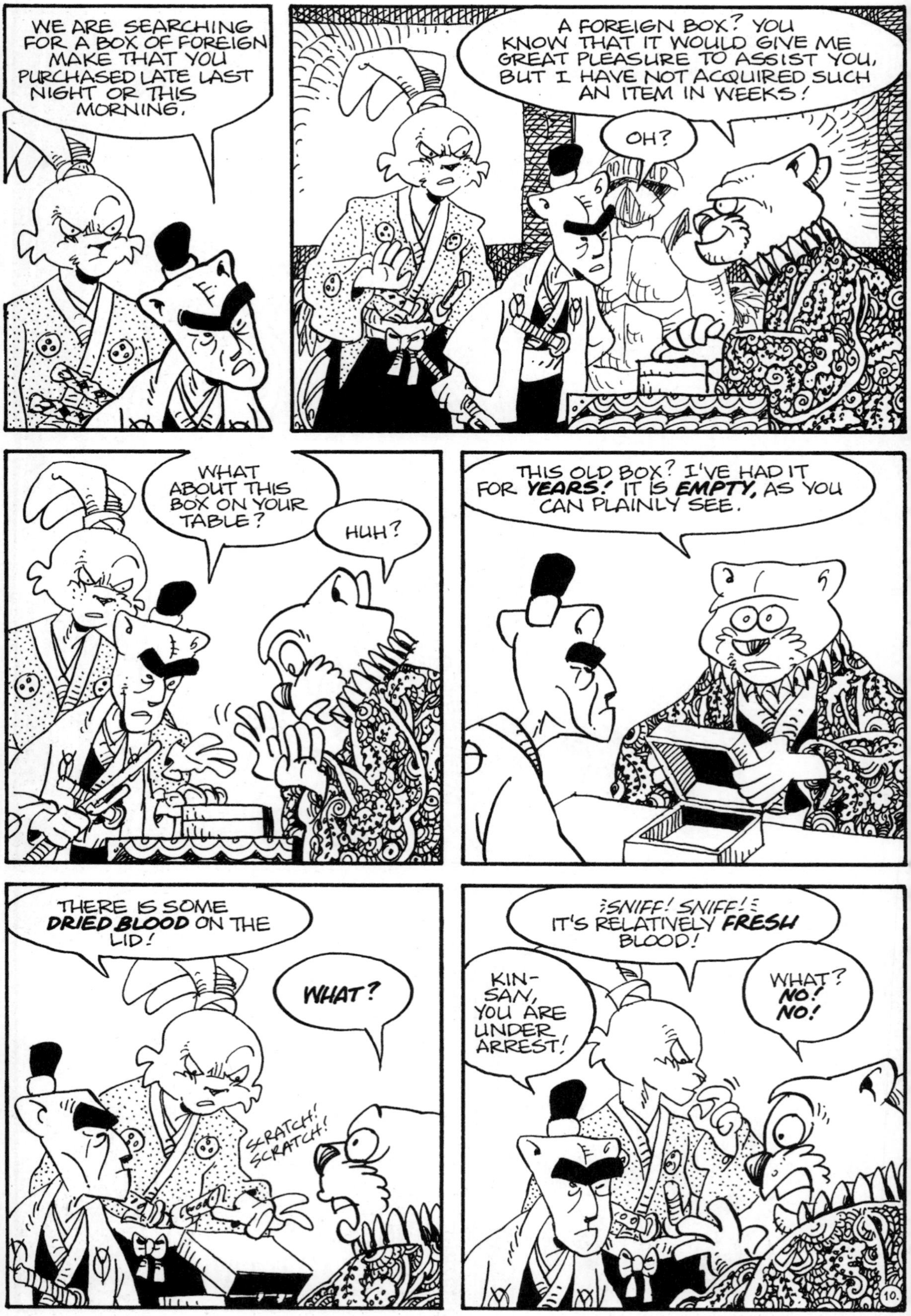
WE ARE SEARCHING FOR A BOX OF FOREIGN MAKE THAT YOU PURCHASED LATE LAST NIGHT OR THIS MORNING.
A FOREIGN BOX? YOU KNOW THAT IT WOULD GIVE ME GREAT PLEASURE TO ASSIST YOU, BUT I HAVE NOT ACQUIRED SUCH AN ITEM IN WEEKS!
OH?
WHAT ABOUT THIS BOX ON YOUR TABLE?
HUH?
THIS OLD BOX? I'VE HAD IT FOR YEARS! IT IS EMPTY, AS YOU CAN PLAINLY SEE.
THERE IS SOME DRIED BLOOD ON THE LID!
WHAT?
SCRATCH! SCRATCH!
SNIFF! SNIFF!
IT'S RELATIVELY FRESH BLOOD!
KIN-SAN, YOU ARE UNDER ARREST!
WHAT? NO! NO!
10

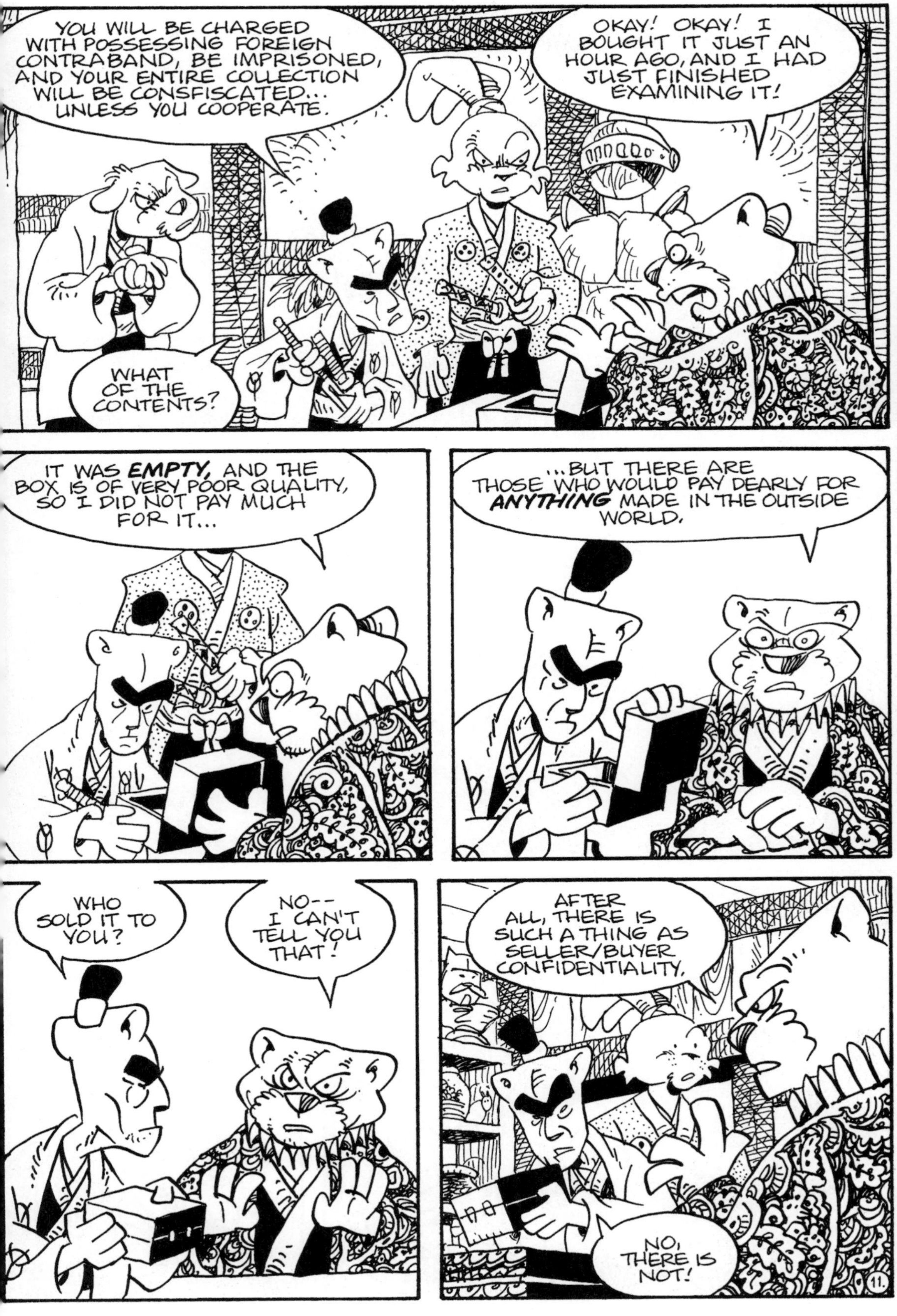
YOU WILL BE CHARGED WITH POSSESSING FOREIGN CONTRABAND, BE IMPRISONED, AND YOUR ENTIRE COLLECTION WILL BE CONSFISCATED... UNLESS YOU COOPERATE.
OKAY! OKAY! I BOUGHT IT JUST AN HOUR AGO, AND I HAD JUST FINISHED EXAMINING IT!
WHAT OF THE CONTENTS?
IT WAS EMPTY, AND THE BOX IS OF VERY POOR QUALITY, SO I DID NOT PAY MUCH FOR IT...
...BUT THERE ARE THOSE WHO WOULD PAY DEARLY FOR ANYTHING MADE IN THE OUTSIDE WORLD.
WHO SOLD IT TO YOU?
NO-- I CAN'T TELL YOU THAT!
AFTER ALL, THERE IS SUCH A THING AS SELLER/BUYER CONFIDENTIALITY.
NO, THERE IS NOT!
11.

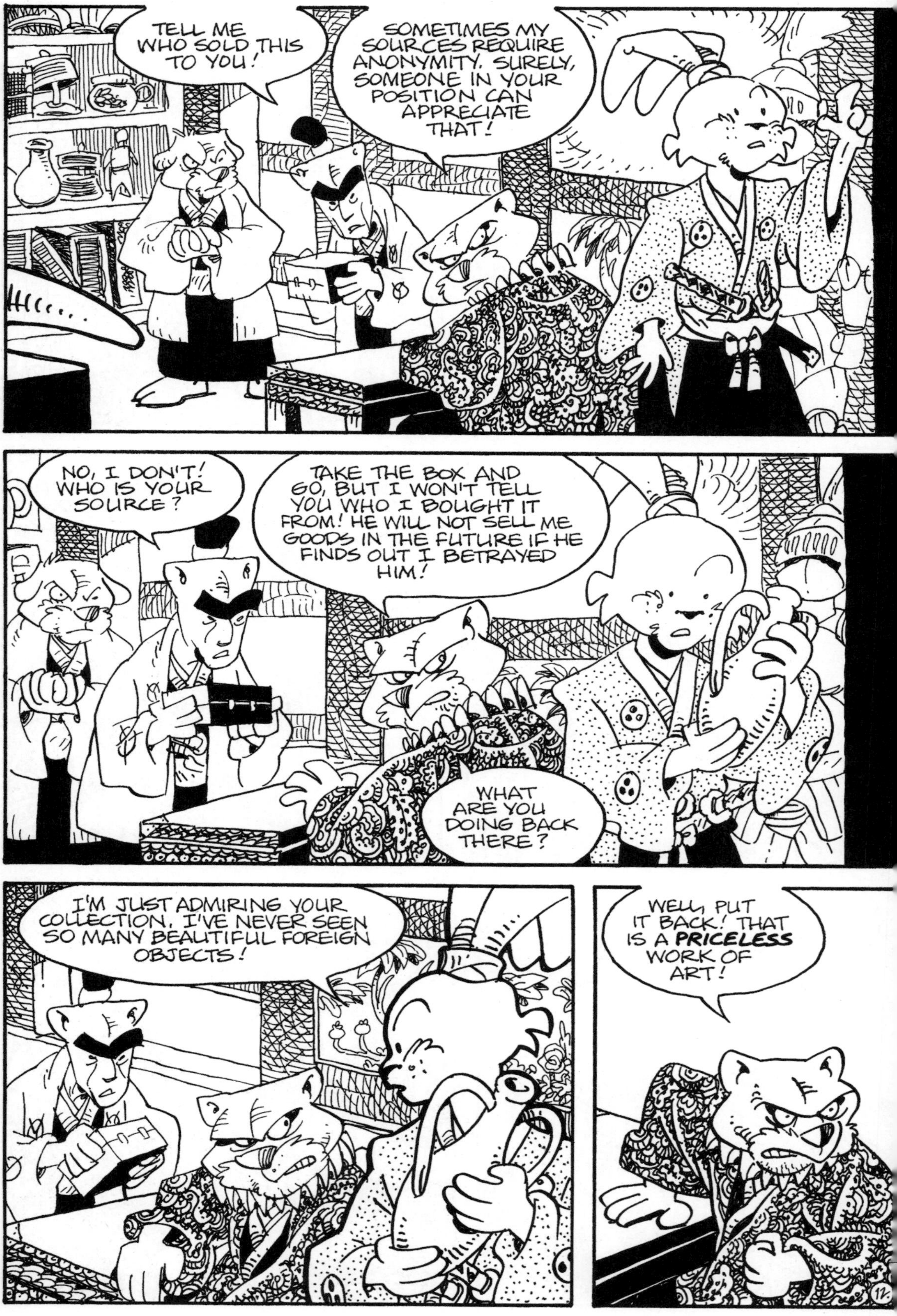
TELL ME WHO SOLD THIS TO YOU!
SOMETIMES MY SOURCES REQUIRE ANONYMITY. SURELY, SOMEONE IN YOUR POSITION CAN APPRECIATE THAT!
NO, I DON'T! WHO IS YOUR SOURCE?
TAKE THE BOX AND GO, BUT I WON'T TELL YOU WHO I BOUGHT IT FROM! HE WILL NOT SELL ME GOODS IN THE FUTURE IF HE FINDS OUT I BETRAYED HIM!
WHAT ARE YOU DOING BACK THERE?
I'M JUST ADMIRING YOUR COLLECTION. I'VE NEVER SEEN SO MANY BEAUTIFUL FOREIGN OBJECTS!
WELL, PUT IT BACK! THAT IS A **PRICELESS** WORK OF ART!
12.

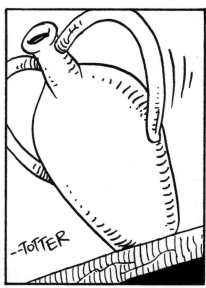

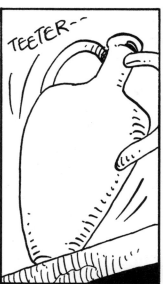

SORRY. I WAS ONLY LOOKING AT IT.

TEETER--

--TOTTER

YAHHH!

OOPS!

ARE YOU CRAZY?! THIS IS IRREPLACEABLE! DO YOU KNOW WHAT I PAID FOR THIS?!

DON'T TOUCH THAT!

I GUESS I'M JUST NATURALLY CURIOUS...

...BUT MAYBE A BIT CLUMSY.

YAH!

WOOPS!

≥ PHEW! ≤ CAUGHT IT!

13.

237

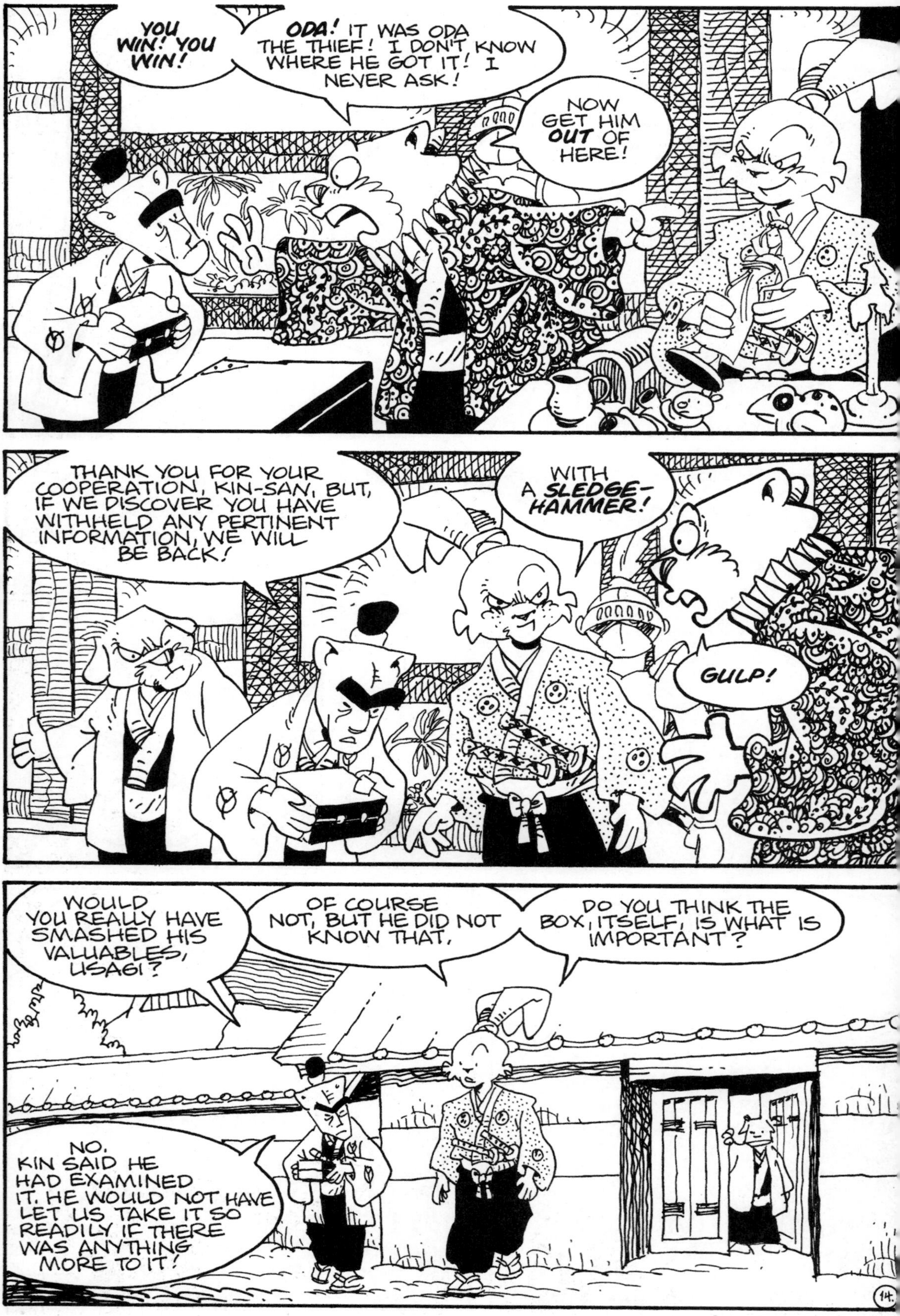
YOU WIN! YOU WIN!
ODA! IT WAS ODA THE THIEF! I DON'T KNOW WHERE HE GOT IT! I NEVER ASK!
NOW GET HIM OUT OF HERE!
THANK YOU FOR YOUR COOPERATION, KIN-SAN, BUT, IF WE DISCOVER YOU HAVE WITHHELD ANY PERTINENT INFORMATION, WE WILL BE BACK!
WITH A SLEDGE-HAMMER!
GULP!
WOULD YOU REALLY HAVE SMASHED HIS VALUABLES, USAGI?
OF COURSE NOT, BUT HE DID NOT KNOW THAT.
DO YOU THINK THE BOX, ITSELF, IS WHAT IS IMPORTANT?
NO. KIN SAID HE HAD EXAMINED IT. HE WOULD NOT HAVE LET US TAKE IT SO READILY IF THERE WAS ANYTHING MORE TO IT!
14.

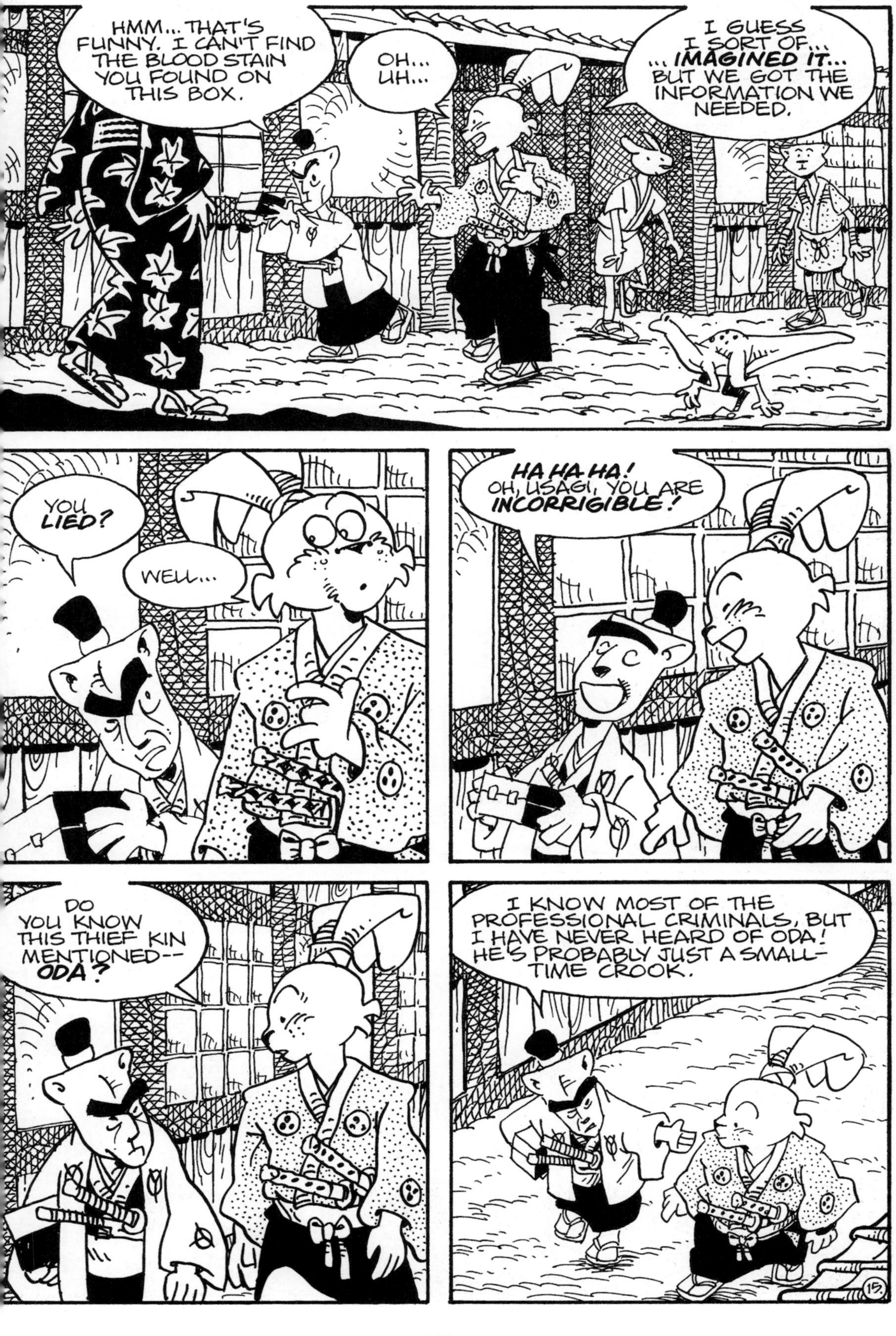
HMM... THAT'S FUNNY. I CAN'T FIND THE BLOOD STAIN YOU FOUND ON THIS BOX.
OH... UH...
I GUESS I SORT OF... ...IMAGINED IT... BUT WE GOT THE INFORMATION WE NEEDED.
YOU LIED?
WELL...
HA HA HA! OH, USAGI, YOU ARE INCORRIGIBLE!
DO YOU KNOW THIS THIEF KIN MENTIONED-- ODA?
I KNOW MOST OF THE PROFESSIONAL CRIMINALS, BUT I HAVE NEVER HEARD OF ODA! HE'S PROBABLY JUST A SMALL-TIME CROOK.
15.

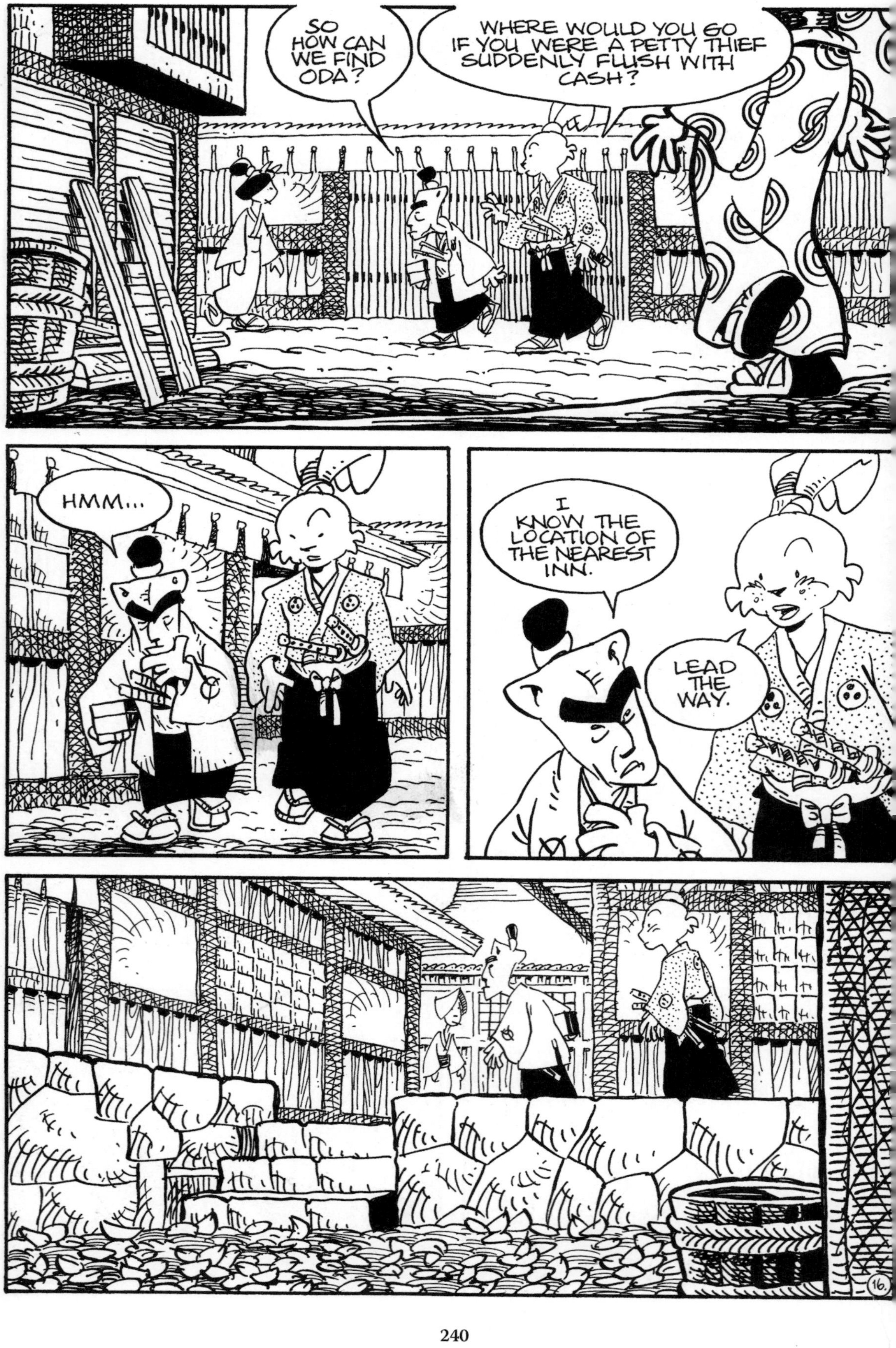
SO HOW CAN WE FIND ODA?
WHERE WOULD YOU GO IF YOU WERE A PETTY THIEF SUDDENLY FLUSH WITH CASH?
HMM...
I KNOW THE LOCATION OF THE NEAREST INN.
LEAD THE WAY.
16.

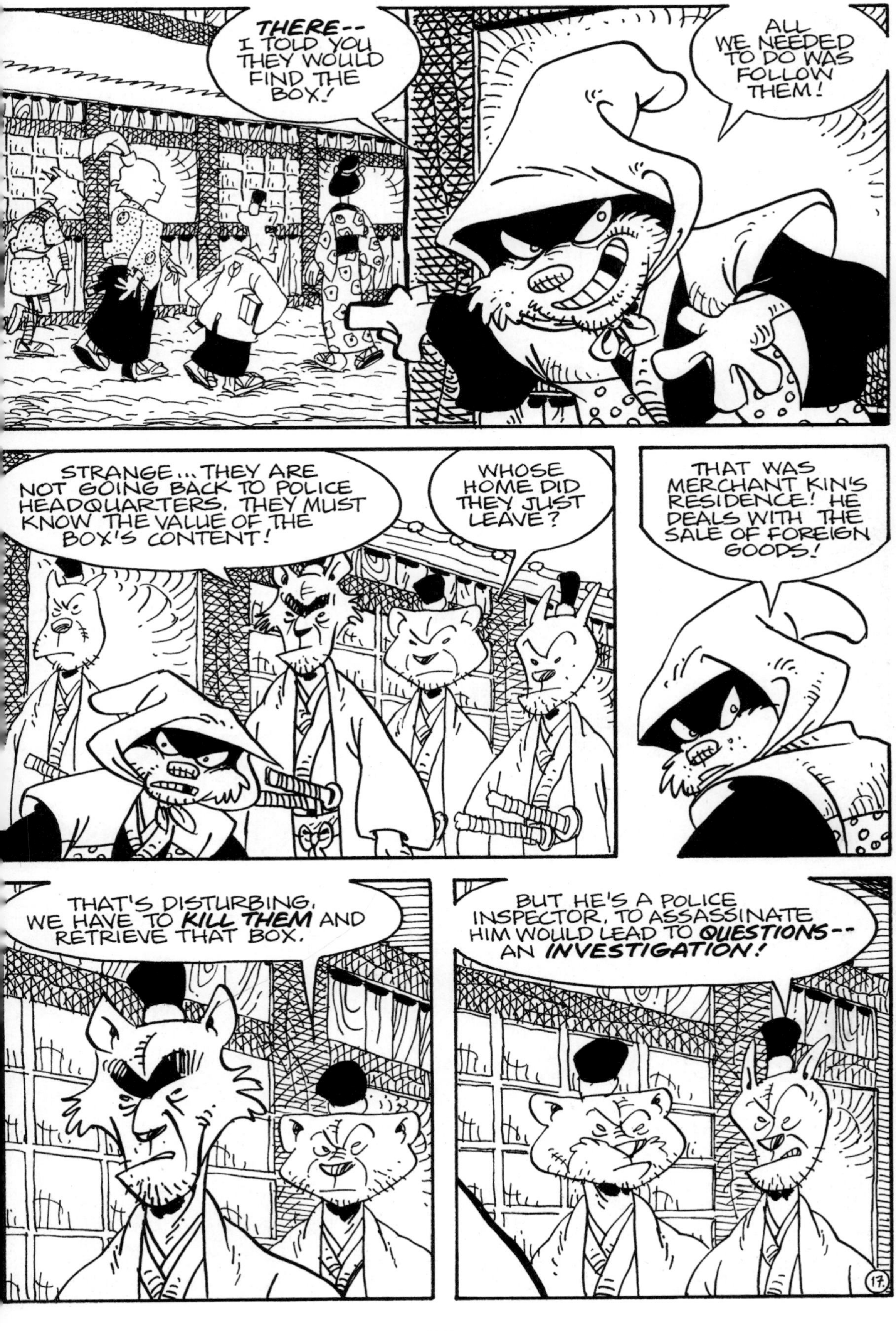
THERE-- I TOLD YOU THEY WOULD FIND THE BOX!
ALL WE NEEDED TO DO WAS FOLLOW THEM!
STRANGE... THEY ARE NOT GOING BACK TO POLICE HEADQUARTERS. THEY MUST KNOW THE VALUE OF THE BOX'S CONTENT!
WHOSE HOME DID THEY JUST LEAVE?
THAT WAS MERCHANT KIN'S RESIDENCE! HE DEALS WITH THE SALE OF FOREIGN GOODS!
THAT'S DISTURBING. WE HAVE TO KILL THEM AND RETRIEVE THAT BOX.
BUT HE'S A POLICE INSPECTOR. TO ASSASSINATE HIM WOULD LEAD TO QUESTIONS-- AN INVESTIGATION!
17.

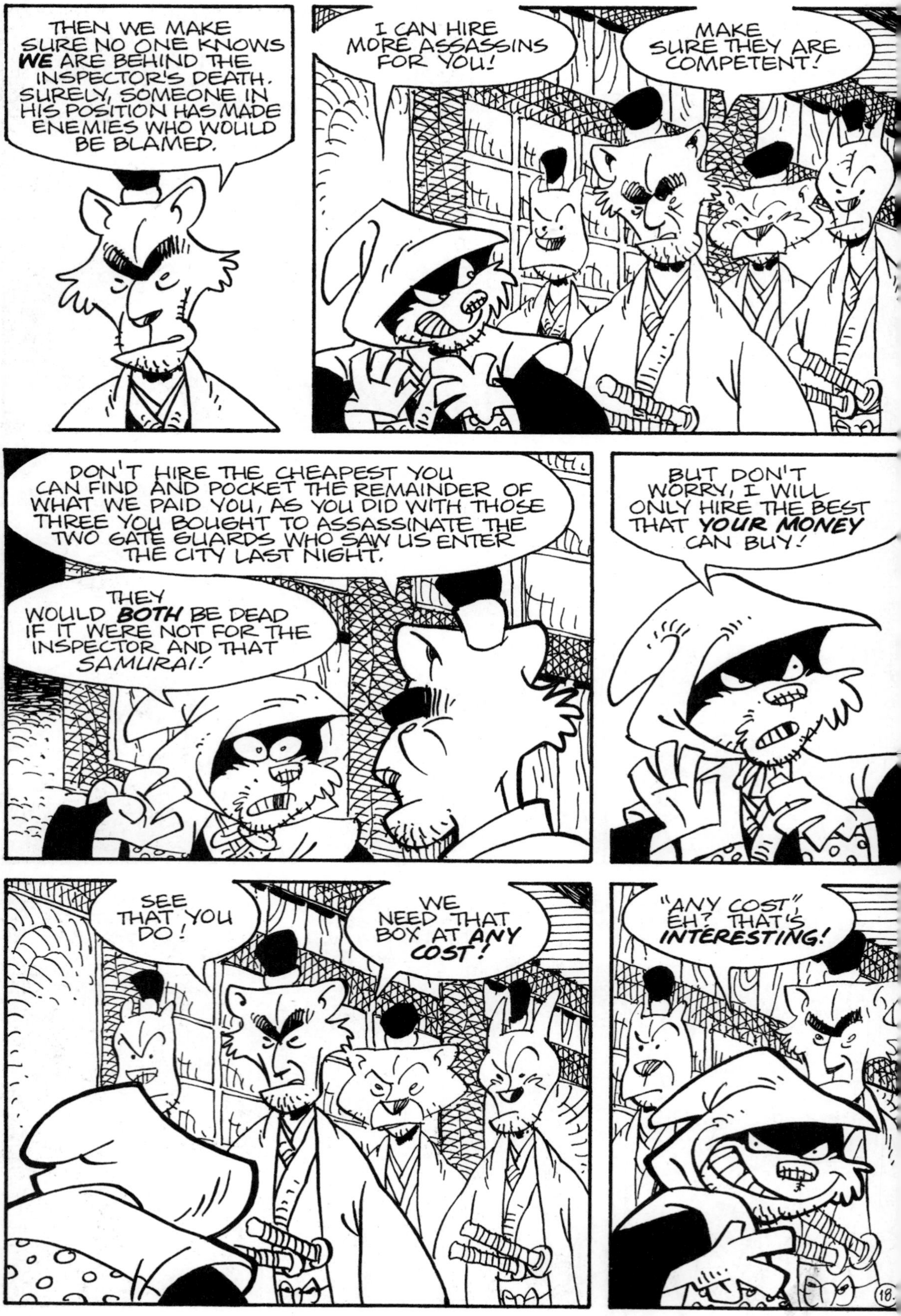
THEN WE MAKE SURE NO ONE KNOWS WE ARE BEHIND THE INSPECTOR'S DEATH. SURELY, SOMEONE IN HIS POSITION HAS MADE ENEMIES WHO WOULD BE BLAMED.
I CAN HIRE MORE ASSASSINS FOR YOU!
MAKE SURE THEY ARE COMPETENT!
DON'T HIRE THE CHEAPEST YOU CAN FIND AND POCKET THE REMAINDER OF WHAT WE PAID YOU, AS YOU DID WITH THOSE THREE YOU BOUGHT TO ASSASSINATE THE TWO GATE GUARDS WHO SAW US ENTER THE CITY LAST NIGHT.
THEY WOULD BOTH BE DEAD IF IT WERE NOT FOR THE INSPECTOR AND THAT SAMURAI!
BUT DON'T WORRY, I WILL ONLY HIRE THE BEST THAT YOUR MONEY CAN BUY!
SEE THAT YOU DO!
WE NEED THAT BOX AT ANY COST!
"ANY COST," EH? THAT'S INTERESTING!
18.

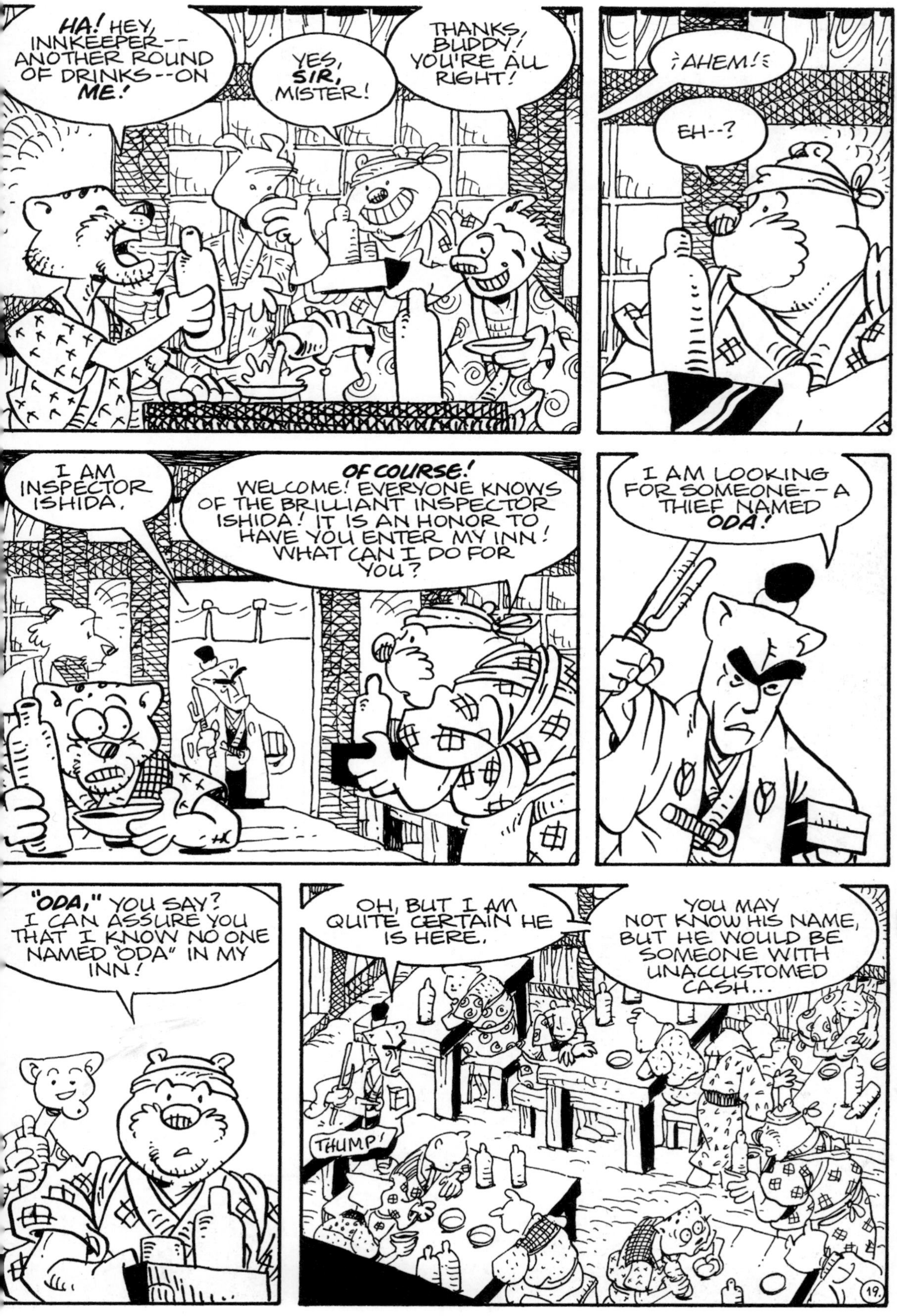

HA! HEY, INNKEEPER-- ANOTHER ROUND OF DRINKS--ON ME!
YES, SIR, MISTER!
THANKS, BUDDY! YOU'RE ALL RIGHT!
AHEM!
EH--?
I AM INSPECTOR ISHIDA.
OF COURSE! WELCOME! EVERYONE KNOWS OF THE BRILLIANT INSPECTOR ISHIDA! IT IS AN HONOR TO HAVE YOU ENTER MY INN! WHAT CAN I DO FOR YOU?
I AM LOOKING FOR SOMEONE-- A THIEF NAMED ODA!
"ODA," YOU SAY? I CAN ASSURE YOU THAT I KNOW NO ONE NAMED "ODA" IN MY INN!
OH, BUT I AM QUITE CERTAIN HE IS HERE.
YOU MAY NOT KNOW HIS NAME, BUT HE WOULD BE SOMEONE WITH UNACCUSTOMED CASH...
THUMP!
19.

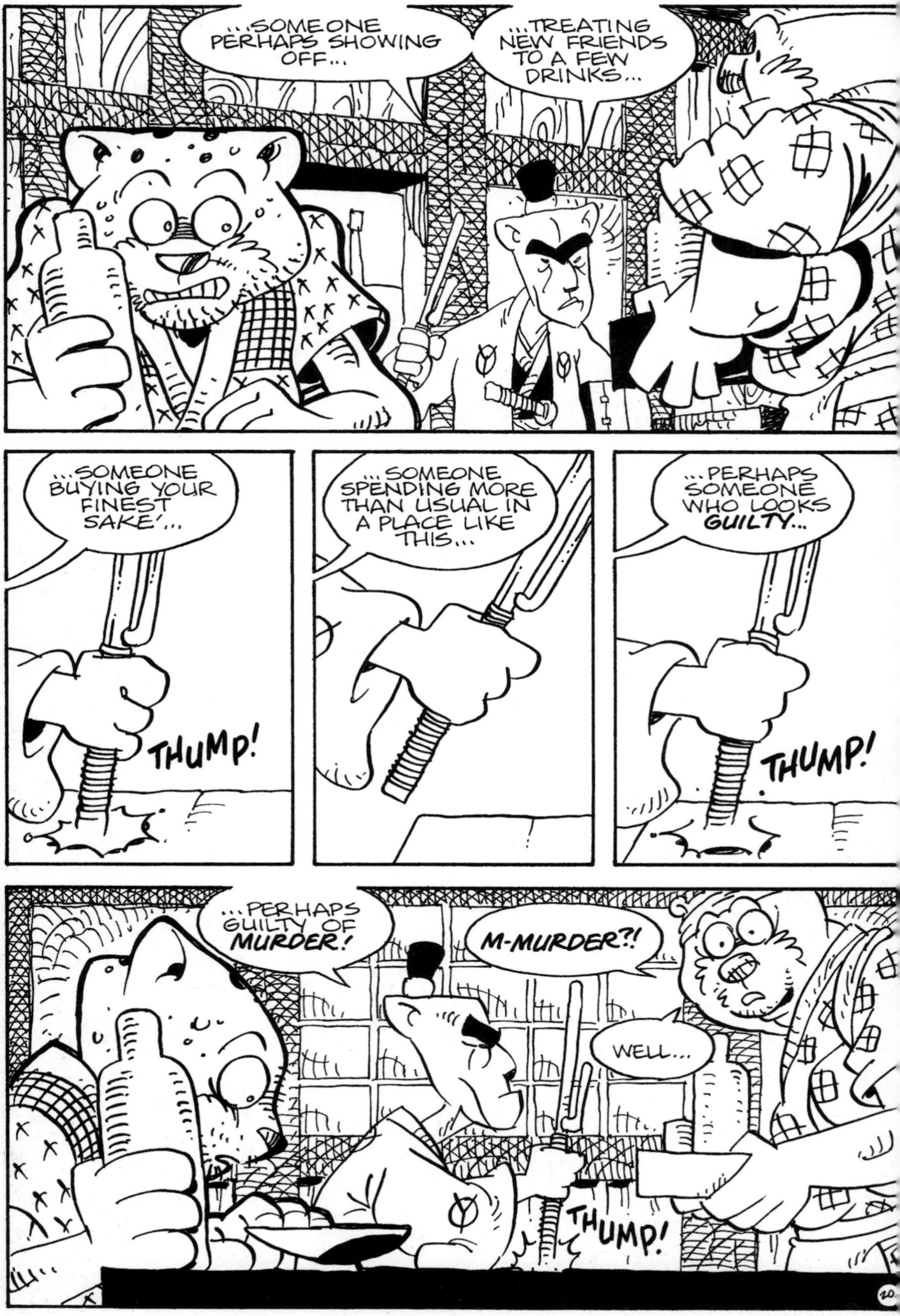
...SOMEONE PERHAPS SHOWING OFF...
...TREATING NEW FRIENDS TO A FEW DRINKS...
...SOMEONE BUYING YOUR FINEST SAKE'...
THUMP!
...SOMEONE SPENDING MORE THAN USUAL IN A PLACE LIKE THIS...
...PERHAPS SOMEONE WHO LOOKS GUILTY...
THUMP!
...PERHAPS GUILTY OF MURDER!
M-MURDER?!
WELL...
THUMP!
20

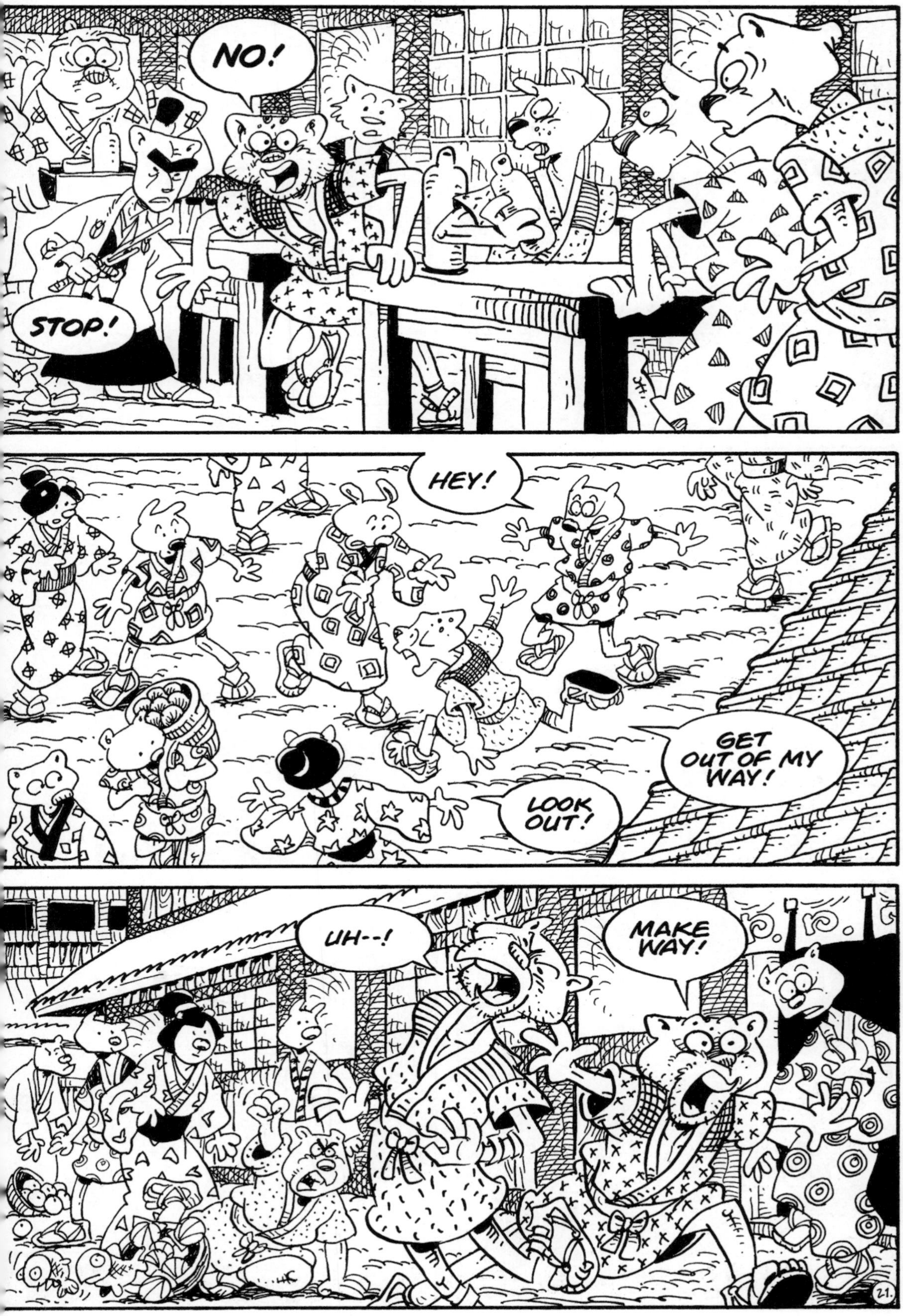
NO!
STOP!
HEY!
GET OUT OF MY WAY!
LOOK OUT!
UH--!
MAKE WAY!
21.

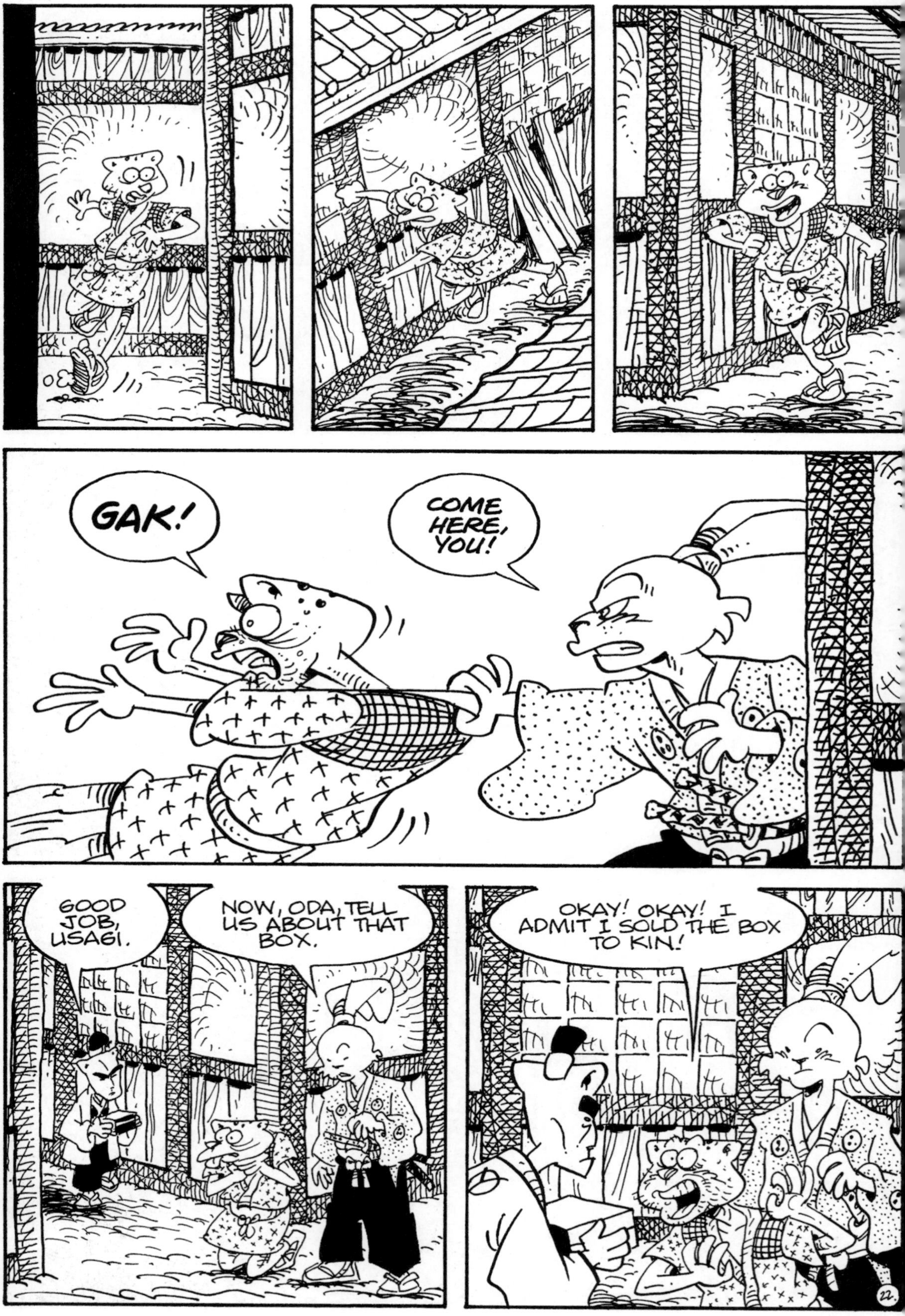
GAK!
COME HERE, YOU!
GOOD JOB, USAGI.
NOW, ODA, TELL US ABOUT THAT BOX.
OKAY! OKAY! I ADMIT I SOLD THE BOX TO KIN!
22.

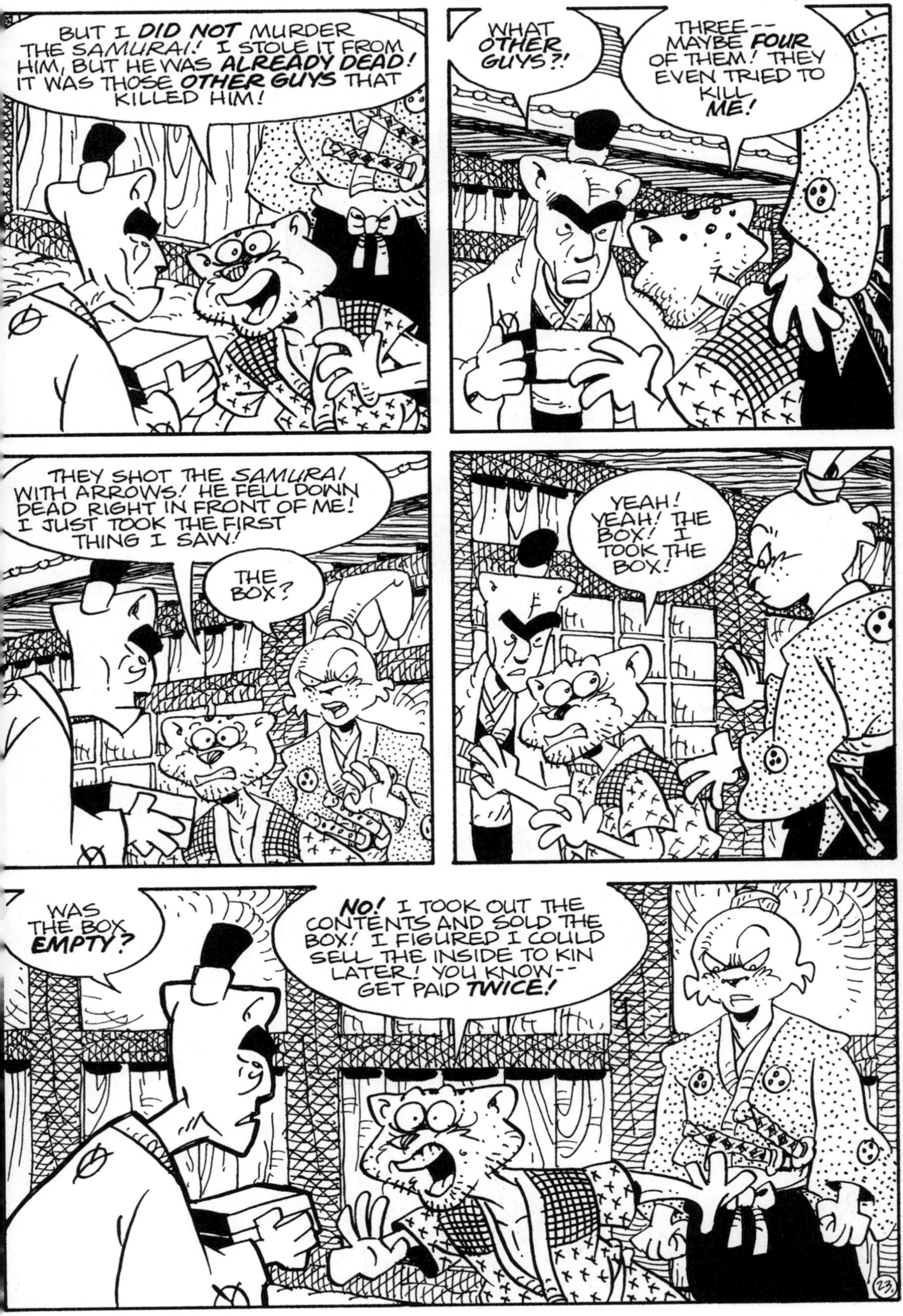
BUT I DID NOT MURDER THE SAMURAI! I STOLE IT FROM HIM, BUT HE WAS ALREADY DEAD! IT WAS THOSE OTHER GUYS THAT KILLED HIM!
WHAT OTHER GUYS?!
THREE-- MAYBE FOUR OF THEM! THEY EVEN TRIED TO KILL ME!
THEY SHOT THE SAMURAI WITH ARROWS! HE FELL DOWN DEAD RIGHT IN FRONT OF ME! I JUST TOOK THE FIRST THING I SAW!
THE BOX?
YEAH! YEAH! THE BOX! I TOOK THE BOX!
WAS THE BOX EMPTY?
NO! I TOOK OUT THE CONTENTS AND SOLD THE BOX! I FIGURED I COULD SELL THE INSIDE TO KIN LATER! YOU KNOW-- GET PAID TWICE!
23

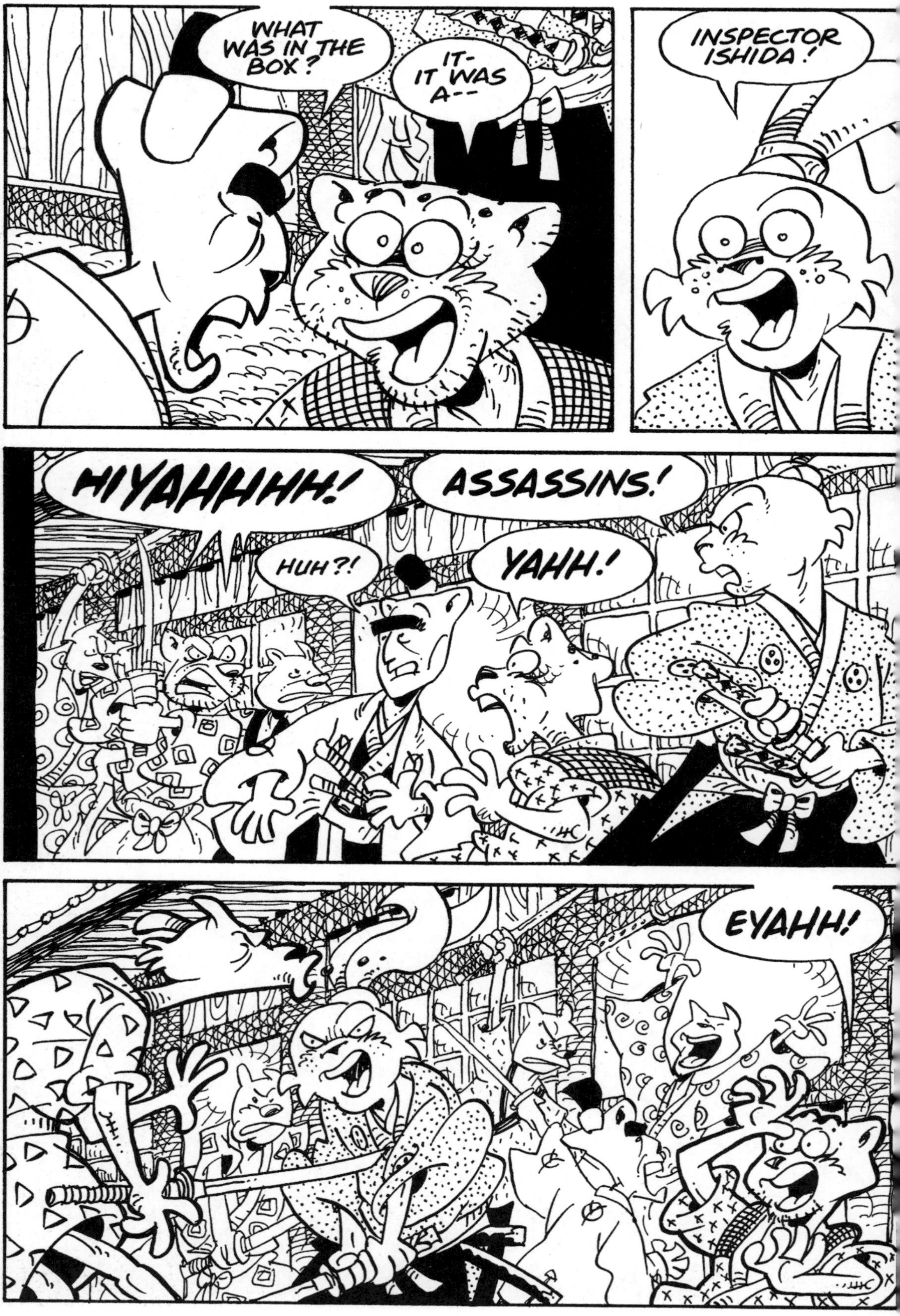
WHAT WAS IN THE BOX?
IT- IT WAS A--
INSPECTOR ISHIDA!
HIYAHHHHH!
ASSASSINS!
HUH?!
YAHH!
EYAHH!

THE HIDDEN PART FOUR

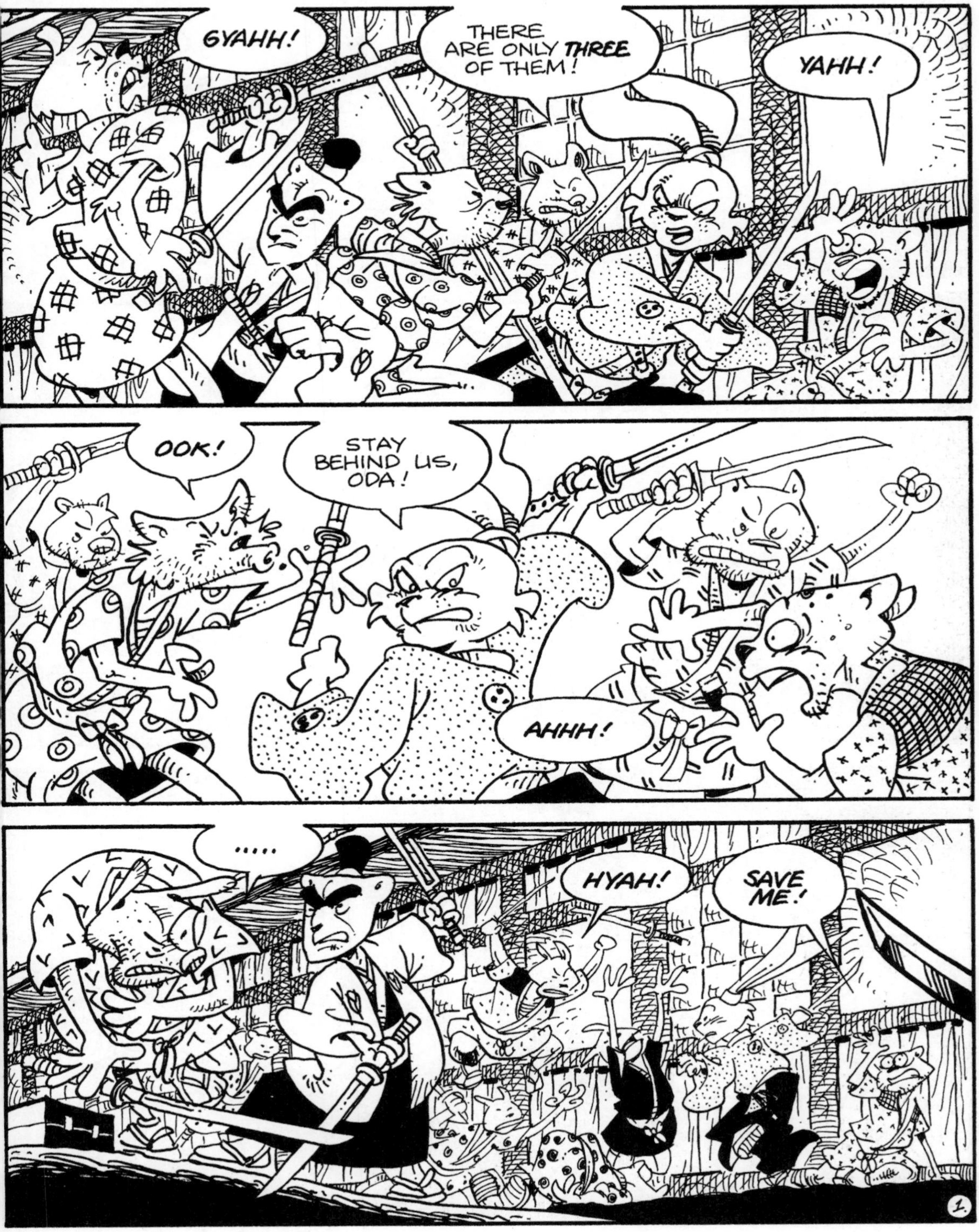
GYAHH!
THERE ARE ONLY THREE OF THEM!
YAHH!
OOK!
STAY BEHIND US, ODA!
AHHH!
.....
HYAH!
SAVE ME!
1.

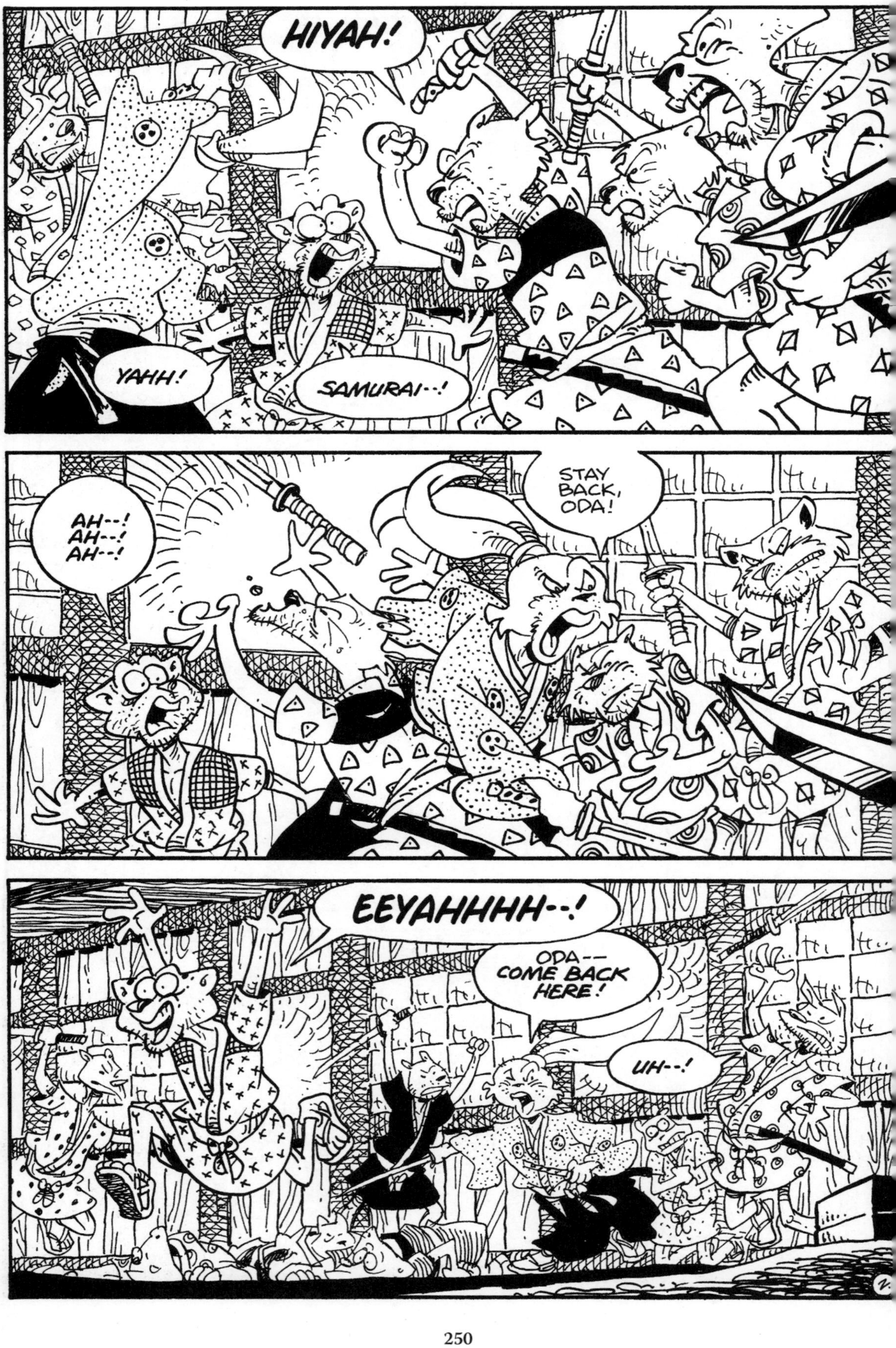
HIYAH!
YAHH!
SAMURAI--!
AH--! AH--! AH--!
STAY BACK, ODA!
EEYAHHHH--!
ODA-- COME BACK HERE!
UH--!

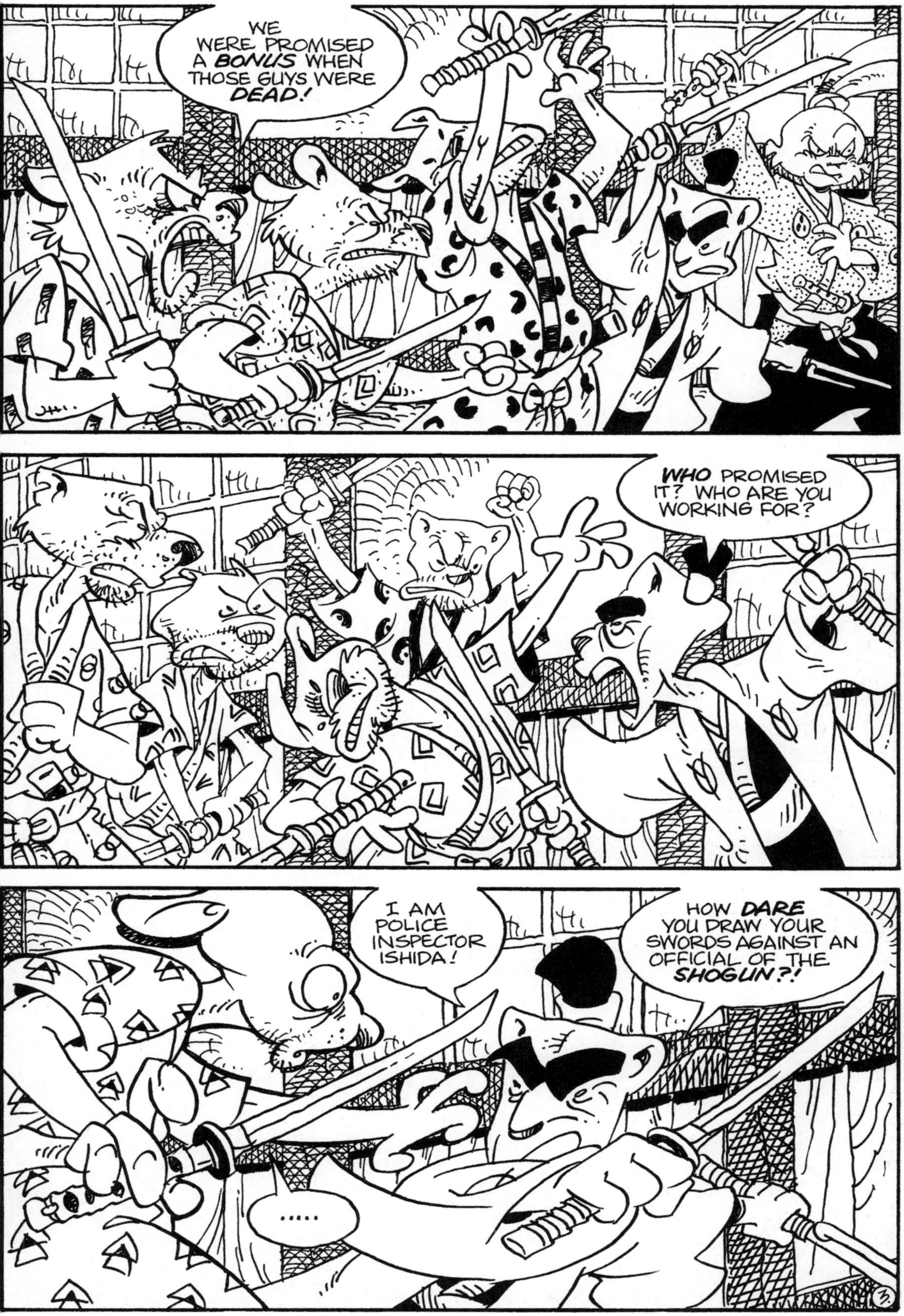
WE WERE PROMISED A BONUS WHEN THOSE GUYS WERE DEAD!
WHO PROMISED IT? WHO ARE YOU WORKING FOR?
I AM POLICE INSPECTOR ISHIDA!
HOW DARE YOU DRAW YOUR SWORDS AGAINST AN OFFICIAL OF THE SHOGUN?!
.....
3.

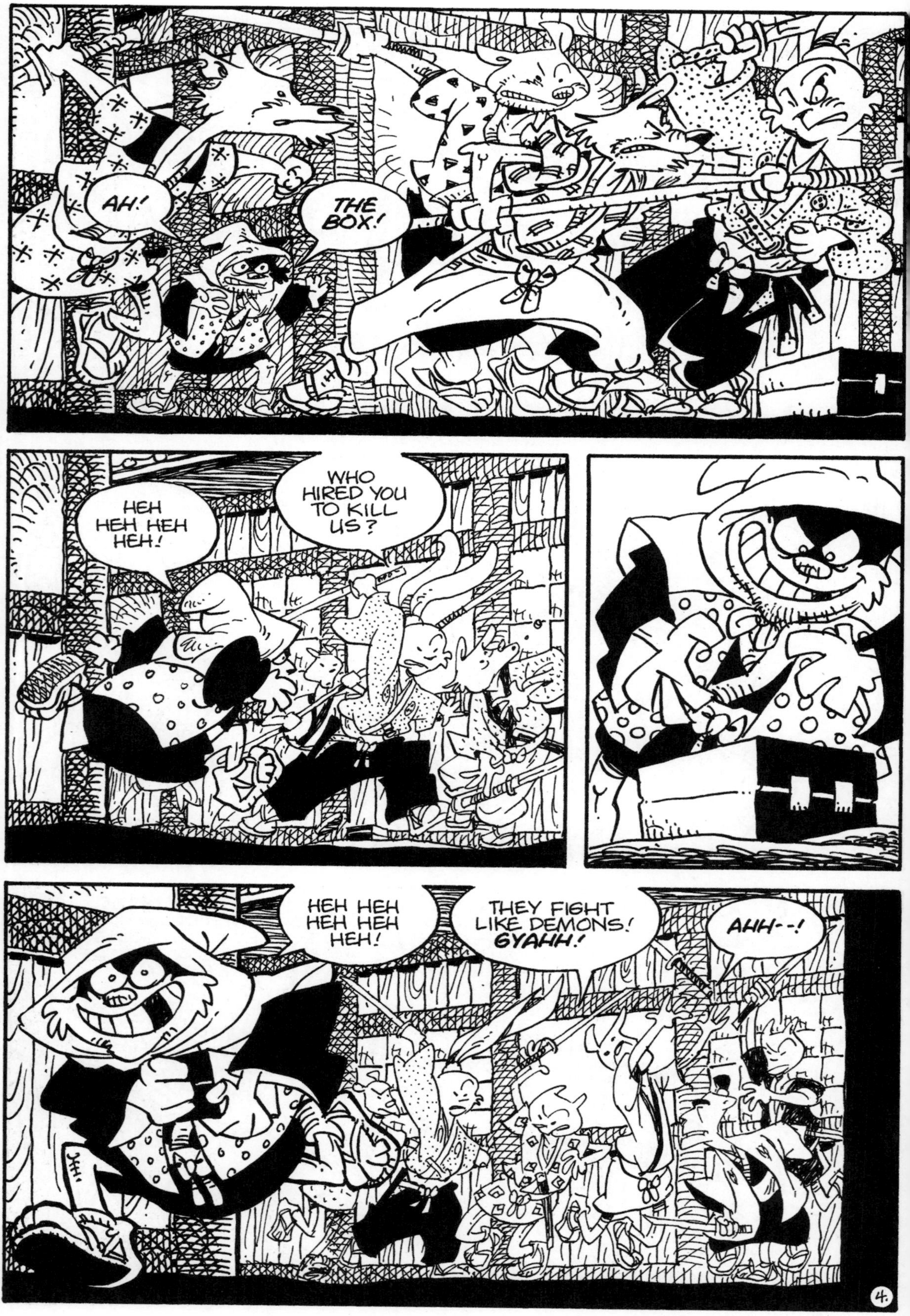
AH!
THE BOX!
HEH HEH HEH HEH!
WHO HIRED YOU TO KILL US?
HEH HEH HEH HEH HEH!
THEY FIGHT LIKE DEMONS! GYAHH!
AHH--!
4

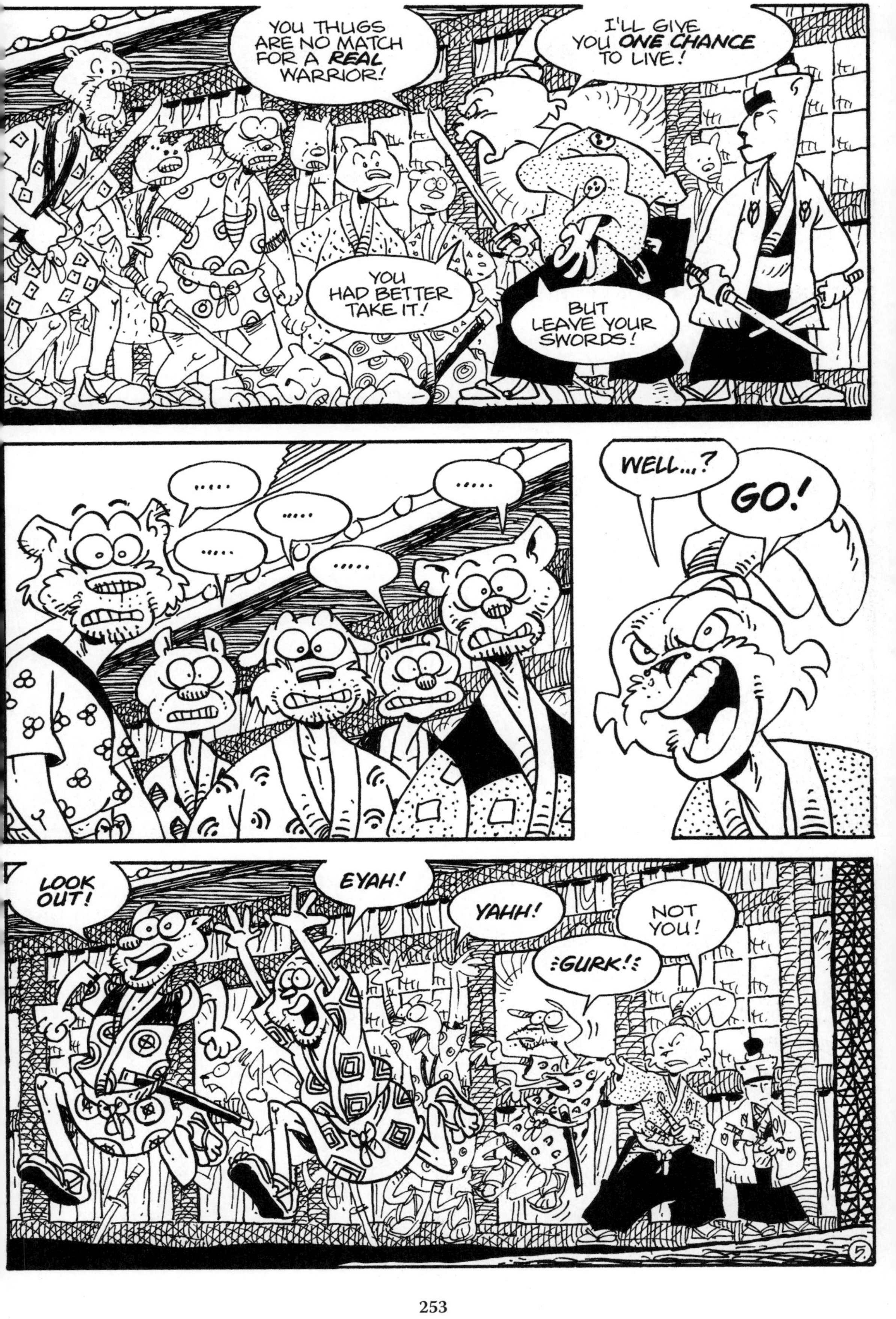
YOU THUGS ARE NO MATCH FOR A REAL WARRIOR!
I'LL GIVE YOU ONE CHANCE TO LIVE!
YOU HAD BETTER TAKE IT!
BUT LEAVE YOUR SWORDS!
.....
.....
.....
.....
.....
WELL...?
GO!
LOOK OUT!
EYAH!
YAHH!
NOT YOU!
GURK!
5

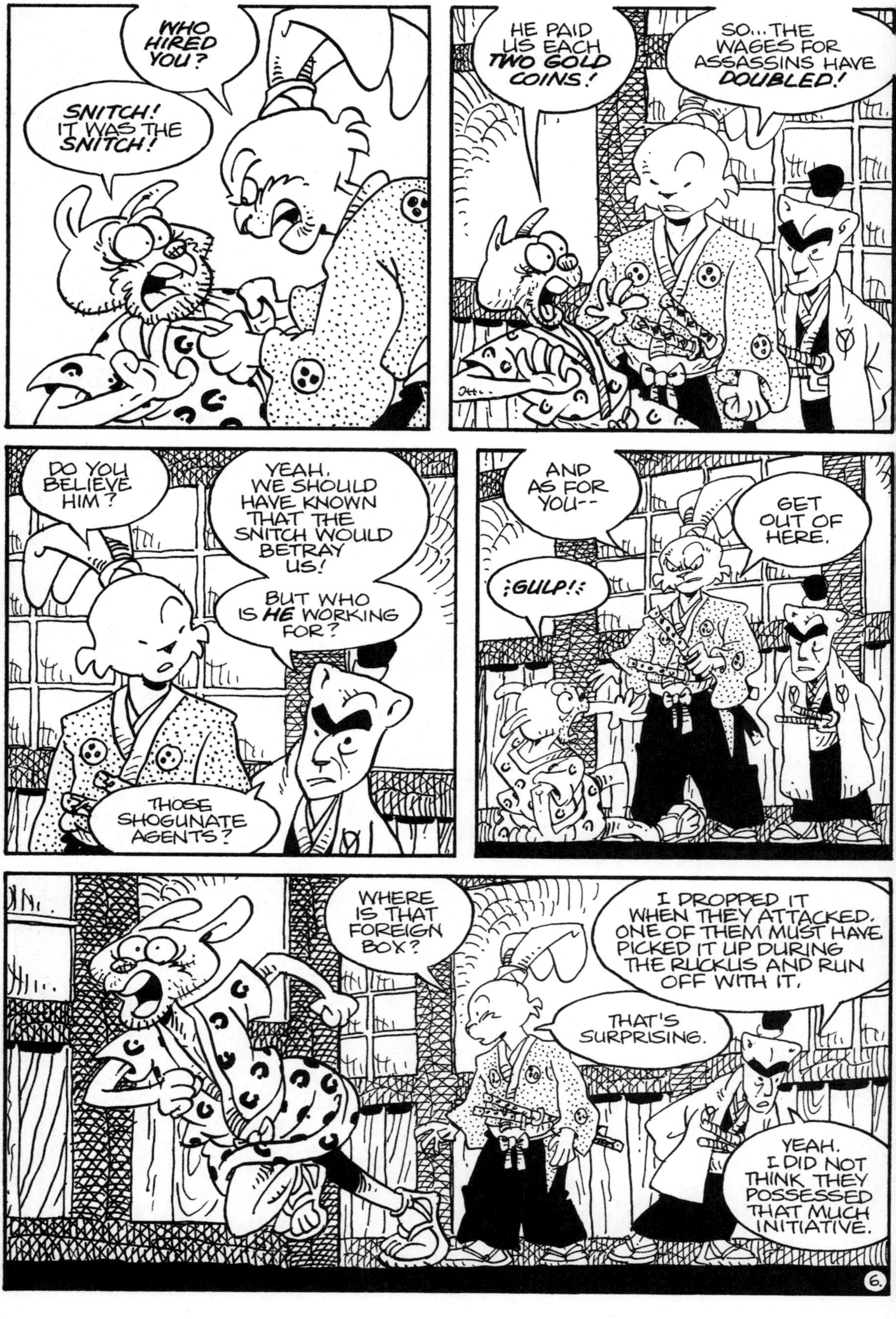
WHO HIRED YOU?
SNITCH! IT WAS THE SNITCH!
HE PAID US EACH TWO GOLD COINS!
SO... THE WAGES FOR ASSASSINS HAVE DOUBLED!
DO YOU BELIEVE HIM?
YEAH. WE SHOULD HAVE KNOWN THAT THE SNITCH WOULD BETRAY US!
BUT WHO IS HE WORKING FOR?
THOSE SHOGUNATE AGENTS?
AND AS FOR YOU--
GET OUT OF HERE.
GULP!
WHERE IS THAT FOREIGN BOX?
I DROPPED IT WHEN THEY ATTACKED. ONE OF THEM MUST HAVE PICKED IT UP DURING THE RUCKUS AND RUN OFF WITH IT.
THAT'S SURPRISING.
YEAH. I DID NOT THINK THEY POSSESSED THAT MUCH INITIATIVE.
6.

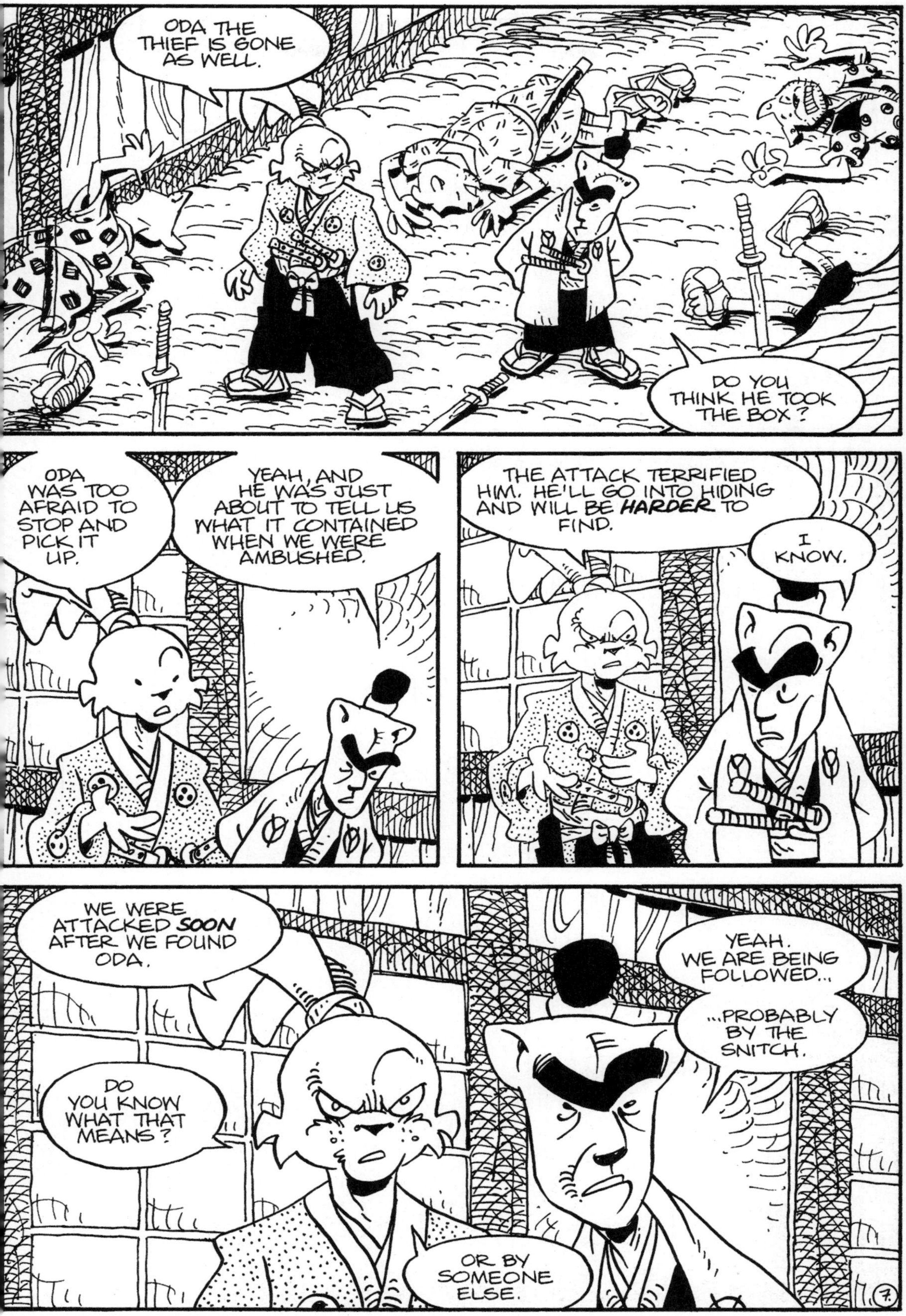
ODA THE THIEF IS GONE AS WELL.
DO YOU THINK HE TOOK THE BOX?
ODA WAS TOO AFRAID TO STOP AND PICK IT UP.
YEAH, AND HE WAS JUST ABOUT TO TELL US WHAT IT CONTAINED WHEN WE WERE AMBUSHED.
THE ATTACK TERRIFIED HIM. HE'LL GO INTO HIDING AND WILL BE HARDER TO FIND.
I KNOW.
WE WERE ATTACKED SOON AFTER WE FOUND ODA.
DO YOU KNOW WHAT THAT MEANS?
YEAH. WE ARE BEING FOLLOWED...
...PROBABLY BY THE SNITCH.
OR BY SOMEONE ELSE.
7.

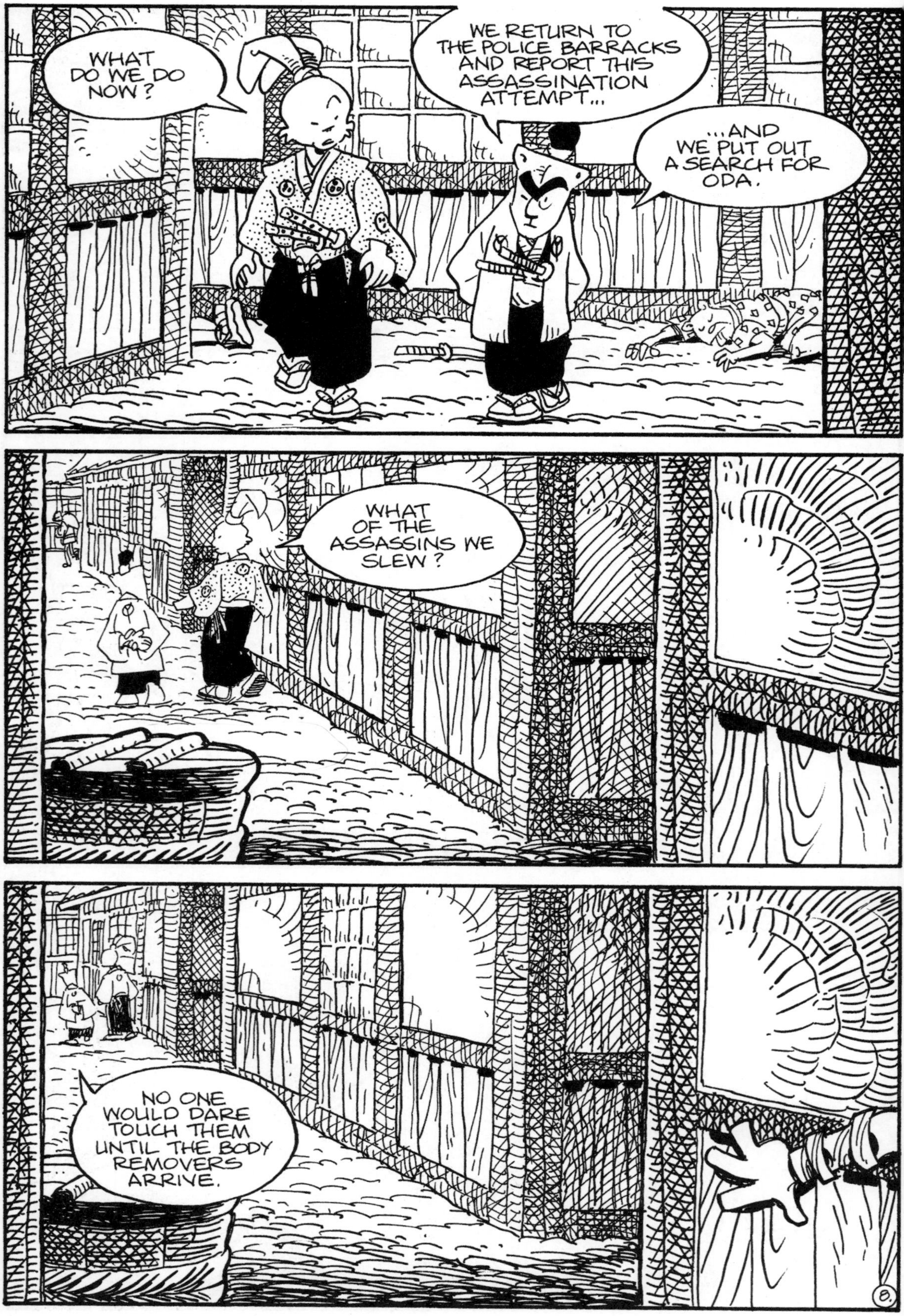
WHAT DO WE DO NOW?
WE RETURN TO THE POLICE BARRACKS AND REPORT THIS ASSASSINATION ATTEMPT...
...AND WE PUT OUT A SEARCH FOR ODA.
WHAT OF THE ASSASSINS WE SLEW?
NO ONE WOULD DARE TOUCH THEM UNTIL THE BODY REMOVERS ARRIVE.
8.

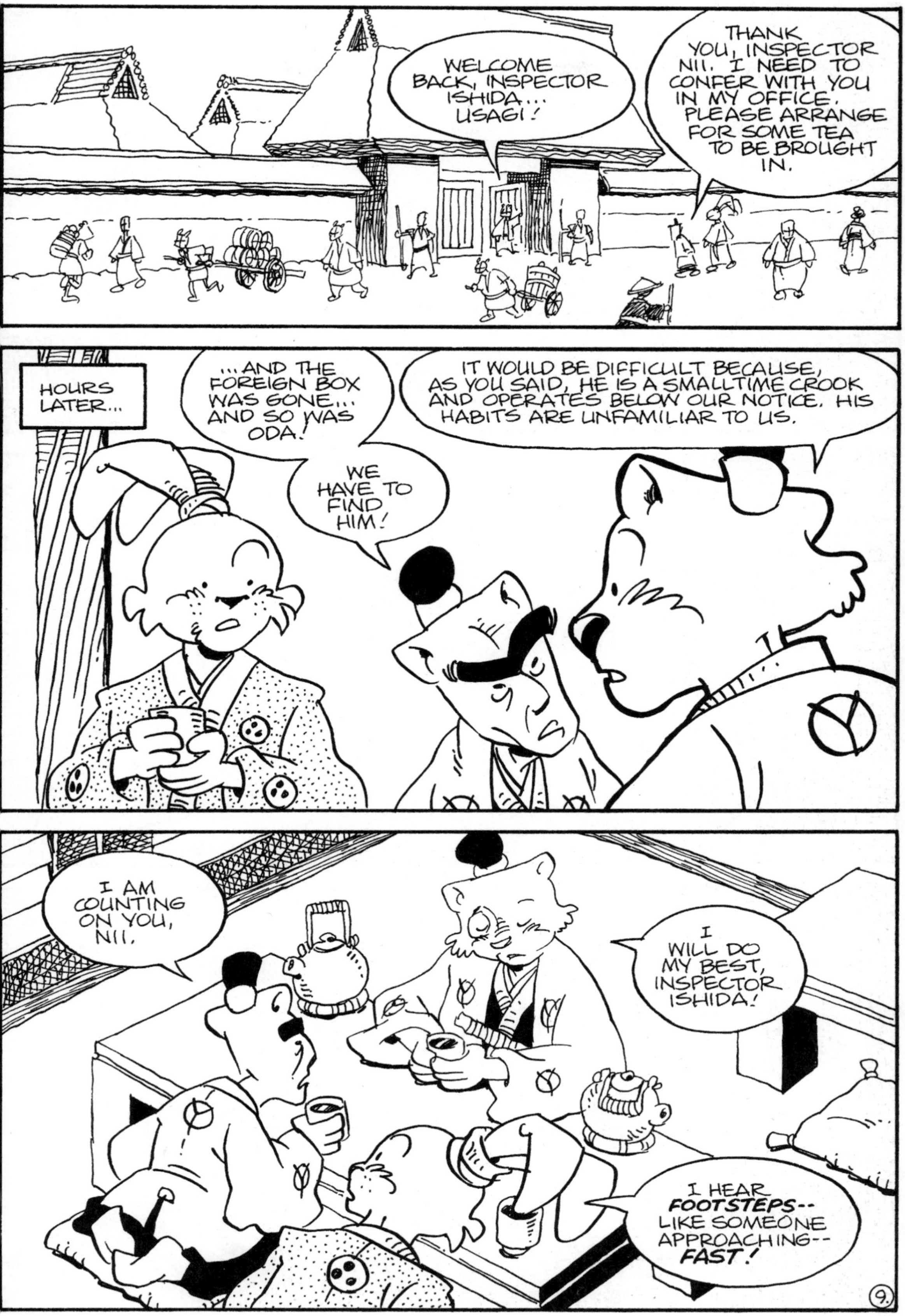
WELCOME BACK, INSPECTOR ISHIDA... USAGI!
THANK YOU, INSPECTOR NII. I NEED TO CONFER WITH YOU IN MY OFFICE. PLEASE ARRANGE FOR SOME TEA TO BE BROUGHT IN.
HOURS LATER...
...AND THE FOREIGN BOX WAS GONE... AND SO WAS ODA!
WE HAVE TO FIND HIM!
IT WOULD BE DIFFICULT BECAUSE, AS YOU SAID, HE IS A SMALLTIME CROOK AND OPERATES BELOW OUR NOTICE. HIS HABITS ARE UNFAMILIAR TO US.
I AM COUNTING ON YOU, NII.
I WILL DO MY BEST, INSPECTOR ISHIDA!
I HEAR **FOOTSTEPS**-- LIKE SOMEONE APPROACHING-- **FAST**!
9.

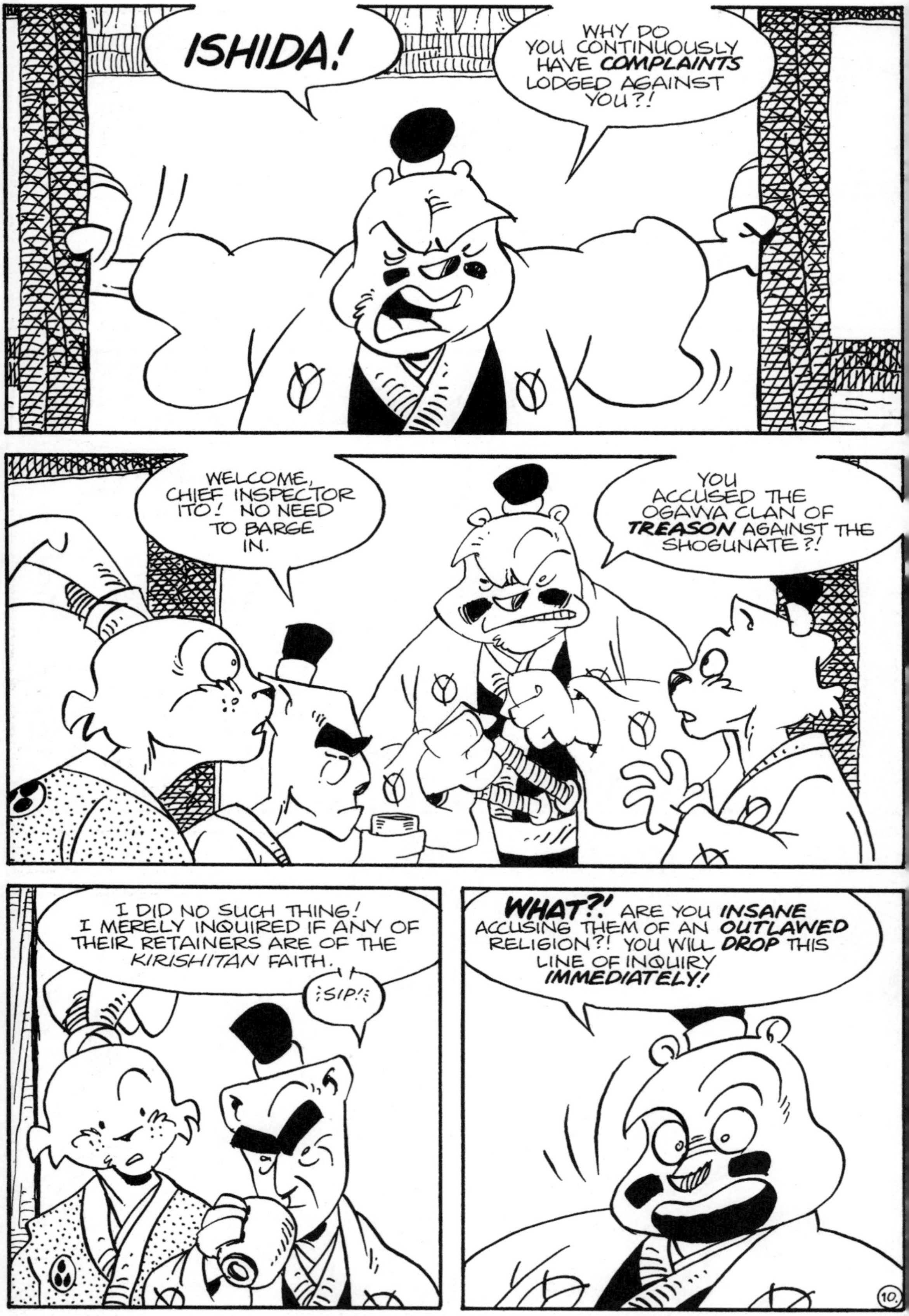
ISHIDA!
WHY DO YOU CONTINUOUSLY HAVE COMPLAINTS LODGED AGAINST YOU?!
WELCOME, CHIEF INSPECTOR ITO! NO NEED TO BARGE IN.
YOU ACCUSED THE OGAWA CLAN OF TREASON AGAINST THE SHOGUNATE?!
I DID NO SUCH THING! I MERELY INQUIRED IF ANY OF THEIR RETAINERS ARE OF THE KIRISHITAN FAITH.
SIP!
WHAT?! ARE YOU INSANE ACCUSING THEM OF AN OUTLAWED RELIGION?! YOU WILL DROP THIS LINE OF INQUIRY IMMEDIATELY!
10.

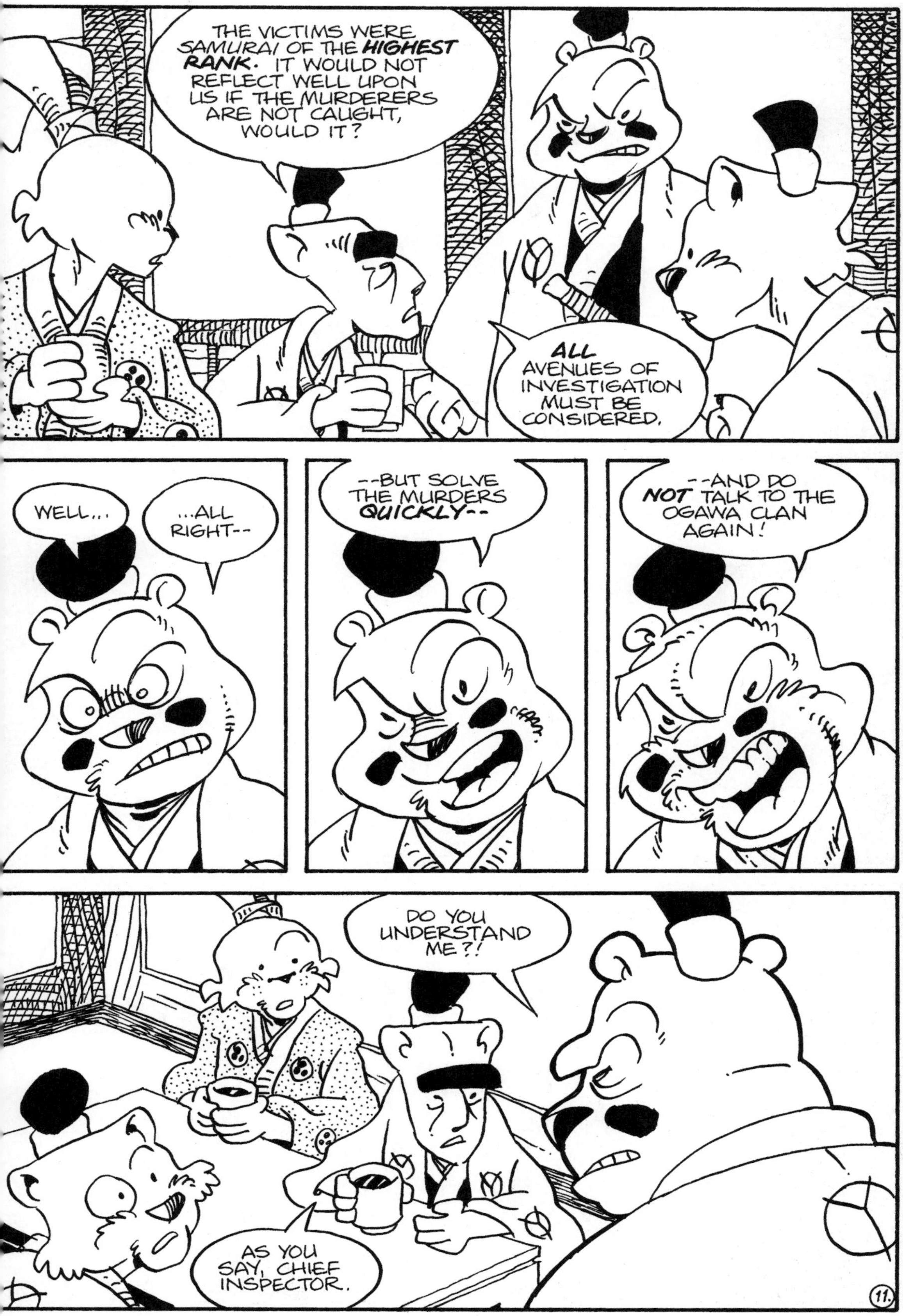
THE VICTIMS WERE SAMURAI OF THE **HIGHEST RANK**. IT WOULD NOT REFLECT WELL UPON US IF THE MURDERERS ARE NOT CAUGHT, WOULD IT?
ALL AVENUES OF INVESTIGATION MUST BE CONSIDERED.
WELL...
...ALL RIGHT--
--BUT SOLVE THE MURDERS **QUICKLY**--
--AND DO **NOT** TALK TO THE OGAWA CLAN AGAIN!
DO YOU UNDERSTAND ME?!
AS YOU SAY, CHIEF INSPECTOR.
11.

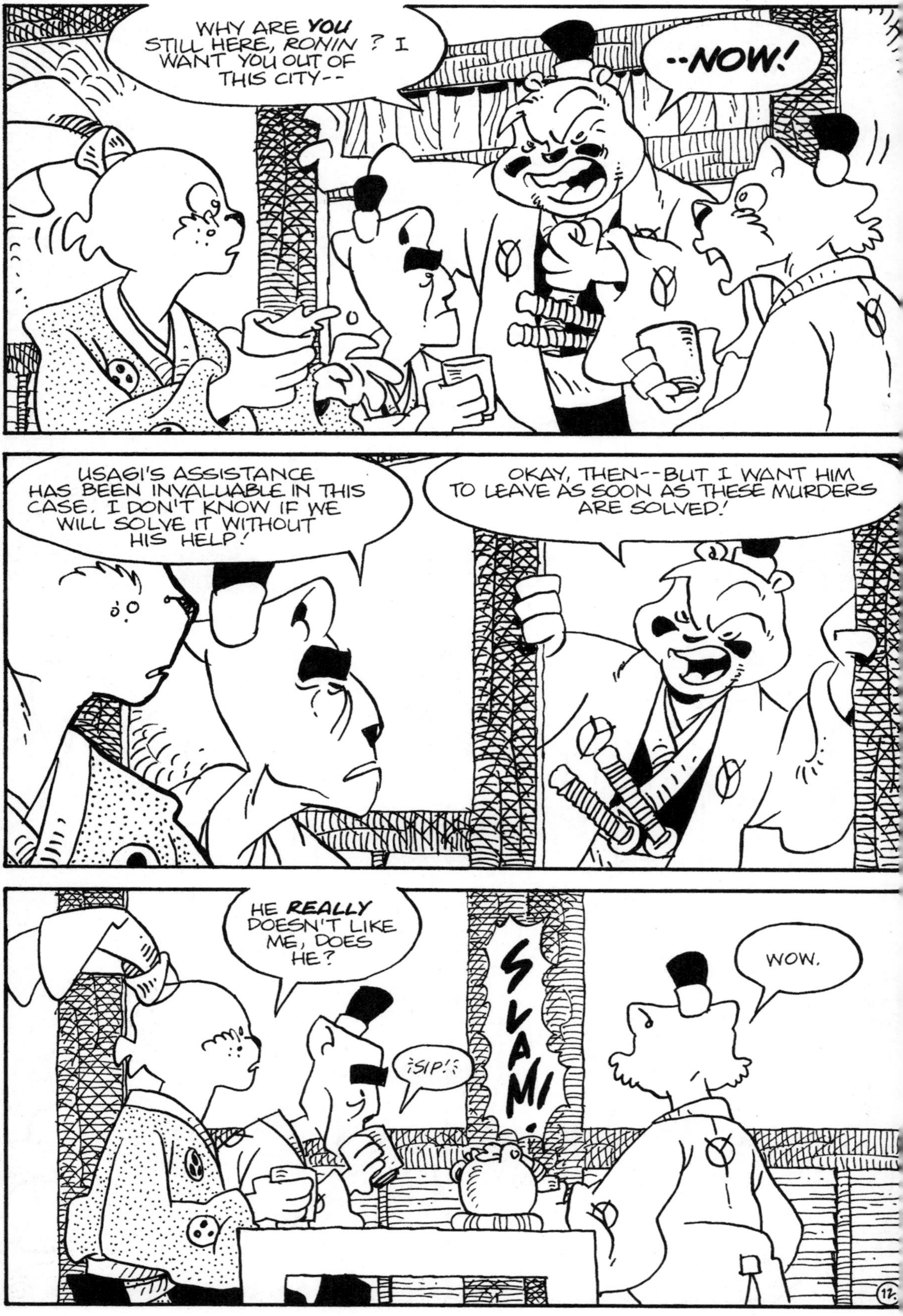
WHY ARE *YOU* STILL HERE, *RONIN* ? I WANT YOU OUT OF THIS CITY--
--NOW!
USAGI'S ASSISTANCE HAS BEEN INVALUABLE IN THIS CASE. I DON'T KNOW IF WE WILL SOLVE IT WITHOUT HIS HELP!
OKAY, THEN--BUT I WANT HIM TO LEAVE AS SOON AS THESE MURDERS ARE SOLVED!
HE *REALLY* DOESN'T LIKE ME, DOES HE?
SIP!
SLAM!
WOW.
12.

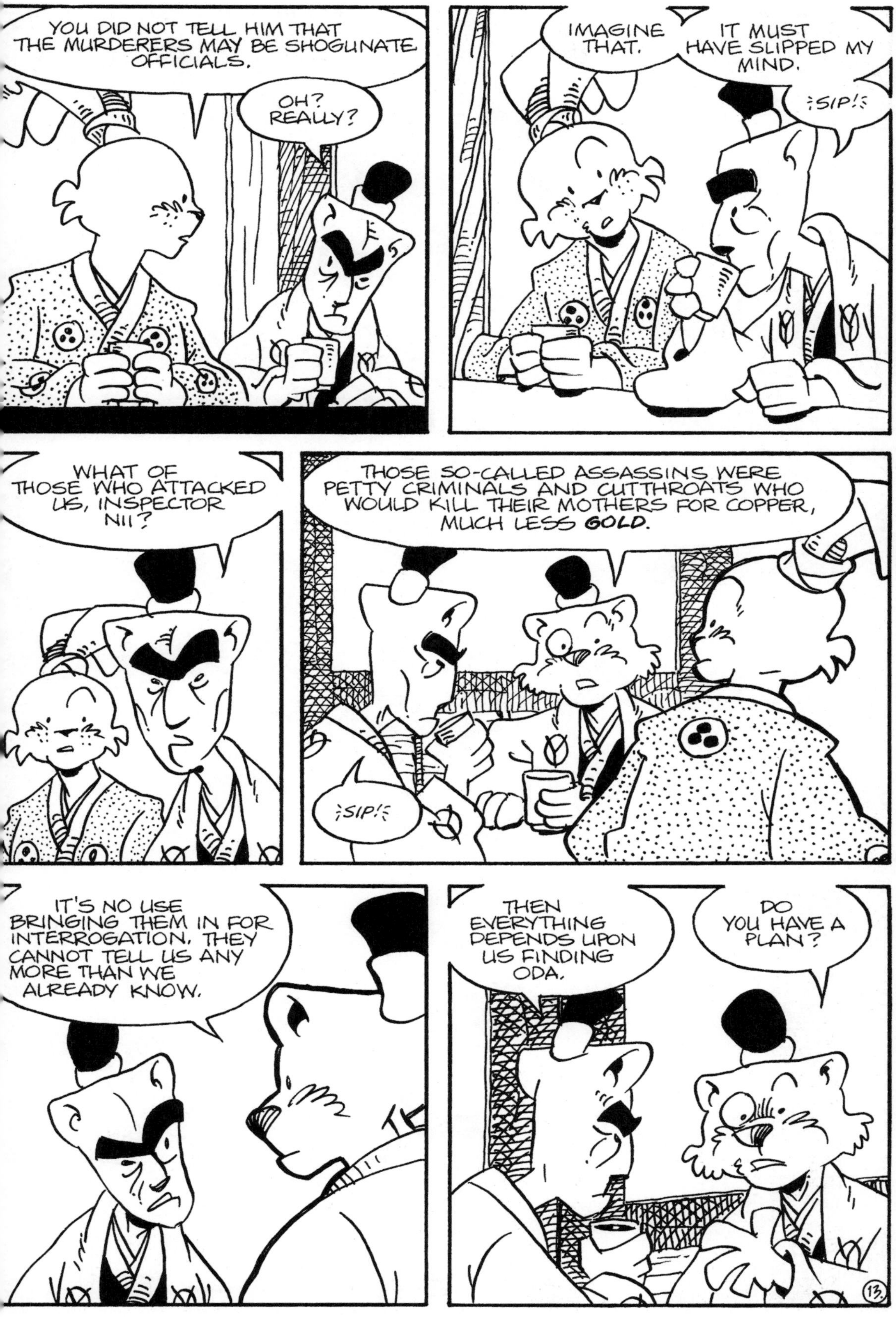
YOU DID NOT TELL HIM THAT THE MURDERERS MAY BE SHOGUNATE OFFICIALS.
OH? REALLY?
IMAGINE THAT.
IT MUST HAVE SLIPPED MY MIND.
¡SIP!
WHAT OF THOSE WHO ATTACKED US, INSPECTOR NII?
THOSE SO-CALLED ASSASSINS WERE PETTY CRIMINALS AND CUTTHROATS WHO WOULD KILL THEIR MOTHERS FOR COPPER, MUCH LESS GOLD.
¡SIP!
IT'S NO USE BRINGING THEM IN FOR INTERROGATION. THEY CANNOT TELL US ANY MORE THAN WE ALREADY KNOW.
THEN EVERYTHING DEPENDS UPON US FINDING ODA.
DO YOU HAVE A PLAN?
13.

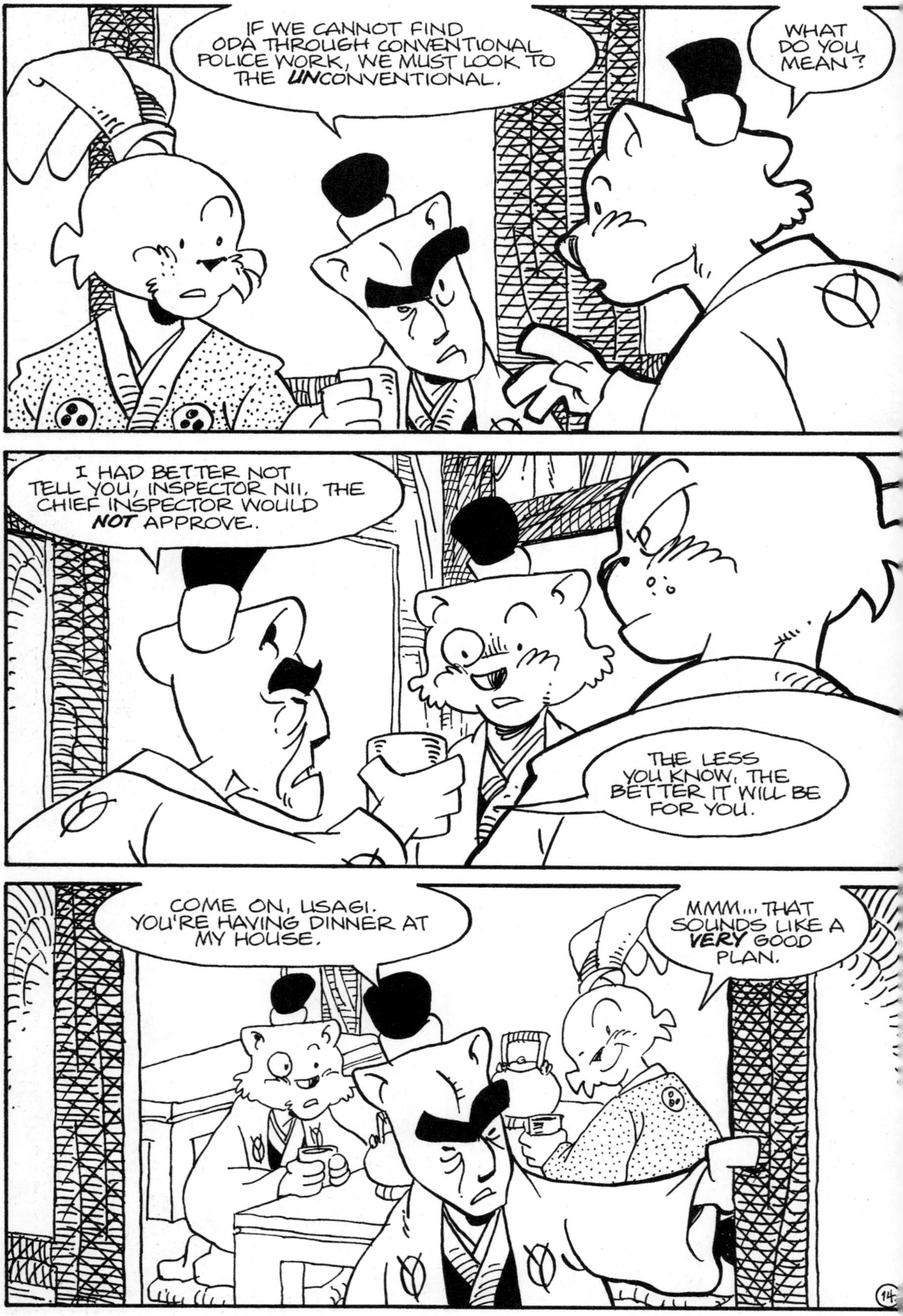
IF WE CANNOT FIND ODA THROUGH CONVENTIONAL POLICE WORK, WE MUST LOOK TO THE UNCONVENTIONAL.
WHAT DO YOU MEAN?
I HAD BETTER NOT TELL YOU, INSPECTOR NII. THE CHIEF INSPECTOR WOULD NOT APPROVE.
THE LESS YOU KNOW, THE BETTER IT WILL BE FOR YOU.
COME ON, USAGI. YOU'RE HAVING DINNER AT MY HOUSE.
MMM... THAT SOUNDS LIKE A VERY GOOD PLAN.
14

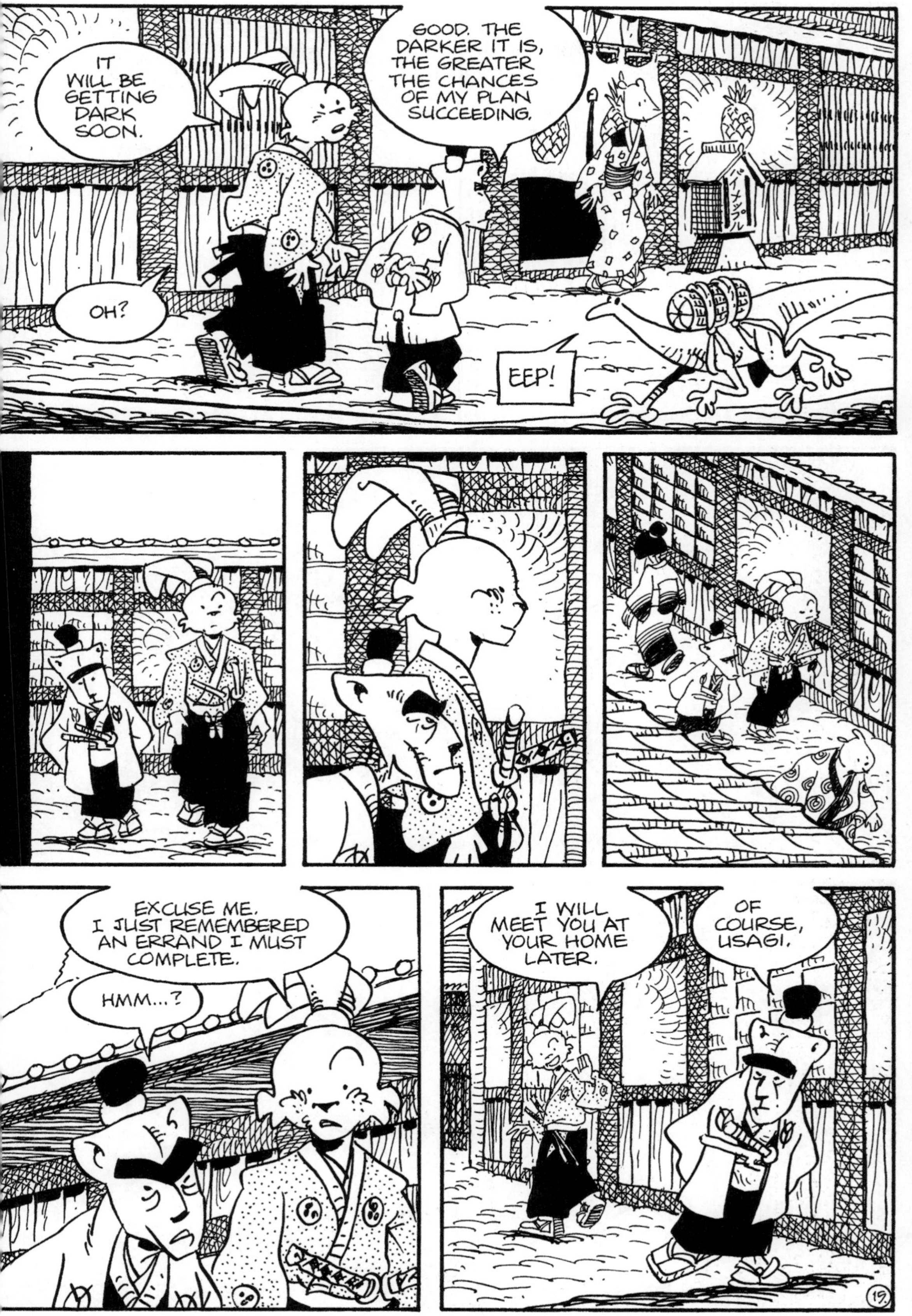
IT WILL BE GETTING DARK SOON.
GOOD. THE DARKER IT IS, THE GREATER THE CHANCES OF MY PLAN SUCCEEDING.
OH?
EEP!
EXCUSE ME. I JUST REMEMBERED AN ERRAND I MUST COMPLETE.
HMM...?
I WILL MEET YOU AT YOUR HOME LATER.
OF COURSE, USAGI.
15.

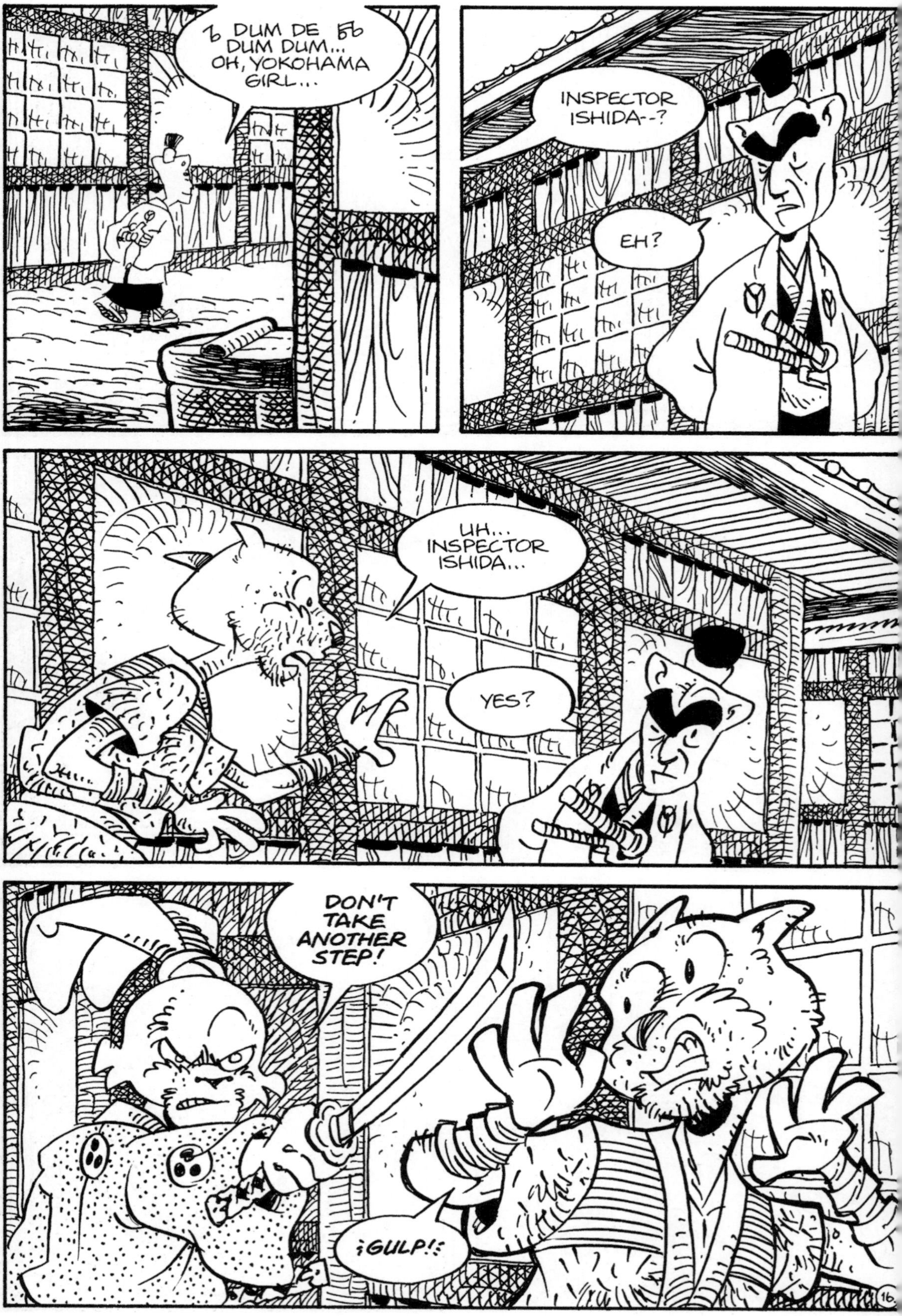

DUM DE DUM DUM... OH, YOKOHAMA GIRL...
INSPECTOR ISHIDA--?
EH?
UH... INSPECTOR ISHIDA...
YES?
DON'T TAKE ANOTHER STEP!
¡GULP!¡
16

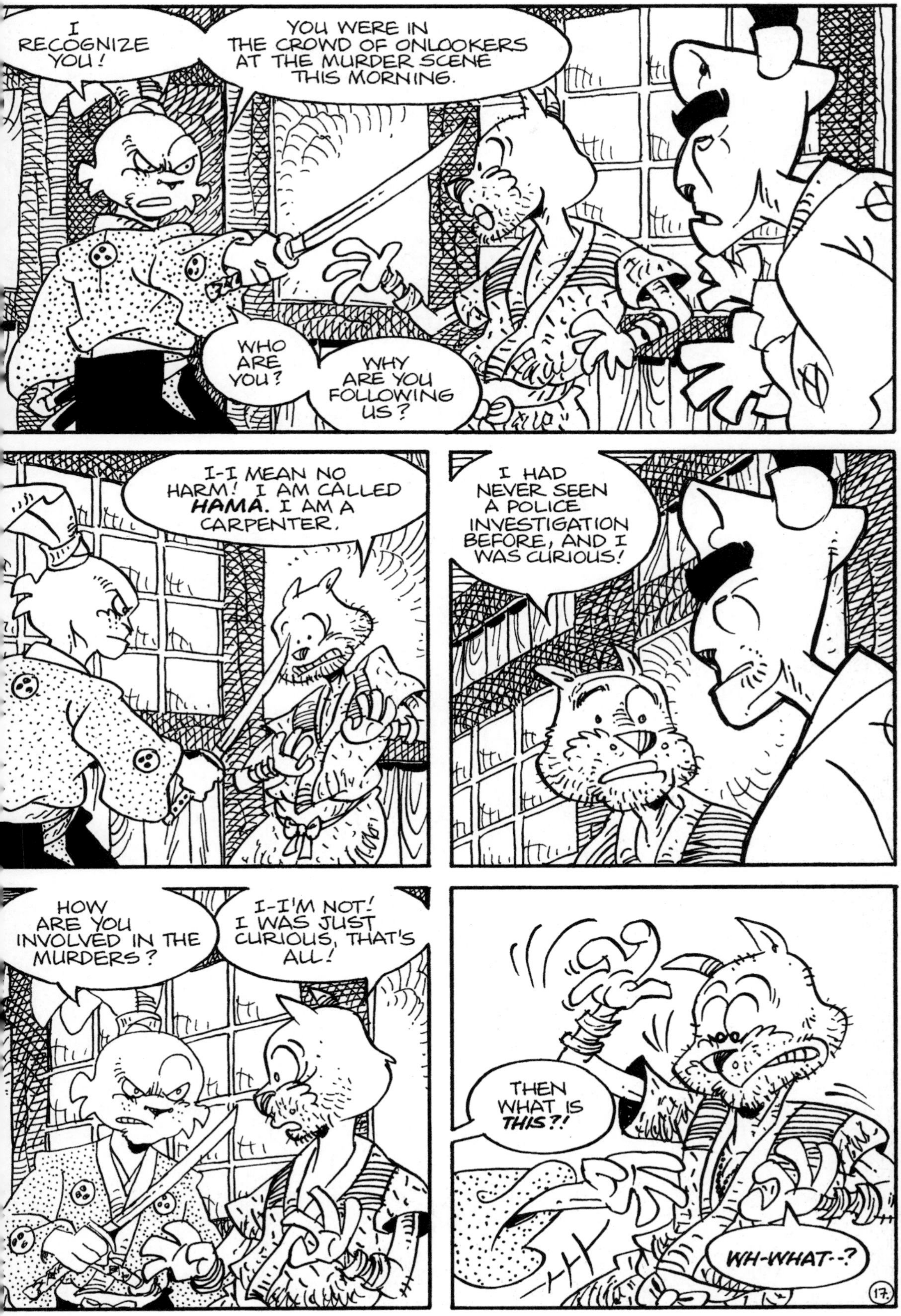
I RECOGNIZE YOU!
YOU WERE IN THE CROWD OF ONLOOKERS AT THE MURDER SCENE THIS MORNING.
WHO ARE YOU?
WHY ARE YOU FOLLOWING US?
I-I MEAN NO HARM! I AM CALLED **HAMA.** I AM A CARPENTER.
I HAD NEVER SEEN A POLICE INVESTIGATION BEFORE, AND I WAS CURIOUS!
HOW ARE YOU INVOLVED IN THE MURDERS?
I-I'M NOT! I WAS JUST CURIOUS, THAT'S ALL!
THEN WHAT IS ***THIS?!***
WH-WHAT--?
17.

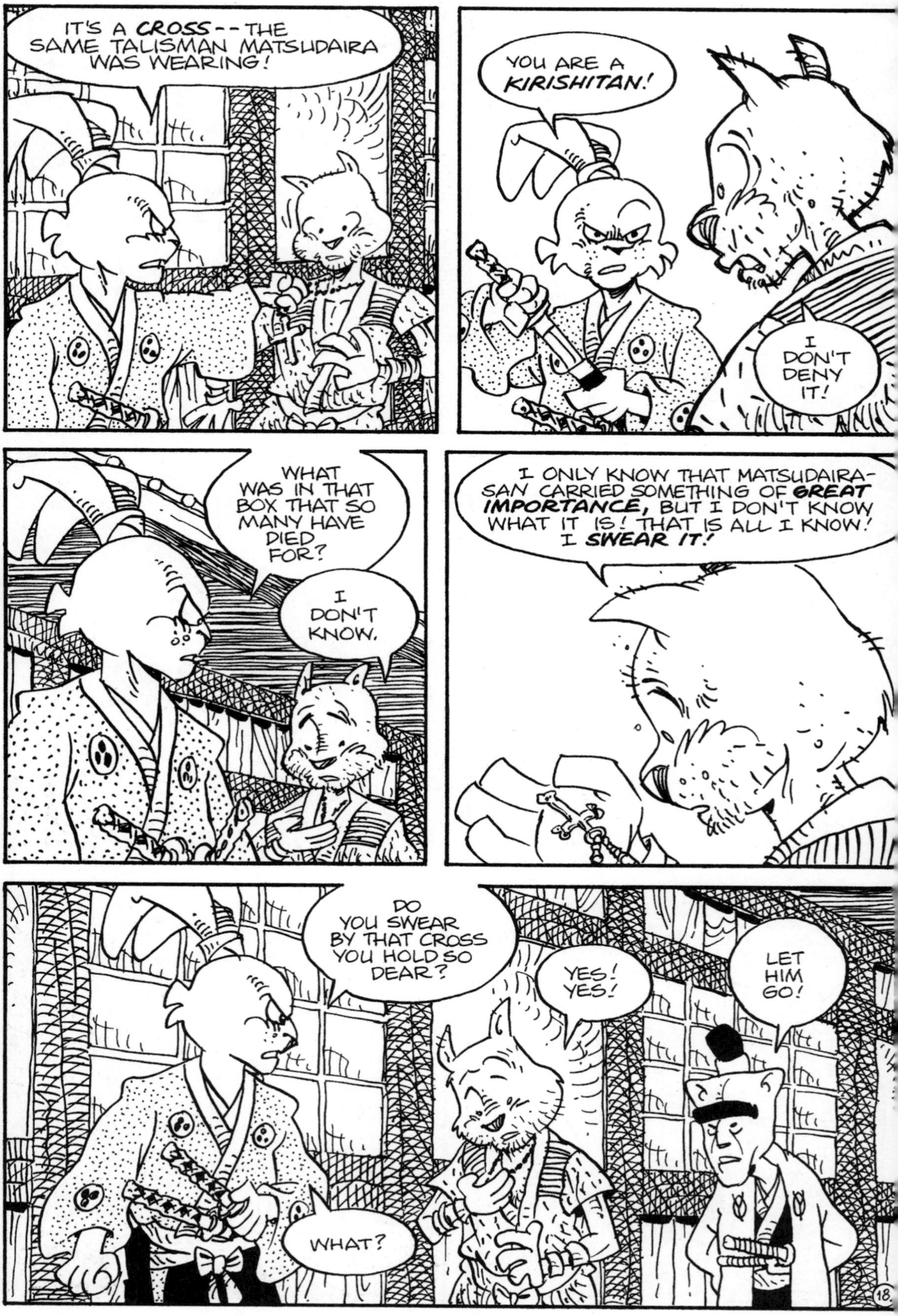
IT'S A CROSS--THE SAME TALISMAN MATSUDAIRA WAS WEARING!
YOU ARE A KIRISHITAN!
I DON'T DENY IT!
WHAT WAS IN THAT BOX THAT SO MANY HAVE DIED FOR?
I DON'T KNOW.
I ONLY KNOW THAT MATSUDAIRA-SAN CARRIED SOMETHING OF GREAT IMPORTANCE, BUT I DON'T KNOW WHAT IT IS! THAT IS ALL I KNOW! I SWEAR IT!
DO YOU SWEAR BY THAT CROSS YOU HOLD SO DEAR?
YES! YES!
LET HIM GO!
WHAT?
18

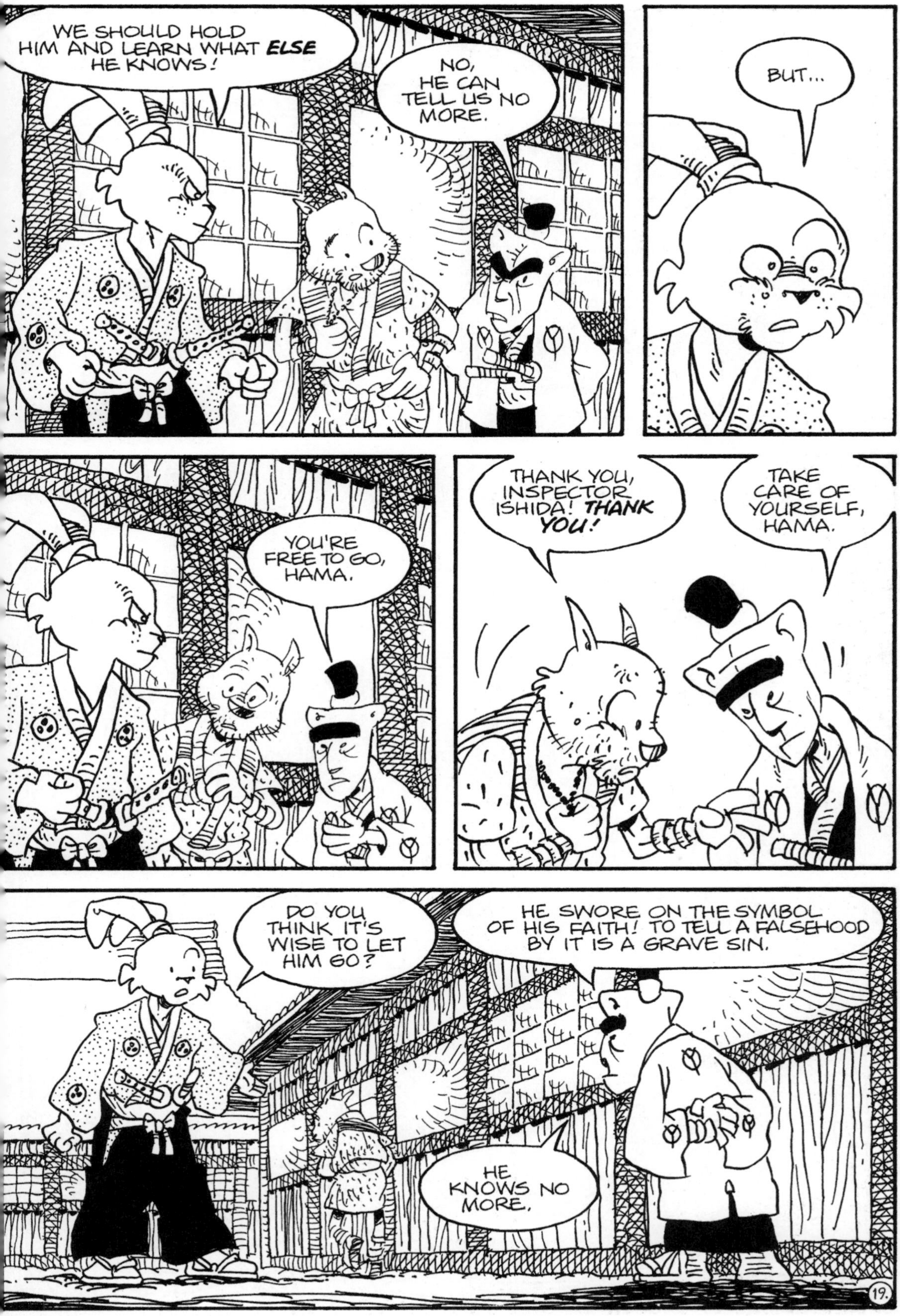
WE SHOULD HOLD HIM AND LEARN WHAT ELSE HE KNOWS!
NO, HE CAN TELL US NO MORE.
BUT...
YOU'RE FREE TO GO, HAMA.
THANK YOU, INSPECTOR ISHIDA! THANK YOU!
TAKE CARE OF YOURSELF, HAMA.
DO YOU THINK IT'S WISE TO LET HIM GO?
HE SWORE ON THE SYMBOL OF HIS FAITH! TO TELL A FALSEHOOD BY IT IS A GRAVE SIN.
HE KNOWS NO MORE.
19.

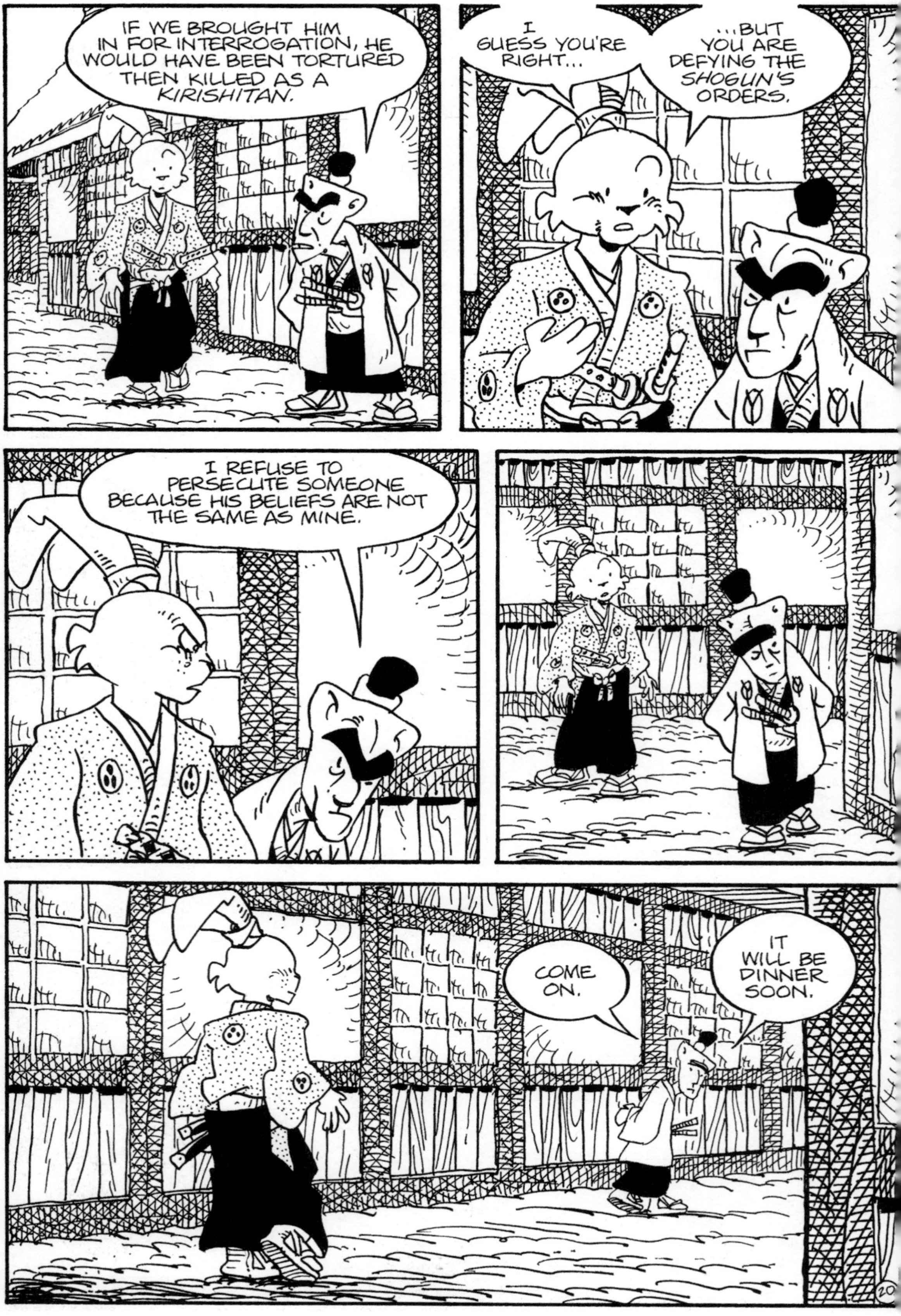
IF WE BROUGHT HIM IN FOR INTERROGATION, HE WOULD HAVE BEEN TORTURED THEN KILLED AS A *KIRISHITAN.*
I GUESS YOU'RE RIGHT...
...BUT YOU ARE DEFYING THE *SHOGUN'S* ORDERS.
I REFUSE TO PERSECUTE SOMEONE BECAUSE HIS BELIEFS ARE NOT THE SAME AS MINE.
COME ON.
IT WILL BE DINNER SOON.
20

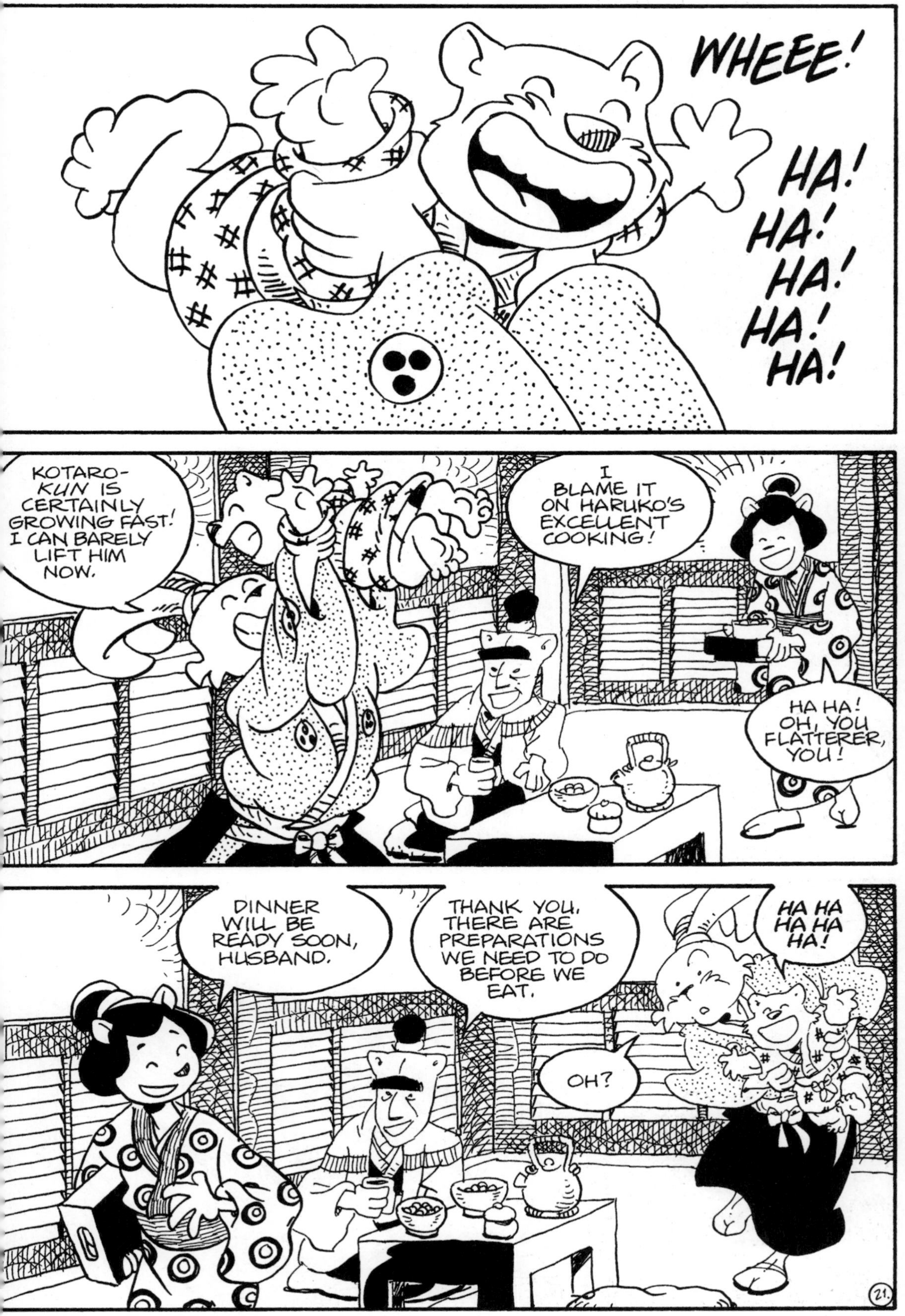
WHEEEE!
HA! HA! HA! HA! HA!
KOTARO-KUN IS CERTAINLY GROWING FAST! I CAN BARELY LIFT HIM NOW.
I BLAME IT ON HARUKO'S EXCELLENT COOKING!
HA HA! OH, YOU FLATTERER, YOU!
DINNER WILL BE READY SOON, HUSBAND.
THANK YOU. THERE ARE PREPARATIONS WE NEED TO DO BEFORE WE EAT.
HA HA HA HA HA!
OH?
21.

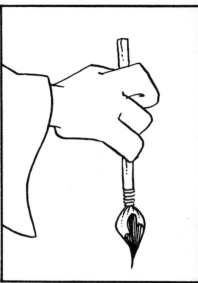
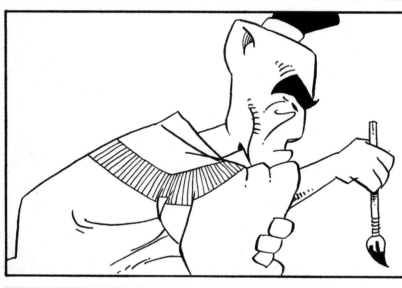

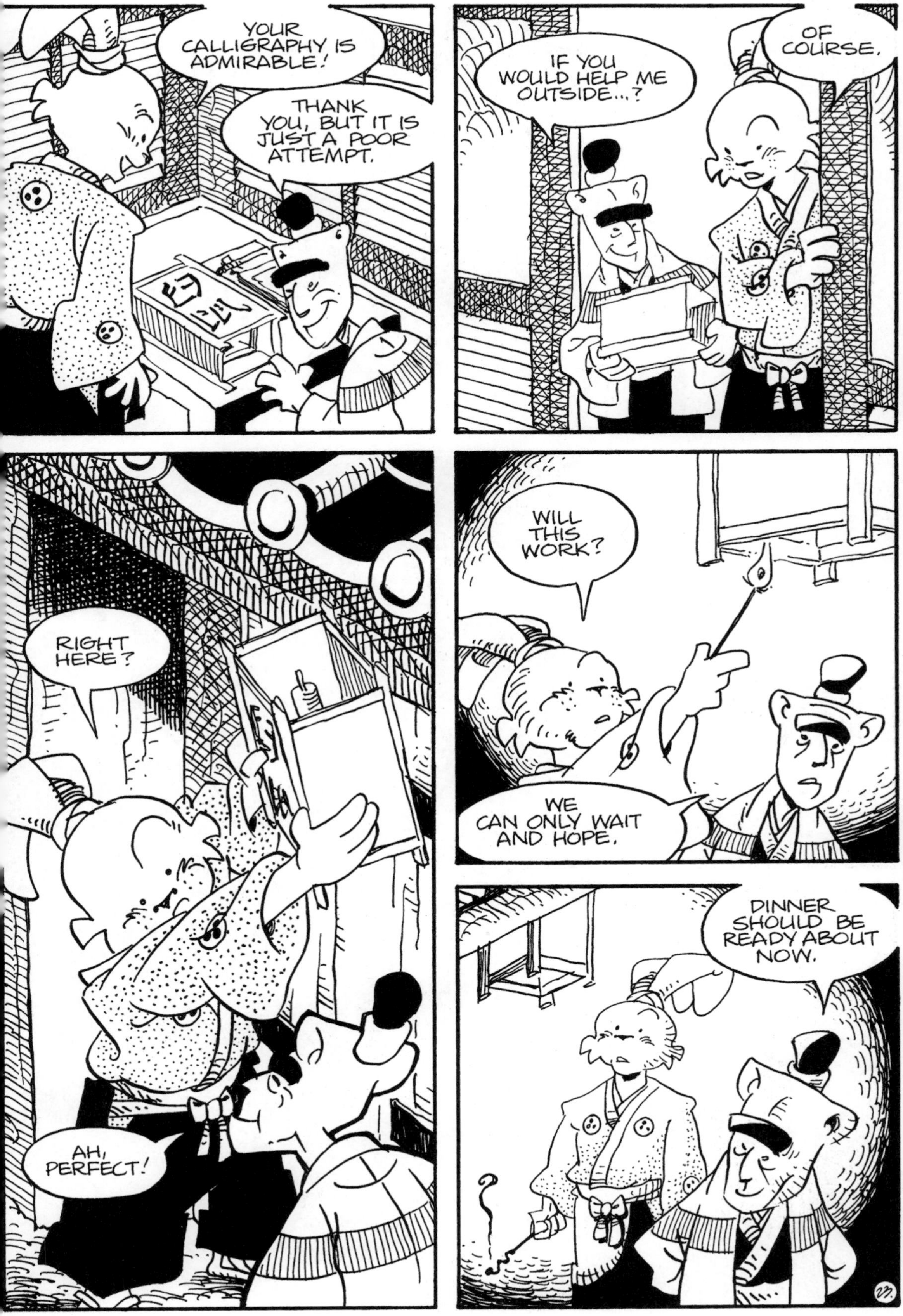
YOUR CALLIGRAPHY IS ADMIRABLE!
THANK YOU, BUT IT IS JUST A POOR ATTEMPT.
IF YOU WOULD HELP ME OUTSIDE...?
OF COURSE.
RIGHT HERE?
AH, PERFECT!
WILL THIS WORK?
WE CAN ONLY WAIT AND HOPE.
DINNER SHOULD BE READY ABOUT NOW.
23.

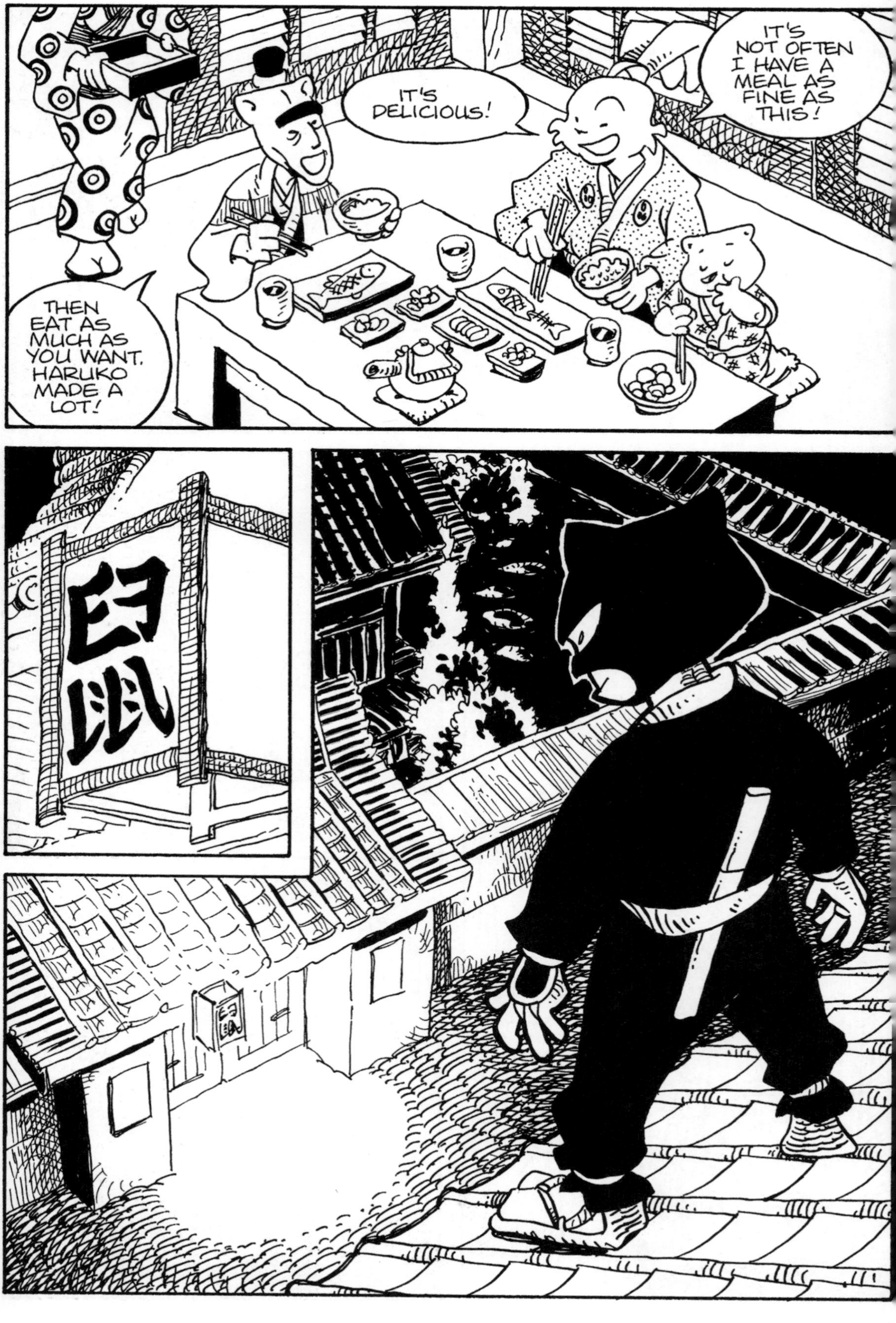
IT'S DELICIOUS!
IT'S NOT OFTEN I HAVE A MEAL AS FINE AS THIS!
THEN EAT AS MUCH AS YOU WANT. HARUKO MADE A LOT!

THE HIDDEN PART FIVE

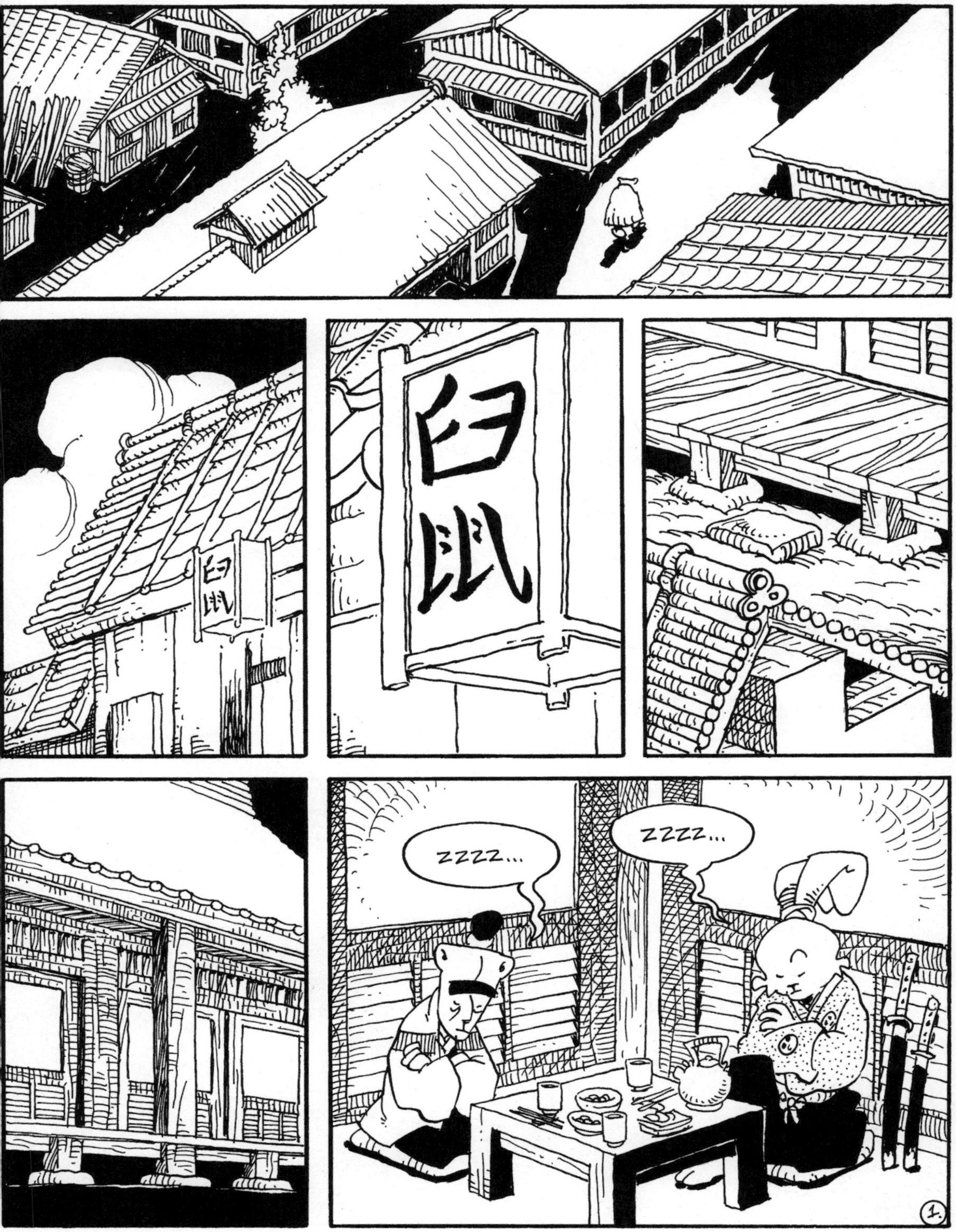
ZZZZ...
ZZZZ...
1.

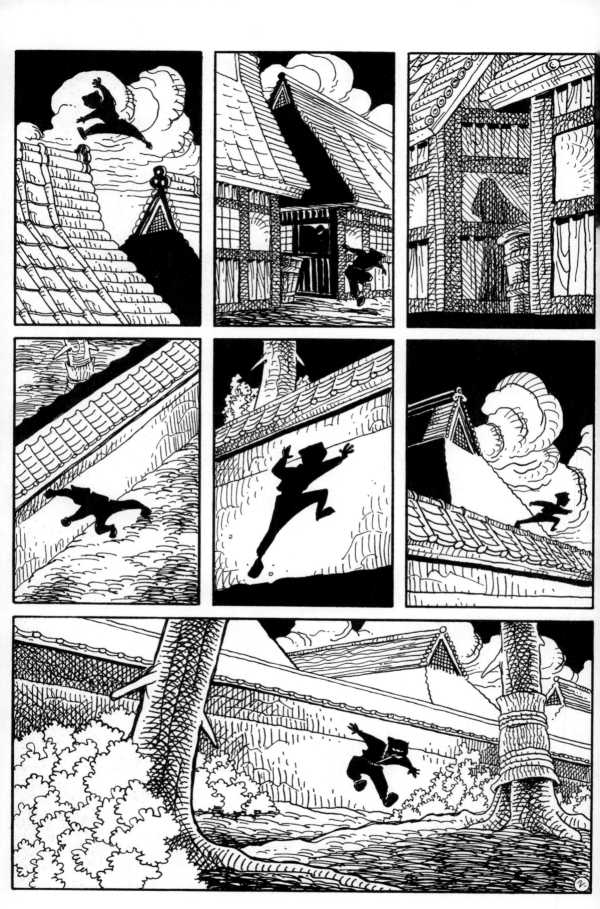

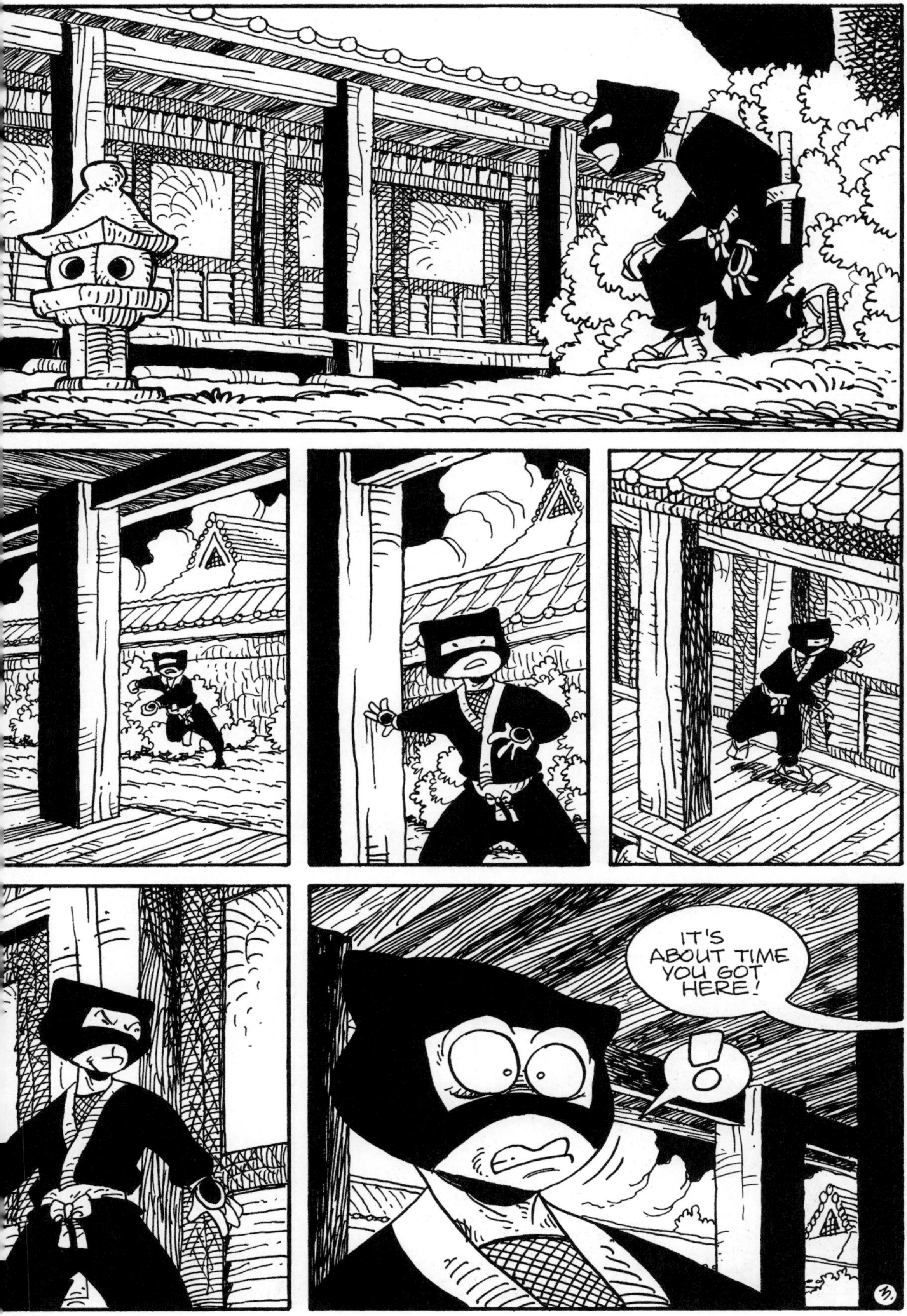
IT'S ABOUT TIME YOU GOT HERE!
!

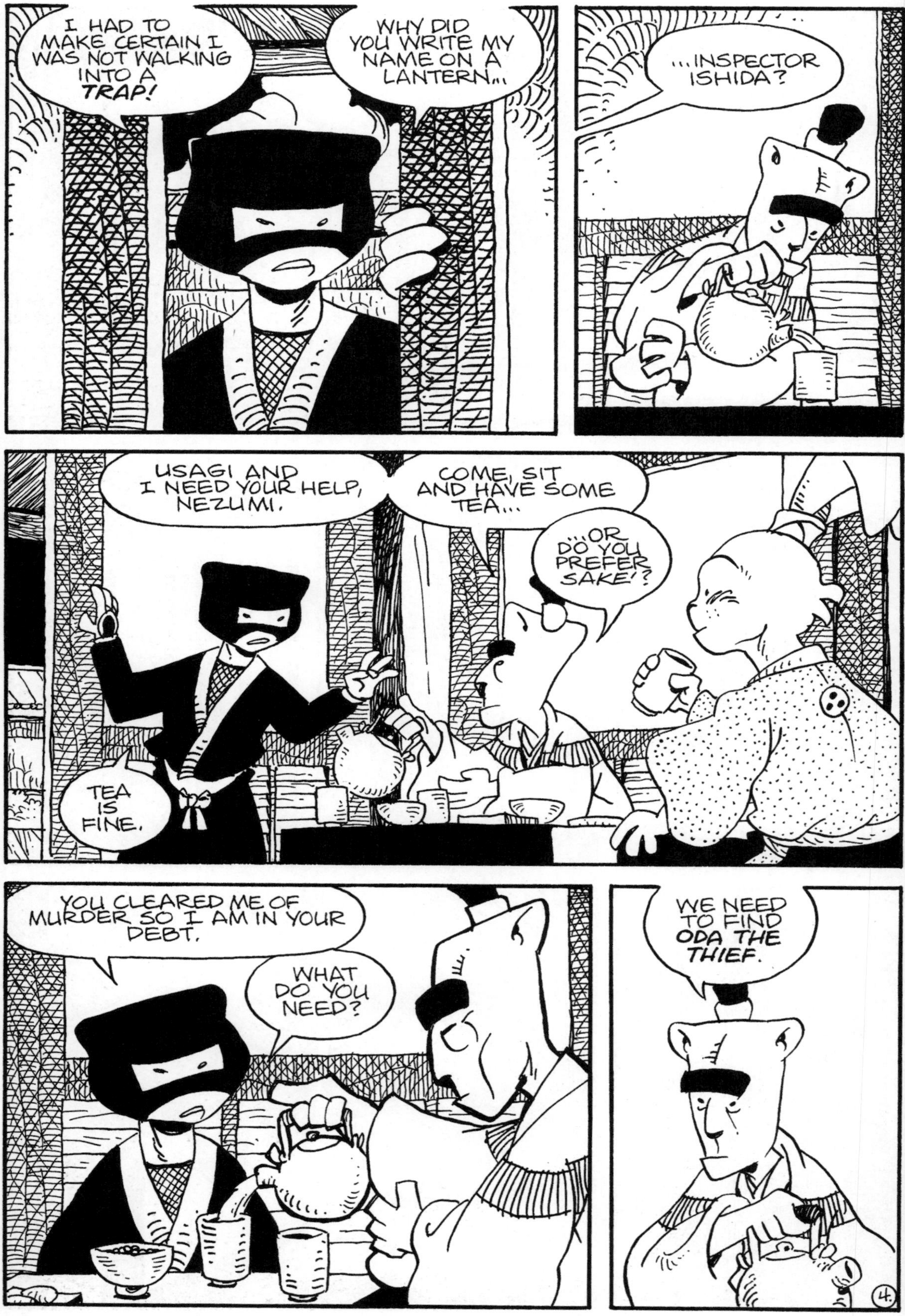
I HAD TO MAKE CERTAIN I WAS NOT WALKING INTO A TRAP!
WHY DID YOU WRITE MY NAME ON A LANTERN...
...INSPECTOR ISHIDA?
USAGI AND I NEED YOUR HELP, NEZUMI.
COME, SIT AND HAVE SOME TEA...
...OR DO YOU PREFER SAKE!?
TEA IS FINE.
YOU CLEARED ME OF MURDER SO I AM IN YOUR DEBT.
WHAT DO YOU NEED?
WE NEED TO FIND ODA THE THIEF.
4.

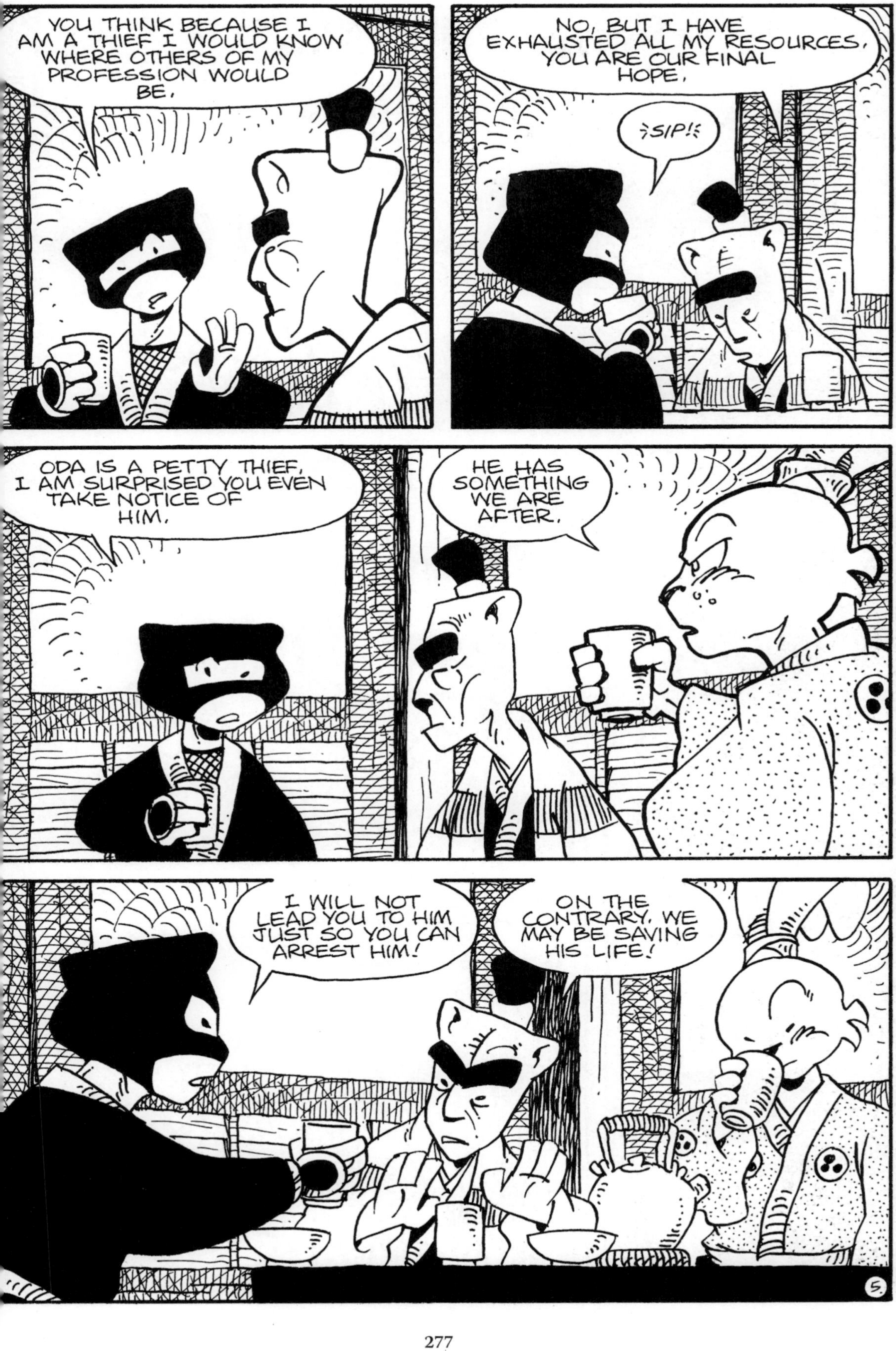
YOU THINK BECAUSE I AM A THIEF I WOULD KNOW WHERE OTHERS OF MY PROFESSION WOULD BE.
NO, BUT I HAVE EXHAUSTED ALL MY RESOURCES. YOU ARE OUR FINAL HOPE.
SIP!
ODA IS A PETTY THIEF, I AM SURPRISED YOU EVEN TAKE NOTICE OF HIM.
HE HAS SOMETHING WE ARE AFTER.
I WILL NOT LEAD YOU TO HIM JUST SO YOU CAN ARREST HIM!
ON THE CONTRARY. WE MAY BE SAVING HIS LIFE!
5.

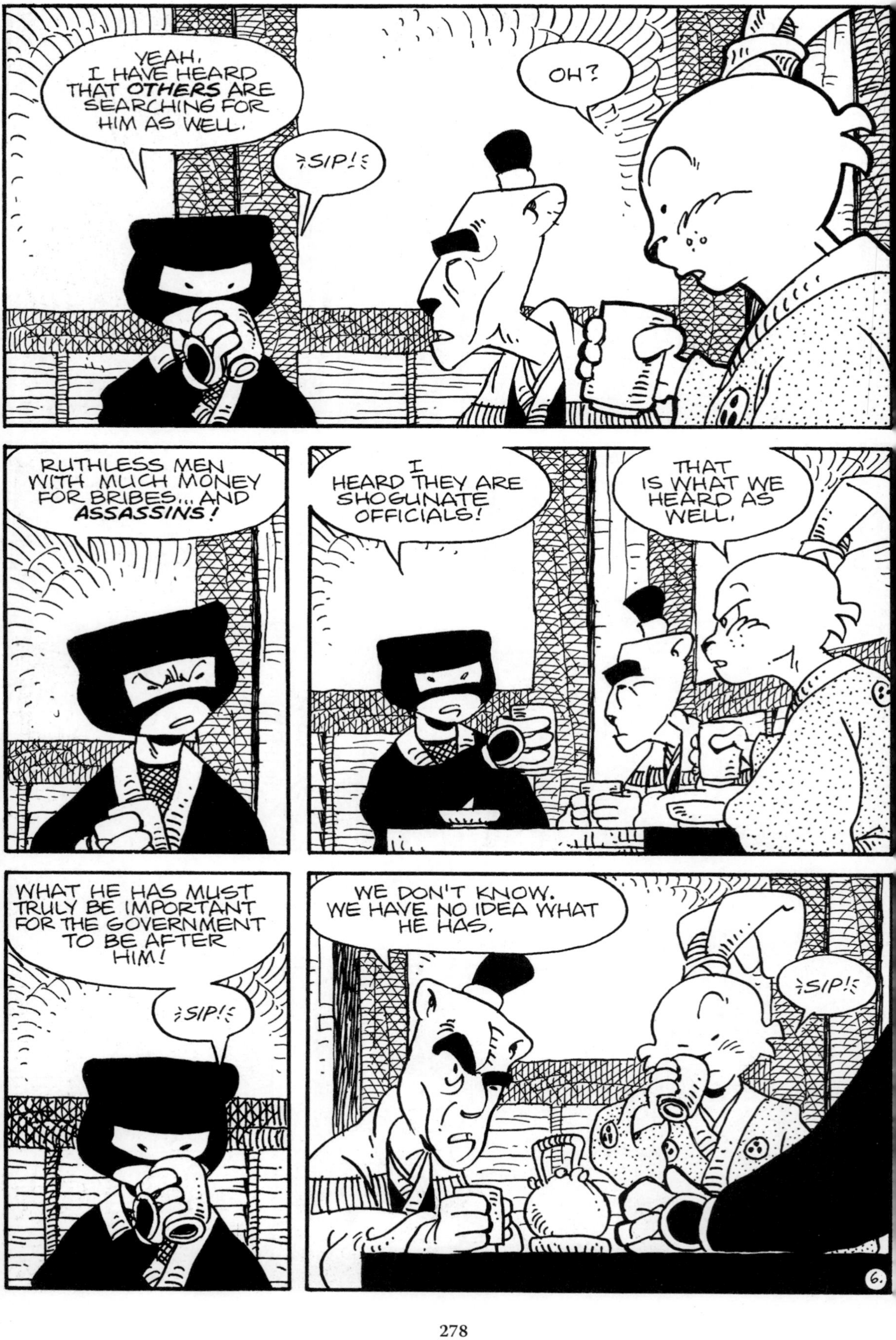

YEAH, I HAVE HEARD THAT OTHERS ARE SEARCHING FOR HIM AS WELL.
SIP!
OH?
RUTHLESS MEN WITH MUCH MONEY FOR BRIBES... AND ASSASSINS!
I HEARD THEY ARE SHOGUNATE OFFICIALS!
THAT IS WHAT WE HEARD AS WELL.
WHAT HE HAS MUST TRULY BE IMPORTANT FOR THE GOVERNMENT TO BE AFTER HIM!
SIP!
WE DON'T KNOW. WE HAVE NO IDEA WHAT HE HAS.
SIP!
6.

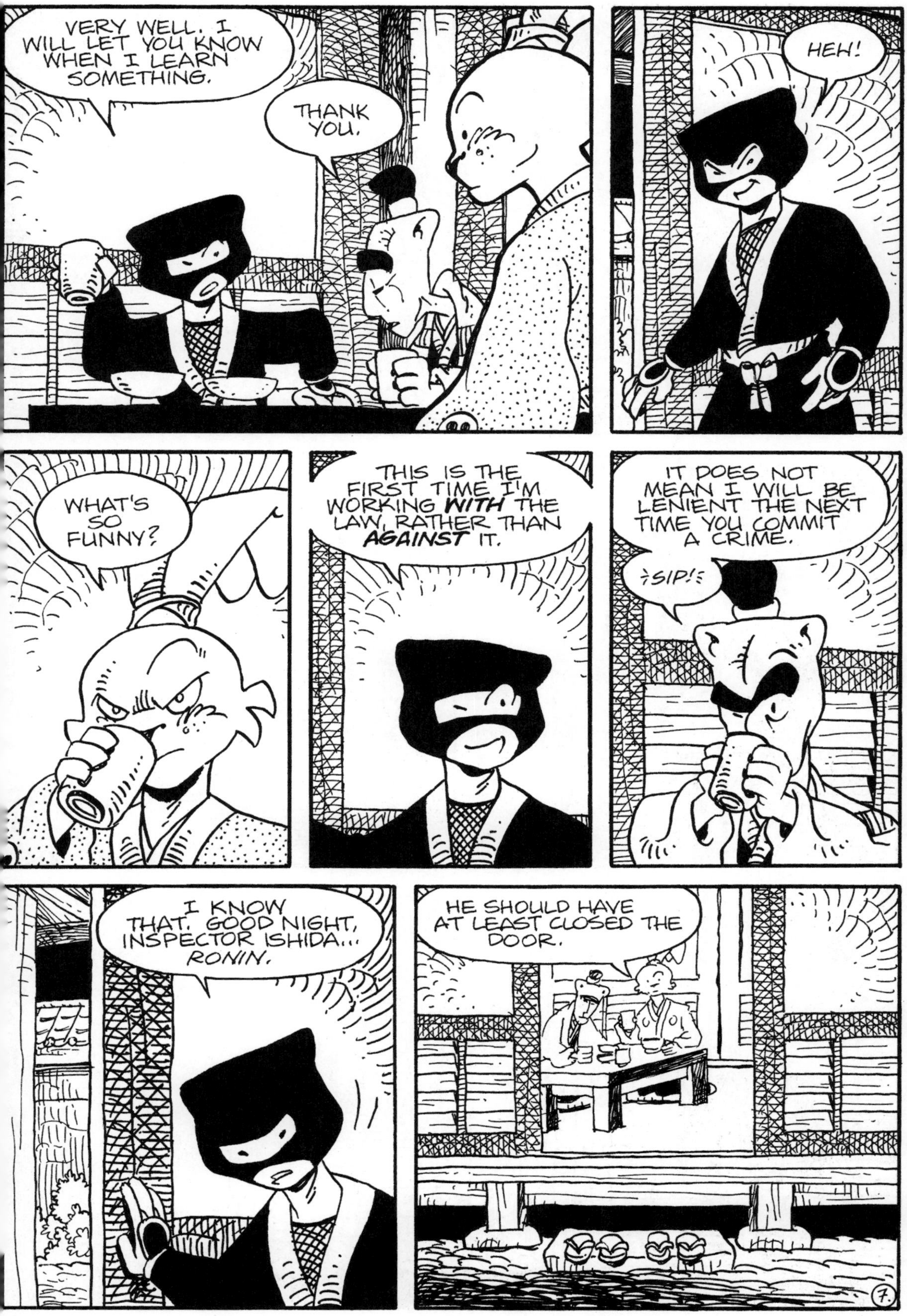
VERY WELL. I WILL LET YOU KNOW WHEN I LEARN SOMETHING.
THANK YOU.
HEH!
WHAT'S SO FUNNY?
THIS IS THE FIRST TIME I'M WORKING **WITH** THE LAW, RATHER THAN **AGAINST** IT.
IT DOES NOT MEAN I WILL BE LENIENT THE NEXT TIME YOU COMMIT A CRIME.
SIP!
I KNOW THAT. GOOD NIGHT, INSPECTOR ISHIDA... *RONIN.*
HE SHOULD HAVE AT LEAST CLOSED THE DOOR.
7.

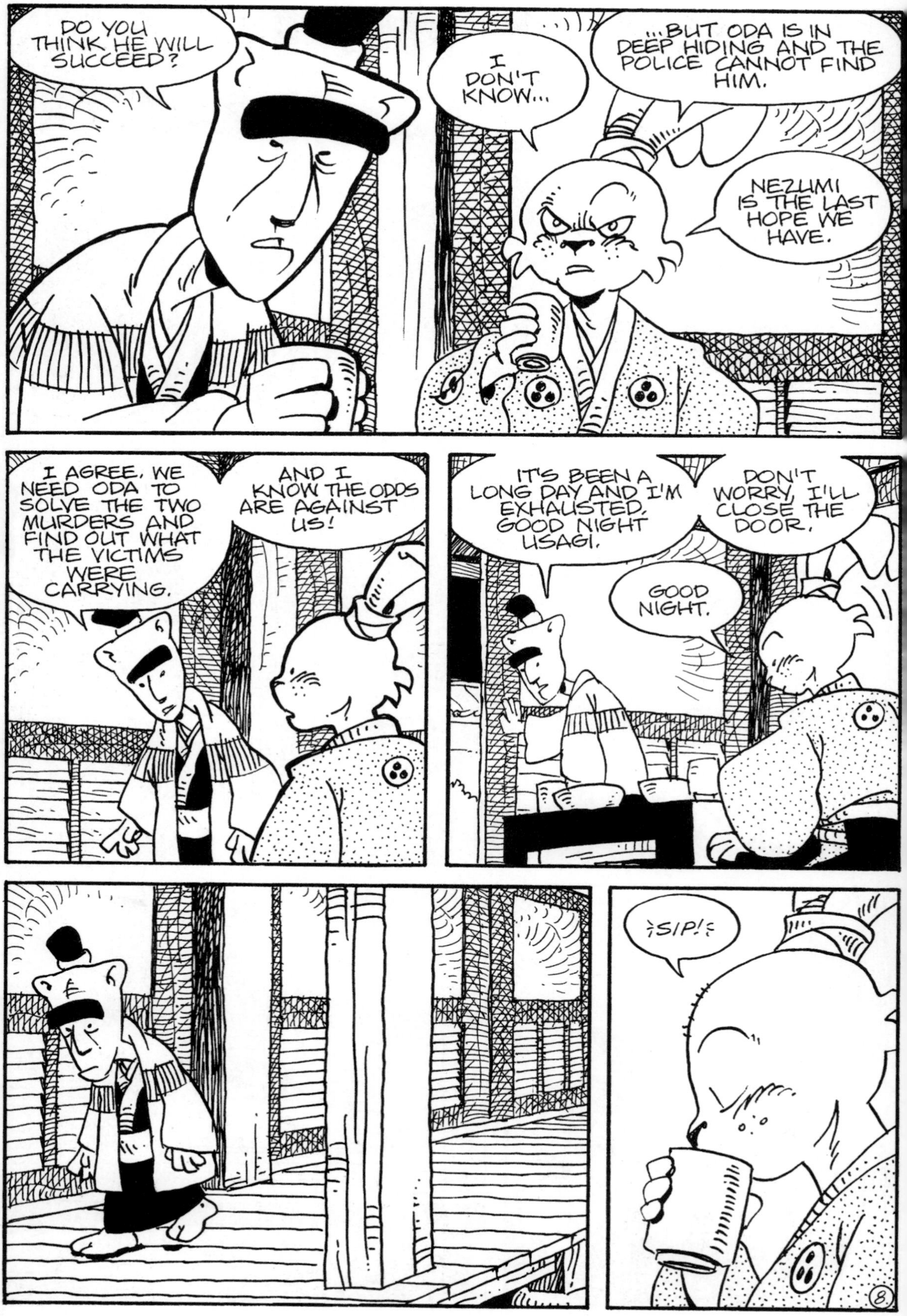
DO YOU THINK HE WILL SUCCEED?
I DON'T KNOW...
...BUT ODA IS IN DEEP HIDING AND THE POLICE CANNOT FIND HIM.
NEZUMI IS THE LAST HOPE WE HAVE.
I AGREE. WE NEED ODA TO SOLVE THE TWO MURDERS AND FIND OUT WHAT THE VICTIMS WERE CARRYING.
AND I KNOW THE ODDS ARE AGAINST US!
IT'S BEEN A LONG DAY AND I'M EXHAUSTED. GOOD NIGHT USAGI.
DON'T WORRY, I'LL CLOSE THE DOOR.
GOOD NIGHT.
SIP!
8

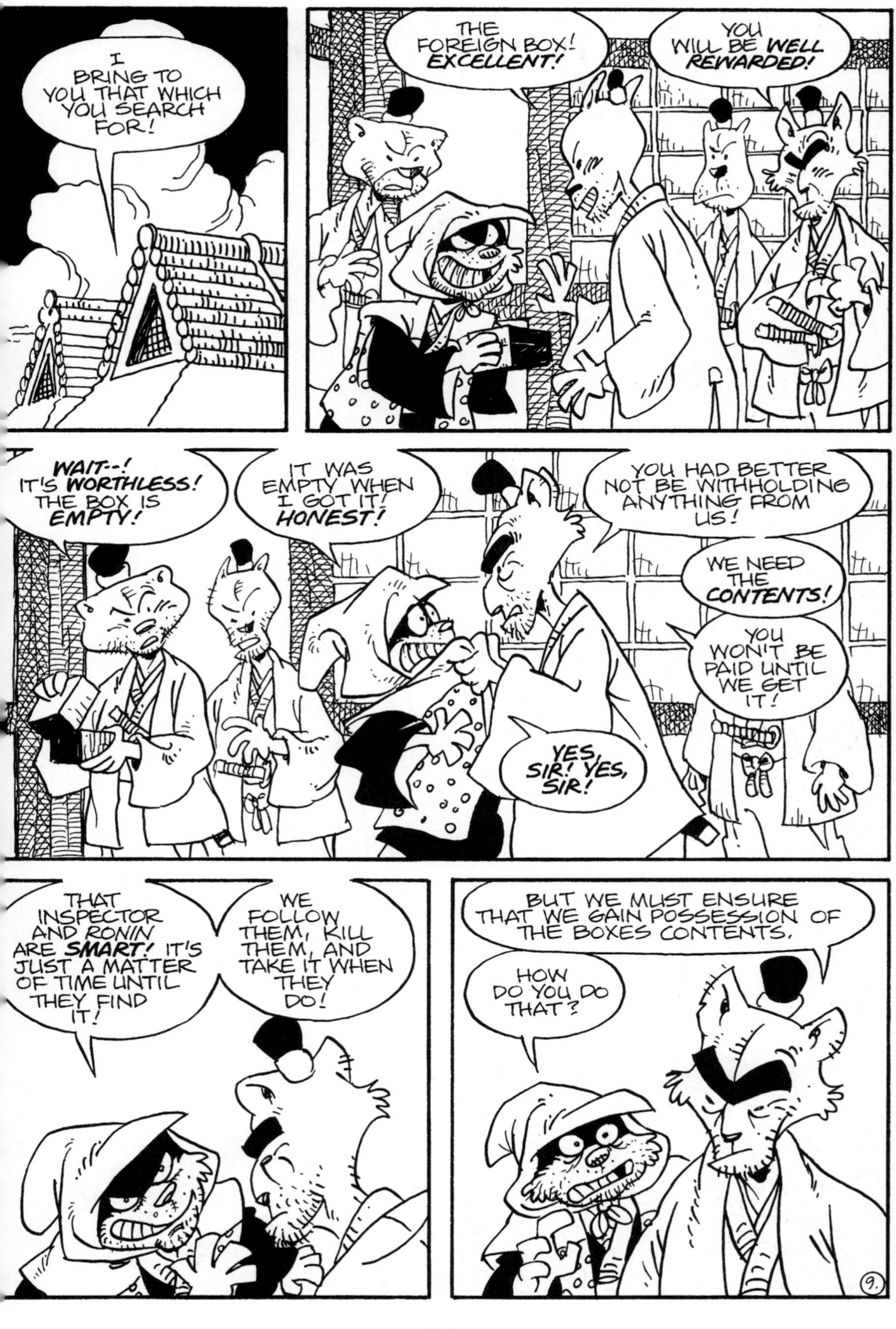
I BRING TO YOU THAT WHICH YOU SEARCH FOR!
THE FOREIGN BOX! EXCELLENT!
YOU WILL BE WELL REWARDED!
WAIT--! IT'S WORTHLESS! THE BOX IS EMPTY!
IT WAS EMPTY WHEN I GOT IT! HONEST!
YOU HAD BETTER NOT BE WITHHOLDING ANYTHING FROM US!
WE NEED THE CONTENTS!
YOU WON'T BE PAID UNTIL WE GET IT!
YES, SIR! YES, SIR!
THAT INSPECTOR AND RONIN ARE SMART! IT'S JUST A MATTER OF TIME UNTIL THEY FIND IT!
WE FOLLOW THEM, KILL THEM, AND TAKE IT WHEN THEY DO!
BUT WE MUST ENSURE THAT WE GAIN POSSESSION OF THE BOXES CONTENTS.
HOW DO YOU DO THAT?
9.

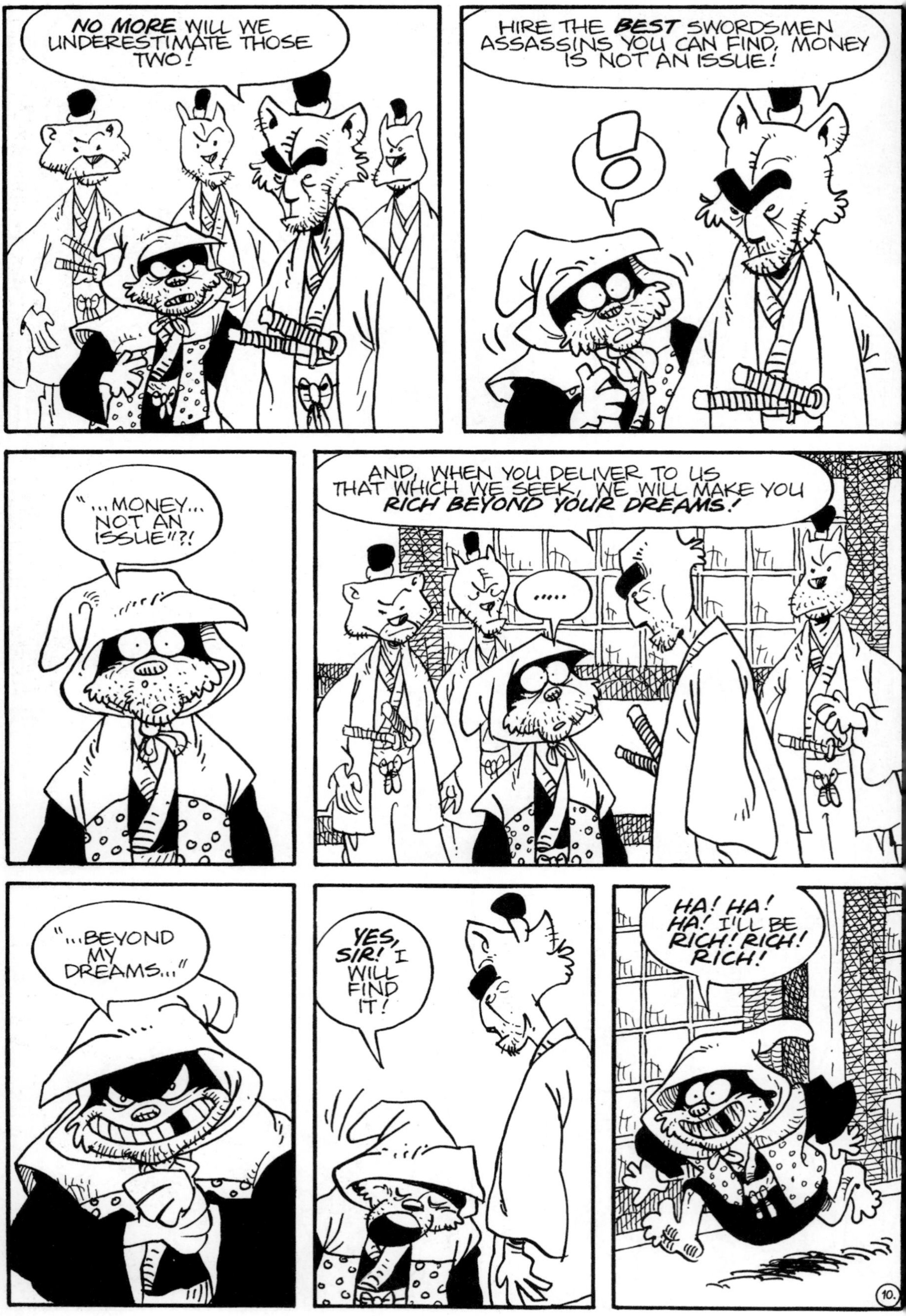
NO MORE WILL WE UNDERESTIMATE THOSE TWO!
HIRE THE BEST SWORDSMEN ASSASSINS YOU CAN FIND, MONEY IS NOT AN ISSUE!
!
"...MONEY... NOT AN ISSUE"?!
AND, WHEN YOU DELIVER TO US THAT WHICH WE SEEK, WE WILL MAKE YOU RICH BEYOND YOUR DREAMS!
.....
"...BEYOND MY DREAMS..."
...
YES, SIR! I WILL FIND IT!
HA! HA! HA! I'LL BE RICH! RICH! RICH!
10.

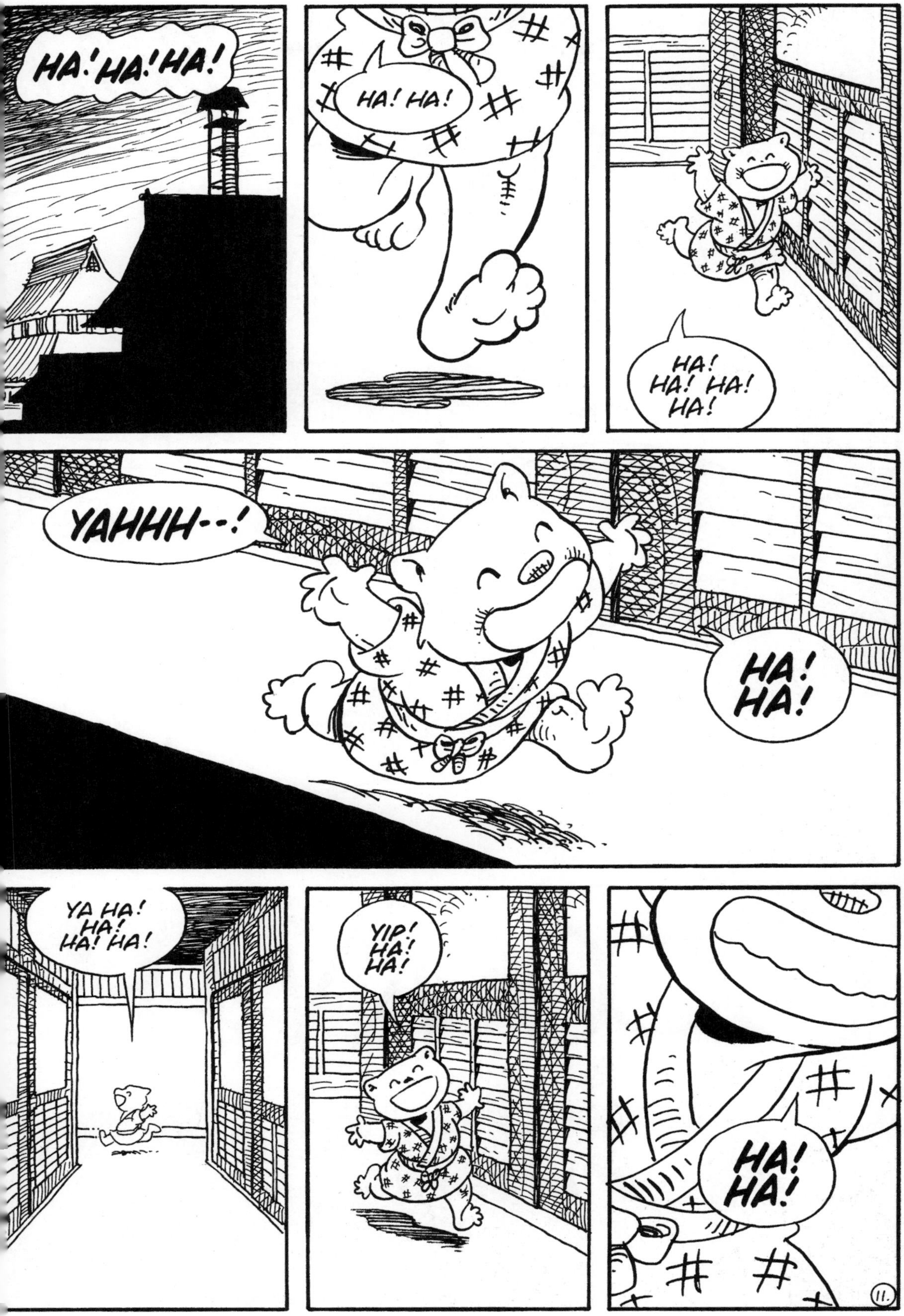
HA! HA! HA!
HA! HA!
HA! HA! HA! HA!
YAHHH--!
HA! HA!
YA HA! HA! HA! HA!
YIP! HA! HA!
HA! HA!
11.

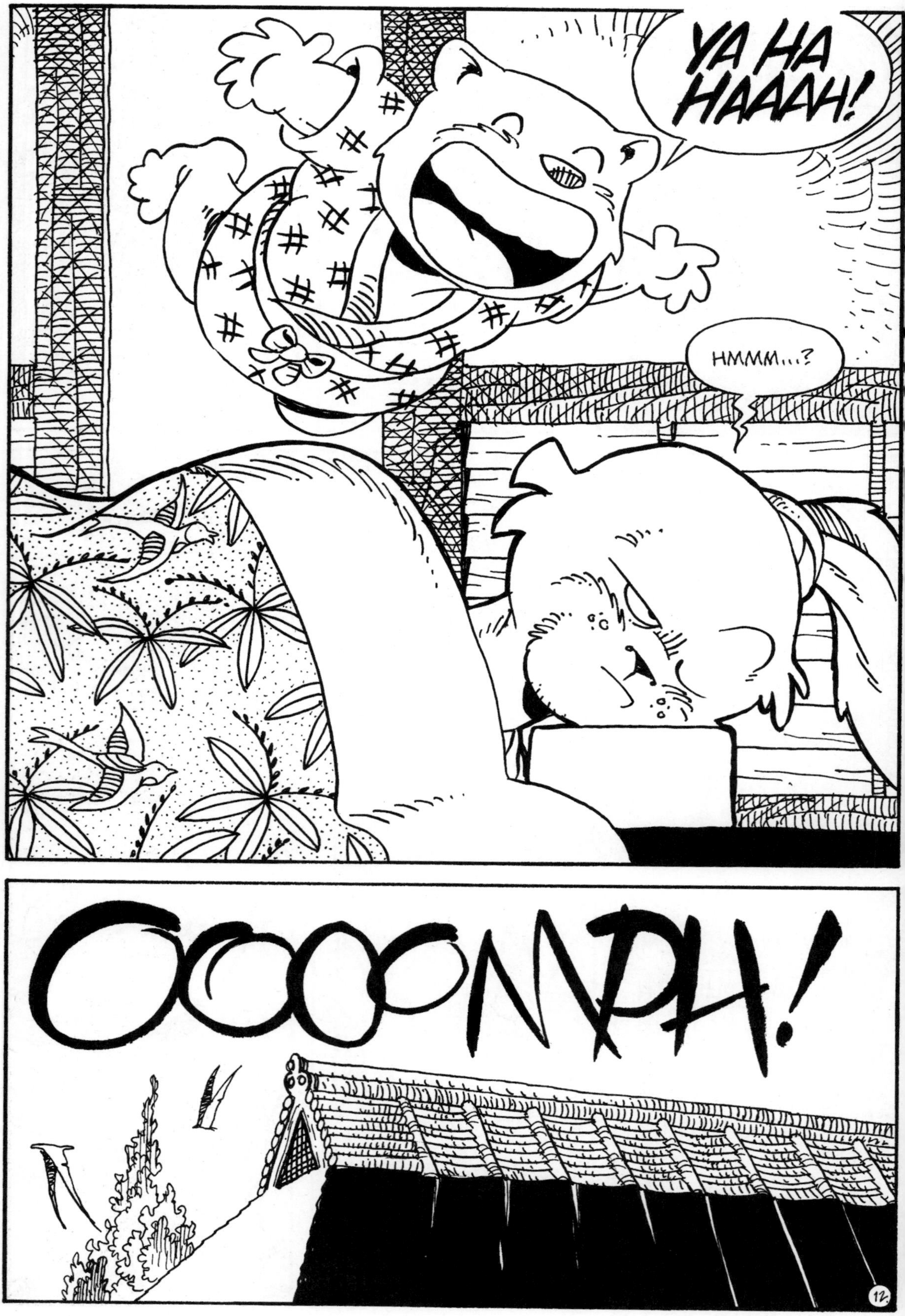
YA HA HAAAH!
HMMM...?
OOOOMPH!
12.

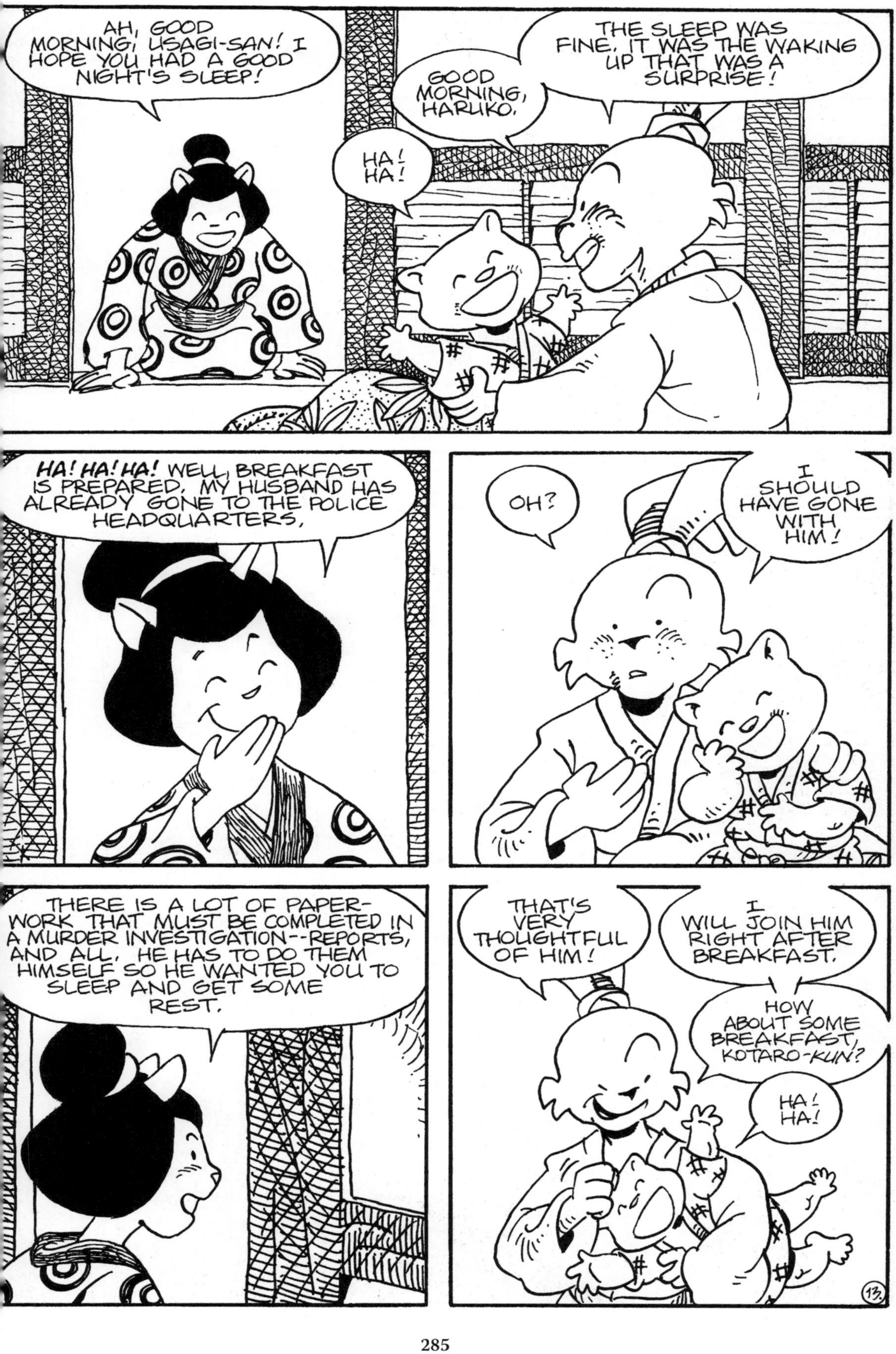
AH, GOOD MORNING, USAGI-SAN! I HOPE YOU HAD A GOOD NIGHT'S SLEEP!
GOOD MORNING, HARUKO.
THE SLEEP WAS FINE. IT WAS THE WAKING UP THAT WAS A SURPRISE!
HA! HA!
HA! HA! HA! WELL, BREAKFAST IS PREPARED. MY HUSBAND HAS ALREADY GONE TO THE POLICE HEADQUARTERS.
OH?
I SHOULD HAVE GONE WITH HIM!
THERE IS A LOT OF PAPER-WORK THAT MUST BE COMPLETED IN A MURDER INVESTIGATION--REPORTS, AND ALL. HE HAS TO DO THEM HIMSELF SO HE WANTED YOU TO SLEEP AND GET SOME REST.
THAT'S VERY THOUGHTFUL OF HIM!
I WILL JOIN HIM RIGHT AFTER BREAKFAST.
HOW ABOUT SOME BREAKFAST, KOTARO-KUN?
HA! HA!
13.

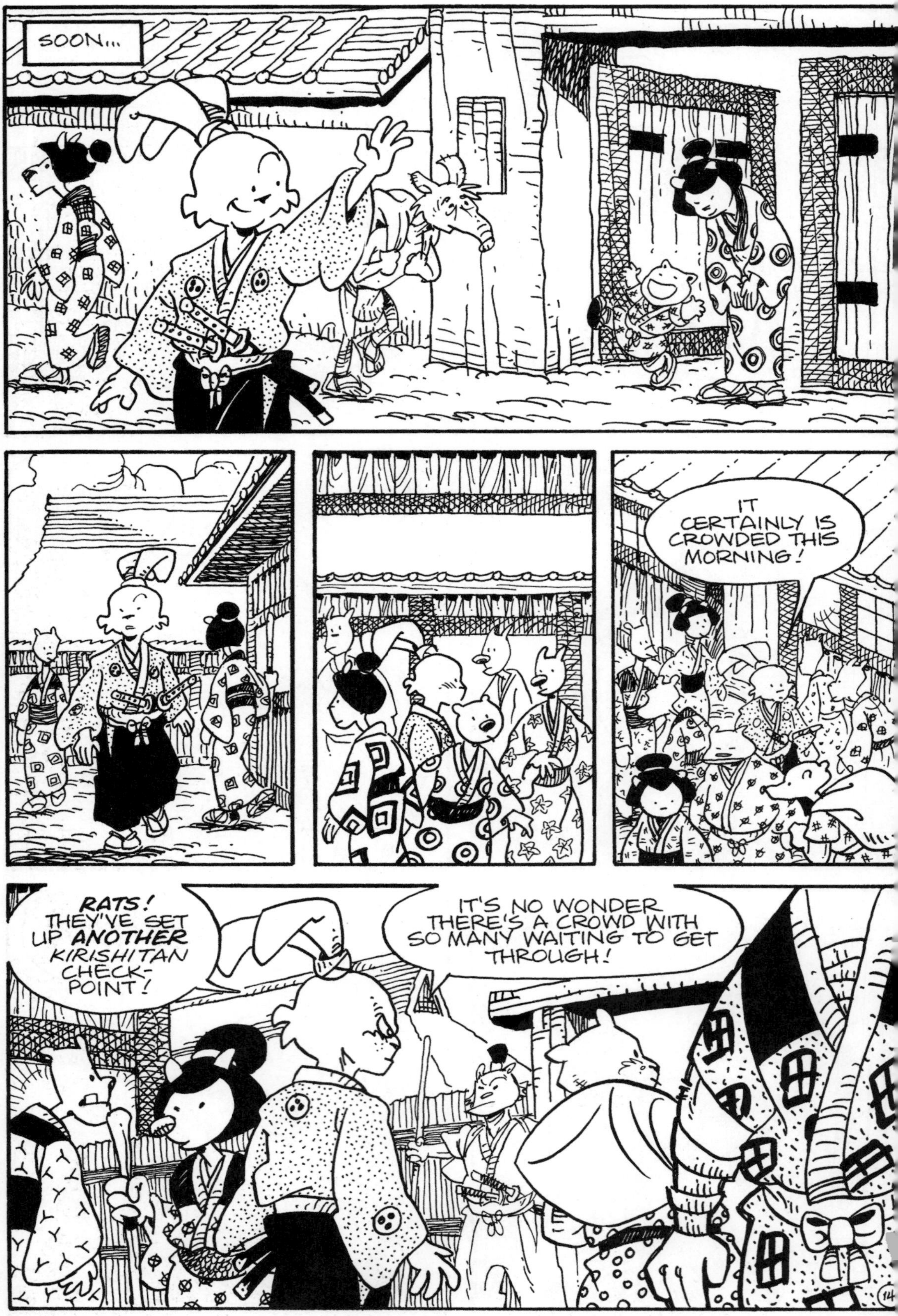
SOON...
IT CERTAINLY IS CROWDED THIS MORNING!
RATS! THEY'VE SET UP ANOTHER KIRISHITAN CHECK-POINT!
IT'S NO WONDER THERE'S A CROWD WITH SO MANY WAITING TO GET THROUGH!
14

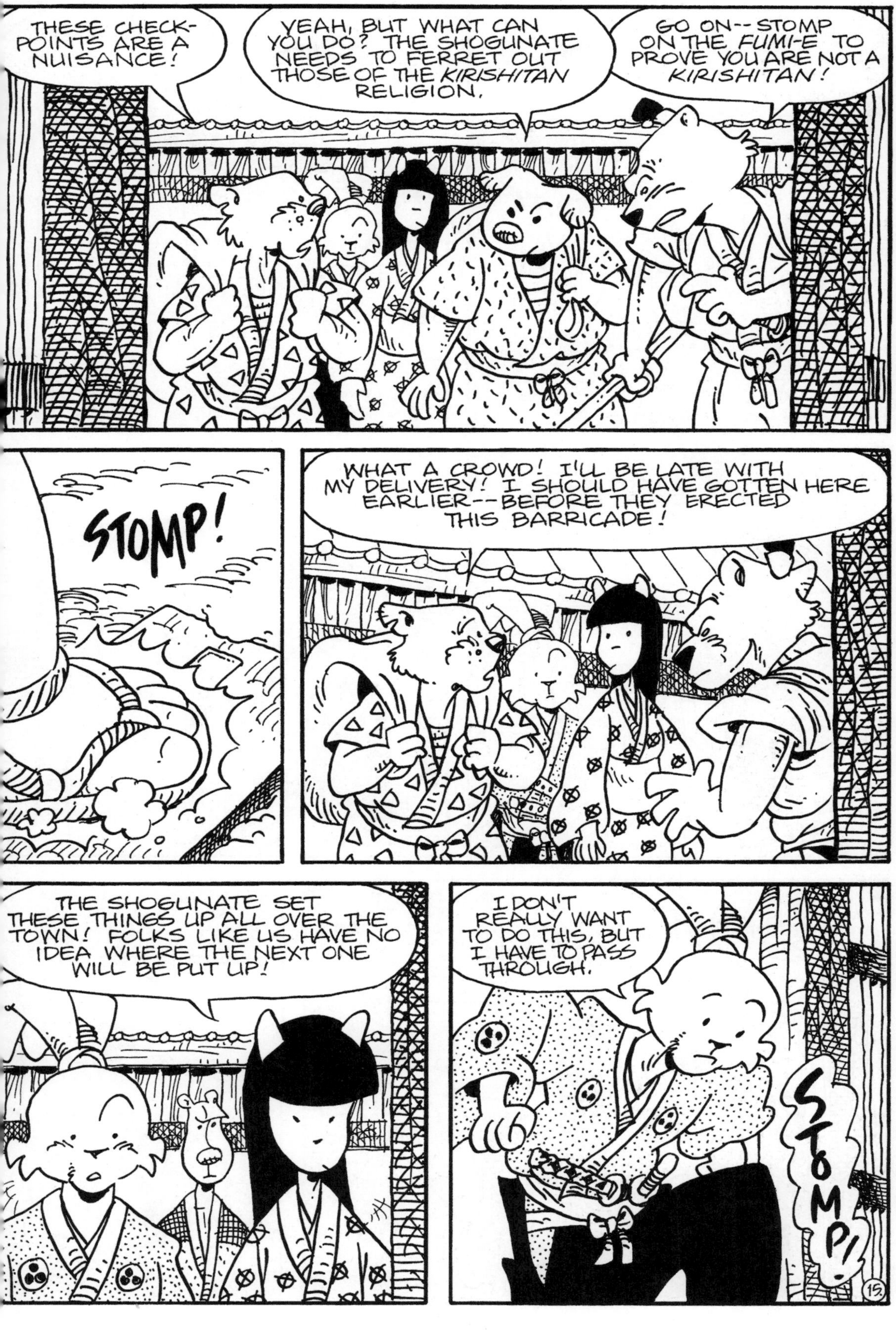
THESE CHECK-POINTS ARE A NUISANCE!
YEAH, BUT WHAT CAN YOU DO? THE SHOGUNATE NEEDS TO FERRET OUT THOSE OF THE *KIRISHITAN* RELIGION.
GO ON-- STOMP ON THE *FUMI-E* TO PROVE YOU ARE NOT A *KIRISHITAN*!
STOMP!
WHAT A CROWD! I'LL BE LATE WITH MY DELIVERY! I SHOULD HAVE GOTTEN HERE EARLIER--BEFORE THEY ERECTED THIS BARRICADE!
THE SHOGUNATE SET THESE THINGS UP ALL OVER THE TOWN! FOLKS LIKE US HAVE NO IDEA WHERE THE NEXT ONE WILL BE PUT UP!
I DON'T REALLY WANT TO DO THIS, BUT I HAVE TO PASS THROUGH.
STOMP!
15.

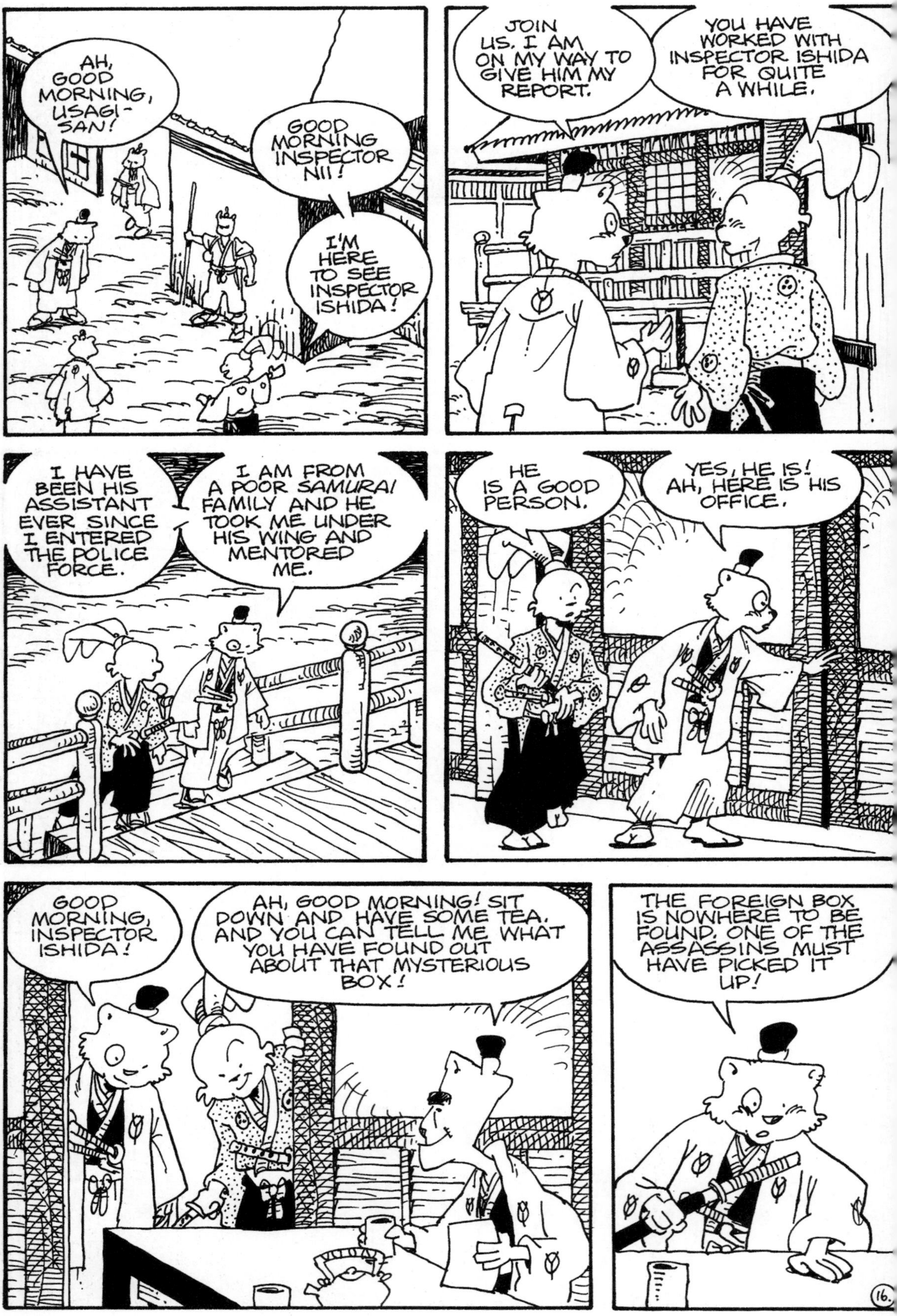
AH, GOOD MORNING, USAGI-SAN!
GOOD MORNING INSPECTOR NII!
I'M HERE TO SEE INSPECTOR ISHIDA!
JOIN US. I AM ON MY WAY TO GIVE HIM MY REPORT.
YOU HAVE WORKED WITH INSPECTOR ISHIDA FOR QUITE A WHILE.
I HAVE BEEN HIS ASSISTANT EVER SINCE I ENTERED THE POLICE FORCE.
I AM FROM A POOR *SAMURAI* FAMILY AND HE TOOK ME UNDER HIS WING AND MENTORED ME.
HE IS A GOOD PERSON.
YES, HE IS! AH, HERE IS HIS OFFICE.
GOOD MORNING, INSPECTOR ISHIDA!
AH, GOOD MORNING! SIT DOWN AND HAVE SOME TEA. AND YOU CAN TELL ME WHAT YOU HAVE FOUND OUT ABOUT THAT MYSTERIOUS BOX!
THE FOREIGN BOX IS NOWHERE TO BE FOUND. ONE OF THE ASSASSINS MUST HAVE PICKED IT UP!
16.

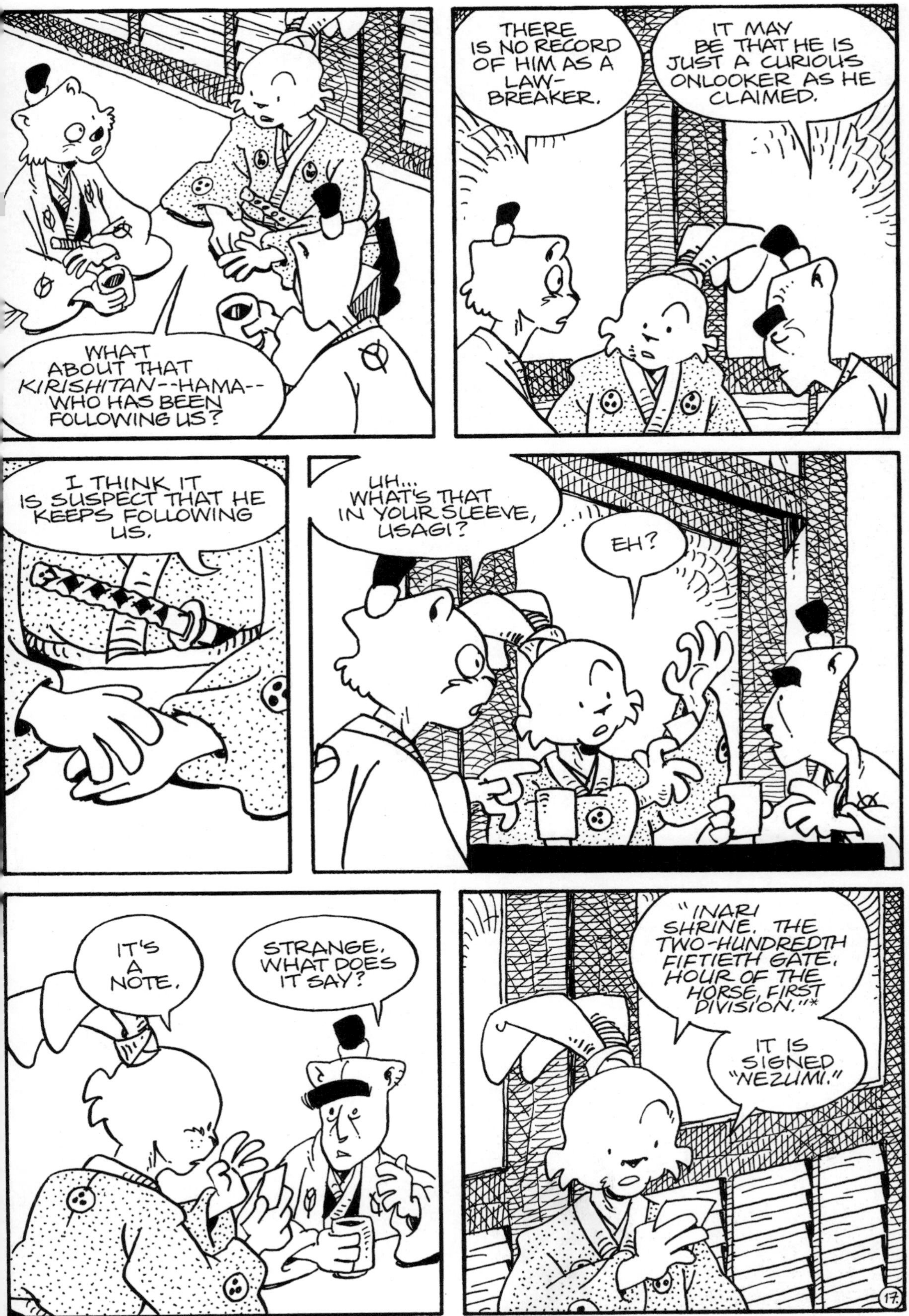
WHAT ABOUT THAT KIRISHITAN--HAMA--WHO HAS BEEN FOLLOWING US?
THERE IS NO RECORD OF HIM AS A LAW-BREAKER.
IT MAY BE THAT HE IS JUST A CURIOUS ONLOOKER AS HE CLAIMED.
I THINK IT IS SUSPECT THAT HE KEEPS FOLLOWING US.
UH... WHAT'S THAT IN YOUR SLEEVE, USAGI?
EH?
IT'S A NOTE.
STRANGE, WHAT DOES IT SAY?
"INARI SHRINE. THE TWO-HUNDREDTH FIFTIETH GATE. HOUR OF THE HORSE, FIRST DIVISION."*
IT IS SIGNED "NEZUMI."
17.

*11:00AM–11:30AM

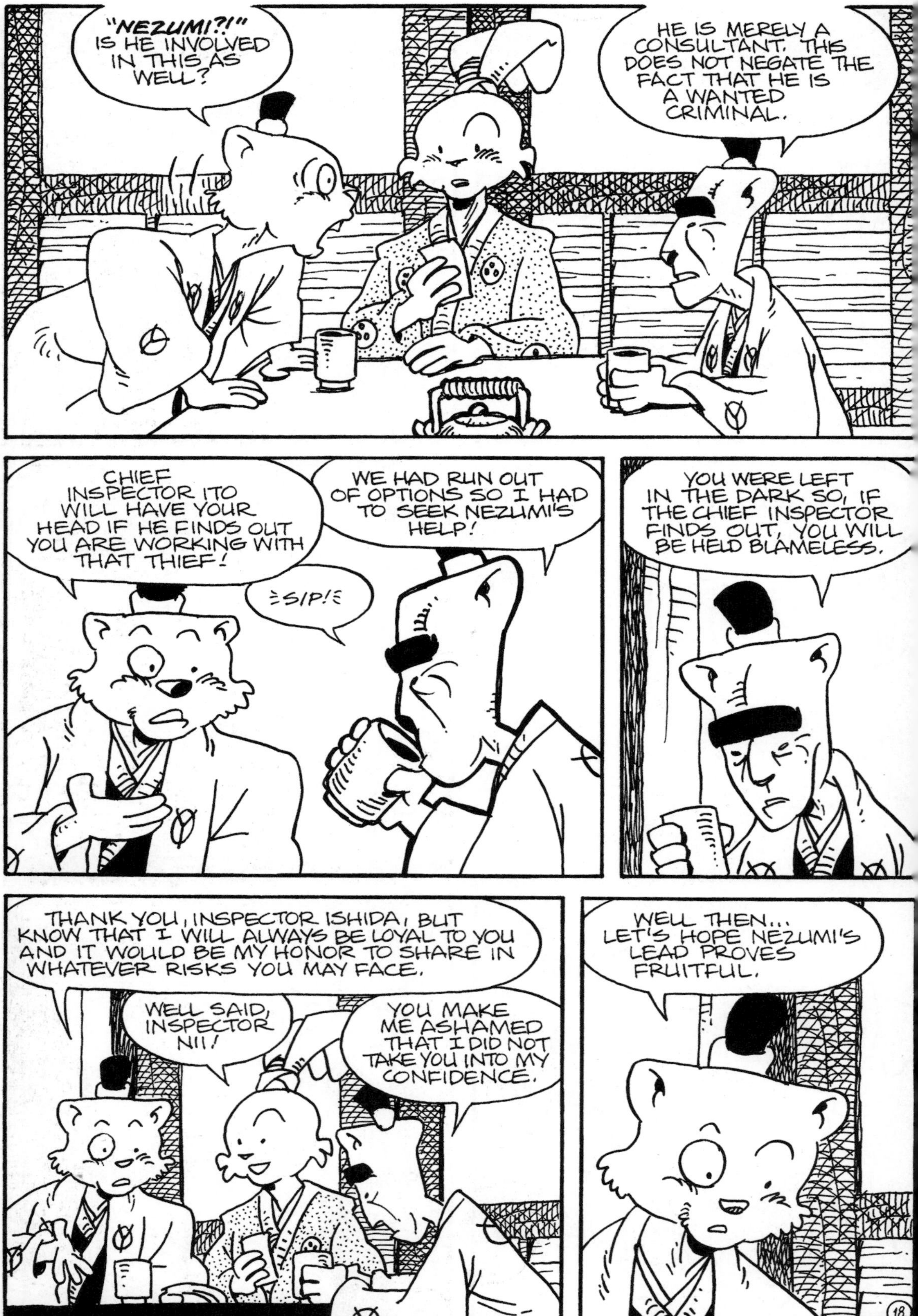
"NEZUMI?!" IS HE INVOLVED IN THIS AS WELL?
HE IS MERELY A CONSULTANT. THIS DOES NOT NEGATE THE FACT THAT HE IS A WANTED CRIMINAL.
CHIEF INSPECTOR ITO WILL HAVE YOUR HEAD IF HE FINDS OUT YOU ARE WORKING WITH THAT THIEF!
WE HAD RUN OUT OF OPTIONS SO I HAD TO SEEK NEZUMI'S HELP!
SIP!
YOU WERE LEFT IN THE DARK SO, IF THE CHIEF INSPECTOR FINDS OUT, YOU WILL BE HELD BLAMELESS.
THANK YOU, INSPECTOR ISHIDA, BUT KNOW THAT I WILL ALWAYS BE LOYAL TO YOU AND IT WOULD BE MY HONOR TO SHARE IN WHATEVER RISKS YOU MAY FACE.
WELL SAID, INSPECTOR NII!
YOU MAKE ME ASHAMED THAT I DID NOT TAKE YOU INTO MY CONFIDENCE.
WELL THEN... LET'S HOPE NEZUMI'S LEAD PROVES FRUITFUL.
18.

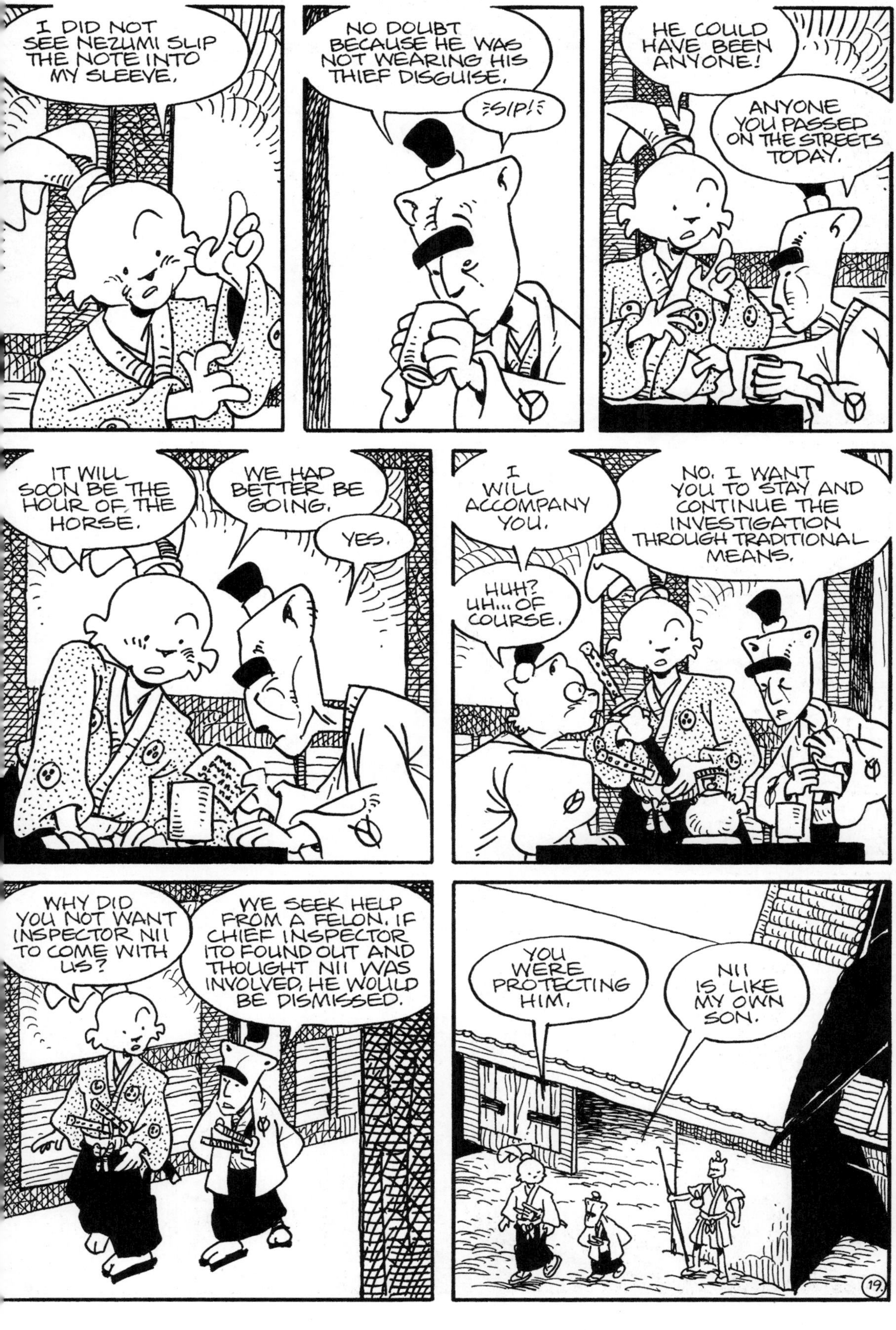

I DID NOT SEE NEZUMI SLIP THE NOTE INTO MY SLEEVE.
NO DOUBT BECAUSE HE WAS NOT WEARING HIS THIEF DISGUISE.
SIP!
HE COULD HAVE BEEN ANYONE!
ANYONE YOU PASSED ON THE STREETS TODAY.
IT WILL SOON BE THE HOUR OF THE HORSE.
WE HAD BETTER BE GOING.
YES.
I WILL ACCOMPANY YOU.
NO. I WANT YOU TO STAY AND CONTINUE THE INVESTIGATION THROUGH TRADITIONAL MEANS.
HUH? UH... OF COURSE.
WHY DID YOU NOT WANT INSPECTOR NII TO COME WITH US?
WE SEEK HELP FROM A FELON. IF CHIEF INSPECTOR ITO FOUND OUT AND THOUGHT NII WAS INVOLVED, HE WOULD BE DISMISSED.
YOU WERE PROTECTING HIM.
NII IS LIKE MY OWN SON.
19

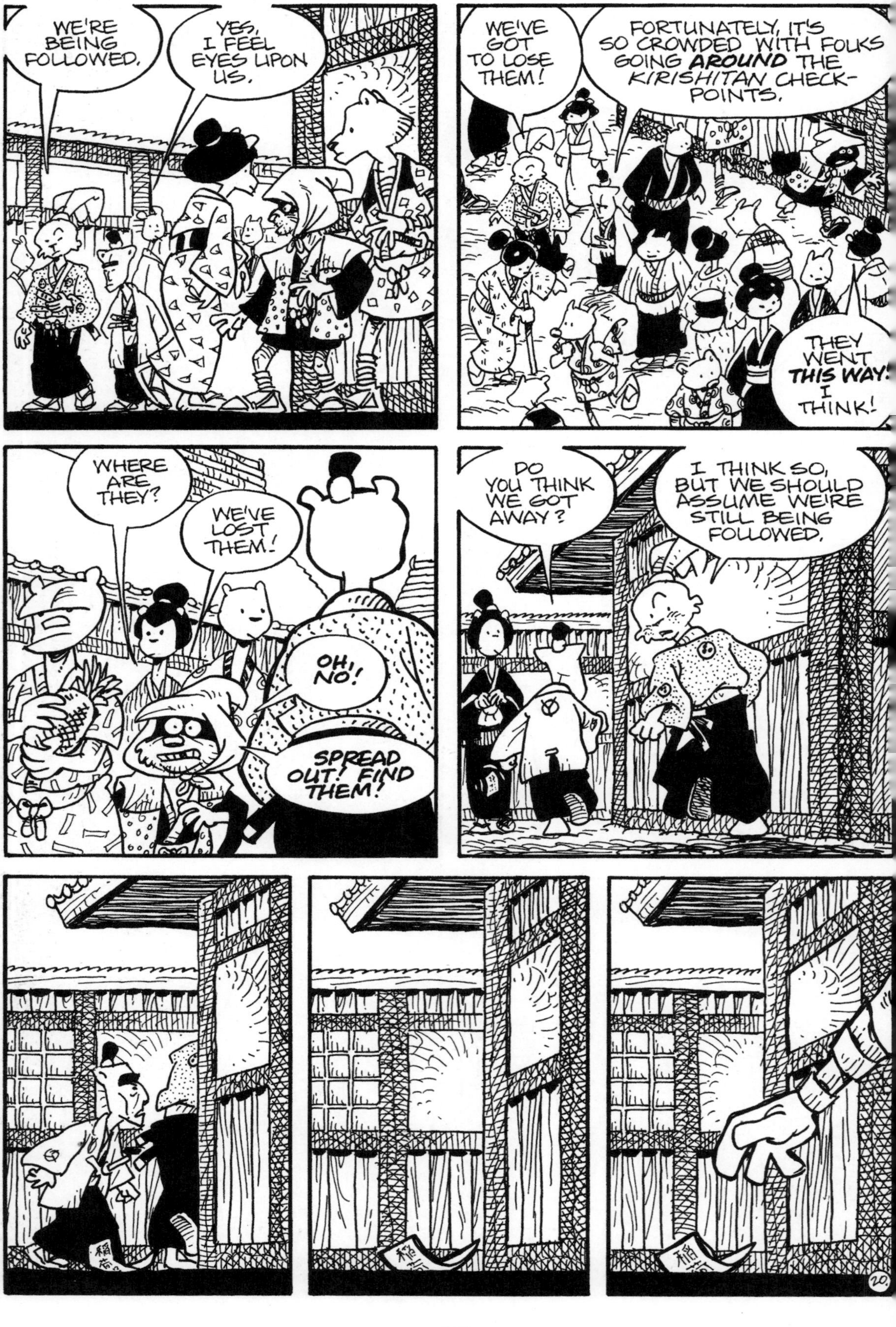
WE'RE BEING FOLLOWED.
YES, I FEEL EYES UPON US.
WE'VE GOT TO LOSE THEM!
FORTUNATELY, IT'S SO CROWDED WITH FOLKS GOING **AROUND** THE *KIRISHITAN* CHECK-POINTS.
THEY WENT **THIS WAY!** I THINK!
WHERE ARE THEY?
WE'VE LOST THEM!
OH, NO!
SPREAD OUT! FIND THEM!
DO YOU THINK WE GOT AWAY?
I THINK SO, BUT WE SHOULD ASSUME WE'RE STILL BEING FOLLOWED.
20.

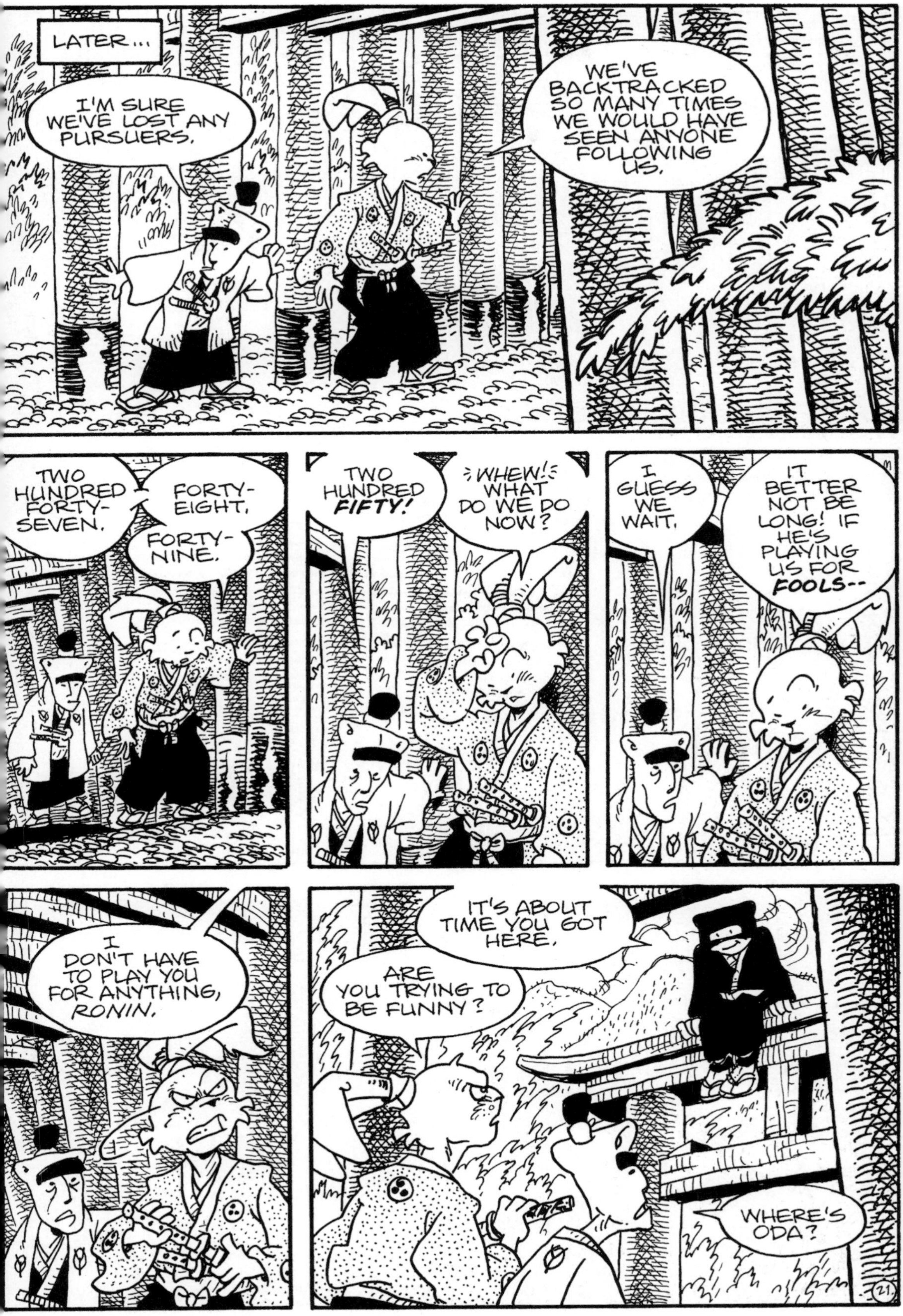
LATER...
I'M SURE WE'VE LOST ANY PURSUERS.
WE'VE BACKTRACKED SO MANY TIMES WE WOULD HAVE SEEN ANYONE FOLLOWING US.
TWO HUNDRED FORTY-SEVEN.
FORTY-EIGHT.
FORTY-NINE.
TWO HUNDRED FIFTY!
WHEW! WHAT DO WE DO NOW?
I GUESS WE WAIT.
IT BETTER NOT BE LONG! IF HE'S PLAYING US FOR FOOLS--
I DON'T HAVE TO PLAY YOU FOR ANYTHING, RONIN.
IT'S ABOUT TIME YOU GOT HERE.
ARE YOU TRYING TO BE FUNNY?
WHERE'S ODA?
21

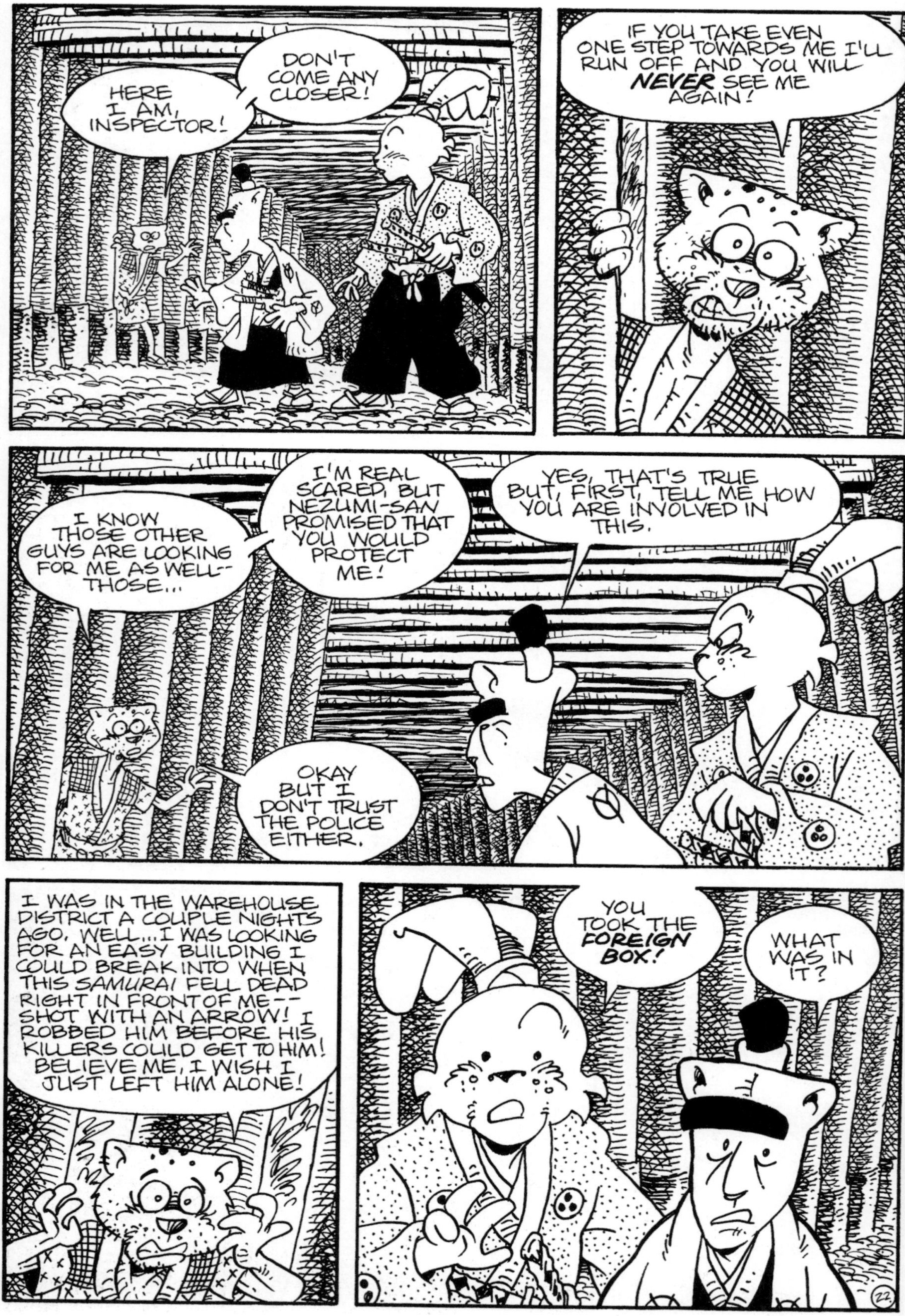
HERE I AM, INSPECTOR!
DON'T COME ANY CLOSER!
IF YOU TAKE EVEN ONE STEP TOWARDS ME I'LL RUN OFF AND YOU WILL NEVER SEE ME AGAIN!
I KNOW THOSE OTHER GUYS ARE LOOKING FOR ME AS WELL-- THOSE...
I'M REAL SCARED, BUT NEZUMI-SAN PROMISED THAT YOU WOULD PROTECT ME!
YES, THAT'S TRUE BUT, FIRST, TELL ME HOW YOU ARE INVOLVED IN THIS.
OKAY BUT I DON'T TRUST THE POLICE EITHER.
I WAS IN THE WAREHOUSE DISTRICT A COUPLE NIGHTS AGO. WELL... I WAS LOOKING FOR AN EASY BUILDING I COULD BREAK INTO WHEN THIS SAMURAI FELL DEAD RIGHT IN FRONT OF ME-- SHOT WITH AN ARROW! I ROBBED HIM BEFORE HIS KILLERS COULD GET TO HIM! BELIEVE ME, I WISH I JUST LEFT HIM ALONE!
YOU TOOK THE FOREIGN BOX!
WHAT WAS IN IT?
22

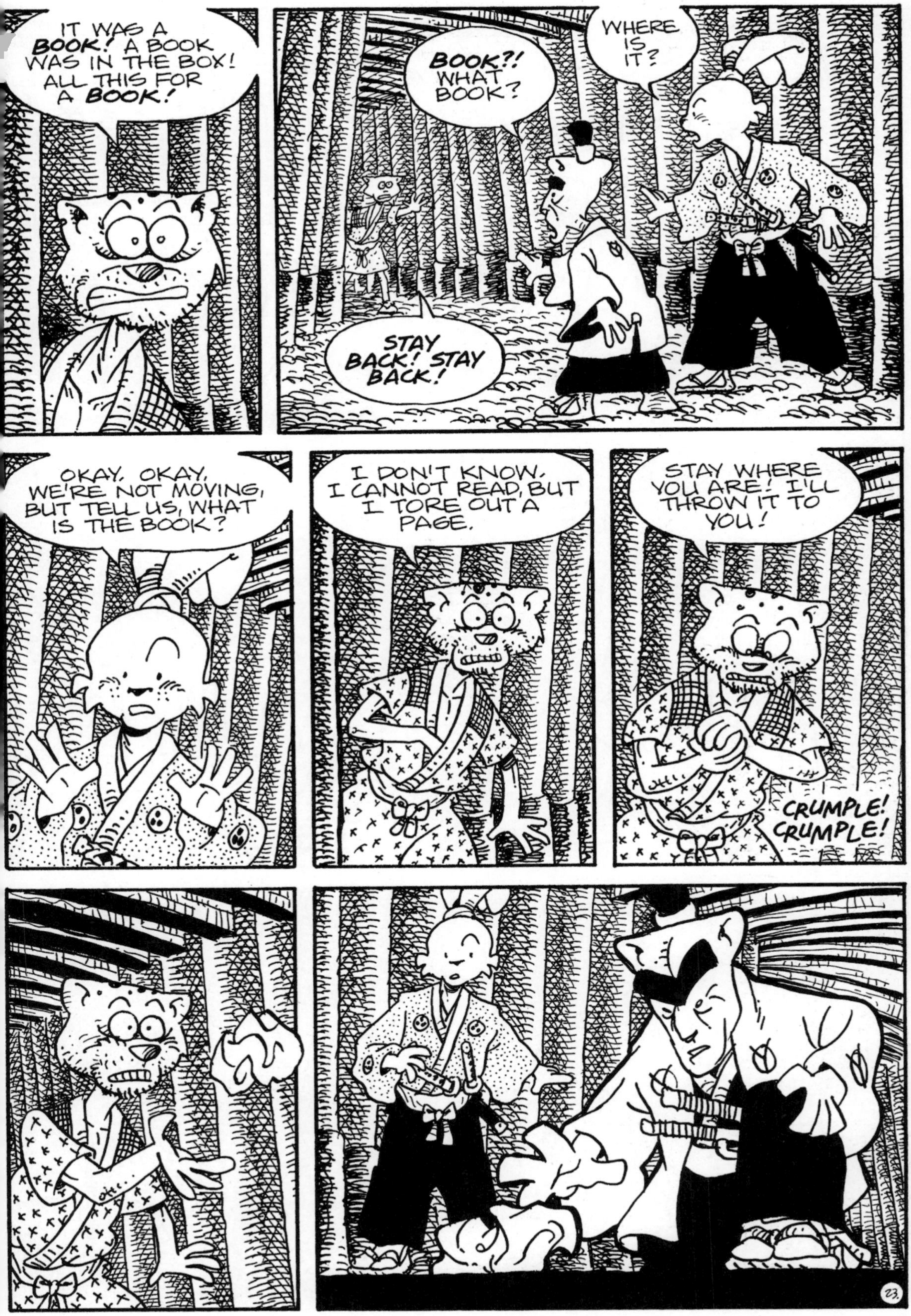

IT WAS A BOOK! A BOOK WAS IN THE BOX! ALL THIS FOR A BOOK!
BOOK?! WHAT BOOK?
WHERE IS IT?
STAY BACK! STAY BACK!
OKAY, OKAY, WE'RE NOT MOVING, BUT TELL US, WHAT IS THE BOOK?
I DON'T KNOW. I CANNOT READ, BUT I TORE OUT A PAGE.
STAY WHERE YOU ARE! I'LL THROW IT TO YOU!
CRUMPLE! CRUMPLE!
23.

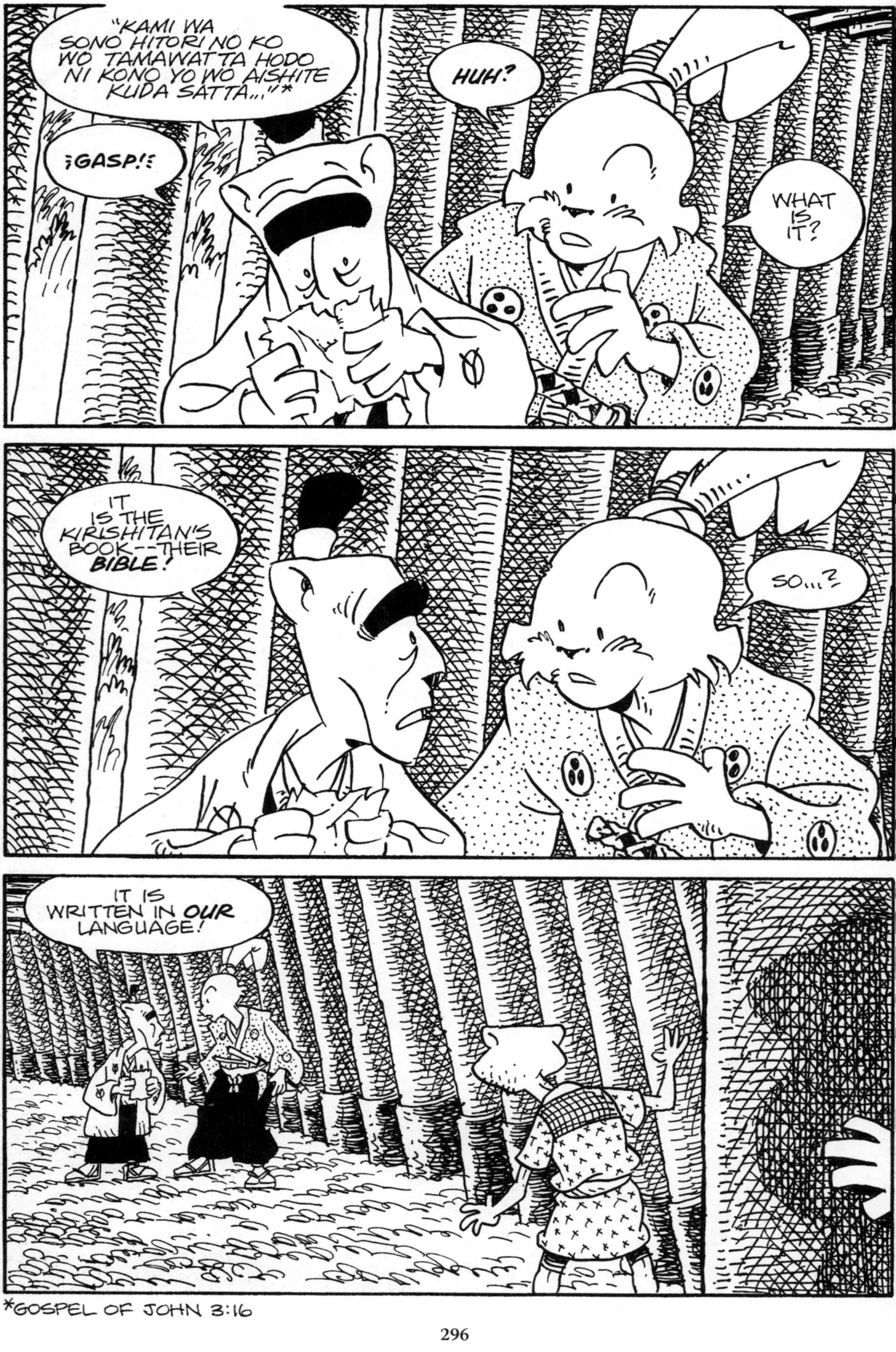
"KAMI WA SONO HITORI NO KO WO TAMAWATTA HODO NI KONO YO WO AISHITE KUDA SATTA..."*
HUH?
¡GASP!¡
WHAT IS IT?
IT IS THE KIRISHITAN'S BOOK--THEIR BIBLE!
SO...?
IT IS WRITTEN IN OUR LANGUAGE!

*GOSPEL OF JOHN 3:16

THE HIDDEN PART SIX

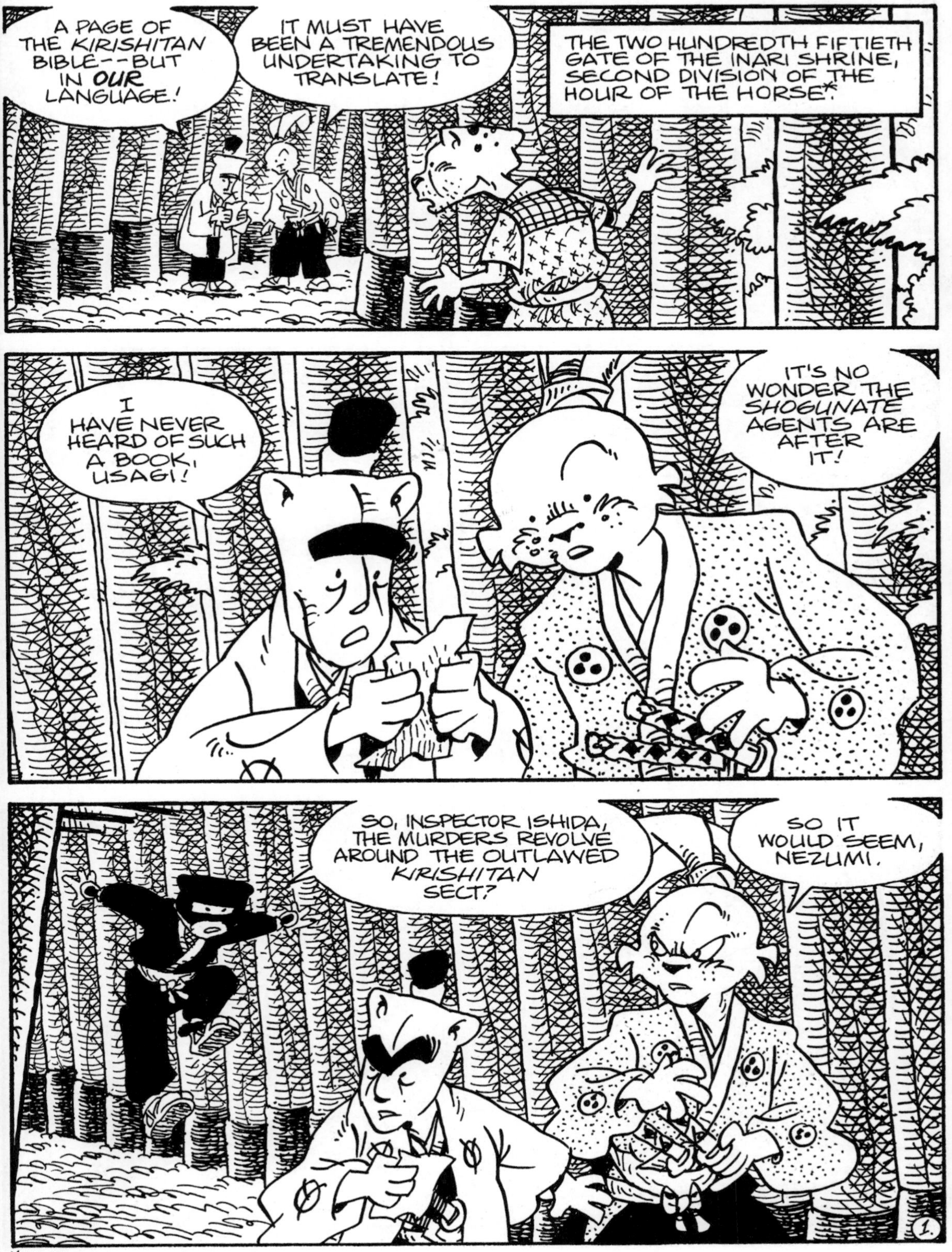
A PAGE OF THE KIRISHITAN BIBLE--BUT IN OUR LANGUAGE!
IT MUST HAVE BEEN A TREMENDOUS UNDERTAKING TO TRANSLATE!
THE TWO HUNDREDTH FIFTIETH GATE OF THE INARI SHRINE, SECOND DIVISION OF THE HOUR OF THE HORSE*.
I HAVE NEVER HEARD OF SUCH A BOOK, USAGI!
IT'S NO WONDER THE SHOGUNATE AGENTS ARE AFTER IT!
SO, INSPECTOR ISHIDA, THE MURDERS REVOLVE AROUND THE OUTLAWED KIRISHITAN SECT?
SO IT WOULD SEEM, NEZUMI.
1.

*11:31 AM–12:00 NOON

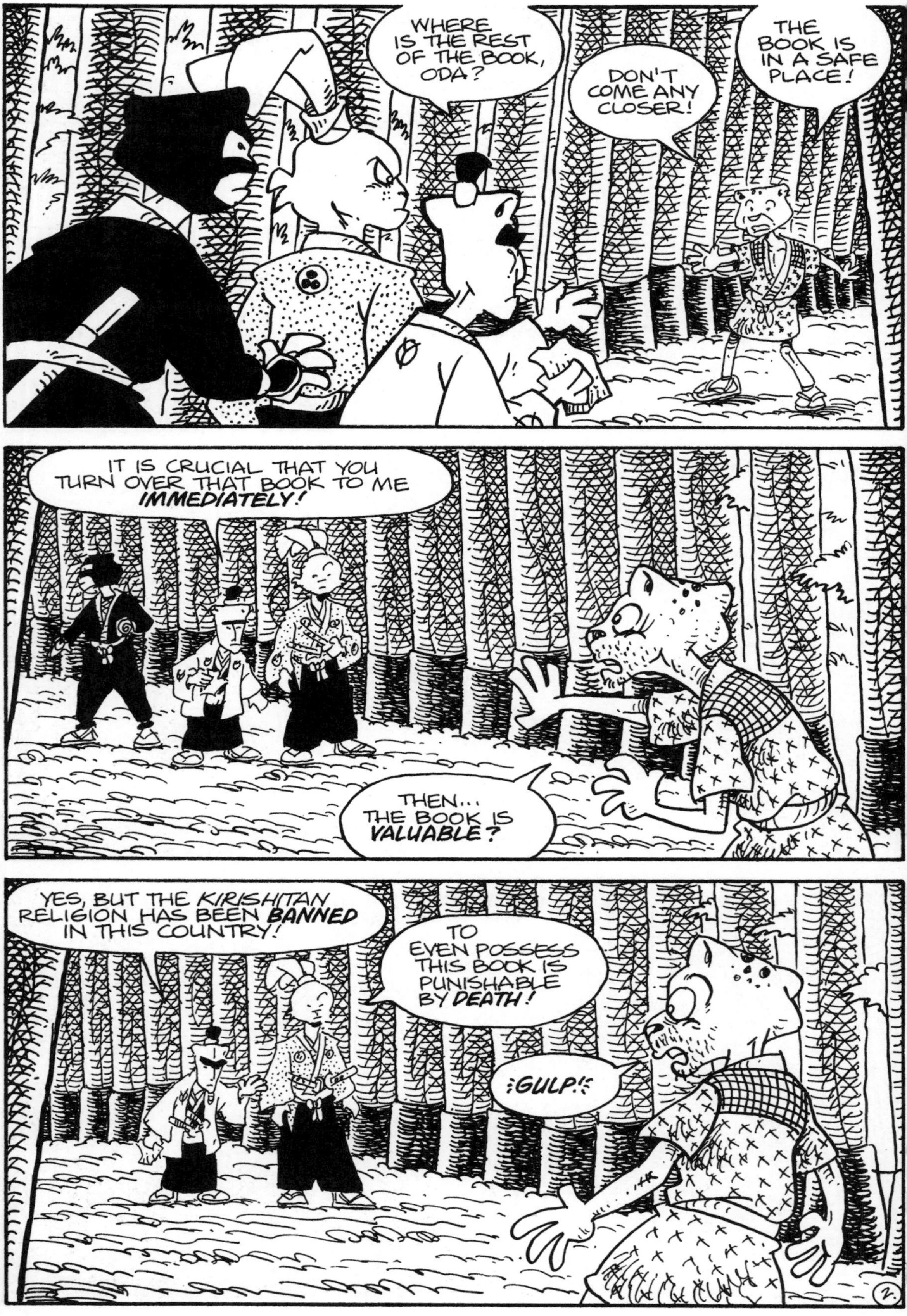
WHERE IS THE REST OF THE BOOK, ODA?
DON'T COME ANY CLOSER!
THE BOOK IS IN A SAFE PLACE!
IT IS CRUCIAL THAT YOU TURN OVER THAT BOOK TO ME IMMEDIATELY!
THEN... THE BOOK IS VALUABLE?
YES, BUT THE KIRISHITAN RELIGION HAS BEEN BANNED IN THIS COUNTRY!
TO EVEN POSSESS THIS BOOK IS PUNISHABLE BY DEATH!
GULP!
2.

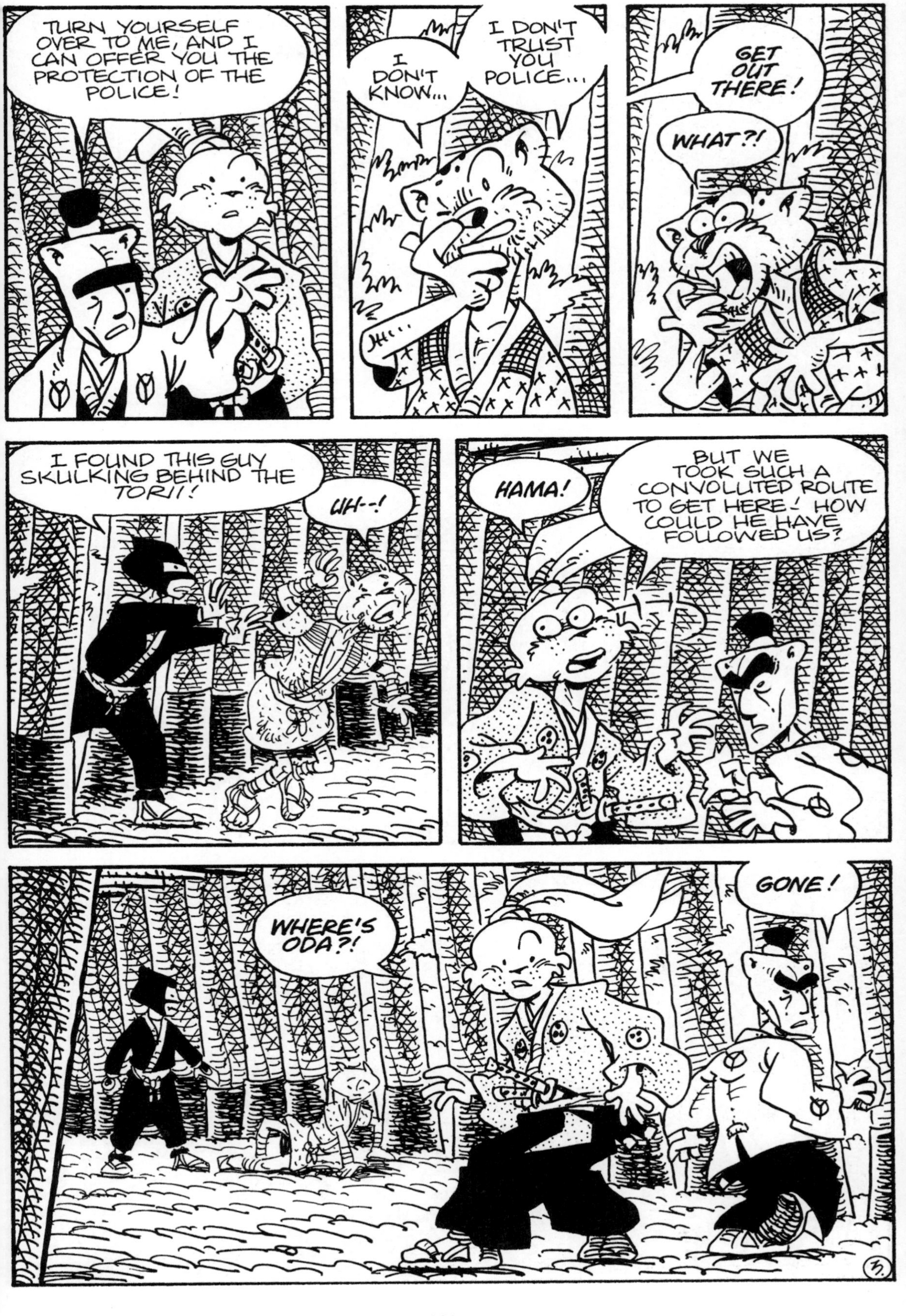
TURN YOURSELF OVER TO ME, AND I CAN OFFER YOU THE PROTECTION OF THE POLICE!
I DON'T KNOW...
I DON'T TRUST YOU POLICE...
GET OUT THERE!
WHAT?!
I FOUND THIS GUY SKULKING BEHIND THE TORII!
UH--!
HAMA!
BUT WE TOOK SUCH A CONVOLUTED ROUTE TO GET HERE! HOW COULD HE HAVE FOLLOWED US?
WHERE'S ODA?!
GONE!

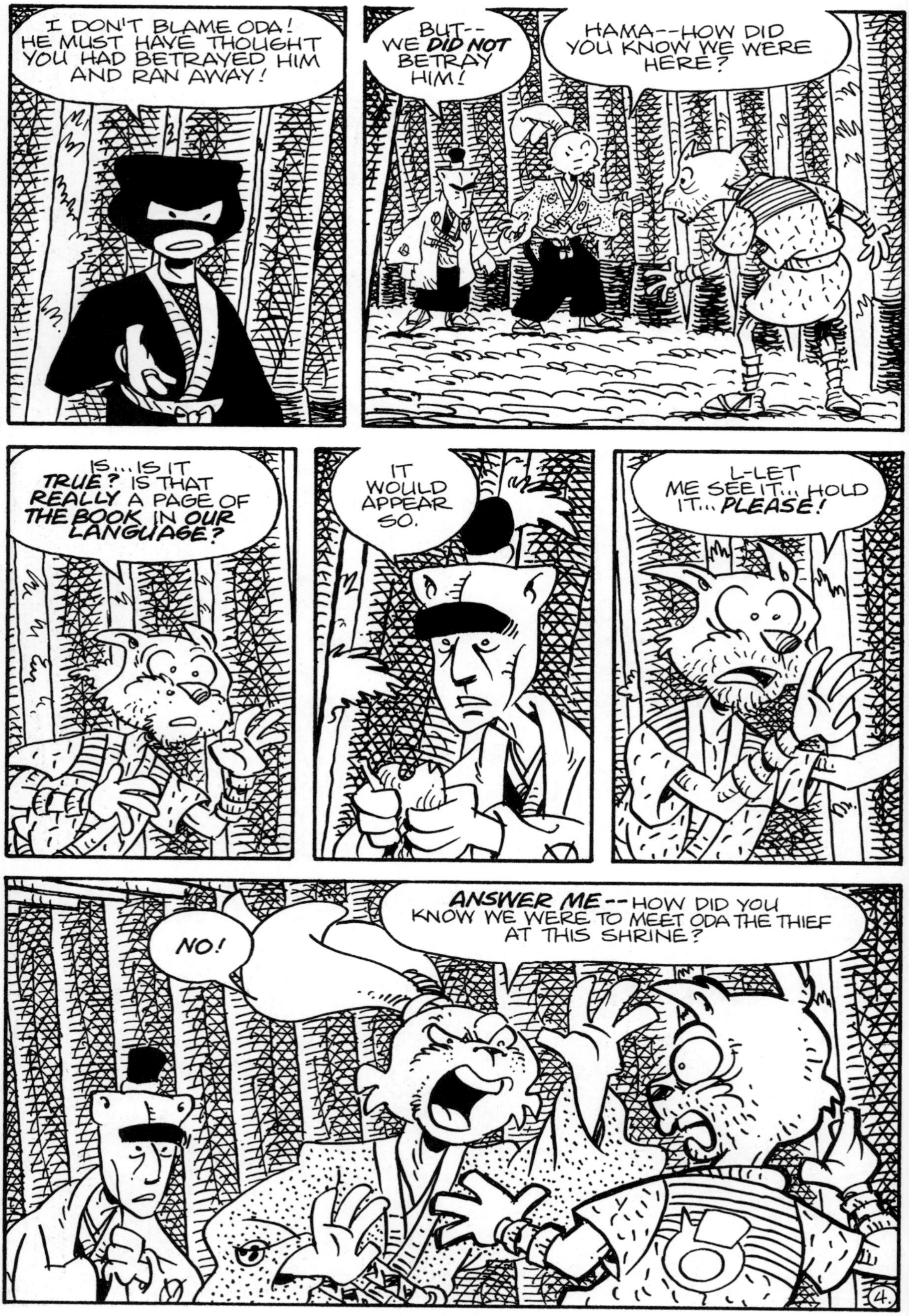
I DON'T BLAME ODA! HE MUST HAVE THOUGHT YOU HAD BETRAYED HIM AND RAN AWAY!
BUT-- WE DID NOT BETRAY HIM!
HAMA--HOW DID YOU KNOW WE WERE HERE?
IS...IS IT TRUE? IS THAT REALLY A PAGE OF THE BOOK IN OUR LANGUAGE?
IT WOULD APPEAR SO.
L-LET ME SEE IT... HOLD IT... PLEASE!
NO!
ANSWER ME--HOW DID YOU KNOW WE WERE TO MEET ODA THE THIEF AT THIS SHRINE?
4.

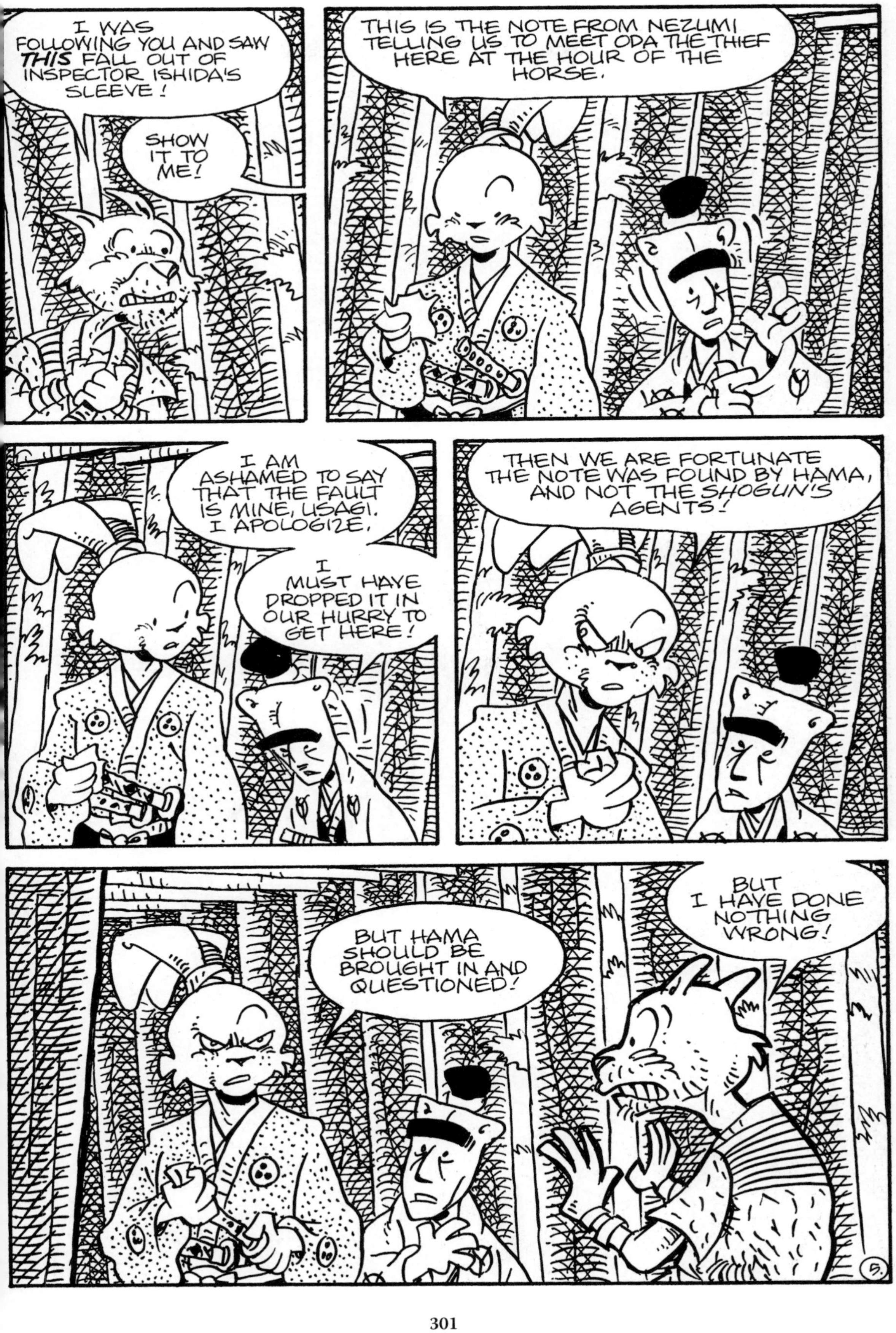
I WAS FOLLOWING YOU AND SAW THIS FALL OUT OF INSPECTOR ISHIDA'S SLEEVE!
SHOW IT TO ME!
THIS IS THE NOTE FROM NEZUMI TELLING US TO MEET ODA THE THIEF HERE AT THE HOUR OF THE HORSE.
I AM ASHAMED TO SAY THAT THE FAULT IS MINE, USAGI. I APOLOGIZE.
I MUST HAVE DROPPED IT IN OUR HURRY TO GET HERE!
THEN WE ARE FORTUNATE THE NOTE WAS FOUND BY HAMA, AND NOT THE SHOGUN'S AGENTS!
BUT HAMA SHOULD BE BROUGHT IN AND QUESTIONED!
BUT I HAVE DONE NOTHING WRONG!
5.

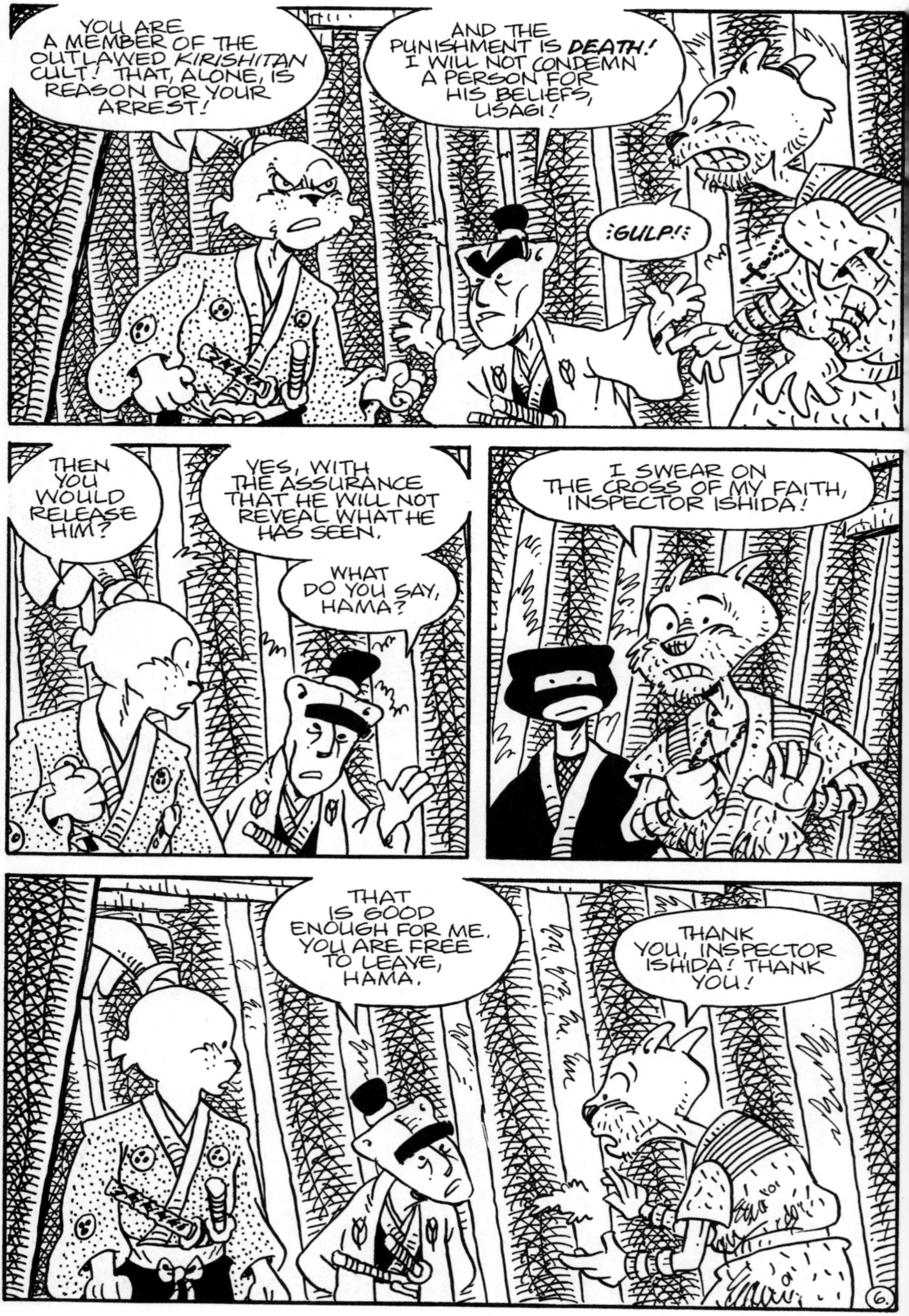

YOU ARE A MEMBER OF THE OUTLAWED *KIRISHITAN* CULT! THAT, ALONE, IS REASON FOR YOUR ARREST!
AND THE PUNISHMENT IS **DEATH**! I WILL NOT CONDEMN A PERSON FOR HIS BELIEFS, USAGI!
GULP!
THEN YOU WOULD RELEASE HIM?
YES, WITH THE ASSURANCE THAT HE WILL NOT REVEAL WHAT HE HAS SEEN.
WHAT DO YOU SAY, HAMA?
I SWEAR ON THE CROSS OF MY FAITH, INSPECTOR ISHIDA!
THAT IS GOOD ENOUGH FOR ME. YOU ARE FREE TO LEAVE, HAMA.
THANK YOU, INSPECTOR ISHIDA! THANK YOU!
6.

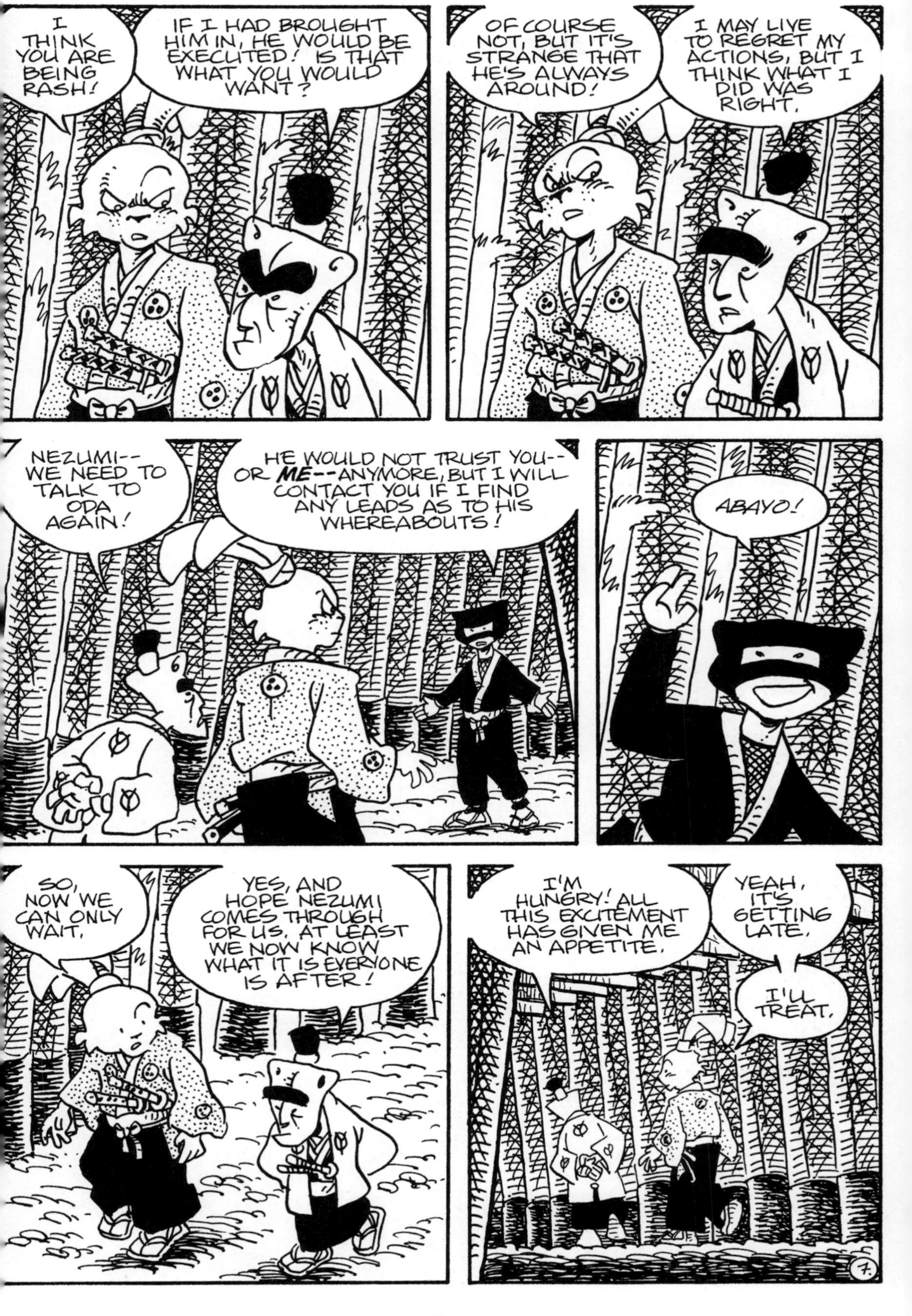
I THINK YOU ARE BEING RASH!
IF I HAD BROUGHT HIM IN, HE WOULD BE EXECUTED! IS THAT WHAT YOU WOULD WANT?
OF COURSE NOT, BUT IT'S STRANGE THAT HE'S ALWAYS AROUND!
I MAY LIVE TO REGRET MY ACTIONS, BUT I THINK WHAT I DID WAS RIGHT.
NEZUMI-- WE NEED TO TALK TO ODA AGAIN!
HE WOULD NOT TRUST YOU-- OR ME--ANYMORE, BUT I WILL CONTACT YOU IF I FIND ANY LEADS AS TO HIS WHEREABOUTS!
ABAYO!
SO, NOW WE CAN ONLY WAIT.
YES, AND HOPE NEZUMI COMES THROUGH FOR US. AT LEAST WE NOW KNOW WHAT IT IS EVERYONE IS AFTER!
I'M HUNGRY! ALL THIS EXCITEMENT HAS GIVEN ME AN APPETITE.
YEAH, IT'S GETTING LATE.
I'LL TREAT.
7.

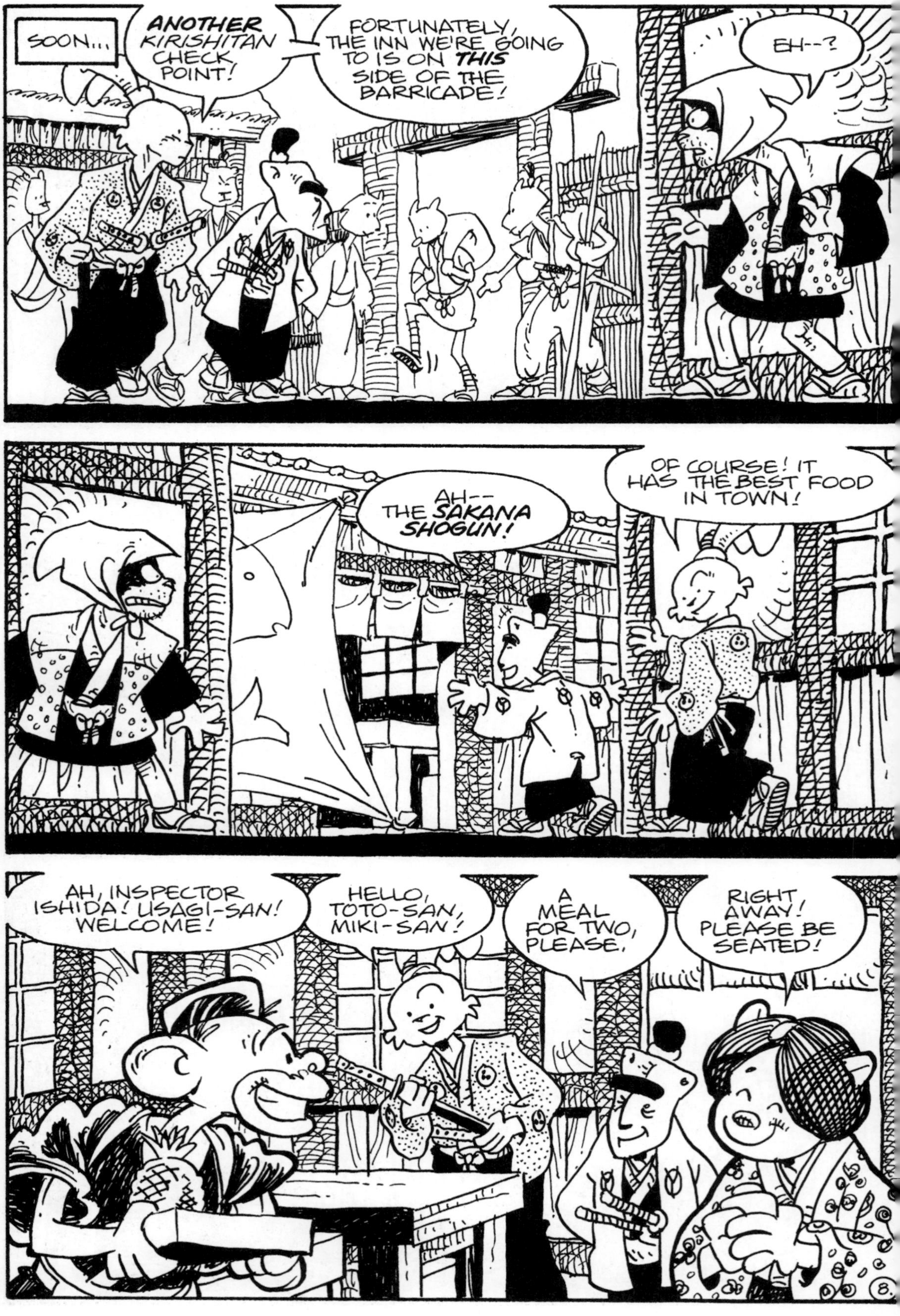
SOON...
ANOTHER KIRISHITAN CHECK POINT!
FORTUNATELY, THE INN WE'RE GOING TO IS ON THIS SIDE OF THE BARRICADE!
EH--?
AH-- THE SAKANA SHOGUN!
OF COURSE! IT HAS THE BEST FOOD IN TOWN!
AH, INSPECTOR ISHIDA! USAGI-SAN! WELCOME!
HELLO, TOTO-SAN, MIKI-SAN!
A MEAL FOR TWO, PLEASE.
RIGHT AWAY! PLEASE BE SEATED!
8.

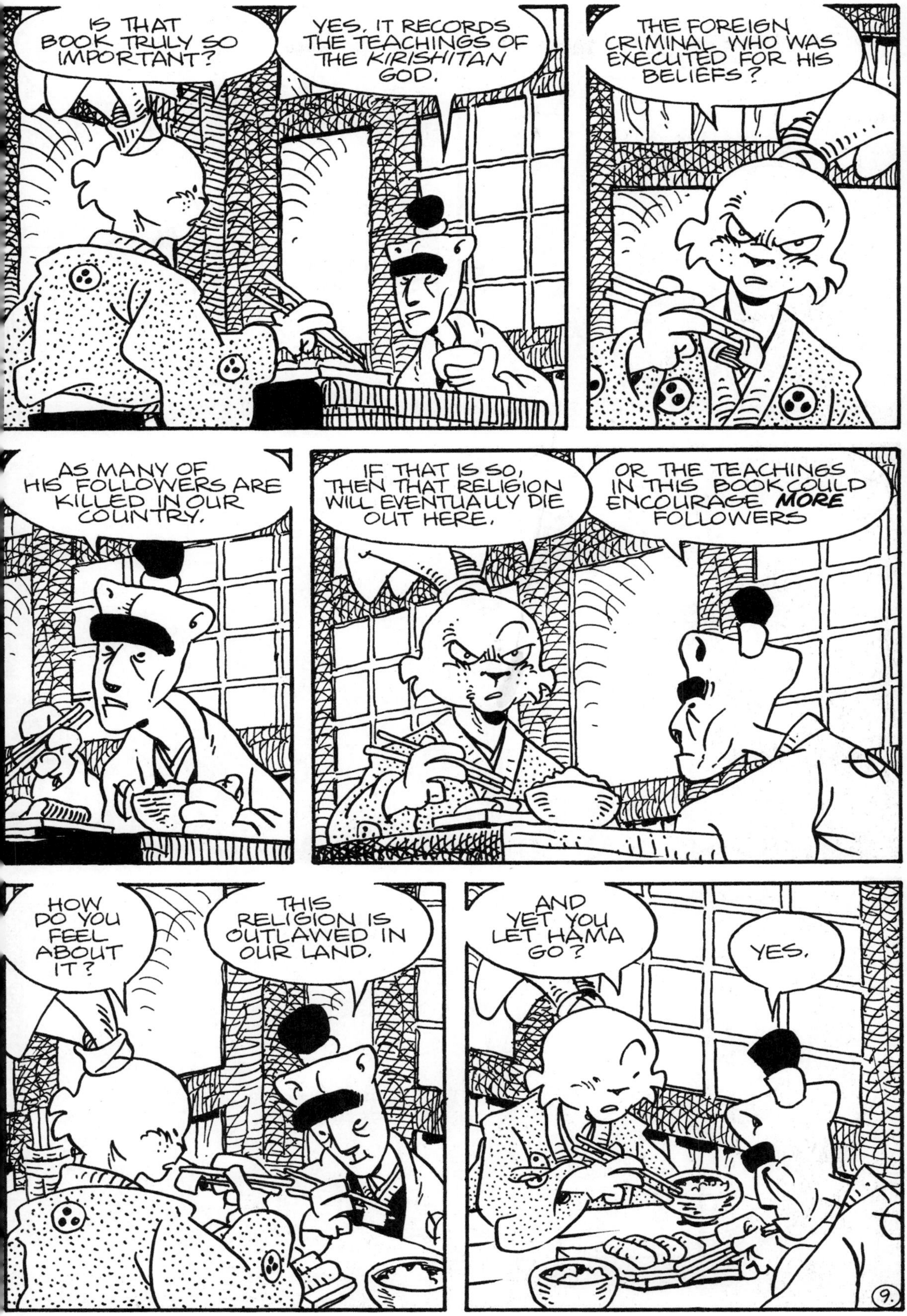

IS THAT BOOK TRULY SO IMPORTANT?
YES. IT RECORDS THE TEACHINGS OF THE *KIRISHITAN* GOD.
THE FOREIGN CRIMINAL WHO WAS EXECUTED FOR HIS BELIEFS?
AS MANY OF HIS FOLLOWERS ARE KILLED IN OUR COUNTRY.
IF THAT IS SO, THEN THAT RELIGION WILL EVENTUALLY DIE OUT HERE.
OR THE TEACHINGS IN THIS BOOK COULD ENCOURAGE ***MORE*** FOLLOWERS
HOW DO YOU FEEL ABOUT IT?
THIS RELIGION IS OUTLAWED IN OUR LAND.
AND YET YOU LET HAMA GO?
YES.
9.

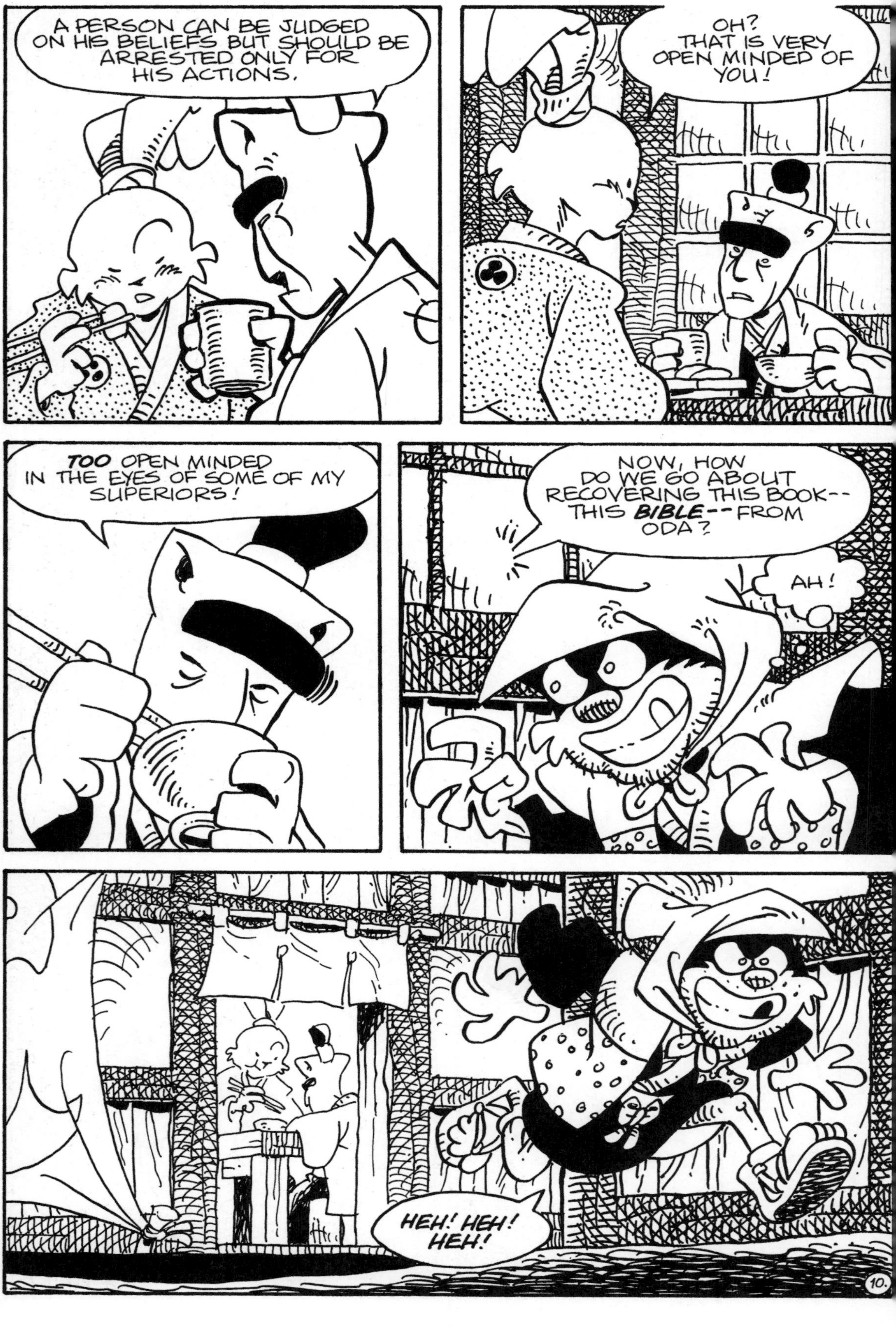
A PERSON CAN BE JUDGED ON HIS BELIEFS BUT SHOULD BE ARRESTED ONLY FOR HIS ACTIONS.
OH? THAT IS VERY OPEN MINDED OF YOU!
TOO OPEN MINDED IN THE EYES OF SOME OF MY SUPERIORS!
NOW, HOW DO WE GO ABOUT RECOVERING THIS BOOK-- THIS BIBLE--FROM ODA?
AH!
HEH! HEH! HEH!
10.

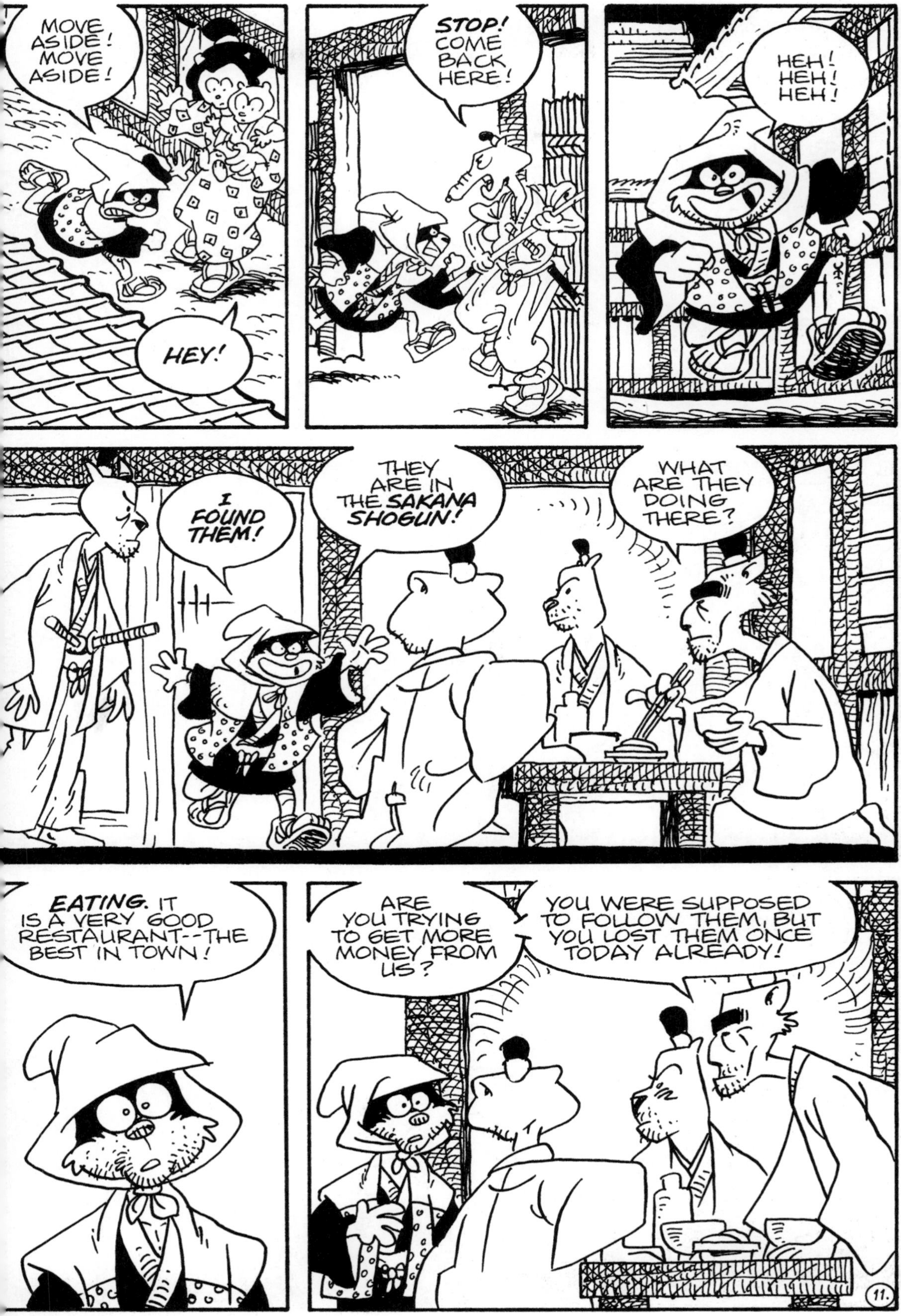
MOVE ASIDE! MOVE ASIDE!
HEY!
STOP! COME BACK HERE!
HEH! HEH! HEH!
I FOUND THEM!
THEY ARE IN THE SAKANA SHOGUN!
WHAT ARE THEY DOING THERE?
EATING. IT IS A VERY GOOD RESTAURANT--THE BEST IN TOWN!
ARE YOU TRYING TO GET MORE MONEY FROM US?
YOU WERE SUPPOSED TO FOLLOW THEM, BUT YOU LOST THEM ONCE TODAY ALREADY!
11.

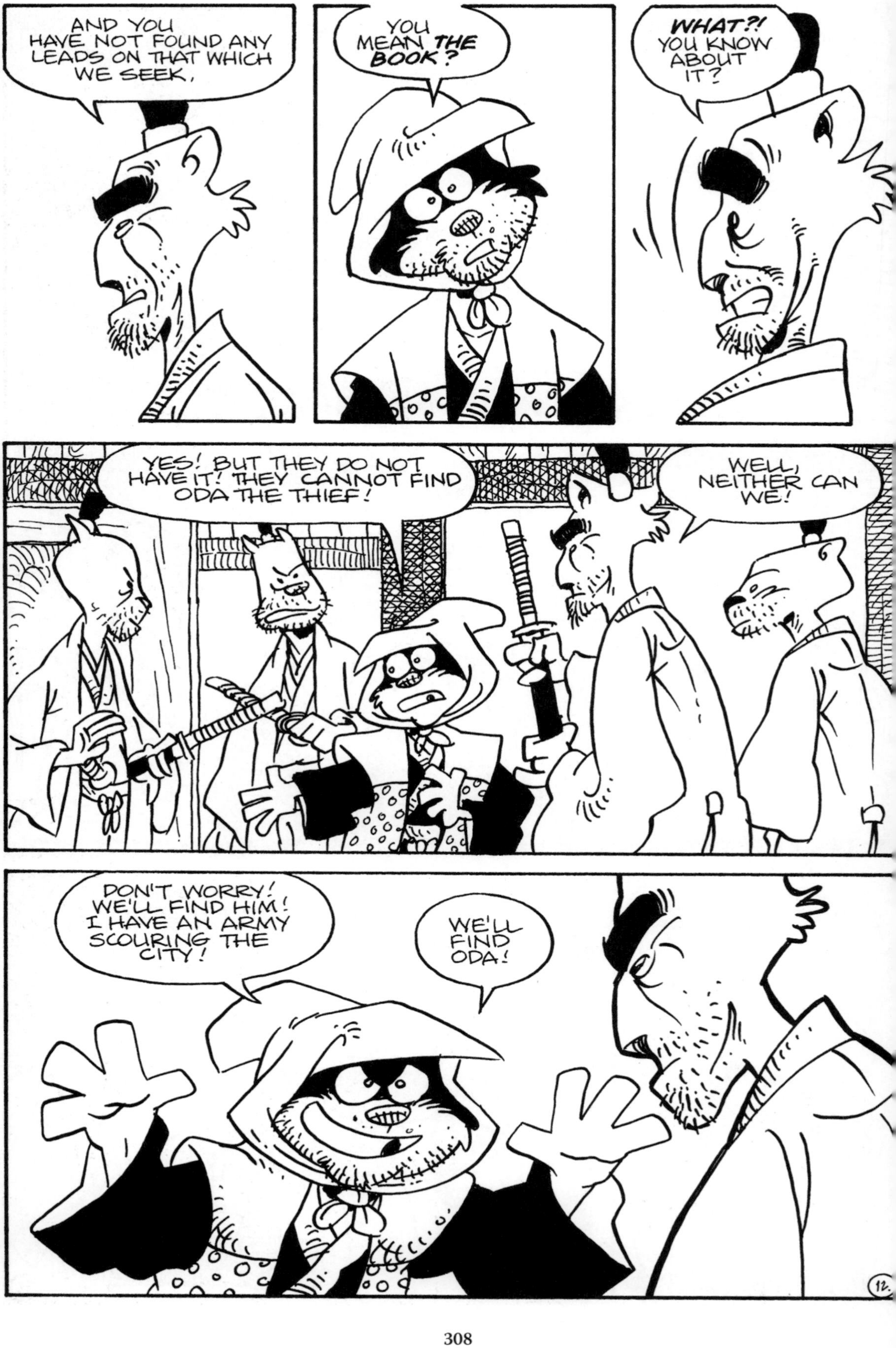
AND YOU HAVE NOT FOUND ANY LEADS ON THAT WHICH WE SEEK,
YOU MEAN THE BOOK?
WHAT?! YOU KNOW ABOUT IT?
YES! BUT THEY DO NOT HAVE IT! THEY CANNOT FIND ODA THE THIEF!
WELL, NEITHER CAN WE!
DON'T WORRY! WE'LL FIND HIM! I HAVE AN ARMY SCOURING THE CITY!
WE'LL FIND ODA!
12.

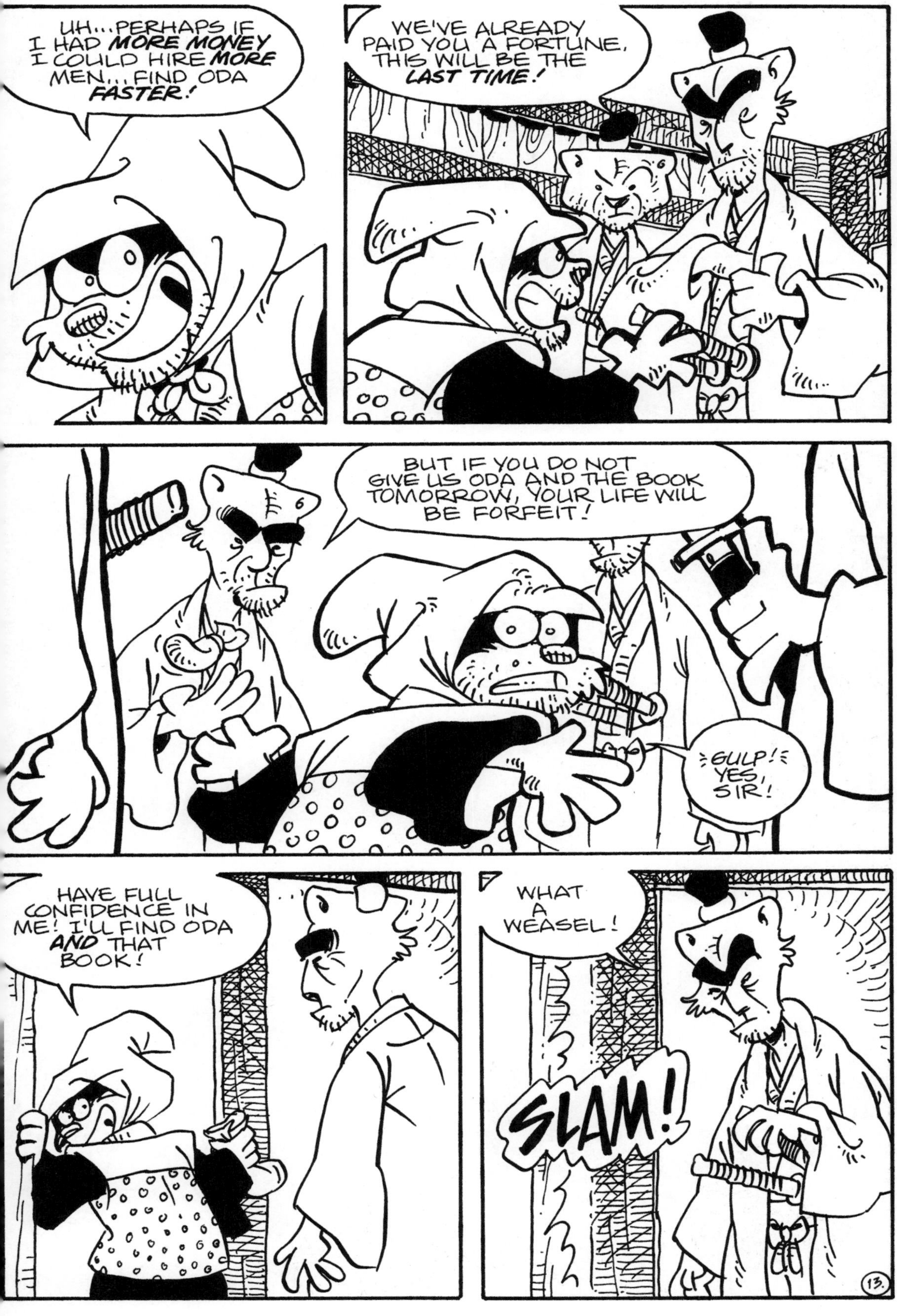
UH...PERHAPS IF I HAD **MORE MONEY** I COULD HIRE **MORE** MEN...FIND ODA **FASTER**!
WE'VE ALREADY PAID YOU A FORTUNE. THIS WILL BE THE **LAST TIME**!
BUT IF YOU DO NOT GIVE US ODA AND THE BOOK TOMORROW, YOUR LIFE WILL BE FORFEIT!
GULP! YES SIR!
HAVE FULL CONFIDENCE IN ME! I'LL FIND ODA **AND** THAT BOOK!
WHAT A WEASEL!
SLAM!
13.

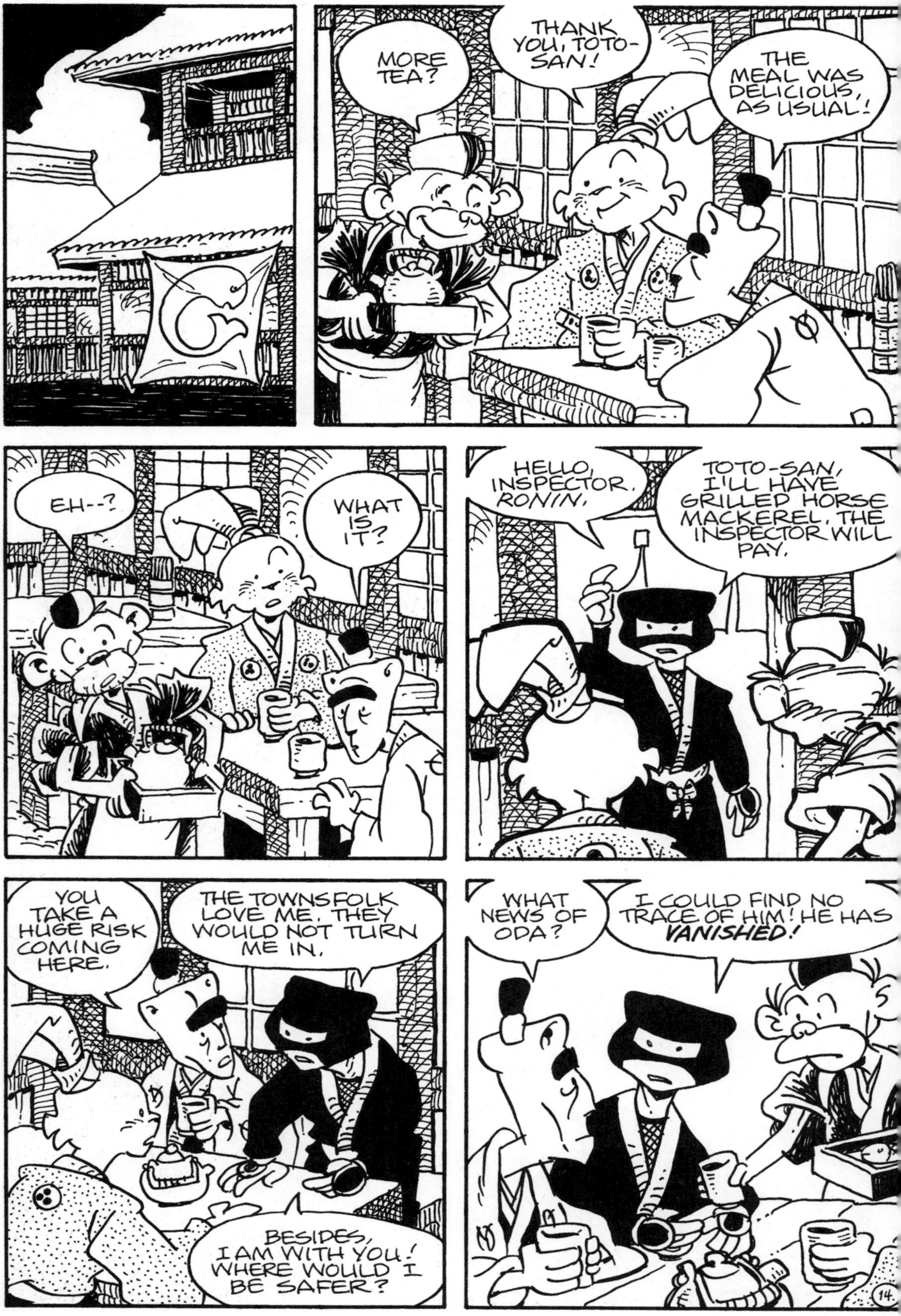
MORE TEA?
THANK YOU, TOTO-SAN!
THE MEAL WAS DELICIOUS, AS USUAL!
EH--?
WHAT IS IT?
HELLO, INSPECTOR RONIN.
TOTO-SAN, I'LL HAVE GRILLED HORSE MACKEREL. THE INSPECTOR WILL PAY.
YOU TAKE A HUGE RISK COMING HERE.
THE TOWNSFOLK LOVE ME. THEY WOULD NOT TURN ME IN.
BESIDES, I AM WITH YOU! WHERE WOULD I BE SAFER?
WHAT NEWS OF ODA?
I COULD FIND NO TRACE OF HIM! HE HAS VANISHED!
14.

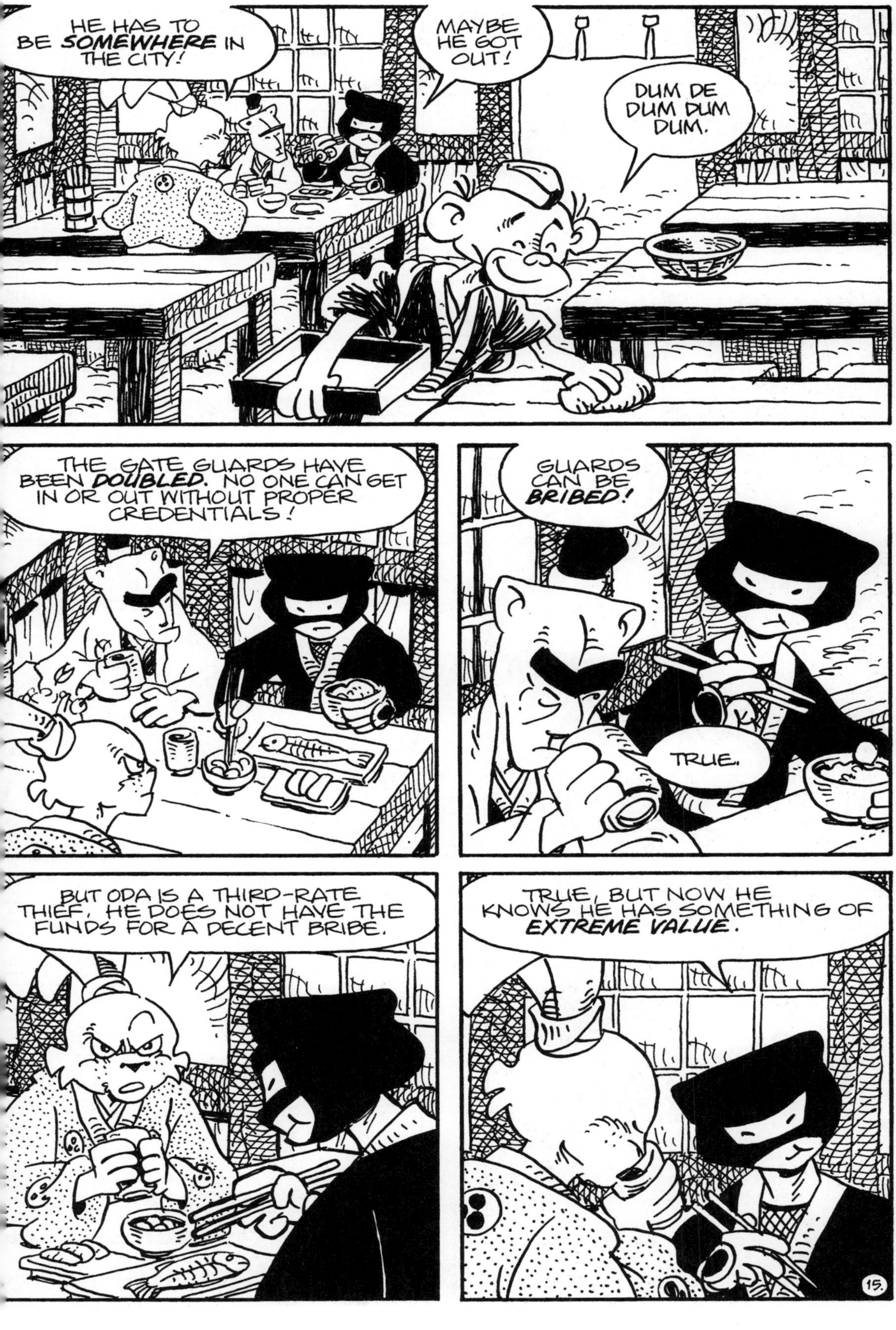
HE HAS TO BE SOMEWHERE IN THE CITY!
MAYBE HE GOT OUT!
DUM DE DUM DUM DUM.
THE GATE GUARDS HAVE BEEN DOUBLED. NO ONE CAN GET IN OR OUT WITHOUT PROPER CREDENTIALS!
GUARDS CAN BE BRIBED!
TRUE.
BUT ODA IS A THIRD-RATE THIEF, HE DOES NOT HAVE THE FUNDS FOR A DECENT BRIBE.
TRUE, BUT NOW HE KNOWS HE HAS SOMETHING OF EXTREME VALUE.
15.

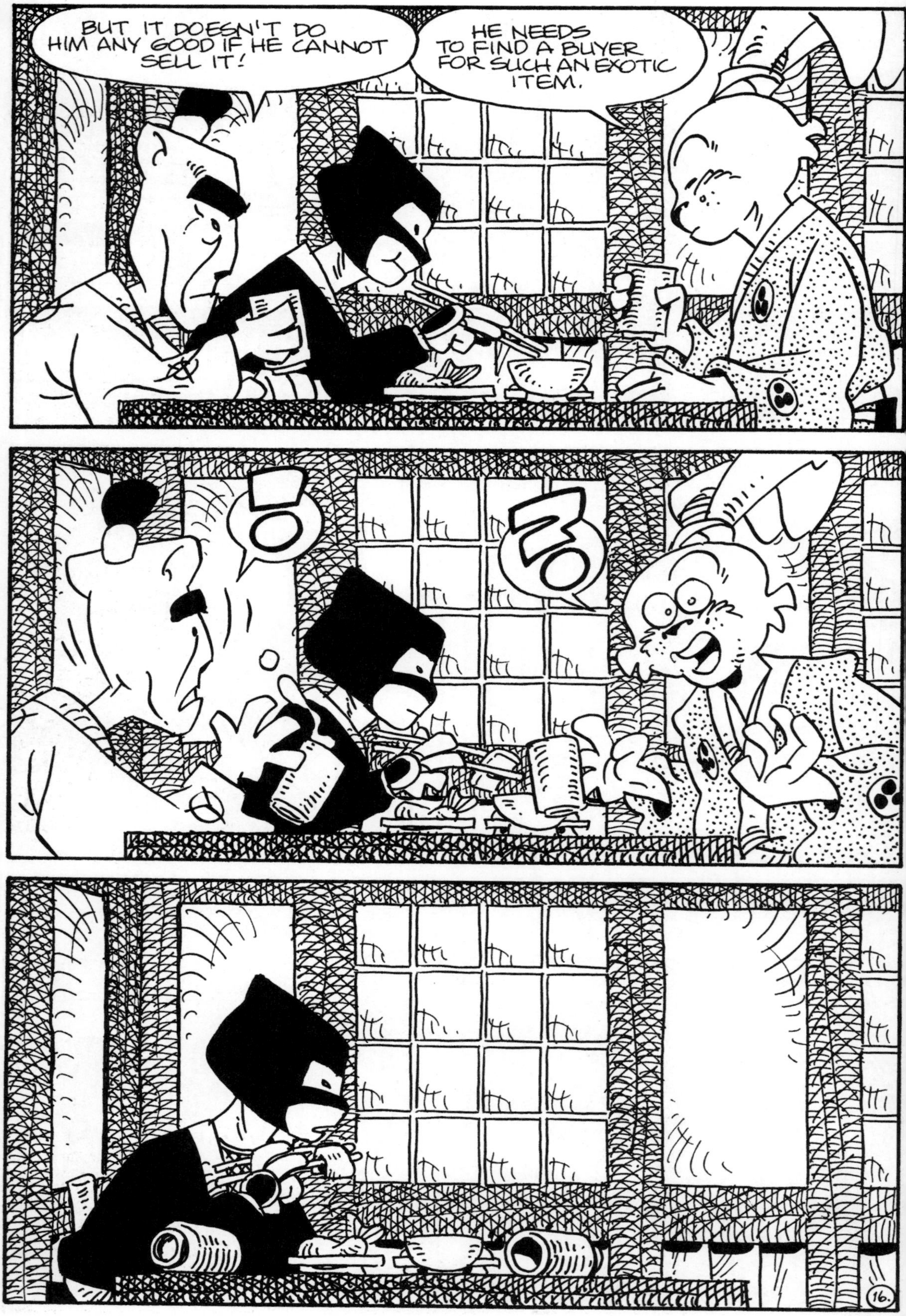
BUT IT DOESN'T DO HIM ANY GOOD IF HE CANNOT SELL IT!
HE NEEDS TO FIND A BUYER FOR SUCH AN EXOTIC ITEM.
!
?!
16.

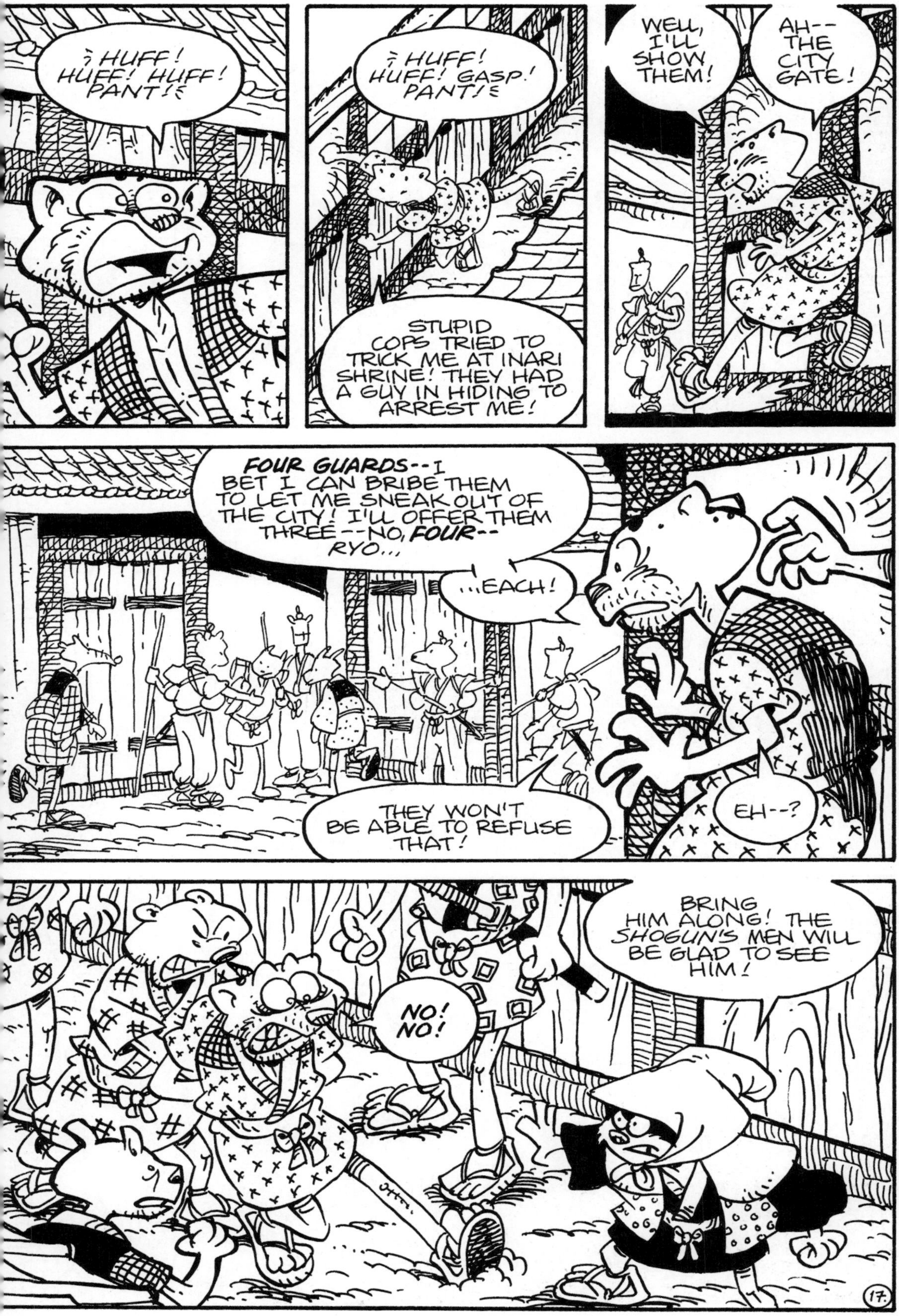
HUFF! HUFF! HUFF! PANT!
HUFF! HUFF! GASP! PANT!
STUPID COPS TRIED TO TRICK ME AT INARI SHRINE! THEY HAD A GUY IN HIDING TO ARREST ME!
WELL, I'LL SHOW THEM!
AH-- THE CITY GATE!
FOUR GUARDS--I BET I CAN BRIBE THEM TO LET ME SNEAK OUT OF THE CITY! I'LL OFFER THEM THREE--NO, FOUR--RYO...,
...EACH!
THEY WON'T BE ABLE TO REFUSE THAT!
EH--?
NO! NO!
BRING HIM ALONG! THE SHOGUN'S MEN WILL BE GLAD TO SEE HIM!
17.

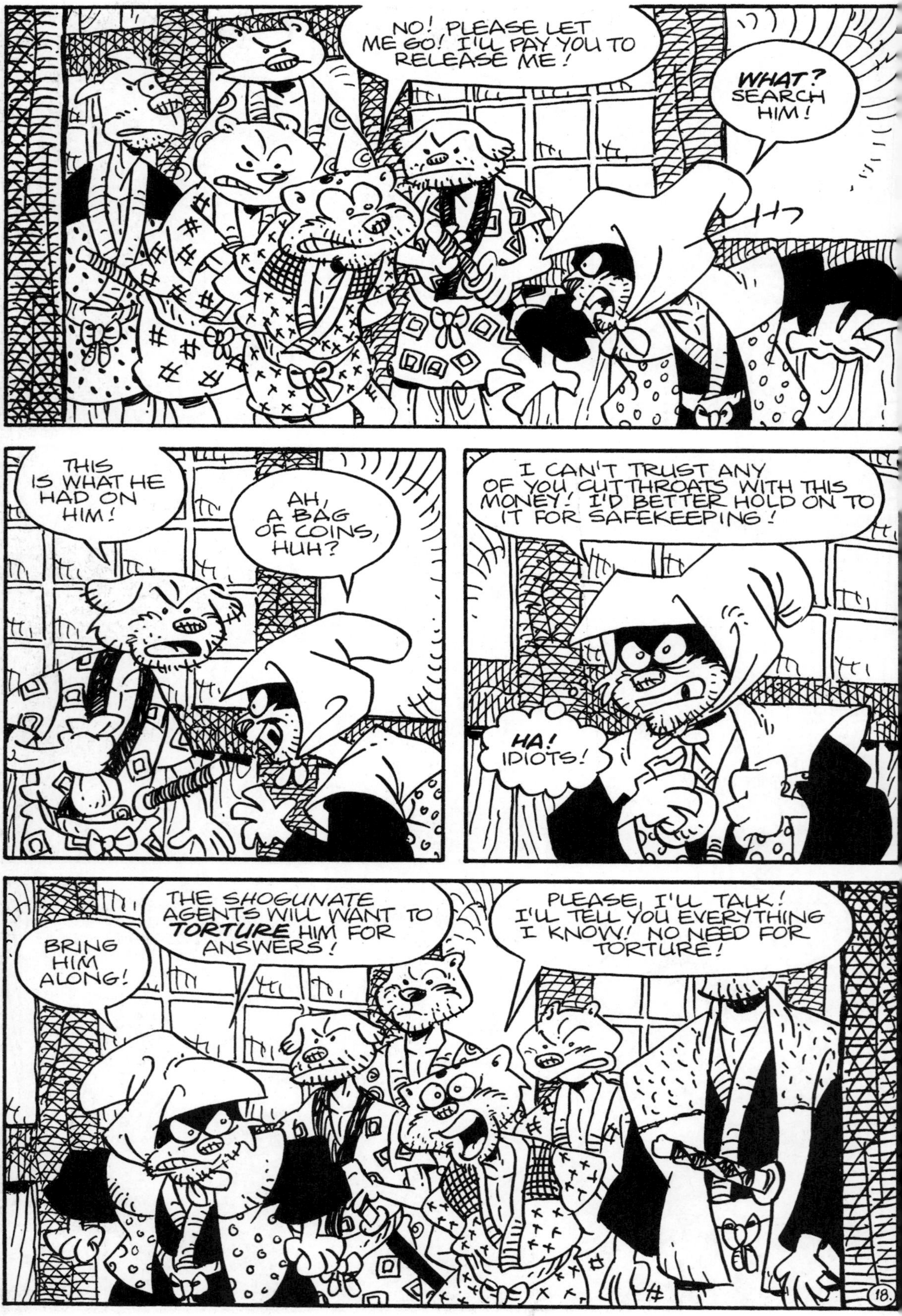
NO! PLEASE LET ME GO! I'LL PAY YOU TO RELEASE ME!
WHAT? SEARCH HIM!
THIS IS WHAT HE HAD ON HIM!
AH, A BAG OF COINS, HUH?
I CAN'T TRUST ANY OF YOU CUTTHROATS WITH THIS MONEY! I'D BETTER HOLD ON TO IT FOR SAFEKEEPING!
HA! IDIOTS!
BRING HIM ALONG!
THE SHOGUNATE AGENTS WILL WANT TO TORTURE HIM FOR ANSWERS!
PLEASE, I'LL TALK! I'LL TELL YOU EVERYTHING I KNOW! NO NEED FOR TORTURE!
18.

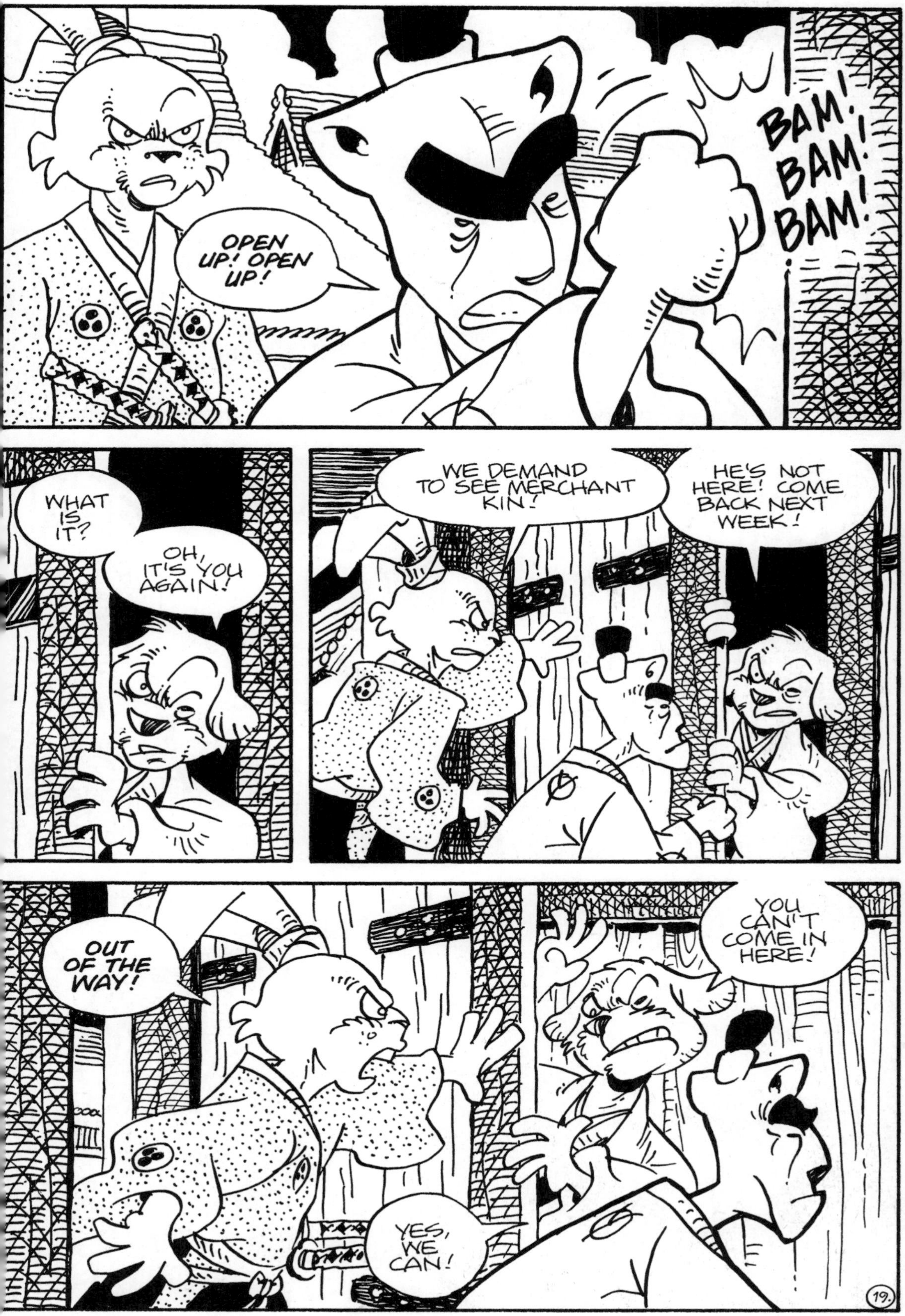
BAM! BAM! BAM!
OPEN UP! OPEN UP!
WHAT IS IT?
OH, IT'S YOU AGAIN!
WE DEMAND TO SEE MERCHANT KIN!
HE'S NOT HERE! COME BACK NEXT WEEK!
OUT OF THE WAY!
YOU CAN'T COME IN HERE!
YES, WE CAN!
19.

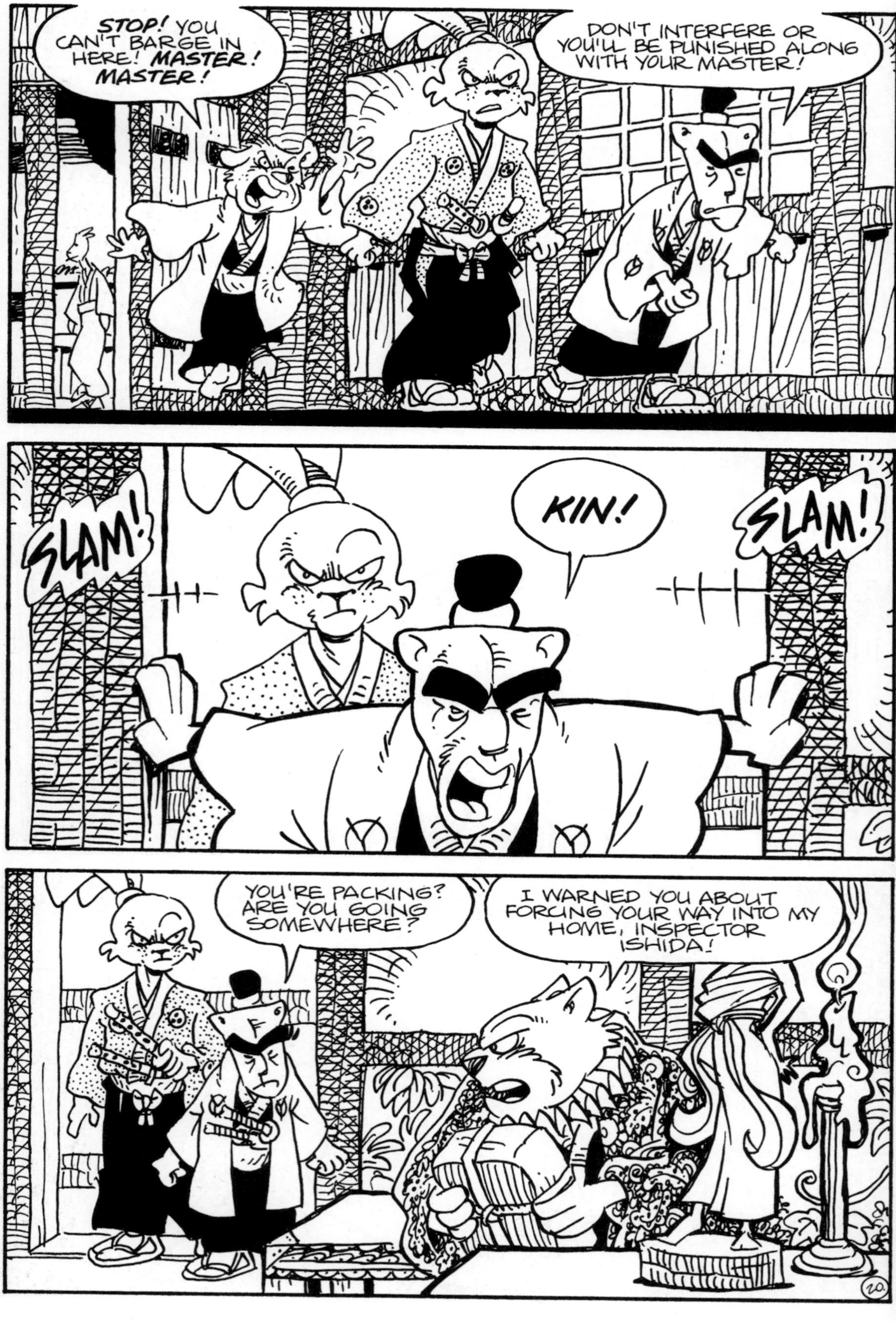
STOP! YOU CAN'T BARGE IN HERE! MASTER! MASTER!
DON'T INTERFERE OR YOU'LL BE PUNISHED ALONG WITH YOUR MASTER!
SLAM!
KIN!
SLAM!
YOU'RE PACKING? ARE YOU GOING SOMEWHERE?
I WARNED YOU ABOUT FORCING YOUR WAY INTO MY HOME, INSPECTOR ISHIDA!
20.

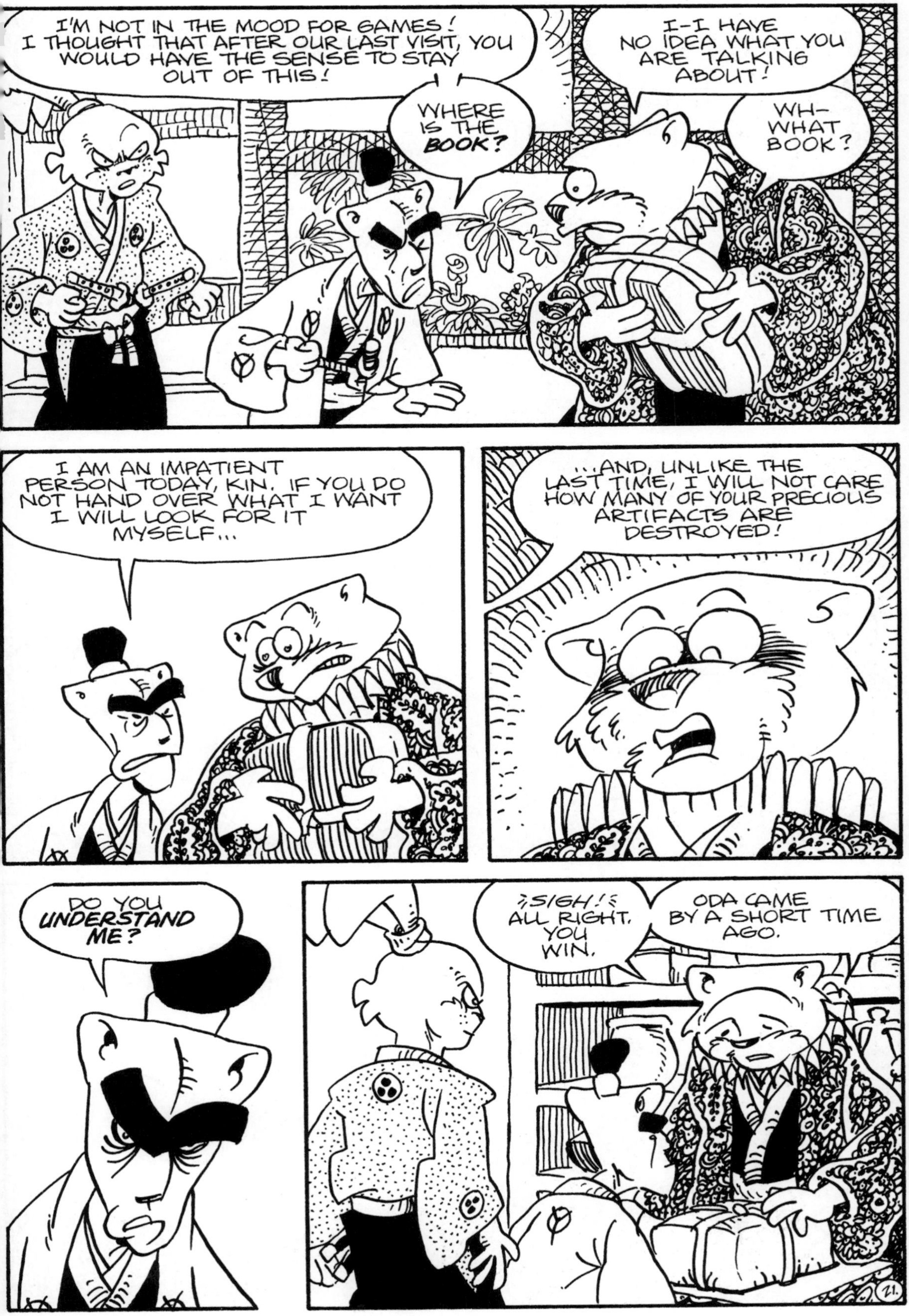
I'M NOT IN THE MOOD FOR GAMES! I THOUGHT THAT AFTER OUR LAST VISIT, YOU WOULD HAVE THE SENSE TO STAY OUT OF THIS!
WHERE IS THE *BOOK*?
I-I HAVE NO IDEA WHAT YOU ARE TALKING ABOUT!
WH-WHAT BOOK?
I AM AN IMPATIENT PERSON TODAY, KIN. IF YOU DO NOT HAND OVER WHAT I WANT I WILL LOOK FOR IT MYSELF...
...AND, UNLIKE THE LAST TIME, I WILL NOT CARE HOW MANY OF YOUR PRECIOUS ARTIFACTS ARE DESTROYED!
DO YOU *UNDERSTAND* ME?
SIGH! ALL RIGHT. YOU WIN.
ODA CAME BY A SHORT TIME AGO.
21.

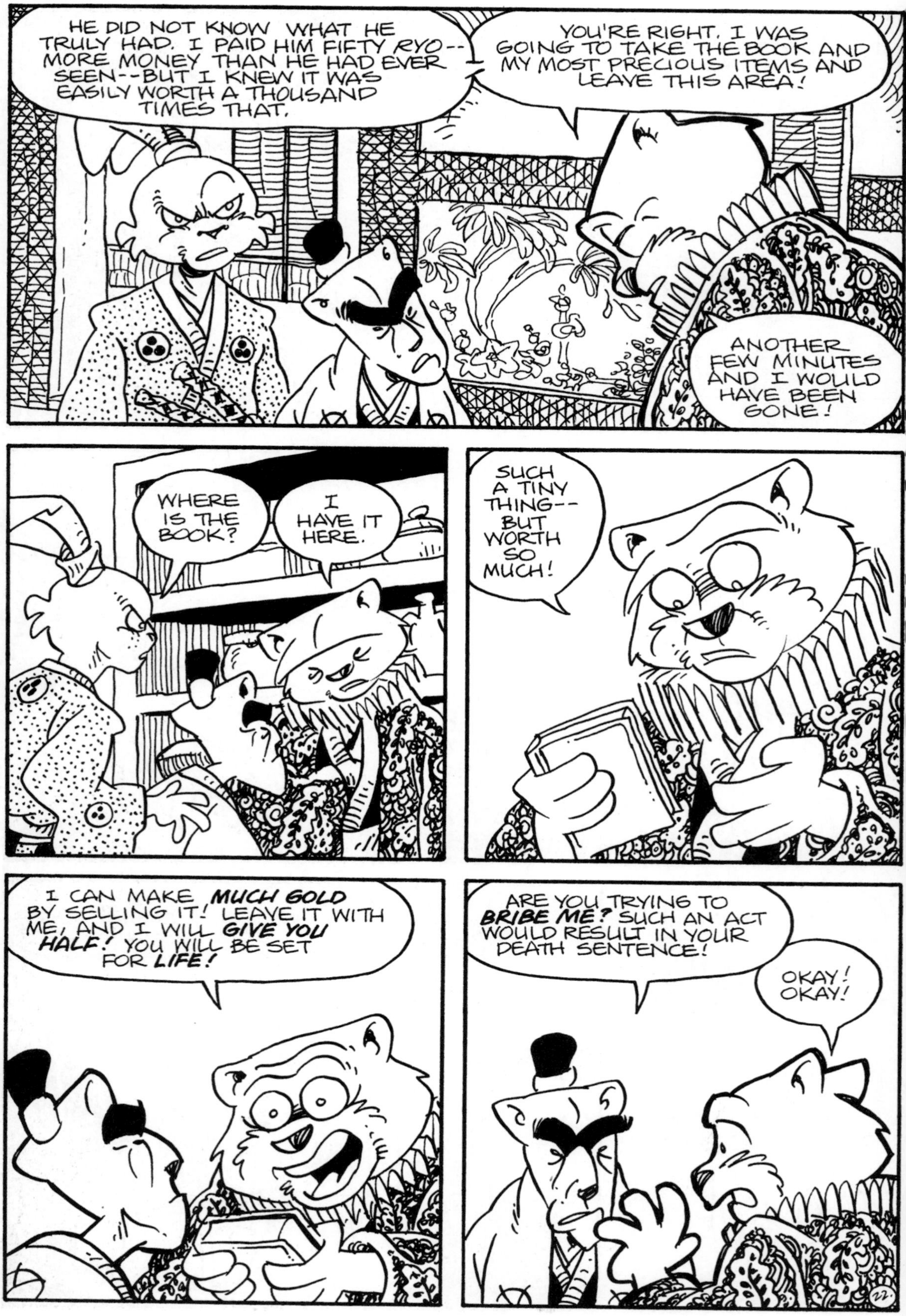

HE DID NOT KNOW WHAT HE TRULY HAD. I PAID HIM FIFTY RYO--MORE MONEY THAN HE HAD EVER SEEN--BUT I KNEW IT WAS EASILY WORTH A THOUSAND TIMES THAT.
YOU'RE RIGHT. I WAS GOING TO TAKE THE BOOK AND MY MOST PRECIOUS ITEMS AND LEAVE THIS AREA!
ANOTHER FEW MINUTES AND I WOULD HAVE BEEN GONE!
WHERE IS THE BOOK?
I HAVE IT HERE.
SUCH A TINY THING--BUT WORTH SO MUCH!
I CAN MAKE MUCH GOLD BY SELLING IT! LEAVE IT WITH ME, AND I WILL GIVE YOU HALF! YOU WILL BE SET FOR LIFE!
ARE YOU TRYING TO BRIBE ME? SUCH AN ACT WOULD RESULT IN YOUR DEATH SENTENCE!
OKAY! OKAY!
22.

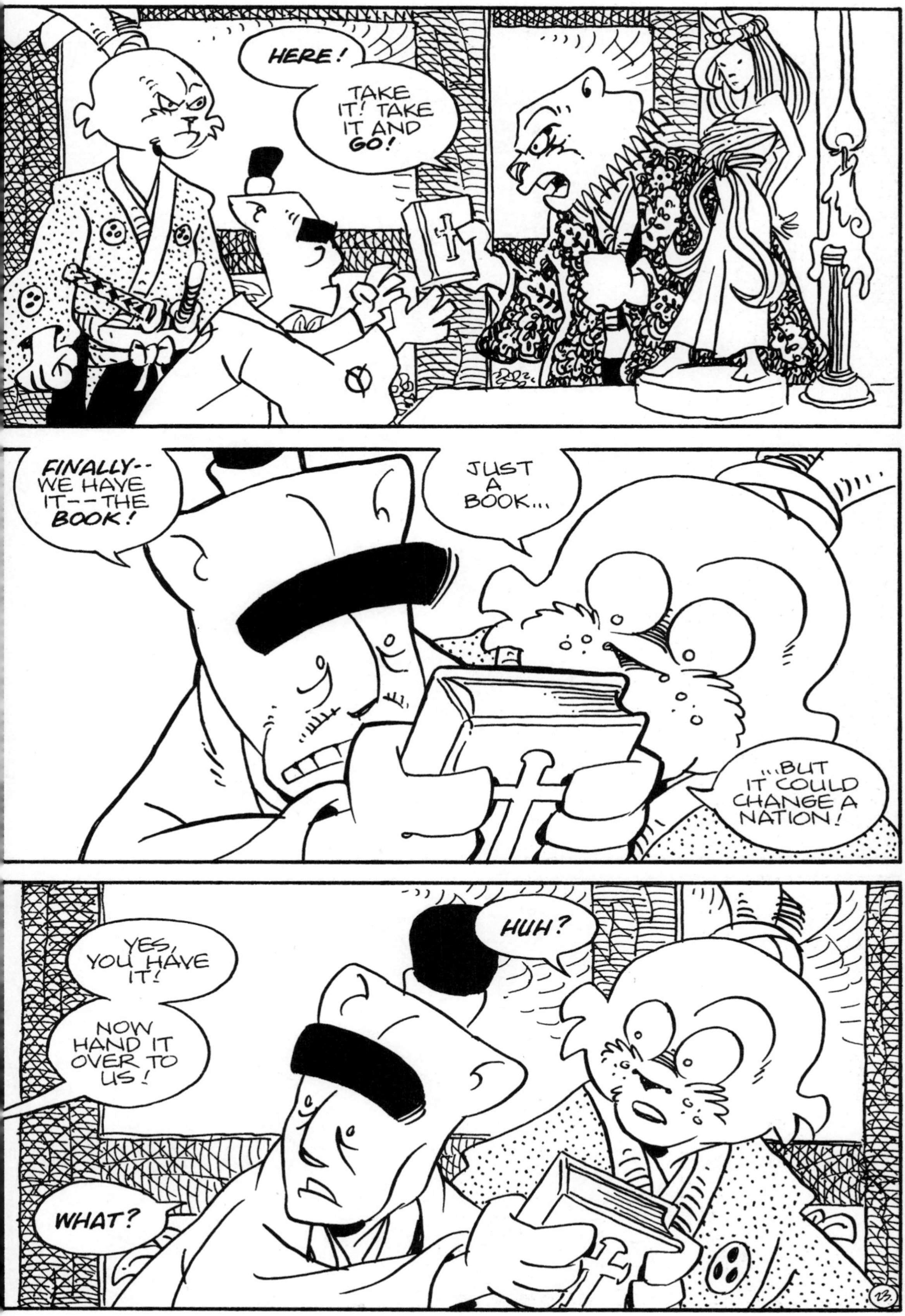
HERE!
TAKE IT! TAKE IT AND GO!
FINALLY-- WE HAVE IT--THE BOOK!
JUST A BOOK...
...BUT IT COULD CHANGE A NATION!
YES, YOU HAVE IT!
NOW HAND IT OVER TO US!
HUH?
WHAT?

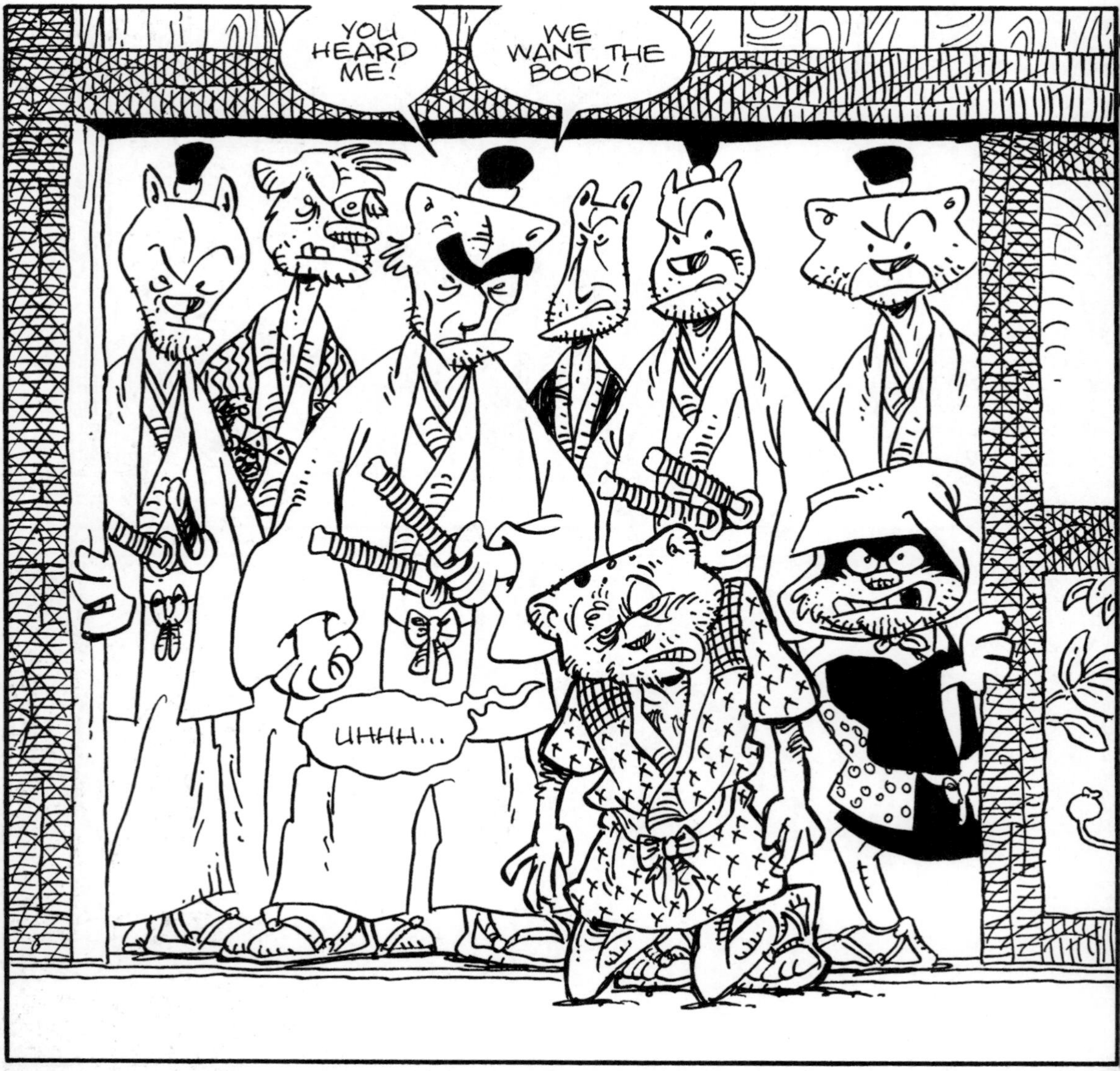
YOU HEARD ME!
WE WANT THE BOOK!
UHHH...

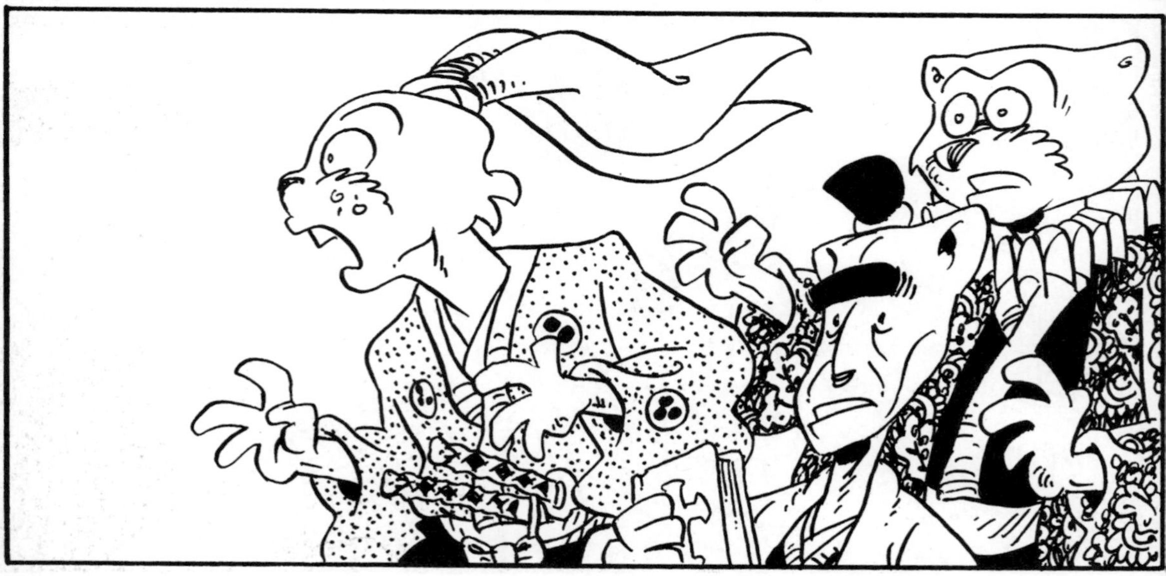

THE HIDDEN PART SEVEN

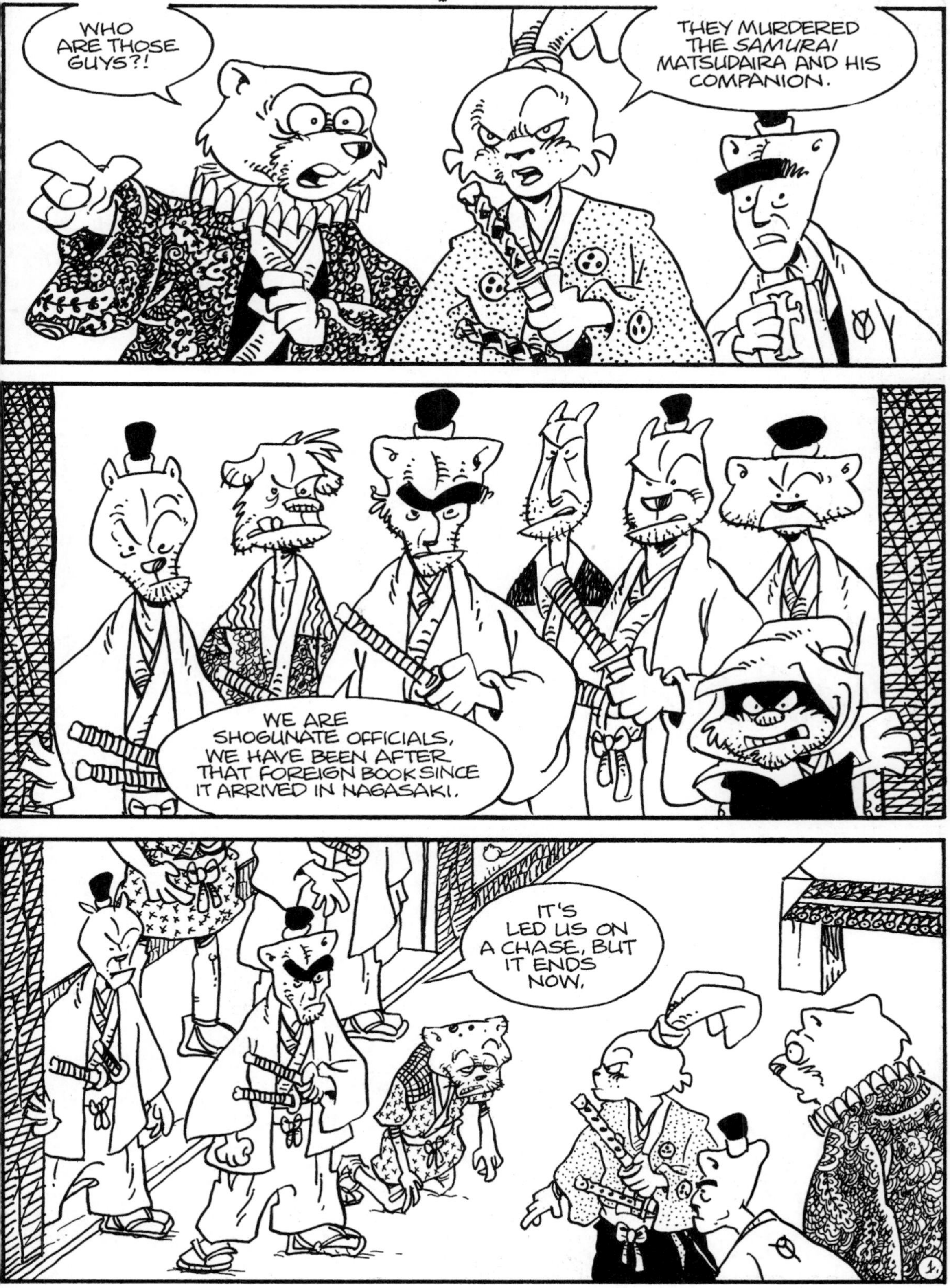
WHO ARE THOSE GUYS?!
THEY MURDERED THE SAMURAI MATSUDAIRA AND HIS COMPANION.
WE ARE SHOGUNATE OFFICIALS, WE HAVE BEEN AFTER THAT FOREIGN BOOK SINCE IT ARRIVED IN NAGASAKI.
IT'S LED US ON A CHASE, BUT IT ENDS NOW.
1.

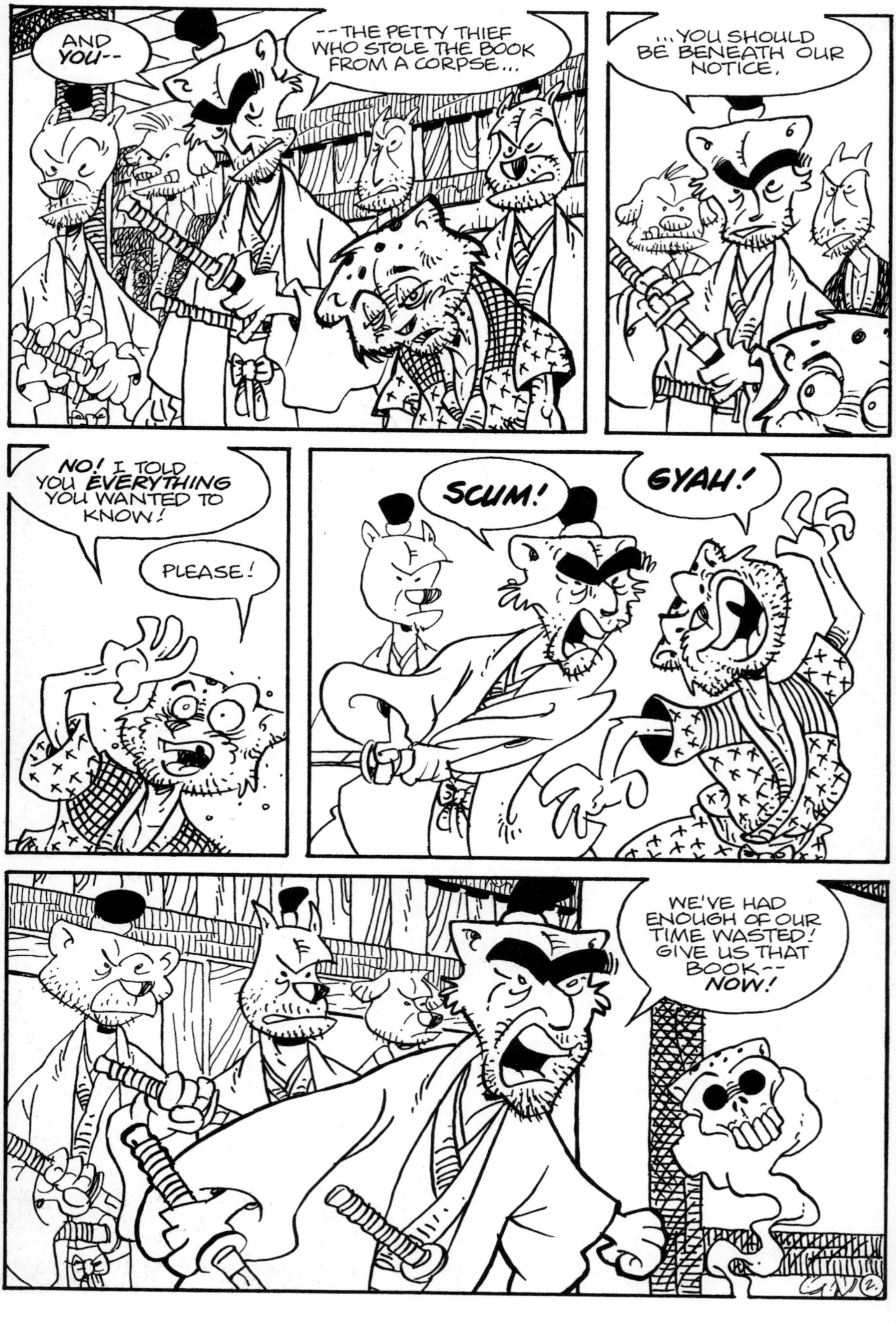
AND YOU--
--THE PETTY THIEF WHO STOLE THE BOOK FROM A CORPSE...
...YOU SHOULD BE BENEATH OUR NOTICE.
NO! I TOLD YOU EVERYTHING YOU WANTED TO KNOW!
PLEASE!
SCUM!
GYAH!
WE'VE HAD ENOUGH OF OUR TIME WASTED! GIVE US THAT BOOK-- NOW!

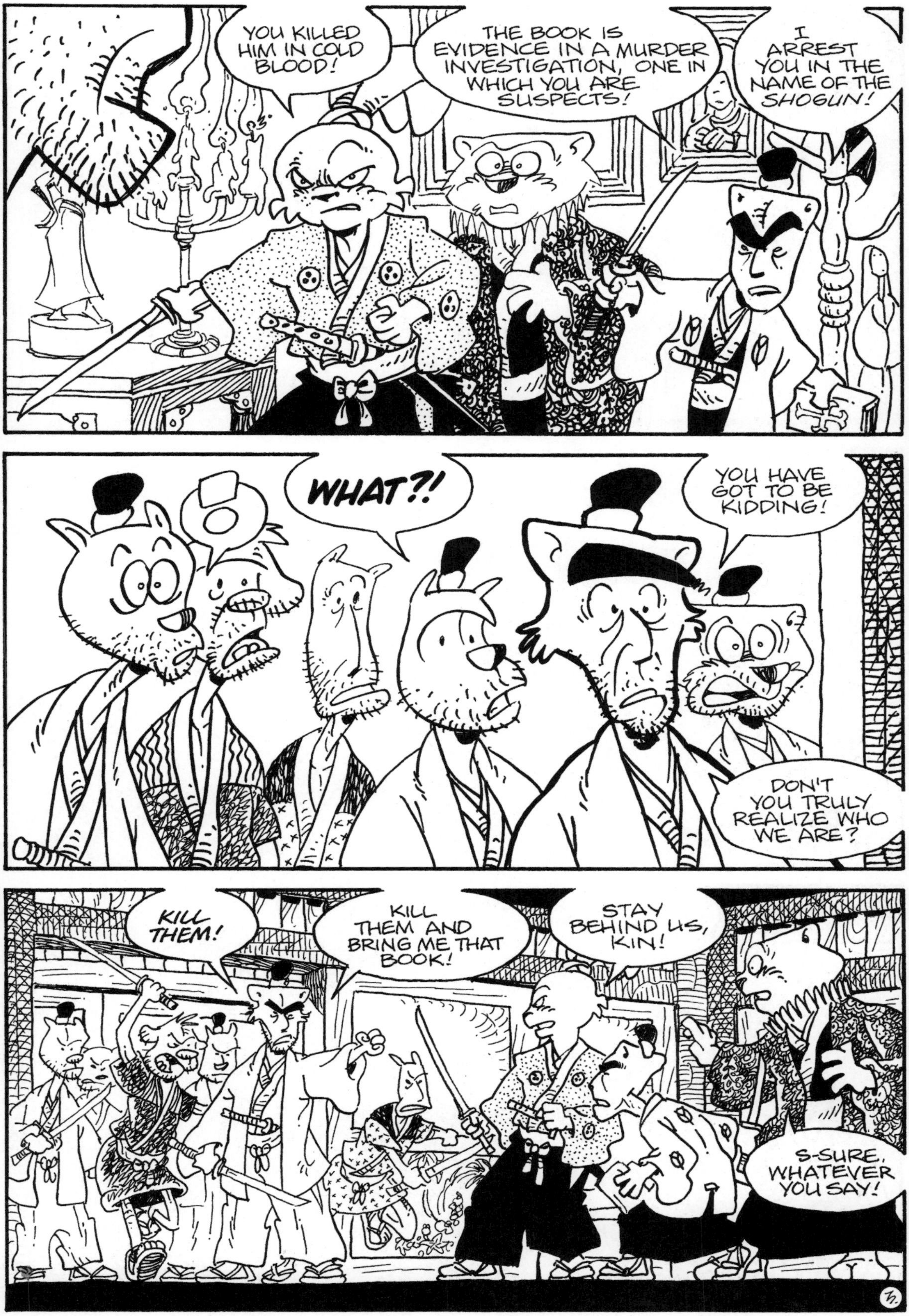
YOU KILLED HIM IN COLD BLOOD!
THE BOOK IS EVIDENCE IN A MURDER INVESTIGATION, ONE IN WHICH YOU ARE SUSPECTS!
I ARREST YOU IN THE NAME OF THE *SHOGUN*!
WHAT?!
YOU HAVE GOT TO BE KIDDING!
DON'T YOU TRULY REALIZE WHO WE ARE?
KILL THEM!
KILL THEM AND BRING ME THAT BOOK!
STAY BEHIND US, KIN!
S-SURE. WHATEVER YOU SAY!

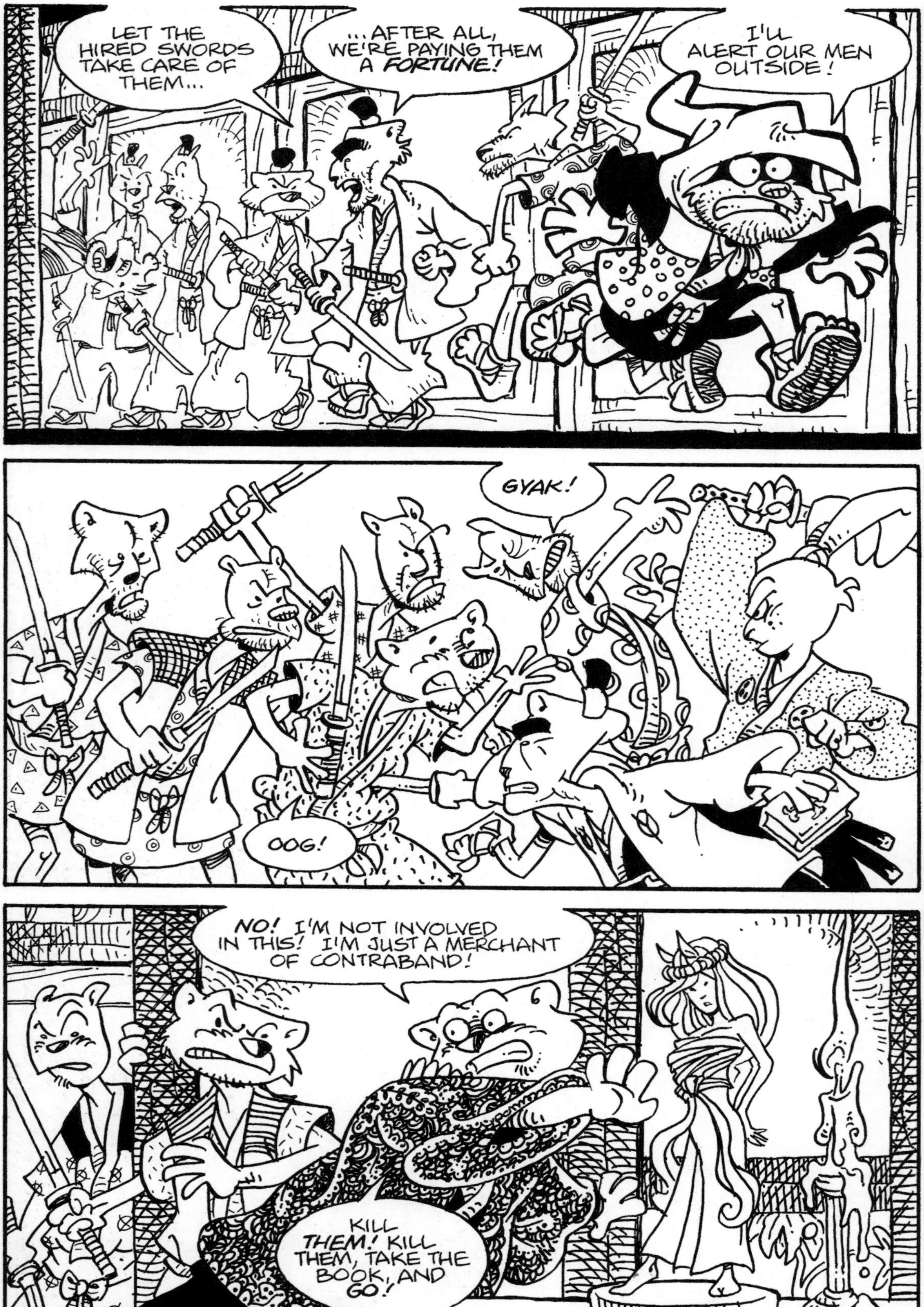
LET THE HIRED SWORDS TAKE CARE OF THEM...
...AFTER ALL, WE'RE PAYING THEM A FORTUNE!
I'LL ALERT OUR MEN OUTSIDE!
GYAK!
OOG!
NO! I'M NOT INVOLVED IN THIS! I'M JUST A MERCHANT OF CONTRABAND!
KILL THEM! KILL THEM, TAKE THE BOOK, AND GO!
4.

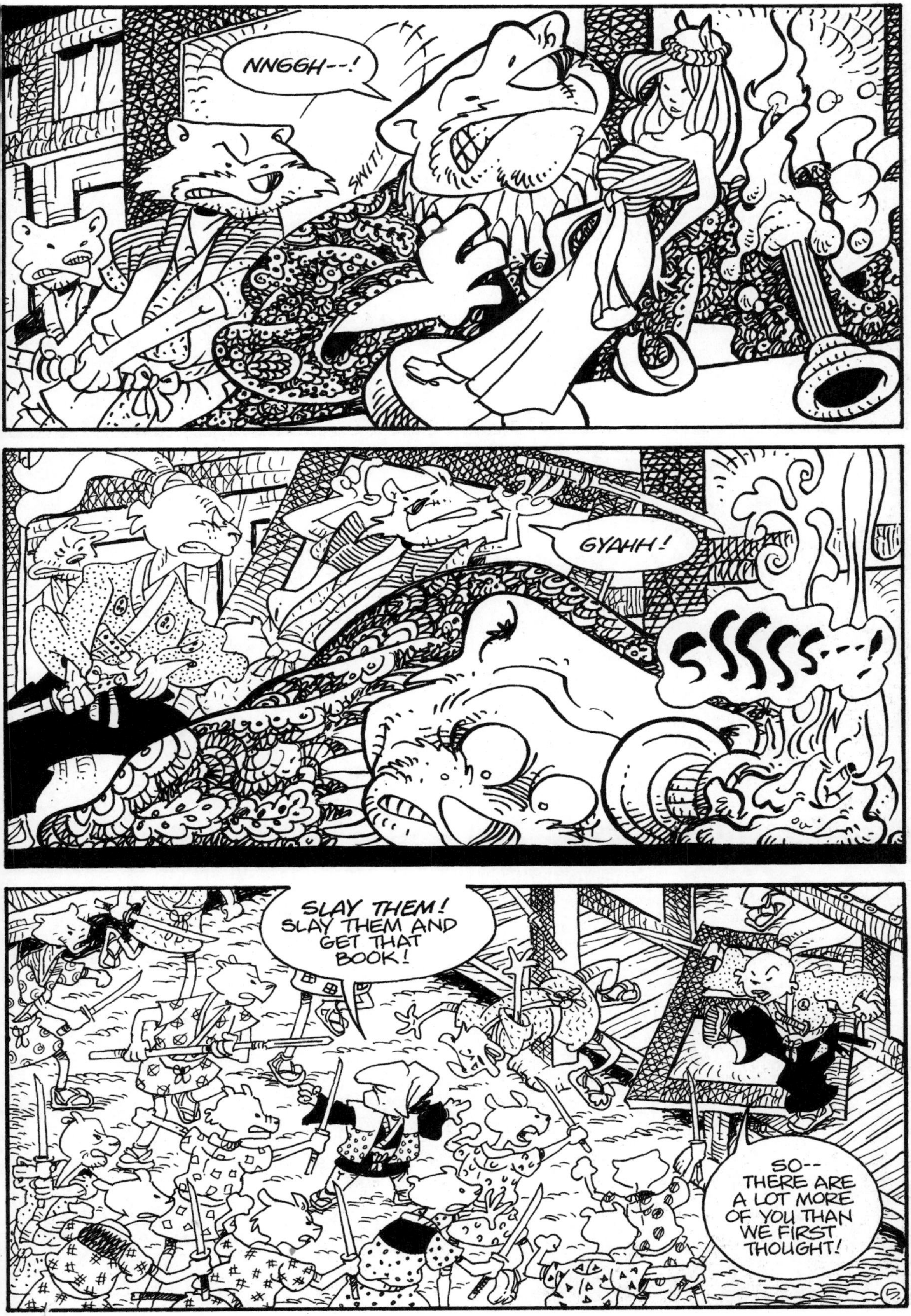
NNGGH--!
SWIT!
GYAHH!
SSSSS---!
SLAY THEM! SLAY THEM AND GET THAT BOOK!
SO-- THERE ARE A LOT MORE OF YOU THAN WE FIRST THOUGHT!

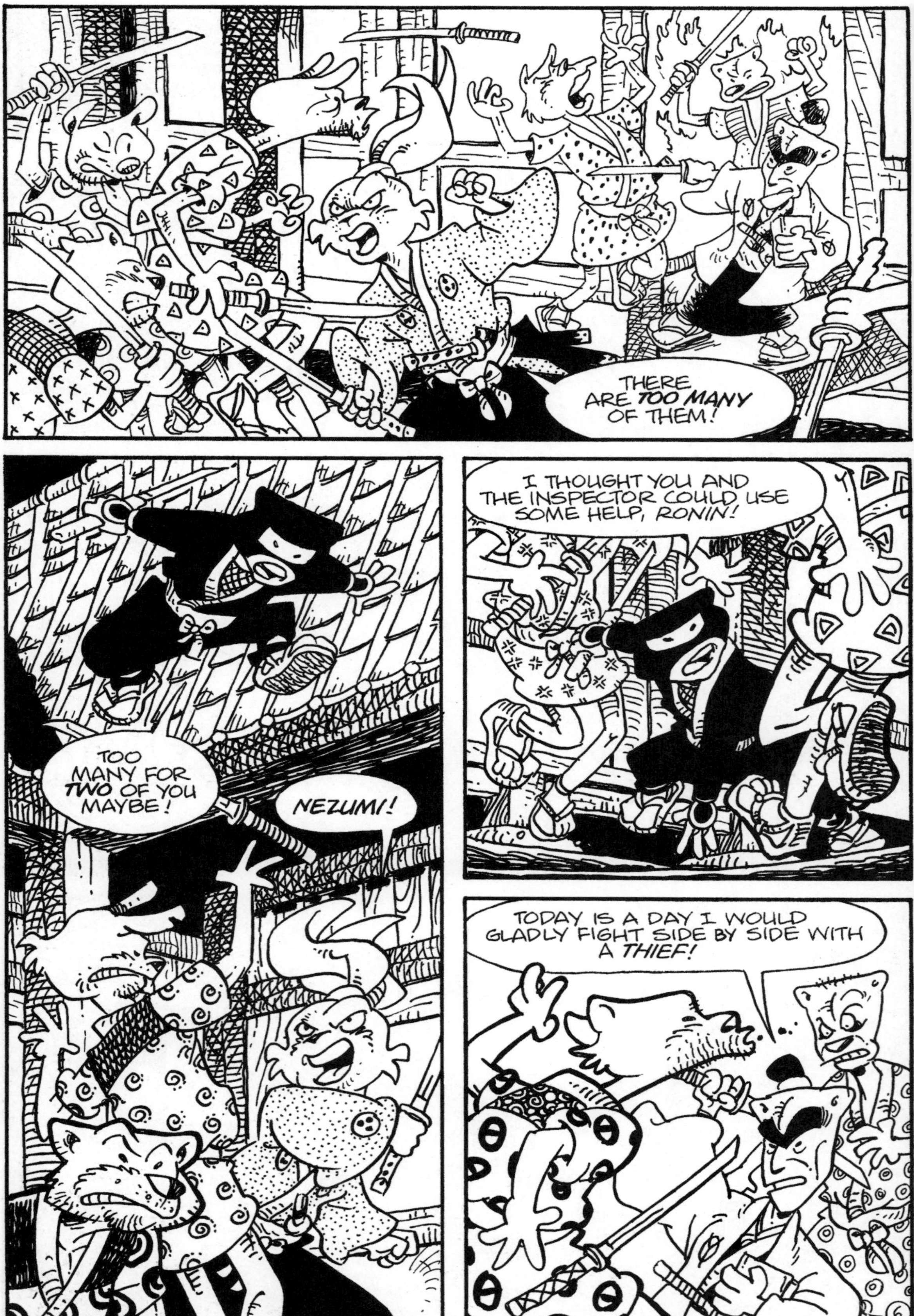
THERE ARE *TOO MANY* OF THEM!
TOO MANY FOR *TWO* OF YOU MAYBE!
NEZUMI!
I THOUGHT YOU AND THE INSPECTOR COULD USE SOME HELP, *RONIN!*
TODAY IS A DAY I WOULD GLADLY FIGHT SIDE BY SIDE WITH A *THIEF!*
6.

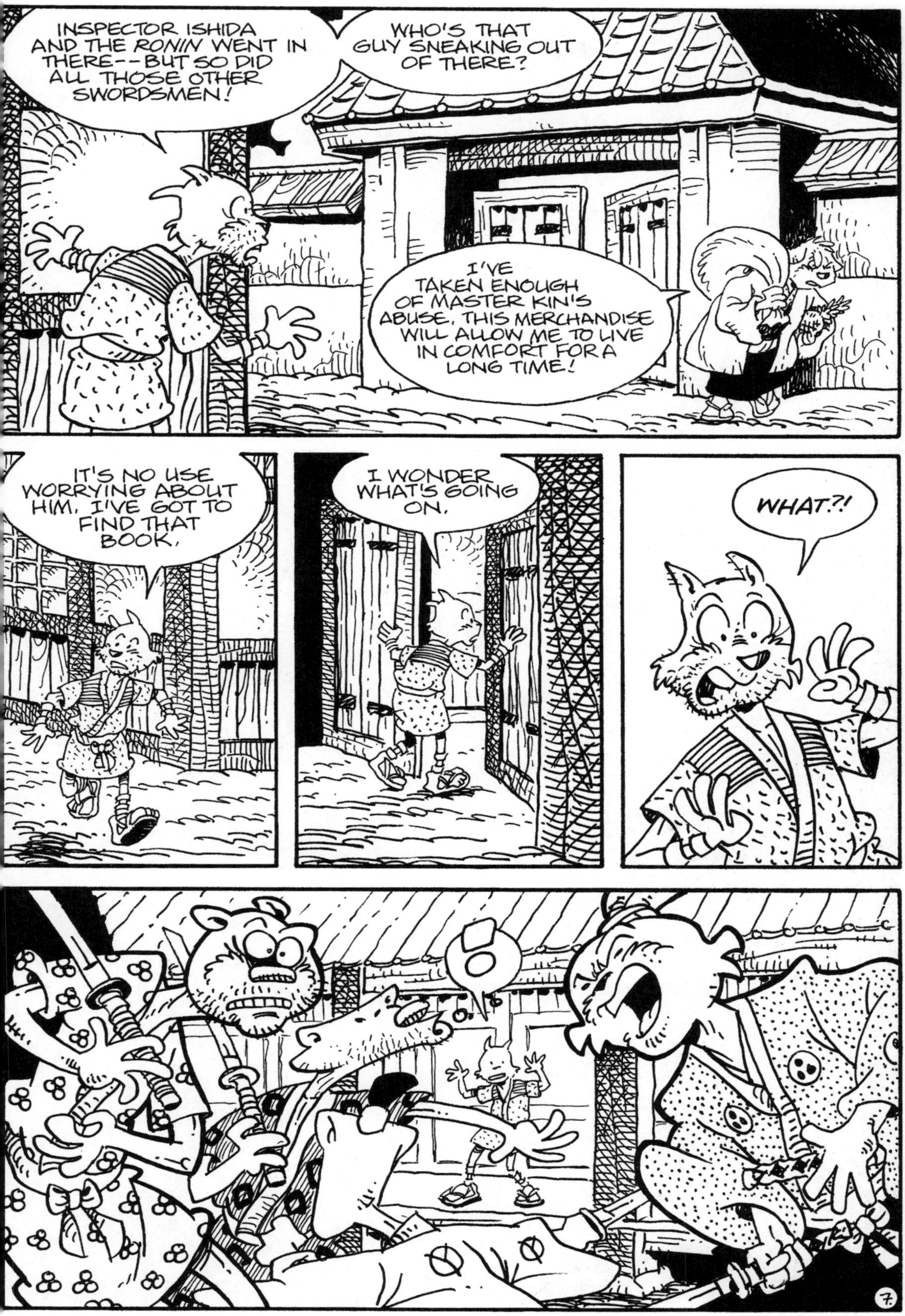
INSPECTOR ISHIDA AND THE *RONIN* WENT IN THERE--BUT SO DID ALL THOSE OTHER SWORDSMEN!
WHO'S THAT GUY SNEAKING OUT OF THERE?
I'VE TAKEN ENOUGH OF MASTER KIN'S ABUSE. THIS MERCHANDISE WILL ALLOW ME TO LIVE IN COMFORT FOR A LONG TIME!
IT'S NO USE WORRYING ABOUT HIM. I'VE GOT TO FIND THAT BOOK.
I WONDER WHAT'S GOING ON.
WHAT?!
!
7.

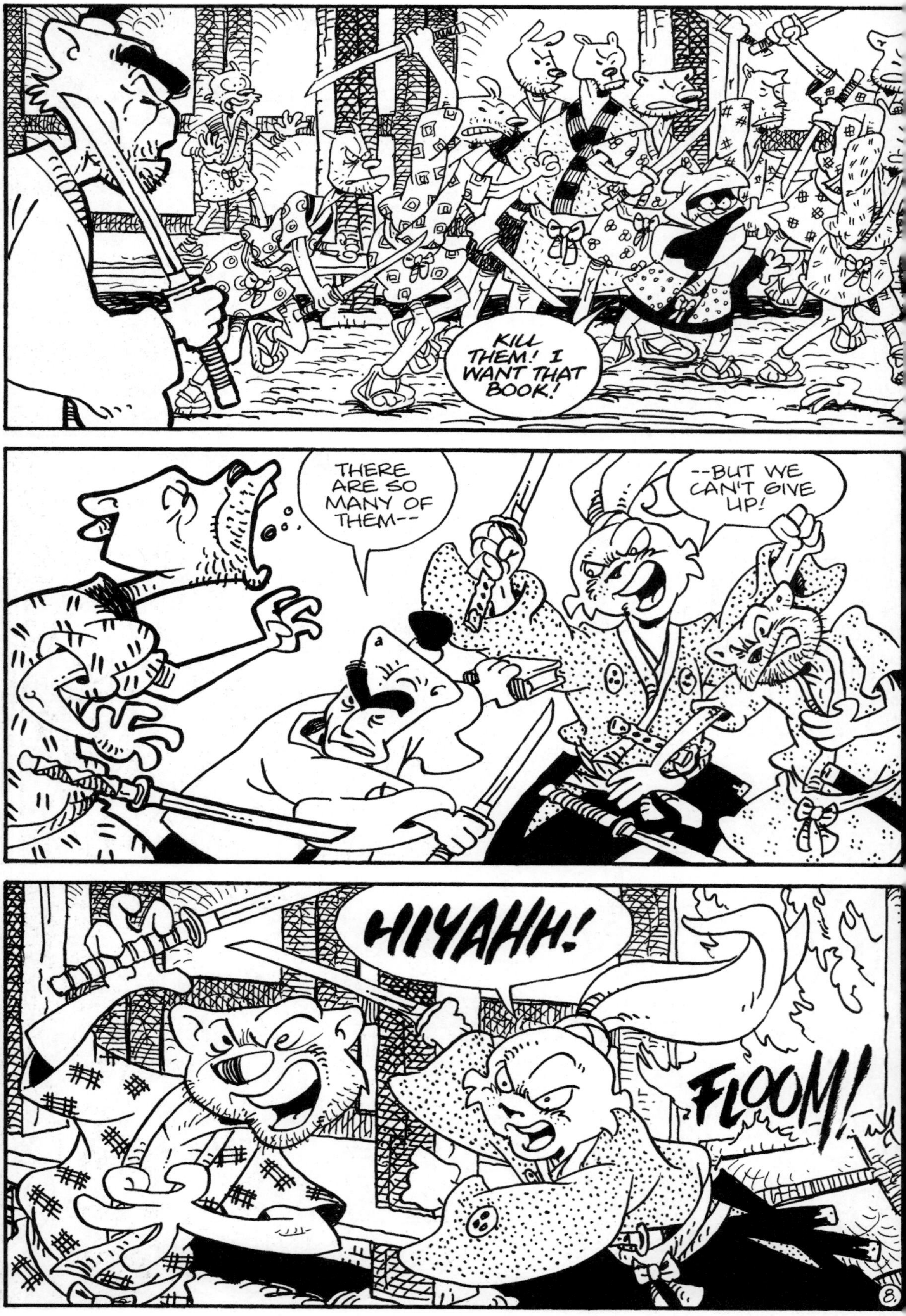
KILL THEM! I WANT THAT BOOK!
THERE ARE SO MANY OF THEM--
--BUT WE CAN'T GIVE UP!
HIYAHH!
FLOOM!
8.

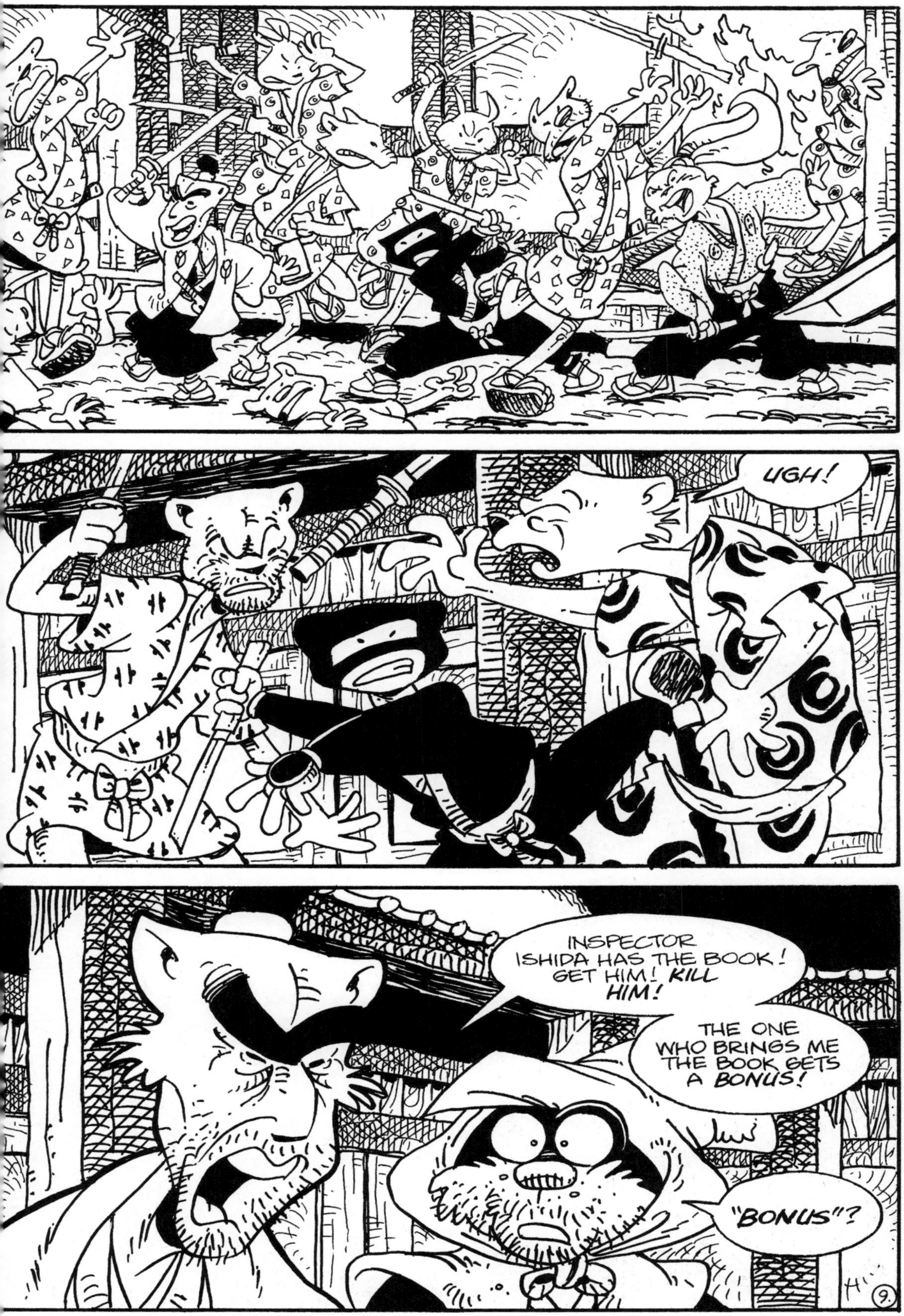
UGH!
INSPECTOR ISHIDA HAS THE BOOK! GET HIM! KILL HIM!
THE ONE WHO BRINGS ME THE BOOK GETS A BONUS!
"BONUS"?
9.

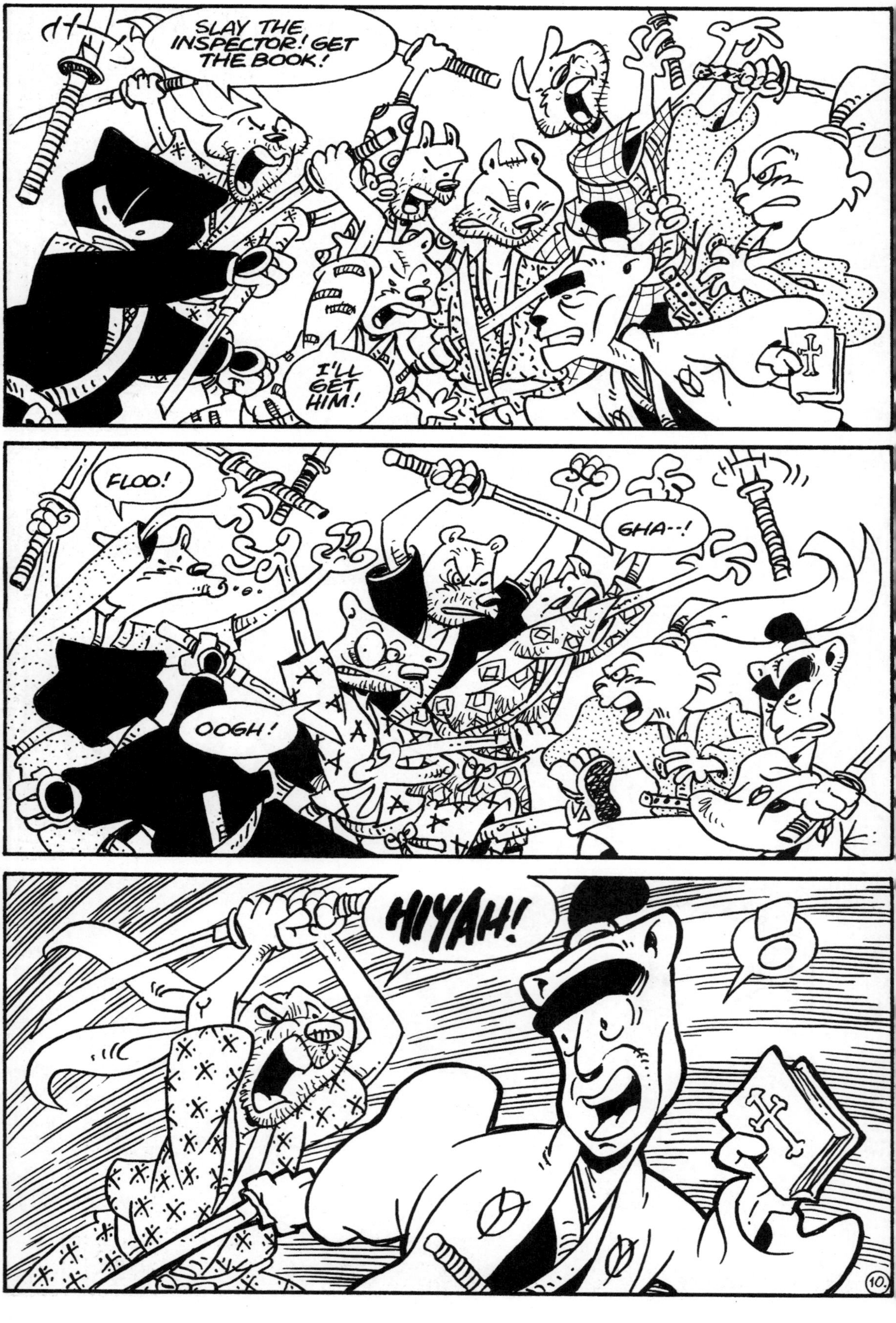
SLAY THE INSPECTOR! GET THE BOOK!
I'LL GET HIM!
FLOO!
GHA--!
OOGH!
HIYAH!
!
10.

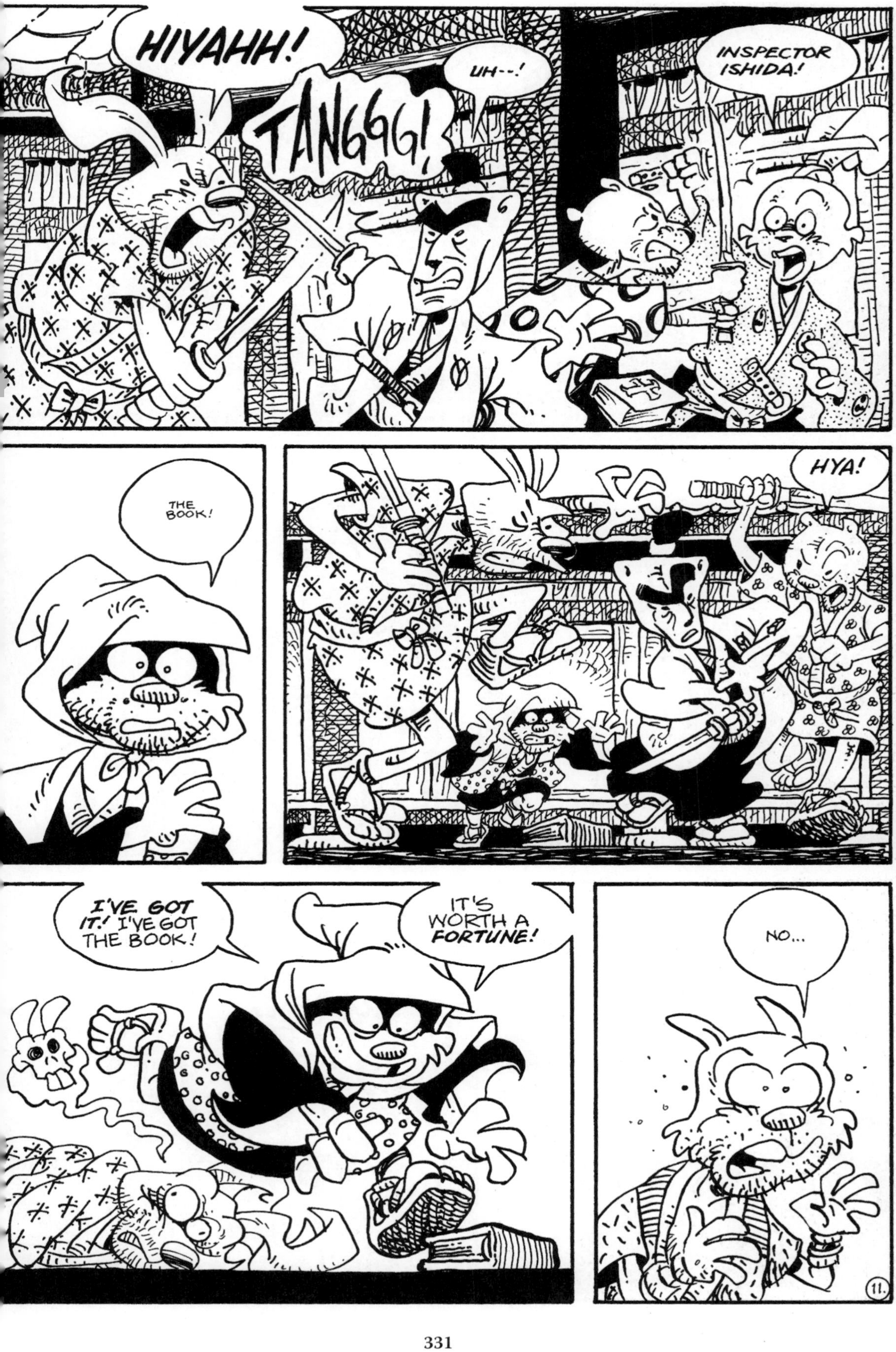
HIYAHH!
TANGGG!
UH--!
INSPECTOR ISHIDA!
THE BOOK!
HYA!
I'VE GOT IT! I'VE GOT THE BOOK!
IT'S WORTH A FORTUNE!
NO...
11.

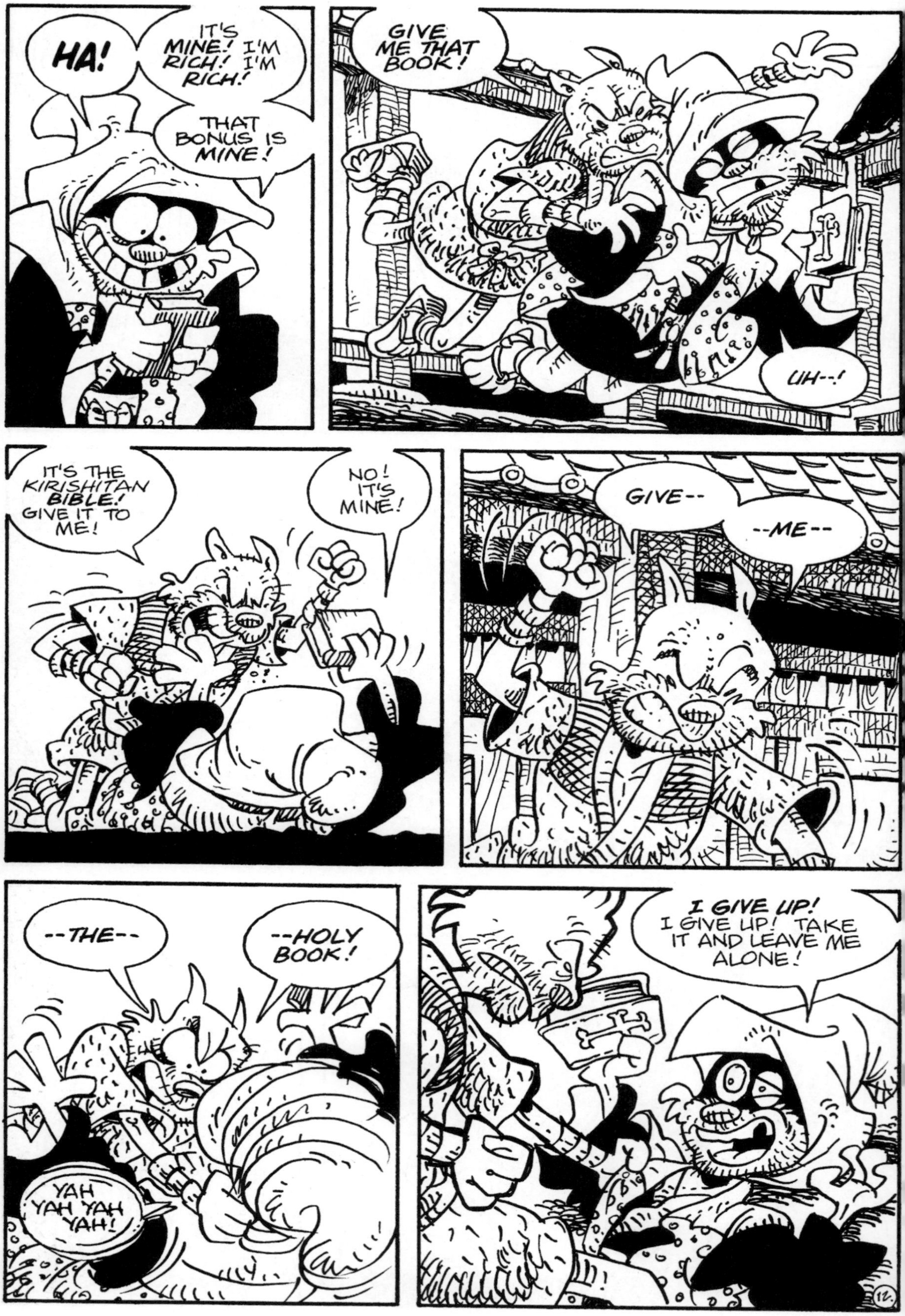
HA!
IT'S MINE! I'M RICH! I'M RICH!
THAT BONUS IS MINE!
GIVE ME THAT BOOK!
UH--!
IT'S THE KIRISHITAN BIBLE! GIVE IT TO ME!
NO! IT'S MINE!
GIVE--
--ME--
--THE--
--HOLY BOOK!
YAH YAH YAH YAH!
I GIVE UP! I GIVE UP! TAKE IT AND LEAVE ME ALONE!
12.

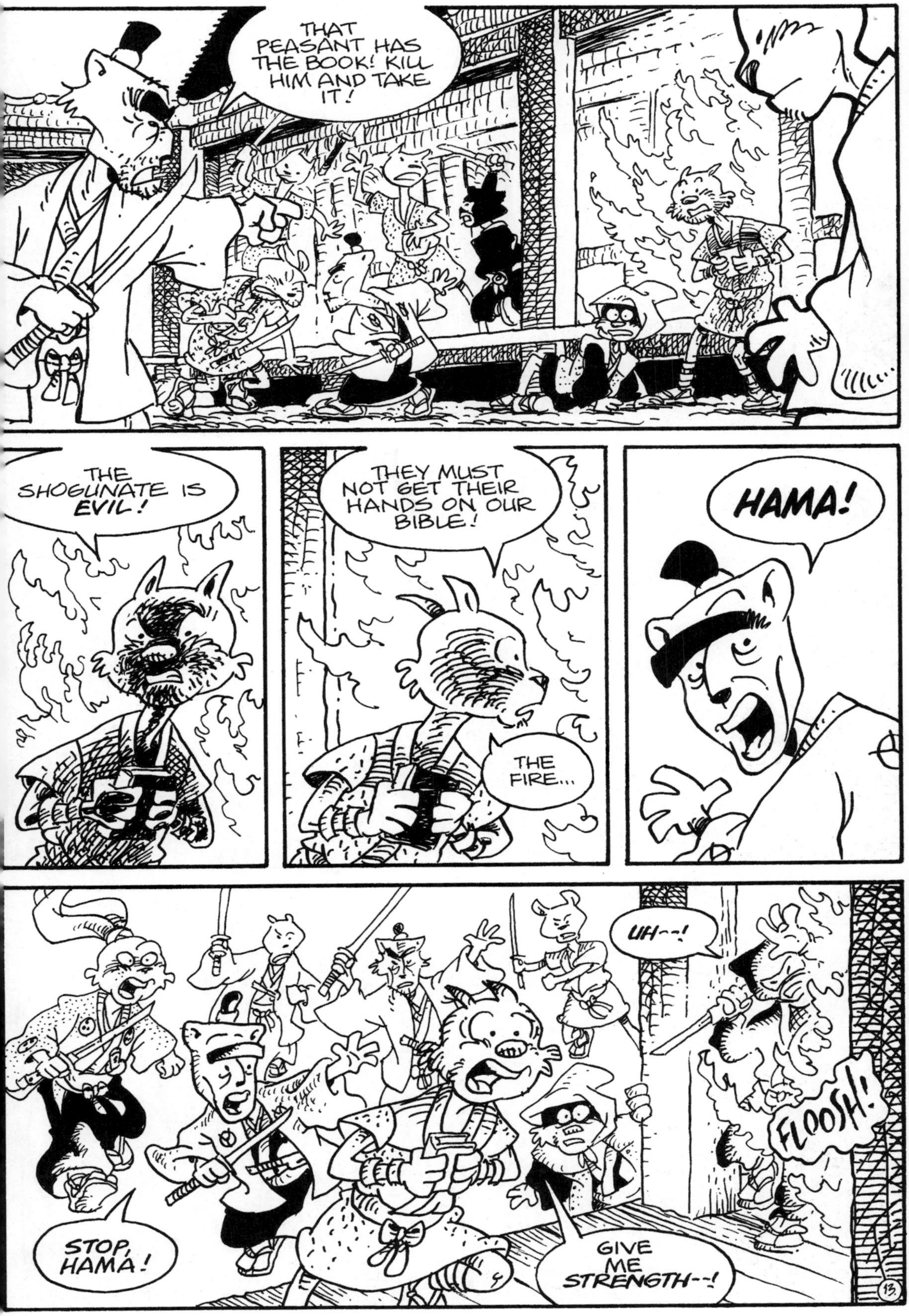
THAT PEASANT HAS THE BOOK! KILL HIM AND TAKE IT!
THE SHOGUNATE IS EVIL!
THEY MUST NOT GET THEIR HANDS ON OUR BIBLE!
THE FIRE...
HAMA!
UH--!
FLOOSH!
STOP, HAMA!
GIVE ME STRENGTH--!
13

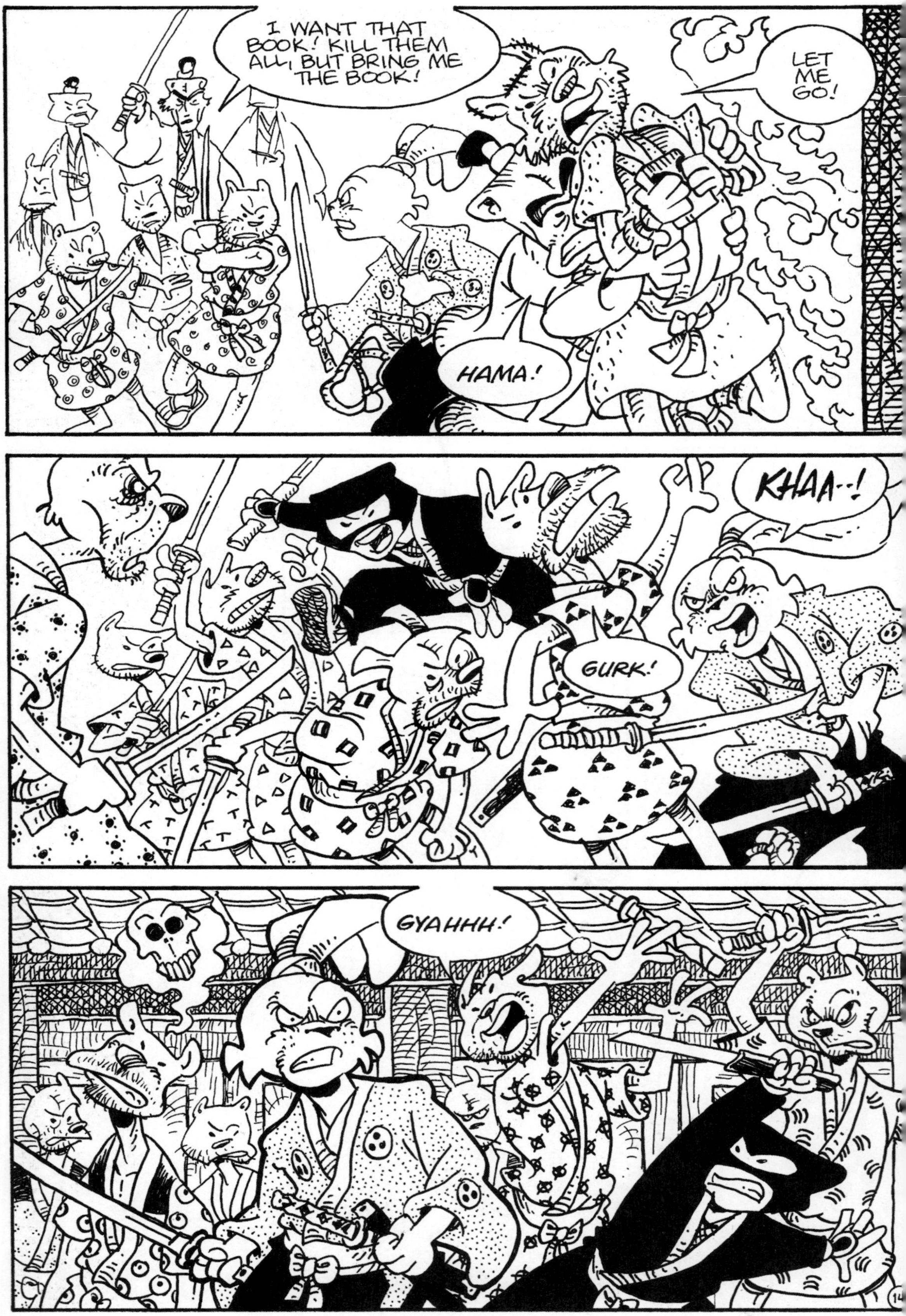
I WANT THAT BOOK! KILL THEM ALL, BUT BRING ME THE BOOK!
LET ME GO!
HAMA!
KHAA--!
GURK!
GYAHHH!

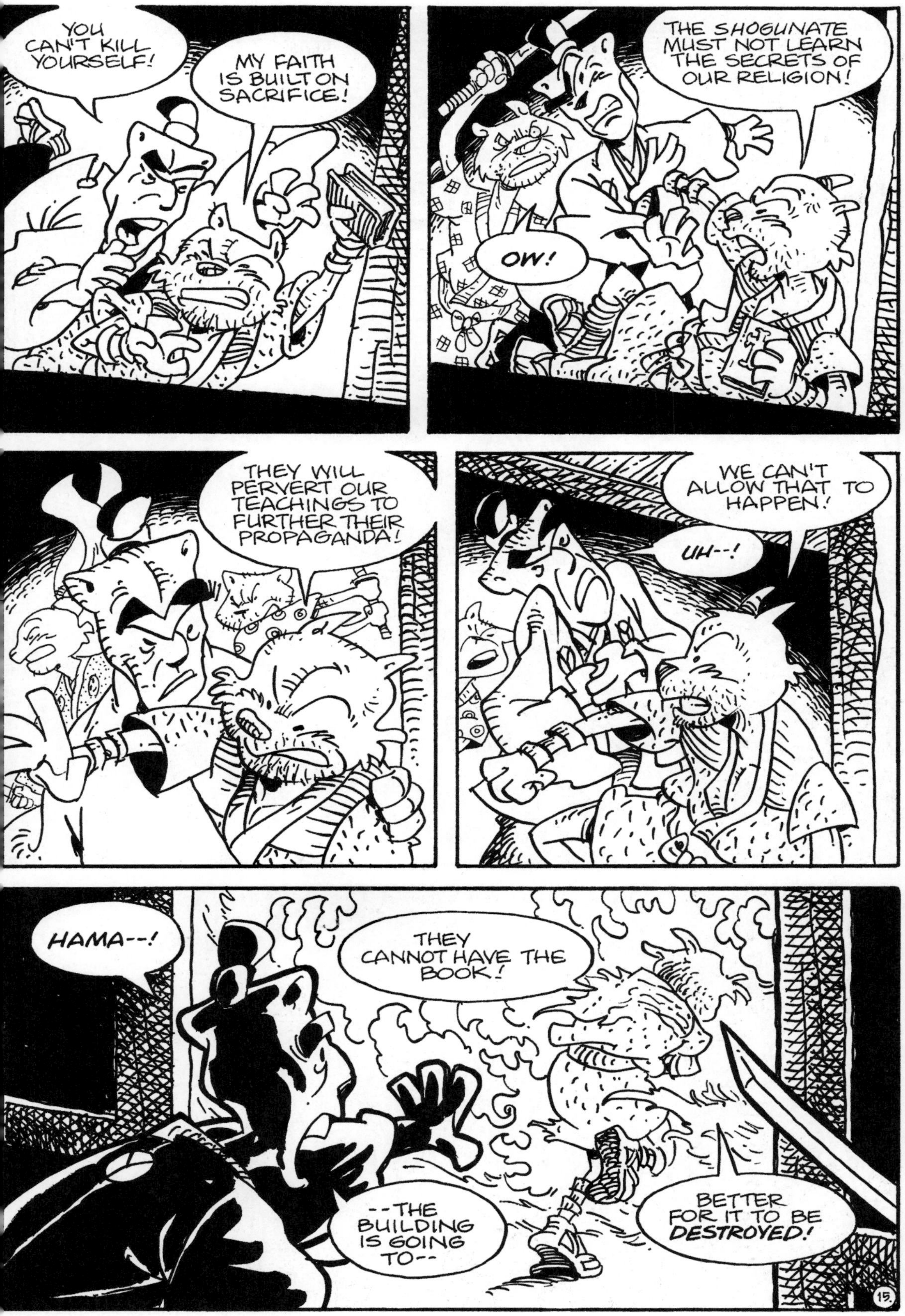
YOU CAN'T KILL YOURSELF!
MY FAITH IS BUILT ON SACRIFICE!
THE SHOGUNATE MUST NOT LEARN THE SECRETS OF OUR RELIGION!
OW!
THEY WILL PERVERT OUR TEACHINGS TO FURTHER THEIR PROPAGANDA!
WE CAN'T ALLOW THAT TO HAPPEN!
UH--!
HAMA--!
THEY CANNOT HAVE THE BOOK!
--THE BUILDING IS GOING TO--
BETTER FOR IT TO BE DESTROYED!
15.

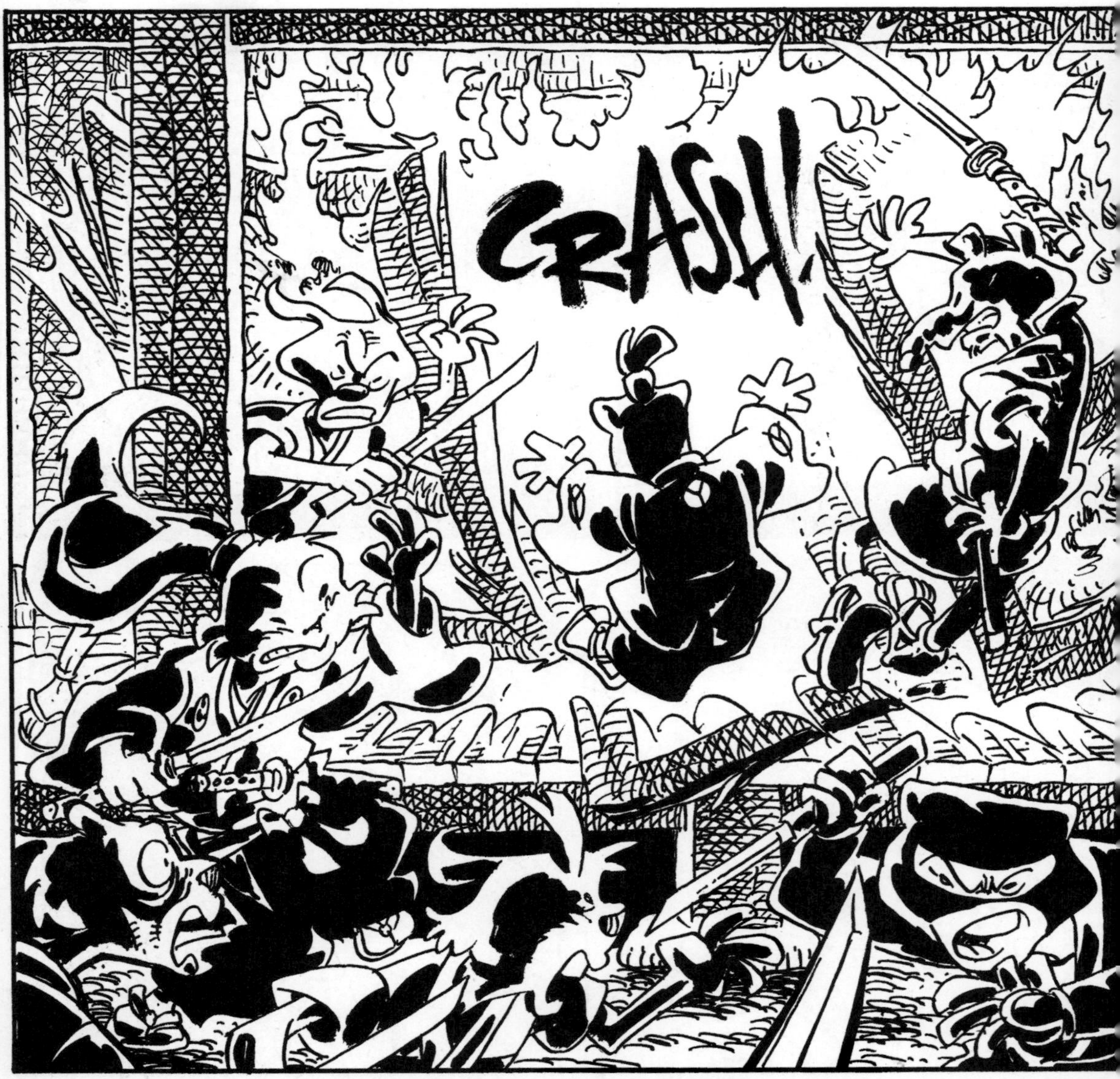
CRASH!

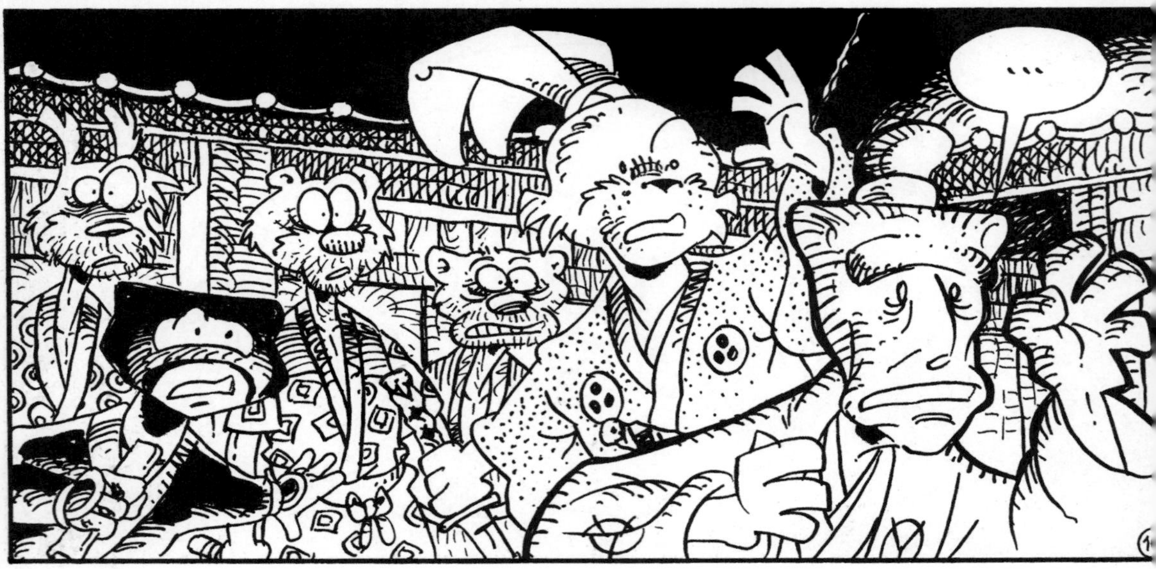
...

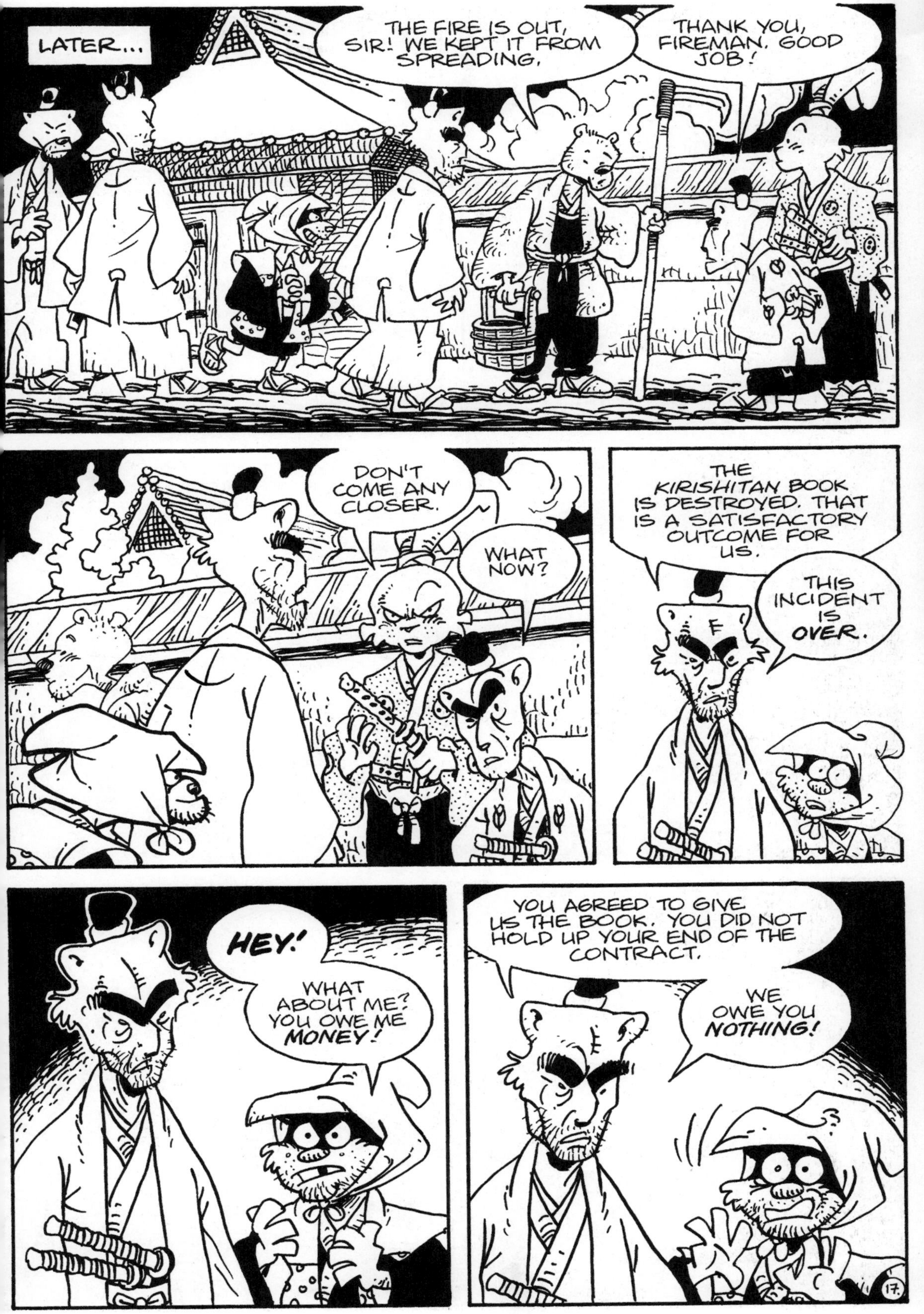
LATER...
THE FIRE IS OUT, SIR! WE KEPT IT FROM SPREADING.
THANK YOU, FIREMAN. GOOD JOB!
DON'T COME ANY CLOSER.
WHAT NOW?
THE KIRISHITAN BOOK IS DESTROYED. THAT IS A SATISFACTORY OUTCOME FOR US.
THIS INCIDENT IS OVER.
HEY!
WHAT ABOUT ME? YOU OWE ME MONEY!
YOU AGREED TO GIVE US THE BOOK. YOU DID NOT HOLD UP YOUR END OF THE CONTRACT.
WE OWE YOU NOTHING!
17.

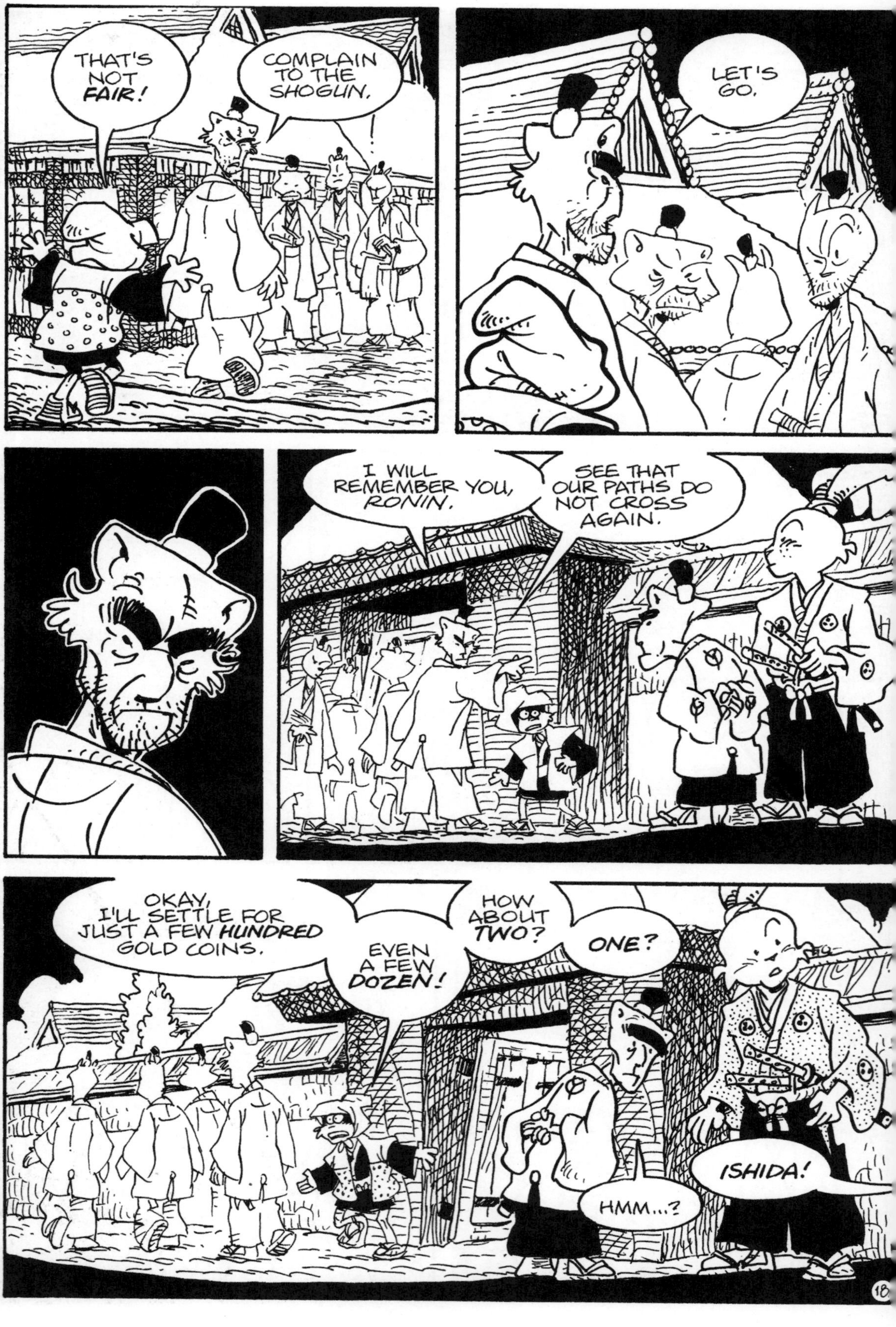
THAT'S NOT FAIR!
COMPLAIN TO THE SHOGUN.
LET'S GO.
I WILL REMEMBER YOU, RONIN.
SEE THAT OUR PATHS DO NOT CROSS AGAIN.
OKAY, I'LL SETTLE FOR JUST A FEW HUNDRED GOLD COINS.
EVEN A FEW DOZEN!
HOW ABOUT TWO?
ONE?
ISHIDA!
HMM...?
18

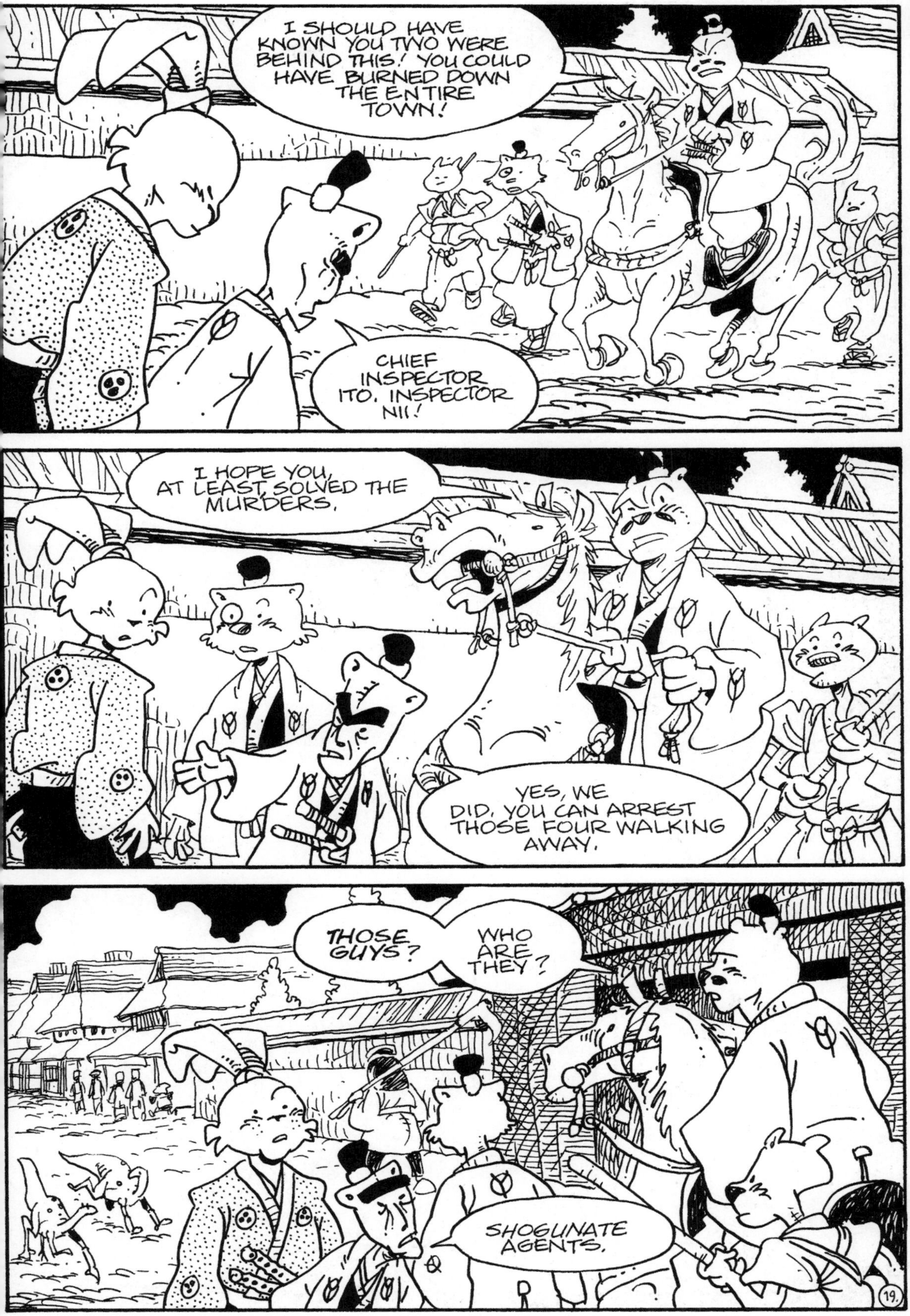
I SHOULD HAVE KNOWN YOU TWO WERE BEHIND THIS! YOU COULD HAVE BURNED DOWN THE ENTIRE TOWN!
CHIEF INSPECTOR ITO. INSPECTOR NII!
I HOPE YOU, AT LEAST, SOLVED THE MURDERS.
YES, WE DID. YOU CAN ARREST THOSE FOUR WALKING AWAY.
THOSE GUYS?
WHO ARE THEY?
SHOGUNATE AGENTS.
19.

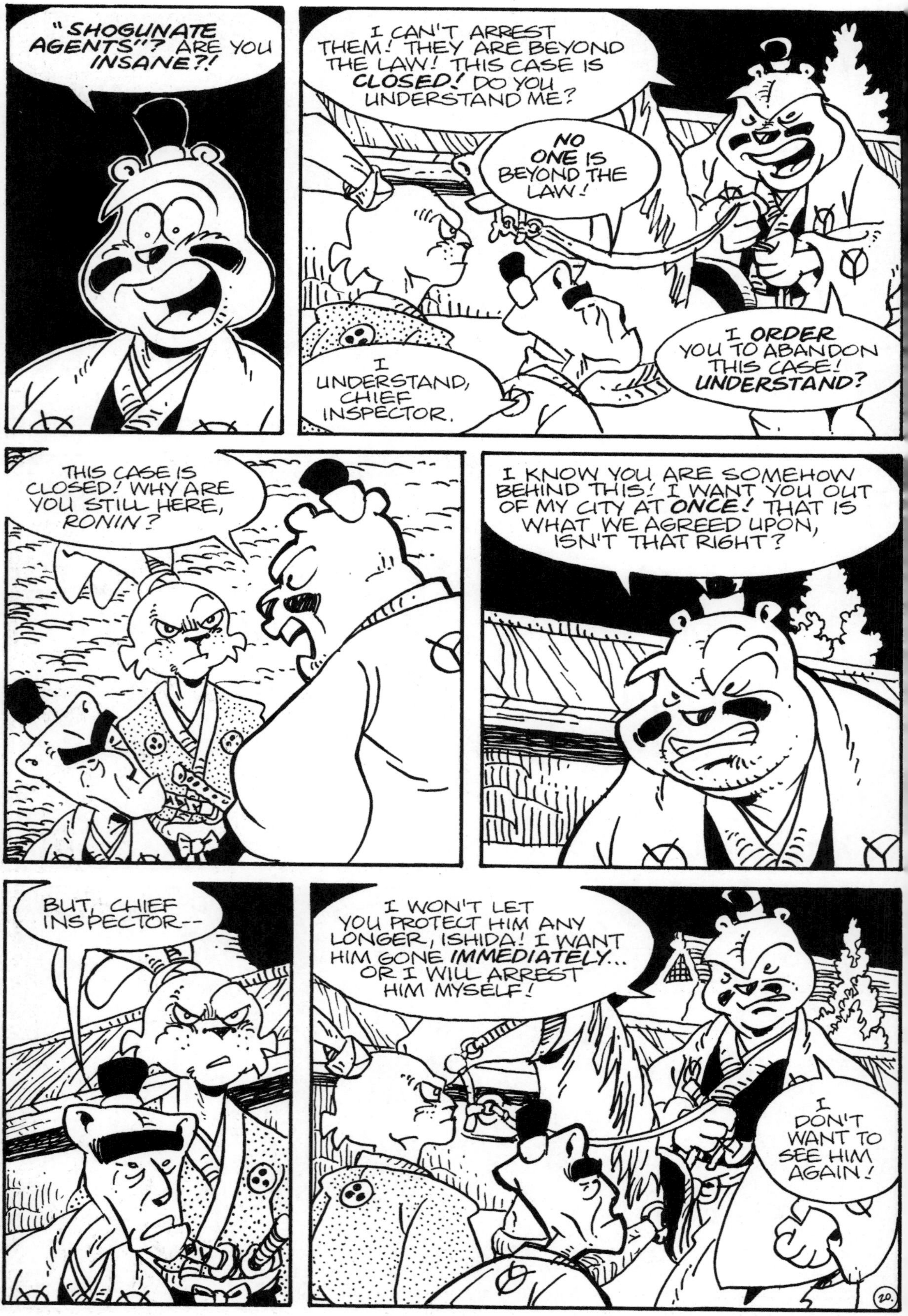
"SHOGUNATE AGENTS"? ARE YOU INSANE?!
I CAN'T ARREST THEM! THEY ARE BEYOND THE LAW! THIS CASE IS CLOSED! DO YOU UNDERSTAND ME?
NO ONE IS BEYOND THE LAW!
I ORDER YOU TO ABANDON THIS CASE! UNDERSTAND?
I UNDERSTAND, CHIEF INSPECTOR.
THIS CASE IS CLOSED! WHY ARE YOU STILL HERE, RONIN?
I KNOW YOU ARE SOMEHOW BEHIND THIS! I WANT YOU OUT OF MY CITY AT ONCE! THAT IS WHAT WE AGREED UPON, ISN'T THAT RIGHT?
BUT, CHIEF INSPECTOR--
I WON'T LET YOU PROTECT HIM ANY LONGER, ISHIDA! I WANT HIM GONE IMMEDIATELY... OR I WILL ARREST HIM MYSELF!
I DON'T WANT TO SEE HIM AGAIN!
20.

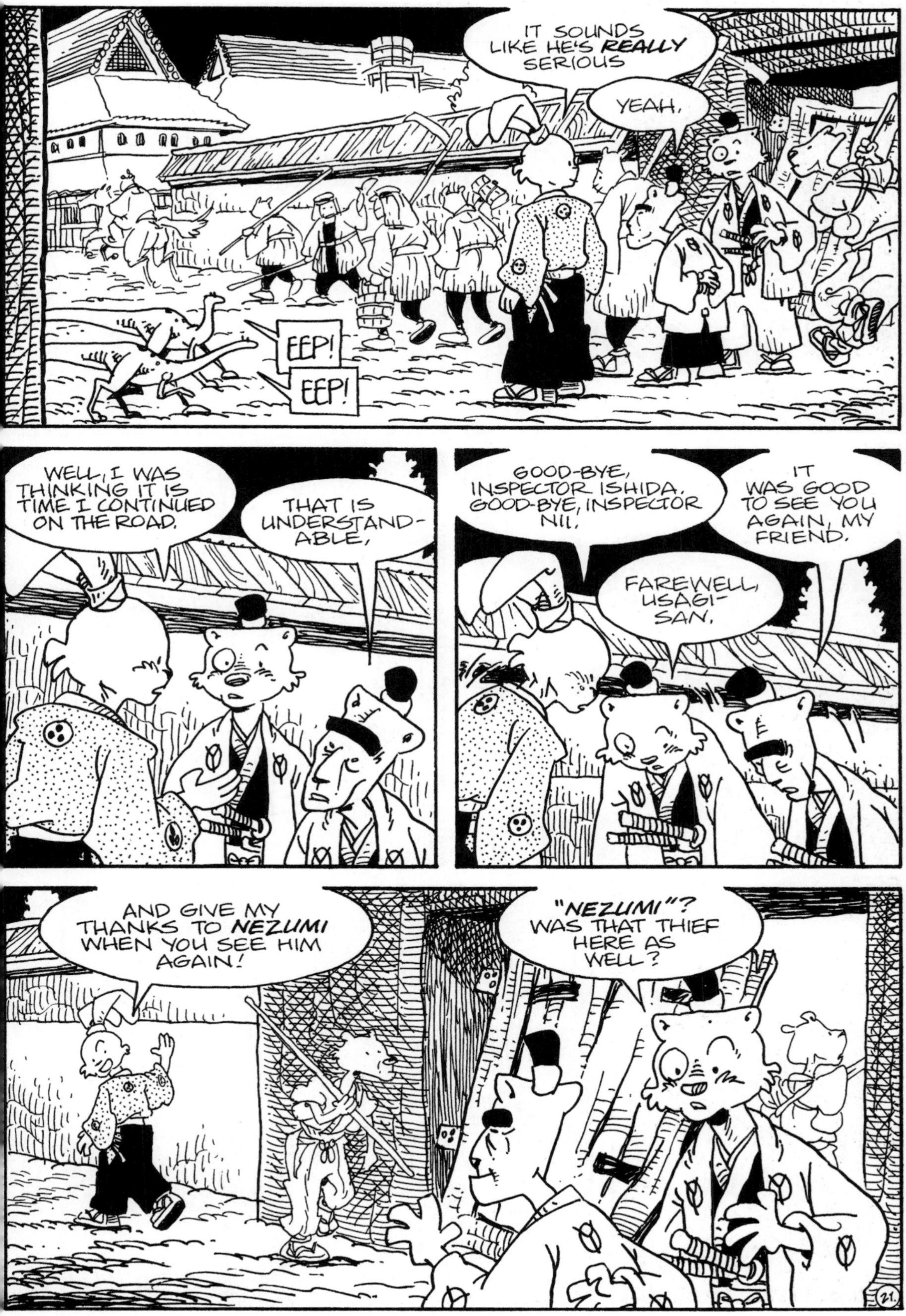
IT SOUNDS LIKE HE'S REALLY SERIOUS
YEAH.
EEP!
EEP!
WELL, I WAS THINKING IT IS TIME I CONTINUED ON THE ROAD.
THAT IS UNDERSTANDABLE.
GOOD-BYE, INSPECTOR ISHIDA. GOOD-BYE, INSPECTOR NII.
IT WAS GOOD TO SEE YOU AGAIN, MY FRIEND.
FAREWELL, USAGI-SAN.
AND GIVE MY THANKS TO NEZUMI WHEN YOU SEE HIM AGAIN!
"NEZUMI"? WAS THAT THIEF HERE AS WELL?
21.

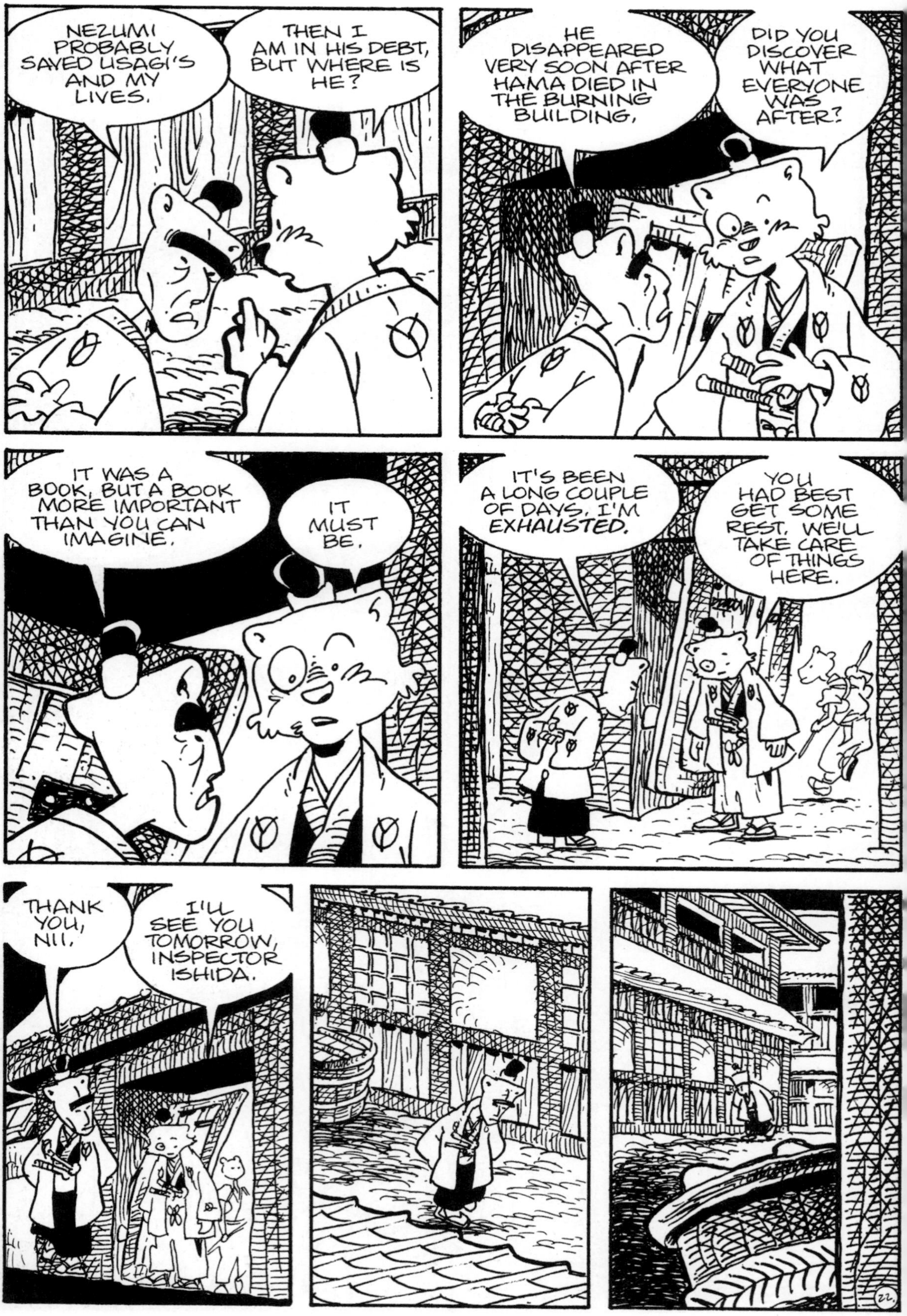
NEZUMI PROBABLY SAVED USAGI'S AND MY LIVES.
THEN I AM IN HIS DEBT, BUT WHERE IS HE?
HE DISAPPEARED VERY SOON AFTER HAMA DIED IN THE BURNING BUILDING.
DID YOU DISCOVER WHAT EVERYONE WAS AFTER?
IT WAS A BOOK, BUT A BOOK MORE IMPORTANT THAN YOU CAN IMAGINE.
IT MUST BE.
IT'S BEEN A LONG COUPLE OF DAYS. I'M EXHAUSTED.
YOU HAD BEST GET SOME REST. WE'LL TAKE CARE OF THINGS HERE.
THANK YOU, NII.
I'LL SEE YOU TOMORROW, INSPECTOR ISHIDA.
22.

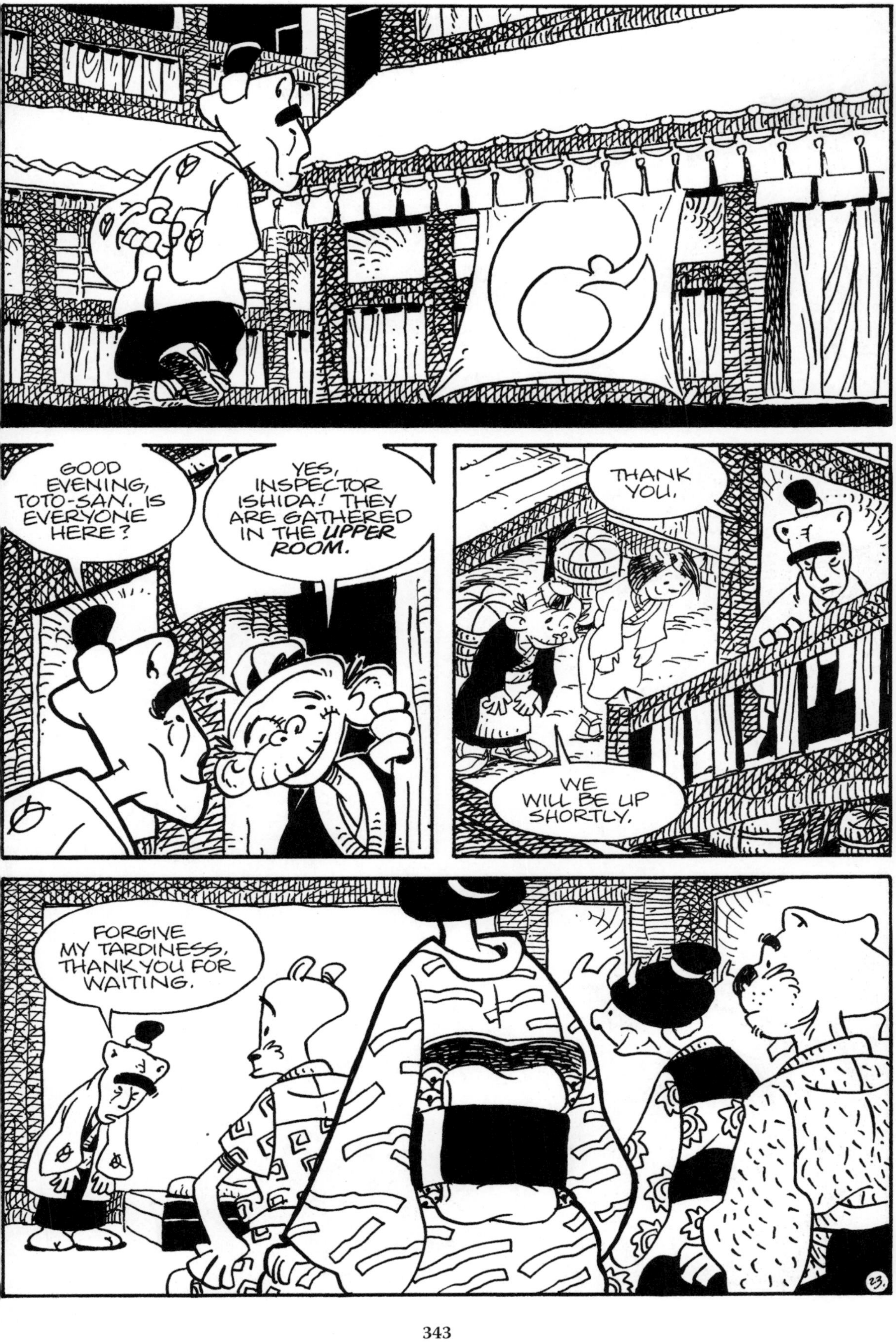
GOOD EVENING, TOTO-SAN. IS EVERYONE HERE?
YES, INSPECTOR ISHIDA! THEY ARE GATHERED IN THE *UPPER ROOM*.
THANK YOU.
WE WILL BE UP SHORTLY.
FORGIVE MY TARDINESS, THANK YOU FOR WAITING.
23.

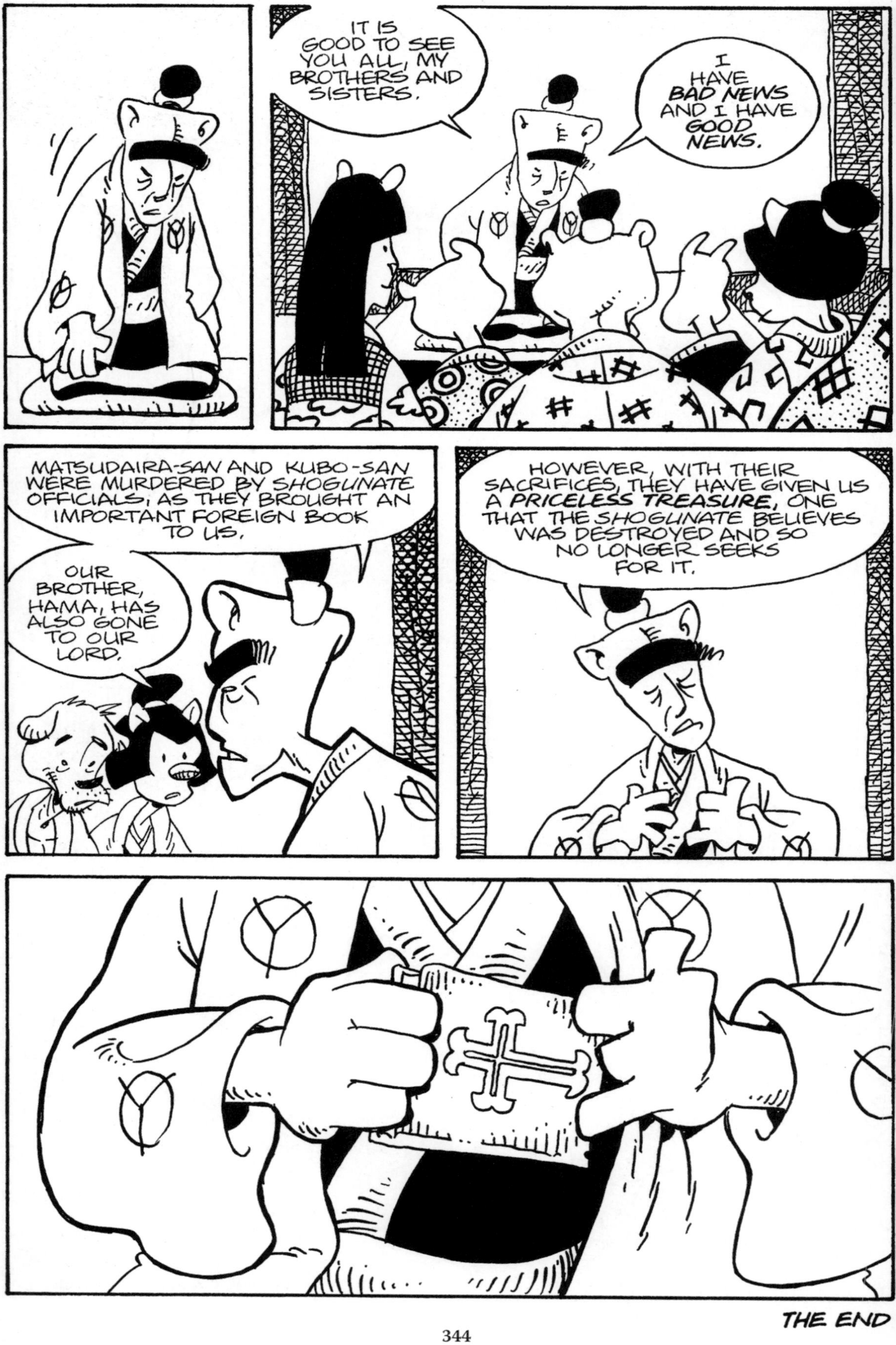
IT IS GOOD TO SEE YOU ALL, MY BROTHERS AND SISTERS.
I HAVE **BAD NEWS** AND I HAVE **GOOD NEWS.**
MATSUDAIRA-*SAN* AND KUBO-*SAN* WERE MURDERED BY *SHOGUNATE* OFFICIALS, AS THEY BROUGHT AN IMPORTANT FOREIGN BOOK TO US.
OUR BROTHER, HAMA, HAS ALSO GONE TO OUR LORD.
HOWEVER, WITH THEIR SACRIFICES, THEY HAVE GIVEN US A ***PRICELESS TREASURE,*** ONE THAT THE *SHOGUNATE* BELIEVES WAS DESTROYED AND SO NO LONGER SEEKS FOR IT.

THE END

THE HIDDEN

The first Europeans came to Japan in 1543. Portuguese sailors landed on Tanegashima, an island far to the south. They had with them matchlock firearms called arquebuses. The Japanese soon copied them and called them *tanegashima* after the island on which they were introduced. This was during the Sengoku period—the Age of Warring States—and within a few years, Japanese armies had musketeers in their ranks. The times of war ended when Tokugawa Ieyasu defeated his enemies and established the Tokugawa shogunate in 1603.

By 1549, Catholic missionaries were common. The first were the Portuguese Jesuits, then later Spanish orders such as the Franciscans and Dominicans arrived. Both Portugal and Spain claimed the Japanese islands. However, because neither could colonize them, they sent missionaries, as the country that would have the exclusive right to propagate their religion would gain the exclusive rights to trade as well. In 1579, Pope Gregory XIII declared that Japan belonged to the Diocese of Macau. In 1588 the Diocese of Funai (Nagasaki) was founded. However, Spanish orders still entered Japan via Manila.

Rather than preach to the commoners, missionaries focused on converting those in influence. As a consequence, many lords became Christians. Many of these early converts did so to gain access to trade goods, particularly saltpeter, which was used to make gunpowder. The area around Nagasaki in the south became the center for Christian activities and trade with Europe.

After Toyotomi Hideyoshi unified Japan, he proclaimed an edict in 1587 outlawing that religion. During this time, Christian lords sold Japanese to the Portuguese as slaves and forced conversions of their subjects. Christians desecrated native temples and shrines and committed many other atrocities. In October 1596, the Spanish galleon *San Felipe* was wrecked off the coasts of Shikoku. To discourage the ransacking of his ship, the pilot tried to scare looters by boasting of the immense power of their king and proclaiming that it was their destiny to conquer the world. He added that it was their practice to first send forth missionaries to proclaim a message of peace so as to leave the Japanese unprepared for conquest. Hideyoshi immediately declared all Christians to be spies. In 1597, as a warning to those who might convert, twenty-six Christians, including six Franciscans, three Jesuits, and seventeen Japanese laymen, were killed by public execution on what is now known as Martyrs' Hill in the center of Nagasaki.

After Hideyoshi's death in 1598, Tokugawa Ieyasu rose to power to become shogun, the military leader of Japan. In 1614, it was proclaimed that Japan was "the land of the gods" and Christianity was no longer welcome. He banned Christianity and expelled all missionaries from

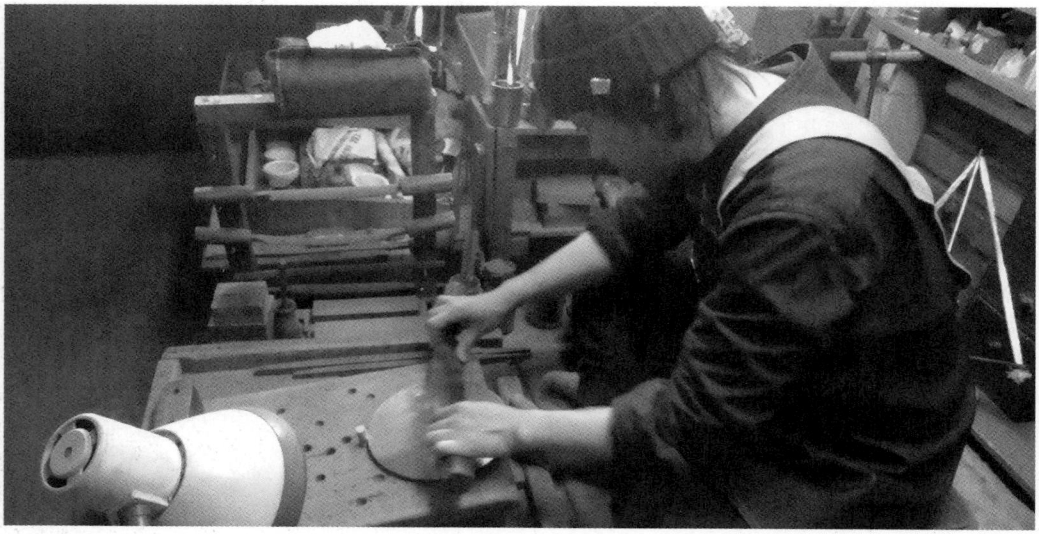

The workshop of mirror maker Yamamoto Akihisa, a designated cultural asset, in Kyoto, Japan.

Japan. He required all subjects to register at their local Buddhist temple, and monuments in Christian graveyards in Nagasaki were torn down. These persecutions were met with resistance from Japanese Christians, forced to practice in secrecy. The government used *fumi-e* images of Christ or the Virgin Mary to identify Christians and sympathizers. Those reluctant to step on the images were taken to Nagasaki. If they refused to renounce their faith, they were tortured. If they still refused, they were executed.

After Christianity was outlawed in the early seventeenth century, *kakure kirishitan*, or "hidden Christians," practiced their faith in secret, using believers' homes as their places of worship. Over time, depictions of saints and the Virgin Mary came to resemble images of Buddha and the bodhisattvas and prayers came to sound like chants. Even crosses on graves became styled after Buddhist imagery. Because copies of the printed Bible were confiscated, "the Book" became an oral tradition and, without the clergy to guide them, Christianity was taught by laymen. As a result, much of their beliefs and traditions changed over the years.

Religious freedom was established in 1873 with the Meiji Restoration, which saw the dissolution of the shogunate and the reestablishment of imperial rule through Emperor Meiji. Christians came out of hiding. They were no longer called "hidden Christians," but *mukashi kirishitan*, or "long-age Christians." Many of these Christians rejoined the Catholic Church, but others separated themselves from its teachings.

In the decades of persecution, they had hidden all signs of their faith, including churches and crosses. We visited Kyoto in April 2017 and were invited to the workshop of Yamamoto Akihisa, a designated cultural asset. He is the last of a line of traditional mirror makers, or *kagami-shi* (masters of mirrors), artisans who hand polish beautifully crafted mirrors. Yamamoto-sensei had an amazing workshop filled with thousands of tools. We were mainly interested in his *makkyo* mirror. These are nickel mirrors with a bronze backing. They reflect an image, as do all mirrors, and the backing is an intricate Japanese motif. However, when a strong light is shined on it, the mirror casts a hidden image onto a wall or other flat surface. In this case, it was Jesus on the cross with worshipers at his feet. It was amazing, and one way for hidden Christians to display their faith without fear of persecution.

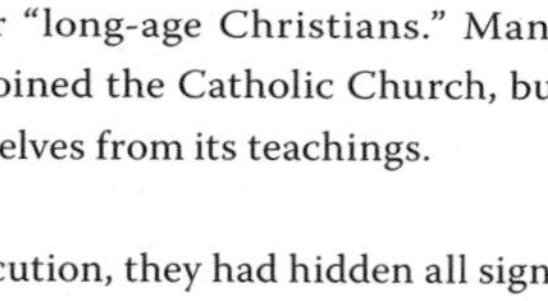
STAN

TEENAGE MUTANT NINJA TURTLES

ONE THING which has always struck me about the crossover stories featuring our Teenage Mutant Ninja Turtles interacting with Stan Sakai's Miyamoto Usagi is how well the combination worked—when, arguably, it should not have.

Consider the essential nature of Stan's *Usagi Yojimbo*. Aside from the occasional element of fantasy, Stan is basically telling realistic stories set in Stan's version of feudal Japan, although instead of humans, this Japan is populated by anthropomorphic animals based on a variety of different species (who generally *act* like humans): Usagi is a rabbit, his friend Gen is a rhinoceros, and so on. The entire world of *Usagi Yojimbo* is populated by anthropomorphic animal characters.

On the other hand, the Teenage Mutant Ninja Turtles are cartoonish anthropomorphic freaks in their world, a modern world full of (mostly) human beings. The Turtles are mutant misfits, wildly altered from their original animal nature and formed by a mysterious alien ooze.

Another "shouldn't have worked" aspect of these *UY/ TMNT* get-togethers relates to the fact that Miyamoto Usagi is a samurai, whereas the Turtles are ninja . . . and samurai and ninja typically are at odds with one another. (I guess it helps that the Turtles are not your typical ninja . . . nor is Usagi your typical samurai.)

These are two qualitatively very different sets of characters, operating in two very different worlds. They shouldn't mesh very well . . .

. . . and yet, they do.

From the beginning, back in the early 1980s, when we first communicated with Stan as fans of each other's independently published black-and-white comics, some kind of crossover seemed inevitable, even given the differences between our universes. Stan showed us that it could work, at least visually, when he sent us a drawing featuring Usagi and the Turtles which we published in an early Mirage Studios *TMNT* comic book—that could be considered the first *UY/TMNT* crossover!

But that was just the beginning, and more substantial team-ups were to come. As you will see in this collection, Stan went on to write and draw a number of terrific comic book crossovers between the Turtles and Usagi, and I contributed a story of my own, "The Crossing," based on one of my favorite Robin Hood tales, in which Robin first meets Friar Tuck on the bank of a river. (While working on this short story, I discovered how difficult it is—well, for me, at least—to draw Usagi. Stan makes it look so easy, with his fluid drawing style and mastery of line.)

One of the things I've always enjoyed about Stan's *UY/ TMNT* crossover stories is how much fun he puts into them. Maybe it's mostly a byproduct of the amazing cartooning abilities he brings to the work, but there is just so much life and energy in these tales. It's also a huge treat to see how Stan takes our often overly rendered characters and converts them into his own clean, crisp cartoon style.

Usagi and Turtles team-ups didn't stay confined to the pages of the comic books. Usagi appeared in two episodes of the original *TMNT* cartoon, then made several exciting appearances in the second *TMNT* animated series, which began in 2003. Part of the joy I had while contributing to that 2003 4Kids *TMNT* show was working with Stan on issues relating to Usagi's guest appearances. Stan was always—like his character Miyamoto Usagi— straightforward and honorable in his dealings with us. (I understand that Usagi has also shown up in the third animated *TMNT* series, though as of this writing I have not seen that.)

And to go along with his animated appearances, Usagi has also joined the Turtles in the various Playmates Toys TMNT action figure lines, where—as with the comics and the animated series—he fits in quite nicely. Maybe when Usagi gets his own long-deserved animated series and associated action figure line, the TMNT could guest star therein. That would make a cool circle!

But action figures and animated series aside, the stories in the book you hold in your hands right now are where all this turtle and rabbit fun began . . . and I hope there's more such fun to come!

PETER LAIRD
NORTHAMPTON, MASSACHUSETTS
FEBRUARY 2018

TURTLE SOUP
AND RABBIT STEW

Written, illustrated, and lettered by

STAN SAKAI

Originally appeared
in *Turtle Soup* #1, published by
Mirage Studios in 1987.

LEONARDO™ MEETS USAGI YOJIMBO™ IN TURTLE SOUP AND RABBIT STEW

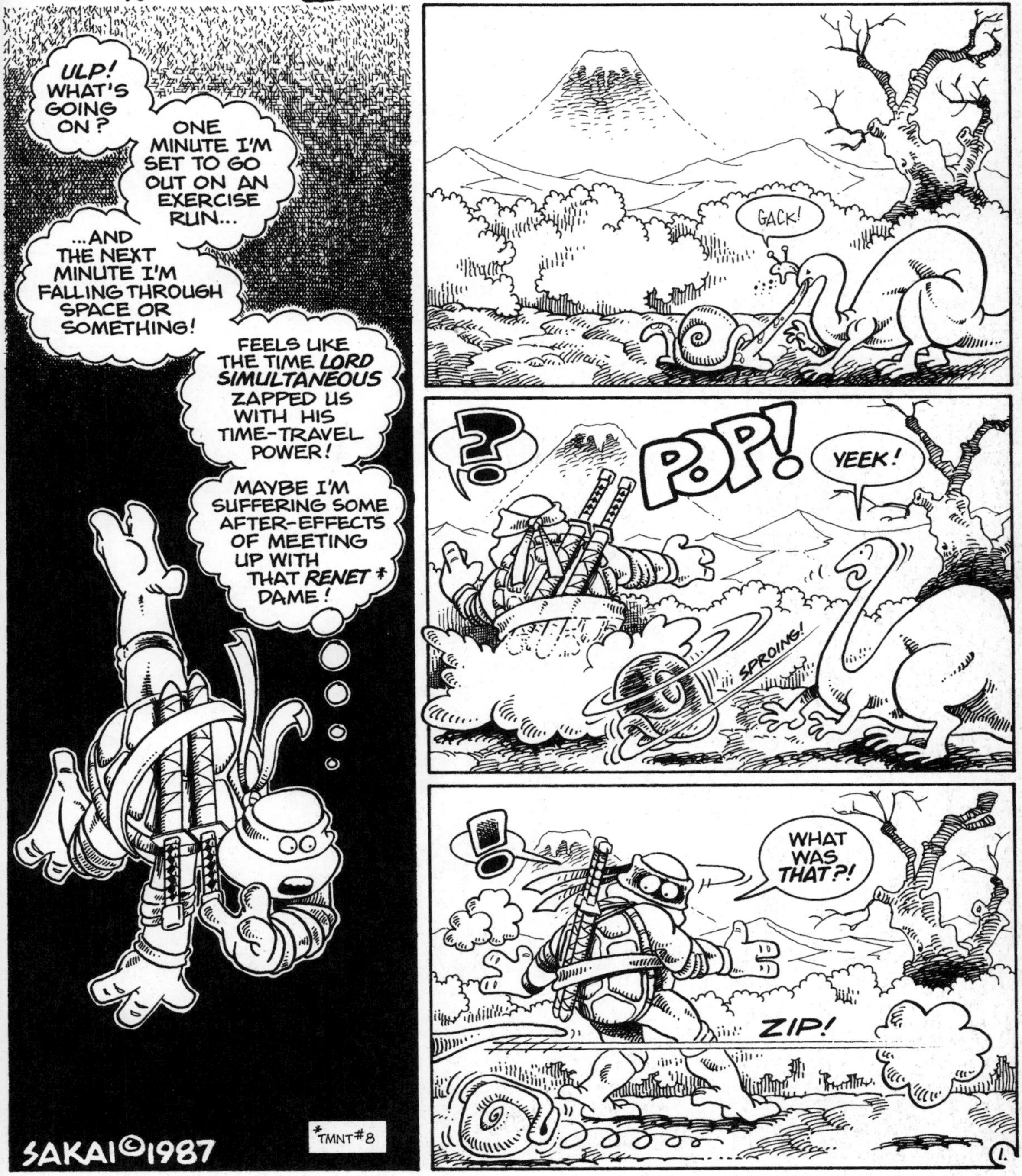

ULP! WHAT'S GOING ON?
ONE MINUTE I'M SET TO GO OUT ON AN EXERCISE RUN...
...AND THE NEXT MINUTE I'M FALLING THROUGH SPACE OR SOMETHING!
FEELS LIKE THE TIME LORD SIMULTANEOUS ZAPPED US WITH HIS TIME-TRAVEL POWER!
MAYBE I'M SUFFERING SOME AFTER-EFFECTS OF MEETING UP WITH THAT RENET* DAME!
SAKAI©1987
*TMNT#8
GACK!
?
POP!
YEEK!
SPROING!
WHAT WAS THAT?!
ZIP!
1.

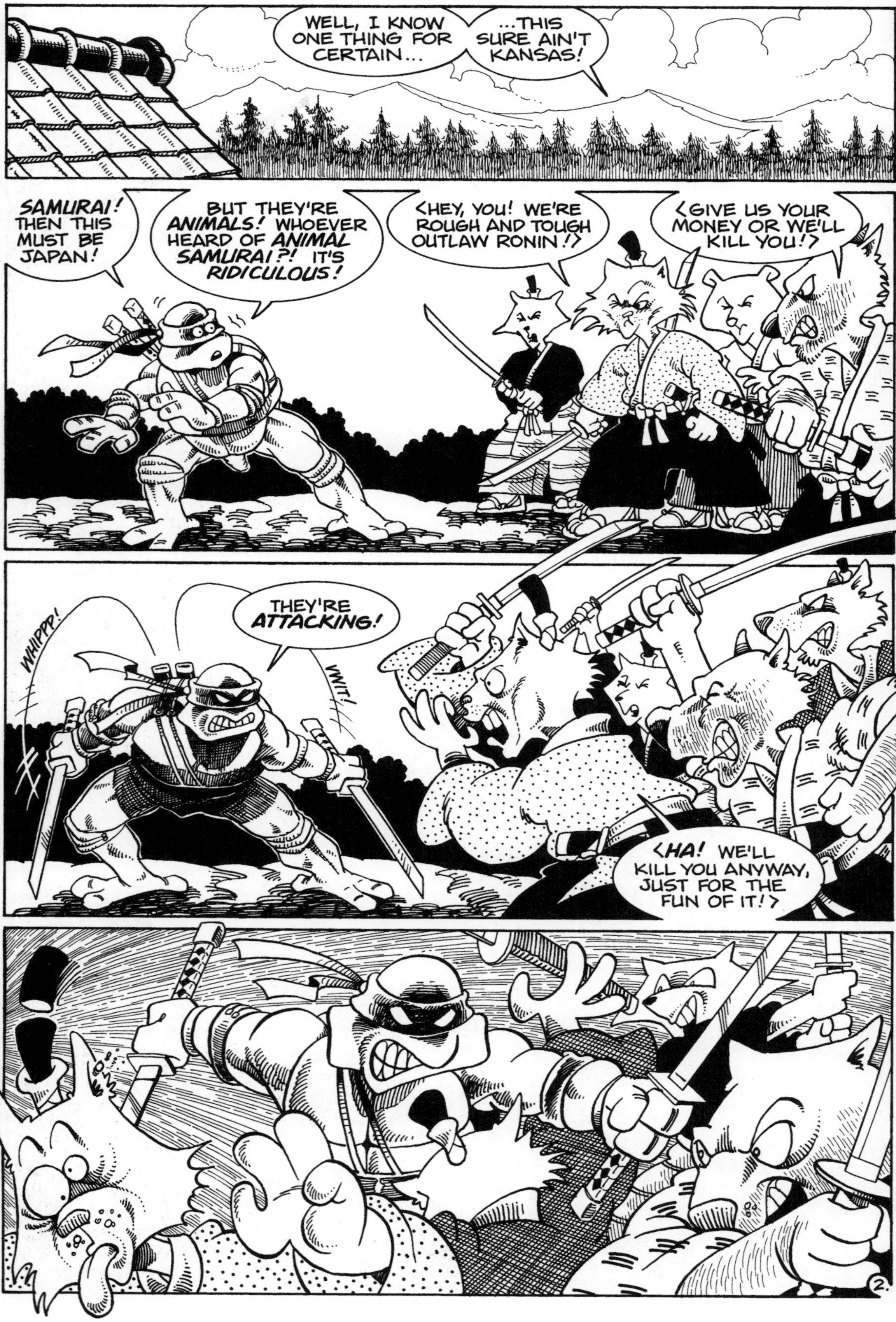
WELL, I KNOW ONE THING FOR CERTAIN...
...THIS SURE AIN'T KANSAS!
SAMURAI! THEN THIS MUST BE JAPAN!
BUT THEY'RE ANIMALS! WHOEVER HEARD OF ANIMAL SAMURAI?! IT'S RIDICULOUS!
<HEY, YOU! WE'RE ROUGH AND TOUGH OUTLAW RONIN!>
<GIVE US YOUR MONEY OR WE'LL KILL YOU!>
WHIPPP!
THEY'RE ATTACKING!
VWIT!
<HA! WE'LL KILL YOU ANYWAY, JUST FOR THE FUN OF IT!>
2.

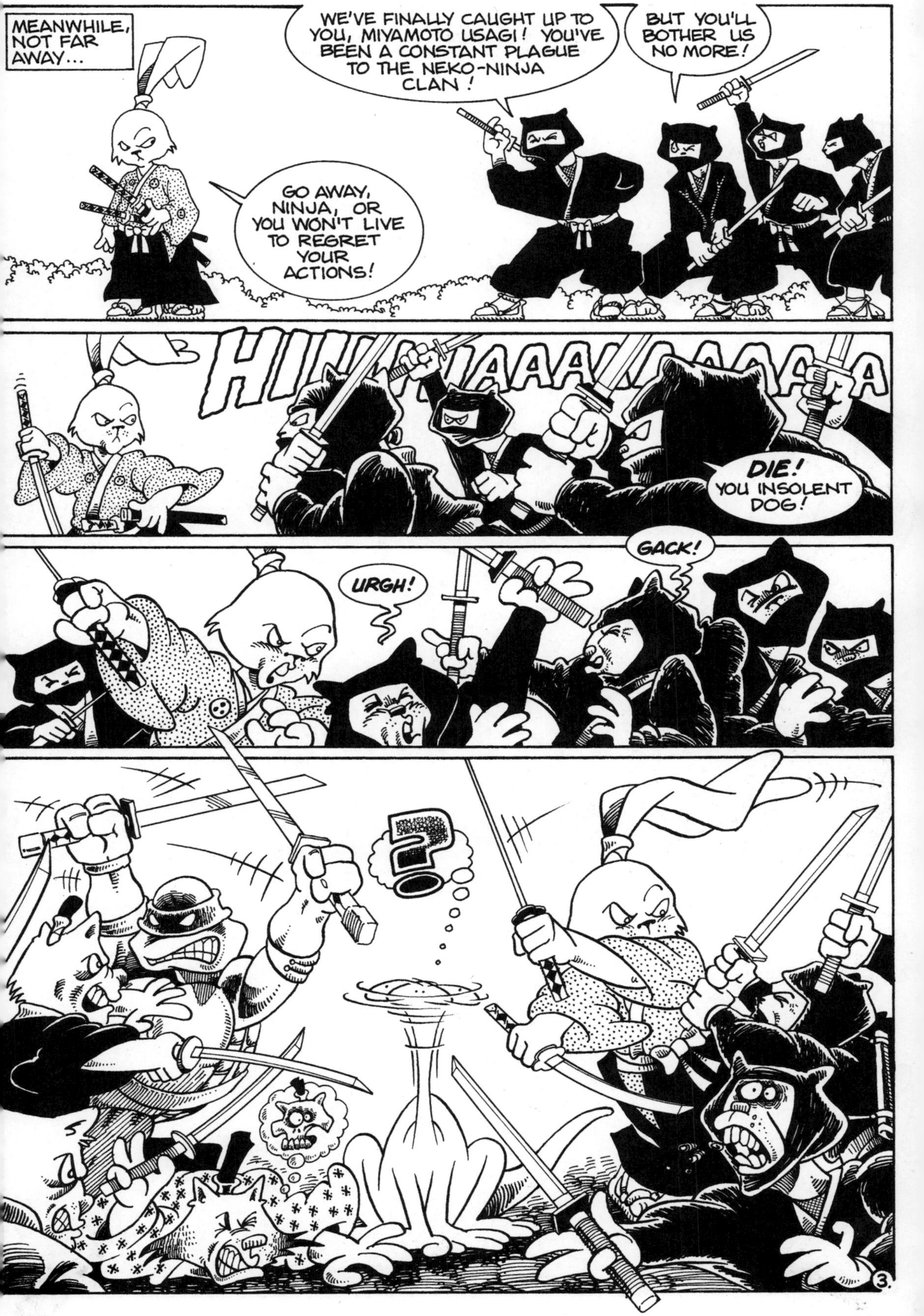
MEANWHILE, NOT FAR AWAY...
WE'VE FINALLY CAUGHT UP TO YOU, MIYAMOTO USAGI! YOU'VE BEEN A CONSTANT PLAGUE TO THE NEKO-NINJA CLAN!
BUT YOU'LL BOTHER US NO MORE!
GO AWAY, NINJA, OR YOU WON'T LIVE TO REGRET YOUR ACTIONS!
HIIIIAAAAAAAAAAA
DIE! YOU INSOLENT DOG!
URGH!
GACK!
?
3.

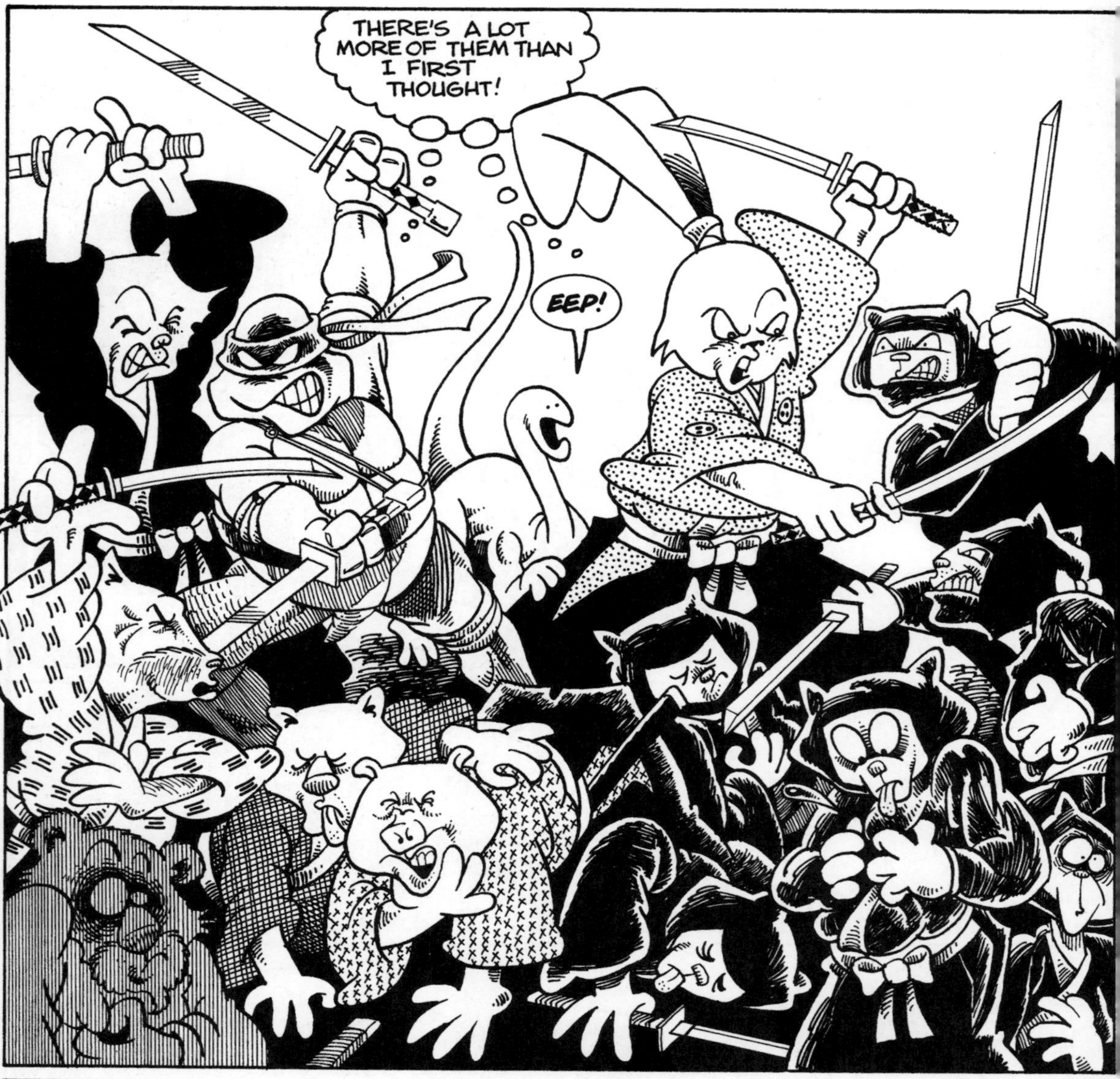
THERE'S A LOT MORE OF THEM THAN I FIRST THOUGHT!
EEP!

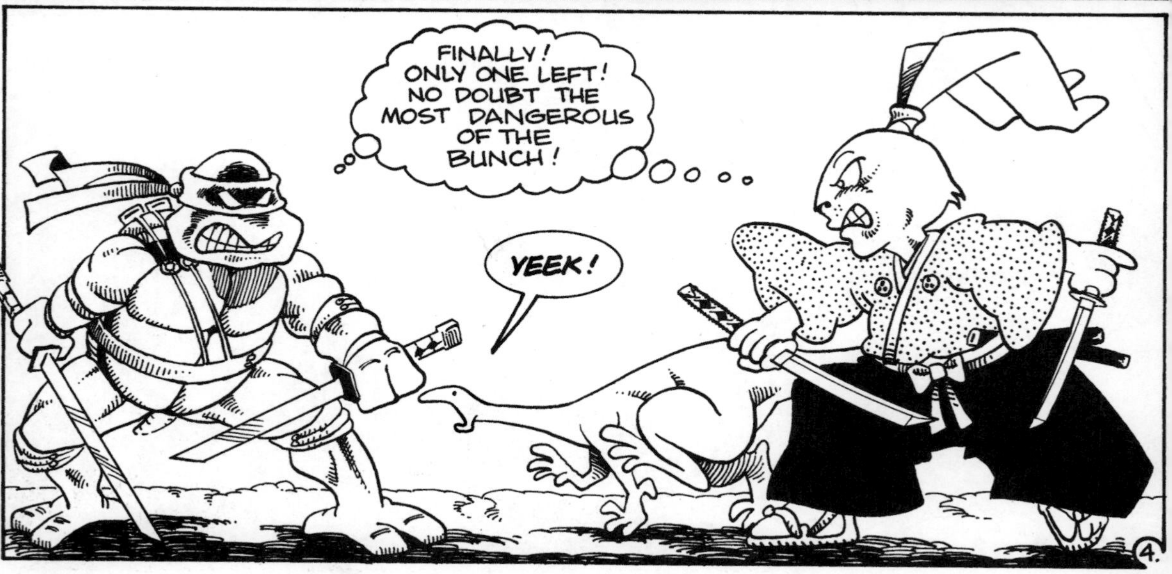
FINALLY! ONLY ONE LEFT! NO DOUBT THE MOST DANGEROUS OF THE BUNCH!
YEEK!
4.

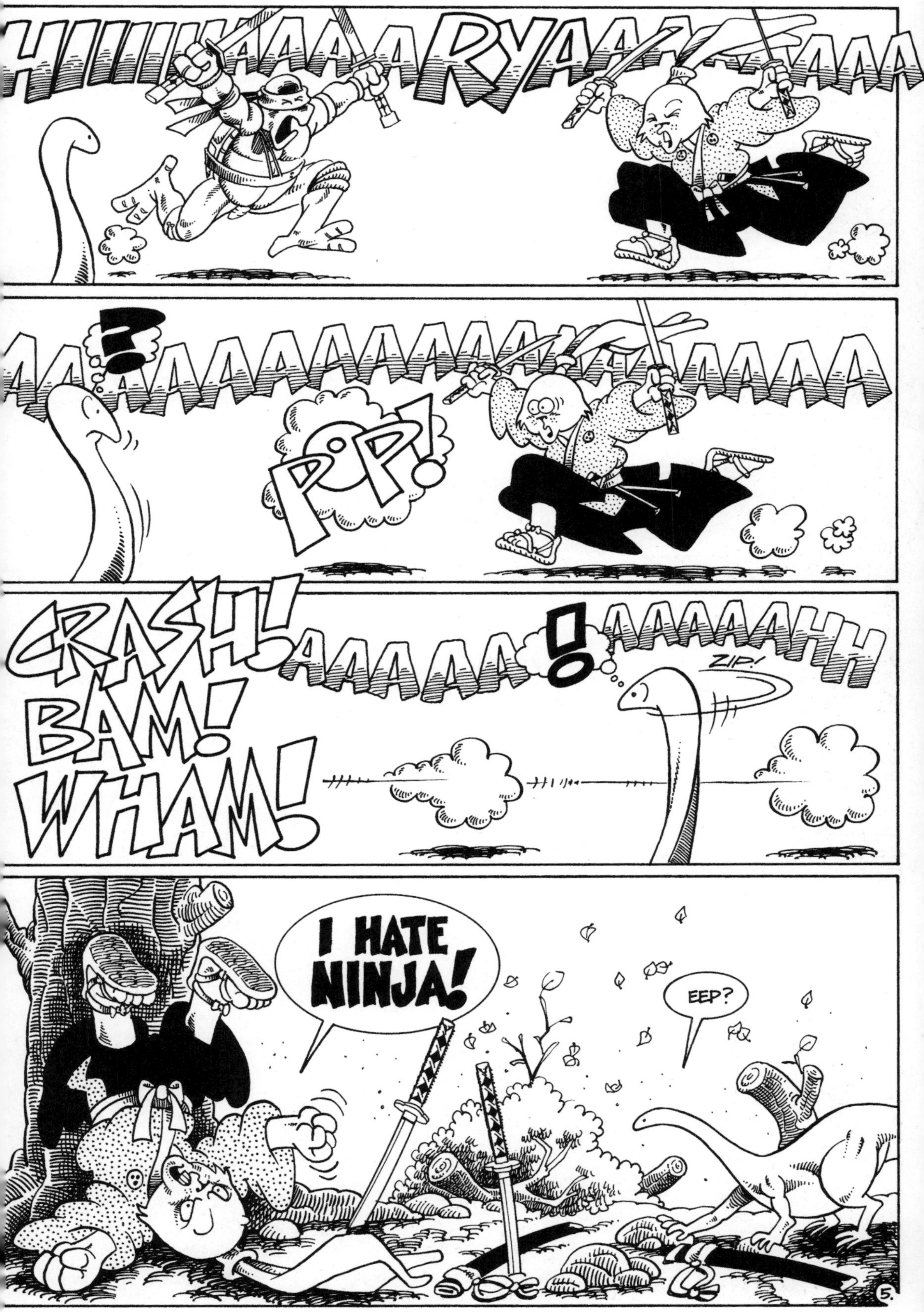
HIIIIIAAAAARYAAAAAAAA
AAAAAAAAAAAAAAAAAAAA
POP!
CRASH! BAM! WHAM!
AAAAAA
AAAAAAHH
ZIP!
I HATE NINJA!
EEP?
5.

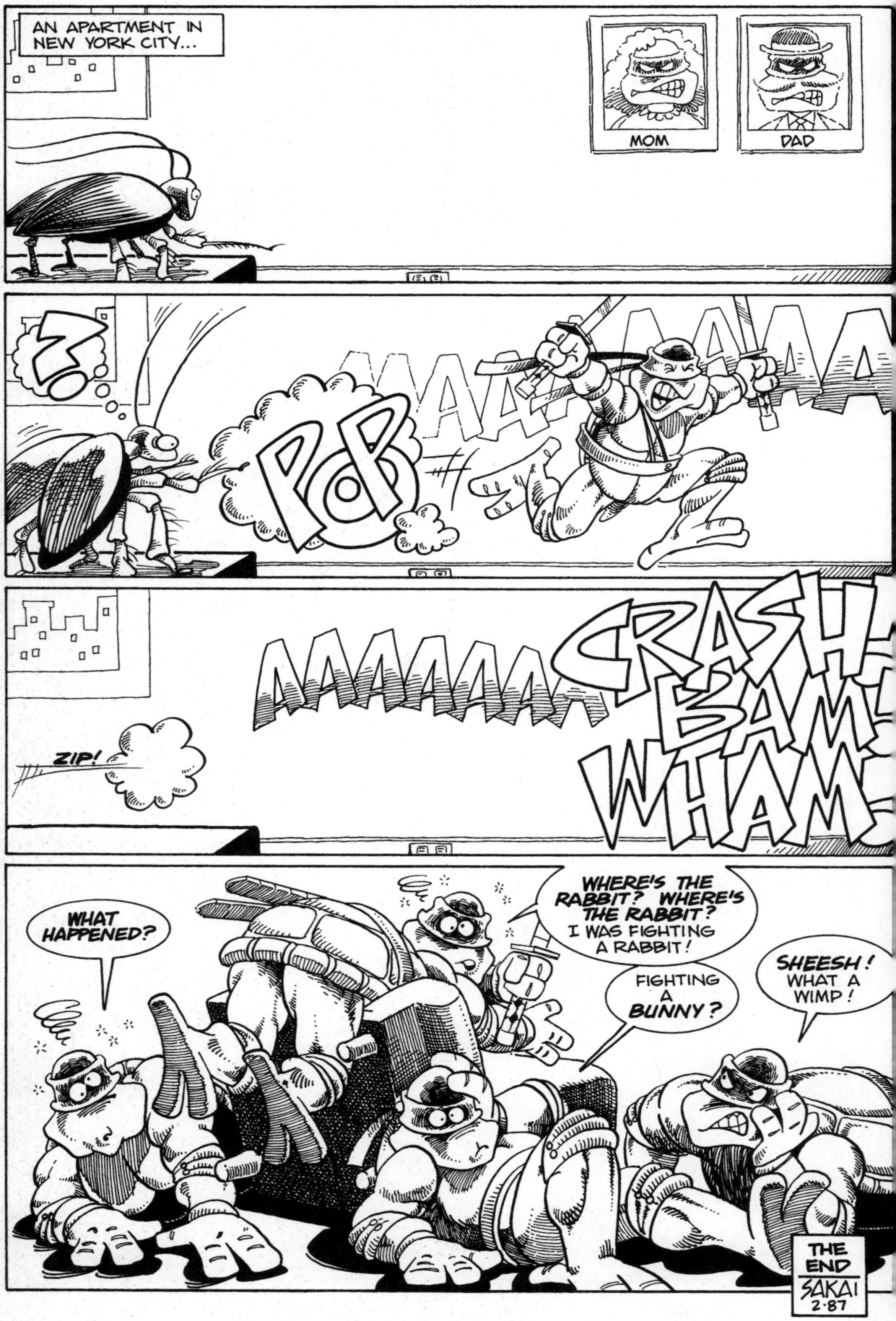
AN APARTMENT IN NEW YORK CITY...
MOM
DAD
Z
POP
AAAAAAA
AAAAAAA
CRASH
BAM
WHAM
ZIP!
WHAT HAPPENED?
WHERE'S THE RABBIT? WHERE'S THE RABBIT? I WAS FIGHTING A RABBIT!
FIGHTING A BUNNY?
SHEESH! WHAT A WIMP!
THE END
SAKAI 2·87

THE CROSSING

Written and illustrated by

PETER LAIRD

Lettered by

LAVIGNE

Originally appeared in
Usagi Yojimbo Volume One #10, published
by Fantagraphics Books in 1988.

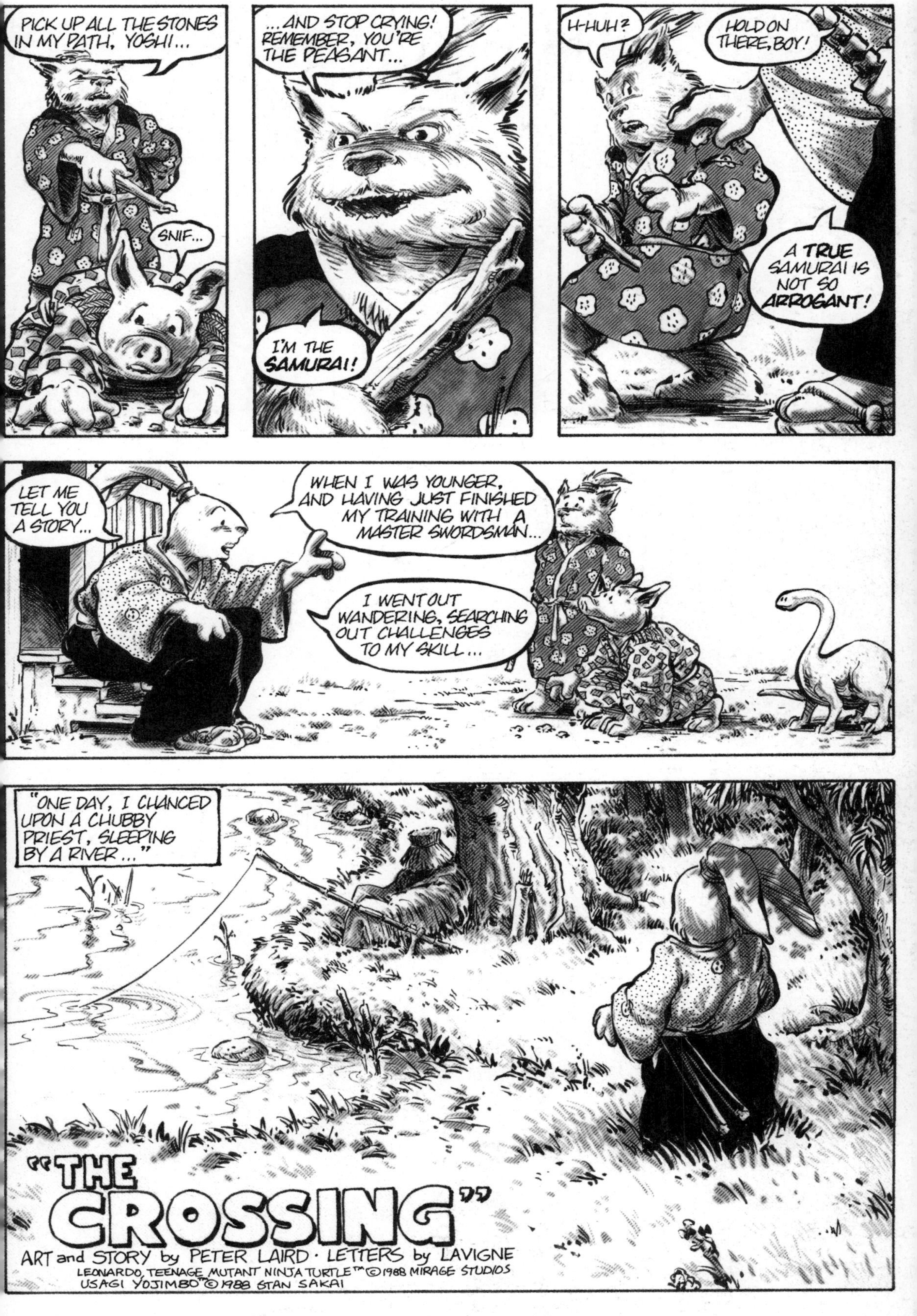
PICK UP ALL THE STONES IN MY PATH, YOSHI...
SNIF...
...AND STOP CRYING! REMEMBER, YOU'RE THE PEASANT...
I'M THE SAMURAI!
H-HUH?
HOLD ON THERE, BOY!
A TRUE SAMURAI IS NOT SO ARROGANT!
LET ME TELL YOU A STORY...
WHEN I WAS YOUNGER, AND HAVING JUST FINISHED MY TRAINING WITH A MASTER SWORDSMAN...
I WENT OUT WANDERING, SEARCHING OUT CHALLENGES TO MY SKILL...
"ONE DAY, I CHANCED UPON A CHUBBY PRIEST, SLEEPING BY A RIVER..."
"THE CROSSING"
ART and STORY by PETER LAIRD · LETTERS by LAVIGNE
LEONARDO, TEENAGE MUTANT NINJA TURTLE™ © 1988 MIRAGE STUDIOS
USAGI YOJIMBO™ © 1988 STAN SAKAI

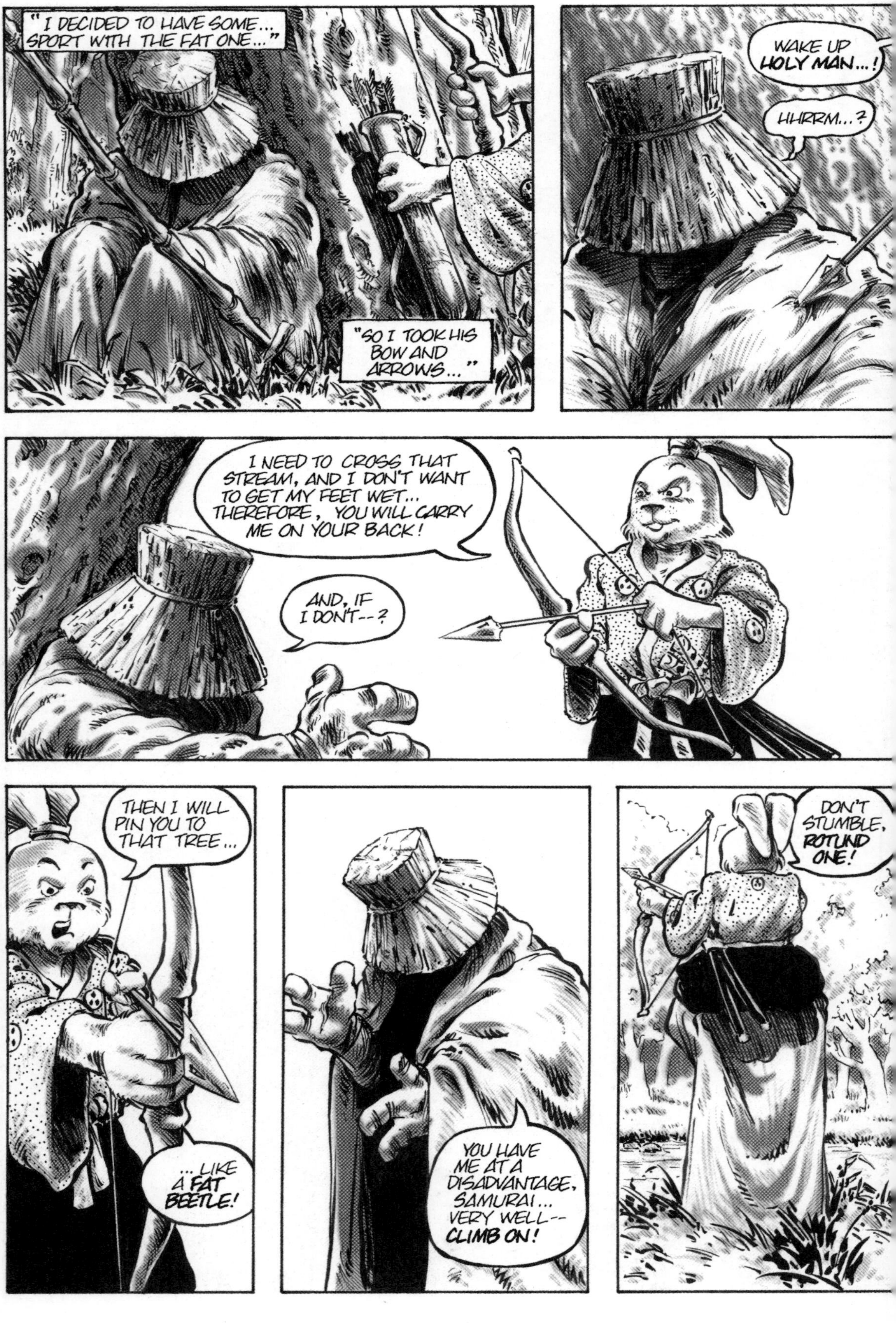
"I DECIDED TO HAVE SOME... SPORT WITH THE FAT ONE..."
"SO I TOOK HIS BOW AND ARROWS..."
WAKE UP HOLY MAN...!
HHRRM...?
I NEED TO CROSS THAT STREAM, AND I DON'T WANT TO GET MY FEET WET... THEREFORE, YOU WILL CARRY ME ON YOUR BACK!
AND, IF I DON'T--?
THEN I WILL PIN YOU TO THAT TREE...
...LIKE A FAT BEETLE!
YOU HAVE ME AT A DISADVANTAGE, SAMURAI... VERY WELL-- CLIMB ON!
DON'T STUMBLE, ROTUND ONE!

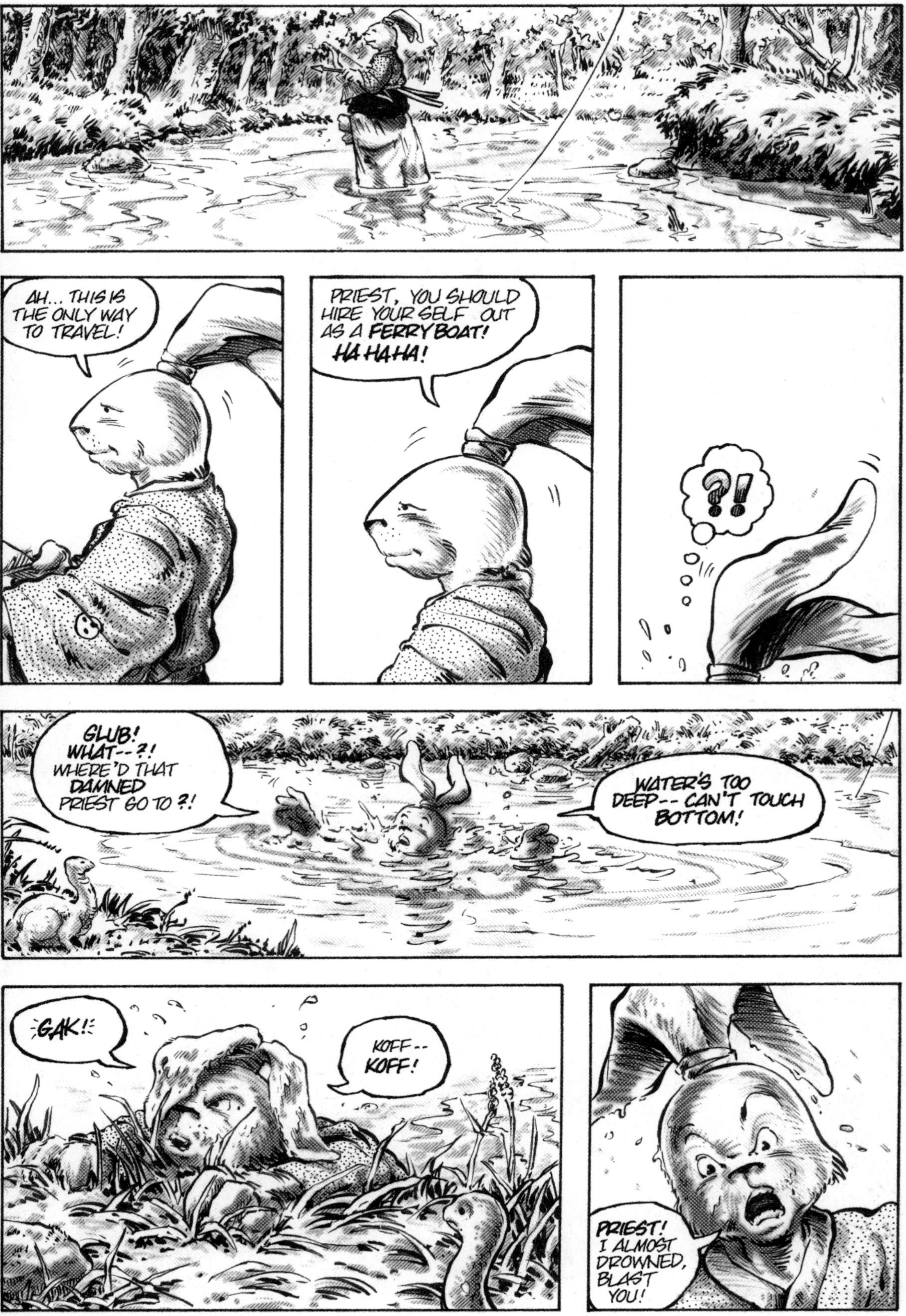
AH... THIS IS THE ONLY WAY TO TRAVEL!
PRIEST, YOU SHOULD HIRE YOURSELF OUT AS A FERRYBOAT! HA HA HA!
?!
GLUB! WHAT--?! WHERE'D THAT DAMNED PRIEST GO TO?!
WATER'S TOO DEEP--CAN'T TOUCH BOTTOM!
GAK!
KOFF-- KOFF!
PRIEST! I ALMOST DROWNED, BLAST YOU!

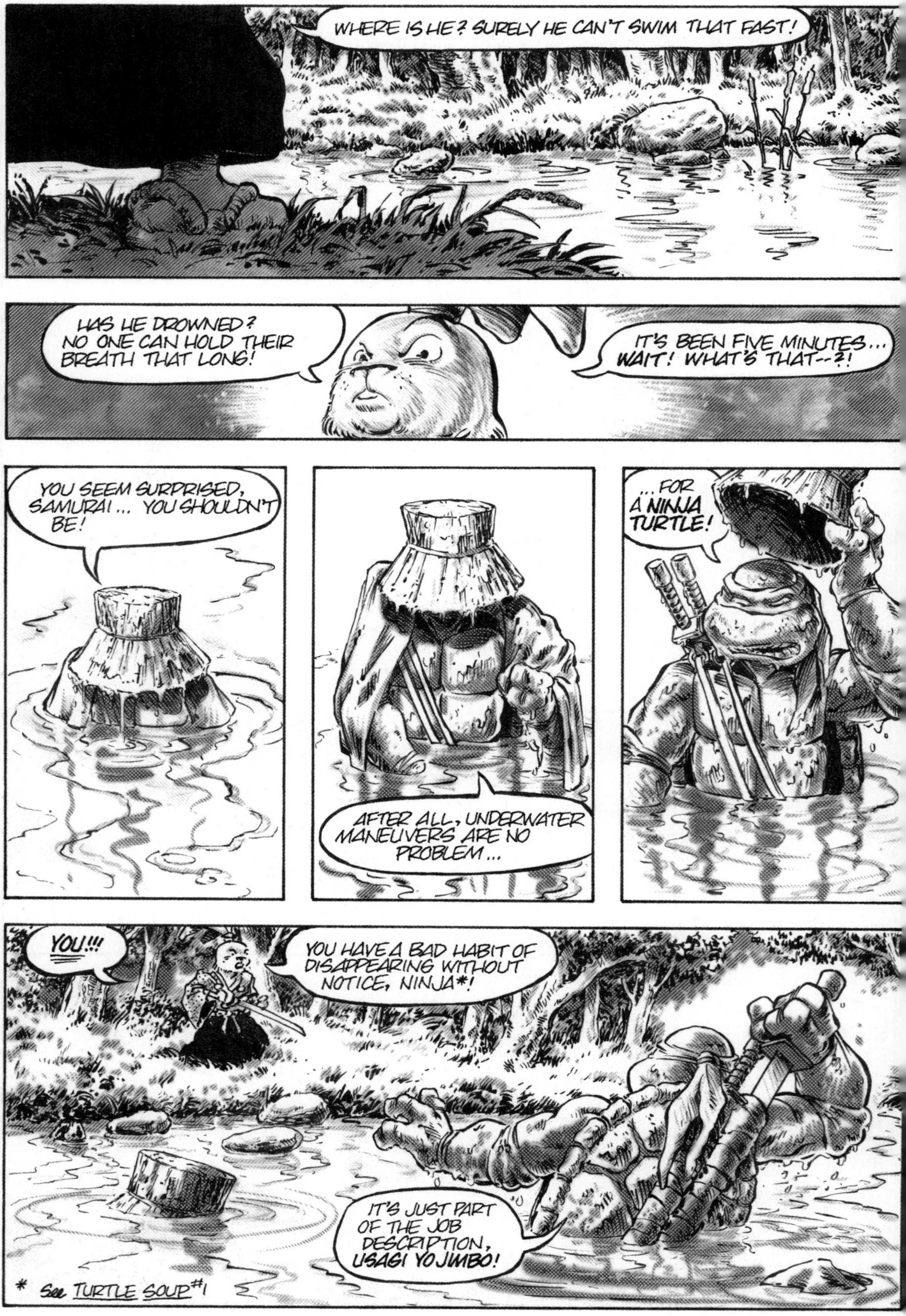
WHERE IS HE? SURELY HE CAN'T SWIM THAT FAST!
HAS HE DROWNED? NO ONE CAN HOLD THEIR BREATH THAT LONG!
IT'S BEEN FIVE MINUTES... WAIT! WHAT'S THAT--?!
YOU SEEM SURPRISED, SAMURAI... YOU SHOULDN'T BE!
AFTER ALL, UNDERWATER MANEUVERS ARE NO PROBLEM...
...FOR A NINJA TURTLE!
YOU!!!
YOU HAVE A BAD HABIT OF DISAPPEARING WITHOUT NOTICE, NINJA*!
IT'S JUST PART OF THE JOB DESCRIPTION, USAGI YOJIMBO!
* See TURTLE SOUP #1

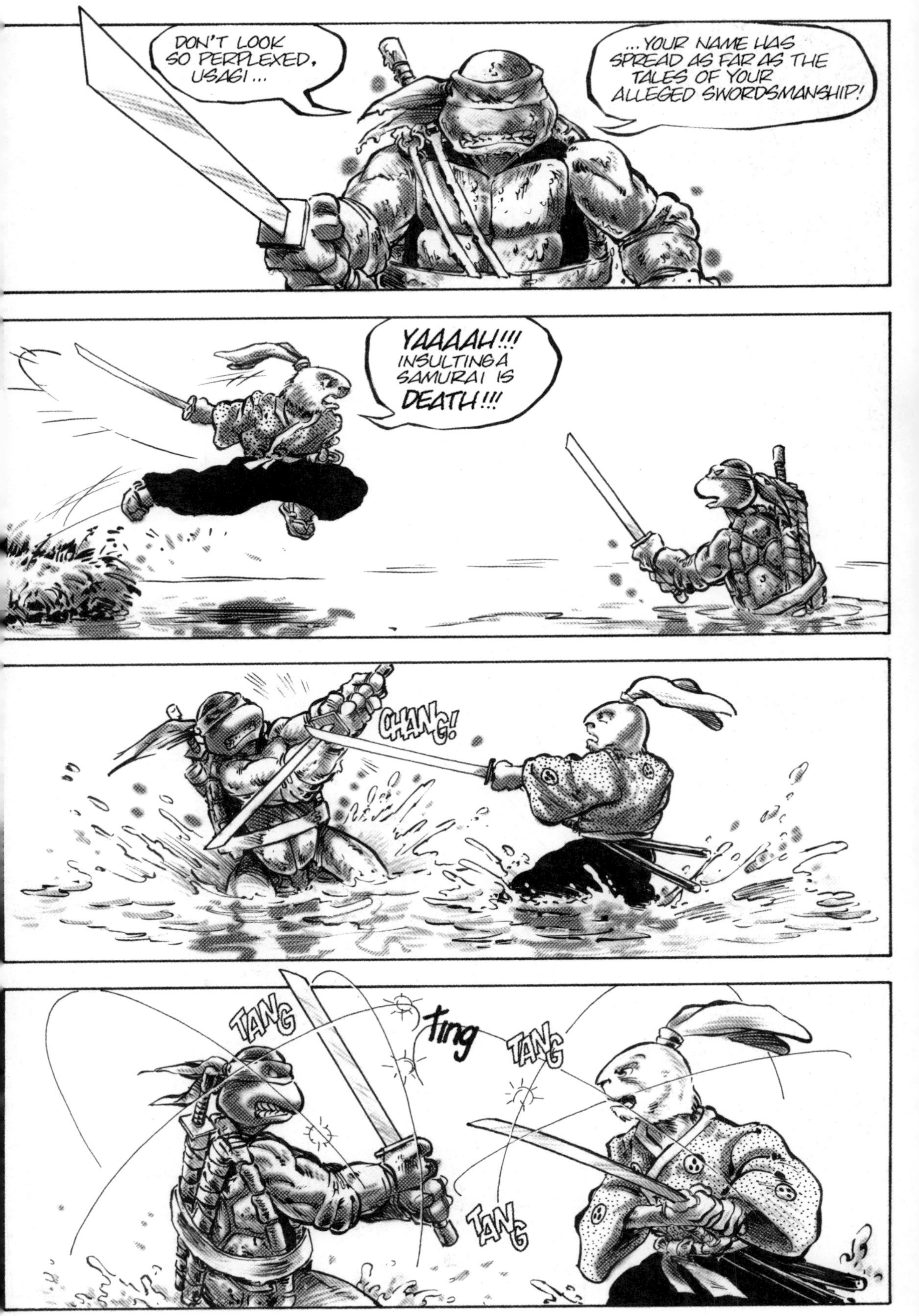
DON'T LOOK SO PERPLEXED, USAGI...
...YOUR NAME HAS SPREAD AS FAR AS THE TALES OF YOUR ALLEGED SWORDSMANSHIP!
YAAAAH!!! INSULTING A SAMURAI IS DEATH!!!
CHANG!
TANG
Ting
TANG
TANG

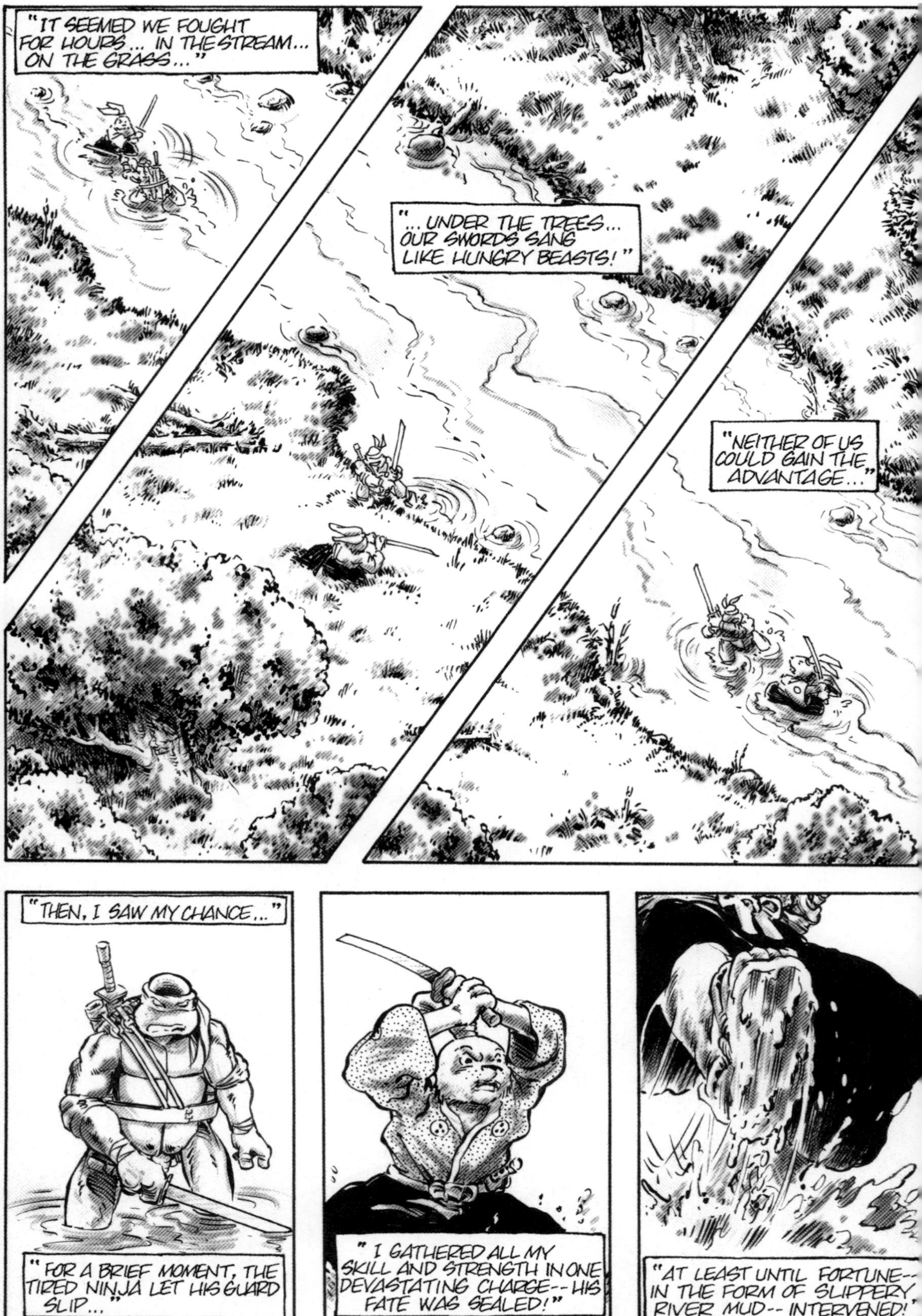
"IT SEEMED WE FOUGHT FOR HOURS... IN THE STREAM... ON THE GRASS..."
"...UNDER THE TREES... OUR SWORDS SANG LIKE HUNGRY BEASTS!"
"NEITHER OF US COULD GAIN THE ADVANTAGE..."
"THEN, I SAW MY CHANCE..."
"FOR A BRIEF MOMENT, THE TIRED NINJA LET HIS GUARD SLIP..."
"I GATHERED ALL MY SKILL AND STRENGTH IN ONE DEVASTATING CHARGE-- HIS FATE WAS SEALED!"
"AT LEAST UNTIL FORTUNE-- IN THE FORM OF SLIPPERY RIVER MUD-- INTERVENED!"

BAD LUCK FOR YOU, SAMURAI... GOOD LUCK FOR ME!

...BECAUSE YOU ARE EVERY BIT AS SKILLED AS I WAS TOLD!

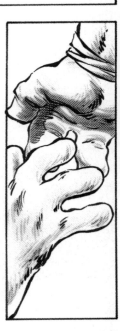

THE NINJA WAS A STRANGE ONE, BUT HE HAD HONOR...

HIS NAME WAS LEONARDO... WE BECAME FRIENDS AND HAD MANY ADVENTURES!

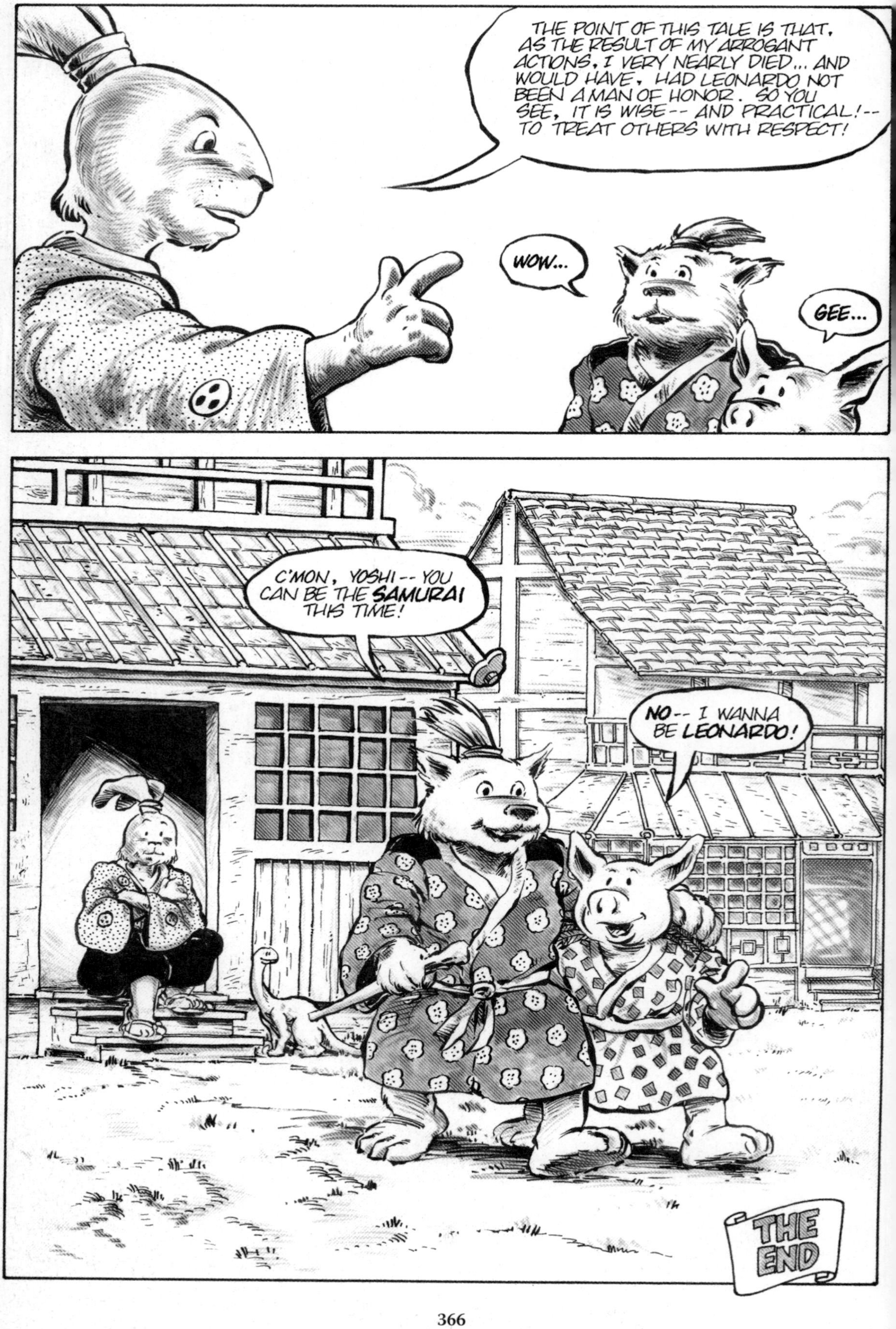
THE POINT OF THIS TALE IS THAT, AS THE RESULT OF MY ARROGANT ACTIONS, I VERY NEARLY DIED... AND WOULD HAVE, HAD LEONARDO NOT BEEN A MAN OF HONOR. SO YOU SEE, IT IS WISE-- AND PRACTICAL!-- TO TREAT OTHERS WITH RESPECT!
WOW...
GEE...
C'MON, YOSHI-- YOU CAN BE THE SAMURAI THIS TIME!
NO-- I WANNA BE LEONARDO!
THE END

THE TREATY

Written, illustrated, and lettered by

STAN SAKAI

Originally appeared
in *Shell Shock*, published by
Mirage Studios in 1989.

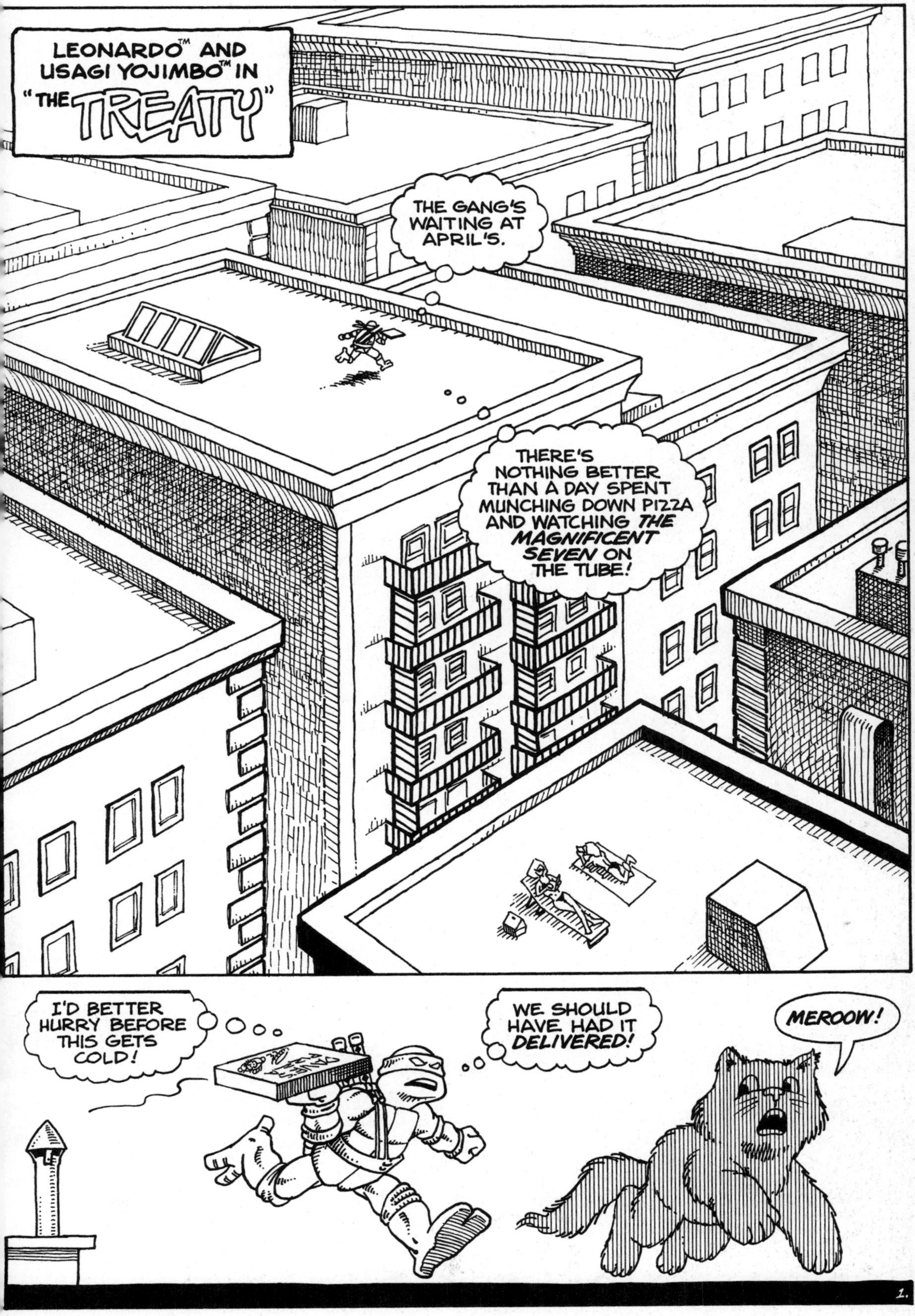
LEONARDO™ AND USAGI YOJIMBO™ IN "THE TREATY"
THE GANG'S WAITING AT APRIL'S.
THERE'S NOTHING BETTER THAN A DAY SPENT MUNCHING DOWN PIZZA AND WATCHING *THE MAGNIFICENT SEVEN* ON THE TUBE!
I'D BETTER HURRY BEFORE THIS GETS COLD!
WE SHOULD HAVE HAD IT *DELIVERED!*
MEROOW!
1.

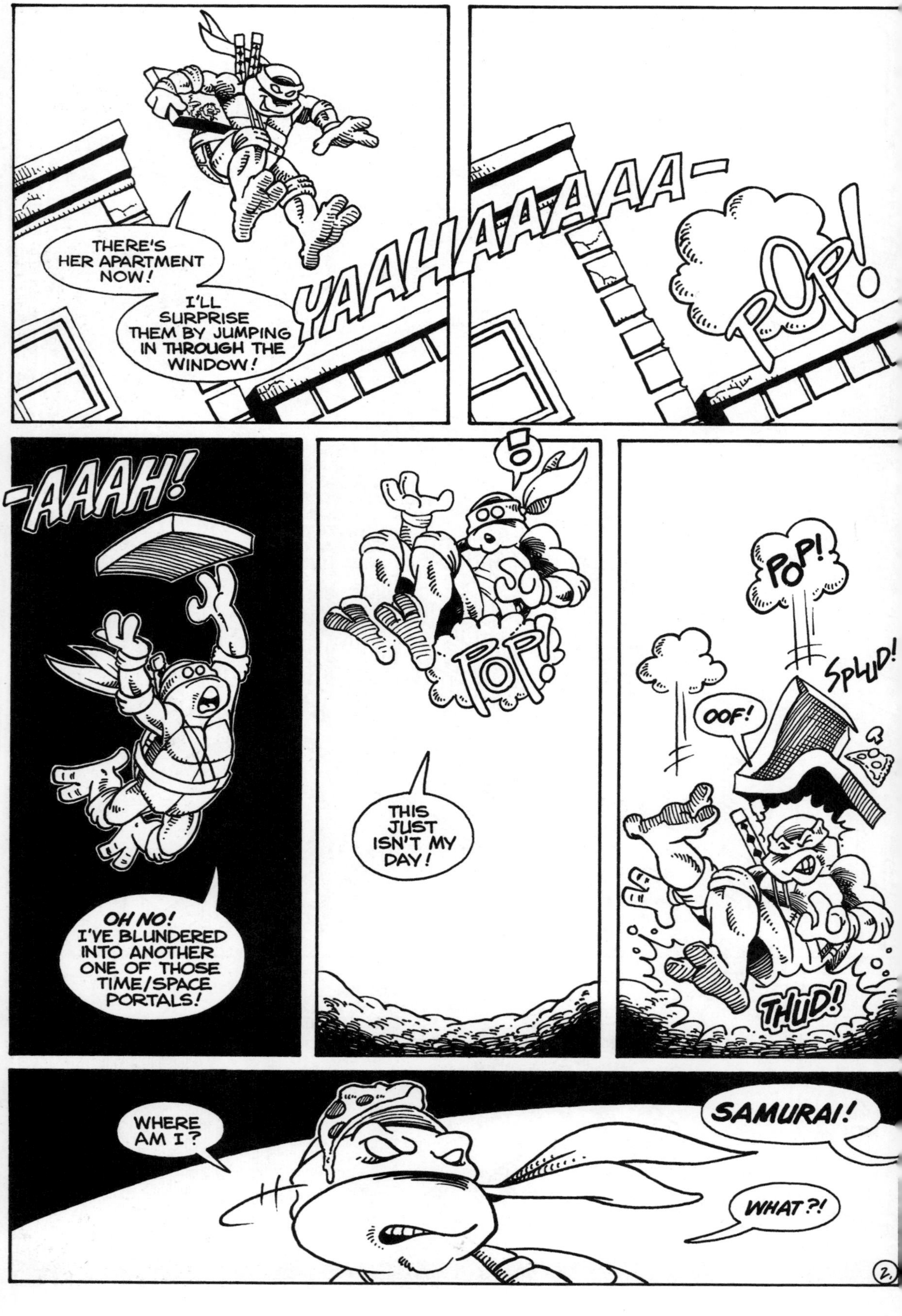
THERE'S HER APARTMENT NOW!
I'LL SURPRISE THEM BY JUMPING IN THROUGH THE WINDOW!
YAAHAAAAAAA-
POP!
-AAAH!
OH NO! I'VE BLUNDERED INTO ANOTHER ONE OF THOSE TIME/SPACE PORTALS!
!
POP!
THIS JUST ISN'T MY DAY!
POP!
SPLUD!
OOF!
THUD!
WHERE AM I?
SAMURAI!
WHAT?!
2.

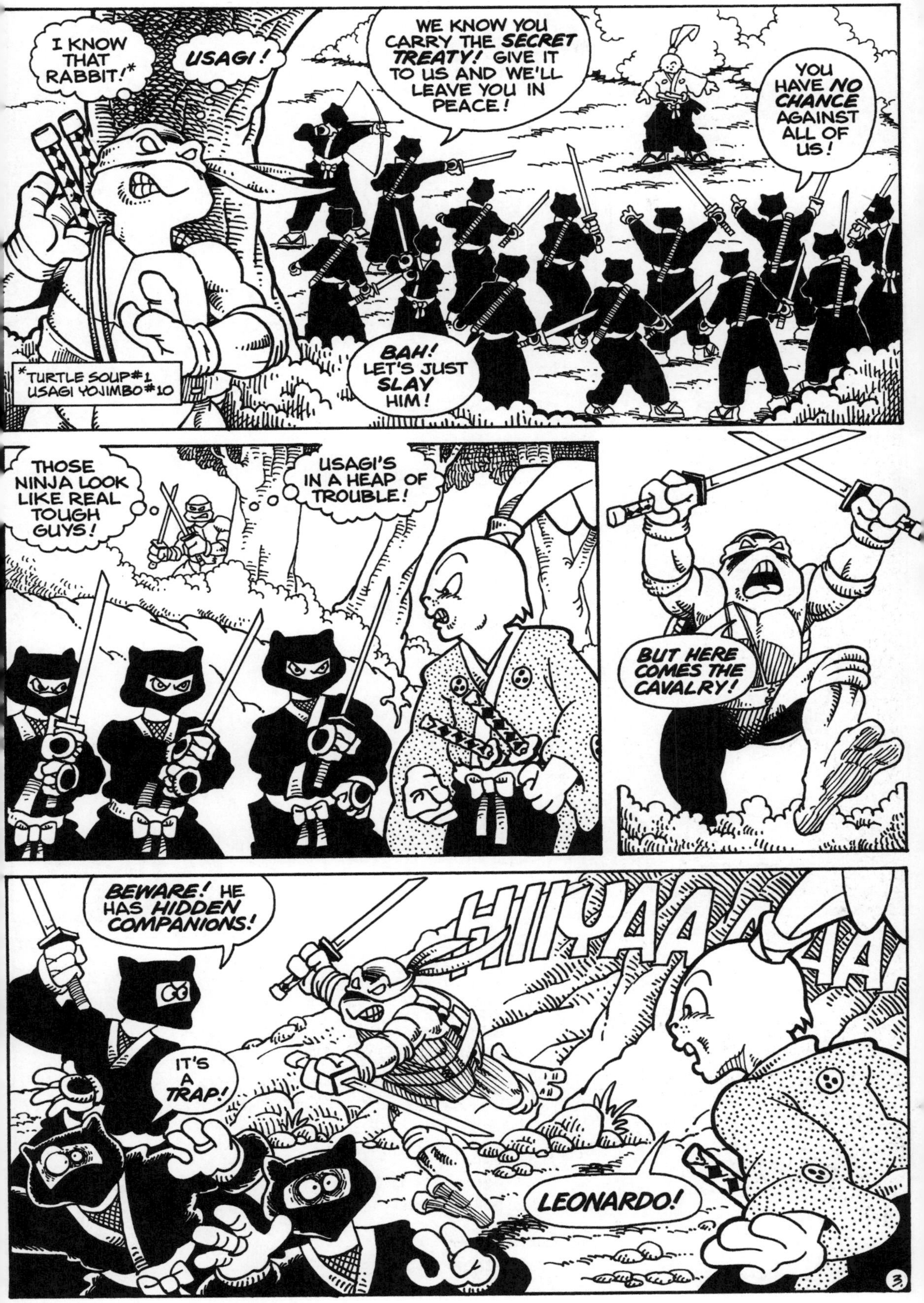
I KNOW THAT RABBIT!*
USAGI!
WE KNOW YOU CARRY THE SECRET TREATY! GIVE IT TO US AND WE'LL LEAVE YOU IN PEACE!
YOU HAVE NO CHANCE AGAINST ALL OF US!
BAH! LET'S JUST SLAY HIM!
*TURTLE SOUP #1
USAGI YOJIMBO #10
THOSE NINJA LOOK LIKE REAL TOUGH GUYS!
USAGI'S IN A HEAP OF TROUBLE!
BUT HERE COMES THE CAVALRY!
BEWARE! HE HAS HIDDEN COMPANIONS!
HIIYAAAAA!
IT'S A TRAP!
LEONARDO!
3.

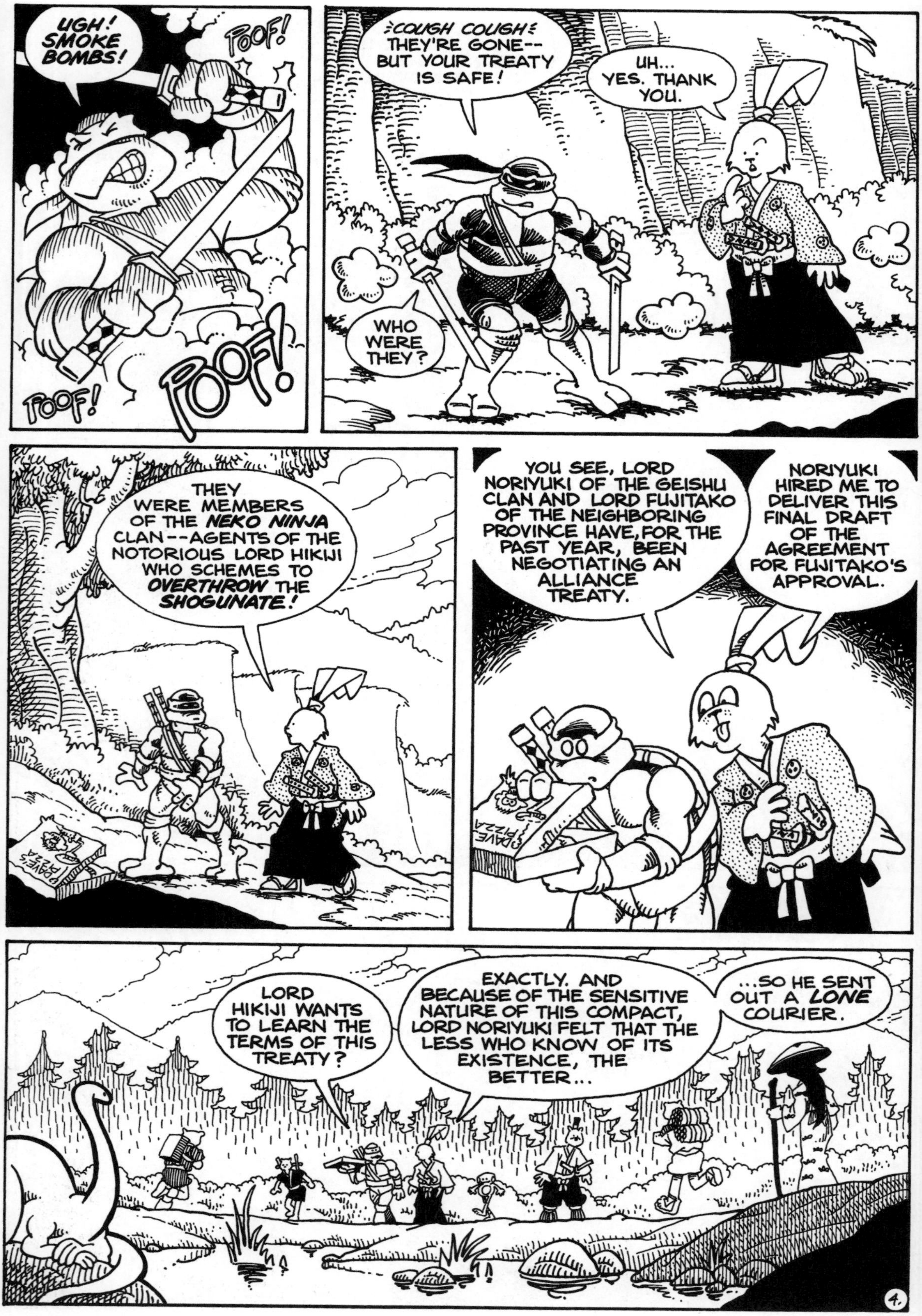
UGH! SMOKE BOMBS!
POOF!
POOF!
POOF!
≤COUGH COUGH≤ THEY'RE GONE-- BUT YOUR TREATY IS SAFE!
UH... YES. THANK YOU.
WHO WERE THEY?
THEY WERE MEMBERS OF THE NEKO NINJA CLAN--AGENTS OF THE NOTORIOUS LORD HIKIJI WHO SCHEMES TO OVERTHROW THE SHOGUNATE!
DAVE'S PIZZA
YOU SEE, LORD NORIYUKI OF THE GEISHU CLAN AND LORD FUJITAKO OF THE NEIGHBORING PROVINCE HAVE, FOR THE PAST YEAR, BEEN NEGOTIATING AN ALLIANCE TREATY.
NORIYUKI HIRED ME TO DELIVER THIS FINAL DRAFT OF THE AGREEMENT FOR FUJITAKO'S APPROVAL.
LORD HIKIJI WANTS TO LEARN THE TERMS OF THIS TREATY?
EXACTLY. AND BECAUSE OF THE SENSITIVE NATURE OF THIS COMPACT, LORD NORIYUKI FELT THAT THE LESS WHO KNOW OF ITS EXISTENCE, THE BETTER...
...SO HE SENT OUT A LONE COURIER.
4.

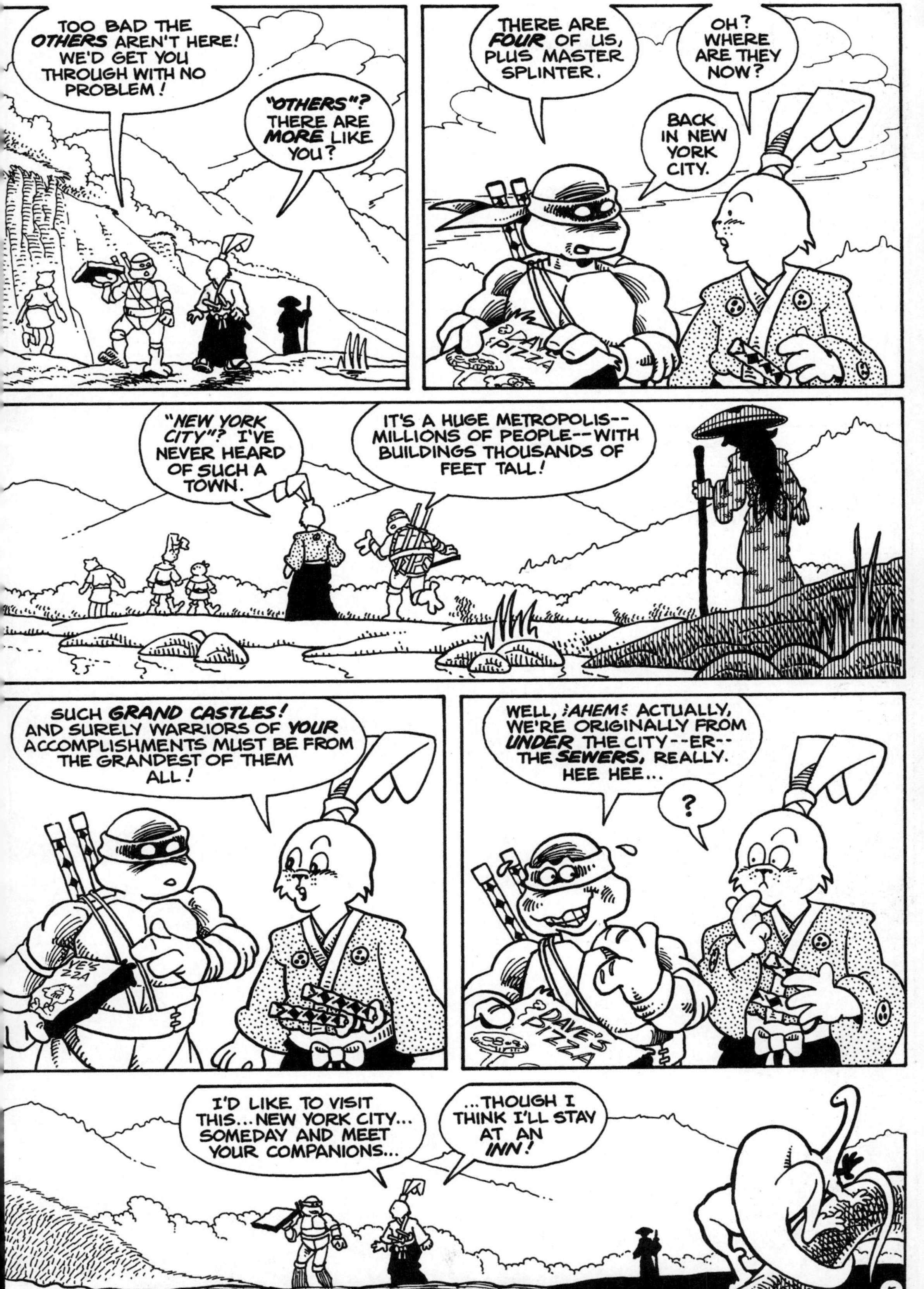
TOO BAD THE OTHERS AREN'T HERE! WE'D GET YOU THROUGH WITH NO PROBLEM!
"OTHERS"? THERE ARE MORE LIKE YOU?
THERE ARE FOUR OF US, PLUS MASTER SPLINTER.
OH? WHERE ARE THEY NOW?
BACK IN NEW YORK CITY.
DAVE'S PIZZA
"NEW YORK CITY"? I'VE NEVER HEARD OF SUCH A TOWN.
IT'S A HUGE METROPOLIS--MILLIONS OF PEOPLE--WITH BUILDINGS THOUSANDS OF FEET TALL!
SUCH GRAND CASTLES! AND SURELY WARRIORS OF YOUR ACCOMPLISHMENTS MUST BE FROM THE GRANDEST OF THEM ALL!
WELL, AHEM ACTUALLY, WE'RE ORIGINALLY FROM UNDER THE CITY--ER--THE SEWERS, REALLY. HEE HEE...
?
DAVE'S PIZZA
I'D LIKE TO VISIT THIS...NEW YORK CITY... SOMEDAY AND MEET YOUR COMPANIONS...
...THOUGH I THINK I'LL STAY AT AN INN!
5.

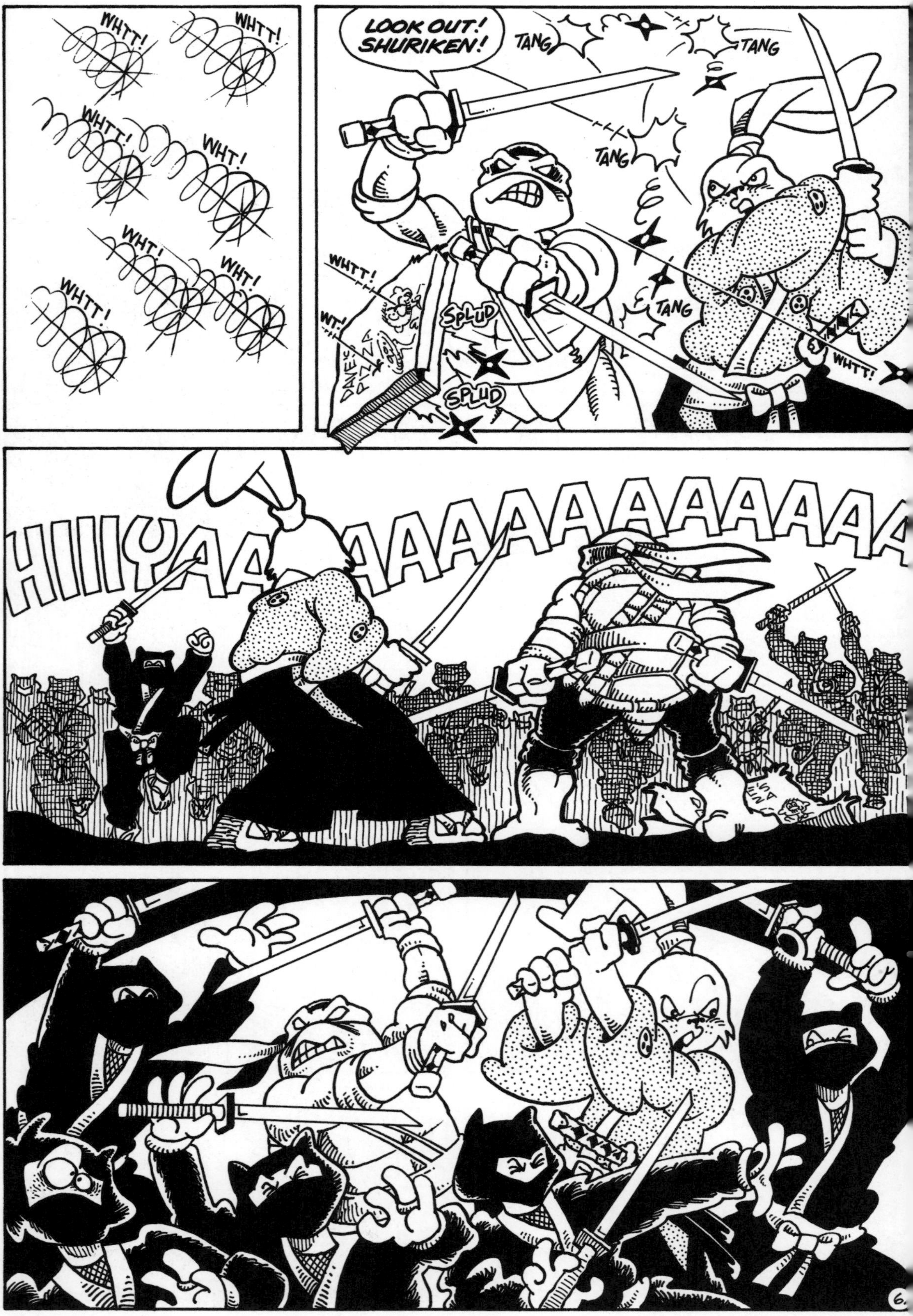
WHTT!
WHTT!
WHTT!
WHT!
WHT!
WHT!
WHTT!
LOOK OUT! SHURIKEN!
TANG
TANG
TANG
WHTT!
WT!
SPLUD
SPLUD
TANG
WHTT!
HIIIYAAAAAAAAAAAAA
6.

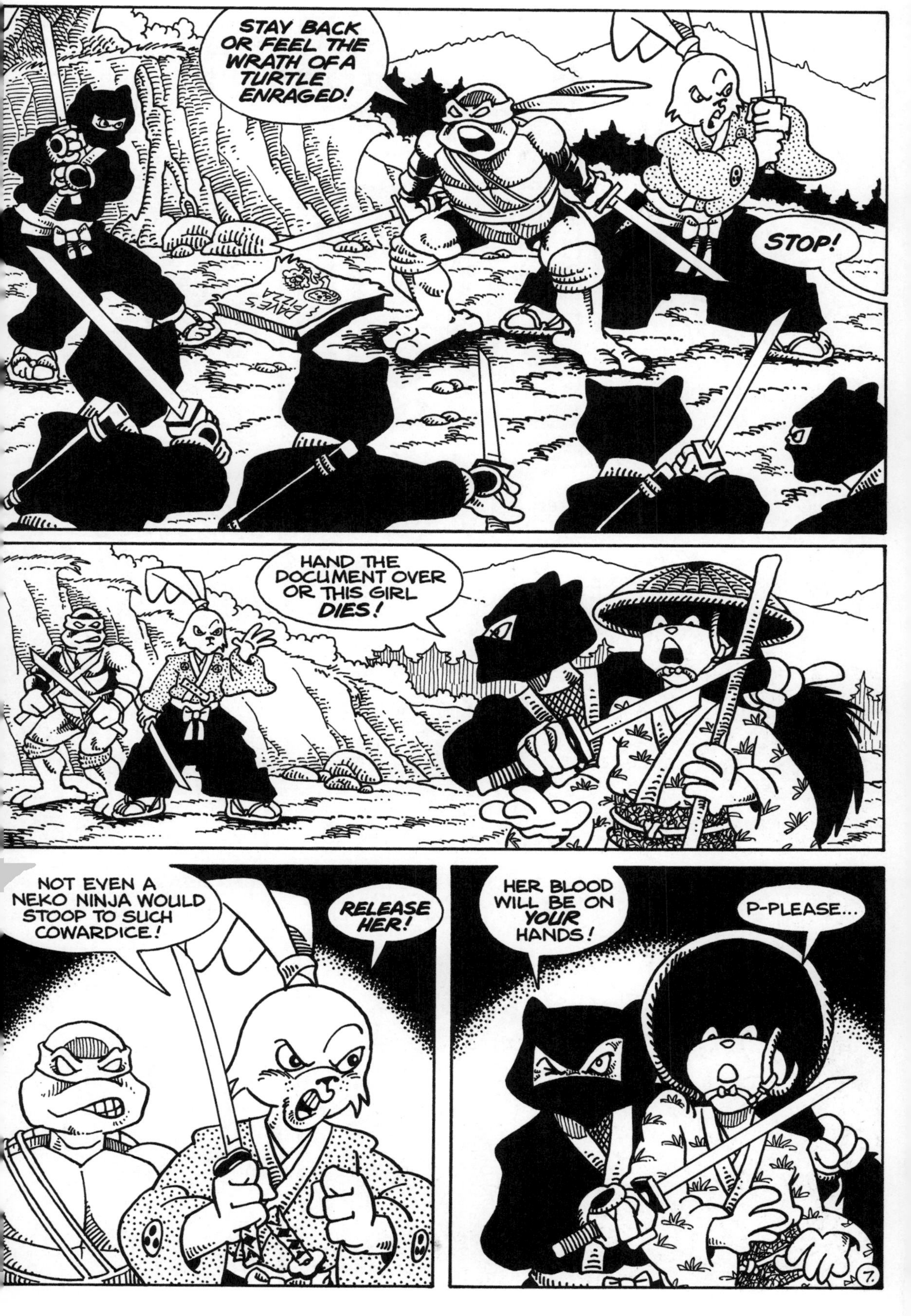
STAY BACK OR FEEL THE WRATH OF A TURTLE ENRAGED!
DAVE'S PIZZA
STOP!
HAND THE DOCUMENT OVER OR THIS GIRL DIES!
NOT EVEN A NEKO NINJA WOULD STOOP TO SUCH COWARDICE!
RELEASE HER!
HER BLOOD WILL BE ON YOUR HANDS!
P-PLEASE...
7.

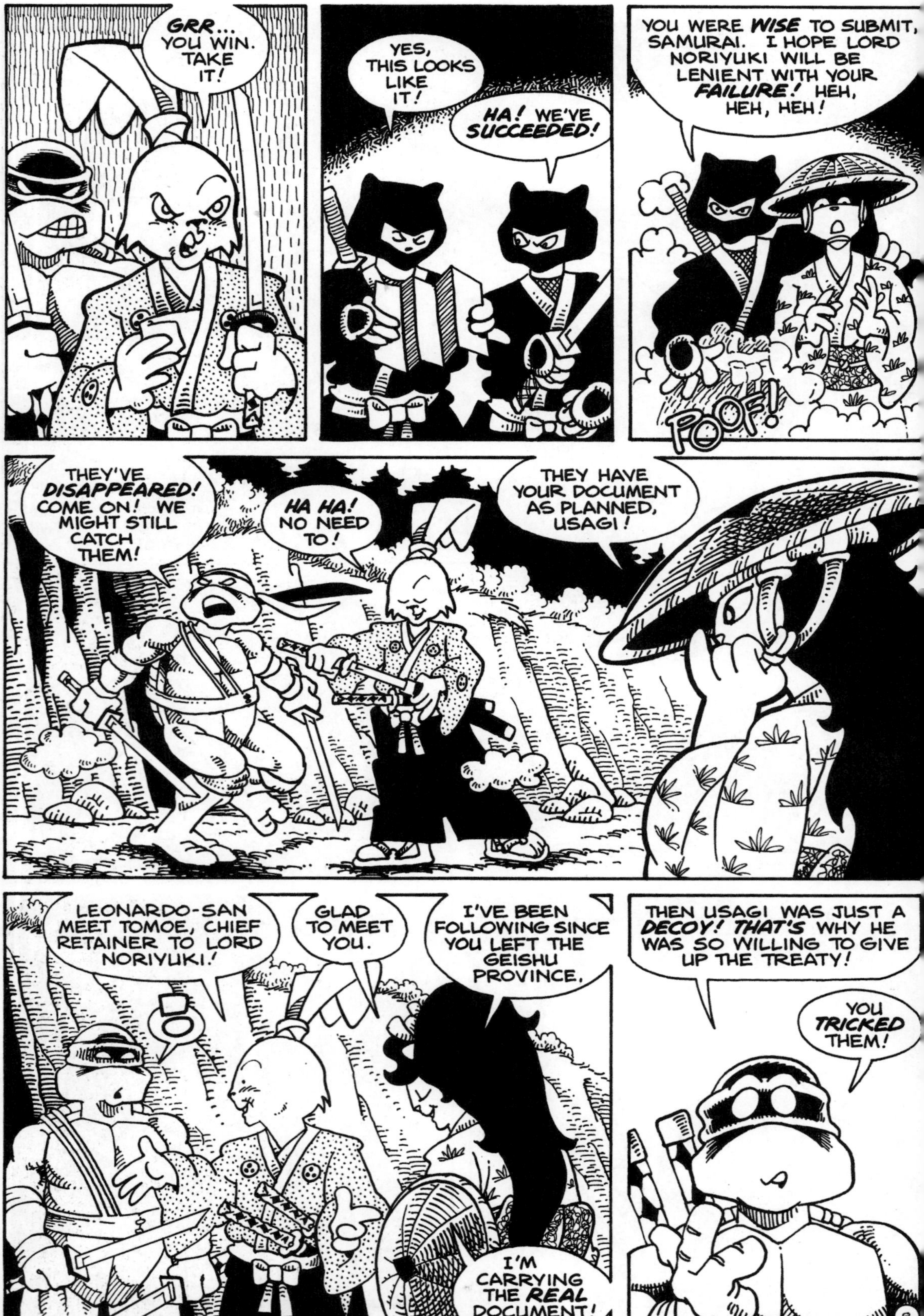

GRR... YOU WIN. TAKE IT!
YES, THIS LOOKS LIKE IT!
HA! WE'VE SUCCEEDED!
YOU WERE WISE TO SUBMIT, SAMURAI. I HOPE LORD NORIYUKI WILL BE LENIENT WITH YOUR FAILURE! HEH, HEH, HEH!
POOF!
THEY'VE DISAPPEARED! COME ON! WE MIGHT STILL CATCH THEM!
HA HA! NO NEED TO!
THEY HAVE YOUR DOCUMENT AS PLANNED, USAGI!
LEONARDO-SAN MEET TOMOE, CHIEF RETAINER TO LORD NORIYUKI!
GLAD TO MEET YOU.
I'VE BEEN FOLLOWING SINCE YOU LEFT THE GEISHU PROVINCE.
I'M CARRYING THE REAL DOCUMENT!
THEN USAGI WAS JUST A DECOY! THAT'S WHY HE WAS SO WILLING TO GIVE UP THE TREATY!
YOU TRICKED THEM!
8.

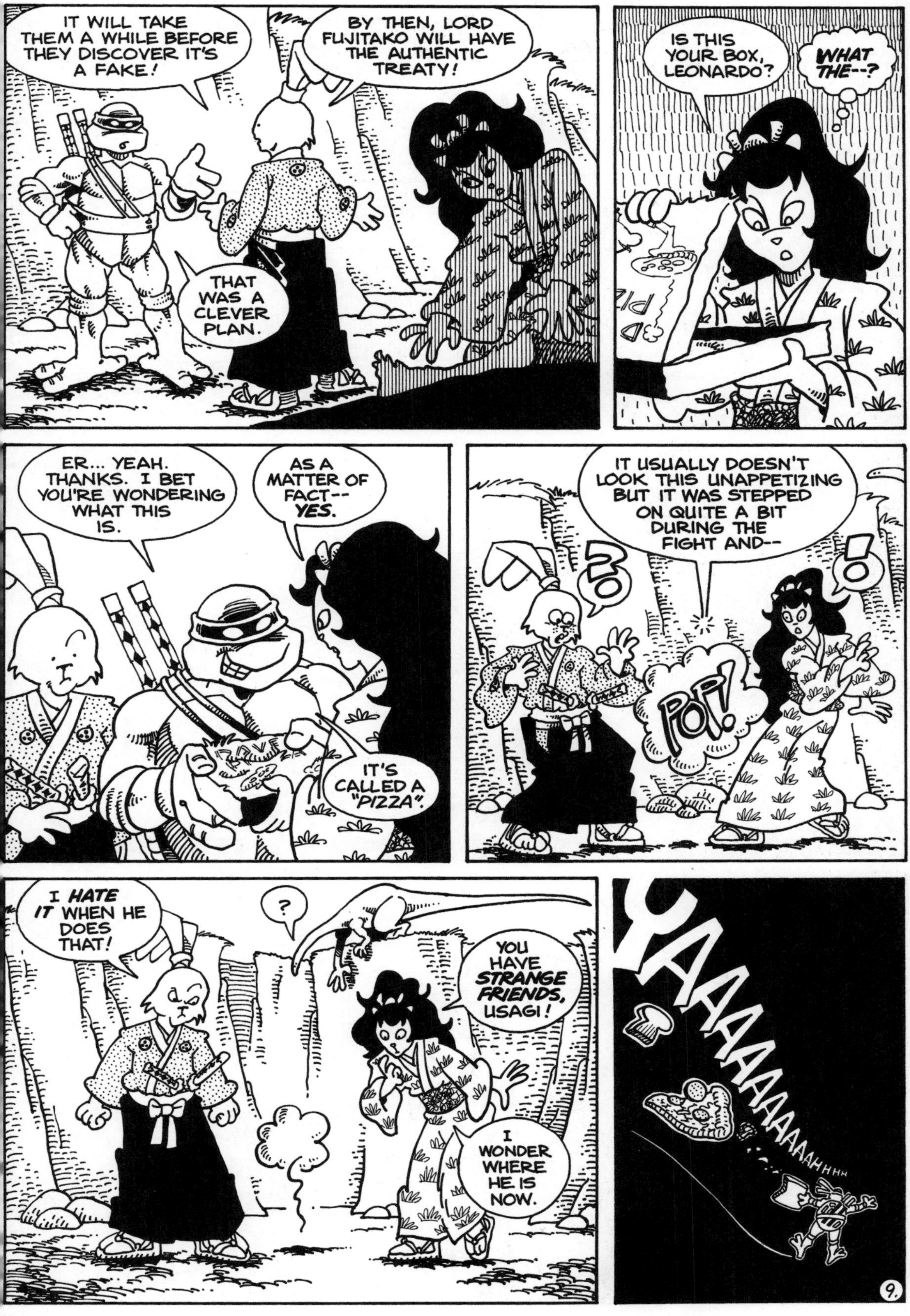
IT WILL TAKE THEM A WHILE BEFORE THEY DISCOVER IT'S A FAKE!
BY THEN, LORD FUJITAKO WILL HAVE THE AUTHENTIC TREATY!
THAT WAS A CLEVER PLAN.
IS THIS YOUR BOX, LEONARDO?
WHAT THE--?
ER... YEAH. THANKS. I BET YOU'RE WONDERING WHAT THIS IS.
AS A MATTER OF FACT-- YES.
IT'S CALLED A "PIZZA".
IT USUALLY DOESN'T LOOK THIS UNAPPETIZING BUT IT WAS STEPPED ON QUITE A BIT DURING THE FIGHT AND--
?
!
POP!
I HATE IT WHEN HE DOES THAT!
?
YOU HAVE STRANGE FRIENDS, USAGI!
I WONDER WHERE HE IS NOW.
YAAAAAAAAAAAHHHH
9.

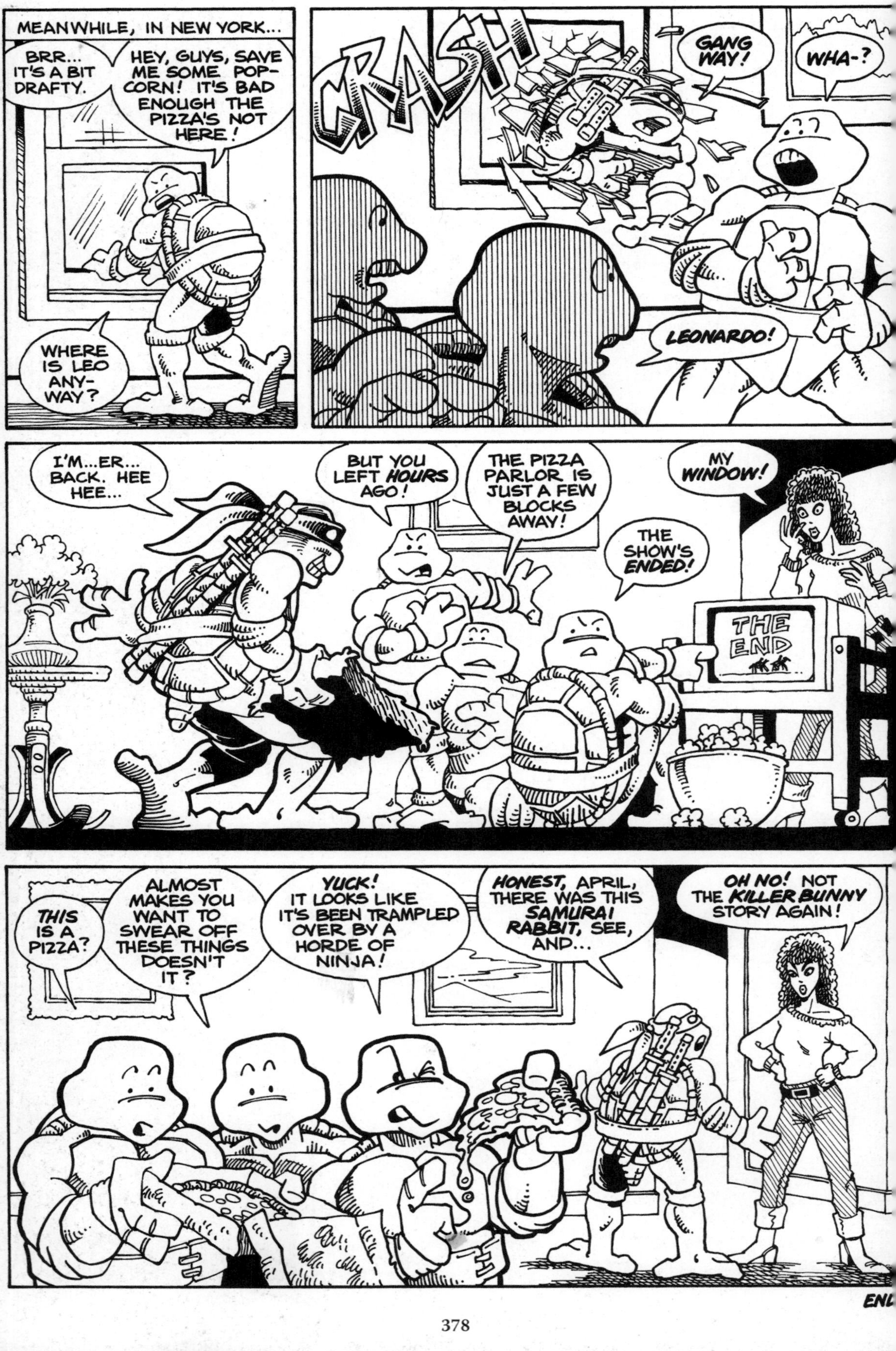
MEANWHILE, IN NEW YORK...
BRR... IT'S A BIT DRAFTY.
HEY, GUYS, SAVE ME SOME POP-CORN! IT'S BAD ENOUGH THE PIZZA'S NOT HERE!
WHERE IS LEO ANY-WAY?
CRASH
GANG WAY!
WHA-?
LEONARDO!
I'M...ER... BACK. HEE HEE...
BUT YOU LEFT HOURS AGO!
THE PIZZA PARLOR IS JUST A FEW BLOCKS AWAY!
MY WINDOW!
THE SHOW'S ENDED!
THE END
THIS IS A PIZZA?
ALMOST MAKES YOU WANT TO SWEAR OFF THESE THINGS DOESN'T IT?
YUCK! IT LOOKS LIKE IT'S BEEN TRAMPLED OVER BY A HORDE OF NINJA!
HONEST, APRIL, THERE WAS THIS SAMURAI RABBIT, SEE, AND...
OH NO! NOT THE KILLER BUNNY STORY AGAIN!

SHADES OF GREEN

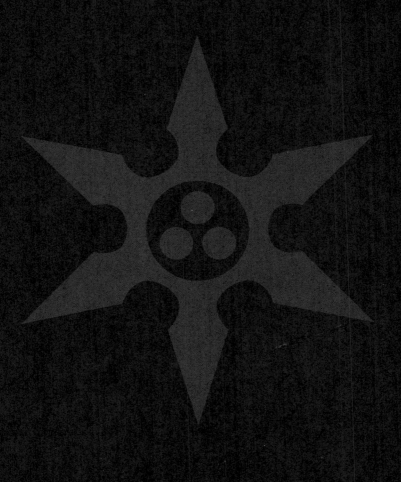

Written, illustrated, and lettered by

STAN SAKAI

Originally appeared in
Usagi Yojimbo Volume Two #1–#3, published by
Mirage Studios in 1993.

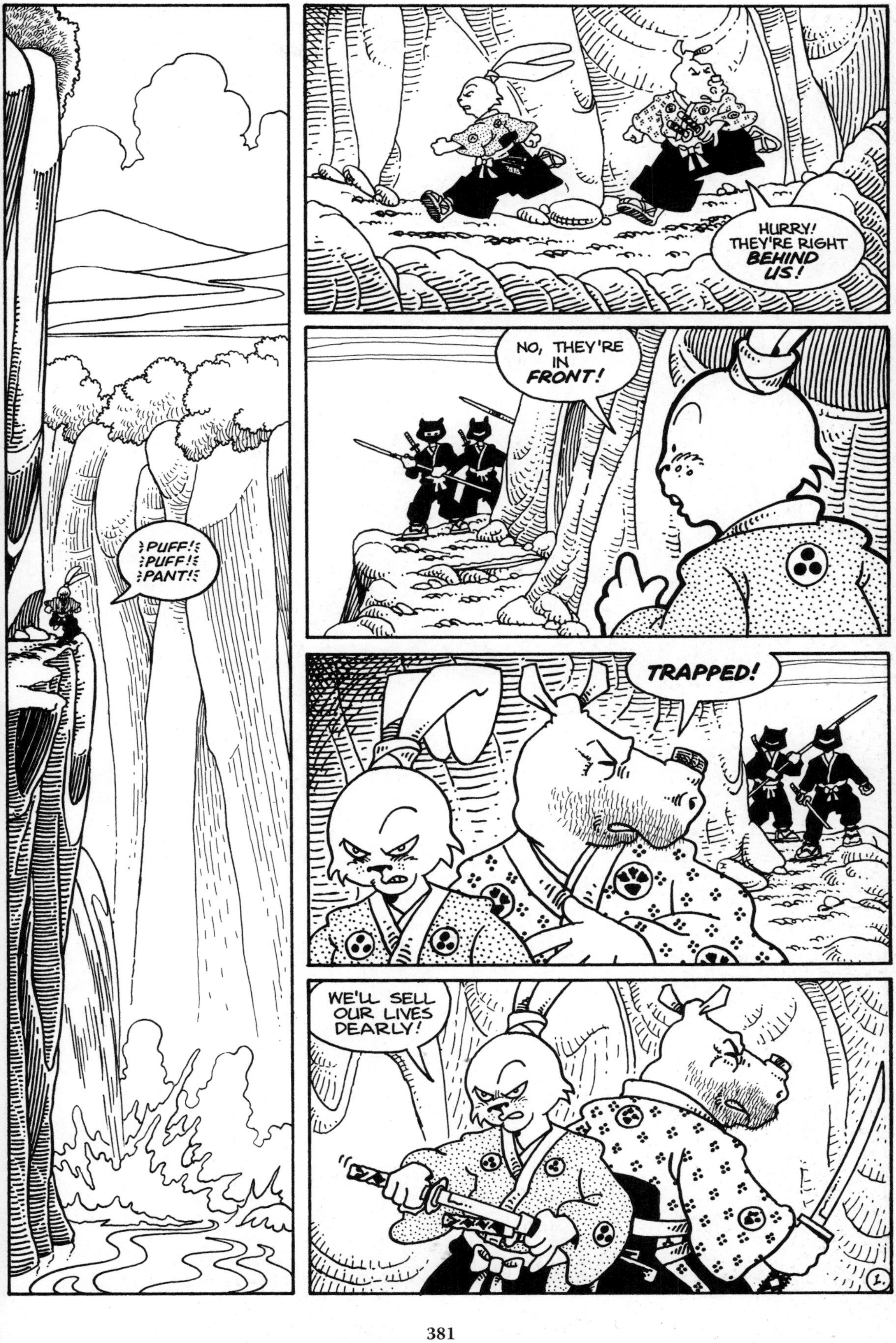
PUFF! PUFF! PANT!
HURRY! THEY'RE RIGHT BEHIND US!
NO, THEY'RE IN FRONT!
TRAPPED!
WE'LL SELL OUR LIVES DEARLY!
2.

SHADES of GREEN

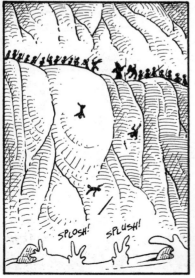

SPLOSH! SPLUSH!

URK!

YAAHH!

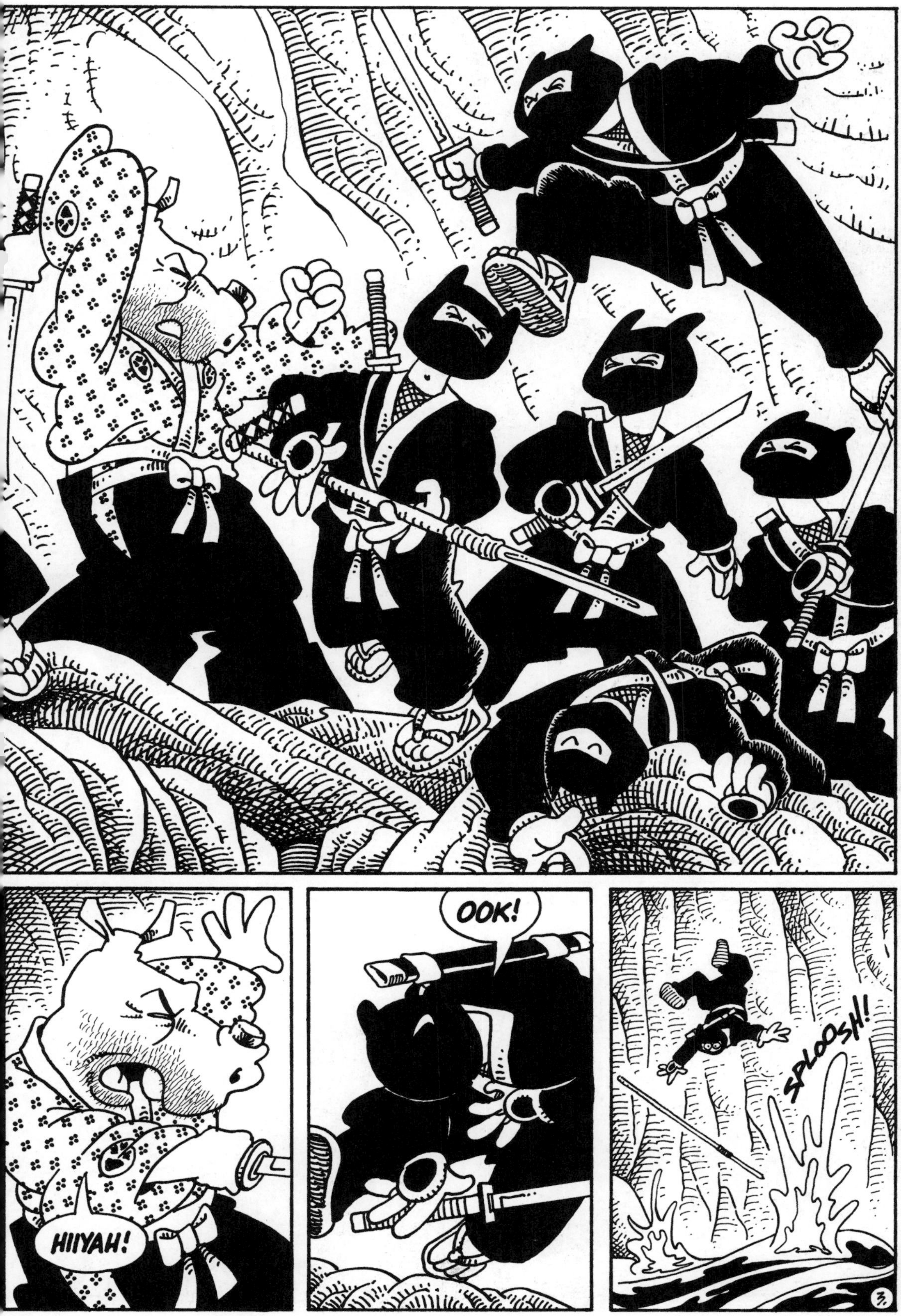
HIIYAH!
OOK!
SPLOOSH!
3

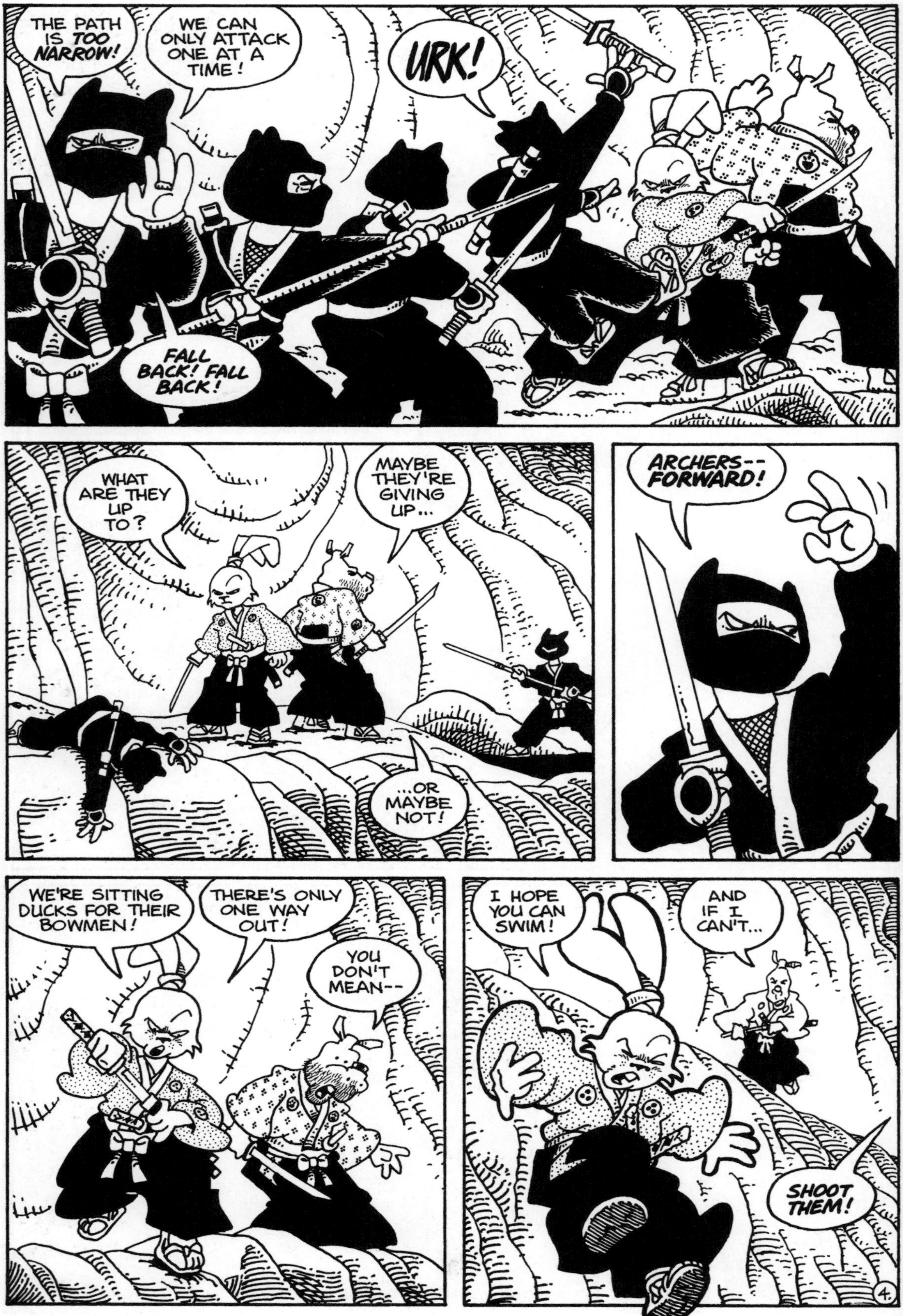
THE PATH IS *TOO NARROW!*
WE CAN ONLY ATTACK ONE AT A TIME!
URK!
FALL BACK! FALL BACK!
WHAT ARE THEY UP TO?
MAYBE THEY'RE GIVING UP...
...OR MAYBE NOT!
ARCHERS-- FORWARD!
WE'RE SITTING DUCKS FOR THEIR BOWMEN!
THERE'S ONLY ONE WAY OUT!
YOU DON'T MEAN--
I HOPE YOU CAN SWIM!
AND IF I CAN'T...
SHOOT THEM!
4.

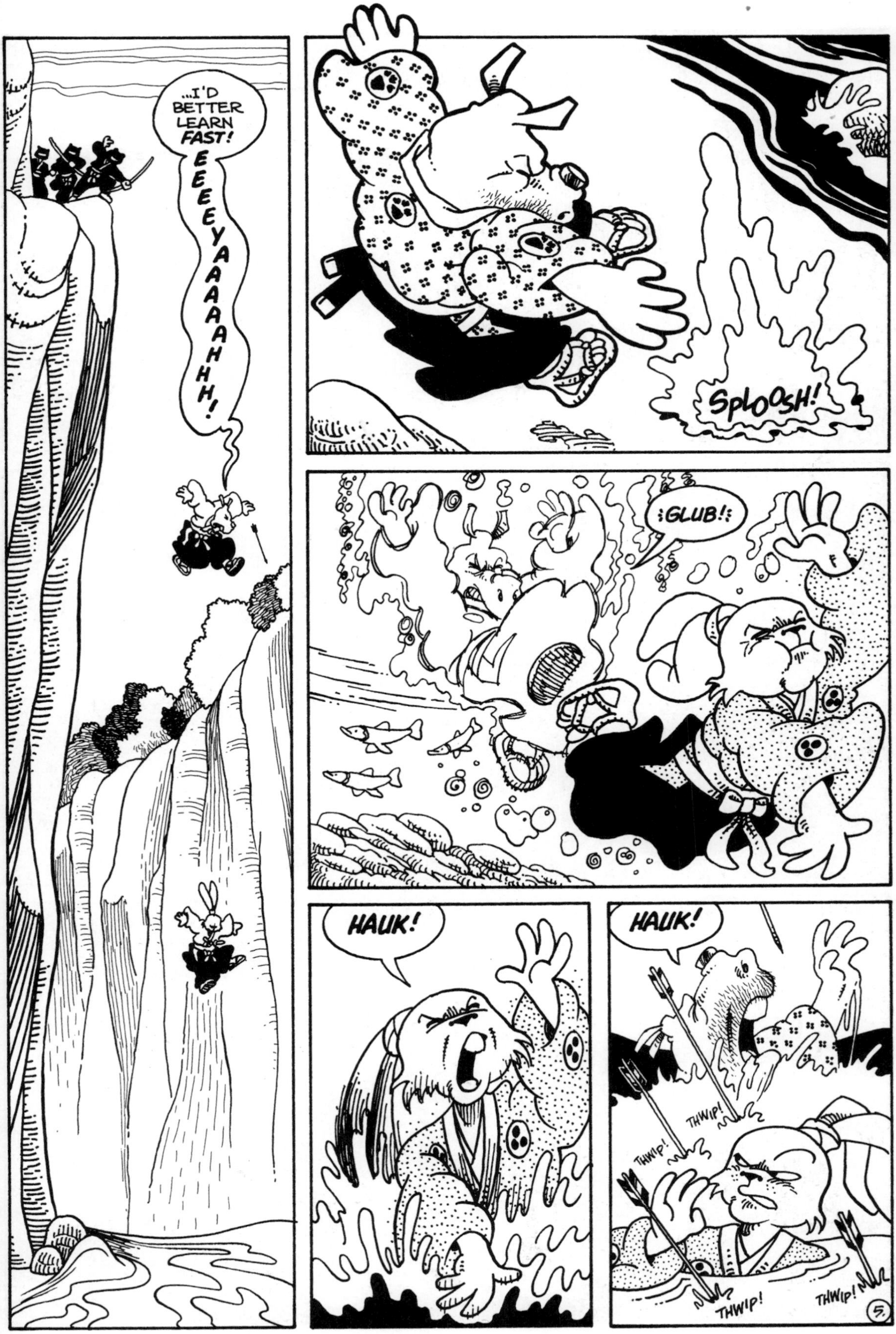

...I'D BETTER LEARN FAST!
EEEEYAAAAAAHHH!
SPLOOSH!
GLUB!
HAUK!
HAUK!
THWIP!
THWIP!
THWIP!
THWIP!
5

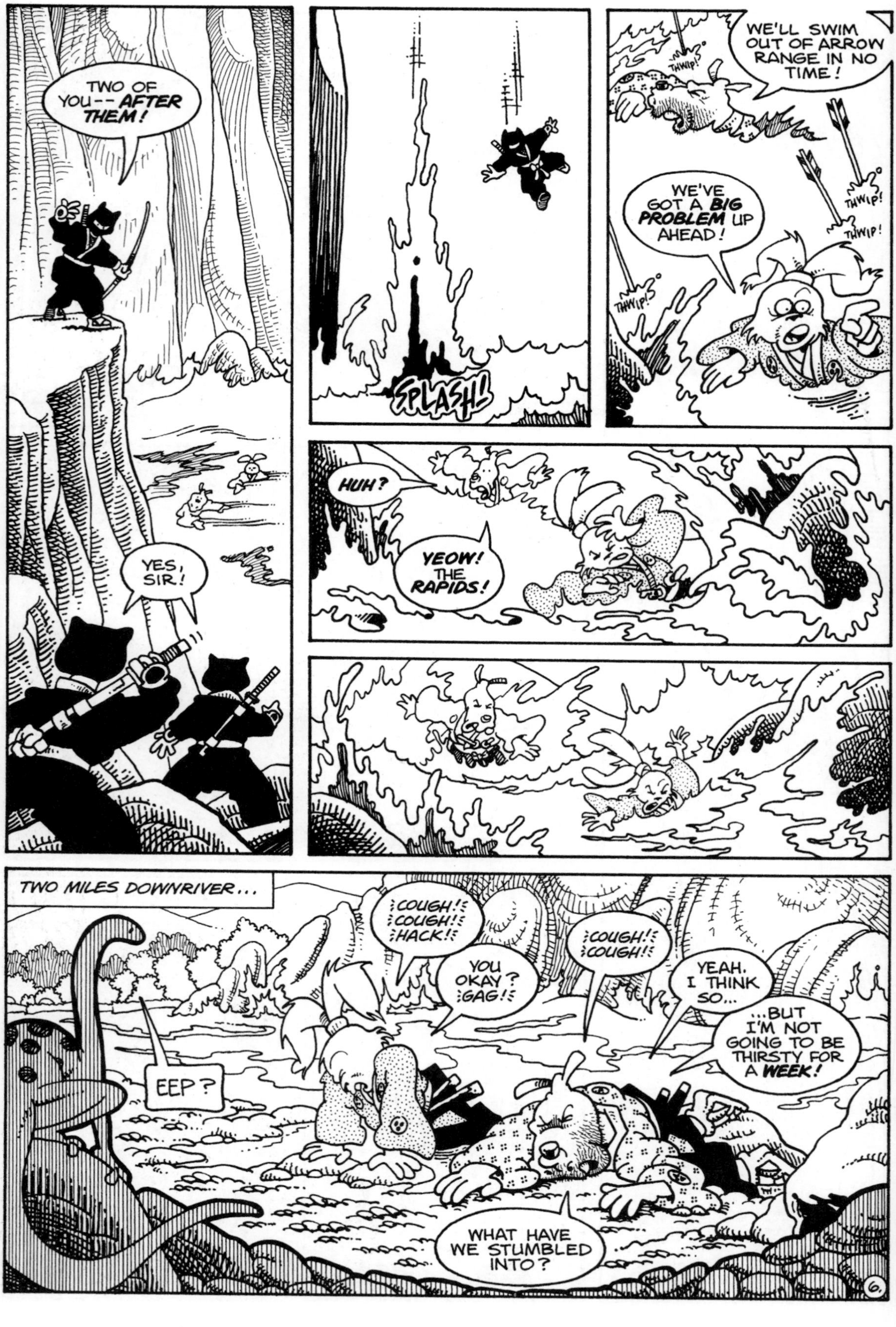
TWO OF YOU-- AFTER THEM!
YES, SIR!
SPLASH!
THWIP!
WE'LL SWIM OUT OF ARROW RANGE IN NO TIME!
THWIP!
THWIP!
WE'VE GOT A BIG PROBLEM UP AHEAD!
THWIP!
HUH?
YEOW! THE RAPIDS!
TWO MILES DOWNRIVER...
EEP?
COUGH! COUGH! HACK!
YOU OKAY? GAG!
COUGH! COUGH!
YEAH. I THINK SO...
...BUT I'M NOT GOING TO BE THIRSTY FOR A WEEK!
WHAT HAVE WE STUMBLED INTO?
6.

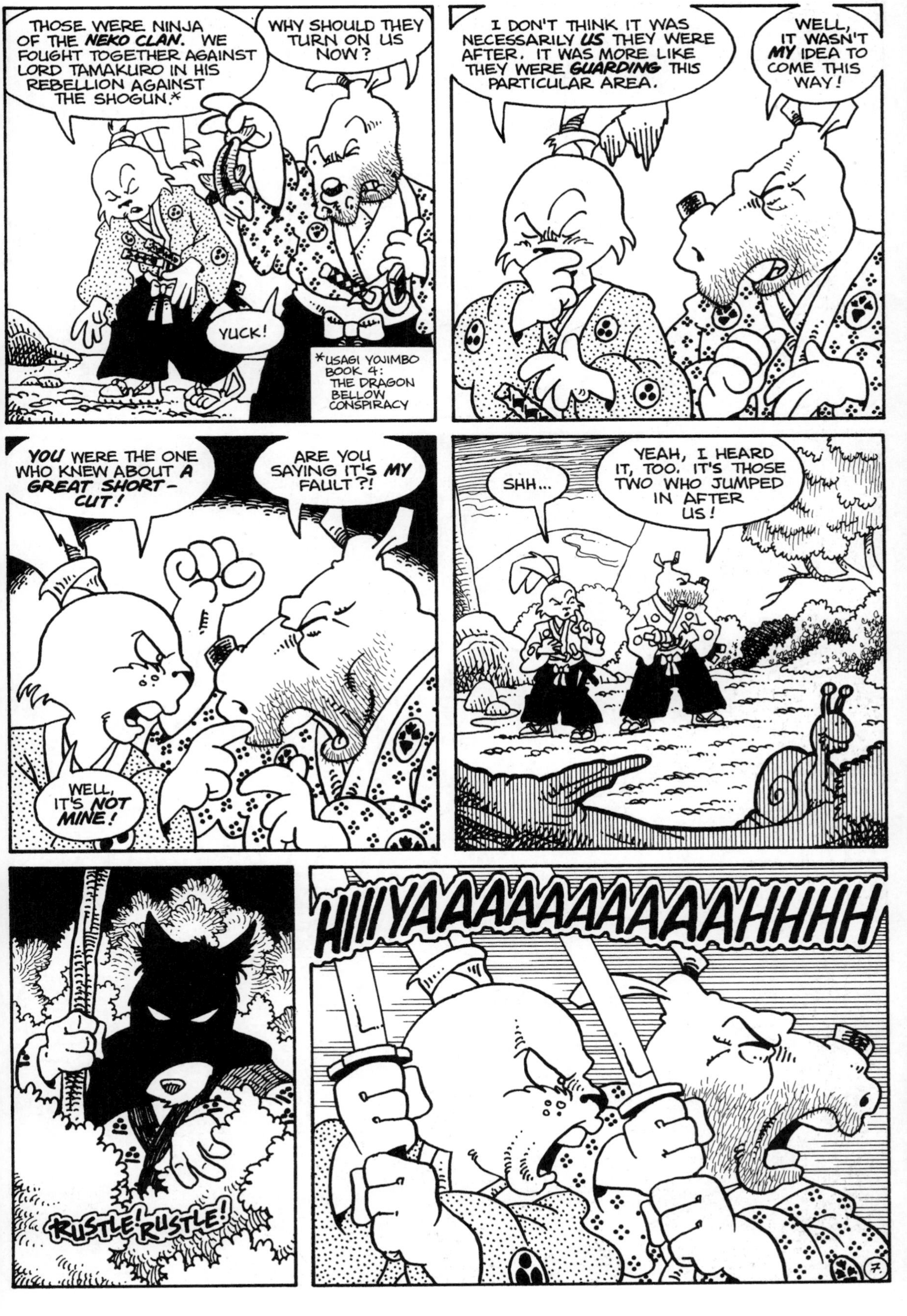
THOSE WERE NINJA OF THE NEKO CLAN. WE FOUGHT TOGETHER AGAINST LORD TAMAKURO IN HIS REBELLION AGAINST THE SHOGUN.*
WHY SHOULD THEY TURN ON US NOW?
YUCK!
*USAGI YOJIMBO BOOK 4: THE DRAGON BELLOW CONSPIRACY
I DON'T THINK IT WAS NECESSARILY US THEY WERE AFTER. IT WAS MORE LIKE THEY WERE GUARDING THIS PARTICULAR AREA.
WELL, IT WASN'T MY IDEA TO COME THIS WAY!
YOU WERE THE ONE WHO KNEW ABOUT A GREAT SHORT-CUT!
ARE YOU SAYING IT'S MY FAULT?!
WELL, IT'S NOT MINE!
SHH...
YEAH, I HEARD IT, TOO. IT'S THOSE TWO WHO JUMPED IN AFTER US!
RUSTLE! RUSTLE!
HIIIYAAAAAAAAAAAAHHHH
7.

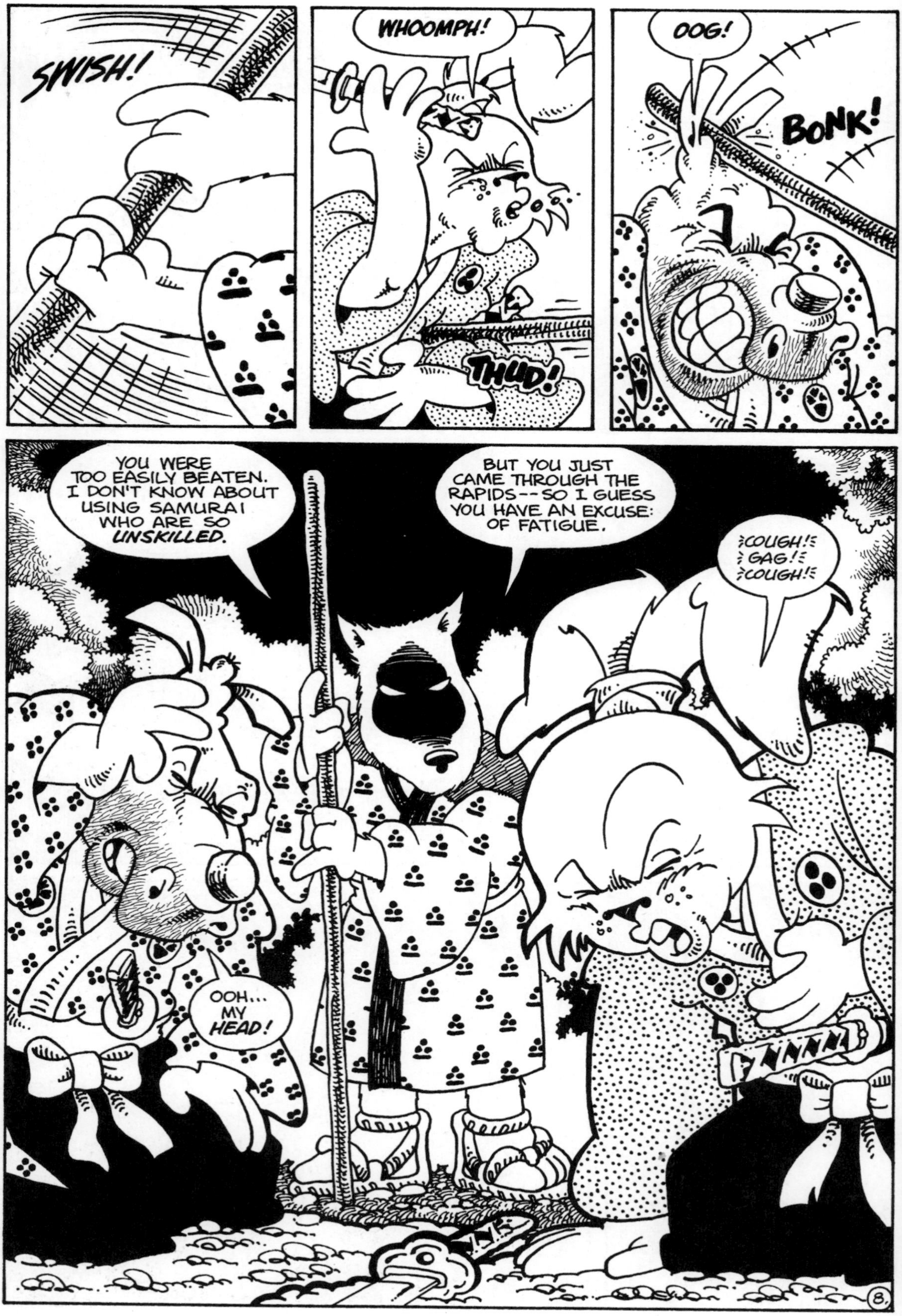
SWISH!
WHOOMPH!
THUD!
OOG!
BONK!
YOU WERE TOO EASILY BEATEN. I DON'T KNOW ABOUT USING SAMURAI WHO ARE SO UNSKILLED.
BUT YOU JUST CAME THROUGH THE RAPIDS--SO I GUESS YOU HAVE AN EXCUSE: OF FATIGUE.
COUGH! GAG! COUGH!
OOH... MY HEAD!
8.

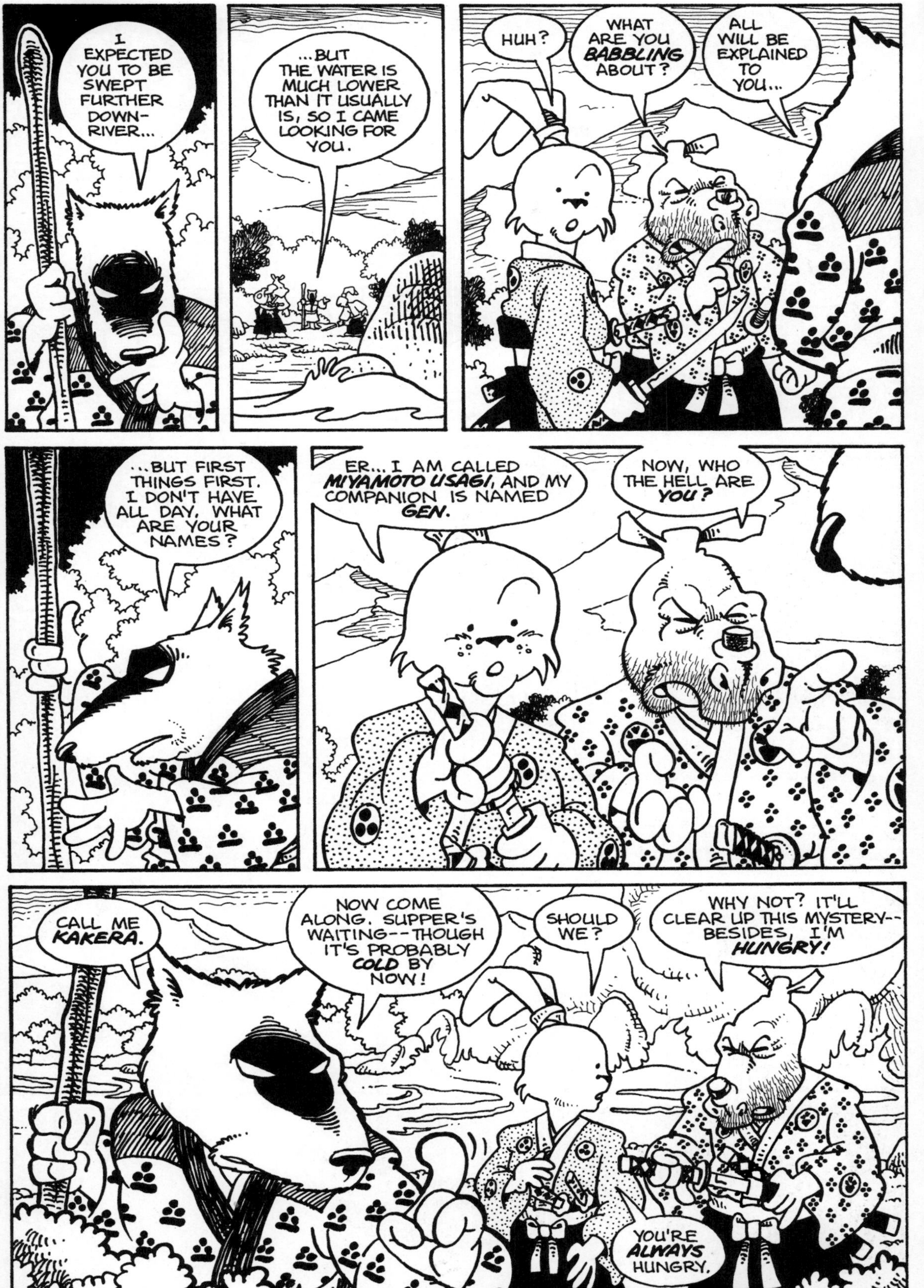
I EXPECTED YOU TO BE SWEPT FURTHER DOWN-RIVER...
...BUT THE WATER IS MUCH LOWER THAN IT USUALLY IS, SO I CAME LOOKING FOR YOU.
HUH?
WHAT ARE YOU BABBLING ABOUT?
ALL WILL BE EXPLAINED TO YOU...
...BUT FIRST THINGS FIRST. I DON'T HAVE ALL DAY. WHAT ARE YOUR NAMES?
ER... I AM CALLED MIYAMOTO USAGI, AND MY COMPANION IS NAMED GEN.
NOW, WHO THE HELL ARE YOU?
CALL ME KAKERA.
NOW COME ALONG. SUPPER'S WAITING--THOUGH IT'S PROBABLY COLD BY NOW!
SHOULD WE?
WHY NOT? IT'LL CLEAR UP THIS MYSTERY--BESIDES, I'M HUNGRY!
YOU'RE ALWAYS HUNGRY.
9.

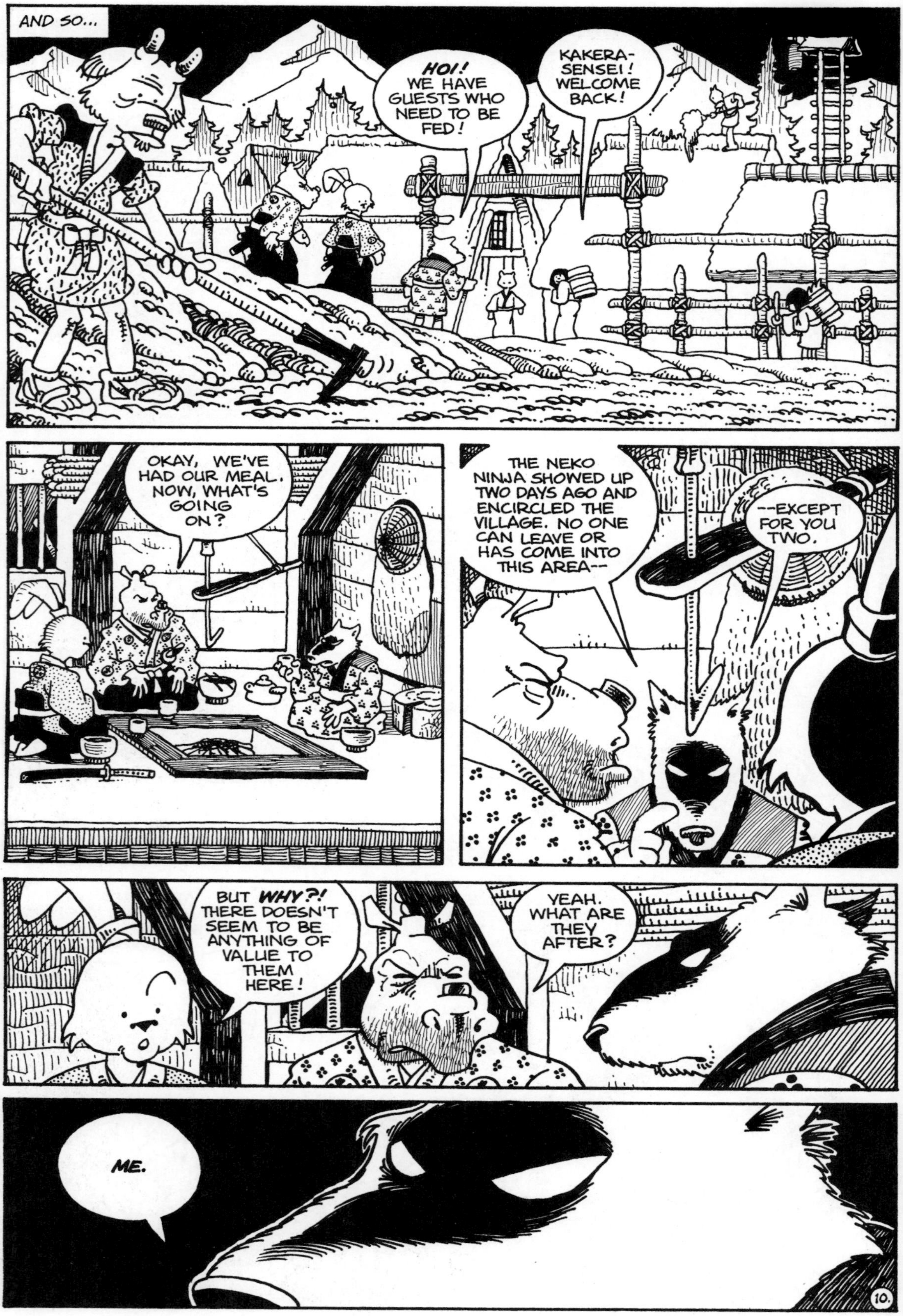
AND SO...
HOI! WE HAVE GUESTS WHO NEED TO BE FED!
KAKERA-SENSEI! WELCOME BACK!
OKAY, WE'VE HAD OUR MEAL. NOW, WHAT'S GOING ON?
THE NEKO NINJA SHOWED UP TWO DAYS AGO AND ENCIRCLED THE VILLAGE. NO ONE CAN LEAVE OR HAS COME INTO THIS AREA--
--EXCEPT FOR YOU TWO.
BUT WHY?! THERE DOESN'T SEEM TO BE ANYTHING OF VALUE TO THEM HERE!
YEAH. WHAT ARE THEY AFTER?
ME.
10.

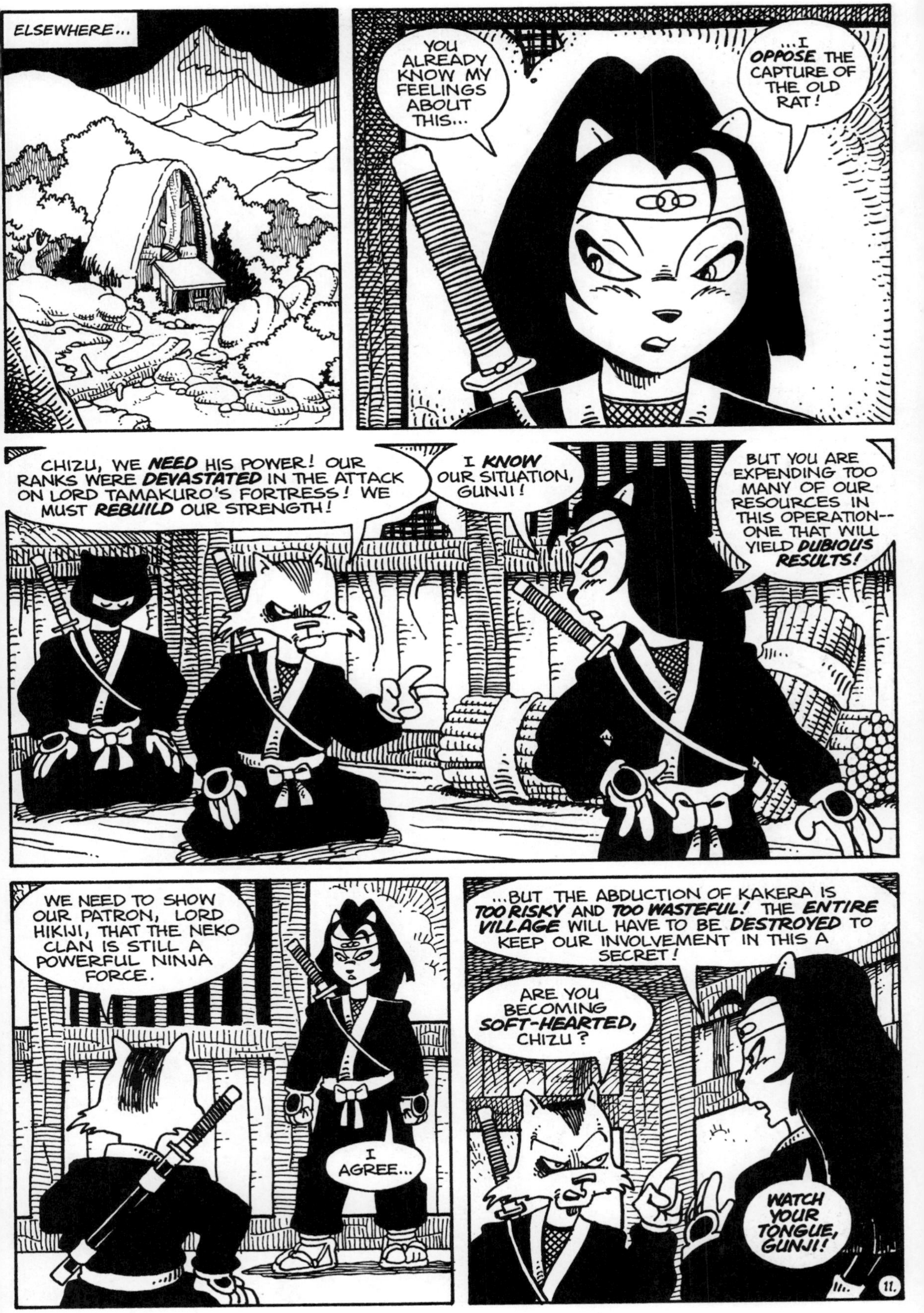
ELSEWHERE...
YOU ALREADY KNOW MY FEELINGS ABOUT THIS...
...I OPPOSE THE CAPTURE OF THE OLD RAT!
CHIZU, WE NEED HIS POWER! OUR RANKS WERE DEVASTATED IN THE ATTACK ON LORD TAMAKURO'S FORTRESS! WE MUST REBUILD OUR STRENGTH!
I KNOW OUR SITUATION, GUNJI!
BUT YOU ARE EXPENDING TOO MANY OF OUR RESOURCES IN THIS OPERATION-- ONE THAT WILL YIELD DUBIOUS RESULTS!
WE NEED TO SHOW OUR PATRON, LORD HIKIJI, THAT THE NEKO CLAN IS STILL A POWERFUL NINJA FORCE.
I AGREE...
...BUT THE ABDUCTION OF KAKERA IS TOO RISKY AND TOO WASTEFUL! THE ENTIRE VILLAGE WILL HAVE TO BE DESTROYED TO KEEP OUR INVOLVEMENT IN THIS A SECRET!
ARE YOU BECOMING SOFT-HEARTED, CHIZU?
WATCH YOUR TONGUE, GUNJI!
11.

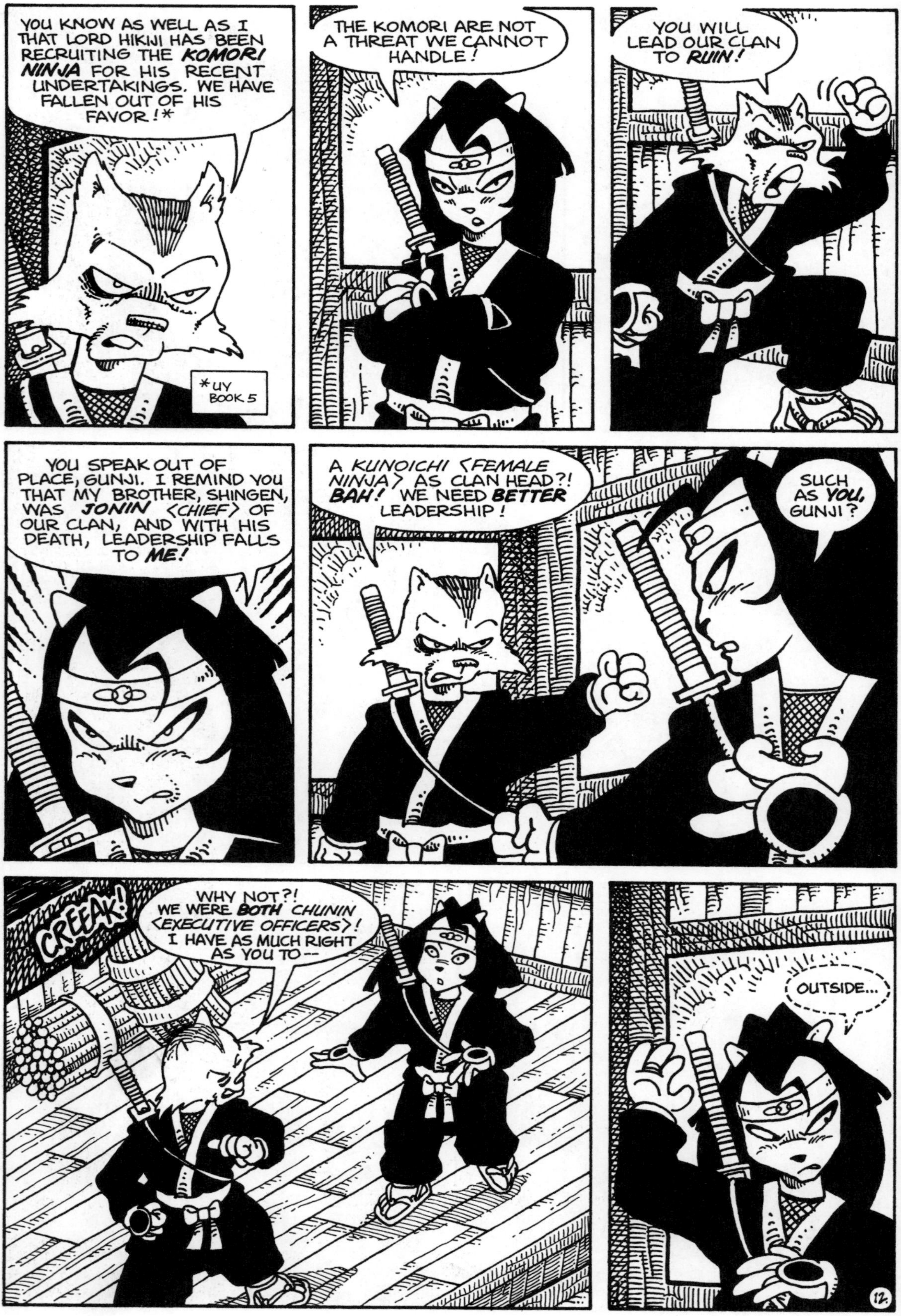
YOU KNOW AS WELL AS I THAT LORD HIKIJI HAS BEEN RECRUITING THE KOMORI NINJA FOR HIS RECENT UNDERTAKINGS. WE HAVE FALLEN OUT OF HIS FAVOR!*
*UY BOOK 5
THE KOMORI ARE NOT A THREAT WE CANNOT HANDLE!
YOU WILL LEAD OUR CLAN TO RUIN!
YOU SPEAK OUT OF PLACE, GUNJI. I REMIND YOU THAT MY BROTHER, SHINGEN, WAS JONIN <CHIEF> OF OUR CLAN, AND WITH HIS DEATH, LEADERSHIP FALLS TO ME!
A KUNOICHI <FEMALE NINJA> AS CLAN HEAD?! BAH! WE NEED BETTER LEADERSHIP!
SUCH AS YOU, GUNJI?
CREEAK!
WHY NOT?! WE WERE BOTH CHUNIN <EXECUTIVE OFFICERS>! I HAVE AS MUCH RIGHT AS YOU TO--
OUTSIDE...
12.

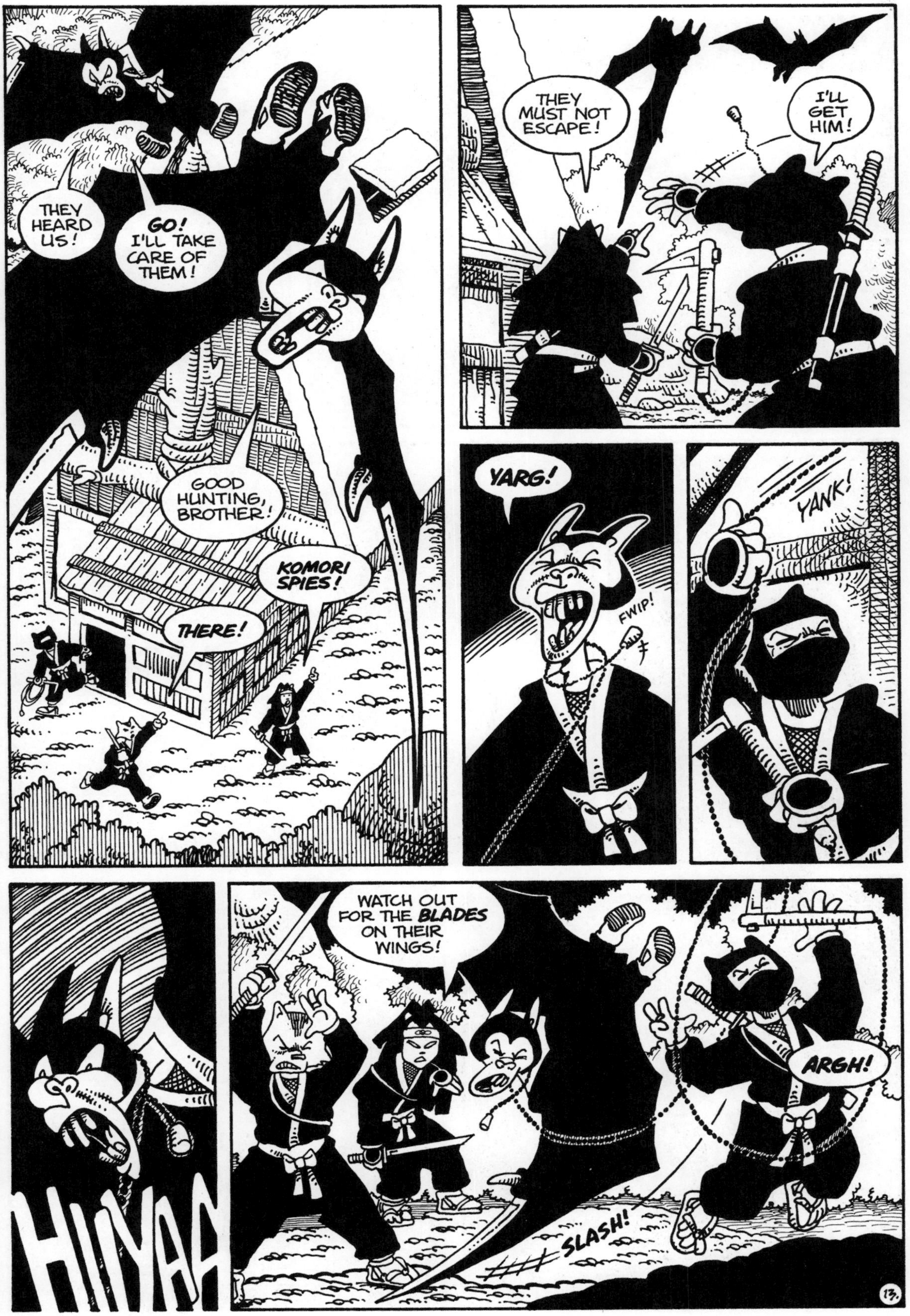
THEY HEARD US!
GO! I'LL TAKE CARE OF THEM!
GOOD HUNTING, BROTHER!
KOMORI SPIES!
THERE!
THEY MUST NOT ESCAPE!
I'LL GET HIM!
YARG!
FWIP!
YANK!
HIIYAA
WATCH OUT FOR THE BLADES ON THEIR WINGS!
ARGH!
SLASH!
13.

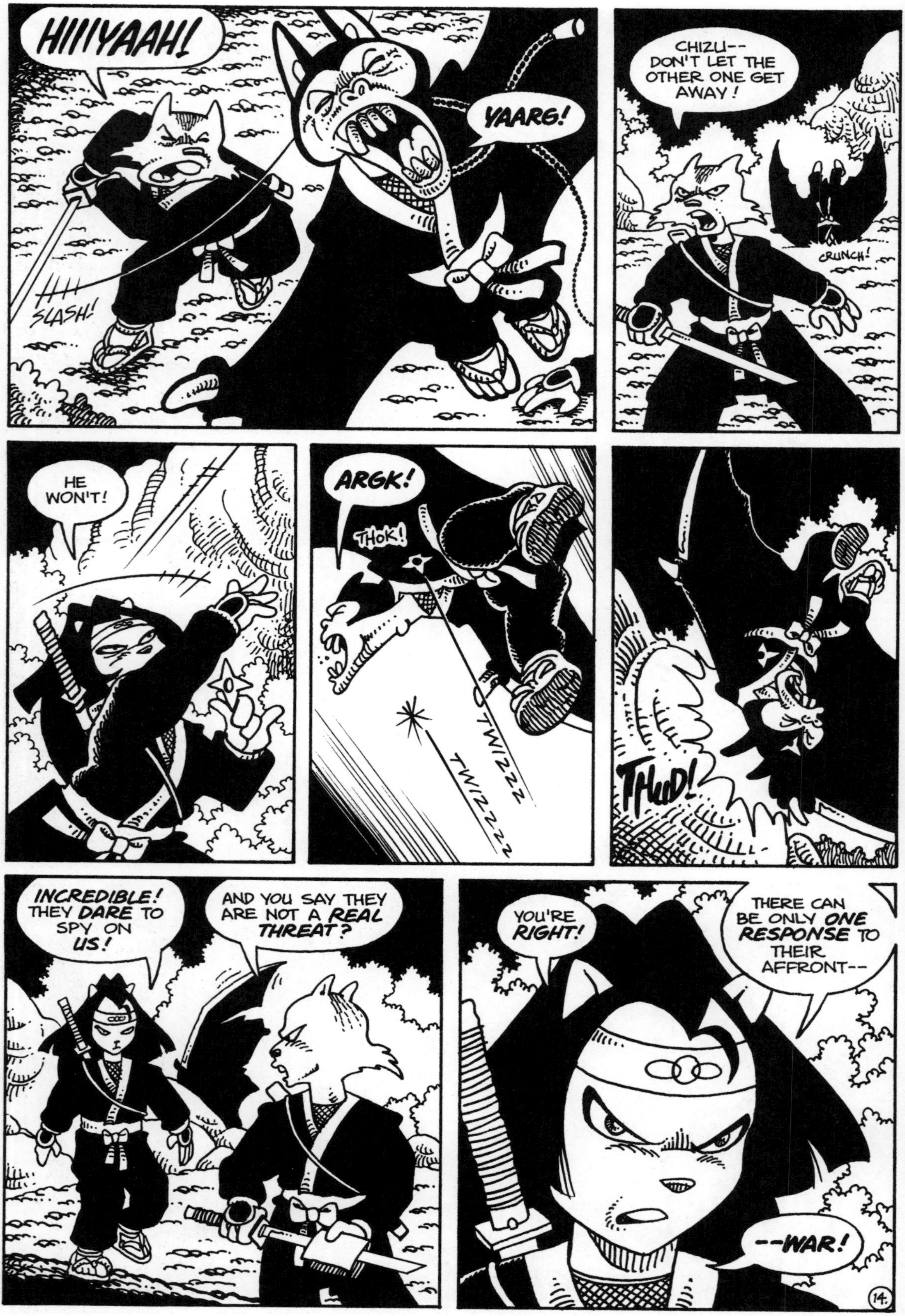
HIIIYAAH!
YAARG!
SLASH!
CHIZU-- DON'T LET THE OTHER ONE GET AWAY!
CRUNCH!
HE WON'T!
ARGK!
THOK!
TWIZZZ
TWIZZZZZ
THUD!
INCREDIBLE! THEY DARE TO SPY ON US!
AND YOU SAY THEY ARE NOT A REAL THREAT?
YOU'RE RIGHT!
THERE CAN BE ONLY ONE RESPONSE TO THEIR AFFRONT--
--WAR!
14.

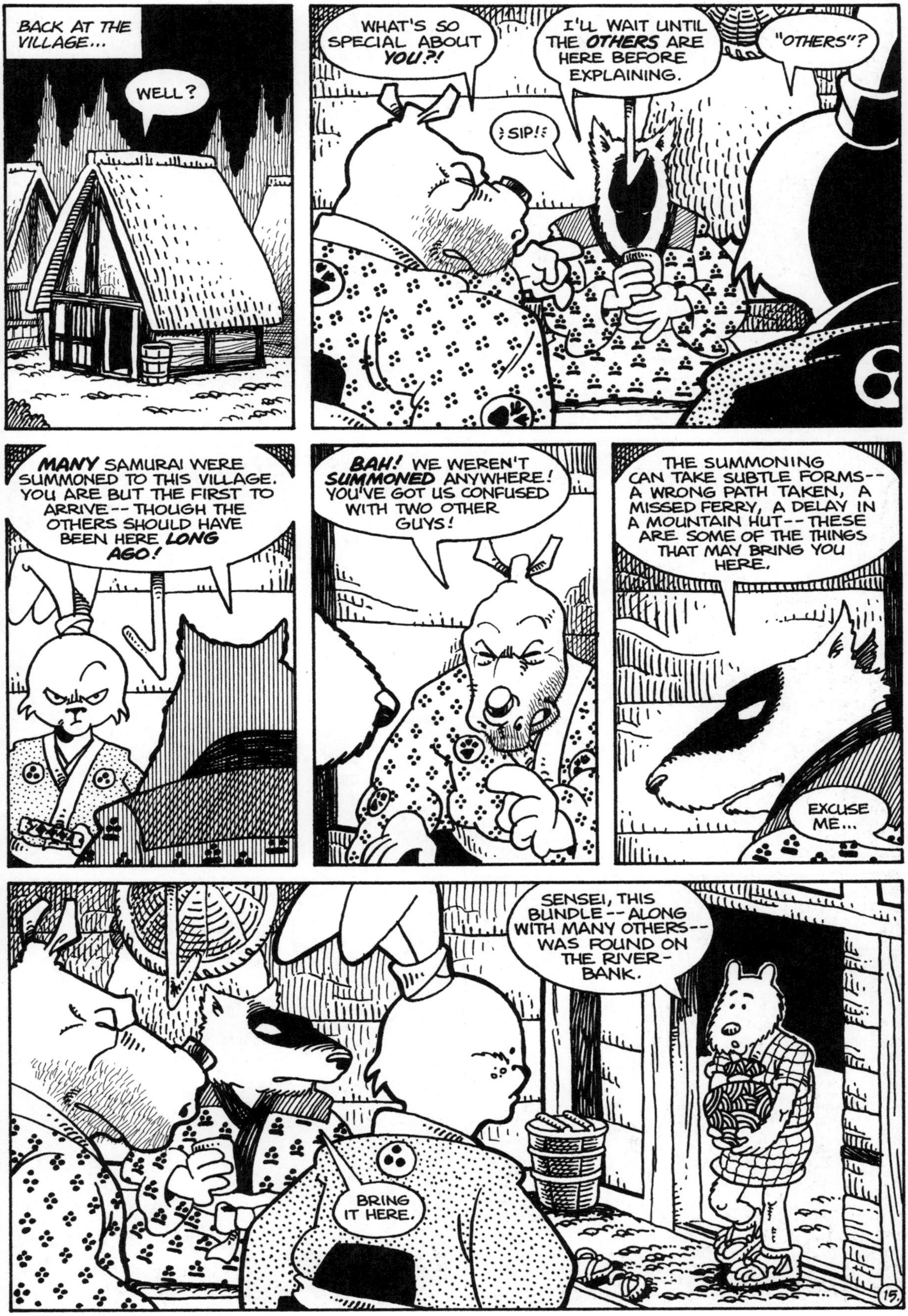
BACK AT THE VILLAGE...
WELL?
WHAT'S SO SPECIAL ABOUT YOU?!
I'LL WAIT UNTIL THE OTHERS ARE HERE BEFORE EXPLAINING.
"OTHERS"?
SIP!
MANY SAMURAI WERE SUMMONED TO THIS VILLAGE. YOU ARE BUT THE FIRST TO ARRIVE--THOUGH THE OTHERS SHOULD HAVE BEEN HERE LONG AGO!
BAH! WE WEREN'T SUMMONED ANYWHERE! YOU'VE GOT US CONFUSED WITH TWO OTHER GUYS!
THE SUMMONING CAN TAKE SUBTLE FORMS--A WRONG PATH TAKEN, A MISSED FERRY, A DELAY IN A MOUNTAIN HUT--THESE ARE SOME OF THE THINGS THAT MAY BRING YOU HERE.
EXCUSE ME...
SENSEI, THIS BUNDLE--ALONG WITH MANY OTHERS--WAS FOUND ON THE RIVER-BANK.
BRING IT HERE.
15.

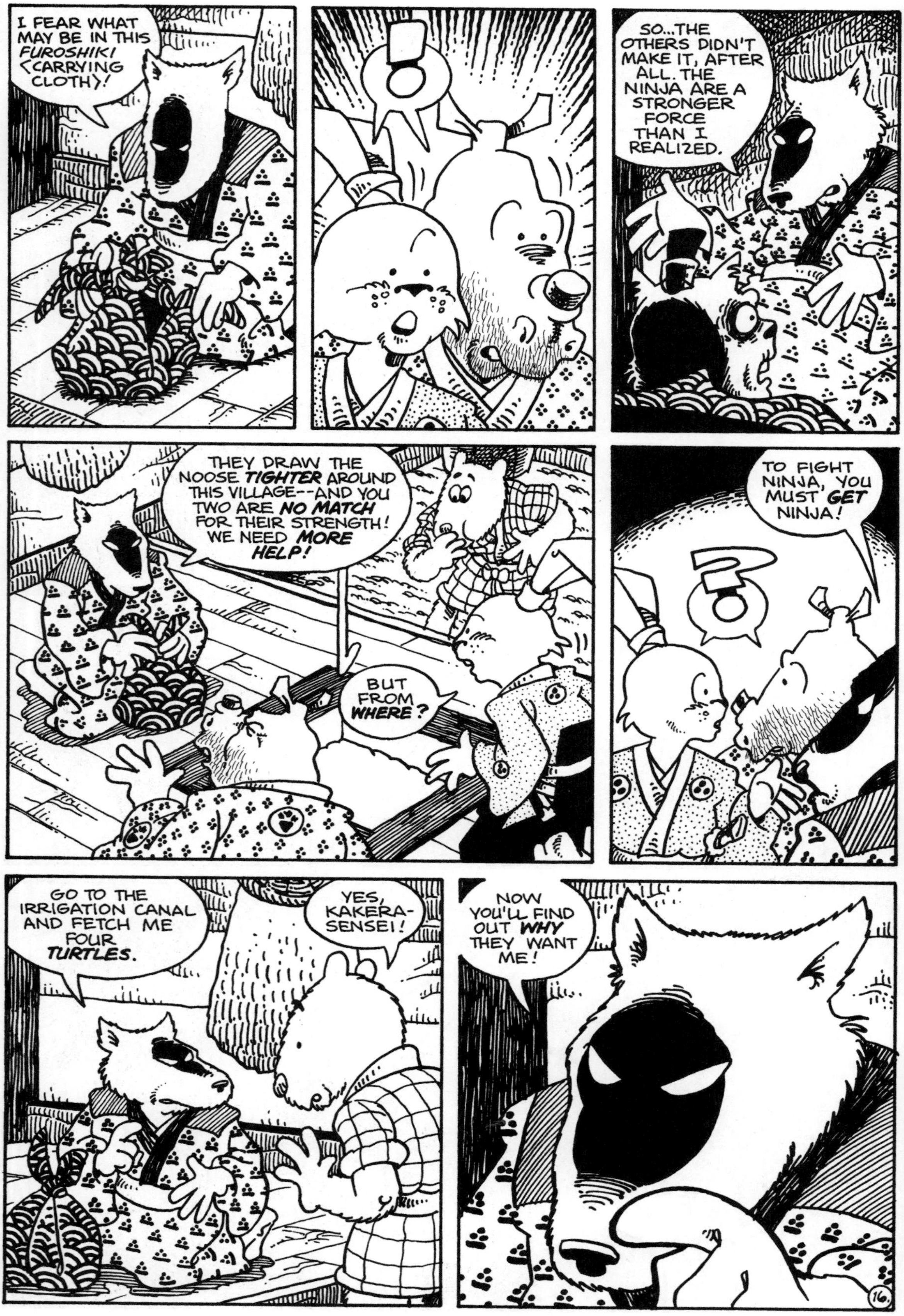
I FEAR WHAT MAY BE IN THIS FUROSHIKI <CARRYING CLOTH>!
!
SO...THE OTHERS DIDN'T MAKE IT, AFTER ALL. THE NINJA ARE A STRONGER FORCE THAN I REALIZED.
THEY DRAW THE NOOSE TIGHTER AROUND THIS VILLAGE--AND YOU TWO ARE NO MATCH FOR THEIR STRENGTH! WE NEED MORE HELP!
BUT FROM WHERE?
TO FIGHT NINJA, YOU MUST GET NINJA!
?
GO TO THE IRRIGATION CANAL AND FETCH ME FOUR TURTLES.
YES, KAKERA-SENSEI!
NOW YOU'LL FIND OUT WHY THEY WANT ME!
16.

AND SO...

OKAY, YOU'VE GOT SOME *WET TURTLES*. SO WHAT?

WHAT'S HE MUMBLING?

mm mm mm mm mm mm m

QUIET, GEN.

THERE'S SOMETHING HAPPENING TO THE AIR! MY FUR IS *PRICKLING!*

SHH...

OH, WOW!

mmmmm mmmm m

≠COUGH!≠ ≠COFF!≠

17.

397

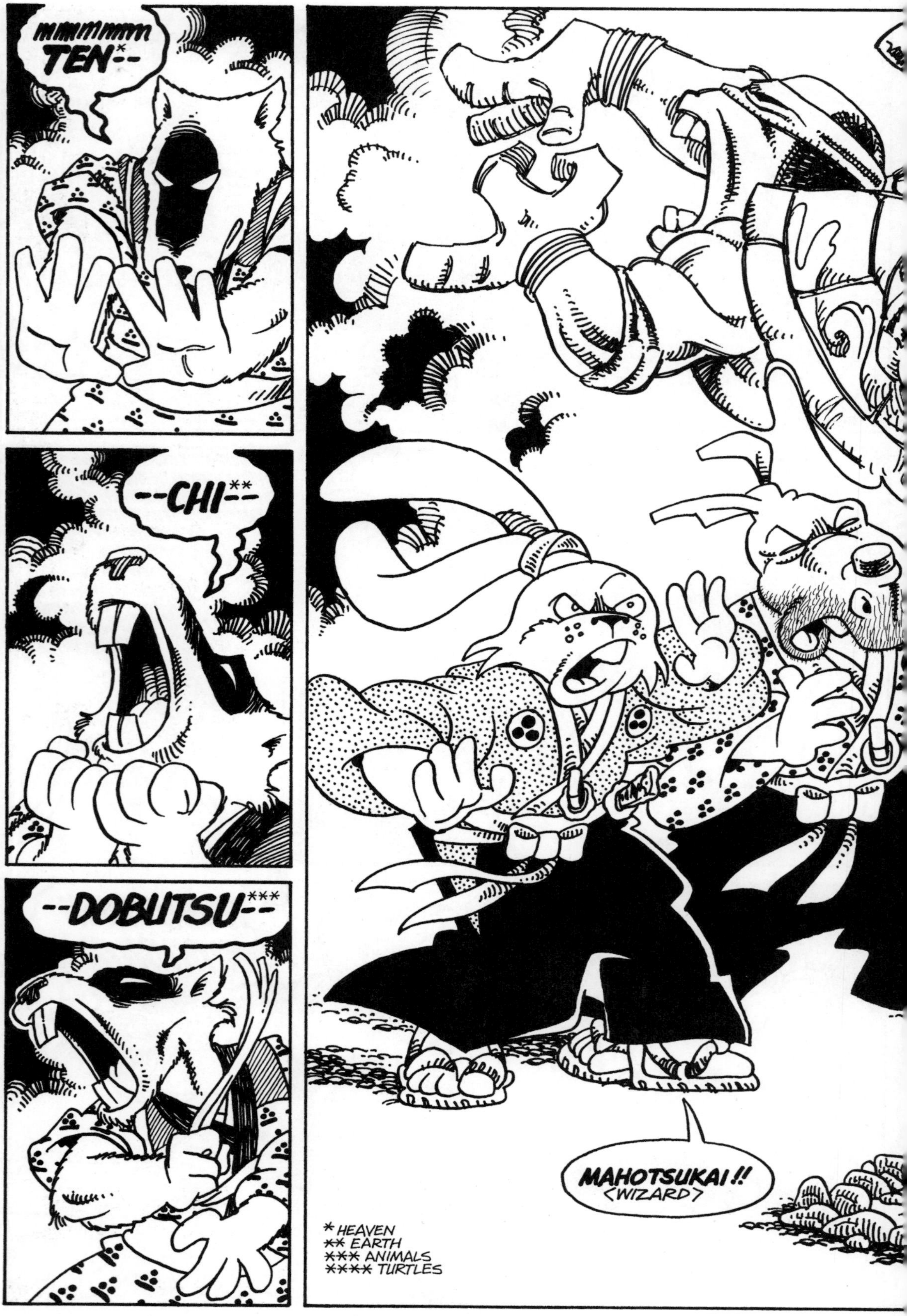
mmmmmm TEN*--
--CHI**--
--DOBUTSU***--
MAHOTSUKAI!! <WIZARD>
* HEAVEN
** EARTH
*** ANIMALS
**** TURTLES

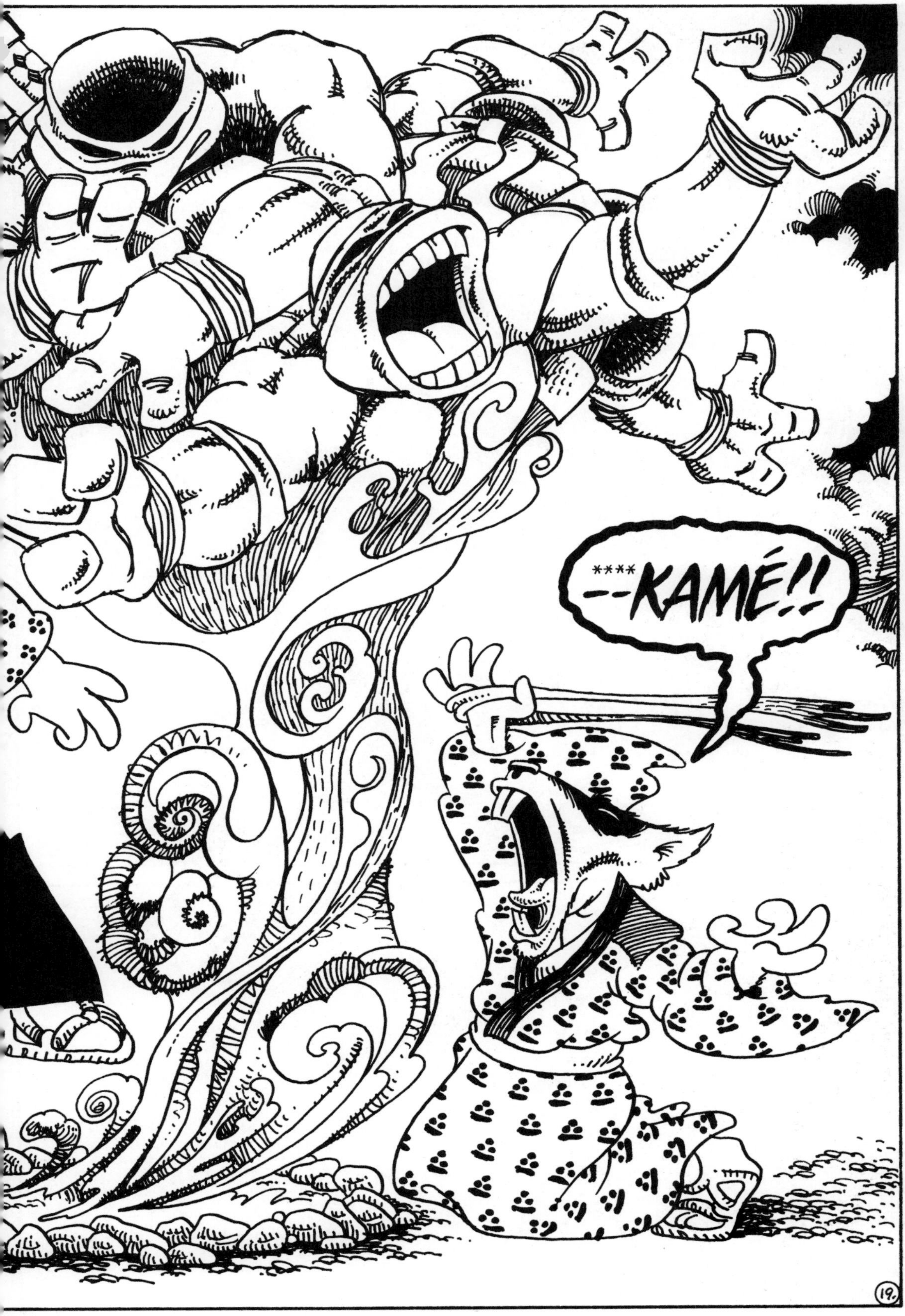
****
--KAMÉ!!
19.

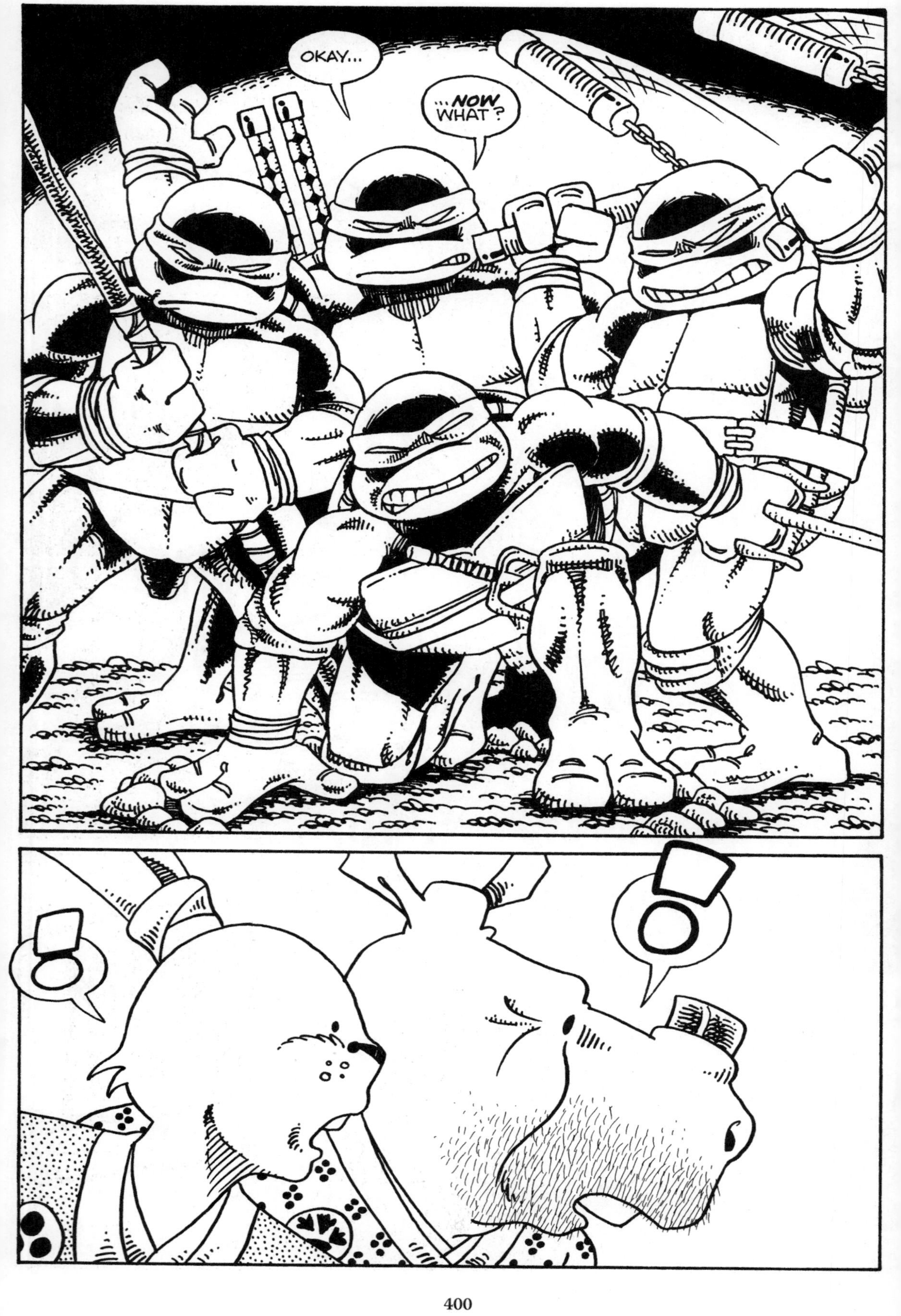
OKAY...
...NOW WHAT?
!
!

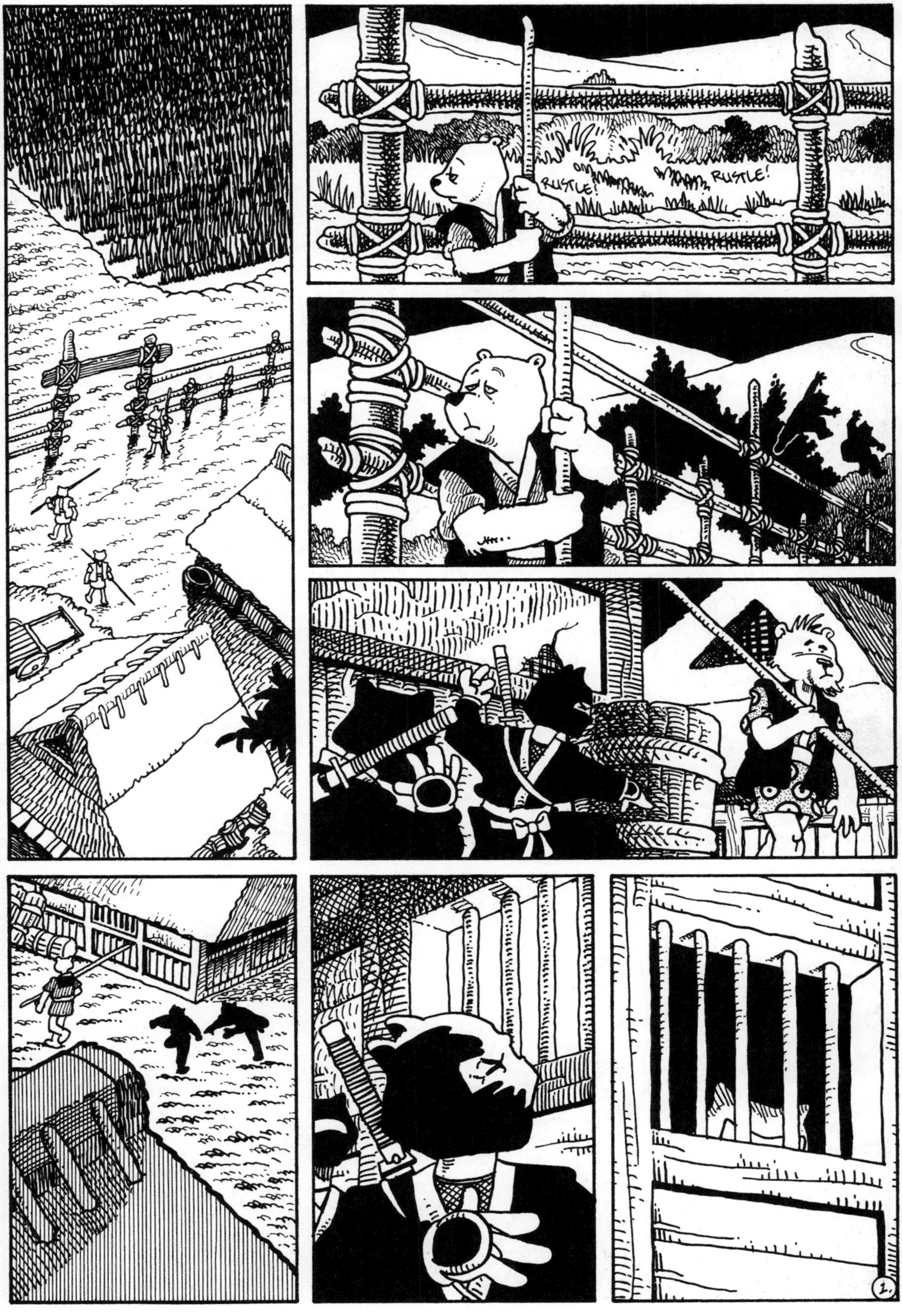
RUSTLE!
RUSTLE!
1.

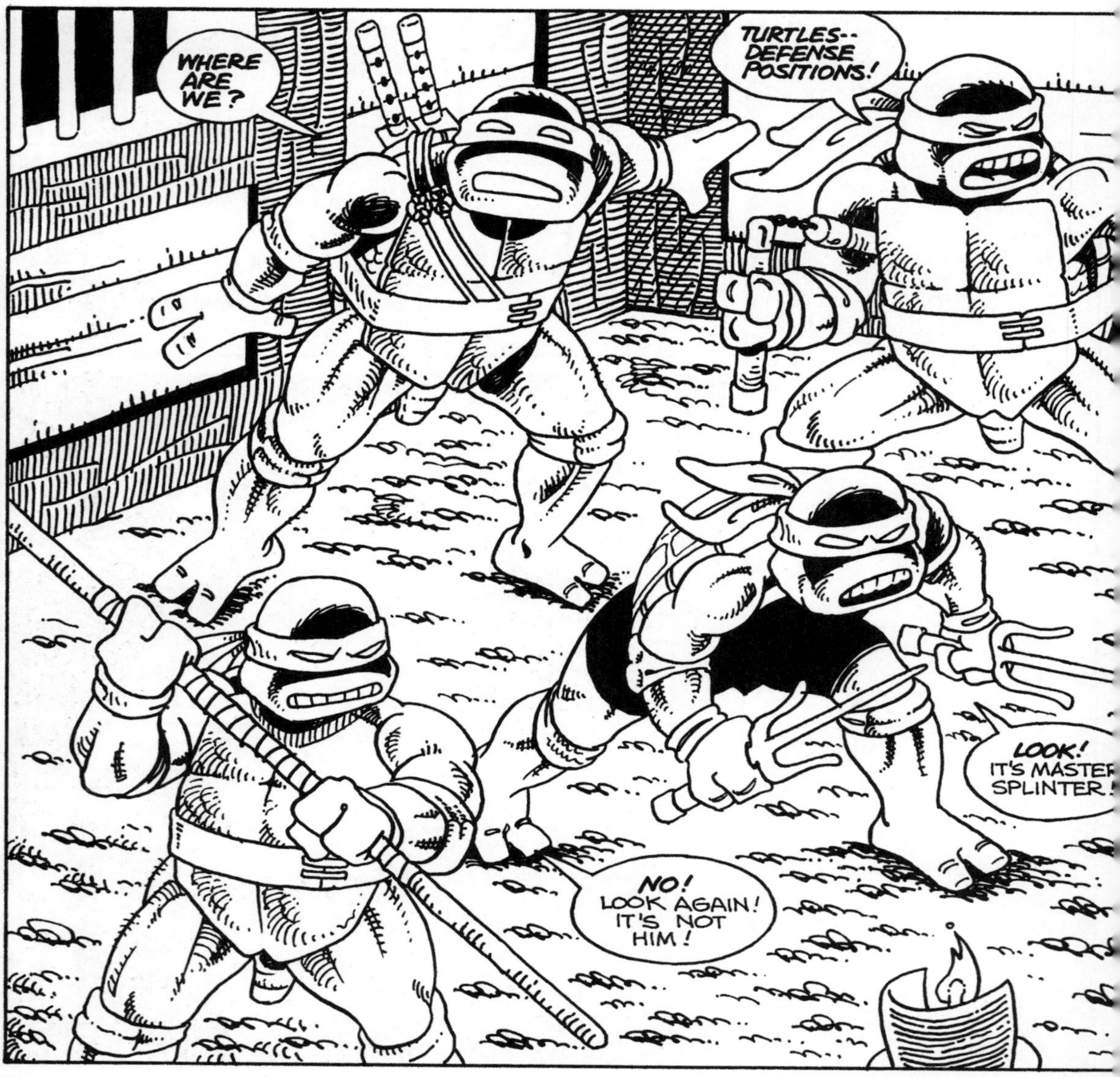
WHERE ARE WE?
TURTLES-- DEFENSE POSITIONS!
LOOK! IT'S MASTER SPLINTER!
NO! LOOK AGAIN! IT'S NOT HIM!

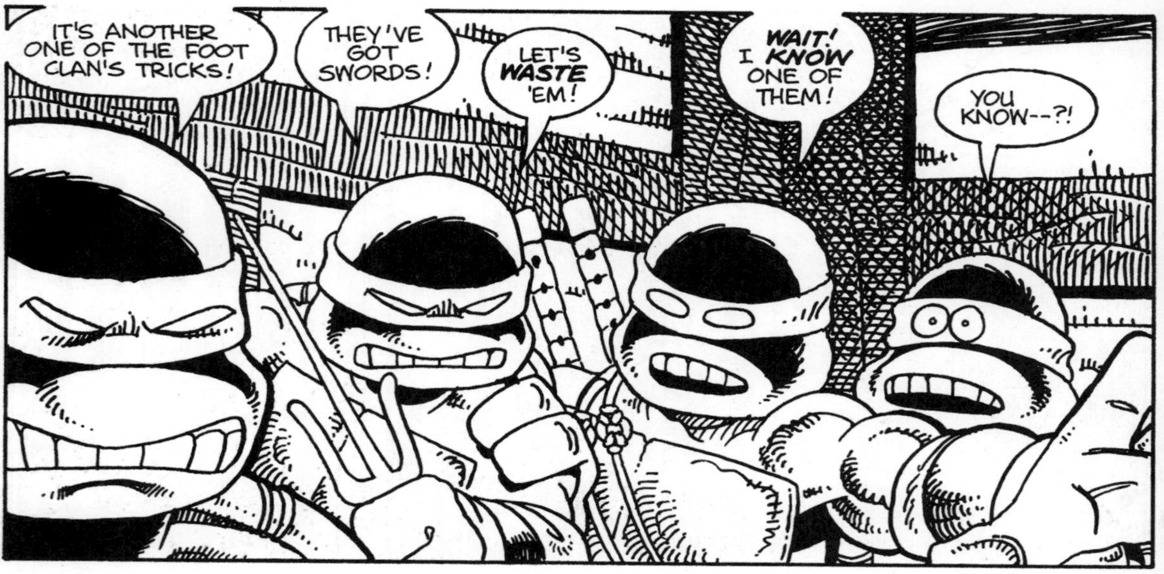
IT'S ANOTHER ONE OF THE FOOT CLAN'S TRICKS!
THEY'VE GOT SWORDS!
LET'S WASTE 'EM!
WAIT! I KNOW ONE OF THEM!
YOU KNOW--?!

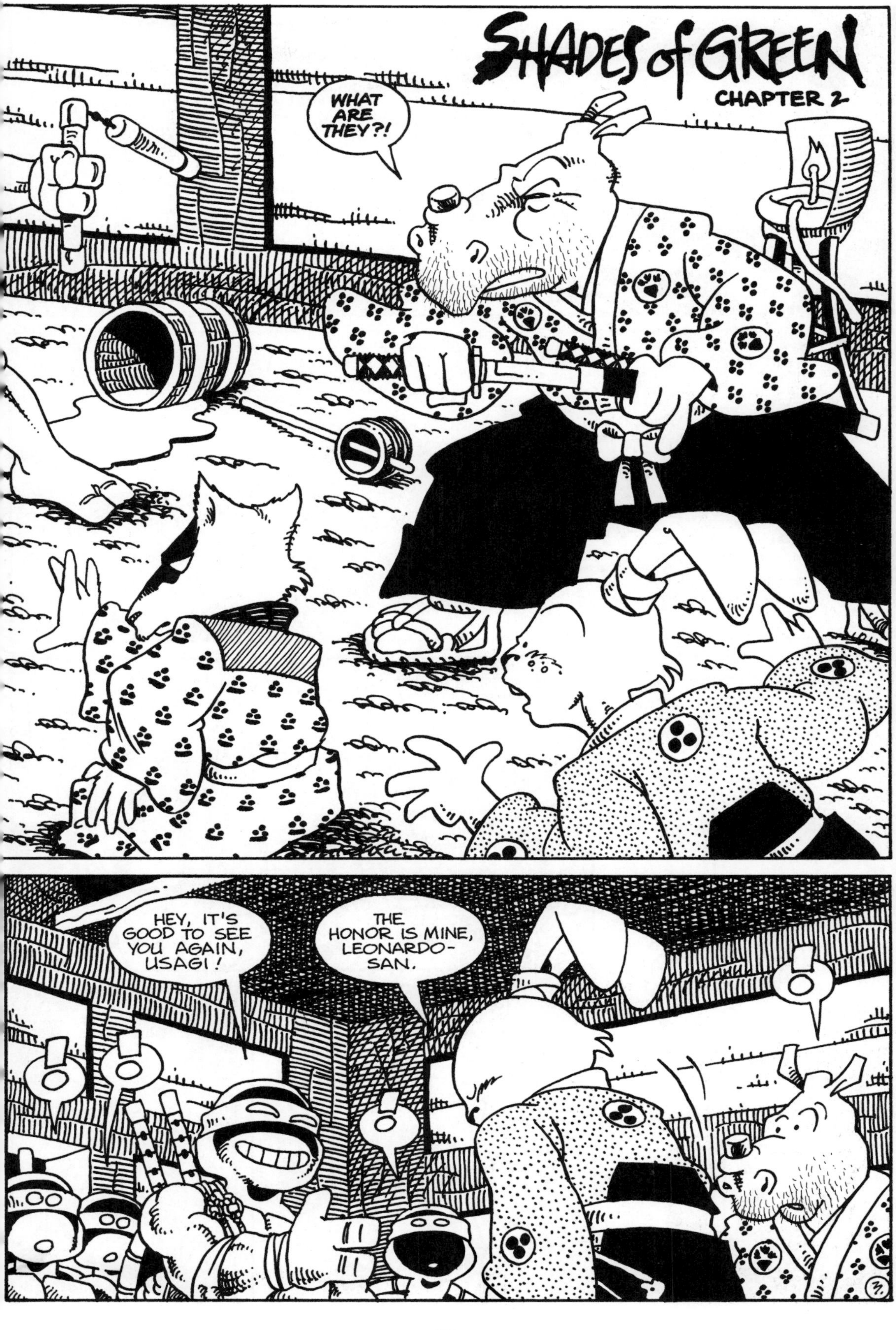
SHADES OF GREEN
CHAPTER 2
WHAT ARE THEY?!
HEY, IT'S GOOD TO SEE YOU AGAIN, USAGI!
THE HONOR IS MINE, LEONARDO-SAN.

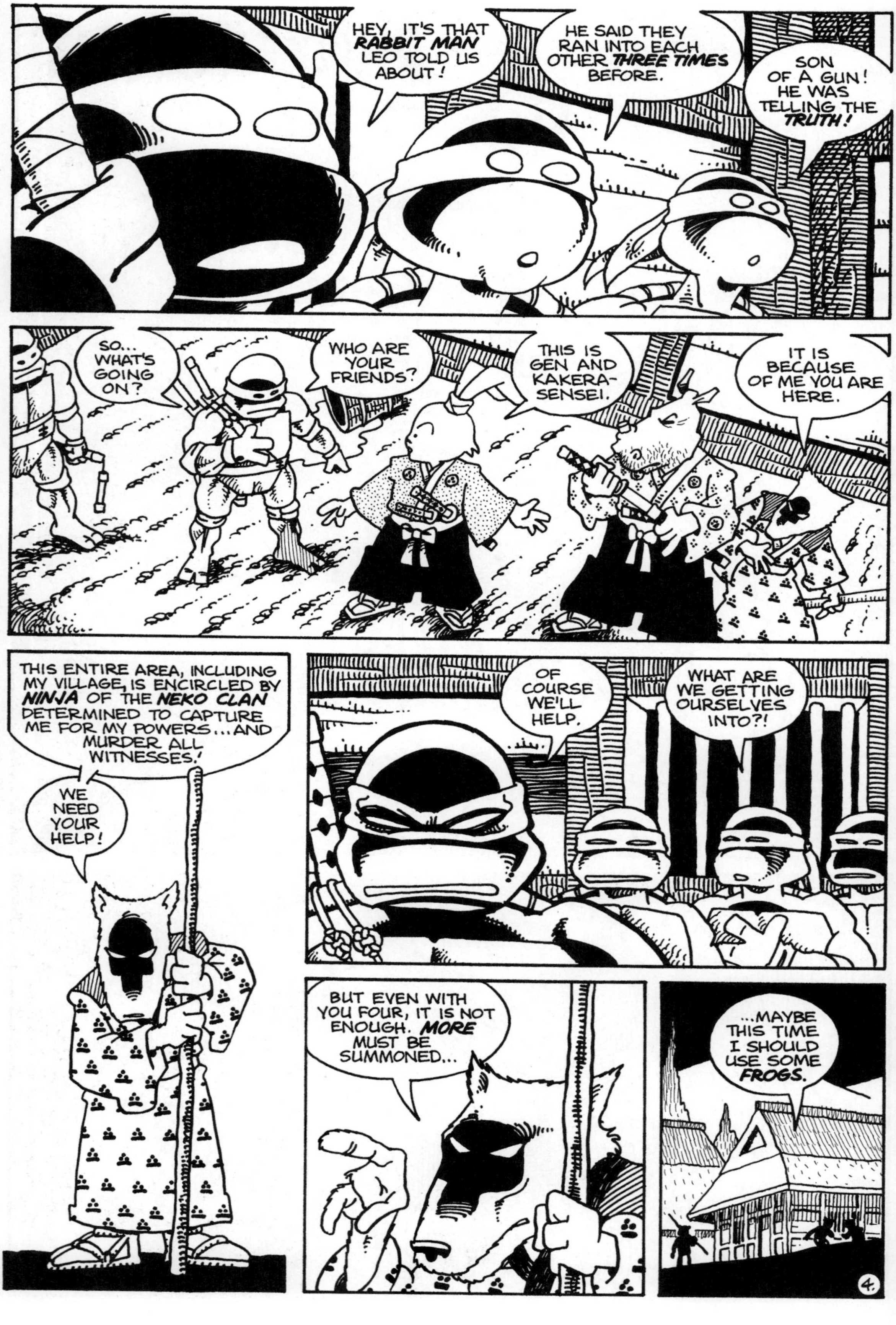
HEY, IT'S THAT RABBIT MAN LEO TOLD US ABOUT!
HE SAID THEY RAN INTO EACH OTHER THREE TIMES BEFORE.
SON OF A GUN! HE WAS TELLING THE TRUTH!
SO... WHAT'S GOING ON?
WHO ARE YOUR FRIENDS?
THIS IS GEN AND KAKERA-SENSEI.
IT IS BECAUSE OF ME YOU ARE HERE.
THIS ENTIRE AREA, INCLUDING MY VILLAGE, IS ENCIRCLED BY NINJA OF THE NEKO CLAN DETERMINED TO CAPTURE ME FOR MY POWERS...AND MURDER ALL WITNESSES!
WE NEED YOUR HELP!
OF COURSE WE'LL HELP.
WHAT ARE WE GETTING OURSELVES INTO?!
BUT EVEN WITH YOU FOUR, IT IS NOT ENOUGH. MORE MUST BE SUMMONED...
...MAYBE THIS TIME I SHOULD USE SOME FROGS.
4.

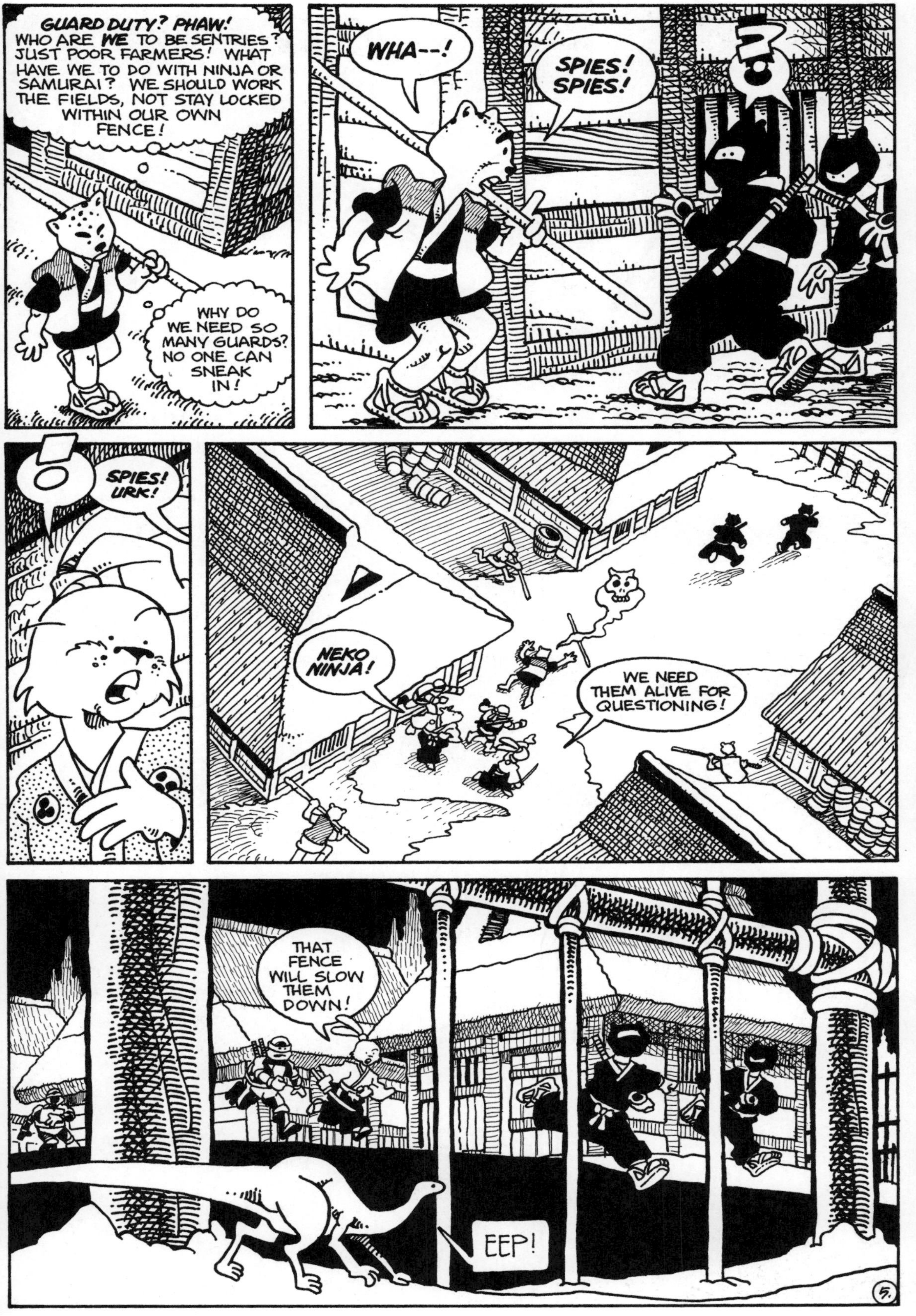
GUARD DUTY? PHAW! WHO ARE WE TO BE SENTRIES? JUST POOR FARMERS! WHAT HAVE WE TO DO WITH NINJA OR SAMURAI? WE SHOULD WORK THE FIELDS, NOT STAY LOCKED WITHIN OUR OWN FENCE!
WHY DO WE NEED SO MANY GUARDS? NO ONE CAN SNEAK IN!
WHA--!
SPIES! SPIES!
SPIES! URK!
NEKO NINJA!
WE NEED THEM ALIVE FOR QUESTIONING!
THAT FENCE WILL SLOW THEM DOWN!
EEP!
5.

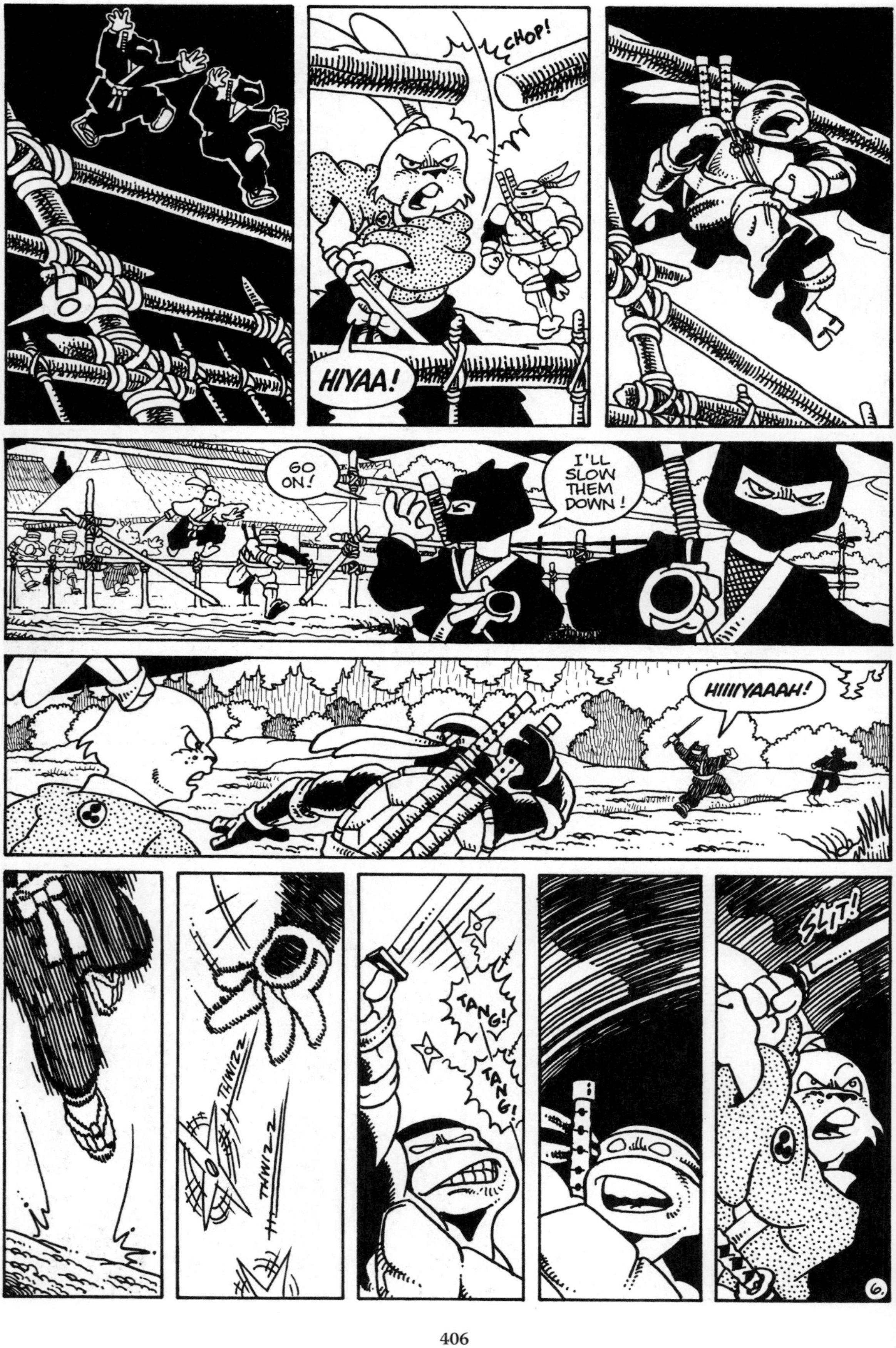
CHOP!
HIYAA!
GO ON!
I'LL SLOW THEM DOWN!
HIIIIYAAAH!
THWIZZ
THWIZZ
TANG!
TANG!
SLIT!
6.

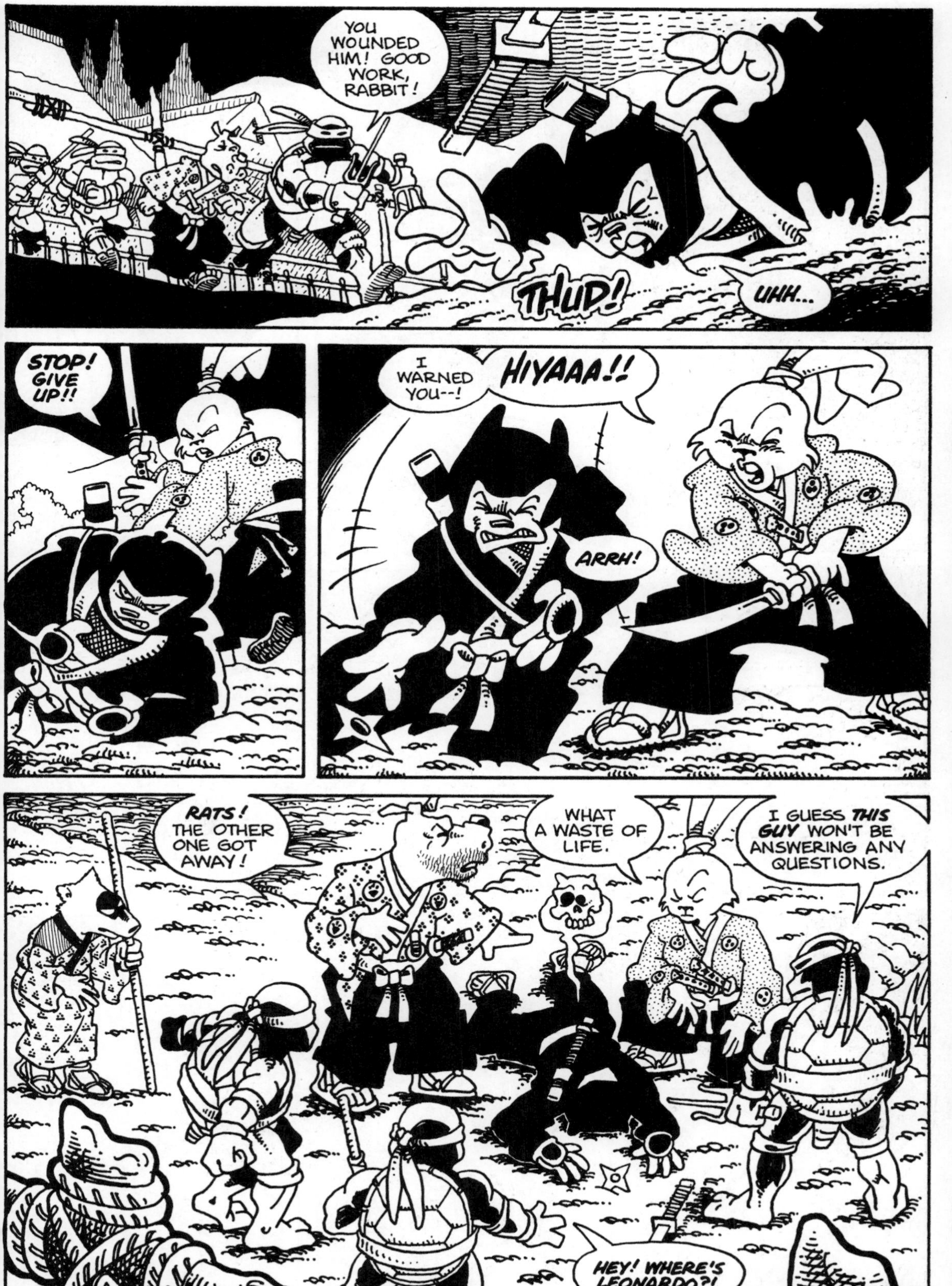

YOU WOUNDED HIM! GOOD WORK, RABBIT!
THUD!
UHH...
STOP! GIVE UP!!
I WARNED YOU--!
HIYAAA!!
ARRH!
RATS! THE OTHER ONE GOT AWAY!
WHAT A WASTE OF LIFE.
I GUESS THIS GUY WON'T BE ANSWERING ANY QUESTIONS.
HEY! WHERE'S LEONARDO?!
7.

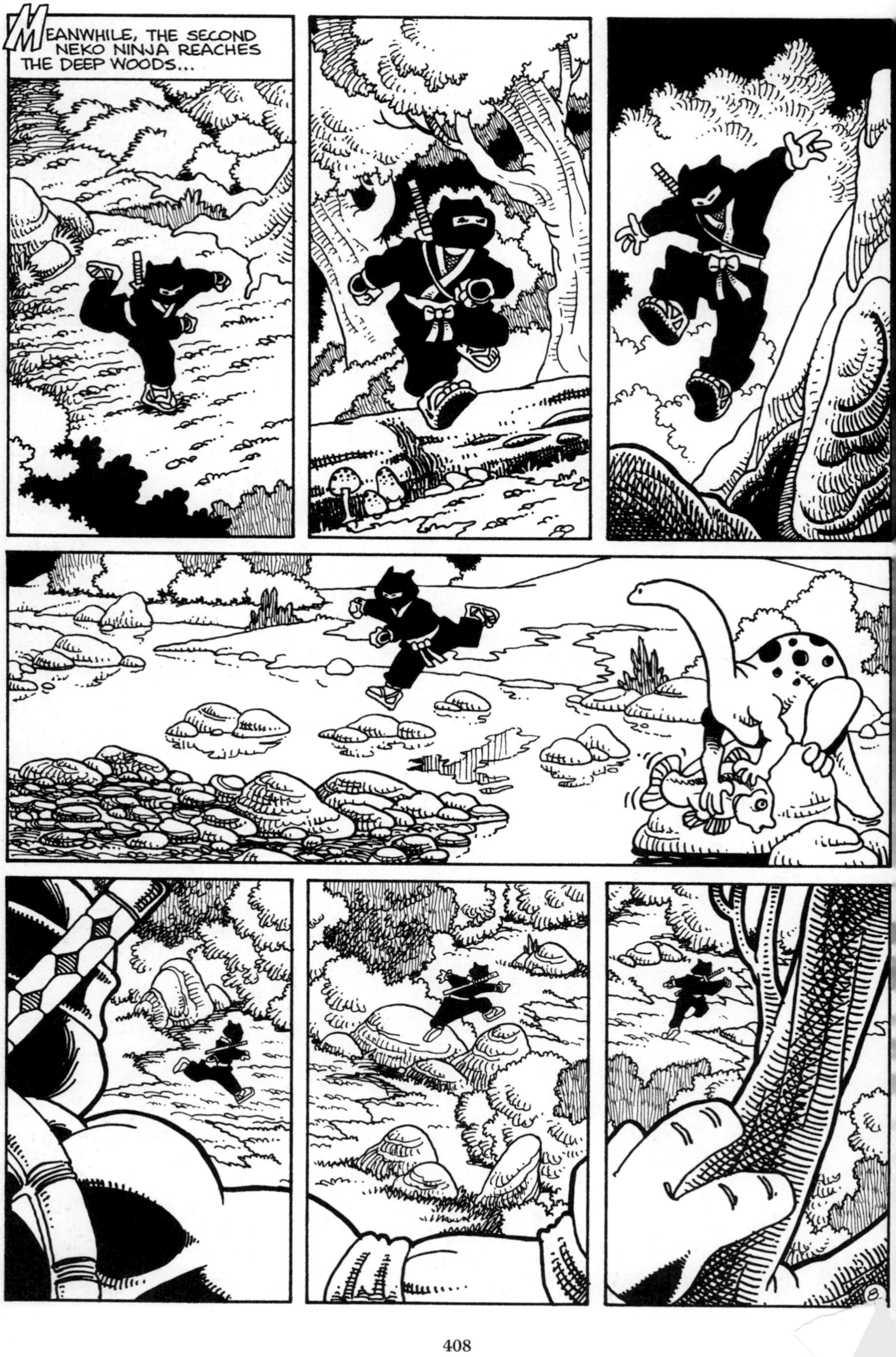
MEANWHILE, THE SECOND NEKO NINJA REACHES THE DEEP WOODS...
8

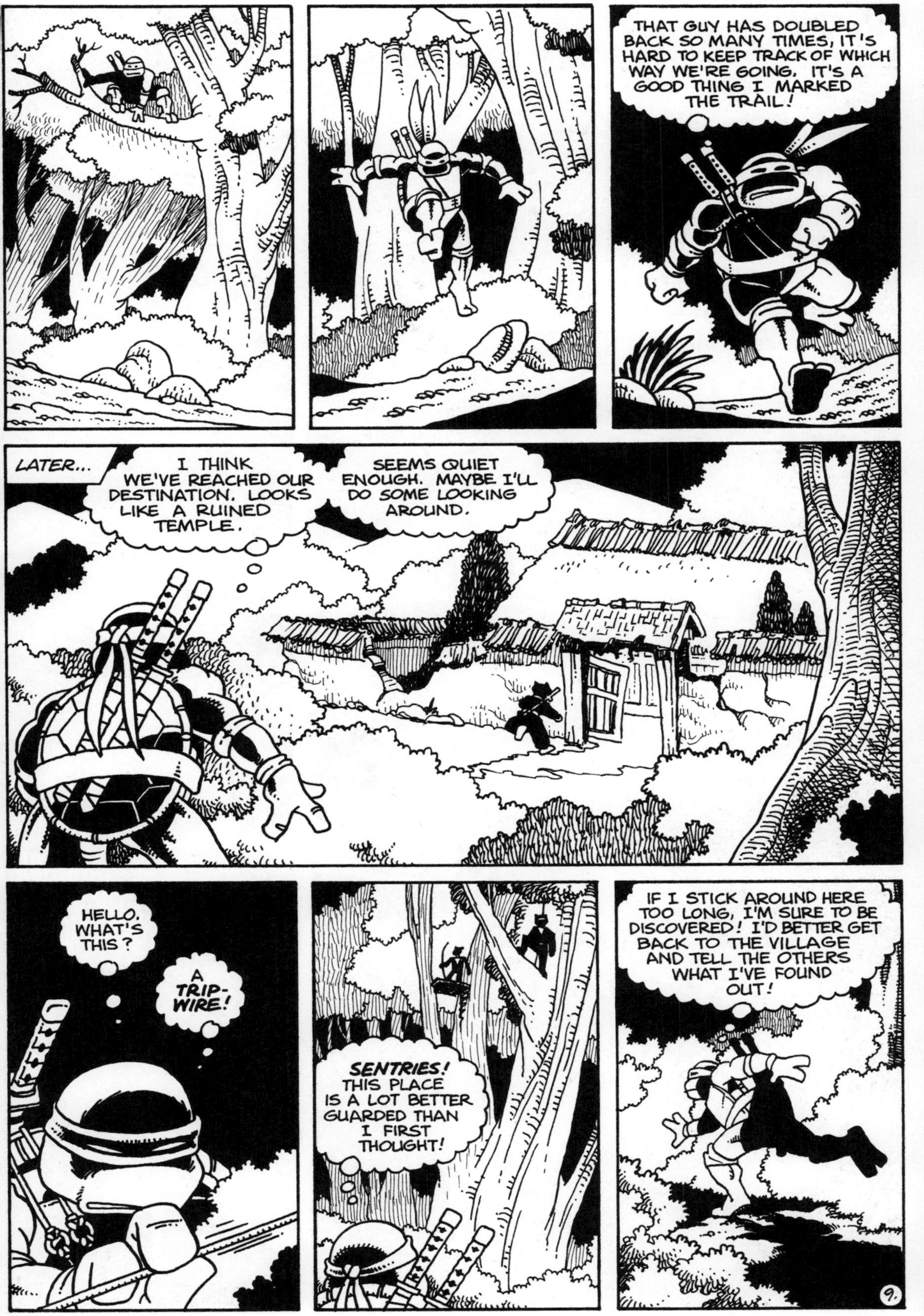
THAT GUY HAS DOUBLED BACK SO MANY TIMES, IT'S HARD TO KEEP TRACK OF WHICH WAY WE'RE GOING. IT'S A GOOD THING I MARKED THE TRAIL!
LATER...
I THINK WE'VE REACHED OUR DESTINATION. LOOKS LIKE A RUINED TEMPLE.
SEEMS QUIET ENOUGH. MAYBE I'LL DO SOME LOOKING AROUND.
HELLO. WHAT'S THIS?
A TRIP-WIRE!
SENTRIES! THIS PLACE IS A LOT BETTER GUARDED THAN I FIRST THOUGHT!
IF I STICK AROUND HERE TOO LONG, I'M SURE TO BE DISCOVERED! I'D BETTER GET BACK TO THE VILLAGE AND TELL THE OTHERS WHAT I'VE FOUND OUT!
9.

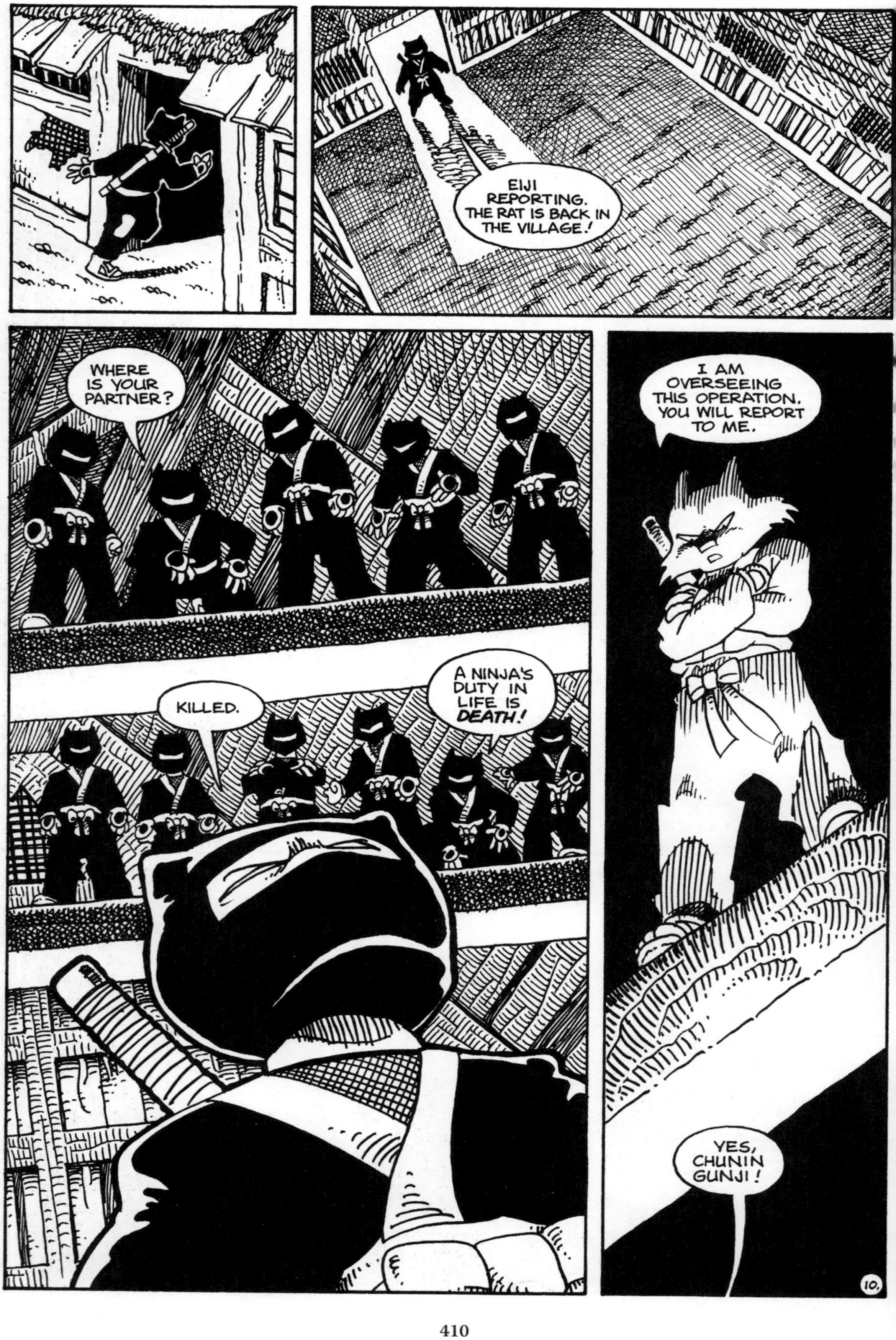
EIJI REPORTING. THE RAT IS BACK IN THE VILLAGE!
WHERE IS YOUR PARTNER?
KILLED.
A NINJA'S DUTY IN LIFE IS DEATH!
I AM OVERSEEING THIS OPERATION. YOU WILL REPORT TO ME.
YES, CHUNIN GUNJI!
10.

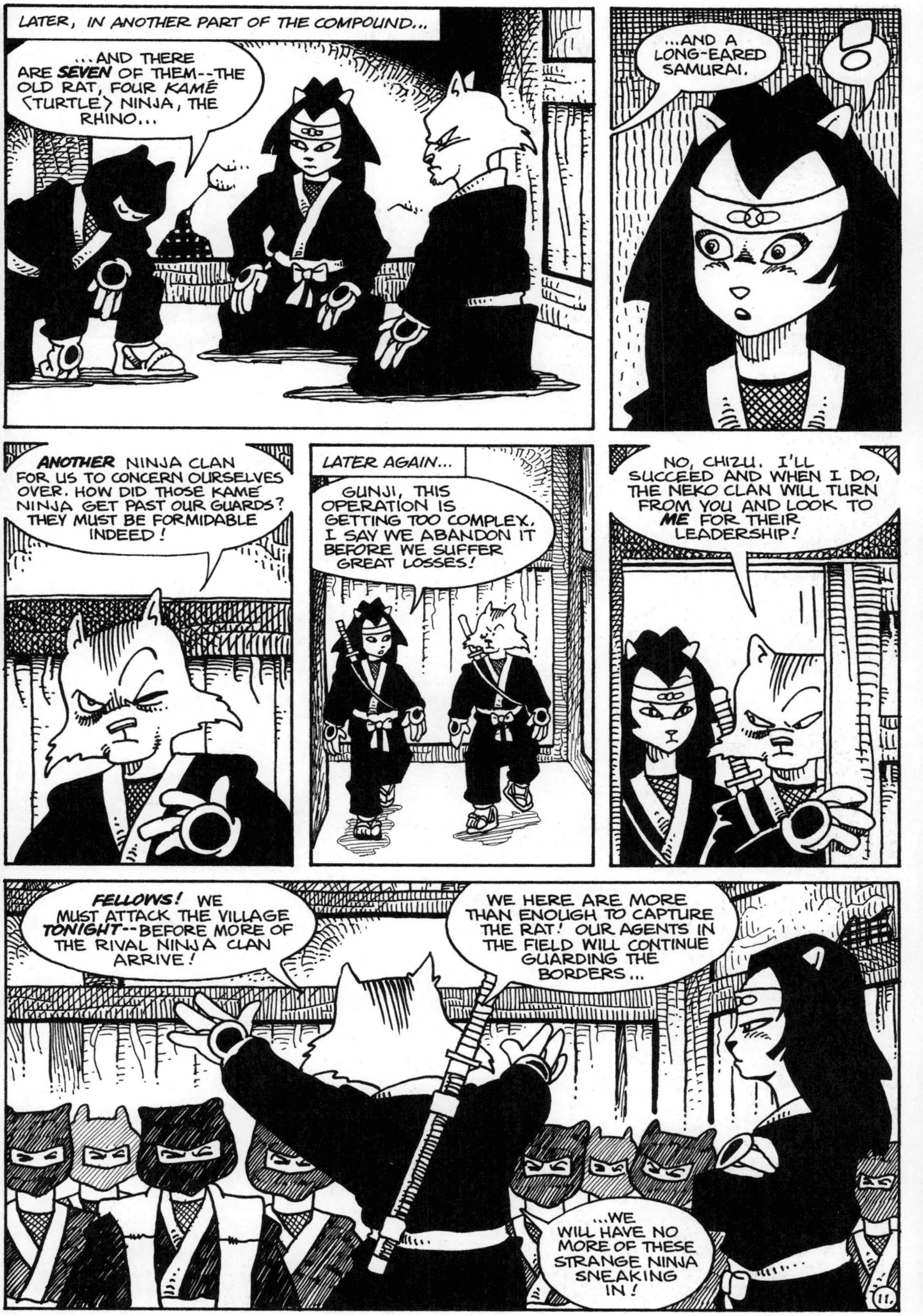
LATER, IN ANOTHER PART OF THE COMPOUND...
...AND THERE ARE SEVEN OF THEM--THE OLD RAT, FOUR KAMÉ (TURTLE) NINJA, THE RHINO...
...AND A LONG-EARED SAMURAI.
ANOTHER NINJA CLAN FOR US TO CONCERN OURSELVES OVER. HOW DID THOSE KAME NINJA GET PAST OUR GUARDS? THEY MUST BE FORMIDABLE INDEED!
LATER AGAIN...
GUNJI, THIS OPERATION IS GETTING TOO COMPLEX. I SAY WE ABANDON IT BEFORE WE SUFFER GREAT LOSSES!
NO, CHIZU. I'LL SUCCEED AND WHEN I DO, THE NEKO CLAN WILL TURN FROM YOU AND LOOK TO ME FOR THEIR LEADERSHIP!
FELLOWS! WE MUST ATTACK THE VILLAGE TONIGHT--BEFORE MORE OF THE RIVAL NINJA CLAN ARRIVE!
WE HERE ARE MORE THAN ENOUGH TO CAPTURE THE RAT! OUR AGENTS IN THE FIELD WILL CONTINUE GUARDING THE BORDERS...
...WE WILL HAVE NO MORE OF THESE STRANGE NINJA SNEAKING IN!
11.

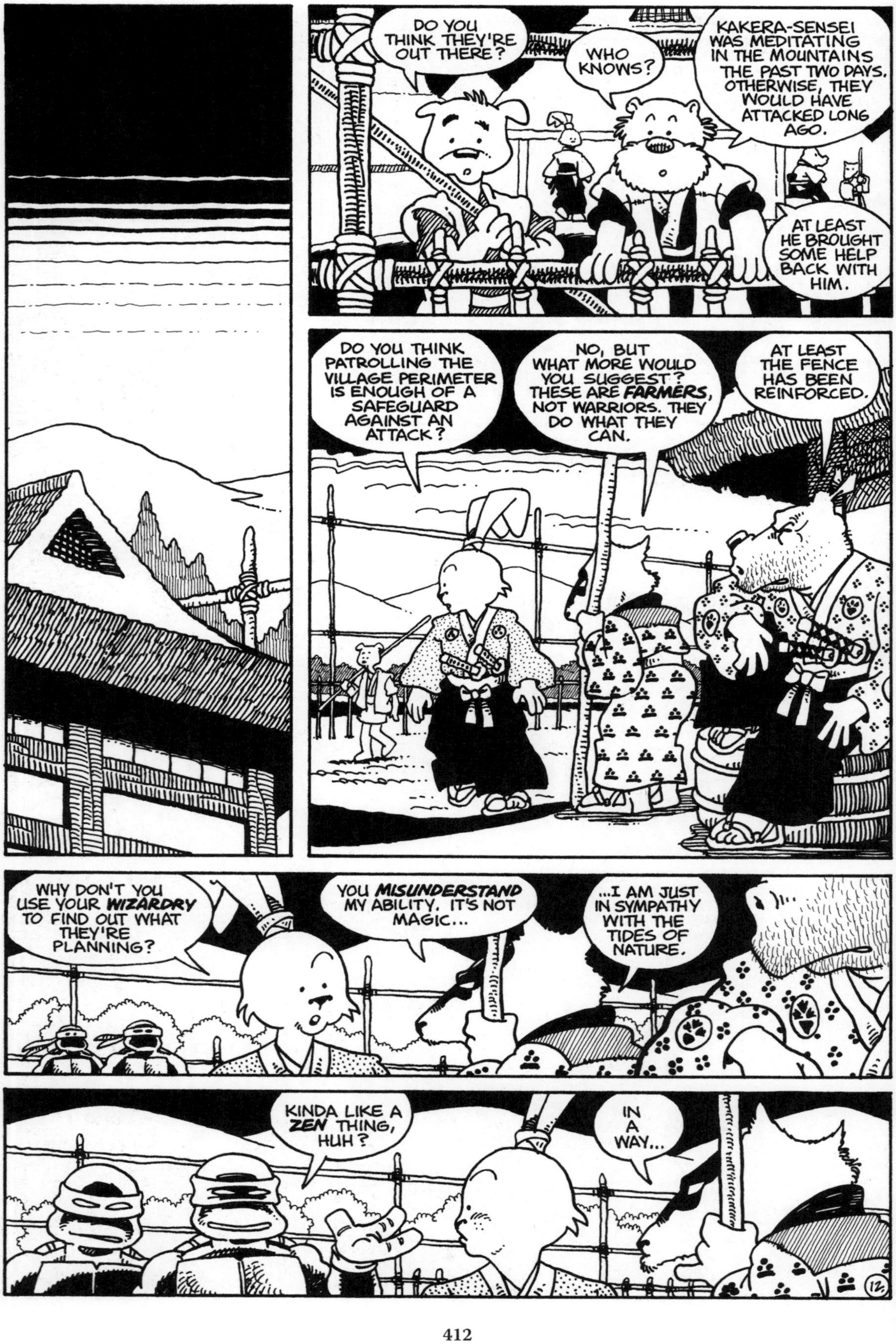
DO YOU THINK THEY'RE OUT THERE?
WHO KNOWS?
KAKERA-SENSEI WAS MEDITATING IN THE MOUNTAINS THE PAST TWO DAYS. OTHERWISE, THEY WOULD HAVE ATTACKED LONG AGO.
AT LEAST HE BROUGHT SOME HELP BACK WITH HIM.
DO YOU THINK PATROLLING THE VILLAGE PERIMETER IS ENOUGH OF A SAFEGUARD AGAINST AN ATTACK?
NO, BUT WHAT MORE WOULD YOU SUGGEST? THESE ARE FARMERS, NOT WARRIORS. THEY DO WHAT THEY CAN.
AT LEAST THE FENCE HAS BEEN REINFORCED.
WHY DON'T YOU USE YOUR WIZARDRY TO FIND OUT WHAT THEY'RE PLANNING?
YOU MISUNDERSTAND MY ABILITY. IT'S NOT MAGIC...
...I AM JUST IN SYMPATHY WITH THE TIDES OF NATURE.
KINDA LIKE A ZEN THING, HUH?
IN A WAY...
12

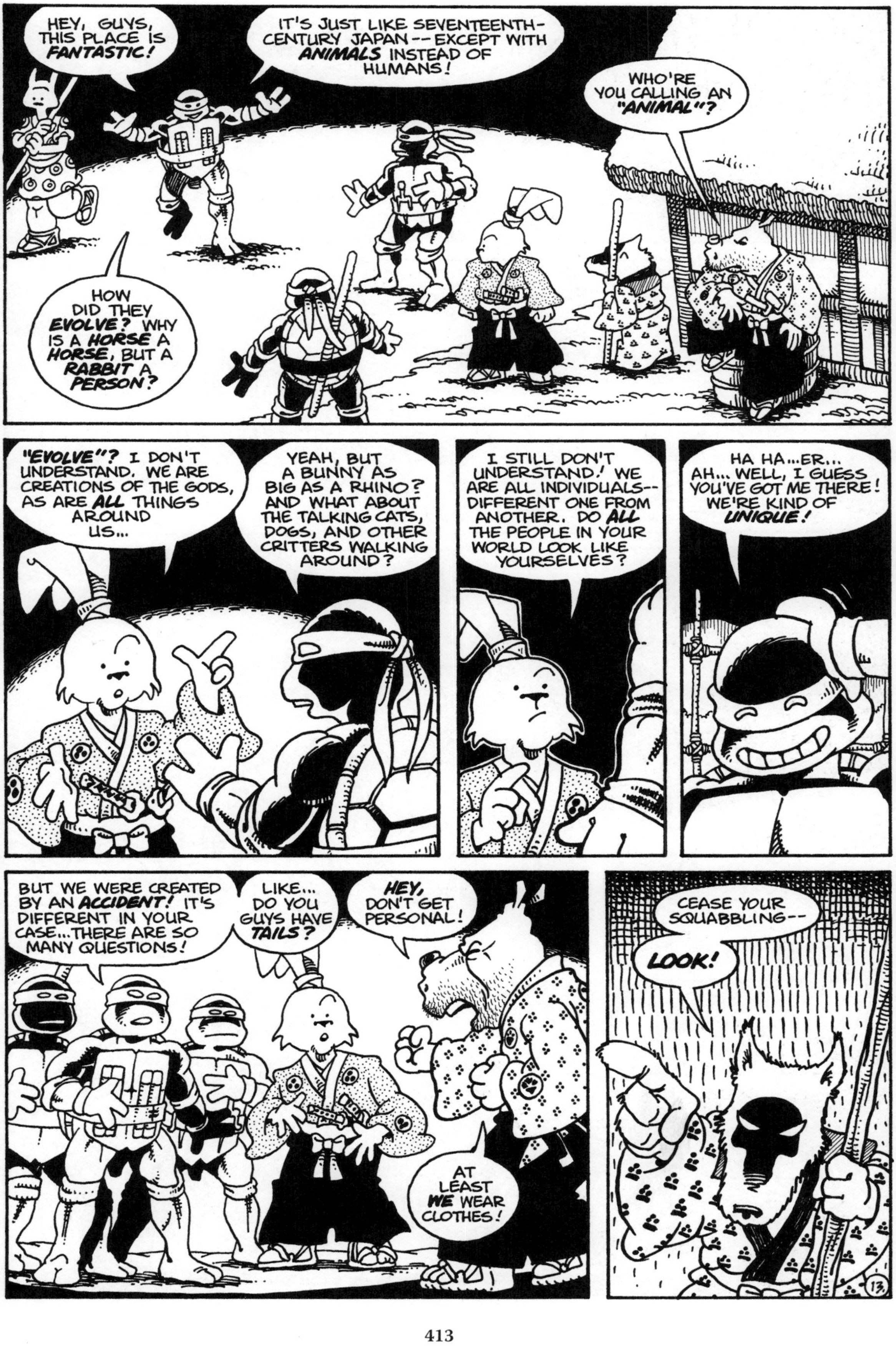
HEY, GUYS, THIS PLACE IS FANTASTIC!
IT'S JUST LIKE SEVENTEENTH-CENTURY JAPAN -- EXCEPT WITH ANIMALS INSTEAD OF HUMANS!
WHO'RE YOU CALLING AN "ANIMAL"?
HOW DID THEY EVOLVE? WHY IS A HORSE A HORSE, BUT A RABBIT A PERSON?
"EVOLVE"? I DON'T UNDERSTAND. WE ARE CREATIONS OF THE GODS, AS ARE ALL THINGS AROUND US...
YEAH, BUT A BUNNY AS BIG AS A RHINO? AND WHAT ABOUT THE TALKING CATS, DOGS, AND OTHER CRITTERS WALKING AROUND?
I STILL DON'T UNDERSTAND! WE ARE ALL INDIVIDUALS-- DIFFERENT ONE FROM ANOTHER. DO ALL THE PEOPLE IN YOUR WORLD LOOK LIKE YOURSELVES?
HA HA...ER... AH... WELL, I GUESS YOU'VE GOT ME THERE! WE'RE KIND OF UNIQUE!
BUT WE WERE CREATED BY AN ACCIDENT! IT'S DIFFERENT IN YOUR CASE...THERE ARE SO MANY QUESTIONS!
LIKE... DO YOU GUYS HAVE TAILS?
HEY, DON'T GET PERSONAL!
AT LEAST WE WEAR CLOTHES!
CEASE YOUR SQUABBLING--
LOOK!
13

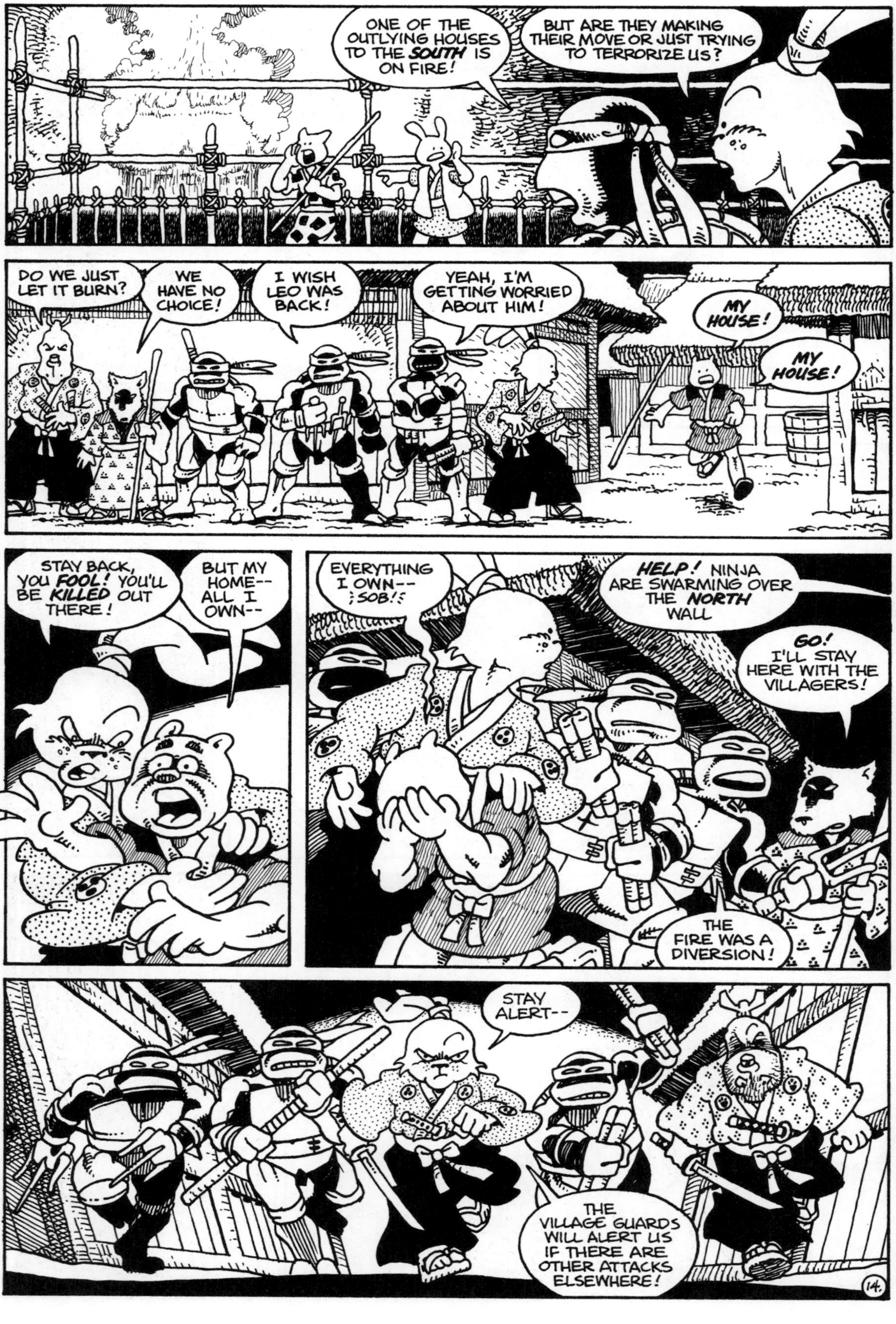

ONE OF THE OUTLYING HOUSES TO THE SOUTH IS ON FIRE!
BUT ARE THEY MAKING THEIR MOVE OR JUST TRYING TO TERRORIZE US?
DO WE JUST LET IT BURN?
WE HAVE NO CHOICE!
I WISH LEO WAS BACK!
YEAH, I'M GETTING WORRIED ABOUT HIM!
MY HOUSE!
MY HOUSE!
STAY BACK, YOU FOOL! YOU'LL BE KILLED OUT THERE!
BUT MY HOME-- ALL I OWN--
EVERYTHING I OWN-- ;SOB!;
HELP! NINJA ARE SWARMING OVER THE NORTH WALL
GO! I'LL STAY HERE WITH THE VILLAGERS!
THE FIRE WAS A DIVERSION!
STAY ALERT--
THE VILLAGE GUARDS WILL ALERT US IF THERE ARE OTHER ATTACKS ELSEWHERE!
14.

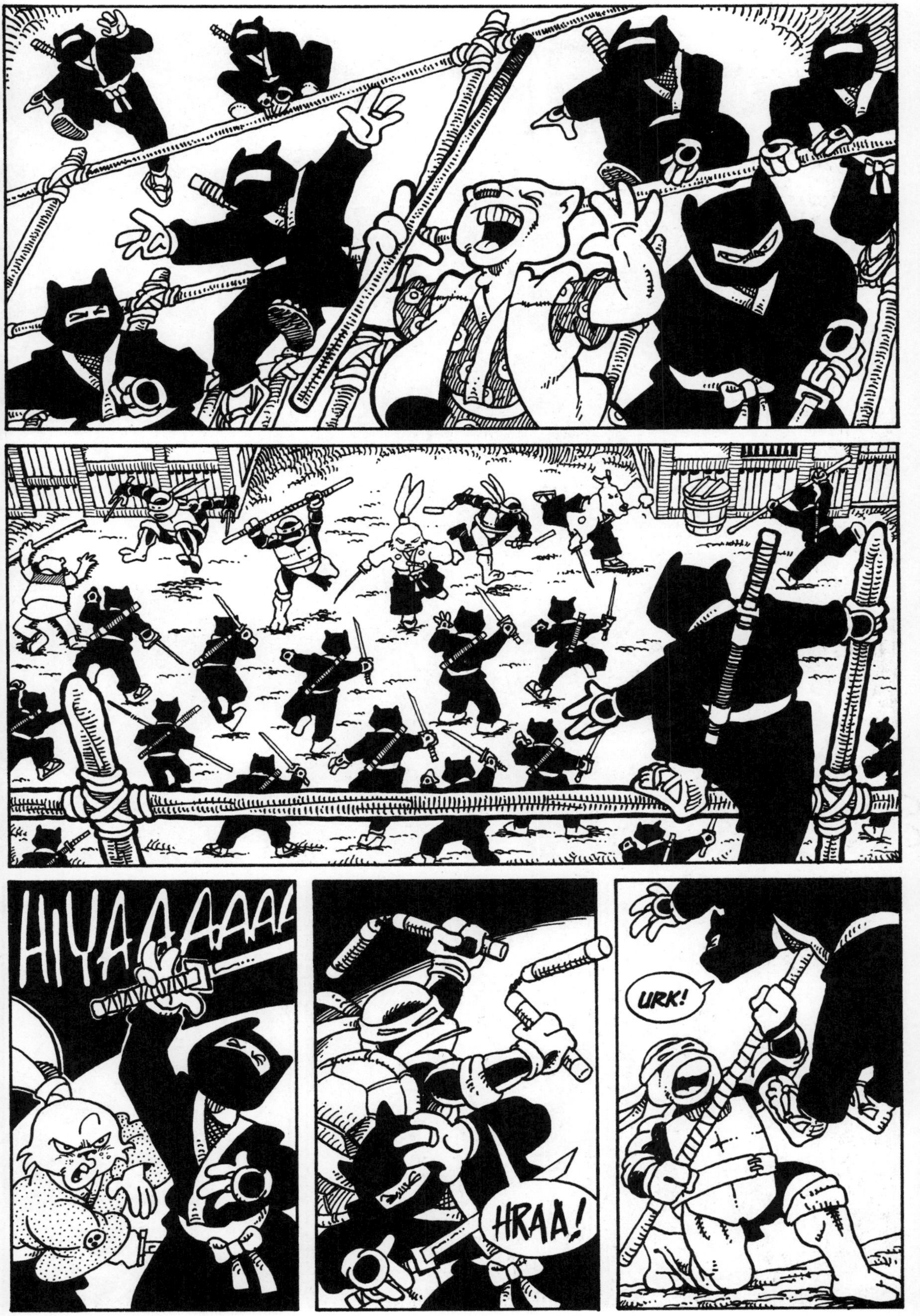
HIYAAAAAA
HRAA!
URK!

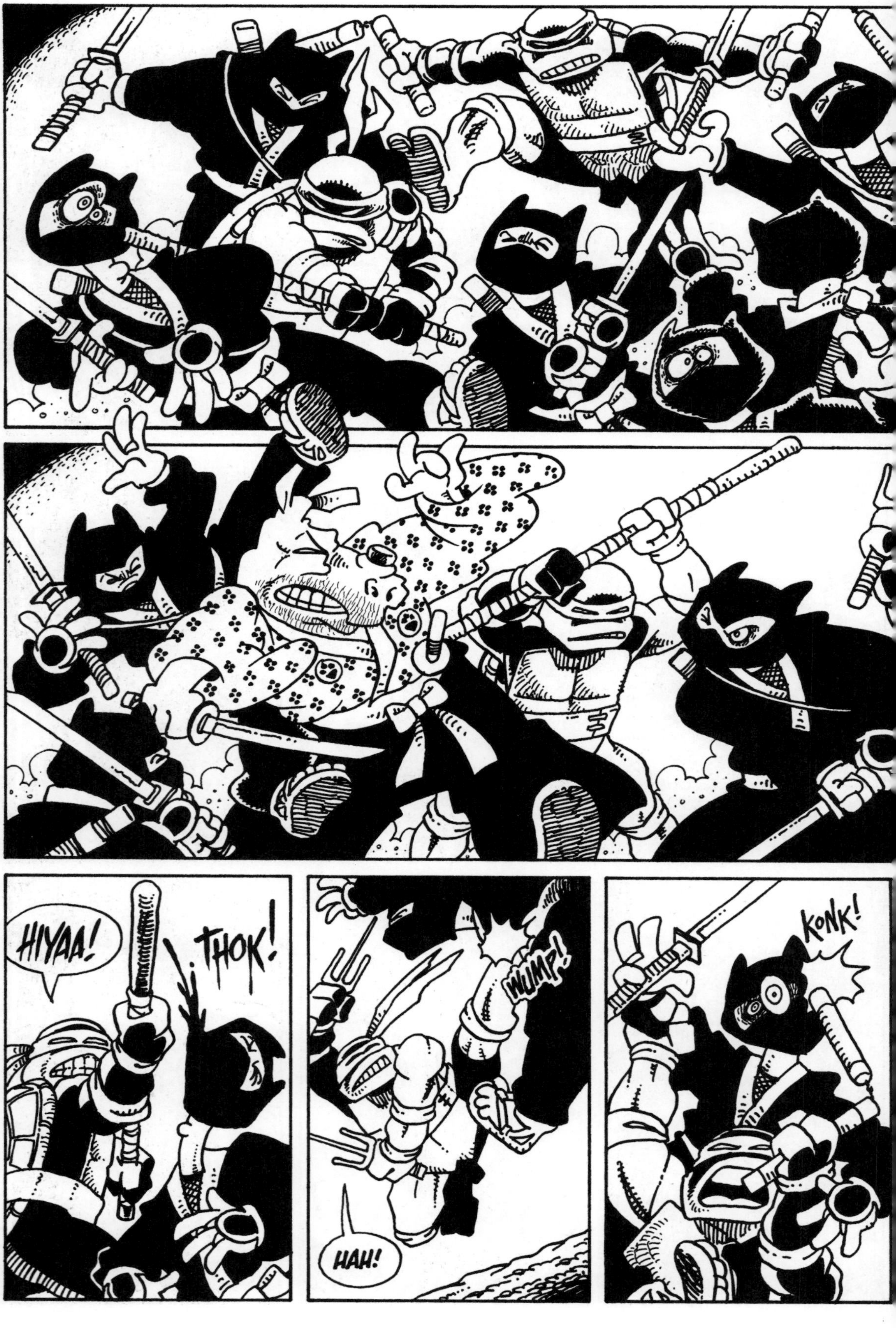
HIYAA!
THOK!
WUMP!
HAH!
KONK!

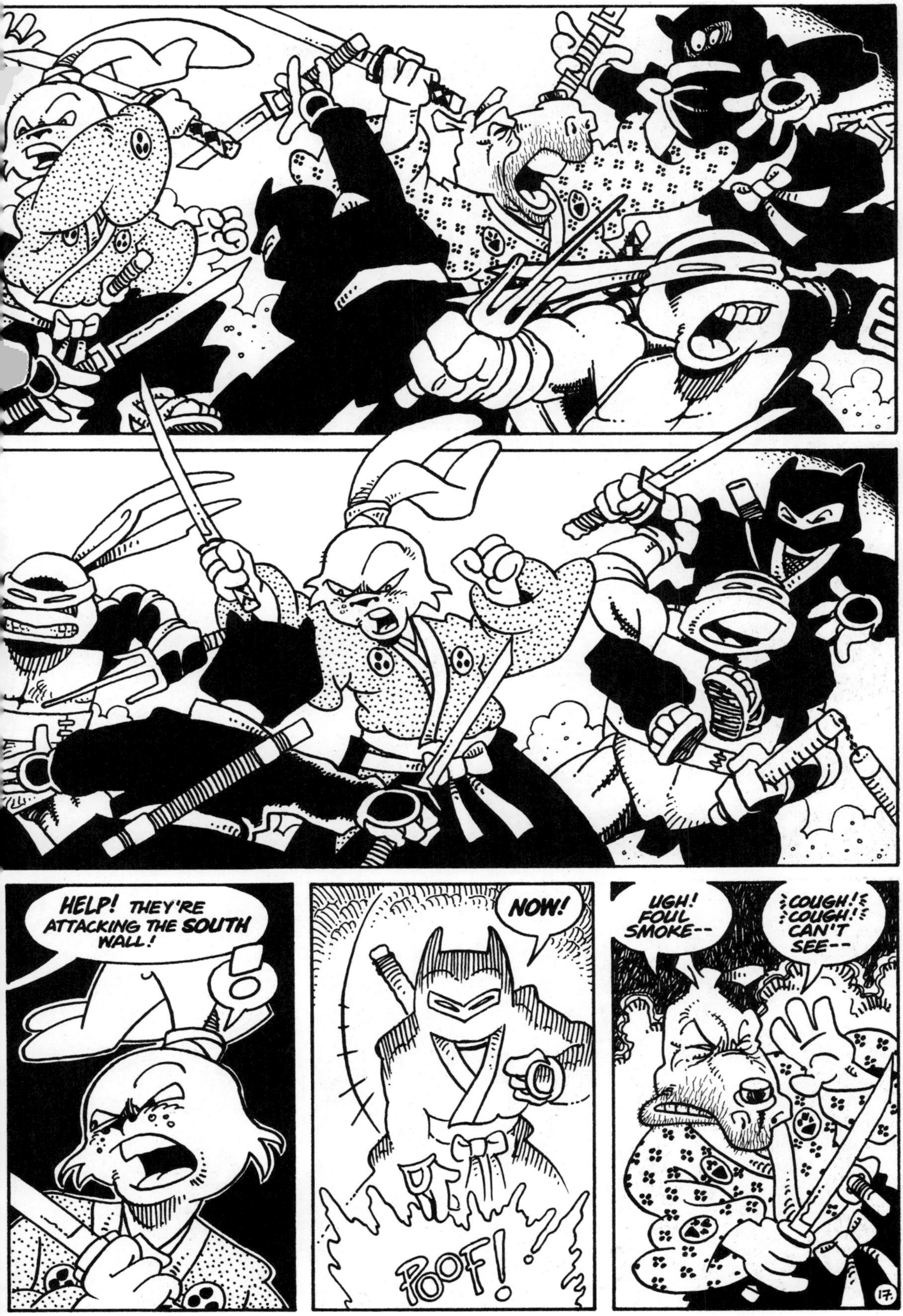
HELP! THEY'RE ATTACKING THE SOUTH WALL!
NOW!
POOF!
UGH! FOUL SMOKE--
COUGH! COUGH! CAN'T SEE--
17

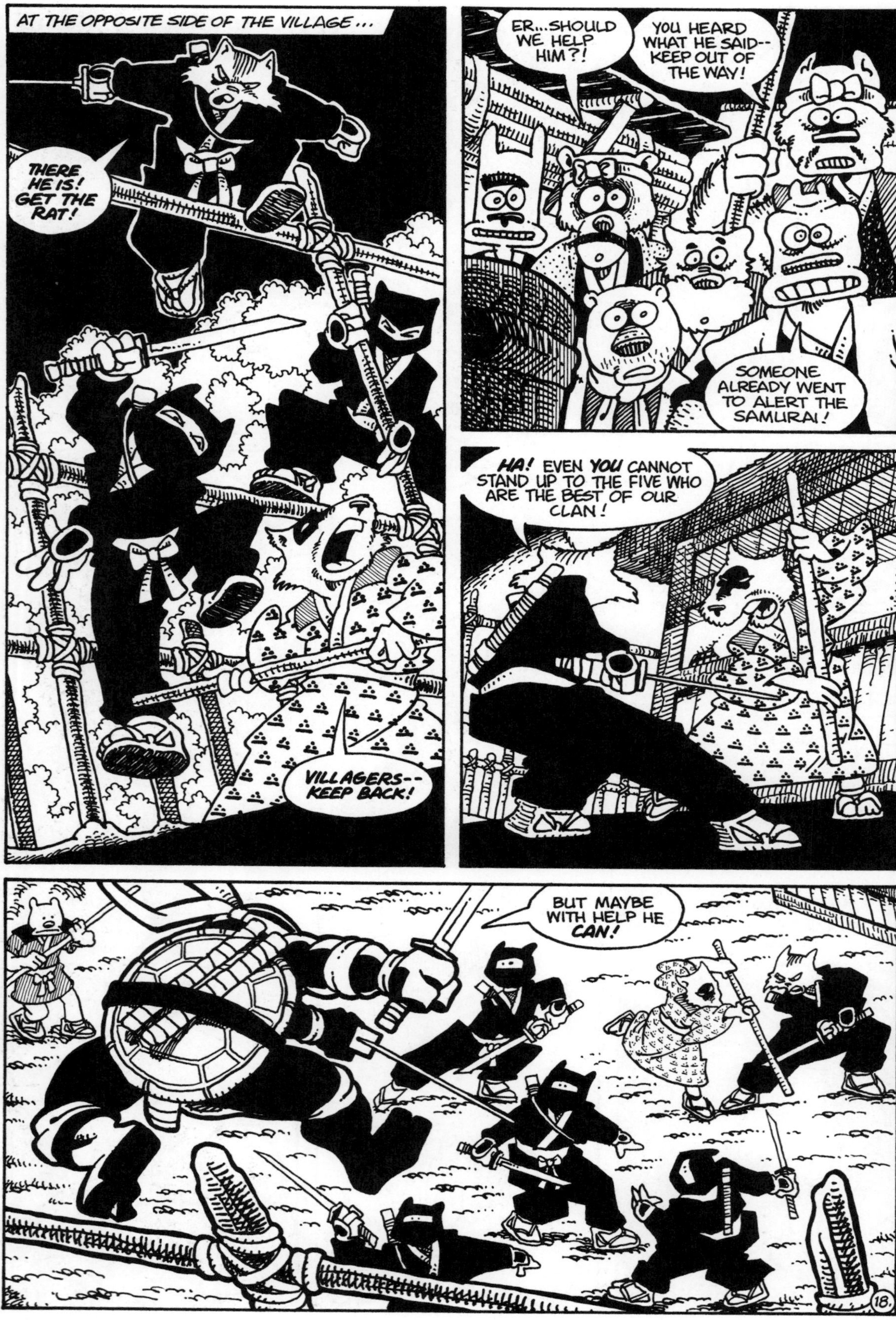

AT THE OPPOSITE SIDE OF THE VILLAGE...
THERE HE IS! GET THE RAT!
VILLAGERS-- KEEP BACK!
ER...SHOULD WE HELP HIM?!
YOU HEARD WHAT HE SAID-- KEEP OUT OF THE WAY!
SOMEONE ALREADY WENT TO ALERT THE SAMURAI!
HA! EVEN YOU CANNOT STAND UP TO THE FIVE WHO ARE THE BEST OF OUR CLAN!
BUT MAYBE WITH HELP HE CAN!
18.

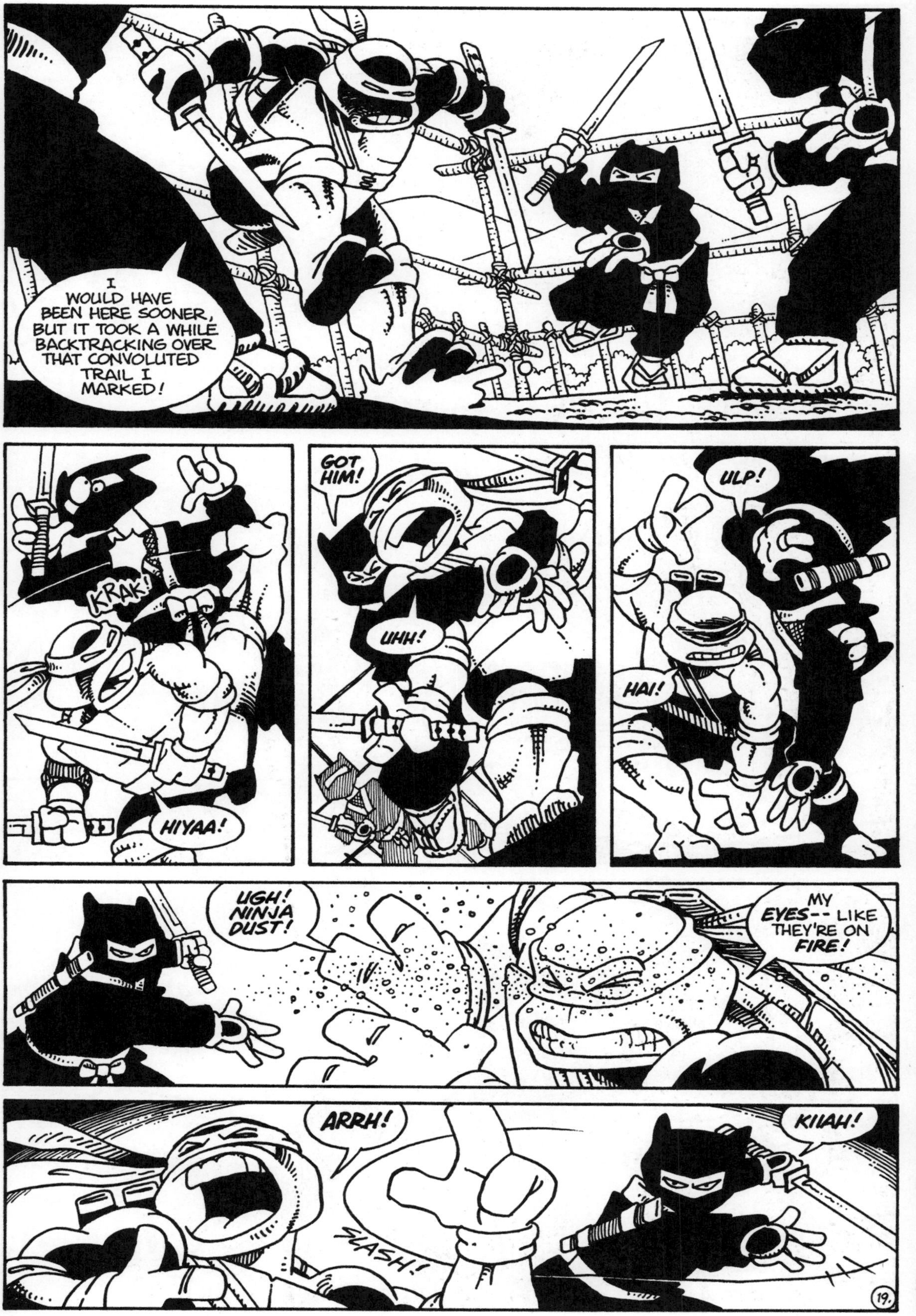
I WOULD HAVE BEEN HERE SOONER, BUT IT TOOK A WHILE BACKTRACKING OVER THAT CONVOLUTED TRAIL I MARKED!
KRAK!
HIYAA!
GOT HIM!
UHH!
ULP!
HAI!
UGH! NINJA DUST!
MY EYES-- LIKE THEY'RE ON FIRE!
ARRH!
KIIAH!
SLASH!
19.

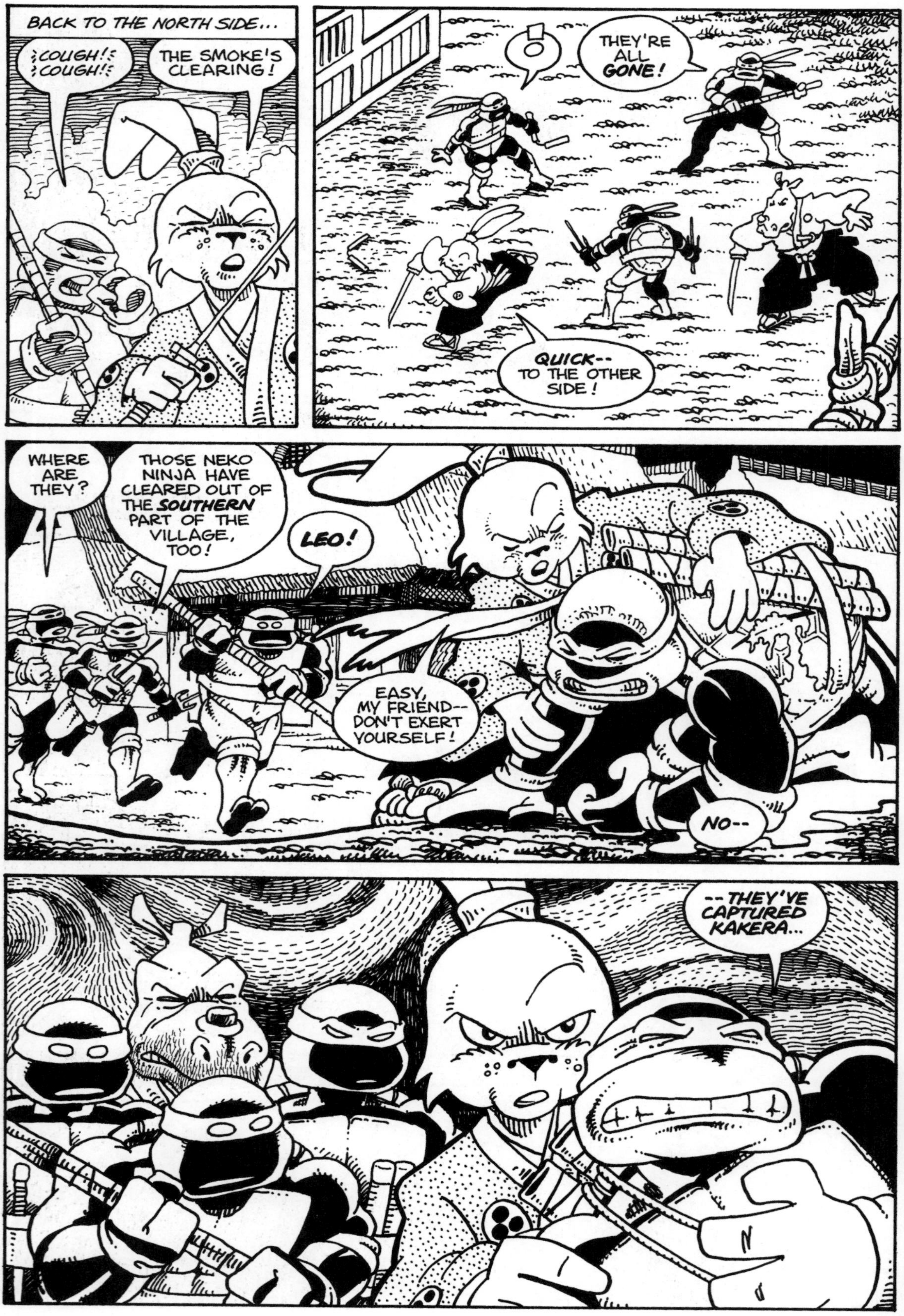
BACK TO THE NORTH SIDE...
COUGH! COUGH!
THE SMOKE'S CLEARING!
!
THEY'RE ALL GONE!
QUICK-- TO THE OTHER SIDE!
WHERE ARE THEY?
THOSE NEKO NINJA HAVE CLEARED OUT OF THE SOUTHERN PART OF THE VILLAGE, TOO!
LEO!
EASY, MY FRIEND-- DON'T EXERT YOURSELF!
NO--
--THEY'VE CAPTURED KAKERA...

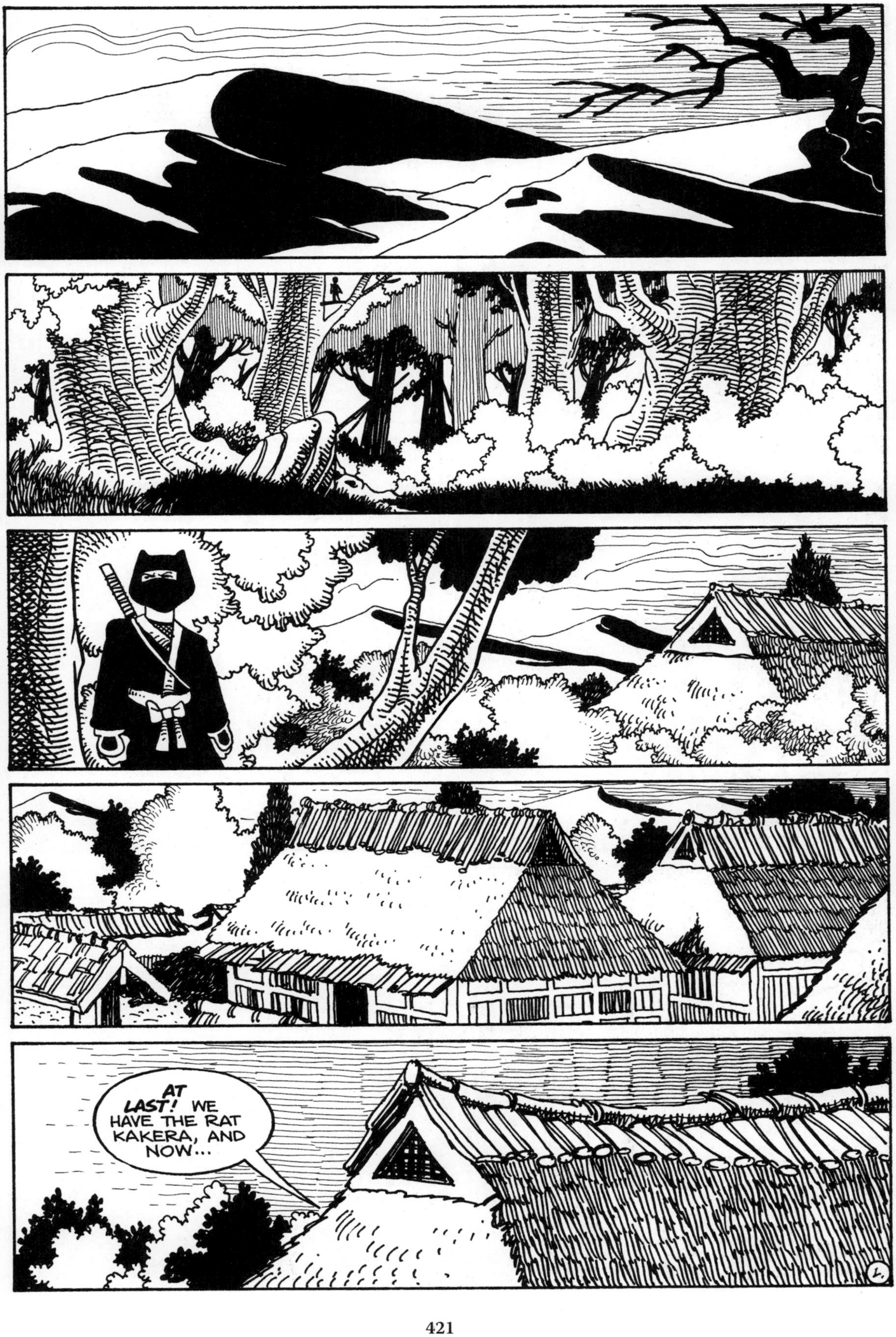
AT LAST! WE HAVE THE RAT KAKERA, AND NOW...

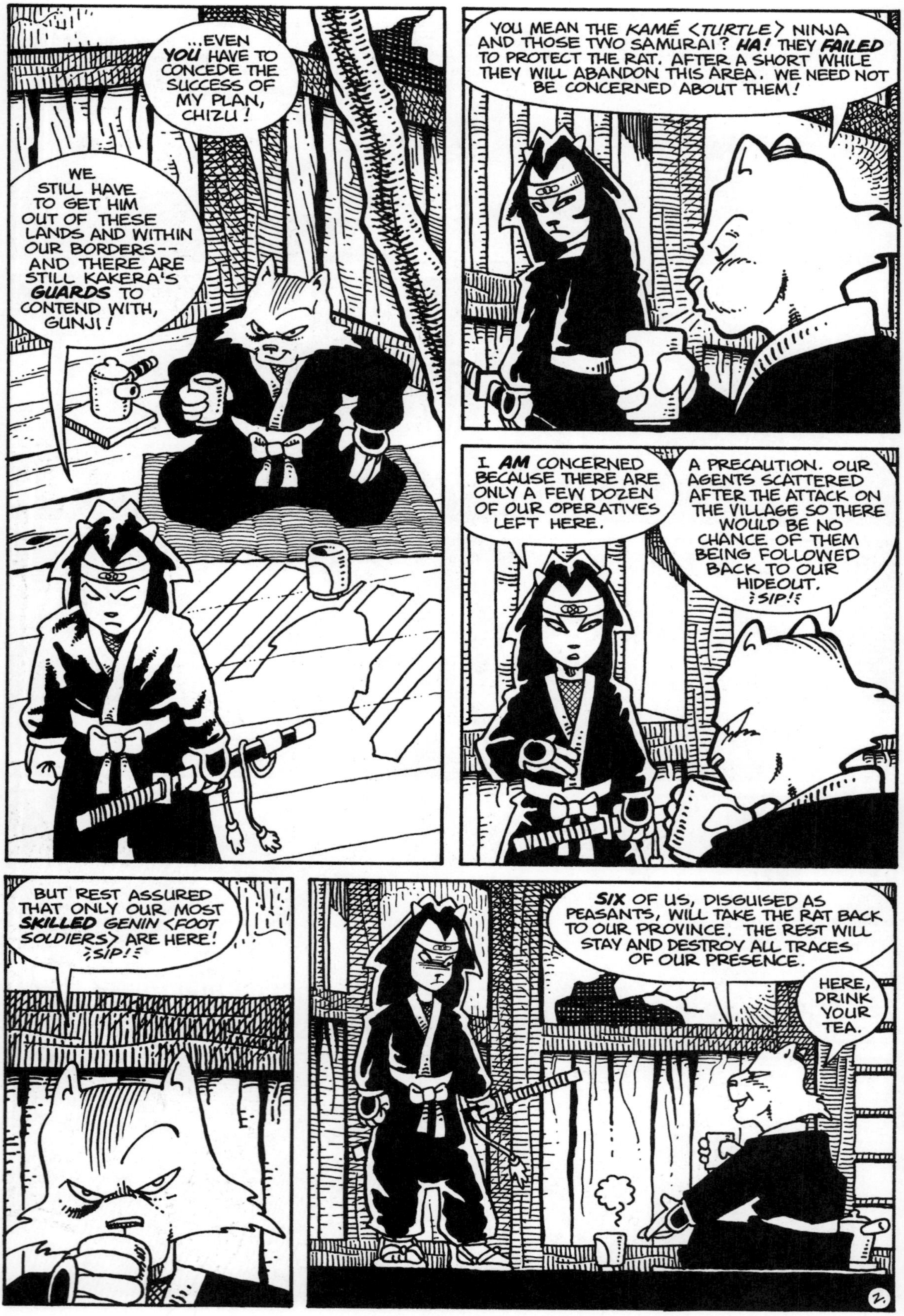
...EVEN YOU HAVE TO CONCEDE THE SUCCESS OF MY PLAN, CHIZU!
WE STILL HAVE TO GET HIM OUT OF THESE LANDS AND WITHIN OUR BORDERS-- AND THERE ARE STILL KAKERA'S GUARDS TO CONTEND WITH, GUNJI!
YOU MEAN THE KAMÉ <TURTLE> NINJA AND THOSE TWO SAMURAI? HA! THEY FAILED TO PROTECT THE RAT. AFTER A SHORT WHILE THEY WILL ABANDON THIS AREA. WE NEED NOT BE CONCERNED ABOUT THEM!
I AM CONCERNED BECAUSE THERE ARE ONLY A FEW DOZEN OF OUR OPERATIVES LEFT HERE.
A PRECAUTION. OUR AGENTS SCATTERED AFTER THE ATTACK ON THE VILLAGE SO THERE WOULD BE NO CHANCE OF THEM BEING FOLLOWED BACK TO OUR HIDEOUT.
SIP!
BUT REST ASSURED THAT ONLY OUR MOST SKILLED GENIN <FOOT SOLDIERS> ARE HERE!
SIP!
SIX OF US, DISGUISED AS PEASANTS, WILL TAKE THE RAT BACK TO OUR PROVINCE. THE REST WILL STAY AND DESTROY ALL TRACES OF OUR PRESENCE.
HERE, DRINK YOUR TEA.
2.

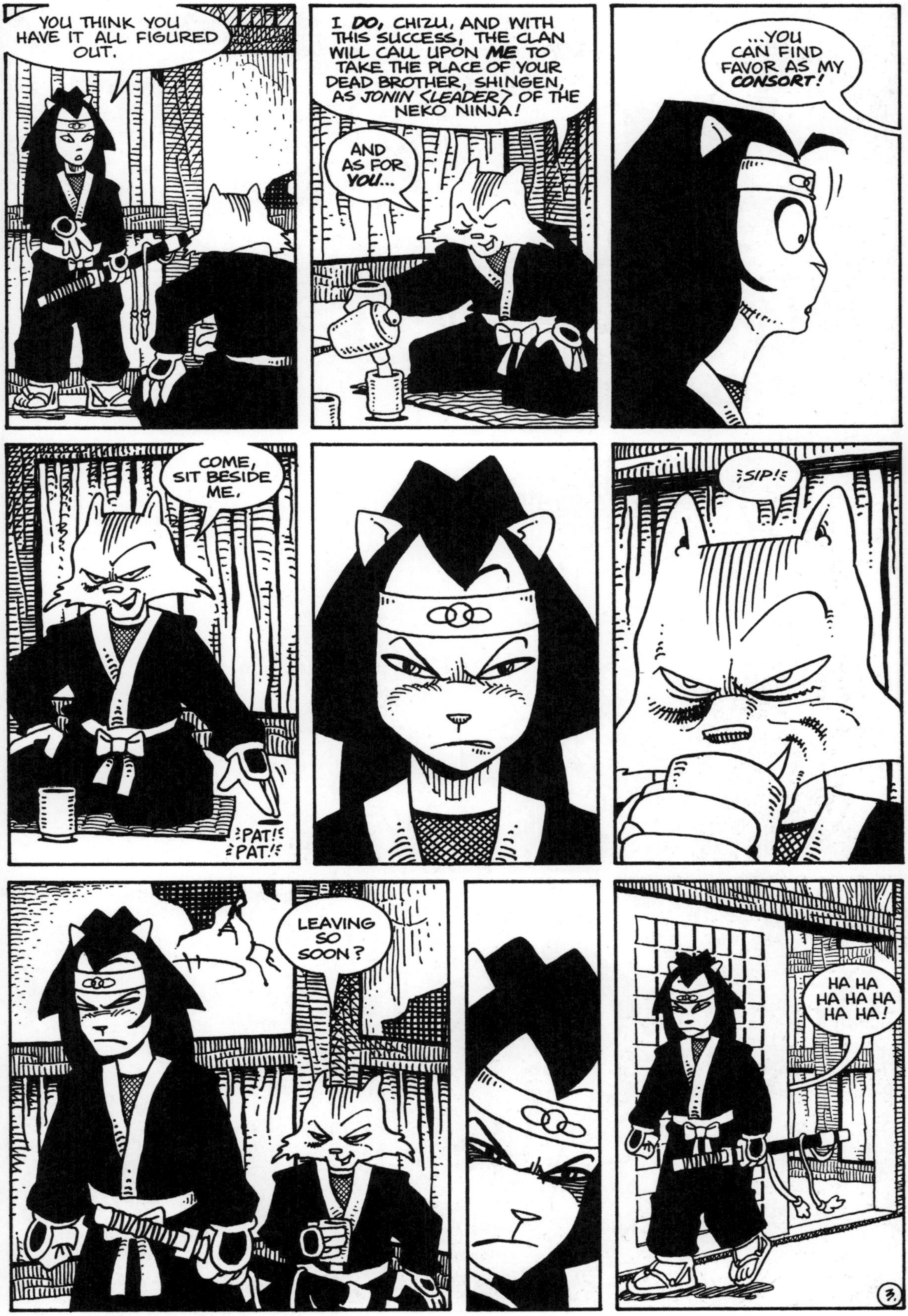
YOU THINK YOU HAVE IT ALL FIGURED OUT.
I DO, CHIZU, AND WITH THIS SUCCESS, THE CLAN WILL CALL UPON ME TO TAKE THE PLACE OF YOUR DEAD BROTHER, SHINGEN, AS JONIN <LEADER> OF THE NEKO NINJA!
AND AS FOR YOU...
...YOU CAN FIND FAVOR AS MY CONSORT!
COME, SIT BESIDE ME.
PAT! PAT!
SIP!
LEAVING SO SOON?
HA HA HA HA HA HA HA!
3.

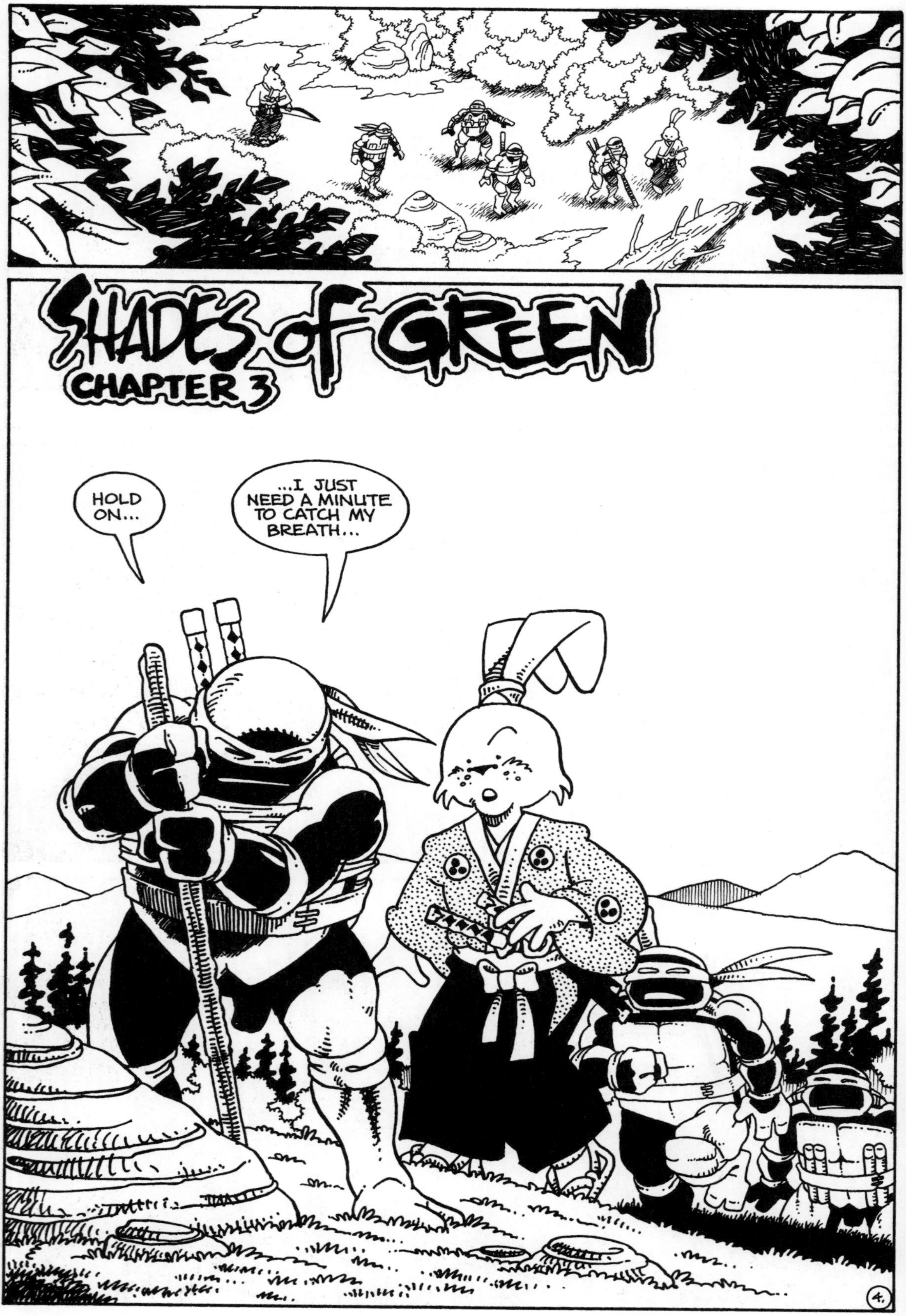
SHADES OF GREEN
CHAPTER 3
HOLD ON...
...I JUST NEED A MINUTE TO CATCH MY BREATH...
4.

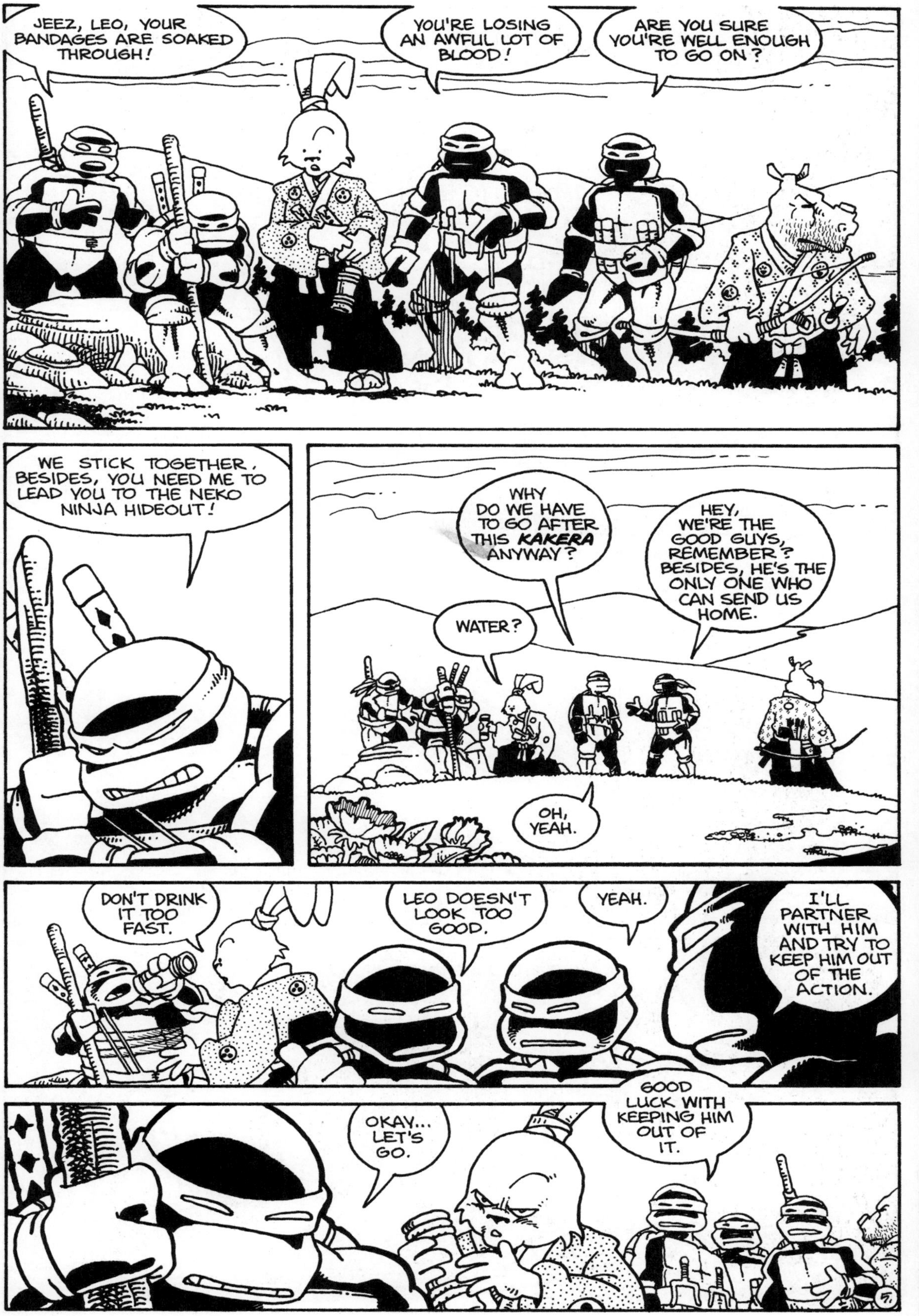
JEEZ, LEO, YOUR BANDAGES ARE SOAKED THROUGH!
YOU'RE LOSING AN AWFUL LOT OF BLOOD!
ARE YOU SURE YOU'RE WELL ENOUGH TO GO ON?
WE STICK TOGETHER. BESIDES, YOU NEED ME TO LEAD YOU TO THE NEKO NINJA HIDEOUT!
WATER?
WHY DO WE HAVE TO GO AFTER THIS KAKERA ANYWAY?
HEY, WE'RE THE GOOD GUYS, REMEMBER? BESIDES, HE'S THE ONLY ONE WHO CAN SEND US HOME.
OH, YEAH.
DON'T DRINK IT TOO FAST.
LEO DOESN'T LOOK TOO GOOD.
YEAH.
I'LL PARTNER WITH HIM AND TRY TO KEEP HIM OUT OF THE ACTION.
OKAY... LET'S GO.
GOOD LUCK WITH KEEPING HIM OUT OF IT.

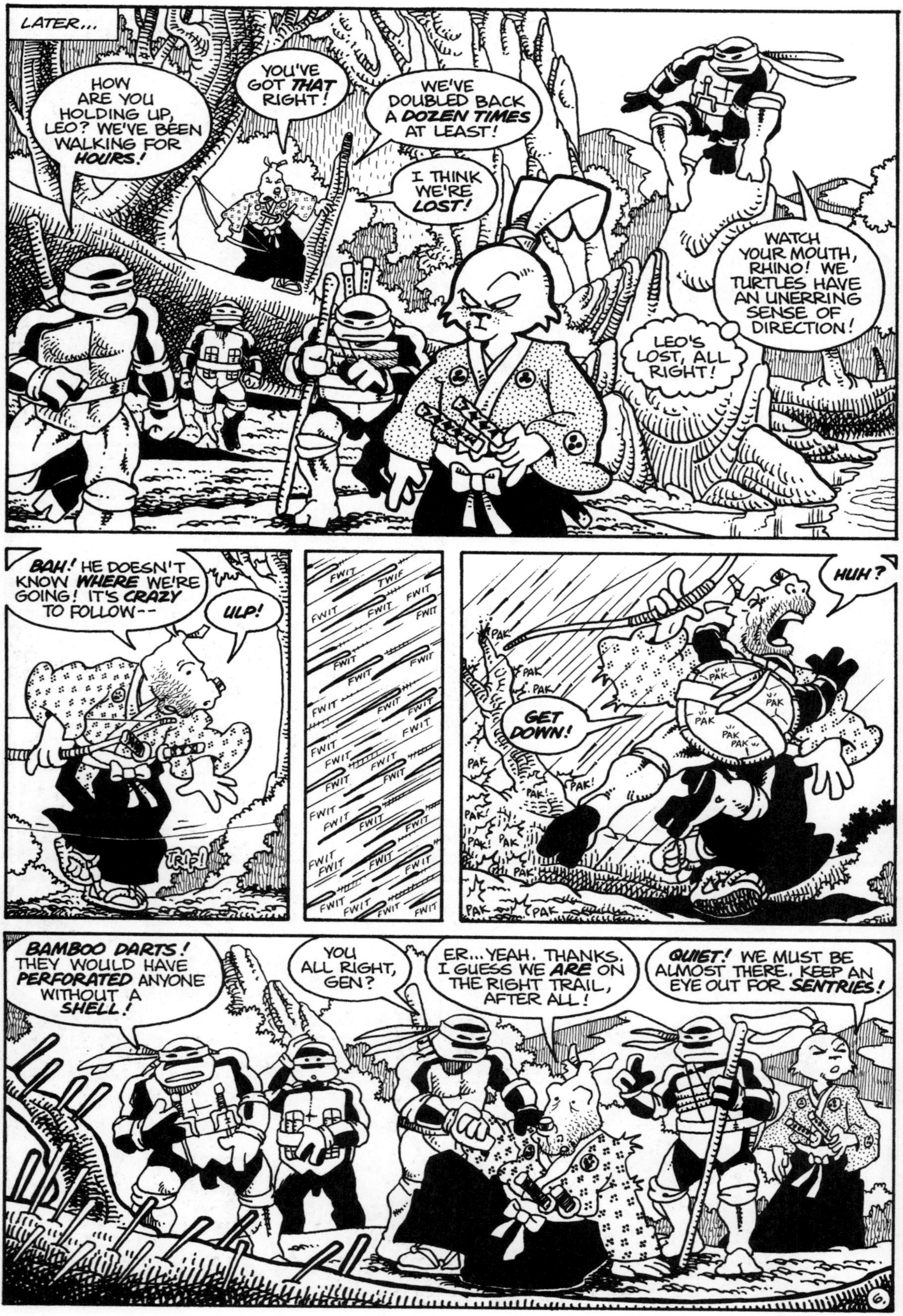
LATER...
HOW ARE YOU HOLDING UP, LEO? WE'VE BEEN WALKING FOR HOURS!
YOU'VE GOT THAT RIGHT!
WE'VE DOUBLED BACK A DOZEN TIMES AT LEAST!
I THINK WE'RE LOST!
WATCH YOUR MOUTH, RHINO! WE TURTLES HAVE AN UNERRING SENSE OF DIRECTION!
LEO'S LOST, ALL RIGHT!
BAH! HE DOESN'T KNOW WHERE WE'RE GOING! IT'S CRAZY TO FOLLOW--
ULP!
TRIP!
FWIT TWIF FWIT FWIT FWIT FWIT
HUH?
PAK PAK PAK
GET DOWN!
PAK!
BAMBOO DARTS! THEY WOULD HAVE PERFORATED ANYONE WITHOUT A SHELL!
YOU ALL RIGHT, GEN?
ER... YEAH. THANKS. I GUESS WE ARE ON THE RIGHT TRAIL, AFTER ALL!
QUIET! WE MUST BE ALMOST THERE. KEEP AN EYE OUT FOR SENTRIES!
6.

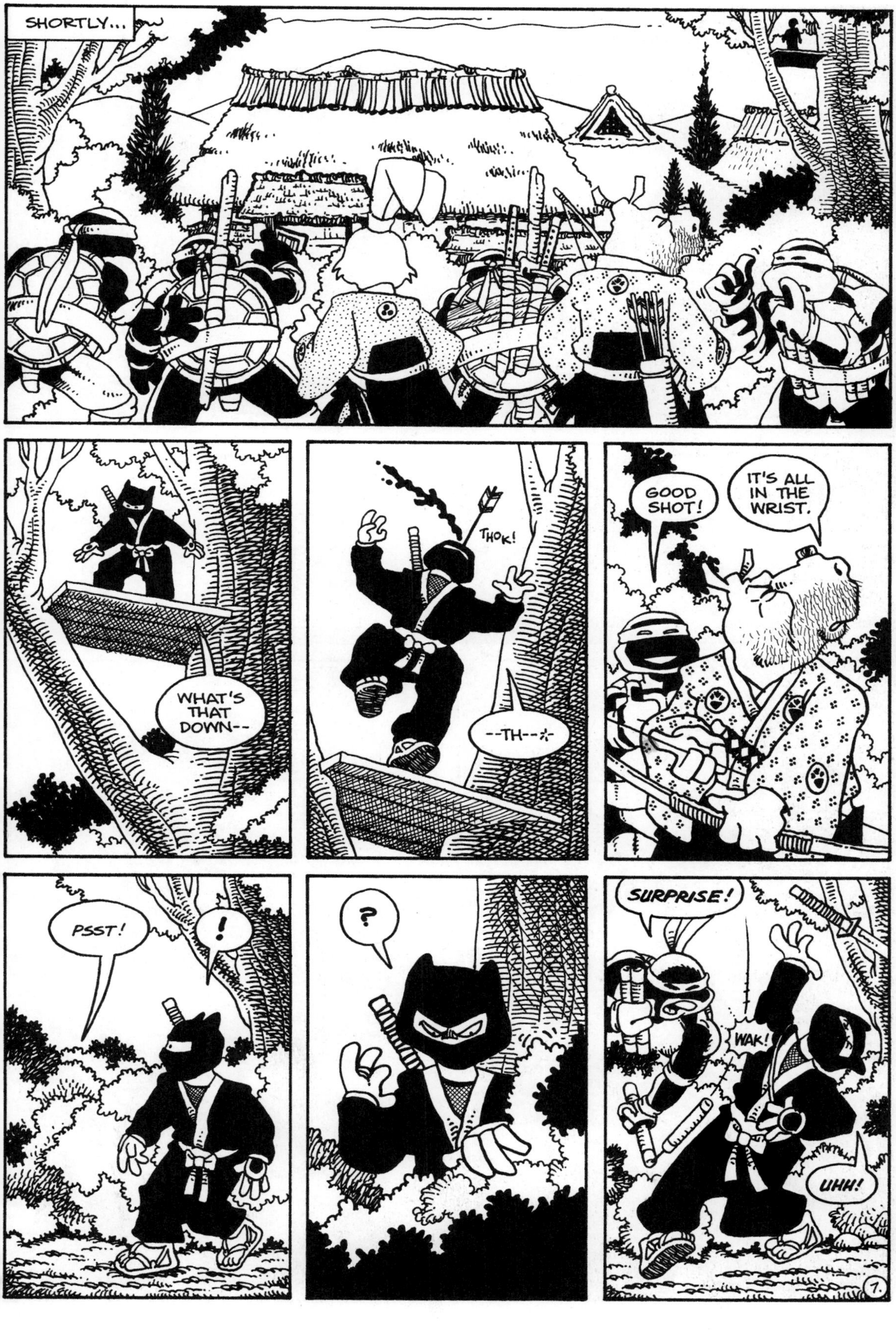
SHORTLY...
WHAT'S THAT DOWN--
THOK!
--TH--
GOOD SHOT!
IT'S ALL IN THE WRIST.
PSST!
!
?
SURPRISE!
WAK!
UHH!
7.

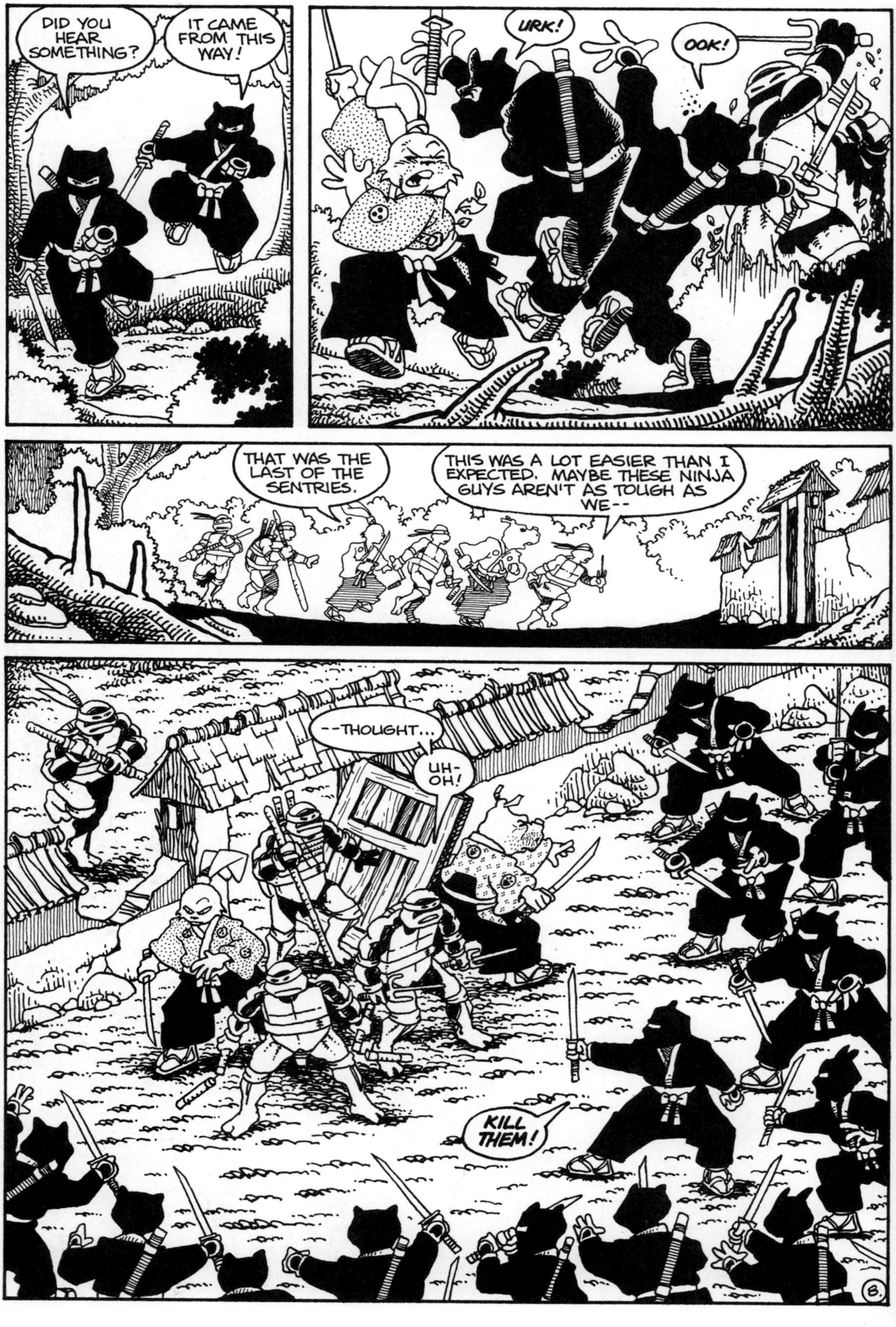
DID YOU HEAR SOMETHING?
IT CAME FROM THIS WAY!
URK!
OOK!
THAT WAS THE LAST OF THE SENTRIES.
THIS WAS A LOT EASIER THAN I EXPECTED. MAYBE THESE NINJA GUYS AREN'T AS TOUGH AS WE--
--THOUGHT...
UH-OH!
KILL THEM!
8.

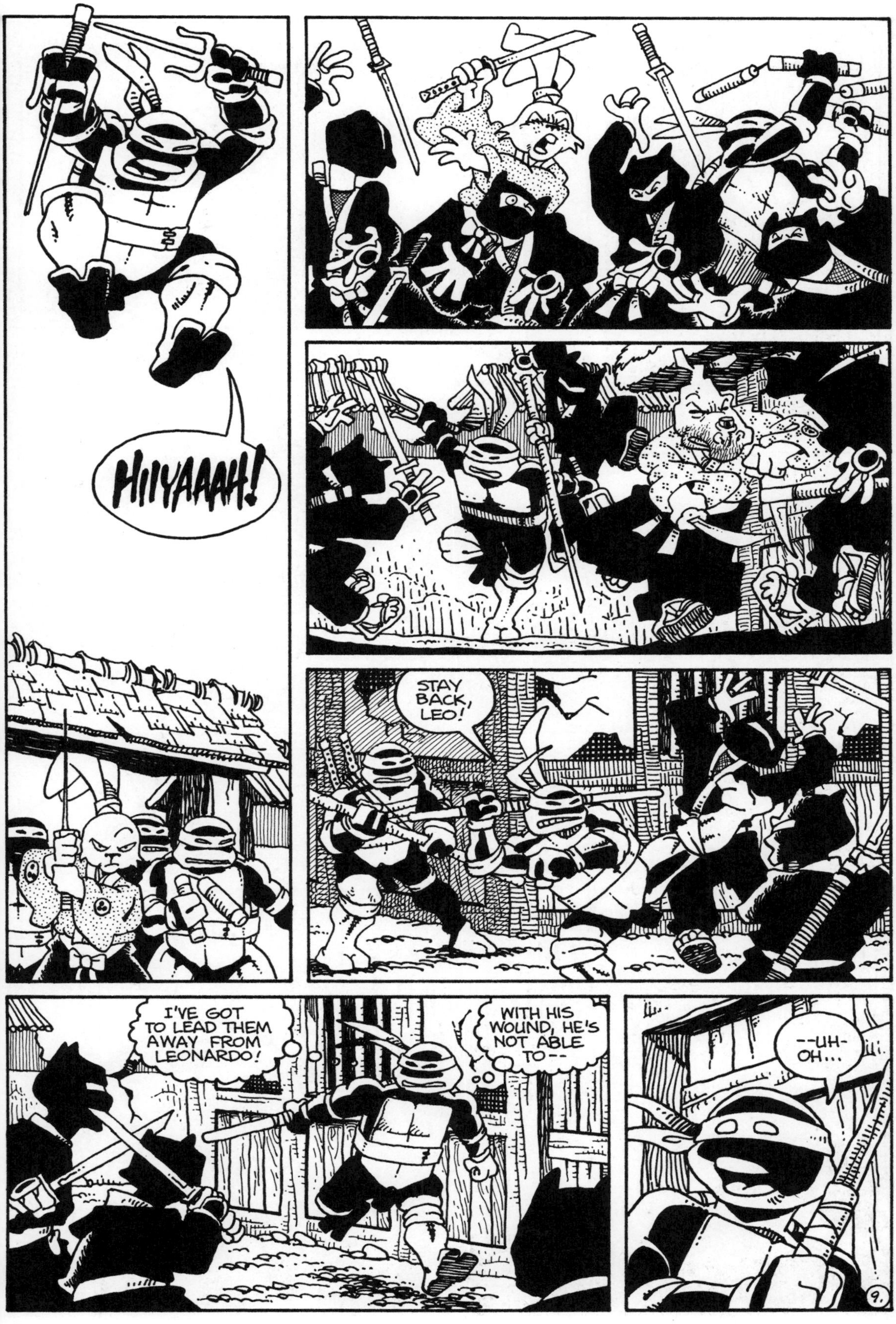
HIIYAAAH!
STAY BACK, LEO!
I'VE GOT TO LEAD THEM AWAY FROM LEONARDO!
WITH HIS WOUND, HE'S NOT ABLE TO--
--UH-OH...
9.

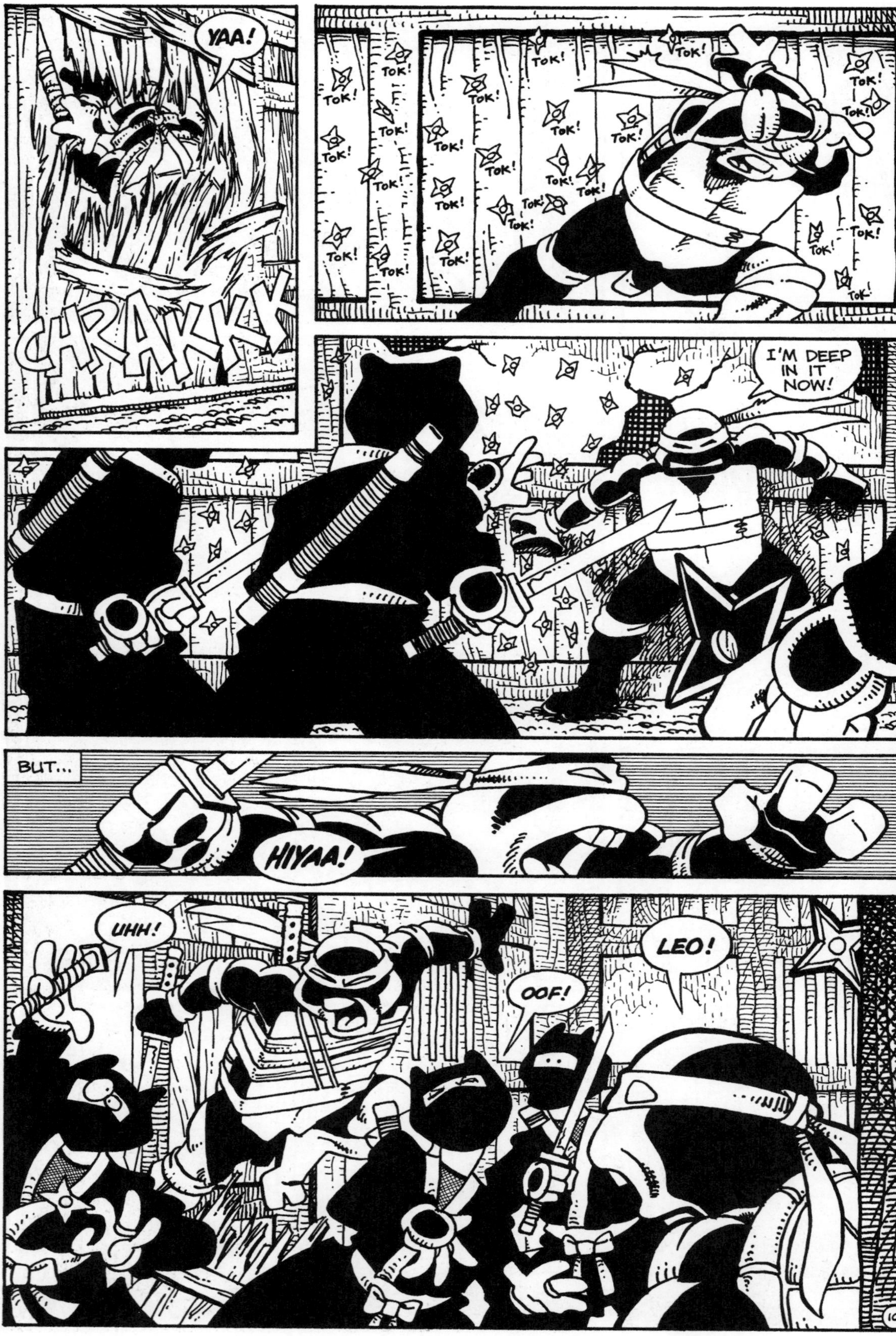
YAA!
CHRAKKK
TOK!
TOK!
I'M DEEP IN IT NOW!
BUT...
HIYAA!
UHH!
OOF!
LEO!
10.

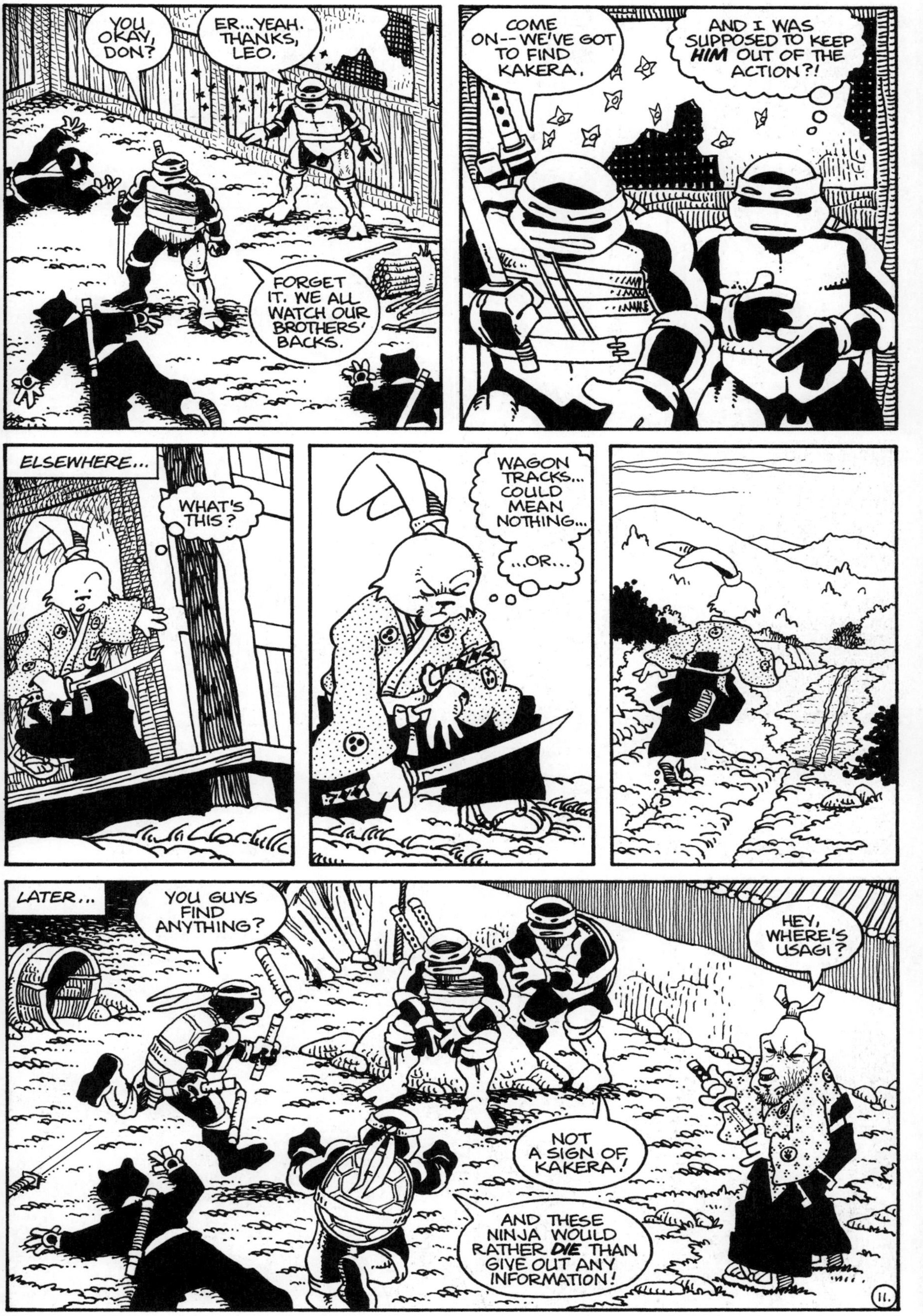
YOU OKAY, DON?
ER...YEAH. THANKS, LEO.
FORGET IT. WE ALL WATCH OUR BROTHERS' BACKS.
COME ON-- WE'VE GOT TO FIND KAKERA.
AND I WAS SUPPOSED TO KEEP HIM OUT OF THE ACTION?!
ELSEWHERE...
WHAT'S THIS?
WAGON TRACKS... COULD MEAN NOTHING...
...OR...
LATER...
YOU GUYS FIND ANYTHING?
HEY, WHERE'S USAGI?
NOT A SIGN OF KAKERA!
AND THESE NINJA WOULD RATHER DIE THAN GIVE OUT ANY INFORMATION!
11.

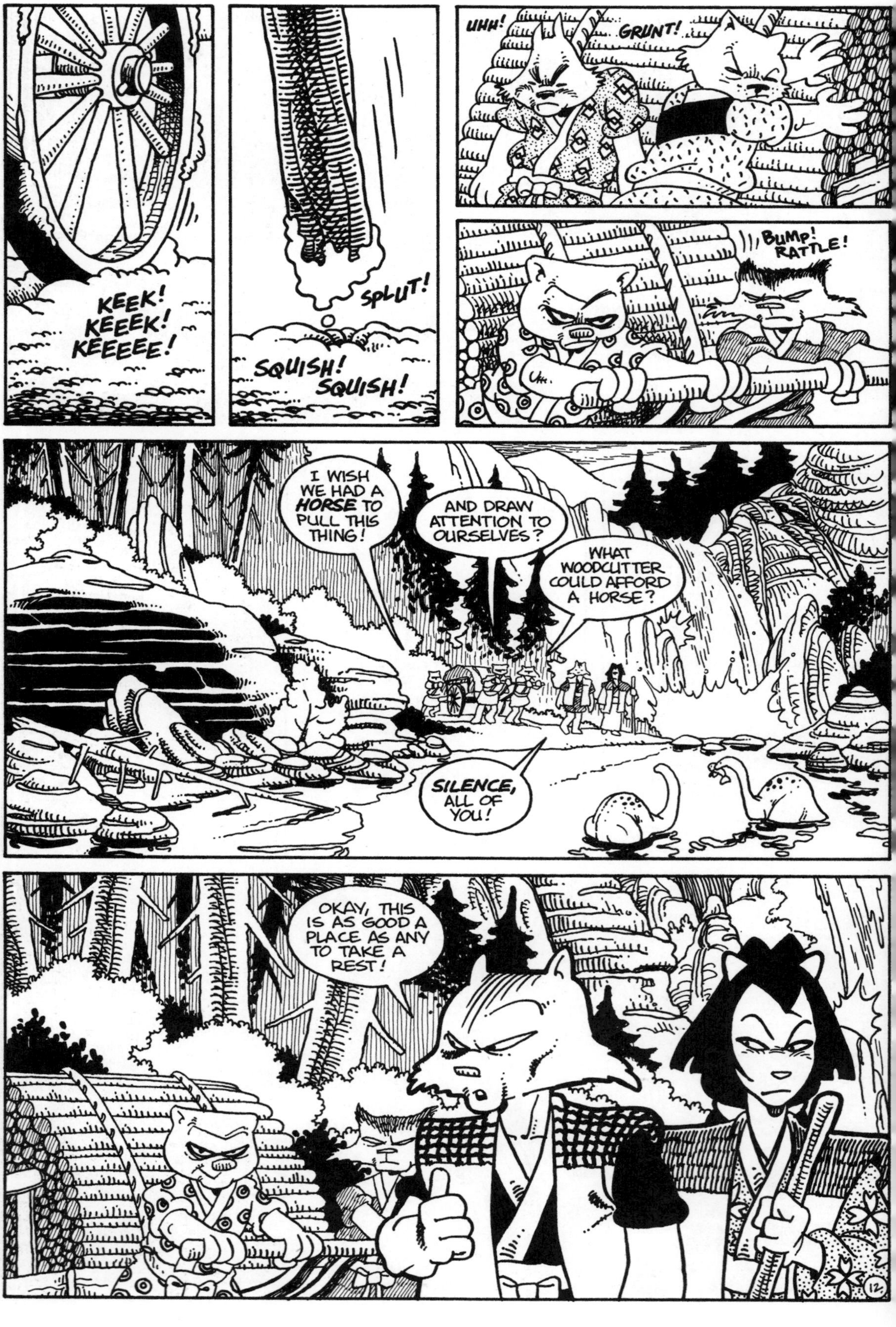
KEEK!
KEEEK!
KEEEEE!
SPLUT!
SQUISH!
SQUISH!
UHH!
GRUNT!
BUMP!
RATTLE!
I WISH WE HAD A **HORSE** TO PULL THIS THING!
AND DRAW ATTENTION TO OURSELVES?
WHAT WOODCUTTER COULD AFFORD A HORSE?
SILENCE, ALL OF YOU!
OKAY, THIS IS AS GOOD A PLACE AS ANY TO TAKE A REST!
12

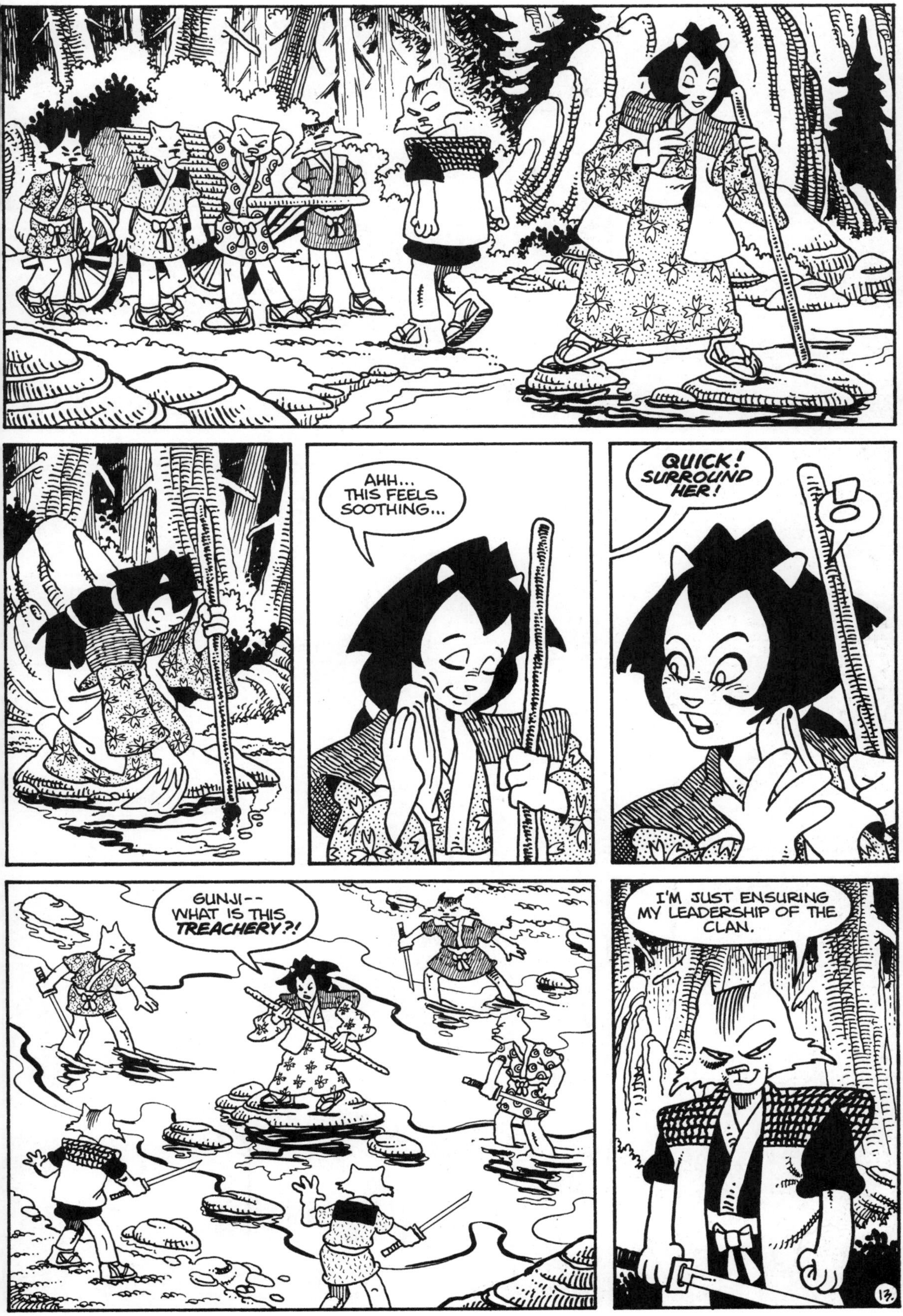
AHH... THIS FEELS SOOTHING...
QUICK! SURROUND HER!
!
GUNJI-- WHAT IS THIS TREACHERY?!
I'M JUST ENSURING MY LEADERSHIP OF THE CLAN.
13.

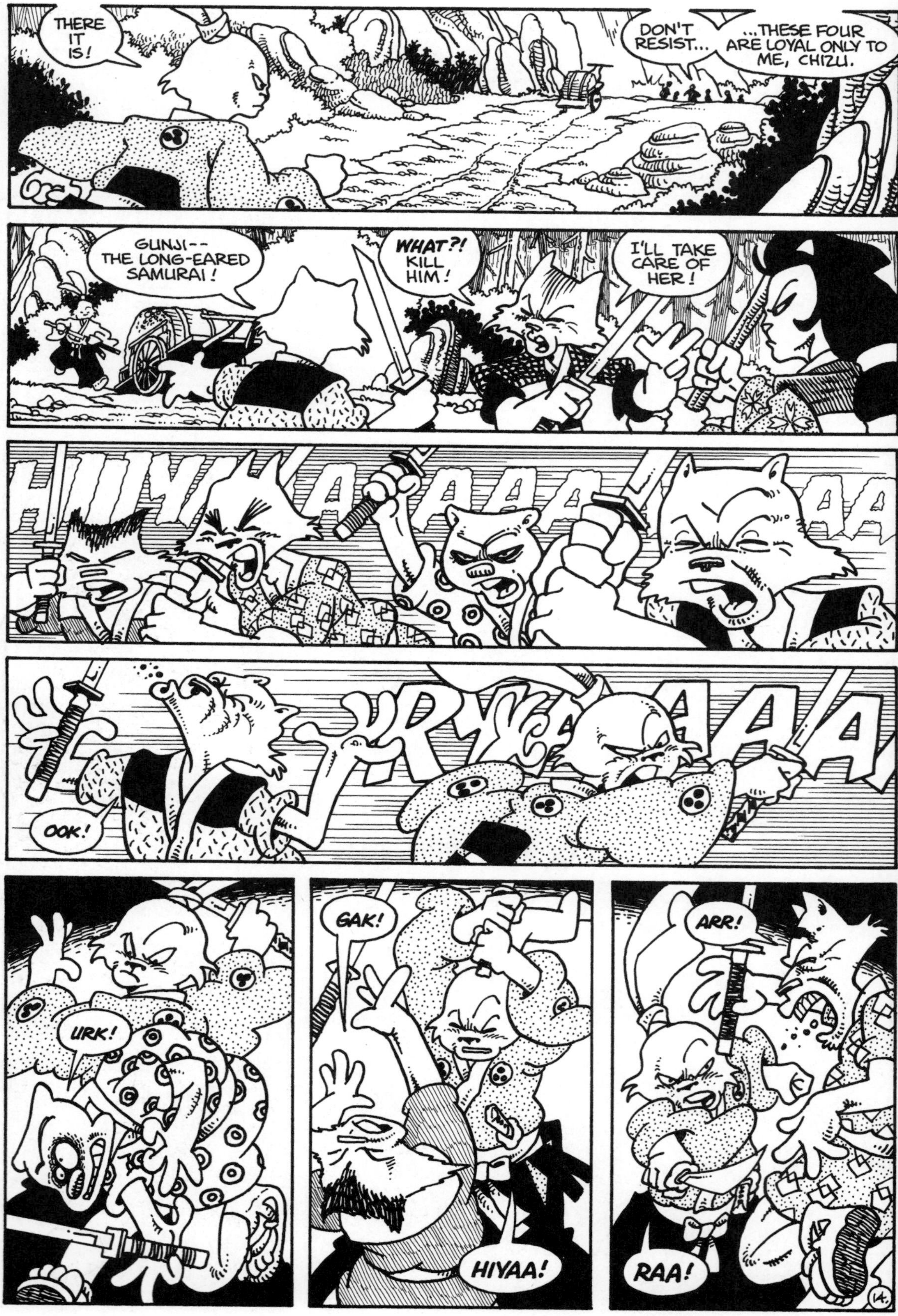
THERE IT IS!
DON'T RESIST...
...THESE FOUR ARE LOYAL ONLY TO ME, CHIZU.
GUNJI-- THE LONG-EARED SAMURAI!
WHAT?! KILL HIM!
I'LL TAKE CARE OF HER!
HIIYAAAAAAA
OOK!
YRYAAAAA
URK!
GAK!
HIYAA!
ARR!
RAA!
14.

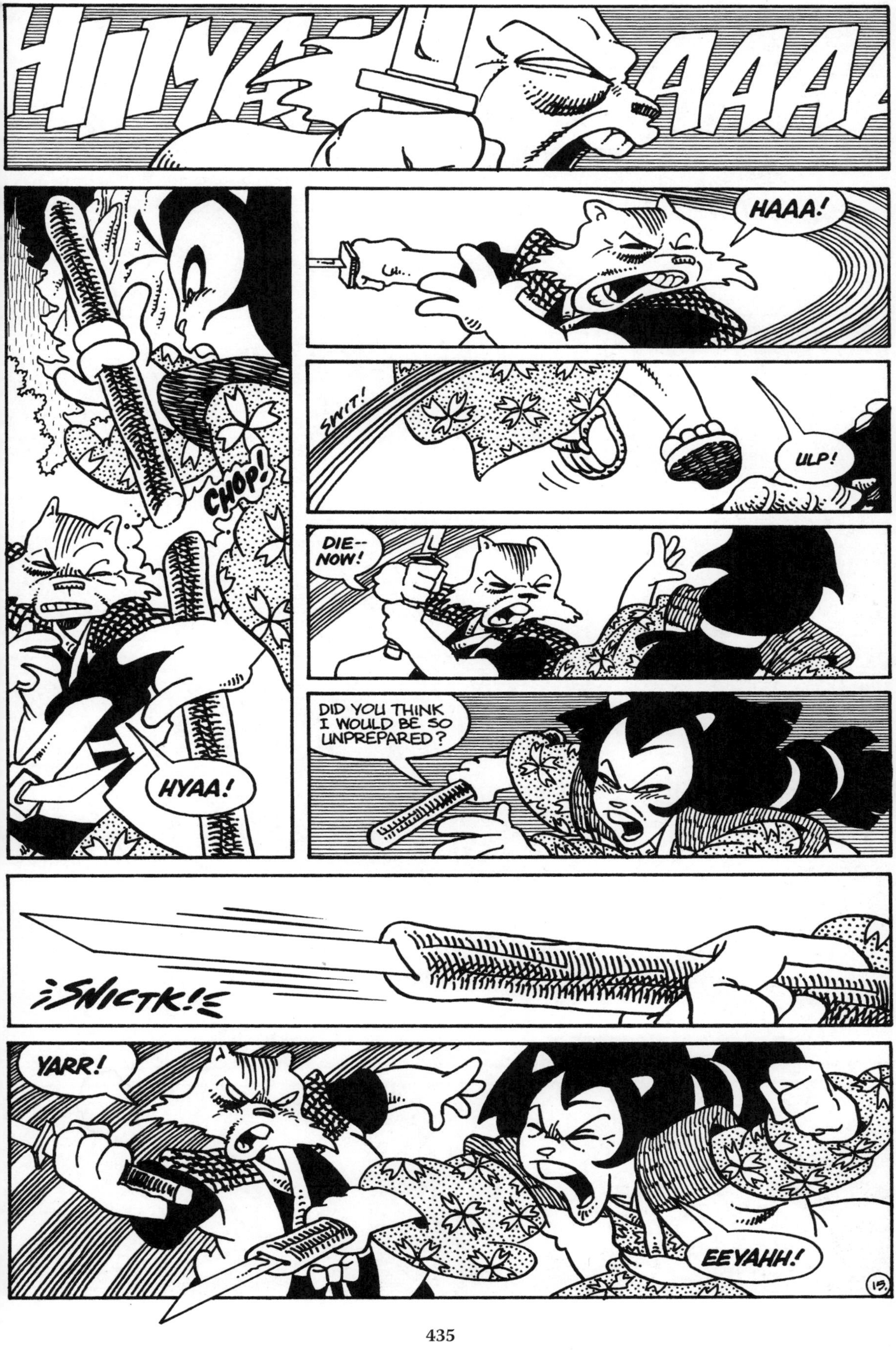
HIIYA-AAAA
HAAA!
CHOP!
SWIT!
ULP!
HYAA!
DIE--
NOW!
DID YOU THINK
I WOULD BE SO
UNPREPARED?
SNICTK!
YARR!
EEYAHH!
15

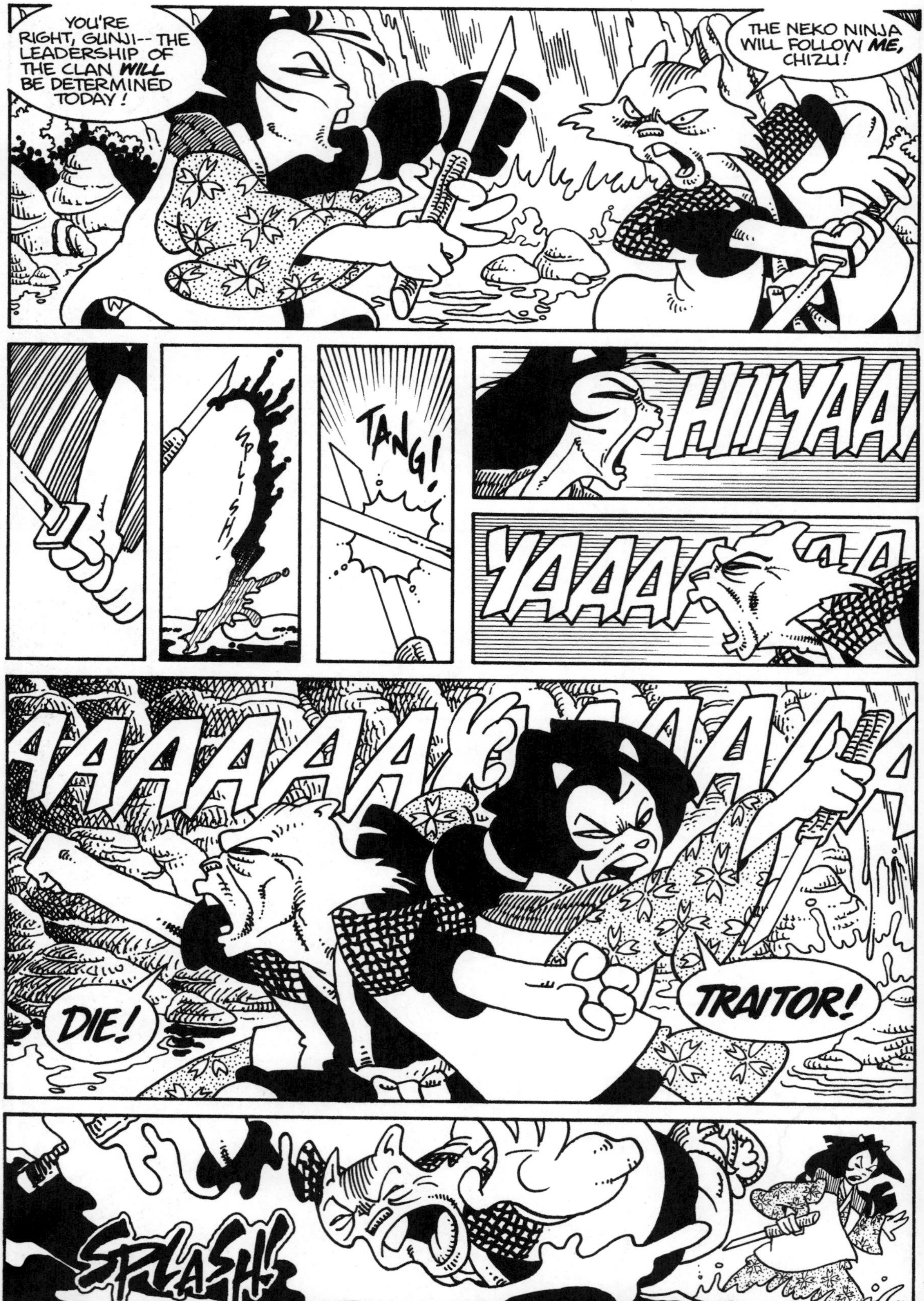
YOU'RE RIGHT, GUNJI-- THE LEADERSHIP OF THE CLAN WILL BE DETERMINED TODAY!
THE NEKO NINJA WILL FOLLOW ME, CHIZU!
SPLISH!
TANG!
HIIYAA
YAAA
AAAAAA
DIE!
TRAITOR!
SPLASH!
16.

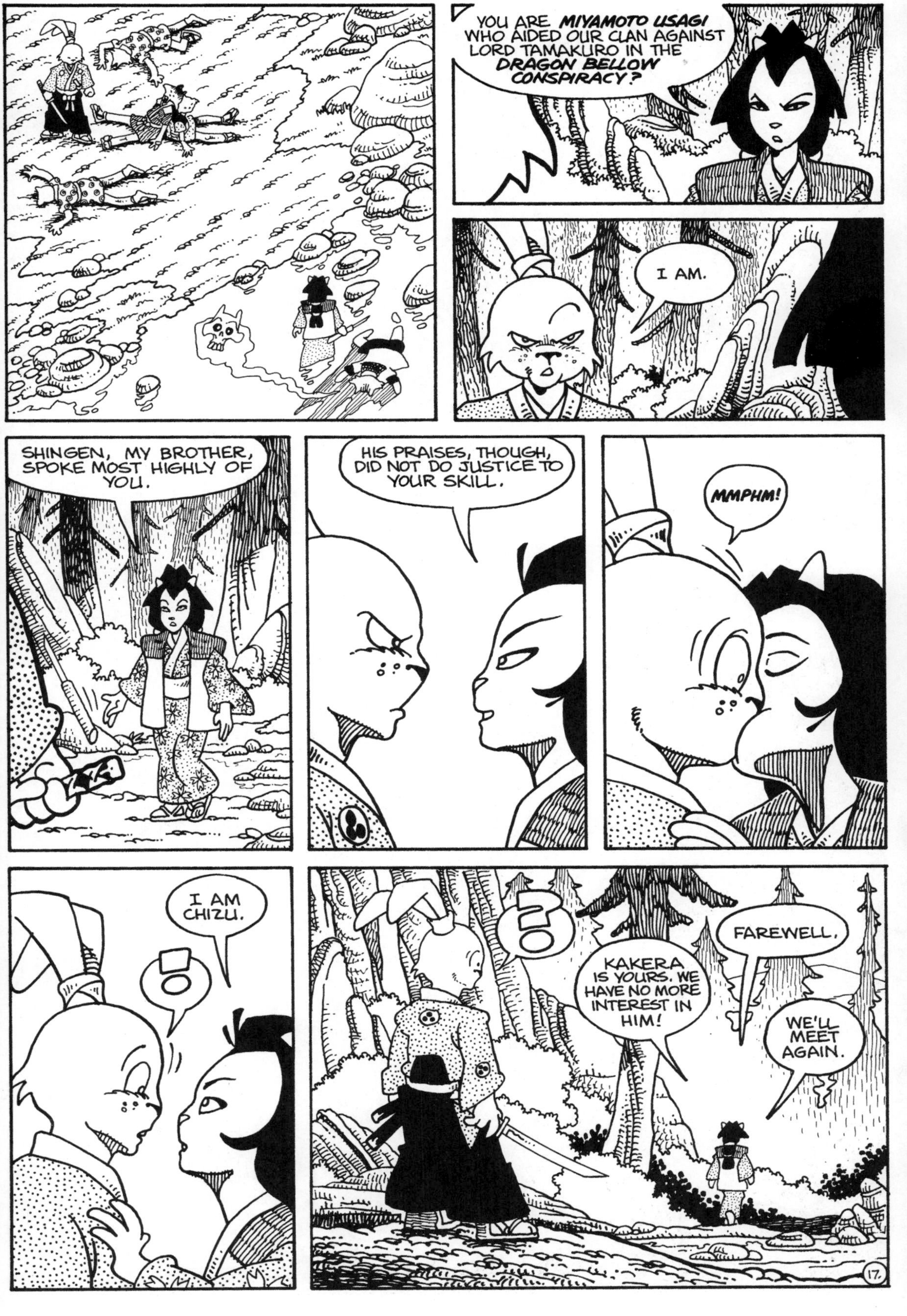
YOU ARE MIYAMOTO USAGI WHO AIDED OUR CLAN AGAINST LORD TAMAKURO IN THE DRAGON BELLOW CONSPIRACY?
I AM.
SHINGEN, MY BROTHER, SPOKE MOST HIGHLY OF YOU.
HIS PRAISES, THOUGH, DID NOT DO JUSTICE TO YOUR SKILL.
MMPHM!
I AM CHIZU.
FAREWELL.
KAKERA IS YOURS. WE HAVE NO MORE INTEREST IN HIM!
WE'LL MEET AGAIN.
17.

SHINGEN'S *SISTER*?

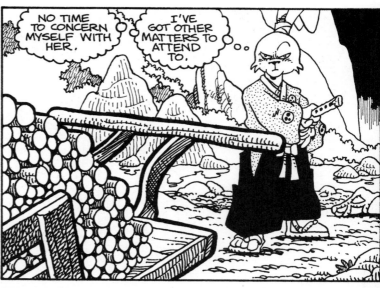

NO TIME TO CONCERN MYSELF WITH HER.

I'VE GOT OTHER MATTERS TO ATTEND TO.

NOW LET'S SEE IF MY HUNCH WAS RIGHT.

A *HIDDEN CHAMBER* IN THE WOOD PILE...

HE'S *DRUGGED* BUT OTHERWISE LOOKS ALL RIGHT.

THERE'S USAGI!

YO!

JIMBO!

I *TOLD YOU* HE FOLLOWED THOSE TRACKS!

DID YOU FIND KAKERA?

YEAH, HE'S SAFE.

18.

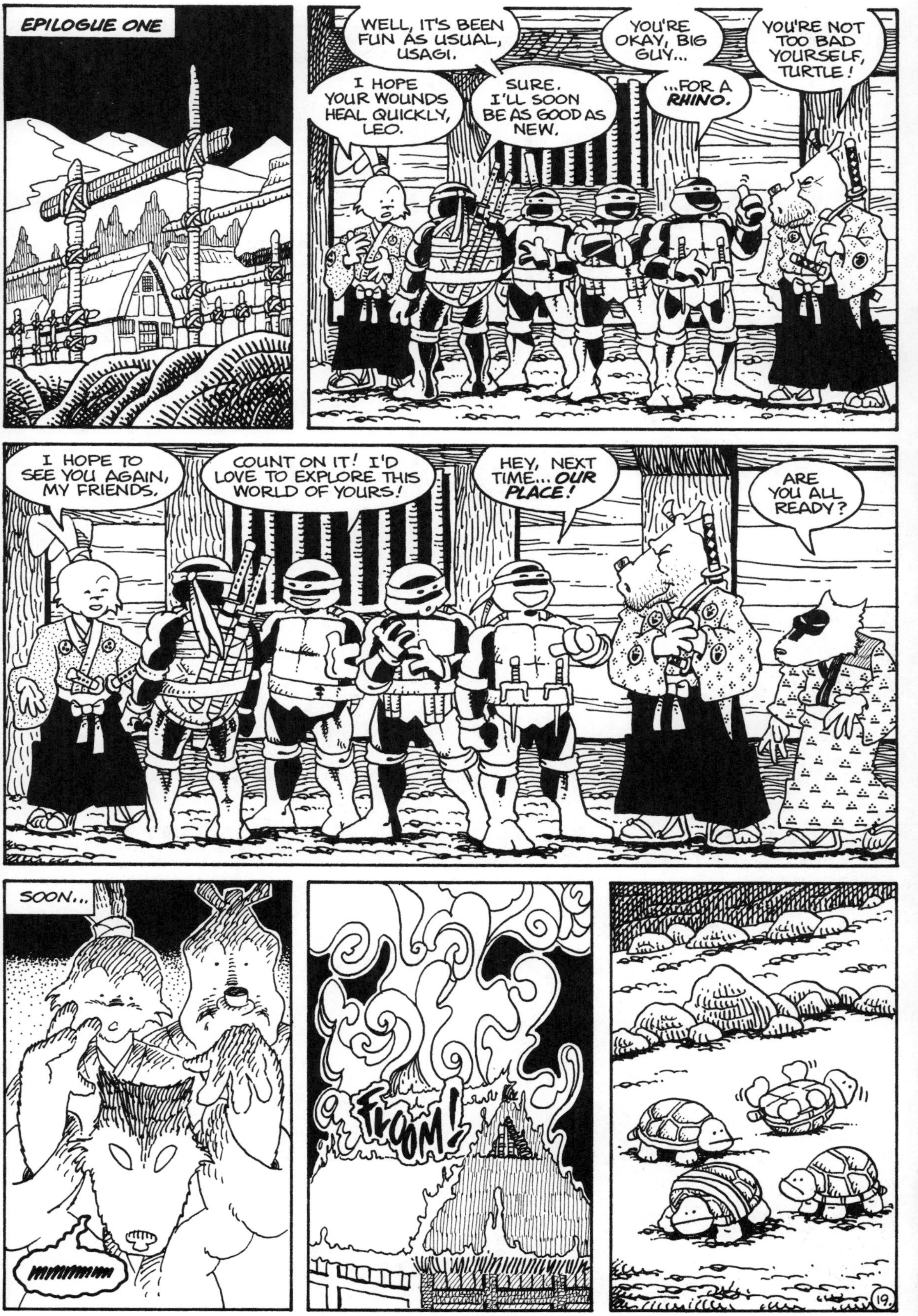

EPILOGUE ONE
WELL, IT'S BEEN FUN AS USUAL, USAGI.
I HOPE YOUR WOUNDS HEAL QUICKLY, LEO.
SURE. I'LL SOON BE AS GOOD AS NEW.
YOU'RE OKAY, BIG GUY...
...FOR A RHINO.
YOU'RE NOT TOO BAD YOURSELF, TURTLE!
I HOPE TO SEE YOU AGAIN, MY FRIENDS.
COUNT ON IT! I'D LOVE TO EXPLORE THIS WORLD OF YOURS!
HEY, NEXT TIME... OUR PLACE!
ARE YOU ALL READY?
SOON...
MMMMMM
FLOOM!
19.

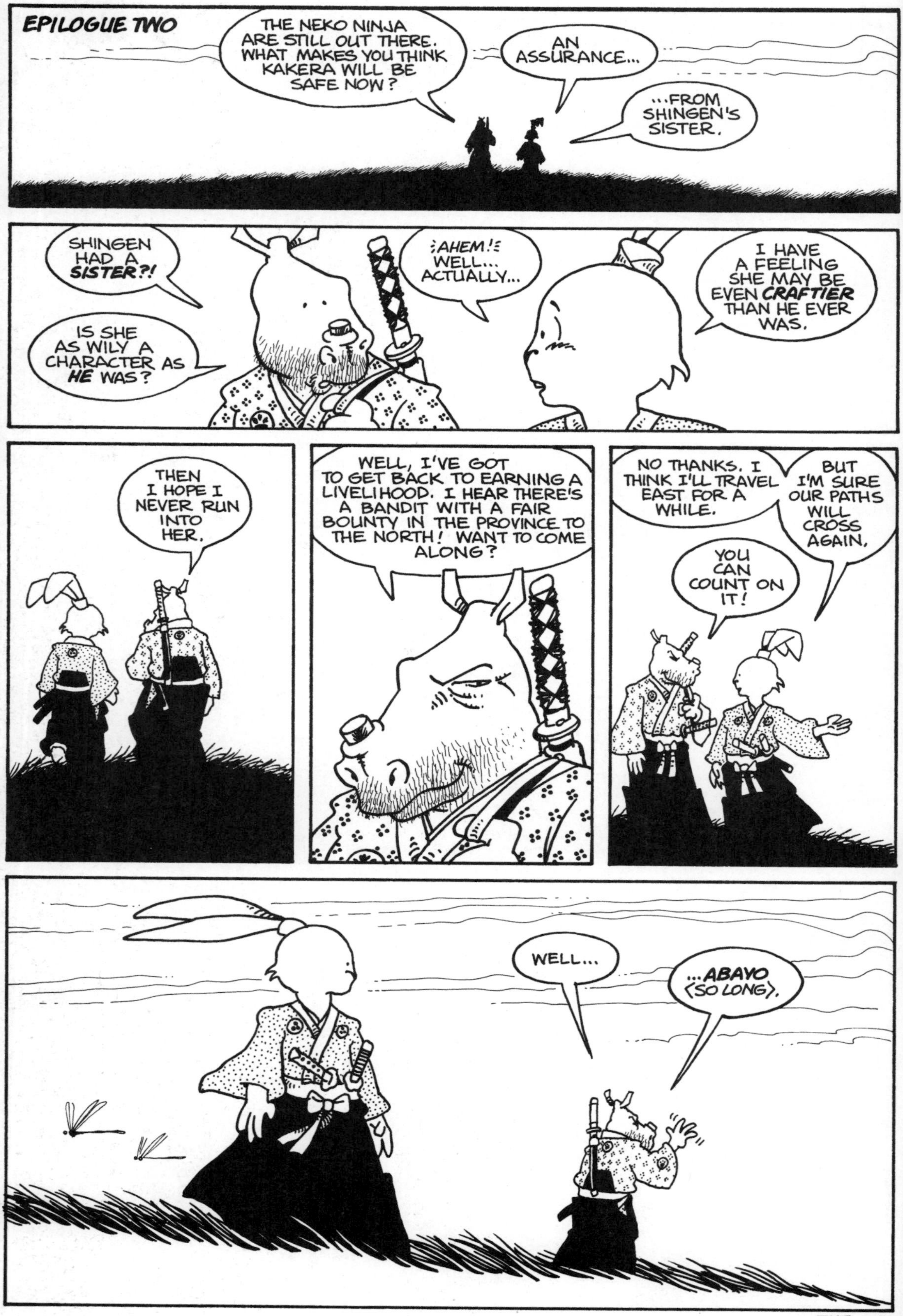
EPILOGUE TWO
THE NEKO NINJA ARE STILL OUT THERE. WHAT MAKES YOU THINK KAKERA WILL BE SAFE NOW?
AN ASSURANCE...
...FROM SHINGEN'S SISTER.
SHINGEN HAD A **SISTER**?!
IS SHE AS WILY A CHARACTER AS **HE** WAS?
AHEM! WELL... ACTUALLY...
I HAVE A FEELING SHE MAY BE EVEN **CRAFTIER** THAN HE EVER WAS.
THEN I HOPE I NEVER RUN INTO HER.
WELL, I'VE GOT TO GET BACK TO EARNING A LIVELIHOOD. I HEAR THERE'S A BANDIT WITH A FAIR BOUNTY IN THE PROVINCE TO THE NORTH! WANT TO COME ALONG?
NO THANKS. I THINK I'LL TRAVEL EAST FOR A WHILE.
BUT I'M SURE OUR PATHS WILL CROSS AGAIN.
YOU CAN COUNT ON IT!
WELL...
...**ABAYO** <SO LONG>.

THE END

NAMAZU

Written, illustrated, and lettered by

STAN SAKAI

Colored by

TOM LUTH

Edited by

BOBBY CURNOW

Originally appeared in
Teenage Mutant Ninja Turtles/Usagi Yojimbo,
published by IDW Publishing in 2017.

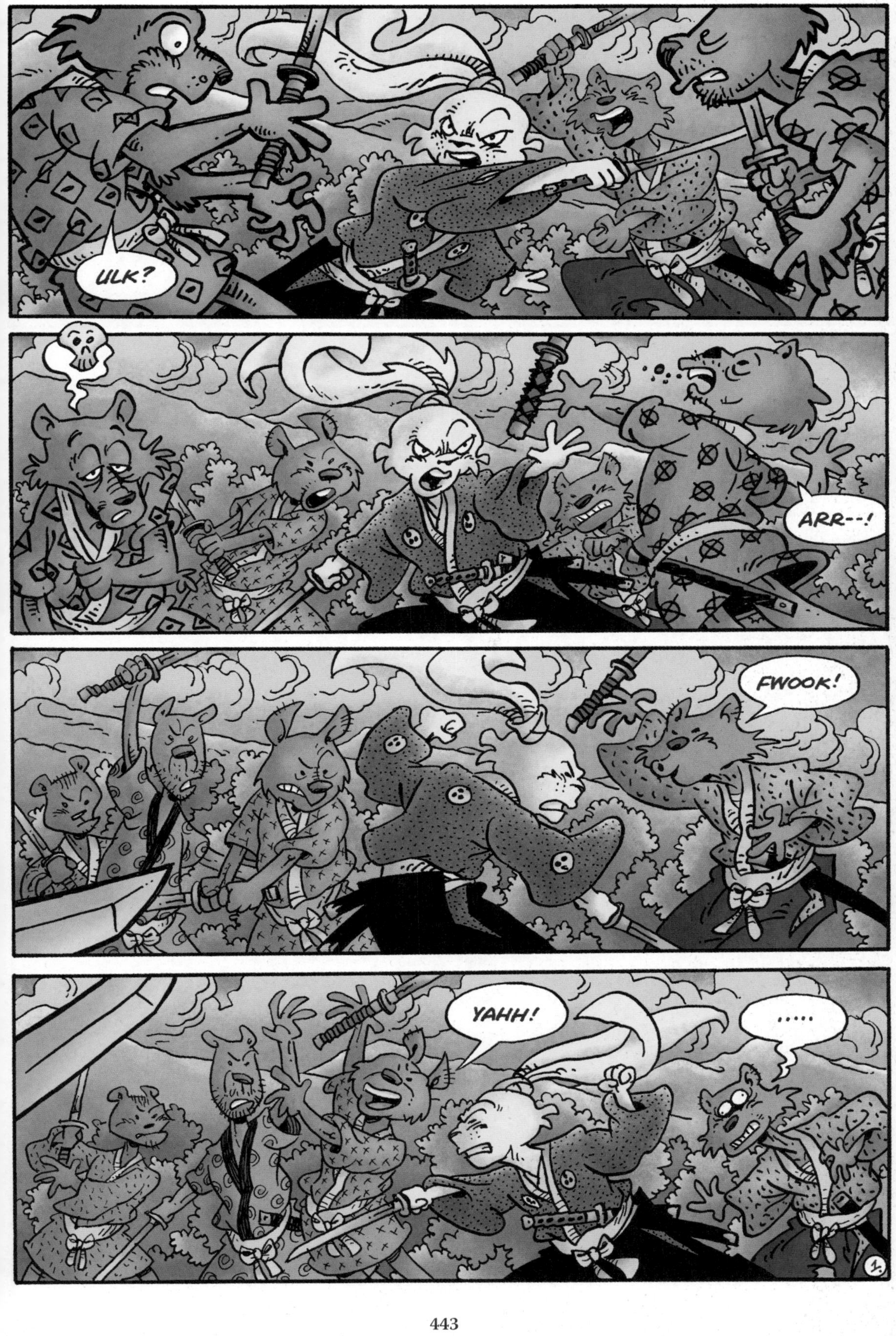
ULK?
ARR--!
FWOOK!
YAHH!
.....
1.

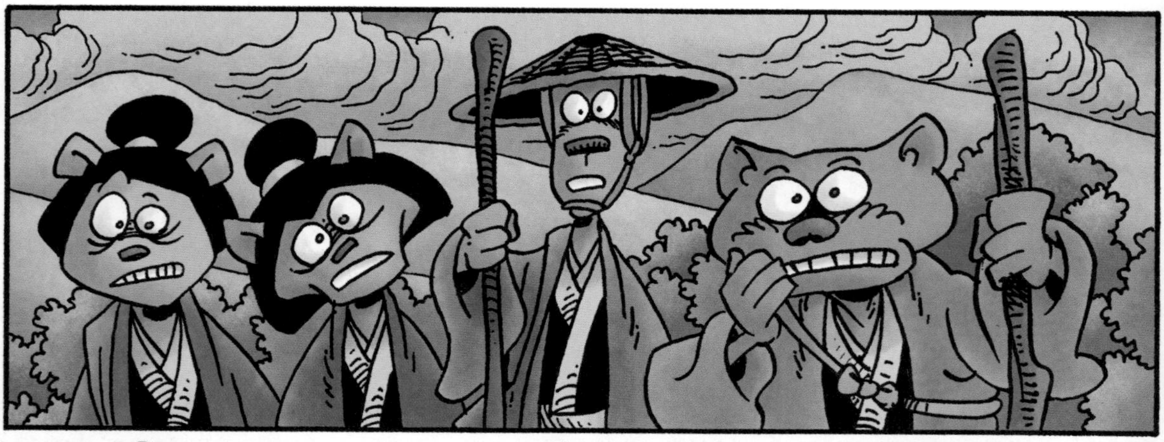

NAMAZU
OR THE BIG FISH STORY

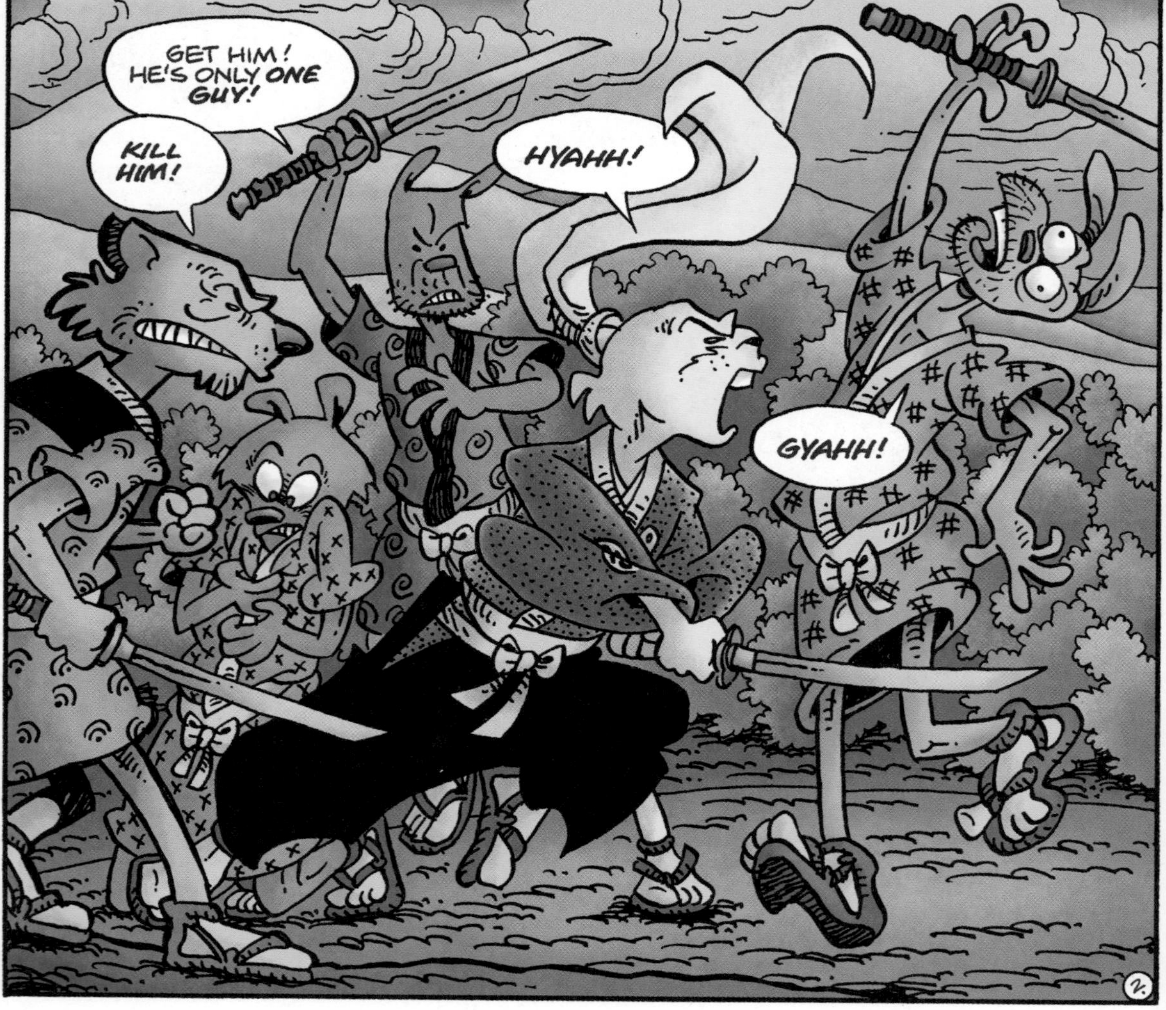
GET HIM! HE'S ONLY ONE GUY!
KILL HIM!
HYAHH!
GYAHH!
2.

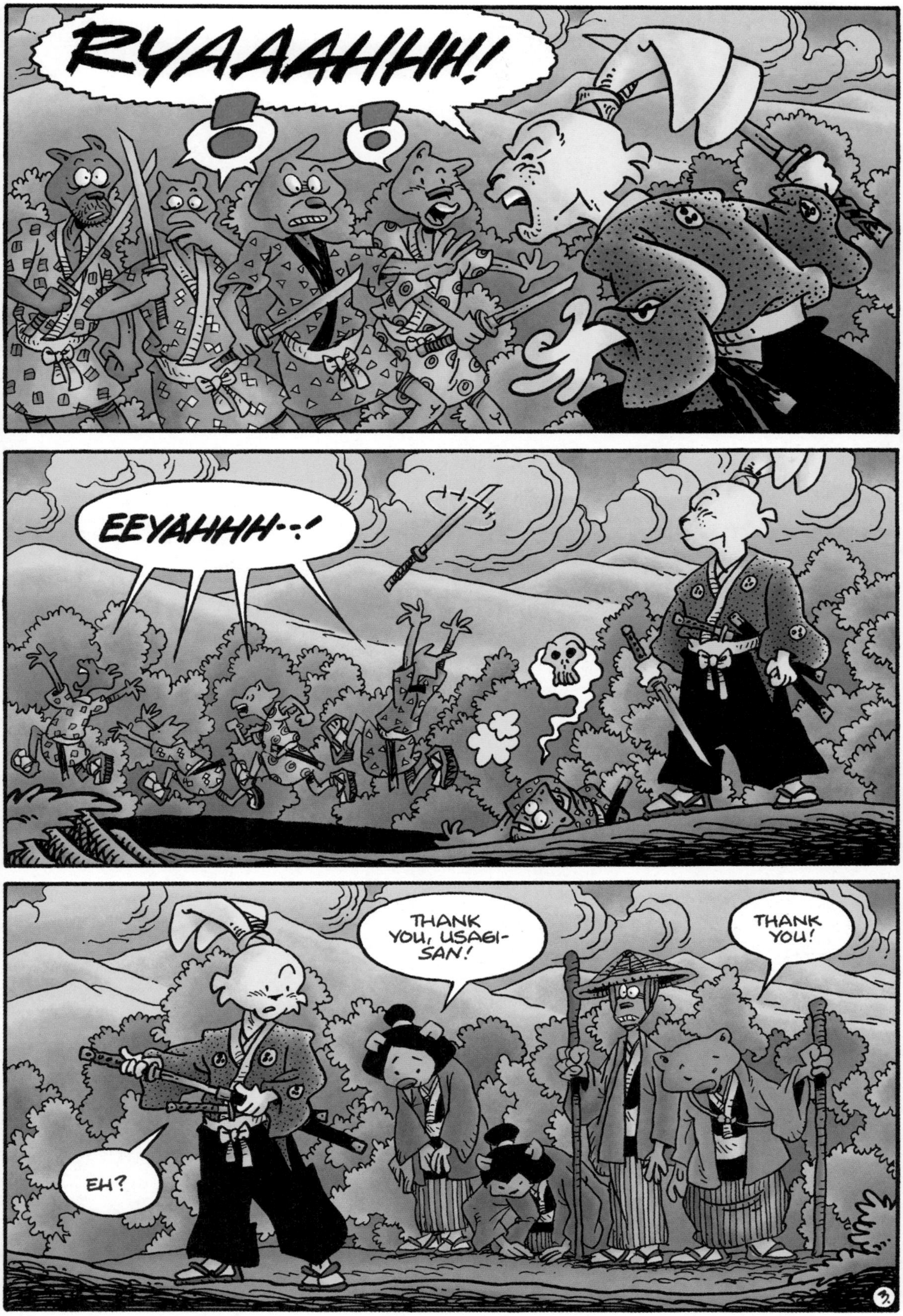
RYAAAHHH!
EEYAHHH--!
THANK YOU, USAGI-SAN!
THANK YOU!
EH?
3

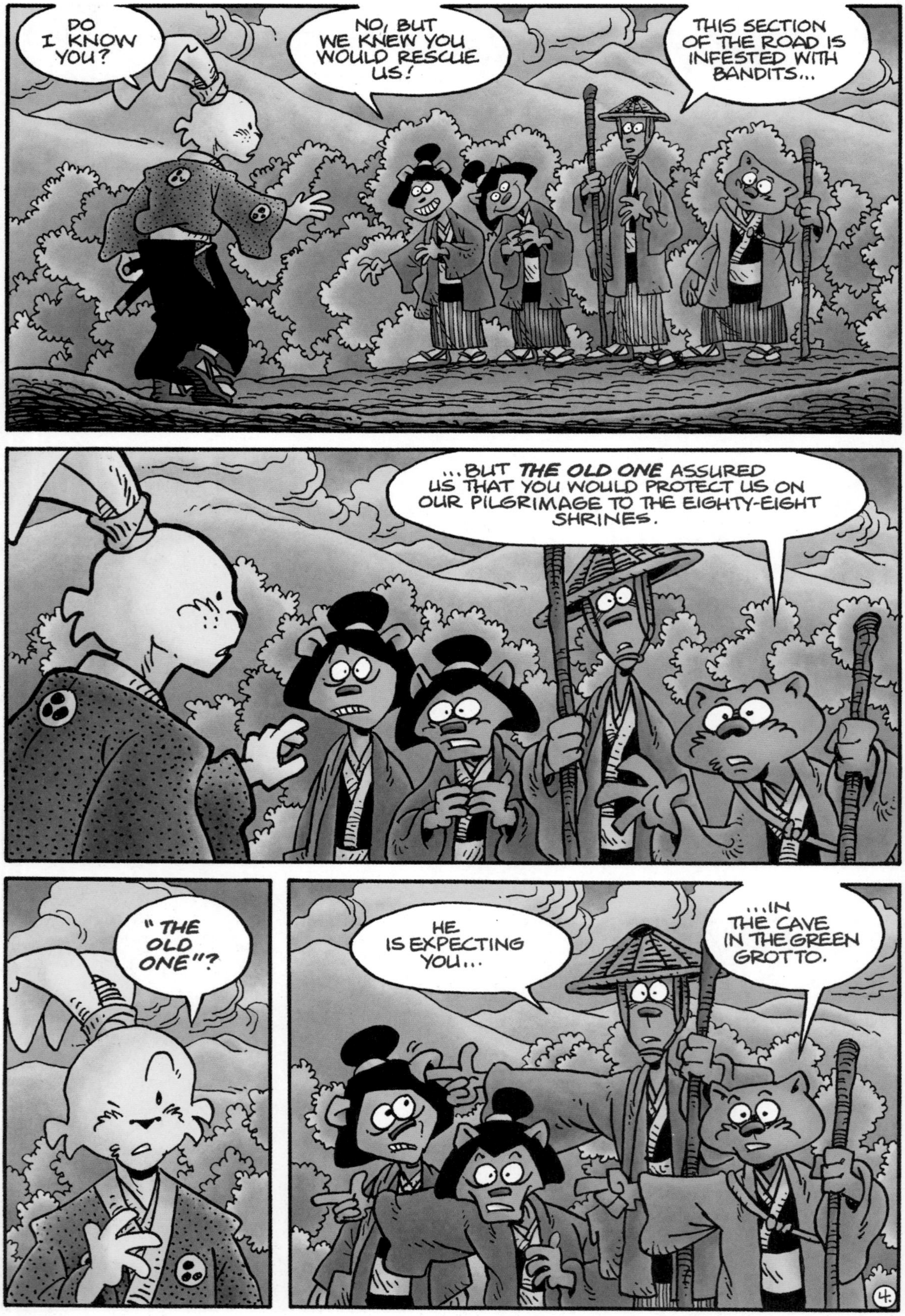
DO I KNOW YOU?
NO, BUT WE KNEW YOU WOULD RESCUE US!
THIS SECTION OF THE ROAD IS INFESTED WITH BANDITS...
...BUT THE OLD ONE ASSURED US THAT YOU WOULD PROTECT US ON OUR PILGRIMAGE TO THE EIGHTY-EIGHT SHRINES.
"THE OLD ONE"?
HE IS EXPECTING YOU...
...IN THE CAVE IN THE GREEN GROTTO.
4.

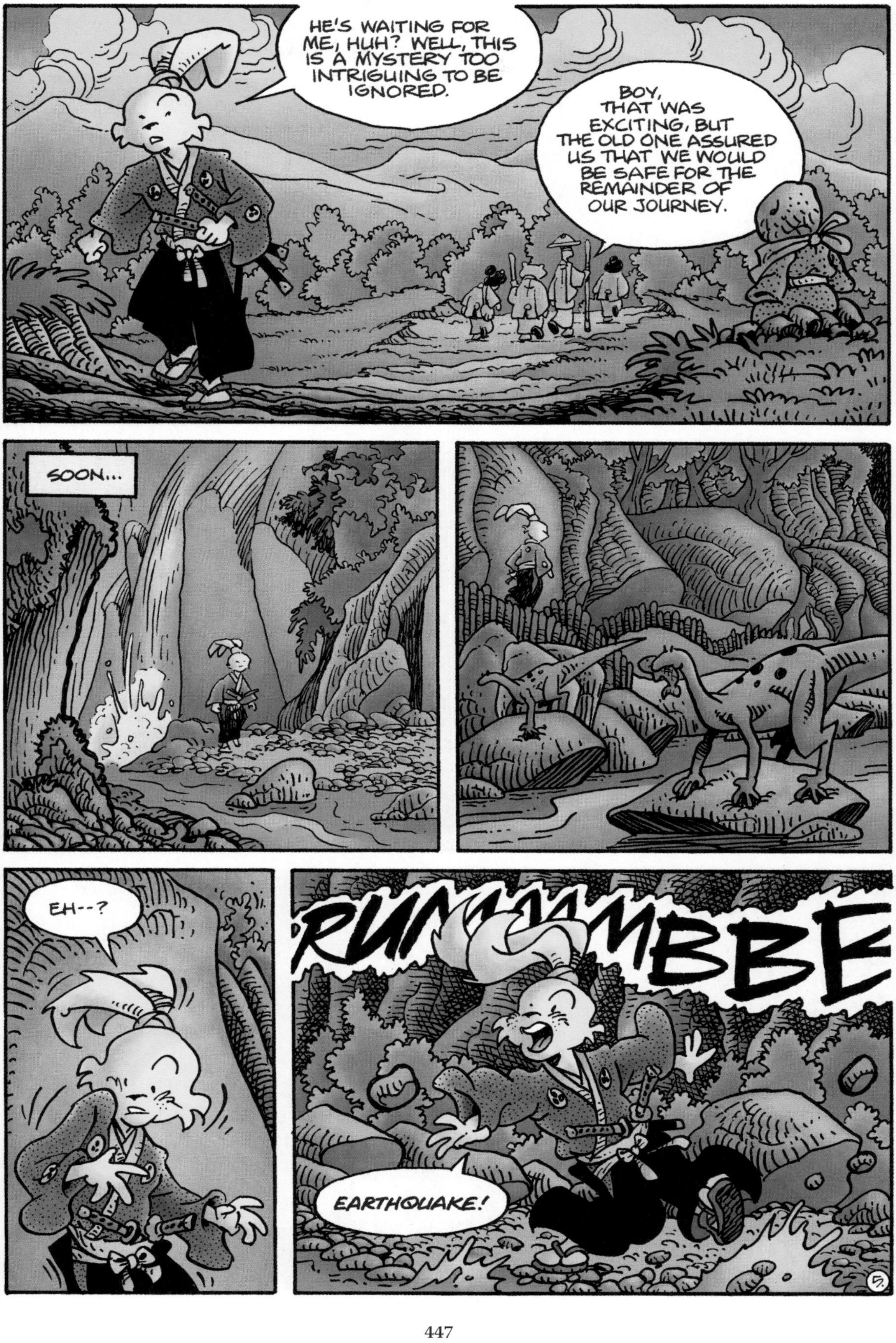
HE'S WAITING FOR ME, HUH? WELL, THIS IS A MYSTERY TOO INTRIGUING TO BE IGNORED.
BOY, THAT WAS EXCITING, BUT THE OLD ONE ASSURED US THAT WE WOULD BE SAFE FOR THE REMAINDER OF OUR JOURNEY.
SOON...
EH--?
EARTHQUAKE!

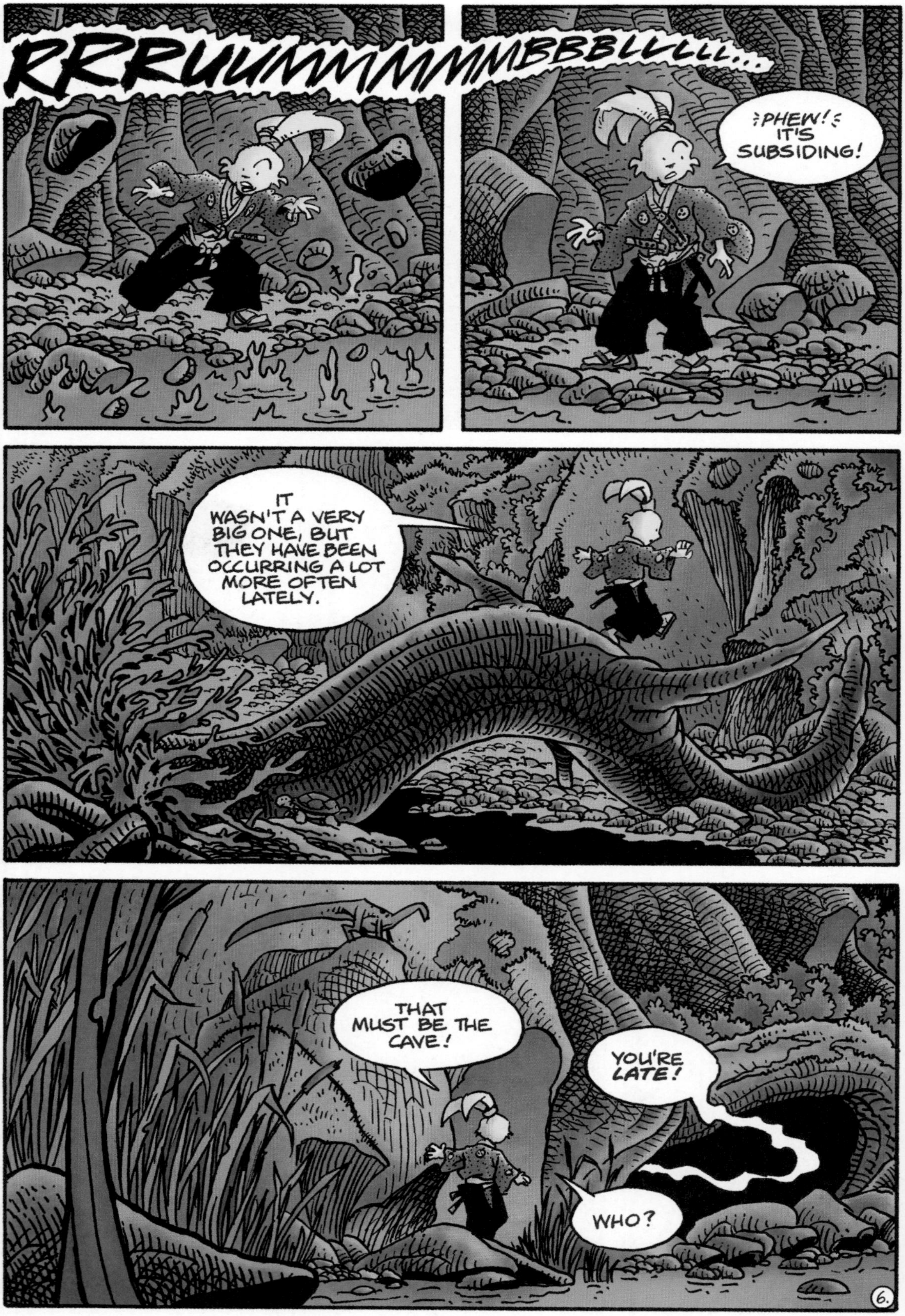
RRRUUMMMMMMBBBLLLLL...
PHEW! IT'S SUBSIDING!
IT WASN'T A VERY BIG ONE, BUT THEY HAVE BEEN OCCURRING A LOT MORE OFTEN LATELY.
THAT MUST BE THE CAVE!
YOU'RE LATE!
WHO?
6.

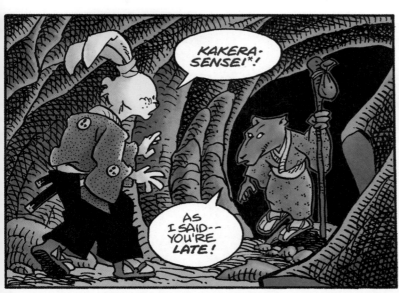

KAKERA-SENSEI*!

AS I SAID-- YOU'RE LATE!

I DID NOT KNOW I WAS EXPECTED.

I REQUIRE YOUR HELP ONCE AGAIN, USAGI.

OH?

I CARRY A MOST VALUABLE OBJECT, WHICH I MUST DELIVER TO TASHIMA SHRINE.

BUT THERE IS ONE WHO KNOWS OF MY MISSION AND WOULD STOP ME!

SO YOU REQUIRE A YOJIMBO**!

* 'SHADES OF GREEN'

** BODY GUARD.

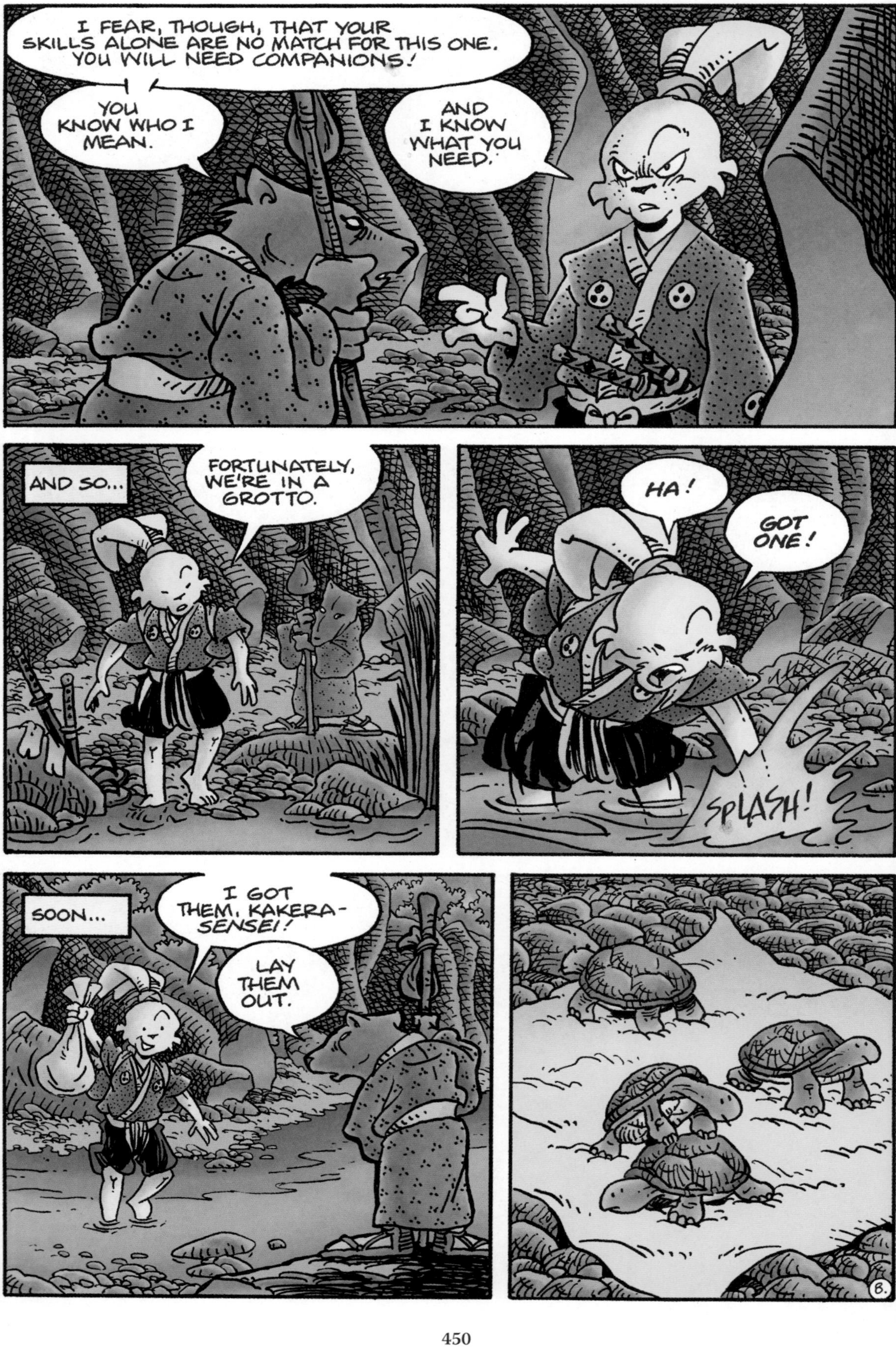
I FEAR, THOUGH, THAT YOUR SKILLS ALONE ARE NO MATCH FOR THIS ONE. YOU WILL NEED COMPANIONS!
YOU KNOW WHO I MEAN.
AND I KNOW WHAT YOU NEED.
AND SO...
FORTUNATELY, WE'RE IN A GROTTO.
HA!
GOT ONE!
SPLASH!
SOON...
I GOT THEM, KAKERA-SENSEI!
LAY THEM OUT.
8.

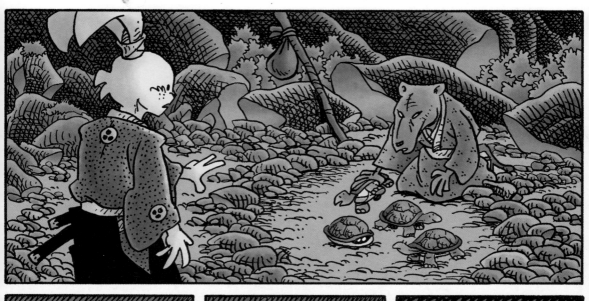

KU*--

KA-***

CHI**--

SUI****--

FU-****

9.

*VOID **EARTH ***FIRE ****WATER *****WIND

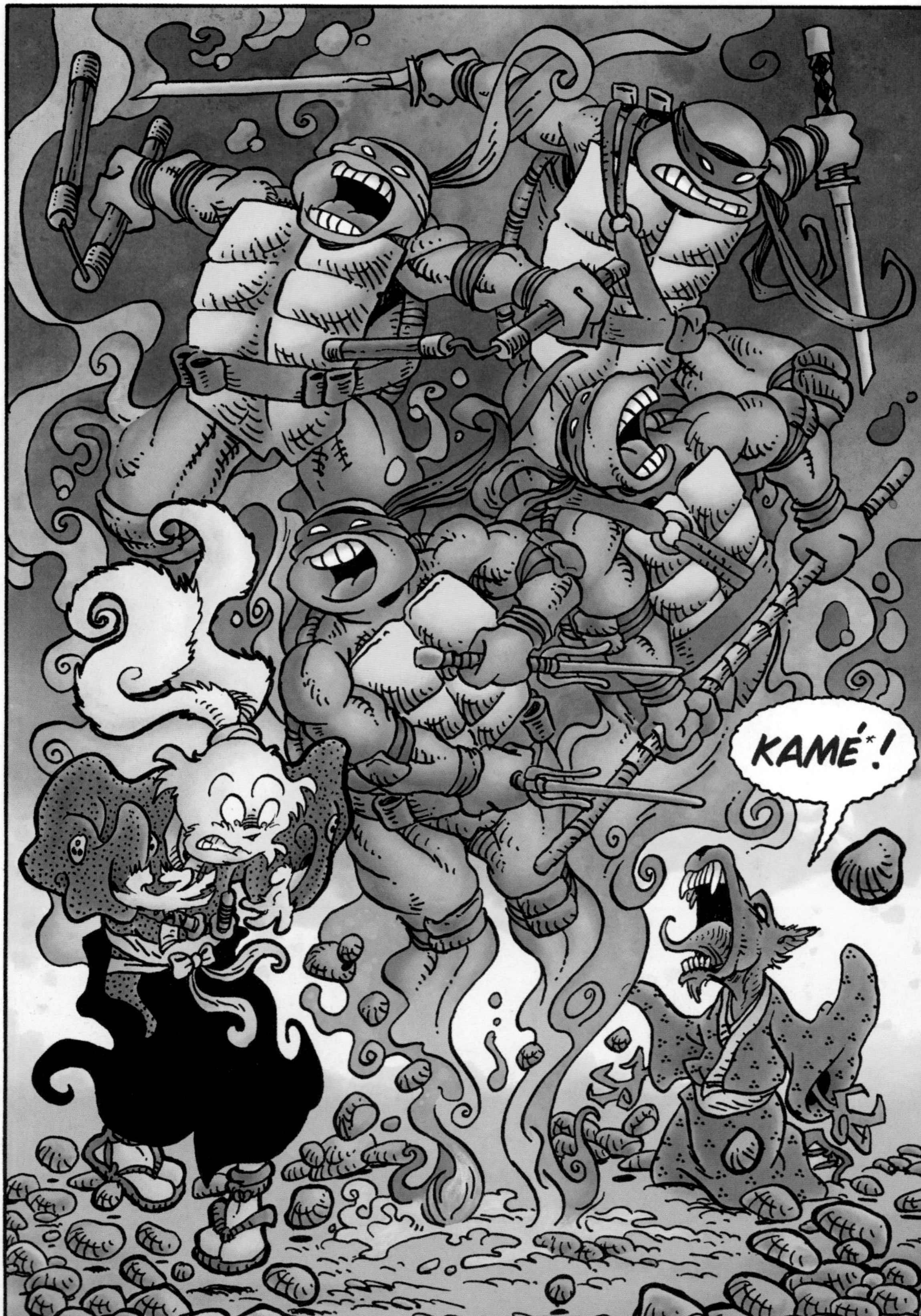
KAME*!
10.

* TURTLES

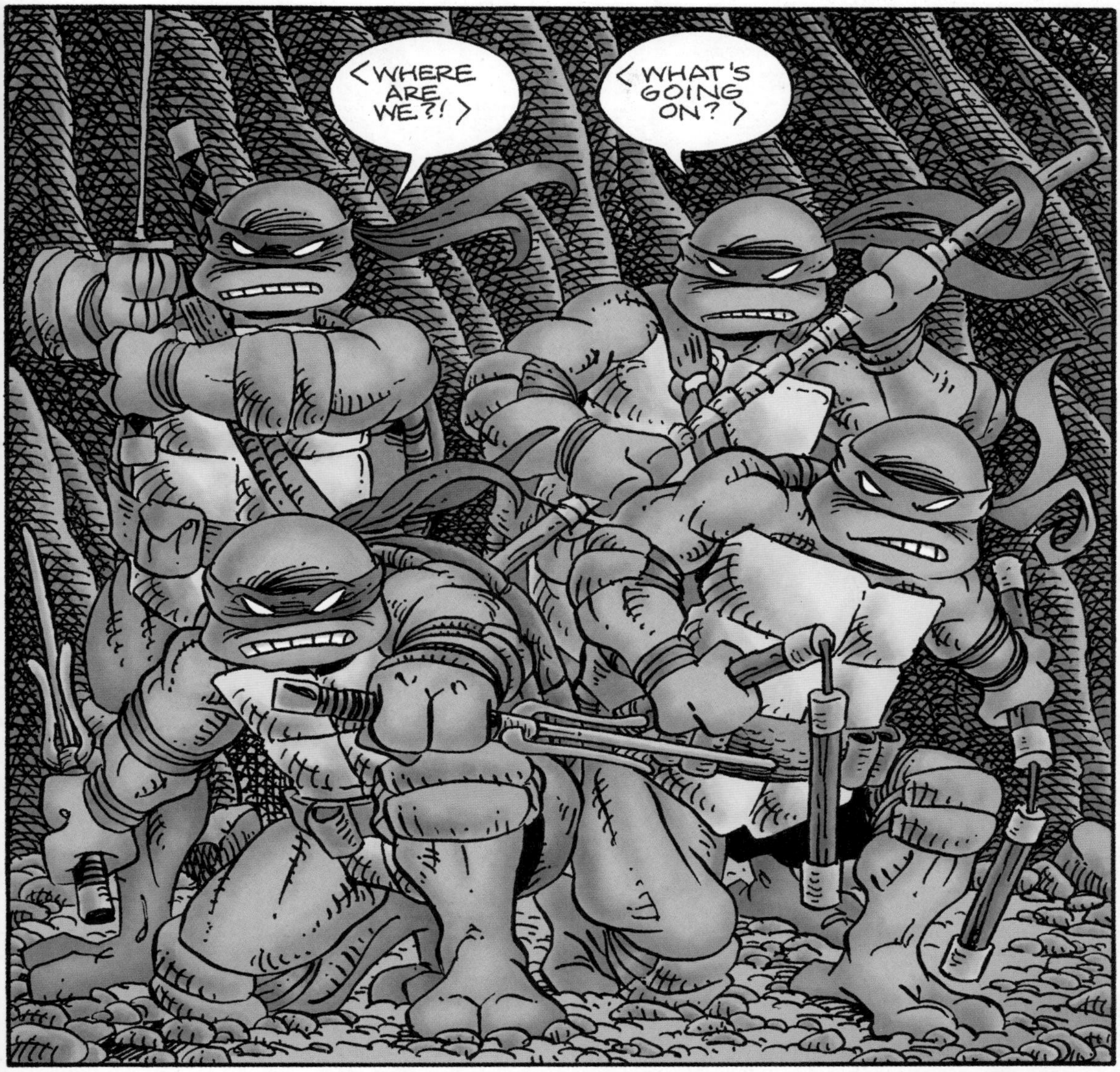

<WHERE ARE WE?!>
<WHAT'S GOING ON?>

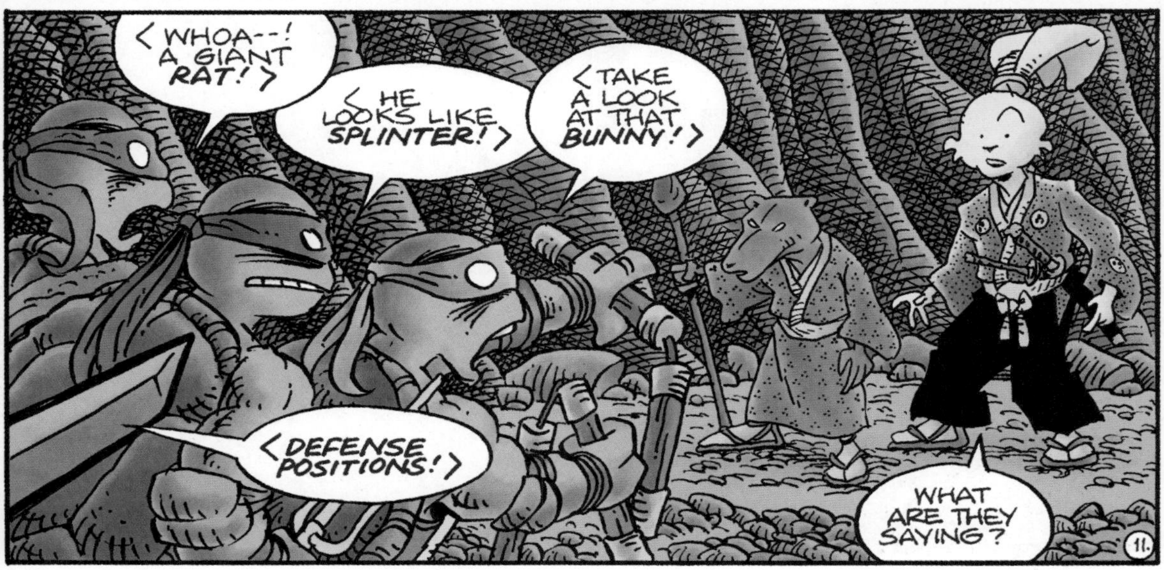

<WHOA--! A GIANT RAT!>
<HE LOOKS LIKE SPLINTER!>
<TAKE A LOOK AT THAT BUNNY!>
<DEFENSE POSITIONS!>
WHAT ARE THEY SAYING?
11.

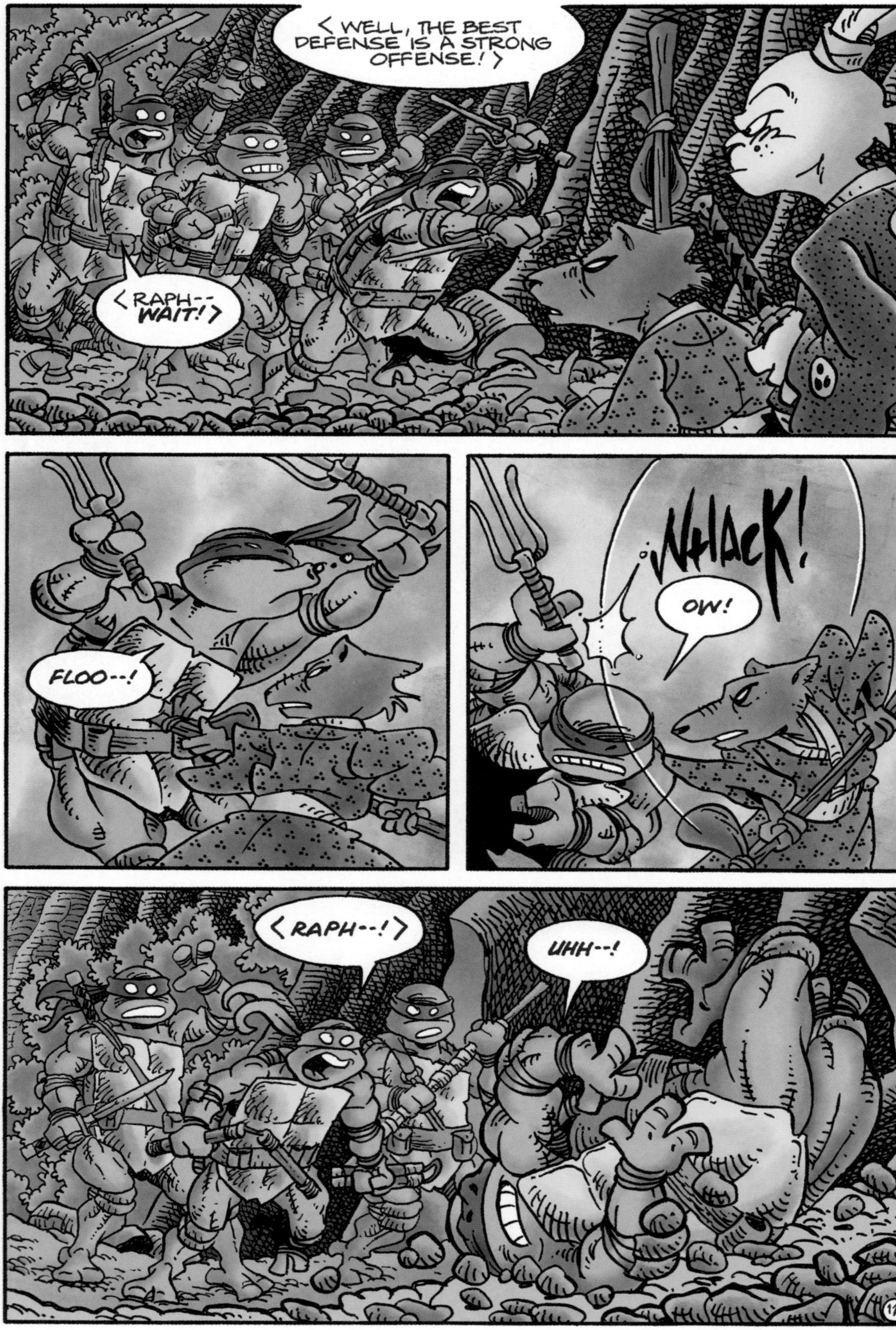

< WELL, THE BEST DEFENSE IS A STRONG OFFENSE! >
< RAPH-- WAIT! >
FLOO--!
WHACK!
OW!
< RAPH--! >
UHH--!
12.

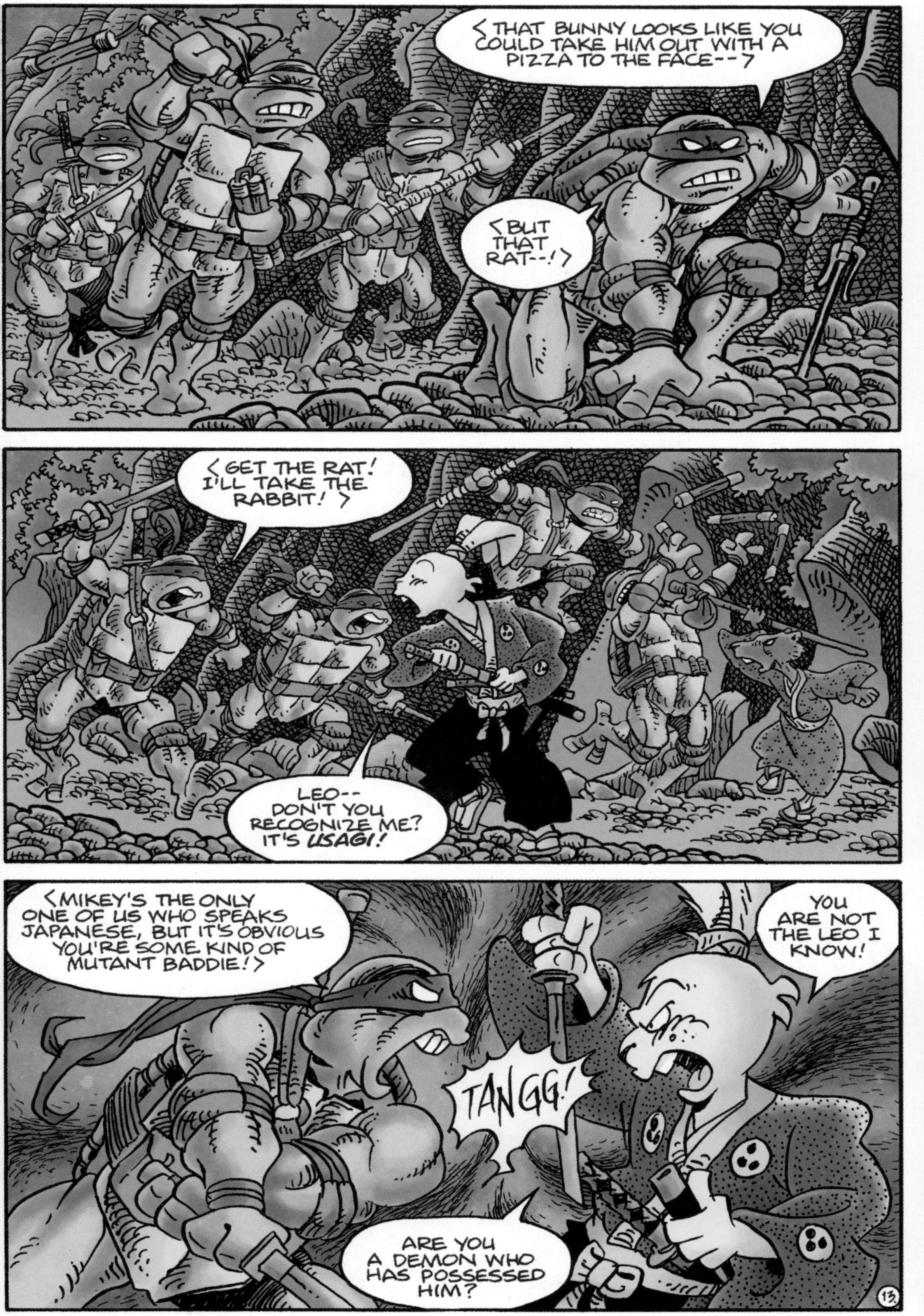
< THAT BUNNY LOOKS LIKE YOU COULD TAKE HIM OUT WITH A PIZZA TO THE FACE-- >
< BUT THAT RAT--! >
< GET THE RAT! I'LL TAKE THE RABBIT! >
LEO-- DON'T YOU RECOGNIZE ME? IT'S USAGI!
< MIKEY'S THE ONLY ONE OF US WHO SPEAKS JAPANESE, BUT IT'S OBVIOUS YOU'RE SOME KIND OF MUTANT BADDIE! >
YOU ARE NOT THE LEO I KNOW!
TANGG!
ARE YOU A DEMON WHO HAS POSSESSED HIM?
13

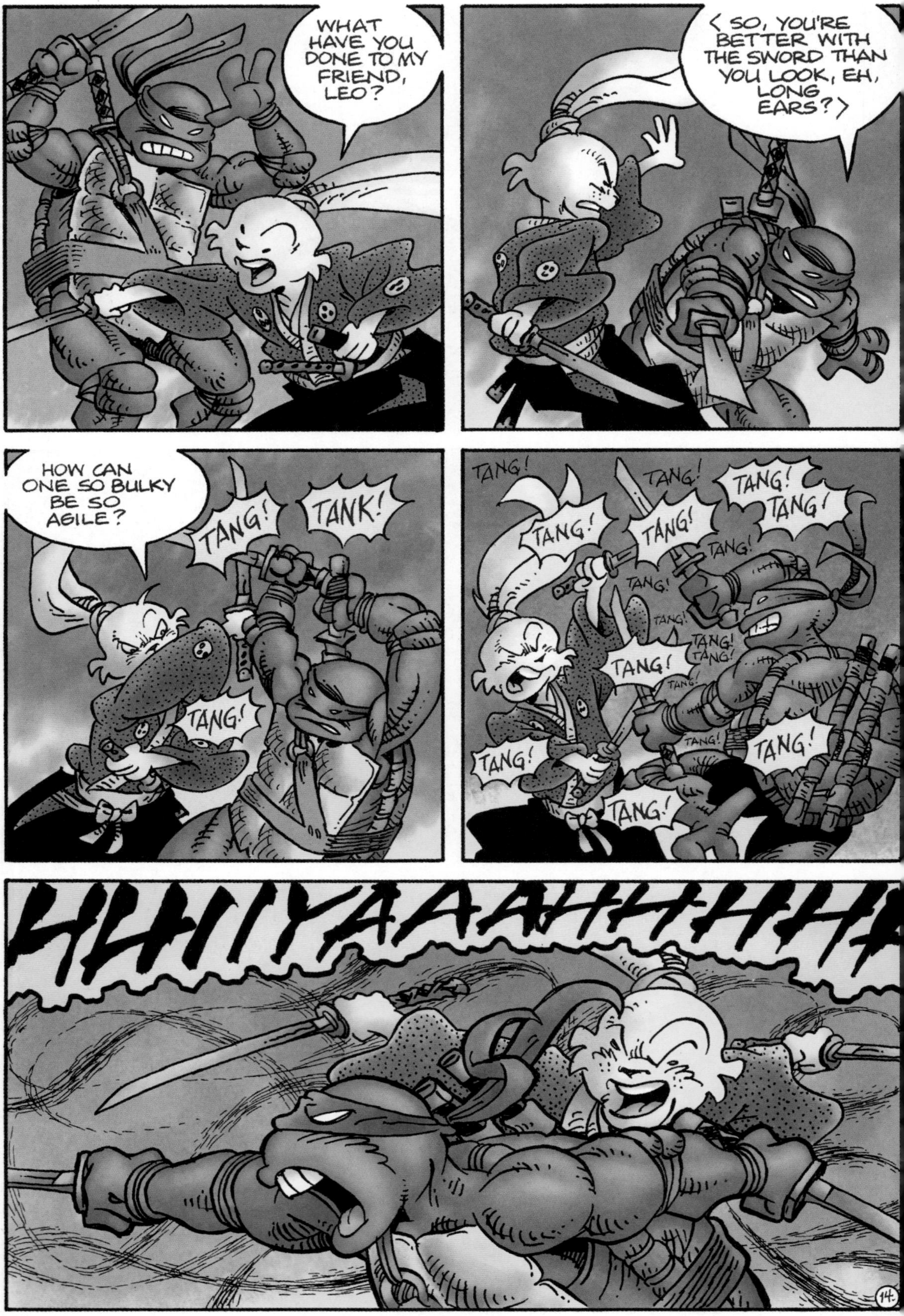
WHAT HAVE YOU DONE TO MY FRIEND, LEO?
< SO, YOU'RE BETTER WITH THE SWORD THAN YOU LOOK, EH, LONG EARS? >
HOW CAN ONE SO BULKY BE SO AGILE?
TANG!
TANK!
TANG!
TANG!
TANG!
TANG!
TANG!
TANG!
TANG!
TANG!
TANG!
TANG!
TANG!
TANG!
TANG!
TANG!
TANG!
TANG!
TANG!
HHIIYAAAHHHHHH
14.

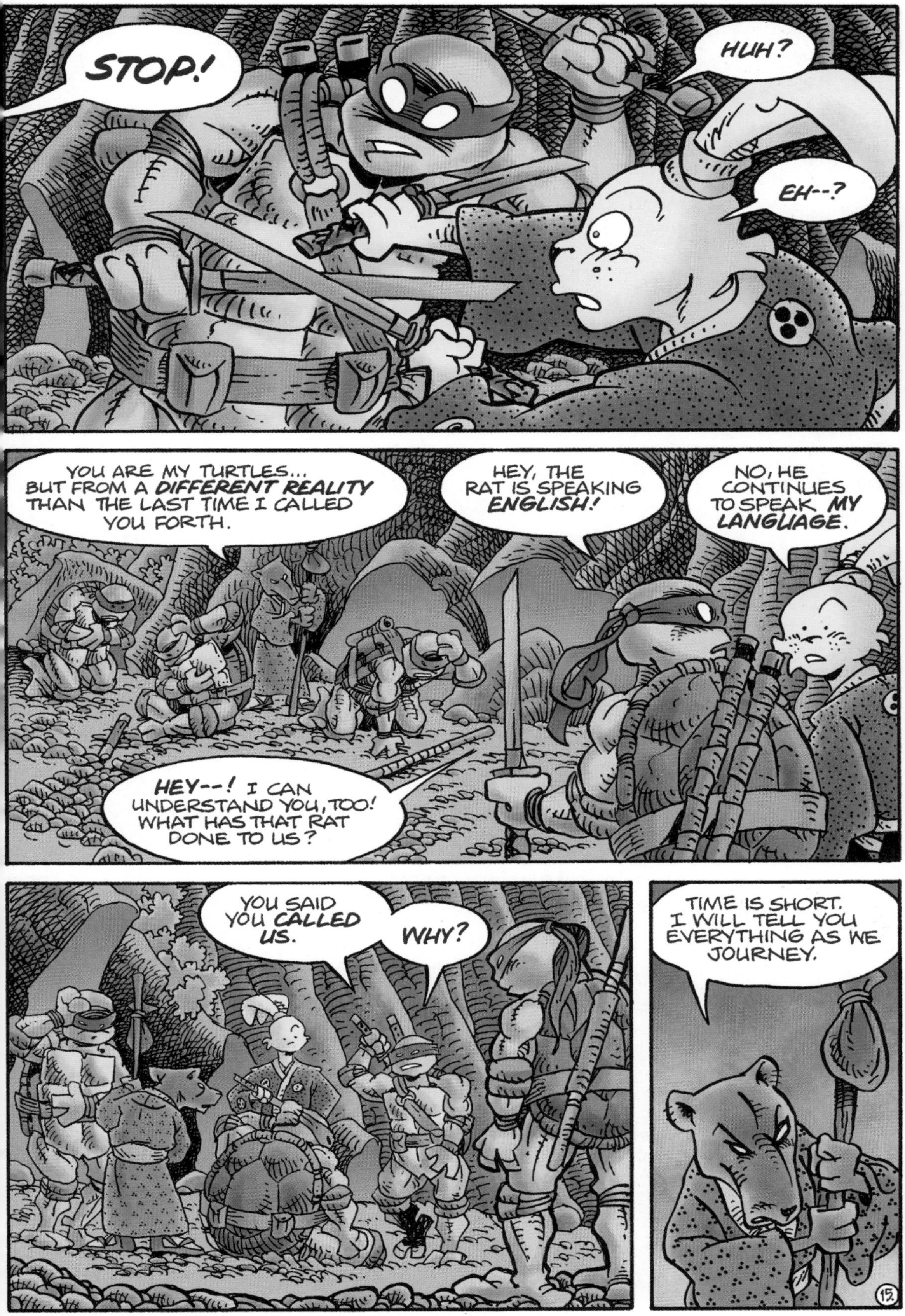
STOP!
HUH?
EH--?
YOU ARE MY TURTLES... BUT FROM A DIFFERENT REALITY THAN THE LAST TIME I CALLED YOU FORTH.
HEY, THE RAT IS SPEAKING ENGLISH!
NO, HE CONTINUES TO SPEAK MY LANGUAGE.
HEY--! I CAN UNDERSTAND YOU, TOO! WHAT HAS THAT RAT DONE TO US?
YOU SAID YOU CALLED US.
WHY?
TIME IS SHORT. I WILL TELL YOU EVERYTHING AS WE JOURNEY.
15.

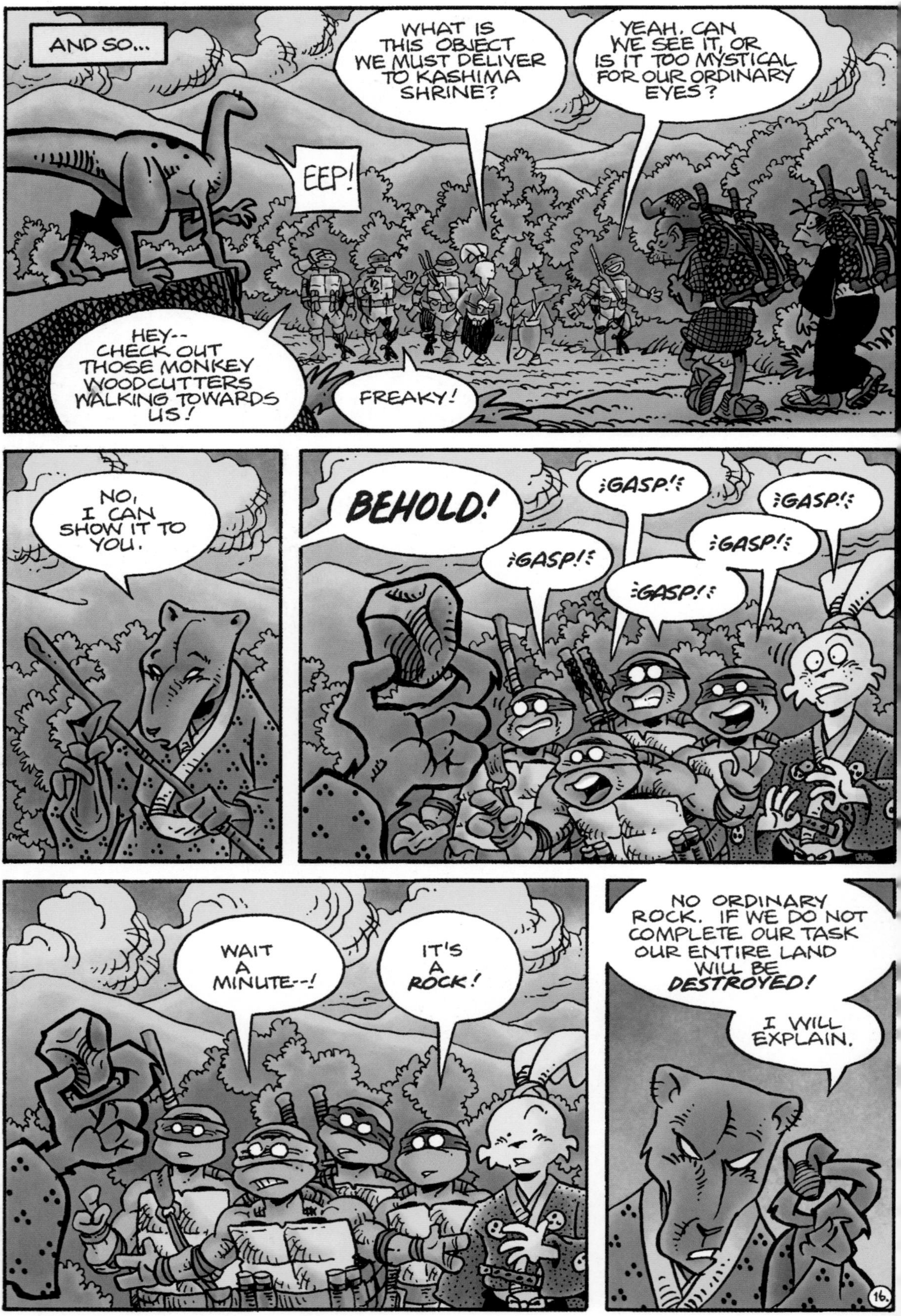
AND SO...
WHAT IS THIS OBJECT WE MUST DELIVER TO KASHIMA SHRINE?
YEAH. CAN WE SEE IT, OR IS IT TOO MYSTICAL FOR OUR ORDINARY EYES?
EEP!
HEY-- CHECK OUT THOSE MONKEY WOODCUTTERS WALKING TOWARDS US!
FREAKY!
NO, I CAN SHOW IT TO YOU.
BEHOLD!
GASP!
GASP!
GASP!
GASP!
GASP!
WAIT A MINUTE--!
IT'S A ROCK!
NO ORDINARY ROCK. IF WE DO NOT COMPLETE OUR TASK OUR ENTIRE LAND WILL BE DESTROYED!
I WILL EXPLAIN.
16.

A GIANT CATFISH NAMED **NAMAZU** LIVES IN THE BOWELS OF THE EARTH UNDER OUR LAND. ANY MOVEMENT, EVEN A SWISH OF ITS TAIL, WILL CAUSE DISRUPTIONS--EARTHQUAKES--ON THE SURFACE.

COUNTLESS CENTURIES AGO, THE GREAT DEITY, **KASHIMA-NO-OKAMI**, THE GOD OF THUNDER, FOUGHT THE GREAT CREATURE.

THE LAND WAS NEARLY TORN APART BY THE STRUGGLE...

...BUT KASHIMA FINALLY SUBDUED NAMAZU, TRAPPING IT UNDER A MASSIVE ROCK CALLED **KANAMEISHI**.

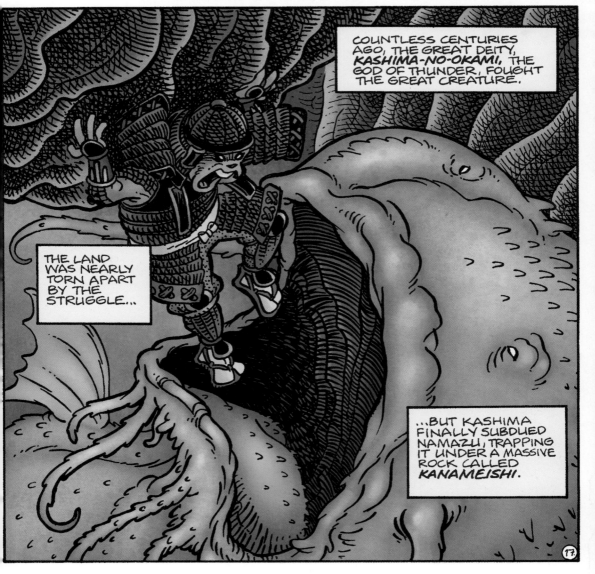

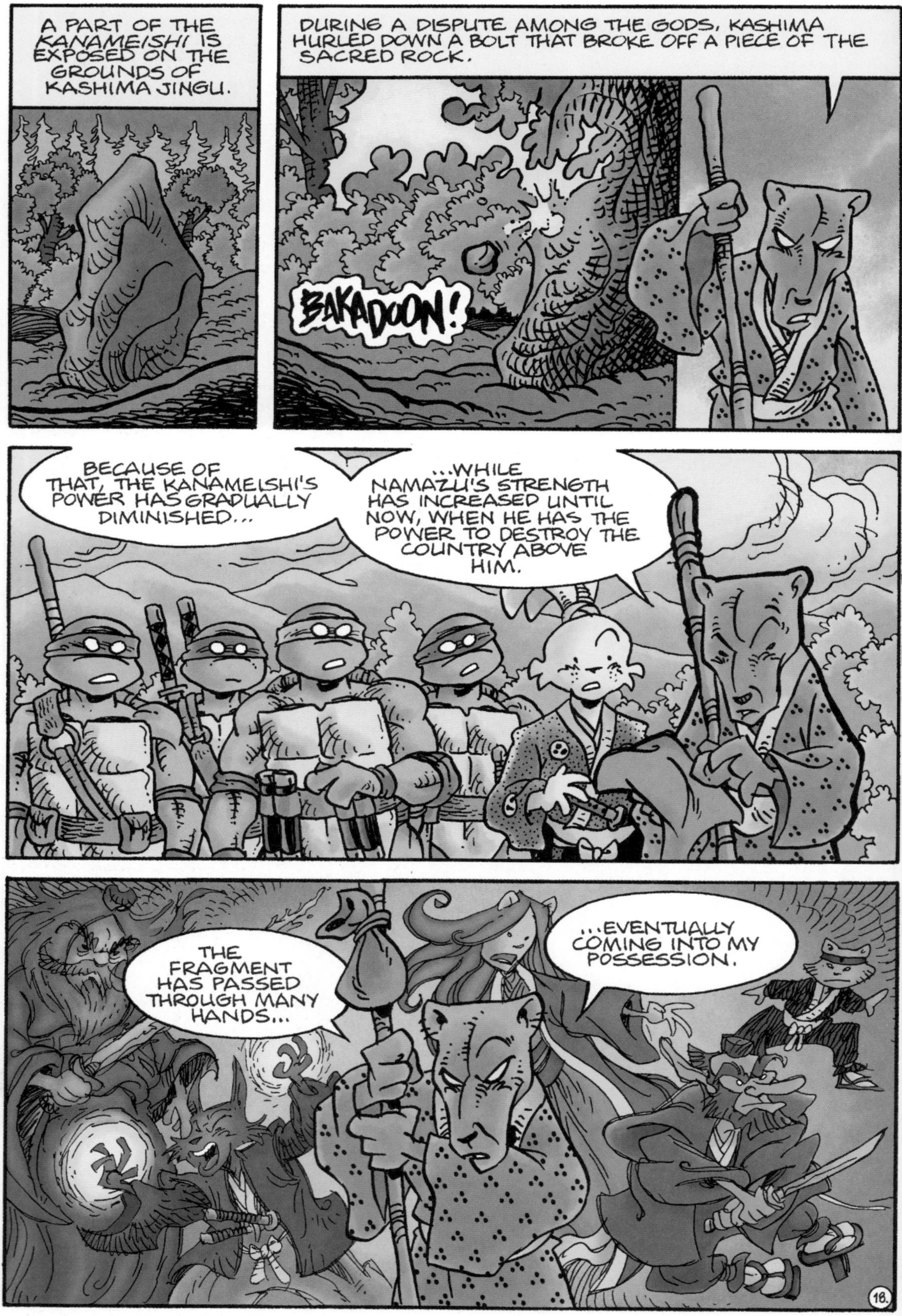
A PART OF THE *KANAMEISHI* IS EXPOSED ON THE GROUNDS OF KASHIMA JINGU.
DURING A DISPUTE AMONG THE GODS, KASHIMA HURLED DOWN A BOLT THAT BROKE OFF A PIECE OF THE SACRED ROCK.
BAKADOON!
BECAUSE OF THAT, THE KANAMEISHI'S POWER HAS GRADUALLY DIMINISHED...
...WHILE NAMAZU'S STRENGTH HAS INCREASED UNTIL NOW, WHEN HE HAS THE POWER TO DESTROY THE COUNTRY ABOVE HIM.
THE FRAGMENT HAS PASSED THROUGH MANY HANDS...
...EVENTUALLY COMING INTO MY POSSESSION.
18.

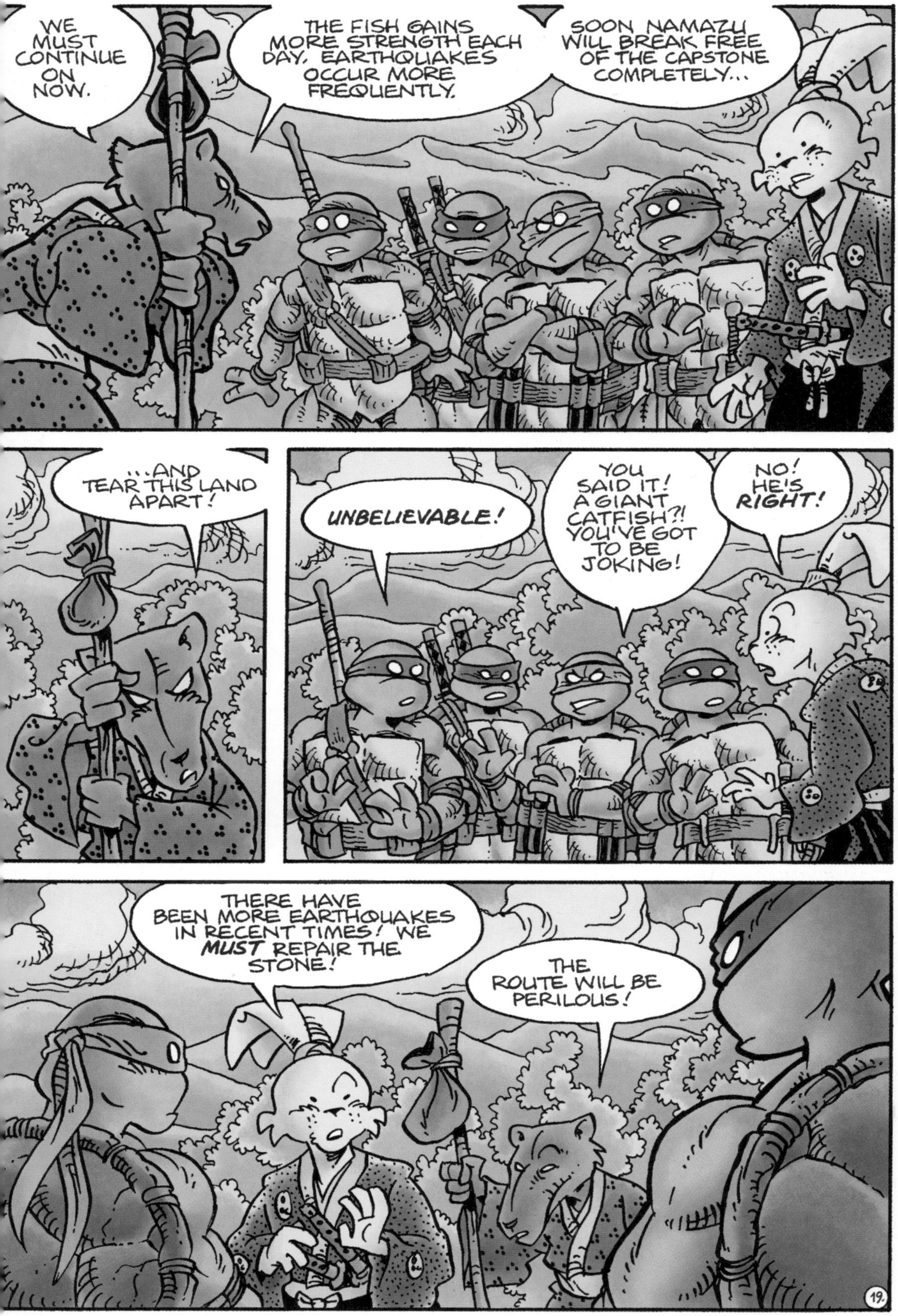
WE MUST CONTINUE ON NOW.
THE FISH GAINS MORE STRENGTH EACH DAY. EARTHQUAKES OCCUR MORE FREQUENTLY.
SOON NAMAZU WILL BREAK FREE OF THE CAPSTONE COMPLETELY...
...AND TEAR THIS LAND APART!
UNBELIEVABLE!
YOU SAID IT! A GIANT CATFISH?! YOU'VE GOT TO BE JOKING!
NO! HE'S RIGHT!
THERE HAVE BEEN MORE EARTHQUAKES IN RECENT TIMES! WE MUST REPAIR THE STONE!
THE ROUTE WILL BE PERILOUS!
19.

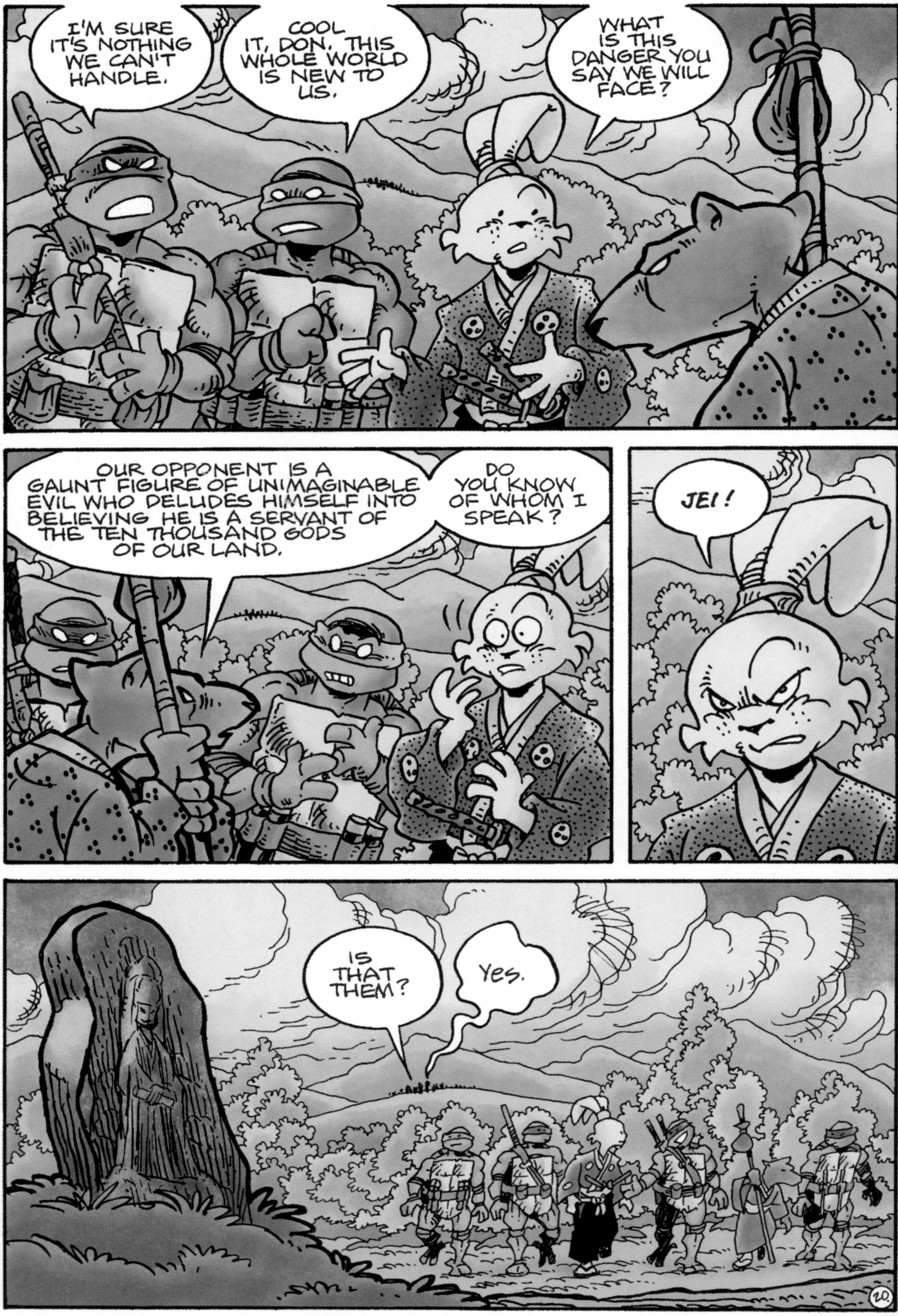
I'M SURE IT'S NOTHING WE CAN'T HANDLE.
COOL IT, DON. THIS WHOLE WORLD IS NEW TO US.
WHAT IS THIS DANGER YOU SAY WE WILL FACE?
OUR OPPONENT IS A GAUNT FIGURE OF UNIMAGINABLE EVIL WHO DELUDES HIMSELF INTO BELIEVING HE IS A SERVANT OF THE TEN THOUSAND GODS OF OUR LAND.
DO YOU KNOW OF WHOM I SPEAK?
JEI!
IS THAT THEM?
Yes.
20.

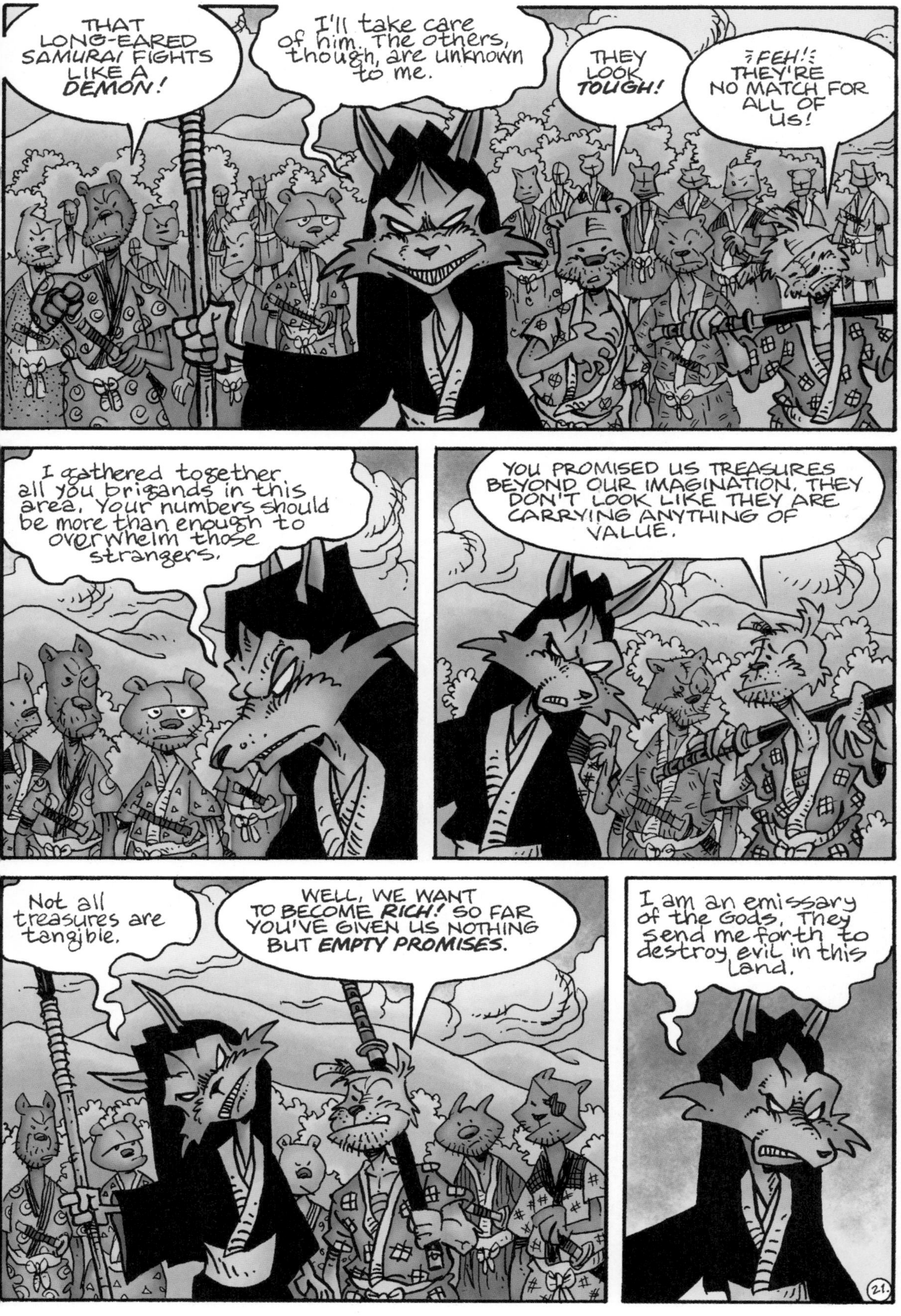
THAT LONG-EARED SAMURAI FIGHTS LIKE A DEMON!
I'll take care of him. The others, though, are unknown to me.
THEY LOOK TOUGH!
FEH! THEY'RE NO MATCH FOR ALL OF US!
I gathered together all you brigands in this area. Your numbers should be more than enough to overwhelm those strangers.
YOU PROMISED US TREASURES BEYOND OUR IMAGINATION. THEY DON'T LOOK LIKE THEY ARE CARRYING ANYTHING OF VALUE.
Not all treasures are tangible.
WELL, WE WANT TO BECOME RICH! SO FAR YOU'VE GIVEN US NOTHING BUT EMPTY PROMISES.
I am an emissary of the Gods. They send me forth to destroy evil in this land.
21.

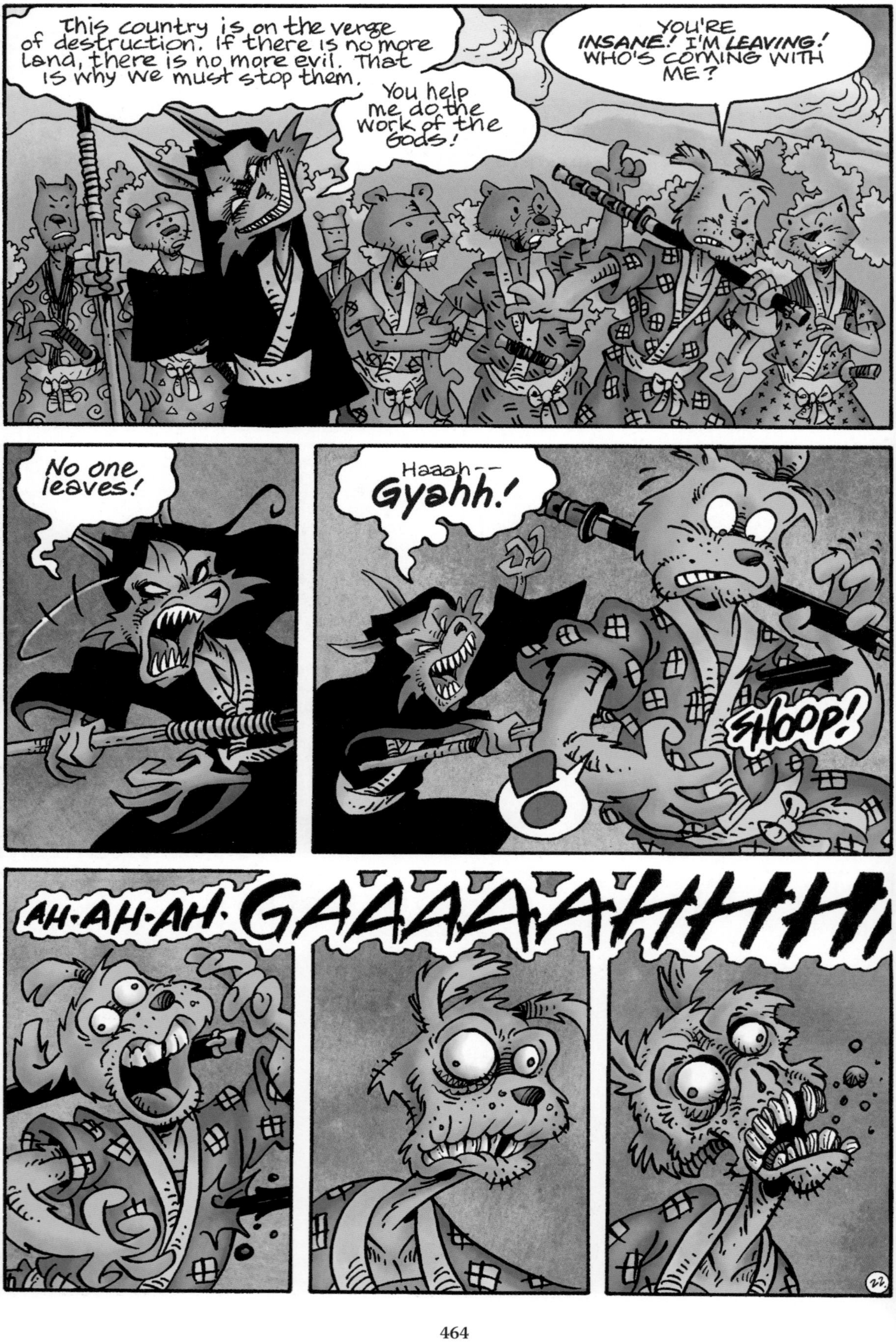
This country is on the verge of destruction. If there is no more land, there is no more evil. That is why we must stop them.
You help me do the work of the Gods!
YOU'RE INSANE! I'M LEAVING! WHO'S COMING WITH ME?
No one leaves!
Haaah-- Gyahh!
SHOOP!
AH·AH·AH·GAAAAAHHHH
22.

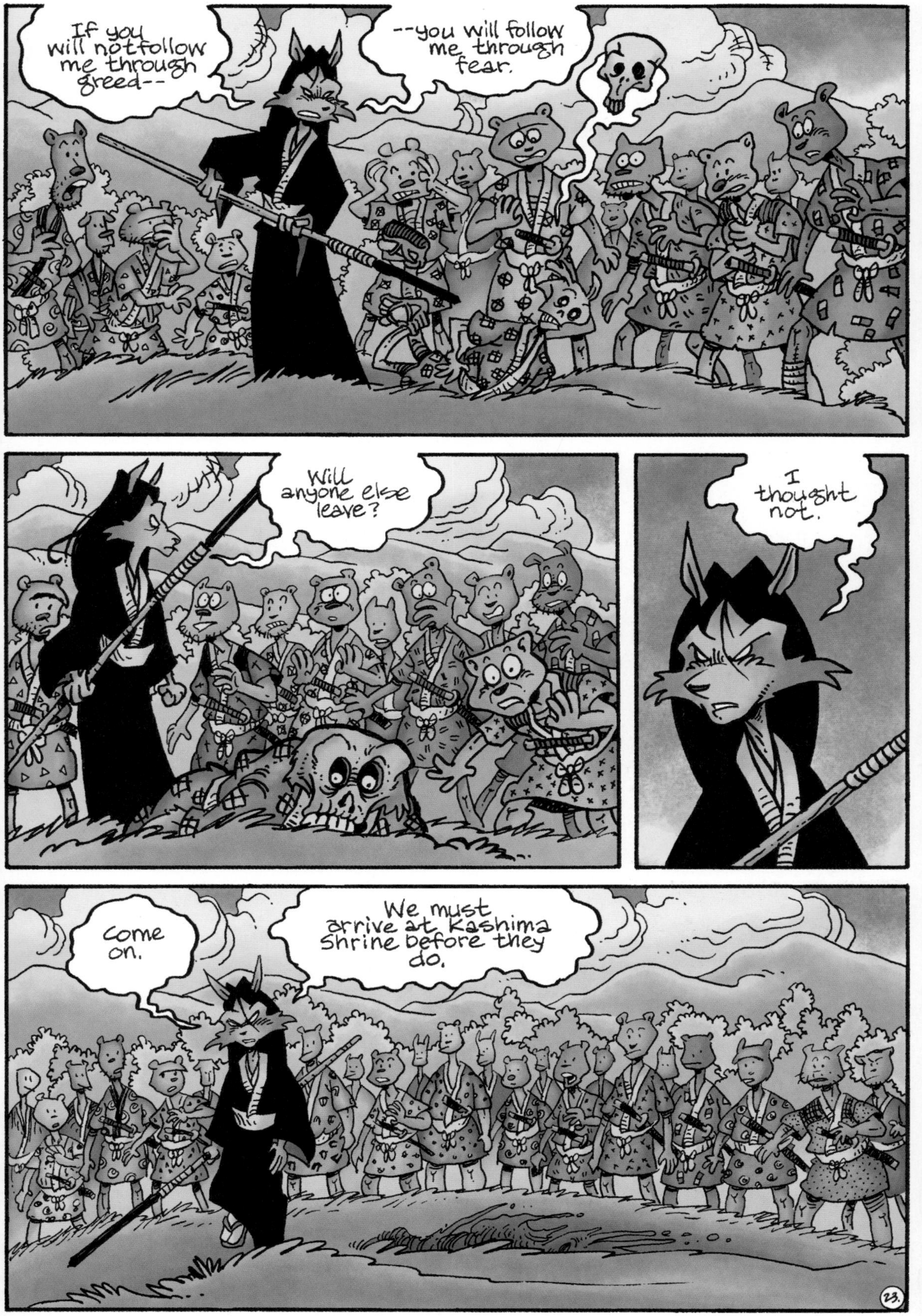
If you will not follow me through greed--
--you will follow me through fear.
Will anyone else leave?
I thought not.
Come on.
We must arrive at Kashima Shrine before they do.
23.

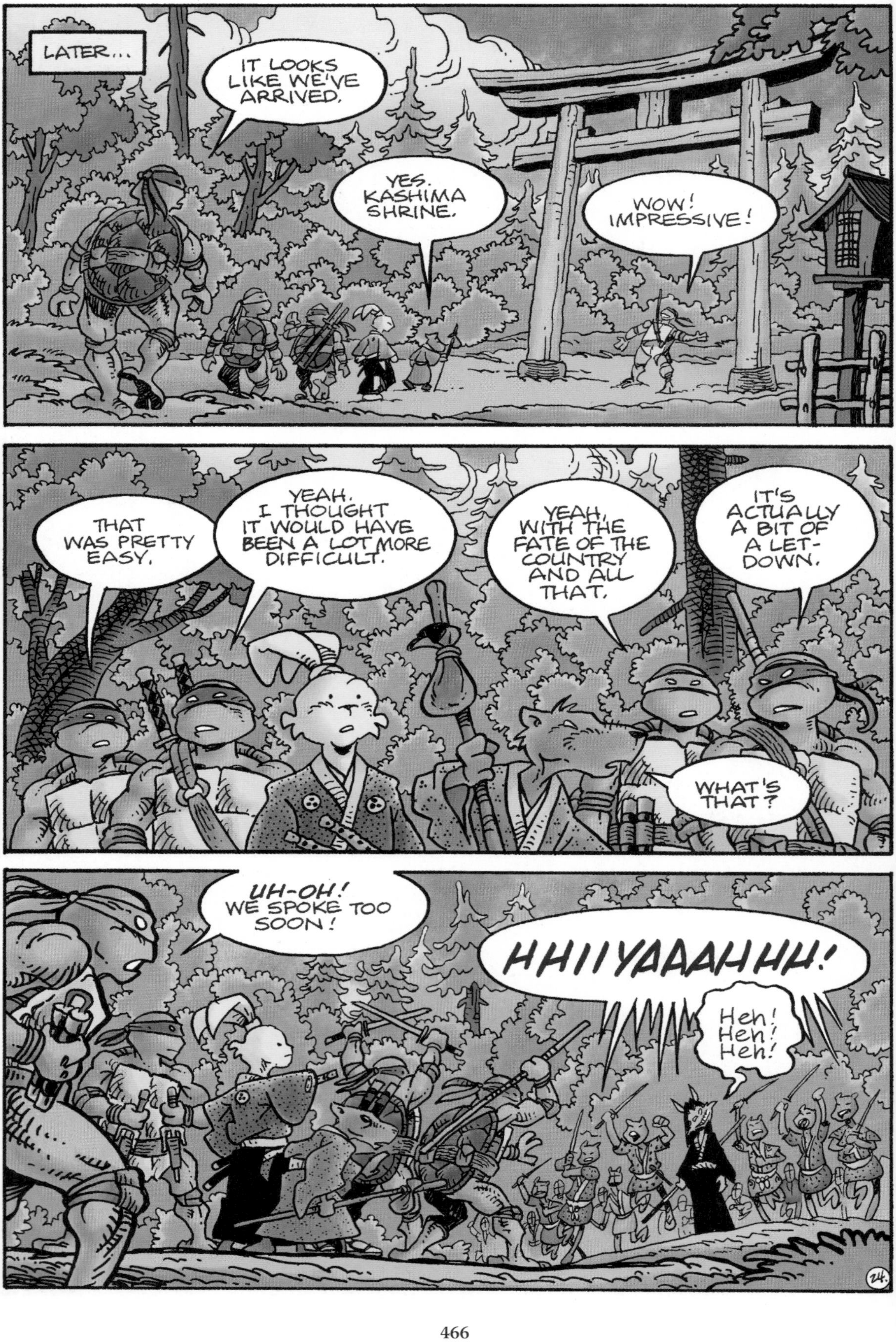
LATER...
IT LOOKS LIKE WE'VE ARRIVED.
YES. KASHIMA SHRINE.
WOW! IMPRESSIVE!
THAT WAS PRETTY EASY.
YEAH. I THOUGHT IT WOULD HAVE BEEN A LOT MORE DIFFICULT.
YEAH, WITH THE FATE OF THE COUNTRY AND ALL THAT.
IT'S ACTUALLY A BIT OF A LET-DOWN.
WHAT'S THAT?
UH-OH! WE SPOKE TOO SOON!
HHIIYAAAHHH!
Heh! Heh! Heh!
24.

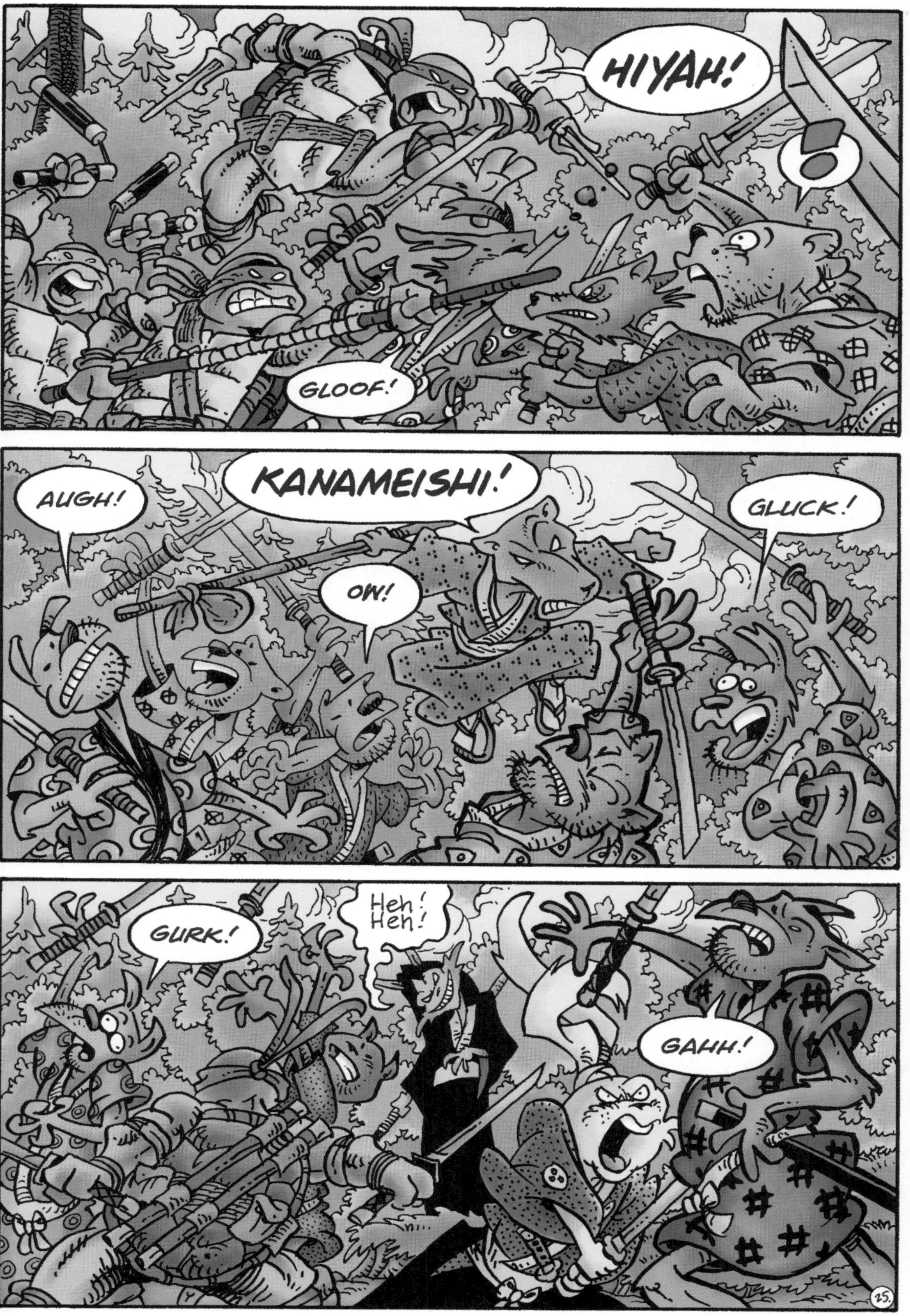
HIYAH!
GLOOF!
KANAMEISHI!
AUGH!
GLUCK!
OW!
GURK!
Heh! Heh!
GAHH!
25.

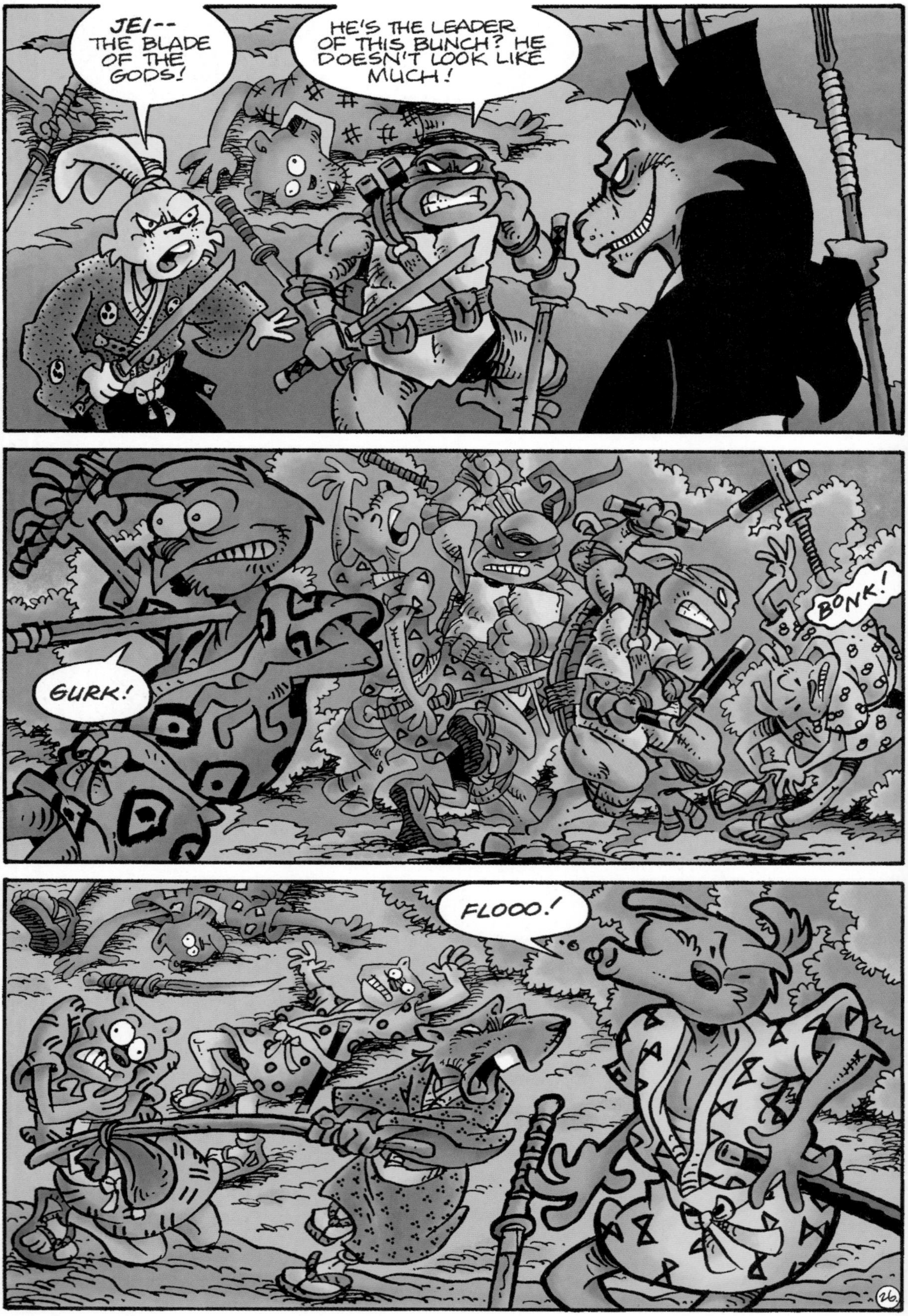
JEI-- THE BLADE OF THE GODS!
HE'S THE LEADER OF THIS BUNCH? HE DOESN'T LOOK LIKE MUCH!
GURK!
BONK!
FLOOO!
26

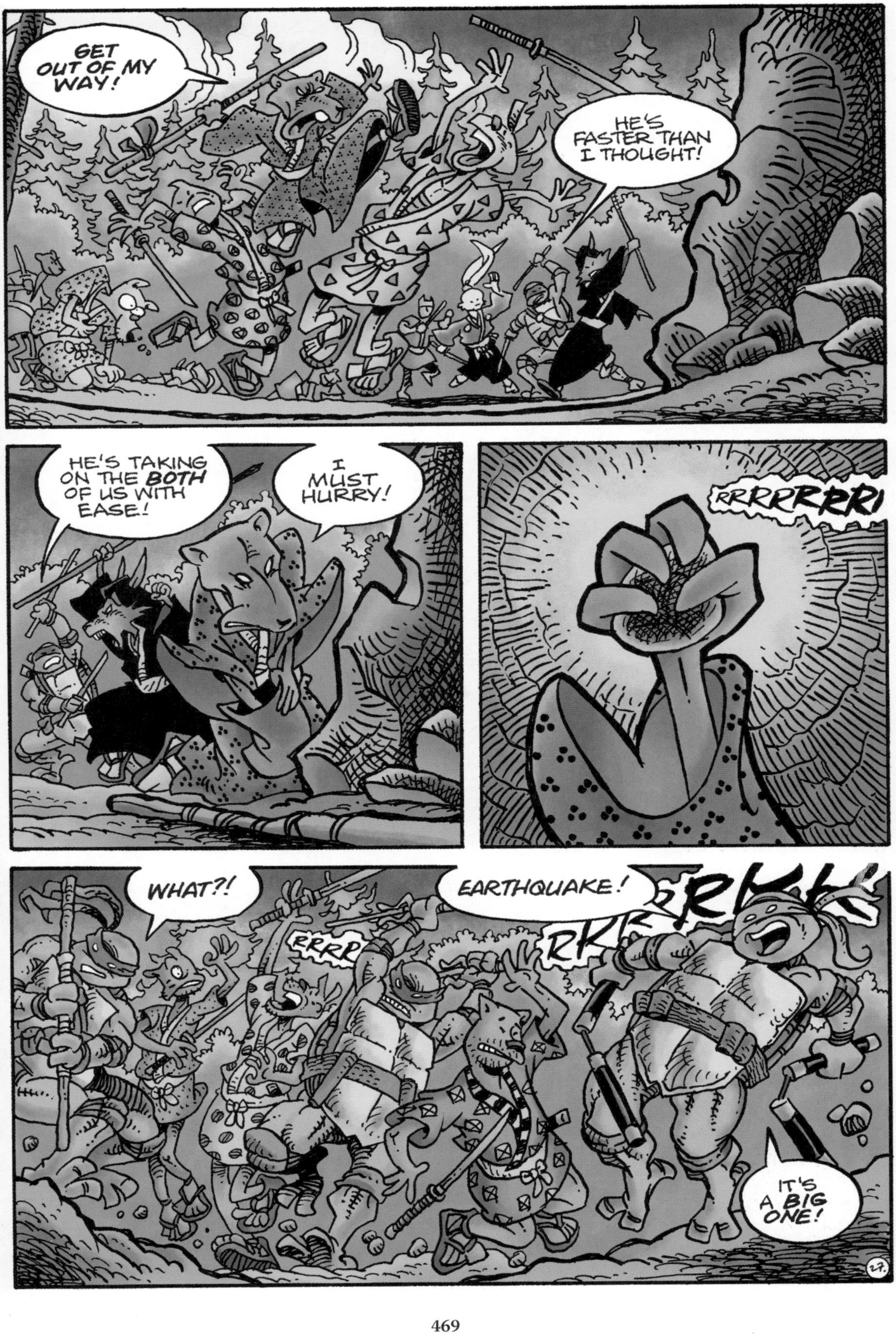
GET OUT OF MY WAY!
HE'S FASTER THAN I THOUGHT!
HE'S TAKING ON THE BOTH OF US WITH EASE!
I MUST HURRY!
RRRRRRRI
WHAT?!
EARTHQUAKE!
RRRR
RRRRMMM
IT'S A BIG ONE!
27.

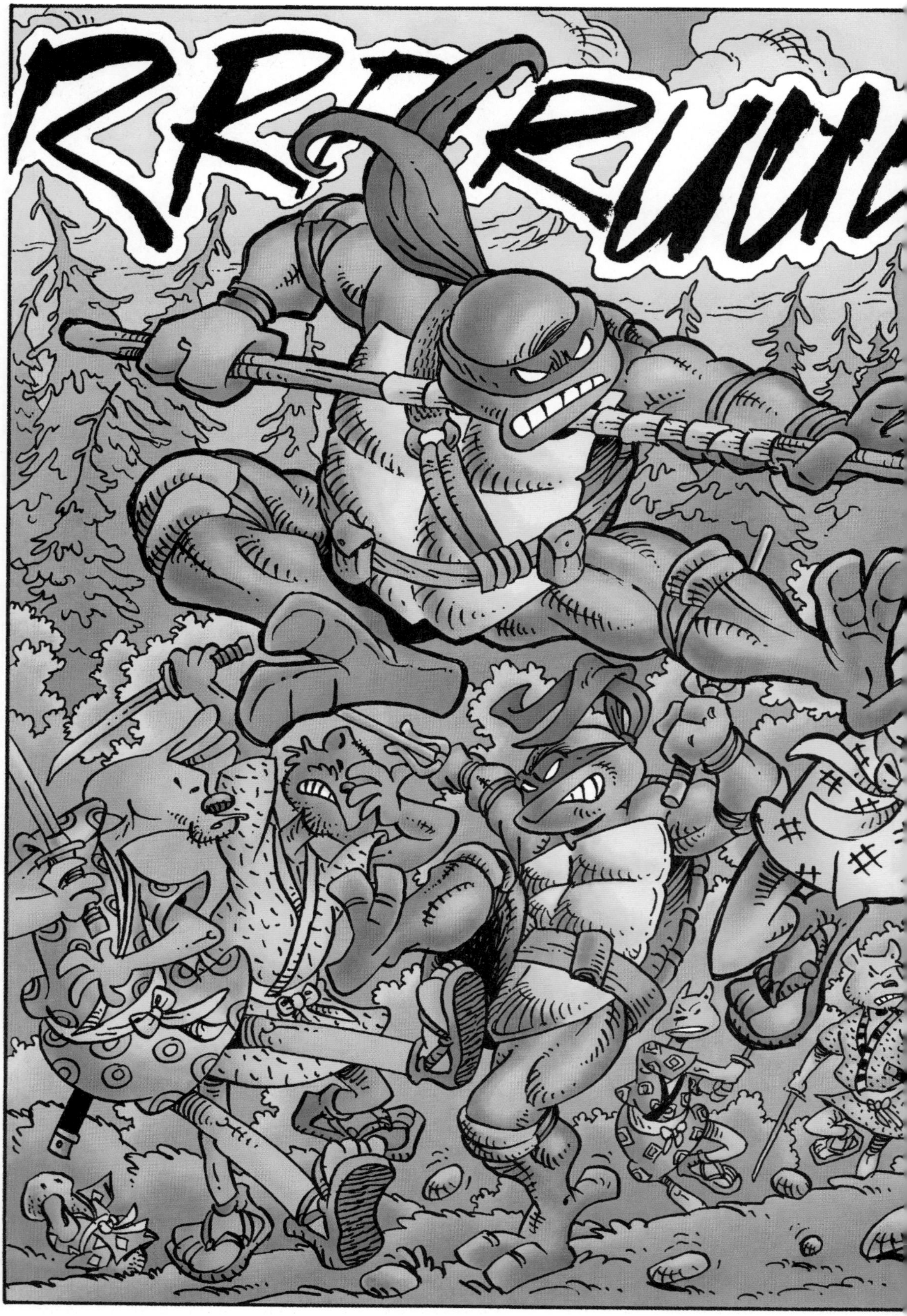

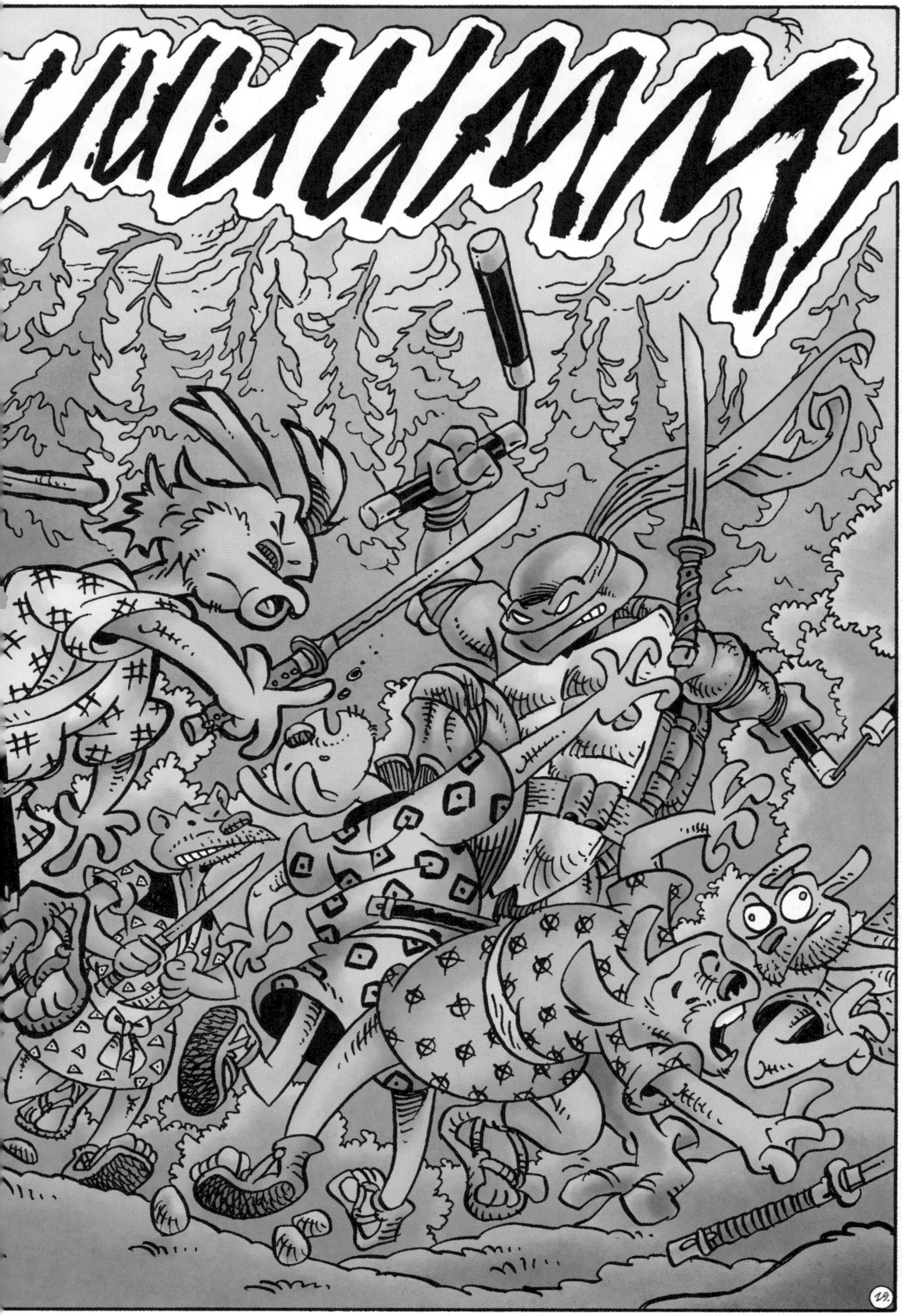

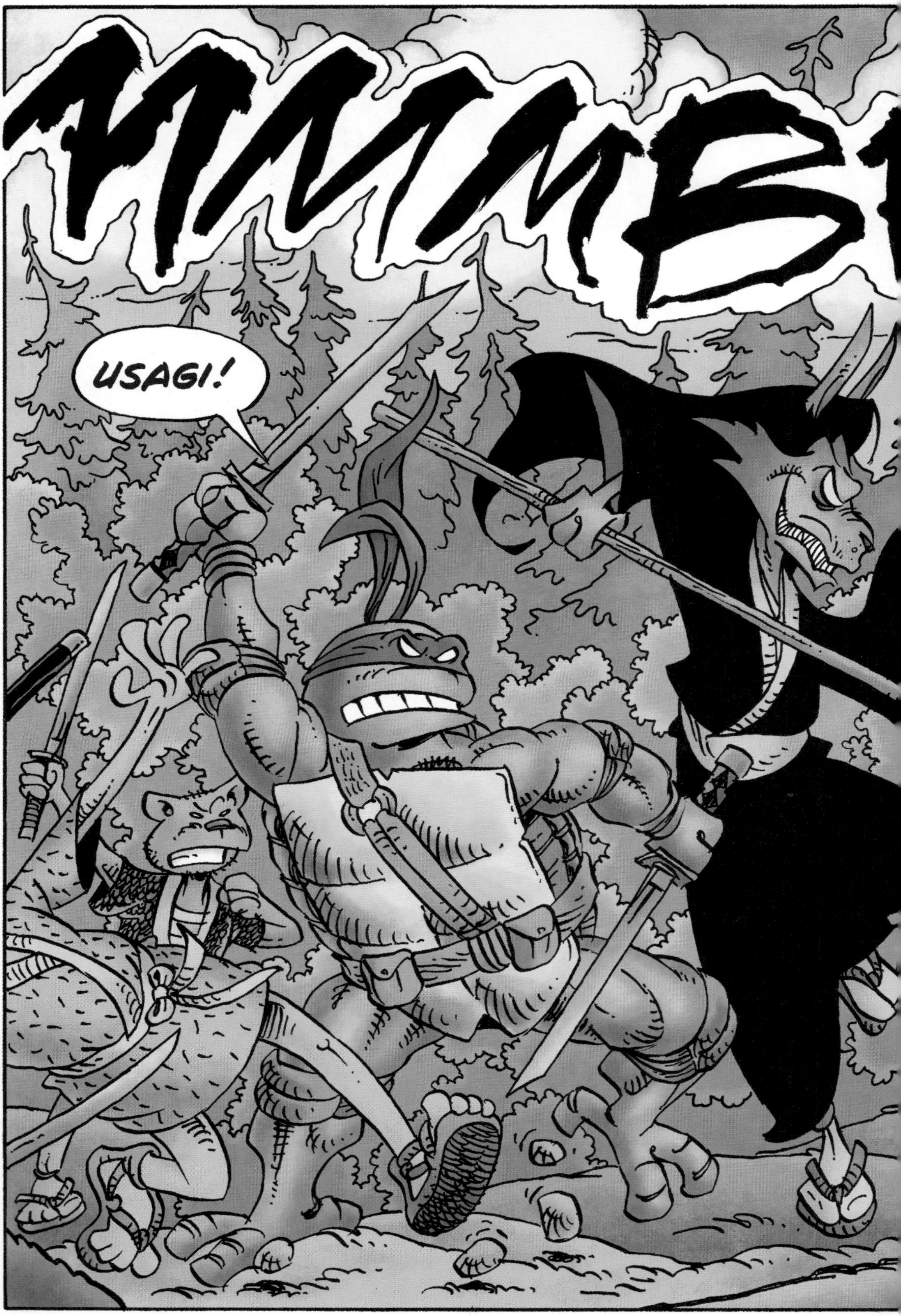
USAGI!

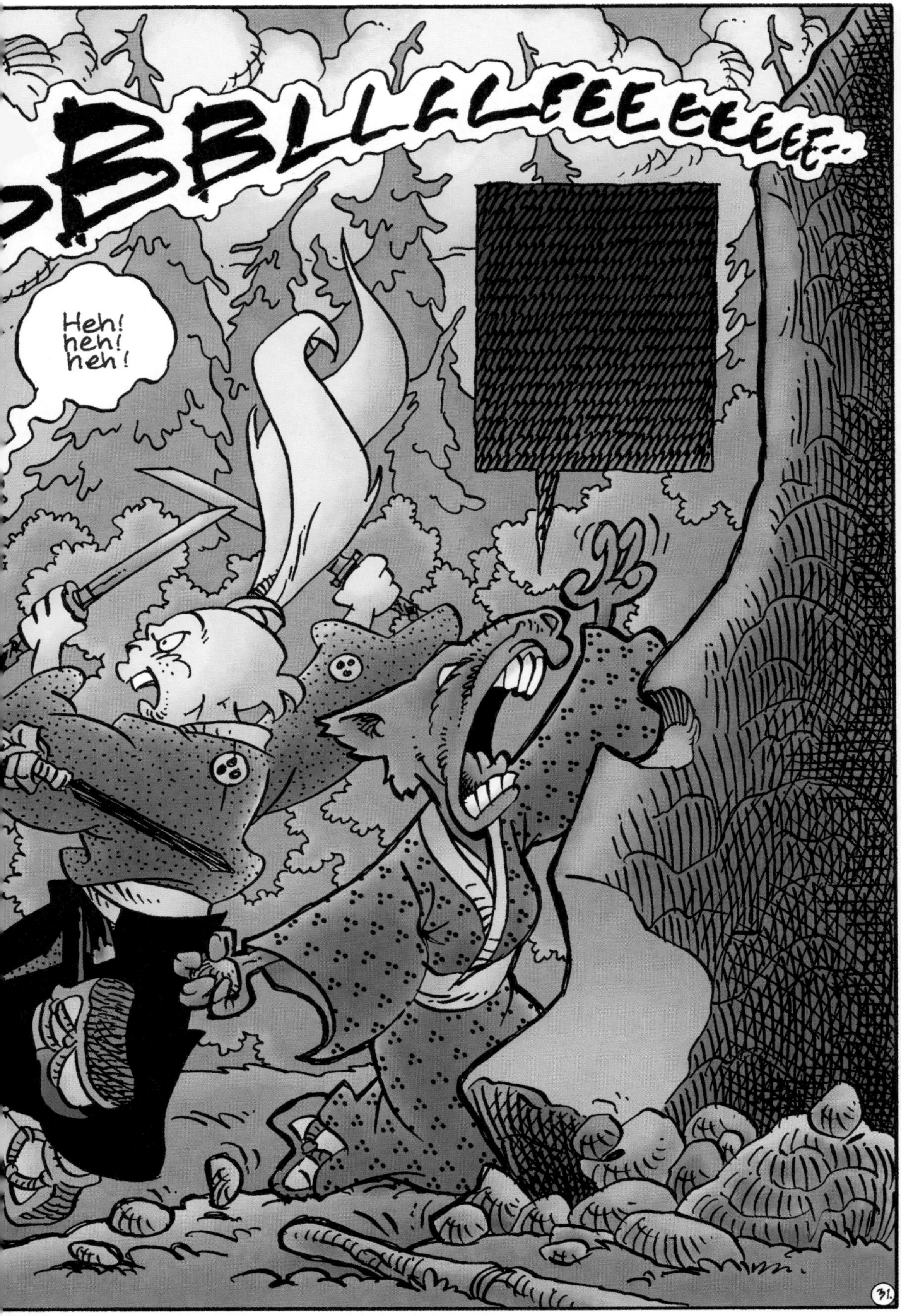
BBLLLLEEEEEEEEE--
Heh! heh! heh!
31.

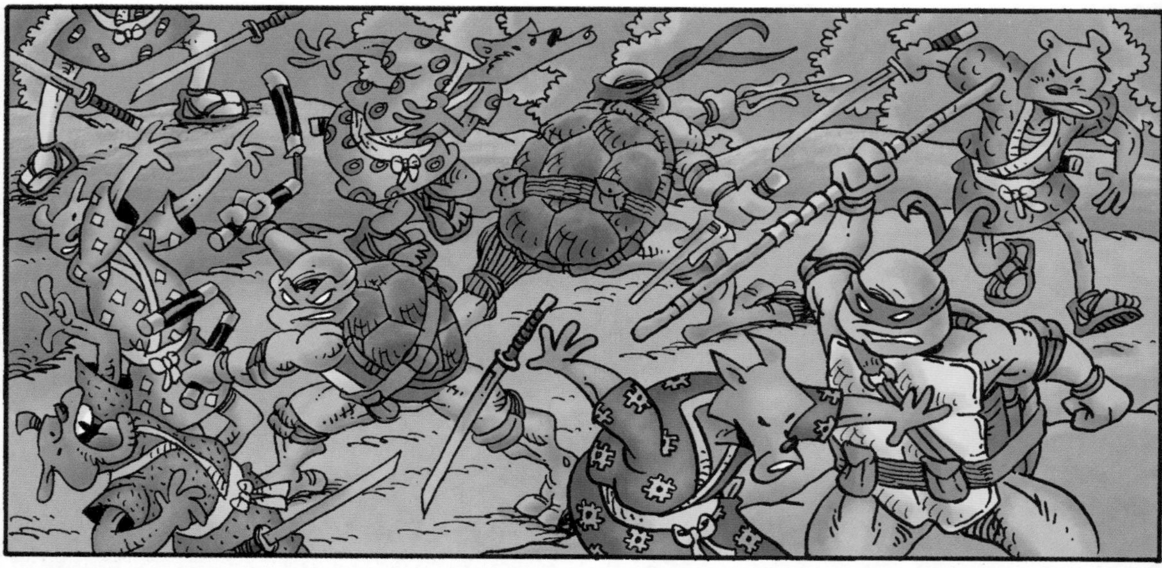

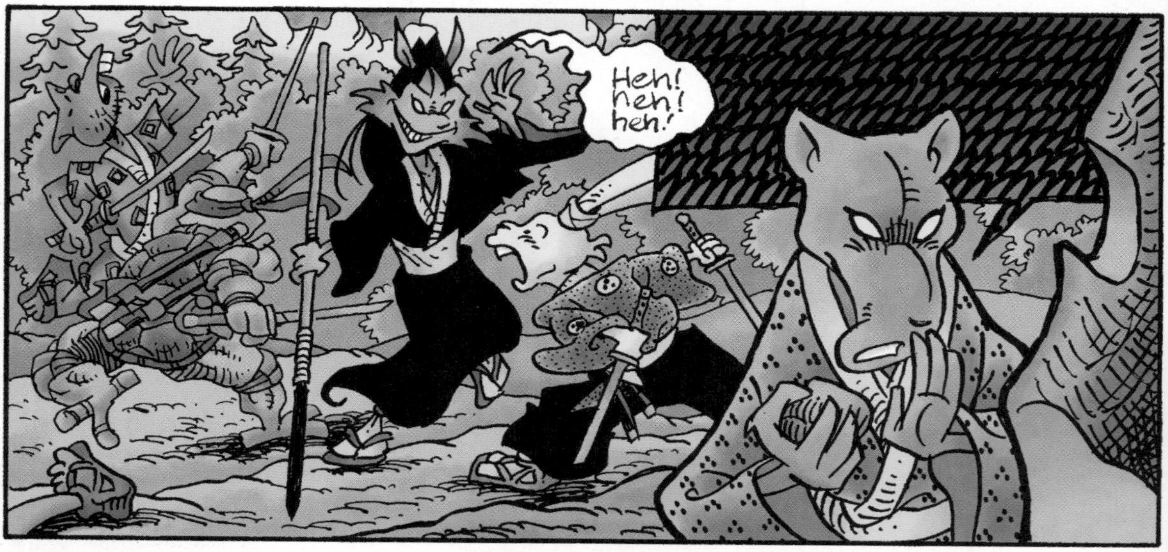
Heh! heh! heh!

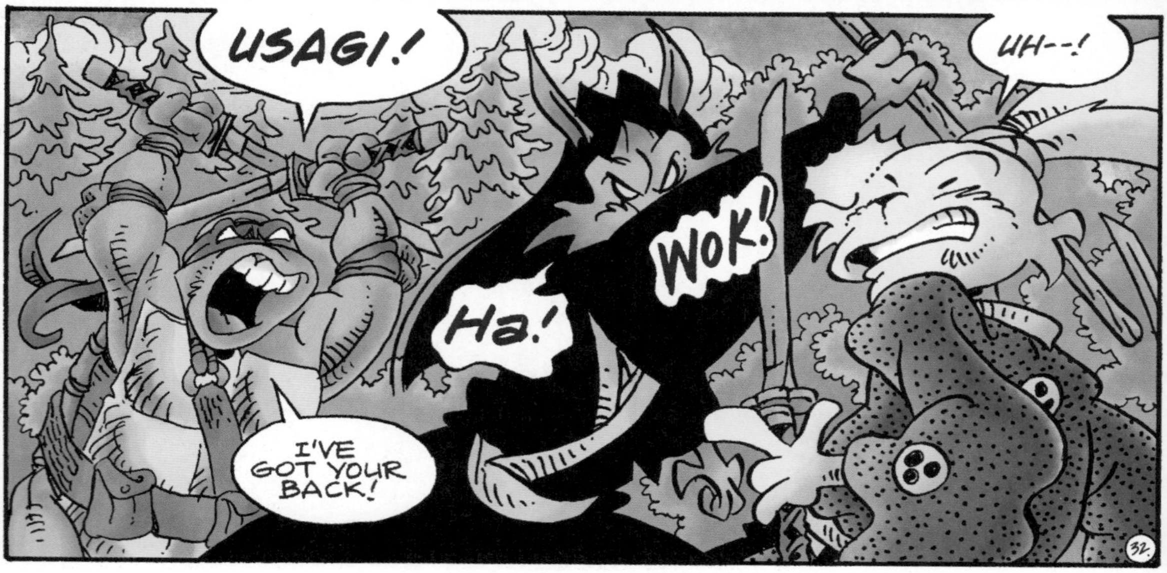
USAGI!
UH--!
WOK!
Ha!
I'VE GOT YOUR BACK!
32

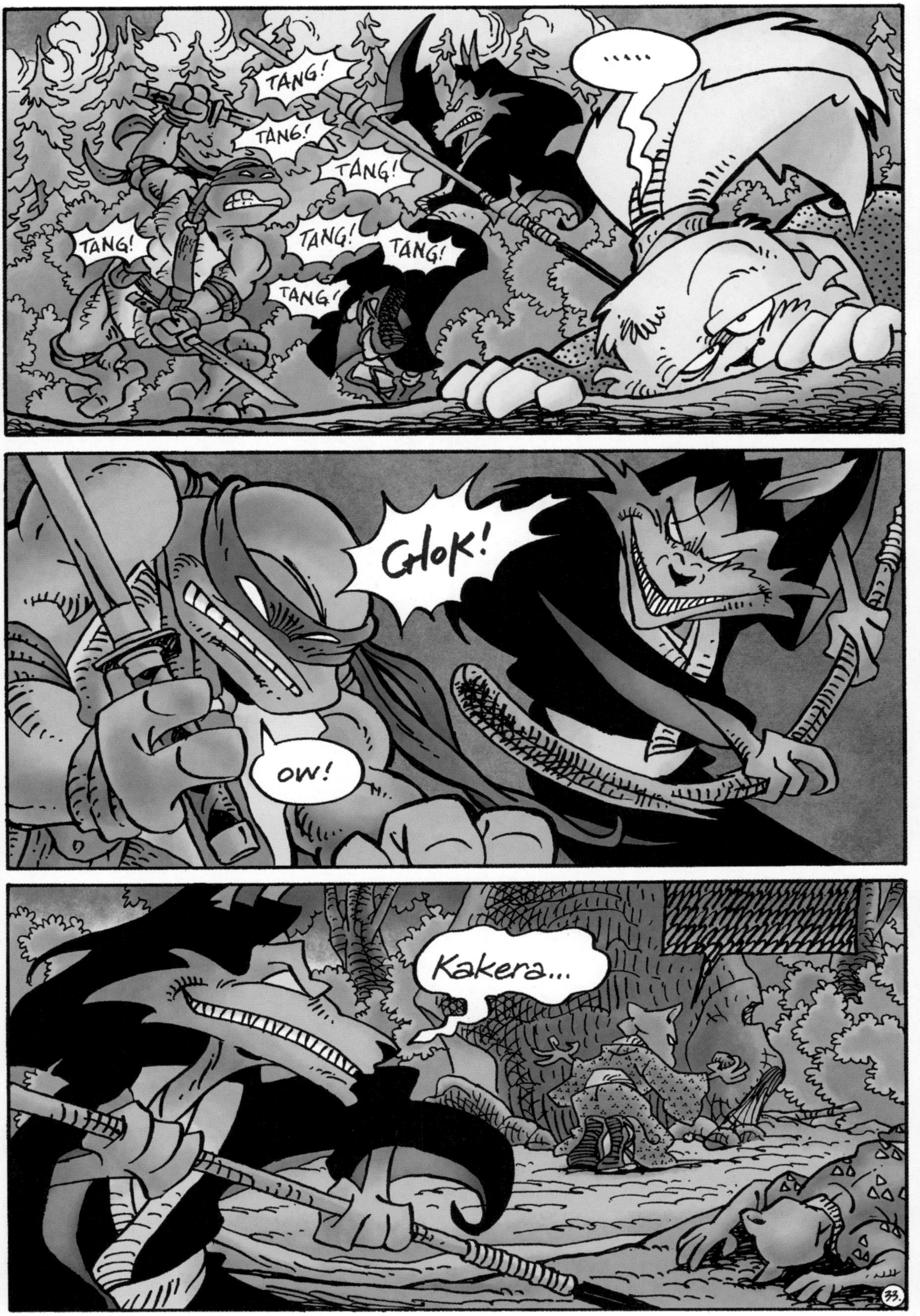

TANG!
TANG!
TANG!
TANG!
TANG!
TANG!
TANG!
.....
GLOK!
OW!
Kakera...
33.

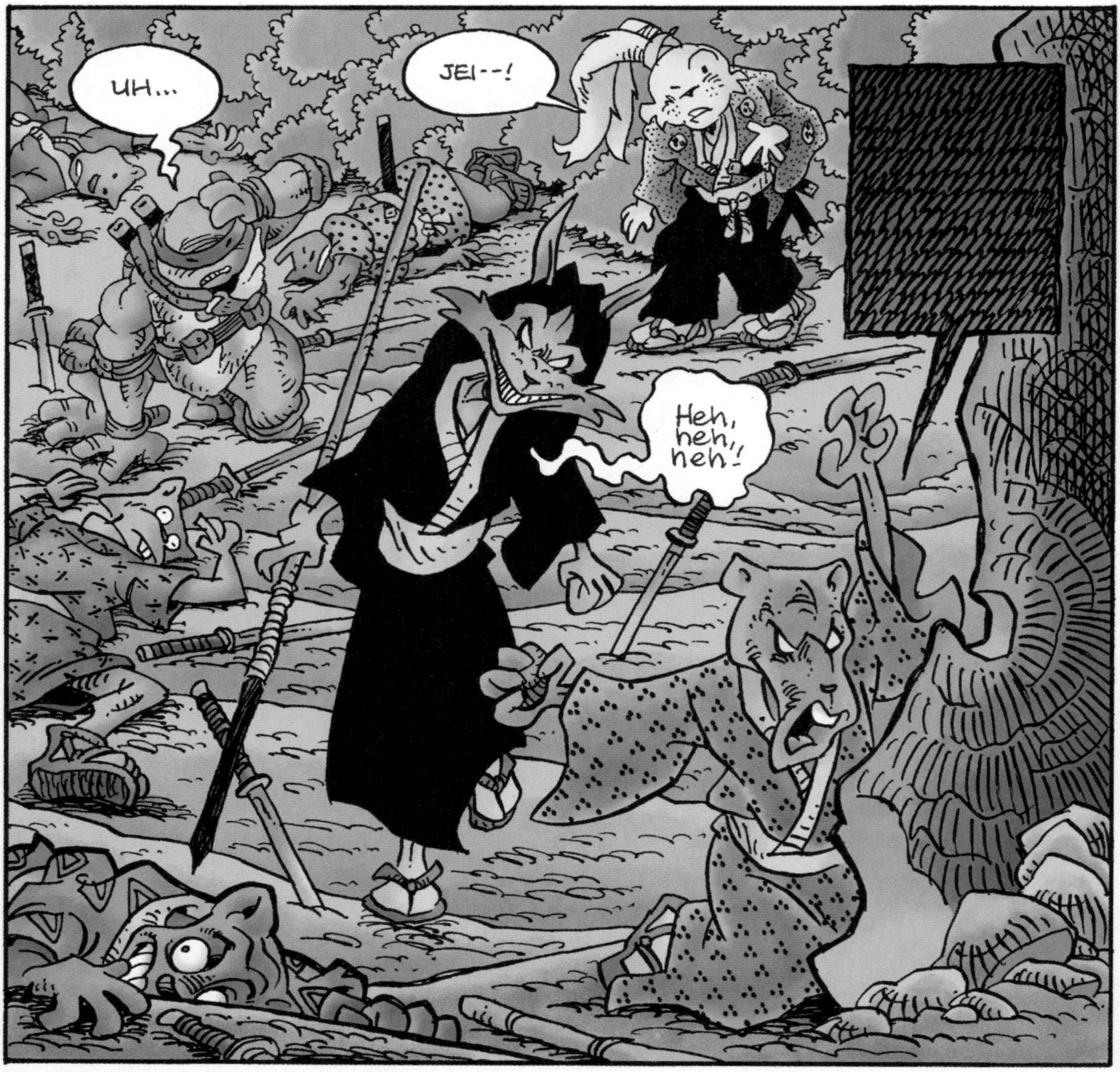
UH...
JEI--!
Heh, heh, heh!!

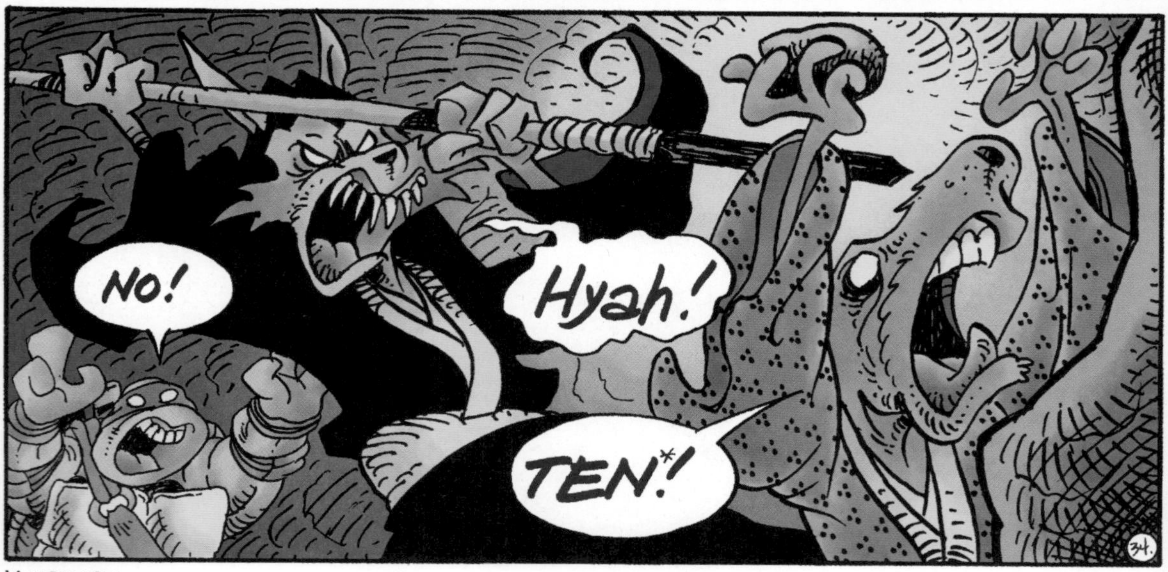
NO!
Hyah!
TEN*!

* HEAVEN

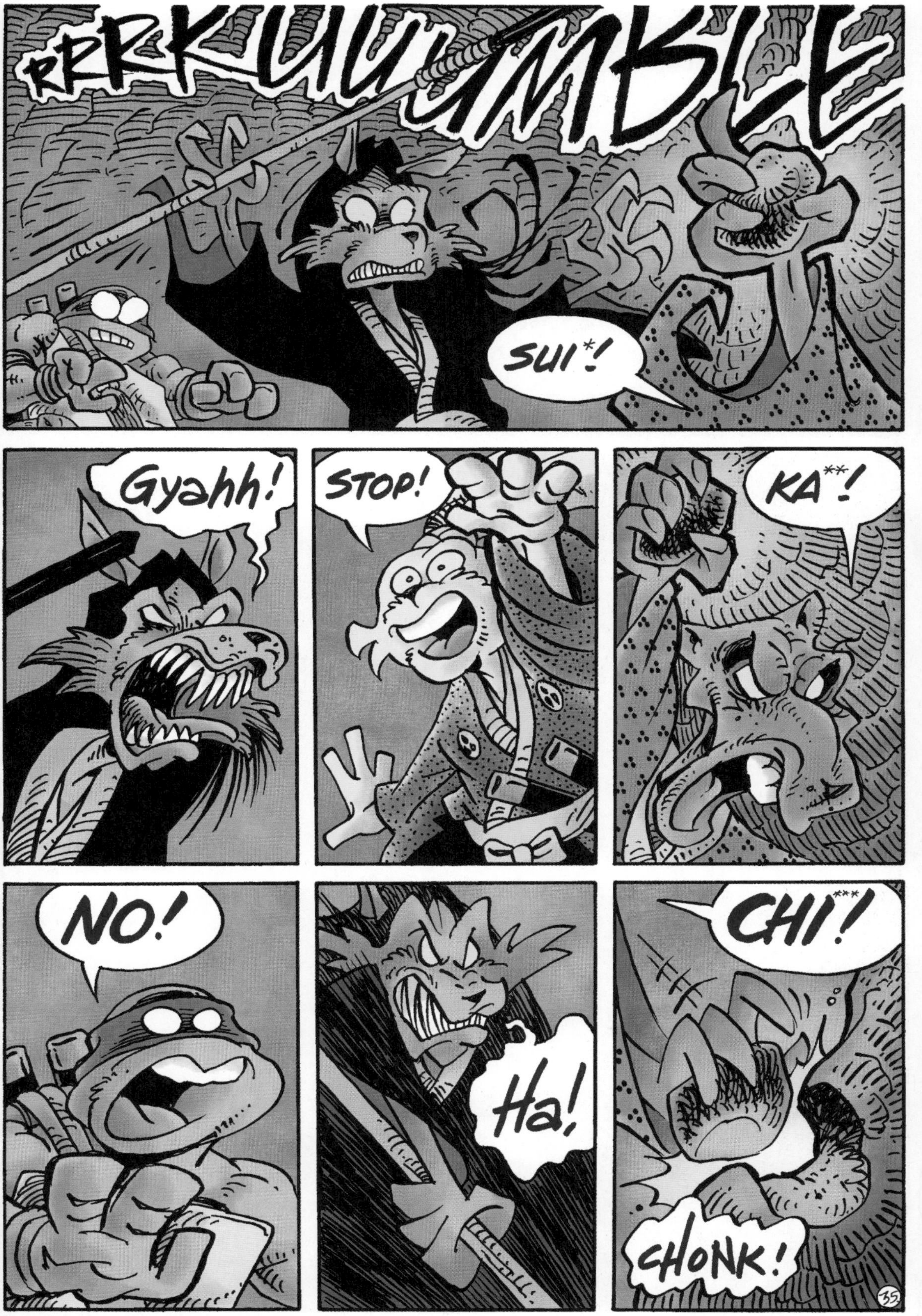
RRRKUUUMBLE
SUI*!
Gyahh!
STOP!
KA**!
NO!
Ha!
CHI***!
CHONK!
35

*WATER **FIRE ***EARTH

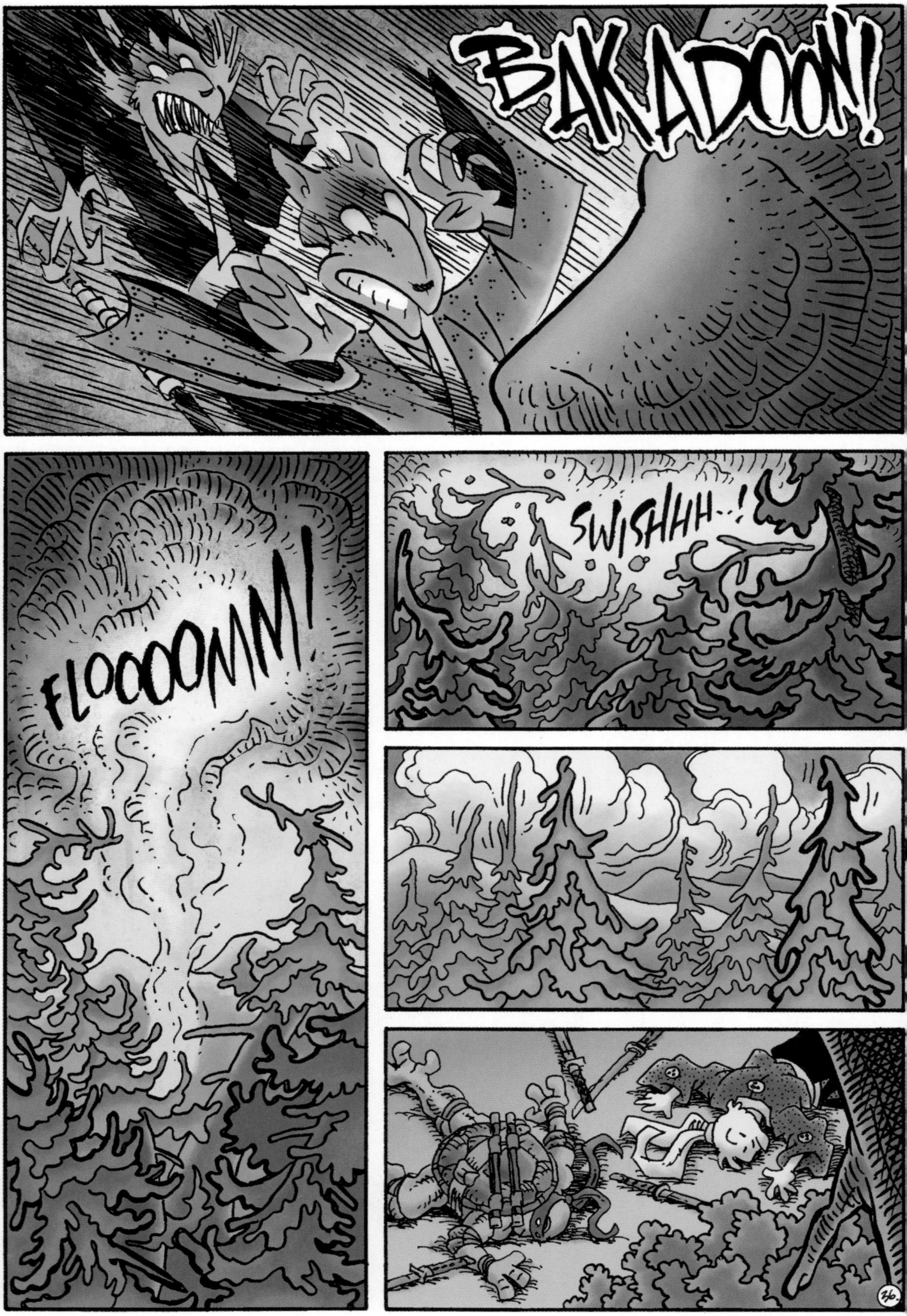
BAKADOOM!
FLOOOOMM!
SWISHHH..!
26.

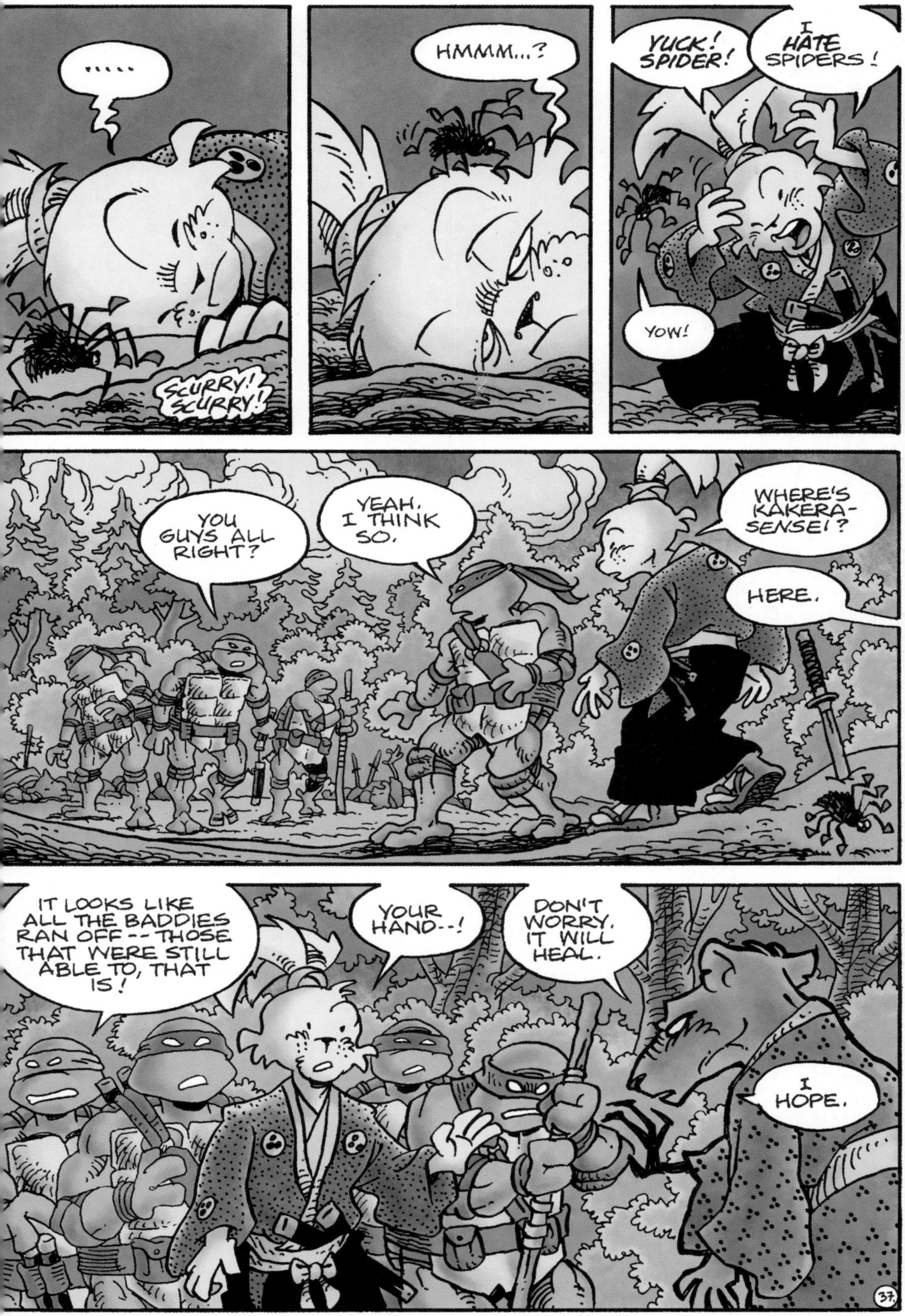
.....
SCURRY! SCURRY!
HMMM...?
YUCK! SPIDER!
I HATE SPIDERS!
YOW!
YOU GUYS ALL RIGHT?
YEAH. I THINK SO.
WHERE'S KAKERA-SENSEI?
HERE.
IT LOOKS LIKE ALL THE BADDIES RAN OFF -- THOSE THAT WERE STILL ABLE TO, THAT IS!
YOUR HAND--!
DON'T WORRY. IT WILL HEAL.
I HOPE.
37.

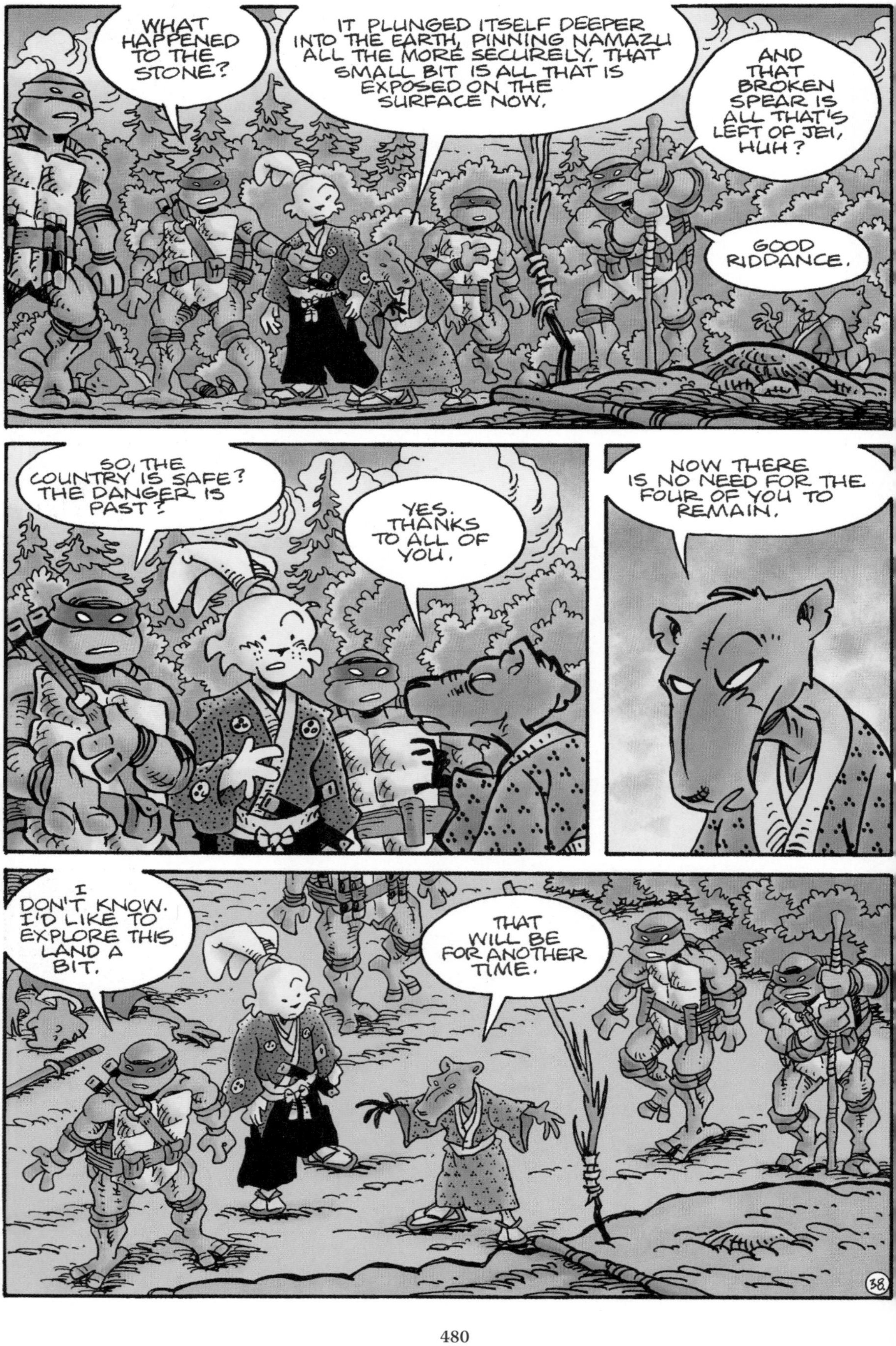
WHAT HAPPENED TO THE STONE?
IT PLUNGED ITSELF DEEPER INTO THE EARTH, PINNING NAMAZU ALL THE MORE SECURELY. THAT SMALL BIT IS ALL THAT IS EXPOSED ON THE SURFACE NOW.
AND THAT BROKEN SPEAR IS ALL THAT'S LEFT OF JEI, HUH?
GOOD RIDDANCE.
SO, THE COUNTRY IS SAFE? THE DANGER IS PAST?
YES. THANKS TO ALL OF YOU.
NOW THERE IS NO NEED FOR THE FOUR OF YOU TO REMAIN.
I DON'T KNOW. I'D LIKE TO EXPLORE THIS LAND A BIT.
THAT WILL BE FOR ANOTHER TIME.
38

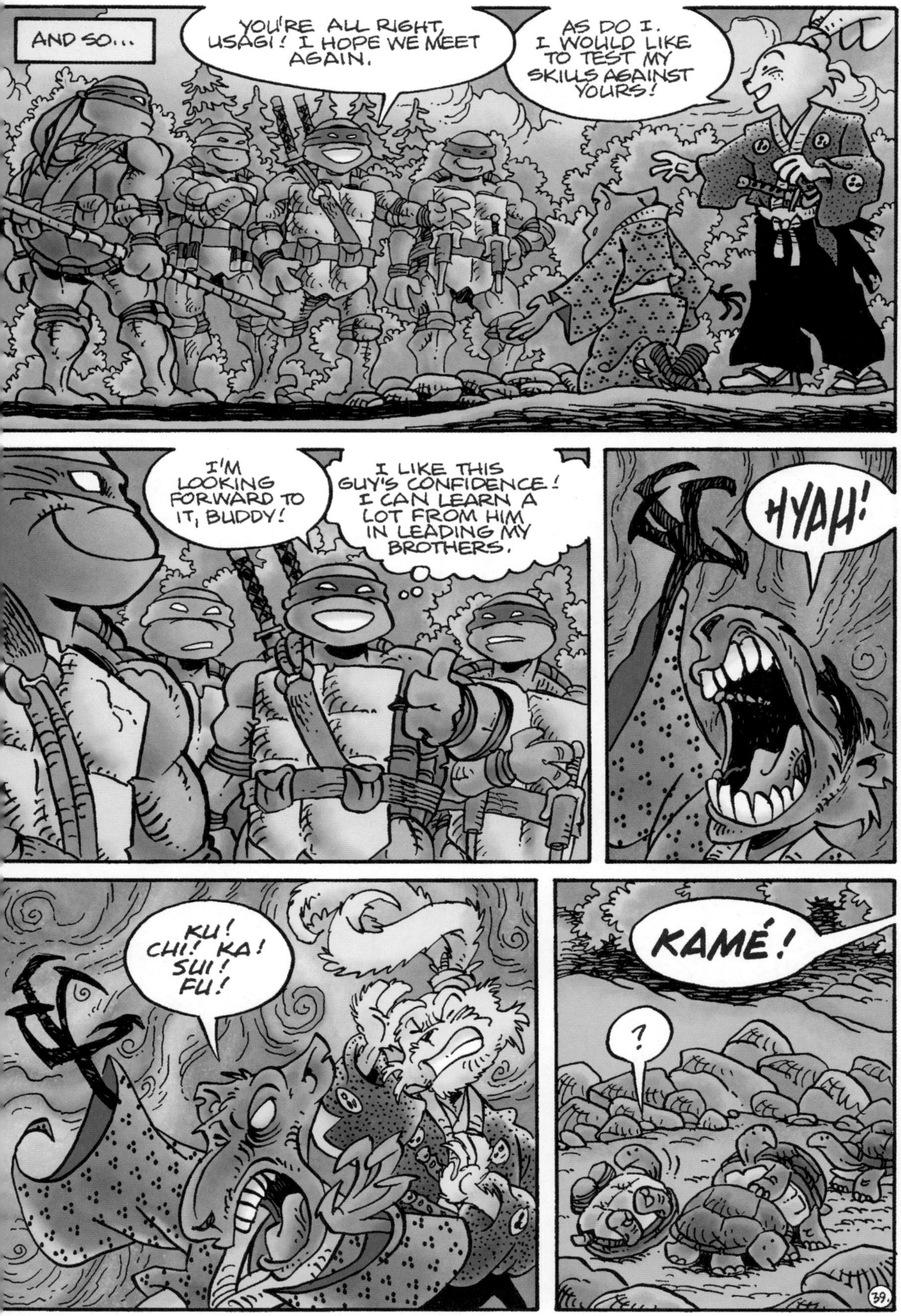
AND SO...
YOU'RE ALL RIGHT, USAGI! I HOPE WE MEET AGAIN.
AS DO I. I WOULD LIKE TO TEST MY SKILLS AGAINST YOURS!
I'M LOOKING FORWARD TO IT, BUDDY!
I LIKE THIS GUY'S CONFIDENCE! I CAN LEARN A LOT FROM HIM IN LEADING MY BROTHERS.
HYAH!
KU! CHI! KA! SUI! FU!
KAMÉ!
?
39.

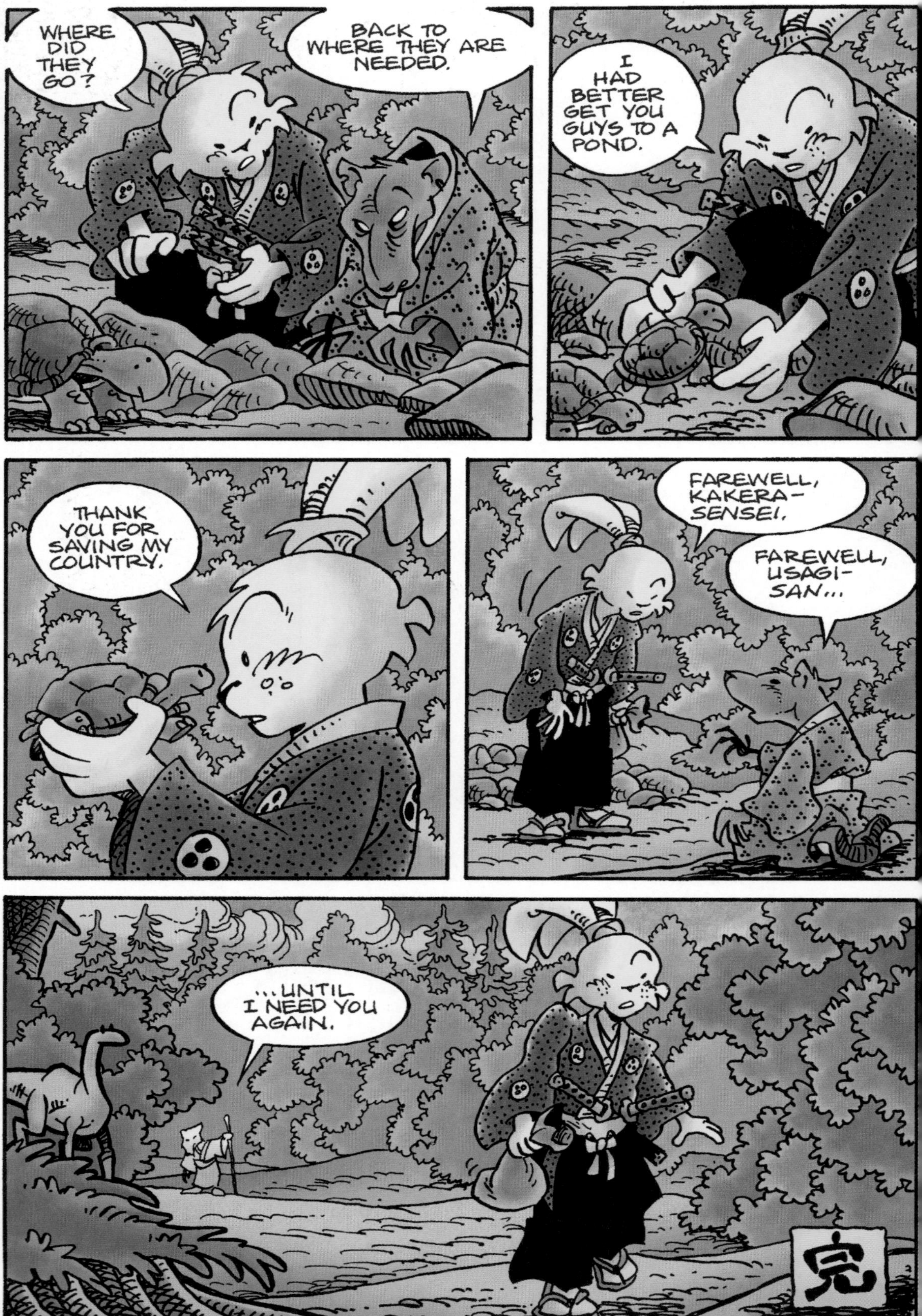
WHERE DID THEY GO?
BACK TO WHERE THEY ARE NEEDED.
I HAD BETTER GET YOU GUYS TO A POND.
THANK YOU FOR SAVING MY COUNTRY.
FAREWELL, KAKERA-SENSEI.
FAREWELL, USAGI-SAN...
...UNTIL I NEED YOU AGAIN.
完

NAMAZU STORY NOTES by Stan Sakai

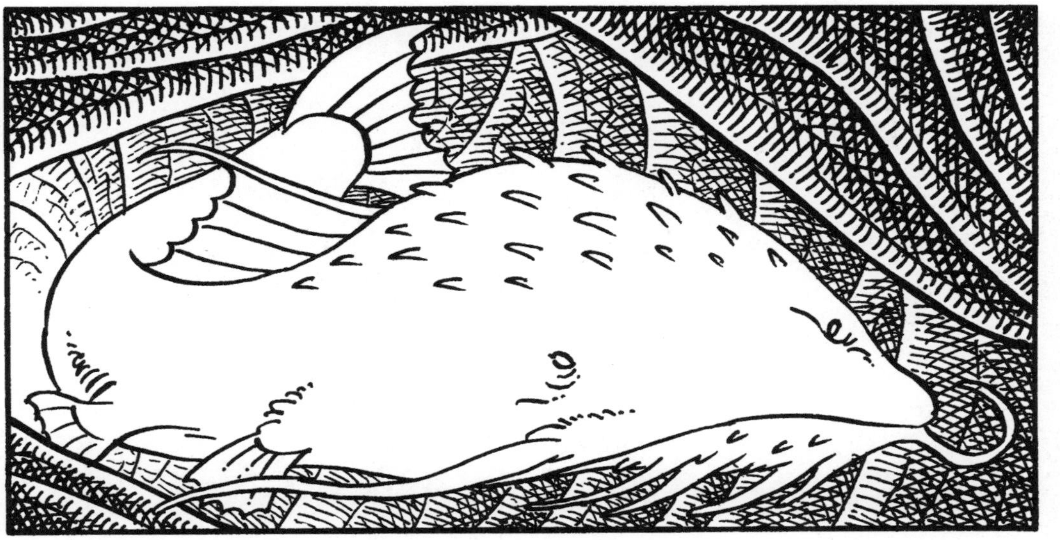

THERE IS A SAYING: "Earthquake, thunder, floods, fire, father—of the five terrors in life, the earthquake is first."

The Japanese islands sit above an area where several continental and oceanic plates meet. The shifting of these plates causes the many earthquakes. The first recorded earthquake occurred in 286 BC, during the fifth year of the reign of Emperor Korei, and legends say that it created Mt. Fuji and Lake Biwa. In 1923 the Great Kanto Earthquake around Tokyo resulted in the deaths of more than one hundred thousand people. On March 11, 2011, the Great East Japan Earthquake, the strongest ever recorded in that nation, killed nearly twenty thousand and caused a nuclear accident at a power plant in Fukushima Prefecture.

A catfish can sense the approach of a tremor and will become more active. Ancient people noticed this activity before a quake and that led them to believe earthquakes were the result of movements by a giant catfish that lives in the mud under the country. The thunder deity Takemikazuchi, also called Kashima-no-kami, trapped the fish under a huge rock, the top of which can be seen on the grounds at Kashima Shrine. He is also noted as being the winner of the very first sumo wrestling match, against a disobedient local deity.

Izanagi, the cocreator of the Japanese islands, beheaded his son Kagutsuchi, the fire deity, after he burned Izanagi's wife to death during childbirth. The blood that dripped from his sword created several gods, including Takemikazuchi.

Kashima Shrine is one of Japan's largest shrines and is located in southeast Ibaraki Prefecture. It was founded during the first year of the reign of Emperor Jimmu, approximately 600 BC. The capstone at Kashima holds down Namazu's head. There is another stone at Katori Shrine in Chiba Prefecture, about eleven miles away, that pins the fish's tail. Just outside Kashima Shrine is a restaurant that dates back to 1897, and which specializes in locally caught catfish.

In another version of the story, it is the god Kadori that subdues the catfish with a magic pumpkin. In some areas Namazu is replaced by a giant eel (Jinshin-Uwo) or a giant bug (Jinshin-Mushi).

A catfish is on pictures of emergency earthquake preparedness programs in Japan, such as the Earthquake Early Warning system.

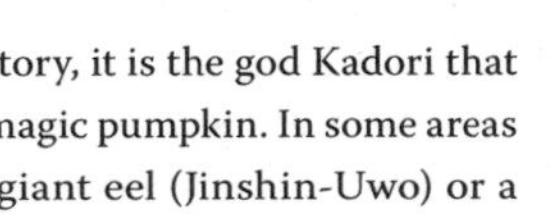
STAN

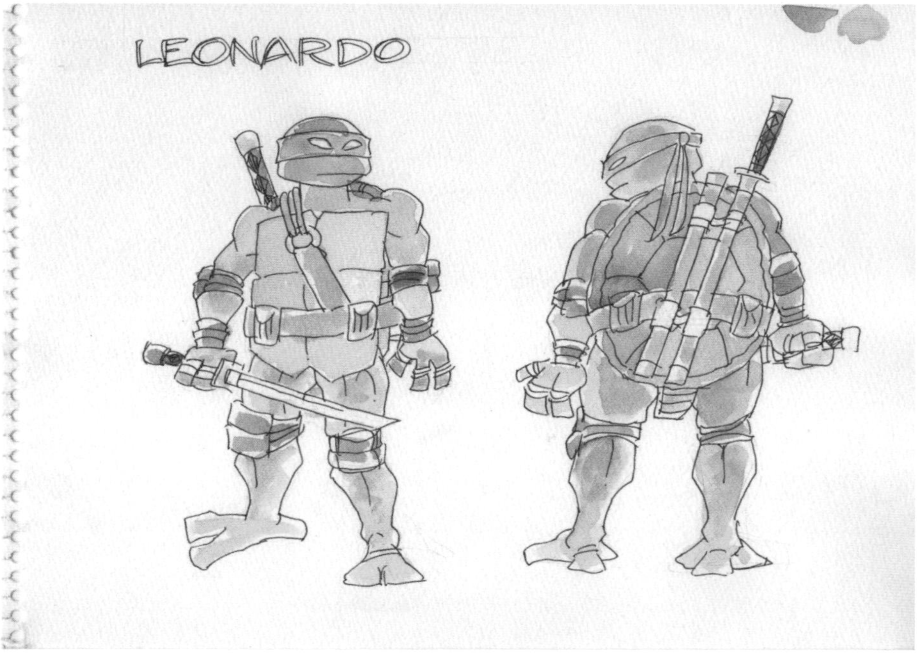
LEONARDO

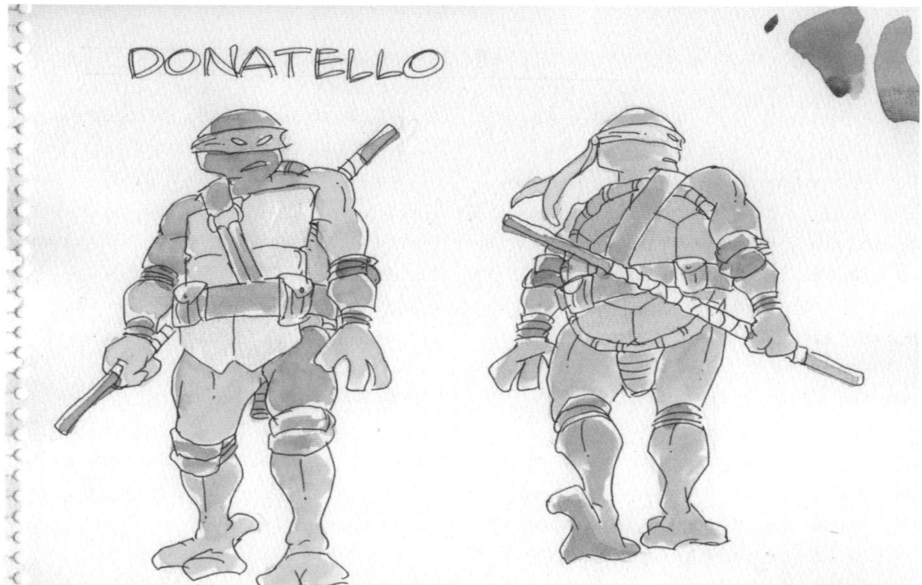
DONATELLO

Character design art for the Turtles by Stan Sakai, created in preparation for "Namazu," in *Teenage Mutant Ninja Turtles/Usagi Yojimbo*.

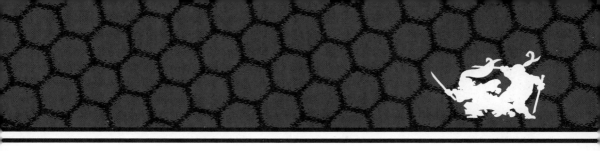

MICHELANGELO

RAPHAEL

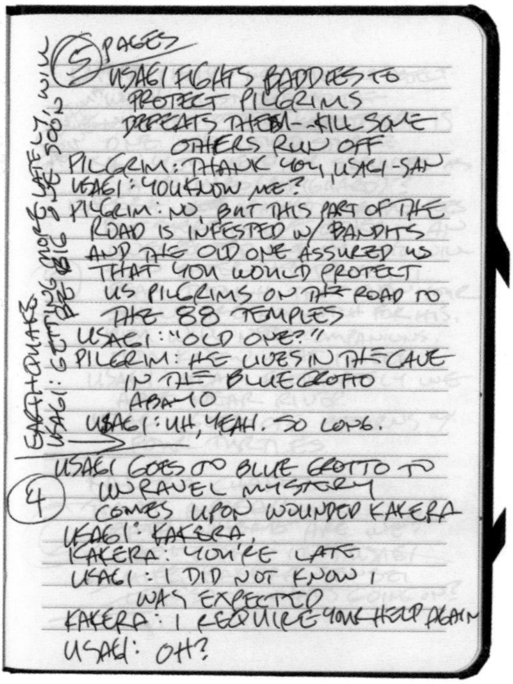

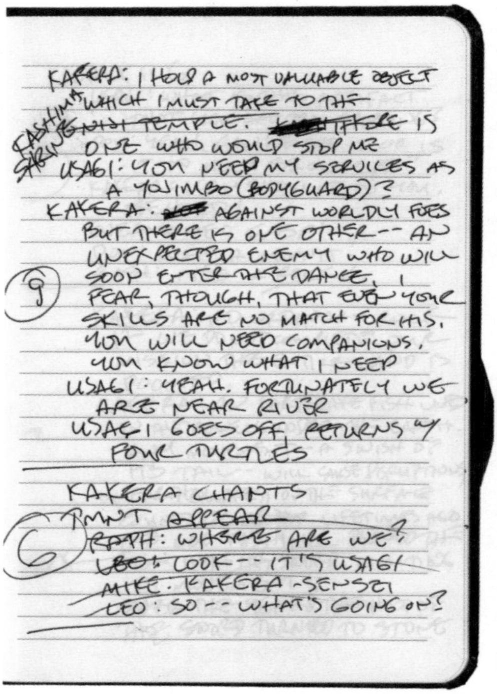

Early story outlines that creator Stan Sakai roughed out in preparation for "Namazu," in *Teenage Mutant Ninja Turtles/Usagi Yojimbo.*

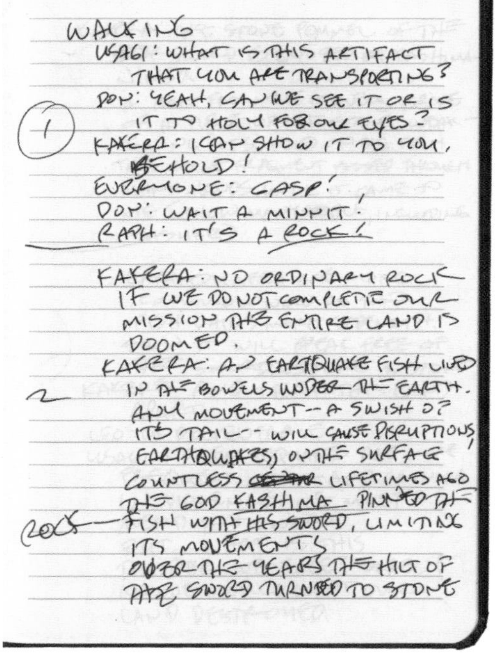

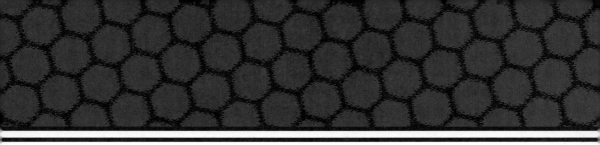

WALKING
USAGI: WHAT IS THIS ARTIFACT THAT YOU ARE TRANSPORTING?
(1)
DON: YEAH, CAN WE SEE IT OR IS IT TO HOLY FOR OUR EYES?
KAKERA: I CAN SHOW IT TO YOU. BEHOLD!
EVERYONE: GASP!
DON: WAIT A MINNIT,
RAPH: IT'S A ROCK!

KAKERA: NO ORDINARY ROCK
IF WE DO NOT COMPLETE OUR MISSION THE ENTIRE LAND IS DOOMED.
KAKERA: AN EARTHQUAKE FISH LIVED IN THE BOWELS ~~UNDER~~ THE EARTH.
2
ANY MOVEMENT -- A SWISH OF ITS TAIL -- WILL CAUSE DISRUPTIONS, EARTHQUAKES, ON THE SURFACE
COUNTLESS ~~[illegible]~~ LIFETIMES AGO THE GOD KASHIMA PINNED THE FISH WITH ~~HIS SWORD~~, LIMITING ITS MOVEMENTS
ROCK
OVER THE YEARS THE HILT OF THE SWORD TURNED TO STONE

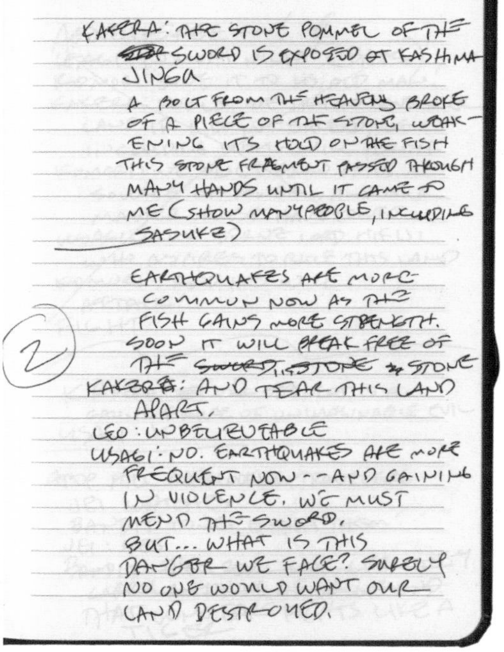

KAKERA: THE STONE POMMEL OF THE ~~[illegible]~~ SWORD IS EXPOSED AT KASHIMA JINGU
A BOLT FROM THE HEAVENS BROKE OF A PIECE OF THE STONE, WEAKENING ITS HOLD ON THE FISH
THIS STONE FRAGMENT PASSED THROUGH MANY HANDS UNTIL IT CAME TO ME (SHOW MANY PEOPLE, INCLUDING SASUKE)

EARTHQUAKES ARE MORE COMMUN NOW AS THE FISH GAINS MORE STRENGTH.
(2)
SOON IT WILL BREAK FREE OF THE ~~SWORD, ITS STONE~~ STONE
KAKERA: AND TEAR THIS LAND APART.
LEO: UNBELIEVEABLE
USAGI: NO. EARTHQUAKES ARE MORE FREQUENT NOW -- AND GAINING IN VIOLENCE. WE MUST MEND THE SWORD.
BUT... WHAT IS THIS DANGER WE FACE? SURELY NO ONE WOULD WANT OUR LAND DESTROYED.

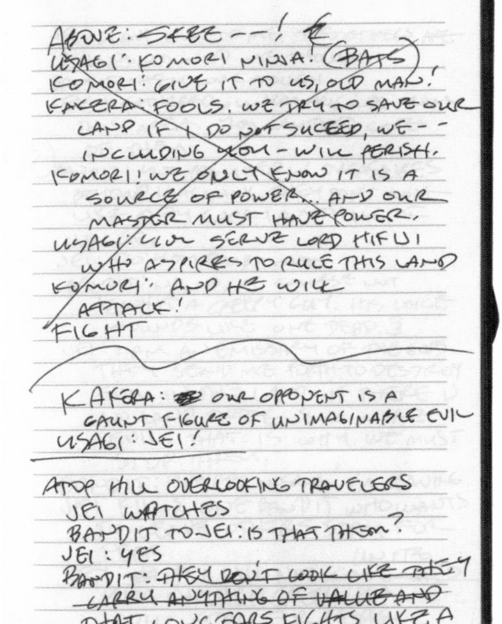

~~ABOVE: SKEE --!~~
~~USAGI: KOMORI NINJA! (BATS)~~
~~KOMORI: GIVE IT TO US, OLD MAN!~~
~~KAKERA: FOOLS. WE TRY TO SAVE OUR LAND IF I DO NOT SUCEED, WE -- INCLUDING YOU - WILL PERISH.~~
~~KOMORI: WE ONLY KNOW IT IS A SOURCE OF POWER... AND OUR MASTER MUST HAVE POWER.~~
~~USAGI: YOU SERVE LORD HIKUJI WHO ASPIRES TO RULE THIS LAND~~
~~KOMORI: AND HE WILL~~
~~ATTACK!~~
FIGHT

KAKERA: ~~[illegible]~~ OUR OPPONENT IS A GAUNT FIGURE OF UNIMAGINABLE EVIL
USAGI: JEI!

ATOP HILL OVERLOOKING TRAVELERS
JEI WATCHES
BANDIT TO JEI: IS THAT THEM?
JEI: YES
BANDIT: ~~THEY DON'T LOOK LIKE THEY CARRY ANYTHING OF VALUE AND~~ THAT LONG EARS FIGHTS LIKE A TIGER

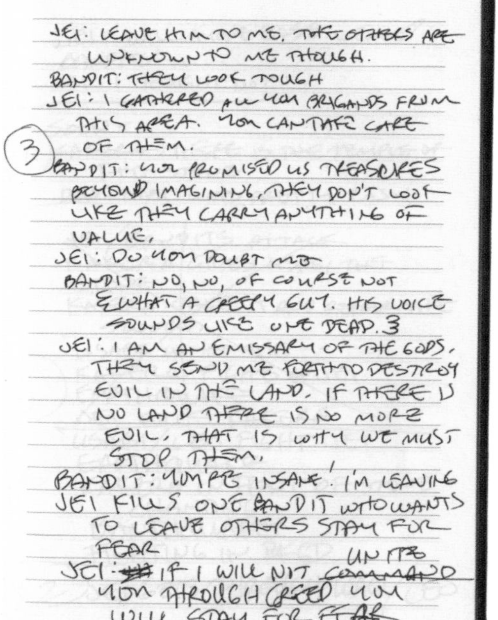

JEI: LEAVE HIM TO ME. THE OTHERS ARE UNKNOWN TO ME THOUGH.
BANDIT: THEY LOOK TOUGH
JEI: I GATHERED ALL YOU BRIGANDS FROM THIS AREA. YOU CAN TAKE CARE OF THEM.
(3)
BANDIT: YOU PROMISED US TREASURES BEYOND IMAGINING, THEY DON'T LOOK LIKE THEY CARRY ANYTHING OF VALUE.
JEI: DO YOU DOUBT ME
BANDIT: NO, NO, OF COURSE NOT
{WHAT A CREEPY GUY. HIS VOICE SOUNDS LIKE ONE DEAD.}
JEI: I AM AN EMISSARY OF THE GODS. THEY SEND ME FORTH TO DESTROY EVIL IN THE LAND. IF THERE IS NO LAND THERE IS NO MORE EVIL. THAT IS WHY WE MUST STOP THEM.
BANDIT: YOU'RE INSANE! I'M LEAVING
JEI KILLS ONE BANDIT WHO WANTS TO LEAVE OTHERS STAY FOR FEAR
JEI: ~~[illegible]~~ IF I WILL NOT ~~COMMAND~~ UNITE YOU THROUGH GREED YOU WILL STAY FOR FEAR

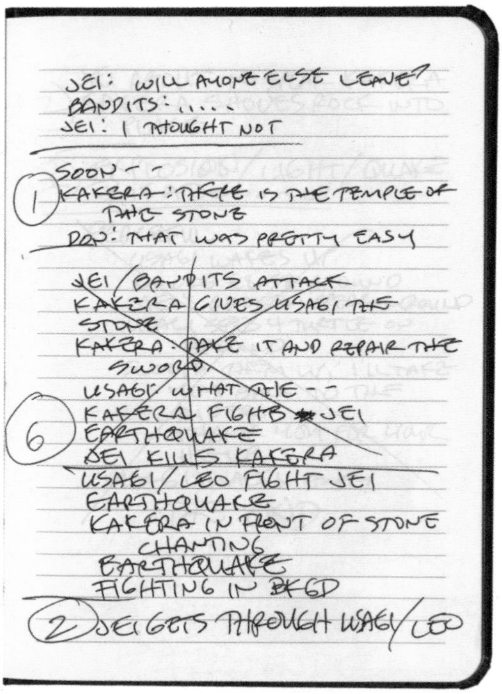

JEI: WILL ANYONE ELSE LEAVE?
BANDITS: .....
JEI: I THOUGHT NOT

SOON--
1 KAKERA: THERE IS THE TEMPLE OF THE STONE
DON: THAT WAS PRETTY EASY

JEI/BANDITS ATTACK
KAKERA GIVES USAGI THE STONE
KAKERA: TAKE IT AND REPAIR THE SWORD
USAGI: WHAT THE--
KAKERA FIGHTS JEI
6 EARTHQUAKE
JEI KILLS KAKERA
USAGI/LEO FIGHT JEI
EARTHQUAKE
KAKERA IN FRONT OF STONE CHANTING
EARTHQUAKE
FIGHTING IN BKGD

2 JEI GETS THROUGH USAGI/LEO

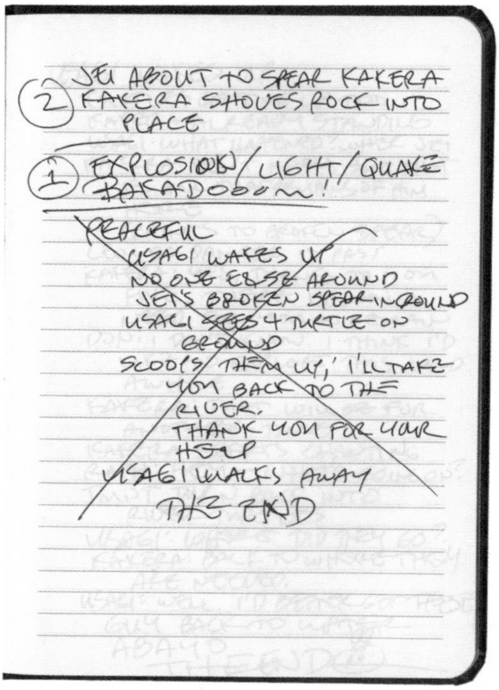

JEI ABOUT TO SPEAR KAKERA
2 KAKERA SHOVES ROCK INTO PLACE

1 EXPLOSION/LIGHT/QUAKE
BAKADOOOM!

PEACEFUL
USAGI WAKES UP
NO ONE ELSE AROUND
JEI'S BROKEN SPEAR IN GROUND
USAGI SEES 4 TURTLE ON GROUND
SCOOPS THEM UP, 'I'LL TAKE YOU BACK TO THE RIVER.
THANK YOU FOR YOUR HELP
USAGI WALKS AWAY
THE END

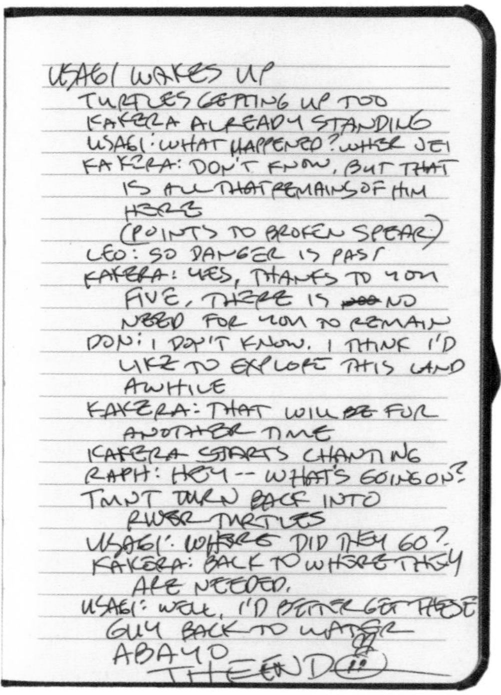

USAGI WAKES UP
TURTLES GETTING UP TOO
KAKERA ALREADY STANDING
USAGI: WHAT HAPPENED? WHERE JEI
KAKERA: DON'T KNOW, BUT THAT IS ALL THAT REMAINS OF HIM HERE
(POINTS TO BROKEN SPEAR)
LEO: SO DANGER IS PAST
KAKERA: YES, THANKS TO YOU FIVE, THERE IS NO NEED FOR YOU TO REMAIN
DON: I DON'T KNOW. I THINK I'D LIKE TO EXPLORE THIS LAND AWHILE
KAKERA: THAT WILL BE FOR ANOTHER TIME
KAKERA STARTS CHANTING
RAPH: HEY -- WHAT'S GOING ON?
TMNT TURN BACK INTO RIVER TURTLES
USAGI: WHERE DID THEY GO?
KAKERA: BACK TO WHERE THEY ARE NEEDED.
USAGI: WELL, I'D BETTER GET THESE GUY BACK TO WATER
ABAYO
THE END

TMNT/USAGI 40page crossover
-1-
UGH!
1
ARR--!
GYAH!
YAK!
2
NAMAZU
OR THE BIG FISH STORY
3
YAHH! RUN AWAY!
THANK YOU, USAGI-SAN! THANK YOU!
EH?
TMNT/USAGI
-2-
DO I KNOW YOU?
4
NO, THIS PART OF THE ROAD IS INFESTED WITH BANDITS...
BUT THE OLD ONE ASSURED US THAT WOULD PROTECT US ON OUR PILGRIMAGE TO THE 88 SHRINES.
"THE OLD ONE?"
HE IS AWAITING YOU IN THE CAVE
IN THE BLUE GROTTO
HE'S WAITING FOR ME, HUH? WELL THIS IS A INTRIGUING TO BE IGNORED.
SOON...
5
EH--?
RUMMMBLLL--...
EARTHQUAKE!
RUMBLLL.....
6
PHEW! IT'S ENDING.
IT WASN'T A BIG ONE BUT THERE HAVE BEEN MORE EARTHQUAKES LATELY.
THAT MUST BE THE CAVE.
HELLO, USAGI
KAKERA-SENSEI!
7
YOU'RE LATE
I DID NOT KNOW I WAS EXPECTED.
I REQUIRE YOUR HELP ONCE AGAIN.
OH?
I CARRY A MOST VALUABLE OBJECT WHICH I MUST TRANSPORT TO KASHIMA SHRINE
BUT THERE IS ONE WHO KNOWS OF MY MISSION AND WOULD STOP ME.
SO YOU NEED A YOJIMBO.
* BODYGUARD.

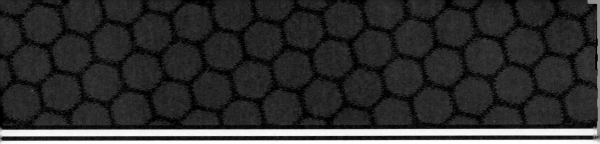

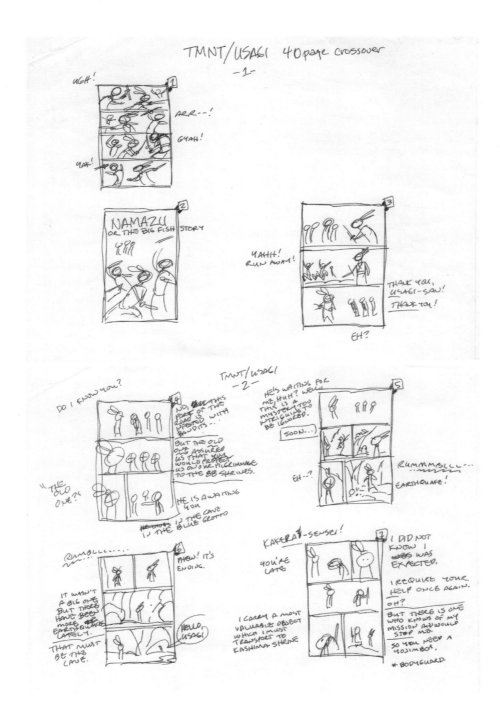

Thumbnail layouts Stan Sakai created in preparation for "Namazu," in *Teenage Mutant Ninja Turtles/Usagi Yojimbo.*

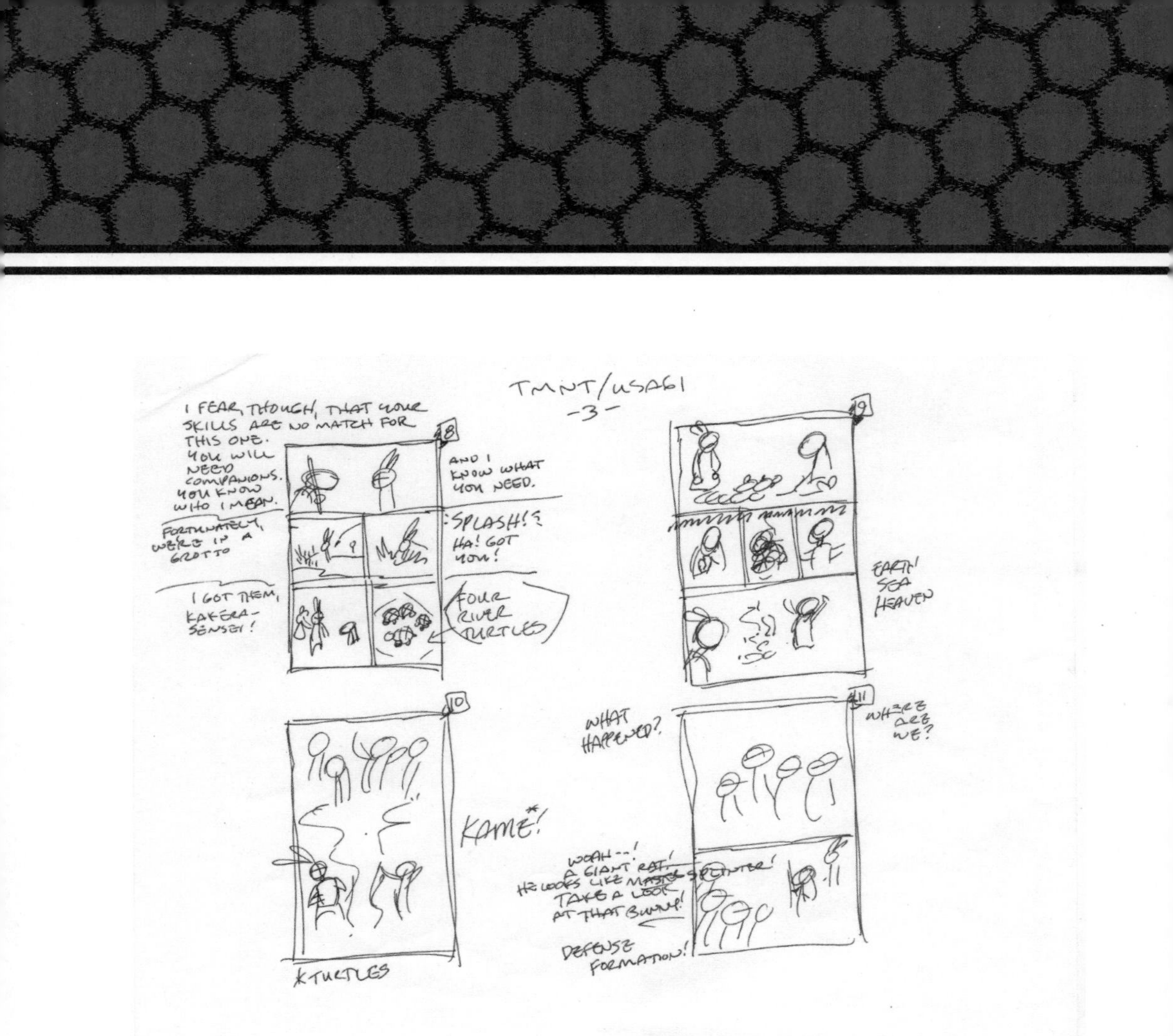
TMNT/USAGI
-3-
I FEAR, THOUGH, THAT YOUR SKILLS ARE NO MATCH FOR THIS ONE. YOU WILL NEED COMPANIONS. YOU KNOW WHO I MEAN.
AND I KNOW WHAT YOU NEED.
FORTUNATELY, WE'RE IN A GROTTO
SPLASH!
HA! GOT YOU!
I GOT THEM, KAKERA-SENSEI!
FOUR RIVER TURTLES
EARTH SEA HEAVEN
KAME!*
*TURTLES
WHAT HAPPENED?
WHERE ARE WE?
WOAH--! A GIANT RAT!
HE LOOKS LIKE MASTER SPLINTER!
TAKE A LOOK AT THAT BUNNY!
DEFENSE FORMATION!

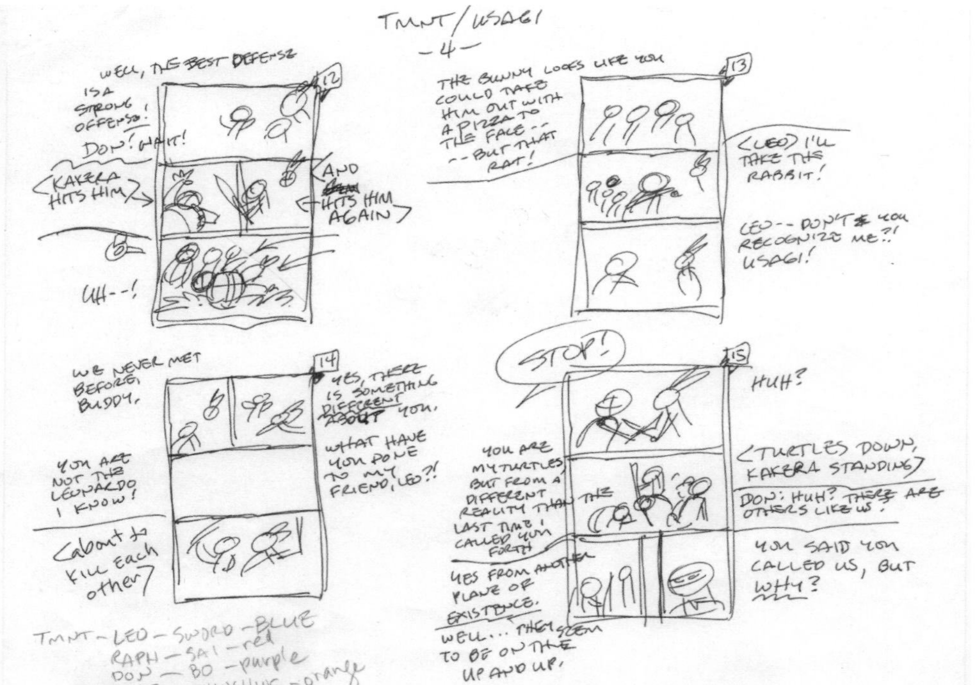
TMNT/USAGI
-4-
WELL, THE BEST DEFENSE IS A STRONG OFFENSE!
DON! WAIT!
<KAKERA HITS HIM>
<AND HITS HIM AGAIN>
UH--!
THE BUNNY LOOKS LIKE YOU COULD TAKE HIM OUT WITH A PIZZA TO THE FACE -- --BUT THAT RAT!
<LEO> I'LL TAKE THE RABBIT!
LEO-- DON'T YOU RECOGNIZE ME?! USAGI!
WE NEVER MET BEFORE, BUDDY.
YES, THERE IS SOMETHING DIFFERENT ABOUT YOU.
WHAT HAVE YOU DONE TO MY FRIEND, LEO?!
YOU ARE NOT THE LEONARDO I KNOW!
<about to kill each other>
STOP!
HUH?
YOU ARE MY TURTLES BUT FROM A DIFFERENT REALITY THAN THE LAST TIME I CALLED YOU FORTH
<TURTLES DOWN, KAKERA STANDING>
DON: HUH? THERE ARE OTHERS LIKE US!
YOU SAID YOU CALLED US, BUT WHY?
YES FROM ANOTHER PLANE OF EXISTENCE.
WELL... THEY SEEM TO BE ON THE UP AND UP.
TMNT - LEO - SWORD - BLUE
RAPH - SAI - red
DON - BO - purple
MIKE - NUNCHUK - orange

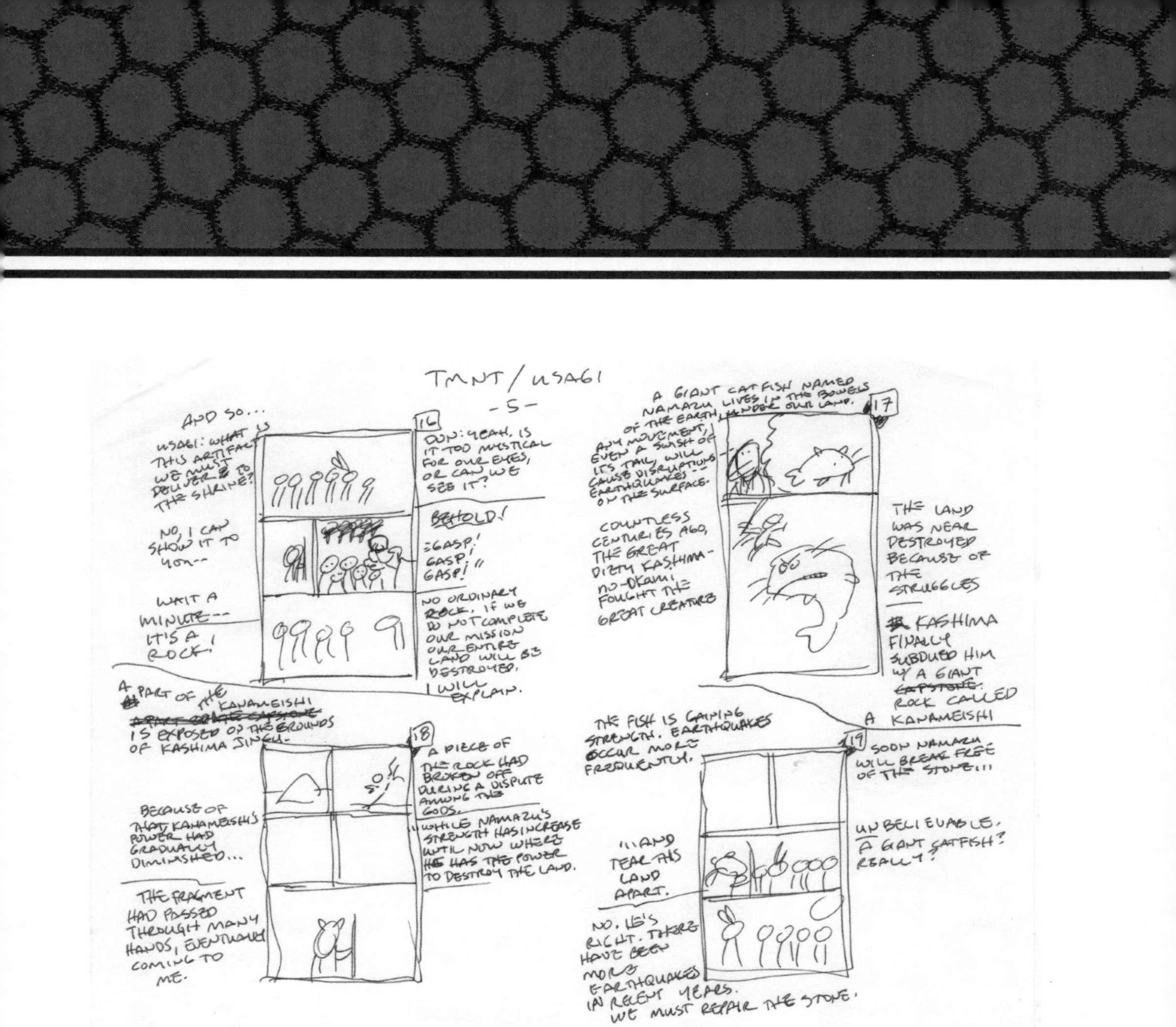
TMNT / USAGI
-5-
AND SO...
USAGI: WHAT IS THIS ARTIFACT WE MUST DELIVER TO THE SHRINE?
16
DON: YEAH, IS IT TOO MYSTICAL FOR OUR EYES, OR CAN WE SEE IT?
NO, I CAN SHOW IT TO YOU--
BEHOLD!
=GASP! GASP! GASP!=
WAIT A MINUTE-- IT'S A ROCK!
NO ORDINARY ROCK. IF WE DO NOT COMPLETE OUR MISSION OUR ENTIRE LAND WILL BE DESTROYED.
I WILL EXPLAIN.
A GIANT CATFISH NAMED NAMAZU LIVES IN THE BOWELS OF THE EARTH UNDER OUR LAND.
17
ANY MOVEMENT, EVEN A SWISH OF ITS TAIL, WILL CAUSE DISRUPTIONS -- EARTHQUAKES -- ON THE SURFACE.
COUNTLESS CENTURIES AGO, THE GREAT DIETY KASHIMA-NO-OKAMI FOUGHT THE GREAT CREATURE
THE LAND WAS NEAR DESTROYED BECAUSE OF THE STRUGGLES
KASHIMA FINALLY SUBDUED HIM W/ A GIANT CAPSTONE ROCK CALLED A KANAMEISHI
A PART OF THE KANAMEISHI IS EXPOSED ON THE GROUNDS OF KASHIMA JINGU.
18
A PIECE OF THE ROCK HAD BROKEN OFF DURING A DISPUTE AMONG THE GODS.
BECAUSE OF THAT, KANAMEISHI'S POWER HAD GRADUALLY DIMINISHED...
WHILE NAMAZU'S STRENGTH HAS INCREASE UNTIL NOW WHERE HE HAS THE POWER TO DESTROY THE LAND.
THE FRAGMENT HAD PASSED THROUGH MANY HANDS, EVENTUALLY COMING TO ME.
THE FISH IS GAINING STRENGTH. EARTHQUAKES OCCUR MORE FREQUENTLY.
19
SOON NAMAZU WILL BREAK FREE OF THE STONE...
...AND TEAR THIS LAND APART.
UNBELIEVABLE. A GIANT CATFISH? REALLY?
NO. HE'S RIGHT. THERE HAVE BEEN MORE EARTHQUAKES IN RECENT YEARS.
WE MUST REPAIR THE STONE.

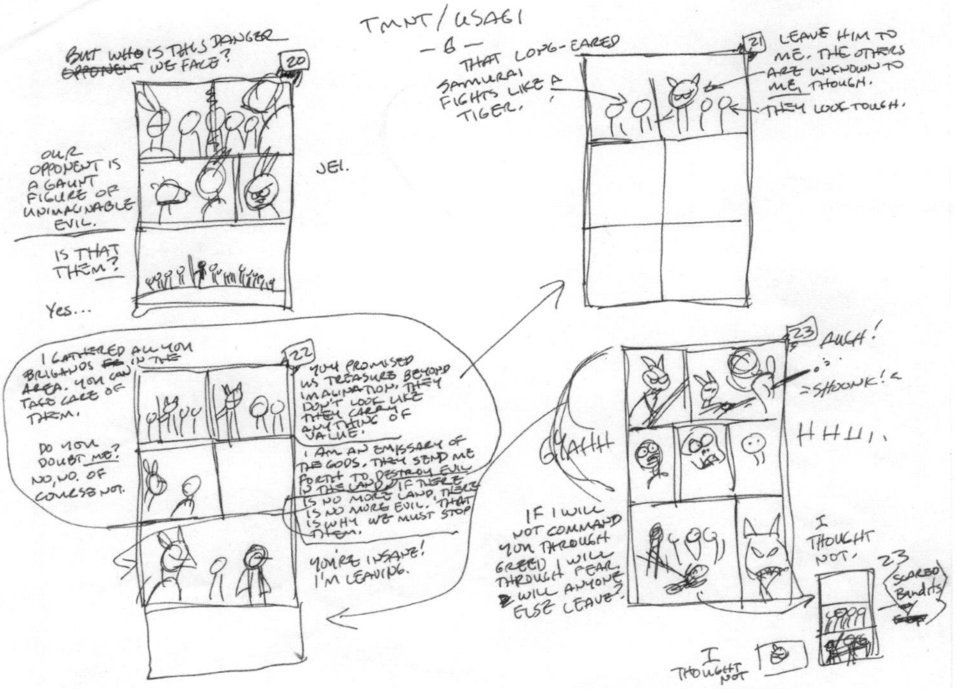
TMNT / USAGI
-6-
BUT WHO IS THIS DANGER OPPONENT WE FACE?
20
OUR OPPONENT IS A GAUNT FIGURE OF UNIMAGINABLE EVIL.
JEI.
IS THAT THEM?
YES...
THAT LONG-EARED SAMURAI FIGHTS LIKE A TIGER.
21
LEAVE HIM TO ME. THE OTHERS ARE UNKNOWN TO ME, THOUGH.
THEY LOOK TOUGH.
I GATHERED ALL YOU BRIGANDS IN THE AREA. YOU CAN TAKE CARE OF THEM.
22
YOU PROMISED US TREASURE BEYOND IMAGINATION. THEY DON'T LOOK LIKE THEY CARRY ANYTHING OF VALUE.
DO YOU DOUBT ME?
NO, NO. OF COURSE NOT.
I AM AN EMISSARY OF THE GODS. THEY SEND ME FORTH TO DESTROY EVIL IN THE LAND. IF THERE IS NO MORE LAND, THERE IS NO MORE EVIL. THAT IS WHY WE MUST STOP THEM.
YOU'RE INSANE! I'M LEAVING.
23
AUGH!
=SHOONK!=
HHH!!
GYAHH
IF I WILL NOT COMMAND YOU THROUGH GREED I WILL THROUGH FEAR. WILL ANYONE ELSE LEAVE?
I THOUGHT NOT.
23
SCARED Bandits
I THOUGHT NOT

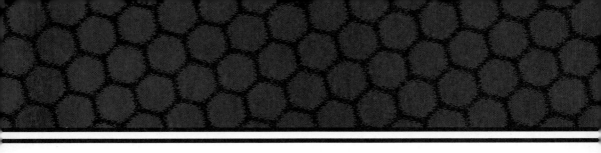

TMNT / USAGI
-7-

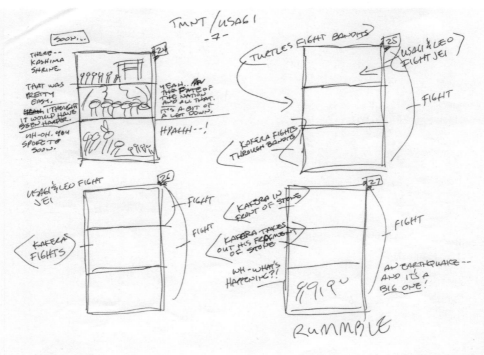

SOON,...

THERE -- KASHIMA SHRINE.

THAT WAS PRETTY EASY.

YEAH, I THOUGHT IT WOULD HAVE BEEN HARDER.

UH-OH. YOU SPOKE TOO SOON.

YEAH.. AN THE FATE OF THE NATION AND ALL THAT. IT'S A BIT OF A LET DOWN.

HYAHH--!

TURTLES FIGHT BANDITS

USAGI & LEO FIGHT JEI

FIGHT

KAFFLA FIGHTS THROUGH BANDITS

USAGI & LEO FIGHT JEI

FIGHT

FIGHT

KAFFLA FIGHTS

KAFFLA IN FRONT OF STONE

KAFFLA TAKES OUT HIS FRAGMENT OF STONE

WH--WHAT'S HAPPENING?!

FIGHT

AN EARTHQUAKE -- AND IT'S A BIG ONE!

RUMMBLE

TMNT / USAGI
-8-

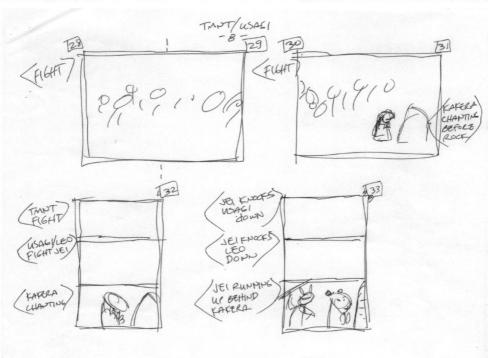

FIGHT

FIGHT

KAFFLA CHANTING BEFORE ROCK

TMNT FIGHT

USAGI/LEO FIGHT JEI

KAFFLA CHANTING

JEI KNOCKS USAGI DOWN

JEI KNOCKS LEO DOWN

JEI RUNNING UP BEHIND KAFFLA

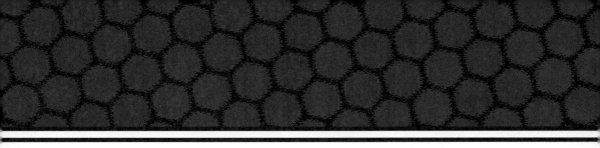

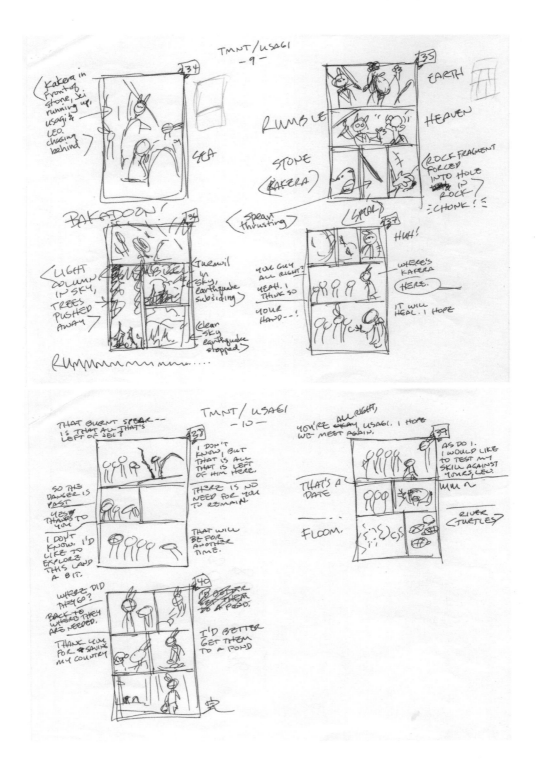

TMNT/USAGI
-9-

[34] Kakera in front of stone, Jei running up, Usagi & Leo chasing behind

SEA

RUMBLE

EARTH [35]

HEAVEN

STONE (KAKERA)

ROCK FRAGMENT FORCED INTO HOLE IN ROCK :CHONK!:

BAKADOON! [36]

LIGHT COLUMN IN SKY, TREES PUSHED AWAY

Turmoil in sky, earthquake subsiding

clear sky earthquake stopped

Spear thrusting

(SPEAR) [37] HUH!

YOU GUY ALL RIGHT? YEAH. I THINK SO

YOUR HAND--!

WHERE'S KAFERA HERE.

IT WILL HEAL. I HOPE

RUMMMMMMM mm mm......

TMNT/USAGI
-10-

THAT BURNT SPEAR-- IS THAT ALL THAT'S LEFT OF JEI? [38]

I DON'T KNOW, BUT THAT IS ALL THAT IS LEFT OF HIM HERE.

SO THE DANGER IS PAST

YES, THANKS TO YOU

THERE IS NO NEED FOR YOU TO REMAIN.

I DON'T KNOW, I'D LIKE TO EXPLORE THIS LAND A BIT.

THAT WILL BE FOR ANOTHER TIME.

WHERE DID THEY GO? [40]

BACK TO WHERE THEY ARE NEEDED.

THANK YOU FOR SAVING MY COUNTRY

I'D BETTER GET THEM TO A POND.

I'D BETTER GET THEM TO A POND

YOU'RE ALL RIGHT, USAGI. I HOPE WE MEET AGAIN.

AS DO I. I WOULD LIKE TO TEST MY SKILL AGAINST YOURS, LEO. [39]

THAT'S A DATE

MMM

FLOOM.

RIVER TURTLES

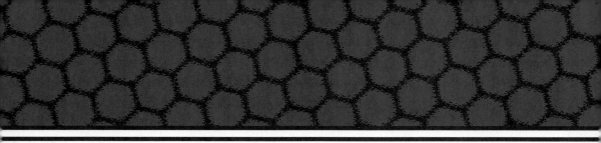

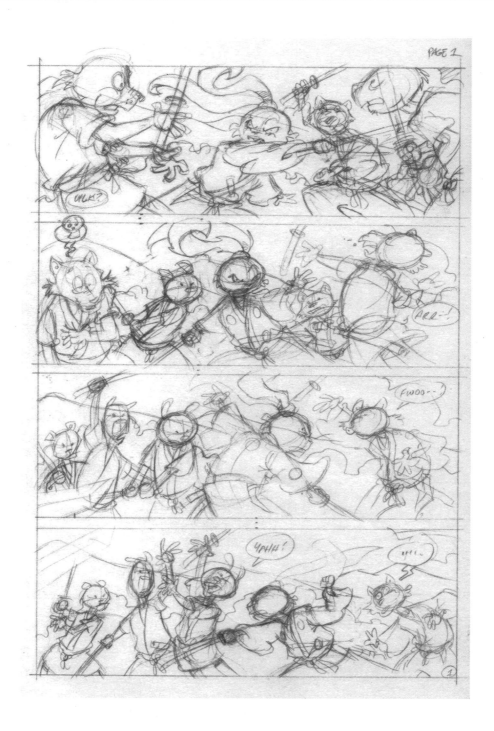

Pencils and inks by Stan Sakai for "Namazu," in *Teenage Mutant Ninja Turtles/Usagi Yojimbo*.

TMNT/USAGI YOJIMBO NAMAZU PAGE 1

ULK?
ARR--!
FWOOK!
YAHH!
.....

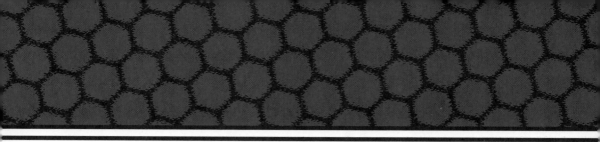

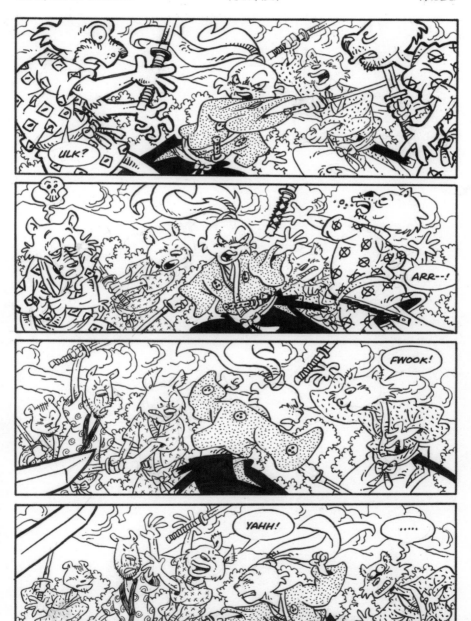

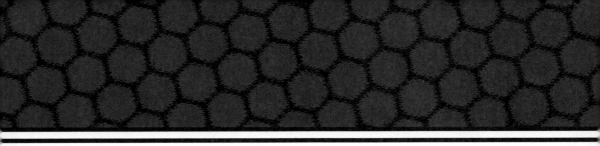

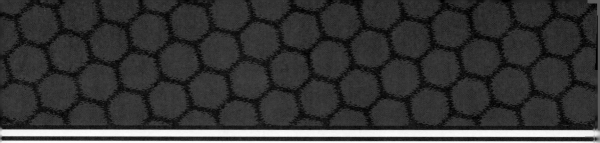

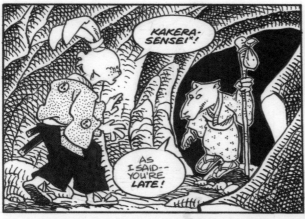

TMNT/USAGI YOJIMBO
NAMAZU
PAGE 7
KAKERA-SENSEI*!
AS I SAID-- YOU'RE LATE!
I DID NOT KNOW I WAS EXPECTED.
I REQUIRE YOUR HELP ONCE AGAIN, USAGI.
OH?
I CARRY A MOST VALUABLE OBJECT, WHICH I MUST DELIVER TO TASHIMA SHRINE.
BUT THERE IS ONE WHO KNOWS OF MY MISSION AND WOULD STOP ME!
SO YOU REQUIRE A YOJIMBO**!
7.
*UY SAGA #1 'SHADES of GREEN'
** BODYGUARD.

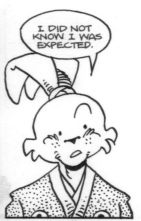

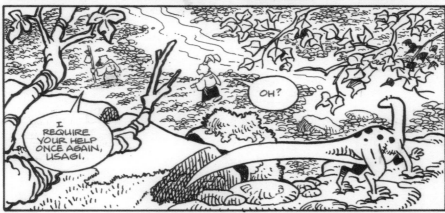

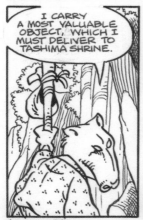

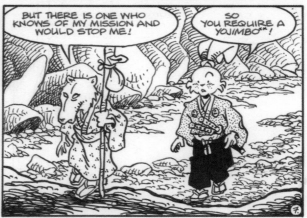

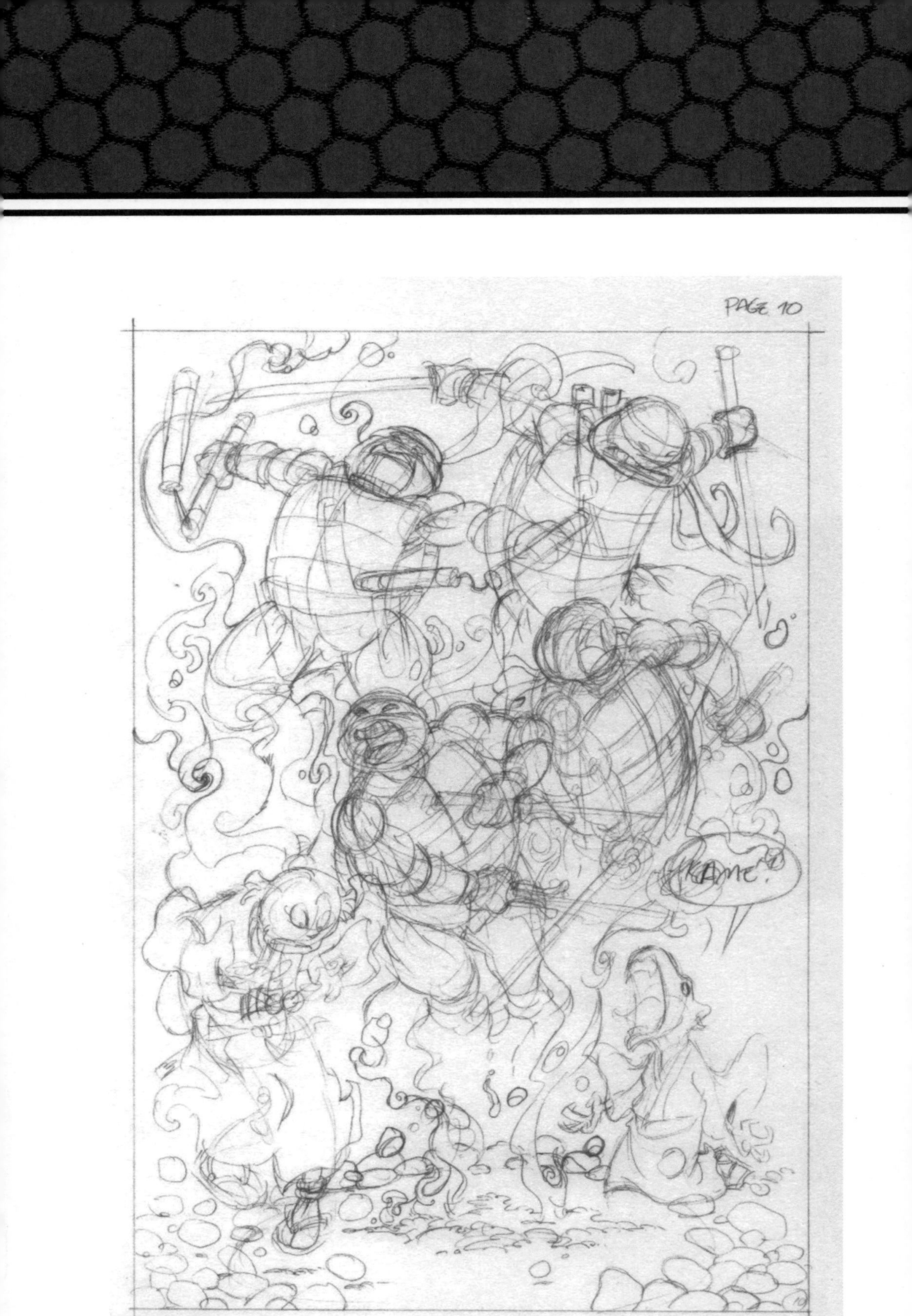
PAGE 10
KAME!
*TURTLES

TMNT/ USAGI YOJIMBO NAMAZU PAGE 10

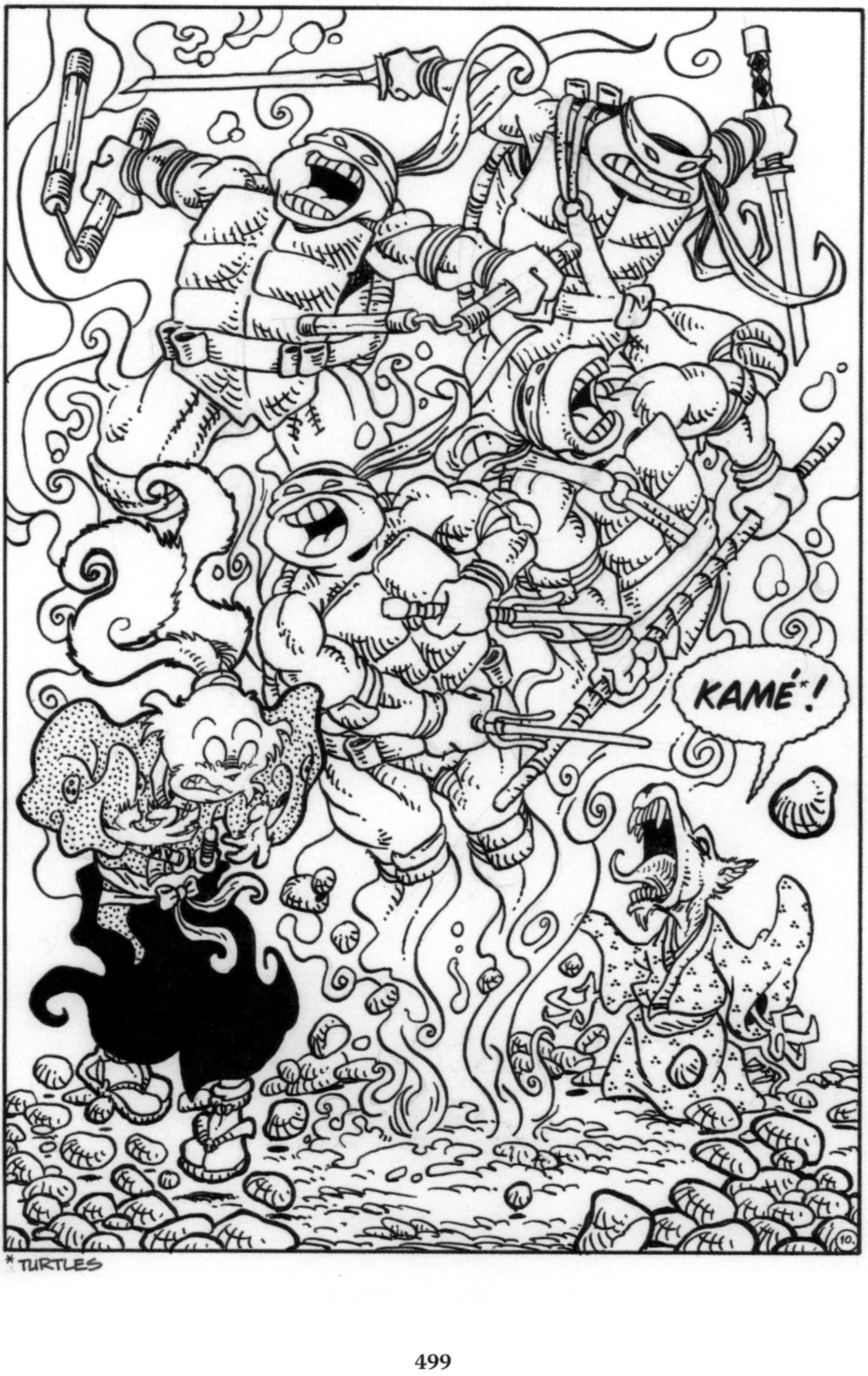
KAME*!
10.

*TURTLES

PAGE 11
<WHERE ARE WE?!>
<WHAT'S GOING ON?>
<WOAH--! A GIANT RAT?>
<HE LOOKS LIKE SPLINTER!>
<TAKE A LOOK AT THAT BUNNY!>
<DEFENSE POSITIONS!>
WHAT ARE THEY SAYING?
11

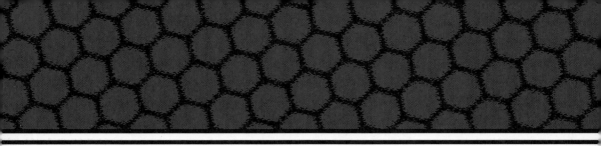

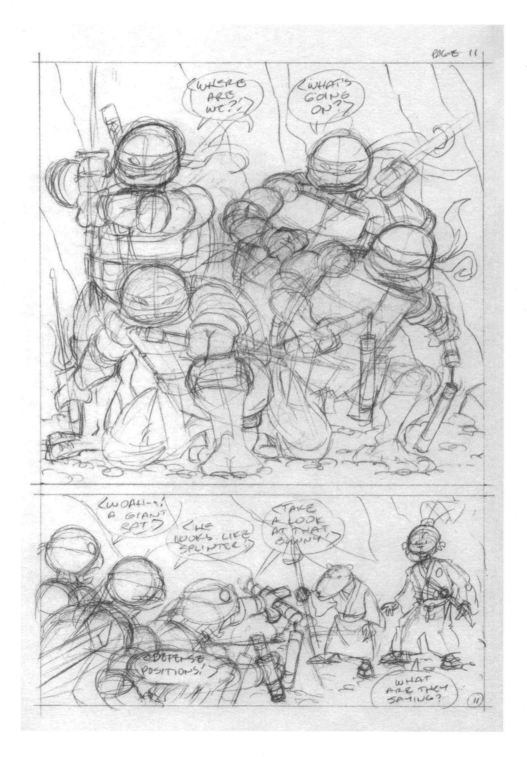

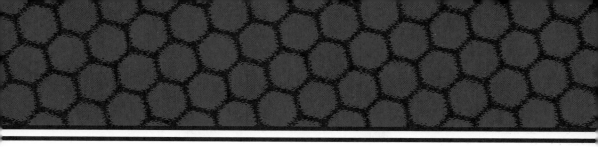

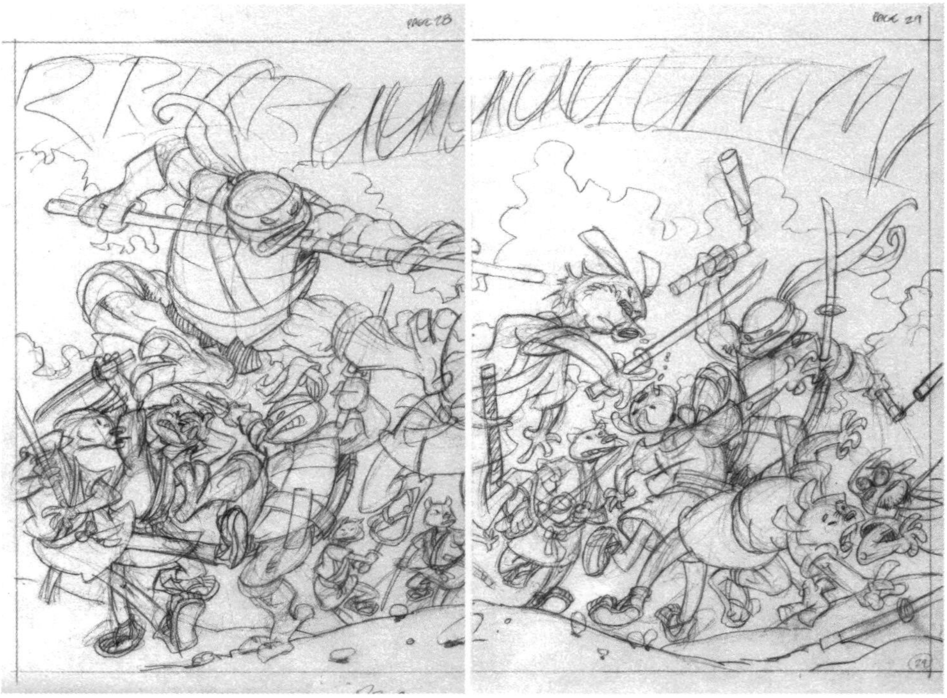

PAGE 28
PAGE 29

TMNT/USAGI YOJIMBO NAMAZU PAGE 28 TMNT/USAGI YOJIMBO NAMAZU PAGE 29

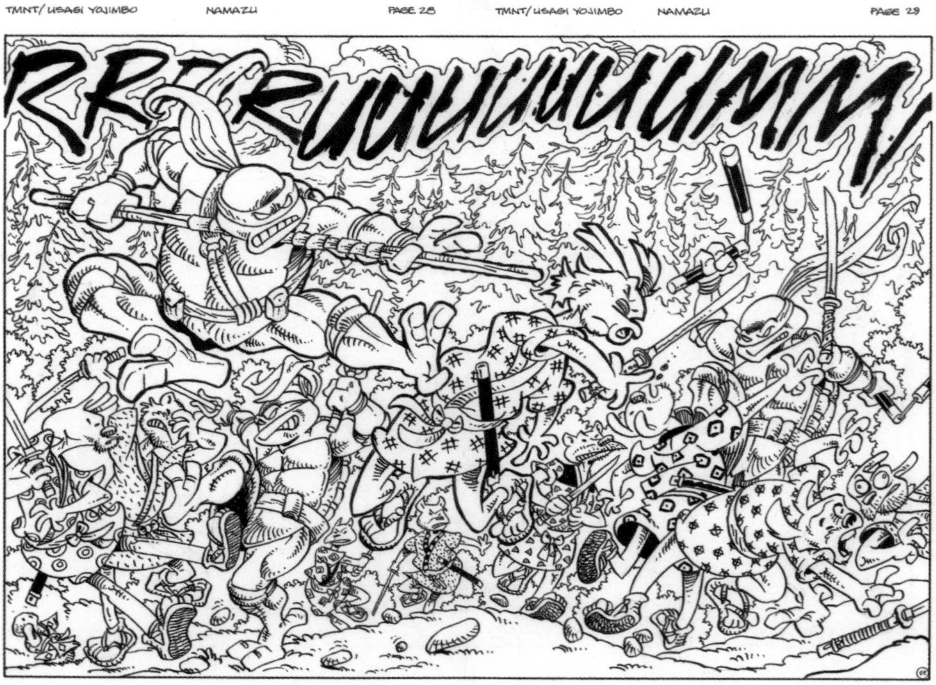

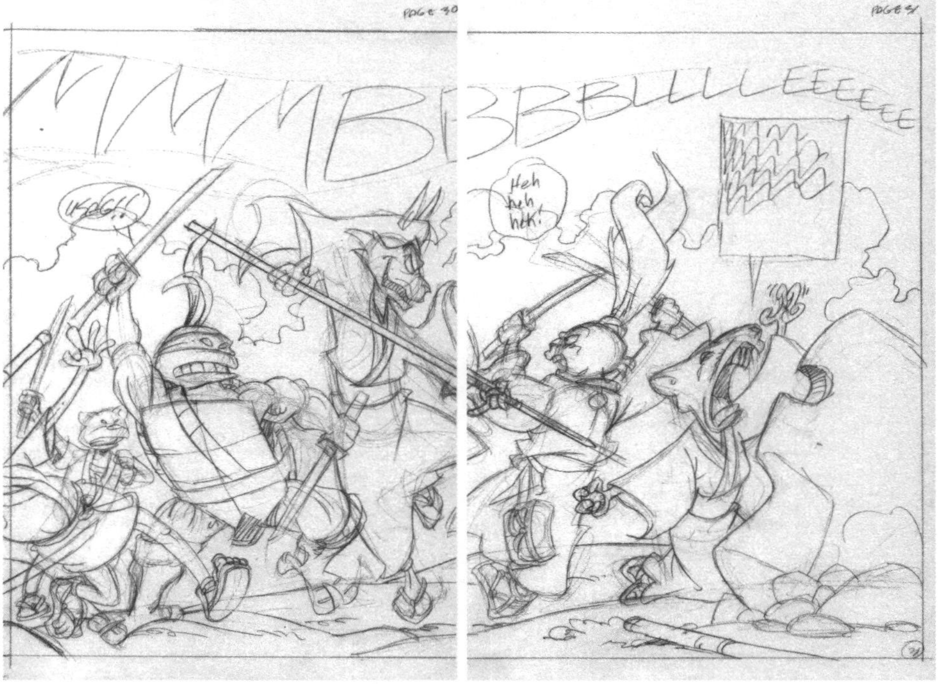
PAGE 30
PAGE 31
USAGI!

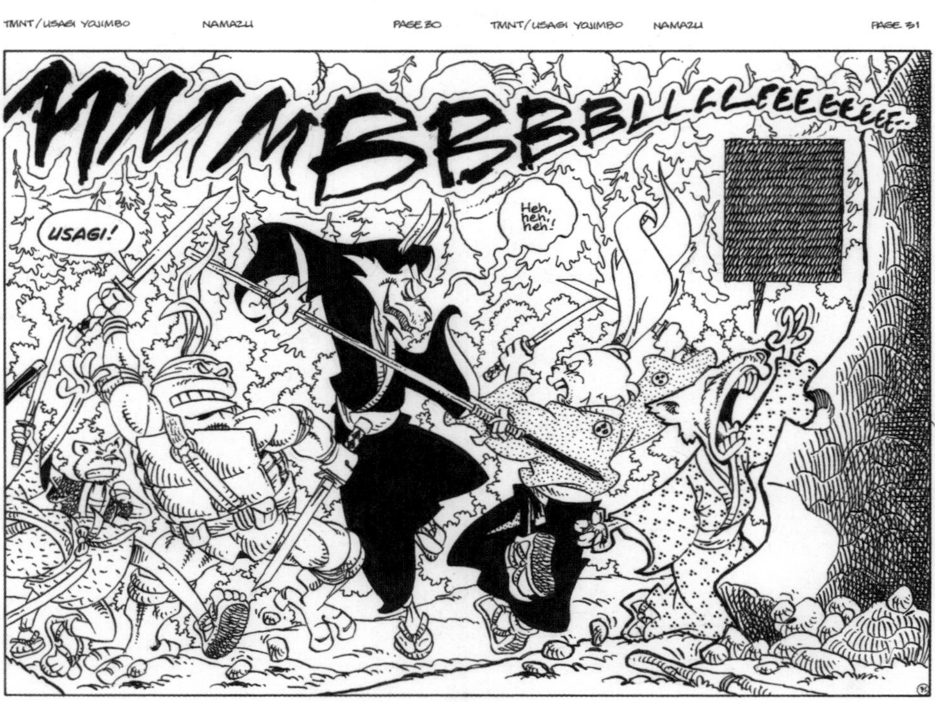
TMNT/USAGI YOJIMBO
NAMAZU
PAGE 30
TMNT/USAGI YOJIMBO
NAMAZU
PAGE 31
USAGI!
Heh, heh, heh!

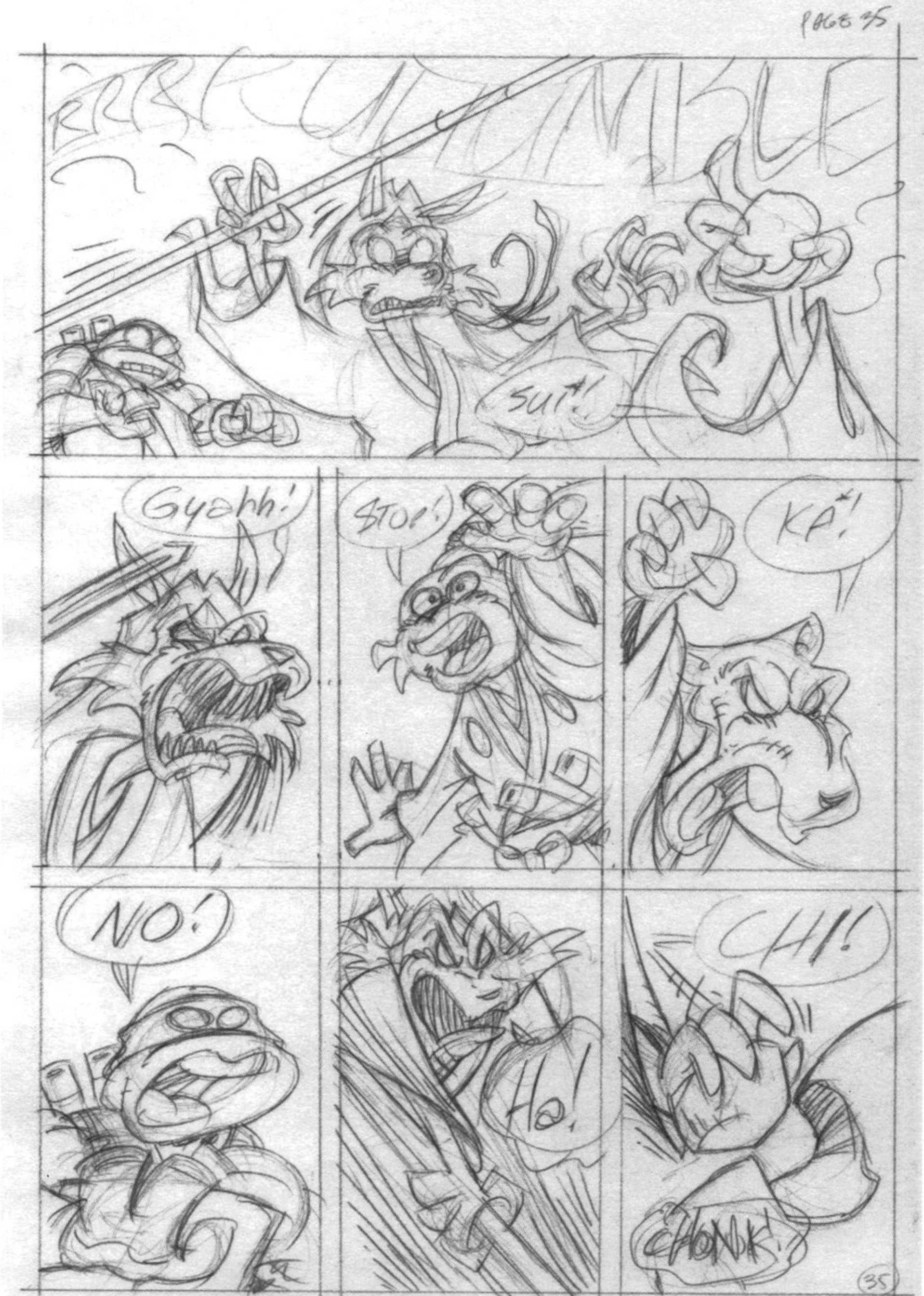
PAGE 35
RRRRUMBLE
SUI*!
Gyahh!
STOP!
KA**!
NO!
Ha!
CHI!
CHONK!
35
*WATER **FIRE

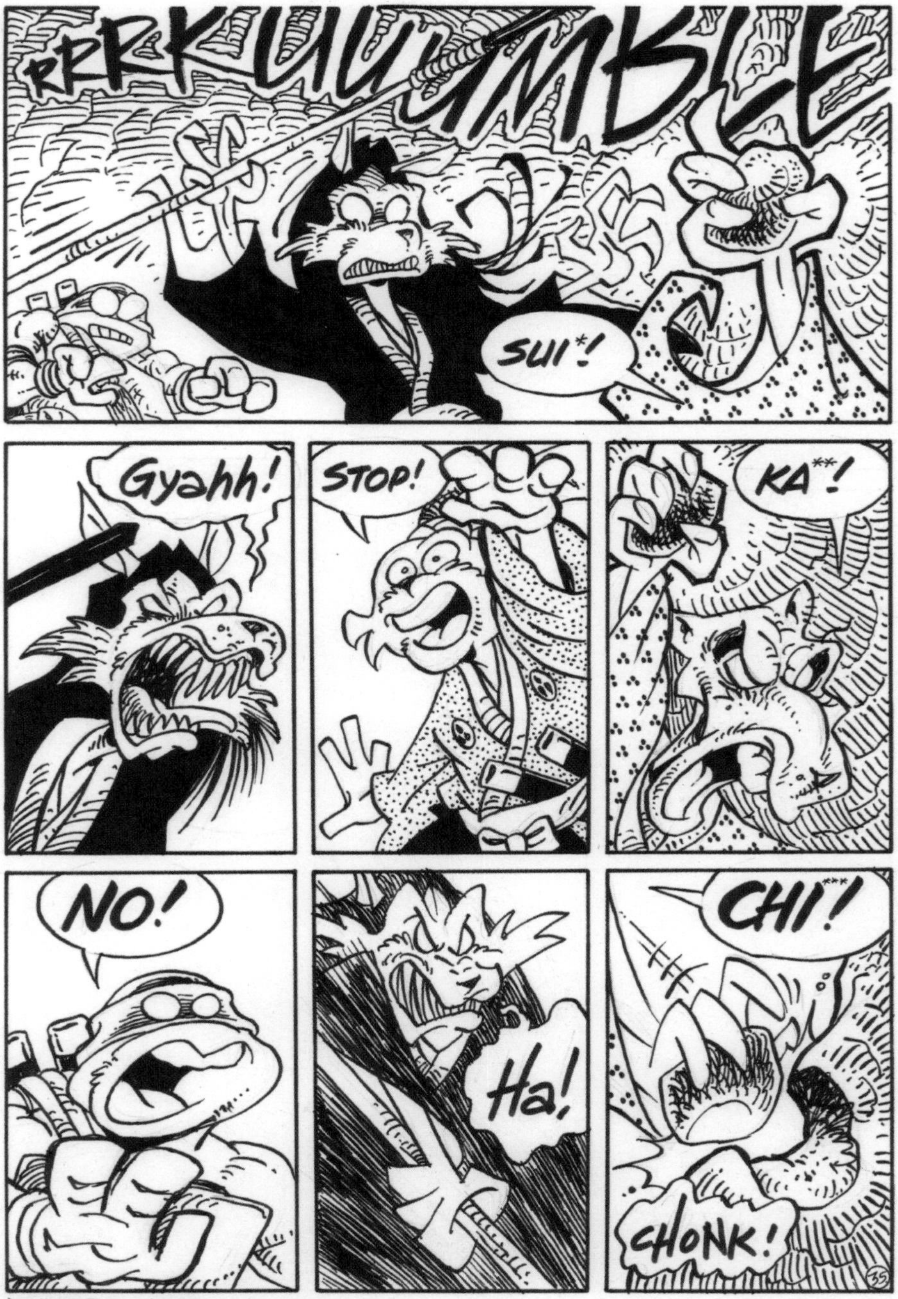
RRRKUUUMBLE
SUI*!
Gyahh!
STOP!
KA**!
NO!
Ha!
CHI***!
CHONK!
35

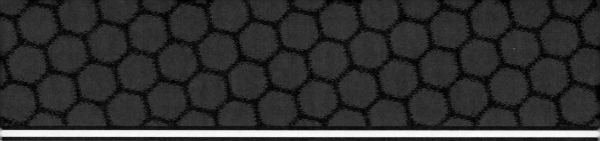

*WATER **FIRE ***EARTH

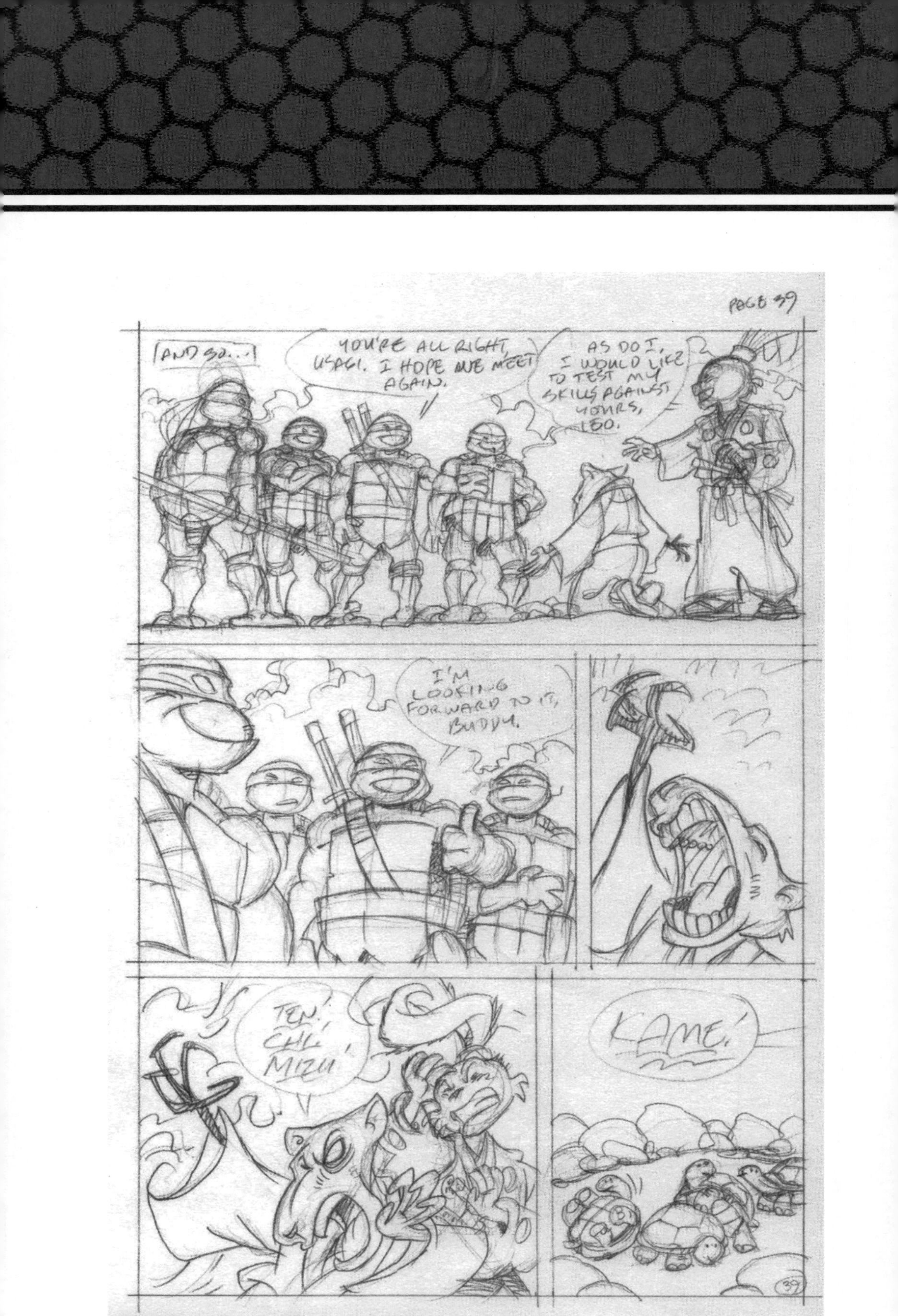
PAGE 39
AND SO...
YOU'RE ALL RIGHT, USAGI. I HOPE WE MEET AGAIN.
AS DO I. I WOULD LIKE TO TEST MY SKILLS AGAINST YOURS, TOO.
I'M LOOKING FORWARD TO IT, BUDDY.
TEN! CHI! MIZU!
KAME!
39

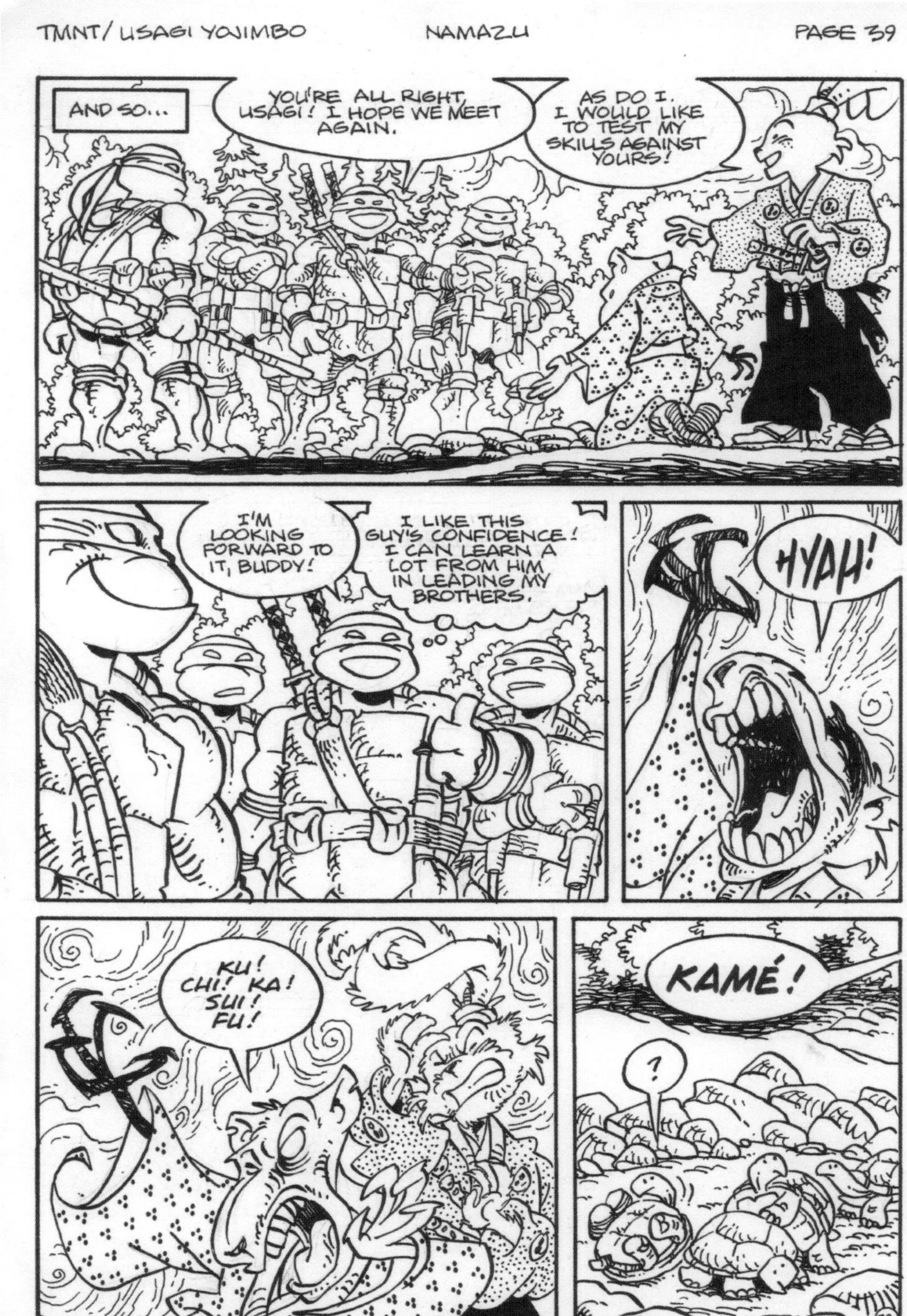
TMNT/ USAGI YOJIMBO
NAMAZU
PAGE 39
AND SO...
YOU'RE ALL RIGHT, USAGI! I HOPE WE MEET AGAIN.
AS DO I. I WOULD LIKE TO TEST MY SKILLS AGAINST YOURS!
I'M LOOKING FORWARD TO IT, BUDDY!
I LIKE THIS GUY'S CONFIDENCE! I CAN LEARN A LOT FROM HIM IN LEADING MY BROTHERS.
HYAH!
KU! CHI! KA! SUI! FU!
KAMÉ!
?
39.

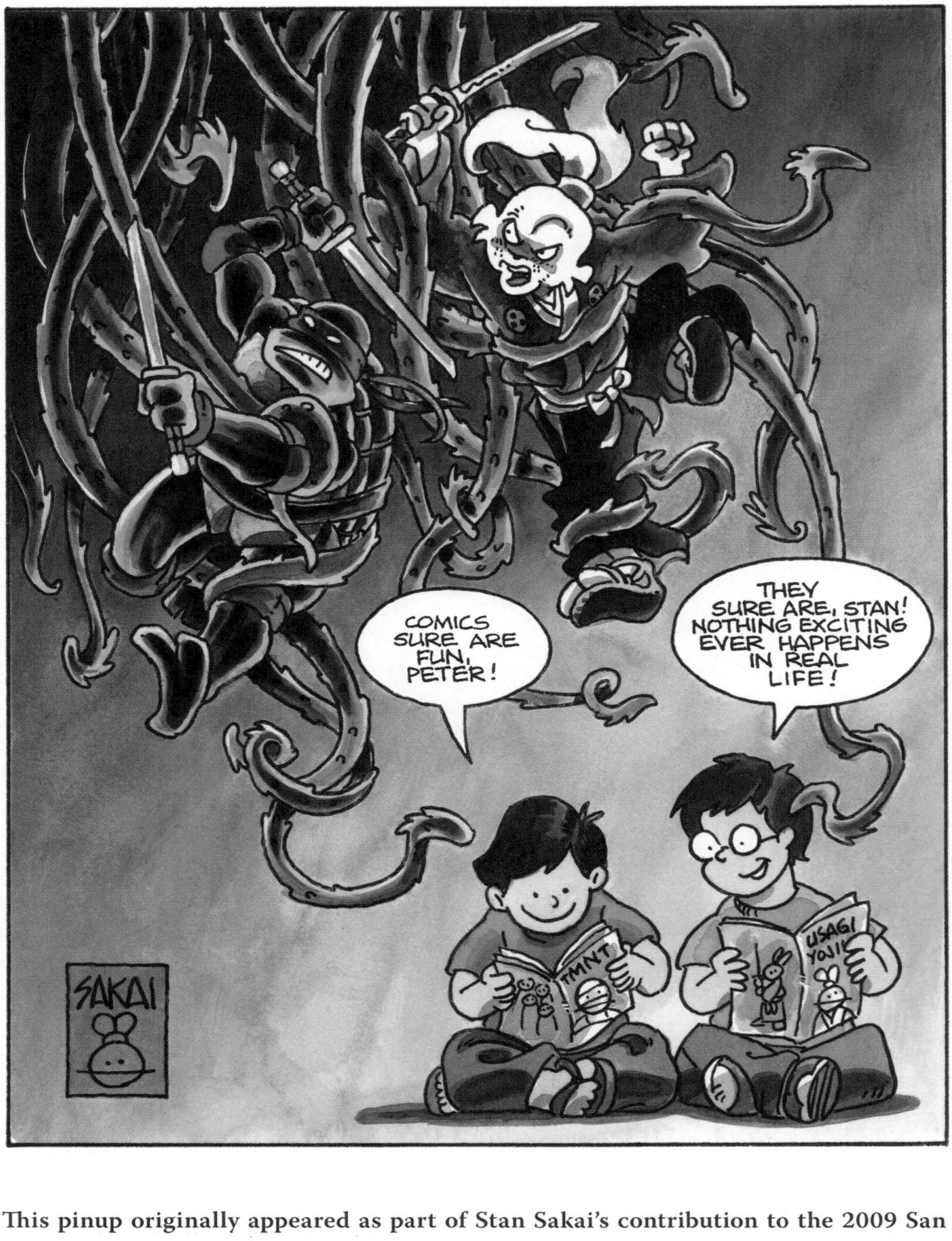
COMICS SURE ARE FUN, PETER!
THEY SURE ARE, STAN! NOTHING EXCITING EVER HAPPENS IN REAL LIFE!
TMNT
USAGI YOJI
SAKAI

This pinup originally appeared as part of Stan Sakai's contribution to the 2009 San Diego Comic-Con souvenir book. It also ran on the back cover of *Usagi Yojimbo Volume Three* #125 in 2009.

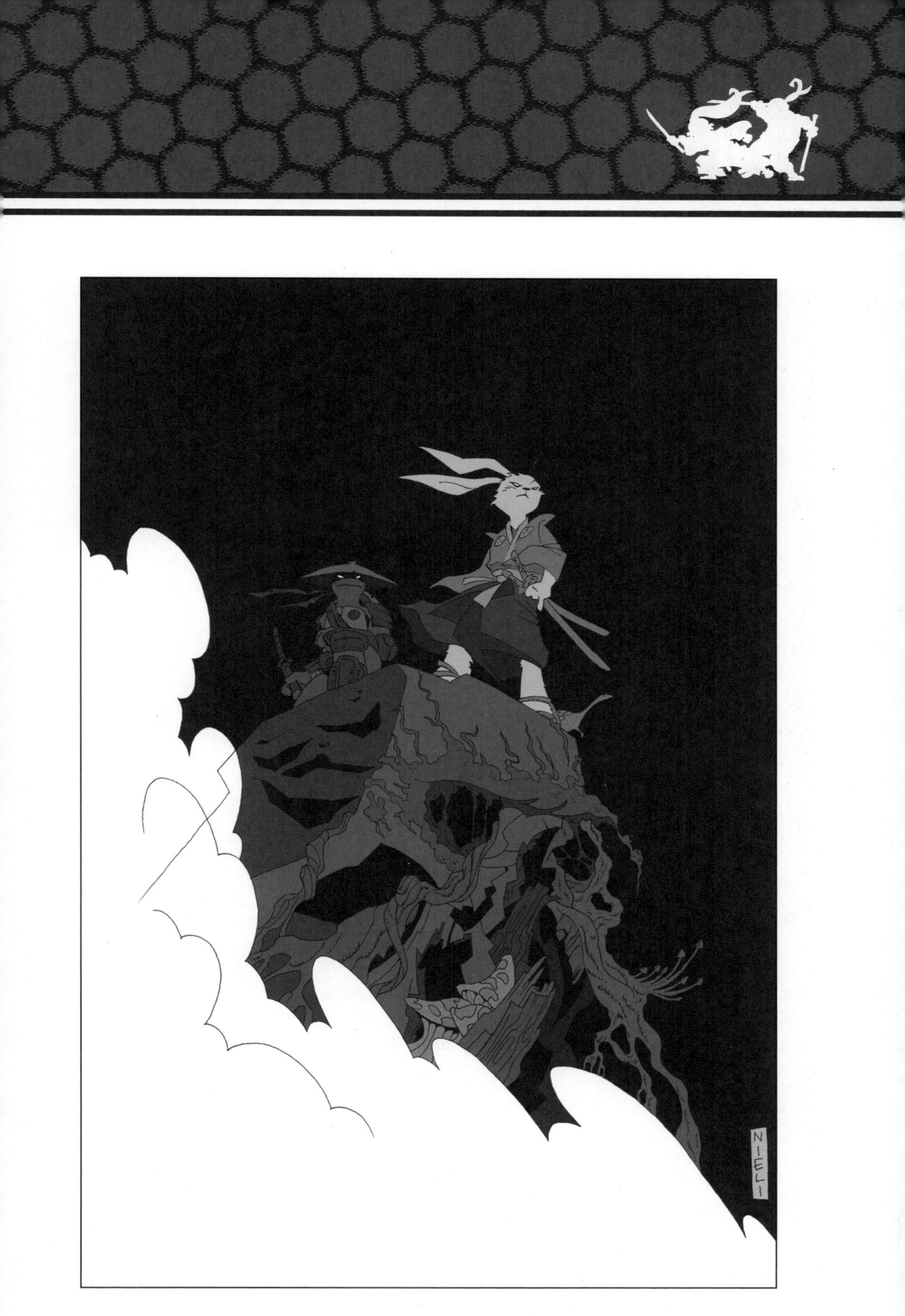
NIELI

Pinup by Ciro Nieli

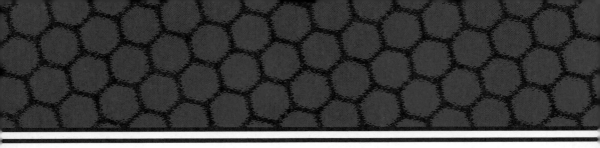

Pinups that Stan Sakai has created featuring his creation Miyamoto Usagi and the Teenage Mutant Ninja Turtles.

SAKAI

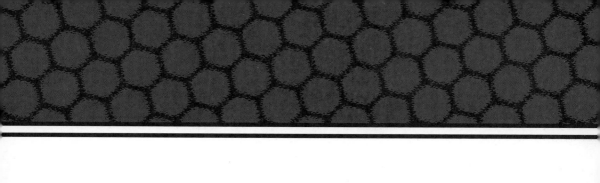

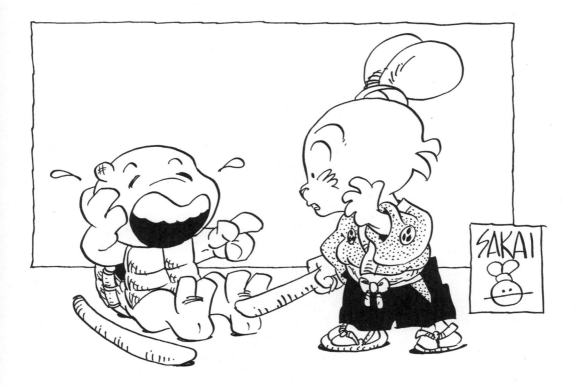

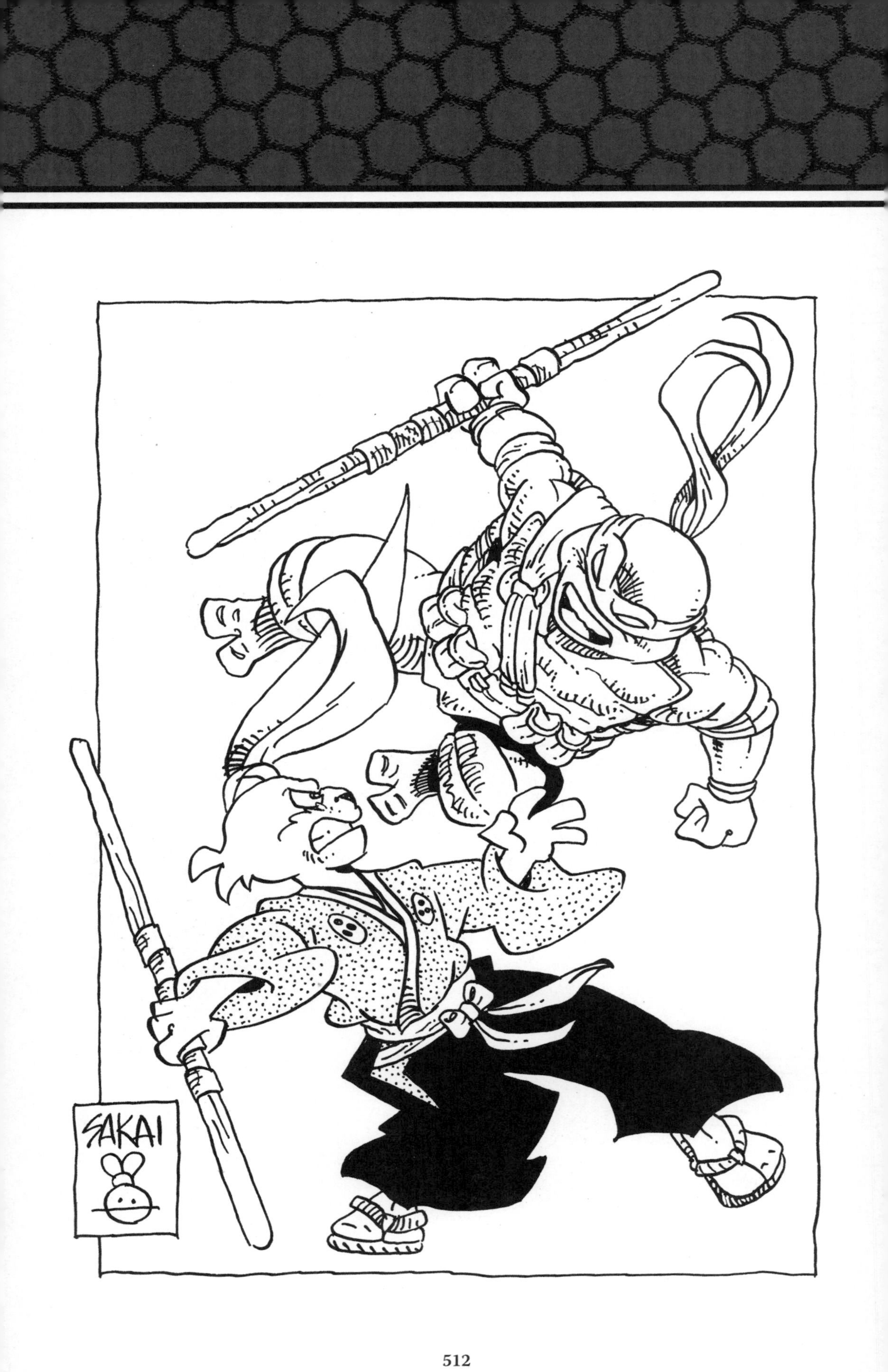
SAKAI

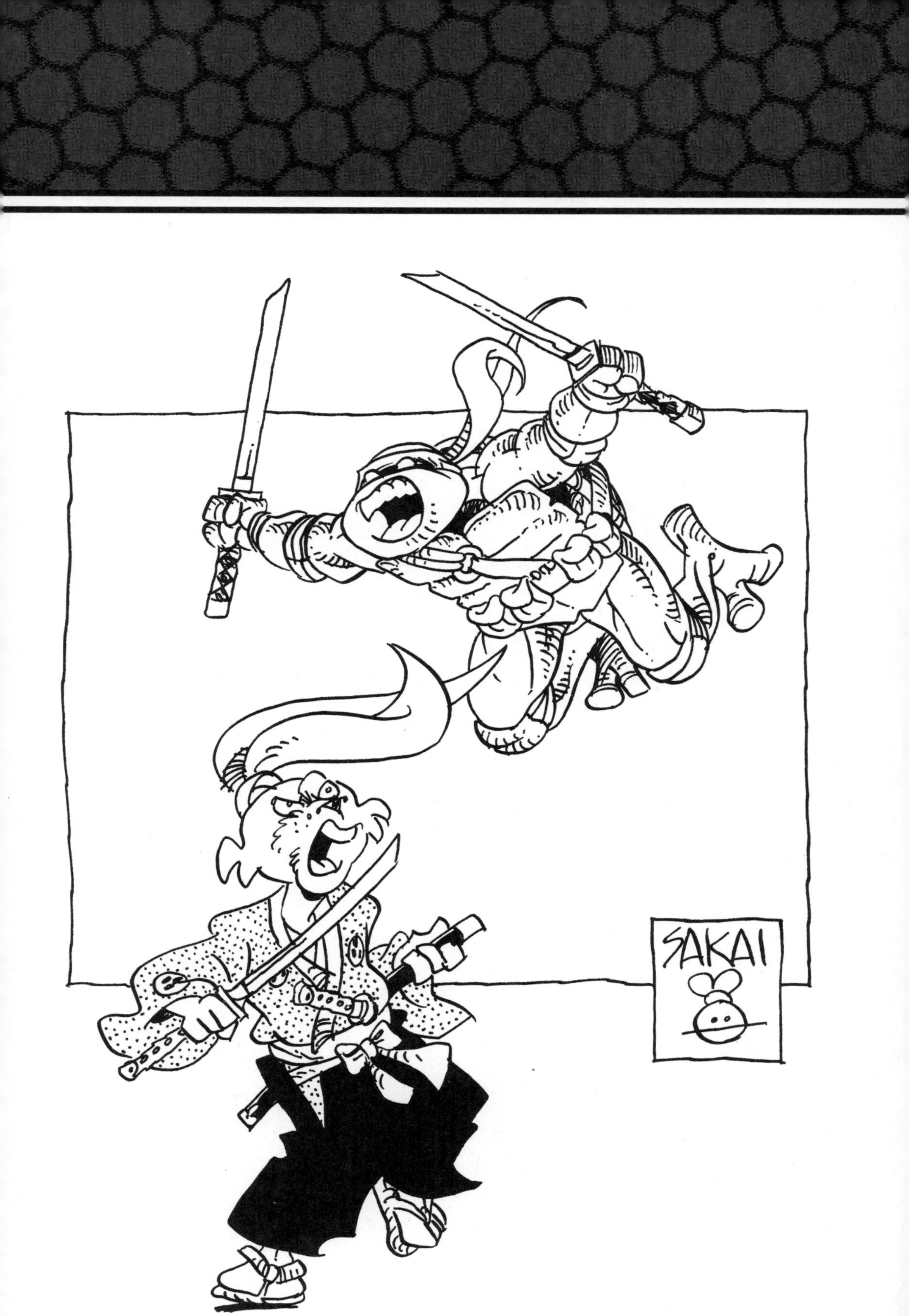
SAKAI

SAKAI

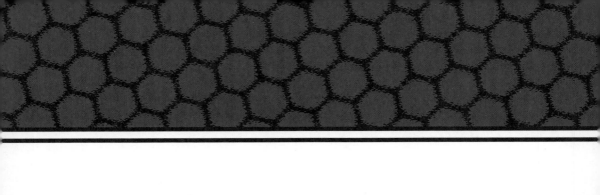

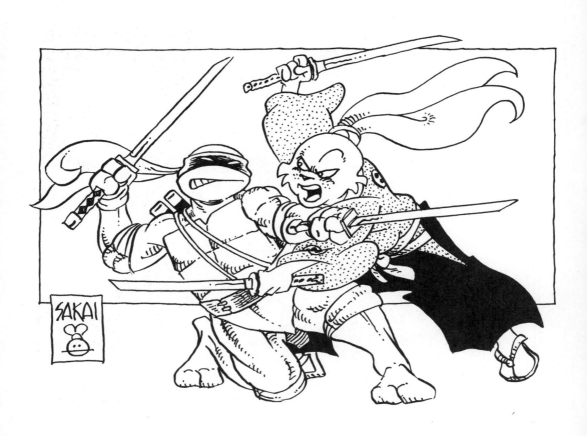

SAKAI

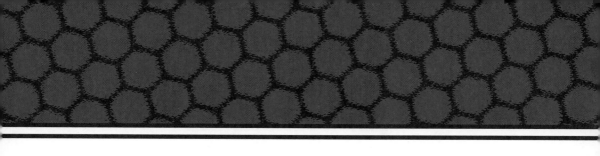

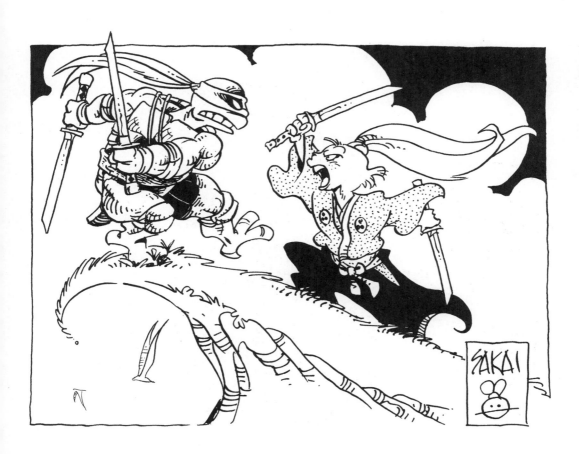

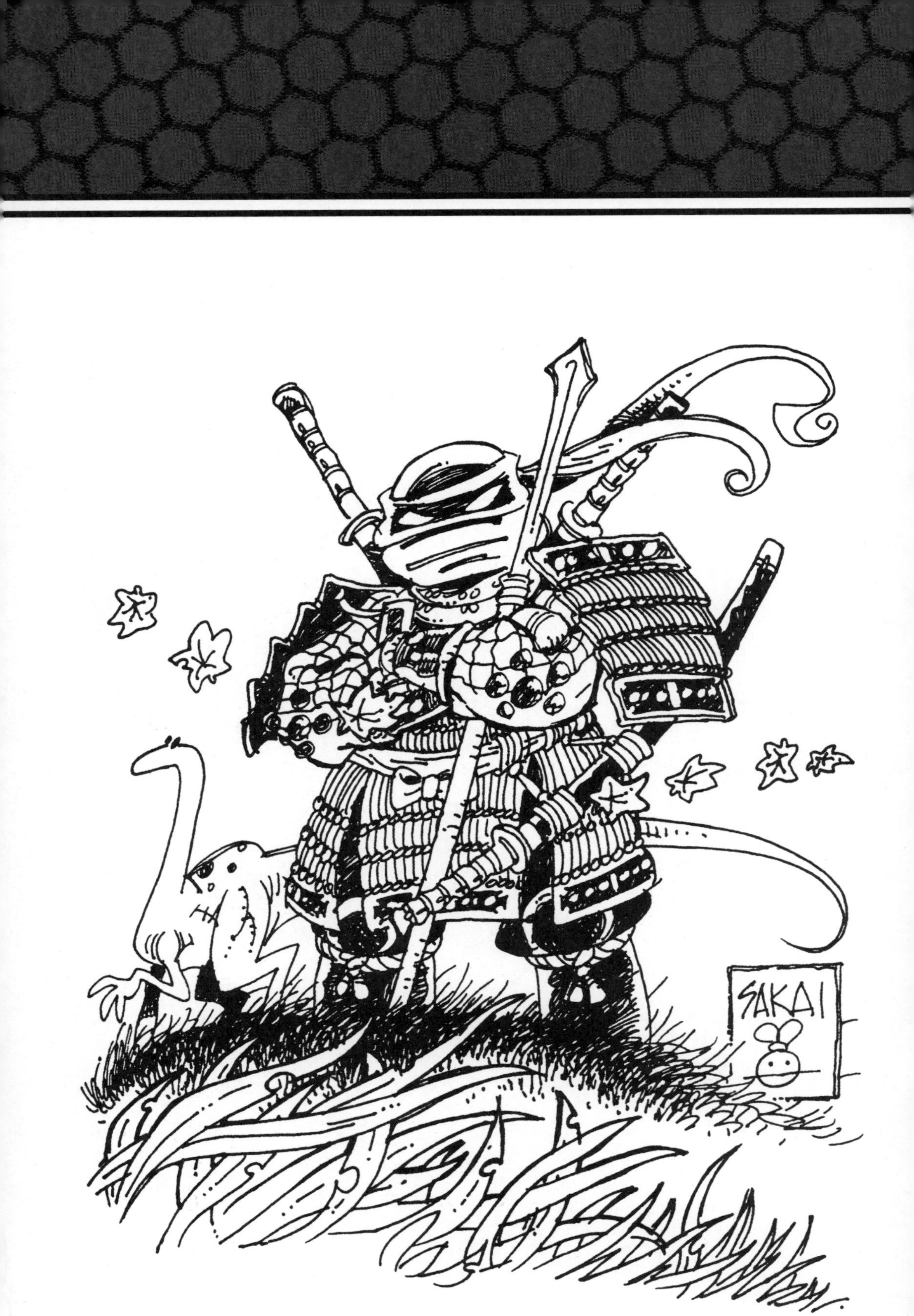
SAKAI

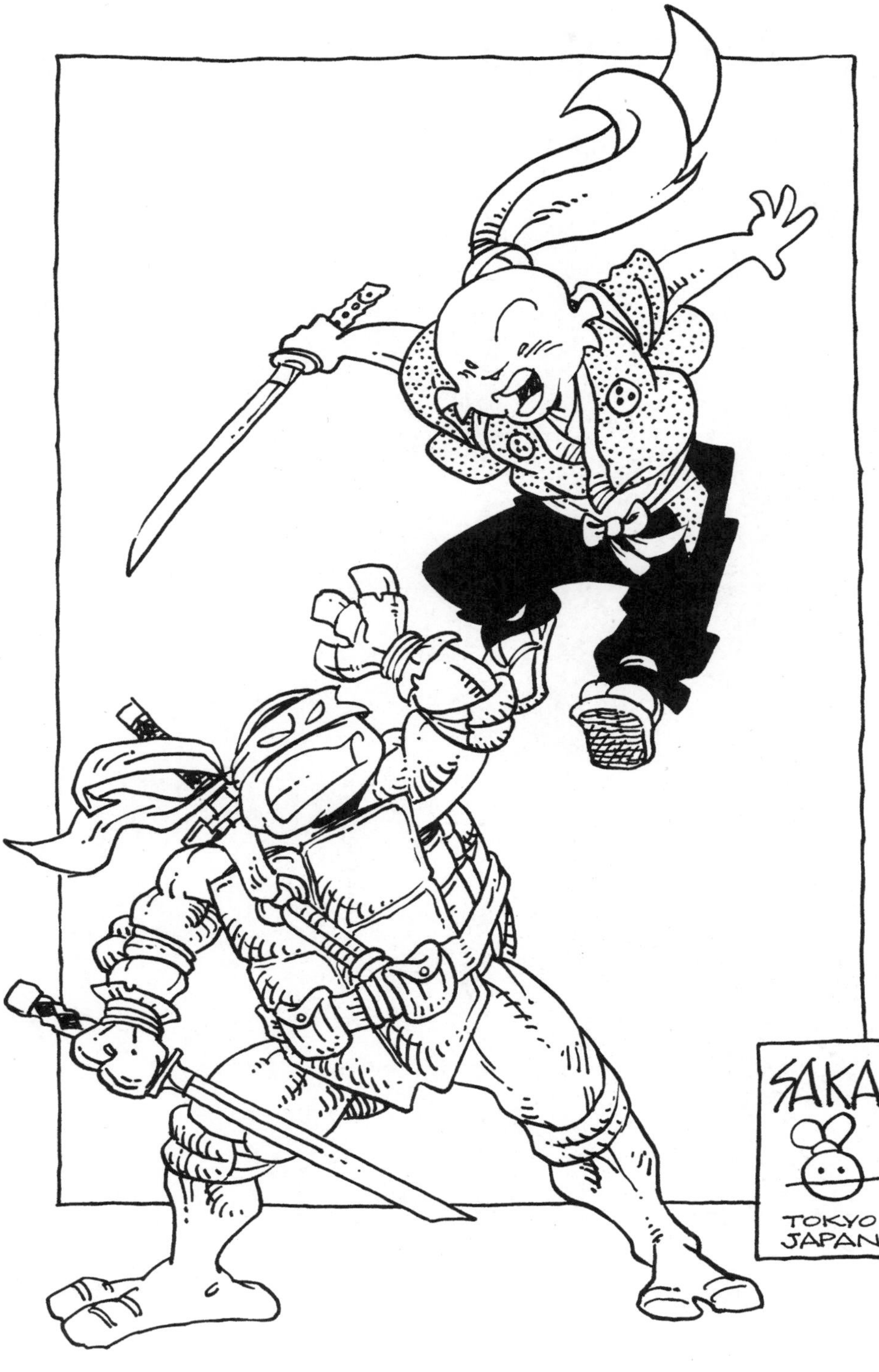
SAKAI
TOKYO
JAPAN

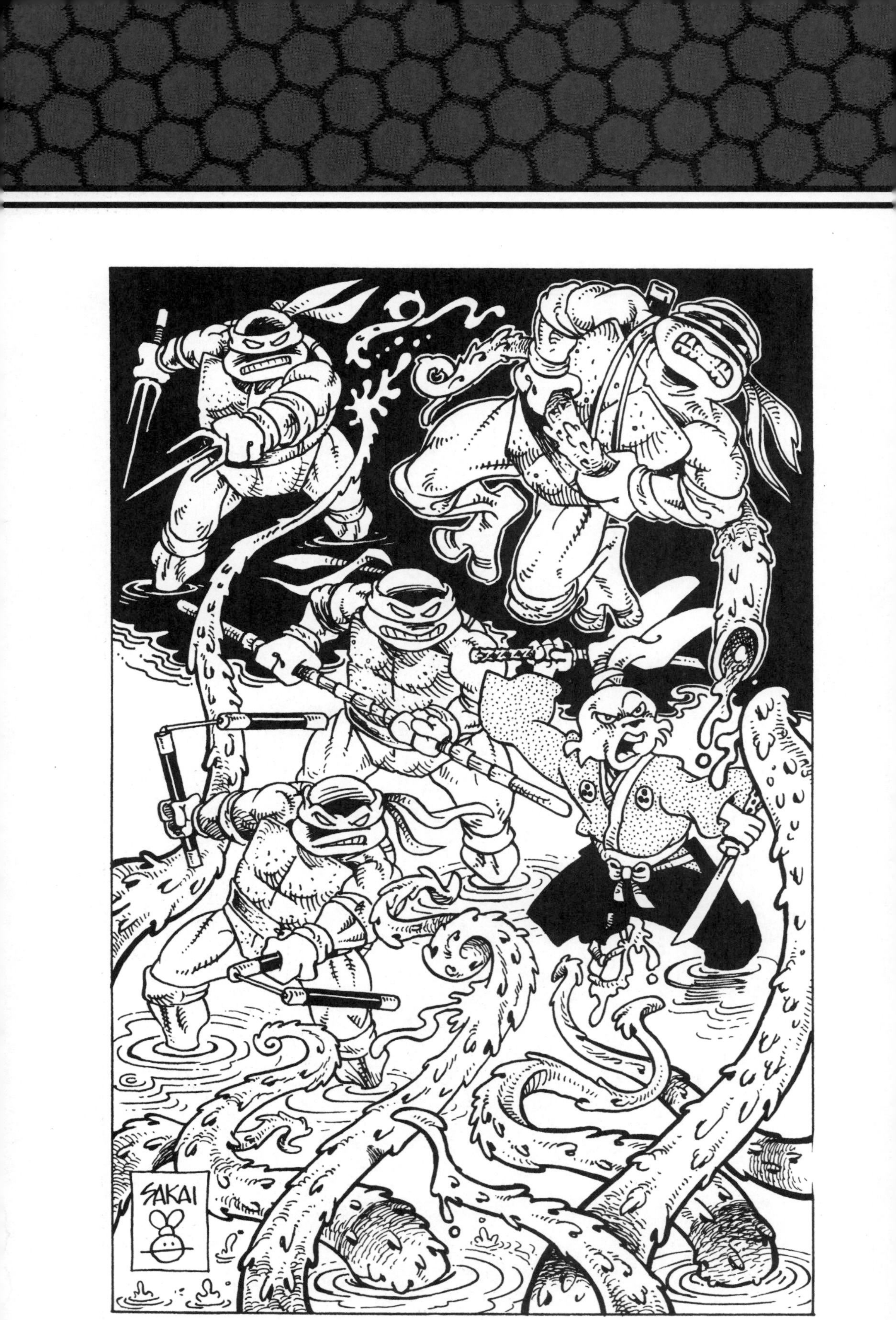
SAKAI

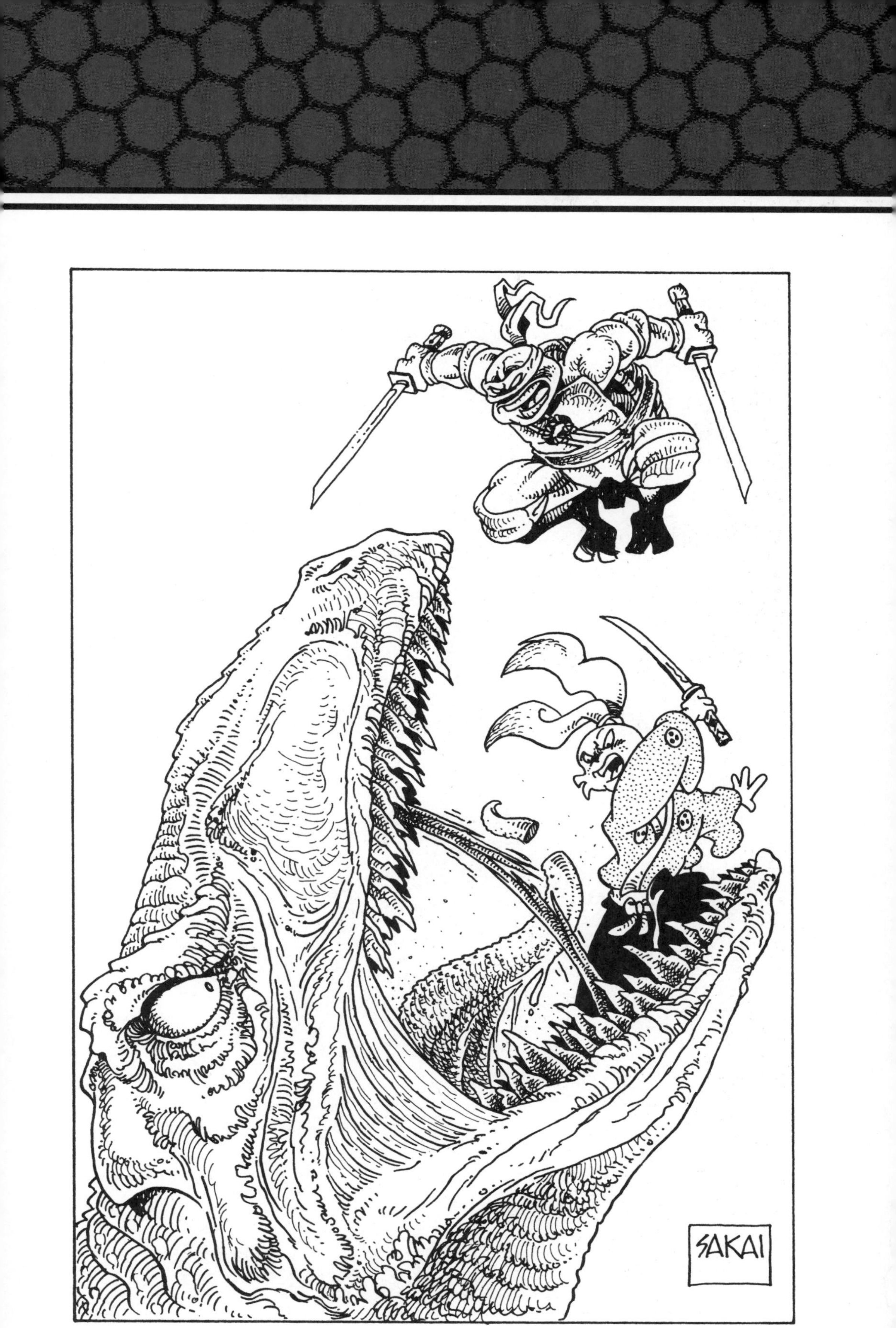
SAKAI

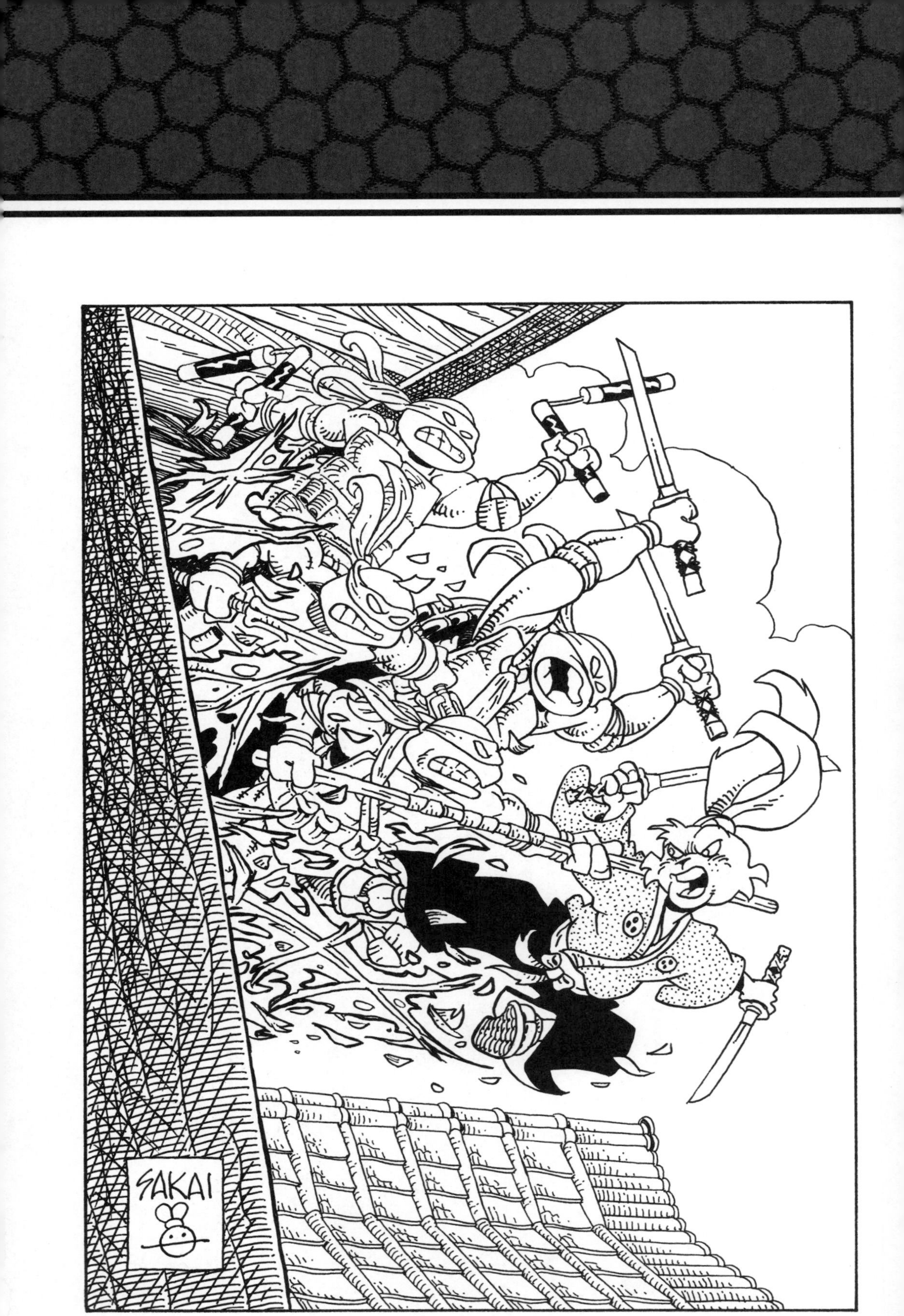
SAKAI

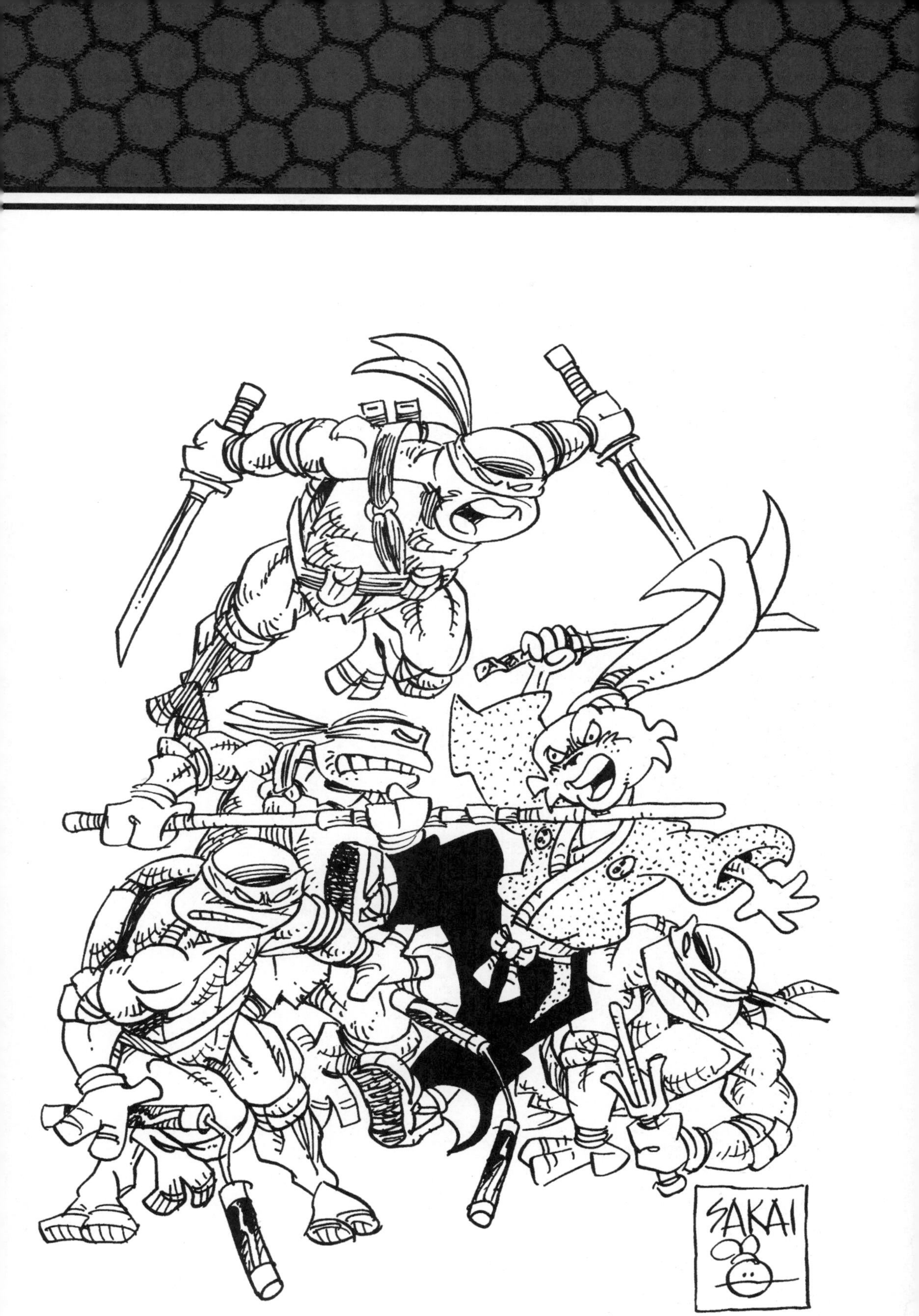
SAKAI

SAKAI

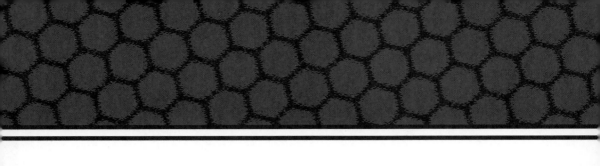

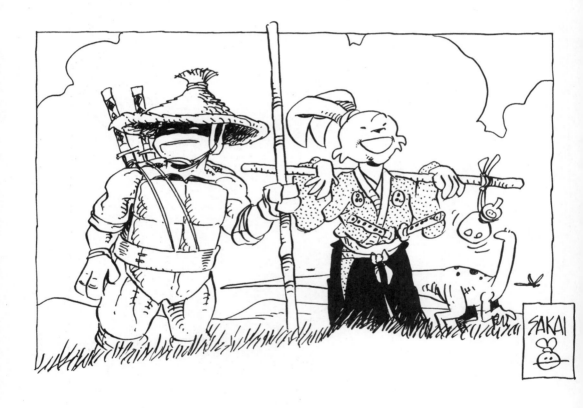

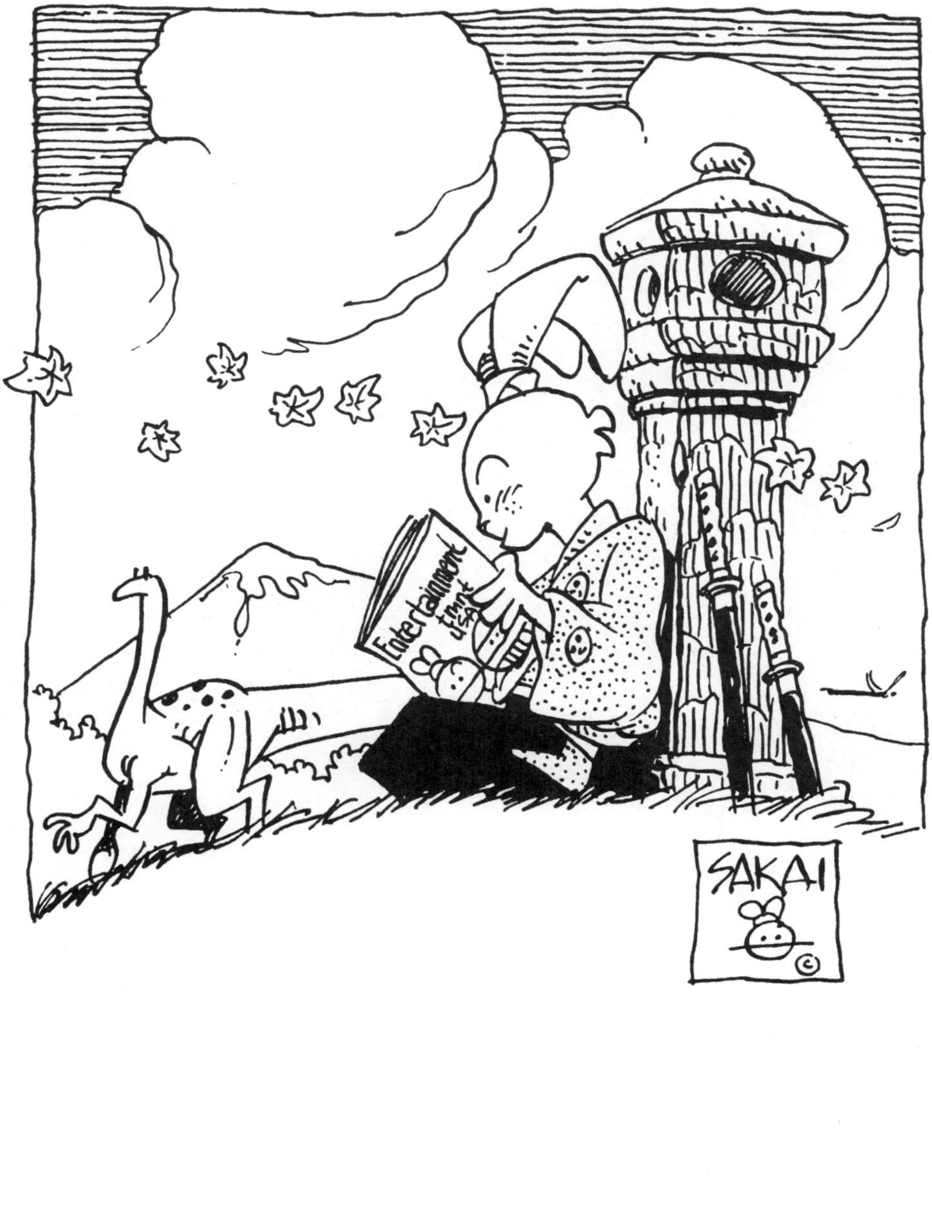
Entertainment
SAKAI

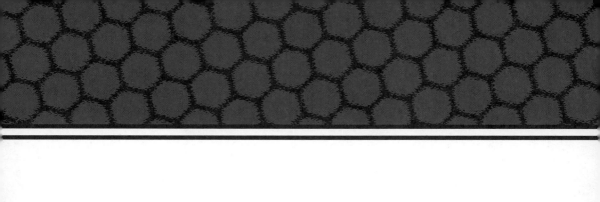

GALLERY

A compilation of front and back cover art by Stan Sakai, along with art by his wife Julie Fujii Sakai, Kevin Eastman, and many more from the issues and collections in this volume.

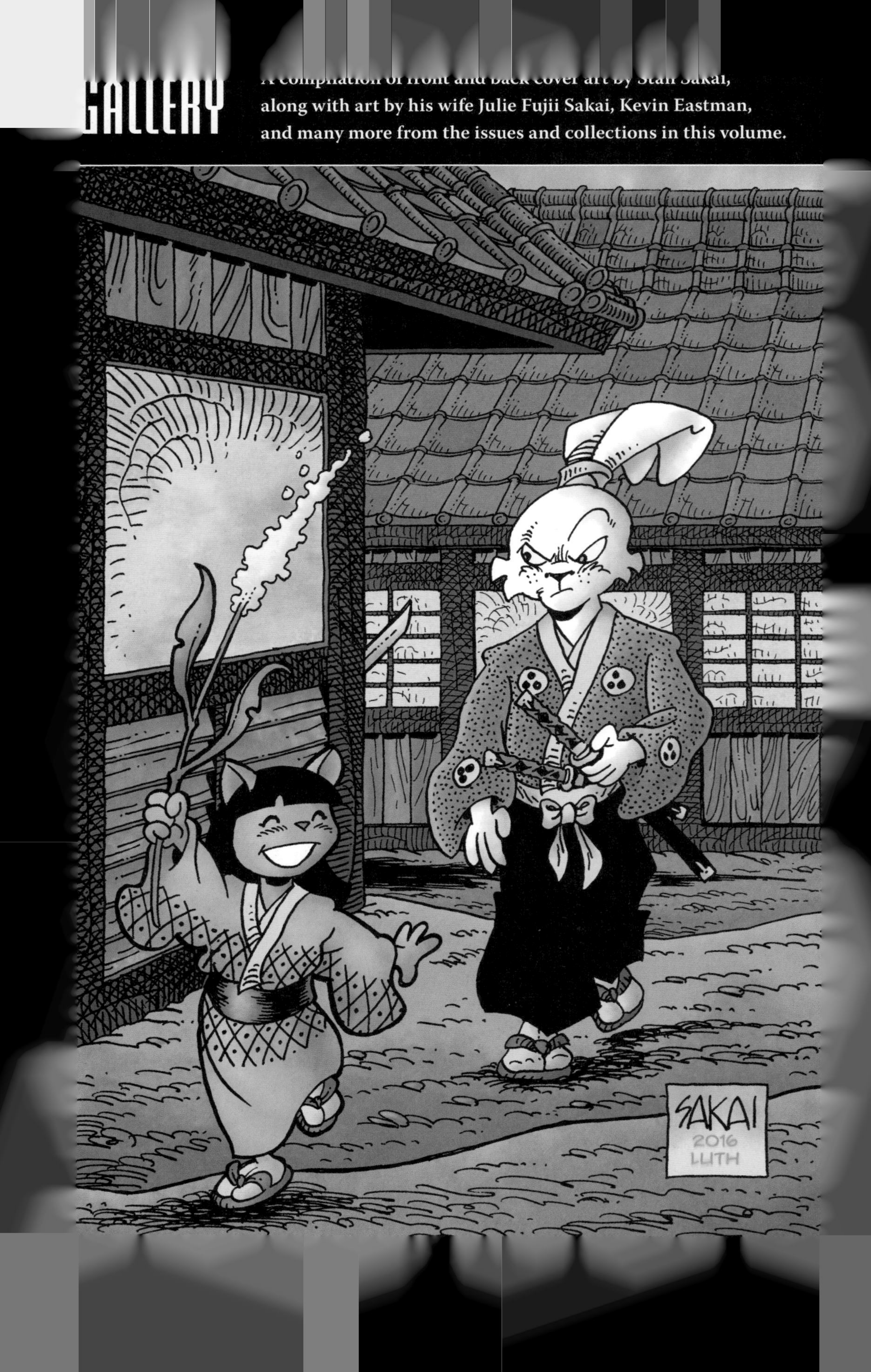
SAKAI
2016
LUTH

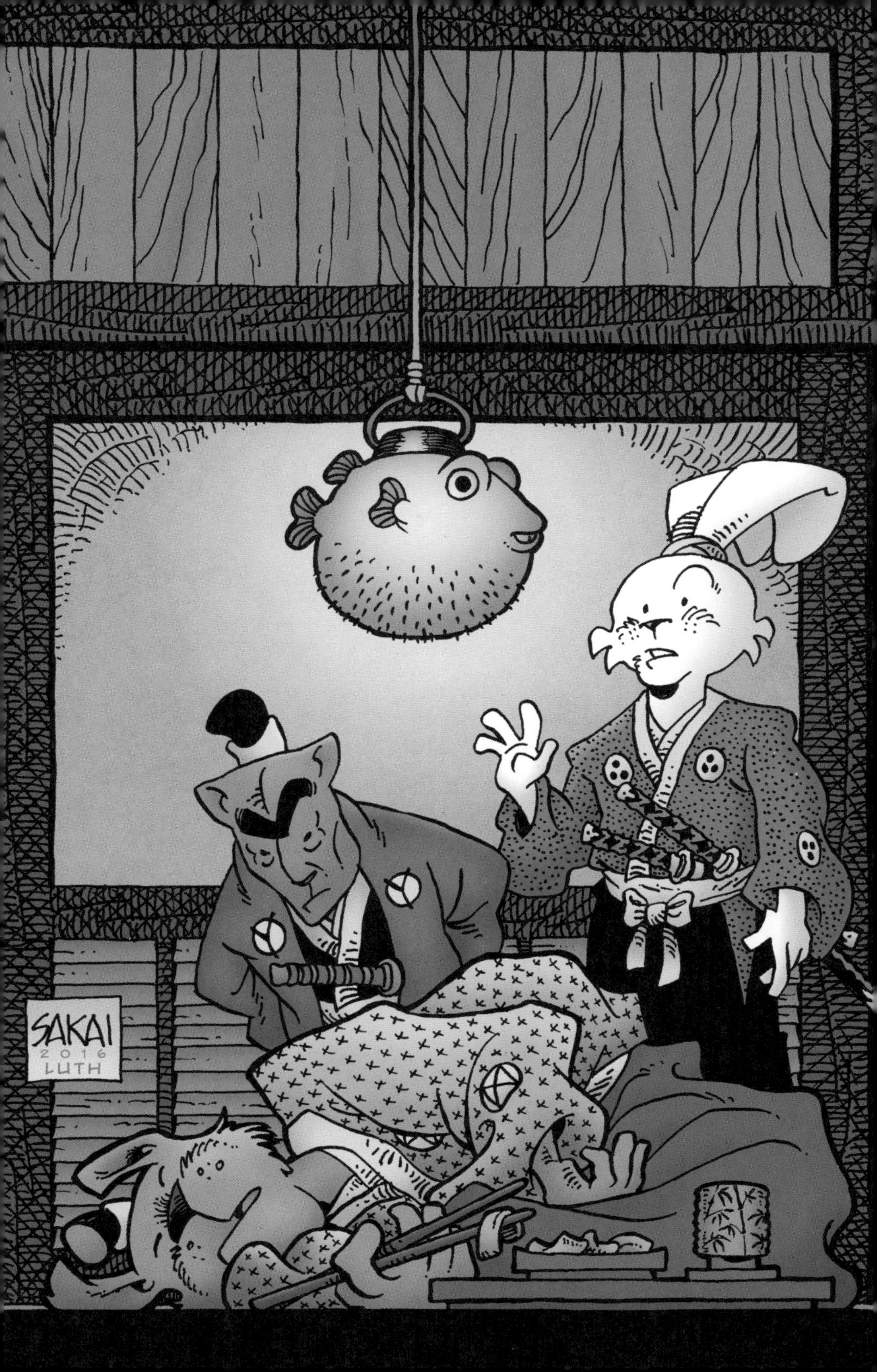
SAKAI
2016
LUTH

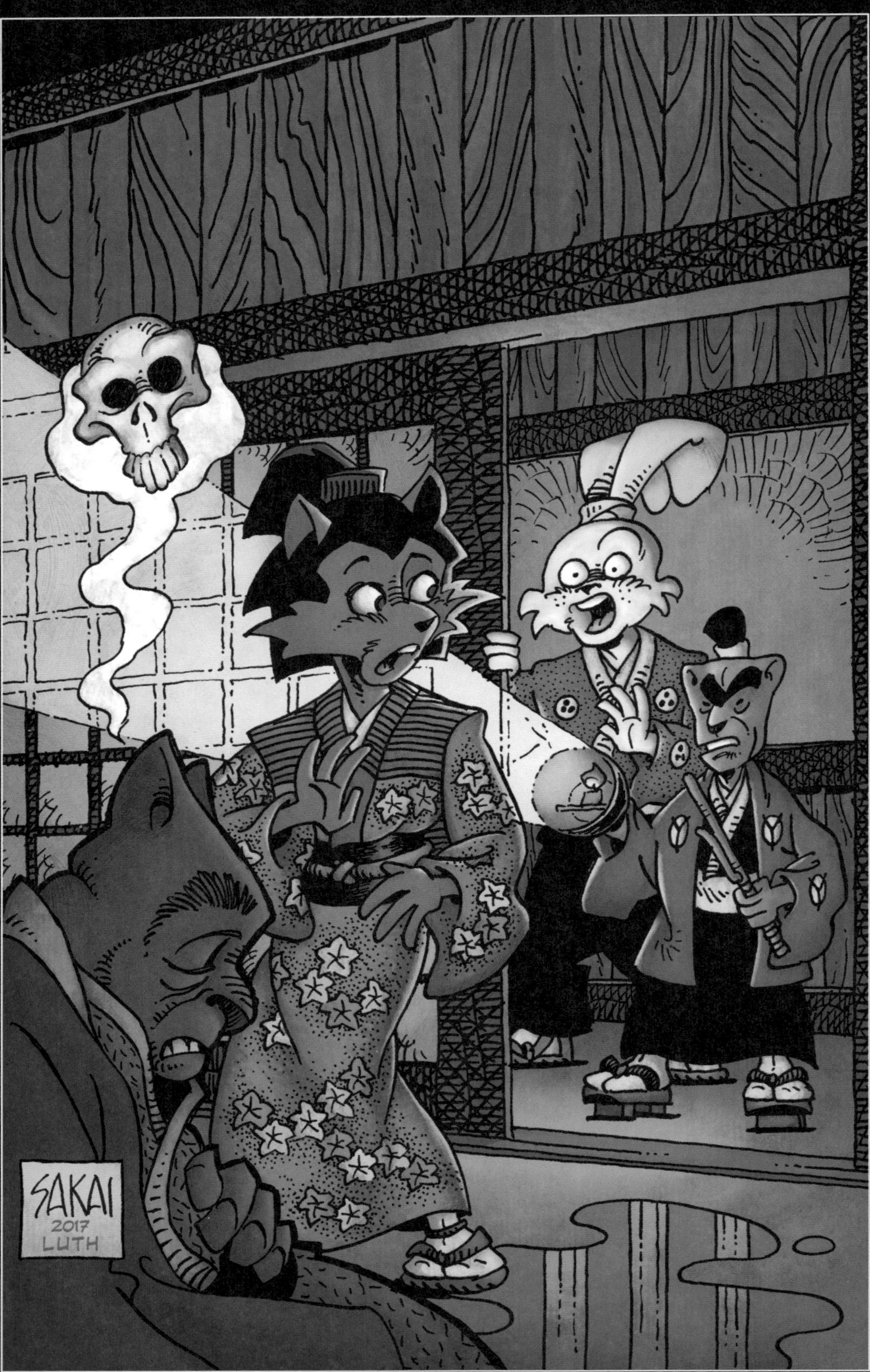
SAKAI
2017
LUTH

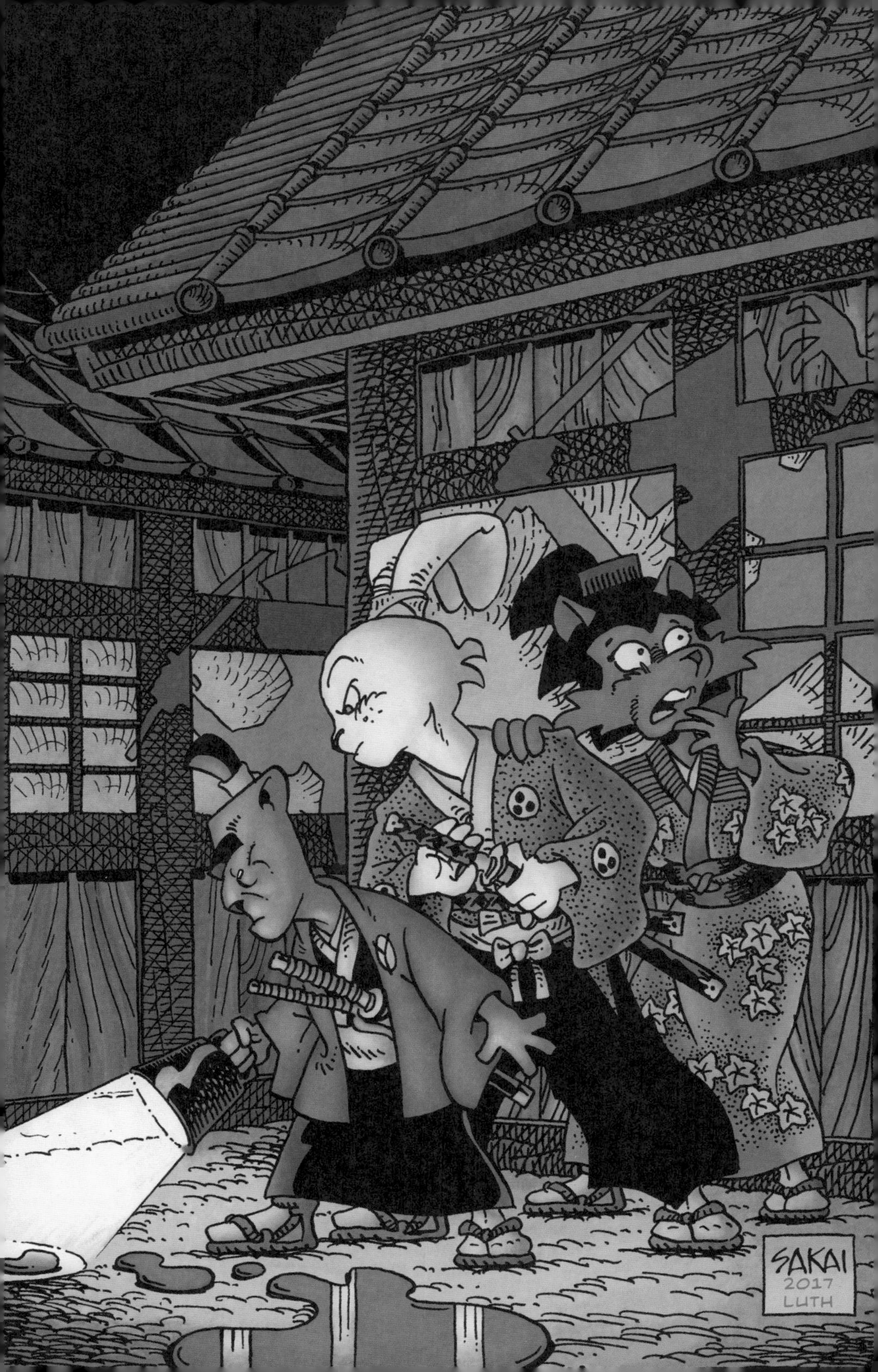
SAKAI
2017
LUTH

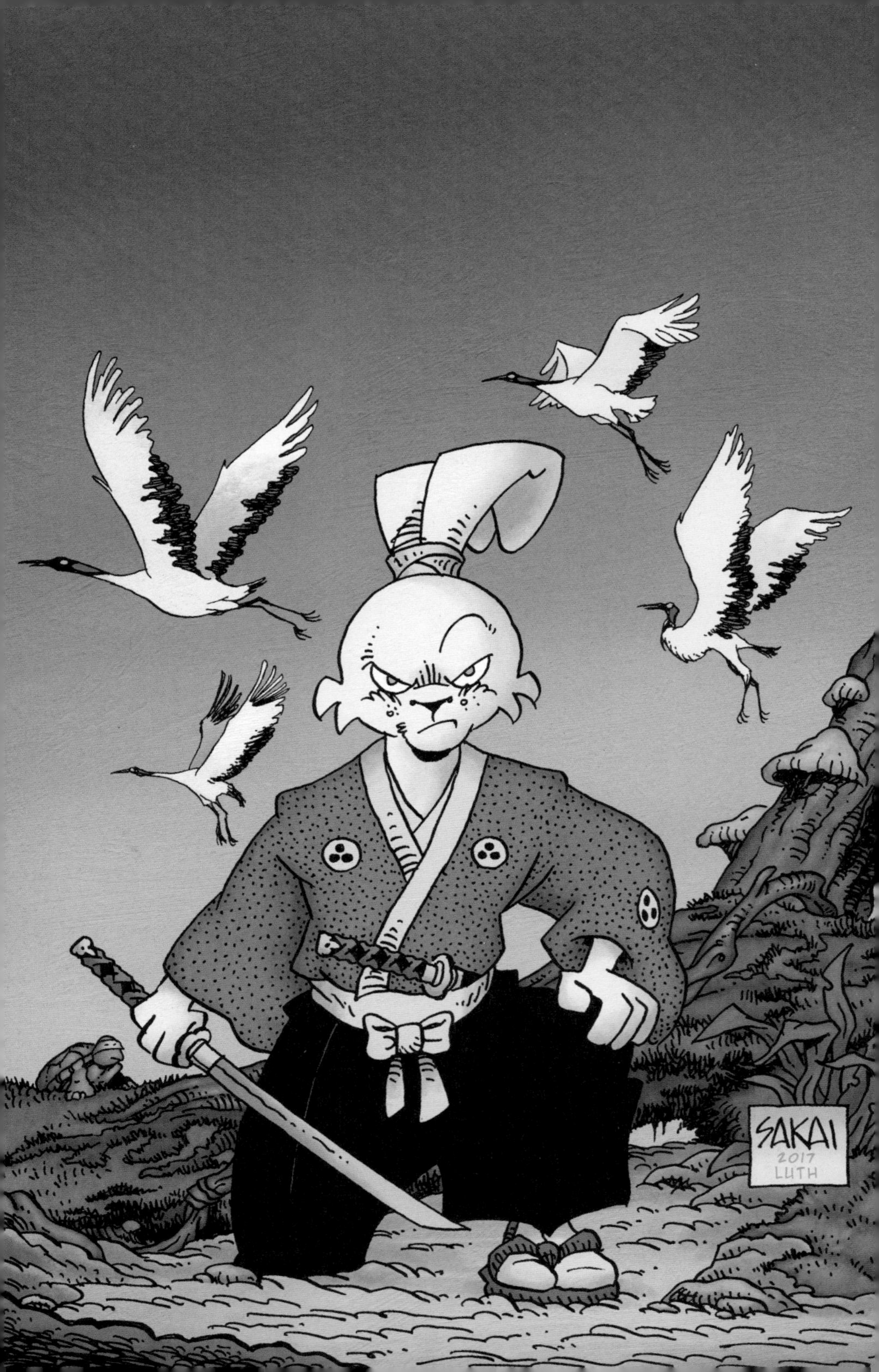
SAKAI
2017
LUTH

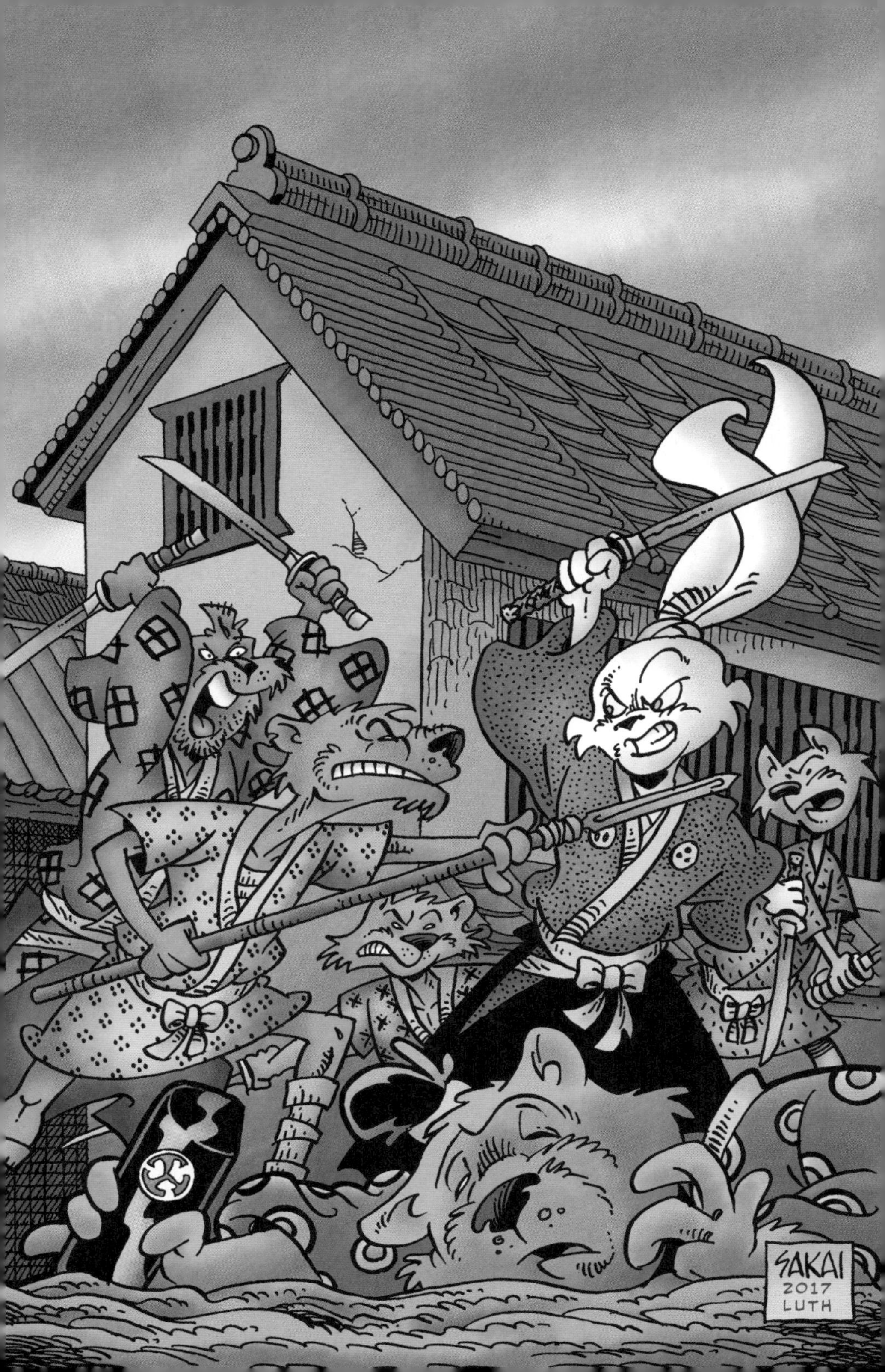
SAKAI
2017
LUTH

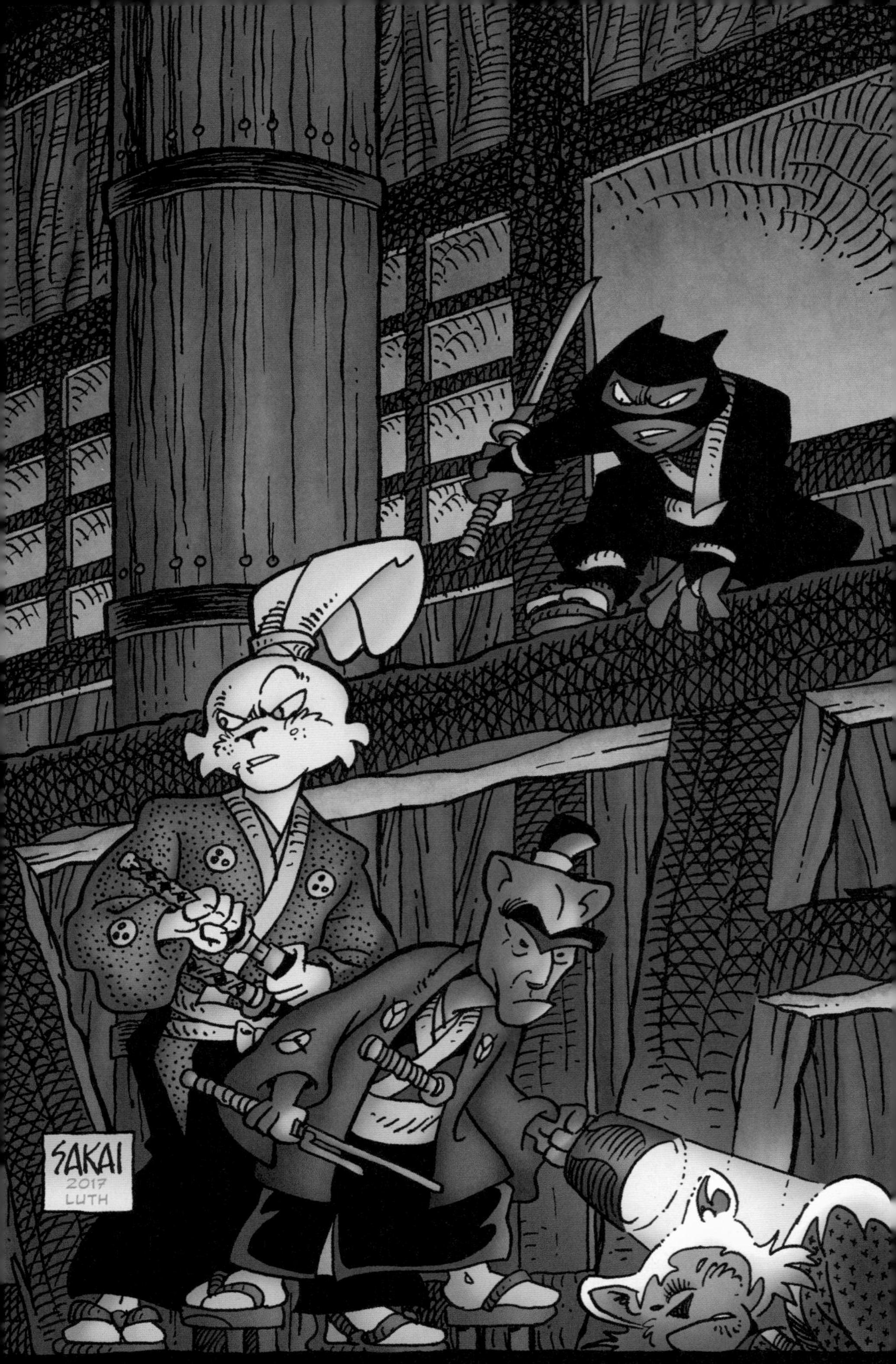
SAKAI
2017
LUTH

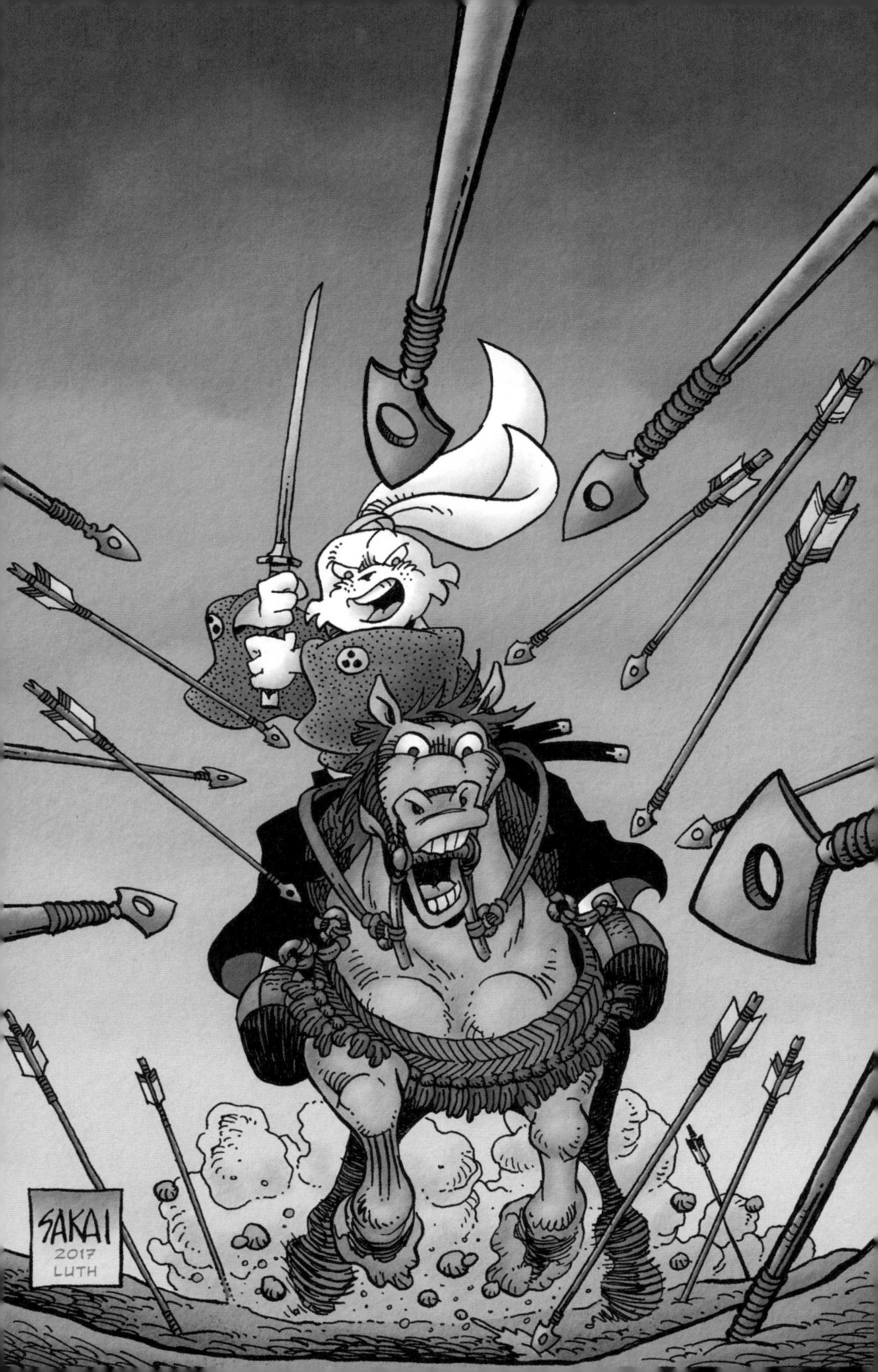
SAKAI
2017
LUTH

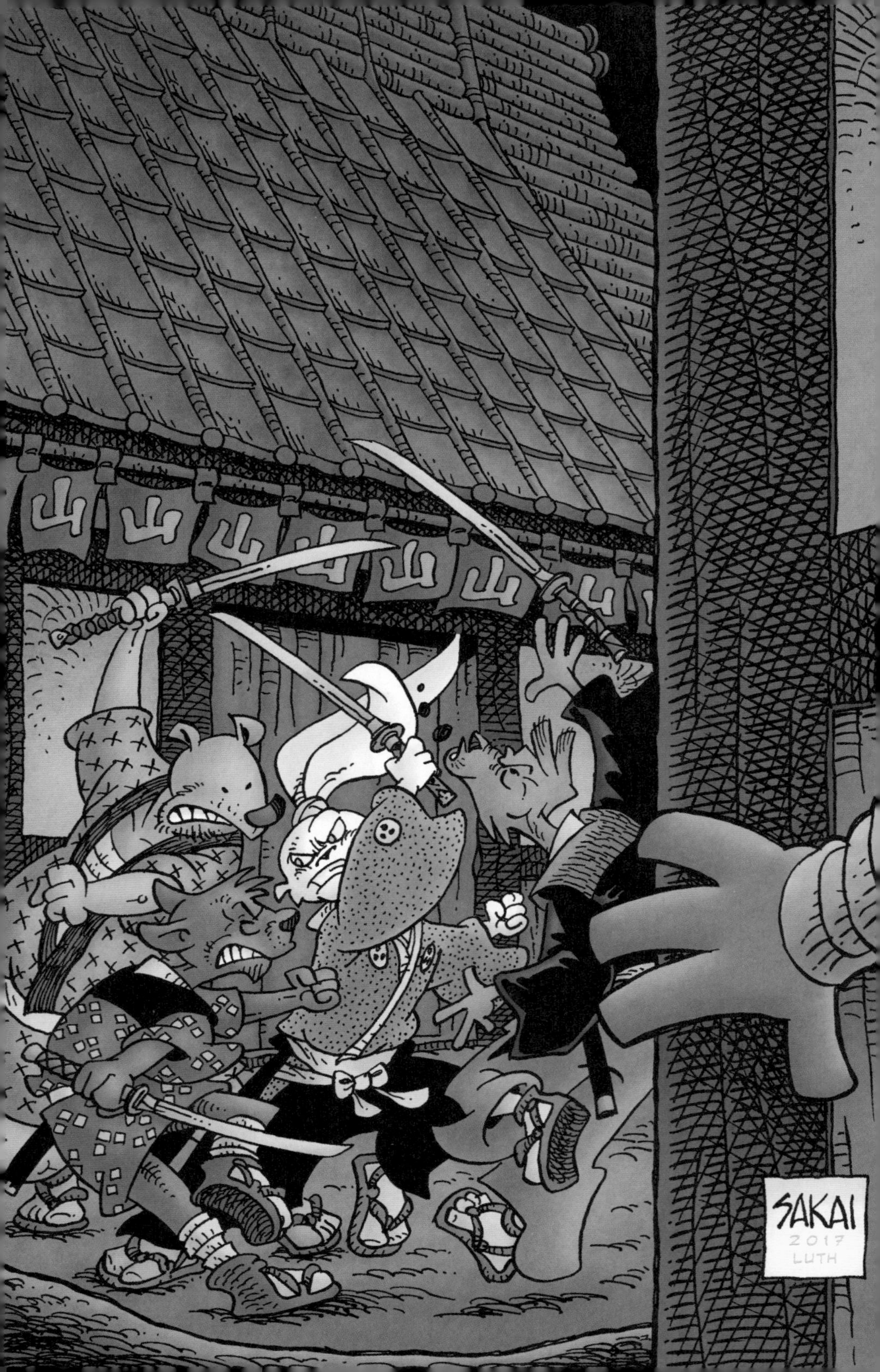
山
SAKAI
2017
LUTH

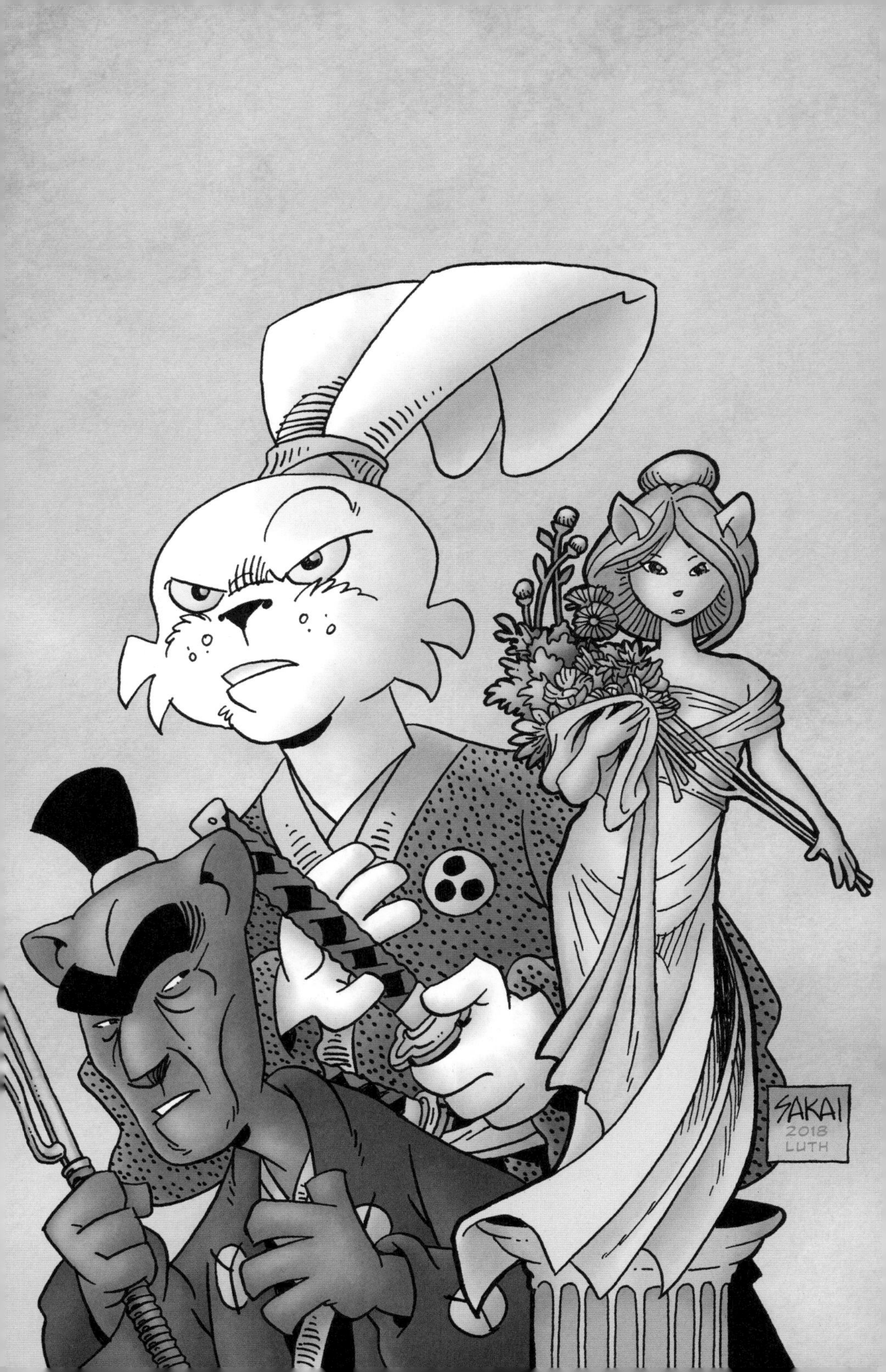
SAKAI
2018
LUTH

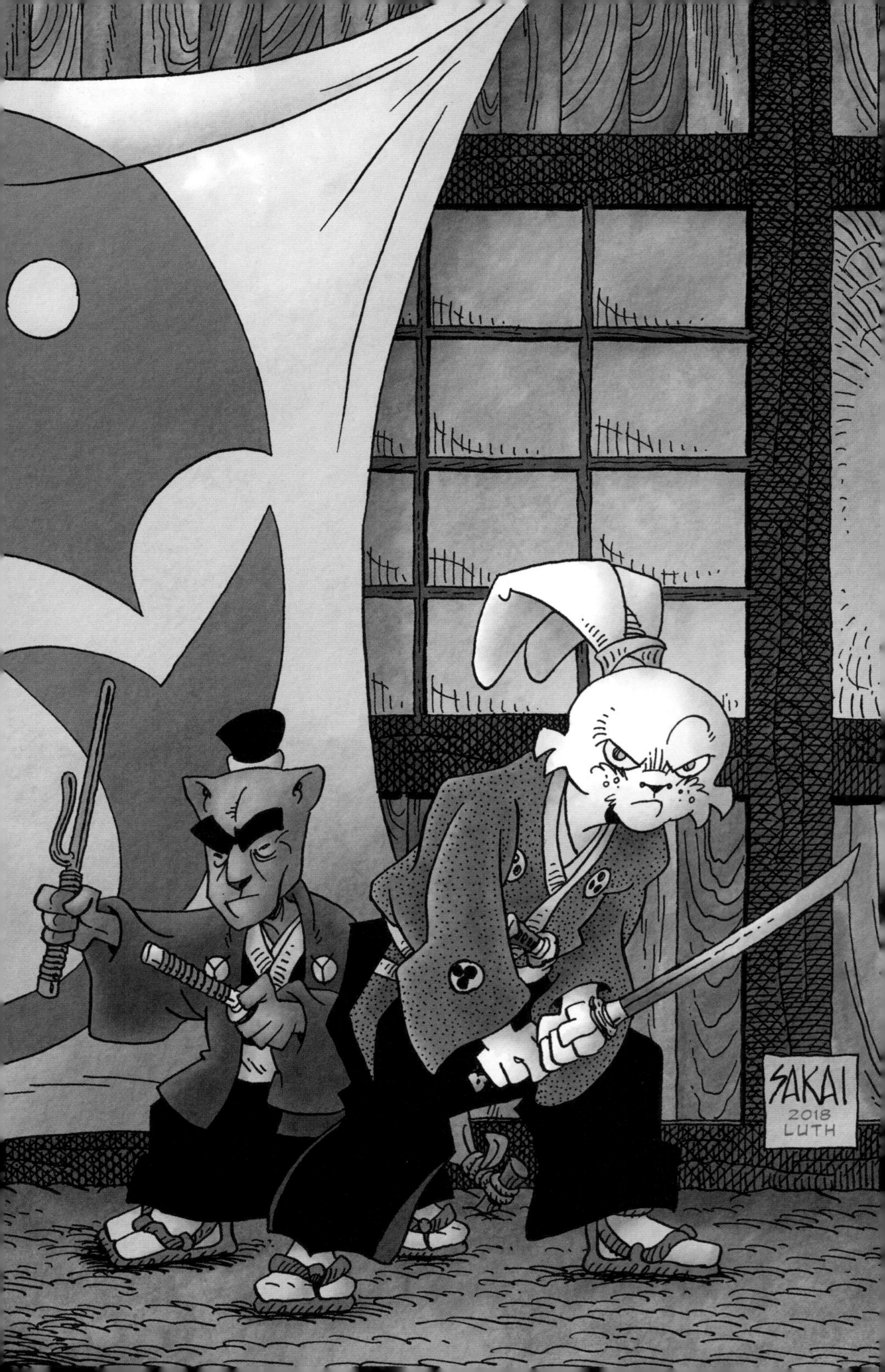
SAKAI
2018
LUTH

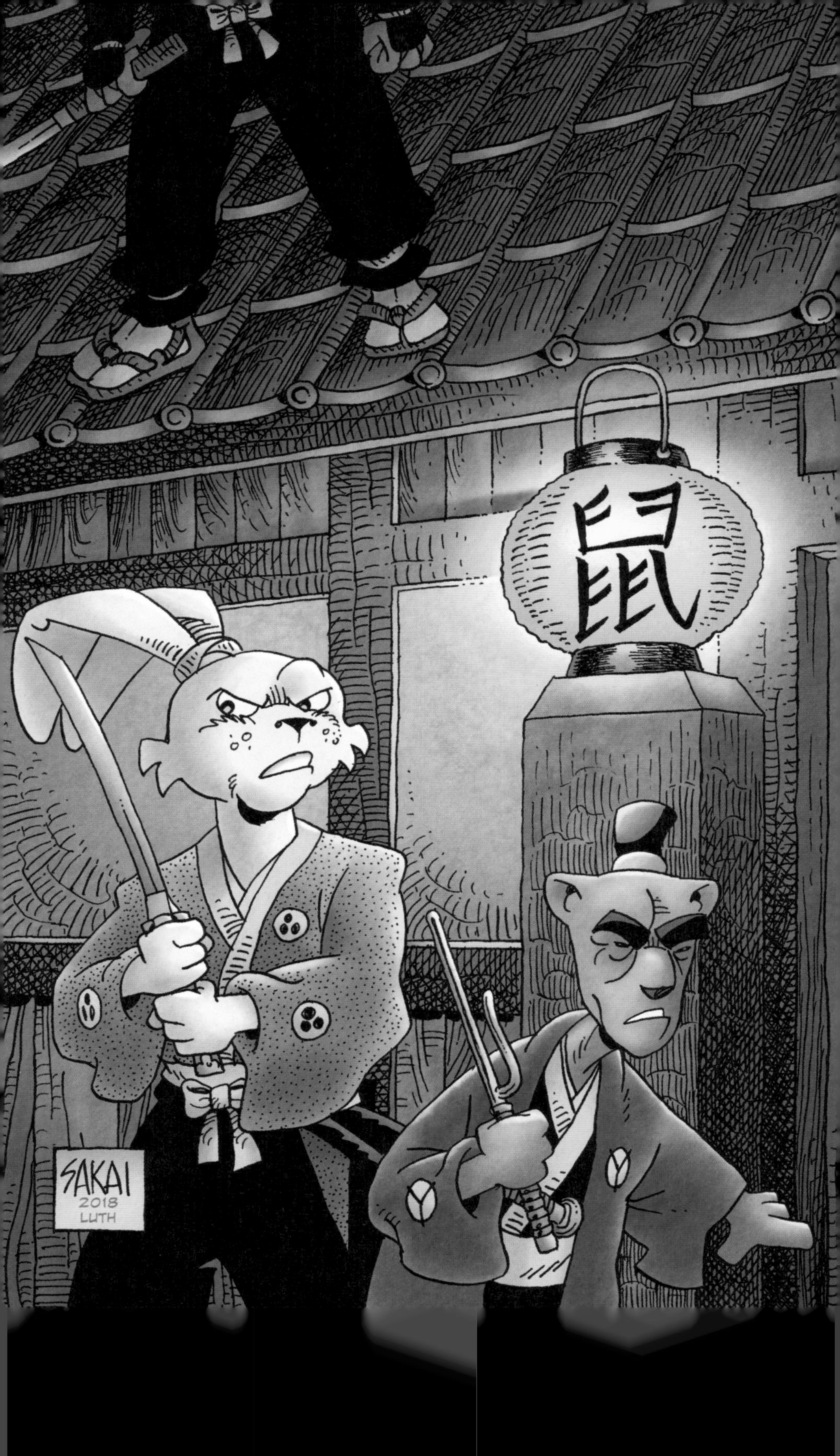
鼠
SAKAI
2018
LUTH

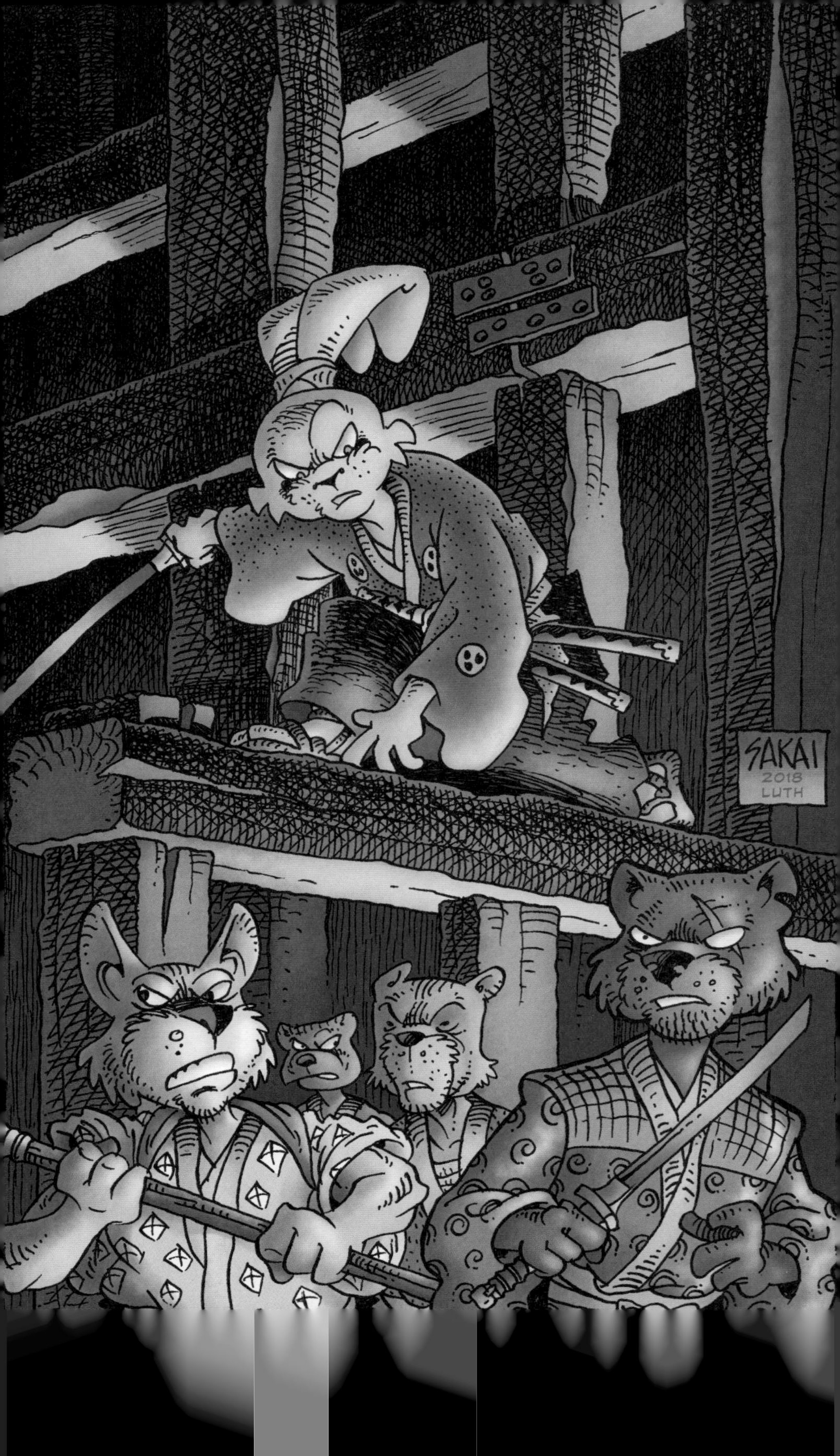
SAKAI
2018
LUTH

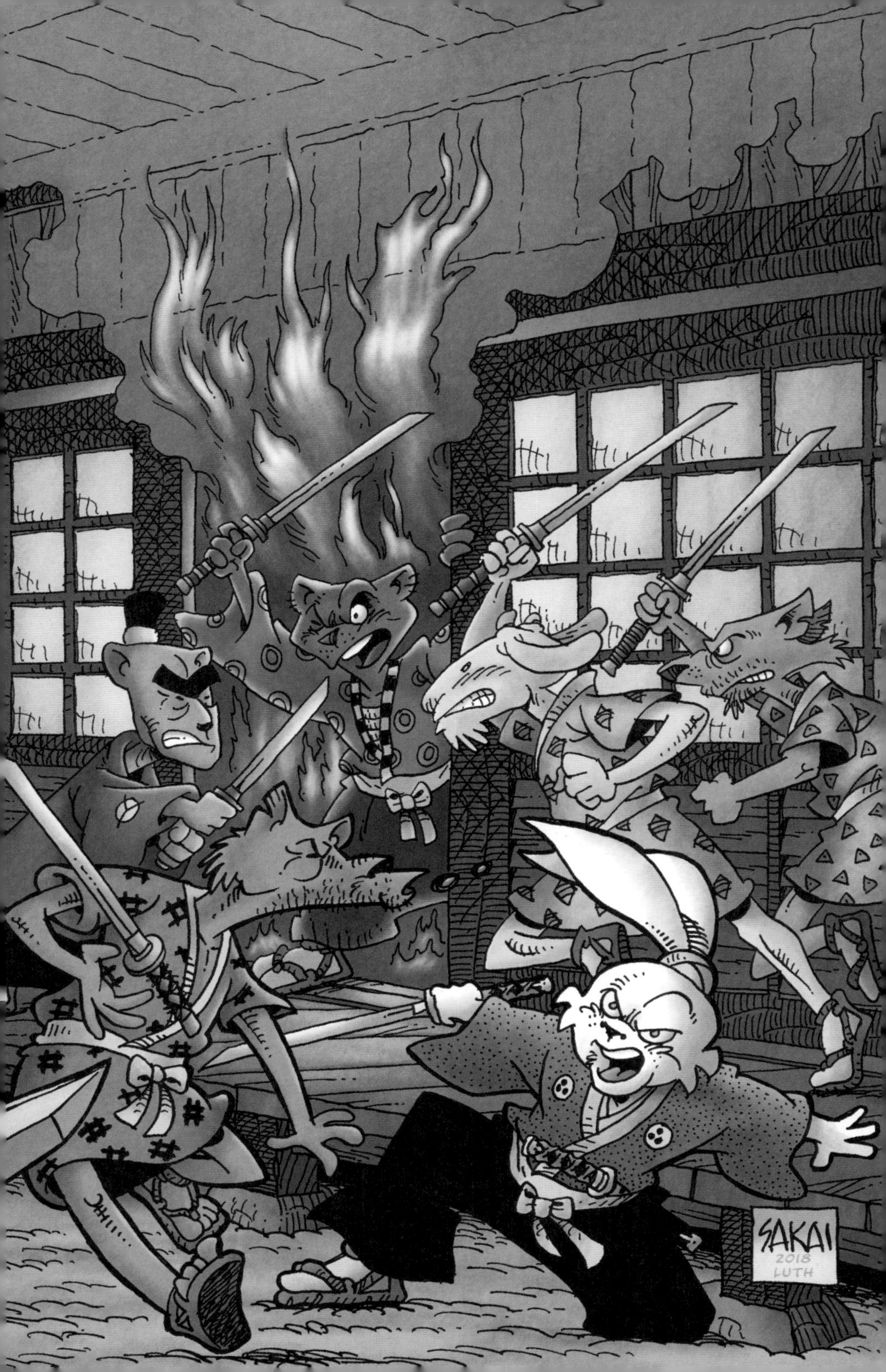
SAKAI
2018
LUTH

Usagi Yojimbo Volume Three #159 Back Cover, by Stan Sakai and Julie Fujii Sakai

Usagi Yojimbo Volume Three #160 Back Cover, by Stan Sakai and Julie Fujii Sakai

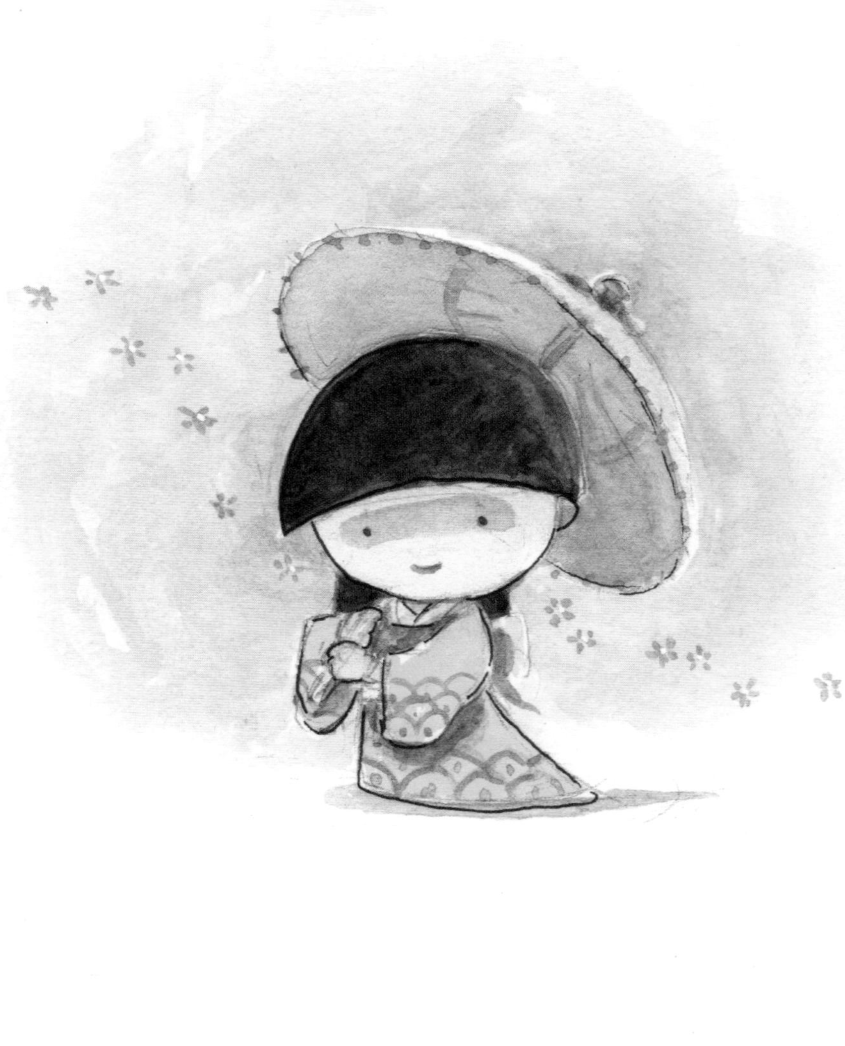

Usagi Yojimbo Volume Three #161 Back Cover, by Stan Sakai and Julie Fujii Sakai

Usagi Yojimbo Volume Three #162 Back Cover, by Stan Sakai and Julie Fujii Sakai

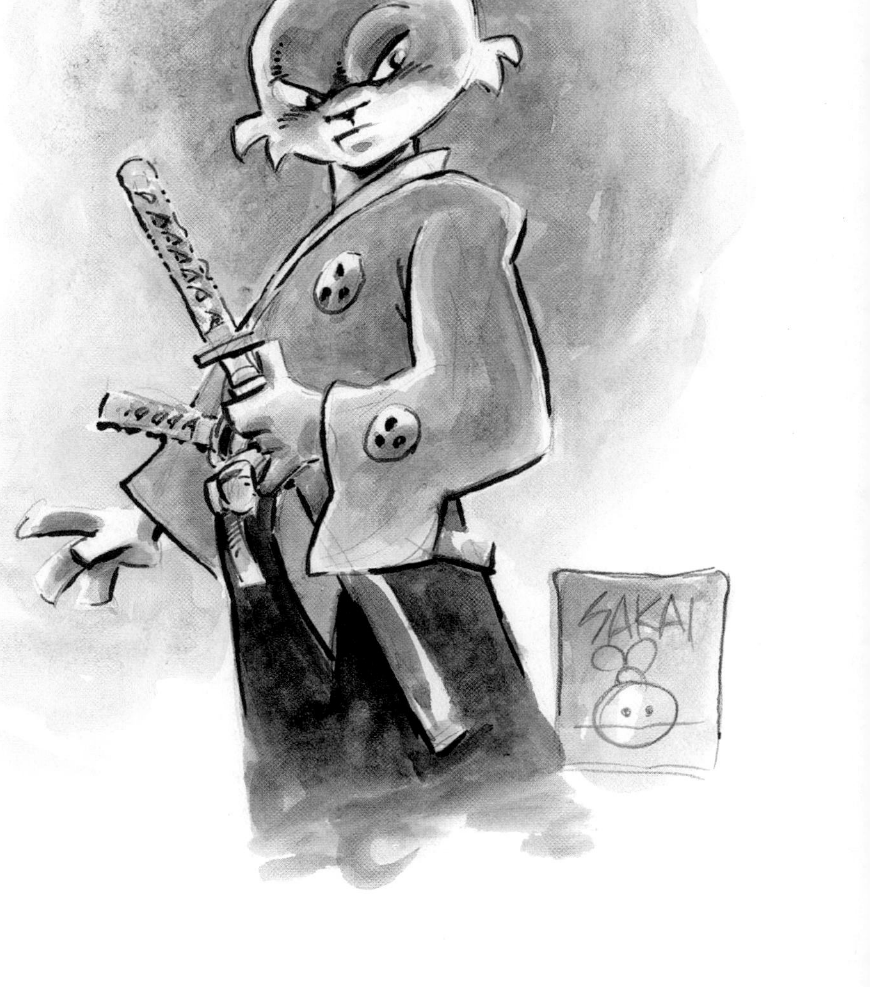
SAKAI

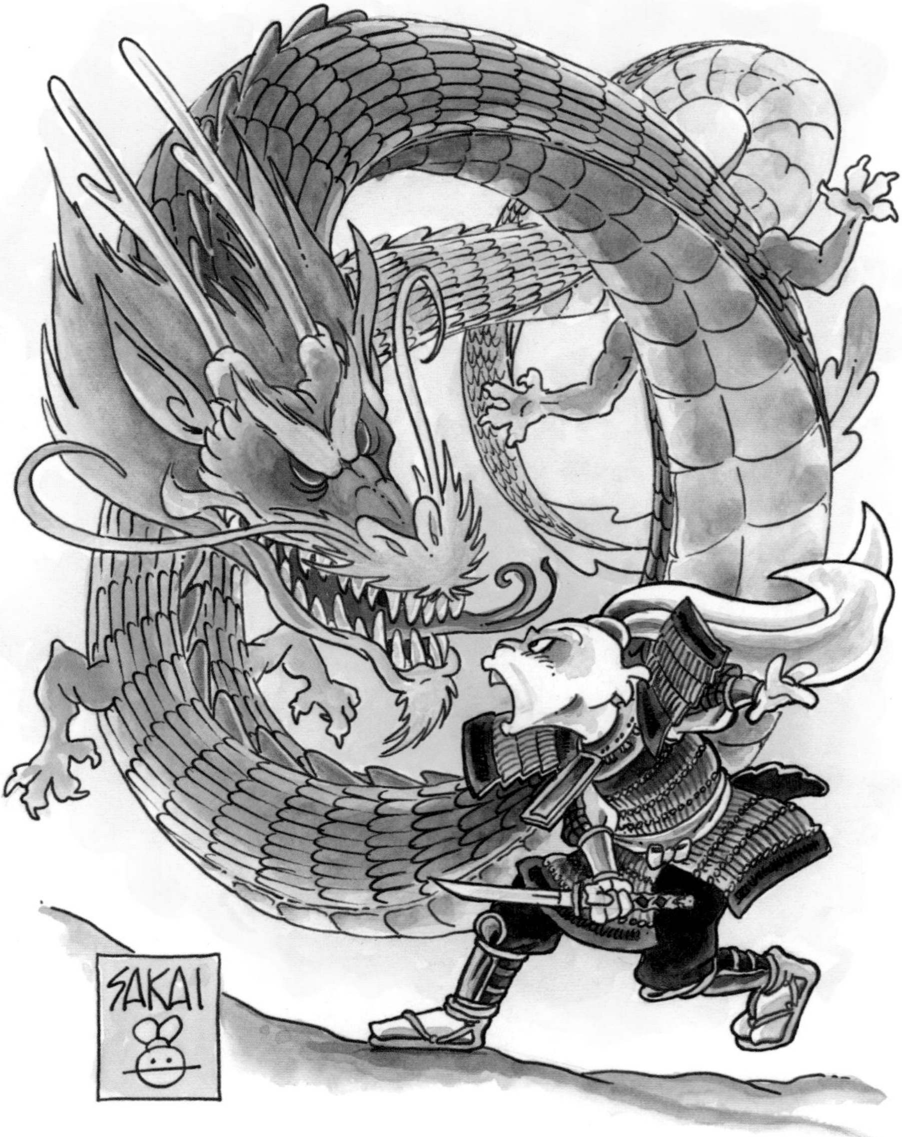
SAKAI

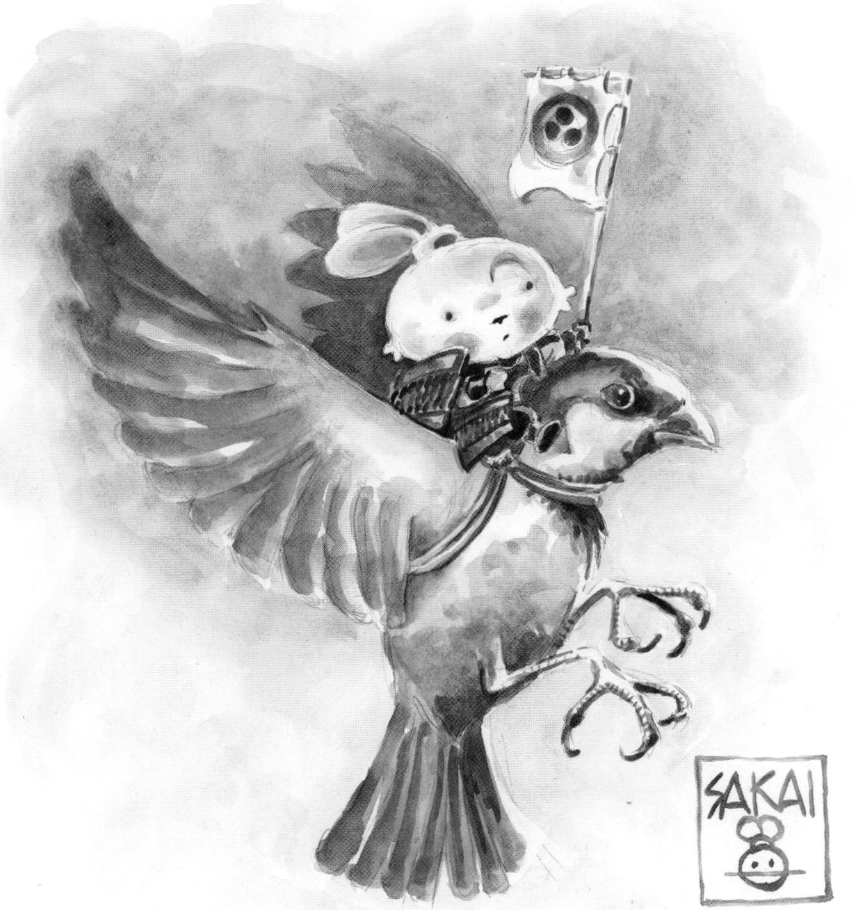
SAKAI

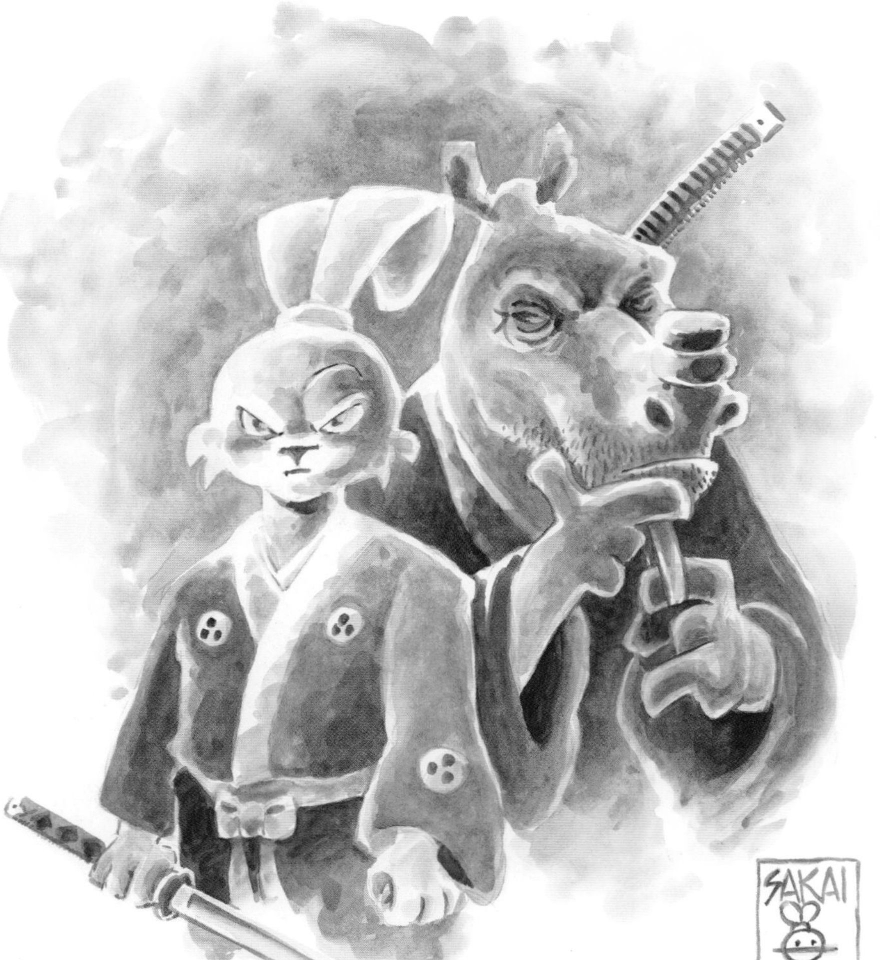
SAKAI

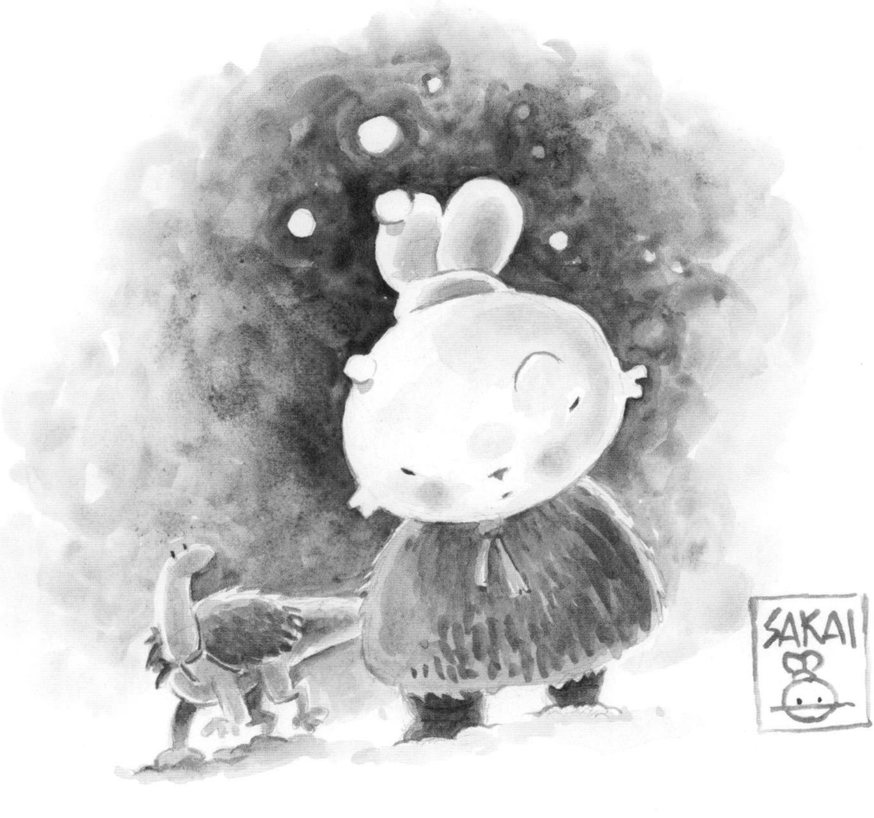
SAKAI

SAKAI

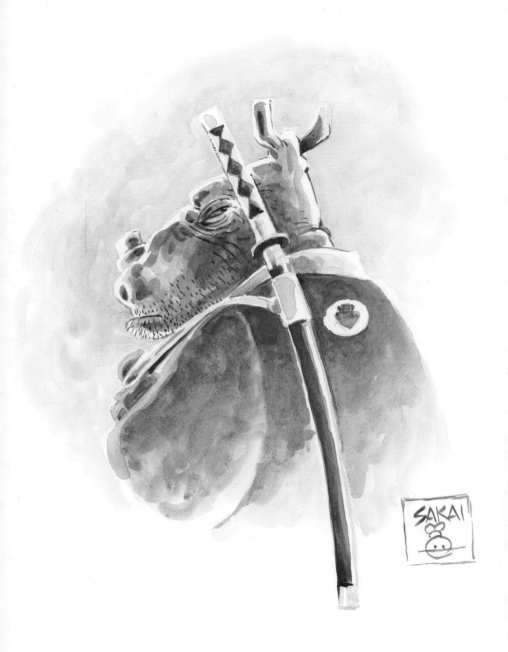

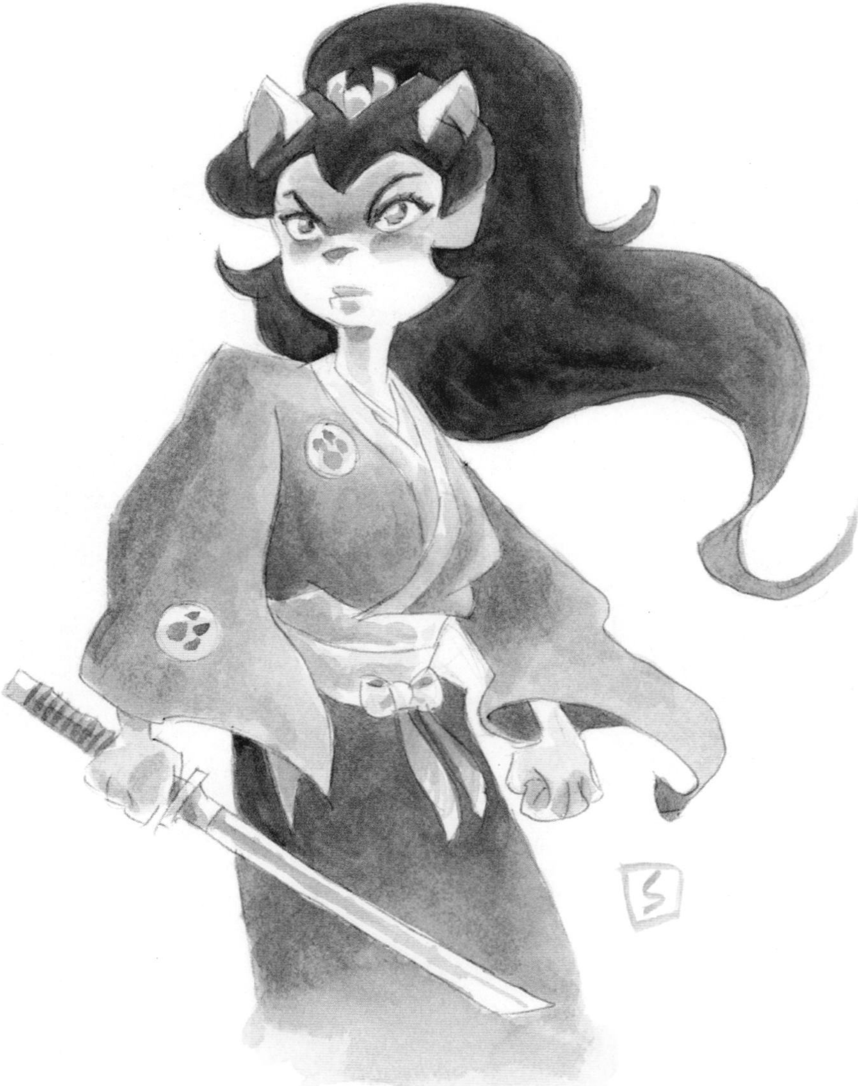

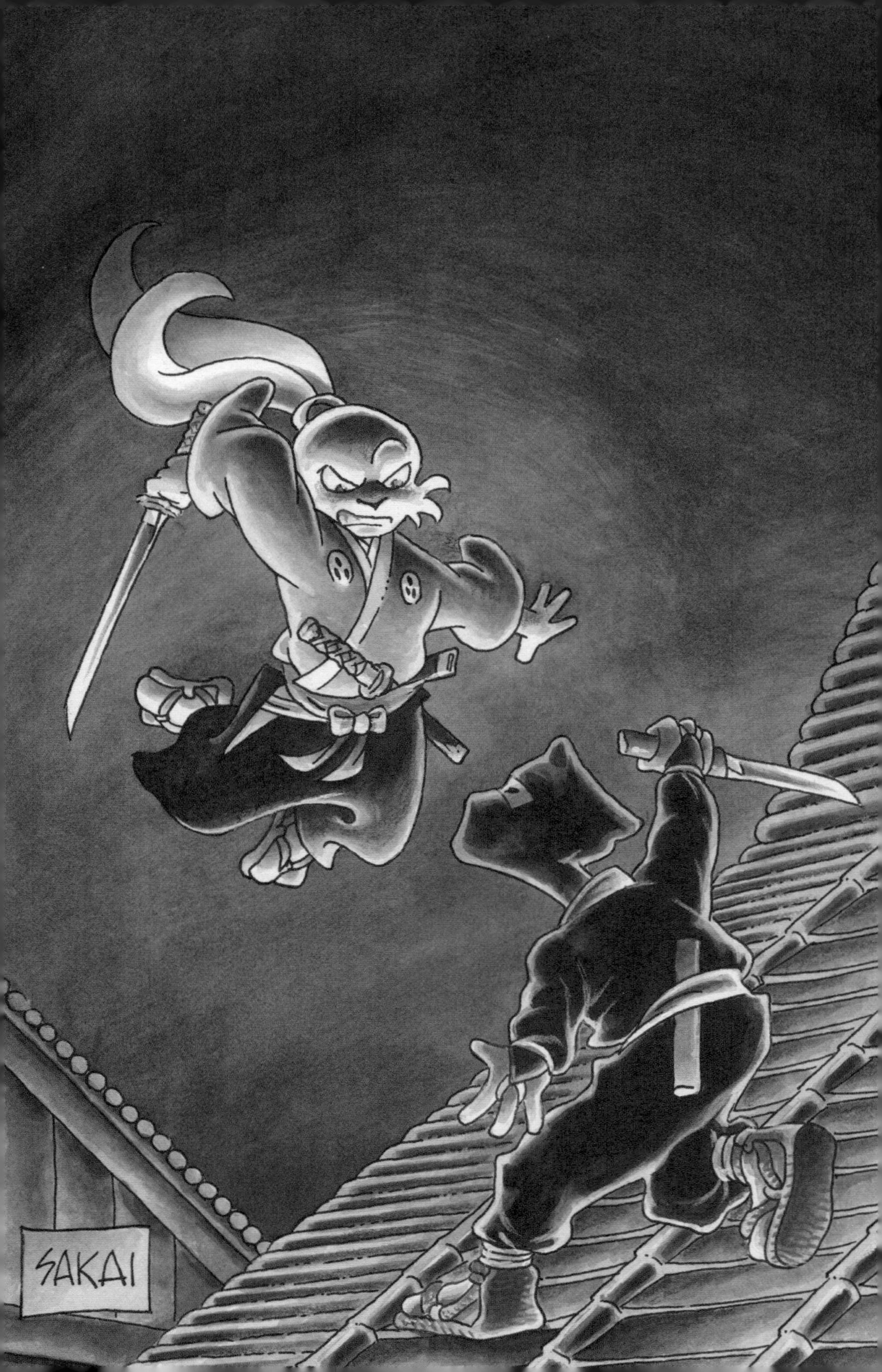
SAKAI

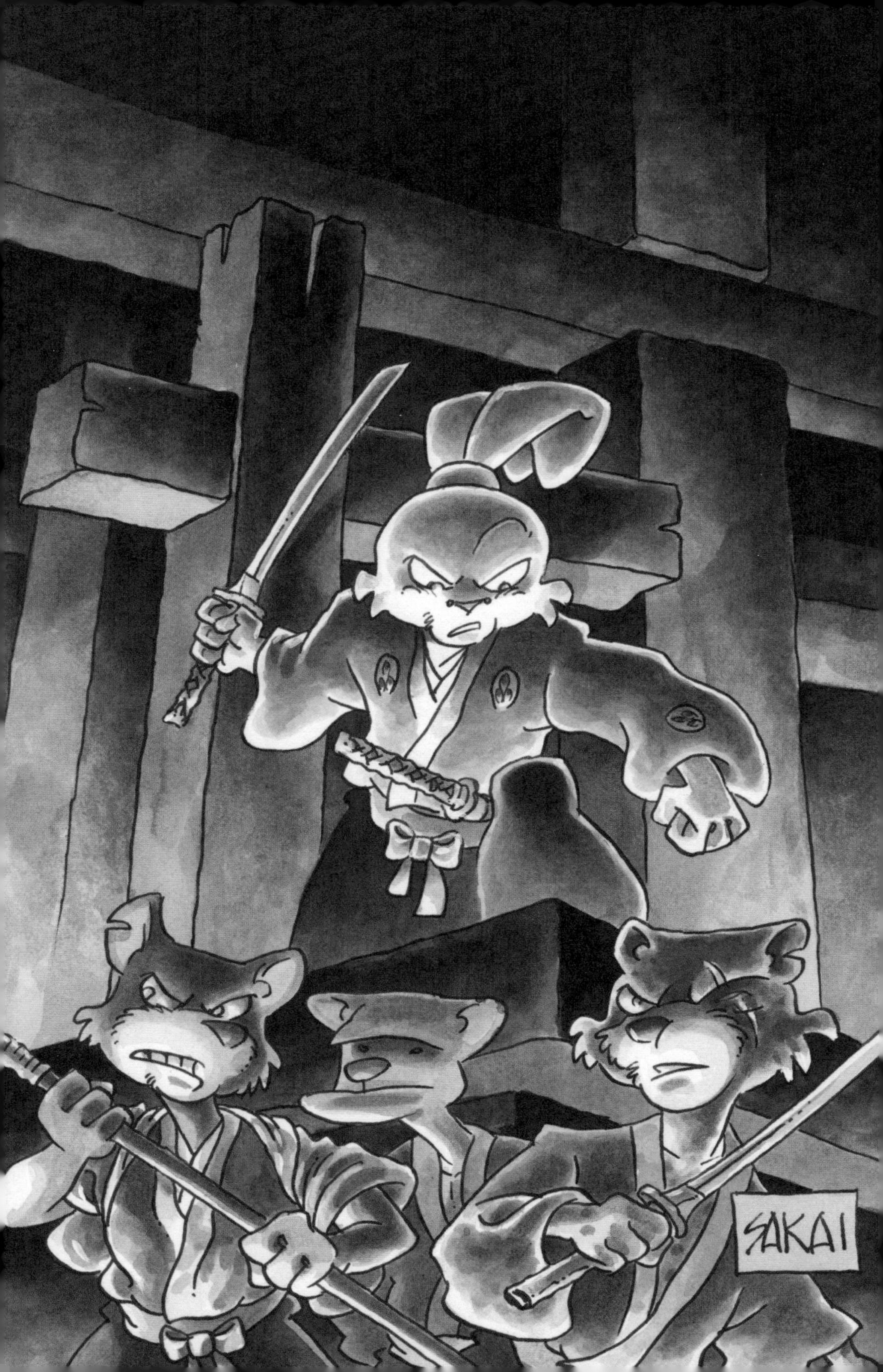
SAKAI

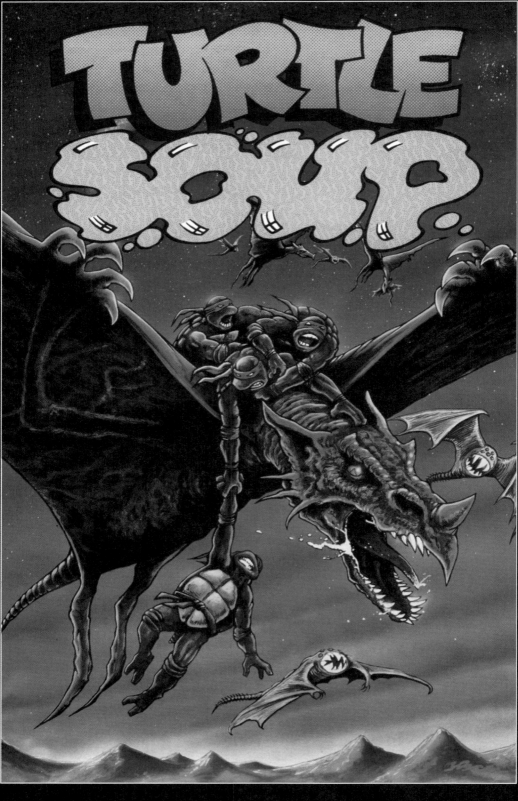

Turtle Soup #1
Art by Steve Bissette and Kevin Eastman

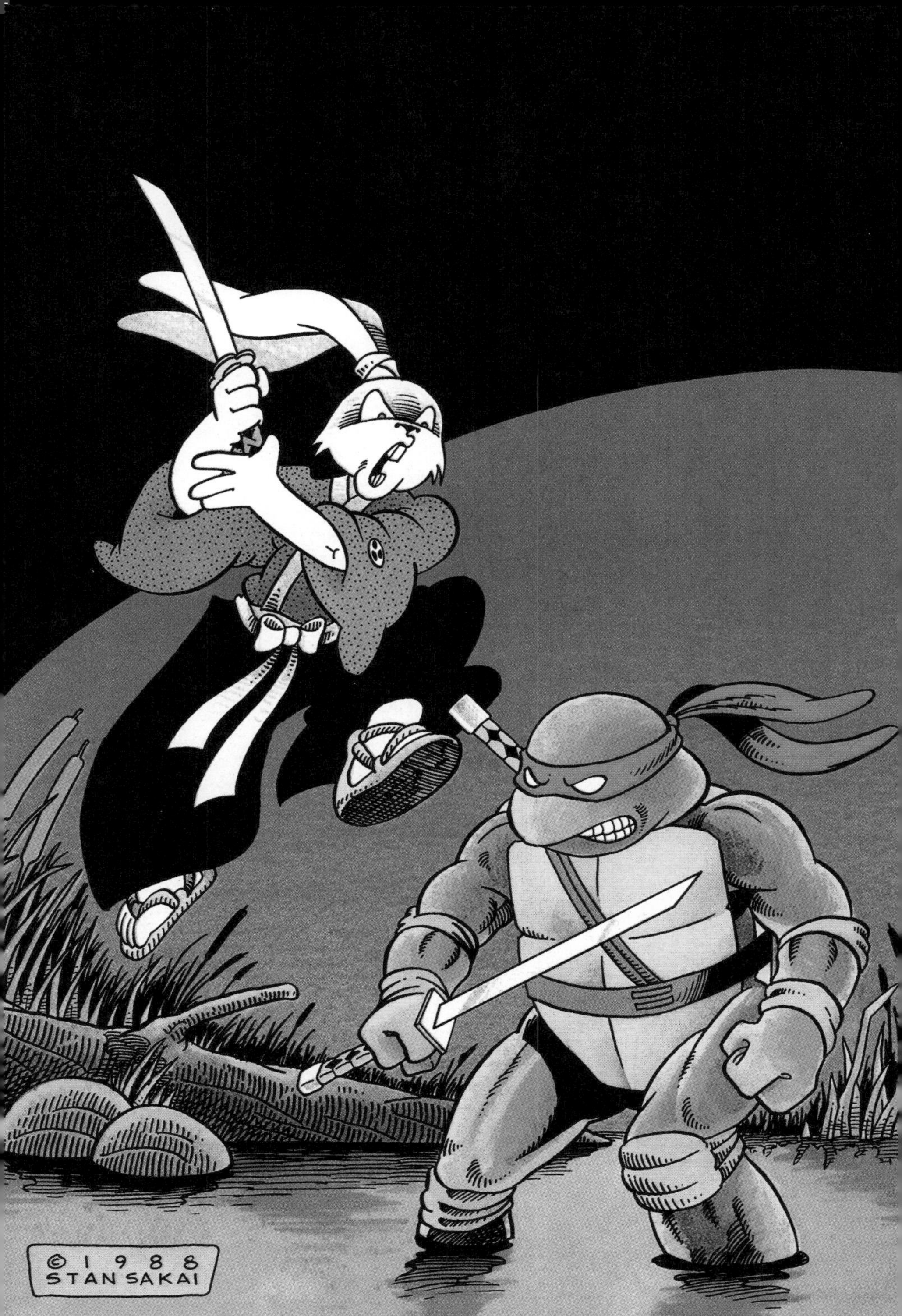
©1988
STAN SAKAI

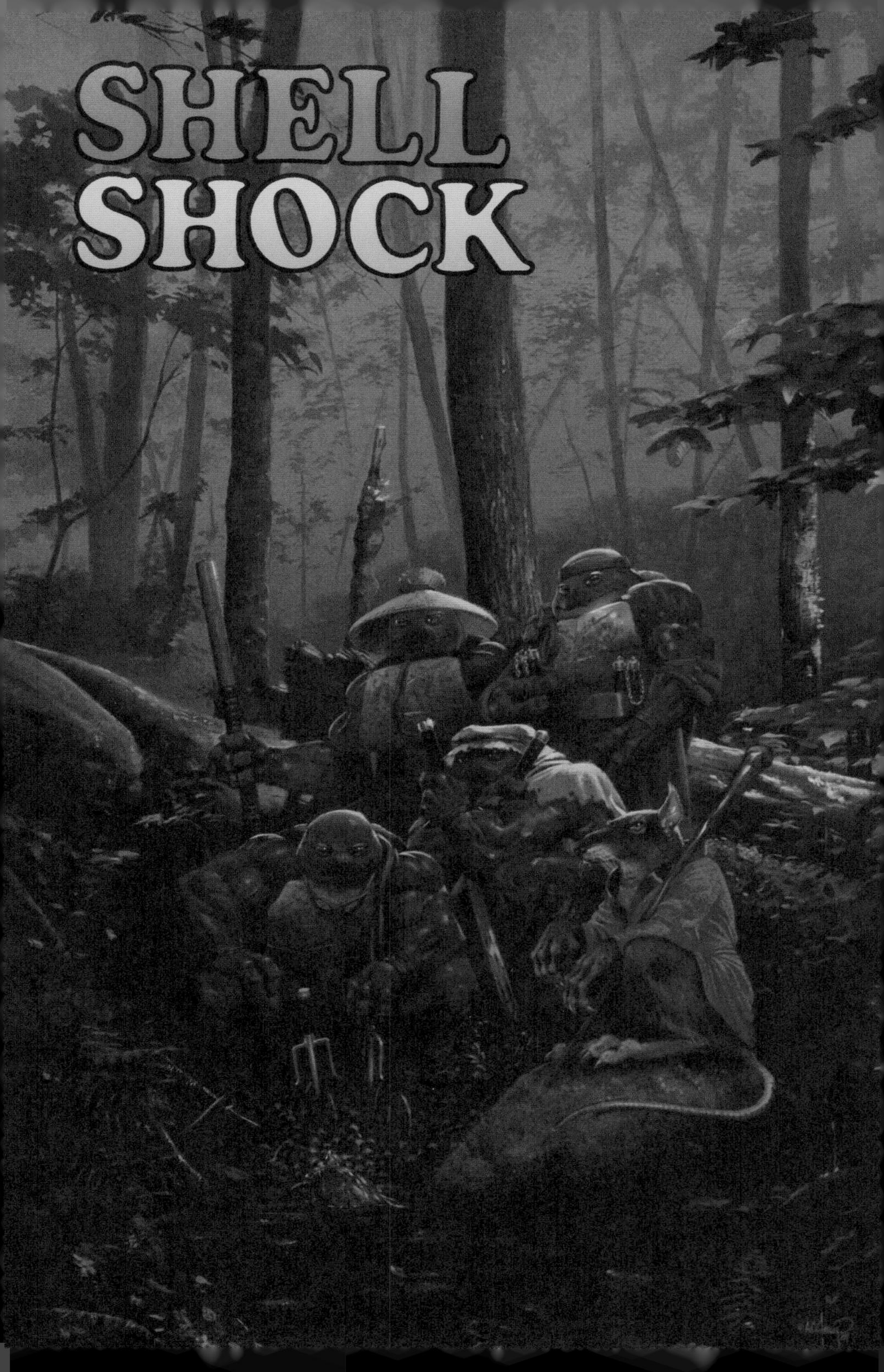
SHELL
SHOCK

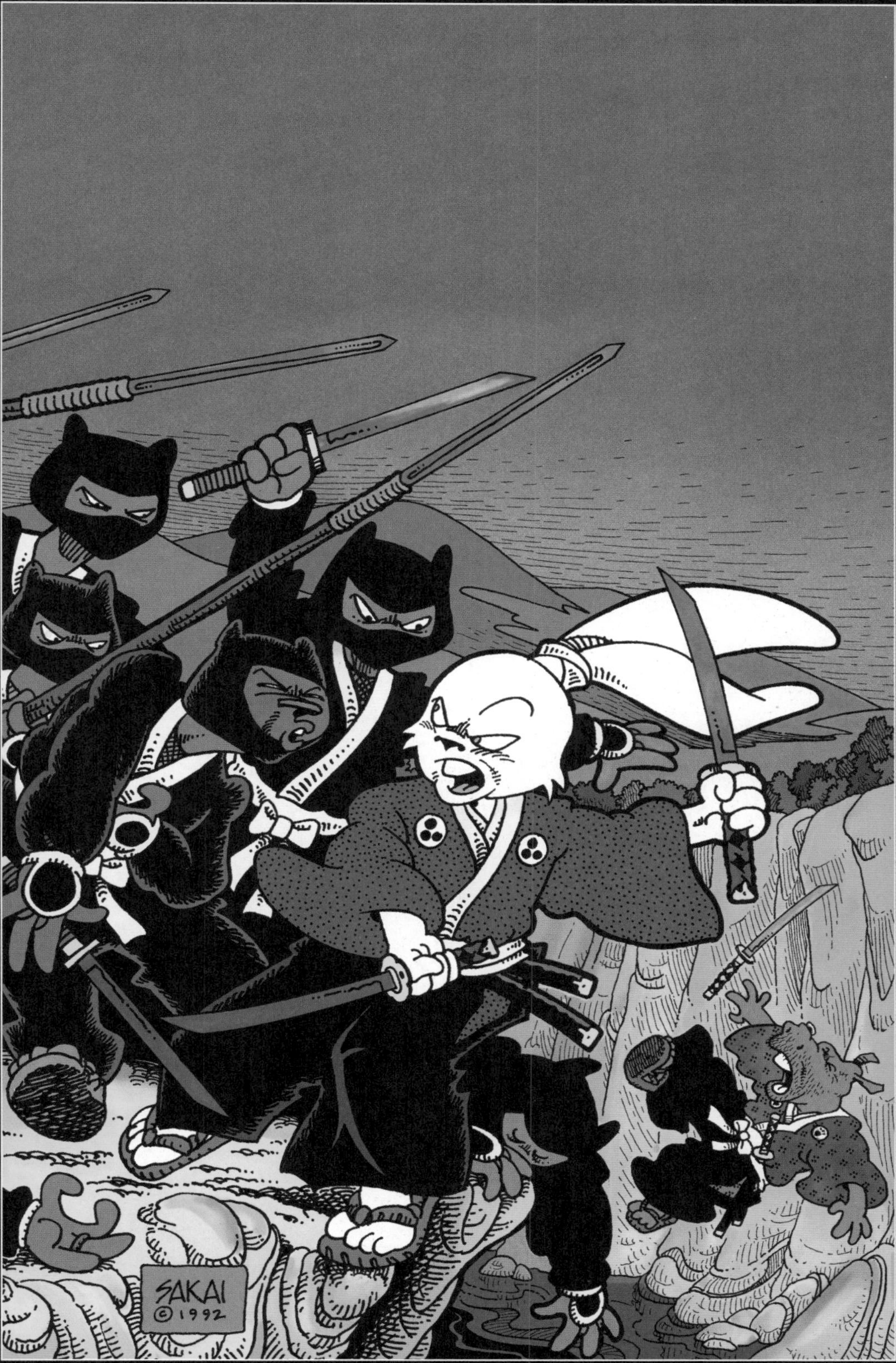
SAKAI
©1992

Usagi Yojimbo Volume Two #1
Art by Stan Sakai, Colors by Tom Luth

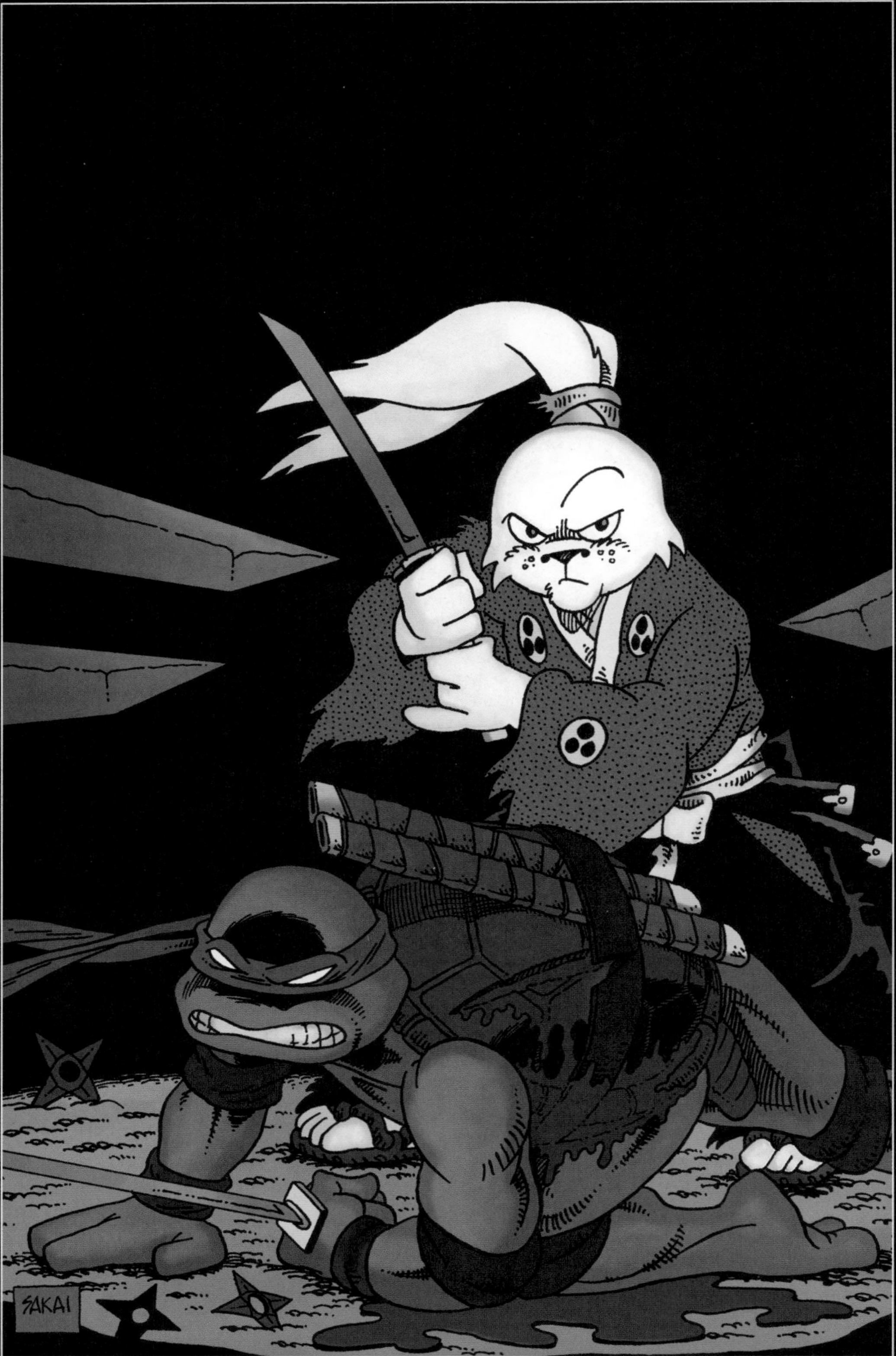
SAKAI

Usagi Yojimbo Volume Two #2
Art by Stan Sakai, Colors by Tom Luth

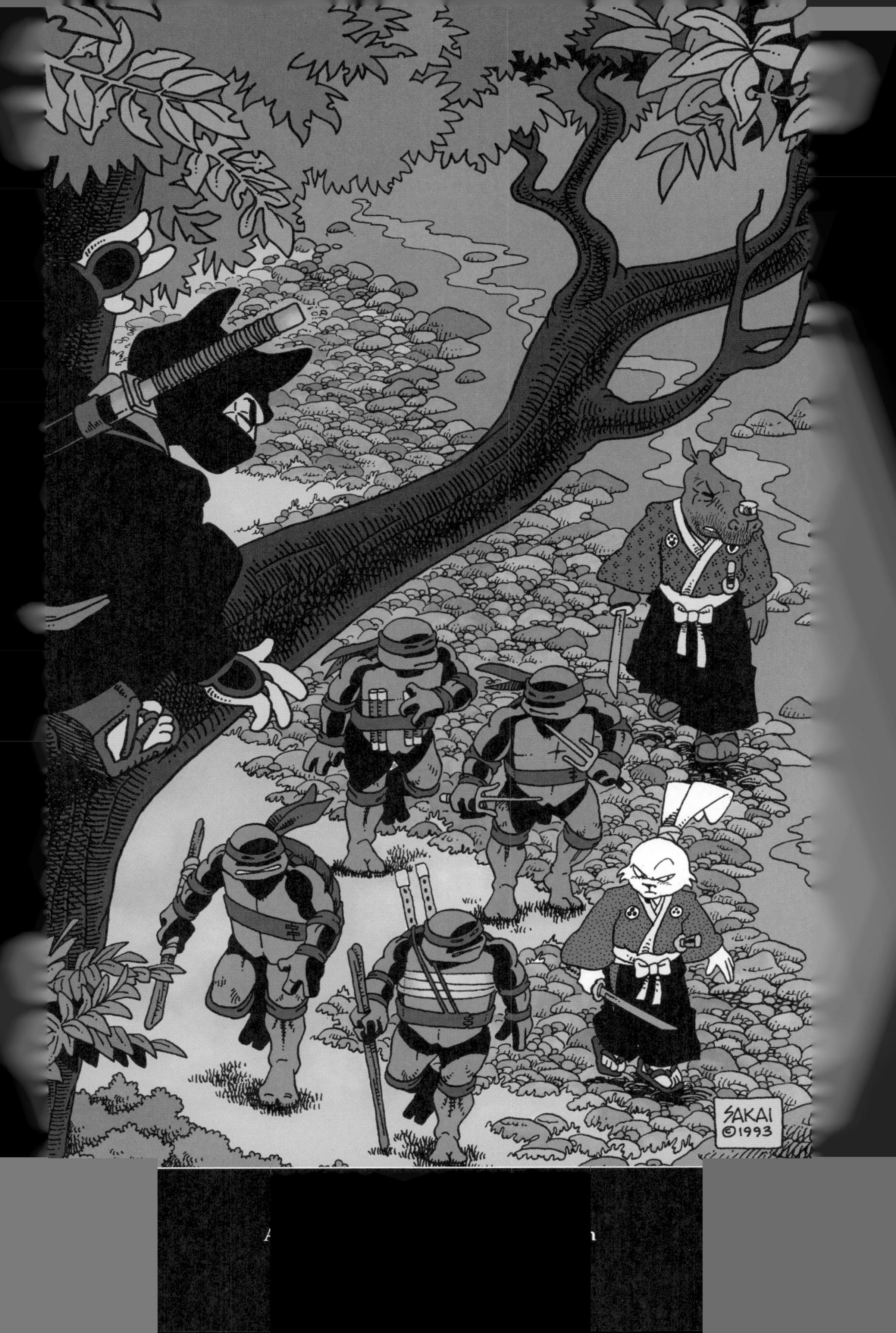
SAKAI
©1993

[redacted]

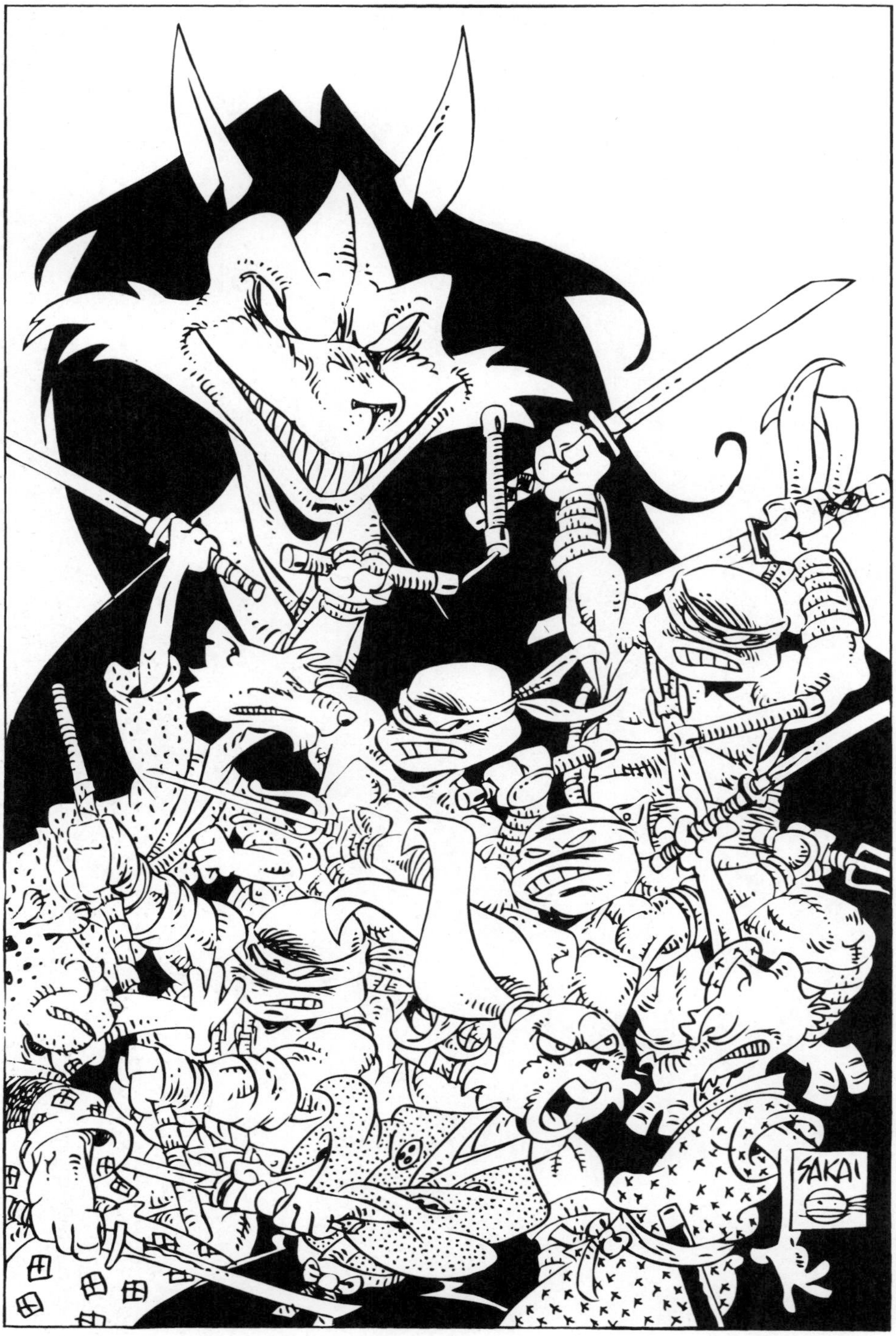
SAKAI

Teenage Mutant Ninja Turtles/Usagi Yojimbo Cover A
Line art by Stan Sakai

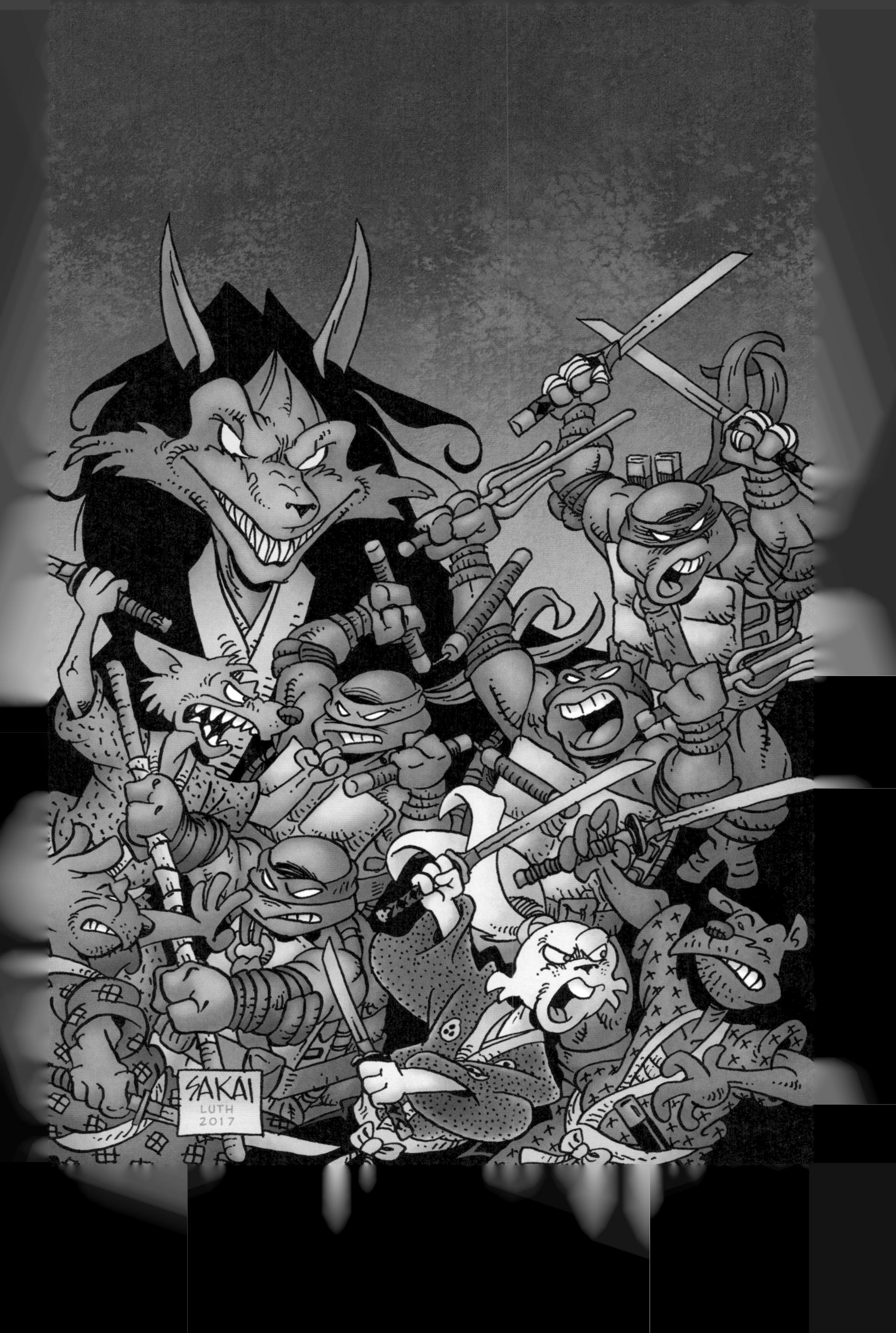
SAKAI
LUTH
2017

TMNT/USAGI YOJIMBO: NAMAZU SAKAI COVER VARIANT SKETCH

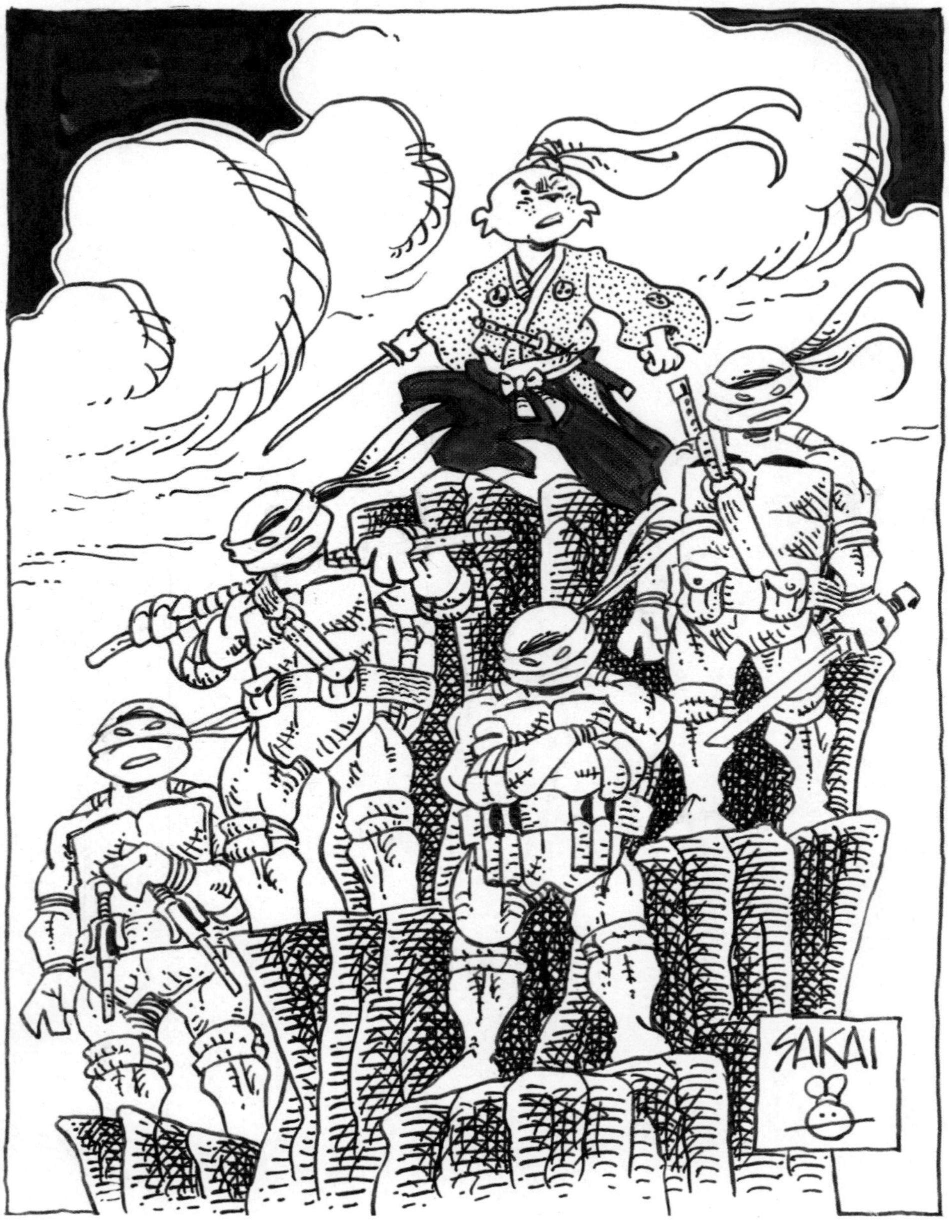
SAKAI

Teenage Mutant Ninja Turtles/Usagi Yojimbo Stan Sakai Variant Cover
Sketch by Stan Sakai

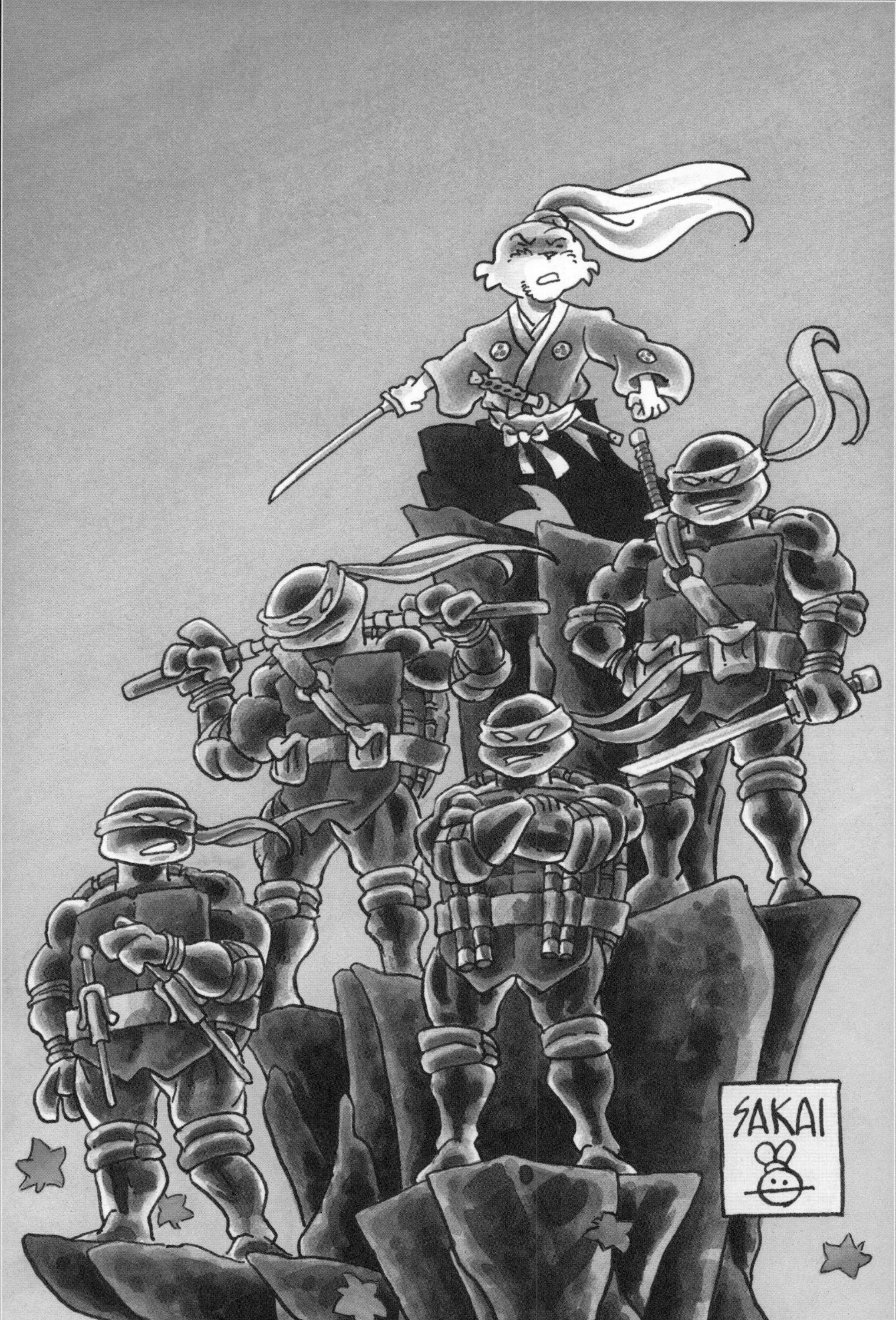
SAKAI

Teenage Mutant Ninja Turtles/Usagi Yojimbo Stan Sakai Variant Cover
Art by Stan Sakai

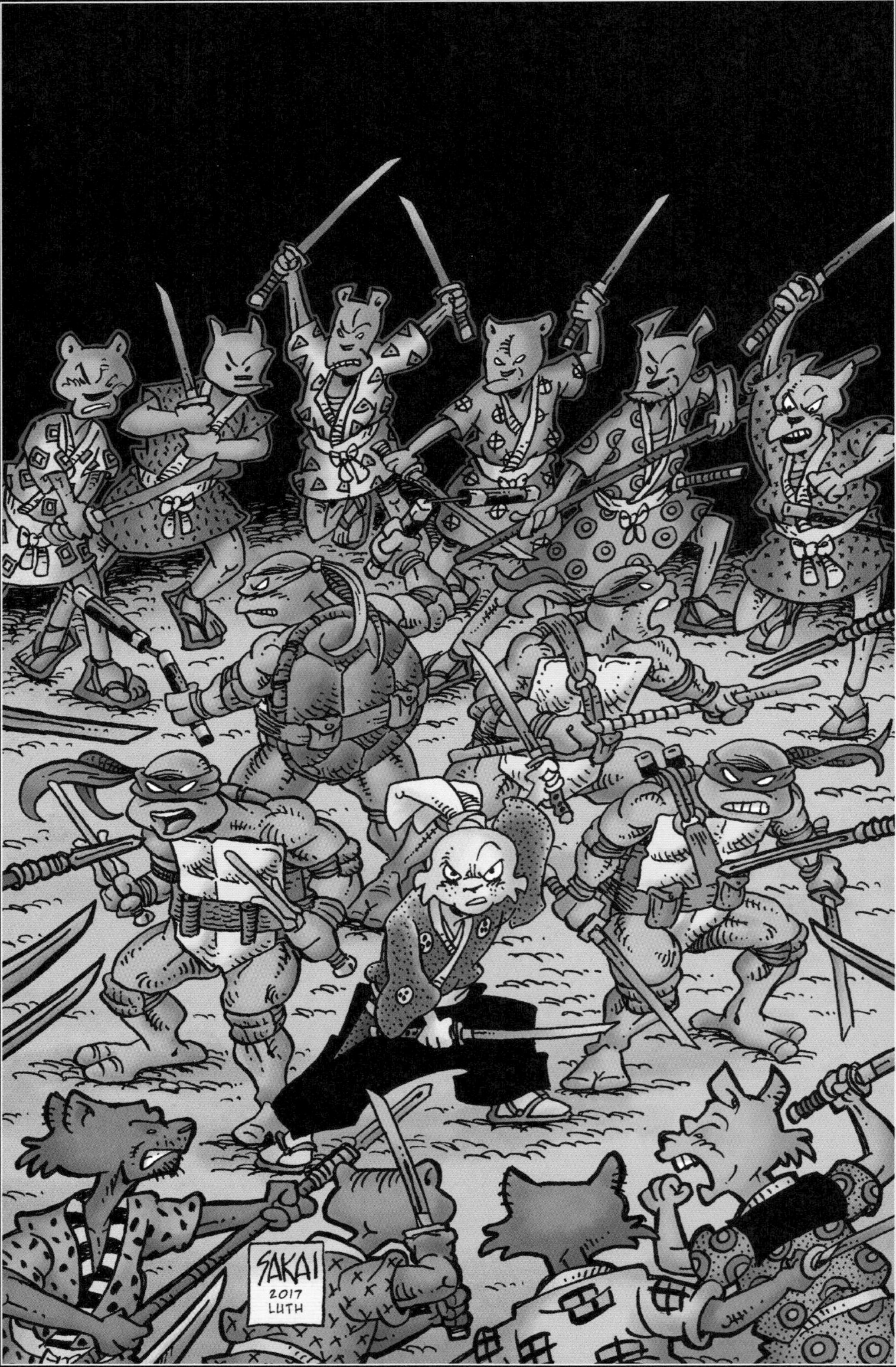
SAKAI
2017
LUTH

Teenage Mutant Ninja Turtles/Usagi Yojimbo **Fried Pie Exclusive Cover**
Art by Stan Sakai, Colors by Tom Luth

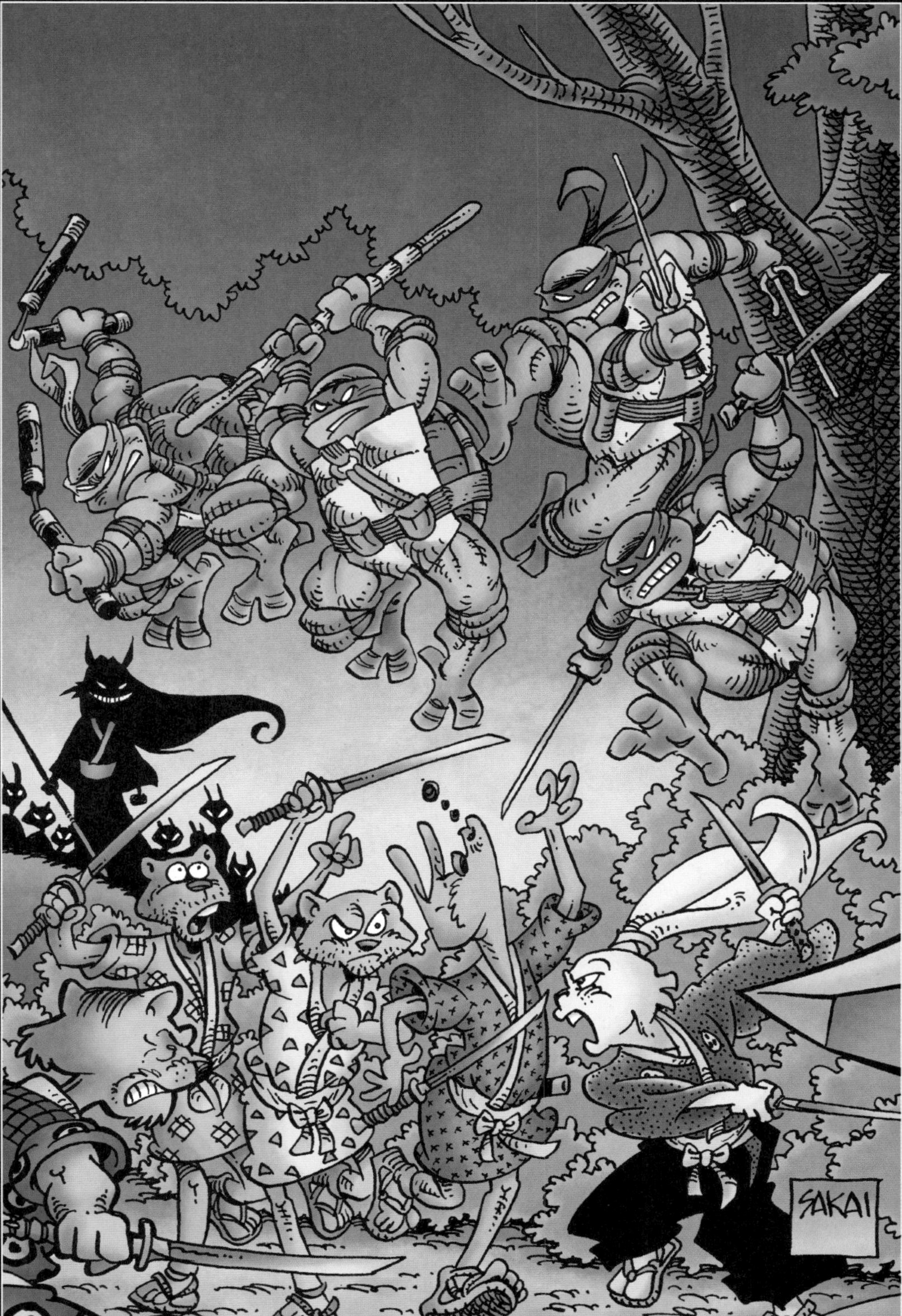

SAKAI

Teenage Mutant Ninja Turtles/Usagi Yojimbo Other Realms Exclusive Cover
Art by Stan Sakai, Colors by Tom Luth

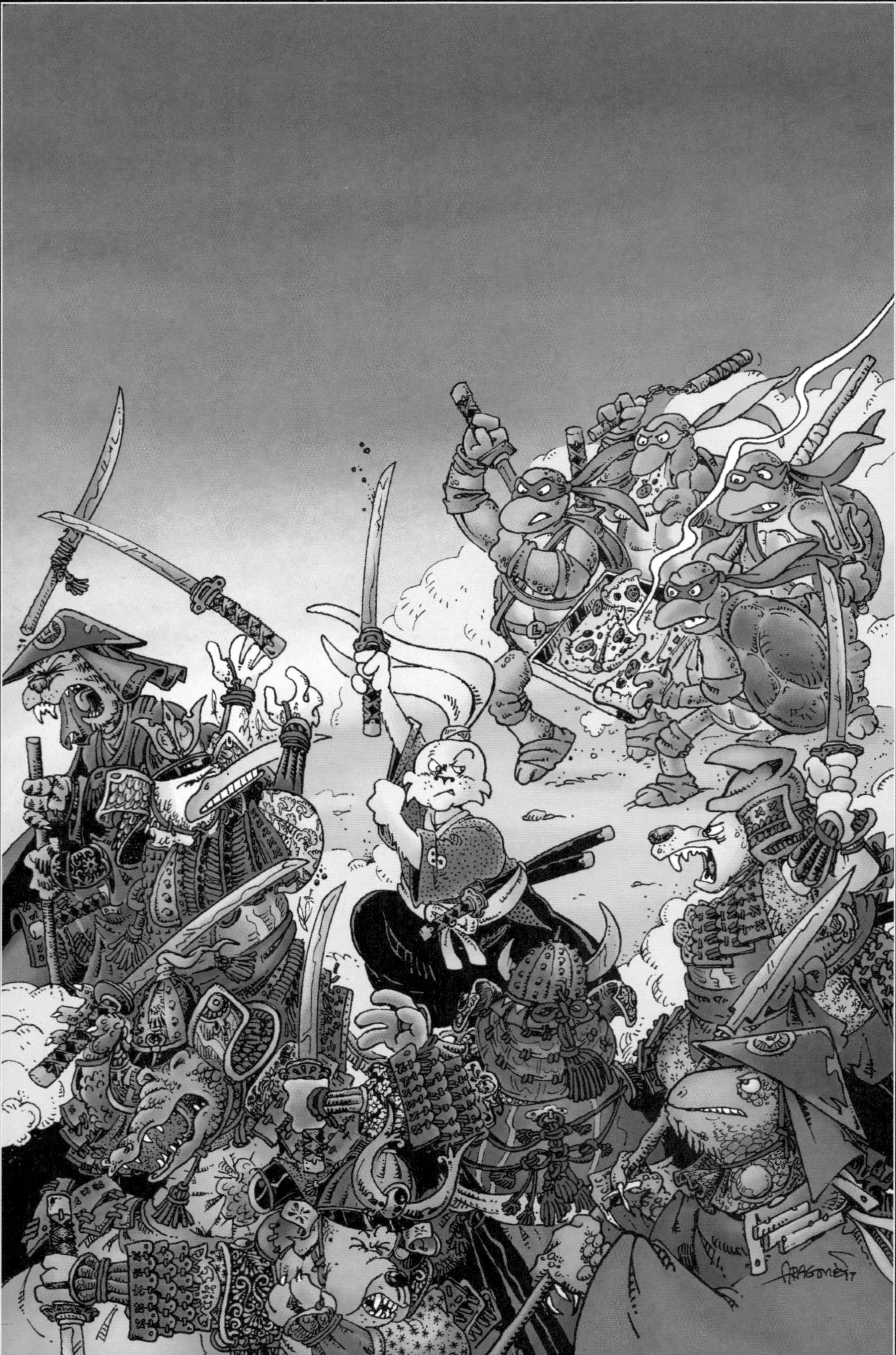
ARAGONÉS

Teenage Mutant Ninja Turtles/Usagi Yojimbo Cover B
Art by Sergio Aragonés, Colors by Tom Luth

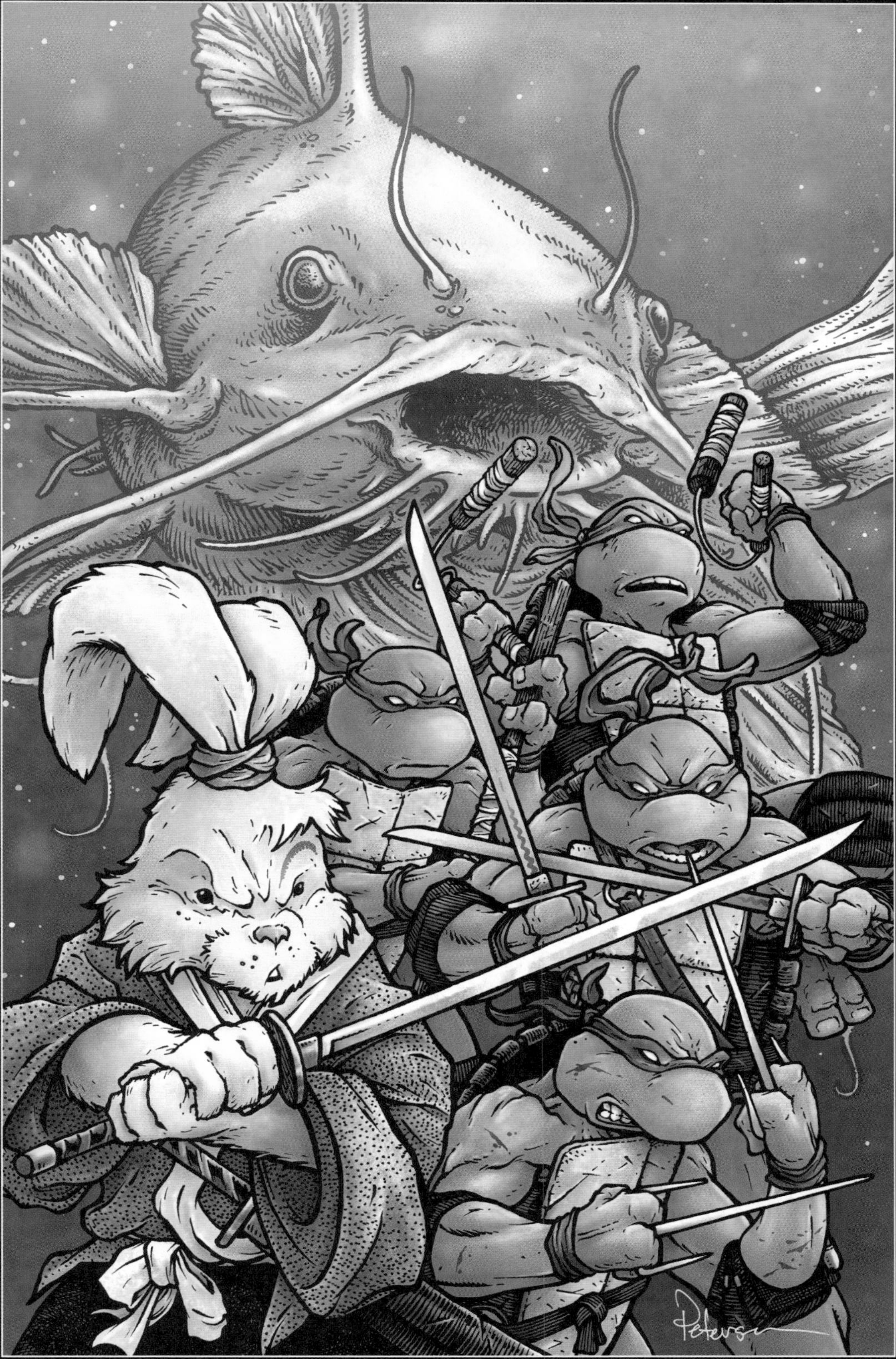
Petersen

Teenage Mutant Ninja Turtles/Usagi Yojimbo Incentive Cover
Art by David Petersen

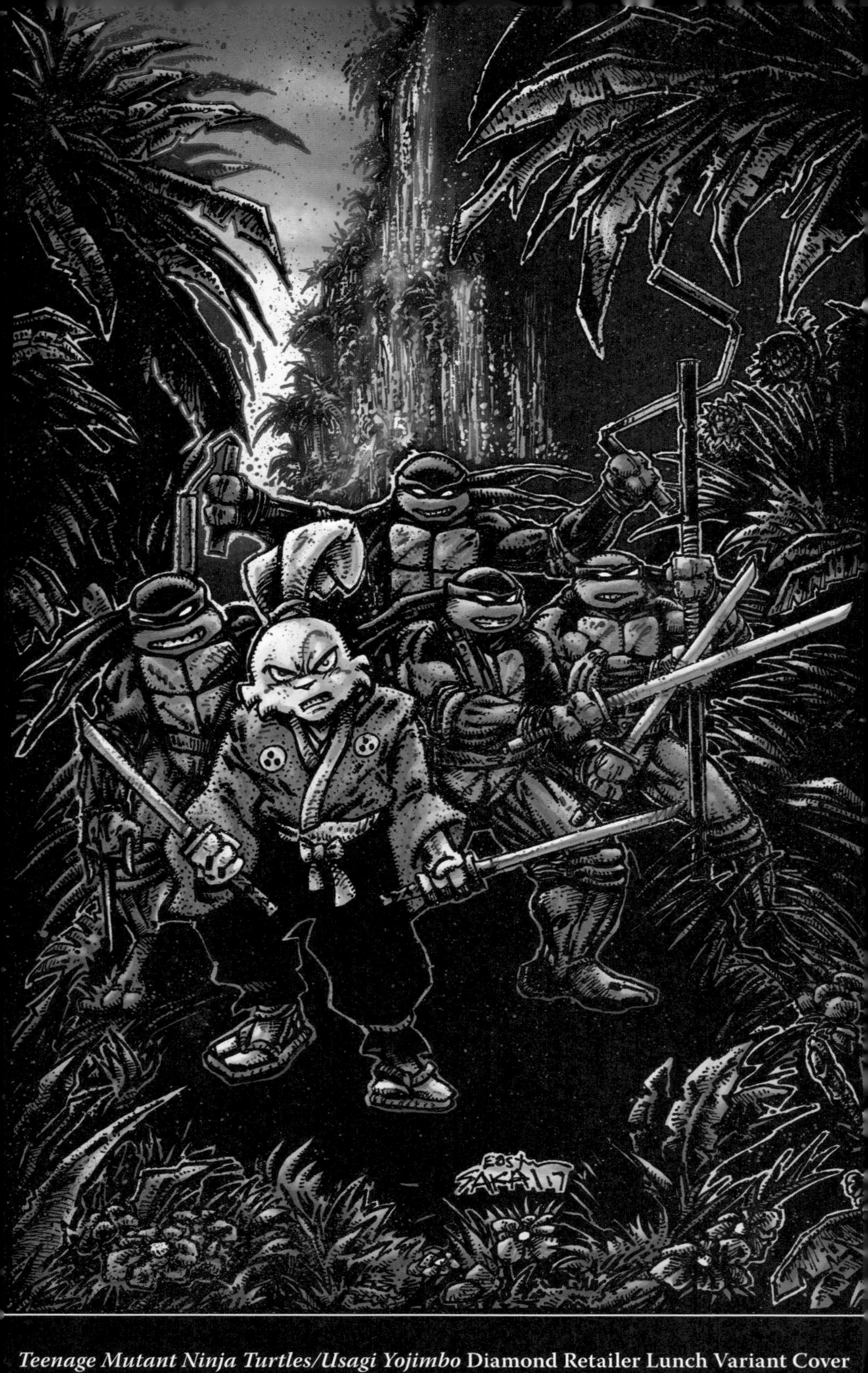

Teenage Mutant Ninja Turtles/Usagi Yojimbo Diamond Retailer Lunch Variant Cover

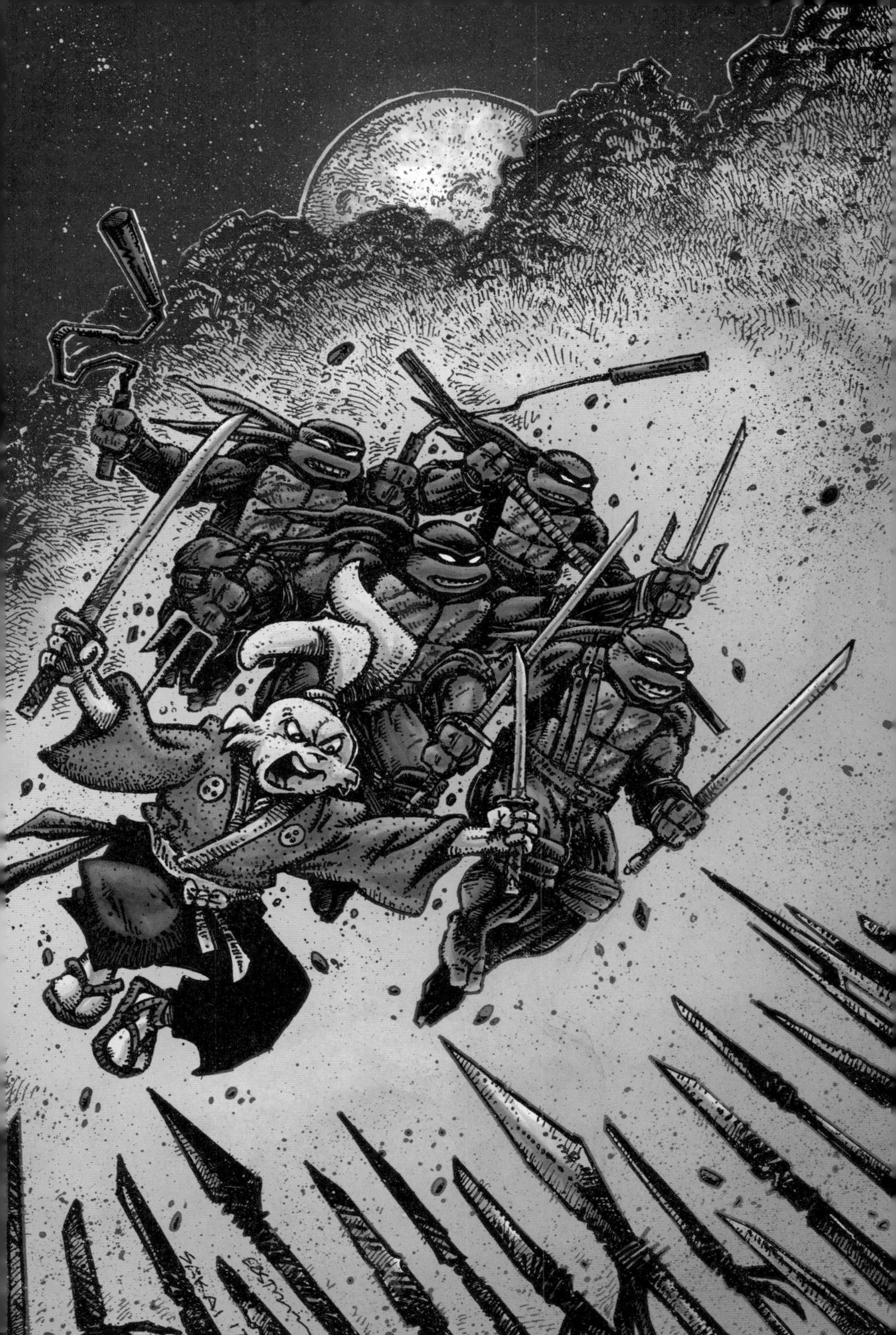

Teenage Mutant Ninja Turtles/Usagi Yojimbo IDW Convention Cover
Art by Kevin Eastman with Stan Sakai. Colors by Tomi Varga.

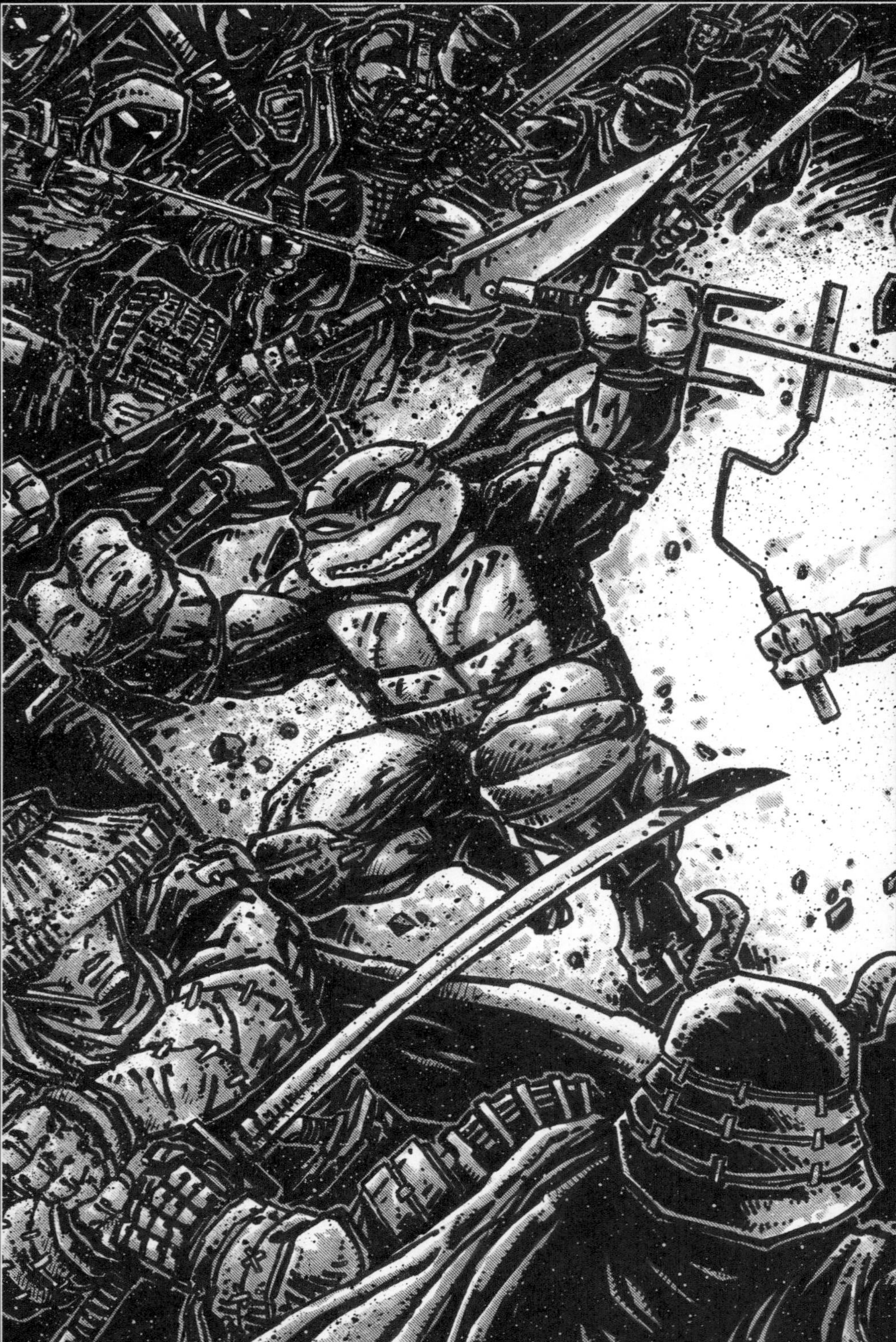

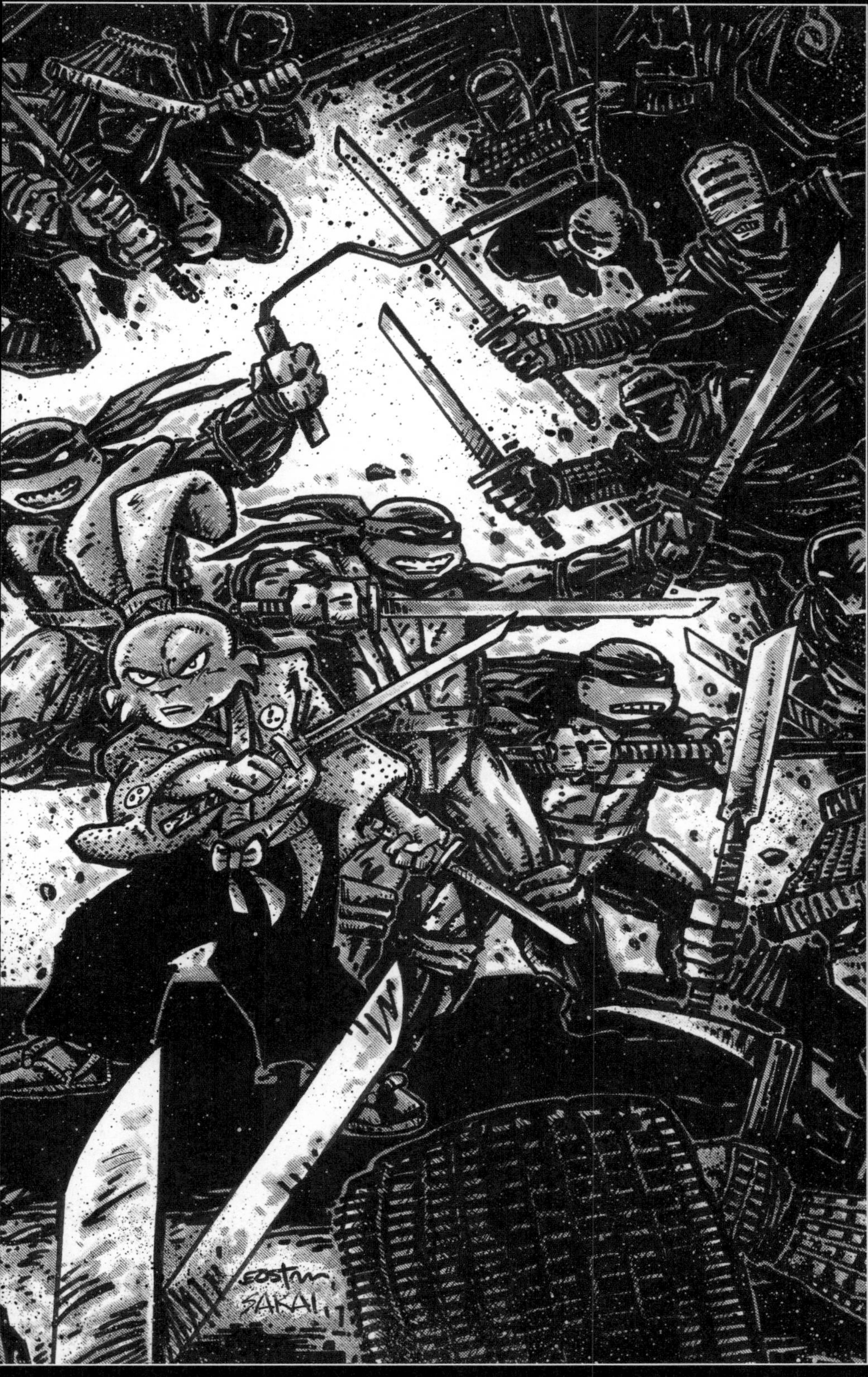

Teenage Mutant Ninja Turtles/Usagi Yojimbo
San Diego Comic Art Gallery Exclusive Cover, Art by Kevin Eastman

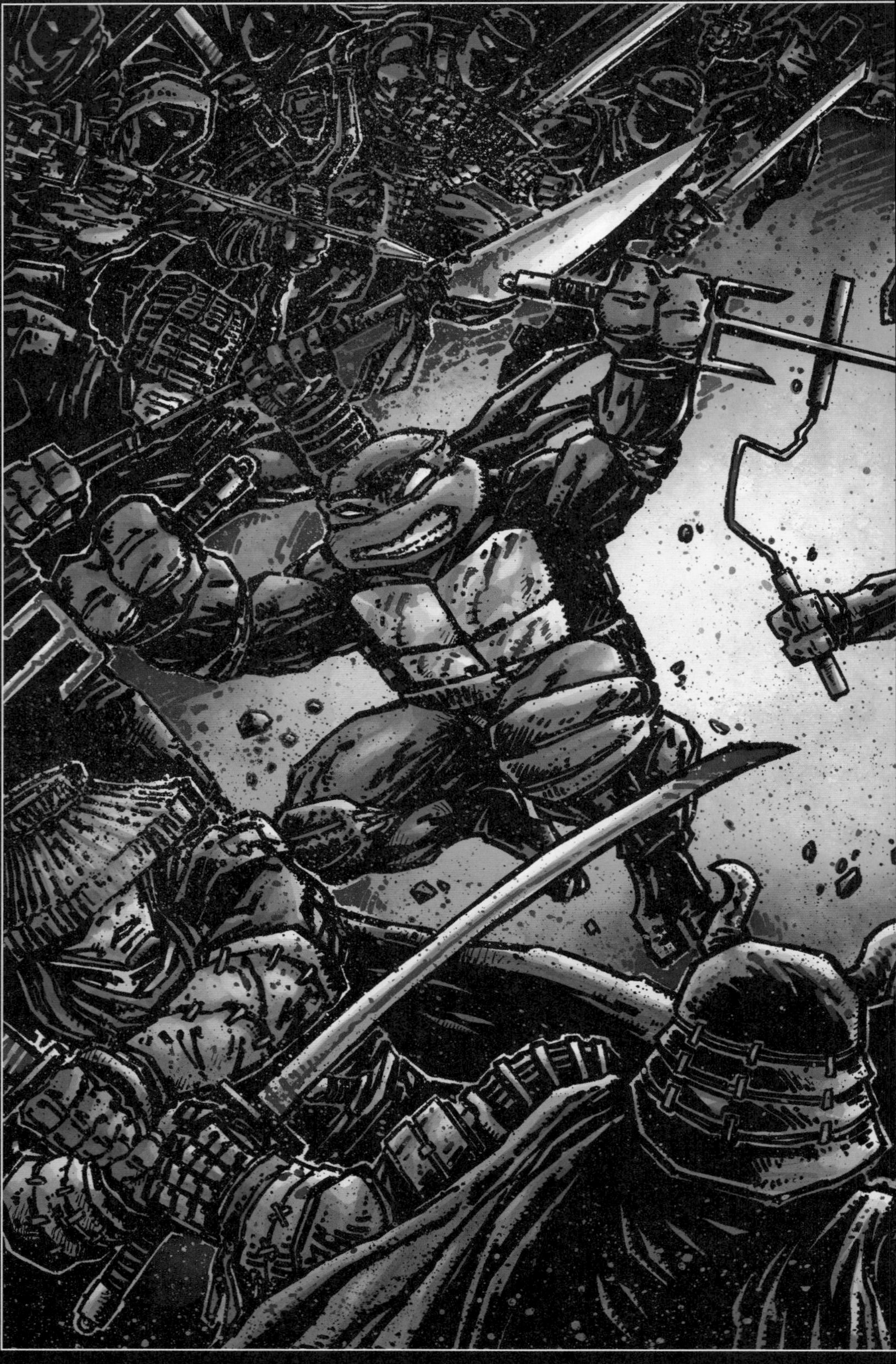

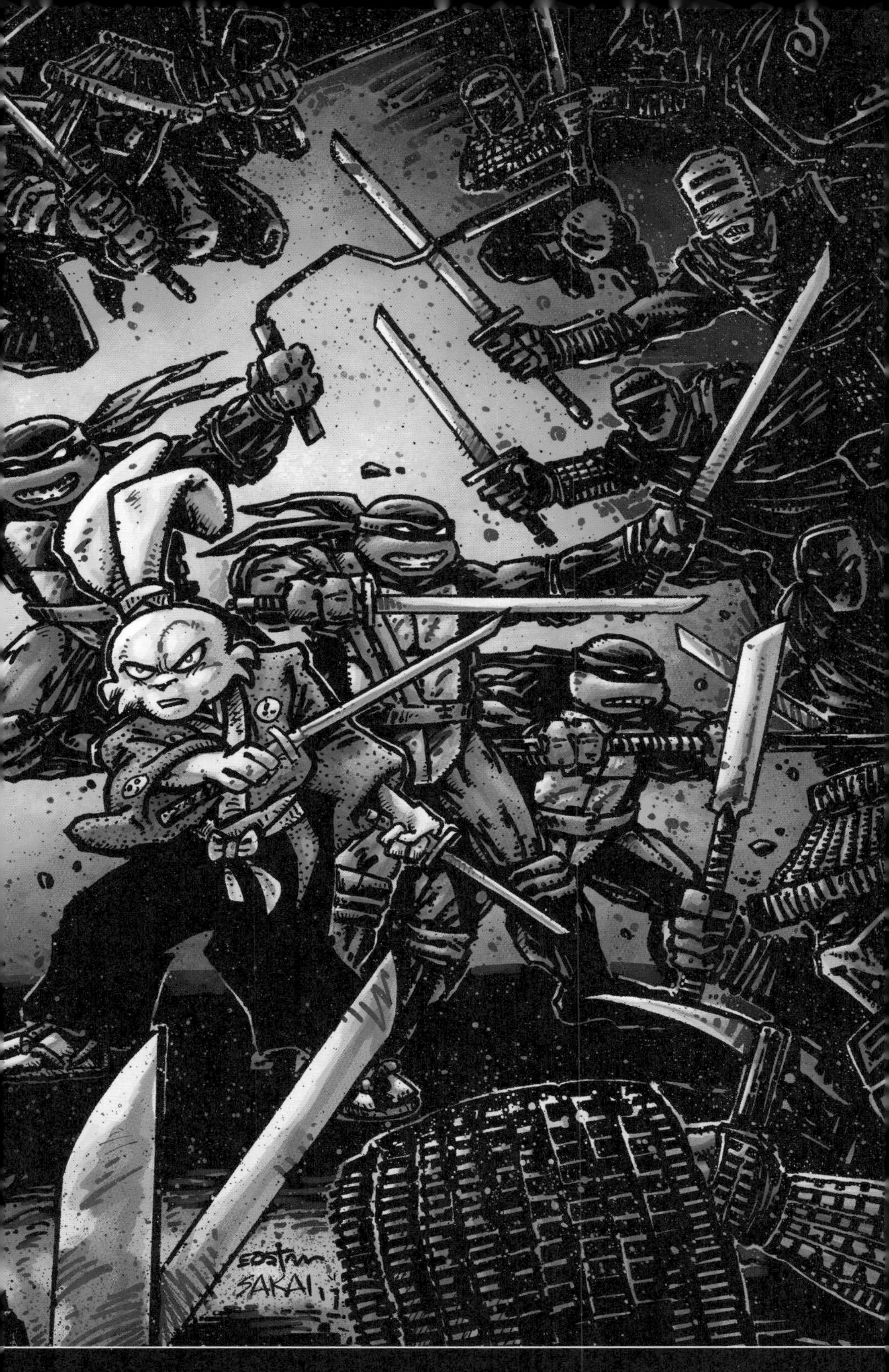

Teenage Mutant Ninja Turtles/Usagi Yojimbo Comics and Ponies Exclusive Cover. Art by Kevin Eastman with Stan Sakai. Colors by Tomi Varga

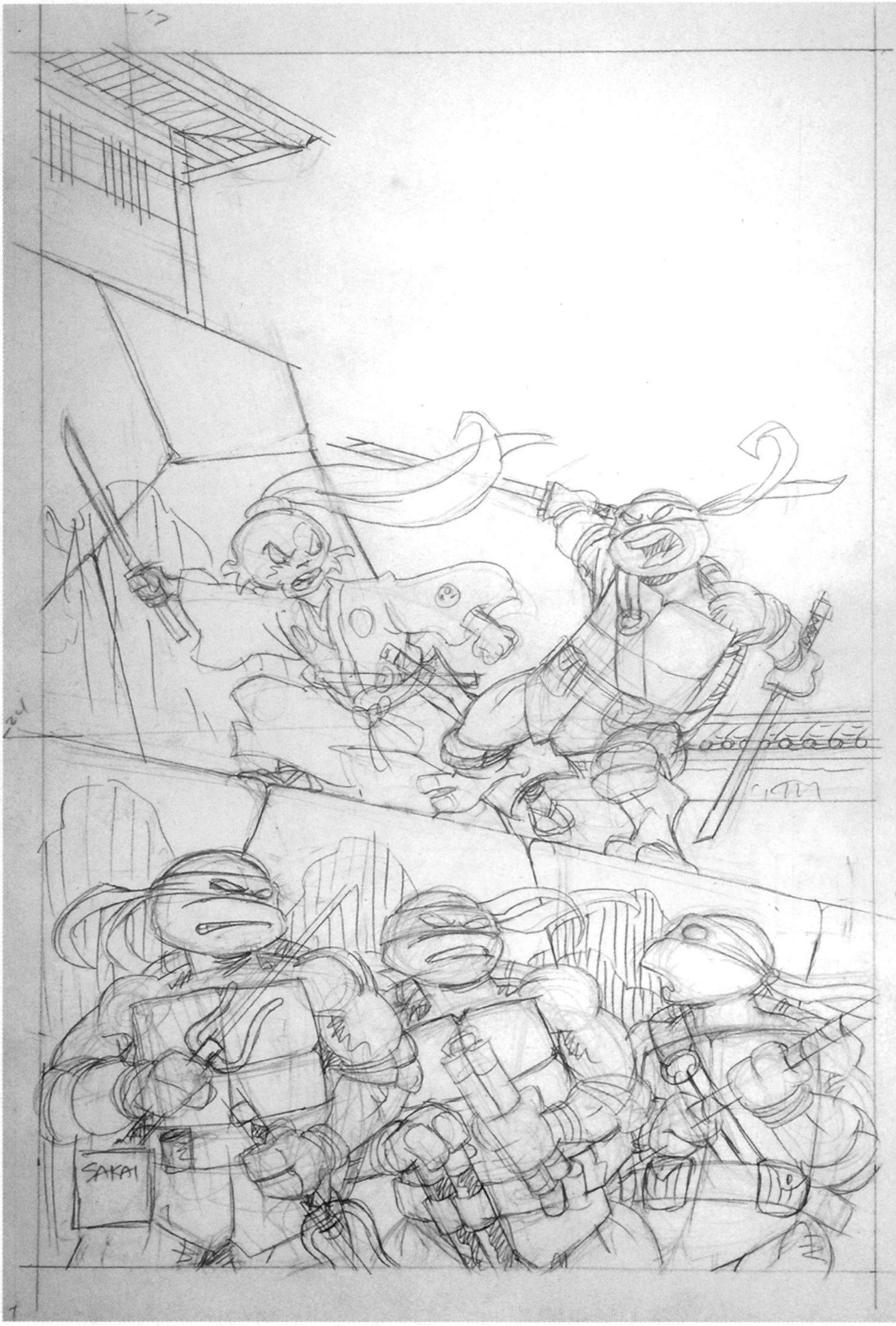
SAKAI

Teenage Mutant Ninja Turtles/Usagi Yojimbo Hardcover
Sketch by Stan Sakai

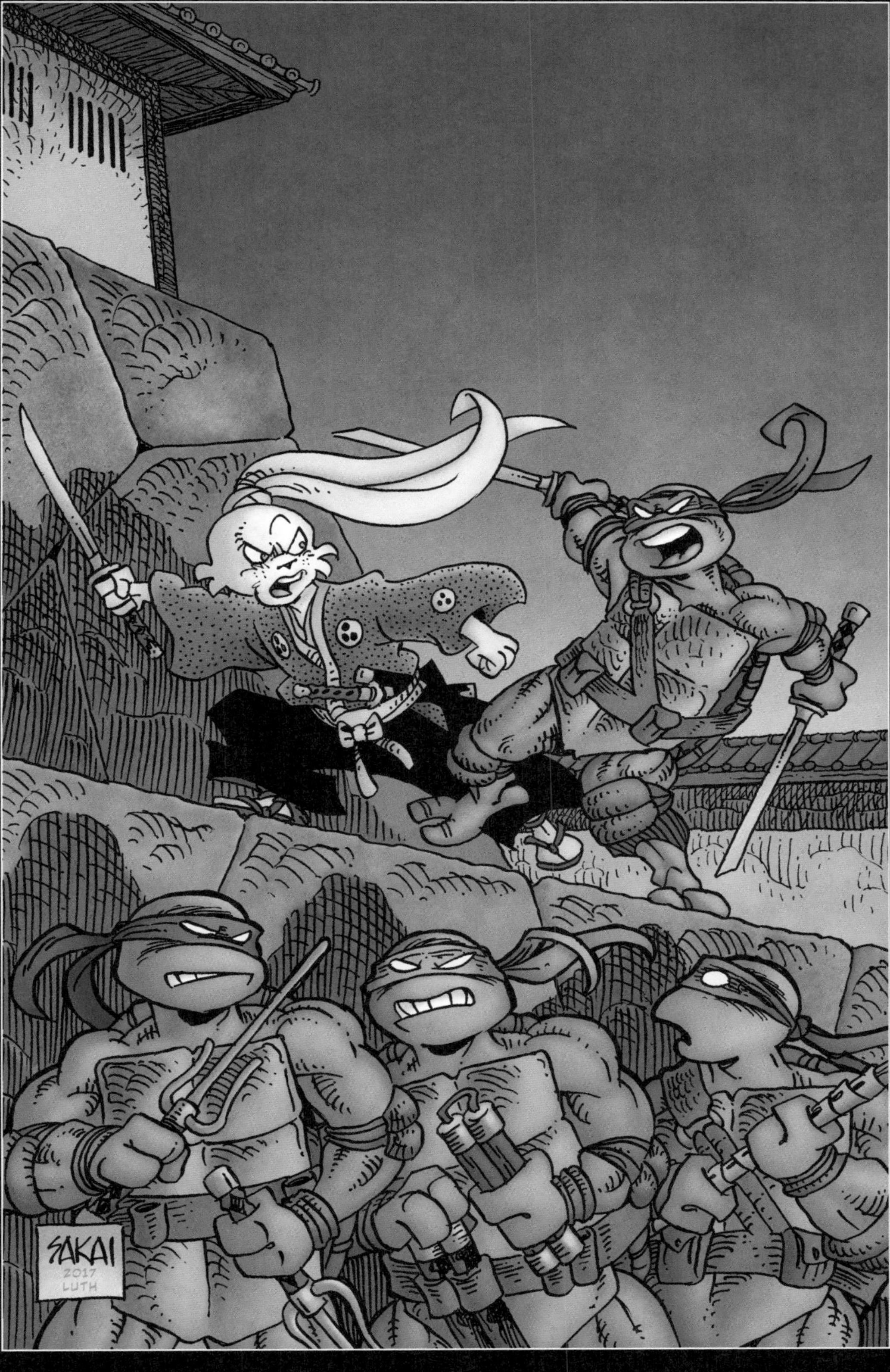
SAKAI
2017
LUTH

Teenage Mutant Ninja Turtles/Usagi Yojimbo Hardcover
Art by Stan Sakai, Colors by Tom Luth

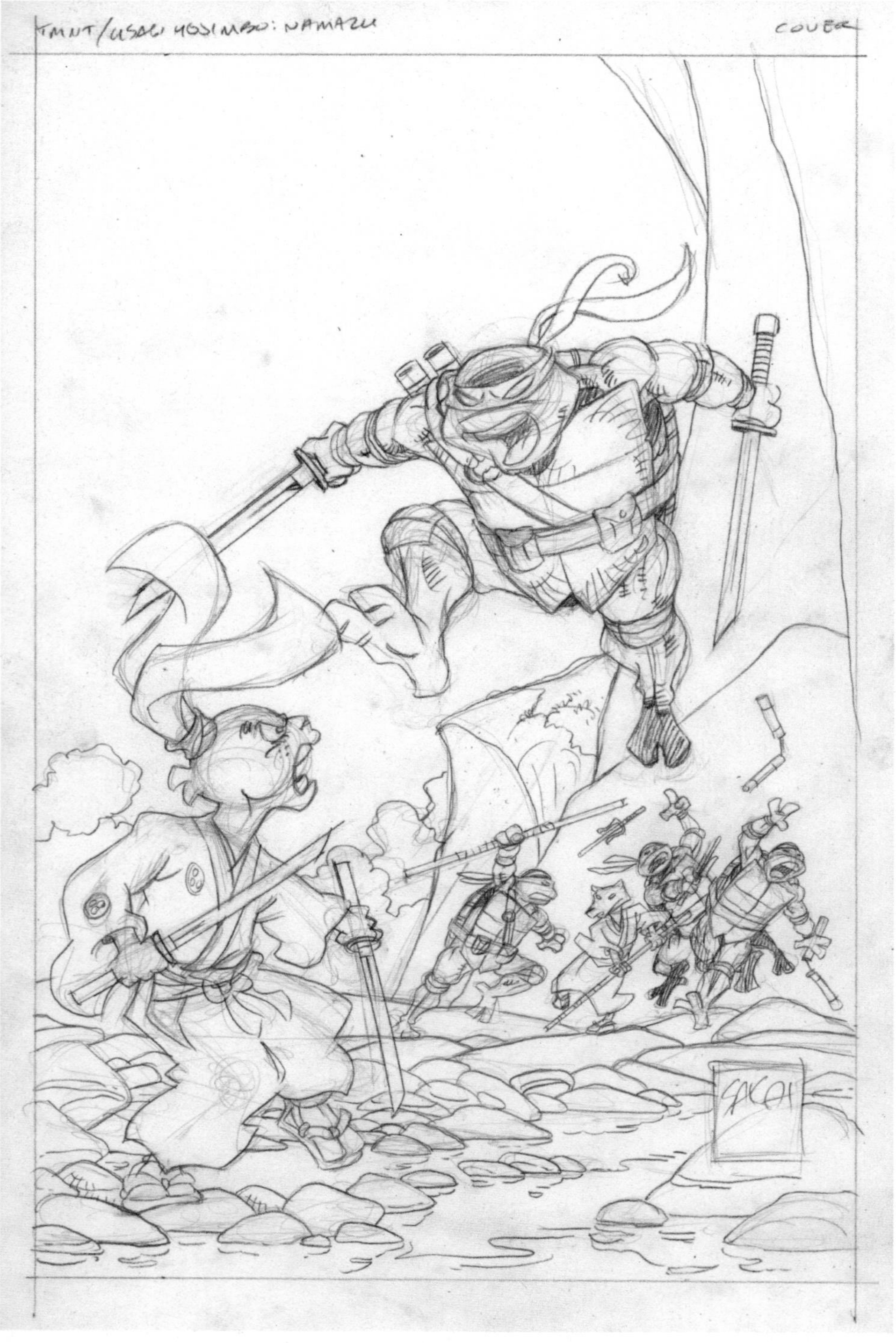
TMNT/USAGI YOJIMBO: NAMAZU
COVER
SAKAI

Teenage Mutant Ninja Turtles/Usagi Yojimbo **Expanded Edition Hardcover**
Sketch by Stan Sakai

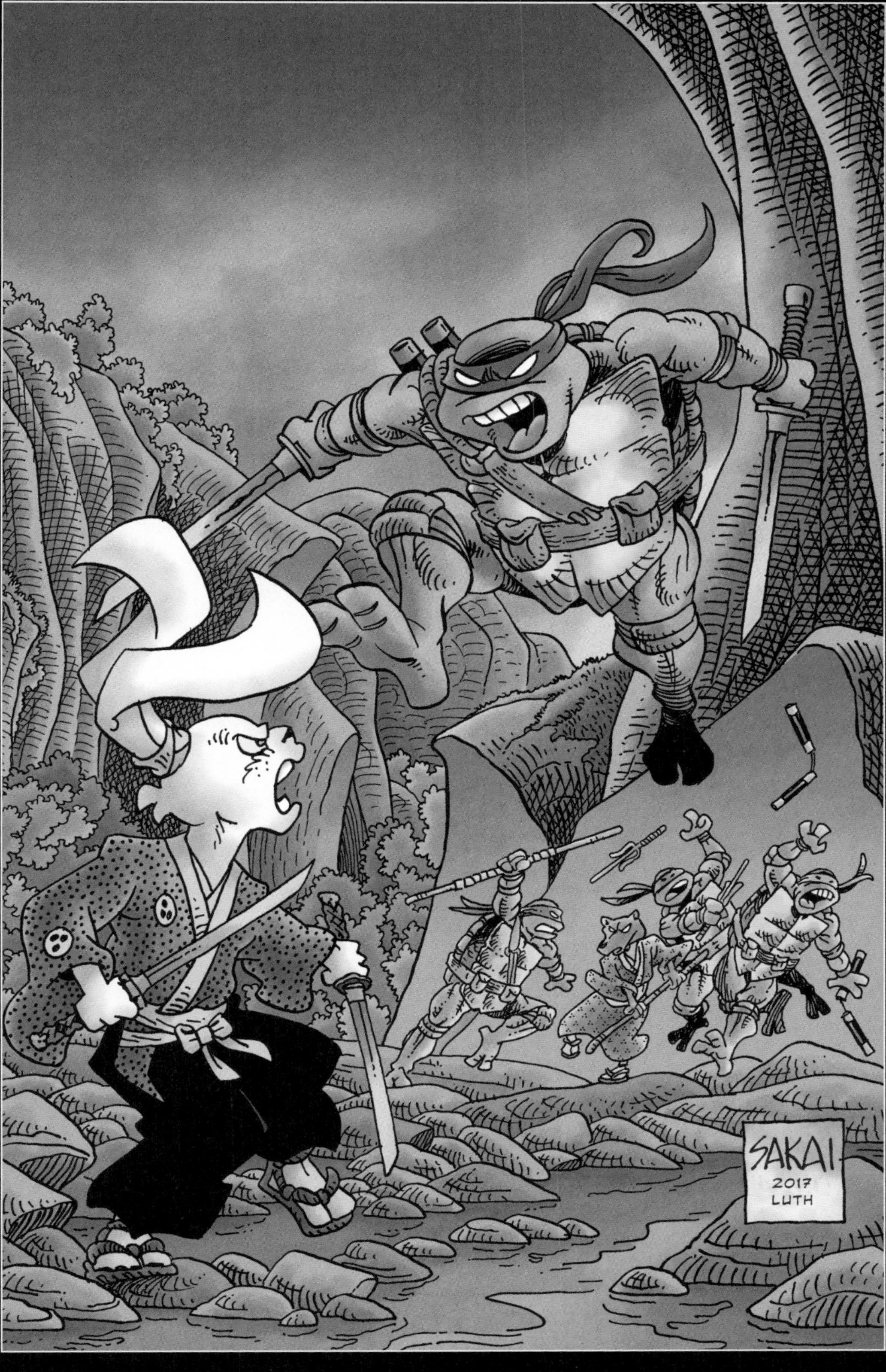
SAKAI
2017
LUTH

Teenage Mutant Ninja Turtles/Usagi Yojimbo **Expanded Edition Hardcover**
Art by Stan Sakai, Colors by Tom Luth

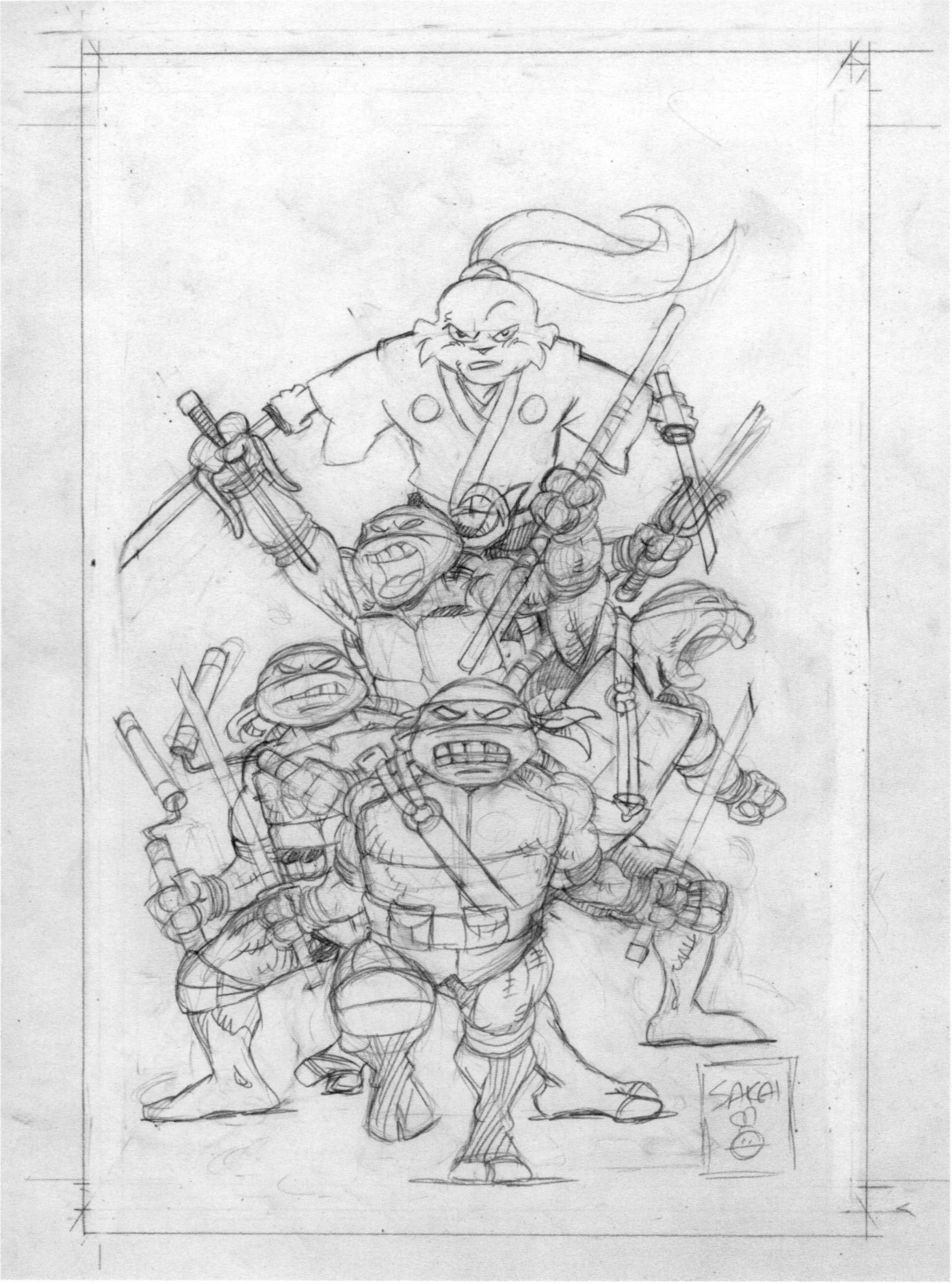
SAKAI

Teenage Mutant Ninja Turtles/Usagi Yojimbo **Expanded Edition Hardcover Variant**
Sketch by Stan Sakai

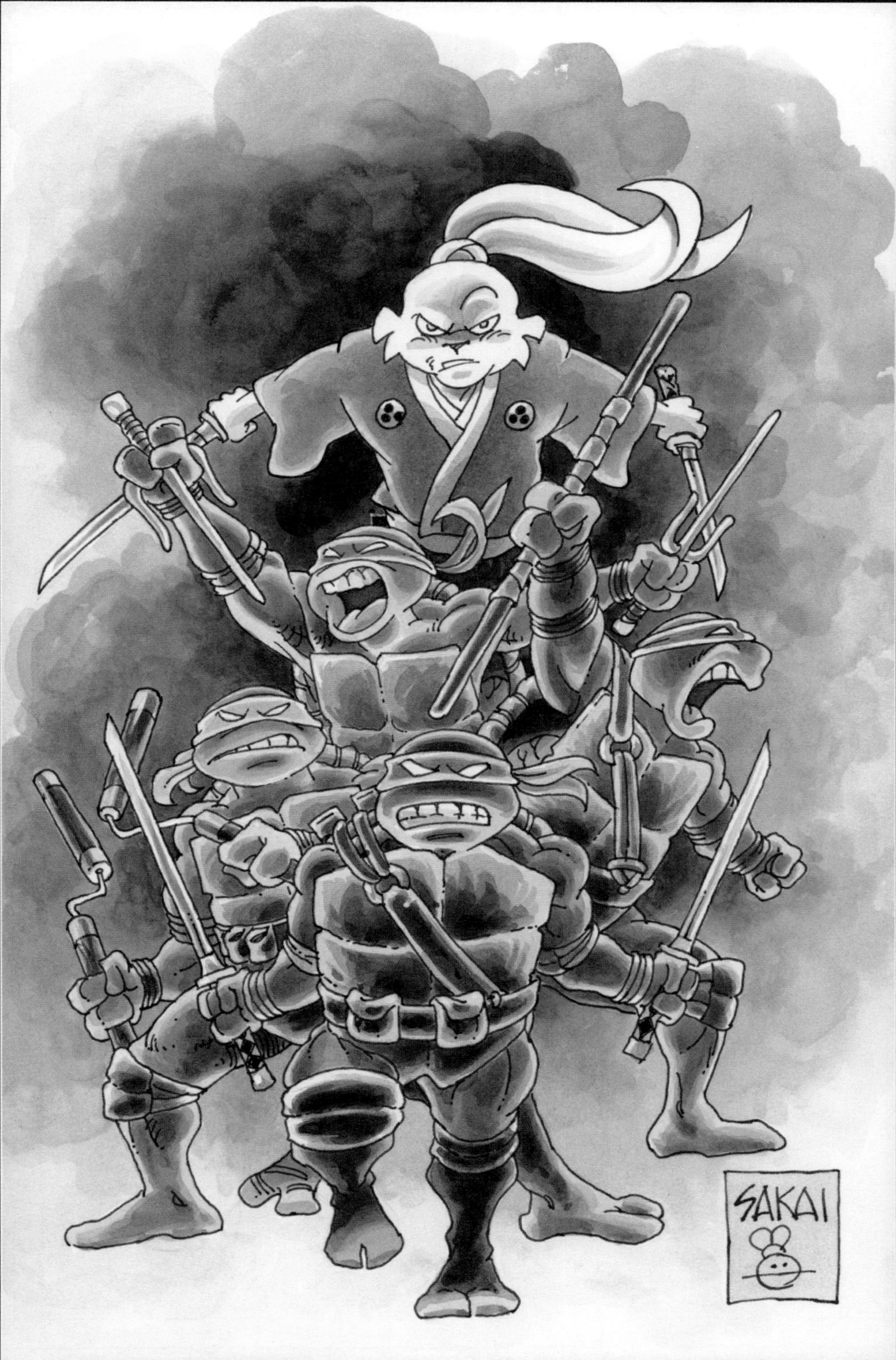
SAKAI

Teenage Mutant Ninja Turtles/Usagi Yojimbo Expanded Edition Hardcover Variant
Art by Stan Sakai

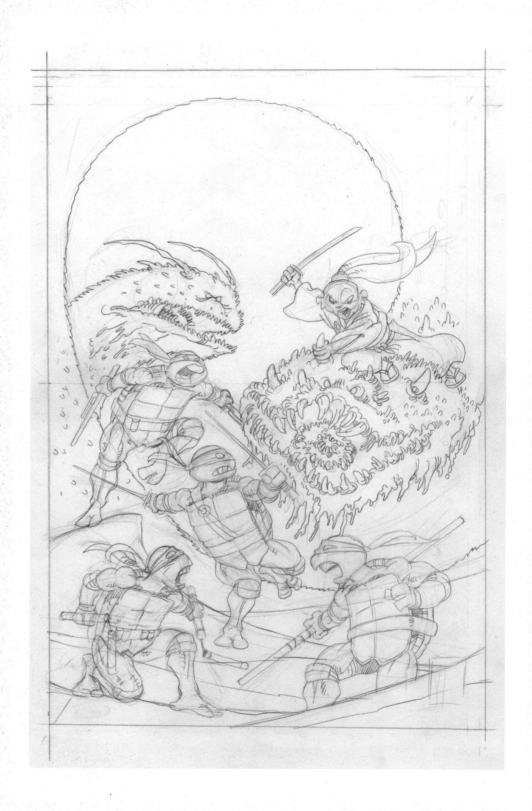

Usagi Yojimbo/Teenage Mutant Ninja Turtles: The Complete Collection Cover
Sketch by Stan Sakai

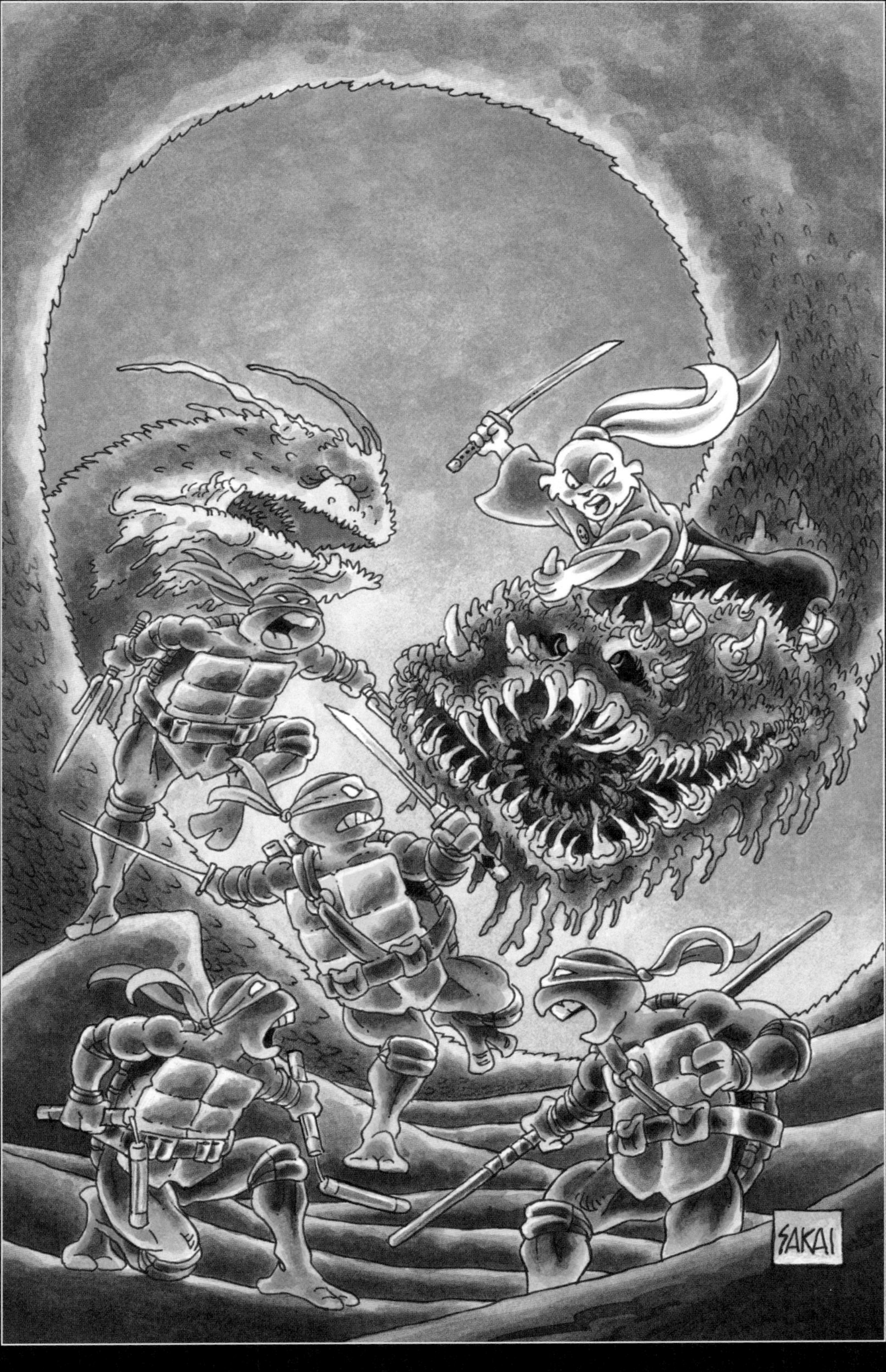
SAKAI

Usagi Yojimbo/Teenage Mutant Ninja Turtles: The Complete Collection Cover
Art by Stan Sakai

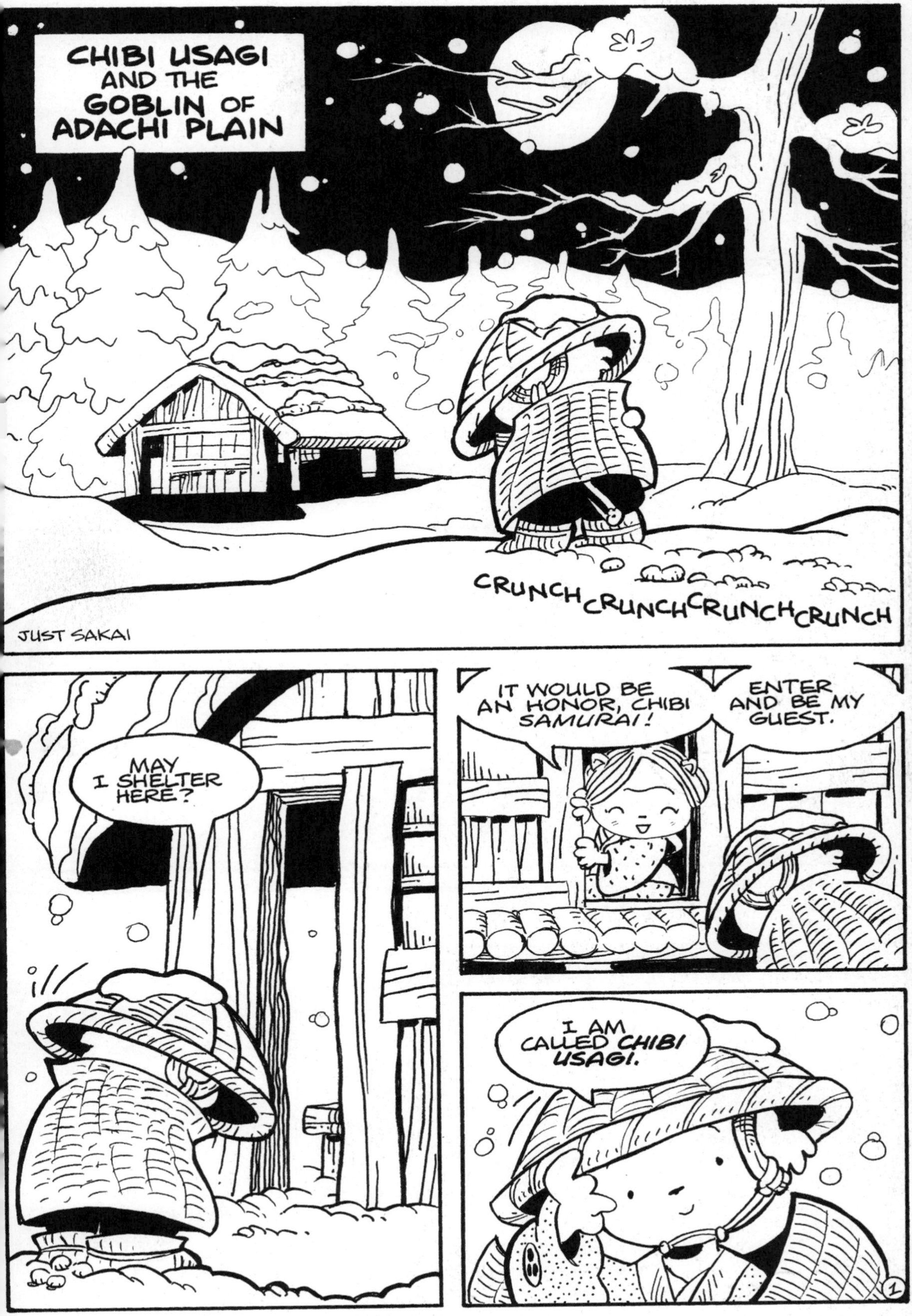
CHIBI USAGI AND THE GOBLIN OF ADACHI PLAIN
CRUNCH CRUNCH CRUNCH CRUNCH
JUST SAKAI
MAY I SHELTER HERE?
IT WOULD BE AN HONOR, CHIBI SAMURAI!
ENTER AND BE MY GUEST.
I AM CALLED CHIBI USAGI.
1

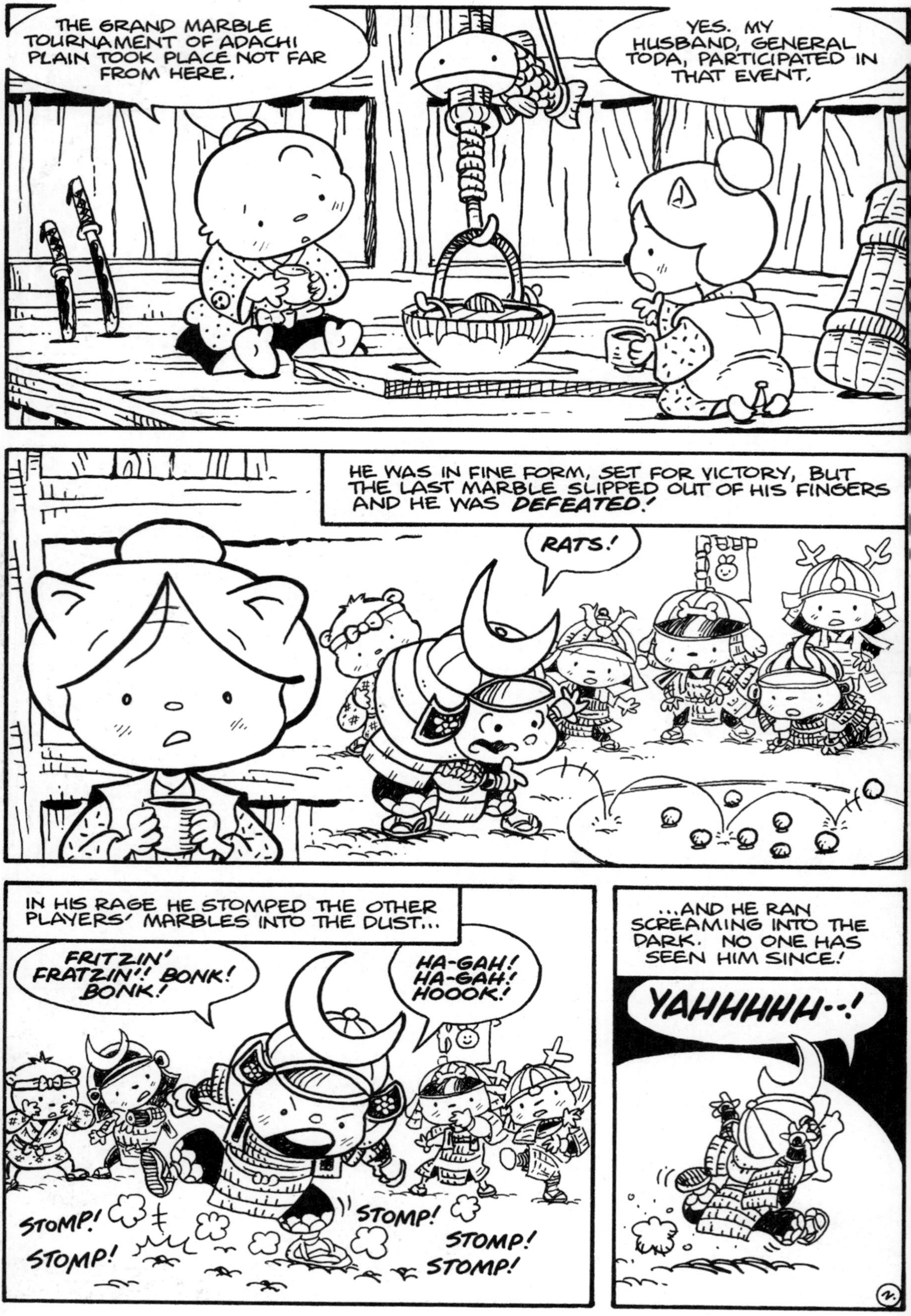

THE GRAND MARBLE TOURNAMENT OF ADACHI PLAIN TOOK PLACE NOT FAR FROM HERE.
YES. MY HUSBAND, GENERAL TODA, PARTICIPATED IN THAT EVENT.
HE WAS IN FINE FORM, SET FOR VICTORY, BUT THE LAST MARBLE SLIPPED OUT OF HIS FINGERS AND HE WAS DEFEATED!
RATS!
IN HIS RAGE HE STOMPED THE OTHER PLAYERS' MARBLES INTO THE DUST...
FRITZIN' FRATZIN'! BONK! BONK!
HA-GAH! HA-GAH! HOOOK!
STOMP! STOMP!
STOMP!
STOMP! STOMP!
...AND HE RAN SCREAMING INTO THE DARK. NO ONE HAS SEEN HIM SINCE!
YAHHHHH--!
2.

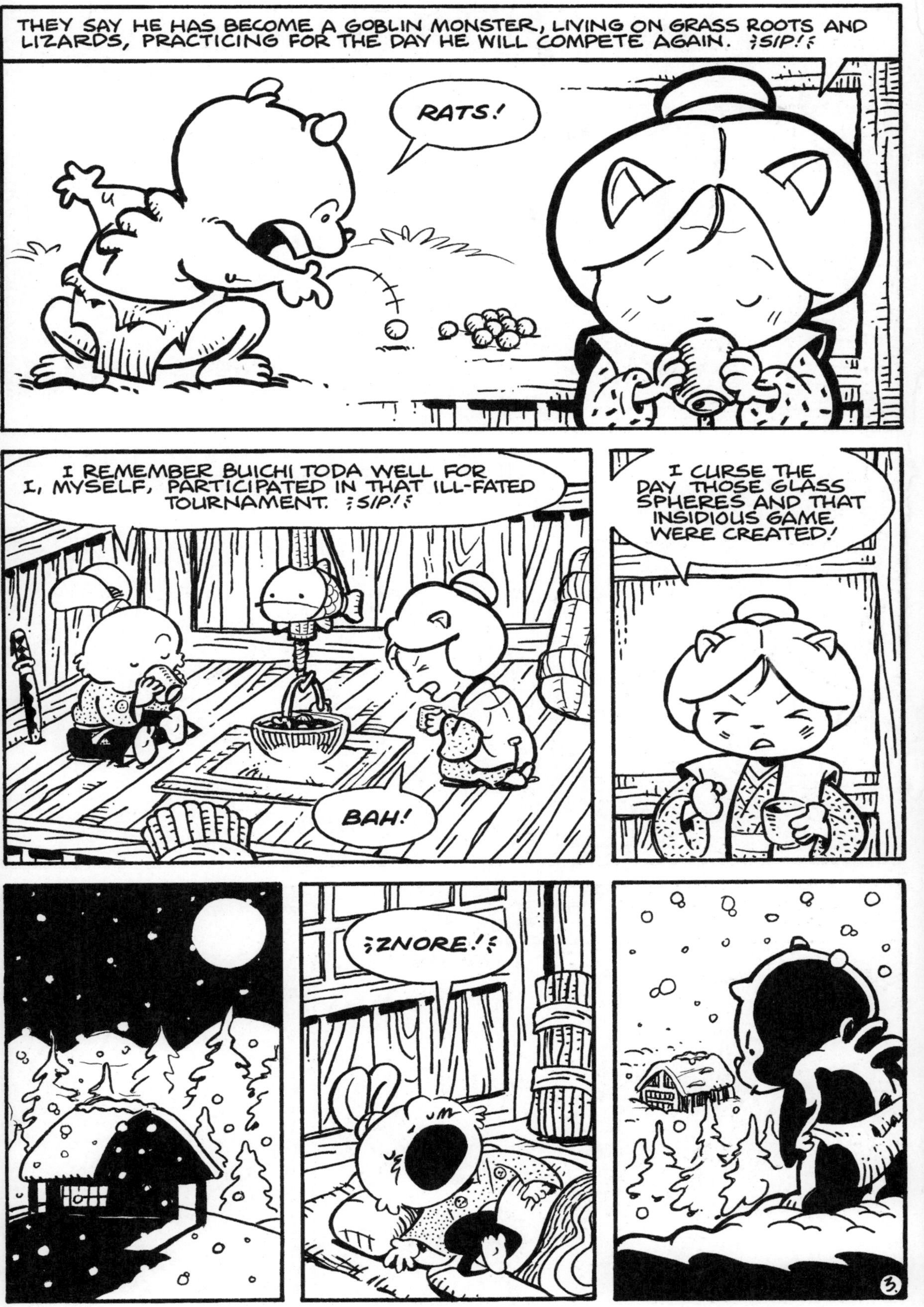
THEY SAY HE HAS BECOME A GOBLIN MONSTER, LIVING ON GRASS ROOTS AND LIZARDS, PRACTICING FOR THE DAY HE WILL COMPETE AGAIN. SIP!
RATS!
I REMEMBER BUICHI TODA WELL FOR I, MYSELF, PARTICIPATED IN THAT ILL-FATED TOURNAMENT. SIP!
BAH!
I CURSE THE DAY THOSE GLASS SPHERES AND THAT INSIDIOUS GAME WERE CREATED!
ZNORE!
3.

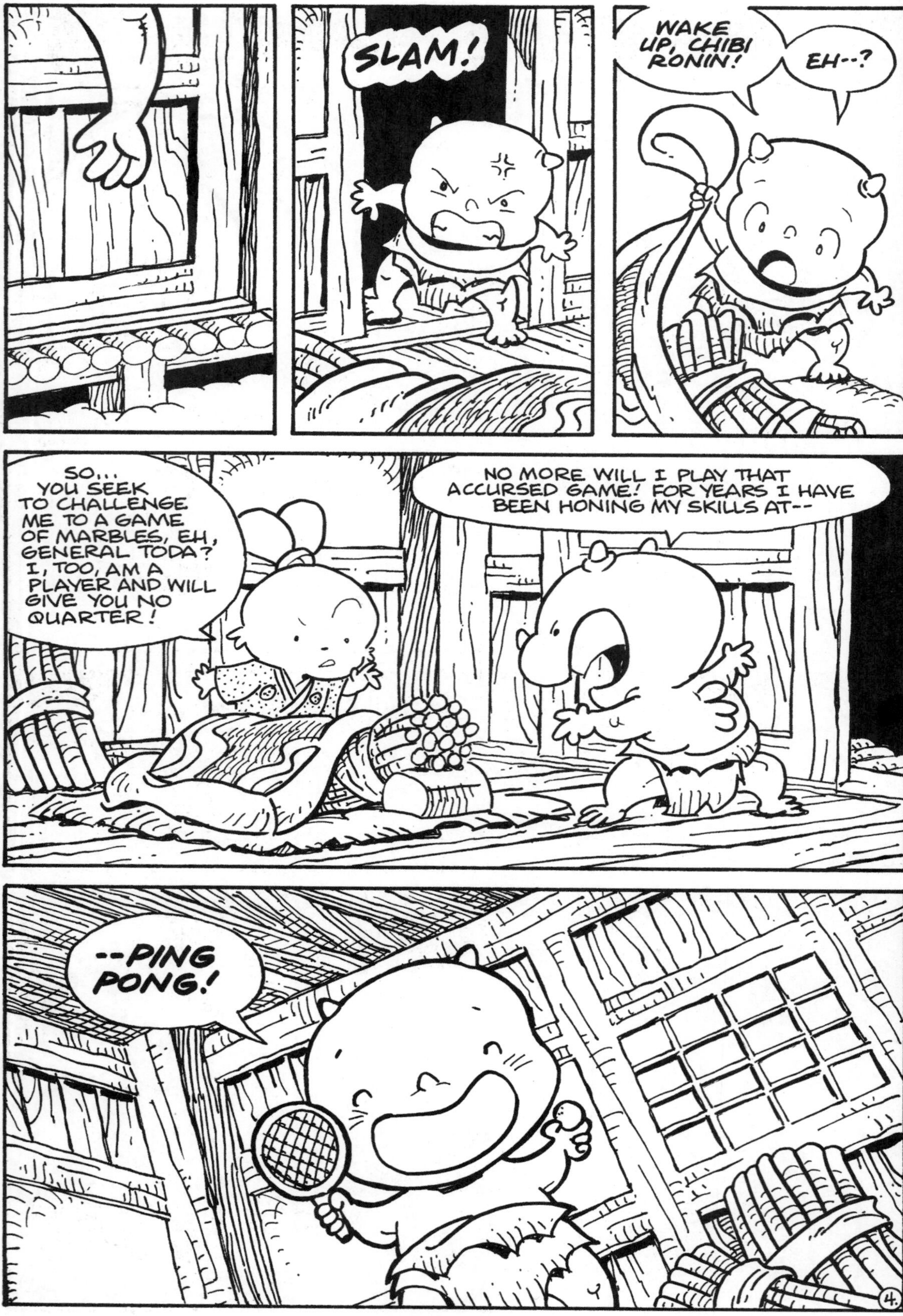

SLAM!
WAKE UP, CHIBI RONIN!
EH--?
SO... YOU SEEK TO CHALLENGE ME TO A GAME OF MARBLES, EH, GENERAL TODA? I, TOO, AM A PLAYER AND WILL GIVE YOU NO QUARTER!
NO MORE WILL I PLAY THAT ACCURSED GAME! FOR YEARS I HAVE BEEN HONING MY SKILLS AT--
--PING PONG!
4.

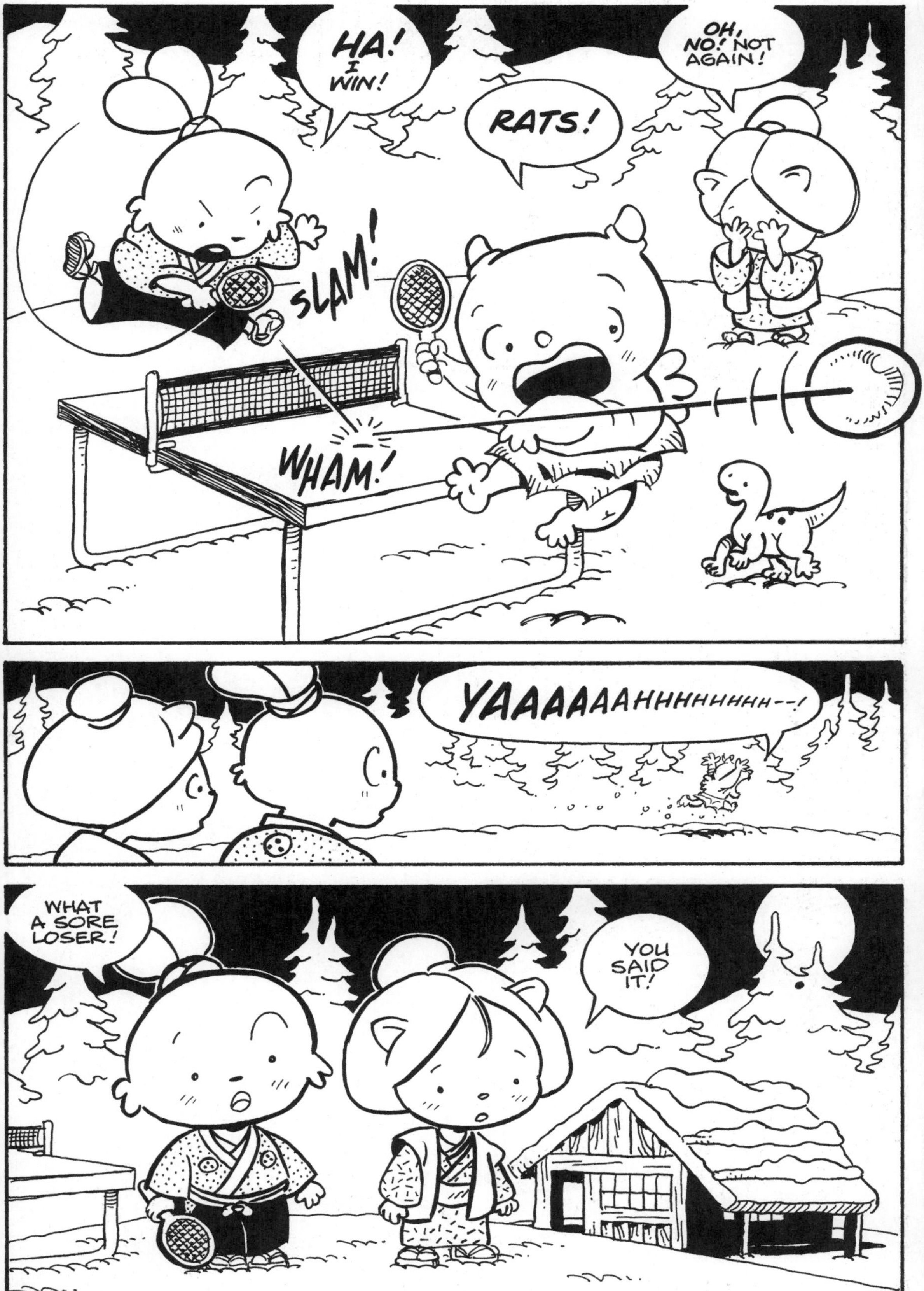
HA! I WIN!
RATS!
OH, NO! NOT AGAIN!
SLAM!
WHAM!
YAAAAAAHHHHHHH--!
WHAT A SORE LOSER!
YOU SAID IT!

THE END

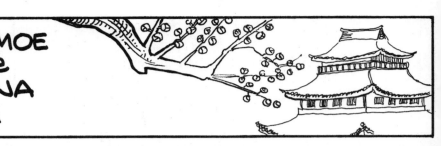

CHIBI TOMOE and the ZŌ NINJA
BY JUST SAKAI

I HAVE HEARD RUMORS OF A NEW NINJA IN THIS AREA, CHIBI-TOMOE!

A *NEW* NINJA? THERE ARE CATS, BATS AND MOLE NINJA!

WHAT COULD BE NEXT, CHIBI-NORIYUKI-SAMA?

I DON'T KNOW, BUT--

¡STOMP! STOMP!¡

WHAT'S THAT NOISE IN THE RAFTERS?

UH-OH!

I THINK SOMEONE IS UP THERE!

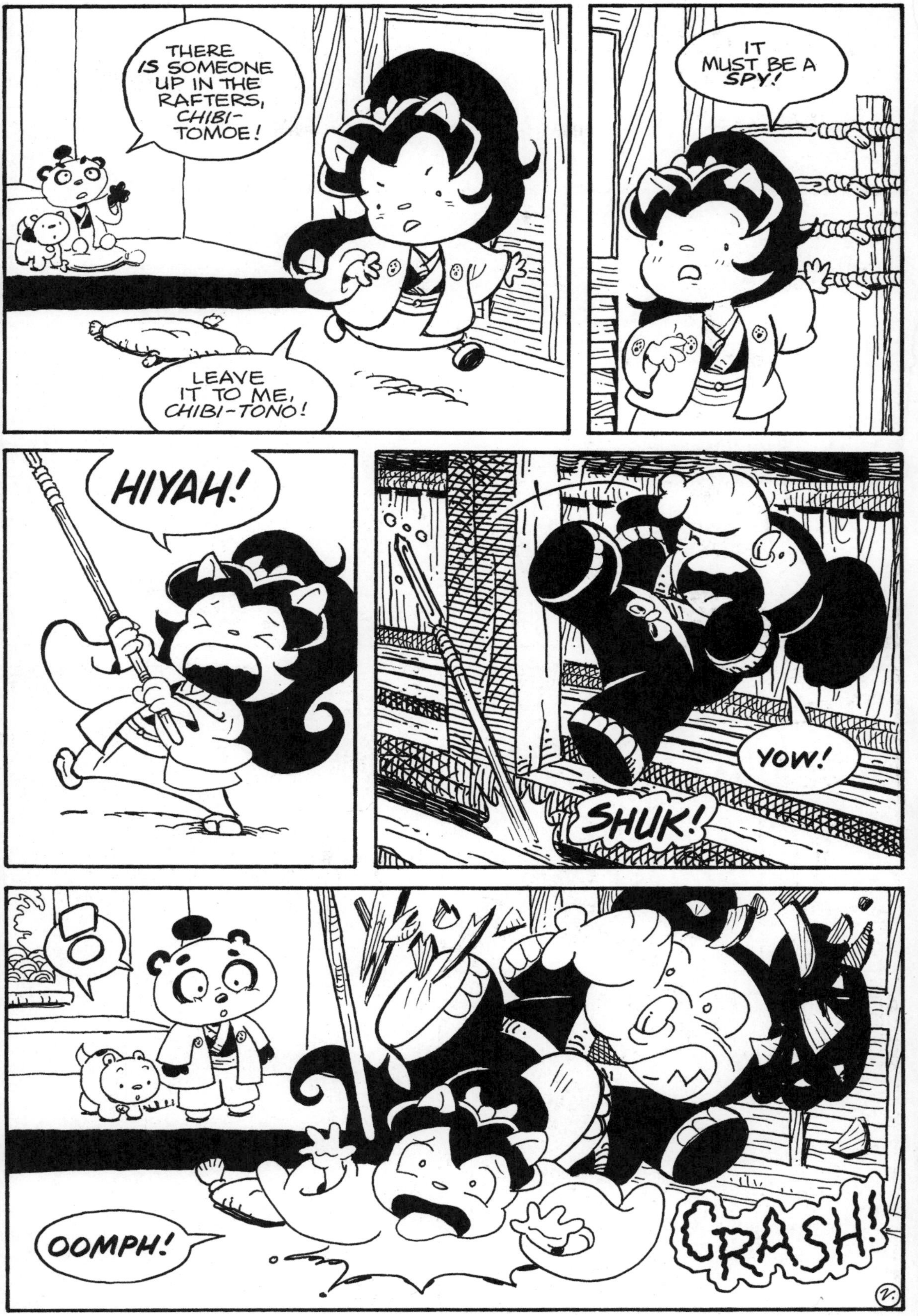
THERE IS SOMEONE UP IN THE RAFTERS, CHIBI-TOMOE!
LEAVE IT TO ME, CHIBI-TONO!
IT MUST BE A SPY!
HIYAH!
YOW!
SHUK!
OOMPH!
CRASH!
2.

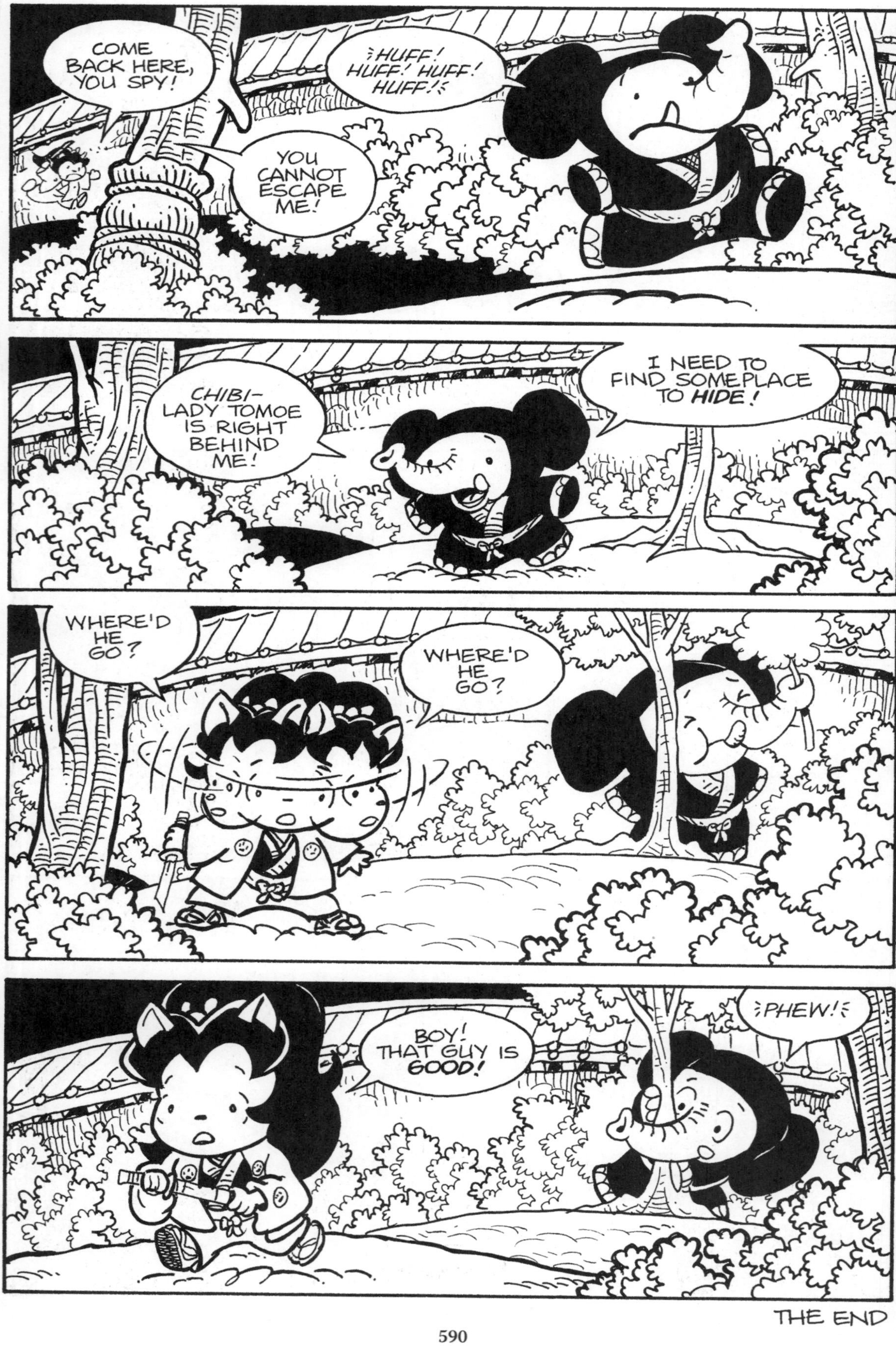
COME BACK HERE, YOU SPY!
HUFF! HUFF! HUFF! HUFF!
YOU CANNOT ESCAPE ME!
CHIBI-LADY TOMOE IS RIGHT BEHIND ME!
I NEED TO FIND SOMEPLACE TO HIDE!
WHERE'D HE GO?
WHERE'D HE GO?
BOY! THAT GUY IS GOOD!
PHEW!

THE END

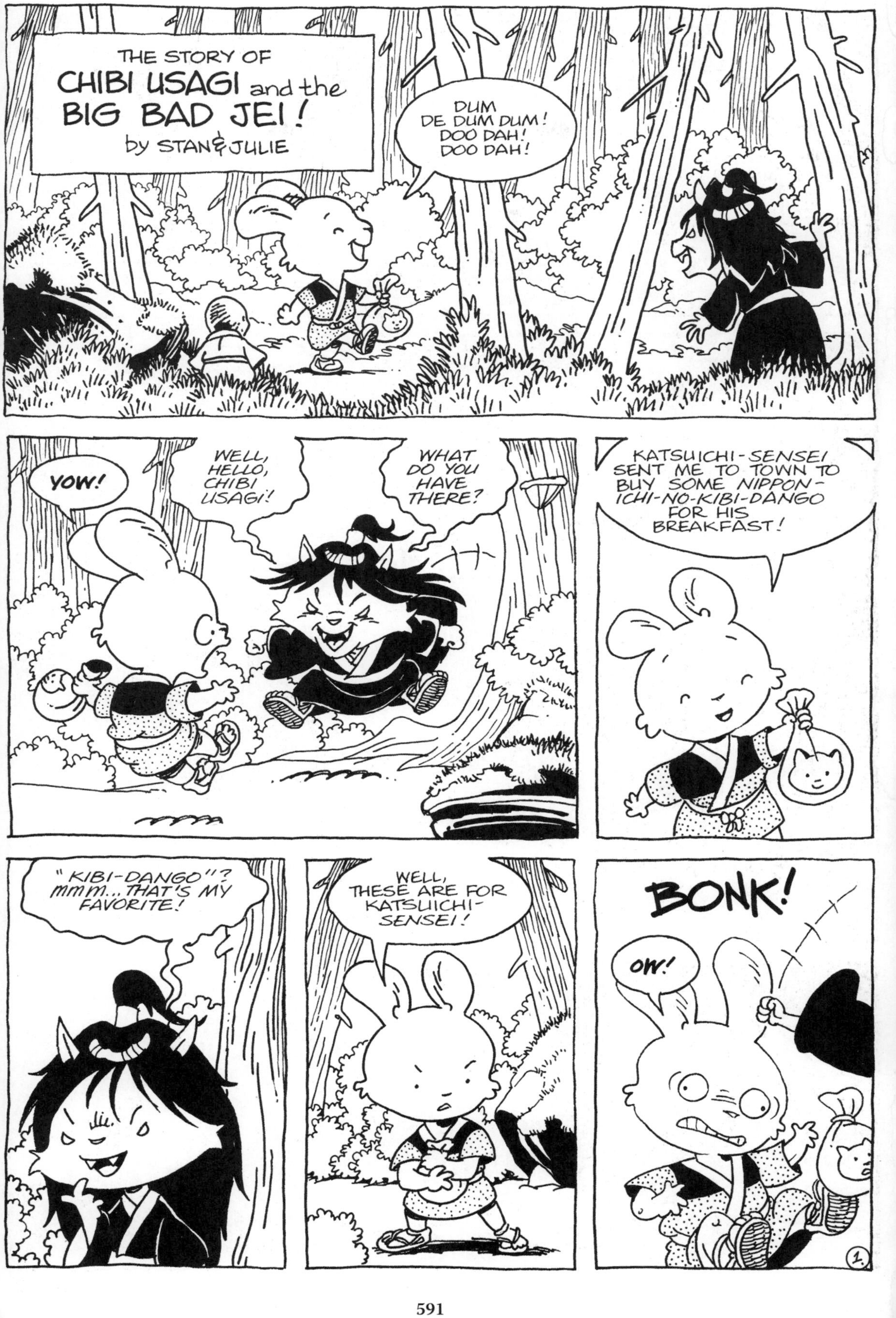

THE STORY OF
CHIBI USAGI and the
BIG BAD JEI!
by STAN & JULIE
DUM DE DUM DUM! DOO DAH! DOO DAH!
YOW!
WELL, HELLO, CHIBI USAGI!
WHAT DO YOU HAVE THERE?
KATSUICHI-SENSEI SENT ME TO TOWN TO BUY SOME NIPPON-ICHI-NO-KIBI-DANGO FOR HIS BREAKFAST!
"KIBI-DANGO"? MMM... THAT'S MY FAVORITE!
WELL, THESE ARE FOR KATSUICHI-SENSEI!
BONK!
OW!
1.

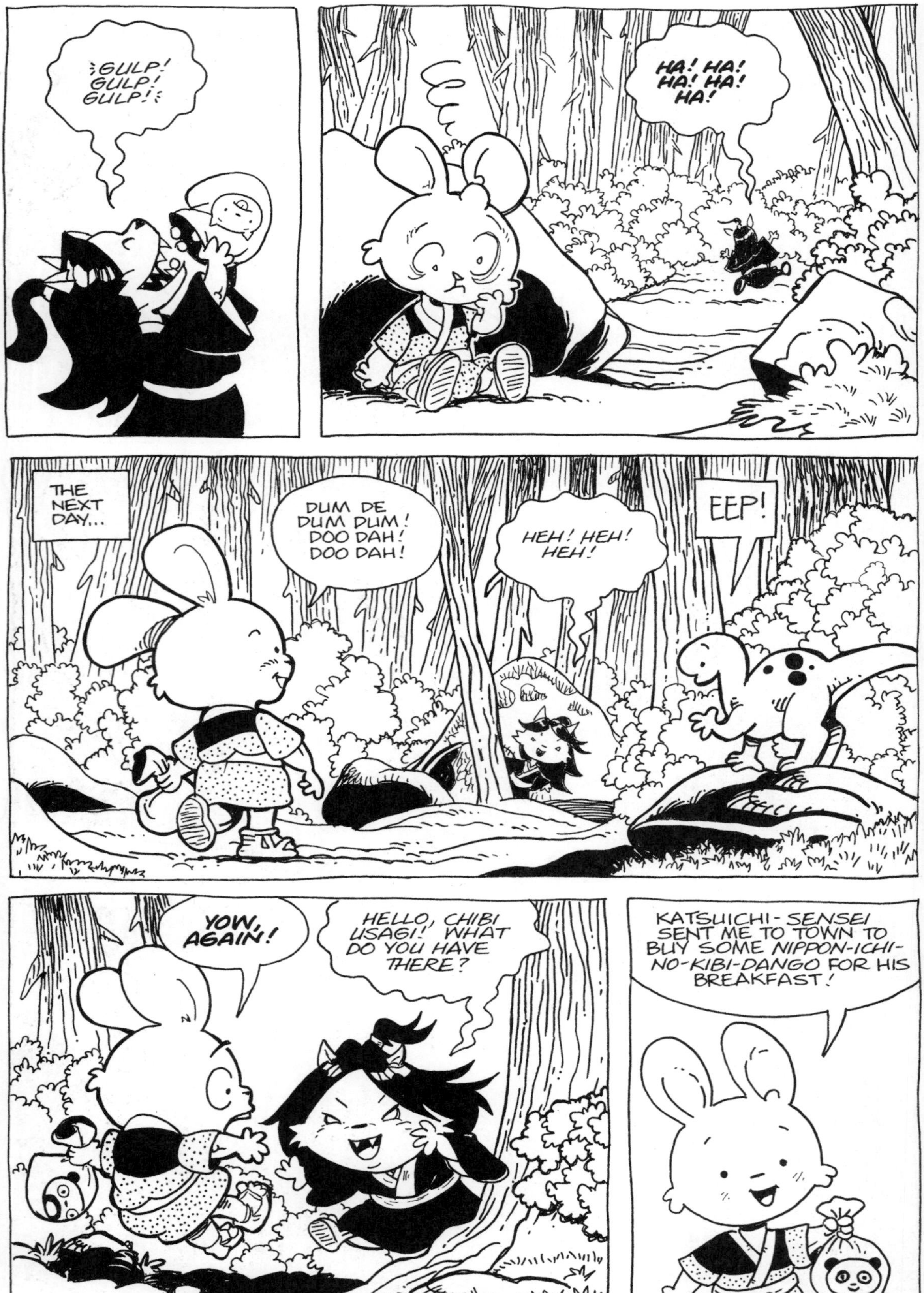

GULP! GULP! GULP!
HA! HA! HA! HA! HA!
THE NEXT DAY...
DUM DE DUM DUM! DOO DAH! DOO DAH!
HEH! HEH! HEH!
EEP!
YOW, AGAIN!
HELLO, CHIBI USAGI! WHAT DO YOU HAVE THERE?
KATSUICHI-SENSEI SENT ME TO TOWN TO BUY SOME NIPPON-ICHI-NO-KIBI-DANGO FOR HIS BREAKFAST!
2.

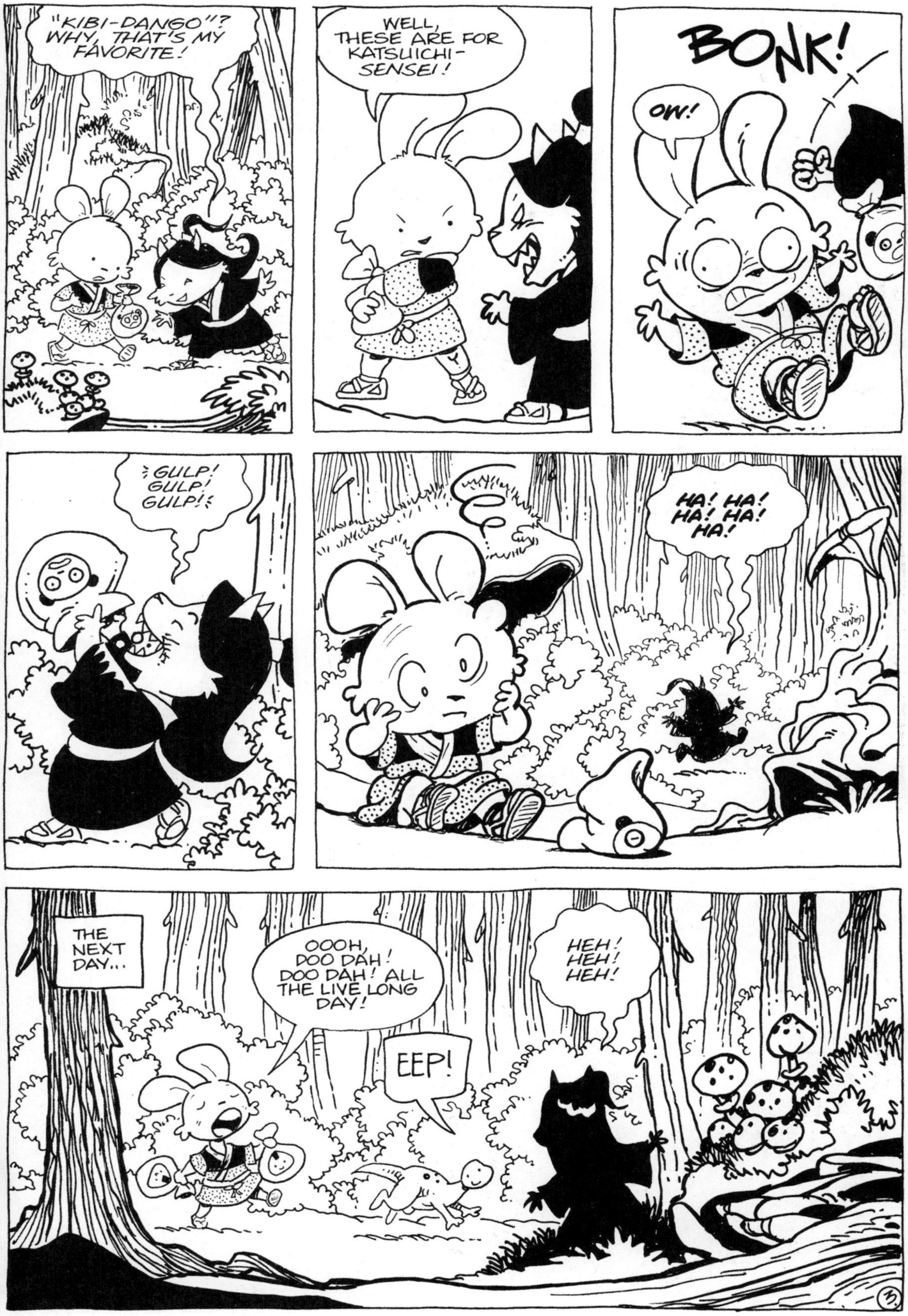
"KIBI-DANGO"? WHY, THAT'S MY FAVORITE!
WELL, THESE ARE FOR KATSUICHI-SENSEI!
BONK!
OW!
GULP! GULP! GULP!
HA! HA! HA! HA! HA!
THE NEXT DAY...
OOOH, DOO DAH! DOO DAH! ALL THE LIVE LONG DAY!
EEP!
HEH! HEH! HEH!
3.

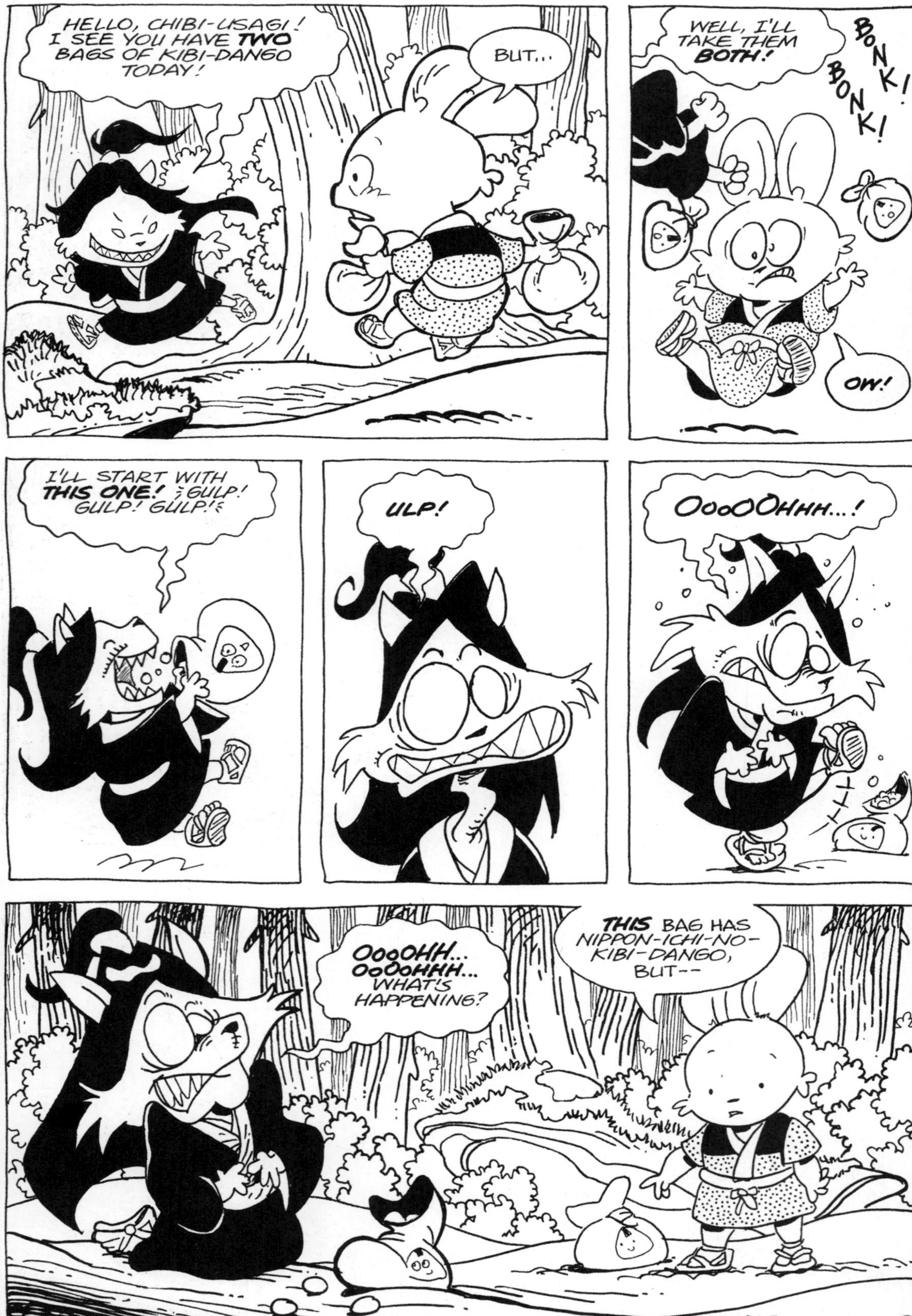
HELLO, CHIBI-USAGI! I SEE YOU HAVE TWO BAGS OF KIBI-DANGO TODAY!
BUT...
WELL, I'LL TAKE THEM BOTH!
BONK! BONK!
OW!
I'LL START WITH THIS ONE! GULP! GULP! GULP!
ULP!
OOoOOHHH...!
OOOOHH... OOOOHHH... WHAT'S HAPPENING?
THIS BAG HAS NIPPON-ICHI-NO-KIBI-DANGO, BUT--
4.

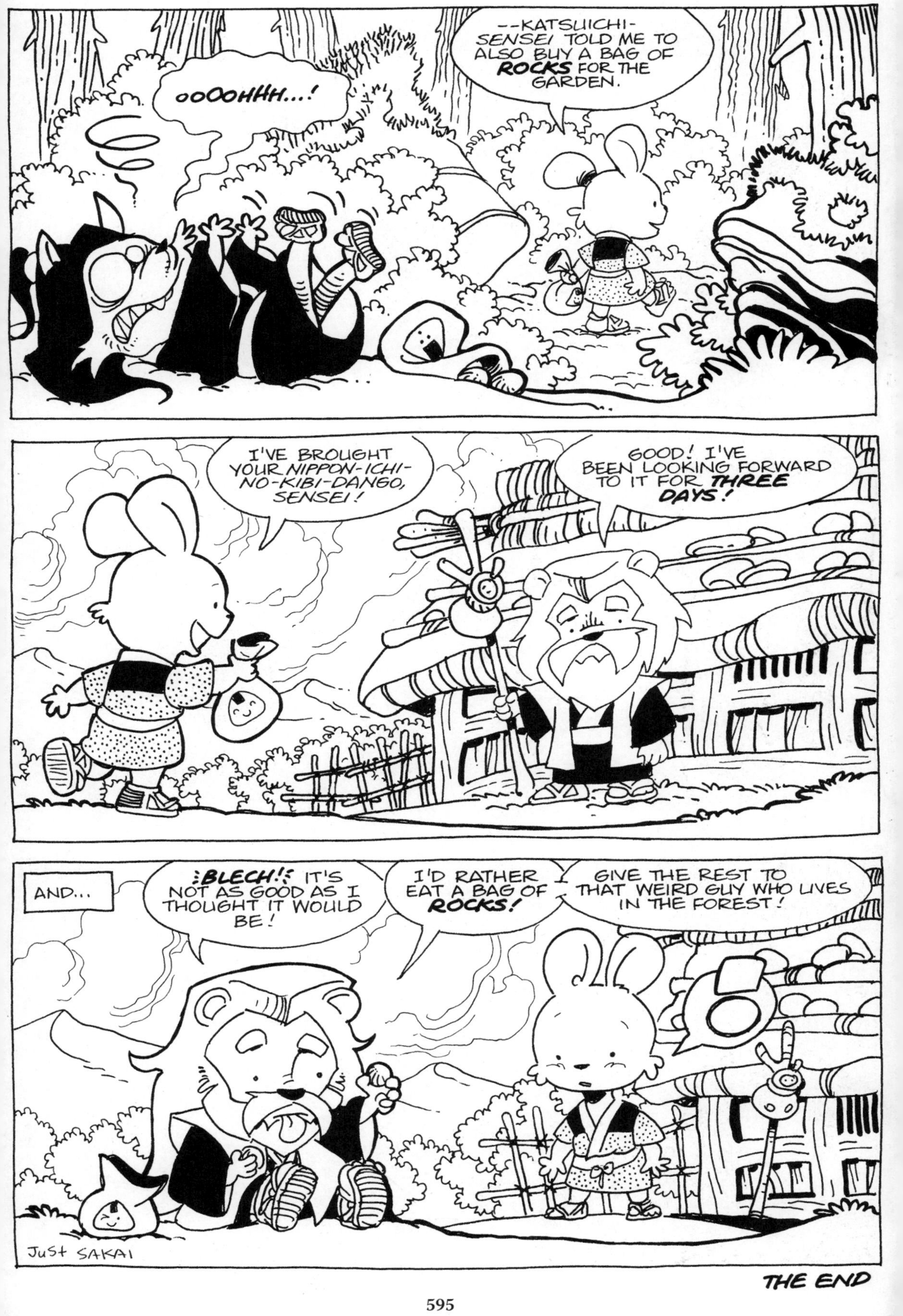
--KATSUICHI-SENSEI TOLD ME TO ALSO BUY A BAG OF ROCKS FOR THE GARDEN.
oOOOHHH...!
I'VE BROUGHT YOUR NIPPON-ICHI-NO-KIBI-DANGO, SENSEI!
GOOD! I'VE BEEN LOOKING FORWARD TO IT FOR THREE DAYS!
AND...
BLECH! IT'S NOT AS GOOD AS I THOUGHT IT WOULD BE!
I'D RATHER EAT A BAG OF ROCKS!
GIVE THE REST TO THAT WEIRD GUY WHO LIVES IN THE FOREST!
JUST SAKAI

THE END

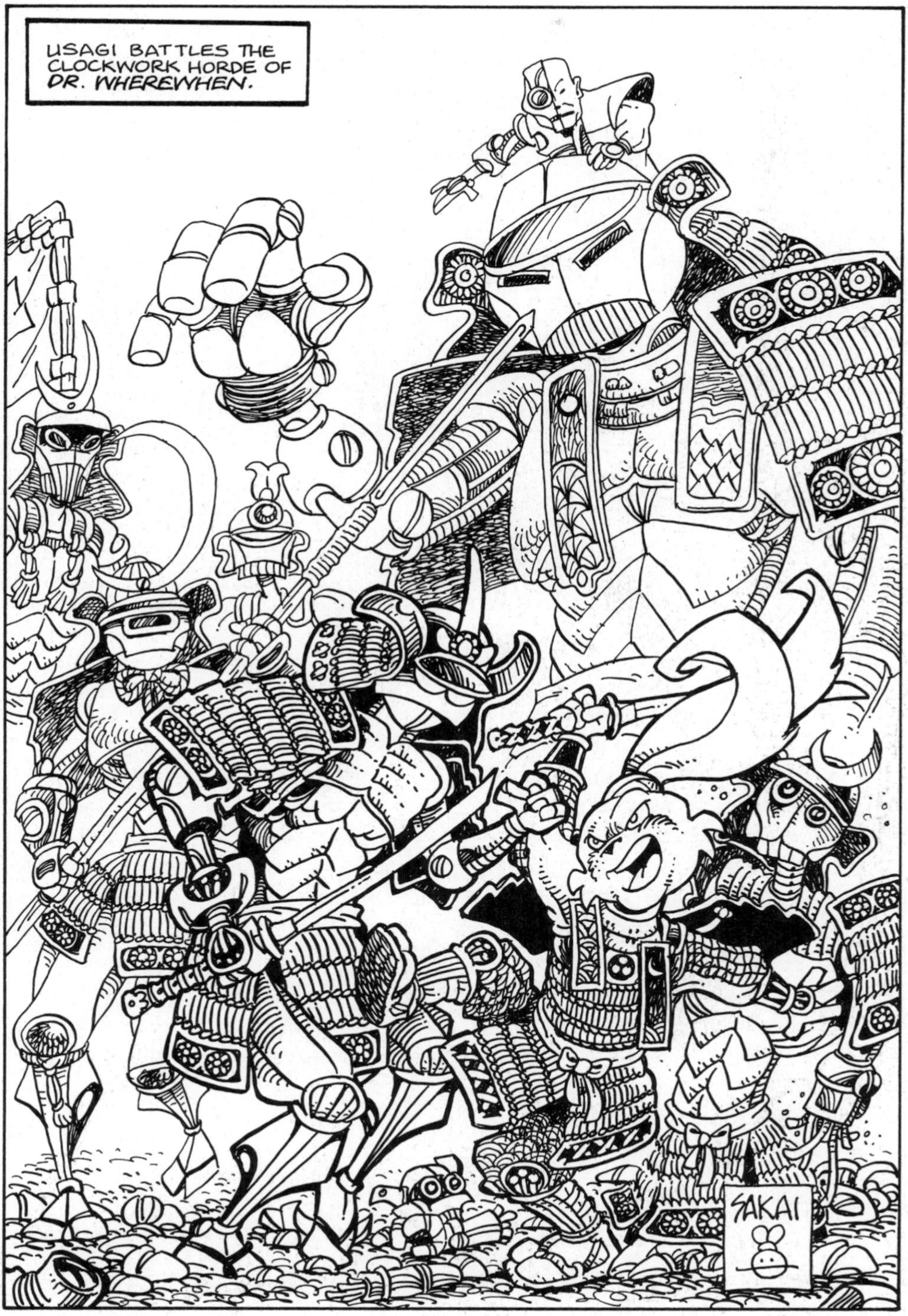
USAGI BATTLES THE CLOCKWORK HORDE OF DR. WHEREWHEN.
SAKAI

ABOUT THE AUTHOR

Stan visiting Old Town Warsaw in April 2019. Photo by Emi Fujii Photography.

STAN SAKAI was born in Kyoto, Japan, grew up in Hawaii, and now lives in California with his wife Julie. He has two children, Hannah and Matthew, and two stepchildren, Daniel and Emi. Stan received a fine arts degree from the University of Hawaii and furthered his studies at the Art Center College of Design in Pasadena, California.

Stan's creation *Usagi Yojimbo* first appeared in the comic book *Albedo Anthropomorphics* #2 in 1984. Since then, Usagi has been on television as a guest of the Teenage Mutant Ninja Turtles and has been made into toys and seen on clothing, and his stories have been collected in more than three dozen graphic novels and translated into sixteen languages.

Stan is the recipient of a Parents' Choice Award, an Inkpot Award, an American Library Association Award, two Harvey Awards, five Spanish Haxturs, eight Will Eisner Awards, two National Cartoonists Society Silver Reubens, and most recently three Ringo Awards, including one for Best Cartoonist in 2020. In 2011 Stan received the Cultural Ambassador Award from the Japanese American National Museum for spreading Japanese history and culture through his stories. Stan was awarded the inaugural Joe Kubert Distinguished Storyteller Award in 2018 and was inducted into the Will Eisner Hall of Fame in 2020. Stan, in partnership with Gaumont USA, is currently developing an Usagi animated series for Netflix.

USAGI YOJIMBO™

Created, Written, and Illustrated by Stan Sakai

Available from Dark Horse Comics

The Usagi Yojimbo Saga Book 1 Second Edition
Collects *Usagi Yojimbo* Books 8–10
$29.99 | ISBN 978-1-50672-490-4

The Usagi Yojimbo Saga Book 2
Collects *Usagi Yojimbo* Books 11–13
$24.99 | ISBN 978-1-61655-610-5

The Usagi Yojimbo Saga Book 3
Collects *Usagi Yojimbo* Books 14–16
$24.99 | ISBN 978-1-61655-611-2

The Usagi Yojimbo Saga Book 4
Collects *Usagi Yojimbo* Books 17–19
$24.99 | ISBN 978-1-61655-612-9

The Usagi Yojimbo Saga Book 5
Collects *Usagi Yojimbo* Books 20–22
$24.99 | ISBN 978-1-61655-613-6

The Usagi Yojimbo Saga Book 6
Collects *Usagi Yojimbo* Books 23–25
$24.99 | ISBN 978-1-61655-614-3

The Usagi Yojimbo Saga Book 7
Collects *Usagi Yojimbo* Books 26–28
$24.99 | ISBN 978-1-61655-615-0

The Usagi Yojimbo Saga Book 8
Collects *Usagi Yojimbo* Books 29–31
$24.99 | ISBN 978-1-50671-224-6

The Usagi Yojimbo Saga: Legends
Collects *Senso, Yokai, Space Usagi,* and more!
$24.99 | ISBN 978-1-50670-323-7

Book 29: Two Hundred Jizo
$17.99 | ISBN 978-1-61655-840-6

Book 30: Thieves and Spies
$17.99 | ISBN 978-1-50670-048-9

Book 31: The Hell Screen
$17.99 | ISBN 978-1-50670-187-5

Book 32: Mysteries
$17.99 | ISBN 978-1-50670-584-2

Book 33: The Hidden
$17.99 | TRADE PAPERBACK: ISBN 978-1-50670-852-2
$59.99 | LIMITED EDITION HARDCOVER: ISBN 978-1-50670-851-5

Usagi Yojimbo/Teenage Mutant Ninja Turtles: The Complete Collection
$17.99 | ISBN 978-1-50670-950-5

The Art of Usagi Yojimbo
$29.95 | ISBN 978-1-59307-493-7

The Sakai Project: Artists Celebrate Thirty Years of Usagi Yojimbo
$29.99 | ISBN 978-1-61655-556-6

Gallery Edition Volume 1: Samurai and Other Stories
$125.00 | ISBN 978-1-61655-923-6

Gallery Edition Volume 2: The Artist and Other Stories
$125.00 | ISBN 978-1-61655-924-3

47 Ronin
Written by Mike Richardson
$19.99 | ISBN 978-1-59582-954-2

The Adventures of Nilson Groundthumper and Hermy
$14.99 | ISBN 978-1-61655-341-8

Available from Fantagraphics Books

fantagraphics.com

Book 1: The Ronin
Book 2: Samurai
Book 3: The Wanderer's Road
Book 4: The Dragon Bellow Conspiracy
Book 5: Lone Goat and Kid
Book 6: Circles
Book 7: Gen's Story

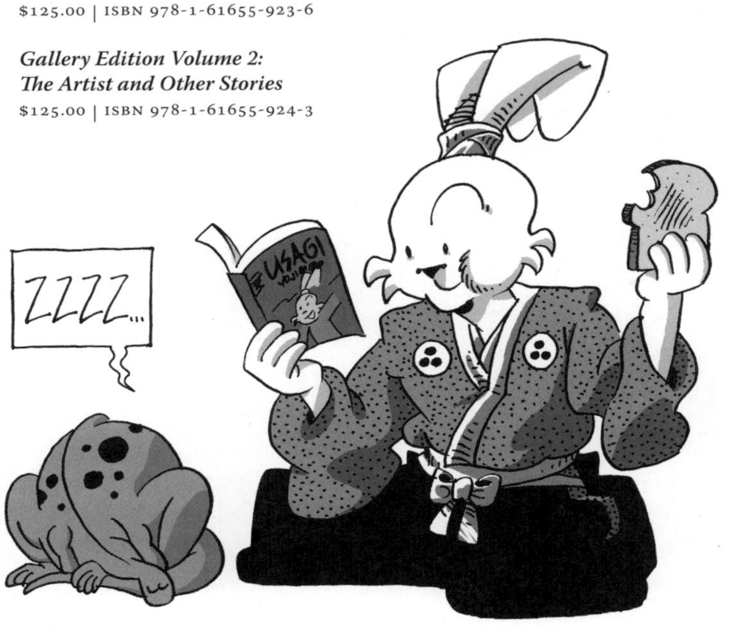
ZZZZ...
USAGI YOJIMBO

AVAILABLE AT YOUR LOCAL COMICS SHOP OR BOOKSTORE
TO FIND A COMICS SHOP IN YOUR AREA, VISIT COMICSHOPLOCATOR.COM.
For more information or to order direct, visit DarkHorse.com or call 1-800-862-0052

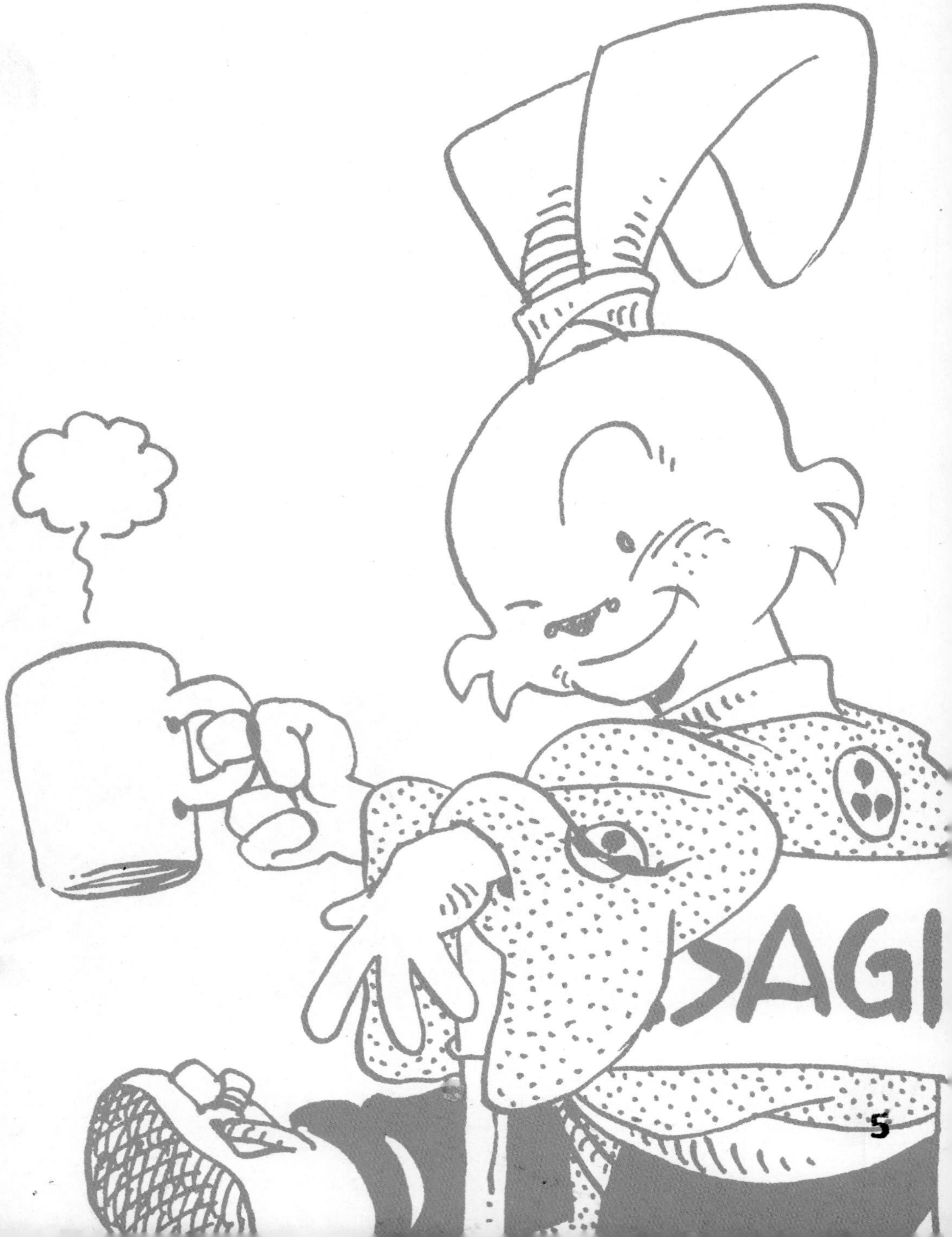
SAGI